"Brown show... remains in the top...
—*Publishers Weekly*, STARRED REVIEW

"Sandra Brown proves herself top-notch."
–ASSOCIATED PRESS

"There are shoot-outs and reformed prostitutes and a no-good hillbilly family, but none of it feels like an empty stereotype.... Combined with Brown's knack for romantic tension and page-turning suspense, [*Blind Tiger*] is a winner."
—*BOOKLIST,* STARRED REVIEW

"BROWN HAS FEW TO ENVY AMONG LIVING AUTHORS."
—*Kirkus*

"A MASTERFUL STORYTELLER." —*USA TODAY*

PRAISE FOR *BLIND TIGER* AND #1 *NEW YORK TIMES* BESTSELLING AUTHOR SANDRA BROWN

"Set in 1920, this superior thriller from bestseller Brown firmly anchors all the action in the plot.... Laurel and Thatcher are strong and inventive characters, and their surprising decisions and evolving relationship will keep readers engaged. Brown shows why she remains in the top rank of her field." —*Publishers Weekly*, starred review

"Brown doesn't often delve into historical fiction territory, but she does here with gusto, and readers will practically taste the dusty streets of Foley and feel every rickety bump of the moonshiners' trucks. There are shoot-outs and reformed prostitutes and a no-good hillbilly family, but none of it feels like an empty stereotype—it's just all a lot of fun. Combined with Brown's knack for romantic tension and page-turning suspense, [*Blind Tiger*] is a winner." —*Booklist*, starred review

"A thrill ride... The historical nature of [*Blind Tiger*] regarding the West Texas setting, the Texas Rangers, and how Prohibition made criminals out of those just wanting a beer is intriguing."

—BookReporter.com

"*Blind Tiger* is a winner." —AARP

"[Brown] is a masterful storyteller, carefully crafting tales that keep readers on the edge of their seats." —*USA Today*

"Suspense that has teeth." —Stephen King

"Sandra Brown proves herself top-notch." —Associated Press

"Brown deserves her own genre." —*Dallas Morning News*

"Bold and bracing hard-boiled crime thriller *Thick as Thieves* [is] perhaps [Sandra Brown's] most ambitious and best-realized effort ever....A tale steeped in noir and nuance that's utterly riveting from the first page to the last." —*Providence Journal*

"A novelist who can't write them fast enough."
—*San Antonio Express-News*

"Brown's storytelling gift is surprisingly rare." —*Toronto Sun*

"Sandra Brown is a publishing icon." —*New York Journal of Books*

"*Outfox* is packed with suspense and love. It is an extraordinarily satisfying and entertaining novel." —*Washington Book Review*

"Sandra Brown just might have penned her best and most ambitious book ever, a tale that evokes the work of the likes of Don DeLillo, Greg Iles, and Robert Stone....*Seeing Red* is an exceptional thriller in every sense of the word, a classic treatment of the costs of heroism and the nature of truth itself. Not to be missed." —*Providence Journal*

"Brown's novels define the term 'page-turner.'" —*Booklist*

"Sandra Brown is a master at weaving a story of suspense into a tight web that catches and holds the reader from the first page to the last."
—*Library Journal*

"Brown has few to envy among living authors." —*Kirkus*

"No one does it better than Brown." —*Romantic Times*

"A master of the page-turning suspense novel." —*Connecticut News*

BLIND TIGER

BLIND TIGER

TIGER

SANDRA BROWN

GRAND CENTRAL
PUBLISHING

NEW YORK   BOSTON

Copyright © 2021 by Sandra Brown Management, Ltd.

Cover design by Anna Dorfman
Cover photos: man © Magdalena Russocka / Trevillion; woman © Jeff Cottenden; door and floor © Allotment Boy 1 / Alamy; lantern from Getty; bar, table, liquor bottles, rifle, and smoke from Shutterstock
Cover copyright © 2022 by Hachette Book Group, Inc.

Grand Central Publishing
Hachette Book Group
1290 Avenue of the Americas, New York, NY 10104
grandcentralpublishing.com
twitter.com/grandcentralpub

Originally published in hardcover and ebook by Grand Central Publishing in August 2021
First trade paperback edition: March 2022

Grand Central Publishing is a division of Hachette Book Group, Inc. The Grand Central Publishing name and logo is a trademark of Hachette Book Group, Inc.

The publisher is not responsible for websites (or their content) that are not owned by the publisher.

The Hachette Speakers Bureau provides a wide range of authors for speaking events. To find out more, go to www.hachettespeakersbureau.com or call (866) 376-6591.

Library of Congress Control Number: 2021939235

ISBNs: 978-1-5387-5197-8 (trade paperback), 978-1-5387-5198-5 (ebook)

Printed in the United States of America

LSC-C

Printing 1, 2022

To my family—Michael, Rachel, Ryan, Pete, Raff, Luke, Lawson, and Cash. Thank you for your unwavering forbearance, encouragement, and love. You are the heroes and heroine of my heart.

BLIND
TIGER

ONE

March 1920

W on't be much longer."

Derby had been telling her that for the past two hours. He said the same four words at intervals that had become so regular she could now predict, to within a minute, the next repetition. His tone was terse and emphatic, as though he were trying to convince himself.

Laurel had stopped responding because whatever she said, he took as an affront. He sat hunched over the steering wheel, his shoulders stacked with so much tension they were nearly touching his earlobes.

They had gotten a late start, not leaving Sherman until past noon. Since the day had been half gone, and daylight with it, she had suggested they wait until tomorrow to set out, but Derby had stubbornly stuck to his plan.

"My old man's expecting us. I didn't spend good money on a telegram telling him when we were coming, only to be no-shows."

It wasn't a trip to be making with an infant just barely a month old. She certainly hadn't expected to be uprooted with only a few hours' notice. But here they were, Derby, her, and baby Pearl, driving through the night. The farther they traveled, the more concerned she became about their welfare.

Derby had told her that his father lived roughly a hundred and fifty miles southwest of Sherman. He had showed her on a map the route they would take. Until today, she had never been on a road trip in an automobile, but she hadn't counted on it taking the six-plus hours they'd been traveling to cover a hundred and fifty miles.

She was huddled inside her coat, the lower half of her face wrapped in a muffler, a cap hugging her head. But even bundled up as she was, she had kept careful track of the highway signs. Freezing precipitation made them difficult to spot unless the T-model's one working headlight caught them at a good angle. They were still on the right highway, but how much farther could it possibly be?

Or maybe, in order to avoid a quarrel, Derby had fudged on the distance.

To be fair, though, neither of them had counted on the abrupt change in the weather. North Texas had enjoyed a reasonably mild winter through Christmas and New Year, but the *Farmer's Almanac* had predicted a spring that would be colder than usual, with hard freezes expected well into mid-March. This was day two of the month, and it had come in like a lion.

They'd just reached the western outskirts of Dallas when the norther had caught up to them. The leading gust of frigid air had broadsided the Tin Lizzy like a runaway freight train.

She wouldn't be surprised to learn that that first buffet had left a dent in the car door. Not that another dent would be noticed. It was already banged up.

The day Derby had driven the car home, she had been flabbergasted by his impulsiveness. When she'd asked where he'd gotten it, he'd told her about a former war buddy who lived in a town nearby.

"He hadn't been in France a month when the poor bastard lost his left leg clean up to here." He'd made a slice across his groin. "Can't work the pedals to drive. He let me have this beauty for a song."

They didn't have a *song*, but she hadn't pointed that out, because, in that boastful moment, some of Derby's rakish charm, which had attracted her to him in the first place, had resurfaced.

He'd swung open the passenger door and made a sweeping gesture with his arm as he bowed. "Your chariot awaits, Miz Plummer." He'd winked and grinned, and she'd seen a flash of the dashing young man who had marched off to fight the Great War, rather than the quarrelsome stranger who had returned from it.

She'd seized on his sudden lightheartedness and had giggled helplessly as he'd driven them through town going faster than he should and needlessly honking at everything and everybody, making her laugh harder. He'd seemed mindless of the jostling, until one pothole sent her bouncing so hard in her seat, she placed her hands protectively over her belly.

"Careful of those chuckholes or the baby might pop out of me like a cork from a bottle."

She had gone into labor that very night. By three o'clock the following afternoon, she was a mother and Derby a father. That had been four weeks ago.

At first Derby had been prideful and happy and solicitous to her and their baby girl. But the newness of fatherhood had soon worn off, and the grinning man who'd taken her on the joy ride retreated once more behind a perpetual scowl she couldn't allay.

In the thirty or so days since Pearl's entrance into the world, Derby had lost another job. He'd spent a lot of time away from the house and snapped at her whenever she'd inquired where he'd been. In a heartbeat, he would become testy and short-tempered. She never knew what to expect.

During supper last evening, out of the clear blue, he'd announced, "We're moving to Foley." He'd avoided looking at her by keeping his head bent over his meal.

Afraid to overreact, she'd blotted her mouth with her napkin. "I think I've heard of it. Isn't it near—"

"It's not *near* anything. But my old man's found me work out there."

She had actually felt a spark of hopefulness. "Really? That's wonderful. Doing what?"

"Does it matter? He's expecting us tomorrow."

The floor, none too level already, had seemed to undulate beneath her chair. "Tomorrow?"

Pearl was a fussy baby who demanded to be nursed several times a night. For a month, Laurel hadn't slept for more than a couple of hours at a time. She was exhausted, worried about Derby's state of mind, worried about their shortage of money, and now . . . this.

Leaving half his supper uneaten, he'd shoved back his chair, left the table, and lifted his jacket off the peg near the back door. "Pack tonight. I want to get away early."

"Wait, Derby. We can't just . . ." Words had failed her. "Sit back down. Please. We need to talk about this."

"What's to talk about?"

She gaped at him with bafflement. "Everything. Do we have a place to live?"

"I wouldn't up and move you and the baby without having a plan, would I?"

"It just seems awfully sudden."

"Well, it's not. I've been thinking on it for a time."

"You should have talked it over with me."

"I'm talking it over with you now."

His raised voice had caused Pearl to flinch where she lay asleep in Laurel's lap. Laurel had lifted her to her shoulder and patted her back. Derby's expression had turned impatient, but whether at her, the baby, or himself, she'd been unable to tell.

"I've got some things to see to before we clear town. Rent's due on this place the day after tomorrow. I'll leave notice of our departure in the landlord's mailbox." He'd reached for the doorknob.

"Derby, hold on." She'd gone over to him. "I welcome the idea of us making a fresh start. I just want it to be a good fresh start. Thought through, not so rushed."

"I told you, I have been thinking on it."

"But making a move to another town seems drastic. When you talked to Mr. Davis, he told you that he might have an opening at his store soon."

"Scooping chicken feed into tow sacks?" He'd made a sour face. "No thanks."

"Something else could—"

"There's nothing for me here, Laurel. Anyway, it's decided. We're leaving." He'd pulled open the door and said over his shoulder as he went out, "You'd better get started packing."

He hadn't returned home until after two o'clock in the morning, disheveled and red-eyed, reeking of bootleg whiskey, too drunk to stand without support. When he'd stumbled into the bedroom, he'd propped himself against the doorjamb and blearily focused on her where she'd sat in the rocking chair next to the bed, nursing Pearl.

"Things ready?" he'd asked in a mumble.

Their duplex had rented furnished, so there hadn't been much to pack except for their clothing and her personal possessions, which were few in number and didn't amount to anything.

In answer to his question, she'd motioned to the two suitcases lying open on the floor. She'd carefully folded his army uniform and laid it on top.

Laurel had eased Pearl away from her breast and tucked it back inside her nightgown. "Couldn't we give this decision a week, talk it over some more?"

"I'm sick of talking." He'd staggered to the bed, crawled onto it, and passed out.

He'd slept late, and had been irritable and hungover when he woke up. Laurel had wished he'd forgotten about their departure, about the whole harebrained idea. But he'd fortified himself with several cups of strong coffee and a dozen hand-rolled cigarettes, and by the time she'd packed them a lunch with what food was left in the icebox, Derby was impatient to be off.

While he was loading their suitcases, putting one in the trunk and strapping down the other on top of it, she'd walked through the duplex one final time, checking to see that nothing belonging to them had been overlooked.

Derby had hung his army uniform back in the closet.

The top on the Ford was up, which kept some of the frozen precipitation off them, but it was open-air. During the whole trip, Laurel had kept Pearl clutched to her chest inside her coat, inside her dress, wanting to be skin-to-skin with her. She was afraid the baby would freeze to death and she wouldn't even know it because she was so numb with cold herself. But Pearl had nursed well her last feeding, and her breath had remained reassuringly humid and warm.

"Won't be much longer."

Laurel held her tongue.

This time, Derby added, "A crossroads is up ahead. He's only a few miles past that."

However, beyond the crossroads, the road narrowed and the pavement gave way to gravel. The surrounding darkness was unrelieved except for the faulty headlight that blinked intermittently like a distress signal from a foundering ship.

So when Laurel caught a flicker of light out of the corner of her right eye, she first thought it was the headlight reflecting off pellets of blowing sleet.

But she squinted through the precipitation and then gave a soft cry of desperate hope. "Derby? Could that be his place?"

"Where?"

"Up there. I thought I saw a light."

He slowed down and looked in the direction she indicated. "Gotta be," he muttered.

He put the car in low gear and turned onto a dirt track formed by tire treads. The sleet made it look like it had been salted. The Model T ground its way up the incline.

At the higher elevation, the north wind was vicious. Howling, it lashed against the car as Derby brought it to a stop.

Whatever relief Laurel might have felt evaporated when she saw the dwelling beyond the windshield. It could be described only as a shack. Light seeped through vertical slits in the walls made of weathered lumber. On the south side of the structure, the roof steeply sloped downward and formed an extension that provided cover for stacked firewood.

She didn't say anything, and Derby avoided looking at her. He pushed open the driver's door against the fierce wind and climbed out. A fan of light spread onto the ground in front of him as the door to the shack came open.

Derby's father was silhouetted, so Laurel couldn't make out his features, but she was heartened by the welcoming tone of his voice as he shouted into the wind, "I'd 'bout given up on you." He waved Derby forward.

Less enthusiastically, Derby approached his father and shook hands. They exchanged a few words, which Laurel couldn't hear. Derby's father jerked his head backward, then he leaned to one side in order to see around Derby and peered at the car.

Derby did a quick about-face, came over to the passenger door, opened it, and motioned Laurel out. "Hurry. It's cold."

Her legs almost gave out beneath her when she stepped onto the ground. Derby took her elbow and closed the car door. Together they made their way to the open doorway, where her father-in-law had stepped aside for them.

Derby hustled her inside, then firmly shut the door.

The wind continued to roar. Or, Laurel wondered, was the roaring in her ears actually caused by the sudden silence, or her weariness and gnawing hunger? All that, she assumed. Plus the alarming and humiliating realization that she and Pearl had not been expected.

"Daddy, this is my wife, Laurel. I'll get the suitcases." With no more ceremony than that, Derby left them.

There was little resemblance between Derby and his father, who was half a head shorter and didn't have Derby's lanky build. The crescent of his baldness was so precise it could have been traced from a pattern.

The hair around it was wiry and gray and grew straight out from his head like brush bristles. His eyebrows looked like twin caterpillars stuck to his forehead.

They assessed each other. She said, "Mr. Plummer." Clearing her throat of self-conscious scratchiness, she added, "Pleased to meet you."

"Laurel, he said?"

"Yes, sir."

"We're kin now, so I 'spect you ought to drop the sir and call me Irv."

She gave him a faint smile, and some of the tension in her chest eased. Pearl squirmed inside her coat, drawing his notice.

"That the baby? What's its name?"

Laurel unbuttoned her coat, lifted Pearl out, and transferred her to the crook of her elbow. "Her name is Pearl."

He didn't step closer, but tentatively leaned forward and inspected what he could see of Pearl, which wasn't much, swaddled as she was, and considering the meager light provided by a kerosene lantern that hung from a hook in the low ceiling.

He appeared to be pleased enough with his granddaughter, because he smiled. But all he said was, "Well, how 'bout that?"

Then he turned away and went over to a potbellied stove. Laurel noticed that he favored his left leg, making his bowlegged gait even more lopsided. He opened the door to the stove and tossed in two split logs he took from the stack of firewood against the wall.

He came back around, dusting his hands. "Y'all are hungry, I 'spect. I've got a rabbit fried up. Fresh killed and dressed this morning. I've kept a batch of biscuits warm. I was waiting till Derby got here to make the gravy."

Laurel's stomach had been growling for the past several hours, but to be polite, she said, "I hate that you've gone to so much trouble."

"No trouble. Coffee's—"

The door burst open, and Derby came in with their suitcases. He dropped them at his sides and pushed the door closed with his heel.

Irv said to him, "Move over there closer to the stove. I'll pour y'all some coffee."

"Got any hooch? Or are you abiding by the new law of the land, even though it's horseshit?"

Looking displeased by his son's crudity, Irv glanced at Laurel, then walked over to a small chest that had only three legs. In place of the missing one was a stack of catalogues with faded, curled, dusty covers. He grunted as he went down on his right knee. He opened the bottom drawer, reached far back into it, and came out with a mason jar that was two-thirds full of clear liquid.

As he heaved himself up, he said, "Sometimes my hip gets to bothering me so's I can't sleep. A nip of 'shine helps."

Derby reached for the jar without so much as a thank you. He uncapped it and took a swig. The corn liquor must've seared his gullet. When he lowered the jar, his eyes were watering.

Laurel was already furious at him. Weren't their present circumstances dreadful enough without his getting drunk? She didn't conceal the resentment in her voice when she told him she needed the necessary.

Irv said, "Around back, twenty paces or so. You can lay the baby down over there." He nodded toward a mattress on the floor in the corner. "Take a lantern, Derby."

Laurel didn't want to leave Pearl, but not having any choice, she laid her on the mattress. The ticking looked reasonably clean compared to the hard-packed dirt floor. She wrapped the baby tightly in her blankets, hoping that a varmint wouldn't crawl into them before she returned.

Between taking sips of moonshine, Derby had lit a lantern. Bracing herself for the brutal cold, Laurel followed him out. It had started to snow, and it was sticking.

She was glad Derby was with her to help her find her way, but she was too angry to speak to him. She went into the foul-smelling outhouse and relieved herself as quickly as she could.

When she emerged, Derby passed the lantern to her. "Get back inside. I'm gonna have a smoke."

"It's freezing out here."

"I'm gonna have a smoke."

"And finish that?" she said, glaring at the fruit jar.

"I'm sick of you nagging me about every goddamn thing."

"As if things aren't bad enough, you're going to get skunk drunk?"

He smirked. "Thought I would." He raised the jar to his mouth, but she slapped it aside, almost knocking it out of his hand.

"Do as I tell you, Laurel. Go inside."

"Your daddy didn't know about Pearl and me, did he?" When he just stared back at her, she shouted, "Did he?"

"No."

Even though she wasn't surprised, hearing him admit it caused her to see red. "How could you do this to me, Derby? To Pearl? To all of us? Why in the world did you bring us here?"

"I had to do something with you first."

"First?"

"You'll thank me later."

He produced a pistol from the pocket of his coat, put it beneath his chin, and pulled the trigger.

TWO

Laurel's father-in-law waited until daylight and the worst of the storm had blown itself out to notify the authorities. Before leaving for town, he made her swear that she would stay inside the shack while he was gone. Listlessly, she agreed to remain inside, having no desire to subject herself to see in the dreary, gray daylight what she had beheld in darkness.

She hadn't even known that Derby owned a pistol.

In Irv's absence, she sat on the mattress near the potbellied stove, where she had endured the long night, benumbed by what Derby had done. She'd held Pearl to her the entire time, her infant being the only thing that seemed real, the one thing she could cling to in this ongoing nightmare.

She couldn't even take comfort in fond memories of Derby. Those she'd cherished had died with him. They'd been obliterated by what would be her final memory of him.

She resented him for that.

Irv returned, followed by the sheriff and the justice of the peace. They came into the shack and spoke to her briefly, but there was little she could say that would make the circumstances any clearer than the gore they'd seen splashed onto the door of the outhouse.

After Derby's body had been removed and taken to the funeral parlor, Irv dismantled the outhouse and burned it. By the early dusk, he had built another enclosure. He probably wouldn't have been so industrious on the day after his son's suicide if it hadn't been for the privacy Laurel required.

Now, less than twenty-four hours after meeting her father-in-law, they were alone in the shack, except for Pearl. He was at the cookstove, preparing food she didn't think she could eat, but knew she must in order to sustain Pearl.

"Thank you for replacing the outhouse."

"Easier to start over than try to clean the old one. He'd made a goddamn mess."

Softly she said, "He wasn't right in his mind."

He turned away from the stove and looked over at her. "Shell shock?"

"I suppose. A light had gone out inside him, and it never came back on. I thought he would get better as time passed. I tried to help him, but he wouldn't even talk about it."

Irv dragged one hand down his creased face. "He was like that after his mama died. Shut down, like. He ever tell you about that?"

"No."

"TB got her. Derby was seven, eight. Had to watch her decline, then die. That's tough on a kid." He paused, lost in thought, then cleared his throat. "After she passed, I couldn't earn a living and look after him at the same time. I had no choice but to put him in a home. For what it was, it was a nice place. Subsidized by the railroad. I'd go see him whenever I could, but..."

He raised his shoulders. "He never forgave me for leaving him. Soon as he was old enough, he went his own way. I'd hear from him off and on. Mostly off. But it seemed to me like he'd found himself again and was doing all right. Then the war came along. If it was as bad as they say, it's a wonder any one of them who survived it haven't done what he did."

He heaved a sigh that invoked Laurel's pity. The wretched memory of Derby's death would stay with Irv until his own final breath.

"Can I help you there?" she asked.

"No thanks. I'm just making some gravy for that rabbit we didn't eat last night. It's almost ready."

Pearl was sleeping peacefully on the mattress. She probably needed to be changed, but in the process, she would wake up. Right now, it was better for Laurel, as well as for the baby, that she remain asleep. Because Laurel needed time to think.

She was viewing her life as a spool of ribbon that had gotten away from her, rolling out of her reach, unwinding rapidly and haphazardly, and she was powerless to stop it.

She shivered, as much from despair as from the cold air that seeped through the cracks in the walls of the shack. She hadn't removed her coat since she arrived. Shoving her hands deep into its pockets, she said, "Right before he...did it...Derby admitted that he hadn't told you about me and Pearl."

Irv set down the long spoon he was using and turned toward her. "He didn't even tell me he'd survived the war."

Derby and she had still been in a honeymoon haze when he had left for overseas. She would have gone crazy if she hadn't received periodic letters from him. Usually they were filled with cryptic references to his misery, but at least she'd known that he was alive. Learning that Derby hadn't extended his father that courtesy made her heartsick for the old man.

"That was terribly thoughtless of him."

"I got one letter telling me he'd been drafted and was going to Europe to kill Huns. I moved around a lot for work, so he'd been long gone by the time that letter caught up with me.

"Armistice came and went without a word from him. I took that as a bad sign, but the military is supposed to let folks back home know when their loved one has fallen or is missing, right?

"So I went up to Camp Bowie, where he'd been stationed before shipping out. After a lot of rigamarole and sorting through red tape, I was told he'd made it back stateside. His last paycheck from the army had been mailed to a post office box in Sherman. I wrote to him there just to tell him where I'd lit in case he ever wanted to find me."

He took in the rustic interior of the shack, as though seeing it from her perspective for the first time. She followed the track of his eyes. Cobwebs laced the rafters that were blackened from age and smoke. A cowhide that looked like it had mange was nailed to the north wall. She supposed that it wasn't so much for decoration as to keep out the elements. The flue of the potbellied stove was piecemeal, forming a leaky and crooked outlet to the hole in the ceiling.

"Ain't much," he said.

Laurel didn't detect any degree of humility or apology in that statement, and she couldn't help but admire him for that.

He gave the simmering gravy a stir. "I didn't hear anything from Derby until the telegram office sent a boy out here day before yesterday. All it said was that he was coming. Nothing more."

Laurel dug at a crack in the dirt floor with the toe of her shoe. "There was no job, no work waiting for him, was there?"

He shifted his weight, redistributing it unevenly, placing more on the right side of his body. "There's work around."

"Of what kind?"

"Same as me."

"Forgive me, Mr. Plummer, but—"

"Irv."

"Irv. What kind of work do you do?"

"I was a railroad man. Over thirty years at it. Went all over, repairing tracks. That's how I got the bum hip." He patted his left leg joint. "Coupler backed into it. Didn't stop me from working, though. Just made it harder.

"But I got old and tired, so I stopped railroading several years ago and settled into this place. Now I do odd jobs in and around town." He looked over at her with something of a grin. "I guess you could say I'm a fix-it man."

"Are there enough things around here that need fixing to keep you busy?" *And solvent?* She wanted to ask that, but didn't.

"I'm stretched pretty thin, all right." He set tin plates and cutlery on the small table, which was not much larger than a checkerboard.

"How much had Derby told you about me? Not much good, I reckon."

"He hadn't told me anything except that you were still living, as far as he knew. He said the two of you weren't close."

He gave a sad nod. "Well, then at least that didn't come as a shock to you."

"What caused the rift?"

He pursed his lips thoughtfully, then said, "His mama died young." He gave the gravy another stir. "What about you? Is your family up in North Texas?"

"Yes. My daddy and uncle grow cotton. Or did. The last three crops got ruined by the boll weevil."

"You'll want to notify your folks of this."

She took a breath, wishing she could postpone this, but reasoned that he needed to know sooner rather than later. "We don't speak."

He came around and studied her for a moment, then asked, "Was it Derby that split y'all up?" He must've seen the answer in her expression, because he said, "Figured."

"The blame wasn't all his. The split was my daddy's doing. He's a hard man. He disapproved of Derby's sinful ways."

"Drinking and dancing?"

She huffed a laugh. "To my daddy's mind, even a game of dominoes will send you to hell. Derby enjoyed egging him on. One day Daddy had enough and put his foot down. He told me that Derby's sinfulness was rubbing off on me, and that if I married him, no one in my family would be allowed to utter my name again. Not ever. It would be as though I'd never been born."

She gazed down at her sleeping daughter, relieved that her stern, intolerant father would never exercise any influence over her. "Fine, I told him. I didn't want to be a member of a family so wrathful and unloving. Both of us meant what we said. Mama, of course, had to go along with Daddy."

Her mother's plight made Laurel sad. She'd been cowed into letting Laurel go without a quibble. But there was no help for that. Her mother, taking seriously her submissive role, had made her bed, and she would die in it.

Suddenly it occurred to Laurel that she unwittingly had been taking that same path. If she hadn't yielded to Derby's irrational decision, hadn't gone dumbly along for harmony's sake, she wouldn't be in this predicament.

Her father-in-law was saying, "Maybe after what's happened, your folks will take you back. I'm happy to drive you up there—"

"No," she said swiftly and firmly. "Thank you for offering, but I won't go back."

Irv rubbed his bristly chin, looked down at Pearl, then at Laurel. "Well then, looks like you're stayin'."

THREE

May 1920

T hatcher had worn out his welcome.

He knew it, although he tried not to act like he did. He lay on his back, using his duffel bag as a pillow, fingers linked over his stomach, fedora covering his face.

He pretended to be asleep. He was far from it. He was acutely aware of everything going on inside the boxcar, the atmosphere of which had turned ripe to the stinking point with hostility.

Beneath him, the wheels of the train rhythmically clickety-clacked over the rails, but their noisy cadence didn't drown out the snores of the three men sharing the freight car with him. Thatcher didn't trust their snorts and snuffles. They were too irregular and loud. Like him, they were playing possum, waiting for an opportunity to spring.

The door to the car had been left partially open to provide them fresh air. The gap was no wider than a few feet. Three, four at best. Once he made his move, he couldn't hesitate. He would get only one chance, so, within a second or two of moving, he'd have to make a clean jump through that slim gap.

If he didn't make it out, a fight was inevitable. Three against one. Bad odds in any contest. Until fate had put them together on this train, they'd been strangers to him and to one another. But last night, somewhere between coastal Louisiana and wherever they were now, the other three had become unified against him.

The last thing he wanted was a damned fight. He'd fought in one. A bloody one. He'd been on the winning side of it, but victory hadn't felt as glorious as people had let on. To his mind, the loss of so many men and women wasn't a fit reason to hold parades.

No, he wouldn't welcome a fight, but if he had to defend himself, he would, and he wouldn't fight fair. He hadn't cheated death in France to die in this railroad car that reeked of its cargo of yellow onions and unwashed men.

One advantage the other three had over him was that they weren't new to riding freights. He was the amateur. But he'd listened to their idle conversation, had paid attention, had sifted the facts out of the bullshit.

They'd jawed about the stationmasters who were charitable and looked the other way when they spotted a hobo, and others who were die-hard company men, "by-the-rules sons o' bitches" who were well known up and down the line for showing no mercy to men they caught hitching a ride.

Thatcher's plan had been to wait until the train began to slow on the outskirts of the next town and to get off before it reached the depot, in case the stationmaster there happened to be one of the less tenderhearted.

But these men, who were seasoned in the art, were probably expecting him to do just that. No doubt *their* plan was to jump him before he could jump from the train.

They were on a track that cut across the broad breast of Texas where towns were few and far between. But within the last few minutes, Thatcher had decided that no matter how desolate the landscape was where he landed, it would be safer than staying in this boxcar and at the mercy of men who didn't have anything left to lose.

Jumping from a moving train couldn't be much worse than being thrown from a horse, could it? He'd been pitched off too many times to count. But he'd never been thrown when it was full dark, when he didn't know his exact location or where his next drink of water would come from.

How long till daylight? He didn't dare check his wristwatch. The army invention was still a novelty to folks who hadn't been issued one during the war. He didn't want to draw attention by consulting the time, which would be a giveaway that he was awake and planning a departure.

As unobtrusively as possible, he used his index finger to raise his hat just far enough to gauge the degree of darkness beyond the opening. Since the last time he'd sneaked a look, the rectangular gap had turned from solid black to dull gray.

Moving only his gaze, he looked toward the men who were a short distance away, lying at various angles to each other. Two were snoring loudly, feigning sleep. One, Thatcher could tell, was watching him through slitted eyelids. Thatcher lowered his finger from the underside of the brim. His hat resettled over his face.

He forced himself to breathe evenly while he counted to sixty. Then in one motion, he lurched to his feet as he popped his hat onto his head and grabbed his duffel bag by the strap. He made it to the opening and hurled his bag out.

Just as he was about to spring, one of the men grabbed his sleeve from behind.

Shit!

Thatcher came around and swung his fist toward the guy's head, but he saw it coming, ducked, and held on to Thatcher's sleeve like a bulldog. Out the corner of his eye, he saw another approaching in a crouch, making wide swipes with a knife.

The man holding on to him threw a punch that caught Thatcher in the ribs. He retaliated by chopping the guy across the throat with the side of his hand. His attacker let go of his sleeve and staggered backward, holding his throat with both hands and wheezing.

Thatcher spun around to the one with the knife. He had less than a second to throw up his hand to protect his face from being slashed. The sharp blade sliced across his palm. Thatcher yelped.

The hobo grinned and charged. With his good hand, Thatcher

caught hold of the vertical iron handle on the door and kicked the knifer in the balls. Dropping the knife, he screamed in agony, grabbed himself, dropped to his knees, then fell onto his side. Thatcher picked up the knife. The third in the group was poised to attack. Thatcher, winded, his cut hand hurting like bloody hell, said, "Call it quits why don't you?"

But the tramp didn't listen. He came up on his toes, preparing to lunge. Thatcher threw the knife end over end. The point pierced through the man's right shoe, nailing his foot to the floor of the boxcar.

Thatcher turned and made a blind leap through the opening. As he went airborne, howled obscenities trailed him into the predawn light as the train rumbled on.

He landed on his feet, but his knees buckled at the jarring impact. Unable to break his fall, he tumbled down the incline, cussing the pounding he was taking from boulders and stumps.

On one of his revolutions, he recognized the shape of a large agave, dead ahead and coming up fast. As he slid downhill toward it, he dug in his heels. They kicked up loose rocks and grit that struck him in the face, but he was able to stop within inches of being impaled by one of the plant's barbed spines.

As the dust settled around him, he took mental stock of himself and determined that none of his limbs hurt bad enough to have been broken. His breathing was hard and fast, but it didn't hurt to suck in air, so no busted or sprained ribs despite the blow he'd taken on one side. He wasn't dizzy, didn't feel like puking.

Accepting that he was basically all right except for his throbbing palm, adrenaline seemed to leak from his pores like sweat. He stayed as he was, lying there on his back, taking in his expansive and unobstructed view of the sky. It was turning paler by the second, causing the panoply of stars to dim, and he thought what a hell of a thing it was that he was still alive and could admire that sky.

Then, as only one who had slept standing up in a trench while rats scuttled across his blood-soaked boots could do, he dropped into a deep sleep.

He woke up to an early sun, but kept his eyes closed against its brightness, basking in the clean warmth of it on his face. He savored the stillness of the ground beneath him. He'd been unsteadily rocking for two days in that mother-lovin' boxcar. It had been almost as bad as the merchant marine freighter requisitioned and re-outfitted to ship troops home from Europe. If he never saw the Atlantic again, or a wave stronger than a ripple in a stock pond, it would be fine with him.

After several minutes, he sat up. His vision was still clear, and he wasn't dizzy, although he had taken a clout to the head during his downhill plunge. A goose egg had formed on his right temple at his hairline.

He took a handkerchief from his pocket and used it to wipe the blood away from the cut across his palm. It wasn't all that deep, but it made his hand ache. He wrapped the handkerchief around it.

By the position of the sun, he figured out the directions. The landscape was dominated by rugged limestone outcroppings, some bare, some with live oak trees or cedar breaks seeming to grow straight out of the rock. Scrub brush, like that wicked-looking agave, dotted the shallow topsoil.

He figured he was somewhere in the hill country. Still hundreds of miles from home.

He stood up and dusted himself off as best he could, then climbed the incline back to the tracks. The wind was southerly and warm, but strong. It had blown his hat off when he'd made the jump, but miraculously it was still there, lying in the railbed.

He clamped it onto his head and pulled the brim down low over his eyes, then started walking along the tracks in the direction from which the train had come, until he reunited with his duffel bag.

Shouldering it, he reversed his direction and continued in the northwesterly direction the train had been traveling. He saw no indication that a settlement of any kind was anywhere close. He didn't even see a road. The only living things he spotted were a small herd of cattle on a distant hill, and three buzzards, circling their breakfast. Or what soon would be their breakfast.

His stomach was gnawing at its own emptiness, but the only food left in his duffel were a few saltine crackers and the last of a hunk of cheddar. Eating them would make him thirsty, so he decided to hold off until he found water.

He hiked along the tracks for an hour before he reached a crossing. A gravel road ran north and south perpendicular to the tracks, extending for seeming miles in both directions without a turnoff. He took the northern route, hoping that he wouldn't have to hoof it for too long before someone came along who would give him a lift.

The road was easier to walk on than the railbed, but the sky was cloudless, and the sun grew hotter than what you'd expect in mid-May. He shucked off his jacket and draped it over the duffel bag, unbuttoned the cuffs of his shirt and rolled them up.

Sighting a thin trail of smoke rising from behind one of the hills, he was tempted to go in search of the source. A ranch house, or even a campsite, could provide him with a drink of water.

But the smoke was swiftly dispersed by the high wind, so he couldn't be certain how far away it was, and he was reluctant to go exploring off the beaten path. He was no stranger to living without a roof over his head, but he wasn't equipped to do so now.

He estimated he'd walked three or four miles before he spotted a structure on the crest of a rise. At first it was only a dark dot, but the closer he got, it began to take shape. He smelled wood smoke, even though he didn't see any coming from the flue sticking out of the roof at an angle. A Model T was parked in front, along with a truck that looked like a junkyard on wheels.

The place didn't look hospitable, but somebody was at home, and he was damned thirsty.

He started up the dirt lane. As he got closer to the house, he saw that it wasn't a house at all, but a line shack, as ill-kempt a one as he'd ever seen. It must belong to a slipshod outfit that instilled no sense of pride in the cowboys who worked for it.

However, it was no cowboy in the yard, but a young woman who was wrestling with a wet bedsheet. She was trying to get it onto a makeshift clothesline strung between the back corner of the shack and the outhouse. The strong wind was hampering her effort, but she was putting up a fight.

He said, "The sheet is winning."

FOUR

=◉=

At the sound of his voice, she spun around, looking at him wide-eyed, her hand slapping against her chest where her breath seemed to have become trapped.

"I'm sorry. I didn't mean to scare you." Thatcher took off his hat.

She recovered enough to close her mouth. In the process of hastily gathering up the flapping sheet, a corner of it dragged through the dirt, which made her frown. She dropped the sheet back into a cauldron of water, obviously her wash pot. As she wiped her wet palms on the skirt of her dress, she looked beyond him toward the road.

Coming back to him, she said, "Who are you?"

"My name's Thatcher Hutton."

"How'd you get here?"

"Train."

"There's no depot within miles of here. Why was the train stopped?"

"It wasn't. I jumped off."

Knowing what that implied about him, she raised her hand and shaded her eyes against the sun as she regarded him with even more wariness. "Out in the middle of nowhere?"

"It was the lesser of two evils."

"What was the other one?"

"The men sharing the boxcar with me bore a grudge."

The admission didn't earn him her favor. "So I see." She looked pointedly at the goose egg on his temple and his bandaged hand. She squared her shoulders and motioned him toward the road. "Well, you lived to tell of it. Get on now."

"I've walked several miles, and your place here is the first sign of civilization I've seen. What's the nearest town?"

"Foley."

He'd heard of it, but had never been there. But he hadn't been much of anywhere before the war. "How far is it?"

"Five miles."

Tapping his hat against his leg, he glanced over his shoulder at the road. "Five, huh?"

"At least."

"I don't suppose you'd be going that way any time soon." He glanced toward the vehicles.

"No. Maybe you should've stayed on the train."

"No, I needed to jump off."

"How many of them were there?"

"In the boxcar? Three."

"How did you get crosswise with them?"

"They got sore at me for taking their money."

"You stole their money?"

He shook his head. "Won at cards."

"Did you cheat?"

"No."

She made a scoffing sound, expressing doubt.

"It's true. I have a knack."

Still frowning with skepticism, she raised her arm and pointed toward the road. "Go north about three miles. At the crossroads go east. It's a state highway that leads straight to town and becomes Main Street."

"Thank you."

"You're welcome. Now move along."

"Could you spare me a drink of water first?"

She glanced toward the shack, seemed to debate it, then tilted her head. "Back here."

He set his duffel on the ground and piled his coat and hat on top of it. She led him past a chicken coop that looked relatively new. Two hens were inside it, nesting. A rooster, strutting outside the coop, ruffled his feathers and challenged him and the woman with an aggressive beating of his wings. She told him to shoo or he'd find himself in a stewpot.

On the back side of the shack, a rough wood bench leaned lengthwise against the exterior wall. A bucket of water was sitting on it, a dented metal ladle hanging on a nail above it.

"Help yourself."

"Thanks."

He lifted the ladle off the nail, dipped it into the bucket, and brought it to his mouth. The water was tepid but it was wet. He wanted to gulp but drank slowly in order to study her.

Her dress was baggy, indicating that either it was a hand-me-down from a woman of more substance or that there used to be more to her than there was now. There was nothing wrong with her shape, though. He'd noticed that each time the wind bonded the ill-fitting dress to her slender frame.

Her hair was honey-colored, lighter around her face, and pulled into a bun worn low on the back of her head. The wind had pulled strands loose, which seemed to aggravate her because she kept impatiently trying to tuck them back in.

In fact, her whole aspect was one of agitation. She was strung up a whole lot tighter than her clothesline.

Before he finished drinking, she lost patience. "I've got to get back to my wash."

He drained the ladle and replaced it on the nail. "Much obliged."

"You're welcome." She turned around and started back the way they'd come. He fell into step behind her. They were nearing the corner of the shack when the rooster came flapping around it with an angry squawk and tried to peck her hand.

She recoiled, bumping into Thatcher. Instinctively, he caught her upper arms. "Did he get you?"

"Not this time."

"But he has?"

"More than once."

The bird charged again. She flinched. Thatcher said, "Git!"

The rooster, having established his superiority, strutted away.

She eased herself free of Thatcher's hands, but turned her head to speak over her shoulder. "He's a wretched bird. I ought to wring—"

Then she winced and came full around to face him. At first Thatcher thought the rooster had pecked her after all, but it wasn't her hand she was grimacing over, it was his. When he'd clasped her arms, the handkerchief had come unwound, exposing the cut on his palm.

She reached for his hand and held it supported in hers as she examined the cut, gently pressing the flesh on either side of it. "You should have that looked at. It could get—"

She broke off when she looked up into his face and realized how close they were standing, how still he'd become, and how fixated he was on her face.

She snatched her hand back, then, with a swirl of her skirt, rounded the corner of the building out of sight.

Thatcher blew out a long breath, wadded up the bloodstained handkerchief and stuffed it into his pants pocket, then followed her back to the wash pot where she was jabbing the contents with a stick as though punishing the soaking sheets. She didn't look at him.

"I'll help you wring out that sheet and hang it on the line. It's my fault it got dirty again."

"No, thank you."

"It's the least I can do."

"No, thank you."

Her words were polite enough, but there was no mistaking her tone. She wanted him gone. He bent down, retrieved his hat, and put it on, then picked up his jacket and folded it over his arm. He lifted his duffel by the strap and was about to haul it onto his shoulder when he saw that he'd earned her notice after all.

She'd stopped what she had been doing and was staring at his jacket where it lay across his arm.

He fingered the torn seam that attached his sleeve, the one grabbed and held onto as he'd made his escape. "It was ripped during the altercation."

She gave her head a slight shake. "It's not the tear. I noticed the buttons."

"Oh. They're keepsakes from off my army uniform."

When he'd mustered out, the army had reclaimed his uniform for reasons never explained. Did they expect another war to break out soon? Were they going to pass down his mud- and bloodstained uniform to the next guy they drafted into service?

He never knew. But before he'd relinquished the uniform, he'd ripped off the dull brass buttons bearing insignias. As soon as he'd acquired a suit of civilian clothes, he'd swapped out the buttons.

He ran his fingertip over the one with an embossed pair of crossed rifles and the capital letter *B*. "The 360th Infantry regiment. All us draftees from Texas and Oklahoma."

"Yes, I know." She spoke with a huskiness to her voice that hadn't been there before. "B Company."

"You know someone who served in it?"

"My husband."

Her eyes flicked up to his, then away as she resumed swishing the water in the cauldron.

"He make it back?"

"Yes."

She kept her head down and didn't elaborate, but he'd had his question answered. He hoisted the duffel bag onto his shoulder. "I'll need a place to stay in town. Any suggestions?"

She was about to shake her head, when she hesitated, as though remembering. "In the window of Hancock's store. There's a sign advertising a room."

"Where's the store?"

"You can't miss it."

"Laurel?"

Startled, she looked in the direction of the shack from where the man's voice had come. "I'm here," she called.

"The baby's coughing again."

Just then a baby's wail could be heard coming from inside. The woman propped her stick against the lip of the wash pot and started toward the door of the shack. As she rushed past Thatcher she said, "Be on your way now."

"Thanks for the water." Before she disappeared inside, he said, "Wait, what was that name again?"

She paused in the open doorway and looked back at him. "Hancock's."

"No. Your name."

"Oh. Laurel. Plummer."

FIVE

As Laurel rushed inside, she nearly ran directly into Irv, who was standing just beyond the threshold but far enough back in the shadows that he couldn't be seen from the yard. He held a double-barreled shotgun crosswise against his chest. He raised his index finger to his lips, signaling for her not to make a sound.

She went over to the crib that Irv had made for Pearl out of scrap lumber he'd salvaged from one of his fix-it jobs. Her daughter's face was near purple from crying and coughing. Laurel picked her up and held her against her shoulder as she firmly patted her back, trying to loosen the phlegm that had made her croupy for more than a week.

Irv remained stock-still, watching the stranger until he had reached the road and headed in the direction Laurel had told him would lead to Foley. Only then did Irv relax his stance. He returned the shotgun to its usual spot, resting it between two hooks mounted above the door.

Laurel said, "He hopped off a freight car and wasn't sure of where he was."

"That's what he told you, anyway."

"Why would he lie?"

"Any number of reasons, and none of them good."

"He startled me, but apologized for it." For reasons she couldn't explain, she felt compelled to defend the stranger. "He was mannerly."

"That's the worst sort. They sneak up on you and act like your friend."

"The worst sort of what?"

"Of anything. How many times have I told you to be suspicious of strangers? Out this far? He could've been up to all kinds of mischief."

"He was only asking for directions and a drink of water."

"He must've had the thirst of a damn camel. What took so long?"

"While we were back there, the rooster made a nuisance of himself."

She thought the less said about that incident, the better. The mean rooster had been the least of it. She'd known what to expect from that damn bird.

Her thoughts lingered now on what had come after. She hadn't touched a man, or vice versa, since Derby's death. Not even Irv. Despite the stranger's leanness, he'd felt as solid as a tree trunk when she'd backed into him. When he'd steadied her with his hands on her arms, she'd had a momentary yearning to lean against him. It hadn't lasted any longer than the flit of a butterfly's wings, so it didn't merit dwelling on now. She forced herself to tune into Irv's grumbling.

"He didn't look like any hobo I ever saw."

Not to Laurel, either. "No, but he looked like a man who'd jumped off a train. His clothes were dusty. He had a ripped sleeve and a bruised bump on his forehead. And a cut on his hand."

She didn't want to think at all about that business with his hand. Any woman in the world would have responded the same way to seeing a nasty cut like that. She'd reacted in a typically female way. Instinctually. Maternally. Although, held in her palm, his hand hadn't felt like that of a child.

"What was that hogwash about saving his army buttons?"

Seeing them had been a bleak reminder of Derby's uniform hanging abandoned in the empty closet. She hadn't told Irv about that, and saw no point in telling him now. It would only make him sad.

"The man was just passing by, Irv," she said. "For heaven's sake. Really, you're making too much of it."

"And you're not making enough. I've lived longer. I've learned to be more cautious, less friendly." He indicated the shotgun. "I'll teach you how to shoot in case a vagrant, who ain't so *mannerly*, comes along when I'm not here watching your back."

She would be unable to reach the shotgun without dragging something over to the door and standing on it. By the time she did that, her throat could have been cut. So not to give Irv another reason to fret, she didn't cite that. Instead, she gave a small nod of acquiescence.

He started for the door. "You tend to Pearl. I'll hang that wash."

"The wash can wait. I want to talk to you."

His shoulders slumped as he turned back to her. "If it's about moving into town—"

"It is. Let's have this out. Sit down. Please."

With obvious reluctance, he went over to a lidded barrel on which he'd placed a cushion to form a seat for himself. He often perched there instead of sitting in a chair. Laurel guessed it was easier on his hip.

She sat down at the small table at which they ate their meals. Pearl's horrible, barking cough had subsided since she'd picked her up. Laurel laid her cheek against the top of Pearl's head. "Her hair's damp. I think her fever finally broke."

"That's good. She coughed all night long."

"I'm sorry."

"Hell, Laurel, I ain't cross over losing sleep." Watching Pearl, he furrowed his brow. "Pains me to hear that cough. Poor little thing."

Unwittingly he had given Laurel an opening. "I want to talk to you about a couple of things. Well, three, actually."

He folded his arms over his middle. "What's the first?"

"Thank you."

That took him aback. "What for?"

"That night we showed up here, you could have sent us on our way. You could have put up a real fuss with Derby for springing us on you.

You didn't. I don't think you'll ever know how much I appreciated your kindness that night and these two months since. You haven't complained once about Pearl and me being foisted off on you."

He snorted. "You could've took one look at me and this place and raised more than a fuss, Laurel. You could've raised bloody hell, and Derby deserved it."

They'd buried him in Foley's municipal cemetery. At the grave site were only the two of them, Pearl, and the undertaker whom Irv had paid an extra fifty cents to read a suitable scripture and say a prayer.

In the weeks following, she and Irv grieved Derby privately, silently, neither speaking of him, because they had no shared memory except for the final few minutes of his life. Neither wanted to reminisce on those.

Laurel's bereavement had been, and still was, far from pure and holy. It was corrupted by outrage. Were Derby's last words to her, "You'll thank me later," supposed to atone for his cowardly, selfish desertion of her and Pearl, his defection from all responsibility?

Willfully, she tamped down the resentment that continued to smolder even now, two and a half months into her widowhood. If ever she allowed it to boil, it would consume her.

She lifted Pearl off her shoulder and placed her facedown across her knees, swaying them slowly from side to side. "Irv—"

"Is this the start of the second thing?"

"Yes."

"Well, let's hear it."

She began by saying that it would be better for all of them to live at least within shouting distance of town. "I'm sure we could find a place to rent. Nothing fancy, but with separate rooms for us. Pearl and I wouldn't always be underfoot. You'd have your privacy back."

She looked at the blankets he'd strung up around the mattress. He now slept on a pallet of old quilts which he'd placed crosswise against the door, as far away from her corner as possible. The makeshift curtain served to keep them out of sight of each other during the night, but it was a fragile barrier against the forced intimacy and each other's humanness.

He didn't argue her point, so she pressed on. "You could take twice as many jobs if you didn't have to drive that ten-mile round trip each day. That takes up valuable time.

"And I worry about that truck of yours breaking down and stranding you on some back road. If you went missing, I wouldn't know where to start looking for you."

"My truck runs just fine."

"Then why are you tinkering on it all the time?" When he didn't answer, she continued. "I'll find something to do that will bring in extra money."

He lowered his bushy brows. "Like what?"

She knew that money would be a primary concern. Rightly so. There were jobs to be had working in the oil patches that were sprouting up in northwest Texas, some not far from here. But an older man with a gimp hip and a woman with an infant hardly qualified them to be roughnecks, even if they desired to be.

She would have to come up with something she could do at home. Take in laundry and ironing. Teach illiterate adults how to read. She wasn't without skills. Or resources.

She decided to admit now that the cash Derby had on him the night of their arrival wasn't all that they'd had to their name. "I have some cash tucked away that Derby didn't know about. I've been saving it for a rainy day, and this is it."

Her father-in-law took umbrage, but not from knowing she'd secreted money from Derby. "I'll have you know that I ain't destitute, and the idea of taking money from a woman, a young widow woman at that, makes—"

"Would you rather Pearl learn to crawl on a dirt floor?"

He scowled and muttered something unseemly under his breath.

"Why do you live here, Irv?"

"Because I like it."

"You couldn't possibly like it."

"It suits me just fine."

"Well, it doesn't suit me. I don't want my daughter growing up in a dilapidated shack with cracks in the walls. Out in the middle of nowhere, cut off from everything and everybody. No telephone or electricity or running water. No other children. No other *people* except for the two of us. What kind of upbringing is that?"

She stopped before she got too fired up. It wasn't her intention to insult or shame him into compliance. More gently, she said, "I'll be forever grateful to you for taking us in, but the baby and I can't go on living like this."

"Weren't so much of a hardship on me having y'all here," he said. "I'd miss you something fierce if you was to leave now. But, I get what you're sayin'."

He thought on it for a time, then said, "You're a pretty girl, Laurel. A bit scrawny, but that hobo was appreciatin' you. Don't think I didn't notice how he was eyein' you. If you fix yourself up a bit, fill out a little, you'll find another husband in no time, is my guess."

She gave a bitter laugh. "I don't want another husband, thank you. Not ever."

"You say that now, but—"

"I'm not looking for a man, Irv, so put that thought right out of your head."

"You gals got the vote, you don't need men no longer?"

She leveled a look on him. "It's way past time we 'gals' got the vote. But you're only saying that to rile me, so I'll drop this subject. I'm not falling for it."

He mumbled more swear words, then sat with arms folded, glowering as he considered his next line of attack. Laurel waited him out. Finally, he said, "A well-heeled family in town would probably give you a roof in exchange for housekeeping and cooking. Like that."

"Not with a baby."

"But if they've got little ones—"

"I don't want to live with another family and take care of their children. Besides, we should stay together. Help each other." She knew better than to remind him that he wasn't getting any younger. "*We're* family."

Laurel gazed at her gruff and scruffy father-in-law, who her own father would consider hell-bound for taking an occasional nip of moonshine for medicinal purposes, but who had been so ungrudgingly charitable.

"You're my family now, Irv. But whether or not you come with Pearl and me, I must leave here and somehow build a life for us."

He drew a deep breath and exhaled it slowly.

"At least tell me you understand my reasoning," Laurel said.

"I ain't dense."

"Then is that a yes? We'll start looking in town for a place to live?"

"I'm thinking on it," he said grouchily. "What's the third thing under discussion?"

"No discussion to it. You're going to teach me how to drive." When she saw that he was about to object, she added, "Today."

SIX

On this Saturday afternoon, countryfolk had come to town. Main Street in Foley was heavily trafficked with automobiles, trucks, and horse- or mule-drawn wagons top-heavy with everything from bales of hay to prolific families.

Hancock's General Goods was a three-story brick building. Its imposing facade dominated a block of the thoroughfare. In one of its four display windows were a pyramid of canned peas and carrots, several unfurled bolts of checked gingham in a rainbow of colors, a rack of Winchester rifles, and an open red metal tool box showing off a set of shiny wrenches.

The merchandise obscured the pale blue card stuck in the bottom corner of the window frame. It looked to Thatcher like it had been there for a while. The black ink had faded to brown, but the printed words were still legible. "Room for Let to single. 312 Pecan St."

Thatcher waylaid a man who was about to enter the store. He was jowly and prosperous-looking. His pocket watch dangled from a thick gold chain threaded through a buttonhole on his vest.

"Excuse me." Thatcher drew the man's attention to the sign. "Can you aim me toward that address?"

The man took a backward step and sized him up. "New to town?"

"Just rolled in."

The gentleman glanced again at the sign. "And apparently planning to stay."

"Till I take a notion to move on."

"What's your business here?"

His challenging aspect didn't sit well with Thatcher, but he said mildly, "Minding my own."

The man frowned and harrumphed, but pointed down the sidewalk. "Three blocks. Take a right on Crockett. Two blocks to Pecan. Hook a left."

"Thanks."

Thatcher brushed the brim of his hat with his fingertips and set off. But something about the man's manner compelled him to look back without being too obvious about it. Sure enough, the man was still watching him with a scowl of distrust. Thatcher couldn't account for it, but he didn't let it bother him overmuch.

Pecan Street was appropriately named. Several of the trees shaded the front lawn of number 312. The house was white with black shutters. Gingerbread trim lined the roof. A lattice with red climbing roses was attached to one end of the deep porch that ran the width of the house.

A picket fence enclosed the property like the frame around a picture of ideal domesticity. Where the fence and an inlaid stone walkway met, a sign hung from an iron post. On it, written in swirly black letters: "Dr. Gabriel Driscoll." Dangling from it by two little brass hooks was another sign: "Out on Call."

Right off Thatcher knew that he couldn't afford any room in this house. It was far too fine. He was seeking more humble accommodations. Just as he was about to turn away, the screened front door opened, and a woman came out onto the porch holding a watering can with both hands.

She tipped the spout toward some purple flowers that bloomed from a wicker stand next to the front door. Noticing him, she paused and broke a friendly smile. "Hello."

He removed his hat. "Ma'am."

She looked in both directions of the street as though wondering how he'd come to be there, much as Laurel Plummer had done.

She said, "The doctor is out making house calls."

"I'm not in need of the doctor. I came to see about the room for let."

The smile with which she'd greeted him faltered. "Oh."

She bent down to set the watering can on the floor and wiped her hands on her apron as she straightened up. She was in the family way. Pretty far along if Thatcher were to guess.

"I had forgotten the sign still was there." She pronounced it "da-zine" in an unmistakably German accent. "We're no longer taking a lodger." Self-consciously she smoothed her hand over her belly.

"Oh. Well, it probably would have been too rich for my blood anyway. Thanks all the same." He replaced his hat and made to leave when she blurted, "Wait. I want to bring you something, to thank you for inquiring."

He gave a dry laugh. "Ma'am, you don't owe me anything."

"No, wait. Please?"

Her eager nodding persuaded him. "Okay."

She beamed a smile. "Come up to the porch. I'll be right back." Leaving her watering can, she bustled inside.

Thatcher pushed open the gate and went up the walk. He stopped at the bottom of the steps leading onto the porch and eased the duffel bag off his shoulder, setting it on the ground. Then he stood there threading the brim of his hat through his fingers as he took a look around.

The house across the street was comparable to Dr. Driscoll's in size and architecture, and was obviously occupied by a snoopy neighbor. He noticed movement behind a lace curtain in one of the front windows before it dropped back into place.

After a minute or two, the lady returned, pushing through the screen door, happily bobbing her head and making the blond curls framing her face bounce. "Fresh baked shortbread. Come."

He left his hat on top of his duffel bag and climbed the steps.

She met him halfway across the porch and extended a plate to him. It was china and lined with one of those white lacy things. On it were two large squares of shortbread, the aroma of which made Thatcher's stomach growl. He'd eaten the last of the cheese and crackers during his five-mile hike from the Plummers' place, but they hadn't gone far.

"Are you Mrs. Driscoll?"

"Mila Driscoll, yes."

"Thatcher Hutton."

"Mr. Hutton. Please." She thrust the plate toward him.

"Thank you, ma'am."

He took one of the squares from the plate and bit into it. It was soft, buttery, sweet, and still warm from the oven. He swallowed the bite. "Delicious."

"My husband's favorite."

Her face was round and rosy, and shiny with perspiration, which she fanned with her apron. The cloth had red and yellow apples printed on it, bordered in a red ruffle. When she smiled, her whole face lit up.

He thought about the tense set of Laurel Plummer's features. He couldn't feature her smiling so unguardedly or wearing that cheerful apron. "Your husband's office is here in the house?"

"Front parlor, yes." She nodded toward a tall bay window that was both functional and ornamental.

"Do you help with his practice?"

"No. Better I don't."

Her cheerful blue eyes took on a sad cast as she glanced behind him toward where he'd left his duffel, which was obviously U.S. army issue. It showed the wear and tear of having been to war and back.

Even before the states got into it, people of German descent were subjected to resentment and suspicion because of a foreign war they'd had nothing to do with. Mila Driscoll's accent was a giveaway to her heritage. Thatcher reckoned she'd experienced a taste of unfair ostracism.

She didn't refer to the war or his obvious service. Instead she asked him if he was moving to Foley.

"No, ma'am. Just staying for a spell."

During the last mile of his journey today, he'd decided that hitching a free ride in freight cars came with risks he was unwilling to take again. His best option at this point was to earn enough money to buy a train ticket to whatever stop would get him closest to the Hobson ranch up in the Panhandle.

Before going off to do Uncle Sam's bidding, Mr. Henry Hobson had told him, "Don't get yourself maimed or killed over there. Your job here will be waiting on you when you get back."

Thatcher had promised that he would be back, but the army had kept him in Germany for over a year after the armistice, so his return had taken longer than he'd counted on. Now on his way, he was eager to get back to his former life.

It was likely to take him a couple of weeks to earn enough to cover the cost of the train ticket and keep himself fed and sheltered. Say a month at the outside. But he needed to be getting at it and find a place to bunk for however long he was here.

He finished the shortbread. "It sure was good, Mrs. Driscoll."

"Take the other."

He hesitated but reasoned she would be disappointed if he didn't. Besides, at his hungriest in the trenches, he'd sworn he would never again turn down food. "Okay. Hold on."

He went down the steps to fetch a spare, clean handkerchief from his duffel so he wouldn't have to wrap the extra piece of shortbread in the bloody handkerchief he'd used to bandage his hand.

When the treat was wrapped and tucked into his pants pocket, he said, "Thank you kindly, ma'am."

He hefted the duffel bag up by the strap and slid it onto his shoulder, then put on his hat. "Do you know anybody in town with a spare room? Doesn't have to be fancy."

"Near the railroad tracks. Room and board. Big yellow house."

"I'll find it."

"I must remember to ask Mr. Hancock to remove the sign."

"It's not that conspicuous. I wouldn't have noticed it if someone hadn't told me where to look."

"Oh? Who was dat?"

"Lady named Laurel Plummer. Lives out a ways."

"Young woman with baby?"

"That's right. I passed their place this morning. She gave me a drink of water. You're acquainted?"

"Only one time I see her. Her baby girl had bad croup. She brought her to my husband for medicine."

Little good it had done, Thatcher thought. "How old's the baby?"

"Infant. Tiny." She held her hands apart, about the length of a loaf of bread. "Poor Mrs. Plummer was very anxious."

With reason. Living in such a squalid place couldn't be good for a sick baby. "I didn't meet her husband. What's he do out there?"

"No husband. Father-in-law."

He scratched his chin with his thumbnail. "That so?"

"Her husband..." Shaking her head, Mila Driscoll tsked. "He died."

Huh. So it had been her father-in-law who'd had his shotgun at the ready. Thatcher hadn't let on that he'd seen him, but he'd caught sight of that side-by-side as the woman had disappeared into the shadows inside the shack.

She'd told him her husband had come back from the war, and that must've been the truth if her baby was that young. He couldn't stop himself from asking, "How long since her husband passed?"

"Two months? Three? The story..." She paused as though reluctant to gossip. Thatcher didn't encourage her to continue, but he hoped she would. He was itching to know why the elder Mr. Plummer was so trigger-happy. Maybe he was just overprotective of the recent widow and his sick granddaughter. Fair to say, too, that a stranger who showed up out of nowhere could be cause for concern to people who lived in such a remote spot.

Mrs. Driscoll overcame her reticence. "The story is that her husband took her and the baby to his old papa out dere, then shot himself the same night."

Jesus. No wonder she'd looked gaunt and wound up.

"Such a shame for her," Mrs. Driscoll said.

"Yes, ma'am, it is." They were quiet for a moment, then he said, "I'd best see if they have any vacancies in that boardinghouse. Thanks again for the shortbread."

"You're welcome. Good luck to you, Mr. Hutton."

He doffed his hat to her, and then, when he reached the street, he tipped it to the busybody who was still observing them from behind the lacy curtain.

SEVEN

The large house near the railroad tracks was indeed yellow. In its day, it might have been considered grand, but Thatcher figured the loud color was an attempt to draw attention away from the overall seediness of the place.

If he planned to stay longer, he would have passed on it. But, reminding himself that the quarters would be temporary and probably affordable, he pulled on the bell at the front door.

Through the screen, he saw a woman walking toward him down the length of a long central hallway. He'd seen scarecrows that were more comely. As she neared, she slung a damp cup towel over her shoulder and peered at him through the mesh. "Whatever you're selling, I ain't buyin'."

Friendlier scarecrows, too. "I'm not a salesman." He stated his purpose and asked if she had a vacancy.

She shifted a toothpick from one side of her mouth to the other. "You railroad?"

"No, ma'am."

"Most of my boarders are railroad men. They rotate in and out."

"I don't plan on being here long term, either."

She pushed open the door, and motioned him inside. "Name's Arleta May. May's the last name. I got one vacant room. Rents by the week. No refund if you cut out early. Three meals a day, but supper is cold, and you serve yourself off the sideboard."

She passed him a piece of paper on which was a badly typewritten list of house rules. He was allowed barely ten seconds to scan it before she took it back. "Basically, no women, no liquor, no cussing, no fighting, no smoking in bed. I've got beans about to boil dry. You taking it or not?"

He took it. She went over to a cabinet, sorted through a drawer full of keys, and exchanged one of them for his first week's rent money. "Third floor, number two. You can find your own way." She shuffled off down the hall from which she'd come.

Thatcher climbed two sets of stairs to the third floor. Room number two met his expectations. The mattress on the rusty iron bedstead sagged in the middle. Water stains spotted the ceiling. The single window was cloudy with grime. He raised it to let in some fresh air.

A set of sheets and a folded towel had been left on the bed. He took the towel with him into the bathroom midway down the hall, used the toilet, washed his face and hands, and returned to his room only long enough to hang the towel on the footboard to dry and to retrieve his hat.

He descended the stairs and followed the aroma of cooking beans to the kitchen. "Uh, Miz May?" She turned to him, scowling. "Sorry to bother you. Is there a public stable in town?"

"Old man Barker's. North side of town, across the bridge."

An advertisement for Goodyear tires was painted on one exterior side of Barker and Son Automobile Parts & Repair. In front were two gasoline pumps, and, even as Thatcher crossed the bridge, he could smell motor oil. Several vehicles were parked both inside and out of the open garage. One was being worked on by a young man in dirty overalls, no shirt.

"Mr. Barker?"

"He's out back." Without even glancing at Thatcher, he hitched his thumb over his shoulder.

Thatcher walked around the building and found an older man lying on his back beneath a milk delivery truck. He was banging metal against metal and cussing a blue streak.

"Mr. Barker?"

The man slid from beneath the truck and shaded his eyes against the sun. "Yeah?"

"Thatcher Hutton." He walked over, bent down, and extended his right hand.

"Never mind that. My hands are greasy." As Barker came to his feet, he pulled a red shop rag from the pocket of his overalls and wiped his hands. "What can I do for you?"

"You stable horses?"

Barker tipped his head toward a large barn about thirty yards distant. "Stable, shoe, groom. Whatever you need."

"I need a job."

The older man scoffed and looked him over. "Doing what?"

"Whatever needs doing."

"You ever seen the inside of a stable, young man?"

"Spent most of my life in one. Before being drafted, cowboying was all I ever did. I mustered out of the army a month ago in Norfolk, Virginia. I've been working my way back up to the Panhandle. The Hobson ranch?"

He posed it as a question to which Barker shook his head. "Don't know it."

"South of Amarillo, along the Palo Duro. I started working for Mr. Hobson when I was eleven years old. I'm handy with horses."

"That may be," Barker said, still looking unconvinced. "But I ain't hiring."

Thatcher glanced over his shoulder in the direction of the garage before coming back around. "Looks to me like you've got more than you can handle on the automotive side of your business. For the next few weeks, I could relieve you of stable chores, free up you and your son to do the other work."

"That nitwit ain't my son. *I'm* the son. My daddy had a smithy and stables at this location for forty years. Henry Ford changed that. I had to adapt or starve."

Thatcher had figured such was the case. "How many horses are you stabling?"

"Currently six. Plus four of my own that I rent out. And one ill-tempered sumbitch that a fellow left here for me to break."

"Yeah? How's that coming?"

Barker shifted his chaw and spat into the dirt.

Thatcher smiled. "That ill-tempered, huh?"

"High-steppin' stallion. Owner won't hear of gelding him yet."

"Let me take a look at him."

"What for?"

"Why not?"

Barker thought it over, then said, "What the hell? I's tired of working on that clutch, anyway." He kicked the front tire of the milk truck as he walked around the hood. "Come on."

Thatcher followed him around the far side of the large stable to a corral of respectable size, but confining to the bay stallion who was running along the encircling fence, making abrupt directional changes, bucking occasionally, demonstrating his anger and frustration over being penned. When he sensed them coming toward the corral, he pinned back his ears, and his nostrils flared.

"I had to put him out here. He kept the other horses stirred up. Especially the mares."

Thatcher chuckled. "I don't doubt it. He's a handsome devil, and he knows it."

He was a large horse, sixteen hands, perfectly formed. He had the classic black points and a deep red coat that would gleam if he were groomed. Thatcher propped his arms on the top fence rail and watched the stallion strut, tail high.

"Does the owner want him trained to race?"

"To ride," Baker said, adding dryly, "for longer than three seconds at a time."

Thatcher smiled at the quip. "Does he have a name?"

"Ulysses."

"I'd be throwing my owner, too." Thatcher shrugged out of his coat and draped it over the fence rail. "How does a dollar and a half a day sound, Mr. Barker?

"Hold it. What are you doing?"

The stallion was snorting and eyeballing Thatcher as he unlatched the gate, slipped through it, and closed it behind himself. The horse didn't like any of it. He became even more agitated, picking up speed on his next go-around of the corral and coming dangerously close to Thatcher who stood stock-still.

Barker said, "Get out of there. You ain't even dressed for this."

"I had to leave my gear behind when I went into the army. But he doesn't know city shoes from boots."

"At least take this rope." Barker lifted a coiled lariat off the top of a fence post.

"Not for our first meeting."

"That bastard'll kick you into next week."

"I'm mindful that he'd like to. But he also wants to know what I'm up to."

"*I* want to know what you're up to."

"Earning my buck fifty." Thatcher calmly walked to the center of the corral.

"I haven't agreed—"

Thatcher said, "Mr. Barker, I don't want him to see me as a threat, but I do want his undivided attention, and, no offense, you're a distraction. If you could back up a little, please."

Thatcher heard Barker spit another wad of tobacco into the ground before muttering, "Your funeral."

There was a lot to be learned about the horse just from watching how he maneuvered. Thatcher faked indifference, but, without appearing to, he studied the stallion's movements as he cantered along the fence, tossing his head, whinnying, stamping, making sudden shifts in direction, asserting himself.

After several minutes, Thatcher spoke softly, "Won't do you any good to keep that up. You'll wear yourself out before I leave this corral."

He partially turned his back to the animal, remaining very aware of where he was, but intentionally keeping his head turned away from him as though uninterested in his arrogant posturing.

"See, I'm not scared of you. And you don't have to be scared of me."

It didn't take long. The horse slowed his gait and eventually came to a standstill. He stomped a couple of times, then turned toward the center of the corral to face Thatcher. "Well, are we going to be friends?" Thatcher made a nicking sound. Not yet ready to concede, the stallion shook his head.

"All right. Stay there and think it over. I can wait. Sooner or later, your curiosity is going to get the better of you." Thatcher stayed as he was, acting nonchalant. "Those mares you've got stirred up. Are they pretty?" The stallion's ears flicked forward. Thatcher made the nicking sound again.

Slowly the stallion walked toward him and came to a stop, head down. "Good boy. We're making strides. Ulysses, huh? Guess you're stuck with it."

The stallion snuffled and jerked his head when Thatcher reached up to stroke his forehead, but after one more rejected attempt, the horse allowed his touch. "Thata boy." Moving slowly, speaking softly, he praised the stallion's cooperation. As Thatcher rubbed the horse's neck, he looked over at Barker. "A dollar and a half a day?"

Barker spat. Thatcher took that as a yes.

After spending another few minutes smoothing his hands over the stallion, building trust, he left the corral and reclaimed his coat. Barker led him into the stable, introduced him to the horses in the stalls, and showed him where tack and supplies were kept.

"I'll have to borrow one of your saddles," Thatcher told him. "Mine's at the ranch."

"Help yourself. What they're there for."

As Thatcher was leaving, Barker told him there was a second-hand clothing store in town. "You might find yourself a pair of boots, at least."

Thatcher got directions to the shop, but it was closed for the day. He had planned on sending Mr. Hobson a letter tomorrow telling him that he could start looking for him in about a month. In the letter, maybe he'd ask Mr. Hobson if he would send him his gear by train and take the expense out of his salary once he was back.

He made it to the boardinghouse before the cold supper was cleared off the sideboard. After finishing his meal, he wandered out onto the porch where several other boarders were chewing the fat.

Laconically, they all introduced themselves and shook hands, but he didn't get the impression that fast friendships were formed among them, probably because of their transiency.

One thumbed through a magazine. One was quietly playing a harmonica. Some puffed smokes. Thatcher noticed that one of the younger among them slid a flask out of his pants pocket, uncapped it, and took a sip.

Another, an older man who had laid claim to a rocking chair, said, "That's against house rules and against the law."

"Now that's a fact," the young man said. "It is." Then, leaning toward the man in the rocker, he whispered, "And teetotaling is against the laws of nature." He took another drink then taunted the older man by smacking his lips and saying a long, drawn-out *ahhhh*.

Sensing the growing tension, the man with the harmonica stopped playing.

The older man didn't let it drop. He said to the young man, "I doubt you respect any rules."

"That's not so," the young man retorted. "I set rules for myself."

"Such as?"

He seemed to ponder it, then snapped his fingers and said, "I only get half as drunk on Sundays."

The others on the porch were equally divided as to who thought that was funny and who didn't. The one in the rocking chair took umbrage. He excused himself, left the rocker, and stamped into the house, letting the screen door slap closed behind him.

The younger man chortled, "He's a barrel of laughs."

Another man, who Thatcher had noticed earlier because of his sporty attire, left the corner of the porch where he'd been smoking in solitude and sidled up to the younger man. "What's your name?"

"Randy Wells. Who's asking?"

"Chester Landry." He motioned to the flask. "Where'd you get the booze?"

Randy cast a wary look around. When his gaze lighted on Thatcher, he squinted suspiciously. "I feel like a stroll." He indicated for Landry to follow him. They went down the porch steps and set off across the yard, talking softly together.

No one said anything for a moment, then the harmonica player picked up his tune where he'd left off, and another commenced to talk about baseball. Thatcher stayed only a few minutes longer before going inside.

He took a turn in the third floor bathroom, then went into his room, undressed, and took the piece of shortbread to bed with him. As he stretched out on the lumpy mattress, he released a sigh of relative contentment.

It had been a damned long day, but he'd accomplished a lot, too. For a start, he'd survived the fight in the freight car and the jump from it without serious injury.

The miles he'd walked had fatigued him, but hadn't completely exhausted him like the long marches he'd made through the French countryside, fully armed, cold, hungry, and hoping an enemy bullet didn't have his name on it.

His landlady, Arleta May, was scary, but he had a roof. The mattress was bad, but still better than wet ground or the floor of the boxcar.

He had a headstrong horse to train, and if he did that successfully, word would get around, and more work could come from it until he'd earned enough to get him the last few hundred miles to home.

All things considered, he had it pretty good.

He polished off the shortbread and licked the crumbs from his fingers before reaching up for the string attached to the bare-bulb light fixture mounted to the wall above the headboard.

When he closed his eyes, an image of Laurel Plummer came to mind. He fell asleep thinking about her in profile, the wind toying with her hair and holding her shapeless dress tight against her front.

EIGHT

S heriff William Amos was awakened by the shrill ringing of his telephone. He squinted the clock into focus and cursed under his breath. Nobody called at three o'clock in the morning to impart good news.

As he threw back the sheet and got up, his wife murmured sleepily. He patted her on the rump, then went to the downstairs hall, where the telephone sat on a small table. He picked it up by the stand and lifted the earpiece from the fork, saying into the mouthpiece, "Bill Amos."

One of his younger, greener deputies identified himself. "Hated to wake you, sir."

"I hated you did, too. What's happened?"

He hoped for nothing more major than rowdy boys being caught painting naughty words on a public building. But he mentally ran through the list of better likelihoods: A still had caught a cedar break on fire. Rival moonshiners had gotten into a skirmish with fists, firearms, or both. Lawmen in a neighboring county, tired of chasing a notable bootlegger, were officially dumping him into Bill's jurisdiction.

Even before Prohibition had become federal law several months back, evangelicals had for generations voted in local laws that had kept many Texas counties dry. Thus the illegal making and selling of corn liquor was the second oldest profession in the state.

All the Volstead Act had accomplished so far was to turn the trade into an even more profitable enterprise. Demand was at an all-time high. Production was up. Competition was stiff. And the moonshiners in Bill Amos's county were among the most industrious in Texas.

"We've got a situation, sir," the deputy said.

"Something y'all can't handle?"

"Thought so when we started out. But things has gone downhill fast."

Bill heaved a sigh. "Somebody must've wound up dead."

"Well, truth is, we don't know yet."

"What's that mean? He's either breathing or he isn't. Is he a Johnson?"

"No, sir. It's Mrs. Driscoll."

With a start, Bill angled his head back and looked at the phone as though the deputy had started speaking in tongues. "Dr. Driscoll's wife? Mila Driscoll?"

"Yes, sir. She's gone missing."

Ten minutes later, Bill entered the sheriff's office, where Dr. Gabriel Driscoll was carrying on like a crazy person. Usually of an austere nature, the physician was clearly unhinged. His hair was standing on end, as though he'd been trying to tear it out. He was pacing in circles and aggressively warding off anyone who attempted to restrain or calm him down.

When he saw Bill, he lunged toward him. "Sheriff, do something! You've got to find her."

Bill hung his hat on a wall rack. "Get us some coffee," he said, addressing one of his deputies who looked relieved to be charged with something besides the physician.

"I don't want any coffee!" Gabe made an arrow of his right arm, pointing to the door through which Bill had just entered. "Get out there and find my wife!"

"Gabe, I can't help you if you don't help me. First off, you've gotta get hold of yourself." He pulled up a chair. "Sit down and tell me what's happened."

"I've told them." The doctor indicated the several deputies watching him with a mix of pity and wariness, much like they would regard a wounded wild animal that hadn't yet died.

"I need to hear everything for myself," Bill said. "So take a breath and brief me on the situation."

"He came and took her," he shouted. "In brief, that's the situation." Then, as though feeling the impact of his own declaration, he collapsed into the chair, planted his elbows on his knees, cupped his bowed head with all ten fingers, and began to sob. "What if it was your wife, Bill? God knows what's he doing to her."

"Who's he talking about?" Bill asked, addressing one of his most trusted men, Scotty Graves.

"I talked to the old lady who lives across the street from the Driscolls."

"Ol' Miss Wise?"

"Yes, sir. She said a man came to their house today, talked to Mrs. Driscoll up on the porch."

"Miss Wise recognize him?"

"No, sir, and she said she knew a stranger when she saw one."

The illogic of that statement caused Bill to run his hand over the top of his head. "Maybe this stranger was sick and looking for the doc."

"The sign was out, saying the doctor was on a call, but Miss Wise said this man stayed for several minutes. He didn't appear to be ailing, either."

"He go inside the house?"

"No, sir. Didn't go no farther than the porch. Mrs. Driscoll gave him something, but Miss Wise couldn't tell what it was."

"Something like what?"

"Something small enough to fit in his pocket."

"A bottle of medicine, maybe? A jar of pills?"

"We thought of that, but the doctor checked his medicine cabinet.

Everything's accounted for. Besides, he keeps the cabinet locked when he's away. Even Mrs. Driscoll doesn't have a key."

"Did Miss Wise describe this stranger? Was he young, old, what?"

"Young. No more'n thirty, she said. Tall, on the slender side, dressed in a dark suit. He had dark hair. He was wearing a fedora, but he took it off while talking to Mrs. Driscoll. He was carrying a bag that looked heavy."

"Salesman's wares?"

"Miss Wise didn't think so. She said it looked like the kind of bag a soldier would have."

"Soldier?"

"That's what she said."

"Yeah, but she's more than half batty," Bill muttered. "Anything else?"

"She said he was cocky."

"How'd she get that? Did she talk to him?"

"No, but he tipped his hat to her."

Bill hooked his thumb in his gun belt. "Maybe he was just being polite."

"She was watching from behind the curtain in her side parlor."

"Out of sight?"

"She thought so, but apparently not."

So, aware of being watched by a nosy neighbor, the young man had mockingly tipped his hat, making himself certain to be remembered. If he'd brought harm to Mrs. Driscoll, he was either incredibly stupid, or he was cocky just like the old maid had said. Bill had rather him be stupid. Someone that cocky usually didn't give a damn, and that was dangerous.

"You boys have scouted the neighborhood?" he asked his men at large.

Scotty answered for the group. "Questioned all the nearby neighbors, searched every outbuilding for blocks around. Mrs. Driscoll was well known. If anybody had seen her, it would've been noted."

"Nobody heard anything suspicious? Shouting? Barking dogs, nothing like that?"

"Nothin' out of the ordinary, no, sir."

"What about Mrs. Driscoll's friends? Have you checked with them?"

"The doc knew of only two people she might visit. One's the preacher of the Lutheran church. He hasn't seen her since last Sunday's service."

The other was the local librarian, who'd told the deputy she hadn't seen Mila Driscoll in a while, but had reassured him that none of the books she'd checked out were overdue.

"What about her family?" Bill asked.

"None closer than down around New Braunfels. Stands to reason."

Stood to reason because it was a predominantly German town. "Have you checked with them?"

"Her parents are deceased. Doc said her uncle is the designated head of the family. We're waiting on a long distance call to go through."

Bill nodded absently and turned back to the doctor, who was still holding his head between his hands and moaning disconsolately. "Gabe." He waited until the distraught man looked up at him. "Do you have any idea who this man was?"

"No."

"Based on the description of him—"

"It could fit a dozen men, Bill. A hundred."

He was right, so Bill didn't press him. "Mrs. Driscoll didn't mention having a visitor today?"

"He came asking about lodging. We used to rent out a room."

"Did she appear afraid, apprehensive, upset?"

Even before he finished the question, the doctor was saying, "No, no. She was her usual self. Maybe a little more subdued than usual, but I think she was sensitive to my mood."

"You were in a mood?"

"Distracted. I ran a rural route today. One of my patients had gone into labor. The baby was breech. Her sister was with her. She told me she'd assisted in breech births before, that she could handle it. I had several other people to see, so I left them.

"But I was worried about the danger to both the mother and child that a difficult delivery like that could be. It wasn't something I wanted to discuss with Mila, not with her being in her condition. As it is, she's nervous, this being her first."

"When's the baby due?"

"Two more months."

Bill took a deep breath. "So she read your mood and was a bit subdued. Anything else out of the ordinary?"

"No. We had supper. I went into my office and did some paperwork. She was crocheting."

"When did you last see her?"

"Around ten o'clock. We were getting ready for bed. I got an emergency call."

"The breech birth?"

"No." He cast a nervous look around the room. "Lefty's. One of the, uh, waitresses got worked over by a customer."

Bill took a visual survey of his deputies, who gave him various versions of a shrug. One said, "First we've heard of it."

"Gert wanted it kept quiet," Gabe said.

Lefty's was a roadhouse that had the best burgers within fifty miles. Also the best whores. Sheriff Amos couldn't vouch for that personally, but that was the general consensus known by everybody.

Lefty flipped burgers while his wife, Gert, oversaw the more lucrative side of the business. A ruckus of one sort or another was frequently incited by one of the "waitresses." Inevitably those incidents resulted in somebody bleeding.

Bill reasoned that Gert wanted this incident kept quiet so not to draw the law's attention to the place. Bill was well aware of the copious amount of bootleg liquor now being served in Lefty's back room. He would need to get out there and deal with that, but it took a back burner to Mrs. Driscoll's disappearance.

"You took care of the girl?" he asked Gabe.

"Yes."

"Is she going to be all right?"

"In time. Can all this wait?"

The doctor's patience was fraying. Bill had to keep him centered. "I've got to establish a time line, Gabe. What time did you get home and discover Mrs. Driscoll gone?"

"Late. On my way back into town, I stopped in to check on the breech birth. The baby had turned at the last minute. The delivery went fine. I checked out the mother and baby." His voice hitched. "While my own wife and baby—"

"Gabe." Bill spoke his name brusquely to keep him on track. "What time did you get home?"

"A little after one o'clock. I was exhausted, but hungry. I made a sandwich and ate it before going upstairs." He looked down at his hands as though they held the answers. "Mila wasn't in bed. Not in the bathroom. I turned the house upside down, searched the yard. When I couldn't find her anywhere, I called here. That's it." When he looked up at Bill, his chin was quivering. "She wouldn't have left on her own."

"I don't think so, either," Bill said, briefly laying his hand on Gabe's shoulder. "But let's not panic. Backtrack a little. Was she in bed when you left for the roadhouse?"

"Yes. She wanted to get up and send me off with a thermos of coffee, but I wouldn't let her. She needed the rest."

"When you got home was there any sign of a disturbance? Broken latch? Anything like that?"

"No."

Scotty chimed in. "We searched the house. Looked like nothing had been touched. No break-in. Led us to believe that Mrs. Driscoll let in whoever snatched her."

Gabe Driscoll lunged to his feet. "Are you implying that my wife invited—"

"He's not implying any such thing, Gabe," Bill said. "Sit down."

"I'm not going to sit down," he shouted. "What's wrong with all of you? Why are you just standing around? Why aren't you out looking for her? She could be hurt. Dying. She could be—"

Suddenly the door was pushed open with a lot of impetus behind it. When Bill saw who filled the doorway, he thought, *Shit!* Drolly, he said, "Mayor."

The Honorable Bernard Croft came inside and shut the door, bristling with self-importance. "Bill, what in hell is going on? Is it true? Mrs. Driscoll is missing?"

On a good day, Bill resented the city official's meddling in the affairs of his department. The mayor had a way of creating a hullabaloo even when one wasn't warranted, for his own aggrandizement.

Bill asked, "How'd you get wind of it?"

"Miss Eleanor Wise called me."

"For what purpose?"

With condescension, Croft replied, "For the purpose of saving Mrs. Driscoll from the man who abducted her, Bill."

"It hasn't been established that—"

"Have you identified him yet?"

"Until you blazed in and interrupted, I was compiling the facts of the case."

"How many facts do you need? Miss Wise described him to a tee."

Everyone in the room gaped at him, Bill included. "What do you know about him?"

"I know I mistrusted him on sight," he said. "I was reluctant to send him over there to your house," he said, addressing Gabe. "But the ad was right there in Hancock's window."

Gabe placed his fingertips to his forehead. "Ad? For the room? I'd forgotten it was there."

"He asked me for directions." Then, in a defensive tone, the mayor added, "If I hadn't told him, the next person he asked would have."

"We stopped taking in a boarder a while ago," Gabe said.

"I'm sure Mrs. Driscoll explained that to him, which means he had to look somewhere else for a place to stay." Bill shouldered past the mayor and reached for his hat. "Scotty, stay with Dr. Driscoll. The rest of you, let's go. Harold, bring a shotgun. Bernie, you can go on home."

"You'll need me to identify him." Seeing that Bill was about to object, the mayor added, "Unless you'd rather take along Miss Eleanor Wise."

NINE

———◈———

When Thatcher had fallen asleep, it never crossed his mind that he would be awakened by having a gun barrel jammed against his cheekbone.

A German infantryman somehow had survived the no-man's-land between his trench and the Americans', and intended to chalk up at least one doughboy to his credit.

Thatcher flung up his hand and slammed the barrel of the shotgun into the soldier's face. Flesh squished. Cartilage crunched. The man hollered.

Thatcher used that instant of the soldier's shock and pain to come up out of the bed and leap over the foot rail, where he barreled into another of the enemy, previously unseen. This one was stocky and strong, but Thatcher had enough momentum to drive him back against a wall.

From behind, another wrapped his arms around Thatcher, pulled him off the stocky one, and wrestled him facedown onto the floor.

But there were more than just these three. Two others joined the melee. The five of them surrounded him, all shouting and grasping at him from every side, trying to secure his arms and legs. One had a hand on the back of his head, holding it down, his cheek against the floor.

He fought them with savage will. They may shoot him, bayonet him, but he was not going to be taken prisoner by these bastards.

He managed to throw off the hand holding his head down and escaped the others' hold long enough to flip onto his back. Instinctually, he thrust his hands straight up into the face of the man straddling him. He had a thick mustache and a white cowboy hat.

Cowboy hat?

There was a five-pointed star badge pinned to his shirt. Engraved on it: Sheriff.

Jesus. The war was over. This wasn't France. He was back in Texas. The men surrounding him weren't German infantrymen. But he sure as hell had been in a life-or-death combat with them.

Before he could surrender himself, the backs of his hands were flattened to the floor on either side of his head. He took stock of the men encircling him. They were all breathing hard from having exerted themselves to restrain him. But even at that, he didn't know what he'd done to warrant their judgmental bearing. They stared down at him with unsettling disdain.

All were strangers save one. Thatcher recognized the gold pocket watch chain strung across his vest. He was the most heavyset. Thatcher figured it had been him he'd crashed into and rammed into the wall.

He was the first to speak. "That's him, all right."

"You're sure?" asked the one wearing the sheriff's badge. He planted his hand on the center of Thatcher's chest and pushed himself off him and to his feet. "What have you got to say for yourself, young man?"

"I woke up with a gun to my face. I was defending myself."

"Or resisting arrest."

"Arrest?"

The only light in the room spilled through the open doorway from the hall. These apparent lawmen cast long shadows across the bed and onto the ugly papered walls, enhancing the menace they conveyed. They meant business.

Thatcher repeated, "Arrest? What the hell for?"

"You're sure this is him, Bernie?"

"Positive," said the man with the gold watch fob. "I recognize him, and I recognize that bag. He had it with him."

He motioned toward Thatcher's army issue duffel bag, which he'd placed on the seat of the room's one chair after deciding last night that he could delay unpacking till morning.

"Gather up all his belongings, put them in the bag, and bring it," said the sheriff.

"You bet." One of the uniformed men turned away to do his bidding.

The sheriff said to another, "Question everyone in the house. See if anybody knows anything about him."

"Yes, sir." That man edged past the footboard and left the room.

Another moved forward and bent over Thatcher. His nose was bleeding. It and his eyes were beginning to swell. He was holding a shotgun, no doubt the one Thatcher had smacked into his face.

The man grinned with malice. "Thought you'd just drift into our town and haul off with one of our women? Think again, hotshot."

Then he flipped the shotgun and smacked the butt of it against Thatcher's skull. The blow hurt like hell and made his vision go dark and sparkly for a moment, but it didn't knock him out.

"Hey, go easy, Harold," the sheriff said. "We need him able to talk."

He extended Thatcher his hand and helped him up. The man who'd struck him—Harold—watched smugly as Thatcher struggled to regain his equilibrium. He made blurry eye contact with the man he recognized by his gold pocket watch. He also was leering with self-satisfaction.

"I'm Sheriff Bill Amos. What's your name?"

"Thatcher Hutton."

The sheriff repeated his name as though committing it to memory, then gathered up the clothes Thatcher had hung on a wall hook before going to bed and passed them to him. "Get dressed."

After he did, he was handcuffed. Then without further ado, the sheriff said, "Let's go."

Thatcher dug his heels in. "I have a right to know what you're arresting me for."

None of them seemed to think so. With the barrel of the shotgun against the base of his spine, he was prodded out of his room and into the hallway.

It seemed that he was the only boarder in the house who'd been taken unawares by the arrival of the posse. Everyone else had emerged from their rooms, all in pajamas or underwear, watching as the procession trooped down the two sets of stairs.

Few of them met Thatcher's gaze directly, but the smart aleck, Randy, who earlier had heckled the older man on the porch, winked at him. And when Thatcher passed the flashy dresser who'd introduced himself to Randy as Chester Landry, he gave Thatcher a sly, speculative look as though they shared a dirty secret.

The landlady stood at the front door, arms crossed over her bony chest, lips tightly pursed. "Don't expect no refund on your rent."

Once outside, the sheriff dispatched all the deputies except Harold to "rejoin the search." Thatcher asked, "The search for what?" but, again, he was ignored.

When Harold manhandled him into the officially marked automobile, he was showy with the shotgun, but careless with his gun belt, which was within easy reach of Thatcher's cuffed hands. However, to go for the deputy's pistol would be foolhardy. They would soon determine that they had the wrong man and release him. Until then, he'd go through the process without making more trouble for himself.

"Mayor, I guess you'll have to ride with us," the sheriff said, and the man Thatcher had met outside Hancock's store—the mayor?—climbed in along with them.

———

Harold drove them to a single-story limestone building that headquartered the sheriff's department. No one said anything during the brief ride. When they piled out of the car, the sheriff gripped Thatcher's arm just above his elbow. Together they entered the building.

It smelled of cigarettes and scorched coffee. The main room was crowded with the standard desks, chairs, and filing cabinets of any law enforcement office. Wall-mounted gun racks were impressively stocked. Two large maps, one of the county, the other of the state, were tacked to the far wall, along with numerous wanted posters and a notice of a missing cow.

Seated in side-by-side chairs were a man in a deputy's uniform and a man with a pale complexion, a dark five o'clock shadow, and wavy hair. The instant he saw Thatcher, he came hurtling toward him like he'd been shot from a cannon. If the deputy hadn't acted swiftly to restrain him, Thatcher thought for sure the man would have gone for his throat.

"Gabe!" the sheriff barked. "None of that business. Scotty, haul him back and keep him back."

"Yes, sir."

Though the man resisted, the deputy managed to wrestle him back into the chair.

The mayor went over to him and laid a hand on his shoulder. "Found him sleeping like a baby, Gabe. Can you believe that?"

Glaring at Thatcher, the man said, "Has he told you where she is?"

"Not yet, but he will." The mayor brusquely signaled the deputy, Scotty, up out of his chair, then the mayor sat down in it.

Thatcher, wanting to ask what the hell was going on, thought better of saying anything just yet. Harold shoved him down into a chair. He pulled a handkerchief from his pocket and wiped at the blood dripping from his now misshapen nose. One of his eyes had almost swollen shut.

Thatcher returned his glare with a mask of indifference and said, "I still owe you for the clout on the head."

The deputy gave him a fulminating look, but he walked away, slung Thatcher's duffel onto a table across the room, opened it, and began to paw through the contents.

No longer wearing his hat, Sheriff Amos drew up a chair and stationed it in front of Thatcher's, pulling it close enough that Thatcher could see the individual whiskers in his thick salt-and-pepper mustache. He said, "Son, save us all a lot of time and trouble. Tell us right now where Mrs. Driscoll is."

TEN

———❖———

Laurel had been awake for most of the night, walking a fussy and feverish Pearl around the shack, trying to soothe her infant even as she fueled her resentment against Derby's selfish suicide, her present plight, her unknown future, and her absent father-in-law.

She had whipped herself into a high snit by the time she heard his truck clattering up the incline shortly before dawn. As soon as he cleared the door, she lit into him. "Where in the world have you been?"

He looked haggard and none too agreeable himself. "That's my business."

"It's my business, too! I was worried to death, afraid something had happened to you, in which case Pearl and I would have been stuck here. What have you been doing all night?"

She was accustomed to his being away most days, all day, often from sunup to sunset. This was the first time he had stayed away all night. Though she would rather die than own up to it, she had been afraid to be alone after the sun went down. With only a sliver of a moon, even the surrounding limestone hills had become indiscernible. She couldn't see the road from the shack. The darkness had been all encompassing, except for the lantern she had kept burning all night.

He plopped down on his seat on top of the barrel and rubbed his bad hip, wincing with discomfort. Mollifying her tone, she said, "I saved you some cornbread and bacon."

"I ain't hungry."

Laurel stood directly in front of him, making it impossible for him to ignore her. "I believe I deserve an explanation, Irv."

"You kept me occupied half the day teaching you how to drive. *Trying* to teach you how to drive."

The series of lessons had been intermittent, carried out during Pearl's brief naps between bouts of coughing. Laurel had never sat behind the steering wheel of an automobile. The sequence of necessary steps one had to perform with both hands and feet had been more difficult to coordinate than she'd anticipated. She was right-handed, so naturally she'd reached for the crank with that hand, when Irv had told her repeatedly to always use her left on the crank unless she wanted her "damn arm broke."

They had wound up being frustrated and fractious with each other.

She asked now, "Did you stay gone all night to punish me for not mastering how to drive?"

He gave her a withering look. "What do you take me for?"

"Then why didn't you come home?"

"I had a project to finish up."

"In the middle of the night?"

"How's Pearl?"

"She's sick, Irv. *What project?*"

"Putting up a wall inside an old house. It was just sold to a family moving here from Waco. The wife wanted to divide one room into two so that her daughter would have a space separate from her brothers."

"You're lying."

He glowered and looked guilty at the same time.

"You went into too much detail," she said. "Just like Derby did when he was lying."

He got up and headed for the other side of the room, but she caught him by the arm.

"What?" he asked, pulling his arm free.

"Do you have a . . . Is there a woman you see?"

He huffed a humorless laugh and continued on his way over to the sink where he pumped water into a glass and took a long drink. Laurel waited until he'd turned back to her before quietly apologizing. "I'm sorry. I had no right to ask that. It isn't any of my business."

He gave that same dry laugh. "I've loved only one woman in my lifetime. Derby's mama. And it damn near killed me to watch her die in misery. Don't go thinking I've got a romance going."

"No project, either, I'm guessing."

Looking done in, he returned to his seat and bent down to unlace his shoes. "No, I had a project all right." He looked up at her from beneath his bushy eyebrows. "That fellow that came here this morning."

"What about him?"

"I don't know, and that's why I'm worried. What the hell was he doing way out here?"

"I told you, he—"

"I know what he claimed, but I ain't buying it. I went around tonight, checked in with people I know, asked if they'd seen him."

"What people?"

"People."

She let his curt reply pass. "Had anyone in town seen him?"

"Nobody I talked to."

"He probably hitched a ride on the highway and is long gone."

"Maybe," he grumbled. "But him snooping around gave me an itch I can't scratch."

"What snooping? He was lost and asking for directions, that's all."

He gave a snort and focused his attention on Pearl, who Laurel had been holding against her shoulder, rocking gently. She'd slept through their conversation.

"You say the baby's sick?"

"She's running a fever again. I want to take her back to the doctor."

"I saw him tonight."

She stopped her swaying motion and looked at Irv with surprise. "You went to see Dr. Driscoll?"

"Naw, naw. He was at the roadhouse, you know, the place where I pick up burgers on occasion?"

"You told me it isn't a respectable place."

"It ain't. But Lefty fries a damn good burger, and he's also a fountain of information. Knows everything happening in and around here. I went to inquire about our visitor today."

"He didn't know anything?"

"Said he didn't. But he was dealing with a problem of his own. One of his, uh, girls got crosswise with a customer. He beat her up pretty bad."

Understanding dawned. "It's that kind of place?"

"It's full service, all right." Irv shook his finger at her. "Don't you ever darken the door of it. It draws all sorts of lowlifes. The girls who work there...Well, let's just say that most are experienced and tough enough to take care of theirselves. Lefty's wife, Gert, is the meanest of them all. When she saw her girl there, beat up and bleeding, she went after Wally—the guy who hurt her—with a meat cleaver.

"Lefty had to literally peel Gert off him. He turned him over to his cousins—them Johnsons cavort in a pack—then tossed the whole sorry lot of them out. They called Doc Driscoll to come patch up the young lady. By the time he got there, Lefty had calmed Gert down. Some. It was quite a scene."

Laurel listened with incredulity to Irv's account of the brawl and marveled at the matter-of-fact way in which he'd related it. She marveled even more to think of Dr. Driscoll's being in such a place.

During her one brief meeting with the doctor, she had thought him to be wholly professional, even a bit cool. Of course, she had been frantic with worry over Pearl, so, by comparison, anyone would have come across as composed and somewhat detached. She couldn't imagine that man tending to a patient in a brothel.

She said, "Despite his late night, I hope he maintains office hours tomorrow. I can't drive well enough yet to go into town. You'll have to take us."

"Sure, sure. Whenever you want to go."

"First thing after breakfast." She hesitated, then asked if he had any fix-it jobs lined up.

"A couple. Why?"

"I was thinking that as long as we're in town, and if Pearl isn't too fussy, we could look around, see what might be for rent."

He gave her a crooked grin. "You're not as smart as you think. I wasn't lying about the old house. I knew of it, sought out the landlord and talked him into meeting me there after he finished his supper. It's a big ol' rambling place, but it's stood empty for years on account of the back of it is built into a wall of limestone."

"Built into the rock?"

He shrugged. "Wouldn't take much to make it habitable. I could do the work myself. But if you don't like it—"

"The least I can do is take a look. Thank you, Irv."

"Don't thank me till you've seen it."

The house couldn't be more of a nightmare than this shack she was living in. She appreciated that her father-in-law had listened to the concerns she'd raised with him this morning, and had taken her ultimatum seriously enough to act on it.

In gratitude, she smiled at him. "You look worn out. Try to get some rest." She then retreated behind the partition with Pearl, who had become restless again and was mewling pitiably.

ELEVEN

———◆———

T hatcher repeated the sheriff's confounding words. "Tell you where Mrs. Driscoll is?" He looked over at the man who'd tried to attack him. "Are you Dr. Driscoll?"

"Yes, you son of a bitch. And I want to know what you've done with my wife."

"Nothing but talked to her. Why? What's happened?"

Sheriff Amos said, "She's missing."

"*Missing?*"

"It's feared she was abducted from her home sometime between ten o'clock p.m. and one o'clock a.m."

Thatcher glanced at the wall clock. It was going on five. He looked at each man in the room in turn, and the reason for their judgmental glowers took on meaning. The hairs on the back of his neck stood on end. "That's why I'm here? You think I know something about it?"

"You were seen talking with her today on her porch."

"I said as much. I was looking for a room to rent. You can ask him." He tipped his head toward the mayor.

"Mayor Croft told us that he gave you directions to their house."

"A decision I regret," the man boomed.

The sheriff, looking irritated, turned his head partially toward the mayor and said in an undertone, "Bernie, I'll handle this." Coming back around to Thatcher, he said, "Where'd you get the bruises, Mr. Hutton?"

"Your deputy Harold there poked me in the face with that pump-action."

Harold, who was still rifling through his belongings, shot him a dirty look over his shoulder.

"Not the bruise on your cheek," the sheriff said, "the one on your noggin."

"Oh." He reached up with his cuffed hands and touched the discolored goose egg at his temple. "I jumped off a freight train, had a hard landing, rolled down an incline."

The sheriff tilted his head and eyed him speculatively. "When was that?"

"This morning. Early. Before dawn."

"Where?"

"Eight, nine miles southeast of here. The middle of nowhere. I walked to town."

"You were bumming a ride?"

Given the circumstances, he felt that admitting to one malfeasance would be to his advantage. "Yes."

"Where were you headed?"

"Amarillo. Or as close to there as the railroad goes these days."

"What's up there?"

He explained his long-time connection to the Hobson Ranch. "I was making my way home, back to the ranch and my job."

The sheriff took it all in, then said, "If you've got a job waiting for you in the Panhandle, why'd you jump off the freight train way down here?"

He came clean about the poker game and the ill will it had created with those sharing the boxcar. "They were sore losers."

"Did you cheat?" Sheriff Amos asked.

"No. I have a knack."

"For winning at cards?"

"For reading people."

The sheriff glanced over at the others as though to verify that he'd heard correctly. Thatcher could tell that they were all skeptical of his boast, as well as of his story, so he didn't volunteer anything else.

When the sheriff came back to him, he said, "What happened when you got to the Driscolls' house?"

"I took one look and knew it was out of my reach." He told them about Mrs. Driscoll's coming out onto the porch and catching him as he was about to leave, and saying she wanted to thank him for coming by. "She called me up to the porch and brought out some fresh shortbread."

The doctor said in a strained voice, "At least that much is the truth. Mila baked it this morning. We ate some after supper."

"She gave me a second piece to take with me," Thatcher said. "I wrapped it in my handkerchief. It left a butter stain. You can check it. Right pocket."

He raised his cuffed hands, inviting the sheriff to withdraw his handkerchief from the pocket of his jacket. When he shook out the folded cloth, a few crumbs fell to the floor. The greasy spot was clearly visible.

"That doesn't mean he didn't go back later and do her harm," the mayor said.

The sheriff frowned. "Doesn't mean he did, either."

Recalling Mrs. Driscoll's friendly smile and hospitality, it bothered Thatcher to think that she was in a direful situation of any kind. "Mrs. Driscoll was as nice a lady as I ever met. We chatted there on the porch while I ate the shortbread. When I took my leave, she suggested I try to find a room at the boardinghouse. I thanked her and left. If something bad has happened to her, you're wasting your time talking to me. You ought to be out beating the bushes, looking for her."

Driscoll surged to his feet. "Or maybe we'll beat the truth out of you." Hands fisted, he made a lunge for Thatcher and took a wild swing.

Sheriff Amos shot out of his chair. "Dammit, Gabe. Sit down, or it'll be *you* I'm locking up."

The mayor took hold of the doctor's arm and dragged him back to his seat. "Can't say as I blame you, Gabe," he said, casting a glare in Thatcher's direction. "It's clear he's lying."

Thatcher didn't give a damn about that blowhard's opinion. The distraught husband was another matter entirely. "I'm telling you the truth, Dr. Driscoll. What call would I have had to repay Mrs. Driscoll's kindness by hurting her?"

The mayor answered for him. "I think you took advantage of her *kindness* and got her to open the door of her house to you tonight."

"I didn't," Thatcher said, but he addressed the denial to the sheriff, not to the mayor.

Harold came stalking across the room. When Thatcher saw what he was bringing with him, his stomach sank. It was a set of postcards that he had brought home from France. Harold had removed the string that bound them.

Smirking at Thatcher, he passed the cards to Sheriff Amos. "Found these in the bottom of his bag."

Each of the cards featured a photograph of a half-naked woman in a provocative pose. The sheriff fanned through them without comment or reaction, then formed a neat stack of them and set it facedown on the nearby desk.

Thatcher didn't offer any apology or explanation for them. Was there a man in the room who wouldn't enjoy taking a peek?

The sheriff leaned back in his chair and tugged at the corner of his mustache while he studied Thatcher. Thatcher wished he knew what was going through the lawman's mind. Apparently, so did the mayor. Above the loud ticking of the wall clock's brass pendulum, he prompted him. "Bill?"

Seeming to be in no hurry to respond, the sheriff waited another fifteen seconds, then indicated the torn shoulder seam on Thatcher's coat. "How'd that happen?"

"One of the men on the train made a grab for me."

"You really believe he jumped off a freight train, Bill?"

That from the mayor, whom the sheriff again ignored. He said, "You could've broken your fool neck. Why didn't you stay on the train and fight it out?"

Thatcher glanced around. All of them were poised, waiting for an answer. He addressed the sheriff. "I did."

"Did what?"

"Fought it out."

"Three against one?"

"Wasn't my choice."

The sheriff reached for his hand and turned it palm up. "How'd you get that cut?"

"One of the men came at me with a knife. I was defending myself."

"Against Mrs. Driscoll," the mayor said.

The sheriff didn't acknowledge the remark. "Back there in your room, you came at us like a vandal."

"I told you. I woke up with a shotgun to my head. I reacted."

"Violently," the mayor said.

The sheriff kept his attention on Thatcher. "Three against one. Five against one. Where'd you learn to fight like that?"

"A bunkhouse."

"He's obviously a dangerous individual, Bill."

"I'm not a danger to a woman," Thatcher fired back at the mayor. "Sure as hell not one in the family way."

The doctor choked back a sob and held his fist against his mouth to contain others.

Thatcher looked directly at the sheriff. "Look, hopping the freight? Guilty. I was just trying to get home, and the army didn't pay me enough to get there. I wasn't looking to fight the men on the train, but they would have killed me if I hadn't fought back. Fought y'all because I've been to war and temporarily mistook you for the enemy.

"The last time I saw Mrs. Driscoll was midafternoon as she was bidding me goodbye. That's the God's truth. I would never raise a hand to a woman or harm one in any way if I could help it."

He flashed to how he'd startled Laurel Plummer as she was hanging out her wash, but decided not to mention that encounter. Approaching two women who were strangers to him, on the same day, might compound their suspicions.

"What did you do after leaving the Driscolls' house?" the sheriff asked.

Thatcher told him about renting the room, then seeking out Mr. Barker. "He hired me."

"As a mechanic?"

"No. He's paying me to train a horse."

The mayor guffawed. "That horse in the paddock behind Barker's place?"

"If you're referring to a bay stallion, yes," Thatcher said.

"He's a brute, Bill. Others have tried. No one can get near him."

"I can," Thatcher said, still speaking directly to the sheriff and trying to ignore the butt-in. "That'll be easy enough to check with Mr. Barker. By the time I left his place, the sun was going down. I stopped by a secondhand store he'd recommended, but it was closed. I got back to the boardinghouse a little before seven o'clock. After supper, I went out on the porch and sat for a spell. A dozen men can vouch for that.

"Mr. Henry Hobson would vouch for me, too. When I left for the army, the ranch didn't have telephone service yet. It was out too far. They may have gotten it by now. If not, by hook or crook you could get word to Mr. Hobson." As an afterthought, he added, "When you do, ask him to please send me my gear. It's locked in a trunk in the bunkhouse. He'll know."

He forced himself to relax his shoulders and sit back in his chair. He'd been as honest and earnest as he knew how to be.

But they locked him up anyway.

For the next two hours, heated discussion filtered through a door that separated the main room from the cell block. Thatcher had been placed in the last cell. He was too far away to catch all the words, but he heard enough to piece together what was happening.

The mayor—Bernie Croft was his name—overstepped the duties

of his office. Sheriff Amos resented his interference and told him so, although it did no good.

Dr. Driscoll cycled between frustration, rage, and despair.

The highway department was alerted to be on the lookout for Mila Driscoll. It would be a hostage situation; she couldn't drive.

It was suggested that the Texas Rangers be brought into the investigation, but none seemed enthusiastic about the prospect and postponed making a decision.

Boats had been launched to search every body of water within a twenty-five-mile radius.

Volunteers on horseback and in motor vehicles, many with dogs, had converged on the sheriff's office, creating chaos and a lot of noise, until they were organized into groups and dispatched to search assigned areas.

Soon after their departure, the deputy named Scotty brought Thatcher a cup of coffee, a biscuit, and a sausage patty from a nearby café. Thatcher thanked him, but the deputy didn't acknowledge it.

Thatcher heard his name repeated hundreds of times beyond the door, but hadn't always been able to discern the context in which he was mentioned. He could guess, though.

On paper, he looked like a stranger of limited means, who'd wandered into town after having been in a fight, and was seen being friendly with a woman who was now missing. It added up.

It adds up had become the mayor's refrain. But the sheriff had been reluctant to act on a supposition, especially since they didn't have a witness to a crime or one iota of evidence on which to base a charge against Thatcher Hutton.

"We don't even know that a crime has been committed," Thatcher had heard the sheriff exclaim.

That had been followed by the doctor's hoarse shout, "Then where is she?"

Now, as Thatcher lay on the bunk staring up at the low ceiling, he heard the telephone ring, but it had been ringing often, so he didn't place any importance on this call until Scotty reappeared and instructed him to put his hands, wrists together, through the bars of the cell.

After being cuffed, he was guided back into the main room. He knew he must look disheveled, but he had fared the intervening hours better than Dr. Driscoll had. There were dark circles under his eyes. His unknotted necktie lay against his chest, which seemed to have been scooped out like a watermelon. He sat stoop-shouldered, his listless hands dangling between his knees, vacant eyes staring at the floor between his shoes.

Thatcher had seen men fresh from a days-long battle looking just like that, like they'd been to hell and back, and were wondering if having survived it was for the better or worse.

Hulking Harold was absent.

The mayor no longer looked smug, but rather like he'd eaten a bad tamale.

Sheriff Amos merely looked tired. He had one hip hitched on a corner of the desk with his nameplate on it. He smoothed his mustache as Thatcher came in. "Mr. Hutton, I just got off the phone with the Potter County sheriff. I explained our situation here. Telephone operator told him there's no line that goes out to the ranch, so he's sending a man to track down Mr. Hobson. He said it's a far piece out there, so it will take a while before we hear back."

Thatcher nodded.

"In the meantime, Fred Barker backed up what you'd told us. So did several men at the boardinghouse. One had noted that you left the porch and went inside at around nine-thirty. He remembered because he used the bathroom right after you and saw you go into your room. No one saw or heard you sneaking out after that."

Thatcher shifted his feet. "So I can go."

"Well," the sheriff sighed, "seeing as we——"

Suddenly the door flew open and Laurel Plummer burst in, clutching a baby to her chest. Wild-eyed, she scanned the room, drawing up short when she saw Thatcher. "*You?*"

The old man who followed her inside looked Thatcher over, noticed the handcuffs, and harrumphed, "Didn't I tell you he was up to no good?"

TWELVE

Considering the short amount of time that Thatcher had planned to be in Foley, he had doubted he would ever see Laurel Plummer again. He certainly never would have predicted their next encounter would be under these circumstances, him in handcuffs, her looking like a woman on the verge of hysteria.

The dress she had on was only a little better than the one she'd been wearing yesterday morning. One of her shoelaces had come untied. Her hat looked as though it might have been an afterthought, put on to conceal how untidy and insecure the bun on her nape was.

The baby was alternately crying and making strangling sounds.

Thatcher guessed the old man who'd followed her in was her father-in-law. Yesterday, all Thatcher had seen of him was his shotgun. He didn't have it with him today, but he was squinting at Thatcher with malevolence. He asked the room at large, "Wha'd y'all get him for?"

The sheriff blinked with surprise. "You know Mr. Hutton?"

"Seen him."

"Where?"

"He came up to our place yesterday morning. He—"

Laurel said, "Never mind that," and rushed across the room to Dr. Driscoll. "Thank God you're here."

The Plummers' sudden and disruptive entrance had roused the doctor from his stupor. He stood up unsteadily. "Mrs. . . . ?"

"Plummer. My baby, Pearl. Remember? You treated her for croup a week and a half ago. I gave her the cough syrup, but it hasn't helped. She's worse. You've got to help her."

He seemed at a loss. "I—"

"We went to your house," she went on. "No one answered the door. An old lady who lives across the street saw us and came over. She told us that your wife disappeared last night. I'm sure she got that wrong, but she said that you would probably be here. You've got to examine Pearl." She'd spoken so rapidly and breathlessly, she had to pause and inhale deeply before adding, "Please."

The doctor didn't react, only looked at her blankly, as though he hadn't sensed her anxiety or understood a word she'd said.

The mayor interceded. "Mrs. Plummer, was it? I'm Mayor Croft. Dr. Driscoll is indisposed. He's not seeing patients this morning. I could recommend several fine physicians who—"

"I tried that," Irv said, interrupting. "She was bent on finding Doc Driscoll on account of he'd treated Pearl before. There was no sayin' no to her. The baby's in a bad way."

"She can hardly draw breath." Laurel looked pleadingly at the doctor, but, as before, he seemed to be in a trance. With a soft cry of desperation, she turned away from him and took in the scene as though just now grasping the significance of the situation she'd barged in on.

"His wife really has disappeared?" She addressed the question to Sheriff Amos.

"Last night. A search is underway, but currently Mrs. Driscoll's whereabouts are unknown."

"The neighbor lady said she'd been abducted."

The mayor loudly cleared his throat. "We're trying to ascertain that. From Mr. Hutton."

When Laurel's gaze moved to Thatcher, embarrassment bloomed hotly inside his chest. She focused on the handcuffs, then looked up into his eyes with misgiving. "I thought surely the old lady was senile, talking nonsense."

Thatcher said quietly, "You told me where to look for the advertisement. I went to the address on the card."

"It was Dr. Driscoll's house?"

"I was seen talking to Mrs. Driscoll."

Laurel's father-in-law made a grunting sound, as though this news was confirmation of the low opinion of Thatcher that he'd already formed.

The sheriff said, "Mrs. Plummer?" She shifted her attention away from Thatcher and back to Bill Amos. "We met on the occasion of your husband's demise. It was such a difficult time for you, I wasn't sure you would remember."

"Of course I do."

He nodded solemnly, then gestured toward Thatcher. "What can you tell me about Mr. Hutton?"

She scooted the baby up onto her shoulder and tried to shush her. "Nothing, except what Irv already told you. He showed up at our place yesterday."

"What time was that?"

She thought on it. "Around eleven, but it could have been thirty minutes either side of that."

"How did he get there?"

"On foot."

"From which direction?"

"I didn't see, but I guess from the south. The railroad is in that direction from us, and he told me he'd jumped off a freight train."

"Did you believe him?"

She hesitated, then said, "It made no difference to me if he was lying or not."

"It did to me," Irv said. "Poking around where he didn't belong."

The sheriff turned to him. "He poked around?"

"No, he didn't," Laurel said, giving her father-in-law a look of asperity. "He asked for a drink of water. I gave him one, and told him how to get to town, then sent him on his way." The baby began to cough. Laurel patted her on the back. "That's all I know, Sheriff Amos. I've got to get Pearl to a doctor."

"A couple more questions. You told Mr. Hutton about the Driscolls' room for rent?"

"I didn't know it was theirs. I just remembered seeing the notice in Hancock's window, and mentioned it to him when he asked if I knew of somewhere he could stay." She cut a glance at Thatcher, then said to the sheriff, "This really has nothing at all to do with me."

Without a blink, the sheriff continued. "Altogether, how long was he there?"

"No more than a few minutes. Ten maybe."

"Did he look beat up, like he'd been in a fight?"

"He had a bump on his head. His hand was wrapped in a hand-kerchief. The shoulder seam of his coat was ripped."

"What was his demeanor, Mrs. Plummer? How did he act toward you?"

She took another quick look at Thatcher, and he figured this was where she would tell them about the rooster's attack and what had happened after. But she didn't relate any of that.

She said, "He didn't act any particular way. He thanked me for the water and the information and left." She pressed her palm against the baby's forehead. "I must go now and find another doctor."

"Doc Perkins is right down the street," Irv said, opening the door. "Come on, Laurel."

She walked quickly to the door, then stopped on the threshold and turned back and addressed the doctor. "When I brought Pearl to your office, Mrs. Driscoll treated me kindly. I'm very sorry for what you're going through. I hope you find her soon. And that she's safe."

Her eyes connected with Thatcher's for a split second, and then she was gone.

After they left, the doctor's knees folded and he dropped back into the chair. The mayor said, "Gabe is exhausted. He can't even stand, much less think straight. He should be allowed to go home for a while and rest."

"No, no," he said. "I want to stay here, be here, in case something…something…" Unable to finish the thought, he rubbed his forehead.

"You see?" the mayor said. "I'll see him home."

"Scotty will see him home," Bill Amos said.

The mayor seemed about to argue, but, instead, bent down and placed his arm around Driscoll's shoulders. In a murmur usually reserved for priests and undertakers, he began reassuring the doctor that he was going to stay on top of things.

The sheriff turned to his deputy and spoke in an undertone, but loudly enough for Thatcher to hear. "Don't let anybody talk to him. There'll probably be a parade of church ladies bearing food. You take it at the door and thank them on behalf of both the doc *and* Mrs. Driscoll. If they start asking questions, say you're not at liberty to talk about an ongoing investigation, and that if you do, I'll have your ass chicken fried and served on a platter. And I will, Scotty."

"I understand, sir."

"Anything turns up, I'll come directly there and inform Gabe of it myself. Anything anyone else tells you, regard as rumor or fabrication."

"Yes, sir."

"Get to it."

Scotty crossed the room and, after nudging the mayor aside, took Driscoll gently by the arm, lifted him up, and guided him toward the door. The doctor went along without objection. He looked like a sleepwalker.

As Scotty pulled the door closed behind them, Mayor Croft

hitched his chin in Thatcher's direction. "What are we going to do with him?"

"You're not going to do anything with him. He's going back to his cell, and I'm going to make some calls."

"To whom?"

"To whomever I damn well please, Bernie. This is my desk, my office, my department, and my investigation." Reining in his anger, he said, "Thank you for your help this morning." He motioned toward Thatcher. "Identifying the suspect."

"It was the least I could do. To my knowledge, nothing like this has ever happened in Foley."

"You can't say that yet because we don't know what's happened."

"I want to be apprised as soon as—"

"News has a way of getting to you, Bernie. I'm sure you'll be among the first to hear of any developments."

"I'm depending on you to see that I do."

The sheriff gave a nod that could have been taken either as acquiescence or could have signified nothing at all, and Thatcher figured the latter.

With self-importance, the mayor headed for the door, but when he came abreast of Thatcher, he stopped. Meeting him eye to eye, he said in a low and sinister voice, "I don't care who you mistook me for. If you ever put your hands on me again, you *won't* live to regret it. Do we understand each other?"

Thatcher met his threatening stare head-on. "Oh, I think so."

Croft held his gaze as he said, "I'll be checking in, Bill," then he strode to the door and left.

The sheriff's relief over seeing him go was obvious, even though that left him alone with Thatcher, who'd been referred to as "dangerous" and "the suspect."

He lifted the metal ring that held the keys to the jail cells off a nail on the wall. "You gonna give me any trouble, Mr. Hutton?"

"No. But I could use the toilet." He'd seen a door at the far end of the corridor marked as such.

"Can't afford you the privacy when I'm the only one here. There's a chamber pot under your bunk." He signaled for Thatcher to precede him.

Once back inside his cell with the door locked, Thatcher stuck his hands between the bars. The sheriff removed the handcuffs.

Thatcher said, "I don't know what's happened to Mrs. Driscoll. I had no part in it."

The sheriff backed up and propped himself against the wall opposite the cell. "Why'd you choose that ratty old shack of Irv Plummer's to stop at?"

"It was the first place I'd come to. I needed a drink of water and directions to the nearest town."

"You ever been to Foley before?"

"No, and I wasn't headed here. Like I told you, I was aiming for the Hobson ranch. But I needed a town to get myself together, earn some money before continuing on."

"You had your poker winnings."

"They didn't amount to much."

"They did to the men who lost."

"If they couldn't afford to lose, then they shouldn't've been gambling."

The sheriff snuffled. "True enough." He studied Thatcher as he thoughtfully stroked his mustache. "Irv seemed to have taken a dislike to you. How come?"

"I have no idea."

"Y'all didn't have a run-in of some kind yesterday?"

"I never even saw him. When I got there, Mrs. Plummer was in the yard hanging out her wash. I didn't know for certain that anyone else was around until he called to her from inside the house. He didn't show himself."

Deliberately he neglected to tell the sheriff about the shotgun, although he couldn't say where his reluctance to mention it came from. "Do you think the baby will be all right?"

"My boy had croup a couple of times when he was little. Sounds worse than it is."

"What's Plummer do for a living?"

"He's a handyman. Drives an old truck."

"It was parked in the yard."

"It's full of tools and gadgets, jangling around. You can hear him coming from a mile away. He's quite a character."

"I gathered." Thatcher debated whether or not to leave it there, but decided to be up-front. "I know that Mrs. Plummer's husband died by his own hand just a few months ago. Mrs. Driscoll told me." He recounted how that conversation had come about. "She didn't go into detail. Told me only that he shot himself."

"He put a Colt forty-five under his chin and pulled the trigger."

Jesus. Thatcher hoped Mrs. Plummer hadn't been the one who found him. "That was an awful thing to do to his family. He leave a note?"

"No." The sheriff lowered his head and stared at a spot on the floor between him and the cell. "When I questioned Mrs. Plummer about it, she told me her husband had come back from the war a different man, that he never recovered from his service over there, and that's what drove him to kill himself."

"It can happen."

The sheriff kept his head down but lifted his gaze to Thatcher, looking at him from under a pair of eyebrows that matched his salt-and-pepper mustache. "Did it happen to you? See, Mr. Hutton, I recognize the buttons on your coat. My boy wore the same uniform."

He lowered his gaze to the floor again. "I know the name of the town in France where he's buried. Can't pronounce it, but I can't see it matters much. I doubt I'll ever get there.

"And, anyway, if I were to, there's a bunch of Company B boys all buried together. They couldn't really tell one from the other, they said. Made separate graves...Well, impractical, I guess."

He coughed behind his fist. Thatcher heard him swallow. Then he raised his head and looked Thatcher in the eye. "Were you witness to atrocities like that?"

"Damn near every day. Even after the armistice, I was left over there to clean up messes that folks who haven't seen can't imagine."

"You didn't feel the effects of seeing things like mass graves stuffed with unidentified body parts?"

"Yes, Mr. Amos, I felt the effects, all right. But they didn't make me lose my mind, or tempt me to blow my brains out, or drive me to abduct women." His hands closed around two of the bars. "Seeing all that death only made me determined to get back home and go on living out the rest of my life as best I can."

Their gazes stayed locked for a time. The sheriff was the first to break away. He turned and started down the corridor. "Try to get some shut-eye."

"How long can you hold me without charging me?"

"I don't think you'll have to worry about it."

"With all due respect, I do worry about it."

Bill Amos stopped and turned. He subjected Thatcher to a long, assessing stare. "There's a lot about you I'm trying to figure out. But it's occurred to me to wonder why you would spend ten minutes or more with a young woman who you thought was all alone way out yonder, and leave politely without laying a hand on her, then walk five more miles, on a hot day that topped eighty, meet another woman who's seven months pregnant, and decide to sneak back in the dead of night and carry her off. On foot."

THIRTEEN

—◦◦◦—

Laurel spent an anxious hour pacing the waiting area of the doctor's office, trying to comfort Pearl. Her coughing spasms were relieved only when she could draw enough breath to wail.

When they finally were called into the examination room, the elderly physician peered at them through his wire-rimmed eyeglasses and asked, "What seems to be the problem?"

Laurel wanted to smack him.

With a maddening lack of urgency, he went about examining the screaming baby while asking Laurel pertinent questions. In the hope of moving things along, she kept her answers brief and precise.

He listened to Pearl's chest and, when he removed the earpieces of the stethoscope, asked if she'd been born early.

"By three weeks."

He ruminated on that, then used a medicine dropper to dose Pearl with powdered aspirin dissolved in water. "This will bring down her fever. And this," he said as he similarly administered a dose of sweet smelling syrup, "will help with her cough." He gave Laurel a small bottle of the cough remedy and a packet of the aspirin to take with her.

Irv had waited in the car. When he saw her coming from the building, he got out to help her and Pearl into the passenger seat. "Is it the Spanish flu?" he asked. "Pneumonia?"

"He didn't say."

He tilted his head and looked at Pearl, who was lying in Laurel's arms. "She seems better already."

"He gave her paregoric."

He frowned. "That's dope, ya know. You'd've been just as well off funneling some whiskey down her throat."

Laurel agreed. Her mother had given her paregoric whenever she'd suffered a stomachache or diarrhea. However, rather than easing her symptoms, the opiate had always nauseated her, making her throw up.

She didn't like the idea of the stuff, and would be very stingy with the doses she gave Pearl for her cough. Now, however, she was grateful that the baby was no longer struggling for every breath. Pearl's eyes were blinking sleepily, and sleep would be as good a remedy as anything.

Laurel kissed her daughter's forehead, then whispered to her, "Things are going to get better, Pearl. I'm going to make them better. I promise." After Irv had started the car and gotten behind the wheel, she said, "I want to see that house for rent."

─────

As they drove through town, Irv reopened the subject of the scene in the sheriff's office. "That fella Hutton. What do you think?"

"I don't think anything."

"I mean in connection with the doc's wife gone missing."

Rather than answer his question, she asked, "How was the mayor involved? Is he a close friend of the Driscolls?"

"Naw, he just sticks his big nose into everybody's business."

"Well, this is his business. He's a public official, and a woman in his city went missing overnight."

"You think that Hutton took her?"

"I don't know, Irv." Her tone reflected how tired she was of his seeming obsession with Mr. Hutton. Since he'd ventured into their yard yesterday, no matter what topic they were talking about, Irv always circled back to him. Every time she'd asked what had made him so suspicious of the man, his answer was usually the same. "Just don't trust a tall, dark stranger who drops out of nowhere."

As now, he muttered, "Don't trust him as far as I can throw him."

He would trust Mr. Hutton even less if he knew that he'd placed his hands on Laurel's arms and held her against him. She'd taken his hand!

By doing so, she'd given him an opportunity to force himself on her if he'd been of a mind to. No, they had to be wrong to suspect him of molesting Mrs. Driscoll in any way. He'd done nothing in the manner that Sheriff Amos's question had suggested, nothing to make her fear that he meant her harm, or that his intentions were dishonorable.

The worst he'd done to her was to make it impossible for her not to think about those moments when they had touched. She feared that seeing him again, even in those circumstances, had prolonged the time it was going to take for her to forget them.

———◆———

The house was as Irv had described: rambling. It appeared to have been broken apart at one point and pieced back together incorrectly. Even more uniquely, it backed up to a sheer wall of limestone.

But it was actually better than Laurel had expected. "Can we see inside?"

Irv wasn't completely sold on the idea of moving into town, but he turned off the truck's motor, grumbling, "Landlord said he'd leave the key under the porch in a sardine tin."

They found the key. The front door's hinges screeched when Irv pushed it open. The interior smelled like mildew with an undertone of dead mouse, but Laurel reasoned that if the front windows were open, the southerly breeze would dispel the odor.

Flanking the central hallway were a parlor to the left and a staircase to the right. Laurel stepped into the parlor. The wallpaper was shabby and stained, but it had tall windows and a pretty Victorian carved wood spandrel that demarcated the parlor from the dining room. A door on the far side of it led into the kitchen.

"The icebox is the old-fashioned kind," Irv said. "You'd have to have ice delivered. But the stove's electric." Gesturing to the rusty faucets in the sink, he added, "It's tapped into the city water. You won't have to pump no more."

"Is there a bathroom?"

Irv led her to it. Obviously a late addition, it was tucked under the staircase. The fixtures needed a good scouring, but she was delirious at the thought of no longer having to use an outhouse.

"Upstairs?"

"Two bedrooms and a sleeping porch. Some of these steps are rotted, so be careful."

The front bedroom faced south. Sunlight shone through the dirty windows, from which she could see the tallest buildings of downtown. Having been isolated for months, the thought of having a view of nearby civilization was comforting. She could make this a pleasant room for Pearl and her to share.

The sleeping porch was a screened-in, long and narrow space. She would have to think on how best to utilize it.

Beyond it was a small, claustrophobic room that had only one east-facing window. The ceiling slanted downward to meet the far wall. "This'll do me fine," Irv said. "I don't require much space."

"But you'll have to climb the stairs," Laurel said. "That won't be good for your hip. I have a better idea."

She led him back downstairs and into the kitchen. "Build a wall on this end of the kitchen to enclose the keeping room. It has a window. It would easily convert into a bedroom."

He scowled. "Where'd you get that notion?"

"From you. You shouldn't have lied about dividing one room into two for a family from Waco."

He swore under his breath, but Laurel could tell that the idea appealed to him. The new room would give him access to the rest of the house without having to use the stairs. The back door leading from the kitchen to the outside would also enable him to come and go freely.

She pointed that out to him, then stood by waiting hopefully as he mulled it over. For an eternity. "If it's a matter of money—"

"It ain't."

"I plan to pitch in."

"I told you, I ain't destitute."

"I still have my money."

"Keep it. I owe you this."

"How so?"

"It was my boy who skipped out on you."

Whenever the subject of money came up, they argued, and Irv was cranky for days after. She supposed it was a blow to his pride for her to question him about finances.

But she suspected his obstinance on the matter went deeper than that. The guilt he felt over leaving Derby in an orphanage weighed even more heavily on him since the suicide. It was too late for him to make restitution to his son. Instead, he had dedicated himself to taking care of Pearl and her.

She was strongly opposed to the idea of being accountable or indebted to anyone, even to her well-meaning father-in-law, but she didn't want to scotch renting the house by quarreling with him now. "When can we move in?"

He hooked his thumbs under his suspenders and ran them up and down as he took a slow look around.

"Well?" Laurel said.

"I'm taking stock."

"You're stalling."

"We don't have any furniture."

"We don't have any now!" she exclaimed, causing Pearl to stir. "Why are you so opposed to this, Irv?"

"I ain't."

"Good. We'll move in tomorrow."

Before he could say anything further, she turned on her heel and left through the front door. By the time he had followed, locked the door, and returned the key to its hiding place, she was in the car—in the driver's seat.

He hobbled around to the passenger side and opened the door. "What do you think you're doing?"

"Pearl's asleep. You can hold her while I drive."

"You need a lot more practice."

"I'll have five miles' worth after driving home. Now get in."

FOURTEEN

———◦◉◦———

Thatcher was confined to the jail cell throughout the day, although after deputies returned, he was allowed two visits to the lavatory. Harold grudgingly provided him with a bar of soap and a towel so he was able to wash up.

He heard people entering and leaving the building where briefings were held in the main room, but for most of the day the door at the end of the hall had remained closed, so he was unable to hear everything that was being said.

The telephone rang frequently. He supposed updates on the search for Mrs. Driscoll were being called in to Sheriff Amos, but Thatcher didn't sense a thunderbolt from any of the incoming information.

Darkness had fallen and the hubbub in the office had died down before Sheriff Amos came through the door. Thatcher hadn't seen him since their conversation that morning.

Apparent to Thatcher immediately was that the stressful day had taken a toll. Bill Amos probably had twenty-five years on Thatcher, but for a man of his age, he was fit. Tonight, however, he looked like he was under a lot of strain and weary to the bone.

Thatcher got up from the bunk and met him at the bars. "Any news?"

"We'll get to it." He hefted a lidded enamel pot by its wire handle. "Hungry?"

"I could do with something."

"Chicken and dumplings." He unlocked the cell and passed Thatcher the pot. "Take it by the handle. It's hot."

Thatcher took the pot, lifted the lid, and sniffed. "From the café?"

"One of Martin's specialities." He took a spoon and napkin from his shirt pocket and passed them through the bars. "Don't dig an escape tunnel with the spoon."

He said it with a smile that Thatcher returned. He carried the pot over to the bunk, where he set it down carefully so not to spill. The sheriff didn't withdraw, but stood just beyond the bars, staring at nothing, thoughtfully smoothing his mustache. Thatcher went back over and waited him out until he was ready to reveal the cause of his furrowed brow.

He began by saying, "There's news only about where Mrs. Driscoll isn't. Nothing about where she is. None of her kin has seen or heard from her. Her uncle and aunt drove up from New Braunfels. They took over for Scotty, staying with Dr. Driscoll."

"How's he doing?"

"At wits' end. Several times he tried to leave his house and join the search. Wrestled with Scotty and the uncle when they stopped him. Last I heard, they'd persuaded him to take a sleeping draught."

"What about me? Are you going to charge me or let me go?"

"The district attorney has taken it under advisement."

"What's that mean?"

"It means that even though we don't have a body or any sign of foul play, Mayor Croft is putting pressure on him."

"What kind of man is the district attorney? Hard or soft?"

Amos snickered. "Flexible."

"The mayor's ready to hang me from the nearest tree. I can't figure why."

Amos took a long, pondering look at him. Thatcher sensed they had arrived at the reason for the sheriff's frown. "Mr. Hutton, how familiar are you with the Anti-Saloon League?"

"Not familiar at all. Must've been formed while I was overseas. But the name sort of explains itself."

"Quite aptly. It's an organization of lobbyists, movers and shakers, zealots."

"Teetotalers."

"They don't merely choose to abstain themselves. Their goal is to rid the earth of every drop of alcohol, along with the people who make it and sell it."

"Then they must've got what they were after when Prohibition was made law."

Bill Amos gave a wry grunt. "Backed by our fire-breathing governor, the League succeeded before that. Last year, Texas passed laws that are stricter than the federal ones. They've made even minor infractions felonies, which carry much stiffer punishments."

"Did that curb consumption?"

Sheriff Amos gave a soft laugh. "Just the opposite. Since these laws went into effect, moonshining and bootlegging have become booming businesses."

Men wanting a drink would find one. Thatcher thought back on the two men at the boardinghouse who'd left together in search of booze. Hell, he remembered soldiers in the trenches fermenting whatever they could, making undrinkable concoctions which they drank anyway.

The sheriff continued. "Some members of the Anti-Saloon League, the governor included, are of the opinion that we local law enforcement agencies and personnel are soft on transgressors, that a large number of us are corrupt, and that we're doing a lousy job of helping them accomplish their goal of making Texas one hundred percent dry. So they've devised a way to 'assist' us in identifying, capturing, and prosecuting offenders."

"How's that?"

"By recruiting what the governor has termed 'innocent bystanders.'"

Thatcher said, "What the hell?"

"In order to convict a bootlegger, state law requires a third party eyewitness to testify to the illegal sale. Since an innocent bystander of such a transaction is rarer than hen's teeth, the League is—"

"Recruiting them."

The sheriff nodded. "Men to work undercover. They infiltrate areas where moonshiners are thriving. They make friends with the culprits, pretend to be one of them, gain their trust—"

"Then rat on them."

"In court and under oath." The sheriff took a deep breath and met Thatcher's gaze. "I think the reason our mayor took an immediate dislike to you is because he suspects you might be one of these official snitches." He raised his eyebrows. "I suspect it, too."

Thatcher gave a short laugh. "Me? I didn't even know there was such a thing. Only undercover agents I've ever heard of were Pinkerton men."

The sheriff stared at him, unfazed by his denial.

"Nobody sent me here," Thatcher said. "When I jumped off that train, I didn't even know where I was. It was dumb fate that I even wound up in this town."

"You're telling me the truth?"

"Damn straight."

"Texas Rangers didn't send you here to make sure I'm square and enforcing the law?"

"No."

"I wouldn't hold it against you."

"Swear to you, sheriff. And I'll tell you something else." He held up his hand, palm out so the cut was visible. "I'll defend myself against a guy wanting to knife me, but I wouldn't tattle on somebody that I'd befriended. That would go against my grain."

Amos assimilated that, then said, "All right, then. I'll take your word for it, and if Bernie ever voices his suspicion again, I'll tell him I already confronted you about it, and you flat out denied it."

"If the mayor suspects I've been sent to rout out local moonshiners, wouldn't he favor that? Why's he hostile?"

"Because he ramrods the most prosperous bootlegging operation in the region."

Thatcher took that news like a clip on the chin. "Son of a bitch," he said under his breath. "Why don't you arrest him?"

The sheriff grimaced. "That'd be messy."

Thatcher didn't press him to elaborate. He felt it possible that arresting the mayor would create a conflict of interest for the sheriff. The ethics of these men were no concern of his. Even if the sheriff dealt dirty on some matters, Thatcher felt that he was a basically good and conscientious man.

"Well, the mayor won't have to worry about me for long," Thatcher said. "I'll be heading up to the Panhandle soon. Assuming you let me go. I thought you'd've heard something from Mr. Hobson by now."

"Sheriff called me back. They had a hell of a sandstorm up there. The deputy dispatched to go out to the ranch got lost."

"I've experienced storms like that," Thatcher said. "You can't see a foot in front of you."

"Well, the fellow turned around and managed to make his way back to Amarillo without crashing into something. He'll try again tomorrow."

That was disappointing. Henry Hobson Jr. had been more than simply the man he'd cowboyed for. He'd been his mentor. Mr. Hobson was a man of his word. A character reference from him would go a long way toward clearing Thatcher of suspicion.

The sheriff was absently plucking at the corner of his mustache. Thatcher had come to recognize the signs. The sheriff wasn't done with him yet. Eventually he said, "There's something niggling me."

Thatcher thought it best not to ask what.

"When we brought you in here and started questioning you, why didn't you tell us you'd stopped at the Plummers' place?"

Thatcher's guard went up. "Didn't seem worth mentioning."

"Bullshit. It was damn worth mentioning because Laurel Plummer could have attested that you had the bruise, the cut, before you ever made it into town and met Mila Driscoll. You relied on Fred Barker to back you up. People in the boardinghouse. But you deliberately omitted mention of her. Why?"

Thatcher shifted his stance, knowing that it probably gave away his uneasiness. "I'd approached two women that day. They were strangers to me, and, best to my knowledge, alone. I thought if y'all knew about Mrs. Plummer, in addition to Mrs. Driscoll, it would look bad."

"It does. It looks bad that you didn't volunteer the information, and I don't think you're being completely honest with me now, are you? What happened out yonder at her place?"

"Not a thing. It was just like she said." She'd left out what had happened out by the water pail. Obviously she was embarrassed by that, and didn't want anybody knowing about it, so Thatcher wasn't going to give it away. But he could tell the sheriff the truth about the rest of it.

"In the short time I was there, it was plain to me that Mrs. Plummer had reached the end of her rope. I got the sense that she'd had more than her fair share of hard knocks lately, and I didn't want to heap on another problem for her."

"You felt compassion for her."

"I guess you could put it like that."

Amos took his measure, then exhaled heavily. "If you're indicted, I advise you against putting it like that. The mayor, the D.A. would pounce on it."

"I don't follow."

"You felt sorry for Mrs. Plummer, so you got your drink of water, your directions into town, and left her alone. Then you met Mila Driscoll. It could be surmised that you felt no compassion for her." He let the implication sink in, then nodded toward the bunk. "Don't let your supper get cold."

FIFTEEN

—◄•()•►—

Wallace Johnson had been born with a pair of jug ears like none other. Not only did they exemplify the term, they sat low on his head and were pointy on top. This manifestation of a problematic gene pool had made him a target for torment by his passel of siblings, by his mother when she got on one of her infamous tears, and by his classmates during all six years of his schooling.

He dropped out at the age of twelve and went into the family business, for which limited literacy wasn't a drawback.

By the time Wally had reached his late teens, the ridicule he'd suffered in his youth hadn't made him timid and fainthearted as one might expect. Instead he was arrogant, aggressive, and meaner than hell.

Somewhere along the way, he had learned to wiggle his ears, making them even more notable. Nowadays, when teased, he used this talent to distract from his reaching for brass knuckles, which he then vigorously applied to the individual who'd insulted him.

One of Gert's whores, who was relatively new to Lefty's and didn't hail from the area, was unaware of Wally Johnson's reputation for a short temper and violent bent.

She was fully aware of it now.

Which was why Gert had left her husband to tend to a middling crowd and had taken back roads out into the countryside to where two clear-running, spring-fed creeks converged, making it an ideal spot for one of the Johnson family's distilleries.

Wally was the family member assigned to operate and protect this particular still. Sometimes a kid cousin helped out with heavy lifting or needed repairs, but Wally preferred to work alone.

He lived in a lean-to tucked beneath a shelf of limestone, which helped shelter him from the elements. The geological configuration also hid the fire required to keep the sour mash cooking at a low boil, thus making the still unlikely to be detected. Wally's great-granddaddy Hiram had chosen the location for just that reason. The still had been producing corn liquor uninterrupted for decades.

When she was still a distance away, Gert rolled her Model T to a halt and blinked her headlights twice, slowly, then three times in rapid succession, signaling that she was a customer and not a hostile competitor or the law.

Wally emerged from his lean-to, cradling a rifle in the crook of his elbow, but, having recognized Gert's vehicle, motioned her forward. She drove up to within yards of where he stood, stopped, and climbed out.

She motioned toward the still. "Why ain't you cookin' tonight?"

"Didn't have a mind to," Wally replied. "You bring my money?"

She planted her hands on her broad hips. "Dammit, Wally, I'm as pissed off at you as I can be at a person, and that's sayin' somethin'."

"What for?"

"What for? I'll tell you what for. Thanks to you, I got a whore who's out of commission."

"You told me to do something that'd guarantee getting Doc Driscoll out to the roadhouse, and that's what I did. Saw him arrive myself."

"I told you to rough up the girl a *little*. You broke her arm, her jaw's out of whack, and her eye's all swole up and ain't sittin' right."

"She told me she'd as soon fuck a bat as me. Which I reminded her of, she said."

Gert gave a snort. "You've heard worse."

He held out his hand, palm up. "Twenty bucks, Gert."

"I ought to subtract what her ruint appearance will cost me in lost revenue." She looked over at his stockpile of moonshine. "But, because I'm a forgivin' person, I'll take a jar for the road, and we'll call it even."

He cursed her under his breath, but went over to a straw-lined crate, lifted out a mason jar of white lightning, and brought it back to her. She screwed off the lid and took a swallow. "You're one ugly son of a bitch, Wally, but you do make good 'shine."

"Twenty bucks." He held out his hand again.

Gert screwed the lid back onto the mason jar and tucked it in her left armpit, then reached into the pocket of her dress, took out a pistol, and shot Wally in the forehead. She bent over his supine form, stuck the bore of the pistol into one of his ears, and fired again.

As she was getting back into her car, she muttered, "Pissant cost me a week's worth of work out of that girl."

SIXTEEN

———◆———

Shortly after noon the next day, Harold came to Thatcher's cell.

His looks hadn't improved since Thatcher had last seen him. He might have explained that he'd mistaken him for a German soldier and apologized for messing up his face, but the deputy radiated so much hostility as he said, "They want to see you" that Thatcher didn't bother.

After being handcuffed, he was prodded out of the cell block and into the main room.

Mayor Croft was standing in front of a window, a position that cast him in silhouette, obscured his face, and made him the most imposing presence in the room, which Thatcher figured was his intention. If he thought Thatcher would be intimidated by either his public office or his bootlegging, he was wrong. Thatcher looked him square in the eye.

Sheriff Amos motioned Thatcher into a chair. "Coffee?"

Thatcher accepted.

The sheriff filled a mug from a pot simmering on a hot plate, then brought it over. When he bent down to place the mug in Thatcher's bound hands, he said under his breath, "Don't volunteer anything."

Then he straightened up, sat down on the corner of his desk, and commenced another interrogation. Beginning with the fight and Thatcher's leap from the freight train, they rehashed Thatcher's account of that day. The sheriff's questions were straightforward. Following his advice, Thatcher stuck to the facts and didn't expand on any of his statements.

Bernie Croft didn't pose any questions, but expressed his skepticism of Thatcher's truthfulness with snorts and harrumphs and dry coughs covered by his fist.

Thatcher finished with, "I went to bed, fell asleep, woke up with a shotgun in my face and y'all surrounding my bed."

The sheriff waited a beat, then looked over at Croft, who had remained in his spot by the window, but was now rocking back and forth on his heels like a man trying to keep his temper under control.

Bill said, "We don't have one iota of evidence implicating him, Bernie."

"Except that he was with Mrs. Driscoll earlier that day."

The sheriff dismissed that with a shake of his head. "Circumstantial. The D.A. has declined to indict him based on that alone."

"Something could still turn up."

"Mrs. Driscoll could still turn up."

"Dead."

"Let's pray that's not the case. But if, after further investigation, we discover something that does implicate Mr. Hutton in any wrongdoing, I'll be on him like a duck on a June bug."

The mayor scoffed. "He'll be long gone."

"He doesn't plan to leave town immediately."

"So he says."

Thatcher said, "Mr. Barker and I shook on me training that stallion before I leave."

"That's hardly a binding contract."

"It is to me."

Thatcher's words fell like four bricks into the room. Croft's face turned red, but he didn't respond. No one said anything. Then Sheriff Amos broke the taut silence.

"I've got to release him, Bernie. But I'll do so with the provision that he doesn't leave town. If not a suspect, he's still a material witness."

"Fine. But you're gambling with your reelection."

"Every damn day I'm in this office."

Because his warning didn't have the desired cowing effect on the sheriff, Croft strode across to the door, yanked his hat off the coat tree, and stormed out, pulling the door closed so hard, it rattled windowpanes.

Amos signaled to Harold. "Uncuff him."

With obvious disgust, the deputy lumbered over and removed the handcuffs.

Sheriff Amos said, "Mr. Hutton, you heard the condition of me letting you go. Don't run off."

"What if Mrs. Driscoll never turns up? I can't stick around here forever. I want to get home. No word from Amarillo?"

"Not yet, but it's early. It'll be a round trip for whoever drives out to the ranch, and you said it was a far piece from the city."

Thatcher acknowledged that, then said, "As much as anybody, I want to know what happened to Mrs. Driscoll. Not just for my sake. I hate to think."

"Me too," the sheriff said. "I've moved past hoping she'll turn up unharmed and with a logical explanation for her absence." Giving Thatcher a keen look, he said, "I'm letting you go. Don't betray my trust." Then he glanced over his shoulder at Harold. "You have his bag ready?"

The deputy carried over Thatcher's duffel and dropped it at his feet. "Everything's there, including the nudie pictures."

Thatcher gave him a sardonic grin. "Good. They're souvenirs I'm taking to the other hands at the ranch." He shouldered the strap of the bag and walked out.

Bill went home for lunch. He was halfway into his meal when the telephone rang. He left the table, went into the hall, and answered.

A deputy identified himself. "Wally Johnson's been found dead. Two bullet wounds through his head."

That was more than enough to spoil Bill's appetite. He pulled his napkin from his shirt collar and blotted his mouth. "Who found him?"

"A cousin."

"Where?"

The deputy described the scene. "The still was intact, there was a stockpile of product, barrels of mash were fermenting. Only thing spoiled was Wally."

"What's the cousin's name? Besides Johnson."

"Elray."

"He owned up to moonshining?"

"Kid's only fourteen. He was scared shitless that whoever did in Wally was going to come after him, too. Said he'd rather be in jail as in Wally's shoes."

"How do I get there?"

The deputy gave him directions. "I'll wait for you at the turnoff. Otherwise you might miss it."

"Has the J.P. been notified?"

"He's on his way. Not that we need an official pronouncement. Wally's deader'n a doornail. Shot through one of his ears."

Sighing over the ill-concealed mirth in the deputy's voice, Bill hung up. But no sooner had he turned away from the telephone than it rang a second time. He picked it up again. "This is Sheriff Amos."

Gabe Driscoll sat at the dining table, force feeding himself from the plate of food Mila's aunt had insisted he eat.

He had met these relatives of Mila's only once before, and that had been on his wedding day. Whenever Mila had gotten homesick for her extended Teutonic family, with whom he had nothing in common, not even language, he would put her on a train and cite a heavy patient load as his excuse for not accompanying her.

Yesterday, these family ambassadors hadn't so much arrived as *descended*. They had been beside themselves with worry over Mila's fate. But it had come as an unwelcome surprise that they were equally worried about him and his fragile condition.

They'd smothered him with platitudes, advice, sympathy, and affection, which he didn't want, and certainly hadn't earned. His only means of escape had been to lock himself in his bedroom with a "sleeping draught," which had been a bootlegged bottle of bourbon.

This morning, when he'd come downstairs looking even more haggard than he had yesterday, the older couple seemed intent on convincing him that whatever had become of Mila, her leaving hadn't been voluntary.

He'd said, "I'll admit that I wondered if she'd had a man in her life before she met me. Maybe she had heard from him and—"

They chorused a swift denial. She hadn't had a serious beau before him. She wouldn't have forsaken him or broken her marriage vows, not their Mila. She loved Gabe dearly and wanted desperately to be a mother. He'd coughed a sob and held his head between his hands. "Of course I know that. I *do*. I'm certain she didn't leave of her own accord."

Now, having eaten enough to pacify the aunt, he thanked her for preparing lunch, excused himself from the dining room, and barricaded himself in his office, where he poured himself a bourbon.

He carried the drink over to the sofa, took off his shoes, and reclined, covering his scratchy, burning eyes with his forearm. He hadn't slept in two nights. His cuffs were loose, his collar button undone, his trousers wrinkled from having been wallowed in.

If he caught a glimpse of himself in a reflective surface, he barely recognized the image. He looked like a bum, bearing scant resemblance to the self-possessed physician who people relied on for healing and succor.

He very much doubted that he would ever regain the high regard and status that he'd had before his wife had gone missing. Even if

Mila had abandoned him of her own volition, her mysterious disappearance would leave a stain on him as permanent as a port wine birthmark.

That distressing thought was interrupted when he heard an automobile approaching. Sheriff Amos? That deputy, Scotty, again? Had they found her?

Heart thumping, he drained his bourbon, rolled up off the sofa, and padded over to the bay window. Peeking around the edge of the drapery, he watched a shiny black touring car come to a stop in front of his house. Around town, it was a familiar automobile. As was the driver, whose name was Jimmy Hennessy. He got out and assisted Bernie Croft from the backseat.

The mayor strutted up Gabe's walkway, chest thrust out like a despot about to watch a parade of his military might.

Hennessy stayed with the car, a daunting, pugnacious presence against the backdrop of Miss Wise's Victorian house and bright petunia beds.

The doorbell jingled. Mila's uncle went to answer. Gabe heard him quietly explaining that the doctor was unavailable to visitors and wouldn't be seeing patients until further notice.

Bernie, of course, was having none of it. He declared that the doctor would see *him*. Over the uncle's objections, Bernie came inside. Gabe followed the sound of his footsteps, which stopped outside his office door.

There was hard knocking. "Gabe, it's Bernie."

Gabe's head dropped forward, and he maintained that helpless pose until the door was rapped on again, this time more imperiously.

"Open up."

Gabe trudged to the door, flipped the lock, and pulled it open. Looking beyond Bernie, Gabe addressed the apologetic uncle. "It's all right. Mayor Croft is a friend."

The uncle retreated. Bernie forged in. Gabe closed the door.

Bernie went straight over to the ledge of the bookshelf where he helped himself to the bottle of bourbon, splashing some into a tumbler. When Bernie turned and extended the bottle toward Gabe, he shook his head.

Noticing the empty glass on the end table beside the sofa, Bernie said, "Just as well, I think. Appears you've already been imbibing."

Gabe didn't reply, but returned to the sofa and slumped against the back cushions. Mila had spent months painstakingly doing the crewelwork on them.

The mayor made himself comfortable in an armchair. "You should open a window, Gabe. You stink. The whole room reeks of you."

He could smell his sour odor himself. Since having to report Mila missing, he hadn't washed, hadn't shaved. With indifference, he'd observed himself becoming more and more disheveled, but had done nothing to stop the deterioration.

"That's what you came to tell me? That I stink?"

Bernie took a sip of whiskey. "The D.A. has declined to indict Hutton. He's been released from custody."

That was hardly surprising, as no evidence had been found to implicate him. But that he'd been eliminated as a suspect wasn't welcome news, which Gabe supposed was the reason Bernie had come to break it to him personally.

"No other persons of interest?"

"None. Of course they're continuing the search. But sooner or later the zeal will begin to flag, and, eventually, they'll stop looking. I'm sure you realize that."

Gabe nodded morosely.

The mayor crossed one leg over the other and propped his glass of whiskey on his knee.

Alerted by the feigned casualness, Gabe sat up straighter. "What?"

"Do you recognize the name Wally Johnson?"

"Of the infamous Johnsons?"

"More infamous than most. It was Wally who beat up that whore at Lefty's. The one you were summoned to treat."

"So?"

"His body was found this morning. He'd been assassinated. My sources in the sheriff's department tell me it was ghastly. Carrion birds and such."

Gabe just looked at him with dispassion.

After an ahem, Bernie said, "The reason I bring it up, this homicide will divert attention from your wife's disappearance. Now that Bill Amos has a murder to solve, and seeing as how it involves a pack of jackals like the Johnsons, he'll be focused on that. The missing person's case will fade into thin air."

Gabe plopped back onto the cushions. "What happens then?"

"You resume your practice. And you begin working for me."

Gabe dug his middle finger and thumb into his eye sockets. He mumbled, "I don't think I can."

Around a soft laugh Bernie said, "You can. You will. Consider this a swift kick in the ass."

Gabe lowered his hand from his eyes. "It's too soon. I'm not over the shock of Mila yet."

"Get over it. Patience isn't my strong suit."

"Look at me, Bernie. I can barely function, much less take on...additional responsibilities."

Bernie tossed back the rest of his whiskey and, with a decisive thump, set the glass beside Gabe's empty one on the end table. "This whining won't do, Gabe."

With desperation, he said, "I can't just snap my fingers and have things return to any kind of normalcy. It's going to take time."

"Of course, you're right." Smiling, the mayor got up and walked over to the sofa. He set a heavy hand on Gabe's shoulder and gave it a paternal squeeze. "You have two weeks."

It was nearly four o'clock in the afternoon before Bill made the return trip to town. It was a long drive, allowing him time to mentally review what he'd observed at the scene of the homicide and what he knew about the Johnson clan.

They were notorious for thumbing their noses at the laws against their industry. If a family member was caught plying his trade, he paid his fine—and, more often than not, a granny fee to empathetic officials. These payoffs were considered a cost of doing business. The additional expense was passed along to the consumer, and the offender and his kinfolk continued making moonshine with impunity.

But in the months since the Volstead Act went into effect, and the ensuing crackdown on offenders, culprits were getting prison time in addition to being fined.

However, the possibility of stiffer punishment hadn't seemed to deter or unduly concern Wally Johnson. Crates of his product were stacked in plain sight outside his hovel, with no apparent attempt having been made to hide it from whomever had killed him. His rifle was still lying in the crook of his arm.

Evidently Wally's young cousin Elray wasn't from the most stalwart branch of the family tree. He blubbered unedited answers to all Bill's questions, providing the names of Wally's friends as well as his sworn enemies.

When asked if he had any idea who would have wanted to murder Wally so ruthlessly, Elray had dragged his sleeve across his snotty nose and replied, "Any of 'em. He wasn't generally liked, ya know. But everybody was mad at him over that girl. It drew unwanted attention."

"What girl?"

"Corrine, I think her name is. Out at Lefty's."

Bill was still mulling over Elray's explanation as he approached the Quanah Parker Creek bridge, a town landmark and one of Mayor Croft's crowning achievements, which he unabashedly advertised.

Fred Barker's auto garage was just this side of the bridge. Guessing he would find Thatcher Hutton there, Bill pulled in. Fred and his assistant mechanic were changing a tire. Seeing Bill approach, Fred wiped his hands on a shop rag and met him halfway.

"What brings ya, sheriff? Hutton?"

Bill noticed the apprehension in the other man's voice and said, "I didn't come with a warrant."

"I'm glad to hear it. A deputy came by yesterday, asked could I back up Hutton's story. I did. Down to the letter. He showed up a while ago, and apologized a dozen times for being two days late for work." Barker chuckled and the sheriff smiled.

"Is he still around?"

Fred told Roger to keep at what he was doing, then struck off toward the stable. Bill fell into step with him.

"Thatcher worked with that ornery stud for a bit," Fred said. "Then asked if he could inventory my tack, see if anything needed repair or replacement. He's conscientious. Not like Roger," he mumbled and spat out a chunk of tobacco. "I saw him come out of the stable a while ago. He's probably back here."

Bill was led around the stable to the corral. Thatcher and the stallion were in the center of it. Thatcher was lightly dragging a wound lasso in an unhurried and unending circuit along the horse's back, down his flank, across his barrel to his shoulder and back up again to his withers. During one of these rotations, the animal got spooked for no good reason Bill could discern. Thatcher spoke softly and stroked him with his hand, settling him before applying the rope again.

He acknowledged their arrival with a glance over his shoulder. "Getting him used to the sight and feel of a rope."

"Never thought I'd see it," Barker said, sounding proud.

"We've got a long way to go," Thatcher told him. "At this point, he trusts me only so far."

Thrasher hung the lasso on his shoulder and rubbed the stallion's neck with both hands while softly commending him for being so cooperative. "But you've had enough for today." He stroked his forehead and muzzle, then left him and joined the men outside the corral.

"Impressive," Bill said.

"You know horses?"

"Know enough to stay off them unless I can't help it."

Thatcher grinned. "I'm happy to give you some pointers."

"Sheriff!"

The three turned in unison to see Harold jogging toward them and Roger rounding the corner of the stable.

The next sequence of events happened with lightning-bolt suddenness.

Thatcher's right hand smacked his right thigh, then, in a single, fluid motion, he jerked the Colt six-shooter from Bill's holster and fired at Harold, who fell back onto the ground.

Fred Barker slapped his hand against his heart.

The stallion went berserk.

Bill heard the report before it had even registered that Thatcher had disarmed him and fired his weapon.

By the time he gathered his wits and realized what had happened, Thatcher had lowered his gun hand. He calmly turned to Bill and extended him the pistol, grip first.

Barker blurted, "What in tarnation?"

The gunshot had stopped Roger in his tracks. Now he ran over to where Harold lay prone and called to them excitedly, "His head's blowed clean off."

SEVENTEEN

Roger bent down and picked up the dead rattlesnake lying within inches of Harold's size thirteen boots. The deputy struggled into a sitting position. Thatcher ran over to him. He didn't even glance at the snake, but gave Harold a helping hand up. "There was no time to warn you. You all right?"

Stupefied, Harold nodded.

Roger was as energized as if he'd been plugged into an electrical socket. "Six feet if he's an inch." He dangled the limp, headless body, looking at Thatcher with bug-eyed admiration. "Never saw shooting like that."

Bill had never seen anything like it, either. Not in all his days. And he'd grown up in a family of excellent marksmen, skilled with both long guns and pistols.

"Can I keep the skin?" Roger asked Thatcher.

"Makes no difference to me."

Assured that Harold was all right, Thatcher went back to the corral and directed his concern to the stallion as he thrashed around the paddock, his eyes crazed, whinnying at a high pitch.

Fred Barker said to Bill, "I've had about all the excitement I can stand for one afternoon. I'll leave you to ask your questions of Mr. Hutton. After witnessing what you just did, you prob'ly have a few more."

He motioned for Roger to go along with him. They walked off together with Roger chattering nonstop about Thatcher's incredible shot and his prize snake skin.

Bill turned to Harold, who still hadn't said a word. Bill guessed he hadn't quite regained his senses, and who could blame him? "What did you come out here for, Harold?"

"Oh, uh, to tell you that the J.P. turned Wally's body over to the undertaker."

"I want to take another look at him before he's embalmed."

"Figured that. I told the undertaker to hold off till you got there." Harold looked over at Thatcher. "Guess I owe him a thanks."

"No, go on. Tomorrow will be soon enough."

Appearing both relieved and humbled, Harold turned and walked off in the direction of the auto shop.

For several minutes, Bill watched Thatcher talking soothingly to the stallion, then walked over to join him. The horse had been kicking at the fence as he bucked and reared. He'd settled down somewhat, but his ears were still flattened back. As Bill sidled up to Thatcher, he asked, "Did he hurt himself?"

"I was afraid he might've. So far, though, no signs he did. I didn't stop to think how the gunshot would booger him."

"You reacted out of reflex."

"I saw Harold about to step right into that rattler and…" He trailed off, raising a shoulder.

"Where'd you learn to shoot like that?"

"On the ranch. Part of the job."

Bill looked at him skeptically. "Quick draw?"

"Never know when you'll have to fend off a predator."

"Of every sort, I would imagine."

"You name it. Wolves. Coyotes. Rattlers."

"Rustlers?"

Thatcher looked at him, his eyes hard and alight with anger. "What? You think I'm a hired gun or something?"

Bill didn't back down. "Are you? Have you ever killed a man, Mr. Hutton?"

"Plenty. I was a hired gunman for Uncle Sam." He spoke with soft but angry emphasis, then turned back to watch the stallion. "I think he'll settle. He just got spooked. I'm calling it a day." As he turned away from the paddock, Bill fell into step with him.

"Did you come straight here from the jail?"

"Yeah."

"Where's your duffel bag?"

"In the stable."

"Get it. I'll drive you."

"No thanks, I'll walk."

"I'll drive you."

———

Once underway, the sheriff said, "Strange day."

It was clear to Thatcher that Sheriff Amos still harbored some suspicion of him. If it hadn't been for that goddamn diamondback...But it had happened, and the sheriff had seen it, and now he'd tossed out a remark that Thatcher didn't think was offhanded. Unsure of how he was expected to respond, he didn't.

"For instance," the sheriff continued, "on my way to the office this morning, I came across Irv Plummer. That old truck of his was pulled off to the side of the road."

"Broken down?"

"Overloaded."

Thatcher was curious, but pretended not to be.

The sheriff said, "He was moving."

"Moving what?"

"Domiciles."

Thatcher looked over at him then. "Domiciles?"

"He's rented a house out on the north side of town. With a sickly grandbaby, he thought it best to be closer in."

"They were moving today?"

"He said his daughter-in-law had put her foot down."

It would be a small foot, but Thatcher could envision her planting it firmly and issuing an ultimatum, spine stiff, chin angled up. It was an image he would enjoy dwelling on if he were alone. He said, "Did he say how the baby's doing?"

"They took her to Dr. Perkins. He gave her some medicine." The sheriff made a right turn and honked at a spotted dog that was trotting down the center of the street.

"Then," he said, picking up where he'd left off, "after releasing you, and while I was at home having lunch, I got two telephone calls. The first was to notify me of a homicide."

Thatcher's heart thumped. "Mrs. Driscoll?"

"No. No sign of her yet, and the search parties are getting weary."

"They can't stop looking."

"My office won't. But volunteers are just that: volunteers. They've got businesses to run, farms to work, cattle to tend. In all truth, Mr. Hutton, we may never know what happened to her."

"People don't just vanish."

"Actually they do."

That was a depressing thought. Not only because of the effect the unsolved mystery could have on his future, but it distressed him that he might never know the kind woman's fate.

"A fellow named Wally Johnson."

Thatcher had to clear his mind of Mrs. Driscoll before the sheriff's words sank in. "Sorry?"

"The murder victim. Well known around here." The sheriff went on to describe the volatile temperament of the deceased and the disreputable family that had spawned him.

Thatcher took it in. "Sounds like you need to find the killer before his kinfolks do. Cream doesn't rise to the top. Bad blood does."

"There you're right. If ever a pack of miscreants adhered to the an-eye-for-an-eye system of justice, it's the Johnsons. If a competing moonshiner is suspected of killing Wally, it'll be like lighting a short fuse to a powder keg. It's happened before. One rival shoots another. People take sides. Old grudges are reignited. Bodies start stacking up. It's all-out warfare until a truce is negotiated."

"Is Bernie Croft one of the Johnsons' competitors?"

The sheriff smiled across at him. "Bernie would never do his own killing." He pulled to a stop near the railroad depot, fifty yards shy of the boardinghouse. "If I took you to the door, it would look official."

"This is fine. Thanks for the ride." Thatcher reached for the door handle.

"The logical conclusion to draw," the sheriff said as he shut off the engine, leaned back in his seat, and began stroking his mustache, "is that another, probably less successful, competitor killed Wally out of jealousy or spite."

Thatcher resettled in his seat, accepting the sheriff's implied invitation for him to stay while he did his thinking out loud.

He looked over at Thatcher, hesitated for a moment, then said, "You're a good listener. I've noticed that about you, because, in that way, you remind me of my boy. Other ways, too."

"Was he your only son?"

"Only child."

Damn. "Did he have a family?"

"Not yet. He was keen on a certain young lady but hadn't declared himself. I heard recently that she's engaged. I'm happy for her, of course, but I can't help wondering, wishing..."

He gave Thatcher a rueful smile, then began to describe the position Wally Johnson's body had been in when found, and the ruthless nature of the wounds. He told Thatcher about the teenaged cousin who'd made the gruesome discovery.

"Elray says he got to the still early this morning prepared to put in a day's work. Saw Wally spread-eagled on the ground. 'Drawing flies,' he said. He drove to the nearest gas station and used the telephone to call it in. I caught up with him and deputies already at the scene. The kid was as skittish as that stallion you're trying to train. Least little sound, Elray would jump three feet."

He paused before continuing. "What I can't figure is this. If it was a competitor, or any perceived enemy, why was Wally found lying flat on his back, holding a rifle that hadn't been fired? The shot to the ear was overkill. He was already dead. The shot that killed him was fired point-blank."

"He and his killer were face-to-face."

"If Wally felt anything at all, it was a split second of shock."

"No resistance?"

"Looks like none."

"Then he knew the person, trusted him to get that close."

"That's what I'm thinking."

"Well, you're probably right, sheriff. I hope you catch the culprit soon. Thanks again for the lift." Thatcher opened the passenger door and put his right foot on the running board, but got no farther before the sheriff waylaid him again.

"None of the Johnsons are geniuses. As book-learning goes, they're ignorant. But they're cagey, wily, and came out of the womb lying. Even so, I believe Elray was telling the truth. Too scared not to, I think. And he told me something that I keep going back to."

"Something niggling you."

"Exactly that." The sheriff gave him a crooked smile and shook his index finger at him. "See? I noted that you're a good listener. Anyway, Elray told me that he and Wally were at Lefty's Roadhouse night before last. You know Lefty's?"

Thatcher shook his head.

"It's a blind tiger."

Thatcher couldn't contain his surprise. "A speakeasy here in Foley?"

"I see you're familiar with the term."

Thatcher shrugged with chagrin and pulled his foot back into the car. "In Norfolk, when we got off the troop ship, some buddies and me were ready to let off steam."

The sheriff smiled in a way that didn't pass judgment. "Your first stop off the boat was a speakeasy."

"One of the ship's crewmen who'd been to this one gave us the password. Never would've known it was there otherwise."

"What was the front?"

"A haberdashery. Family owned, established 1898. There was a black-and-gold sign above the door."

"A family of smart entrepreneurs, it seems. These days booze is selling hotter than tweeds."

Thatcher chuckled. "We didn't go there for tweeds."

"Good stock of liquor?"

"Nobody left thirsty."

"Ladies?"

Thatcher didn't say anything, but he figured his expression was telling enough.

The sheriff chuckled. "Was it a nice place?"

"Nice enough for us. We'd come off a troop ship. We didn't care whether or not it was high-toned."

"Well, Lefty's isn't high-toned. Not by a long shot. It's a roadhouse, a typical diner that serves fat hamburgers. It's also a cathouse. Gert, Lefty's wife—probably common law—oversees that aspect of their business.

"It was a popular watering hole, but since Lefty can't sell liquor legally anymore, customers have to enter through a rear door into a back room. Bootleg booze and locally made moonshine flow as steady as Quanah Parker Creek during a heavy rain."

Thatcher didn't see how any of this concerned him, so he didn't comment.

"Now, I don't meddle in Lefty's business so long as the peace is kept and nobody bleeds overmuch. But Wally died with his brains in the dirt. Approximately twenty-four hours earlier, he was at Lefty's where, according to his cousin, he got a little too amorous with one of the girls upstairs. She didn't favor him, turned him down in terms to which he took exception, and he beat the hell out of her.

"This afternoon, I dropped by there to ask her about the incident, to see if it had any relevance to Wally's murder. He'd bashed in her mouth and broken her arm. In time, those will heal, but she'll be lucky not to lose sight in one eye." He shook his head and made a sound of profound regret. "She's seventeen."

A train came rumbling into the station, spewing steam, its brakes squealing. The sheriff let the noise die down before resuming. "The reason it's bothering me is that Dr. Driscoll went out to Lefty's that night for the purpose of patching up that girl."

Thatcher reacted with a start. "The same night Mrs. Driscoll disappeared?"

"That's why she was alone in the house. Gabe had told me about the incident at Lefty's. He didn't name Wally Johnson as the offender. He might not have known. But that connection is what niggles." The sheriff shrugged. "It's thready, at best. May be nothing. Could be something."

Thatcher turned his head aside and watched passengers disembark from the train. Some were greeted, others not. A porter unloaded luggage. The engineer climbed down from the locomotive and stood on the platform, stretching his back.

The atmosphere inside the sheriff's car had become weighty, although, if pressed, Thatcher couldn't have said why. Sensing that the sheriff was waiting for a response from him, he said, "It's probably just a coincidence."

"Probably. An interesting one, though."

After a lapse, Thatcher said, "Well, my landlady is a stickler for clearing the sideboard on the dot. I don't want to miss supper. Thanks again for the lift."

"Thatcher?"

He'd been about to step from the car, but pulled up short when the sheriff addressed him by his first name, something he hadn't done before. He turned back to him.

"I told you I'd received two telephone calls during lunch. The second was the one you've been waiting on from the sheriff's department in Amarillo. I hate telling you. Truly, I do. Some while back, Mr. Hobson passed away."

EIGHTEEN

—◦—

B ill Amos didn't soft-soap it. Not that it mattered how delicately he broke the news. To Thatcher it came as a heavy blow.

Mr. Hobson had suffered a stroke. His son Henry Hobson III had sold the herd, sold the ranch.

Learning of Mr. Hobson's passing was dismantling enough, but Thatcher listened with disbelief when the sheriff told him that the ranch, his home for fifteen years, no longer existed. "Trey *sold* the ranch?"

"Not the land itself," Bill explained, "but what's under it. Oil leases. Dozens of them. Everybody's punching holes in the ground up there, looking for oil."

Thatcher couldn't bear the thought of the sweeping plains being dotted with drilling derricks instead of beef cattle. But he wasn't surprised that Henry III's eye was on the future rather than the past.

Much to Mr. Hobson Jr.'s disappointment, his son never had desired to take over the ranch and had wanted nothing to do with the operation of it. When Thatcher had left for Europe in 1917, Trey had already moved to Dallas and was serving in a managerial capacity in a bank, on his way up.

"What happened to all the ranch hands?"

"I don't know, Thatcher," the sheriff replied. The intimate conversation had established a first-name basis between them. "I guess they scattered. The deputy who went out there said the place was deserted except for a dog that looked half wolf, and an old Mexican man."

"Jesse," Thatcher said. "He was born on the ranch. His daddy worked for the first Mr. Hobson, Henry senior. His mother cooked for the family."

"Well, Jesse was still out there, living in the bunkhouse. He told the deputy he would stay until somebody forced him off, or he died. He preferred the latter."

That sounded like Jesse.

"He was glad to learn that you'd survived the war," Bill said. "He's been safeguarding your trunk and saddle. He sent the trunk back to Amarillo with the deputy so he could put it on a train. He was reluctant to send the saddle, though. Didn't trust it to arrive undamaged or not at all."

Thatcher nodded absently. He would make arrangements to reclaim it later. In the meantime, he struggled to take in that Mr. Hobson was gone.

"I'm awfully sorry about this, Thatcher," the sheriff said.

Thatcher replied by rote, "Thanks."

He retrieved his duffel bag from the backseat of the sheriff's car and returned to the boardinghouse. He hadn't been back since being hauled out in handcuffs. He ignored Landlady May's glare and the sidelong glances of the other boarders, and, skipping supper, went straight upstairs to his room, where he weathered a sleepless night remembering the kindness and generosity of the man under whose wing he had spent formative years of his life.

The next morning, shortly after breakfast when all the other boarders had cleared out, he used the telephone in the central hallway to place a long-distance call to the bank in Dallas where Trey Hobson worked. He had to wait for five minutes for the local telephone office to get through.

A lady with a smooth and polite voice answered with the name of the bank. Thatcher asked to speak to Mr. Hobson. "May I ask who's calling?"

Thatcher gave her his name. "He knows me. Up till the war, I was a hand on his daddy's ranch. I didn't learn about Mr. Hobson till yesterday. I phoned to tell Trey how sorry I am."

"Please hold on, Mr. Hutton. I'll get him to the phone."

She came back about a minute later, still smooth and polite. "Regrettably, he's in a meeting, Mr. Hutton, and can't talk right now, but he said to tell you that he's relieved and glad to know that you made it back from the war, and that it was very kind of you to call about his father."

"Okay. I have a number here, if he gets a chance to call me back. It's in Foley."

He gave her the information and hung up, disappointed but not surprised that Trey was unavailable to talk to him. Mr. Hobson had shared more interests with Thatcher than he had with his son. Although Trey never would have wanted to switch places with Thatcher, Thatcher felt he might have resented the relationship that had developed between Mr. Hobson and him. But then again, Trey had never warmed to any of the cowhands, regarding all of them as nothing more than hired help.

His trunk arrived two days later. Thatcher picked it up at the depot and opened it in the privacy of his room. He'd placed his most cherished possessions on top, so they were the first things he saw when he raised the lid: a tooled leather gun belt with holster and a shiny Colt revolver with a stag horn grip. They'd been Mr. Hobson's gift to him on his eighteenth birthday. From that day forward, he'd strapped it on every day until he'd packed it in the trunk. The pistol had been what he'd reached for when he saw the rattlesnake poised to strike Harold.

For the next week, he went about his business, but without enthusiasm. He slogged through each day, the finality of his mentor's death catching him at odd times, and he would experience the crushing impact of the news all over again.

The more permanent residents of the boardinghouse continued to be standoffish. He sensed that they still harbored doubts about his innocence regarding Mrs. Driscoll. He didn't mind them keeping their distance. He didn't feel like making meaningless conversation.

However, one evening after supper, he was invited to join a round of poker being played out on the porch. The stakes were diddly, but a dollar was a dollar, so he anted up. He won five hands straight. Then, to avoid antagonizing the others, he lost the next two hands on purpose before excusing himself.

The landlady made no secret of her dislike and mistrust of him, but she accepted his rent money for the second week.

***

Laurel was certain the preacher knew the appropriate scriptures by heart. He was old. No doubt he had performed this rite hundreds of times.

Nevertheless, he held his Bible open in the palm of one hand and pretended to read the passages. Although they came from several books of both the Old Testament and the New, he never turned a single page. It would have been awkward for him even to try. In his other hand, he was holding an open umbrella above his head.

Rain drummed on it so loudly, it made his creaky voice nearly inaudible.

Low, dark clouds had created a false dusk at midmorning. The rain fell straight down in oppressive monotony. Even so, Laurel welcomed the miserable weather. On the day she was burying her daughter, even one ray of sunshine would have seemed obscene.

Pearl had died less than twenty-four hours ago, but there had been no reason to postpone her interment. There was no one to host a wake, and no one to invite even if one had been held. The undertaker had an infant coffin in his stockroom. The plot next to Derby's was available. No purpose would have been served to delay the inevitable.

The preacher closed his Bible. "Please join me in prayer."

Beside her, in spite of the rain, Irv removed his hat before bowing his head. Because she couldn't bear seeing the tiny coffin being pounded by the rain, she bowed her head and tightly closed her eyes as she joined the preacher and her father-in-law in reciting the Lord's prayer.

Two grave diggers hunched inside rubber rain capes had been standing by. They moved in immediately after the amen and began lowering the casket. Laurel, unable to watch it being buried, turned away.

The bleak trio made their way back to their cars. Irv had driven them to the cemetery in her roadster. When they reached it, they thanked the preacher, who looked relieved that the brief service wasn't being prolonged. He made a hasty departure.

Irv and she rode home in silence. Their footsteps echoed in the hollow silence of the house as they let themselves in. "You want me to put the kettle on, make you some tea?"

Laurel wanted to decline the offer, but Irv looked so distraught, she thought that perhaps he needed a task to alleviate his despair. "That sounds nice. Thank you."

She removed her hat and sat down at the table. He brewed her tea. He took his secreted jar of whiskey from the cabinet. "A touch of this wouldn't hurt you."

"No thank you."

He poured some of the moonshine into a glass for himself. "You hungry?"

She shook her head. He sat down across from her. They sipped their beverages. After a lengthy silence, he said, "I was tore up when Derby died. But nothing like this. This hurts something awful."

Looking across at him, she watched his eyes fill.

"Derby died of his own choosing," he said, gulping a breath. "That baby girl didn't."

Then a terrible sound issued from deep in his throat, and he began to cry. Laurel left her chair in a rush, knelt beside his chair, and placed her arms around his shoulders, drawing him to her. They clung to each other as he wept. She murmured to him all the banalities that would cause her to scream and run mad if anyone were saying them to her. Yet he seemed to derive comfort from them.

He cried himself out. As he wiped his wet face with the large handkerchief he always carried in his back pocket, he looked embarrassed.

"I haven't carried on like that since Derby's mother passed. It helped a little to get it out. What can I do for you, Laurel?"

"Nothing, thank you. I'm going up to my room."

"I understand. But you'll let me know if you need anything?"

"I will."

"The hurt will never leave you, but you learn to tuck it away," he said, tapping his heart, "and get on."

She gave him a wan smile. But as she climbed the stairs, she doubted that she would survive the night. She would surely die of grief.

At first, Thatcher had been too aggrieved over Mr. Hobson's demise to give much thought to how it would affect his future. But soon he had to face the reality of his situation and figure out a way to make money. Even living frugally, he'd gone through his poker winnings from the men on the freight train and at the boardinghouse. He couldn't live for long on a dollar fifty a day.

One afternoon, Thatcher approached Fred Barker. "I'm making progress with the stallion. But I've got to scare up more business for myself."

"What's on your mind?"

"You've got five empty stalls that aren't earning you a cent. If I can get some horses to work with, how much will you charge me to stable them here and use your paddock?"

They struck a deal that Thatcher thought favored him. But it wouldn't matter how good the terms were if he couldn't fill the stalls.

He put in another few evenings of poker at the boardinghouse, won the largest pot each night, and invested his winnings in having handbills printed. He spent the next Saturday afternoon going around town nailing them to utility poles.

That's when he spotted Laurel Plummer on the other side of Main Street. Her hair was in a long braid hanging down her back out from under a wide-brimmed straw hat. She was dressed in a dark skirt, a white blouse, and a pair of black gloves. She was trying to secure something on top of the trunk of her Model T with a leather strap. Looked to Thatcher like the strap wasn't cooperating.

He hit the head of the nail he'd been hammering one final time, then, taking the sack of nails, hammer, and handbills with him, he crossed the street. "Need a hand?"

She let go of the strap and whipped around. As before, her features were taut, her expression guarded. They relaxed only slightly when she recognized him. "Oh. Mr. Hutton."

"Hi."

"Hi."

"Seems you're always wrestling with something." He gestured toward the strap. He saw now that she'd been trying to get the ends to meet so she could buckle it.

She looked him up and down, taking in his cowboy hat, faded shirt, and dusty boots, then turned away and resumed pulling on the strap. "My father-in-law told me they had released you from jail."

"They had no reason to hold me in the first place."

"Mrs. Driscoll is still missing."

She yanked hard on the strap as she glanced over her shoulder at him. If she had meant that as an implied accusation, he wasn't going to honor it with a denial. "I heard you moved into town."

"That's right."

"Do you like your new house?"

"It's a far cry from new, but it's better than where we were. How's your hand?"

He held it up, palm out. "Healed. How's your little girl?"

She gave the strap another yank. "She died."

The ground seemed to give way underneath him. Her blunt statement had left him dumbfounded, and she must have sensed it. She stopped grappling with the strap and faced him.

"Please don't feel like you have to say anything, Mr. Hutton. Actually, I would rather you didn't."

"All right."

"It's just that it's difficult for me to talk about."

He nodded. "I can see where it would be."

She wet her lips, then pulled the lower one through her teeth.

He squinted up at the sun and readjusted the brim of his hat to shade his eyes.

After several awkward moments, he set the sack of nails, hammer, and handful of flyers on the hood of the car, then stepped around her and easily buckled the strap over several bundles of what looked like household goods. He gave it a test tug. "That ought to hold."

"Thank you."

"You're welcome."

He looked down at her. The straw brim of her hat cast a patterned shadow over her face that intrigued him. Or, he just liked looking at her. Her eyes were green. And skittish. They looked everywhere except back at him.

A strand of hair had escaped both the braid and her hat. She pushed at it with the back of her wrist, the small knob of which barely cleared the curled edge of her worn leather glove. He didn't remember ever seeing a wrist that delicate or a gesture that feminine.

But if he weren't mistaken, the collarless shirt she wore was a man's garment. It was way too large for her. The sleeves were rolled back, forming bulky cuffs against her thin forearms. The top button had been left open, exposing the triangular hollow at the base of her throat and making it about the most tempting patch of skin on the planet.

Her darting eyes eventually landed on the handbills. She tilted her head in order to read the bold printing upside down. "You break and train horses for a living?"

"Trying to."

"That explains the cowboy clothes." She glanced down at the ground. "The boots make you taller."

Pleased to know that she'd noticed anything about him, he lifted his foot and looked at the scuffed riding heel. "I reckon so. I never thought about the height thing because I've always worn them. Only recently have I been without. These didn't catch up to me until a few days ago, and it was like meeting up with old friends."

He explained about the trunk. "It had been up there waiting on me, but turns out I won't be going back to the Panhandle, after all."

"No?"

"No. Circumstances up there changed while I was gone. Anyhow, these britches are more suited to my occupation." He grinned. "The seat of my suit pants ripped the first time I got thrown."

"Thrown? You mean bucked off?"

"That's what I mean. The horse I'm working with now—his name's Ulysses—is spirited, to say the least."

"Were you hurt?"

"A knock or two. Nothing to speak of."

"He could do it to you again."

"Oh, you can count on it."

"You're not scared?"

He hesitated, then said, "I'm not that easy to scare off. He's a bit touchy, but he'll learn to trust me."

He could tell by the way she dropped her gaze that she'd caught his underlying meaning. "I have to go," she said. "Good luck with Ulysses."

"There's no give in that strap."

"What?"

He tipped his head toward the bundle on top of the trunk. "You're gonna have trouble unbuckling it without some help. If your father-in-law isn't around, I'll be glad to lend you a hand."

"I can manage."

"I don't doubt that, but why turn down my offer to help?"

"Because—" She broke off whatever it was she had been about to say and turned her head aside.

"Oh. I get it." He took a step back. "Mrs. Driscoll is still missing."

She came back around and said quickly, "No, no. That's not the reason. Not at all." She clasped her hands together, then, as though realizing she was still wearing the gloves, took them off, and tapped the pair of them against her palm. "I don't want to be beholden to you, Mr. Hutton."

"You wouldn't be."

"I don't want to be beholden to anybody."

She looked like she meant it, and he didn't want to provoke her by trying to change her mind. He supposed a young widow would be sensitive to becoming indebted to a single man. Though knowing that didn't make him any less sorry that he couldn't get near her without her bristling.

He motioned toward the driver's door. "At least let me crank the motor for you. Climb in." He extended his hand to help her onto the running board.

She hesitated only briefly before setting her hand in his. It was the one with the cut across his palm. She looked into his eyes, swiftly, then reclaimed her hand and stepped into the car.

He went around to the front of it. After she'd adjusted the spark and throttle levers on the steering column, he turned the crank twice. She switched on the battery, and the engine sputtered to life.

He collected his things from the hood, came back to the driver's side, and passed her one of the handbills. "In case you come across anyone with a horse that needs to be taught some manners."

She took the sheet from him and gave him a small smile. "I'll pass it along."

"I'd sure appreciate it. Thank you."

He looked at her for maybe a couple of seconds longer than was easy on either of them. Long before he wanted to, he brushed the brim of his hat. "Take care, Mrs. Plummer." He started back across the street.

"It was pneumonia."

Her blurted statement brought him to a halt. He turned around.

She was off by five degrees of looking him directly in the eye. "Pearl came early. Her lungs probably weren't finished developing, Dr. Perkins said. They were too weak to fight off the infection."

He let his breath out slowly. "You asked me not to say anything. Just as well. I don't have the words."

She did look straight at him then, her expression stark with pain.

Then she bobbed her head, put the car in gear, and drove away.

NINETEEN

———◆———

Bernie stood at one of the four windows in his office. It was on the second floor of City Hall, affording him a bird's-eye view of Main Street. From this advantageous point, he could monitor who was doing what, sometimes to his amusement, sometimes to his consternation.

Presently he was watching Thatcher Hutton make his way along the thoroughfare, going from utility pole to utility pole, nailing a notice to each one.

"What does it say?" Bernie asked and held out his hand.

Hennessy passed him one of the flyers. Bernie scanned it, then said to his bodyguard, "Thanks. That's all for now."

Hennessy left the office and closed the door.

"Does he ever speak?" Bernie's associate asked.

"He doesn't need to."

"No, I guess the scowl does speak for itself. What about Mr. Hutton? What does his handbill say?"

Bernie turned away from the window and sat down at his mayoral desk. "It's an advertisement for his services. Read for yourself." He pushed the printed sheet across his desk toward the man sitting facing it. "This indicates to me that he's sticking around."

"He paid our charming landlady another week's rent."

"What do you make of it?"

Frowning in thought, Chester Landry needlessly straightened his perfectly tied bow tie. "I would suspect, as you do, that he's a spy for the Anti-Saloon League in conjunction with a law enforcement agency. May they all roast in hell. Although, if they get their way, that's where we're destined."

"Bill Amos swears up and down that Hutton appears to be exactly what he claims. A cowpoke without a herd. A straggler of a dying breed."

"Well, the sheriff may be right." Chester told Bernie about the arrival of Hutton's trunk. "He dragged it up two flights of stairs, declining assistance from several who offered, myself included. The following morning, he came down for breakfast wearing common cowboy getup." He dusted an imaginary speck of lint from the knee of his trousers, a lazy gesture Bernie privately regarded with scorn.

Chester Landry fancied himself a dandy. His hair was slicked down with enough pomade to pave the highway from here to El Paso. The side part looked like it had been carved into his scalp. He was always dressed to the nines, favoring patterned vests and brightly colored bow ties that Bernie wouldn't have been caught dead in. The man also had a gold upper molar that glinted whenever he flashed his wolfish smile.

He was Bernie's partner in business. He was also a pain in Bernie's ass. Bernie couldn't get moonshine out of the county and into the speakeasies in Fort Worth and Dallas without it going through Chester Landry's manicured hands. Nor could he get bootlegged liquor smuggled into the county without Landry. He brokered the deals on both ends, and the percentage he demanded for each transaction was downright usurious.

But without him and his "powers of persuasion," Bernie's business wouldn't run as smoothly. Or as covertly. Which brought him to a matter of importance. "Is that loudmouth still at the boarding-house?"

"Randy Wells? Yes. As talkative and obnoxious as ever. His hobby is goading the teetotalers, and the most pious among them can't resist the bait. It results in some lively give-and-take."

"He hasn't told you who he buys his whiskey from?"

"It remains his secret."

"Dammit, Chester, I want to know who it is."

"Well, the choices are limited to either one of the Johnsons or to someone in our organization."

"Or it's a lone wolf who's selling cheaper and undercutting all of us."

"In other words, someone not playing by the rules as set by you."

"You're damn right."

Landry chuckled. "Should we try to unionize?"

"I'm thinking more of monopolizing."

Chester raised his brows. "Hmm. An interesting prospect."

"It would be good for everybody."

"Especially you."

"And you."

Landry conceded that with another languid gesture and sly smile. "Get me the identity of this Randy's source."

"I'm working on it."

Chester's smile remained in place, but his voice suddenly had a bite, and that didn't sit well with Bernie. The bootlegger was a necessary evil, but Bernie never would allow him to get the upper hand. He feared that most of Landry's posturing was just that: posturing. He wasn't nearly as insouciant as he pretended to be.

"These things require finessing, Bernie," he said, speaking smoothly again. "I can't press Randy on it, or seem overeager, and he doesn't want to reveal his source because he's acting as his own middleman. I'm not his only customer. For every jar he sells, he jacks up the price and takes a cut for himself."

"Everybody and his dog takes a cut."

"If you don't like the system, you should have invested in another enterprise."

"As it is now, the *system* is taking money out of my pocket."

The gold tooth flashed. "But by anyone's standards, they're still awfully deep pockets."

Bernie grumbled in response, then said, "It takes only one hotshot like your pal Randy to put all of us in jeopardy. Advise him to keep his fat mouth shut."

"I'll put it more diplomatically, but consider the problem of Randy's loquaciousness solved." With that, he shot his cuffs and straightened his cuff link. "Anything happening toward finding that missing woman?"

"Nothing."

"How's the doctor getting on?"

"He isn't. He's holed up in his house. He hasn't resumed seeing patients." Bernie didn't add that he wanted to throttle the man. Gabe was a veritable wreck. He needed to be brought up to snuff. Soon.

"What was his missus like?"

"You're speaking in the past tense."

Chester shrugged negligently.

Bernie said, "She had butter-colored curls, a round, rosy face, and big jugs. A *fraulein*. So anybody with an axe to grind against the Germans could have wished her harm. Including our sheriff. He lost a son to the war."

"He's cleared Hutton as a suspect."

"He hasn't *cleared* anybody." Frustrated, Bernie got up and moved to the window again. "Speaking of." Across the street, Hutton was engaged in conversation with Irv Plummer's daughter-in-law.

Chester joined him at the window. "Who's she?"

Bernie filled the bootlegger in on what he knew about the woman's history and described the scene that had taken place in the sheriff's office. "Stunned us all that she and Hutton had met, but she backed up everything he had told us about his random arrival here."

"Well, then," Chester said, "I don't think we need to worry about him working undercover."

"I worry," the mayor said. "I live here. I don't flit in and out like you do."

"Flit?" Landry said, taking umbrage. "Don't forget that I represent a line of quality women's shoes. I have a vast sales territory to cover."

Bernie snorted. "Shoes."

"Shoes. Just today, I arm-twisted Hancock into placing his largest order yet. It's not like I come here to relax and enjoy the quaintness of the boardinghouse."

Down below, Thatcher Hutton was helping the recent widow with something on the back of her auto. Bernie thoughtfully fingered the chain on his pocket watch. "How's he act around the other boarders?"

"Polite but not engaging. Keeps his head down. Never offers an opinion unless asked, and then he hedges."

"What do they say about him?"

"They're split down the middle. Half think he was the victim of circumstance and wrongly accused. The other half aren't so sure. But they all agree on one point. No one wants to cross him."

"Has he made a single friend?"

"No."

"Does he socialize at all?"

"He's played cards a couple of times."

"And won big."

Landry looked at Bernie with surprise. "How did you know?"

"He told the sheriff he had a knack." The mayor turned his head and met the bootlegger's gaze. "A knack for reading people."

"An enviable talent."

"A problematic one." Through the window, Bernie focused again on their subject. "When we startled him awake in the boardinghouse, he came up out of that bed as though he'd been catapulted."

"It was quite a commotion," Landry said. "I'm on the second floor. I was afraid the ceiling would collapse."

"It took five of us to subdue him. And have you heard about the rattler?" Chester hadn't. Bernie related the story that had been circulating. "He doesn't get flustered. He fights with ferocity and shoots with awe-inspiring skill."

"He's a surprise to you, Bernie. That's all."

"I hate surprises. I'm not discounting that he's more than an ordinary cowboy, which is why I'm going to keep a close eye on Mr. Thatcher Hutton. And, if you're as smart as I think you are, Chester, you will, too. In fact," he said, smiling, "the man is in want of a friend."

A knock on the door forestalled any rejoinder Landry might have made. Bernie consulted his watch and called out, "Bill?" Sheriff Amos opened the door and came in. "Right on time," Bernie said. "In fact, we were just talking about you."

"Anything good?"

"You tell us." Bernie pointed him into a chair and Landry returned to the one he'd been occupying. As Bernie sat down behind his desk, he thumbed over his shoulder and said to Bill, "We were observing Mr. Hutton out there on the street and speculating on his future."

He picked up the handbill on his desk and pretended to reread it. "As a horse trainer at Barker's? What happened to going home to the ranch in the Panhandle?"

"He suffered a misfortune." Bill took off his hat and set it on his crossed knee. "Finds himself adrift. He knows horses and, until something better comes along, he's got to eat. What were you speculating about?"

Landry said, "Bernie fears that Mr. Hutton is an agent of some sort, who could put a crimp in our, uh, profitable endeavor."

"I asked, he denied it, I believe him."

Bernie said, "I think you're being naïve, Bill."

"And I think you're needlessly fixated on Thatcher Hutton when you should be concerned about Wally Johnson's murder and the hell that's sure to rain down because of it." He was fuming. "You talk about a *crimp*, Mr. Landry? I'm talking about *castration* if Hiram finds out that you two killed him."

Bernie barked a laugh. "Don't be ridiculous. I wouldn't go within a mile of that freak."

"Then who'd you send?"

"Nobody."

"Hennessy?"

"Neither Chester nor I had anything to do with it."

Landry raised his hands. "No blood on these, Sheriff Amos."

"No, but I would swear your nails are buffed," Bernie said. The two of them laughed.

The sheriff, however, didn't find either of them funny. To humor him, Bernie clasped his hands on his desk and spoke with exaggerated seriousness. "Though Hiram would never admit it, he's probably secretly glad that Wally is no longer an embarrassment to the family as a testament to their inbreeding. What motive would I have had for killing him and, in doing so, putting my manhood at risk?"

"Because the Johnson clan is making inroads into markets you covet."

Bernie tried to keep his expression schooled. "True. I'll admit that they've got a relay route up to the oil towns that I wish I had. But it would have been petty to kill Wally over it."

"The more mischief you make for them, Bernie, the more ground you gain. Don't insult my intelligence, or their vengeful mentality."

"I didn't order Wally's execution."

"I haven't heard you sound that sincere since your swearing-in speech." The sheriff snuffled a laugh as he stood up and put his hat back on. "But it's not me you've got to convince. It's the bloodthirsty Johnson tribe."

Supremely annoyed by Bill's amusement as his expense, Bernie said, "Wait a minute, Sheriff Amos. You don't want to forget this."

He opened the bottom drawer on the left side of his desk and took out an unopened bottle of Jim Beam and a letter envelope bulging with cash. He pushed both to the edge of his desk. For ponderous moments, the sheriff stared at both. Then he did something he had never done before.

He took only one of them and left the other.

TWENTY

Laurel hadn't believed she would live through the night after Pearl's burial. She had, but the days and nights that followed were just as difficult to endure. She'd sequestered herself in her bedroom, holding Pearl's baby clothes against her face, inhaling the familiar scent, using the soft garments to muffle her continual keening.

She'd bound her breasts. Eventually her milk had stopped coming.

Irv had checked on her periodically, delivering plates of food she hadn't wanted. Those trips up and down the stairs must have pained his hip, but he didn't complain, and, although he was visibly concerned about her well-being, he didn't admonish her to hurry along her grieving process.

One morning, she had opened her eyes and realized that tears were no longer blurring the sunlight coming through her window. The pain in her heart wasn't as sharp. When she went down and joined Irv in the kitchen for breakfast, his smile was worth the effort it had taken her to bathe and dress.

Later that morning, she'd sealed all Pearl's clothes and baby things inside a box and slid it beneath her bed. That dreaded rite behind her, she'd pushed through the remainder of that day, fearing that if she didn't, she would remain inert and languish until she died.

Damned if she would give Death that satisfaction.

She'd attacked the leased house as though it were an embodiment of all her recent misfortunes. She dipped into her nest egg money to buy items that would spruce it up, then had thrown herself into every chore—scrubbing, painting, repairing—in order to keep her hands busy and her mind from reverting to debilitating heartache.

She'd made the bedroom she had expected to share with Pearl into a retreat for herself, complete with a cozy sitting area. Once Irv had built the wall to enclose the keeping room, she'd made it as comfortable for him as he would let her, although he'd told her repeatedly not to fuss.

He'd brought his barrel seat from the shack. It was an eyesore, but she'd said nothing when he'd rolled it into his room and turned it right side up in a spot of his choosing. He'd declined her offer to make him a new cushion for it.

She'd painted the kitchen cabinetry white, which had brightened the drab room considerably. She'd bought a dining set in a second-hand store and varnished it to a new shine. Irv had complained of the bathroom being so sanitary he was reluctant to do his business in it.

She'd given the parlor and formal dining room thorough cleanings but had left them unfurnished. They weren't needed for living space, because she and Irv each enjoyed spending time alone in their private quarters. When they were together, both were content to remain at the table in the kitchen.

Another area of the house that she'd left alone was the cellar. She'd discovered it one day while trimming a thick honeysuckle vine that blanketed the exterior wall of the kitchen. Behind the dense foliage was a door, which she'd had to use a crowbar to pry open.

She'd lit a lantern before venturing down an unstable set of steps. The cellar was musty-smelling, but not as damp as one would expect. The dirt floor was well-packed and firm. Cobwebs clung to the ceiling, and a few castoff articles had been abandoned there, but otherwise the space was remarkably unlittered. It attached the house to the limestone hill. The far wall was solid rock, the edges of it sealed with a clay-like matter.

That evening she'd told Irv about her discovery. "Did you know it was there?"

"Landlord mentioned it, but he didn't take me down there."

Nothing more had been said about it.

Day by day, the house had become more livable. Eventually Laurel had completed all the projects she had planned for herself and had begun nagging Irv to finish the list of undertakings she'd assigned to him.

This night, as she was clearing the table after their meal, she asked him for the third time to repair an electric light fixture in the ceiling of the central hallway. She said, "If I need the bathroom during the night, I have to feel my way."

"You could carry down a lamp."

"And you could fix the electric light."

"Can't tonight. I've got something else to do."

Her impatience boiled over. She shook her handwritten list at him. "If I could do these things myself, I would. I can't reach the ceiling, even with a ladder. I tried."

"You got up on that rickety stepladder? It's a wonder you didn't fall and break your neck."

"Well, I didn't. Don't change the subject."

He ran a hand over his bald pate. "I'm keeping food on the table by repairing other people's light fixtures, Laurel. Work is a blessing, and in my whole life I've never backed down from it, but I've got more than I can handle right now, and I'm tuckered out of an evening."

She piled their dishes in the sink and turned on the taps, muttering, "Not too tuckered out to leave and stay gone for hours on end."

"What was that?"

She turned off the water and faced him. "I hear you sneaking out three or four nights a week, Irv. Where do you go?" When he remained stubbornly silent, she pressed on. "Keeping an eye out for Mr. Hutton is an excuse that no longer holds."

"It should," he retorted. "They haven't found nary a trace of that woman."

"They didn't find nary a trace of evidence against him, either."

Irv gave a grunt of distaste.

Immediately after her encounter with Thatcher Hutton on the street, she had regretted having told him the circumstances of Pearl's death.

Even Irv, who'd had that one crying jag following the burial, avoided talking about it with her. Perhaps he sensed that her sorrow was too raw, too personal to be shared.

Which was why she hated herself for exposing it to Mr. Hutton. Now he would look at her with pity, when she didn't want him looking at her at all.

Each of their chance meetings, the last one in particular, had left her discomfited. On the surface, they spoke as courteous strangers, their dialogue commonplace and harmless. But it seemed as though they were actually communicating in an unspoken language which he understood, but which escaped her.

She couldn't fault his behavior or criticize his manners. He was just too observant for her to feel comfortable around him. When he looked at her, she feared he was detecting more about her than she was willing to reveal.

Fortunately, there would be few, if any, opportunities for them to cross paths. Her last sight of him might very well be of his walking away, the straps of his braces forming a large letter Y tapering from his shoulders and down his lengthy spine, his walk the slightly bow-legged saunter of a man who had spent most of his waking hours astride a saddle.

That retreating image of him was scandalously stirring. She conjured it with irritating frequency, and it always brought with it an ache that was paradoxically pleasurable. Averse to acknowledging that forbidden sensation for what it was, she always forced it from her mind.

As now when it had distracted her from finishing this squabble with her headstrong father-in-law.

"I'm not going to argue with you about Mr. Hutton, Irv. In fact,

I'm not going to argue with you at all." She turned back to the sink and braced herself against the rim of it. "I'm tired, too."

"Tired, hell. You're exhausted. You tear around here every day like your hair was on fire, paintin' this, scrubbin' that, wearin' yourself to a frazzle."

"Yes. I do." Feeling tears welling in her eyes, she kept her back to him and began to wash the dishes with ruthless efficiency.

He sighed. "Where'd you leave that damn ladder?"

An hour later, with her holding the ladder steady for him, he twisted a new bulb into the repaired fixture, flooding the hallway with light. "Leave the ladder here," he said as he climbed down. "I'll take it out in the morning."

"Thank you." He waved off her thanks, but she touched his arm to keep him from dismissing her. It was important to her that he knew how genuine her gratitude was. "I apologize for being short-tempered, Irv. It's not you I'm mad at. It's—"

"Life. I know. I'm sorta put out with it myself." His smile was empathetic. "I'll get around to those other chores, Laurel. I promise. But I do have something else to do tonight."

He left and didn't return until the wee hours.

Only a few days after their spat over his mysterious nighttime excursions, Laurel learned of something else he'd been keeping from her: a money shortage.

Because she shopped in Hancock's store so frequently, she'd come to know the head cashier by name. Mr. Hamel was always chatty and friendly. Today, when she placed the items she wished to purchase on the counter, he looked askance, stammered a greeting, then hastily excused himself.

At least two minutes went by while other customers ready to check out stacked up behind her. She became hotly self-conscious of their malcontent over the delay she was causing.

Mr. Hamel returned, followed by another of the store employees, who took over the register, while he drew Laurel aside. He wore an agonized expression and spoke in an undertone.

"I'm terribly sorry, Mrs. Plummer, but Mr. Hancock refuses to extend further credit until your father-in-law brings his account current. It's months in arrears."

"What? You must be mistaken."

"I'm afraid not."

Her cheeks flamed. "I'm certain it's an oversight."

"Oh, I'm certain of that, too," he said hastily. "As is Mr. Hancock. It's just that..." He wrung his hands. "You understand."

"Of course. Of *course*."

She asked the amount of the balance due, and when he told her, her knees went weak. She opened her pocketbook and removed the small change purse in which she carried her nest egg money when she was on an errand.

She rapidly counted the bills folded inside it. They covered only half the amount owed to the store, but she gave what she had to Mr. Hamel. "I'll bring you the rest later today."

Still looking pained, he said, "Should I restock the goods on the counter?"

Aware of people nosily staring, she forced herself to smile. "I wouldn't have you go to all that trouble. If you'll please sack them up, I'll pay cash for them when I return." Then, with as much dignity as she could muster, she exited the store.

As promised, she returned with cash in an envelope addressed to Mr. Hancock. In it, she included a note of apology and assured him that it would never happen again.

But getting current with Hancock's had taken a huge bite out of her nest egg.

She was loaded for bear when Irv came home for supper. But he looked weary to the core, and, without her even asking, he undertook the first to-do task on her list.

She didn't have the heart to relate the humiliating experience she'd suffered, or to demand an explanation for the embarrassing delinquency. Perhaps he'd bitten off more than he could chew by renting the house. If so, whose fault was that? Hers.

Although it wasn't like Irv to be absentminded, maybe the unpaid account *had* been a mere oversight. That night she went to bed praying that was the case.

However, the next day while he was away working, she entered his sanctum and opened the lidded cardboard box he referred to as his filing cabinet. To her dismay, several recent bills had balances carried over from previous months.

How had he gotten them into these straits? When he went out at night, was he gambling? He could have been lying when he denied seeing another woman. Was he supporting a mistress in addition to Laurel?

She couldn't tell him how to live his life. But—to hell with his pride—she would relieve the financial burden she had become.

To supplement Derby's paltry income from the army while he was overseas, she'd taken a job clerking in a drugstore. She'd enjoyed the sense of purpose and independence employment had given her.

But once Derby got back, he'd insisted she resign. He was the breadwinner, he'd said. Taking care of him would be her full-time job, he'd joked. After Pearl was conceived, the issue was never again addressed, not even when he couldn't hold a job for more than weeks, sometimes days, at a time.

She was *not* going to give up another home in order to spare a man's ego. If Irv couldn't afford for them to live here on what he earned, then she would subsidize the household income. And not only for the short term, not just long enough to bring their bills current. She must begin thinking long range, to the time when Irv was too old and infirm to provide for her to any extent. She must plan for a future without him.

Without *anybody*.

Because she had resolved never again to hand over the reins of her life to someone else, as she'd done with Derby. She would be self-supporting, thank you.

Making that resolution was one thing, implementing it quite another, and she had no time to waste. Days passed, bills piled up. Without Irv's knowledge, she went around to local vendors, paying them out of her nest egg only enough to pacify them and buy herself a little more time.

In secret, she began perusing the local newspaper's want ads. She wasn't qualified to teach school. The telephone company had more applications for operators than they had switchboards.

Other jobs open to women required secretarial skills like typewriting and shorthand. She could learn to do both, but not without Irv's knowledge, and she didn't want to raise the subject with him until she had something already in place, giving him no opportunity to argue with her about it.

She also began keeping count of the nights he left the house and how long he stayed away. He was entitled to a private life, of course. He was a man, after all. But if he was gambling money away, or spending it on a woman, or women, instead of keeping their household bills current, she had a right to her say-so on the matter.

She planned and prepared to follow him at a moment's notice the next time he slipped out the back door.

The night arrived. When she heard the back door closing behind him, she hurried downstairs and watched him from the kitchen window as he climbed into his truck and drove away.

She rushed outside, frantically cranked up her car, and, miraculously, it started the first time. She followed the taillights of Irv's truck, never getting too close. He had repaired the faulty headlight, so she didn't have to worry about a winking one giving her away.

Once he cleared the streets of town, he took the familiar highway that led to the shack. Maybe he simply missed his solitude and came out here to be alone. But when they reached the drive leading up to the old place, he drove on past.

The farther they got from town, the more uneasy Laurel became. Where on earth was he going?

When he turned off the highway, Laurel dropped farther back and switched off her headlights before carefully taking the same turn. But her ploy didn't work. She topped a rise, and, there in the middle of the road, was Irv's truck. He was standing in front of the tailgate with his hands on his hips. She pulled to a stop.

He walked up to her car, scowling. "Did you think I wouldn't notice I was being followed?"

"Where are you going?"

"Dammit, Laurel!"

"*Where are you going?*"

He stewed, cursed under his breath, then said, "You want to know so bad? Come on then."

He stalked lopsidedly back to his truck, climbed in, and pushed it into low gear. After a couple of miles, he turned onto another road, narrower and more rutted than the previous one. It wound its way between the hills. As they rounded a curve, Laurel saw flickering firelight ahead.

Irv pulled his truck off the road and drove cross-country toward the fire. The old truck jounced over the rugged ground, its headlight beams eerily bouncing off stands of cedar trees and rock formations. Laurel, with her teeth clenched to keep them from being jarred loose, followed and pulled up behind him when he braked and killed his engine.

He got out of his truck and waited as she picked her way over the rocky ground to join him. He extended his arms from his sides. "Well? Satisfied?"

She looked beyond him at the glow of the fire. "You camp out here?"

"Damn, girl. Wha'd'ya think? I'm making whiskey."

TWENTY-ONE

Muttering imprecations, Irv turned and led her toward the contraption being attended by a man she'd never seen before. As Irv and she approached, he stayed where he was, but stopped what he'd been doing and gaped at the two of them, slack-jawed.

He was holding onto a long stick that extended out of a pear-shaped metal vat, the rounded bottom of which was nestled in the center of a manmade stone pit. An opening had been left in the pit's base in order to stoke and fuel the fire smoldering inside it. The fire's smoke drifted out of a flue on the back side of the pit and curled up the face of a limestone outcropping, which formed a natural backdrop for the still, which seemed to Laurel to have been haphazardly engineered.

"Meet Mr. Earnest Sawyer," Irv said. "Ernie, this is my *nosy* daughter-in-law, Laurel."

The other man let go of the stick and doffed the brim of his newsboy's cap. "Ma'am. I've heard a lot about you."

"Me and Ernie worked together on the railroad," Irv said. "Known and trusted each other for years. He's from Kentucky. Knows everything there is to know about making corn liquor. So, when I retired, Ernie said to hell with the railroad and quit, too. We partnered up—"

"This is why you've been sneaking out at night?"

"You thought I was seeing a woman, didn't you?"

"You're making moonshine?"

"Good moonshine."

"It's illegal!" Her voice echoed off the surrounding hills, making both men cringe.

"Pipe down," Irv said. "Sound carries out here. And, yes, it's illegal, but it's a living. A damn good one. How do you think I'm affording that rent house?"

She was presently too flabbergasted to cite the past due bills. She took in her immediate surroundings, which, by all indications, was a permanent encampment. In addition to the components of the whiskey-making apparatus, a tent had been erected at the edge of the clearing. It was dark in color and camouflaged by cedar boughs.

She took a closer look at Ernie Sawyer. He was as thin as a string bean; his overalls hung straight from the shoulder straps, seeming to touch him nowhere else. He wasn't nearly as young as she, but not nearly as old as Irv. He was watching her with misgiving.

"You stay out here in the tent, Mr. Sawyer?"

"Yes, ma'am."

"All the time?"

"Mostly, yes, ma'am. Always when we're doing runs."

Laurel looked to Irv for clarification.

"A run is the process that starts with cooking the mash and ends with a jug of distilled whiskey. Ernie oversees the making of, I distribute. We split the revenue fifty-fifty."

The pride with which he spoke left Laurel at a loss for words. Resuming her survey of the area, she noticed a number of metal barrels lined up. "What's in those?"

"Mash. Fermenting till it's ready to cook."

"And all that?" She indicated a pile of what appeared to be building supplies.

"Materials to make our second still," Irv said. "We're duplicating this one, based on Ernie's great-granddaddy's design. It would already be assembled and doubling our production, but I had a *list*."

She let that shot pass without comment. "What about your fix-it business?"

"A front. Don't get me wrong. I fix plenty, I'm good at it and in demand. But driving around hither and yon, going from job to job, allows me to—"

"Distribute your product."

"Secret-like. There's a false floor in the bed of the truck. You can't hear the jars clinking together with all my tools rattling around. Plus, I'm old and have a crippled hip."

"He plays that up," remarked Ernie.

Irv shot him a dirty look, then said to Laurel, "I've got the perfect cover."

Still disbelieving, she rubbed her forehead, wet her lips. "It's not only against the law, it's dangerous. A local moonshiner was murdered recently. At his still. I read about it in the newspaper."

"Wally Johnson," Irv said with a snort of disdain. "The world's better off, believe me."

"They's all sorry, them Johnsons," Ernie said. "Sorry and mean. We're smart enough not to cross 'em."

Earnest was befittingly named. He spoke with perfect conviction. However, Laurel questioned his smarts. "Why didn't you set up shop in Kentucky?" she asked him. "Isn't it known for moonshining?"

Irv spoke up ahead of his partner. "So's this area. Texas's best held secret. There's stills all over these parts." He made a broad sweep with his hand. "Lot of hills to hide them in. Unlimited cedar and oak for the fires. Cedar gets it to going good, oak keeps it burning low and even.

"Hear that gurgle?" He angled his head toward the wall of limestone. "A natural spring flows out of that. Unlimited supply of cold, clean water, filtered by Mother Nature herself. You gotta have good water to make good 'shine."

He pointed toward a wooden barrel with a spout close to the bottom which emptied into a glass jug with a funnel acting as a stopper. "Ernie's great-granddaddy preached filtering and testing. First, filtering makes the whiskey smell and taste better. Testing prevents accidents."

Ernie chimed in. "No Sawyer in my branch of the family tree has ever poisoned or blinded nobody. We don't turn out popskull, neither."

"Popskull is—"

"I don't care what it is, Irv," Laurel snapped, cutting him off. Then she took a deep, calming breath. Her father-in-law and his crony had obviously lost their marbles, to say nothing of their morality. She must make them see reason. "The consequences of what you're doing could be dire."

"Dire?"

"Dire. Who owns this land? Tell me it's not government property."

"No, me and Ernie own it. He chose this spot, saying it was as ideal a place for a still as he'd ever seen. The previous owner, a cotton farmer who'd lost three crops in three years straight to the boll weevil, was happy to get rid of some of his land that wasn't fit to grow nothing. Ernie and me pooled our savings and relieved him of ten acres.

"The tract is long and skinny. Shaped sorta like a fishhook." He drew one in the air. "We're here, at the bottom of the bend. The shack is up here on top."

She'd never thought to ask about who owned the shack and the plot it was on. "It seems farther than that."

"Nope. The road loops and meanders around. But as the crow flies, the shack is just over that hill. Didn't you ever notice the smoke coming from this direction?"

"I thought it was another house." She'd had distractions, God knew, but her own gullibility fanned her temper. "You could get caught, Irv."

"Haven't yet, and we've been at it going on five years."

"Yes, but now Prohibition is in effect."

"Increasing the demand for whiskey," he said, giving her a shrug that emphasized the practicality. "That's why we want to double our production."

"You could go to jail!"

"Not for the first offense. We'd be fined, is all."

She flung her hand back toward their vehicles. "You drive around in that rattletrap, which is always breaking down, and it's loaded with jars of moonshine? That's...that's begging to be found out."

"I stage most of the truck's breakdowns, so all its rattling is convincing. As for being found out, I'm in plain sight every day. People are used to seeing me."

"Who do you sell to?"

"I have a route of regular customers that I keep supplied."

"Someone, anyone, who buys from you could turn you in."

"What kinda damn fool getting corn liquor delivered straight to his door would turn me in? Wives, now, are another thing. Gotta be careful of them, but that ain't my problem."

Infuriated by the logic of his arguments, she lashed out, "I should turn you in myself!" She pivoted and gave the two of them her back, hugging her elbows to her body.

Ernie hissed, "Shit, Irv. Have you gone plumb crazy, bringing her out here?"

"I didn't bring her. She followed me," Irv whispered back. Apparently both had forgotten how well sound carried.

On top of Derby's suicide, on top of Pearl's cruel death, on top of everything, *THIS*? Her father-in-law was committing a federal crime, with nonchalance and no shame, and for months she had been living off the profits of it, oblivious.

Dear God! When would enough be enough? What was she supposed to do about this?

"Laurel?" Irv said softly and with hesitation, "Are you gonna—"

She raised her hands, fingers spread, in an unspoken but emphatic demand that he not say another word. He fell silent.

She looked above at the panoply of stars. There was only a fingernail moon. The sky was very black. Somewhere in the distance a coyote yapped. While living out here in the shack, she'd gotten used to hearing them.

Now that she thought about it, it was remarkable how much she had gotten used to in the months she had been here. She was a different person from the woman who had left Sherman, clinging to the fragile hope that Derby and she would be happy together, or at least that their situation would improve. How naïve she'd been about love, loyalty, life, about a lot of things.

She looked down at the ground, pressed a loose rock deep into the chalky soil with the toe of her shoe, then turned her head and looked back at the still.

It was an odd configuration; all the separate parts of it looked crudely assembled, wrongly angled, and disjointed. She wandered over and went up the slight incline toward the limestone backdrop where Ernie had resumed using the long stick to stir the contents of the cooker.

Still regarding her with apprehension, he said, "It's just beginning to bubble. We'll be capping her soon."

Laurel peered down into the simmering mixture, then looked over at the empty glass jug sitting on the ground beneath the spout of the barrel, waiting to be filled with a product in huge demand. She thought of the "file cabinet" full of unpaid bills.

She met Ernie's nervous gaze, then turned to Irv.

"What's the recipe?"

TWENTY-TWO

When Sheriff Amos strolled into the stable late one afternoon, Thatcher was in the center aisle grooming a mare that had been brought to him the day before.

"Another bucking bronco?" Bill asked.

"No, this one just needs to be taught that it's not up to her when she's ridden. Her owner has to chase her down. She has him trained, not the other way around."

"I've seen your handbills all over town."

"They've paid off. I've got only one empty stall."

"Good for you. When you're done there, let's take a walk."

Thatcher lowered the currycomb and looked over at the sheriff, whose grave expression indicated that this wasn't a social call. He asked the first question that came to mind. "Has she been found?"

"No."

Thatcher waited, but when the sheriff didn't expand on that, he said, "Time to quit anyway."

After returning the mare to her stall and putting away the grooming utensils, he walked with Bill toward the bridge. They didn't cross. Instead the sheriff led him down the grassy embankment to the water's edge. The creek's current was sluggish.

Bill removed his hat and fanned his face. "This spot isn't as cool as I thought it would be. Not much of a breeze."

"Doesn't bother me if it doesn't bother you."

The sheriff turned his head and gave Thatcher several moments of intense scrutiny. "Does anything bother you, Thatcher?"

"Lots of things."

"You don't show it."

Thatcher raised a shoulder, not knowing how else to respond.

"What about people's opinion of you?"

Thatcher shifted his stance and tilted his head to one side. "One thing that bothers me is for someone to beat around the bush."

"All right." Bill hiked up his gun belt and took a deep breath. "I officially called off the search for Mila Driscoll today. It's been three weeks. Volunteers have petered out. I can't spare the manpower to keep up the search.

"I informed Gabe in person. I promised to hop on any leads that turned up, but I'm not hopeful there'll be any. The case remains open-ended."

Thatcher was quick to catch on to the reason for this visit. "This leaves me the one and only suspect."

The sheriff backed up to a butt-high boulder, propped himself against it, and folded his arms. "I don't think you had anything to do with it, Thatcher. None at all. But people are funny."

"It'll be like a shadow of doubt following me around."

"I hope not, but people—"

"Need somebody to blame."

"It's human nature."

Thatcher knew Bill was right. An unsolved mystery was like a sore tooth. It couldn't be left alone. He was the logical solution to this mystery, and, no matter what he did, in the back of some folks' minds, he would continue to be.

He supposed he could leave town as suddenly as he'd arrived, but that would look like running and only justify suspicion. And where would he go? He could probably be hired on at another ranch, but that would somehow seem disloyal to Mr. Hobson. City life held no allure for him.

Wildcatters were actively soliciting for roughnecks to work in the new oil patches, promising good pay. But he'd be living in a men-only camp and doing a dirty and dangerous job. If that lifestyle had held any appeal for him, he would have stayed in the army.

For the time being, staying in Foley was his best option. But he knew the prejudice he would come up against every day, and that rankled. "Damn. There'll always be those who think I'm guilty, won't there?"

"Until proven otherwise. What do *you* think happened to her?"

"What difference does it make?"

"Venture a guess."

"What for?"

"Why not?"

Thatcher hesitated, then squatted down, picked up a rock, bounced it against his palm a few times before pitching it overhanded into the creek. The plop sounded loud in the still air.

He squinted up at the sheriff from beneath the brim of his cowboy hat. "My guess? I'd say the doc had her with him when he left the house that night."

The sheriff assumed a contemplative expression. "She wasn't with him at Lefty's. Or with him when he made the stop to check on that breech delivery."

"Breech delivery?"

"I haven't mentioned that to you?" Bill explained Dr. Driscoll's second stop that night. "All had gone well, but because of that additional delay he didn't get back home until after one o'clock when he discovered that Mrs. Driscoll wasn't in their bed where he'd left her."

"Nobody can vouch for that."

"Except for the old biddy across the street who put Mayor Croft on to you. She says she saw their bedroom light go off around nine-thirty. That's consistent with what Gabe told me about their bedtime. The light came back on around ten, then went back off only a few minutes later. Eleanor Wise saw him collecting his medical bag from his office. That light went off. He backed his car out of the driveway a few minutes after that."

"Is watching other people all that old lady does?"

"Apparently."

Thatcher looked out across the creek to the opposite bank where a black-and-gray-striped cat was stalking something in the tall grass. "Did the old lady see the doctor walk from the house and get into his auto?"

"He keeps it parked around back."

Thatcher brought his gaze back to the sheriff, but he didn't say anything.

Bill said, "You're thinking Mrs. Driscoll was dead, and he carried out her body without Eleanor Wise seeing him."

"I'm not accusing anybody of anything."

"Understood, understood. We're just talking off the top of our heads here."

Thatcher didn't contradict him, but the truth was, he'd given this a lot of thought. Based on what he knew for fact and not scuttlebutt, he'd dismissed the various theories that had been disproved already or were too outlandish to put stock in.

The process of elimination always left Thatcher with only one plausible explanation for Mila Driscoll's disappearance.

"If she'd died accidentally," Bill said, musing aloud, "like if she'd fallen down the stairs, something like that, Gabe would have reported it."

"Um-huh."

"If they'd had a quarrel that got out of hand, if he flew off the handle and struck her—"

"A quarrel between them wouldn't have gone that far."

Bill's sharp look invited Thatcher to explain why he thought that.

He said, "When she talked about him, her cheeks turned rosier than normal."

"A woman in love."

"A woman who worshiped the ground her husband walked on," Thatcher said.

"Do you have a lot of experience in that area?"

Thatcher smiled. "No. Just wish I had a woman light up when she talked about me like Mrs. Driscoll did when she told me how fond her husband was of her shortbread. I doubt she ever said a cross word to him. But if they did have a squabble, she would've given in early. It would never have reached the boiling point."

Looking troubled, the sheriff ran his hand over his mouth and mustache. "Here's the thing, Thatcher. If a man kills his wife, it's usually in a fit of passion. Fed up with her nagging about his multiple failures, he loses his temper and, while teaching her a hard lesson in who's boss, he kills her, intentionally or not.

"Or a husband finds his beloved in bed with another man, goes blind with rage, kills them both. Afterward, he feels either justified for doing it—'They had it coming. I'd kill them all over again.'— or mortified, and he lives out the days till they hang him eaten up with regret.

"Of course some wife-killings are plotted. Another woman catches a man's eye, he disposes of the spouse who's blocking his path to greener pastures."

Bill paused and took a breath. "Over the course of my career, I've seen all that many times. What I haven't seen is a man killing his *pregnant* wife, his *very* pregnant, devoted wife who thought the sun rose and set in him. Not accidentally, not in a burst of violent rage, but with cold calculation. To take her life as well as his unborn child's, to do that with aforethought, would call for a total absence of soul. I just can't feature it."

Not wanting to interrupt the sheriff's thought process, Thatcher held his peace. He picked up another rock and tossed it from hand to hand.

"And anyhow," Bill went on, "it couldn't have been premeditated. The doc didn't know he was going to get called away from the house that night."

"It would help to know the length of time between the emergency call from the roadhouse and his arrival there."

"No more than half an hour, Lefty said."

"What's it usually take to drive it?"

"Roughly that. Gabe would have had to plan a perfect murder and implement it in a matter of minutes before racing out to treat the young prostitute who got beat up."

Thatcher looked at him intuitively. "You already asked this Lefty about the timing of the doc's arrival?"

Bill nodded.

"So this isn't a sudden notion of yours. It had crossed your mind that the doc had a hand in Mrs. Driscoll's vanishing."

Bill's sigh was as good as an admission. "He's the one link between Mrs. Driscoll's disappearance and Wally Johnson's homicide. The more I thought about it, the less coincidental it seemed."

"I thought so all along," Thatcher said.

"So did I."

"I just didn't want to say so."

"Me either." Glumly, Bill added, "I wish you'd scoffed at the idea. Doesn't make me feel any better to learn that it had occurred to you, too."

"Are you going to arrest Driscoll?"

"Without any evidence? No. It's still all speculation."

"That didn't stop you from arresting me."

The sheriff put his hat back on and slapped his thighs as he stood up. "I had that coming."

"You sure as hell did." Thatcher also came to his feet.

"Cut me some slack. Hauling in a drifter for questioning is one thing. Hauling in a highly respected pillar of the community is another." The sheriff started up the embankment. "But I could make it up to you. That is if you're willing."

"Willing?"

When the ground leveled off, the sheriff took advantage of the shade cast by the steel grillwork of the suspension bridge. "I've thought of a way to relieve you of suspicion."

"How's that?"

"I'll deputize you."

Thatcher laughed. "Come again?"

"You heard me. It would be a show of the faith I have in your innocence. If you wore a badge, folks would start looking at you in a different light."

Still amused, Thatcher shook his head. "Thanks for the offer, and the show of faith, but I don't want to be a lawman."

"You've got a natural aptitude for it. You're cool-headed. You listen more than you talk, and you yourself boasted of having a knack for reading people."

"In a game of poker."

"Bluffing at cards is a form of lying. Detecting it is a talent. You'd sense when a witness or suspect was giving me the runaround."

When he saw that Thatcher was about to argue, he held up a hand. "Besides all that, Mrs. Driscoll's fate is eating at you. You want to know what happened to her."

"So does everybody."

"But not everybody has a personal stake in solving the mystery. You've dwelled on it."

"In my idle time."

Bill grinned. "That speaks volumes. I'm headed out to talk again with that woman who had the breech birth. Maybe she'll provide some insight into the doc's frame of mind that night. Why don't you come with me, listen in? Give it a trial run."

Thatcher shook his head. "It won't do any good to go on about it. I appreciate your trying to improve people's opinion of me, but I don't want to be a deputy. All I know is ranching and horses."

"You could still do your horse training. You wouldn't be on staff. Just, you know, every once in a while, I could use an extra set of eyes and ears and—"

"And?"

"I've seen you shoot." After the blunt statement, he waited a beat. "I count on needing extra firepower soon, because I fear all hell's about to break loose. The Johnsons have sworn vengeance for Wally. I've heard rumblings that they're going to start sniffing out their competitors, and they're going to keep at it until they find and execute Wally's murderer."

"How will they know when they've got the right man?"

"When they've killed all of them."

He couldn't have hammered his point home any harder, and Thatcher felt the impact of it. Nevertheless, he had no aspiration to wear a badge. "I hope it doesn't turn into a bloodbath, Bill. But a war between moonshiners isn't my fight, and I'm staying out of it."

The sheriff held his gaze for several seconds. "We'll see."

They walked back to the stable together but said nothing more until they parted there with exchanged goodbyes.

As Thatcher watched the sheriff walk away, the words *we'll see* echoed in his head. He wasn't struck by the words themselves so much as by the way Bill had said them. Not with disappointment over being unable to change Thatcher's mind. But with the shrewd confidence that he would.

TWENTY-THREE

———◆———

The morning following her discovery of the still, Laurel plunged headfirst into her study of the centuries-old art of making sour mash whiskey. The more product they had to sell, the more money they could make, and the sooner she could settle their outstanding accounts.

In addition to the pressing financial necessity propelling her was a personal goal: As long as she was embarking on an illicit business, she wanted to excel at it.

Under pain of death, Ernie confided in her his family's recipe for the mash: unsprouted corn kernels, malted barley, water, sugar, yeast, and pot-tail.

"But," he warned, "you gotta know how much of each ingredient to add. You gotta know what stage to add it, and it has to be the right temperature. You gotta know when the mash has reached the perfect stage of fermentation. If your mash ain't good, your whiskey ain't gonna be."

"How do you know when it's fermented long enough?"

"When it gets foamy on top. But I dip my finger in and taste it just to be sure."

Many of his instructions went that way. "What's pot-tail?"

"Also called slop. It's what's left in the cooker at the end of the run."

"And when is the run at an end?"

"When the liquor breaks at the worm and won't hold a bead. After that it's distilling less than a hunerd proof liquor. You stop cookin' and pour out the pot-tail right then so it won't burn. Hogs love it if you want to use it for feed. Chickens, too. But save some to start another batch of mash."

"Oh. Like sourdough bread."

"I reckon. Never heard of that. Is it like cornbread?"

She had a lot to learn, beginning with Ernie's vast glossary of moonshining terminology. Thumper. Backings. Goose eye. Popskull. "That's low-quality 'shine that gives you headaches for days on end," Ernie explained.

A swab-stick was what he'd been using to stir the mash as it had begun to cook. It was different from a stir-stick, which had a forked end with a wire strung between the points. That was used to stir the mash as it was fermenting, which usually took four to five days. "Longer when the weather's cooler."

The referred-to "worm," she learned, was slang for the copper tubing coiled inside the wooden barrel she'd noticed the night before. The hot vapor created by the cooking mash rose up to the cap and made its way through the cap arm into the worm, where the steam was cooled by circulating water inside the barrel. The condensed result that funneled out of the worm into the container outside the bottom of the barrel was corn liquor.

Because of his down-home way of speaking, Laurel's first impression of Ernie was that he was simple. Most would still have that impression of him. In actuality, Earnest Sawyer was a chemist, who prided himself on the quality of his product.

"You only gotta poison one or two customers and your business is did for." To guard against contaminants or toxins, he held to a rigid standard of filtering their moonshine three times before bottling it. Grinning widely, he'd told her, "I sample each run my ownself just to be sure."

He walked and talked her through their next run, letting her observe the entire process. She asked a lot of questions. She even took one sip of the white lightning. Ernie and Irv laughed at the face she made. Eyes watering, coughing, she said she would leave them in charge of testing their whiskey's quality.

Although she had no intention of taking over the distilling process, she'd wanted to have a rudimentary understanding of the science behind it.

Of course, it was also essential to learn how not to get caught. That was a science she must master.

One evening when Irv skipped going out to the still, she brought up her fear of being found out. The two of them were seated at the kitchen table enjoying a coconut meringue pie she had baked earlier that day.

Around a bite of pie, he said, "You don't have to be fearful, just careful. There's dyed-in-the-wool abstainers, sure. But a lot of folks around here turn a blind eye to moonshining because they understand the farmer's plight brought on by the boll weevil. They switched from cotton to corn because corn is a boon market. And that's because of whiskey-making. It's basic economics."

"It's basic crime."

"Yeah, well, tell that to a sod buster trying to keep his kids from going hungry. These people aren't outlaws, Laurel. They're hardworking, poor folk striking while the iron is hot."

"I don't think you take the potential dangers seriously enough, Irv."

"All right, I'll admit that things have clamped down since Prohibition. Before it, many lawmen ignored the illegal whiskey trade. Others adhered to 'if you can't beat 'em, join 'em.' They lined their pockets with bribes. Now, though, they're getting squeezed by federal revenue officers and the Texas Rangers."

He raised his fork for emphasis. "That bunch is serious about upholding the law, no matter how unpopular it is. They can muscle their way past local and county officials, clean or crooked.

"Rumor is," he continued, "the Rangers and other agencies are recruiting men to snitch, and typically these snitches are former moonshiners and bootleggers who know the business inside out. They swapped sides in exchange for clemency. Or maybe they found religion and reformed. Who knows? What I do know is that it's happening.

"Which is why I was leery of that Hutton when he showed up at the shack, what with our whiskey still being just over the hill. He raised the hair on the back of my neck."

"You still suspect him of being one of those snitches?"

"He looks the type."

"What type?"

"Like Pinkerton agents. I used to see them in depots. Could spot 'em a mile off. All had the same traits. Polite. Quiet. Calm. Deadly."

"*Deadly?*"

"One of my regular customers? His boy Roger works for Fred Barker who has the auto garage and stable just across the bridge from downtown."

That was where Mr. Hutton's handbills said he did his horse training. But she hadn't told Irv about their meeting on the street, so she said, "I know the place."

"Well, Roger saw this Hutton, if that's his real name, shoot the head off a rattlesnake poised to strike a deputy sheriff. Faster than a blink, Roger said."

He described the incident to Laurel as it had been told to him. "They were all dumbfounded, none more than Sheriff Amos, who'd been disarmed before he realized what was happening. The deputy had dirty drawers.

"But Roger claims Hutton took it in stride, never broke a sweat, like he was accustomed to beheading rattlers with one shot from twenty yards, firing a pistol he'd never touched before." After taking another bite, he'd added, "This is damn good pie, Laurel. Save some for Ernie."

"Of course."

She wished he would elaborate on Thatcher Hutton without her having to prompt him with questions. However, he said no more about him, and returned to the topic of avoiding detection.

Days ago she had proposed to her partners that she take over half of Irv's "regulars" route, giving him more time to work on the new still. "It only makes sense," she had argued, stressing that she had time on her hands, and that the new still was essential to increasing their production. After a lengthy back-and-forth with the two men, she'd gotten them to agree.

But since she was now an active participant, actually transporting the product, Irv seized every opportunity, like tonight, to emphasize how careful she must be to avoid pitfalls.

"Don't make a track that leads off-road. Lawmen look for them. One of Ernie's cousins got caught by creating a trail with his truck that led through the woods straight to his still."

"But to get to our still, we have to drive over ground."

"So never turn off at the same place twice. Also, lawmen are on the lookout for anybody buying copper. It's a dead giveaway. I was lucky to sneak in mine for the new still. Bought the copper sheets from an outfit in Weatherford, then smuggled them in on the bottom of my truck."

He had already explained that the purchase of the copper had coincided with their leasing the house. That was why their other bills had gone unpaid. He had planned to make up the temporary shortfall soon by doubling whiskey production. Her "list" had limited his time to work on it.

"You trust the copper seller not to report you?" she asked now.

Irv laughed out loud. "He ain't gonna tell. He's supplying every moonshiner west of Fort Worth. See? The business is good for everybody."

"How's the still coming along?"

"About finished. Soon's the cap passes Ernie's inspection. He's persnickety about the tapering. Says even before it's sealed during a run, it's gotta fit into the cooker as tight as a..." Clearing his throat, he'd left the analogy unspoken and simply said the fit had to be airtight.

He then circled back to other giveaways. "Don't be caught with a stockpile of mason jars or sugar. Nobody needs twenty or thirty pounds of sugar at a time unless they're making moonshine."

"Where do you buy your supplies?"

"From my trusted suppliers, who will remain nameless."

"Nameless to me?"

"Especially to you. For your own safety as well as theirs. They're making money hand over fist, too, but they can't be too obvious about it and jeopardize their legitimate businesses."

"They could trust me."

"The system doesn't work that way, Laurel. Their trust in me doesn't rub off on you. You'll have to earn it yourself."

"All right. But what's the risk to me?"

"Competition for goods is fierce. Men have had knock-down-drag-outs over bags of Dixie Crystals. That might've been what got Wally Johnson killed."

"The man who was murdered?"

"Gossip is that he hijacked a hay wagon loaded with contraband sugar that was meant for somebody else. I don't know if it's true, but it stands to reason. His family have recently upped their production to meet the demand in Ranger and Breckenridge."

"Oil boom towns."

"Yep. Populated by hundreds of thirsty men that the Johnsons intend to keep quenched."

"Not you, though."

"Hell no," he said. "Those are lucrative markets, all right, but they come with risks Ernie and me aren't willing to take. The men working on those drilling rigs are a tough crowd. They'll shoot each other over a roll of dice, a perceived insult, or a whore. Pardon the mention."

"I can hardly take offense, Irv. I'm a moonshiner, in no position to judge how another woman makes her living."

"Well, around here they don't walk the streets like in the boom towns. Mostly they ply their trade at Lefty's."

"The roadhouse."

"That's why I told you not to go near it. If a man is so inclined, he can take his pleasure in the rooms upstairs. Or get skunk drunk in the back room. Lefty's is a regular den of iniquity. A blind tiger."

"A what?"

He'd explained the term, and she was astonished.

"A speakeasy? *Here?* Where there's a church on every corner?"

He snuffled. "Me and Ernie, and every moonshiner around, love nothing better than a tent revival that goes on for days. We raise more spirits selling corn liquor on the parking lot than the preachers raise under the tent. Make more money than what's dropped in the offering plate, too."

They laughed together before he turned solemn again. "When this new still is up and running, I'd like to expand the business. But those boom towns...naw," he said, shaking his head. "I'm too old for all that rowdiness. And, if I was to poach on the Johnsons' territory, they'd cut out my heart and feed it to a mad dog.

"Just as scary," he went on, "are the government agents on the hunt for bootleggers and moonshiners. And it's open season. They patrol every road going in and out of those oil towns, armed to the teeth. More and more of them are getting those new submachine guns. And even if it weren't for the guns, Ernie and me don't have a vehicle fast enough to outrun theirs."

They fell into a ponderous silence, each lost in thought. Laurel picked up a piece of pie crust left on her plate and crumbled it between her finger and thumb. Her mother had taught her the technique of making it flaky. She remembered standing on a footstool in the kitchen, watching as her mother combined the ingredients and added cold water, one drop at a time, until the dough was the perfect consistency to roll out on the floured surface.

She often felt a wave of nostalgia for her mother. But never for her father. The condemnation he would heap on his daughter, the moonshiner, perversely deepened her determination to succeed at it.

"Tell me more about Lefty's," she said.

"It does a brisk business. Folks come from all round."

"Who keeps him stocked?"

"A bootlegger out of Dallas. Or so I'm told. He's talked about, but not by name. Lefty also supports the local economy, though."

Laurel raised an inquisitive eyebrow.

All Irv said was, "Lefty and me have an understanding and do just fine by each other."

"Who else does he have an understanding with?"

"That's his business."

"It's *our* business, Irv. Our bills are caught up, but I don't want to be just caught up. I want to make money, and my stock-in-trade is moonshine whiskey." She leaned forward across the table. "Maybe Lefty—what's his last name?"

Irv scratched his cheek. "You know, I don't recall ever hearin'. It's always just been him and his wife, Gert.

"Could Lefty be enticed to buy more from you if you discounted the price per jar?"

"Jug."

"He buys by the jug?"

"He does, and I'm leaving well enough alone, missy. We'll make enough profit without taking a baseball bat to a hornets' nest." He ended on that note, pushing back his chair and announcing that he was beat. "Thanks for the pie. I don't think I've ever had better."

She wished him a good night. He retreated to his bedroom and shut the door, but Laurel was too keyed up to go to bed. Over the course of their lengthy conversation, several things had become crystal clear to her.

One. The new still would double their production, but it was unlikely that Irv's regulars would correspondingly double their consumption—especially under the watchful eyes of their wives. In order for the new still to pay for itself, they must increase their customer base.

Two. Ernie's talent was distillation and controlling the quality of their product. Thus far Irv had proved to be a crafty and capable distributor of it. However, neither thought like an entrepreneur. Growing the business would be her contribution, and she was eager to start.

It galled her to think that the Johnsons had a foothold in the boom towns. But any attempt to compete with cutthroat big-timers like them would be foolish and potentially hazardous.

And, realistically, neither Irv, nor Ernie, nor she could make the long and dangerous trips up and back to the oil patch towns, hauling hooch. In newspapers, they were portrayed as fertile fields for every form of wickedness. One was either a purveyor of it, or a victim, but no one was immune to peril.

If the immoral climate and fearsome competition weren't enough cause for trepidation, there were the heavily armed lawmen who couldn't be outrun.

Surely there was a safer, saner way to conduct business. But how, when the manufacturing and selling of their product were illegal? These inherent dangers wouldn't abound if they were making and selling hat pins, or sachets, or...

She drew focus on the coconut meringue confection in the center of the table.

Eight hours later, she was still seated at the table, but the pie had been replaced with the scattered contents of the recipe box her mother had given her when she married. She'd filled sheets of paper with scribbled notes, jotting down ideas as they occurred to her. Various lists had grown longer as the night had stretched into morning.

"What the hell's all this?"

Not having even noticed that Irv had emerged from his bedroom, dressed and expecting breakfast, Laurel looked at him and declared, "I'm going to need more than twenty or thirty pounds of sugar. A lot more."

TWENTY-FOUR

For days after his discussion with Bill Amos at the creek, Thatcher couldn't shake everything they'd talked about. He accepted that suspicion would shadow him until it was confirmed that someone else had abducted Mrs. Driscoll. His bet was on the doctor. Sheriff Amos was leaning that way, too.

But Thatcher was no crime-solver, and he rejected having to pin on a badge in order to convince skeptics of his innocence.

Nevertheless, the specter of suspicion continued to weigh on him.

At least on this night, he had something to take his mind off of it for a while. He was going out to dinner. It would be a distraction, but not one he particularly looked forward to.

After work, he washed up and changed into a fresh white shirt, dark tie, and his black suit. He'd had it dry-cleaned, the tears in his pants and shoulder seam sewn up, and his shoes shined. He put on his fedora.

The cracked mirror above the dresser in his room reflected a man who looked like he had a lot on his mind, but one presentable enough to go to supper with Mr. Chester Landry.

The shoe salesman's invitation had taken Thatcher off guard. Except for renting rooms in the same boardinghouse, he and the city slicker from Dallas had nothing in common that Thatcher could see.

But when Landry had approached him the night before and invited him to join him for a dinner out, he'd felt obliged to accept.

Landry was waiting for him out on the porch. He too was wearing a dark suit, but his bow tie was the color of bile and his satiny vest was striped. Thatcher caught a glimpse of a gold jaw tooth when the salesman smiled in greeting and informed Thatcher that he would drive them to the café.

As they motored through the streets of Foley, Landry kept the conversation flowing, commenting on aspects of the town and how it compared to others on his sales route.

Thatcher wasn't the least bit interested in either women's footwear or the salesman's travels, but he listened attentively and made polite inquiries that encouraged Landry to keep the chitchat on himself and off Thatcher, which was precisely Thatcher's intention.

Most of the locals stuck to the more agrarian schedule with which they'd been reared and tended to eat their larger meal at noon. Consequently, Martin's Café wasn't all that crowded at the dinner hour.

But parked in front of it was a long, black Ford, the most expensive of this year's models. As Landry pulled in beside it, he said, "I see the mayor is dining here tonight."

"That's his car?"

"It is."

"You know him?"

"We've met. Chamber of Commerce meeting, I believe it was. I attended as a guest of Mr. Hancock."

Seated in the driver's seat of the town car was a man with the bill of a newsboy cap pulled low over his eyes. Thatcher asked, "Who's that?"

"Mayor Croft's *chauffeur*," Landry said, adding tongue-in-cheek, "and if you believe that, I'll sell you the Brooklyn Bridge."

They alighted from Landry's car. As they walked toward the entrance of the café, Thatcher got a closer look at Croft's chauffeur. He had bulky shoulders and the face of a boxer who'd gone a thousand rounds.

As Thatcher and Landry reached the door of the café, Bernie Croft emerged from it. Upon seeing them, he pulled up short. His eyes sawed between them, lighting on Landry. "Mr. Landry, isn't it?" He stuck out his hand and Landry shook.

"Thank you for remembering, Mayor Croft. Allow me to introduce—"

"I know who he is." Croft settled a brittle gaze on Thatcher. "Mr. Hutton."

Thatcher tipped his head.

Croft hooked his thumbs in the pockets of his vest. "Your companion is well known for his derring-do, Mr. Landry. And his amazing skill with a six-shooter." Then to Thatcher, "I heard you saved a deputy's life."

"A lot of agony, anyway."

"Well, splendid marksmanship."

"Thanks."

Landry stepped in. "What do you recommend from the menu, Mr. Croft?"

"You can't go wrong with the fried chicken." He doffed his hat. "Enjoy, gentlemen. 'Evening."

Landry murmured a response, then entered the café. Thatcher followed, but as he stepped inside, he looked over his shoulder to see the chauffeur holding the rear seat door open for Bernie Croft. Both were looking back at him.

Clyde Martin was a rotund and cheerful man who took obvious pride in his establishment and its longevity. It had occupied the same corner on Main Street since the turn of the century, serving breakfast through dinner. Salt, pepper, and sugar shakers, along with bottles of ketchup and Tabasco, were kept on the tables.

Mr. Martin welcomed the new arrivals personally and ushered them to a table. Thatcher took the chair with its back to the wall, giving him a view of the entire room. This was his habit. But also, from the moment he'd noticed Landry loitering in the dark corner of the boardinghouse porch, unobtrusively observing the others as he smoked, Thatcher had determined that he would never turn his back to this man.

Was it Landry's sly grin and oily manner that put him off? His pomaded hair? Was it the gold tooth, tucked into his jaw like a kernel of secret knowledge waiting to be exposed and used to someone's disadvantage?

Thatcher also had gotten the sense that he was better acquainted with Bernie Croft than either had let on.

Thatcher couldn't specify what it was that caused him to question Landry's integrity, but on matters as important as trust, he relied on his gut. The salesman's friendly overtures toward him seemed a little too polished to be genuine or spontaneous.

Now, as Landry cut into his thick slice of fried ham, he said, "I am as tired of the other boarders as I am of Mrs. May's uninspired cooking."

"Why do you room there then?"

"It's cheap. But the company is dull. Their conversation isn't exactly scintillating, is it? Or even interesting."

"You seem to get on with Randy all right."

He smiled. "He isn't bad company. He can tell a good dirty joke. He's just young."

"Outgoing."

"Yes, he's gregarious. But underneath all the braggadocio, he's as shallow as this pool of redeye gravy." He dipped the slice of meat into it. "Unlike you."

Thatcher had chosen a T-bone. "Unlike me?"

"The strong, silent type." Landry intoned the statement like a stage actor.

Thatcher speared a bite of steak and put it in his mouth.

His failure to comment didn't deter Landry. "You keep your own counsel, Hutton." He wagged his fork at Thatcher. "You never give away what's going through your mind."

"Usually because it's not worth knowing."

"Oh, I doubt that. I seriously do." He appraised Thatcher as he broke off a piece of dinner roll and spread it with butter. "Tell me about yourself."

Thatcher gave him a sketchy biography, sharing nothing of importance. "Mustered out, was making my way back, wound up here."

"Where you got stuck and now plan to stay for a while. Is that about it?"

"Just taking it one day at a time."

"A man with no plan."

"In the trenches I saw men die in mid-sentence. Planning your next breath is a wasted effort."

"Strong, silent, *and* a philosopher."

Flashing the wily grin that instilled Thatcher with dislike as well as mistrust, Chester held his stare a beat longer, then continued eating. When he was done, he leaned back in his chair, patted his stomach, and sighed with contentment.

"Must say, that was tasty. I'll have to trust the mayor's endorsement and try the fried chicken next time."

"Have you had a hamburger at Lefty's?"

The salesman cocked his head. "Lefty's?"

"It's a roadhouse. Out a ways. I've heard the burgers are worth the drive."

Thatcher couldn't say what had prompted him to drop a mention of the roadhouse into the conversation. It had been a gambit, like placing a large opening bid only to see how the other player at the table would react.

Chester Landry didn't take the bait. He gave a *hmm* of disinterest, and signaled to Mr. Martin that they were finished. Thatcher noticed that they were the only two diners remaining. They passed on dessert but ordered coffee.

As Mr. Martin served it, he said, "Take your time, gentlemen. There's plenty in the pot for a refill."

Thatcher sipped his coffee piping hot and black. Landry added cream and sugar to his and stirred it for longer than necessary. When he lifted the spoon from the cup, he clinked it against the rim several times.

He said, "It's such a shame that you were—associated—with the investigation into the missing woman. That couldn't have been a pleasant experience."

"It didn't last long."

"Even so."

Thatcher sipped his coffee, saying nothing, hoping the subject would die.

Landry wagged his spoon just as he had his fork earlier. "See, Hutton? That's what I'm talking about. Most men would be furious, railing at the sheriff, at everybody who would listen about the unfairness of your detention. You act unaffected, but I wonder if behind the steely veneer, you're seething. Or are you truly this slow to rile?"

Before Thatcher could answer, motion toward the back of the café drew his attention. The swinging door into the kitchen was being pushed open. By Laurel Plummer. By Laurel Plummer's bottom. Her very shapely bottom.

She was attempting to wedge through the door with both hands raised, each supporting what looked like a baking dish draped in a dish towel. It was a precarious balancing act.

In an instant, Thatcher was out of his chair. Mr. Martin was late to respond because he'd been behind the counter matching the day's receipts with the money in his till.

Thatcher pulled wide the door.

"Thank you, Mr. Martin," she said as she was turning. "I shouldn't have tried to—" She came to an abrupt stop and blinked up at Thatcher. Several seconds passed without either of them speaking, then she mumbled a thank you and sidestepped to go around him.

He reached for the dish in her left hand. "Let me take this one."

"No thank you. I've got them."

Mr. Martin rushed around the end of the counter. "Mrs. Plummer, forgive me. My people working in back were supposed to tell me when you got here."

"It's quite all right. They were busy." She took a breath and gave a shaky smile. "As ordered, a pecan pie and a peach cobbler."

She handed them to Mr. Martin in turn. He set the baked goods side by side on the counter and whisked off the muslin towels with the flourish of a magician over a top hat. "Ah, they look scrumptious. Beautiful, too. My wife, God rest her soul, always got the crust too brown."

Laurel looked pleased but self-conscious over the compliment. "I hope your customers approve."

"I've got two gents here now who turned down dessert, but I'll bet they'll reconsider." He winked at her. "Gentlemen, Mrs. Plummer has started baking for me, and her pies are out of this world. The cobbler is still warm. Can I tempt you? I'll add a scoop of ice cream on the house."

"You've sold me," Chester Landry said. He had pushed away from the table and was standing with his napkin in his hand. "Mrs. Plummer, Chester Landry." He touched his chest and gave her a nod.

"How do you do."

"Actually, I regretted that my dinner partner—oh, forgive me. This is Mr. Thatcher Hutton."

The introduction required her to acknowledge him again, something she had avoided doing since her stunned reaction to another unexpected meeting with him. Having recovered, she now said coolly, "Mr. Hutton."

"Mrs. Plummer."

Landry said, "As I was saying, to my disappointment, Mr. Hutton had declined dessert, so I felt compelled to do likewise. Thank you for coming to my rescue."

"I hope you enjoy the cobbler."

Landry pulled an empty chair from beneath the table. "Would you care to join us?"

"No." Then, as though realizing how curtly she'd answered, she added, "I can't. I have other deliveries to make."

She turned back to Mr. Martin and spoke to him in an undertone. Thatcher didn't catch her words, but Martin said, "Of course, of course," and bustled back around the counter to the cash register.

Laurel meticulously folded the dish towels and tucked them beneath her arm. When Mr. Martin returned to her, she extended her hand, and he counted out bills into her palm. She slipped the money into a pocket of her skirt. "Do you want to place an order for Thursday, Mr. Martin?"

"Can you do another apple? And people are still raving about the lemon meringue."

"I could make another lemon, of course. Although..." She dragged out the word, capturing the café owner's attention. "I also do a chocolate meringue."

"One apple, one lemon, one chocolate."

She reached across the counter to shake his hand. "Thank you. I'll see you before closing on Thursday."

She turned and gave Chester Landry a nod, which looked token to Thatcher. He outdistanced her to the swinging door and pulled it open for her. "I'll walk you out."

"No thank you. I'm in a hurry."

He suspected her of fibbing about having more deliveries to make, but there was no way to gracefully call her on it.

"Then good night, Mrs. Plummer."

"Good night."

He watched her wend her way through the kitchen, where two women were washing dishes, and a man was chopping up raw chickens. After Laurel disappeared through the rear exit, Thatcher let the door swing shut. Mr. Martin was behind the counter spooning Landry's cobbler into a bowl.

Landry himself had remained standing, his hand on the back of his chair, smarmy smile in place. Thatcher walked over and resumed his seat.

As Landry sat down, he said, "I was wrong."

"About what?" Thatcher sipped his cold coffee.

"One sometimes *can* guess what's going through your mind." He cocked an eyebrow in a one-man-to-another leer.

Thatcher gave him a long, unwavering stare from which most men would back down. Landry's grin only widened enough to reveal his gold tooth.

Thatcher badly wanted to knock it out.

Instead he called over to Mr. Martin, "I'll have a slice of the pecan pie, please. No ice cream."

His attempt to deflect Landry's interest only seemed to amuse the man more. But the salesman didn't pursue the subject of Laurel Plummer. Instead he asked Thatcher about his horse training technique.

Each bite of the rich pie melted in Thatcher's mouth.

As they left the café, Thatcher declined the ride back to the boardinghouse. "I need to stretch my legs. I'm going to walk back." Giving Landry no opportunity to quibble, he stuck out his right hand. "Thanks for dinner."

Chester Landry shook hands. "Don't get used to it. Next time it's Dutch treat."

Thatcher, planning for there never to be a next time, smiled as expected, then turned and headed down the street in the opposite direction from which he intended to go.

He waited until Landry's car was out of sight, then doubled back. He looked in Hancock's storefront window. The advertisement was still there.

He continued on, following the directions Bernie Croft had given him that first day.

Along the way, he kept to the shadows. Five minutes later, the picturesque facade of the Driscolls' house came into view. Lights were on in some of the downstairs rooms, including the parlor with the bay window, the doctor's office.

Aware of Miss Eleanor Wise's seemingly uninterrupted vigilance, Thatcher didn't go any farther, but took cover behind the catty-corner neighbor's detached shed. He slid down the exterior wall of it, worked his butt around until he'd created a depression for it in the ground, and settled in to wait.

What he was anticipating, he couldn't say. The sudden reappearance of Mrs. Driscoll? A surefire giveaway of the doctor's guilt?

He was irrationally annoyed with Bill Amos for lending credibility to his notions about the physician. If the sheriff had instead laughed himself silly over them, Thatcher wouldn't be sitting here in the dark, swatting at mosquitoes, accomplishing nothing.

Time passed. He whiled most of it away thinking about Laurel Plummer. She'd charmed Mr. Martin into increasing his order, and had seemed damned pleased with herself for having done so. Her features hadn't looked as strained as they had the other times Thatcher had seen her. The smile she'd given the café owner looked genuine.

She'd been dressed different, too. Her skirt was shorter than any he'd seen her in before. It was nipped in at the waist. And, right off, he'd noticed the good fit of her blouse.

He wished he'd thought of an excuse to touch her during the brief time she'd been in the café.

As mouthwatering as her pie had been, Thatcher was certain her mouth would be even more delicious.

He'd enjoyed the sight of her bottom wiggling its way through that door, and couldn't help thinking back onto what it had felt like when it had bumped up against his front during the rooster episode, as he'd come to think of it.

The contact hadn't lasted more than a few seconds, but it had flooded him with lust then, and remembering it did now, not for the first time. He meant no disrespect. He had no control over the fantasies about her that came to his mind, some so vivid and arousing they justified Landry's insinuating grin.

He wished he'd punched that sly mug.

As the lights in the Driscoll house began to go out, he pushed the image of Laurel from his mind. The last light to be turned off was on the second floor, the bedroom no doubt.

Thatcher stood up and looked toward the old busybody's house. "I guess we can get to bed now."

He slipped out of the cover of the shed and headed toward the boardinghouse, hoping he wouldn't be spotted walking the streets where he didn't belong, skulking around in the dark, like a criminal returning to the scene of his crime.

TWENTY-FIVE

Laurel pulled her Ford into the gravel drive that led around to the back of the house. Irv had told her always to park facing out toward the street in case she ever had to leave in a hurry. "It'll probably never happen, but...you know."

Tonight may be the night when taking the precaution would pay off.

Although it wasn't something easily done, she executed the three point turn and killed the headlights. She reached beneath the seat for the pistol Irv had insisted she begin keeping with her. She couldn't feature an instance where she would actually fire it, but it was a comforting weight in her hand now.

Her heartbeat thumped as she made a rapid sweep of her surroundings, then took more time to probe the shadows for a possible ambush, seeking out anyone who might have followed her from Martin's Café, which had been the last stop on tonight's round despite her claim of having more deliveries to make.

As she'd pulled away from the alley behind the café, she'd had no indication that she was under anyone's surveillance. Nevertheless, during the drive home, she'd half expected someone to roar up behind her.

She waited inside her car for several minutes longer, but no one showed himself, nothing stirred. Weak with relief, she dropped the pistol in her lap, placed both hands on the steering wheel, and pressed her damp forehead against the backs of them. She took deep breaths.

Of all people to happen upon: the perceptive Mr. Thatcher Hutton. While standing face-to-face with him, one of Mr. Martin's cooks was out back retrieving four jars of moonshine from the trunk of her car.

At the sight of Mr. Hutton, her heart had almost burst. But, despite the unexpectedness of their near collision, she'd recovered reasonably well, she thought now. Mr. Martin had kept his head and had given nothing away. Of course, he wasn't the novice that she was. Since the county had been dry for decades, Clyde Martin had been pouring illegal alcoholic beverages for drinking customers for as long as he'd been in business. Or so Irv had informed her.

Neither Mr. Hutton nor the man with him, whose name now escaped her, had seemed the least bit suspicious of her transaction with Mr. Martin, or of the order he had placed for three pies, which, in the coded language they'd worked out between them, translated to that many pies, plus twice that number of jars of corn liquor.

She'd taken her money and run, getting a nod from the cook on her way through the kitchen that the transfer of fruit jars from her car to a hidden compartment in the kitchen had been conducted without detection. Nothing had gone awry.

All the same, she felt she had escaped a close call.

Deciding it was safe to do so, she turned off the engine and got out. She let herself into the house through the back door and went directly upstairs to her bedroom, relieved that she didn't have to explain her shakes to Irv, who was helping Ernie at the still tonight.

As she entered her room, she left the light off, being more fearful of light than of the dark. She acknowledged that was standard criminal behavior.

Hands still unsteady, she set the pistol on the dresser. The handgun was small enough to fit in her palm, but Irv had assured her that the business end of it would give pause to anyone with harmful intent. He'd also assured her that it wasn't the one Derby had used to kill himself.

Feeling claustrophobic, she hastily undressed. When she was down to her chemise, she poured water from the pitcher into the wash bowl and sponged off a film of nervous sweat. Then, moving to the bed, she sat on the edge of it and bowed her head, if not in prayer, certainly in relief.

Over the past several weeks, she had become so wrapped up in her exciting new enterprise, that, at times, she had to pause and remind herself that she wasn't playing a high stakes game where she was merely trying to out-trick an opponent. She was breaking the law. If caught, the penalty was steep. She did not want to go to jail. Nor did she want to be responsible for Irv and Ernie being incarcerated.

When she'd first laid out her idea to use bakery goods as a cover for moving moonshine, Irv had responded with guffaws. Then he'd put up stubborn resistance, followed by pessimistic predictions. But after talking herself hoarse, she'd finally won his grudging support to try it.

"Just for a time. If it doesn't work, I'll stop."

He'd retorted, "If it doesn't work, we'll all be behind bars."

Clyde Martin, the restauranteur, had been the logical choice for their first prospective client.

"He used to keep a bootlegged stock," Irv had told her. "So long as it was only a state infraction, and a fine if caught, he poured bourbon and scotch on the sly and called it 'Mama's sweet tea.' He bought his moonshine from me. But the new law spooked him. He stopped buying, and, as far as I know, has gone completely dry. I don't figure he's a convert to abstinence, though. Might be worth me going to see him."

"Let me."

Irv had argued, but ultimately relented. "All right. But... Don't take this wrong, Laurel. When you go soliciting, wouldn't hurt if you girlied up some."

"Girlied up? What does that mean?"

"You know what it means. Every woman in the world knows what it means."

"I'm not soliciting at Lefty's."

"All's I'm saying is, you might want to throw away those baggy old shirts of Derby's and fix yourself up to be more...girlified."

She'd spent that evening taking in the waistlines of garments that she'd let out during her pregnancy. As an afterthought, she'd also taken up the hemlines an inch and a half. She'd ironed a blouse with a front placket flanked by strips of lace, and had dusted off her best hat.

She'd timed her arrival at the café during the lull between the mid-day meal and dinner. She gave the busboy her name and asked to see Mr. Martin. After getting clearance, he'd escorted her to a cramped office off the kitchen.

When she'd walked in, Clyde Martin had been standing behind his desk, looking the picture of benevolence. "Mrs. Plummer. I'd like to express my sincere condolences for your—"

She'd cut him off. "You're losing money, Mr. Martin."

"I...I beg your pardon."

"Try this." She'd taken a mason jar of moonshine from her tote bag, strode forward, and set it on the paper-littered desk.

"And this." Also from the tote, she'd produced a slice of apple pie wrapped in wax paper and set it beside the jar. "You need to be offering both in your café. I'll come back tomorrow to work out the particulars of a deal. Have a pleasant afternoon." She'd left him with his mouth agape.

When she'd returned the following day, Mr. Martin had been eager to negotiate terms. He'd soon learned that she was no shrinking violet, further weakened by grief. Settling on a price, he'd placed an initial order for two pies and 4 jars of moonshine. "I'll come by twice weekly to deliver the products and take your next order," she'd told him.

As they shook hands on the deal, he'd said, "I thought you were going to apply for a waitress job."

"This pays better."

Initially, Irv had kept up his route and the handyman cover, but once the new still was in operation, she'd suggested that she take over his deliveries. "I could drive your route on the days I don't bake."

"You can't drive my truck."

"Why not?"

"It's a truck."

She'd given him a roll of her eyes. "I could drive it, but you make a valid point. It would attract unwanted curiosity. Instead, what if you built some kind of false floor in my car, the way you did in your truck?"

He'd fashioned a false bottom in her trunk, creating a hidey-hole underneath, which she padded with an old quilt. Thus outfitted, she'd begun driving his route. As she became better acquainted with the roads and back roads in the area, she'd gone further afield, scouting for new opportunities.

She'd picked up two cafés in two different towns, both of which had been customers of Irv's before becoming gun shy of the Prohibition law. In addition to delicious pies, cobblers, and corn whiskey, she'd promised her customers utmost discretion.

As Irv was leaving one evening to work at the still, she'd approached him with another idea. "What about Logan's Grocery?"

"What about it?"

"As a possible broker."

"Hell'd freeze over first. A nicer man you'll never meet. Logan extends credit even to folks he knows will take a long time paying. But he's a staunch teetotaler. His wife was the standard bearer for the local temperance society."

"Does he sell fresh baked goods in his store?"

"Not that I know of."

"He should, don't you think? I'll pay him a call and take samples."

"I just told you, Laurel, he—"

"I saw a notice in his window that he offers delivery service for a small charge."

"That's recent."

"Who makes the deliveries?"

"A couple of young men. Twins, in fact. Davy and Mike O'Connor."

"Are they teetotalers?"

He'd scoffed. "They worked in the pool hall until it was forced to shut down. A campaign led by Mrs. Logan, by the way. I guess Logan felt bad about the twins losing their livelihood. He hired them to deliver groceries."

"Hmm."

It took several days for her to secure an interview with the busy grocer. As Irv had said of him, he was extremely polite, and highly complimentary of the samples of pie she'd brought for him to try. Even so, he'd declined.

"I would like to stock them, Mrs. Plummer, but the problem is a shortage of shelf space. I'm at full capacity."

She'd made a sound of regret. "That is unfortunate. Because I notice that all the baked goods you carry are factory-made and packaged." After a strategic pause, she'd added, "There's nothing wrong with that, of course."

At that, his smile had slipped a bit.

The next day, she'd gone back and told him, with rehearsed animation, that she had slept on his dilemma and believed that she had a solution.

"I could make up a menu of my pies. You display it and take orders. The pies will be delivered from my kitchen directly to the customer. You never have to touch the goods, and they won't take up your valuable shelf space."

"How would you get the orders?"

"You could telephone them in to me."

"Do you have a telephone?"

"I will by tomorrow." Her cheekiness had made him smile. "I think this idea is growing on you, Mr. Logan."

"You certainly have my interest, and I admire your initiative, which is rare in a young and recent widow."

"But?"

"But we haven't yet talked terms."

Acting *girlified*, she'd smoothed her hands over her skirt nervously, then had pretended to summon the courage to open the bidding. "For each pie order you submit, I'll give you ten percent."

"Fifteen."

"*Fifteen?*"

"My two deliverymen are kept busy during store hours. Your deliveries will have to be made after closing. I'll have to pay them extra."

After-hours deliveries were what she'd hoped for, but she'd pursed her lips as though she hadn't considered this stumbling block. "Perhaps just one could work overtime. Perhaps they could swap off."

"They're twins. Inseparable, and they work as a unit. One drives their truck and waits, while the other runs the delivery to the customer's door. It's a very efficient system. With the two of them working together, it takes only half as long to make the deliveries. Because they're paid by the hour, it's actually more economic to have both on the payroll."

She'd appeared impressed by his business savvy, but crestfallen by how it affected their deal. "I see. Well, I'll give you two percent more to cover that expense. For a total of twelve."

"Fifteen."

"Thirteen."

"Fifteen."

She'd been prepared to give him twenty. Her cash crop wasn't pies. It was whiskey. "You drive a hard bargain, Mr. Logan. I'll agree to fifteen percent."

He beamed.

Then she'd jerked the rug out from under him. "But we haven't yet shaken on it. There is a matter that concerns me, because I can't take any chances with my reputation as a businesswoman. I'm sure you understand."

"Of course. What's the nature of your concern?"

"Your deliverymen. My father-in-law told me they used to work in a pool parlor. Are they presentable? Do they have integrity? Can I trust them?"

"What Mr. Plummer told you is correct. They went through a wild phase, as young men are wont to do, but they've been tempered by my influence and that of Mrs. Logan. I've received no complaints from customers about their comportment. I wouldn't have them in the store if I thought they were dishonest. I'll summon them right now so you can meet them."

"No, if they know employment is riding on the introduction, they'll be on their best behavior, won't they? I'd rather see them in action, when they don't know it's an audition. As I leave, I'll pick out some grocery items and opt to have them delivered. If I approve their service and manner, you'll get your fifteen percent."

She'd straightened her backbone. "But if in my opinion they're unsuitable for any reason, I'll hire someone else and pay him out of my share, in which case, your percentage will be reduced to thirteen percent. That's the deal, Mr. Logan. Nonnegotiable."

"I'm agreeing because I'm confident that the O'Connor twins will work well for you."

Laurel had been confident of that herself.

That evening, Davy O'Connor had showed up at her front door, a box of groceries balanced on his shoulder. He flashed her a winning smile. "Mrs. Plummer, good evening. Whenever you come into the store, the very sight of you makes my day. But in this gloaming light, you look a vision. Your—"

"Cut it out. Mr. Logan went for it. Have Mike drive around to the back. I baked a strawberry and rhubarb pie for our celebration."

Her deal with the O'Connor brothers had been struck even before she had approached Logan.

Irv had been downright apoplectic when she'd advanced her idea to use the twins. "They're crazy kids. Rambunctious and reckless. Wish I'd never told you about them."

"Well you did. Please arrange a meeting."

Davy and Mike would have been interchangeable except for Davy's front tooth, which at some point in his boyhood had been chipped by a fist thrown by Mike. Both were handsome, flirtatious, and devilishly witty. Laurel liked them instantly.

Irv had informed them that the meeting was to discuss the peddling of moonshine. Already enticed, the two had been eager to hear what Laurel had in mind. Gathered around the kitchen table, she'd gotten down to business. "We need runners to move our product. You seem qualified."

"Count us in," Davy had said, winking at her. "We like excitement, right, brother?"

"We only went to work in that bloody store because we need to eat."

Laurel had explained why they would need to continue working at the store. "At least for the time being. We need the cover of a legitimate business."

The twins had looked at each other, obviously troubled. Speaking for both, Davy had said, "You know the Logans walk the straight and narrow."

"I've told her that," Irv had said.

"Mrs. Logan is trying to save our souls." Mike had grinned when he said that. "Being Catholic is failing in that regard, according to her."

"So when I approach Mr. Logan I should—"

"Act the prude, lady Laurel."

"I'll keep that in mind." When she'd told them her plans for expanding the business, they'd surprised Irv and her by contributing ideas of their own.

"All those men who used to hang out at the pool hall have worked up powerful thirsts, Mrs. Plummer. We can sell them your whiskey, whether or not they buy the baked goods."

"But we'll push your pies, too," Mike had said as though pledging fealty.

As hoped, Mr. Logan's customers had gone wild for Laurel's pies. The twins delivered them after hours and, while at it, peddled moonshine to standing customers. Two weeks into their sideline, the twins had asked for another meeting with Irv and Laurel.

Davy had acted as spokesperson. "One of our friends from the pool hall is working up in Ranger. He says if we deliver your pies up there, he could sell them for a dollar a slice."

Irv had dismissed that with a harrumph. "That ain't worth the bother or the price of gasoline. It's seventy miles one way."

Mike had said, "If, along with the pies, we delivered five gallons of whiskey—"

"Five *gallons?*"

"Every other day." Davy had turned to Laurel and winked.

Irv and she had given the O'Connors the go-ahead. Wearing their Saint Christopher medals for protection, they'd begun making trips to places where angels feared to tread. Irv and Ernie had difficulty keeping up with the demand.

And so had Laurel. A second oven had become necessary. She'd applied at the First National Bank for a loan. The bank officer, a long-standing customer of Irv's moonshine, had approved the note. To accommodate the new appliance, Laurel had moved their dining table from the kitchen into the unfurnished dining room.

Between making deliveries and baking, she'd become so busy that hours would go by without Pearl crossing her mind. Her marriage to Derby seemed to have belonged to another woman in another life far removed from the one she was living. But as exhilarating as this venture was, it came with constant threats to her newfound independence, even to her life. She'd had a shocking reminder of that tonight when, once again, she'd crossed paths with Thatcher Hutton.

Recently, on a trip out to the still to deliver supplies to Ernie, as they passed the cutoff to the shack, she'd casually remarked to Irv that it seemed a long time ago since Mr. Hutton had wandered into the yard asking for directions.

Irv had said, "*If* he wandered, and *if* it was directions he was after."

Her father-in-law still had Thatcher typed as a man who was polite, quiet, calm. And deadly.

Now, as she huddled on the side of her bed, Laurel wondered if the cowboy who broke horses was a guise for a government agent who broke up stills.

On the front page of today's newspaper had been a picture of a still in northeast Texas near the Arkansas line that had been discovered and destroyed by state and federal law enforcement officers, unsmiling men with firearms and stern resolve.

They'd been grouped around the disassembled still and busted casks, spilled corn liquor pooling around their boots and the handcuffed men sitting on the ground. The photograph had been staged to make a point, to send a warning to current or aspiring distillers of illegal whiskey.

Was Thatcher Hutton one of the snitches that Irv had warned her to be wary of? Had he come to the shack that day looking for a still? Did he suspect her of doing precisely what she was doing? Was that why he always regarded her with such intensity?

Despite the summer heat that had collected in her bedroom during the afternoon, her arms broke out in gooseflesh. She clumsily removed the pins from her bun and let it unfurl down her back. Ordinarily the release felt good. But tonight the scene in the café had left her nape and shoulders knotted with tension.

She folded back the bed covers and slid in beneath the top sheet. She settled her head on her pillow, closed her eyes, and tried willing herself not to dwell on the encounter.

But her mind replayed the incident anyway. Had she done anything that might have given her away? Should she tell Irv about it? No. Absolutely not. He would make far more of it than it warranted. He would say that she hadn't just bumped into any man during a delivery, she'd bumped into *that* man.

As reluctant as she was to admit it, her father-in-law would be right.

Whatever else he was, Thatcher Hutton was no ordinary man.

And neither was her middle's flighty reaction to the very sight of him.

TWENTY-SIX

———◆———

W hat are you doing out here?" Randy asked as he clomped up the front steps of the boardinghouse.

"Too early to go to bed. Just taking in the air," Chester Landry replied. He lazily fanned himself with a folded newspaper. "You appear to be drunk."

Randy laughed and plopped down into the chair beside Landry's. "As a skunk."

"Fun evening?"

"Fun and frolic, my friend." He chortled over his alliteration.

Landry shushed him. "Lower your voice. Everyone else has turned in for the night." Everyone except for him, Randy, and Thatcher Hutton, who'd yet to return to the boardinghouse since they'd bade each other good night at the café.

Landry couldn't help but wonder if his dinner guest had cut out on him in order to follow the widow home. He made a mental note to pursue that later, but, right now, his focus was more on the indiscreet and talkative Randy Wells.

"Who were you frolicking with?"

Randy leaned across the arm of his chair and crooked his finger. Landry moved closer. Randy said, "The public library hosts a Bible study every Tuesday night for young singles."

"What's to whisper about?"

Randy giggled. "What's to whisper about is what happens after Bible study."

Landry pretended that was the most delicious piece of information he'd ever heard. "Do tell."

"Those young ladies who sing in church choirs on Sunday are just dying to be led astray on Tuesday. So me and some other guys—"

"Like who?"

"Davy and Mike O'Connor? Know them?"

"I don't believe so."

"You'd know if you did. They're twins. Anyhow, they've joined the Bible study because they work for Deacon Logan, and his wife is practically a missionary. She…" He hiccupped, then waved his hand. "Doesn't matter. Tonight, we treated a few of those young ladies to all the sin they could handle."

"You and these O'Connor brothers?"

"They are my kind of folk. If you know what I mean?" He bobbed his eyebrows.

"Drunk and disorderly?"

Randy roared with laughter.

"Shhh!"

"Oh, sorry." He pressed his index finger vertically against his lips.

"You know what?" Landry said, as though he'd had a sudden inspiration, when actually he'd been planning this since his talk with Mayor Croft about Randy and his loose tongue. "I could use some diversion. I had a rather dull evening tonight with Mr. Hutton."

"Tight-lipped, isn't he? Good at cards, though. Do you think he cheats?"

"If he does, he's good. I haven't caught him at it."

"No, me neither. Lost five bucks to him."

Landry pushed out of his chair. "Come on."

Randy stood up swaying. "Where're we going?"

"For a drive. Did you sinners drink all your hooch?"

"Still have half a jar under the seat of my car."

"Then let's go in it." He threw his arm across Randy's shoulder. "But I'll drive."

TWENTY-SEVEN

———◦◉◦———

Dusk was easing into full-blown darkness when Bill Amos came out of his headquarters and headed toward his car. Thatcher had been waiting for this opportunity to speak to him in private.

"Bill?"

The sheriff turned as Thatcher materialized out of the wide band of shadow under the eaves of the building. "Hey, Thatcher. What's doing?"

"Got a minute?"

Bill glanced back toward his office, hesitated, then asked, "Have you had supper?"

"No."

"Me neither, and Mrs. Amos is hosting bridge tonight. Get in."

Thatcher went around to the passenger side. Once on the road, he asked, "What's your wife's name?"

"Daisy. Her bridge club meets one night a month."

"Does she know how to play poker?"

Bill laughed. "Not with you, she doesn't." After a beat, he said, "I'm glad she's having the group at the house tonight. She doesn't entertain as often as she used to."

That had sounded like a loaded statement. Thatcher waited for him to expand.

Bill cleared his throat. "Daisy isn't always up to socializing. She has...declines. A heart condition."

"I'm sorry to hear that."

"Yeah, well, you know. Life." He gave Thatcher a weak smile. "How's it been treating you lately?"

"Can't complain. Me and Ulysses have finally resolved our differences. His owner is picking him up later this week."

"Will he take to another rider?"

"We'll see."

Bill chuckled. "I wouldn't want to be the first to try. Did you fill that last stall?"

"I've got a waiting list."

Bill removed his pocket watch and checked the time. "I have a hankering for a juicy hamburger. Have you been to Lefty's yet?"

Thatcher shook his head.

"Then you're past due." He tucked his watch away and settled into his seat. "Did you wait in the dark to see me so you could ask my wife's name?"

"Naw." Thatcher exhaled heavily and propped his elbow on the door ledge. "I was wondering if you had talked to that woman, Dr. Driscoll's patient who had the breech birth."

Bill gave him a sharp look, swerving in the process. The driver of an oncoming vehicle tooted a warning. Bill waved an apology as he passed a jalopy of a truck with two young men inside.

"Mrs. Plummer's delivery boys."

Thatcher reacted with a start. "Her delivery boys?"

Bill told him about the arrangement Laurel had made with Logan's Grocery. Although Thatcher turned his head aside and pretended to be absorbed in the passing scenery, he listened with avid interest.

"I hear her pies are selling like hot cakes," Bill said. "No pun intended."

"I knew she'd gone into the business. One night last week, I had supper in Martin's Café. While I was there, she came in to deliver an order."

"Really? To Clyde?"

"Um-huh."

"Huh."

"What?"

"Nothing. Just that Clyde has always used his own cooks for everything."

"I guess he prefers her pies to theirs."

"Guess so. Have you sampled her wares yet?"

Thatcher looked over to see if there was an innuendo behind the question, but Bill had his head turned away, signaling to make a left turn. "I had a slice of pecan pie."

"Was it good?"

"Damn good."

Bill had turned onto a road leading away from town. "We've got a ways to go before we get to Lefty's," he said. "Tell me why you asked about Gabe Driscoll's patient."

"I've been watching his house every night for a week."

Bill looked across at him with both consternation and curiosity. "What for?"

Thatcher started by telling him about his dinner out with Chester Landry. "He's a shoe—"

"I know who he is and what he claims to be."

"Claims to be?"

"Are y'all pals?"

"Hell, no," Thatcher said. "I don't trust that grin of his."

"So why'd you go to dinner with him?"

"I didn't have a reason not to."

Bill gave him a knowing glance. "You want to find out what he's hiding behind that grin."

He was right, but Thatcher didn't want to admit it. "Anyway, that's why I was in the café when Mrs. Plummer came in. By the time Landry and I had finished our desserts, I'd had about all of his company

I could stomach. I opted to walk back to the boardinghouse. But I didn't go straight there. I circled around to the Driscolls' place."

"Again, what for?"

"Shit, I don't know. But after you and I talked about the doc, the coincidences that took place that night, I couldn't get it off my mind. I just felt led to go over there, take a look-see. I didn't really expect to uncover anything, didn't even know what I was looking for. But I went back the next night, and I've been going back." He paused. "Did you question that woman again?"

"Her name is Norma Blanchard, and, yes, I went straight from our conversation by the creek to talk to her about that night."

"And?"

"Have you changed your mind about becoming a deputy?"

"No."

"Then I shouldn't be discussing an open investigation."

"You called it open-ended. Doesn't mean the same as active, does it?"

Bill waved that away with annoyance. "Speak your mind, Thatcher."

They were in the countryside now. They passed barbed wire–fenced pastures with horses and cattle grazing, farmhouses lit by lamps and lanterns instead of incandescent bulbs, chalky rock formations.

Thatcher took time to choose carefully what he was going to say and how he was going to phrase it. He turned slightly in his seat to better address Bill and gauge his reactions.

"Describe Norma Blanchard."

"Late twenties, I'd say. Dark hair, parted down the middle, all knotted up in back. Not pretty, but...Just say men would take to her better than women would."

"She came to the doc's house last night."

Bill gnawed on that as Thatcher figured he would. "After office hours?"

"At eleven twenty-eight."

He shrugged. "Could've been an emergency."

Thatcher said nothing, just looked at him.

"But you don't think so."

"No, I don't, Bill. She was dropped off at the street, and seemed in perfect health, best as I could tell by the way she walked."

"How'd she walk?"

"Like she owned the place. Knocked on the door the same way. The doc was up, or at least his bedroom light was on. Drapes were drawn but there was light around the edges of them, which was why I hadn't left yet.

"He came to the door in his pajamas and a bathrobe. It appeared to me that he wasn't altogether happy to see her. In fact, when she tried to step inside, he blocked her. They didn't raise their voices, or tussle, but there was a lot of angry gesturing. Eventually, he let her in."

Bill kept his eyes on the road and didn't comment, so Thatcher continued. "I don't know where they spent their time while inside, because no other lights in the house came on. If she'd come for medicine or something, they'd've gone into his office, don't you think?"

"How long did she stay?"

"Almost an hour. The car came back at twelve-fifteen. She walked out to it and got in, it drove off. A few minutes later, the upstairs bedroom light went off."

"She didn't have the baby with her?"

"No. Could have been in the car, I guess."

"Did you see who was driving?"

"Another woman."

"Her sister, no doubt. Patsy Kemp. They live together. Mrs. Kemp's husband is off working somewhere. Montana, Alaska, somewhere like that. Which is why Norma is living with her, I guess."

"Norma isn't married?"

"I didn't ask, but she wasn't wearing a wedding band and no reference was made to a husband."

"Did you see the baby?"

"He was sleeping there in a basket in the living room. She showed him off to me. If he was born out of wedlock, she gave no sign of being ashamed about it."

"What did she tell you about Dr. Driscoll?"

"What she'd told Scotty when he questioned her, which matched what Gabe had told us. He paid her a house call earlier in the day while she was still in labor. On his way home from Lefty's, he stopped there again to check on her. In the meantime, she'd given birth and all was well."

Thatcher took off his hat and ran his fingers through his hair. "I feel like a damn peeping Tom."

"It feels like that sometimes."

"What feels like that?"

"Detective work."

"That's not what I was doing."

"Then you are a peeping Tom. Swear to God, Thatcher, I ought to arrest you again."

Thatcher shot him a look.

"Well then, tell me what's compelled you to go over there every night for the past week?"

"I wish now I hadn't. I wish I'd left it alone."

"No you don't."

Thatcher gave him another hard look, which didn't dent Bill in the slightest. He said, "If you had wanted it left alone, you wouldn't have told me about Norma's late-night visit."

Thatcher didn't have a chance to form a comeback. They had arrived at the roadhouse. There were twenty or thirty vehicles parked around it, and yet only weak light shone through the screened windows. Built of unpainted clapboard, the structure was as square as a box of saltines and totally without character. A set of warped wood steps led up to the entrance.

It looked nothing like the speakeasy Thatcher had been to in Norfolk, which had had the classy veneer of the haberdashery and an aura of intrigue.

"You seem let down," Bill remarked.

Thatcher shrugged. "Doesn't have much atmosphere."

"Oh, it's got atmosphere." He reached beneath his car seat and came up with a Colt revolver. "A hostile atmosphere."

TWENTY-EIGHT

——◈——

B ill passed the pistol to Thatcher. "It's loaded."

"Will I need it?"

"Depends." He didn't say on what.

Even though Thatcher had been told the gun was loaded, he checked the cylinder before pushing the pistol into his waistband and buttoning his jacket over it.

He and Bill got out of the car and walked toward the porch steps where two men sat smoking. As they went around them in order to reach the door, Bill addressed the men by name. They kept their heads down and replied to his greeting with surly mumbles.

The instant they stepped inside, the low rumble of conversation died. Bill acted as though he didn't notice and pointed Thatcher toward an empty table. They sat in adjacent chairs, both facing out into the room, their backs to the wall.

Thatcher was about to take off his fedora, when Bill said, "Leave it on. Bad manners, I know, but the brim shades your eyes. Nobody can tell where you're looking."

Following Bill's example, Thatcher left his hat on. Once his eyes had adjusted to the dim interior, made even foggier by tobacco and grease smoke, he surveyed the place, trying not to noticeably move his head.

The bar ran almost the full length of the back wall, but behind it, the shelves were stocked with bottled soft drinks only. A gramophone in the corner emitted scratchy, tinny music. Only a few of the tables were occupied.

Thatcher remarked on the small crowd. "Doesn't match the number of vehicles outside."

"And you say you're no detective."

A steep staircase was attached to the far wall. Thatcher noticed a hulking figure leaning against the bannister halfway up, smoking a cigarette, and staring at him through the haze.

Bill said, "I see you've captured Gert's attention."

"That's Gert, the madam?"

"What did you expect? A red velvet dress and hourglass figure?" Lowering his voice, Bill added, "Careful how you answer. Here comes her other half."

The man approaching their table had the proportions of a praying mantis and the lips of a lizard. They formed a tight seam between his beak of a nose and pointed chin. A smile would have looked out of place on such a face, but, in any case, he didn't fashion one.

"Sheriff. Been a while."

"Hello, Lefty. How're things?"

He jutted his chin toward Thatcher. "Who's he?"

"Meet Thatcher Hutton. He's new to town."

"Hutton. You're the one what shot the snake."

"He's a horse trainer," Bill said amiably.

"Horse trainer." He said it like he'd been told that Thatcher performed a high-wire act in the circus. "Well, welcome to Lefty's."

Thatcher didn't say anything, just gave a bob of his head.

Bill placed their order for two hamburgers and cold Coca-Colas.

"Comin' up."

Thatcher watched Lefty's progress back across the room. Midway, he was intercepted by his wife. They had a brief exchange, then

Lefty continued on toward the grill behind the bar while Gert made her way toward their table. Through the soles of his boots, Thatcher could feel the vibration of her heavy tread.

Unlike her husband, who looked like he could be snapped in two as easily as a toothpick, Thatcher didn't think Gert could be knocked over with a tank like those he'd seen on the battlefront.

When she reached them, she sized him up. "Thatcher, huh?"

"Yes, ma'am."

"Never knew nobody with that name. Who're your people?"

"You wouldn't know them."

"Try me."

He gave her a one-sided smile that didn't show teeth. "*I* wouldn't know them."

Still appraising him, she took a drag of her cigarette, then leaned over and ground it out in the ashtray in the center of their table. She blew a plume of smoke out of the corner of her mouth.

Turning her attention to Bill, she said, "What are you doing here?"

Bill, who'd checked his watch again, pocketed it. "Hello to you, too, Gert. I'm here for a hamburger. Also to ask after the girl."

"Which?"

"You know which, Gert."

She huffed a gust of stinky breath. "That Wally Johnson. Jug-eared little bastard ruint her face, her arm's healing all crooked, and she cain't see out one eye."

"Is she still here?"

She hitched a thumb over her shoulder. Thatcher and Bill looked in the direction she'd indicated. A young woman with her arm in a sling was flipping meat patties on the grill while Lefty was uncapping Coke bottles.

Gert was saying, "Her name's Corrine. Out of the goodness of my heart I'm keeping her on even though she ain't much use to me upstairs no more. But some men if they're that hard up ain't all that particular about looks." She gave Thatcher a sly glance. "You interested? You can have half an hour at a cut rate."

Bill said, "Gert, if you openly solicit, I'll slam down your operation upstairs." He spoke in a low voice that thrummed with warning.

Her eyes, set in folds of ruddy fat, narrowed to slits. "Lessen you forgot, you and me have a deal, sheriff."

"Only as long as we both keep up the pretense that this isn't a low-rent whorehouse."

"Beg your pardon. It ain't low-rent."

"All I'm saying is, don't forget the terms of our deal, or I'll forget we have a deal. I'll close you down, and you'd lose a shitload, what with all the roughnecks racing down here from Ranger every Saturday night." He looked over at Thatcher. "They've struck oil up there."

"Yeah, I've heard."

"Despite the distance they have to drive, the oil field workers have been a boon to Gert's business."

"I don't know what you're talking about," she said.

Bill snickered. "The hell you don't. They're a wild bunch, those boys. I hear you've got them lining up in the hall and making them bid on who goes next. That's begging for trouble." Then, after a beat, he said in a steely undertone, "Keep things under control, Gert, or our deal is off."

She took a challenging stance. "I got iron control."

"You didn't the night Wally battered that girl." Bill eyed her keenly. "Or *was* that under your control?"

Looking up at her from beneath the brim of his hat, Thatcher noticed an instantaneous slackening of the woman's smirk, her rapid blinking. Bill had struck a nerve, but she recovered quickly.

"Chew good, sheriff. It'd be a damn shame if you choked to death on your burger." She looked again at Thatcher. "Any of my girls would be tickled to see you." She turned and lumbered off.

"Why, Thatcher. I think she took a shine to you," Bill said. He was still laughing under his breath when Lefty brought over their food.

After one bite, Thatcher understood why the burgers had earned their reputation. He'd polished his off in no time and was about to comment on the tastiness, when the crack of a gunshot silenced him.

Reflexively he dropped sideways out of his chair onto the floor and pulled the pistol from his waistband.

Much more calmly, Bill stood up and drew his weapon. "That was only the warning shot, Thatcher. But any from now on, you should take seriously."

"Warning shot?"

"We're raiding the back room."

Bill left him and began swimming upstream of all the patrons who were hotfooting it toward the entry. "I could use some help," he shouted back at Thatcher.

Thatcher was furious at Bill and at himself for being so goddamn gullible, but he followed, pushing people aside before they could trample him.

When he and Bill drew even with the staircase, Gert leaned over the bannister and screamed, "I won't forget this, sheriff! Fuck you!"

Ignoring her, Bill slid into a narrow space behind the bar that accessed a door. He knocked on it twice with the butt of his gun. It was opened by Harold, who was breathing heavily. "Hell's broke loose."

From beyond the doorway came the sounds of pandemonium: swearing and shouting, grunts of pain, the splintering sound of breaking furniture, glass shattering.

Bill turned and slapped his hand over Thatcher's chest. "Pin that on and consider yourself deputized."

Thatcher fumbled the star-shaped badge, pricking his finger on the pin. "You son of a bitch."

"Well, I guess I am, but—"

A barrage of gunshots drowned out the rest.

"Dammit!" Bill barged through the open doorway.

Thatcher slid the badge into the breast pocket of his jacket as he followed the sheriff. Holding the Colt at shoulder level, barrel toward the ceiling, he entered the fray.

Scotty had the man obviously responsible for firing the gunshots pinned facedown on the floor. Bill was trying to wrestle away the man's handgun before he could fire another round.

Harold was dodging the uncoordinated jabs of a broken beer bottle wielded by a man so drunk he could barely stand. Thatcher rushed over and bonked the drunk on the back of his head with the grip of his pistol. The man dropped the broken bottle and landed on the floor like a sandbag, face first.

Harold said, "That's twice I owe you. Thanks." Then he dashed off to help other deputies whom Thatcher recognized but didn't know by name. They were swapping blows with some of the angrier, drunker customers.

Others trying to avoid arrest were overturning tables, chairs, and each other in their mad scramble to exit through the single door at the back of the room. Some were making their escape by jumping through windows. Along with their male counterparts, a few women were kicking and clawing their way toward the nearest way out.

A dozen or more people had bottlenecked at the exit. Thatcher noticed in the midst of them a familiar head of hair, so pomaded it looked like it had been painted onto his scalp. No sooner had he identified Chester Landry than the man managed to squeeze through the congested exit to the outside.

Thatcher fought his way toward the door. Harold, he realized, was following in his wake, apprehending the people Thatcher shoved back toward him.

When Thatcher reached the door, he bolted outside and tried to catch sight of Landry. Mad confusion was made even worse by the darkness, and by the sudden blinding glare of headlights as people made it to their cars and peeled out in every direction.

A car without headlights came speeding out of the darkness, missing Thatcher by a hair. Thatcher saw two autos collide in their haste to leave the area. Some drove over ground in the opposite direction of the road, leaving clouds of dust that further obscured vision.

He didn't catch sight of either Chester Landry or his automobile, which Thatcher probably couldn't have identified anyway. But one vehicle did catch his eye, and it caused his heart to lurch. He ran over to it; no one was inside.

He replaced the Colt in his waistband and ran full-out back into the building, where the chaos continued. The deputies and Sheriff Amos were trying to restrain those still bent on escaping and to keep corralled those they'd halted. Above the cacophony, Gert was bellowing profane threats. Lefty was swinging a full bottle of whiskey at the head of a man he was calling a goddamn snitch, which his victim was frantically denying as he ducked each hazardous arc of the bottle.

On his first sweep of the room, Thatcher didn't see whom he sought, but there were several men down, lying on the floor either wounded or dead of gunshot. He rushed over to the first, who was cursing and clutching his thigh.

He yelled, "I'm shot!"

Thatcher squatted down and took a look. "It would be spurting if it had clipped an artery. You have a handkerchief?"

The man nodded.

"Use it as a tourniquet. Tie it tight. You'll be all right."

"I'm dead," he wailed.

"You're not going to die."

"Hell I ain't. My wife's gonna kill me."

Thatcher left him and moved to another person lying motionless nearby. He was on his side, facing away from Thatcher. Fresh blood was spreading a dark blotch on the back of his shirt.

There was no mistaking the bald pate, as round and shiny as a cue ball, fringed by wiry gray hair. Thatcher knelt and eased Irv Plummer onto his back.

His eyelids fluttered open, but when he saw Thatcher, he scowled. "Did you shoot me?"

"Where're you shot?"

"Under my arm." He raised his left arm, or tried to. But pain drained his face of color and he gnashed his teeth. "Hurts like a son of a bitch."

"Put your right arm around my neck."

"I can make it my ownself."

Thatcher swore at him, then hooked Irv's right arm around his neck, put his shoulder to Irv's middle, and stood up with Irv draped over him. He felt the old man go limp. He'd fainted.

Thatcher wove his way through the overturned tables and chairs toward the door, but it was slow going. The floor was littered with broken glass, and slick with spilled liquor and blood. He'd almost reached the exit when, "Thatcher!"

He turned to face Bill Amos, who asked, "Irv Plummer? Is he dead?"

"No, but he's been shot."

"How bad?"

"I don't know. I'll take him to a doctor."

"Put him in my car."

"His truck is outside. I'll drive him in that. Can't leave it here, it's his livelihood."

"Thatcher, he—"

"I'm driving him." He turned to go, but Bill caught his sleeve.

"When you told me that this wasn't your fight and that you were staying out of it, I knew better."

Thatcher didn't waste time arguing with him. He pulled himself loose and left through the door. Most everyone had cleared the area. Only a few stragglers remained. He carried Irv over the rough ground with as little jostling as possible.

When he reached the truck, he opened the tailgate and eased Irv off his shoulder and into the bed of it. Thatcher shook him slightly. "Where's your key?"

Irv groaned, but he'd understood the question and patted his right pants pocket. Thatcher fished out the key, then adjusted Irv's legs and feet to clear the tailgate.

"I saw you sittin' with the sheriff."

Thatcher turned quickly. Standing behind him was the young prostitute in the arm sling. She said, "You law?"

"No."

"Gert said you prob'ly was."

"She's wrong." The badge in his breast pocket seemed to be branding him through his shirt.

With a tip of her head the girl indicated Irv, who was moaning and muttering incoherently. "Is he gonna die?"

"I don't know."

"If you'll take me away from here, I'll help you with him."

"No thanks."

"I'm a good helper."

"Thanks, but—"

"Don't make me go back to Gert, mister. Please."

Thatcher took in her misshapen jaw and the damaged eye. He mouthed a vulgarity used frequently in the trenches. "Get in."

TWENTY-NINE

Laurel was accustomed to Irv's truck clanking into the drive at all hours of the night, so when it did now, her subconscious registered that he had made it home, but she didn't fully wake up until there was thunderous knocking on the back door.

She threw off the sheet, grabbed her housecoat, and pulled it on as she rushed downstairs. She didn't even bother to turn on the kitchen light before running to the back door and yanking it open.

Even having been certain that the knocking didn't bode well, she still wasn't prepared for the sight that greeted her. Thatcher Hutton stood on the other side of the threshold. He was wearing the familiar black fedora, a bloodstained Henley undershirt, and dark trousers with a pistol stuck in the waistband. He was carrying Irv over his shoulder.

"Your father-in-law has been hurt."

Laurel stepped around him to better see Irv, who hung limply, his arms dangling lifelessly. "Irv?" She turned his face toward her and repeated his name. When he didn't respond, she cried out in alarm.

"He's not dead, just unconscious."

"He's bleeding!"

"He was. I stanched the wound."

"*What wound?*"

"He was shot."

Aghast, Laurel looked down at the pistol in his waistband.

"Not by me," he said. "Let's get him inside, see how bad it is."

"We already know it's bad. He needs a doctor."

"He refused a doctor."

"Refused? How could he refuse if he's unconscious?"

"Where should I put him?"

"Back in his truck. I'll drive him myself."

He took a breath, then in a voice that brooked no argument said, "Where to?"

He seemed immovable. Realizing that further argument would be a waste of valuable time, she motioned. "The room behind the kitchen."

Thatcher stepped inside and headed in that direction. She reached out to close the door, but a young woman with her arm in a sling was coming through. "The old man threatened to chop off Mr. Hutton's pecker if he took him to a doctor."

She scuttled past Laurel and followed Thatcher into Irv's room. Laurel shut the door, then rushed to follow them, reaching the room just as the girl switched on the overhead light. Thatcher eased Irv off his shoulder and lowered him onto his back on the bed.

Out of sheer desperation, Laurel prayed, "God, please no." She elbowed Thatcher aside and sat down on the edge of the mattress. She took hold of Irv's hand, squeezed it tightly, and exhaled in relief when he opened his eyes.

"Hi, Laurel."

"What in the world happened?"

"Ain't Hutton told you?"

"You need a doctor."

"It ain't gonna be that bad."

"You don't know that."

"Fetch that jar of 'shine from my dresser drawer."

"Which drawer?" Thatcher asked.

"Bottom."

On his way over to the dresser, he pulled the pistol out of his waistband and set it on the cushion atop Irv's barrel, then took off his hat and placed it over the gun. He eased his braces off his shoulders and let them fall to form loops over his hips.

He found the jar of corn liquor, brought it over to the bed and screwed the lid off, then held it against Irv's lips while he sipped.

After a few swallows, Irv relaxed his head on the pillow. "Don't fret, Laurel. Pour some of this whiskey in the bullet hole, smear it with a little coal oil, and cover it with a bandage. In a day or two, I'll be right as rain."

"Coal oil?"

"Cures everything." Irv gave her a woozy grin and helped himself to another sip of moonshine when Thatcher pressed the rim of the jar to his lips, then gave a grunt of satisfaction and closed his eyes. "Get on with it."

Thatcher turned to the girl. "Corrine, think you can put a kettle on to boil?"

"Sure."

"While you're waiting on it, gather up some things. Towels, tweezers, rubbing alcohol, bandages, some—"

"I don't have any bandages," Laurel said, interrupting him. She resented his taking charge of *her* emergency with *her* father-in-law in *her* house. "You'll have to cut strips of bedsheets," she said to the girl. "Fresh ones are in the cupboard in the upstairs hallway." She rattled off where the girl could find the other items.

The girl repeated the instructions to make sure she'd gotten them all, then turned to leave. In her haste through the door, she bumped into the jamb. Laurel had noticed that her right eye was swollen and partially closed. She was curious about her, but for the time being, she shelved her curiosity and asked the question uppermost in her mind.

"How did this happen?" She was afraid that Irv had been assaulted at the still. What of Ernie?

Irv made a limp motion with his hand, ceding the explanation to Thatcher, who asked her, "Do you know about Lefty's?"

She gave a brusque nod.

"The back room?"

"I've heard about it."

"Well, the sheriff raided it tonight. It was bedlam. Someone started shooting."

"At Irv?"

Although his eyes remained closed, Irv answered, "No."

Laurel looked to Thatcher for confirmation. He said, "I don't know for sure, but I think it was random. He caught a wild shot. I got him out of there quick as I could."

"I appreciate that, Mr. Hutton. Thank you for seeing to him, but you don't have to stay. I'll take over from here."

"You'll need help."

"I'll manage."

"I don't think the bullet is still in there, but the wound needs to be cleaned out. Have you ever dug around in a bullet hole?"

The thought of it made her queasy. She gave a tight shake of her head.

"It's nasty business," he said, "and through some of it, he'll probably have to be held down."

Laurel was still clutching Irv's hand, though his had gone slack. His face was ashen. She understood that Mr. Hutton was right. Giving in to him smarted, but it wasn't only her pride at stake here. Irv's life was at risk. "All right. I accept your offer to help."

"Good."

She swiveled her head to look up at him. "But I don't like it."

"I know. You don't want to be beholden." His gaze stayed steady on hers for several beats, then he turned his attention to Irv. "Let's get him out of his shirt."

The cloth had turned stiff with drying blood, front and back. Whenever they had to readjust his position to work his arms free of the sleeves, he hissed through clenched teeth. When the garment was off, Laurel wadded it up and tossed it into a corner.

"This isn't going to be pretty," Thatcher said.

He lifted Irv's left arm and removed a balled-up shirt from his armpit. It was more blood-soaked than Irv's had been. "Yours?" she asked, as she sent it the way of the other.

"It was the only thing I had handy." He gave his shirt no heed as he assessed the raw, gaping wound. "This is where the bullet came out."

"And went in where?"

"On the back of his arm. Help me roll him over."

Following his directions, she went around to the other side of the bed and helped him turn Irv toward her. Her father-in-law wasn't too drunk to spew some colorful expletives.

"Sorry," Thatcher said to him. "Bullet went straight through a fleshy part of your arm. Best I can tell, it missed bones. All told, you're lucky."

"Told ya it weren't gonna be bad. But right now, I ain't feelin' so lucky," Irv grumbled. "Where's the whiskey at?"

The girl moved like a whirlwind. She made several trips in and out of the room, depositing everything that she'd been sent to scavenge. She placed them on a table that Laurel had cleared for that purpose and had moved close to the bedside.

Thatcher put the tweezers and scissors in a washbowl and poured boiling water over them. While he organized the things they would need, Laurel stayed at Irv's side and plied him with moonshine from their own still.

At one point, as Thatcher was packing towels beneath Irv's left side, he said to her, "Go easy on that whiskey. We'll need it for later."

"There's plenty more." Then, realizing her slip, she added, "He keeps another jar hidden in the bottom of that barrel. He doesn't know that I know."

Thatcher gave her a wry grin. "Before we're done, you and I may need a swig."

"Don't be giving away my whiskey, Laurel," Irv mumbled into his pillow. "Or my secrets."

She leaned down and whispered directly into his ear, "*Our* secrets. And I won't."

When everything was ready, and Irv was good and looped, Thatcher and she bathed their hands with rubbing alcohol. They worked on the entry wound first since it was the minor one. Irv remained stoic.

But when they repositioned him on his back, placed his arm above his head, and began to clean the exit wound, Thatcher had to restrain him while Laurel tweezed out a scrap of his shirt fabric from deep inside. Irv yelped, swore, then fainted. He remained blessedly unconscious while they continued.

At last, Thatcher said, "I think that's the best we can do."

"We're going to leave the wounds open?"

"You want to close them with stitches?"

She shuddered. "I dread the thought, and I'm not sure closing them would be best anyway."

"I don't advise it," he said. When she looked up at him, he gave a small shrug. "One time one of the ranch hands got shot by a rustler as we were chasing him. The boss, Mr. Hobson, sent for a doctor. The doc got the bullet out and wanted to stitch up the hole. Mr. Hobson wouldn't let him. He said the cowboy might survive the blood loss, but then die of infection."

"Did he live?"

"Yeah, he did fine. Well, until he tried to ride a bull on a dare. He got gored. Bled to death after all."

Laurel looked over to see if he was joking, but his brow was furrowed with concentration as he flooded Irv's wound with rubbing alcohol.

She stood by to blot up the runoff, then covered the bullet holes with folded patches of cloth. Only then did the tension drain from her shoulders.

Thatcher must have felt similar relief. He leaned against the wall and wiped his perspiring hairline with the back of his hand. "He's a tough old coot."

"He is." Laurel regarded the sleeping Irv with affection as she sponged dried blood off his arm and torso. "But I don't know what I would have done without him."

Thatcher let that hover for a moment, then said, "Tomorrow when you change the dressing, it probably wouldn't hurt to apply a little coal oil."

"I planned to," she said around a light laugh, "but I wasn't going to admit it. My mother swore by its healing properties."

"Keep the moonshine handy, too."

"I also planned to do that." She used a clean towel to dry Irv's damp skin where she had washed.

"Ready to wrap?" Thatcher asked.

The girl had left them with neatly stacked bands of cloth. Together she and Thatcher began winding them around Irv's torso, being as gentle as possible when they rolled him from one side to the other.

The room Irv had created for himself wasn't that spacious, but the quarters had never seemed small to Laurel. Until now. When sharing it with Thatcher Hutton.

As they wound the bandage, their movements were so in sync they could have been choreographed. Or perhaps they were just keenly attuned to each other, so attuned they read each other's mind.

Occasionally their fingertips brushed. When even a whisper of contact was made, she felt his eyes on her, but she didn't have the nerve to look into his. She kept her head down and pretended that her concentration was solely on their task.

But her awareness of him was breath-stealing. The five-button placket on his undershirt was open, revealing a wedge of dark chest hair that looked soft. The long sleeves had been rolled up to above his elbows, tightly cuffing his arms just beneath his biceps. Plump veins ran down his forearms all the way to the backs of his hands, which she watched now as long, strong fingers tied a knot to secure the bandage.

"It's snug," he said, "but keeping pressure on it tonight will keep the bleeding down."

"Thank you for stanching it when you did." She glanced over at his discarded shirt on the floor in the corner. "I'll wash it for you."

"It isn't a favorite."

"That one is worse for wear, too."

He looked down at the streaks of blood on his undershirt. "It'll soak out."

Looking away from him, she rested her hand on Irv's forehead. "He doesn't feel hot now, but I'll keep checking for fever."

"If the wounds get red and puffy, or start to stink, call in a doctor. Only, please don't tell Irv I was the one who suggested it."

Remembering what Irv had threatened to do if Thatcher took him to a doctor, Laurel bit back a smile.

THIRTY

Laurel had learned that the girl's name was Corrine. She had been very useful, eagerly fetching and carrying, handling everything with remarkable efficiency considering that she had the use of only one arm and limited eyesight.

She reentered Irv's room now. "There was a pie in the pie safe. I cut each of y'all a piece and started a pot of coffee. Take a breather, I'll sit with the old man. Irv's his name? Never mind that bloody water in the washbowl. I'll pitch it out the winda."

"Did you help yourself to some pie?" Laurel asked.

"It looked too good to pass up. I hope you don't mind."

"Not at all. You've been extremely helpful tonight. Thank you."

Corrine shrugged off the thanks, and with her free hand made a shooing motion for Laurel and Thatcher to leave the room. Irv was snoring loudly through his open mouth. Laurel didn't think she would be missed.

Thatcher followed her into the kitchen. When they were out of earshot of Corrine, she asked quietly, "Who is that girl? Where did she come from?"

"She works at Lefty's."

Laurel looked toward Irv's room, then back at Thatcher. "Not upstairs, surely?"

The look he gave her said otherwise.

"She's just a girl."

"Seventeen."

She was about to say more, ask more, but then remembered that Thatcher had been at Lefty's tonight when it was raided, and that what he was doing in the company of a teenage prostitute was none of her business.

He stood there, looking down at her as though waiting for her to pose questions she had thought better of asking. Then, stepping around her, he said, "I'll be right back," and went out through the back door.

She loaded a tray with the slices of pie Corrine had prepared, cups of coffee and the fixings, and carried it into the dining room, where she laid two place settings on the table. Since she and Irv had begun eating their meals here, she'd bought a secondhand sideboard. At each end of it, she'd placed matching kerosene lamps with milk-glass chimneys. Preferring their glow to the glaring overhead electric light, she lit them now.

As she leaned down to adjust the flame, her long braid swung forward. *Lord!* Throughout the ordeal with Irv, she'd lost sight of the fact that she was in her nightclothes, barefoot, her hair plaited for bedtime.

But it was too late to correct these oversights. The back door squeaked open. She made certain her housecoat was fully buttoned, flipped her braid over her shoulder, and called, "In here, Mr. Hutton."

He must have gone to Irv's truck to get his suit jacket. He'd put it on over his undershirt. His braces were no longer lying loose against his hips, so she assumed he'd pulled them back onto his shoulders. He might also have smoothed down his hair, although it seemed to have a will of its own. In spite of the bloodstains on his undershirt, he looked more respectable and suitable to the setting than she did.

They sat down across from each other. She tucked her bare feet beneath her chair, then pulled it closer to the table in a belated attempt to hide her dishabille.

She placed a napkin in her lap. As she poured a dollop of cream into her coffee, she noticed that he hadn't yet started on his pie. His hands were loosely fisted on either side of the plate, and he was studying it. "You don't like peach?"

"Oh, a lot. I was just wondering how you get the crust to wave like that at the edge."

"I flute it."

He raised his head and looked over at her.

"Like this." She used her fingers to demonstrate. "To the dough."

"Huh." He picked up his fork and began to eat.

After a full minute of strained silence—at least to Laurel it seemed strained—she asked, "Have you been thrown from a horse again?"

"Only once today."

"I was being serious."

He gave a lopsided grin. "So was the horse."

She laughed softly and shook her head. "I don't know how you do that."

"Well, I don't know how to flute pie dough."

They smiled across at each other, then she set her fork on the rim of her plate and clasped her hands in her lap. "You were right, Mr. Hutton. I—"

"Why won't you call me Thatcher?"

For a moment she was thrown by his interrupting her to ask that. She picked up her fork. Set it back down. "It wouldn't be appropriate for us to use first names."

"How come?"

"Because we're not that well acquainted."

"Using first names would be a start in that direction, wouldn't it?"

All things taken into account, not the least of which was the privacy of this moment, relaxing the rules of etiquette was a risky step she was unwilling to take. Once a boundary was breached, it was difficult, if

not impossible, to reestablish. Breaching boundaries with him seemed particularly chancy.

"I think we should leave things as they are."

He didn't respond immediately, but ultimately made a gesture of concession with his shoulder. "You were saying?"

It took a moment for her to remember what she'd been saying. "I apologize for the curt way I turned down your offer to help with Irv. I couldn't have adequately tended to him by myself. Thank you for getting him home; thank you for staying."

"You're welcome, Mrs. Plummer."

He didn't smile, but his eyes—the bluish-gray color of storm clouds—glinted with humor. His amusement made her feel silly and prudish for making first names an issue. But it would take on greater significance if she amended her position on the matter now.

Instead, she changed the subject. "I grew up on a farm. The nearest doctor was ten miles away, at least. Accidents happened frequently. Even as a girl, I patched up cuts and scrapes, bound up sprains, things like that. I don't faint at the sight of blood. But I never had to deal with a bullet wound before. I hope I never have to again."

"How ammunition can rip through a body can be ugly, all right."

"You're referring to the war? I'm sure you saw some horrific things on the battlefield."

"And in the hospital. Some of the men brought in might've been better off dying on the front. In the hospital, they were just made to suffer longer."

"You were wounded?"

He shook his head. "Spanish flu. I was laid up with it for three weeks. Three miserable weeks."

"I lived in constant fear of Derby being blown to bits, or dying of exposure to mustard gas, something war-related. But I was just as scared that he would die of flu."

"Thousands did."

"In some ways that seems a crueler death than being killed during a battle. Little glory. Less heroic."

"More of a waste." He focused on tracing the curved handle of the coffee cup with his fingertip. "I'm sorry about your husband."

His somber tone indicated that he knew how Derby had died. Foley was a small town. Through someone, he would have heard the circumstances by which she'd become a widow. She nodded an acknowledgment of his condolence, then gestured to his empty plate. "Would you care for another piece?"

"No thanks. Sure was good, though."

"I'm glad you liked it. The peaches came from Parker County. It's famous for them."

"I didn't know that. They must be special if you went all that way to buy them. How long a drive is it?"

When she realized the dangerous territory she'd carelessly wandered into, her throat seized up. "Well, I didn't go myself."

"You sent Irv?"

"No. A couple of young men who deliver my bakery items were up in that area several days ago. They stopped at a roadside stand and brought a bushel of freestones back for me. It was very sweet and thoughtful of them."

"Hmm."

She could kick herself for bringing that up, and then for blabbering on about it. Hadn't she warned Irv that telling too much was the best way to get caught lying? Although she'd essentially told the truth. The O'Connor twins *had* brought her back a bushel of peaches, but their primary errand had been to deliver several gallons of whiskey to the man in Weatherford who'd sold Irv the copper to make the new still.

Mr. Hutton seemed to detect that she was nervously dancing around something. He continued to stare at her over the rim of his cup as he drank the last of his coffee. He returned the cup to the saucer. "Your father-in-law is going to mend."

She smiled. "I'm relieved."

"He'll be ornery for a week or so."

Her smile broadened. "I expect so. He's fiercely independent and doesn't like to be fussed over."

"I got that about him."

He shifted in his seat, stretched out his long legs at an angle to the table, then drew them back beneath it. He turned his head aside and studied the spandrel with much more absorption than it warranted.

Evidently he wanted to say something, but was hesitant. She waited.

Finally, his meandering gaze came back to her. "I hated having to give you a scare tonight."

"You mean when you arrived?"

"I knew it would shock you, seeing your father-in-law like that, the blood and all, but there was just no way to make it easy. At least, I couldn't think of a way."

"No, there wouldn't have been an easy way. My heart was in my throat."

"You must've thought the worst had happened."

"'Not Irv, too.' That's what flashed through my mind."

"I saw the fear in your face."

"Was it that obvious?"

"It was to me."

The four words, softly and solemnly spoken, had an immediate and noticeable effect on the atmosphere. He said nothing more, for which she was glad. Except that, moments into the ensuing silence, during which they just sat there looking at each other, she wished for more dialogue, or a movement, no matter how slight, anything to relieve her awareness of him, which had become both terrible and tantalizing.

Her nightclothes were made of summer-weight cotton, old and soft from so many washings, but they began to feel like chain mail against her chest, equaling the pressure collecting behind her breastbone.

When she could stand it no longer, she said, "I had better check on Irv." She pushed back her chair and came out of it so quickly, she tripped on the hem of her housecoat.

She hadn't quite made it out of the dining room when he touched her arm from behind. "Laurel, wait."

She didn't upbraid him for using her first name. Of greater consequence was that he had covered the distance from the table in half the time she had and was now standing close behind her. So terrible and tantalizing that she kept her back to him.

"What, Mr. Hutton?"

"Why didn't you ask me about Corrine?"

"I did ask you about her."

"You wanted to know more."

"No, I didn't."

"Yes you did." He reached for her hand and turned her around, then kept his fingers clasping hers as they faced each other. "Why didn't you ask how come she was with me?"

"Because it isn't any of my business."

"Yes, it is."

He drew on her hand, bringing her closer to him, close enough for her to feel his body heat. Denying to herself that she felt anything at all, she kept her head lowered and whispered insistently into the open placket of his undershirt, "No, it *isn't*."

"Well, it's about to be."

With his other hand, he tipped her chin up. His eyes moved over her face, pausing momentarily on each feature. He brought his hand up to her cheek and rested it there. His thumb stroked her chin, coming close enough to her lips to make them tingle. He lowered his head, then more, more still, until his face filled her field of vision and she felt his breath drift warmly over her lips.

Her eyes closed.

His lips met hers softly, whisking back and forth, sipping gently, teasing her so maddeningly that she came up on tiptoes to secure the connection.

He made a low sound as his arm curved around her waist. The hand against her cheek slid beneath her chin, supporting her jaw and neck as he tilted her head and realigned their lips.

His were parted. Hers responded in kind.

Tongues touched, shyly and fleetingly, but electrically. Breaths caught and were suspended. He waited. For her it was agonizing, this indecision, this self-denial, this wanting, wanting, but fearing.

But then he spoke her name on a ragged breath, and something inside her that had been fettered for a long time broke free and took flight.

He sensed it immediately and deepened the kiss with hunger and heat, a low growl, his tongue searching. His arm tightened around her waist until their bodies met where his was straining and hers was aching.

He nudged the dip between her thighs, and stayed, and pressed, and still it wasn't close enough. She placed her hands on his chest, clutched handfuls of his jacket...

And then gave a cry of sudden pain.

He released her immediately and backed away. "God, Laurel. What's the matter?"

She looked down at her right hand where a drop of blood beaded up out of her palm. "I don't know." Mystified, she looked up at him. "Something in your pocket?" She reached into his left breast pocket and came up with a star-shaped badge.

She gaped at it, then dropped it as though the pin had pricked her again. The badge clinked against the hardwood floor. She looked up into his face, her breath rushing in and out. "You're a deputy sheriff?"

"No. Not officially."

She backed away from him, drawing her housecoat more tightly around her. "Were you in on that raid?"

"Not by choice."

"Either you were or you weren't," she said, raising her voice. "If there hadn't been a raid, Irv wouldn't have gotten shot."

"If he hadn't been in Lefty's back room, he wouldn't have gotten shot."

"You're blaming *him*?"

"No. All I'm saying is that he was at the wrong place at the wrong time, and so was I."

"Oh, were you? If Irv hadn't been shot, would you have arrested him?"

"Wasn't up to me. I didn't arrest anybody. I hauled your father-in-law out of there, carried him to his truck, and drove him home."

"For which I've thanked you. Now I want you to leave."

"It wasn't my doing, Laurel."

"Don't use my name!"

"I got railroaded into taking part, *Laurel*. Sheriff Amos—"

"I don't care."

"Sounds like you do. Sounds like you care one hell of a lot."

"Will you just go?"

"What difference does it make to you if I was official or not?"

"None. Absolutely none. You…your…nothing you do is any of my business. Or didn't I make that clear to you not three minutes ago?"

He leaned forward and said with emphasis, "It was an eventful three minutes."

True. With desire spreading through her like warm syrup, all sorts of *events* had taken place in intimate places. To cover her mortification, she went on the offensive. "Why did you keep that badge concealed? It makes me wonder what else you're hiding."

"Yeah? Then that makes two of us. Because I don't think it was the kiss that has got you coming apart."

Anger and fear were potent emotions. In the throes of either, one could speak ill-advisedly. In the grips of both, one would be foolish to say anything at all. She'd gone far beyond that, but if she didn't stop now, she could dig herself in much deeper.

Drawing herself up to her full height, she said, "You prevented Irv's condition from getting much worse. Possibly you even saved his life. Thank you. But I want you to leave now and, from now on, stay away from us. Away from me."

He remained as he was just looking at her, then bent over and scooped the badge up off the floor. "Thanks for the pie." He turned and disappeared around the corner into the kitchen. The back door was soundly pulled shut.

Laurel walked backward over to the table, groping blindly for her chair, and when she located it, landed hard in the seat. She squeezed her eyes shut and covered her mouth with her hand. Her lips were still damp from his kiss. She could taste him. Her breasts felt heavy, full, tingly. She didn't know whether to scream with fury, wring her hands with anxiety, or weep because she could never be near him again.

"Miss Laurel?"

She started. Corrine was standing only a few feet away, looking at her with uncertainty. "Did he leave me here?"

Laurel laid her forehead on the table and hiccupped a sob tinged with hysteria. "So it would seem."

THIRTY-ONE

—◄●►—

"... and like a damn fool, I believed every word out of his lyin' mouth and ran off with him." Corrine finished a slice of bacon and licked the grease off her fingers. "It was romantic and excitin' and all. I kept tellin' myself that Mama and Daddy wouldn't miss me, that they'd be glad to have one less mouth to feed. There's eleven of us kids. I'm second oldest.

"Anyhow, on the night Jack and me had set, I snuck out of the house and walked to the crossroads where he was waitin'. We hit the open road, laughin' and carryin' on, waitin' to see where destiny would take us. It took us to Lefty's. You gonna finish that?"

The sudden question, asked out of context, roused Laurel from her woolgathering. "Pardon?"

"You gonna eat what's left of your breakfast?"

"Oh. No. Help yourself." She pushed her plate across the table. Corrine broke a biscuit in half, spooned jam onto it, and popped it into her mouth. At least that silenced her for several seconds.

Laurel didn't know where the girl found the energy or wherewithal to chatter. Both of them had been up for most of the night, taking turns sitting with Irv, waiting and watching to see if he would take a bad turn. He was in obvious pain, but he'd showed no signs of worsening. Except for some spotting on his bandage, there'd been no further bleeding, no fever.

At sunup, Laurel had gone to her room to wash and dress for the day. She'd undone her braid and brushed her hair, then plaited it again and wound it into a bun on her nape. As though her loose braid were responsible for her lapse in good judgment last night, this morning she had mercilessly jabbed the hairpins in to secure it.

What other excuse did she have for allowing Mr. Hutton to kiss her like that? The crisis with Irv had left her emotionally vulnerable, yes. But she'd always disparaged members of her sex who blamed stupid behavior on frayed emotions.

When she had returned downstairs, Corrine was in the kitchen frying bacon. Biscuits were baking. Laurel had been embarrassed by the girl's industry, because she felt completely wrung out.

When she'd murmured an apology to that effect, Corrine had said, "You got saddled with me. I'll make myself useful till you kick me out."

When Corrine had been left behind in the middle of the night, Laurel would never have insisted she leave. But now she didn't know what to do about the girl. Or really what to do about any aspect of her predicament.

Throughout the night, Irv's condition had been her primary concern. However, dawn had brought with it jarring realizations. He'd survived the gunshot, thank God. But the repercussions of it, chiefly his convalescence, created practical problems to which Laurel must find solutions. Soon.

"...so what I think is that he outright sold me to that old bitch."

Laurel's thoughts were so deeply troubling, her attention had again drifted away from Corrine's running monologue. "Sorry?"

"Gert," Corrine said. "When I came back after a visit to the outhouse, Jack was gone. He'd hightailed it as soon as my back was turned. Gert said I could stay, but I'd have to earn my keep and pay back her 'investment' in me.

"I caught on quick, though. I could spend the rest of my life on my back, and I would never make enough to earn my 'keep' plus repay whatever chickenshit amount of money she'd given Jack. But I didn't have nowhere else to go, so..."

She gave a shrug which, to Laurel's amazement, conveyed more resignation than rancor. The girl seemed to have accepted being prostituted better than she herself had being intentionally widowed.

"Most of the time it wasn't so bad," Corrine continued, "but after the hullabaloo that creep Wally Johnson caused, Gert—"

"Wally Johnson? The man who was murdered?"

"Yeah. The night after he did this to me." She pointed to her face and patted her arm in the sling. "The sheriff came out to Lefty's and asked did I know anything about his killing. I told him nothing except I was glad he was dead."

Laurel remembered Irv telling her that he had seen Dr. Driscoll at the roadhouse, attending a girl who'd been beaten. Things had come full circle.

"Anyhow," Corrine continued, "all ol' Gert cares about is money, money, money. I thought she was gonna beat the tar out of Wally for ruinin' what she called my 'earnin' capacity.' Now he's dead, she's takin' it out on me that my face is messed up and my eye has gone wonky. She's gotten meaner by the day. So, last night, when I saw a chance to get away from her, I took it."

"With Mr. Hutton."

"Um-huh. He sure is nice. Handsome, too. I clapped eyes on him the second he walked into Lefty's. I thought to myself, now there's a man that might be worth droppin' drawers for. Gert must've thought so, too. The bitch pounced, offerin' her wares, I'm sure. He didn't go upstairs, though.

"Then, after the shootin' started, I ran outside like everybody else. I saw Mr. Hutton come out carryin' the old man. He laid him in the back of the truck. I ran over, took in what was happenin', offered to help if he'd let me tag along. He cussed somethin' fierce. You know how a man does when he's had about all the aggravation he can tolerate? But then he said okay and told me to get in the truck.

"I didn't give him time to think twice. I hopped in, put your daddy-in-law's head in my lap, so it wouldn't be bangin' around while we was driving. Along the way, though, he started bleedin' real bad. I hollered at Mr. Hutton to stop. He came back, took a look, and that's when he pulled off his shirt and stuffed the bullet hole with it. Are y'all sparkin'?"

These sudden questions of Corrine's continued to throw Laurel. When she realized what the girl was asking, she replied with a definitive *no*.

Corrine giggled like she knew otherwise, then scooted her chair back. "You go see to Irv. I'll clean up the kitchen."

"Really, Corrine, you don't have to do that. I don't expect anything from you."

"Neither did Mr. Hutton, which is why I think he's right decent. And real serious like, ain't he? Go on now, before the ol' man gets cranky. I took him some breakfast. He's probably finished it by now."

Laurel tapped once on Irv's bedroom door before pushing it open. He was half sitting up, a tray on his lap. His lined features were compressed into a frown.

As Laurel entered, she asked, "Are you hurting?"

"I've felt better," he groused, "and that girl didn't put enough sugar in the oatmeal."

"I know that you know her name. You failed to mention she was the one brutalized by Wally Johnson and treated by Dr. Driscoll."

"You didn't ask."

Laurel removed the tray from his lap and set it on the dresser. Despite his complaint, she noticed he'd eaten everything. She went back over to the bed and laid her palm against his forehead. He didn't feel feverish. "Have you used the chamber pot?"

"The girl's already emptied it."

"Did you have trouble getting out of bed?"

"No. I'm limber as a ballerina. Did a coupla twirls while I was up." At her look, he added, "What do you think? Yes, I had trouble. Took twenty minutes to take a piss."

He was way past cranky. "I'll bring you a jar to use in the bed."

"The girl already offered. I told her hell no. I'm not an invalid."

Laurel restrained herself from commenting on that. "I need to change your bandage."

"That can wait." He motioned toward the end of the bed. "Sit down so I don't have to crane my neck. We gotta talk."

She did as requested. "What's on your mind?"

"You have to ask?"

He would become even more irascible if she pretended not to know what they needed to talk about, so she went straight to the point. "I don't know how we're going to manage things while you're recovering. I haven't figured it out yet."

"You're already toting more than your fair share, Laurel. Damn me for getting my fool self shot."

"It wasn't your fault, but what were you doing at Lefty's?"

"Negotiating that new deal you proposed."

"Did he go for it?"

"He listened, but we hadn't shook on it before the deputies came busting in. One fired a pistol into the air. He got everybody's attention, all right. Caused a stampede."

"You could've been killed."

"Well, I wasn't. But it served as a reminder to me that you're in constant danger."

"So are you."

"But I've been at it longer, and I'm old. If I got killed, some would say it was past time. But if something was to happen to you, I'd never forgive myself. This ain't a lark, you know."

"I do know that, or I wouldn't have agreed to carry a pistol. I realize the dangers and accept them as part of the venture."

"What about him?"

"Who?"

He lowered his chin and looked at her from beneath his bushy eyebrows.

She somehow kept herself from squirming. "If you're referring to Mr. Hutton, nothing about him. He extended us a kindness. I think he would have done the same for anyone."

"He didn't, though, did he? There were others hurt. Several shot. I was the only one he slung over his shoulder and brought home. Why do you think he singled me out?"

"Well, not because he suspects something. To him you were just another customer having a drink in Lefty's back room."

"He said that?"

"He didn't say otherwise."

"That's not quite the same, though, is it? In fact, I've noticed he doesn't say much of anything unless it's called for. Did he tell you that he was there with Sheriff Amos?"

"He mentioned him."

"Strange that he was out there with the sheriff at that particular time."

"He said he got railroaded into it."

"Railroaded into what?"

"Into...I don't know, Irv." It irritated her that her father-in-law was fixated on the one subject she definitely did not wish to talk about. "Never mind him. Let's focus on us."

"All right, I'll drop it for now. And, anyway, we won't have to worry about secret agents or incarceration if we don't make and sell product."

"Exactly. It'll take weeks for you to fully recover."

"Only one."

"At least two, possibly three."

"Well, we'll see. In the meantime, our daytime activities will continue pretty much as they have been. You'll keep baking and delivering as usual."

"I can certainly do that."

"How big's our stockpile of product in the cellar?"

"Fair. But with the business the O'Connors are generating, it won't last long."

"Ernie's got some inventory stashed away," he said. "You trust those twins enough to send them out there for it?"

She liked the young men. They were charmers, and had given her no reason to mistrust them. But she didn't trust them enough to reveal the location of the stills. "No."

"Me neither. One's moony over you."

"Davy."

He looked surprised that she knew. "Has he professed himself?"

"No. I've sensed that he's infatuated, but pretended not to notice. Please, can we get back to the subject? I'll go out to the still today, bring back Ernie's stash, and transfer it to the cellar. It'll have to last until you're back on your feet and we resume production."

"*Resume* production? *Resume?* We ain't shutting down, Laurel. Not for any length of time. As of yesterday, we've got twenty barrels of mash fermenting. You planning on just pouring it out, wasting it?"

"All right. Ernie can do a run when a barrel becomes ready, but until you're up and about we won't mix more mash, and we'll cut back to just one still."

Irv shook his head. "We've got customers to keep supplied. New ones that you yourself courted. If we stop delivering as promised, they'll start buying from someone else."

His arguments against shutting down were considerations she had already taken into account. "I'll have to help Ernie then. But on the nights I'm at the still, I worry about leaving you here alone and helpless if anything were to happen."

"What could happen?"

"The house could catch on fire, and it takes you twenty minutes to use the chamber pot."

"Well, you can't be baking all day and then driving back and forth to the still in the dead of night, either."

"Why not?"

"Because I said so."

"Irv—"

"Laurel, we're not arguing over this. I'd bust up both stills myself before I'd put you at risk like that. What I propose," he said before she could raise another objection, "is this." He grimaced as he shifted his position. "Situate the girl out there."

"Corrine?"

"Set her up in the shack. It'll look like you've taken her on as a charity case. You rescued her from a life of iniquity. She's young and spry. She could walk back and forth over that hill between the shack and the still with no problem at all. She can help Ernie."

"Help him make moonshine? That's not rescuing her from a life of iniquity, it's setting her up to commit a crime."

"What she's been doing at Lefty's is a crime."

"That was imposed on her."

"All the more reason this arrangement will be better."

Laurel rubbed her forehead, which had begun to throb. "Does she know anything about making whiskey?"

"Haven't asked her yet. I wanted to run the idea past you first. Whether she does or not, she can stir mash. She can seal jars. She can box them."

"With a broken arm?"

"It's almost healed. She took her sling off and showed me how she can rotate it. As for the process, she'll catch on quick enough with Ernie teaching her. She can't read, but she's bright enough."

"She can't read?"

"No, but she can talk. Damn can she ever. She's got magpie in her blood. Before I told her to put a sock in it, I heard her whole life story."

"Why can't she read?"

"No schooling. She had to stay at home and help her mother tend the brood. Her two ambitions in life are to learn to read and to see a moving picture show. Anything else you want to know?"

"Yes. Why aren't you worried about her safety at the still the way you're worried about mine?"

"Because she ain't my kin, and because she's had to live by her wits, and, considerin' how young she is, she's fared pretty good, survivin' Wally and Gert and all. You can't bake your pies in that old stove at the shack, and if you weren't seen around town, everybody would wonder where you went off to. Especially that Hutton. I'd bet my left nut on him being first to ask where you was at. And you hate that shack."

It was a speech that sounded suspiciously rehearsed. "You have given it some thought."

"Wasn't nothin' else to do last night except to hurt and think. I don't see another solution. Now, send the girl in here. I'll lay it out for her, but I know she'll jump at the chance. She's scared you're gonna cast her out for being a fallen woman."

"I wouldn't do that." She went over to the dresser and picked up the tray. "I'll be back shortly to change your bandage."

"First," Irv said, "you need to drive out to the still and tell Ernie what's happened. He was expecting me out there last night after my visit to Lefty's. He'll be worried."

"That'll take me an hour."

"My arm ain't gonna rot off in that amount of time." To make his point, he tried to raise it and winced. In a growl, he said, "Next time you see that Hutton fella, tell him I'm grateful. I don't trust him, but I owe him my thanks."

"I won't be seeing him anymore."

But when she walked into the kitchen with the tray, he was standing on the back door threshold in conversation with Corrine.

THIRTY-TWO

———◦◉◦———

The tcher wasn't feeling too gracious toward Laurel this morning, and when she saw him, he could tell by her sour expression that the feeling was mutual.

The tray she was carrying was set on the drainboard with a dish-rattling thud. "Corrine, Irv wants to talk to you." Her tone didn't invite discussion or argument.

"Can't wait to hear what he's gripin' about now." Corrine shot Thatcher a parting smile, then scuttled around Laurel and out of the kitchen.

Laurel waited until Irv's bedroom door was closed, then said in an angry whisper, "I told you to stay away from us."

"Only reason I'm here is to get what I left behind last night."

She propped her hands on her hips. "Corrine?"

He didn't blame her for being mad about that. He'd been so miffed when he left, he'd forgotten all about the girl until he'd reached the boardinghouse. He sure as hell wasn't going to come back for her then. "I didn't mean to dump her on you."

"What *did* you mean to do with her?"

"Well, I really didn't have time to mull it over. What with keeping your father-in-law from bleeding and all."

"Tell me, deputy, did you save him last night only so you could arrest him this morning?"

To hell with this. He had things to do that didn't include swapping snide remarks on her doorstep. "I came for the pistol. I could've bought another hat, but the gun isn't mine. I need to return it to its owner."

"And who is that?"

"Can I have it back, please?"

She stood there seething, then said, "It's been in safekeeping. Wait here."

She went into the dining room. He heard her open one of the sideboard's drawers then slam it shut. She reappeared with his hat in one hand and the Colt in the other. She thrust them at him.

He caught them both against his chest. "Thanks." He placed his hat on his head and pushed the pistol into his waistband.

"You're going to walk around town with it poking out like that?"

"No. I'm going to ride around town with it poking out like that."

"Ride?"

He thumbed over his shoulder toward her backyard where he'd hitched a gelding to a post of her clothesline. She glanced past him, saw the horse, and remarked, again snidely, "He doesn't look like a bucking bronco to me."

"Far from it. He's lazy. His owner hired me to pump some spirit into him. Riding him over was a lesson in obedience."

"For him or for you?"

"I got him up to a canter. For me, it beat walking."

The scornfulness in her expression was replaced by one of sudden realization. "When you left last night...?"

"Yeah, I was afoot. But I'm used to walking." He didn't see a need to belabor the point. "Corrine and I will ride double. Go get her, and we'll be out of your hair."

She hesitated, tugging at her lower lip with her teeth, and damn if he didn't want to be doing that. Sore as he was at her in his head, other parts of him hadn't gotten the message.

She said, "Did Corrine express a desire to go with you?"

"You mean just now? No. She was bringing me up to date on Irv. Sounds like he's doing okay."

"Ornery, as you predicted, but holding his own."

"Have you changed the bandage?"

"Not yet. But he isn't running a fever, so I don't think the wound is infected."

"Want me to stay while you check, then help you wrap him up again?"

"No, I wouldn't want to inconvenience you any more than you already have been." She clasped her hands at her waist and avoided looking him in the eye. "In fact, Irv asked me to tell you—on the outside chance that you and I met again—that he's grateful for what you did and to give you his thanks."

"He said that?"

"Specifically."

He propped his shoulder against the doorjamb and folded his arms. "Now I wonder who that pained the most? You for having to pass along his thanks? Or him for owing me his thanks in the first place?"

"My gratitude is sincere, Mr. Hutton. So is Irv's."

"Then he's changed his opinion of me?"

"Why would you say that?"

"When you two came into the sheriff's office while I was in custody, the second he saw me he said, 'Didn't I tell you he was up to no good?' Meaning that before he'd even met me, before he ever looked me in the eye, he'd drawn that conclusion and shared it with you."

He uncrossed his arms and pushed off the door frame to face her squarely. Watching closely to see how she would react, he added, "Which I guess is why he went for his shotgun that day I wandered into your yard."

"Shotgun?"

"No sense in lying. I saw him. Why'd he have that shotgun at the ready?"

Noticeably uneasy, she said, "He's leery of strangers."

"Overmuch, I'd say."

"He kept a shotgun handy as a precaution. To protect Pearl and me if the need arose."

"But I hadn't done anything out of line. You said so yourself. You told the sheriff that—"

"I know what I told him."

"Then why did your father-in-law feel he had to stand guard?"

His persistence had turned her uneasiness into annoyance. "Maybe it's your overall manner, Mr. Hutton."

"What manner is that?"

"The way you look at a person. Like you're trying to figure them out."

"Sometimes I am."

"Well, it's rude and unnerving. It makes people uncomfortable."

"You especially, I think."

Dander up, she said, "Not at all."

"Then why'd you go all jumpy last night?"

"I didn't go *jumpy*."

He snuffled. She'd played right into his gambit.

When she realized it, she looked away from him, then turned and looked behind her toward Irv's bedroom before coming back around to him. Her expression was now as prim as a nun's.

"You deliberately got us off the subject of Corrine," she said. "In good conscience, I can't send her back to the roadhouse and that Gert who has been so cruel to her."

"She wanted out of there, all right. But where can she go?"

"I'm willing to take her in. She'll have a place to live, and I'll pay her a modest salary to work for me. With Irv incapacitated, I could use the extra help with my business. Corrine is eager to improve her lot in life."

"Sounds good all around, but it seems sudden."

"Well, she was suddenly foisted on me, wasn't she? I thought you would be relieved. This will free you from any responsibility you feel toward her."

"Not entirely." He hitched his chin toward the bedroom. "How's Corrine feel about this arrangement?"

"Irv is talking it over with her now. He's confident that she'll jump at the chance, and so am I. It's certainly preferable to the situation she was in at Lefty's."

"How'd she wind up there? Did she tell you?"

"She was naïve and trusting of a man. She's paying the consequences of having stars in her eyes. They can be blinding." She looked down at her open palm and ran her other thumb over the pinprick in the center. Then she dropped her hand and hid it in a fold of her skirt, as though she'd been caught with it in the cookie jar.

"I shouldn't have let you kiss me last night, Mr. Hutton. But neither should you have taken advantage of me when I was in such a state, so we were both at fault for things getting out of hand. Don't even think of it ever happening again. The incident will never be mentioned. We'll pretend that it didn't happen. No, we'll *forget* that it happened."

He didn't say anything. She didn't look into his face but continued to stare straight ahead at the button on his shirt to which she'd issued the ultimatum about pretending and forgetting. He waited her out. Finally, she tilted her head back and met his eyes. "That's how it's going to be."

"Is that right?"

She went rigid with indignation and made a sound of disgust. "I knew you'd be difficult about it."

She elbowed him aside and went out into the yard. She strode over to the horse. The gelding shied, taking several cautious steps backward. She untied the reins from around the post, then tugged on them until the reluctant horse went along as she led him over to Thatcher.

"Here." She held out the reins. "Goodbye."

Thatcher took the reins, then caught her hand and walked her backward until she came up against the gelding's side, the back of her head resting against the seat of the saddle. Thatcher cupped the horn with his left hand and placed his right on the cantle, bracketing her with his arms.

He could tell the action shocked her, but he didn't give her time to counter. "You've said your piece, now I'm going to say mine. I like the look of you. Have since I first laid eyes on you. That soft spot right there where your lips meet was the first place I wanted to kiss."

He homed in on that spot, then his eyes trailed down her front and back up again. "I like the size and shape of you. I like everything. Even your sass. Mostly your sass," he said, his gaze dipping briefly to her lips again before returning to her eyes.

"As for not thinking about that kiss ever happening again, I've already thought about it. And more. I think about you unbuttoned and unhooked and with your hair loose. I have dreams where we're lying down together, and I hate like hell waking up."

He shifted his stance, still not touching her, but coming awfully close, and it was hard as hell not to give in to the urge to bring them flush like they'd been last night. "Now, Laurel, I've never t   ha advantage of a woman in my life. You damn well know that I didn't take advantage of you last night, and I won't. Ever."

He dropped his voice so she'd have to listen really close to this last part, because it was an ultimatum of his own. "But if you genuinely don't want me coming at you again, be careful you don't dare me."

He gave the words seconds to sink in, then lowered his hands from the saddle, moved her aside, put his boot in the stirrup, and swung up. He nudged the gelding with his knees and rode out of the yard without looking back.

Thatcher had another difficult encounter ahead of him this morning. He'd said what he'd wanted to say to Laurel, but in doing so had probably offended her beyond any hope of ever making amends. But if he had it to do over again, he'd say the same.

He feared things wouldn't go any better with Bill Amos.

The sheriff's car wasn't parked out front of the department, but Thatcher went inside to check if he was there. Three personnel were inside, but Harold was the only one Thatcher knew by name. All stopped what they were doing when he walked in.

Harold said, "Sheriff's not here."

"Do you know where he is?"

"At home."

"I have business with him."

"What kind of business?"

Harold had covered his back last night during the raid, but the resentment persisted, it seemed. "The kind that won't wait. Where does he live?"

The Amoses' house wasn't as picturesque as Dr. Driscoll's, but the second story roofline sported gingerbread trim. It overhung a deep porch with two wicker rocking chairs. The yard was shaded by a massive pecan tree loaded with clusters of green shucks that promised a good harvest come fall. Thatcher secured the gelding to a fence post, made his way up the limestone walk, and knocked on the front door.

The upper half of it had an oval glass pane through which Thatcher and the sheriff made eye contact as he approached. He was in shirtsleeves and seemed a bit thrown to see Thatcher at his door. He greeted him by name with a question mark behind it.

"I stopped by your office first. Harold told me where you lived. Can I have a minute?"

The sheriff turned his head and glanced up the staircase attached to the right wall of the vestibule. He came back around, smoothing his mustache. "All right. Come in."

Thatcher took off his hat and stepped inside. On the wall opposite the staircase was a gallery of framed photographs, but the foyer was dim, and Thatcher couldn't make out who was in the pictures.

"How bad off is Irv Plummer?" Bill asked.

"He'll live. The bullet entered the back of his arm, here." Thatcher illustrated. "Came out through his armpit. Lost blood, but it wasn't as nasty as it could have been. What about the other injured?"

"Bloody noses and scraped knuckles, one broken finger. Four were shot, including Irv. None of the wounds were fatal or permanently crippling. Thank God."

"Who was the shooter?"

"Local boy. Preacher's kid. Stupid and blind drunk. He panicked, overreacted. Broke down and cried when we told him that his wild shots had found flesh. More scared of his daddy's punishment than jail time. We've got a dozen in the cell block sleeping it off until they can be arraigned later today. Lefty's lawyer has already posted bail for him and Gert. Routine," he said with a shrug. "How was Mrs. Plummer when you got Irv home?"

"Scared at first, seeing the blood. But once the shock wore off and she realized the wound wasn't fatal, she was fine."

"Third crisis in a row for that young lady."

"Another would be having the old man sent to jail. Do you plan on arresting him?"

"Not this time. But he should learn his lesson from getting shot and stay out of Lefty's."

Thatcher didn't comment on that. He pulled the pistol from his waistband and extended it to Bill by the barrel. "Wasn't fired. Wasn't needed after all."

"Why don't you keep it, Thatcher?"

"No thanks."

"Why not?"

"I've already got one. It was a gift. This one comes with strings."

With a sigh of resignation, Bill took the Colt and set it on the lengthy table that ran along the wall under the picture gallery. "Look, I can tell that you're upset about—"

"I'm not upset, Bill, I'm pissed off. You roped me into something I wanted no part of, and it's not like I hadn't told you flat out that I wanted no part of it."

"Guilty. But last night you only proved that you—"

"Bill?"

The feminine voice came from above. Thatcher looked up the

staircase where a woman hovered halfway down. She was of comparable age to Bill, maybe fifty. She was wearing a dressing gown and bedroom slippers. Her long, pale hair hung loose and tangled almost to her waist. She looked like a disheveled angel, a remarkably beautiful angel.

And she was regarding Thatcher with as much awe as he was regarding her.

With gentleness, Bill said, "Daisy, go on back upstairs. I'll be there in a sec."

She eased her grip on the bannister and continued her descent, but it was as plain as day to Thatcher that she was drunk or high on something. Her tread was so unsteady that if Bill hadn't bounded up to assist her down the last few steps, she surely would have fallen.

When they reached the bottom, she shuffled toward Thatcher, bringing with her a waft of whiskey. She laid her frail hand against her chest as she gazed up at him with a yearning that made Thatcher uncomfortable. He looked over at Bill, who was watching his wife with sorrow, pity, and love. The raw and tragic kind.

"Daisy, this is Thatcher Hutton. Remember I told you about him?"

In a breathy voice, she said, "For a moment there, I thought... With the light behind him, the angle of his jaw, he looked..." She trailed off, and, turning away from Thatcher, said to her husband, "They do make mistakes. I've read stories."

Bill placed his arm around her shoulders. "I don't think it's a mistake, Daisy."

She looked toward the photo gallery, then pressed her face into Bill's shirtfront, and began making keening sounds that made chills run down Thatcher's spine.

Bill shushed her, then turned with her toward the stairs, saying to Thatcher over his shoulder, "Wait for me on the porch."

Thatcher quietly slipped through the front door. *Fucking hell.* This was turning out to be some morning.

He sat down in one of the rocking chairs and stared at the gelding whose head drooped in the midmorning heat. He was too lazy even to graze at the patch of grass within nibbling distance. Thatcher actually preferred a horse that would stamp and rear and buck him off a dozen times to one he had to light a fire under.

Neither he nor the horse moved much in the ten minutes before Bill came through the door, pulling it closed behind him. He avoided looking at Thatcher as he dragged the other rocking chair over and lowered himself into it, settling heavily. He rested his head against the back of it and closed his eyes, his bearing one of utter despair and defeat.

Thatcher took his cue from Bill and remained silent.

After a time, Bill sat forward and placed his forearms on his thighs, linking his fingers between his knees and staring at the floor planks under his boots. "Daisy has a heart condition. You see? Her heart is broken. Shattered, actually.

"The 'declines' I told you about are actually drinking binges. When I got home late last night, she was passed out. I couldn't wake her up. Scares me shitless when I find her like that. I stayed home this morning, waiting for her to wake up, bathe, to eat something…" He made a rolling motion with his hand. "You get it."

Thatcher nodded, but Bill had yet to look at him, so he didn't see the nod. He said the first thing that came to mind, and it was in earnest. "She's beautiful."

Bill gave a sniff of rueful humor. "First time I saw her, swear to God I don't think I took a breath for five full minutes. It was at a community picnic on the Fourth of July. She had on a white dress and carried a parasol. I drew her attention by winning a shooting contest. She strolled over to congratulate me on my blue ribbon. I don't remember what we said to each other. I doubt I made a lick of sense."

He paused and smiled at the recollection. "Anyhow, I started courting her the next day. A few months later, I asked for her hand, and she said yes. I thought for sure she was taunting me, but no, she was in earnest. I marched her to First Methodist before she could change her mind. Our son Tim was born nine months later, almost to the day of the wedding."

During his next pause, his smile faded. "But after Tim, she couldn't conceive. That boy became the light of our lives. We loved him. Most everybody who met him did. The good die young, they say." He gulped, and it took a while for him to continue.

"We never saw his body, didn't have a casket. We put up a marker in the cemetery, but Daisy can't accept that he's gone. I know it was eerie for you, the way she was staring. I apologize. She thinks she sees Tim in every young man who's the right age and of similar build. You do resemble him that way.

"She drinks herself into stupors. Some last hours. Some for days. Every once in a while, she can pull herself together and make an effort to be her old self, the belle of the ball. But not often."

Thatcher shifted in his seat. "Have you thought of taking her to a sanatorium?"

"A thousand times a day. But I can't bring myself to do it, Thatcher. I can't do that to either of us. Being locked up might send her over a cliff to where I couldn't reach. I wouldn't have anything of her, and I'd rather have this than nothing."

"Where does she get the hooch?"

He looked over at Thatcher then, and in his eyes was a shameful confession. "That's why I told you it would be messy if I tried to charge our mayor with bootlegging. Not just messy, but hypocritical. He supplies me with the good stuff from Kentucky."

"He might not if he knew it wasn't for you, if he knew it was Mrs. Amos who was drinking it."

"Oh, he knows. He takes perverse pleasure in her addiction and our sad, sad circumstance." He gave Thatcher another rueful smile. "He was Daisy's escort to the picnic."

THIRTY-THREE

Chester Landry was in conversation with Mr. Hancock and one of his female customers. She was effusively extolling the quality and styling of her recently purchased shoes. With matching effusiveness, Landry complimented her on how well she wore them.

She simpered, Mr. Hancock suggested she buy an additional pair, and Landry's eye was caught by Jimmy Hennessy, who was paying for a purchase at the cash register. Croft's bodyguard tipped his head toward the door.

Landry excused himself from the merchant and the woman, telling them how badly he regretted being unable to stay longer, and exited the store. Hennessy was staring into one of the store's display windows and didn't even turn his head in Landry's direction as he said, "He wants to see you."

Five minutes later, Landry entered the municipal building through a back entrance and took a private staircase that led to a side door of the mayor's office, bypassing his secretary. This door was used only by Bernie's inner circle and individuals like Sheriff Amos who came to pick up their graft.

Landry tapped on the door and was told to come in. Concealing his

displeasure over being marshaled, he said, "Good morning, Bernie."
He walked over to his customary chair and took a seat.

Bernie, seated behind his desk, was fiddling with a sterling silver
letter opener. Landry got the sense he was testing its worth as a
weapon. He said, "I understand there was some excitement at Lefty's
last night."

"Yes. Rip-roaring."

"Why didn't you tell me?"

Landry's head went back an inch. He cocked an eyebrow. "If you
know, then obviously you didn't need me to tell you."

"I want to hear your account of it, Chester."

He raised his shoulders. "It was a raid. Typical in execution and
response. People scattered and fled. Heads were knocked. I'm sure
there were some arrests, but I have a lot of practice at avoiding arrest,
and I succeeded in doing so last night."

"In company?"

"I was there by myself. Prior to the bust-in, I chatted with Lefty.
He placed his standard order, but you'll be pleased to hear that I
talked him into taking an extra case of that expensive Canadian." He
paused, then said, "You still look perturbed."

"Thatcher Hutton was at Lefty's last night."

"Hutton? He wasn't in the back room, I'm certain."

"No, he was out front."

"He must've taken his own recommendation."

"Explain that."

"At dinner last week, he said he'd heard Lefty's hamburgers were
good. I guess he decided to try one."

"He didn't go for a hamburger. He was there with Bill Amos."

That took Landry by surprise. "Are you sure?"

"Yes, I'm sure," Bernie replied testily. "Hutton took part in the raid,
on the side of the sheriff's department. Not all of Bill's men are happy
about it, either. There's grousing in the ranks. First Hutton is in cuffs,
now he's in our sheriff's back pocket."

"And the sheriff is in yours," Landry returned mildly.

This was a development he hadn't foreseen. Last week, Hutton had claimed that he had no plans, that he was taking things one day at a time. His sudden change of course needed to be explored, but in a coolheaded manner. Bernie was fuming, and that bothered Landry. First because his anger was so apparent, and secondly because angry people made rash decisions in order to put a quick end to an unexpected problem.

He needed to talk him down. "Actually, Bernie, you should be relieved."

"Why in hell?"

"Because if Hutton is wearing a badge and carrying out raids, he isn't working undercover."

"Not necessarily."

"But improbably."

"Well, I don't like it. I don't like him. You two live in the same boardinghouse. Keep an eye on him."

"Hmm." Landry steepled his fingers and tapped them against his chin. "He's no fool, Bernie. He won't be as easily manipulated as Randy was."

"I'm confident you'll handle him with your usual finesse."

"I'm glad we agree on that."

Landry got up and went to the door. Hand on the knob, he turned back. "You were entirely right to tell me about Hutton's new status. I needed to know. But I disliked being summoned. I'm not one of the good ol' boys you have at your beck and call, Bernie. Don't ever send that mick lummox of yours after me again."

THIRTY-FOUR

Gabe Driscoll was appalled by Norma's recklessness. "What the devil are you thinking, showing up here in broad daylight?"

"I suggest you let me in. It wouldn't do for your nosy neighbors to see you refusing to examine a pediatric patient, no matter how closeted you are."

He glanced down at the bundle in her arms. "The baby's sick?"

"He's as healthy as a horse, but they don't know that." She shoved past Gabe and entered the house.

He took a furtive look up and down the street. Norma's sister's automobile was the only one in sight, but Patsy wasn't in it. He shut the door. "You drove yourself?"

"I wanted us to be alone." Without invitation, Norma went into the parlor. "This room is like a dungeon. Why don't you raise the shades and open the drapes?"

"Never mind the drapes, Norma. I told you not to come here."

"You gave me no choice. You haven't kept your promise to come see Arthur and me."

"I couldn't get away."

"What's keeping you occupied? Not your practice. The sign out front says you're still closed."

"People are watching me."

"People?" she said, sputtering a laugh. "What people?"

"All people," he shouted. "My every move incites speculation on what really happened to Mila."

"You're imagining things."

He chewed the inside of his cheek. "Maybe. To an extent. But we have to be discreet, Norma. Why can't you understand that?"

"I do understand it. I just hate being apart." She came toward him, her gait that of a stalking predator. He was easy prey. He swelled inside his trousers just as he had the first time he saw her.

Patsy had been suffering a wracking cough, and Norma had brought her to him for treatment. While he'd been pressing his stethoscope against her sister's chest and listening to her wheezing lungs, Norma had been toying with the strand of beads lying against her own chest and drawing his attention to her voluptuous, well-defined breasts.

When they left, Patsy had gone ahead of her. Hanging back, Norma had glanced toward the kitchen where Mila could be heard humming. Looking up at him provocatively, Norma whispered, "I hope the medicine doesn't work, and we'll have to come back soon. Or maybe," she'd purred, "you should spare my ailing sister the trip into town and make a house call."

The following day, he'd done that. He'd spent five minutes examining Patsy, then had spent an hour in Norma's cluttered bedroom examining every inch of her dusky nudity. She was without shame or modesty. She was exotic and carnal and sexually industrious, so unlike Mila and her conventional wholesomeness that he became besotted.

Or bewitched.

Because even now, when he was irritated with her, he was incapable of breaking the spell she had cast over him that first day. Sandwiching the baby between them, she leaned in and breathed against his lips. "I'm tired of doing without you, Gabe. I'm burning. I want us to be together all the time."

He placed his hands on her shoulders, squeezing. "We will be. Be patient. Please. Just a little longer."

"How much longer?"

"Until our being seen together won't arouse suspicion. We've come this far. We can't get careless now."

Beneath his hands, her shoulders relaxed. "Of course. You're right. I'm being selfish." She backed away, then went over to the divan, sat down, and opened the light flannel blanket wrapped around the infant. "Come say hello."

Gabe sat down beside her and looked at his son, whose dark eyes were open and alert. Gabe stroked his cheek. "He is a fine-looking boy."

"More than fine. He's perfect. I adore him."

"He does appear to be the picture of health."

"He eats well." Her eyes linked with Gabe's, she unbuttoned her dress, pushed down her chemise, and put Arthur to her breast. When the baby latched onto her nipple, the lust that surged through Gabe was rampant and consuming. During the past year, and with only token resistence from him, his sexual appetite for her had taken control of his reason. It had procured his soul.

He couldn't pinpoint the precise moment he had decided that he must kill his wife, but it had been around the time that Norma told him she was pregnant. His spontaneous reaction was to suggest an abortion. "I could send Mila to her kinfolks for a visit and perform the procedure in the office while she's away."

He'd done D and Cs following miscarriages, but had never aborted a living fetus. He wasn't certain that when the time came, he could go through with it. But his ambiguous reaction to the prospect was mild compared to Norma's tumultuous one.

She had collapsed on the spot. She'd wept bitter tears. Once he'd calmed her down, he'd determined that it wasn't their unborn child he needed to be rid of, it was Mila. She was the impediment.

Even Mila's pregnancy, which she had informed him of with unbridled joy, hadn't deterred him. Whenever his conscience got a tenuous toehold, Norma reminded him that their baby had been conceived first. His loyalty must be to it, not to the product of his loveless marriage. Wouldn't he choose true love over duty?

On the day he'd irreversibly chosen love, he had returned home from his rural route in time for supper. He hadn't entered the house thinking that this was the night he would commit murder. Mila had greeted him with a kiss on the cheek, her unsuspecting smile, and a glass of iced tea.

He'd relaxed in the parlor and read the newspaper while she'd puttered in the kitchen putting the finishing touches on their meal. When it was ready, she'd called him into the dining room. There was a bouquet of flowers in the center of the table. The linen napkins smelled of starch. From a china tureen, she'd served him pork roast with potatoes and carrots.

He remembered these small details later. That evening he'd taken them for granted.

While they ate, she'd kept up her happy prattle, telling him about the first shoots springing up in the vegetable garden, the fabric she thought would do nicely for the nursery curtains, and the man who had stopped by to inquire about the room to let.

"I think he was hungry. I had just taken da shortbread out of dee oven. I gave him two pieces. Are you ready for your dessert?"

He remembered looking down at his empty plate, surprised to find that he'd eaten his whole portion without tasting it. His mind had been on Norma and his infant son whom he had stopped by to see that day. Arthur had been born a month earlier, not that day. His birth had been easy, not a difficult breech. Those were lies he'd later told the sheriff.

During that afternoon's visit, Patsy had left him and Norma alone to admire their son. They lay on the bed with Arthur between them. Norma had wanted to make love, but he'd told her it was too soon for her after giving birth. She'd settled for playfully stroking his penis through his trousers and lauded it for the ideal son it had provided, a child untainted by foreign blood.

That was one of Norma's familiar refrains: His wife's German heritage continued to cost him patients even this long after the Armistice.

That's what had reeled through his mind that evening as Mila left the dining table carrying their plates into the kitchen, keeping up her running monologue about mundane topics. He didn't give a fuck about what color she'd chosen for the nursery curtains when he was stiff with the anticipation of fucking Norma again.

He'd gotten up from the dining table and walked into the kitchen. Mila had her back to him, cutting slices of shortbread for their dessert. He hadn't been nervous or hesitant. He hadn't paused to think: *I'm going to kill her now.*

He simply picked up a clean iron skillet from off the stove and swung it at the back of her head. The blow didn't even break the skin, but he heard the crunch of bone as her skull caved in. Never having known what had hit her, she'd gone silent and fell to the floor.

Later, he didn't recall how long he'd stood there staring at her inert form. Eventually he'd knelt down and checked to make sure her scalp hadn't bled. It hadn't. Not one drop. He'd felt her carotid. No pulse. No *breath*. Utter stillness. That's when he'd realized the magnitude of what he'd done, and he experienced a paroxysm of panic. He'd thrown up his dinner in the sink.

Even after retching until he was empty, he was dizzy. His ears were buzzing. His mind was spinning with possible explanations. But he couldn't land on one that sounded plausible. None would be believed. He would be charged and tried. During the trial, his affair with sexually unrestrained Norma would be exposed as an unquestionable motive. He would be sentenced to hang.

He'd witnessed a hanging once. His father had thought it would be good for his ten-year-old self to see firsthand the wages of sin. It had been ghastly. He didn't want to die shitting his pants and twitching at the end of a rope.

Clutching his head between his hands, he tore at his hair, and sobbed.

Then as spontaneously as the panic had seized him, it vanished, and was replaced with an incredible calmness. He thought through the idea that had suddenly occurred to him. He inspected it, looking for pitfalls. It wasn't without risks, certainly. But he didn't want to hang.

He'd stepped over Mila's body, went into his office, and picked up the telephone to call Mayor Croft.

"Gabe?"

The sound of his name jerked him back into the present. Arthur was no longer nursing, but sleeping on his stomach beside Norma on the divan. She frowned. "You were miles away. Were you thinking about *her*?"

"No."

She knew he was lying. The first night she had showed up on his doorstep, unexpectedly and near midnight, they had fought over the guilt eating at him. Then, after pitching a temper tantrum, she had cried and begged him to forgive her for being insensitive to his plight.

"You have a reputation to protect. You must preserve it. It's just that I miss you so much," she'd whispered into his neck.

That smoky seductiveness was in her voice now as she ran her fingers through his hair. "Thinking about it only distresses you. You did what was necessary for us to be together, Gabe. You see that, don't you?"

"Yes."

"It's done. We have Arthur. We have each other." Her lower lip began to tremble. "Would you want to change things back to the way they were before? With her?"

"No. God no. Of course not."

"Then stop punishing yourself. Instead, take advantage of the reason you did it." She unbuttoned her dress the rest of the way and laid it open. Except for the chemise wadded up around her waist, she was bare.

"We can't, Norma. It's too soon after the baby."

She gave him a sultry smile and drew him to her. "Mama needs you."

Afterward, when they separated, they were damp and listless and breathing heavily. Gabe slid to the floor and sat between her legs. He rested his cheek on her lap. "Did I hurt you?"

"Yes." At his start, she pressed his head back down and laughed huskily. "It was marvelous."

"Tease." He turned his face into her belly.

"You came like a fire hose. I hope it cleared your thoughts of Pointer's Gap."

He ceased the nuzzling and looked up at her with horror. "*What?*"

"Pointer's Gap. Where your dead wife is buried."

He gave his head a violent shake as though to deny hearing what she was saying. "How did you...Nobody knows that except me."

"And Bernie Croft."

Gabe forced himself to swallow before he choked. "He swore to me...swore that nobody would ever know."

She smiled placidly and stroked his cheek. "Surely you didn't think that 'nobody' included me."

THIRTY-FIVE

With Corrine assisting, Laurel changed the dressings on Irv's wounds. They showed no sign of festering, but, for good measure, she dabbed on some coal oil before wrapping him in a fresh bandage.

Once that was done, she left him to rest while she prepared to make the necessary trip to the still and to get Corrine settled in the shack. There was no question of her happiness over her new position. She celebrated by dancing a little jig.

They raided the pantry and icebox for foodstuffs that would last her for several days. As they carried the parcels from the house, Laurel said, "Don't forget your things. Did you leave them in Irv's truck last night?"

"What things?"

Laurel stopped and looked at her. "Your belongings."

Corrine swept her hand down her front. "What I got on is what I've got to my name. When Mr. Hutton stopped cussing and told me to get in, I got in. And anyway, there was nothing at the roadhouse I wanted bad enough to go back for."

"Clothes?"

"This is what I was wearing the night I ran off with Jack. Gert gave me some castoff dresses, but she's probably passed them on to another girl by now. Besides, I wouldn't want them back. They were whores' clothes."

Laurel motioned toward her auto. "Climb in."

She drove them to Hancock's, where she bought Corrine three changes of clothes, undergarments, and basic toiletries. Once on their way out of town, Corrine said repeatedly that she'd never before owned things so fine, and Laurel believed her. The girl clutched the package to her chest, often peering into it as though she feared the merchandise might disappear.

Laurel was touched that she took such delight in simple necessities. Their moonshining business might yet fail, but she was confident in her decision to rescue Corrine.

The girl was even inordinately pleased with the shack. "I've never had a place all to myself. Can I fix it how I want it?"

"Certainly."

She unwrapped her new hairbrush and other grooming items and lined them up just so on Irv's old three-legged bureau. Then, "What's this?" She pulled a tablet from the bottom of the package.

"What does it look like?"

"A schoolbook."

Laurel had added the purchase in secret before leaving the store. "That's right. It's a primer used to teach people the alphabet. Irv told me you wanted to learn to read. The first step is to learn the alphabet."

The girl ran her hand over the workbook's cover as though it were the costly first edition of a classic. "What if I'm too stupid?"

"Nonsense. I'll teach you. Let's start with your name."

"Right now?"

"There should be a box of pencils in the package. I asked the store clerk to sharpen them for us."

Fifteen minutes later, Corrine had followed the guidance of Laurel's hand to print her name. "Two of them?" she said, pointing to the r.

"That's right. You must practice printing all twenty-six letters as you see them in the example. Capitals and lower case. Next time, we'll go over the sound each letter makes."

"I'll practice. I promise."

"When Ernie doesn't need you. He'll be putting you to work, you know."

Corrine rubbed her hands together. "I'm ready."

Rather than drive to the still, Laurel left her Ford at the shack and showed Corrine the shortcut over the hilly, rocky terrain. Along the way, she dispensed advice.

"As the crow flies, it's about a mile, so if time is a factor, allow yourself at least half an hour to walk it. After dark, always bring a lantern with you, but only light it if you must. You don't want to signal someone that you're making this trip back and forth. I'll ask Ernie if he can spare you a firearm."

"To shoot at what?"

"You might come upon wildlife."

"Or them Johnsons."

"Same thing," Laurel said under her breath. "Alter your route a little each time so you don't create a noticeable path. If you see anyone showing an interest in the shack, or the same vehicle frequently driving past, be sure to caution Ernie."

"What's he like?"

Laurel hesitated. "Rustic."

Following their introduction, the moonshiner and the former prostitute sized each other up, and it was clear to Laurel that both found admirable traits lacking in the other.

Ernie had reacted to the news about Irv with the expected concern. Laurel had assured him that his friend would heal. "But I'm afraid it will be several weeks before he regains full use of his arm, if ever. While he's out of commission, Corrine will be assisting you in the distillation and bottling process."

A taut silence followed that announcement. Then Ernie said, "She whut?"

"It's a temporary arrangement," Laurel said. "She'll work with you only until Irv is able."

Corrine piped up. "Don't forget that he's old and already has a bum hip."

"I ain't forgot," Ernie snapped.

Laurel could have done without Corrine's contribution and Ernie's retort. She said, "The point is, his convalescence can't be rushed, Ernie. You wouldn't want him to return to work too soon and do further damage to himself."

"'Course not." He picked up a stir-stick and moved it around in a barrel of mash. He aimed his pointy chin in Corrine's direction. "Does she know squat about making whiskey?"

"I've got ears," Corrine said, "and I'm standing right here. You want to know something, ask me d'rectly."

"Do you know squat about making whiskey?"

"Irv said it was up to you to teach me. That's what Laurel said, too."

He harrumphed. "It ain't as easy as it looks."

"It don't look easy at'all. In fact, I've never seen a more rickety pile of junk as that still."

"It's my great-granddaddy's design."

Before Corrine could comment on that, Laurel stepped in. "Ernie, let me stir the mash. You walk Corrine through the process."

It took him an hour to explain all the still's components and their various functions. Lesson over, Corrine asked to be excused to seek a private spot to relieve herself.

Ernie said to Laurel, "Wouldn't have taken half as long if she hadn't asked so many dadgum questions."

"They were good questions, Ernie, about things she needs to know."

"She always rattle on that much?"

"You'll get used to it."

"I doubt it. What happened to her eye?"

"She took a beating from the late Wally Johnson."

He looked in the direction Corrine had gone. "She's the whore?"

"Don't use that word again." After her sharp rebuke, she set her hand on his arm in conciliation. "Listen, Ernie, when Mr. Hutton brought Irv home last night, I thought he was dead. I'm sure you were fit to be tied when he didn't show up for work. It was a rough night on all of us. Fair to say, we're feeling the strain?"

He nodded.

"I'm sorry to spring Corrine on you," she continued, "but it was actually Irv's idea, and at first even I was resistant to it." She recapped for him the conversation she and Irv had had early that morning. "We've got to keep up production or we'll soon be out of business. In fact, our supply is already low. I'll walk back to the shack and bring the car around. Irv said you had some crates stashed away. I need to take them back with me."

"They was stole."

Her breath escaped her. *"What?"*

"I wasn't gonna tell you, didn't want you worrying."

She backed up to an upended crate and sat down. "Well, I'm worried now. When were they stolen?"

"Night before last. I'd added a crate to the stash that day. Went back yesterday to add another one. They's all gone."

"How many?"

"Ten."

One hundred and twenty jars of one hundred proof. She did the math. Her heart sank over the amount of the loss.

Ernie said, "I would've told Irv last night, only he got shot." He raised his bony shoulders.

"Where was this stash hidden?"

"Over in that cedar break."

She looked in the direction he'd pointed. "That nearby?"

"Thirty yards, maybe. I'd dug a hole big as a grave, thought I had it covered up good with brush."

"Who could have gotten that close without your knowing?"

Another shrug. "I wasn't doing a run that night. Did some tinkering on the new still. Shored up the firebox with more rock. Crawled into the tent pretty early. Never heard a thing." He pushed his hands into the deep pockets of his overalls. "You trust those twins?"

"Yes." Then she gave a shrug of her own. "I suppose."

"Irv says they're half drunk half the time. Randy as goats. Lightning rods for trouble."

"Maybe, but we need them."

"What about that Hutton fella?"

"What about him?"

"How was it he brought Irv home from Lefty's?"

"It's a long story." She didn't want to mention the deputy's badge.

"Irv thinks—"

"I know what Irv thinks." Her brittle tone stopped him from taking that subject any further. *Be careful you don't dare me.*

"Well," Ernie said, "somebody found out where we're at. If it'd been lawmen, they'd've poured out the hooch and busted up the stills."

"Unless it was corrupt lawmen."

"Could be. But..."

"But what, Ernie?"

"You don't need this on top of Irv."

"Don't spare me bad news. I hate surprises. Recent ones have been calamities."

"Well then, what I think? Whoever stole the 'shine was giving us a warnin'. It was somebody's way of saying we know who you are and where you're at, and you got off light with us just taking off ten crates instead of ten fingers and toes."

"The Johnsons?"

"So long as we're small timers, they'll leave us be. But if we start horning in on their profit..."

Again he didn't finish, but she got the message. "Maybe I shouldn't involve Corrine after all. What if they come back?"

"I've got two rifles, a side-by-side shotgun, a six-shooter, and a trap."

"A trap?"

"Jaw spring. Big enough to trap a bear. If some sorry sumbitch sticks his hand in that hidey-hole again, he'll come up with a stump."

Corrine reappeared. Both observed her as she walked toward them. When she got nearer to them, she stopped and put her hands on her hips. "Why are y'all lookin' at me like that?"

"Can you shoot a rifle?" Ernie asked.

"Damn good. Back home, I helped keep food on the table."

"You ain't back home, and you got only one good eye."

"Then I might have to use you for target practice."

Looking at Laurel, he mumbled, "I'll give her the shotgun. Tell Irv to take it easy and not worry about things. That mash needs stirrin'." He skulked off.

Laurel and Corrine watched him go. Laurel said, "Are you comfortable with me leaving you here?"

"Sure."

"Will you have trouble finding your way back to the shack?"

"I made note of things along the way. With my one good eye," she added with a scowl aimed at Ernie.

"Irv and I are counting on you to make yourself useful. Do you think you can do that without picking silly fights with him?"

Corrine looked over at Ernie as he dipped the stir-stick into the barrel. "One thing I can do is put some meat on his bones," she said. "I never saw a man who needed feedin' more'n him."

When Laurel came upon the road sign, she slowed down then rolled to a full stop. She stared at the sign's uneven, hand-painted lettering, which was familiar because she'd passed it many times before. But the sign now had new, and more personal, significance.

She calculated how long she'd been away from the house, leaving her infirm father-in-law alone. She thought about the deal he had failed to cement with Lefty before the raid. She thought about Corrine and the abuse she'd suffered.

Before she could talk herself out of it, she made the turn. Earlier today, she'd been told she had sass. This would be a test of just how much.

The road was as corrugated as a washboard. Her tires kicked up dust as fine and white as talcum powder. It swirled around the Model

T when she brought it to a stop. As the dust settled, she studied the uninviting structure. It looked deserted.

She hesitated, thinking that perhaps this wasn't a good idea at all. She patted her pocket and, after feeling the reassuring weight of the Derringer, pushed open the car door and got out.

Warped steps led up to an equally uneven porch. The heels of her shoes tapped loudly on the planks and echoed in the crawl space beneath. The screen on the outer door was rusty and jaggedly torn in places, as though someone had taken a dull can opener to it. The wooden frame supporting it was splintery. It slapped against the solid door behind it when she knocked.

She heard muffled voices from within, and then a thudding tread as someone came to answer.

The individual who opened the door had to be Gert, because she was the female counterpart of an ogre. A cigarette was anchored in the corner of her lips, the smoke from it curling up around her face. She squinted against it, making her eyes appear even more hostile.

"We're closed."

"Not closed. Shut down."

"Then what are you doing here?"

"To discuss business with Lefty."

Gert took away the cigarette and barked a sound that was half laugh, half phlegmy cough. "I think your business is with me. You must've heard about the girl I lost to the raid. You figuring on taking her place?" She looked Laurel up and down. "There's men who don't mind small ones. What's your name?"

"Laurel."

"Pretty."

"Plummer. And my business isn't with you. It's with your husband. Is he here? Or in jail?"

"I'm here." A stick figure of a man materialized out of the dark and murky interior. "Plummer, you say? Kin to Irv?"

"His daughter-in-law."

"Huh. Heard your husband blew his brains out."

Laurel ignored Gert's cruel remark and focused on Lefty. "May I have a moment of your time?"

"What for?"

"It would be in your best interest."

Gert repeated the statement, mimicking the modulation of Laurel's voice. "Who do you think you are, a fuckin' Rockefeller?"

"Back off, Gert." Reaching past her, Lefty pushed open the screen door. "Come on in, but I already told Irv no deal."

"That's not what Irv told me," Laurel said as she stepped inside. "One of you is lying." She gave the hatchet-faced man an arch look. "I suspect it's you."

He turned and crossed the large room to the bar, where he motioned her onto a stool. He sat down, leaving an empty stool between them. Laurel pretended not to notice the shotgun lying on the bar.

Gert lowered herself into a chair at one of the nearby tables and lit a fresh cigarette. By the time she'd smoked it down all the way, Laurel and Lefty were sealing a new deal with a handshake.

As Laurel stood to leave, she asked, "Do you know the O'Connor twins?"

"Don't everybody?"

"Since Irv was wounded in the fracas last night, one or both of the O'Connors will take over making your deliveries. They'll know the terms of our agreement. Don't try to cheat me."

"Wouldn't think of cheating a lady," he said, grinning. If that's what you could call the exposure of his crooked teeth when he peeled his lips back.

"When do you think you'll be able to reopen?"

"Tonight," Gert said as she ground out her cigarette butt in the chipped ashtray on the table. She heaved herself out of her chair. "Smarty-pants, you keep undercutting people in this business, you're gonna start pissing them off."

"Thank you for the warning." Laurel headed for the door.

"You got gumption. I'll say that for you. If moonshining don't work out, I could always use you upstairs."

Laurel didn't acknowledge that. Rather, she kept walking until she reached the door, and only then turned and confronted Gert. "You didn't lose Corrine to the raid. She took advantage of the commotion to escape her imprisonment here."

Gert's face became bloated with rage. "That ungrateful little slut. Where's she at? If you know, you'd better tell me. She owes me money."

"While in your charge, she was disfigured, maimed, and half blinded. The only thing you're owed is contempt." She turned and stalked out.

The screen door banged against the exterior wall as Gert barged through it, but Laurel didn't turn to look back. Gert was bellowing obscenities, most of which Laurel didn't even know the meaning of.

She kept her head high and walked toward her car with purpose, although she was mindful of that handy shotgun. At any moment a blast from it could be the last thing she ever heard.

She made it to her car and thanked God that it started on the first crank. She drove away unscathed except for the blistering her ears had taken from Gert's profanity.

But midway to the highway, when no longer in sight of the road-house, fear and trembling caught up with her. Like the night she'd escaped from Martin's Café without being exposed as a moonshiner, she broke a cold sweat.

She braked her car, rested her forehead on the steering wheel, and gasped for breath as she willed her heartbeat to slow down. Hearing another vehicle approaching, she jerked her head up and looked behind her. But the sound was coming from ahead, not from the direction of the roadhouse.

She pulled out of the middle of the road, allowing the other vehicle to pass her. It was a newer model than hers by several years, the shiny black paint defiant of the powdery road, but she was relieved to see that it didn't have an official seal stenciled on the side.

She continued on her way and blessed the second she reached the highway without anyone in pursuit. Still shaken, but calmer than she had been, she pointed herself toward town.

THIRTY-SIX

A fter leaving Bill Amos to deal with his situation at home, Thatcher rode the gelding back to Barker's, then put in a long day of work, exercising every horse in the stable and trying to correct whatever bad habit or stubborn trait each had.

He kept his distance from Fred and Roger. The youngster had developed a case of hero worship since the incident with the rattlesnake and often trailed Thatcher around like a puppy. Today the two picked up on his desire for solitude and stayed away from the stable and corral.

Learning of Bill's circumstances had left Thatcher with conflicting emotions that were equally strong and unshakeable. Throughout the day, he fluctuated between being angry and resentful over Bill's manipulation, while also feeling compassion for his personal torment.

And prior to that distressing conversation with Bill, he'd had the set-to with Laurel.

He was ready to see an end to this day.

He returned to the boardinghouse in time to fill a plate with what was left of the cold supper and ate alone in the dining room, even as the landlady was clearing the dishes and utensils off the long table with more clatter than necessary. When finished eating, he dodged the residents seeking companionship and headed for his room.

He'd almost reached the third floor when he was called to from below. "Hutton."

Chester Landry was rounding the landing on the second floor. His gold tooth caught the light from a wall fixture as he smiled up at Thatcher. "Hold up."

Shit. Chester Landry's intrusion was the perfect top-off to this crappy day.

He replied unenthusiastically to the salesman's greeting and was tempted to continue on to his room, but, in spite of himself, he was curious to see if Landry would refer to the roadhouse raid.

Landry reached him and took a moment to catch his breath. "You'd think I would be conditioned to climbing these infernal stairs by now." He inhaled deeply, then asked, "Am I keeping you from anything?"

"Bed."

"That kind of day?"

"And then some."

"Would you consider going out for a little refreshment? Grab a Coca-Cola at the filling station?"

"No, thanks. I'm ready to hit the hay."

"Well then, another time." He slid his hands into the pockets of his trousers. "I feel at loose ends tonight."

"Ask your buddy to go with you."

"Buddy?" He tipped his head and looked at Thatcher with puzzlement, which Thatcher thought was faked. "Oh, you mean Randy? He's moved on."

It occurred to Thatcher only now that he hadn't seen the young man around lately. "Where'd he go?"

"God knows. Greener pastures, I guess." He shrugged. "I missed seeing him around and inquired about him. Mrs. May said he left without notice. She went up to collect his rent, which was a day late. He'd cleared out in the dead of night." He chuckled. "Sounds like something impulsive and irresponsible he would do."

Thatcher thought Landry's dry laugh also seemed faked. When Thatcher didn't join in, Landry must have sensed his reserve. He glanced down the staircase to make certain no one else was around. No one was. Nevertheless, he lowered his voice to a confidential level.

"We're avoiding the subject we're both dying to talk about."

Thatcher just looked at him.

"Come on, Hutton." For the first time ever, some of Landry's polish dimmed and he showed annoyance. "I didn't see you, but I heard you were there last night."

"I saw you, running away."

"Yes, our perspectives were entirely different. We were on opposite sides of the bedlam." When Thatcher didn't respond, Landry said, "No comment on that?"

"What do you want to know?"

"From kidnap suspect to deputy sheriff is a very broad leap. You covered it in a matter of weeks. How did you manage to curry the sheriff's favor and become a deputy?"

"I didn't."

He declared it as a fact, but that damn badge was still in his breast pocket. After listening to Bill's tragic tale, witnessing the heartache, sorrow, and despair that he lived with daily, Thatcher hadn't had the heart to return the badge with the stern put-down he'd rehearsed.

"What I heard was that you were in the thick of it with the sheriff's men."

"I went for a hamburger, and got caught up in it." He stopped there, not feeling a need to explain or justify anything he did to this popinjay. "What were you doing there, Landry? Fitting the soiled doves with new shoes?"

Thatcher got a flash of the gold tooth when Landry threw his head back and laughed. "You have a sense of humor after all. I was beginning to wonder." Recovering from his laughter, he said, "God help any man who goes near one of those girls. I'm sure they're petri dishes for VD.

"No, I went only for a hamburger, too, but couldn't resist the enticement of a drink. You were the one who told me about the place, remember? Did you know about the back room?"

"I'd heard rumors." Thatcher paused, then asked, "That was your first time there?"

"Rotten luck to choose last night to try it out, huh?"

"I'd say."

"Having to escape arrest wasn't the worst of it. In the melee, I lost my pocket watch. I went back today to see if it had been found and turned in. The madam..." He raised his eyebrows. "...denied having seen it. I doubt that's true, but there was a shotgun within her reach, so I wasn't about to question her honesty."

"Good call."

Landry shuddered. "Lord, she's a species unto herself. To make the unpleasant encounter even worse, she was already in a foul temper when I arrived. I hope her ire wasn't provoked by Mrs. Plummer."

Thatcher felt like a bolt of lightning had shot through him, from the top of his head to the soles of his feet. Every nerve ending in his body sizzled. "Laurel Plummer?"

Landry grinned and winked. "The charming lady of the pies. She was leaving as I was arriving."

"Leaving Lefty's?"

"We met on the road. She pulled over so I could pass."

"You must have mistaken somebody for her."

Landry tapped him in the chest with the back of his hand and winked again. "Come now, Hutton, who could mistake that face?"

Thatcher wanted to lift him bodily and pitch him headfirst over the bannister. But he knew he was being baited, and that a volatile reaction was what this slick dude was after, so he forced one corner of his mouth to tilt up. "A blind man, maybe."

"There's an appealing air of refinement about her, too." Landry made a spiraling motion with his hand. "I can't picture her going to that ratty roadhouse for any reason other than it having something to do with her father-in-law getting shot."

"You're well informed, Landry."

"Small-town scuttlebutt," he said. "I couldn't go anywhere today without hearing about the raid and the fallout from it. It's all anyone was talking about."

Thatcher remained noncommittal and tried to look bored with the subject. He covered a yawn with his hand. "Sorry. As I said, I was off to bed."

Landry gave him a little bow. "Then don't let me detain you any longer. Good night."

"Good night."

"Sleep tight."

Landry's mocking lilt set Thatcher's teeth on edge. He went into his room, but not to sleep.

Laurel led the O'Connors down the steps into the cellar and set the lantern on the dirt floor. She gestured toward the stacked wooden crates. "The theft hurt us. That's our stockpile."

"That's it? No jugs?" Davy asked.

"As you see," she said. "Ernie had hidden ten crates of jars. Even those would barely have covered our orders. Now, they're gone."

"Thieving bastards," Davy muttered.

She had gauged the brothers' furious reaction to the news of the theft and didn't believe they would have stolen from her even if they'd known where the crates had been buried. They seemed to understand and appreciate that their enterprise was in dire straits due to the loss of product simultaneous with Irv's being incapable of working to replace it.

"Ernie is doing a double run tonight," she said. "In the meantime, this is the supply we have on hand."

Mike did a quick calculation. "Seventy-two jars. Those roughnecks will have that drunk before we get halfway back from delivering them."

"I can't help it, Mike. Nobody counted on these setbacks."

Davy sighed. "Let's get the haul into the car, brother, and make the best of it."

"When you have everything loaded, join me inside. There's another development to tell you about."

A few minutes later the two came inside. Davy was about to speak when Laurel put her index finger to her lips. "Softly, please. Irv was restless and grumpy all afternoon. I know he's in pain, but he's also fretting over our situation. I let him drink enough to tranquilize him. He's asleep, and I hope he'll stay that way till morning."

They carried cups of coffee into the dining room and gathered around the table. She served the twins slices of cherry pie. "None for you?" Davy asked.

"I was up all night last night. I've been baking since I returned from the still." While there, she'd made the trek over the hill twice, but she didn't tell them that. "My feet are tired, my back is aching, and the last thing I want to see is a piece of pie."

They looked at her with sympathy but dug into theirs.

As she watched them shovel in bites, humming enjoyment, she pushed her fingers into her hair and held her head. "It's just occurred to me that I should be putting up jars of pie filling while fresh fruit is in season." It was an exhausting thought, but their moonshining business was reliant on her pie trade as a cover. "But that's a worry for another day."

Lowering her hands, she met the twins' expectant gazes. "You don't have to tell me *how* you know her, but are you acquainted with a girl named Corrine who worked at Lefty's?"

"The whore?" Mike said.

Davy kicked his brother beneath the table. Mike drew back his fist.

Laurel held up her hands. "Stop it! We don't have time for that, but don't ever refer to Corrine that way again. Within or outside of my hearing."

Davy said, "We know she's the poor girl Wally Johnson beat up."

"That's right, and she's still suffering the effects. By a set of bizarre circumstances, she's now a member of our group."

The twins gaped at her with identical expressions of incredulity.

"Never mind how it came about. She arrived here last night with Irv. She proved herself helpful in any number of ways, and that gave Irv an idea." She went on to tell them about the present arrangement at the stills. "Ernie will teach her how to do the simpler tasks, and I trust her to work hard so that our shortfall will be made up for soon. And—"

"Jesus," Mike said. "There's an and?"

Laurel gave him a look. "*And*, I went to Lefty's today to renegotiate terms."

"You went to Lefty's?"

"Alone? Are you daft, Laurel?"

"Irv had laid the groundwork of a new deal with him, and I couldn't let that opportunity pass, especially in light of the theft. I got Lefty to triple his usual order."

"Bloody lot of good it'll do us, though," Davy said. "We've got no whiskey to sell, and Lefty's is shut down."

"Only until dark tonight." She glanced out the window at the darkened sky. "By now, they should be back in full swing."

"He greased somebody's palm," Mike said. "Somebody high up."

"I'm sure he did," Laurel said.

The twins cut glances at each other, but neither said anything.

"What?" she asked.

Davy shifted in his seat and cleared his throat. "Have you ever considered...uh..."

Mike cut in. "What numb-nuts is trying to ask is, have you ever thought of *approaching* someone who has *influence* to persuade him to be a tad less *influential?*"

"You mean pay him not to be? Absolutely not."

"It's the way business is done, darlin'," Davy said softly.

Mike added, "In order to stay in business, the owner of the pool hall had to give graft to damn near everybody."

"Look how far it got him," she snapped. "I won't stoop to bribery. And, anyway, we can't afford it." She pushed back her chair and stood up.

"This new order of Lefty's is a good one, and, as long as *he* continues to bribe officials, it'll be a standing order.

"All the more reason why Corrine's help is essential until Irv can resume his duties. Now, you need to be on your way to Ranger, and I must go to bed before I drop. Any questions?"

The brothers looked at each other again. Laurel braced herself for what might be coming this time, but Davy flashed her a boyish grin. "Can we take a piece of pie for the road?"

She gave them half the pie for themselves, and sent them off with the others she had baked and boxed that day. As he carefully placed the last one in their truck, Mike said, "We'll have them there well before breakfast. The men working the night shifts on the rigs love having pie for breakfast."

"And moonshine for dinner," Davy said.

The three were laughing together as she walked them out to their truck. She admonished them to drive carefully, but fast enough to return in time to start their shift at Logan's store. "You can't get fired."

"Ah, we won't," Mike said. "We're Mrs. Logan's pet project."

"She's urging us to get baptized," Davy explained. "She fears our infant baptism didn't take."

The three of them began laughing again, but there was no levity in Mike's voice when suddenly he asked, "Who is that?" and simultaneously pulled a pair of brass knuckles from his pants pocket.

THIRTY-SEVEN

Alarmed, Laurel turned.

Just outside the fan of light provided by the kitchen windows, Thatcher was propped against the clothesline post where he'd hitched his horse that morning. To Laurel's dismay—and outrage—her heart thumped at the sight of his tall, lean silhouette.

She wanted to rail at him for not making his presence known, but she needed to defuse the O'Connors, who were a hairsbreadth away from a catastrophic overreaction. "It's okay," she told them in a murmur, then, "Mr. Hutton. You startled us."

He pushed himself off the post and strolled forward, but his seeming nonchalance didn't fool Laurel, and she doubted the O'Connors would be deceived by it, either. Beneath the brim of his cowboy hat, his eyes shifted from one twin to the other.

She was almost certain that Thatcher had seen the brass knuckles now bridging Mike's fingers, and surely he'd also noticed that Davy's right hand was at the small of his back, where she knew he carried a small pistol similar to hers.

When the twins first began delivering to the boom towns, she'd expressed concern for their safety. They'd shown her their weapons and assured her that they would never be without a means of protecting themselves. However, this was the first time she'd seen just how willing they were to act first with violence and ask questions later. The two weren't all smiles and blarney.

Thatcher stopped within five yards of them, planting his feet firmly, causing her to wonder if he was still toting the pistol he'd retrieved from her this morning and was about to draw it like a gunslinger in a dime novel.

He said, "I came to ask how your father-in-law is faring, but I saw that you had company and didn't want to break up the party."

She injected a lightness into her voice that she was far from feeling. "No party. These are the O'Connor brothers, Davy and Mike." She pointed out which was which. "They work for me."

"They brought you the peaches," he said.

"That's right. I'd forgotten I'd mentioned that." But he hadn't, and that was disconcerting. "Davy, Mike, this is Thatcher Hutton. He was the Good Samaritan I told you about, who brought Irv home last night after the raid."

Thatcher leaned forward only far enough to shake hands with the twins in turn, then all three of them returned to their guarded stances.

Mike looked him over. "Are you a cowpoke, Mr. Hutton?"

He asked it as a put-down, but Thatcher replied blandly, "You could say."

Laurel said, "He breaks and trains horses."

"Does he?" Again, his question sounded deprecating.

Davy shot his twin a warning look, then addressed Thatcher with a smile. "So, you were at Lefty's last night. Things were exciting, I hear. How did you avoid arrest, Mr. Hutton?"

"I wasn't in the back room."

"Occupied upstairs then," Mike said.

Thatcher slanted him a glance, but didn't even blink. "I was having a hamburger in the front room."

"Ah," Davy said, "what fortunate timing for you that was."

When Thatcher didn't respond, and no one else spoke, Laurel turned to the twins. "The night isn't getting any younger, and you have deliveries to make."

As boss, she really gave them no choice except to depart. With noticeable reluctance, they retreated to their truck. As they got in, the backward glances they gave Thatcher were blatantly hostile.

As soon as their truck had cleared the drive, Laurel turned to face Thatcher, feeling hostile herself and ready with an accusation of snooping.

He, however, got the jump on her. "Kind of late to be making deliveries, isn't it? Where are they off to?"

To equivocate would only make them all look guilty. "Ranger."

Obviously he was familiar with the town's reputation. His eyebrow arched. "That explains the hardware they're carrying."

"To be used only in self-defense."

He looked skeptical of that. "They go all the way up there to deliver pies?"

She resisted the impulse to rub her damp palms against her skirt. "It's worth the trip. The markup per pie is three times what I get here. Seems every roughneck has a sweet tooth."

"And a taste for other things, too." He waited a beat, then said, "Are the O'Connors always on edge like that, spoiling for a fight?"

"Yes, especially with each other." She gave a soft laugh.

Thatcher didn't join in. "What were you doing at Lefty's roadhouse today?"

She couldn't conceal her astonishment over his knowing that, and it robbed her of speech.

"So it *was* you he saw."

Although her mouth was dry, she attempted to swallow. "Who saw?"

"Chester Landry."

"Who is . . . Oh, your friend with the plastered hair."

"He's no friend of mine, Laurel, and I don't think he's one to you, either."

"I don't even know him."

"Well, he knows you, and he made a point of telling me about your visit to the roadhouse."

"Why would he do that?"

"I'm wondering that, too. Why would he?"

Trying not to appear bothered by his probing stare, she shrugged. "Would he need a reason? He knows we're acquainted. He saw me today and mentioned it to you in passing."

"Un-huh. He climbed three flights of stairs, huffing and puffing, to tell me." He came forward, crowding in on her, but she held her ground. "What the hell were you doing at Lefty's?"

"What business is it of yours?"

He lowered his head, bringing his face to within inches of hers. "Asking for another demonstration? I warned you not to dare me."

The thought that perhaps she was subconsciously angling for another kiss mortified her. Relenting on her resolve not to back away from him, she did, but only by one step. "I went out there to implore them not to give the sheriff Irv's name."

"Them?"

"Lefty and that horrid woman, Gert."

"What made you think they would give Irv over?"

"Based on what Corrine and Irv have told me about that pair, they're without scruple. I was afraid that if they were pressured to rat out anyone who was there last night in exchange for leniency, they would do it in a heartbeat. I went for Irv's sake, to plead on his behalf."

She'd made up the explanation as she'd gone along, but to her it had sounded perfectly plausible. She hoped it would to him. He was watching her in that incisive way of his.

After a moment, he said, "You could have saved yourself the trip. Irv isn't going to be arrested."

"How do you know?"

"I asked the sheriff myself."

"You did?"

"This morning. Directly after leaving here, I went to see him to give back his Colt and the badge."

"You really aren't a deputy, then?"

"No."

She inhaled deeply, but her relief was short-lived.

"But if I was," he said, "what would it matter?"

"It wouldn't."

"It did."

It had. She groped for a logical reason. "If you had shown me the badge, explained it...But you didn't, and that seemed underhanded. I like to know where I stand with people."

"Yeah, I like that, too."

There was no winning this argument, and she would only sink herself in deeper if she continued trying. She fixed her gaze on the loose knot that secured a bandana around his neck. "I appreciate your intervening for Irv with Sheriff Amos."

"He said maybe getting shot taught Irv a lesson." He looked beyond her toward the house. "How's he doing?"

"He was hurting all day, and that made him grouchy. This evening I let him sip his moonshine until he fell asleep."

"Sleep is the best thing for him."

She nodded. "I hope he sleeps through the night."

"Who does he buy his moonshine from?"

That was the second question he'd asked out of the blue. As before, she was momentarily dumbfounded before mumbling, "I'm not supposed to tell."

Thatcher just stood there looking at her, silently pressing for a more satisfactory answer.

The one that sprang to her mind was evasive, but actually the God's truth. "He doesn't have to buy it. A friend gives it to him in exchange for handiwork."

"Hmm," he said. "Well, Irv and his friend need to be careful. Obviously local law is cracking down on offenders."

"I'll pass along the warning, but I'm afraid Irv won't change his ways."

"I'm afraid of that, too."

It was a solemn and weighty statement, not a quip. The intensity of his stare held her captive without force, without even a touch. Perhaps Irv's sixth sense about him had been correct. Perhaps Thatcher Hutton was something other than the loose-limbed cowboy he played, someone who represented a threat, not only to her, but to the people whose welfare depended on her.

But no sooner had that upsetting possibility entered her mind than he relaxed his shoulders and eased away from her. "How's Corrine? Did she go for your idea?"

"Wholeheartedly. Just as I thought." She hoped he wouldn't ask to speak to Corrine or ask for details about living arrangements, etcetera. Lying to him had become increasingly hard on her conscience, and standing this close to him in the dark made it hard to breathe.

That inability became even more constricting when he took yet another step closer to her. "Those twins."

Bravely, she tilted her head up in order to look into his face. "What about them?"

"You seem friendly with them."

"I am. Why shouldn't I be?"

He frowned at her flippancy. "You know what I'm asking you."

She did know. "They're charming boys."

"They're men."

"And I'm a widow."

"A young and pretty widow."

"A very recent widow, who has morals and a reputation to uphold." Her cheeks went hot. She dipped her head. "Which makes my lapse last night all the more incomprehensible."

He didn't say anything for the longest time, then, "The O'Connors are troublemakers."

Her head came up. "Says who?"

"Sheriff Amos. He pointed them out to me last night as we were on our way to Lefty's. He called them a wild pair."

She didn't want to read too much into the sheriff's notice of her deliverymen, but it gave her a twinge of concern. "Davy and Mike can get into mischief, I'm sure. But they're hardworking and, at heart, decent. If I didn't believe in their integrity, I wouldn't have them working for me."

"It's not all work, though, is it?" He looked aside, staring into the empty darkness. "You were laughing."

"What?"

"You were laughing," he said, turning back to her. "I heard you all the way out here. They make you laugh."

"Sometimes." The hushed tone in which she'd spoken the word made it sound like what one would admit only in a confessional.

He bobbed his chin once and looked aside again, his jaw working. He took off his hat and tapped it against his thigh as the fingers of his other hand raked through his hair. He said a swear word under his breath.

She didn't dare try to guess what these manifestations of male agitation implied. Actually, she was afraid she knew. "It's late. I'd better go in, so I can—"

"Run away from me."

"I'm not running away."

"Those twins make you laugh. I make you nervous. You've been wound up since you saw me here."

"Yes! Lurking in the dark!"

"Are you jittery because of what I said to you this morning?"

Unbuttoned. Unhooked. Us lying down together. "I don't remember what you said this morning." Her voice lacked conviction and substance, and instead sounded raspy with desperation.

"You remember."

"No I don't."

He didn't grab her. She didn't even see him move. She had no warning at all before he was just there, his hands encircling her waist, his fingers tensing and drawing her against him. Flush against him. Fitting them together. He felt solid and strong, an ensuring and durable presence, safe except for the quickening in her center that he incited and the unchecked recognition with which her body responded.

His breath was damp and warm against her neck as he sighed her name, the one she had forbidden him to use but which sounded so sweet now as he nuzzled her ear and whispered, "Stay away from Lefty's."

She couldn't believe she'd heard right. She jerked her head back. "What?"

"Keep away from there, Laurel. It isn't safe."

She tried to escape his hands, but he held her fast. "Let go of me."

"Not until you listen. Don't go out there again."

"You're overstepping, Mr. Hutton." She pried his hands from her waist, but before she could move away, he cupped them around her face, bringing it up and close to his own.

"You're right, I am, and I'll tell you why. Chester Landry claimed that last night was his first time to go to Lefty's, but I don't believe that for a second."

She turned her head aside and was about to shout at him how little she cared, but he talked over her.

"He told me he went to Lefty's today to recover a pocket watch he'd lost during the raid. He's the flashiest dresser I've ever come across, but I've never once seen him sporting a pocket watch."

It finally sank in that he hadn't insulted her carelessly or maliciously. He'd wanted to secure her attention because what he was telling her held importance, at least to him.

She placed her hands over his where they still pressed against her cheeks. "Why are you preoccupied with this man you obviously dislike, and how does it relate to me?"

He withdrew his hands gradually, as though fearing that as soon as he released her she might sprint into the house. Which she probably should do. And bar the door. But when he said, "Just hear me out," she stayed where she was and gave a small nod.

"Landry palled around with a young man in the boardinghouse. A show-off. Obnoxious. Named Randy. One night, he up and moved out without notice, without telling anybody."

"So?"

He raised a shoulder. "Maybe nothing, but…" He raked his fingers through his hair again. "Landry made light of it. Shrugged it off. But I got the impression he knew exactly what had happened to Randy."

"If they were friends, maybe Randy had asked him to cover his trail."

"Maybe," he said, but it lacked backbone. "He claims to be a shoe salesman. He boasts of a wide territory he covers on a routine basis, but he's rarely away from the boardinghouse for more than a couple of days at a time."

"Men often exaggerate their success."

"True, but I think Landry downplays his. I think he's very successful, but not at selling women's shoes. He's dealing in something else."

"Like what?"

"Liquor. He's bootlegging."

Her heart skipped a beat, but when he paused to give her time to comment, she didn't say anything.

"There's money to be made," he said, "and a lot of it, but it's a dangerous occupation. There are few game rules and no such thing as honor among thieves. Double-crossers, poachers, and loudmouths— like Randy—usually wind up dead."

He paused and focused even more sharply on her. "If I'm right about Landry, he wouldn't want to be seen at a well-known speakeasy the night after a raid when it was closed to business. But he *was* seen. By you."

She took all that in and thought how closely it correlated to what Irv had told her about the hazards of the illegal liquor trade. But she couldn't tell Thatcher she'd heard it all before in cautionary sermons from her father-in-law. She carefully weighed how she would respond.

"The only two people I saw were Lefty and Gert. Not even a sign of the girls. On my way out, before I got to the highway, a car passed me on the road. I didn't see the driver. Even if I had, and had recognized Mr. Landry, I wouldn't have given it a second thought because I don't know him, and how he earns his living makes no difference whatsoever to me. So even assuming you're right and his business dealings are illegal, he has absolutely nothing to fear from me."

"But see, Laurel, you may have a lot to fear from him."

THIRTY-EIGHT

—◆◆—

G ert knew that eyes had been on her since she'd turned off the highway. From the crevices of boulders, from behind foliage, from underneath the collapsed roof of a disused barn, she was being watched, probably through the sights of deer rifles.

Her arrival had been charted, but when she reached the house, it was in total darkness, and there was no one to greet her, not that she'd expected a welcoming committee.

A pack of mongrels was standing sentinel. They weren't barking, but she could hear their bloodthirsty growls as they stood alert and eager for the signal that would send them charging her.

She heaved herself out of her auto and moved to stand in the beam of her headlight where she could be seen. Cupping her hands around her mouth, she hollered, "Call off your mutts and your militia and invite me in."

Nothing happened. She stayed as she was, knowing that the head of the clan was taking his sweet time just to piss her off. "I ain't leavin' till we talk, Hiram."

From around the corner of the house, a Johnson materialized out of the darkness. She couldn't make out any distinct features except for the shotgun he held aimed at her.

"You're trespassing," he said. "Be on your way."

"Or what? You'll pull the trigger?"

"You make a sizable target. I couldn't miss with both eyes closed."

"If you shoot me, you'd just be provin' what everybody knows, and that's that all Johnsons are stupider than they are ugly, and that's sayin' somethin'."

"What do you want?"

"Like I said, to talk to the ol' man. Unless he's dead."

"He ain't."

"Figured that was too much to hope for. Tell him to show hisself or *he*'ll never know what *I* know about Wally's killin'."

Seconds ticked past. Then, no doubt acting on a cue from inside the house, the young man lowered the shotgun. The dogs backed down, whimpering in disappointment over being denied a mauling. The screen door squeaked open and a young woman came out onto the porch. "He says come on in."

Lamps flickered to life inside as Gert made her way toward the house. She paid the dogs no mind as she stomped past them and up the steps. The young woman lit a cigarette, eyeing Gert sourly as she shook out the match. "He's waitin'."

Gert pulled open the screen door and went inside.

It was a large, rectangular room. The collective glow from the recently lit lamps didn't reach the ceiling. Loitering around the perimeter of the room were a passel of Johnsons of both sexes spanning at least three generations, from a bald-headed baby straddling his mother's hip to a withered, toothless old woman, who Gert recognized as the reigning matriarch.

Gert muttered with scorn, "To think I'm related to this bunch."

"We ain't so proud to claim you, neither."

This from the man holding the place of honor in the corner of the room where he sprawled in an overstuffed chair. He held a coffee can propped on one knee. Looking at Gert, he raised it to his mouth and spat a string of tobacco juice into it.

Hiram Johnson had inherited his position as head of the clan from his father, and for the last four decades had ruled the family with an iron fist. His face was as crinkled as a dry creek bed in August. He had a dingy gray beard that covered his chest to the third button of his flannel shirt. A jar of moonshine and a flyswatter sat on the windowsill within easy reach of him. His bare right foot, missing toes and striated white with petrifaction, was propped on a footstool. A large, leather-bound Bible lay open in his lap.

"But I don't hail from the inbred branch of the family," Gert said.

Eying her with malevolence, Hiram spat into the can again and wiped stained spittle from his beard with the back of his hand. "Gettin' raided is bad for business, cousin."

"Couldn't tell it by the crowd we got tonight," Gert said. "The place was hoppin' when I left."

"You had some product stashed?"

"Enough for tonight, but the raid made a dent. I come to buy."

"Tup." Hiram raised his index finger to one of his offspring whose chair was propped against the wall, front legs raised. He was stropping a hunting knife. At the signal from the old man, the chair legs hit the floor. The man addressed as Tup came to his feet and slid the knife into a scabbard at his waist.

"Load her up," Hiram said to him.

He was on his way to the door when Gert said, "Ten gallons less than what we usually take."

Tup looked to Hiram for direction. Gert kept her expression blank. Never taking his eyes off her, Hiram said, "You heard her." Tup pushed open the screen door and went out, calling to someone unseen to come help him.

"How come you're cuttin' back?" Hiram asked.

Gert took a slow look around the room, as though taking inventory of the assembled relatives. They all appeared indolent and uninterested, but she knew better. They all had the trademark big ears, but not necessarily in the physical sense.

Hiram, grasping that she wanted to talk to him privately, flipped his hand at the room at large. "Git."

His offspring began to scatter, some going outside, others disappearing into other rooms. A teenaged girl helped the old woman out of her chair and supported her as she hobbled out.

Watching her leave, Gert said, "I thought she'd've died by now. You, too. And why don't you spare us all that stink and cut that damn foot off?"

Ignoring that, Hiram repeated his question about her order.

Gert seated herself in one of the vacated chairs. "While your boys have been keeping the roads hot between your stills and the oil patches, small-timers have been taking up the slack locally. You're losing ground, Hiram. You're being undercut."

"Nobody would dare."

"Fine. Don't believe me. But Lefty struck a deal today. I's sittin' right there when they shook on it. More hooch for a lot cheaper than you charge us."

"Rotgut."

"Nope. Good stuff."

"Labeled liquor?"

Gert shook her head. "'Shine."

"Whose?"

"I'll get to that. Let's talk about Wally."

He slapped his palm onto the open Bible in his lap. "God as my witness—"

"Which he ain't."

"—we're gonna get the sumbitch what killed Wally."

Gert crossed her arms over her massive chest. "You made any headway in that direction?"

"We'll get him."

"That means you got no idea who done it."

Temper sparked, Hiram leaned forward, nearly tipping over his spit can. "If you know something, you'd better tell me, or being my second cousin thrice removed won't mean shit. Kinship won't save your fat ass from being flayed."

She huffed an exhale. "The night before Wally was murdered,

he tore into one of my girls." No doubt Hiram had heard about it because he didn't dispute or defend it. "She weren't much count as a whore, but she was handy helping Lefty on the grill and serving drinks in the back room, so I kept her on."

"You're sayin' *was*. She die after all?"

"No. The ungrateful hussy run off last night, still owing me money for her upkeep. Slipped off during the raid. Today, I learned she's been took in."

"By who?"

"By the moonshiner who persuaded Lefty to squeeze you out of ten jugs per order." She leaned forward and tapped her temple. "I put two and two together. One bullet was fired into Wally's head for stealing that truckload of sugar and causing a shortage. The second bullet was payback for whippin' up on that whore."

Hiram picked up the Bible and brandished it. "He's dead meat."

Gert's smiles were as infrequent as blood moons. She gave Hiram Johnson a smug one now. "Ain't no he."

THIRTY-NINE

———◦◉◦———

Irv scowled up at Laurel from his pillow. "Hutton dropped that on you, then just left?"

"Without another word." Now part of their morning routine, she tied a knot to secure the fresh bandage around his chest. "There."

"Does it have to be so tight?"

"Yes, because you work it loose as the day goes on. But the wound looks better today than yesterday, and it will continue to get better if you *rest*."

"I've done nothing besides lie in bed."

"And fret. Your mind needs rest, too. Stop worrying so much."

"First you tell me that Ernie's secret stash has been stolen, then that you took it upon yourself to go *alone* to Lefty's, and lastly about this doomsday message from Hutton. Now you tell me to stop worrying?"

"Do you know Chester Landry?"

"How would I know a guy who sells ladies' shoes?"

"Maybe more than shoes."

"What's he look like?"

She described him to the best of her recollection. "I only saw him that one time in the café, and I wasn't really paying attention." She'd been distracted by Thatcher.

Irv scratched his bristly chin. "I know the fella you're talking about. I've seen him in town."

"Where?"

"Here and there."

"At Lefty's?"

"No, and I think I would remember, considering those duds he wears."

"If you haven't seen him there, then it's possible Mr. Hutton's hunch about him is wrong."

"Just as possible that he's right, though, Laurel. Remember, I told you it was rumored that a bootlegger from Dallas was a big-time operator around here? Could be Landry's him. Hutton must think so, or he wouldn't've gone out of his way to tell you."

"That wasn't all he came to tell me. You'll be glad to know that Sheriff Amos is letting you off the hook, this time, in the hope that you've learned your lesson."

"And I hope you've learned yours." He shook his finger at her. "Out at Lefty's, you're in danger of more than bootleggers. Don't go there again."

"I won't." When he looked sternly doubtful, she stressed that she wouldn't. "I only went to seal your deal. The O'Connors will be making the deliveries."

"Larger deliveries."

"Which is what we were going for, Irv. Remember?"

"There's nothing the matter with my memory. But our gain represents a loss to competitors. I'm all for increasing our business, but not if it means that one or all of us will meet with bodily harm."

"I'll be doubly discreet and careful."

"Warn those twins not to be so damn cocky, but don't tell them why. Keep it general."

"You still don't trust them."

"Never have trusted men with dimples."

She laughed. "What do you have against dimples?"

He went on as though she hadn't interrupted. "Ernie and Corrine need to be put on watch, too."

"Because of the theft, Ernie is already on alert."

"How'd Ernie take to Corrine?"

She hedged. "She'll grow on him."

He barked a laugh. "Don't count on it. He's used to his own company and silence. God knows he'll have precious little of that."

Laurel smiled. "I have pies to bake today, but I'll drive out and check on them tomorrow. Hopefully they'll have several crates of whiskey ready for me."

"Speaking of, I could do with a nip."

"At bedtime."

"I just woke up."

"At bedtime."

"I'm hurting now."

"Part of the healing process." She stood up and straightened the cover where she'd been sitting at the foot of his bed. He was idly scratching his chin again. "Your stubble is itching. Would you like a shave?"

"No."

"I'm happy to do it."

He waved off the offer. "I'm thinking, is all."

"Something's gnawing at you, Irv. What?"

"You say you introduced Hutton to the twins? How'd that go?"

"All right. After they shook hands, I sent the twins on their way."

In giving Irv an account of last night's visit from Thatcher, she had omitted certain details, one being the hostility that had crackled between him and the O'Connors. She also didn't tell him that Thatcher had questioned her about the deliveries the twins made to Ranger, or that Sheriff Amos had pointed the O'Connors out to Thatcher while referring to them as wild. Nor did she mention that Thatcher had asked who supplied Irv's moonshine.

Unabridged honesty could set his recovery back for weeks, which was how she justified those omissions. Even so, his forehead remained furrowed.

"This warning from Hutton about Chester Landry worries me," he said. "It should worry you, too, Laurel. My advice is to steer clear of the man."

"I plan to, whether or not he's into bootlegging."

Irv peered up at her through his lowered brows. "I wasn't referring to Landry."

Bernie Croft had eaten a late breakfast at Martin's Café. Rather than ride to his office, he'd chosen to walk the short distance and was almost there when a deranged individual lunged at him from out of a narrow alleyway.

He was grabbed roughly by the lapel of his suit coat, jerked into the space between the two buildings, and forcefully pushed against a brick wall. Hands closed around his neck and began to choke him.

Dr. Gabe Driscoll was barely recognizable. His eyes were bloodshot. His bared and clenched teeth looked feral. But his fingers were like steel clamps around Bernie's throat. "I'm going to kill you."

Bernie gasped, "Jesus Christ, Gabe." He planted his hands on the physician's chest and pushed with all his might.

Obviously in a weakened state, Gabe wasn't that hard to dislodge. He reeled backward and landed against the opposite brick wall, his shoulder catching the brunt of the impact. He clapped his hand over his rotator cuff and yelped in pain.

Hennessy came bounding in from the end of the alley. Bernie held up a hand. The bodyguard skidded to a halt. "I'm all right," Bernie said. "But don't let anybody wander in here."

Hennessy looked at Driscoll with misgiving. Bernie patted the air. "It's fine, Jimmy." Hennessy backed out of the alley and posted himself at the entrance to it.

Bernie returned his attention to Gabe, whose ferocity had

evaporated. He was slumped against the wall. "What the hell is wrong with you?" Bernie hissed. "It's ten-thirty in the morning, and you're pissing drunk!"

"Why did you tell?"

"Tell what?"

Gabe glared at him with maddened eyes. "You want me to yell it out loud? You want me to shout it out so everybody will know about Pointer's Gap?" Unmindful of Hennessy, he stumbled toward the street.

Bernie reached out, clutched a handful of his jacket, and yanked him back. Despite his rancid body odor and days-old breath, Bernie held him by the lapels and got right in his face, speaking softly, but with emphasis. "Nobody knows."

"You promised me that no one would, but you told Norma Blanchard. Why? *Why?*"

Bernie instantly released him and took a step back. He felt like his head might explode. Every blood vessel in his body began to throb with wrath. But he clenched his teeth in order to keep his features rigid and his expression impassive. He tugged on the hem of his vest, shot his cuffs, assumed his customary intimidating, confident posture, and said blandly, "Insurance."

Gabe blinked several times. "How did you even know about her and my...our..."

"Your grubby, adulterous affair? I make it my business to know who's fucking whom. It comes in handy on occasions just such as this, Dr. Driscoll. I've got you by the balls, you see. You killed your wife in order to take up with your mistress and bastard child."

Gabe flinched and gulped back a sob. "I came to you that night for help."

"You came to me panicked, beyond any hope of getting yourself out of a nasty fix without my assistance. You were out of your mind with desperation and fear, and I responded immediately."

"We made a vow."

"Yes, we did. We made a vow to help each other. Quid pro quo.

I held up my end of our bargain in a matter of hours. You, by contrast..." He sniffed with disdain. "Look at you. You're a wreck, a disgrace."

Gabe wiped his dripping nose with the back of his hand. "You swore to me that no one would ever know."

"But did you think that a man in my position would volunteer to get rid of your problem without holding some collateral? Did you think that, Gabe? Did you really? Are you that naïve? That dim?"

The man's shoulders sagged. His head dropped forward as though the pin of a hinge holding it onto his neck had been pulled.

Bernie let him suffer in humiliation and silence for several moments, then said, "I assume Miss Blanchard is using this information for leverage of her own?"

"She's come to the house twice," Gabe mumbled. "Once in the middle of the night. I lectured her on how foolhardy that was, but she came back. In daytime, no less. She even brought the baby. She wants us to be together."

Bernie made a sound of regret and sighed. "Typical female behavior. She's wanting to nest."

"It's too soon. People would become suspicious."

"Rightfully," Bernie said. "You must drill that home to Miss Blanchard. Or would you rather I speak with her on your behalf?"

Gabe raised his head and looked at Bernie with bleary eyes. "No, I'll do it."

Bernie gave Gabe's arm a fatherly squeeze of support. "I suggest that before you go calling on your ladylove, you get sober, take a bath, and shave. Get a haircut. Buy Miss Blanchard something nice. Take the baby a play-pretty."

Gabe nodded assent, but Bernie could tell that his heart wasn't in it.

With vexation, he said, "I gave you two weeks to sort yourself out, Gabe. Instead you've lost ground, and your time is up. You start tomorrow."

"What?"

"Hang out your shingle. Resume making house calls. Dispense pills, set broken bones, administer enemas. And, as agreed, begin your work for me."

"Smuggling bootlegged liquor on my rounds."

Bernie tugged on his lower lip. "Actually, since our last conversation, I've determined that any able-bodied person with half a brain can do that. I have plenty of them already on my payroll. You would be a wasted asset doing manual labor.

"No, what I have in mind for you now, Gabe, is something more complex, more suited to an austere and respected man who has a knowledge of science and the healing arts."

Befuddled, Gabe said, "What are you talking about, Bernie?"

"Poison."

FORTY

Thatcher was working late. The sun had already set, making it dark enough in the stable to require a lantern. He moved it from stall to stall as he replenished water and feed for each of his charges.

The mare who had caused him to work overtime snuffled and tossed her head when he entered her stall. She had a bad reputation for kicking, so he waited for her to settle before closing himself in with her.

"I saved you for last because we need to have a talk." He moved to stand where she could see him. He stroked her forehead. "You kick another board out of Mr. Barker's fence, he may kick both of us off his property. I'd lose money. Your owner, who's already put out with you, would send you to the glue factory."

Her ears twitched. She was listening.

"What he would rather do is breed you with that handsome stallion he's got. If you keep acting unladylike, you'll miss out. He's hung like a racehorse," he whispered. "He *is* a racehorse. The other mares would give their eye teeth. Think it over."

He lifted a coiled lasso from a hook and began rubbing it over her with one hand while smoothing her coat with the other. Dryly, he said, "Of course, I'm nobody to be giving advice in that department."

He'd spent three restless nights since he'd gone to Laurel's house and had seen her with the O'Connor brothers. She thought they were charming. They had the gift of gab. They made her laugh.

This was Thatcher's first experience with jealousy, but it had sunk its claws in deep. He understood now how it could cloud a man's judgment and cause him to behave irrationally. But jealousy aside, he didn't see anything good coming from Laurel Plummer mixing with hell-raisers the likes of them.

Thatcher knew—damn his knack for reading people—that she didn't always tell him the whole truth. Some of that wiggling around certain topics and giving less than direct answers could be passed off as part of her prideful nature. She was fiercely determined to stand on her own. But he suspected that her sidestepping pertained to something besides protecting her privacy.

And that bothered him, because he didn't think she had taken his warning about Chester Landry seriously.

To get her to listen, to try and impress upon her how important it was that she heed his warning, he had held her and made out like he was going to kiss her again. The instant he'd put his hands on her, he'd gotten her attention, all right, but she'd for damn sure gotten his, too.

He'd counted on feeling a stiff corset or whatever it was women wore under their clothes to narrow this and plump that. But all he'd felt through Laurel's dress was Laurel.

Her waist had been giving, each dainty rib delineated. The heel of his hand had brushed the underside of her breast. Not to cup that soft crescent in his palm... He deserved some kind of medal. He—

The mare's ears twitched, and she restlessly bobbed her head at the exact moment that Thatcher heard a noise coming from the front of the stable. He lowered the lariat, but continued to run his hand over the mare's withers to keep her calm.

A rustle. The faint crunch of straw underfoot. Maybe some kind of critter? Mouse, rat, cat, possum?

Then a clangor that would raise the dead. An animal might

knock over an empty feed bucket, but it wouldn't cuss a blue streak when it did.

The mare began to stamp and neigh, as did the other horses in their stalls. Thatcher hooked the lariat over his shoulder, unlatched the stall door, and slipped through. But he had to take the time to latch it back so the mare wouldn't get out. Once it was secure, he ran to the wide stable door. As he cleared the opening, he caught sight of a fleeing male figure. Thatcher bolted after him.

It was full-on dusk, but Thatcher spotted the intruder skirting around the corral and running for the creek. Thatcher went after him, uncoiling the lariat as he ran. As the man began to slide down the steep embankment, Thatcher tossed the rope and lassoed him with ease, neatly dropping the loop over his head and trunk, pinning his arms against his torso.

The man gave a sharp cry as he was jerked backward and off his feet. When he landed butt-first on the rocky ground, he let fly another round of colorful profanities.

Thatcher walked toward him, taking up the slack in the rope as he went. The face that glared up at him was that of a young man still in his teens, about Roger's age.

"Fuck you, cowboy."

Thatcher planted the sole of his boot against the youngster's chest and pushed him onto his back, holding him down with his foot. "You know what happens to horse thieves?"

Still glaring, the boy remained stubbornly silent.

"They're hanged from the nearest tree."

The young man's rebellious, hostile expression wavered. "What I said, I didn't mean nothin' by it."

"Sounded to me like you did."

The kid peered up through the gathering darkness into Thatcher's face. "Heard about some cowboy who shot the head off a rattlesnake here in town. You him?"

"Um-huh."

"Oh, shit."

"Roger tell you?"

"Don't know no Roger. Just picked up word of it somewhere."

Thatcher tipped his head back toward the stable. "Horse thieves are a sorry lot."

"I was just lookin' around, is all."

"Bald-faced liars are just as bad." Thatcher removed his foot and hauled the kid up. "Before you kicked over that bucket and gave yourself away, you figured on helping yourself to a horse, didn't you?"

"I kicked over that goddamn bucket on my way out. I'd changed my mind about *borrowing* a horse."

"You saw my lantern?"

"Saw the horses. I thought they'd be saddled."

In spite of himself, Thatcher chuckled. "A sorry, thieving numbskull. What's your name?"

Thatcher's insults had put the chip back on his shoulder. "What's it to you, Billy the Kid?"

Thatcher looked around, his gaze landing on a large live oak. "That lowest branch ought to do." He started toward it, yanking on the rope, pulling the kid along behind.

He dug his heels in. "Wait! Wait! Hold it! It's Elray. My name is Elray Johnson."

Recognizing the name immediately, Thatcher stopped and turned back. The sheriff had told Thatcher about Elray Johnson's fearfulness following the murder of his cousin, Wally. Elray looked ready to jump out of his skin now. "Why were you trying to steal a horse, Elray?"

With no cockiness left in him, the kid choked up and gave a hard shake of his head. "You can hang me, mister, but I ain't tellin'."

Bill was summoned from home by Scotty. The deputy didn't share much information over the telephone except to say that the matter had to do with Elray Johnson. That didn't bode well.

When Bill walked into the department ten minutes later, he wasn't met with the chaos he'd expected. The wall clock's pendulum ticked loudly in the otherwise quiet room. Scotty was filing paperwork.

He said, "Sorry to bring you from home."

"What's the trouble? Where's Elray?"

"He's got him back there in a cell."

"Who does?"

"Your boy wonder."

Bill rebuked that remark with a stern look. "I assume you're referring to Thatcher."

"Are the rest of us supposed to consider him official?"

"Good question," Bill muttered as he hung up his hat. He entered the cell block where all the barred doors stood open. In the first cell, Thatcher was leaning with his back to the wall, one foot flat against it, his knee raised. He had a bead on Elray, who was sitting on the cot gnawing at his fingernails and jiggling his knees.

When he saw Bill, he shot to his feet and aimed an accusing finger at Thatcher. "He roped me like a damn calf. He was gonna hang me!"

Bill looked at Thatcher, who said, "He sneaked into Barker's stable to steal a horse. He bungled it, and I caught him. But that's not why I put him in here."

"Okay," Bill said, "I'm listening."

"He said he would rather me hang him than tell me why he needed a horse."

Bill hadn't seen Thatcher since the morning he'd come to the house. During their conversation on the porch, he'd told Thatcher more than was comfortable about his and Daisy's personal life, but he knew instinctually that his secrets were safe with this man of few words.

He also knew that Thatcher wouldn't have hanged the Johnson kid, but had scared him into thinking he would. Apparently Thatcher also had perceived that Elray's desperation might signify a need to flee. Bill thought Thatcher was probably right.

Elray had dropped back down onto the cot. His knees were bobbing again at a frantic rate. Bill asked, "What's going on?"

"Nuthin'."

"Did you intend to steal a horse?"

"Naw."

Thatcher said, "He admitted he was until he realized they didn't come already saddled."

Wanting to laugh, Bill managed a strict tone. "That true, Elray?"

Glowering at Thatcher, he said sullenly, "He didn't have to rope me and jerk me to the ground. It's a miracle my butt bone ain't broke. I'd've stopped running if he'd've asked me nice."

Bill said, "Where were you planning to go on horseback?"

"Just ridin'. I hadn't thought that far ahead."

Bill went over to the cot, motioned for Elray to scoot to the other end of it, and sat down where the boy had been. "My supper's getting cold on your account, and you dare to bullshit me? Now, where were you off to that was so important you'd steal a horse to get there?"

Elray's face muscles began working like a child's on the brink of tears. "Somewhere, anywhere, to lay low for a while."

"Why do you need to lay low?"

He choked on a sob. "If they find out I was here talking to y'all they'll . . . they'll . . . no telling what they'll do to me."

"Who?"

"Cain't say."

"Your family?"

Elray wiped his dripping nose on his sleeve. "Goddamn Wally."

"What about him?"

"He was always stirrin' up trouble, then skippin' out, leavin' it to everybody else to clean up his mess."

"Is that what's happening now? A cleanup?"

Elray didn't answer.

Bill said, "Has something come to light about who killed Wally?"

Elray's eyes darted between Bill and Thatcher, then he lowered his head and shook it *no*.

"Then why were you hoping to get away?"

"Just tired of everybody being all worked up over it, is all." He sat up straighter, gave a belligerent roll of his shoulders, and looked across at Thatcher before coming back to Bill. "He don't know what I wasn't at the stable only to take a gander at the guy who shot that rattler. I weren't in there more'n a few seconds and didn't steal shit. Anyhow, I got nuthin' more to say."

Bill looked over at Thatcher, who raised a shoulder and said, "He's not worth the trouble it would take to hang him. I doubt Mr. Barker would want to bother with pressing charges of trespassing."

"Then what do you suggest?"

He gave another laconic shrug. "Notify his kin to come take him off your hands."

Bill recognized it as a bluff, but Elray didn't. He surged to his feet again. "No!"

Bill grabbed him by the waistband of his britches and jerked him back down onto the cot. "What's got you scared, son? You tell me, or I'll hand-deliver you to your great-granddaddy. What's Hiram up to? Vengeance for Wally?"

Elray hiccupped several times, then said, "He's been on a rampage. He ordered all us to comb the hills. Every square inch we could cover. Any stills we found, tear 'em up, he said. 'Wreak havoc on anybody making moonshine who ain't a Johnson' is how he put it."

He made another swipe at his nose. "The other night one of my cousins—we call him Tup. Don't ask why. Me and him were explorin' and picked up the scent of wood smoke. We followed it to a still. Two, actually, but only one man was camped out there. What had drawn us was the smoke from his cookfire. He weren't doin' a run, just tinkerin' around.

"We watched him hide a crate of 'shine in a hole in the ground. After he went into his tent, we waited to make sure he was down for the night, then snuck up to the hidin' place, and took his whiskey."

"How much?" Bill asked.

"Ten crates."

"Ten *crates*?"

"It was a deep hole. Like a grave, only covered up good with brush. Had to make several trips to get it all back to our truck."

"Did you know the man?"

"Don't think so, but it was dark so I couldn't see him good."

"Do you think he saw you?"

"I know he didn't. He had firepower within reach. If he'd've seen us, he would've used it. We got away clean."

Stroking his mustache, Bill mulled that over. "Sounds to me like Hiram ought to be happy with you and your cousin." When Elray didn't respond, Bill asked, "Or isn't that the end of the story?"

Thatcher hadn't moved or taken his eyes off the boy. He said, "I don't think it is, sheriff. He's spooked."

"Is he right, Elray?" Bill asked.

"Things is gettin' crazy," he said, his voice cracking.

"This path of vengeance Hiram is on?"

Elray nodded several times. "Old Hiram—he ain't my great-grandaddy, he's my great uncle—he told Tup and me that those two stills we happened on sounded like easy pickin's. The 'shine we stole was quality, too."

"He wouldn't like that," Bill said. "Competition."

"Yes, sir. He told us to go back, steal all the liquor that was bottled, dump out the barrels of fermentin' mash, bust up the stills, and..." He lowered his voice. "And hurt whoever was there. Make 'em sorry they'd ever heard the name o' Johnson, he said."

"Wreak havoc."

"Yes, sir."

"You jumped to carry out his orders to hurt people?"

"I weren't given no choice, sheriff. And Tup, who has a mean streak a mile wide, was looking forward to it. So we went back last night."

"Who'd you hurt and how bad? Did you kill the moonshiner?"

"No! Tup and me waited till late and snuck up, same as before. Nobody was around. The cookers weren't thumping, and the cookfire had burned down to coals. We crept over to where the hole's at. Tup reached into the brush covering it and—" He stopped and swallowed several times. "I ain't ever heard a scream like that, not from nobody, not even from a woman."

"What happened to him?"

"Bear trap. Damn near chomped his arm in two. Then the shootin' started."

"How many shooters?"

"I didn't stick around to count. I ran like hell." His voice cracked again. "I got to our truck and took off, but after a few miles, I left it and struck off on foot."

"Afraid you'd be followed by the man at the still?" Thatcher asked.

He shook his head. "He already had Tup. He might've shown me mercy if I'd of given his whiskey back. But I knew that Uncle Hiram, all them, was gonna be wonderin' why me and Tup hadn't come back. I ran out on him, and that's somethin' a Johnson won't forgive, running out on kin. If they find me, they'll kill me. Slow and in misery."

Bill feared the boy was right. He and Thatcher exchanged a glance, and Bill could tell that he was of the same mind.

Elray's head was down. He was staring at the loose cuticle that he'd picked at until it had bled. "I've been hidin' all day, working my way into town, waiting for it to get dark. I counted on hopping a freight, but missed the last one out till tomorrow morning." He raised his head and looked at Thatcher. "I was gonna steal a horse so I could get the hell away from here."

Bill asked, "Do you think your cousin is dead?"

"Don't know. The shootin' stopped, but his screaming didn't. I could hear him all the way back to the truck. He might've died or been killed after I left."

He thought on it for a moment, then added, "Like I said, he's got a cruel temper, especially when he's drunk, which is usually, but I'm a damn coward for leavin' him. That's what Hiram will say, and what that ol' bastard says is law."

"Not in this office, it isn't." Bill stood up. "You sit tight while I call in some deputies, then we'll be on our way."

Elray sniffed back dripping snot and looked at him dumbly. "On our way where?"

"You have to guide us to those stills, Elray."

His eyes went wide and wild. "Please don't make me. Anyhow, I'd lose my way. I don't remember where they're at."

Ignoring that, Bill tipped his head toward the door into the main room and started moving in that direction. "Thatcher."

Thatcher pushed himself upright. "Hold on a sec." As he walked toward Elray, the boy shrunk back against the wall behind the cot. Frantic, he looked over at Bill. "Don't leave me by myself with him."

Thatcher stood over him. "Relax, Elray. If I'd've wanted to hurt you, I would have strung you up."

"Then what'chu want?"

"I want to know what you're lying about."

"I ain't. I owned up to stealing that whiskey, leavin' Tup, and—"

"Not all that."

"Then whut?"

"What's come to light about who killed Wally?"

FORTY-ONE

Laurel turned off the highway and started up the familiar rutted drive to the shack, where she was dropping off supplies for Corrine before driving the remainder of the way to the stills to pick up product.

It didn't surprise her that the dwelling was barely detectable in the darkness. Corrine spent most of the nighttime hours working with Ernie at the still, rarely returning until daylight. But on the nights she was in the shack, it still looked unoccupied from the road.

Not wishing anyone to know that it was inhabited, Laurel had purchased a bolt of thick, black cloth from the general store in another town. Corrine and she had draped the shack's few windows with it, and tacked it over the interior walls to keep light from leaking through the cracks. Corrine used the cookstove as infrequently as possible to keep smoke at a minimum. When the season changed, and the potbellied stove was needed for heat, they would have to make adjustments, but Laurel had a few months to figure it out.

She pulled her car around to the rear of the building, out of sight of the road, and retrieved her parcels from the floorboard. It was a moonless night, but she knew where there were obstacles to avoid as she made her way.

One of them was the chicken coop, which reminded her of that malicious rooster. Before moving into town, she had made good on her threat to throw him into a stewpot—Ernie's. She'd given the laying hens to an old folks' home, the staff of which had been most grateful for the contribution.

Thinking of the rooster reminded her of the altercation she'd had with him the day she'd met Thatcher. And the reminder of Thatcher made her "truculent." That was the word Irv had used to describe her mood since their last encounter.

She'd neither seen nor heard anything further about Chester Landry, either to substantiate or dispel Thatcher's warning. When she'd asked the twins if his name was familiar to them, they'd told her they'd heard of the shoe salesman through their friend Randy. But Randy hadn't been around lately, and they'd never met his pal Chester.

The twins had begun delivering to Lefty's, so far without incident. Although, they'd told Laurel, since the raid, the sheriff's department had begun patrolling the roads around the roadhouse with regularity. Lefty had complained about the increased vigilance keeping customers away.

Since that night in the yard, Thatcher hadn't sought her out.

She considered the matter closed.

Out of politeness, she tapped on the door to the shack and softly called Corrine's name. Getting no response, she pushed open the door and went inside. As expected, Corrine wasn't there. Laurel set the parcels she'd brought on the table, leaving it to Corrine to put away the items where she wanted them.

On her way out, Laurel noticed two things about Irv's old bureau. To support the legless corner, Corrine had replaced the stacked catalogues with blocks of wood. And on top, along with her hairbrush and other personal articles, was the primer Laurel had given her.

She thumbed open the cover and was pleased to see that Corrine had been practicing. She'd copied several lines of the alphabet on the first page. The letters were imperfect, but by page three she was showing improvement. On page four she'd doodled a drawing. Beneath it, she'd printed ERNIE.

Laurel laughed softly. Maybe Corrine's drawing was an indecipherable death threat. Their relationship was still prickly.

She returned the primer to its place on the bureau, then stepped out and pulled the door closed. As she was retracing her way to the back, she heard the sound of an approaching automobile on the road. A set of headlights topped a hill. Another set of lights followed close behind the first. Then a third vehicle. All were traveling fast, maintaining their distance from each other, looking very much like a convoy with a mission.

Laurel's heart lurched and didn't stop pounding until they had passed the turnoff to the shack. She could easily have talked her way around being here. It was still Irv's property. She could say she had come to retrieve something he had left behind when they'd moved.

But then, a worse thought occurred to her: If the shack hadn't been their destination, where were they going in such an obvious hurry? Beyond here was no-man's-land, nothing out there except—

Not thinking twice about it, she began running toward the hill behind the shack. She forgot all the safety precautions she had hammered into Corrine. Her pistol was in her pocket, but she didn't have a lantern, and she wouldn't have lit it if she did. She didn't tread carefully. She didn't think about turning her ankle or slipping on loose rocks and plunging down a steep incline into a crevice where she could die of thirst before being found.

She heard the yap of a coyote, but it was far away, and the only predator that concerned her was Man. Lawmen. Or angry competitors. She didn't know which posed the greatest threat, and was loath to speculate on the consequences of the stills being discovered by either element. If indeed that's where the convoy was headed, she had to get there first. The stills might have to be abandoned, but Corrine and Ernie could escape.

Over the months that she'd been making this trek, she'd found routes that weren't so steep, that curved up the incline gradually. But they meandered and took more time, and she was aware of time running out. She went straight up.

She stumbled once and fell to her knee. Her skirt and petticoat helped to pad her kneecap, but she'd struck it hard enough to jar her teeth. She would bear a bruise.

Losing her footing a second time, she reached for a bush to break her fall. The brittle foliage scraped her arm. A night bird swooped low directly in front of her, its screech causing her to cry out in fright despite the need for stealth.

Her lungs began to burn, her heart felt near to bursting, but she pushed on, upward. If she was wrong, they would all have a good laugh over her frantic climb later. Much later.

But for now she must assume that her friends were in danger of being caught, captured, punished to the extreme. If she arrived too late, they might even pay with their lives.

Even in the darkness, she knew she was approaching the crest that overlooked Ernie's camp. She was panting hard as she scrambled up the last several yards. Sweat dripped into her eyes, causing them to sting. As she topped the hill, she closed her eyes to blink away the sweat, but also to postpone, even for a millisecond, what she would see below.

Praying for the best, expecting the worst, she opened her eyes.

What she saw caused her to stagger backward. She gasped for breath through her mouth, which hung open in disbelief.

Because there was nothing to see below. The clearing was empty.

FORTY-TWO

The sheriff stood at the edge of the clearing with his hands on his hips in a pose of disgust. He watched while deputies used flashlights to search the area, which obviously had been recently vacated.

"Goddamn it."

Thatcher came alongside him in time to overhear his muttered blasphemy. "They just left with Tup. His given name is Thomas."

"How's he doing?"

"Hanging on. Doc Perkins gave him a shot of morphine. But up to that point he was vocal. Very. Cursed the sons of bitches who had laid the trap, cussed his sorry-assed cousin who'd abandoned him." Thatcher paused, then added, "Honestly, when we arrived, and there was nothing here, I thought Elray had been lying about all of it, even the stills."

Elray's memory of the stills' location had been miraculously restored when Bill again threatened to turn him over to his great-uncle Hiram. Shortly thereafter, three sheriff's department vehicles, one with Dr. Perkins as a ride-along, had set out from town with Elray giving directions. Because the night was so dark, he'd mistaken landmarks several times, and they'd had to double back in order to find turnoffs previously missed.

The various roads they traveled became progressively narrow and rutted, winding through hills that all looked the same to Thatcher. He had begun to suspect Elray of leading them on a wild-goose chase, when the kid had suddenly sat forward and pointed through the windshield.

"Over there. Behind them cedars."

Tup Johnson had been found in the grave-like hole that Elray had described. He was still alive, but if he didn't die of gangrene or sepsis, he would surely lose the limb, which was half-severed already, grotesquely dark and swollen, and had jagged broken bones protruding from it.

As Bill and his deputies had fanned out to investigate the scene, he asked Thatcher to remain with Tup and try to get from him as much information as he could. Apparently it had slipped the sheriff's mind that Thatcher had declined to become a deputy. But none of this would be taking place if he had let Elray go. So, having only himself to blame for his involvement, he'd done as Bill requested.

"No, Elray wasn't lying, Thatcher," Bill said now. "There were stills here, all right. Two, just like the kid claimed. You ever seen one before?"

"Only pictures."

"Those stacks of rocks are the fireboxes. Some of the charred wood is still smoldering."

"Cookers sat on top?"

"Right. Scotty figured the flues were backed up to the cliff face there, an old trick to disperse the smoke, keep it from being easily spotted."

"What about the man Elray and Tup saw working here?"

"Not a trace. All we know for sure was that he wasn't a Johnson."

"He had a partner," Thatcher said, bringing Bill around to him. "Yeah. Tup says there were two of them, but he never got a glimpse of either. While he was writhing on the ground, they came up behind him and put a burlap sack over his head. He thought for sure they would put a bullet through it. But one held his good arm while the other released the trap."

"No sign of it," Bill said. "Retrieved to use another day, no doubt."

"They lowered Tup into the pit. None too gently, he said. But they left him with a canteen of water and a full jar of moonshine. He admits that he yelled and screamed and cried for his mama. They ignored him and went about breaking camp. He managed to uncap the jar with one hand, drank all the whiskey, and eventually passed out.

"This morning when he came to, he knew they were gone. Dead silence, he said, except for the gurgling of the spring."

"Moonshiners capable of assembling a still are just as capable of rapidly taking it apart and relocating."

Thatcher smiled. "Not to a spot as good as this one. According to Tup, this is an ideal place."

"He would know."

Together, they watched deputies pick through a clump of dead brush to see what it might yield, but nobody cried *Eureka*.

Bill said, "Tup didn't see them, but what about their voices?"

"Never spoke a word. Neither of them."

"All night?"

"That's what he said."

"Huh. Moonshiners clever enough to keep their mouths shut."

"I guess."

"Anything else he remembers?"

Thatcher rubbed the back of his neck. "They were light-footed." He got another questioning look from the sheriff. "I don't know what to make of that, either, but Tup said they both had a light tread."

"So our suspects are clever, mute, light-foots." Bill sighed. "At least we know Elray was telling the truth."

"About this."

"You still think he's lying?"

"About something."

"How sure are you?"

"Royal flush sure."

Bill gave a grunt.

Thatcher watched the flickering flashlight beams sweeping across the ground. "The clearing has been pretty much covered. Has anybody checked for tracks leading away from it?"

"A couple of the men tried, but got nowhere. Are you any good at tracking?"

"Stray cows. Wolves, coyotes, bobcats."

Bill handed him a flashlight. "You're not looking for scat or paw prints. Don't venture too far in the dark. I don't want to have to search for you, too. I need to get home."

"How's Mrs. Amos?"

Bill turned away. "Meet me back at the car in ten."

Thatcher rejoined him in under ten minutes and returned his flashlight. "Too dark to see much."

"I'll send a team out after daylight, but I have a feeling our bear trappers are too savvy to leave an easily followed trail."

Elray had been so fearful of Tup's wrath, he'd pleaded with them to let him stay in the car to avoid being seen. He'd been hunched down in the backseat under a deputy's guard. Bill dismissed the deputy, then got into the driver's seat.

"Y'all find anything?" Elray asked. "I mean, except for Tup."

Bill didn't answer. Neither did Thatcher as he climbed into the back with Elray.

"I'm not ignorant enough to jump out of a moving car, Mr. Hutton. You don't have to ride back here with me."

At some point over the course of the night, the kid had begun addressing Thatcher respectfully, which amused Thatcher. He didn't think Elray was a genuinely bad sort, or ignorant, but more hapless than anything, like he'd had the rotten luck to be born into a family where he didn't truly fit. Which was probably why he was coming to like the kid.

But now, he followed Sheriff Amos's lead and gave Elray the silent treatment as he settled in beside him. He didn't feel like talking just now, anyway.

Their silence must've been unnerving, because Elray began to chatter. "Only law I broke was to steal another moonshiner's whiskey, and how can that be a crime? I won't see a nickel from that. Plus, I was actin' under orders to cause pain, but I didn't raise a hand to nobody."

When neither Thatcher nor the sheriff responded, he continued.

"Them stills was hid so good, weren't for me, y'all never would've found 'em. Y'all should be thankin' me, not..." He swallowed. "Not whatever y'all're plannin'.

"What I think is, what y'all ought to do, is keep me locked up in jail, maybe a jail in a faraway town. Just till the dust settles around here. Better yet, put me on that freight train tomorrow morning, and you'll never have any trouble out of Elray Johnson again. I have a hankering to see Arkansas."

Bill drove in stony silence.

Thatcher gazed out the window.

Elray gave up on engaging them and lapsed into a brooding silence.

Although by now they were on the main highway, there was little to see. When they passed the Plummers' place, Thatcher looked up toward the shack, but it was barely discernible against the black sky.

The day he'd come upon Laurel wrestling with the wet sheet, the sky had been purely blue behind her. She'd made quite a sight, one engraved on his memory. He figured he would think back on it for the rest of his life.

Under his breath, he cursed her.

"Dammit, Laurel. Your pacing is making me dizzy."

"The whiskey is making you dizzy."

Irv lifted the jar toward her. "You should have a snort. Maybe it would calm you down."

"I can't afford to be calmed down."

Since returning home and waking him up to report what she'd

seen—and hadn't seen—she'd been beside herself, unable even to sit. "You don't know what it was like, looking down and seeing nothing there. Everything just *gone*."

While she had been trying to grasp that her friends, the stills, the tent, everything had vanished, out of the corner of her eye she'd caught headlight beams sweeping across the smooth face of a nearby hill.

Not having had time even to fully regain her breath, she'd turned away from the abandoned site and had begun the return trip to the shack in a flat-out run. Most likely, whoever was in those approaching vehicles would spend more time than she trying to figure out what had happened there, and what the implications were. But that was a supposition, not something she could count on, and it was imperative that she not be caught in the vicinity. Not by anyone.

She'd also been frantic to share this news with Irv, who might possibly have some information unknown to her. Her most earnest hope was that he could provide an explanation for the site having been abandoned.

But, to her dismay, after she'd shaken him awake, he had listened to her breathless recitation of facts with astonishing and infuriating calmness. For the past hour, while she'd been whipping herself into a froth, he had grown increasingly mellow by sipping from a jar of moonshine.

"I'm sure Ernie's got it under control."

She spun around to him. "If you say that one more time, I'm going to hit you with something. You can't be sure of anything. They might have gotten away. They might even have gotten away with most of the equipment. But how far could they have gone carting all that?"

"Ernie's old truck—"

"Yes, Ernie's old truck." She stopped in her tracks and turned to face him, hands fisted at her sides. "Why wasn't I ever told that Ernie had an old truck?"

"Because we had no call to tell you."

"Until tonight!" she shouted. "If his truck is so well hidden in the hills, maybe they couldn't get to it. Carrying all that paraphernalia? How could they possibly?

"If the people in the three vehicles I saw launch a search... God!" She resumed pacing and wringing her hands. "Ernie and Corrine could be in custody. Or worse, dead. And any minute now so could we be."

"I'm sure Ernie's got it—"

Her glare silenced him.

He used the jar of moonshine to point at the article lying at the foot of his bed. "I still think that could be a message of some sort."

She picked up Corrine's workbook and slapped it against her palm. "Of what sort? It's squiggles and lines."

"Then why'd you'd bother going in after it and bringing it back? You must've thought those hen scratches the girl made meant something."

The return jaunt to the shack had seemed more hazardous because it was mostly downhill, and she'd run like the devil was chasing her, which she feared he was. By the time she'd reached the shack, her entire body had been about to give out on her. Muscles, lungs, heart, had been taxed to their limit. She'd collapsed against her Model T, her arms outstretched across its hood, hugging it like a pilgrim at a shrine.

She'd allowed herself one precious minute to slow her heartbeat and breathing. Partially restored, she'd willed herself to move and get into the Model T.

"I was backing into a turn so I could drive out when I remembered seeing this primer on the dresser. I honestly don't know what urged me to stop and get it."

She opened the workbook to the page where Corrine had drawn what looked like absentminded scribbles. She realized now that the printing of Ernie's name seemed beyond Corrine's present capabilities.

"Is Ernie literate?"

"Yes. He's no scholar, but he can read good enough to get by."

"Then maybe this is his doing, and Corrine left the primer where she knew I would see it."

"Let me take another look."

She rounded the bed where Irv was semi-reclined and handed him the primer. He studied the crudely drawn etching, tilting both his head and the workbook to various angles. Then a laugh began deep inside his chest before burbling out.

"What? What is it?"

He closed the primer and passed it back to her. "Go to bed, Laurel."

"Not on your life!"

"Turn out the light. Everything's fine. I know where they're at."

———

He refused to talk about it further, saying that morning would come soon enough. Frustrated, but exhausted, Laurel turned out his bedroom light and pulled the door shut on her way out.

Bone-weary as she was, she took a bath before retreating upstairs to her room, where she pulled on a fresh nightgown, took the pins from her hair, and gave it a good brushing. She plaited it loosely into her customary bedtime braid. She was about to extinguish the flame in the lamp when she saw his reflection in her dresser mirror.

Gasping, she spun around, her hand at her throat.

FORTY-THREE

—◦◉◦—

"Don't raise a ruckus."

"What do you think you're doing? Get out of here!"

Thatcher came into the room and quietly closed the door.

"If you don't leave in two seconds, I'll shoot you."

"With what? You keep your pistol in the pocket of your skirt."

"How do you know that?"

"I've noticed you're always patting at it."

Intending to mend and wash her tattered and soiled skirt in the morning, she'd left it on a hook on the back of the bathroom door, her pistol forgotten in the pocket. She didn't believe Thatcher meant to harm her, but she wished she had the Derringer to reinforce her point about his audacious intrusion.

"As you're well aware, Irv has a shotgun," she said. "He's right downstairs."

"Sawing logs. I could hear his snores as I passed through the kitchen."

"If you don't leave now, I'll yell for him."

"No, you won't. You don't want me confronting him with this."

"This what?"

He didn't answer. Instead, he took off his well-worn black felt cowboy hat and set it on a table. Then he took off his jacket and folded it over the back of a chair.

"Pick those right back up," she said. "I did not invite you to stay. In point of fact, I'm sick of you sneaking around me and my house. What gives you the right to do that, to show up at all hours of the night?"

"When you always seem to be awake. Awake and wound up like a top. I wonder why that is."

"If I'm wound up it could be because you appear out of nowhere and catch me unfit to receive a visitor." Yes, this was twice, wasn't it, that he'd caught her wearing only—

She didn't finish that thought, because, somewhat recovered from the shock of his being in her house, her bedroom, she realized that his demeanor was particularly solemn.

His gray eyes shone in the lamplight beautifully, but reflecting bleakness. His face was drawn, his expression taut, emphasizing the sharp ridges of his cheekbones. He looked as though he were about to undertake a dreaded task, like someone designated to deliver tragic news. She felt twinges of alarm. Why *was* he here?

It was then she noticed that his boots had been ghosted over with a fine, chalky dust, and she realized where he had been tonight before coming to her. Though her breathing turned quick and uneven, she struggled to keep her features schooled. She even managed to ask aloud the troubling question in her mind. "Why are you here?"

He reached down to his coat and took something from the breast pocket, then walked over and set it on the dresser. Instantly recognizing a silver barrette, her heart seized up. She swallowed. "I must've lost it in the yard."

Speaking quietly, he said, "I didn't find it in your yard, Laurel."

She didn't need to ask where he had found it. She knew. But she brazened it out and made an offhanded gesture. "Then it probably isn't mine."

"I've seen you wear it in your hair."

"Lots of women have that same clip. Hancock's sells them. Six to a card. You didn't need to bother to return it."

"Actually, I did."

"Why?"

"Because I've got something to tell you."

"About a hair barrette?"

"Have you seen Chester Landry around?"

The question was out of context. She replied with exasperation. "No. I told you it was doubtful I would." Thatcher didn't look convinced. She added, "I don't know the man. How many times do I have to tell you?"

"Was the O'Connors' trip up to Ranger successful?"

He was intentionally trying to rattle her. She couldn't allow being caught off guard. "Very."

"They didn't encounter any problems?"

"In fact they did. They sold out of pies in a matter of minutes and left some of the roughnecks disgruntled. I need to bump up production." If her flippant answer annoyed him, he didn't show it.

"How's Corrine working out?"

Involuntarily, she glanced at the barrette and could have kicked herself for doing so. "She'll be able to do more when her arm gets stronger."

She could tell by the way Thatcher was looking at her that he knew she was hedging every answer to these questions. On the surface they might seem casual and random, but she knew they weren't.

"Do you know Elray Johnson?"

That query genuinely threw her. "His name is vaguely familiar. Is he one of the—"

"Notorious clan, yeah. His cousin Wally was murdered recently. Elray discovered his body."

"That's it. I remember reading his name in the newspaper. What about him?"

He told her about the teen's aborted attempt to steal a horse from Barker's stable. "I took him to the jail and summoned the sheriff."

"That doesn't seem fair. You caught him before he stole anything."

"But I sensed that he had something else on his conscience. Turned out, I was right. He confessed to stealing crates of corn liquor from a competing moonshiner."

Those twinges of alarm became outright pangs. She was trembling on the inside, but managed to keep her voice steady. "From what I understand, that happens routinely."

"This theft might've been routine if it had stopped at that. But it didn't."

"What happened?"

"Last night, Elray and his cousin, Tup, went back to the same still. A decision they came to regret. There was an incident."

Her heart in her throat, she asked, "What kind of incident?"

"One that warranted investigation. Tonight, when Sheriff Amos organized a team of deputies to return to the scene with Elray, I was more or less recruited to go along."

That was the convoy she'd seen. Thatcher had been among those who'd discovered the location of their stills, and there he'd found the barrette she'd given Corrine.

Feeling that her silence might be a giveaway to her mounting anxiety, she said, "Like at Lefty's. You were roped into taking part in the raid."

He gave a mirthless smile. "Literally this time." He told her about lassoing Elray. "But that's neither here nor there. He was pressured into leading us to the site. Seemed like we covered miles of wilderness on roundabout roads. I thought the kid had been lying. But no, we found Cousin Tup."

"At the still?"

"In a hole in the ground with his arm mangled so bad you couldn't identify it as a human part." His eyes holding steady on hers, he said, "It had been snared in a bear trap."

By now her heart was pumping so hard, she thought she might faint. By a sheer act of will, she contained a sob pressing at the back of her throat. "That's horrible," she said hoarsely. "Was he dead?"

"Last I heard, he was still alive but short one arm."

The strength to stand up deserted her. She sank down onto the end of her bed and hugged her elbows close to her body. "How awful."

Thatcher sat down in the rocking chair in which she had planned to spend hours rocking Pearl in her lap, reading to her from storybooks, loving her. She had attached a cushion to the chair's back, so she'd have something to lean her head against during nighttime feedings that had never taken place.

Thatcher placed his head on that cushion now and closed his eyes. "Whoever was operating the stills—there were at least two of them—had cleared out, taking everything with them. Setting that trap to catch a man stealing moonshine seemed extreme, a cruel thing to do.

"But," he continued on a sigh, "Tup had stolen from them, and had gone back with every intention of stealing again and then destroying their property. He and Elray had been ordered by the family head, Hiram, to rain down hell on them. If they hadn't caught Tup in that trap, if they hadn't cleared out, chances are good they would be dead."

He rocked two or three arcs. "I used to think the difference between right and wrong was clear-cut. Law and justice meant the same thing. But I'm not sure of that anymore."

She studied him for a time. He looked like an everyday cowboy who lived from one day to the next, accepting and dealing with the vagaries of life without giving them much thought. Not so, Thatcher Hutton. Perhaps he thought too much, saw too much. "Who are you?" she asked in a hushed tone that conveyed her mystification. "Who are you, really? Where did you come from?"

He stopped rocking and looked over at her. "What do you mean?" She didn't say anything, only continued to search his face. Finally, he said, "I'm nobody."

"Parents?"

He went back to rocking, but rested his head on the cushion again and gazed into near space. "Well, I didn't hatch, but I don't remember either of them. I was told my father worked in a smithy, shoeing horses mostly. He was accused of laming a horse on purpose because he held a grudge against the owner. The horse had to be put down. My dad was tried and sentenced. He didn't survive prison. I never knew what exactly he died of."

"Is your mother still living?"

"I don't know. She ran off with my daddy's accuser days after he was convicted. They were never seen or heard of again." He glanced over at her and asked dryly, "Do you reckon that story about the lame horse might've been made up?"

Laurel was dismayed. "She just left you?"

"Appears so."

"Who took care of you?"

"I was placed with a family. Decent people. They took in orphans, kids like me. We were expected to do chores on their place, but they saw that we got schooling.

"When I was eleven, thereabouts, I heard that a Mr. Henry Hobson, who had a large spread, was looking for hands to drive his sizable herd to the nearest railhead, which at that time was Fort Worth. Mr. Hobson's age requirement for trail hands was thirteen, but I passed for that. He signed me on."

He smiled with one corner of his mouth. "Years later, he told me he knew I'd fudged on my age, but he saw how bad I wanted the job. Anyhow, after the drive, he made it permanent. I lived and worked on his ranch for the next fifteen years, till I was drafted into the army."

"Why haven't you gone back?"

"Nothing to go back to." He told her the circumstances, his gaze pensive and sad when he talked about his mentor's death and the change of fortune it had wrought for him.

"Mr. Hobson was the finest man I've ever met. I called his son up in Dallas and left word how to reach me. Haven't heard from him, though, and I don't expect to. Don't see that it makes much difference. Not now."

"Now?"

He broke his distant stare and turned to her. "Things have changed, Laurel."

"What things? Since when?"

"Since tonight."

He left the rocker and made a circuit of the bedroom. Pausing at one of the windows, he drew the curtain aside and looked out, before resuming his restless prowling. Ordinarily she would have resented his prying and this invasion of her personal space and would have told him so. However, being unsure of his reason for coming here, and made timid by his broodiness, she held her tongue.

He said, "Before they took Tup away, I had a chance to talk to him. He told me what he remembered about the two people working those stills. One trait he recalled was they were both light-footed." Now standing in front of her dresser, he looked down at the barrette he'd set there. "Where's Corrine?"

Believing it would benefit her to stick as close to the truth as possible, she said, "She's staying at the shack."

He turned and fixed his gaze on her.

"She was afraid if she didn't pull her weight, I'd kick her out, although I had assured her I wouldn't. But she was doing too much and not giving her broken arm time to heal properly. I took her out there to stay for a while."

"We drove past the old place tonight. Twice. The shack was pitch black dark both times."

"I guess she had turned in."

He came toward where she sat on the end of her bed. "If I went back out there right now, would she be there?"

"Why are you asking me all these questions?"

He captured her head between his hands, tilted it back, and brought his face close to hers. "Because I'm afraid we're gonna wind up on opposite sides of a bitter and bloody fight."

"What fight?"

"You know damn good and well what fight, Laurel. Why did I find your hair clip at the site of a still?"

She tried to look down, but he held her head, disallowing her to look away and making it impossible for her to lie to him anymore. With a catch in her voice, she implored him, "Please don't ask."

He stamped a hard kiss on her lips. "Please don't answer."

He placed his knee on the bed and took her down with him as he stretched out across it. He dug his fingers into her hair as his thumbs brushed across her cheeks. Looking into her eyes, he said, "You knew this was coming, didn't you?"

Understanding what he meant by "this," she whispered roughly, "Since that day we met on the street."

"I knew sooner than that. Also knew it was a bad idea. You're the damnedest, most complicated woman I've ever met. But I can't stop wanting you."

He kissed her again. This time it started out tender, but almost at once turned tempestuous. When she responded with the same degree of ardor, he placed one arm around her shoulders while the other encircled her waist. She folded her arm around his neck and clung.

Moaning unintelligible words of arousal, he wedged his knee between hers and pushed it up to separate her thighs, then splayed his hand over her bottom and secured her against him. She felt his want, hard and imperative, assertively male. Every feminine inclination in her being yearned to have that potency inside her.

When he began undoing the buttons down the front of her nightgown, she said faintly, "The lamp—"

"Stays on." He opened her neckline, slid his hand inside and lifted her breast clear of her nightgown. "Jesus." His warm breath drifted over her, as did his fingertips, feather-light. He lowered his head and rubbed his lips against her nipple, then swept it with his tongue.

She whispered his name and tunneled her fingers into his hair. He hadn't gotten it cut since she had met him. It was longer, thicker than then, and she loved the feel of it sliding between her fingers.

When he drew her nipple into his mouth, she closed her fingers, clutching at his hair. He tilted his hips and began moving against her. She arched up to meet the evocative thrusts.

Air stirred against her skin as he raised her nightgown up over her hip. He cradled the back of her knee in his palm, squeezed it with strong fingers, then began stroking her inner thigh. His touch was gentle but bold, dictating adjustments in position as he worked his hand up to where she lay open.

His exploring caresses brought her into stunning awareness of her own feverish, full achiness, of how wet she was. When he pressed a finger into her, she flinched. But reflexively she clenched, signaling a desire for more. He withdrew his finger, but where he touched her next caused her body to jerk in response.

He began drawing fluid circles upon that spot. When at the same time, his mouth tugged on her nipple, her body began to tingle throughout. It was wonderful. It terrified her.

She gasped, "What are you—?"

And then all control spun away from her. Her throat arched, her hips came up off the bed, seeking the cursive design of his strokes. If he stopped, she would die. If he continued, she would die. She ground against his hand in her desire to be engulfed by this tidal wave of sensation, even as she feared being drowned by it.

She panicked and cried out, "Stop!"

He did so instantly. He pulled his hand from beneath her night-gown and braced himself above her on one arm. "Laurel?"

"Don't." Using hands and heels, she madly pushed herself from beneath him, moving all the way up to the brass headboard. She crammed the hem of her nightgown into the vee of her thighs, grabbed a pillow and held it against her bared breasts. Her nipples were pinpoints of sensation.

Thatcher was looking at her with bewilderment and concern. "What?"

She couldn't speak for the currents that continued to ripple through her. Even as they ebbed, her breathing remained choppy.

"Did I hurt you?"

She shook her head and managed a gruff "No." She pulled down her nightgown to cover her legs. "I'm not like the French girls, that's all."

He frowned. "What?"

"I know about them. Derby told me. He admitted that he had been with a few women while he was over there. Only because of the horrible things he saw. I couldn't hold it against him, could I?"

He opened his mouth to speak, but she cut him off before he could.

"He told me the girls over there do things that are unheard of in America. Against the law, even. Not only prostitutes. Regular girls. I'm sure you had your share of them."

He looked down at the floor and ran his hand around the back of his neck. "Laurel—"

"Of course you did. That's none of my business, just don't expect me to be like them and do...things." She raised her chin toward the bedroom door. "Please be enough of a gentleman to leave now."

He looked like he wanted to argue, to say more, but he exhaled heavily and turned away from the bed. He picked up his hat and put it on, then pulled on his jacket. He went to the door but didn't open it. Looking back at her, he said, "I didn't finish my story."

"I don't want to hear it."

"Well, you need to."

"It doesn't concern me."

"I hope to God not. I really hope to God not, Laurel." He paused. "See, when we got back to the jail, the sheriff left straight for home. I volunteered to escort Elray inside and lock him up. Deputies were piling out of the other car. Some lit up smokes and jawed about the expedition, others went inside. I hung back with Elray and seized the opportunity to ask him in private what he'd been lying about."

"He'd told you the truth."

"But not all of it. I knew he was holding something back about Wally's murder, something that had recently come to light. He hem-hawed around but finally told me that a tip had come from none other than Gert. According to her, a competing moonshiner had done Wally in."

"That's not at all surprising."

"I didn't think so, either. But I sensed that Elray was still with-holding something. I kept pressing him about the identity of this bloodthirsty competitor, and he finally gave up what he knew."

"Which was?"

"It's a woman."

Laurel's breathing was suspended for a full fifteen seconds before Thatcher continued.

"I doubted him. I told him that either Gert was lying or she'd been misunderstood. Elray swore he was there when Gert named the culprit to his great-uncle Hiram. Naturally, I encouraged him to give me her name. And I believe he eventually would have. Except that somebody shot him through the head from the roof of the bank building."

Laurel exhaled in a burst. "Oh, my God, Thatcher."

He stared at her for several beats. "He was standing no more than a foot away from me. I saw his eyes go dead before he dropped."

She covered her mouth with a shaking hand. "I'm sorry."

"Yeah, so am I. He wouldn't have been there if it weren't for me."

He put his hand on the doorknob and addressed it rather than her. "Sheriff Amos predicted that there was going to be a bloody moonshine war. He said he could use an extra deputy and offered me the job. I turned him down, told him it didn't have anything to do with me, that it wasn't my fight, and I wouldn't be taking sides. That's the thing that changed tonight."

He reached into his pocket, took out the now familiar badge, and, looking back at her, pinned it to his lapel.

Irv was standing in the kitchen, holding the shotgun aimed at the door through which Thatcher had to pass on his way out. When he saw Irv, he stopped. The two squared off, and when Irv spotted the badge, his scowl deepened.

He said, "Badge or not, I could shoot you for trespassing."

"You could. But just so you know, I'm unarmed. To a jury that might look like murder."

"I could murder you for messing with my daughter-in-law."

"I'd be dead. Laurel would be left to suffer a scandal."

"It's Laurel now, is it?"

"Yes." Thatcher walked forward until the barrel of the shotgun was inches from his belly. "It's Laurel. And hear me, Plummer. If you and your moonshining get her killed, I'm going to kill you."

He allowed time for the words to sink in, then he stepped around the old man and left through the back door.

FORTY-FOUR

<hr>

Norma was seated on a stool at her vanity table plucking her eyebrows when Patsy sauntered into the bedroom. "You're not even dressed yet?"

Norma yanked out the last wayward hair, dropped the tweezers onto the vanity, and swiveled around. "What's your rush?"

"I'm not in a rush. The man at the bank is, and he keeps bankers' hours."

"What is the problem?"

"Something to do with a signatory card. He was expecting us at one o'clock. It's thirty minutes after."

"Can't you handle it alone? I don't want to get Arthur up just to traipse in and out of the bank."

Five minutes later, Patsy left the house more noisily than necessary, probably in a spiteful attempt to wake Arthur from his nap. But he slept peacefully in his bassinet. Earlier Norma had placed it near the open living room window that provided a gentle southern breeze.

She was returning to her bedroom when she heard an auto braking out front. Thinking that Patsy must have forgotten something, she muttered, "Not a moment's peace around here."

But when she looked out the window, her irritation evolved into apprehension. Bernie Croft was climbing out of an unfamiliar automobile. It wasn't his long touring car, but a much smaller roadster. For once, his chauffeur, whom she secretly feared, wasn't with him.

She overlapped the sides of her silky, floral-patterned robe and tied the belt tightly around her waist. It was almost back to what it had been before the baby. Her curvy figure was coveted by women and lusted after by men. Arthur had been worth the temporary bloating, but she was glad to have her notable figure restored.

As Bernie neared the door, she opened it and, with more bravado than she felt, said, "This is a surprise."

"A good one, I hope."

"A delightful one."

She stood aside; he came in.

This being his first time ever to come here, he took a look around. Like the rest of the house, the main room was shabby overall. The wallpaper was faded. The window curtain sagged unevenly. There were stains on the rug.

In these surroundings, Bernie looked all the more immaculate and imposing.

"I'm a mess," she said. "Give me a sec?"

"Of course."

Norma rushed into her bedroom and inspected herself from the different angles provided by the tri-panel mirror. Dammit, she didn't look her best. Although it was after lunchtime, she'd spent a lazy morning and hadn't even powdered her nose. There wasn't time to pin up her hair, so she fluffed it around her shoulders. Grabbing a tube of lipstick, she applied a coating, then turned toward the door as Bernie strode in and tossed his hat into a chair piled with discarded clothing.

Embarrassed over the bedroom's messiness, she made a self-conscious gesture of helplessness. "The baby keeps me so busy, I don't have time to do much else." Then around a nervous laugh, she added, "Not that I've ever been much of a housekeeper."

"You weren't expecting company."

"Especially not such important company."

His affectionate smile relaxed her. Gabe wouldn't have been fool enough to tell Bernie that she was in on their secret about Pointer's Gap.

"Would you like something? Maybe some iced tea?"

"Nothing, thank you. Except privacy."

He shut the bedroom door with his elbow. She would have preferred that it be left open a crack so she could hear Arthur if he stirred, but Bernie was having to bat away the articles of clothing hanging on the back of the door that had swung outward and swiped his face, so she let it go.

"Did you see Arthur?"

"I took a look," he said, "but you're who I came to see."

Responding to the suggestiveness of his tone, she moved her shoulder enough to make the robe slip off it. "I hope you don't mind that I didn't consult you on the baby's name. Do you like it?"

"It'll do."

"Well, I couldn't name him after you, could I?"

He laughed. "God, no."

"He has your wide brow. I hope no one notices the resemblance."

"No one will be looking for one," he said. "If they look for resemblances to anyone, it will be Gabe."

"Yes, our marriage coming so soon after his wife's disappearance may raise a few brows, but I've come up with a tragic love story." She placed the back of her wrist to her forehead and struck a dramatic pose. "Arthur's father was taken too soon, I'll say, and give a delicate sniff-sniff. He never got to see his son, but he would be pleased to know that his child's stepfather is a prominent physician, a loving man who treats Arthur as his own."

He grinned. "You've got it all planned."

"I am a planner. But I do like surprises." She leaned back against her vanity table, letting her robe fall open, baring her legs.

Appreciating the view, Bernie walked toward her. "You're no pious-looking madonna, Norma."

She fluttered her eyelashes. "Thank you for saying so."

"How is motherhood?"

"Sleep-depriving. But I adore Arthur. He's a good baby."

Bernie fingered the silk lapels of her robe, then impatiently pushed them apart. "Are you a good mother?"

"I think so. I want to be."

"I'm sure you are." He covered her breasts with his wide hands and squeezed. "With these titties? I'm sure you excel. Arthur's a lucky little bastard."

She recoiled. "Don't call him that."

"That's what he is."

"It's an ugly word."

"I agree." He looked up from her breasts into her eyes. "So is *whore*."

Her lips parted in shock.

"And that's what you are, Norma."

"I'm not!"

"The word fits you to a tee."

His squeezes had become painful pinches. She pushed his grasping hands away and pulled her robe together. "You had better leave. Gabe wouldn't like knowing that—"

"That I was fucking you on the night he called me in a panic over killing his wife?"

"He never has to know about us."

"Maybe he should."

"No! Anyway, that phase of my life is over. I got what I wanted."

"A well-to-do husband with a lovely home."

"Yes."

"Respectability."

"Yes."

"Gabe hasn't married you yet."

"Soon, though."

"But the blushing bride-to-be welcomes me, naked except for that cheap, tacky robe and red lipstick."

"Before I knew you were going to be so horrid."

"You thought we would end our affair on a sweeter note."

"Yes."

"I hate to disappoint."

He pulled back his fist and slammed it into her face.

The pain was so excruciating she didn't even feel the center mirror of her vanity shattering against her back when she fell into it. He hit her in the face again, this time hard enough to knock her to the floor. She groped for the vanity stool to try and pull herself up and attempt some kind of defense, but he kicked the stool out of her reach.

She crawled on all fours in an effort to escape his hammering fists and the vile things he was saying to her and about her. Worse, he didn't shout the insults in outrage. He spoke them in a soft but repugnant parody of sweet nothings.

He kicked her in the ribs. Then he stopped and stood over her, breathing heavily. She thought that perhaps that was the end of it. He'd vented his rage. He was through.

But then he stamped on her, and the pain was unimaginable. She screamed.

He pulled her up by her hair and pushed her face-first onto the bed. He held her head down with one hand and used the other to shove her robe up above her waist.

He clamped the tops of her thighs and forced them apart. She tried to scream again, but the mattress beneath her battered face muffled the sound. She couldn't draw in sufficient air through either her nose or her split and bleeding lips. She feared suffocating.

But in a black and distant part of her mind, she wished she would.

His thrusts were brutal. His hands held her with bruising strength. His language was obscene, vicious, abasing. It seemed to go on forever.

Then, heaving and hot, he collapsed on top of her, leaden, compressing her lungs, making spears of the ribs he'd broken. But he lifted his hand from her head, allowing her to turn it aside and try to suck in air through her mouth, but nothing was functioning right. His sweat had combined with the cloying scent of his cologne, making her gag. She choked on blood.

Finally he pushed off of her. Standing beside the bed, he righted himself. She heard the rustle of his clothing, the jingle of his belt buckle, the clink of his watch fob. The floorboards creaked under his weight as he crossed the room toward the door. It whooshed open, the clothes hanging on the back of it swishing.

In a voice that was eerily detached, he said, "*If* you have the misfortune of surviving, and *if* you breathe a word of this, I'll tie that brat of yours in a sack and throw him in the Brazos."

He walked out of the bedroom. He left the house.

Norma was too benumbed to move.

FORTY-FIVE

———⋘◉⋙———

Laurel baked all day. Recollections of what had happened between Thatcher and her last night were persistent distractions, and her feelings about them ranged from delirium to despair. Work helped to keep those troubling thoughts from swamping her, but they lurked at the fringes of her mind, teasing and tormenting.

While her last batch of pies was cooling, she delivered Clyde Martin's order to the café. By dusk when the O'Connors showed up, she had pies boxed and ready for them.

"Where's the whiskey?" Davy asked.

"We're fresh out. There's been some trouble. Our distiller had to shut down and relocate in a hurry. I'm hopeful he'll do a run tonight, but at this point, I just don't know. In the meantime, we're in the pie business exclusively."

The twins took the news with a surprising lack of despondency. "Don't worry yourself, lovely Laurel," Davy said. "In view of our recent shortfall, we've been courting another supplier to keep us in moonshine should another shortage occur. Which it has. Once we're up and running again—"

"Wait. What other supplier? Who?"

"Now, Laurel, you know better than to ask," Mike said. "We can't give you his name any more than we'd give him yours. It's all very discreet."

"Is he reliable?"

"Yes," Davy said, "but reliability is expensive."

"How expensive?"

They told her the terms of the deal they'd negotiated, and they were reasonable. Nevertheless, she was leery. "I don't like having to buy moonshine in order to sell it."

"A temporary necessity," Mike said.

His brother added, "And a smaller profit is better than none."

"Is his whiskey any good?"

"We thought so," Mike said.

His glazed eyes indicated that he had had more than a sampling, which reassured Laurel not at all. Dividing a stern look between them, she said, "You're sure of this?"

Davy answered for both. "We wouldn't let you down, sweetheart."

Reluctantly, she counted out the currency they would need to purchase the moonshine. "Just this once."

Before they set off, she pleaded with them, "Please, please be careful. A young man was killed last night right in front of the sheriff's office."

"Ah, we heard about that. Tragic for sure. But it's rumored that it was a family dispute. Nothing to do with us."

She could have argued that it wasn't any ol' family's dispute, it was a Johnson family dispute, and that if they discovered that it was her still where their kinsman Tup had been maimed, the clan would be gunning for her.

The less the twins knew of that, the better. She also didn't want them knowing that she was consorting with a lawman. Further discussion of Elray's slaying might lead to mention of Thatcher, a subject best avoided.

But no sooner had she thought that than Mike said, "Did you hear about your Good Samaritan Mr. Hutton?"

"What about him?"

"Ah, he was talking to the young man when it happened. A second shot missed Hutton by a hair."

Davy picked up. "But he took off running to the building where the shots came from. Couldn't be stopped, they said."

Laurel's hands had gone clammy. "Who said?" she asked huskily.

"The sheriff's deputies trying to hold him back, because he wasn't even armed. But that didn't stop him sprinting to the bank building. He was mad to catch the shooter. Those there said he never uttered a word, but that the look in his eyes was positively feral."

"He didn't catch him?" she asked.

"No," Mike said. "Lucky for the murdering Johnson."

Laurel put up a disinterested front, but she couldn't wait for the twins to be on their way. After they left, she felt more forlorn than she had since Derby's suicide and Pearl's death. She'd had no control over either of those life-changing events.

But rather than surrender to feelings of defeat, she had resolved never to be that defenseless against fate again. With sheer determination, she had persevered, had built a life and livelihood for herself.

Now, she felt control of that also slipping away.

Recent events had played out on their own, without her knowledge or oversight. Irv had been wounded. A man had lost his arm. A boy had lost his life. Ernie and Corrine and the stills were unaccounted for. Where had her tight grip on control been when all that was happening?

And when she was with Thatcher? Last night he'd come to her after what surely had been one of the worst experiences of his life. But his concern had been for her, not for himself. She recalled the sorrow in his eyes when he'd told her about his mentor's death and Elray Johnson's murder. She also remembered the determination in his demeanor when he'd pinned on the badge.

Some might mistake his reticence for indifference, or a steeliness against emotion, but he felt things more deeply than anybody she'd ever met.

She'd fought her attraction to him every step of the way, but last night she'd been helpless against it. She'd been overtaken by the look and feel of him, the desperation in his voice when he'd said, "Please don't answer."

Unlike anything she'd ever experienced, the groundswell of sexual sensation brought on by his caresses had completely undone her. The control had belonged to him, not to her, and that loss of herself had been terrifying.

But also thrilling. If the climb had been that incredible, what would the cresting have felt like? She couldn't help but wonder, and regret—

"Laurel?"

Nearly jumping out of her skin, she whipped around to find Irv standing behind her and dressed to go out. "You were a million miles away, girl. What were you thinking about?"

"Nothing."

"Huh. Didn't look like it to me." He watched her for a moment. "I threatened to shoot him. If you want me to, I will."

Ignoring that, she patted her pocket to make certain she had her pistol. "Are you ready?"

———

Laurel insisted on driving even though they were taking Irv's truck. He gave in way too easily, leaving Laurel to believe that even though the bullet wound had closed and healed well enough for him to leave his bed, his arm remained infirm.

He brought Ernie's map with him, although he claimed to know where his partner had likely relocated their stills. "He showed me the place once, bragged on it being nearly perfect like our other spot."

"Is it on your property?"

"Barely." When she shot him a doubtful glance, he added defensively, "Barely counts."

They drove for half an hour. When they saw a flicker of firelight in the distance, Laurel slowed down. "They may start shooting before they realize it's us."

"Honk the horn three times. That's the signal."

The new location had the natural attributes of the original. Ernie and Corrine had both stills reassembled, and both were cooking. Over cups of coffee they told Laurel and Irv about the harrowing night they had spent moving everything.

Ernie said, "Soon's we got the trap off that fella's arm and put him in the hole, I ran for my truck, brought it to the site, and started loading everything up. Even with a gimp arm, she did aw'right," he said, looking over at Corrine.

"I like to've wore myself out," she said. "But, in a way, it was good we had to take everything apart and put it back together here. I learned a lot. But I don't want to do it again anytime soon."

"We wasn't sure you'd get the map," Ernie said. "It was her idea to leave it."

Laurel told them about her seeing the convoy from the shack and racing over the hill to beat it. "Although, at the time, I didn't know it was lawmen. It could just as well have been rival moonshiners. Imagine my shock to see the place deserted and not knowing what had happened to you."

She finished telling the rest of it. "I can't explain what inspired me to get the primer. Irv figured out what the drawing meant."

Ernie tossed the dregs of his coffee into the dirt and watched as it was absorbed. "Was the thief I trapped a Johnson?"

Laurel nodded. "He and a younger cousin."

"He die in the hidey-hole?"

"Miraculously, no, but his arm was amputated."

He nodded solemnly. "Then he pro'bly won't be stealing no more."

"Probably. But that was a big price to pay for a few crates of moonshine."

"Yep, it was, Miss Laurel. But given the chance, he'd've killed us without blinkin'."

Thatcher had reasoned the same. She said, "It's believed that was his intention."

"What about the cousin who ran out on him?"

"Shot and killed last night," Laurel said. "They feel for sure by his own kin." She related the circumstances, but didn't refer to Thatcher by name, only as "a deputy" who was seeking information about Wally's murder.

As though reading her mind, Corrine asked, "You seen any more of Mr. Hutton?"

Irv harrumphed and kept his head down, poking at the logs in the cookfire with a stick. Laurel said, "He came by one evening to check on Irv's progress." Quickly changing the subject, she asked Ernie about their renewed production. "Can you step it up?"

"We brought six barrels of mash with us that were close to ready. The rest, we had to pour out. Luckily we had enough supplies to mix up more yesterday and today."

"We've got two crates you can take with you," Corrine said with pride. "I got 'em ready myself while Ernie was mixing the mash."

Two crates wouldn't have excited Laurel a few days ago, but now she was glad to know she had them. She didn't tell the others about the O'Connors buying from another moonshiner, knowing that they, particularly Irv, who mistrusted the twins, would disapprove. *She* disapproved.

They discussed more about the operation, then Laurel expressed her misgivings. "Tup and Elray Johnson found our stills. How well hidden are you here, Ernie?"

"Pretty good, I reckon, or I wouldn't've moved us here." He glanced around at the others. "But about them Johnsons finding us..."

"What?" Irv said.

"Just seems unlikely is all," Ernie said. Without looking directly at anyone, he added, "Unless they were keeping an eye on the shack."

"Why would they be doing that?" Laurel asked.

He shrugged his bony shoulders. "If somebody was to've tipped 'em off."

Laurel's ears began to roar as Thatcher's words came back to her in a surge. *Elray swore he was there when Gert told his great-uncle Hiram who the culprit was*. The culprit meaning the female moonshiner.

Gert knew Laurel was dealing in whiskey. She had been there when Laurel and Lefty had sealed their deal. She'd been livid to learn that Laurel had sheltered Corrine. Narrowed down, that would be in one of two dwellings: their house in town, or the shack.

If it had been discovered that Corrine was living in the shack, if she'd been seen going on foot over the hills, if she'd been followed to the still, Gert would have had the perfect setup for revenge against both Corrine and Laurel.

Good God. Everything that had happened in the last forty-eight hours was a consequence of Laurel's going to the roadhouse that day. Thatcher had said he was afraid they would wind up on opposite sides of a fight. He wasn't afraid of it at all. He already knew that she was moonshining, and last night he'd warned her that, thanks to the vengeful Gert, the Johnsons did, too.

"Corrine, things have become dangerous. You have to come back to town with Irv and me," she said. "You're too far from the shack to be going back and forth on foot."

"Ernie and me done talked about it," the girl said. "I'll stay here and help him do runs till we catch up."

"Ernie?" Irv asked. "What do you think of that plan?"

He shifted self-consciously. "When she ain't blabbing, she's handy."

Laurel came to her feet. "It doesn't matter what Ernie thinks. It matters what I think."

The three of them looked up at her like she'd lost her mind, and very possibly she had. She walked away from them, pressing her fingers against her temples where her pulse was beating fast and hard. There had to be a way out of this, not to save her own skin, but to protect these three and the twins.

The logical solution to all their problems would be to shut down completely. But then what?

She couldn't stop Ernie and Irv from carrying on as they had before her interference. Corrine, having shown an enthusiasm for making corn liquor, would likely join them.

The twins were young, daring, and resourceful. They obviously had other contacts in the illegal liquor trade. With their winning personalities, they would prosper.

She would bake and sell pies.

The dreariest part of that prospect would be that Gert would continue to thrive, turning victims of mistreatment and misfortune into prostitutes for her gain.

Laurel slowly came back around to three pairs of eyes looking at her expectantly. Corrine would actually be safer out here than she would be in town where she was much more likely to be seen by someone who would return her to Gert. But this was hardly a Garden of Eden.

"Corrine, are you sure you want to stay here?"

"Oh, I don't mind at'all. I'm enjoyin' bein' out in the open."

Irv and Laurel looked to Ernie for his opinion. "She's proved herself to be right smart," he said. "Nimble and quick, too."

"All right," Laurel said, but not without reluctance. "For the present, she stays. Please get the crates loaded into the truck."

Although Irv couldn't be of much help, he accompanied Ernie.

Laurel stayed behind with Corrine. "I'll be back the day after tomorrow." She glanced over at the tent. "By then, if you've changed your mind about your situation here, you can come back to town with me. You'll have a home with Irv and me."

"I know what you're askin' without coming right out with it. Ernie treats me regular, not like a whore."

"You were never a whore, Corrine. You were a victim of circumstance."

"Well, anyway, Ernie has his cranky moments, usually over my jabberin', but he's nice. Even without me asking, he dug a latrine for my private use."

Laurel tried to contain her smile. "That was thoughtful of him."

The men came back for the other crate. As soon as they were out of earshot again, Laurel said, "Corrine, the morning after Irv got shot, and you and I were having breakfast, you talked to me about Gert and how upset she'd been with Wally Johnson for the beating he gave you."

"Upset? I'll say. She carried on something fierce."

Laurel remembered what Corrine had told her that day, but she wanted to hear it from her again. "What made Gert so angry?"

"'Cause I looked like roadkill, and she wouldn't be making any money off me, and money is all she cares about.

"She was so mad at Wally, her face turned purple. She hollered cuss words, threatened him with a meat cleaver, and ordered him to get his ugly self out of her place."

Laurel patted the girl's shoulder. "Ernie needs help, and you seem content to be here. But I'm worried about your safety."

"You got no call to be."

"Yes, I do, Corrine. Believe me."

"Ernie's protective."

"I'm sure. But he may not always be around. You need to protect yourself."

"I will, Miss Laurel. I promise."

"Well, I want to make sure of that."

FORTY-SIX

The landlady called Thatcher away from the supper buffet to the telephone in the hall. "Keep it short," she said as she handed him the earpiece. "There's others who use it, too, you know."

Thinking it might be Trey Hobson at long last, he leaned into the mouthpiece mounted on the wall. "This is Thatcher."

Bill Amos said, "Can you get over to Doc Perkins's office?"

"Right now?"

"Right now."

"Who's sick?"

"Just come. Don't say anything to anybody."

The sheriff disconnected. Thatcher hung up, stared at the telephone in puzzlement for several seconds, then, responding to Bill's urgency, ducked back into the dining room to take his hat from the rack.

The crabby Mrs. May said, "Are you eatin' or not?"

"Not." He was aware of Chester Landry's interest in his abrupt departure, but he didn't acknowledge the man as he rushed out. He feared the emergency pertained to Daisy Amos.

Having to walk several blocks, he was winded by the time he reached the professional building on Main Street where he'd been told the elderly doctor had a clinic that took up half the third floor. It was past quitting time for anyone else who had office space there, but the main entrance was unlocked. Thatcher went in and climbed the stairs two at a time.

A door with the doc's name printed on it opened into a waiting room where a woman was seated near a small table, smoking a cigarette. She was unkempt. There were blood smears on her dress. Her eyes were red-rimmed, her expression harsh. "Who are you?"

He took off his hat. "Thatcher Hutton."

"What are you doing here?"

Before he could reply, Bill Amos opened a door with "Examination Room" stenciled on it. "I called him," he said to the woman, then hitched his head, indicating for Thatcher to join him in a small room with glass-fronted supply cabinets on two walls. The center was dominated by the examination table.

"Through here," Bill said as he led Thatcher through yet another room into an operating room. He drew up short when he saw the table on which a female person lay.

A white sheet covered her from toes to chin. All that showed was a mass of thick, dark hair and her face, which looked like it had had a head-on collision with a locomotive.

Wearing a white lab coat, Doc Perkins was washing his hands at an industrial-size porcelain sink. Thatcher recognized the strong smell of antiseptic from his days in the army hospital.

Bill said, "That's Norma Blanchard."

Stunned, Thatcher remembered the pretty, shapely woman with the saucy walk whom he'd seen going into Gabe Driscoll's house late one night. "She dead?"

"As of when I called you. I wanted you to see her to get an idea of what we're dealing with here."

Thatcher wanted to object to the plural pronoun. In his mind, he'd taken a stand against the likes of the violent Johnsons, but he hadn't been sworn in as a deputy yet, and he wasn't wearing the badge. However, now wasn't the time to go into all that.

Thatcher said, "Who's the woman outside?"

"Miss Blanchard's sister. Patsy Kemp."

She was no doubt the woman who'd chauffeured Norma to Gabe Driscoll's house, but Thatcher hadn't gotten a good look at her face that night and wouldn't have recognized her.

Bill said, "I asked her to stay, so we could talk to her about the assault."

"Assault? This wasn't an accident?"

"No. Mrs. Kemp brought Norma to Dr. Perkins around four o'clock. She was barely alive. He evaluated her condition and called me right away. She never regained consciousness." To the doctor, he said, "Give him a run-down. No medical jargon, please. Plain talk."

The doctor unhooked the wire stems of his eyeglasses from behind his ears, removed them, and began polishing them with the towel he'd used to dry his hands.

"Her nose is broken. Pulverized, actually. Fractured cheekbone, broken jawbone, three loose teeth. A flap of scalp about an inch in diameter had been ripped away. I sewed it back, but that's the least of it."

He replaced his glasses and looked down at the draped figure. "The back of her torso appears to have been pummeled repeatedly, I suspect with fists. I also tweezed out several shards of mirror glass that had sliced through her garment." He pointed to a silky dressing gown wadded up in a chair.

"I detected three broken ribs. Others may have been cracked. She might have survived, in time, and under the care of physicians better trained and skilled at treating the more serious of her injuries."

"What were they?"

"She has a sizable bruise and swelling above her left kidney. It's so precisely placed, it appears the organ was targeted. Perhaps by the heel of a shoe. I suspect the blunt force caused internal hemorrhaging. She bled to death."

The doctor's eyes looked apologetic behind the round lenses of his glasses. "I did what I could, but I'm a country doctor, unqualified to deal with something like this. Perhaps Gabe Driscoll would have been a better choice."

Bill glanced at Thatcher, then turned to the doctor. "Tell him the rest."

The doctor bowed his head and addressed the floor. "She was raped. Barbarically. Considerable damage was done to tissue."

The men stood silent, looking neither at each other, nor at Norma Blanchard's still form. After a moment, the doctor covered her face.

In a quiet voice, Bill said, "Her injuries are of such a sensitive nature, I'd like to keep the details between us, doc."

"Of course."

"Do you mind if we use your waiting room to talk to Mrs. Kemp?"

"Not at all. I'll stay with Miss Blanchard until the ambulance arrives."

"Ambulance?" Thatcher asked.

"I want the autopsy done in Dallas," Bill said. "They have a lab, forensic specialists."

Thatcher took a last look at the sheet-draped figure then followed Bill from the surgery and back out into the waiting room. Patsy Kemp hadn't changed her position since Thatcher had come in.

Bill pulled a chair over closer to her and motioned for Thatcher to do the same. When they were seated, Bill said, "I'm awful sorry this terrible thing has happened, Mrs. Kemp."

She gave him a curt nod.

"This is Thatcher Hutton."

"So he said."

"He's new to my department. We'd like to ask you some questions, gain as much information as we can, in an effort to catch the person who assaulted your sister."

She sat stony-faced.

Bill asked softly, "Where's her baby?"

"I dropped him off with a lady I buy fresh eggs from. She has a baby close to Arthur's age. She'll wet-nurse him and look after him until I can pick him up."

"Good." Bill paused, then said, "You know the extent of what was done to your sister?"

"I found her, remember?"

"Do you know who attacked her?"

"No."

"At any point, was she conscious?"

"Conscious but out of her head."

"Did she say—"

"Did you see her mouth? She couldn't talk."

Bill eased away from her, as though sensing, as Thatcher did, that pressuring her wasn't the tack to take. "Tell us what happened today."

"Do we have to do this now?"

"Do you want us to catch the man responsible?"

Bill won the stare-off. She took a deep breath. "Today started out like any other. I did chores while Norma tended to Arthur."

"You told me earlier that the assault took place while you were away from the house."

She told them about receiving a telephone call from First State Bank. "I don't remember the man's name. He asked me to come in and take care of a matter. Something I needed to sign. Arthur was down for a nap. Norma was primping. It was easier to go without her than to wait for her to get ready. She was very particular about her appearance."

She glanced toward the examination room. Her eyes turned watery. "Norma wouldn't have wanted to live looking like that. Jesus God." She shook a cigarette from her pack. When she had difficulty striking the match, Thatcher struck it for her and held it to the tip of the cigarette.

She gave him a nod of thanks.

The men allowed her time to compose herself and take a few puffs before Bill asked, "What time did you leave the house?"

"One-thirty. I was trying to beat it to the bank before it closed. But when I got there, nobody knew anything about a phone call. There wasn't a problem with my account. I didn't know what to make of the mix-up, but rather than waste a trip to town, I stopped in Logan's for some groceries." Her voice trembled. "I'll never forgive myself for not going straight home."

Thatcher noticed that her hand was shaking when she flicked an ash into the ashtray she was holding on her knee.

"I could hear Arthur screaming the minute I pulled up to the house. Norma wouldn't let him whimper without picking him up, so I knew something was wrong. I ran into the house. Arthur was still in his bassinet, where he'd been when I'd left. He was wet and hungry, but otherwise okay.

"Norma..." She choked up and had to force the words out. "She was facedown on her bed. She wasn't moving. There was blood. I would have thought she was dead, except that she was making sounds like...like...I don't know...a wounded animal."

She took another drag off her cigarette. "I'm not sure she knew it was me who was handling her. She flailed her arms, trying to fight me off. I liked to have never gotten her into the car."

"No sign of who had been there?"

"Don't you think I would have told you by now?"

"Was anything missing that you noticed?"

"I didn't take the time to look, sheriff."

"I ask only because if the house had been ransacked, it could have been a vagrant."

"The house hadn't been ransacked."

"You sister's bedroom?"

"It was a mess, but it always is. The vanity stool was overturned, the mirror had been shattered. Glass was everywhere."

"When you left for your errand, had you locked the front door?"

"Yes."

"Was it locked when you returned?"

She had to think for a second, then said, "No."

"Was the lock damaged?"

"I think I would have noticed if it had been broken."

"Then it's possible that Miss Blanchard knew her attacker and let him into the house."

She bent her head down and massaged her forehead.

Bill cleared his throat. "Where is Mr. Kemp?"

"His name is Dennis. He's in Colorado."

"What's he do there?"

"Sets dynamite. He blasts through mountains for railroad and highway construction." She raised her head and gave Bill a baleful look. "Is this important?"

"When did you last hear from him?"

"Barking up that tree will be a waste of your time. Every two months I go to see him. He hasn't come home since Norma moved in with us."

"They didn't get along?"

"Couldn't stand each other. She called him a bore. He called her silly and conceited." In a mumble, she added, "Among other things."

"If there's so much animosity between them, why did she come to live with you?"

She hesitated, looking resentful of the question. Finally she said, "Because the man she had been living with in Austin kicked her out for cheating on him. She had no money, no job, nowhere else to go."

Bill asked her to write down the name of the company her husband worked for. She did. The sheriff tucked it into his breast pocket.

"What about the father of her son?"

She smoked, saying nothing.

Bill prompted. "Had Norma been asking him for money? Demanding that he marry her? Something like that?"

Having smoked her cigarette down, she ground it out. "I wouldn't know, Sheriff Amos, because I don't know who Arthur's father is."

She caught the skeptical look Thatcher and Bill exchanged. "You don't believe that? It's true. Swear to God, I don't know." She turned to Thatcher. "You're young and good-looking. Were you acquainted with my sister?"

"No, ma'am. But I saw her once."

"Did your eyes pop out of your head?"

He gave a shy smile, and she snuffled.

"Norma had that effect on men." Turning back to the sheriff, her momentary mirth disappeared. "She used her looks to her advantage. She had a lot of men. But to be dragging her name through the dirt while her body is still warm just doesn't sit right with me."

Before Bill could respond, Thatcher said, "It isn't right. But neither is a brutal, fatal assault. What Sheriff Amos is trying to do is find out who did it. The more information you give him, the better chance he has of catching the man and seeing him punished."

Patsy's chest caved in a little. Her hostility cooled. As she thought over what Thatcher had said, she picked at the loose stitching on the handbag in her lap. "Norma had been carrying on an affair with Dr. Gabe Driscoll."

She looked at Bill and Thatcher in turn. He wondered if she noted that neither was surprised to hear this.

Bill asked, "For how long?"

"Close to a year."

"Where did they rendezvous?"

"He always came to the house. Or did. He hasn't been there since the night his wife disappeared. Norma wasn't happy about not seeing him."

"Up until Mrs. Driscoll's disappearance, how often did they meet?"

"Two or three times a week. He would come by while he was out making rural calls. But he isn't Arthur's father. Norma was already pregnant when she met him. She only passed the baby off as his to reel him in. She set her sights and went after him."

Watching her closely, Bill tugged at the corner of his mustache. "Did they conspire to get rid of Mrs. Driscoll?"

"I don't think Norma had anything to do with it."

"Mrs. Kemp—"

"I'll tell you why," she said, cutting Bill off. "Norma didn't consider Gabe's missus competition. She had convinced herself that Gabe would ultimately choose her and Arthur over 'that fat German cow,' as she called her.

"She had big plans for Gabe to move her and Arthur into that large, pretty house. As his wife, she would become a society maven. I told her she was delusional. But I also saw how besotted Gabe was with her." She shrugged. "Maybe he gave in to her impatience."

"Gabe claims to have been at your house twice on the day his wife went missing. Once in the afternoon, once late that night."

"He was, but not to help with Arthur's breech birth, because Arthur was already a month old. Gabe came that afternoon. He held the baby for half an hour and spent another thirty minutes in the bedroom with Norma. They were lovey-dovey. She begged him to stay longer and was pouty when he left.

"When he came back that night, it was a different story. He was frantic. I mean berserk. Batshit crazy. I had to deal with him myself because Norma was out."

"Out where?"

Thatcher could tell she was reluctant to answer, but finally she did. "There was someone else. Before Gabe, and the whole time she was with him."

"The baby's father?"

"That would be my guess, but I don't know. It was a very secretive affair. She always went to him. She was with him that evening of Mrs. Driscoll's disappearance. When she got back home, Gabe was there, but he was too distraught even to ask where she'd been."

"What time did she get home?"

"Midnight or better. Honestly, I believe Gabe is rather thick. She smelled of sex. He's a doctor, right?" She snorted with derision. "Arthur was a hefty newborn. Any fool could see he was too big to be six weeks early, as Norma claimed. But Gabe never raised a question about his size or seemed to doubt that he was the father. In my opinion he's a loser."

Bill said, "But you covered his lie about the breech birth."

"I did, yes. Norma insisted that we back him up, for Arthur's sake, she said."

"Did Gabe kill his wife, Mrs. Kemp?"

"I swear to you I don't know."

"Did you ever question Norma about the convenient timing of Mrs. Driscoll's disappearance?"

"No," she replied in her wheezy smoker's voice, "I didn't want to know the answer."

Bill sighed. "When two people share a secret like that, it tends to erode the relationship, whether it's between siblings, husband and wife, illicit lovers. If it turns out that Gabe Driscoll assaulted your sister today—"

"Then all bets are off. I'll dance naked at his hanging. But..." She shook another cigarette from the pack. Thatcher lit it for her.

Bill said, "You were about to say, Mrs. Kemp?"

"I'm not sure Gabe has it in him to do that. I told you she was pouty when he left that afternoon. It was because he wouldn't make love to her. Our walls are thin. I could hear her trying to seduce him. He refused, saying it was too soon after the baby for them to have sex. So the way she was violated today just doesn't seem like him. Murder maybe, but not that."

"Not even if he'd found out the baby isn't his?" Bill asked. "Maybe he realized that he'd been duped, suckered into killing his wife and his own unborn child for another man's. That could have motivated him to fly into a blind rage."

She said, "Then they ought to hang the bastard twice."

Fifteen minutes later, the ambulance from Dallas arrived. Bill directed it to the back of the building, where Norma Blanchard's body was loaded. Patsy was going to follow in her car. She told Bill that her husband had family in Dallas, and that she had arranged to stay with them until her sister's body could be released for burial.

"Please remember that you're a material witness in two crimes," Bill said. "I'll need to reach you."

"I understand." She gave him her relative's telephone number and address.

As they watched her departure, Bill said to Thatcher, "She could also face charges of obstruction if Mila Driscoll suffered the fate I suspect. But I didn't want to tell her that."

They returned to the doctor's office so Dr. Perkins could sign off on departmental paperwork. Thatcher remained in the waiting room. He noticed that Patsy had left her last cigarette smoking in the ashtray. He went over and stubbed it out, then he and Bill left the office together and started downstairs.

Bill slipped a small stoppered bottle into the pocket of his jacket, and when he saw that Thatcher noticed, he said, "For Daisy."

"Is she all right?"

"For the past few days, she's had a stomachache. Doc said this would settle it."

Thinking of the picture gallery in the Amoses' foyer, Thatcher said, "I wonder if Mrs. Kemp has a picture of Norma."

"Lots. I saw them in the house when I went to interview them."

"That's good. When the boy gets older, he'll want to know what his mother looked like." Bill gave him an inquiring look, but he pretended not to see it and returned to the topic of the attack on Norma Blanchard. "I've been thinking about something."

"Don't hold back."

"A man in a blind rage would have killed her outright. Whoever attacked that woman wanted to punish her to death. There's a difference."

Bill took that in, then gave him a wry smile. "Don't talk yourself out of that badge, Thatcher. You were born for this." He continued on his way down the stairs. Thatcher followed.

As they exited the building Bill cursed under his breath. Bernie Croft was between them and the sheriff's car, waiting for his dog to finish peeing against a utility pole.

FORTY-SEVEN

***

H ello, Bill. Hutton."

"Bernie," Bill said.

Thatcher didn't believe that the mayor's being here at this precise time was coincidental with his dog's bladder. He was right. When the dog lowered his leg and wandered off to sniff at a patch of weeds growing against the side of the building, Croft strolled along the boardwalk to join them.

He looked Thatcher over. "I heard you actively participated in the raid on Lefty's."

"Who'd you hear that from?"

"A mutual acquaintance of ours." Thatcher figured he referred to Chester Landry but didn't remark on it.

Croft turned to Bill. "This young man is practically your shadow these days."

"Thatcher is no one's shadow, Bernie. But if I can twist his arm, I'm going to sign him on as a deputy."

"That will raise eyebrows."

"It's certainly raised yours. Now, if you'll excuse us."

"I saw the arrival of an ambulance from my office window."

He looked across the street toward the second-story windows on the facade of city hall. Bill had told Thatcher that those office windows overlooking Main were to Bernie what the pope's balcony was to His Eminence.

He was saying, "If I read the insignia correctly, the ambulance came from Dallas. Who was it for?"

"Doctor-patient privilege, Bernie," Bill said. "You know I can't divulge the—"

"Was it someone I know? Why was he shuttled off in secrecy behind the building? Was it the Johnson boy? What was his name again?"

"Elray," Thatcher said.

Croft turned to him. "Elray, yes. I heard you tried to chase down his assassin. In fact, you seem to be Johnny-on-the-spot since you came to Foley. One can find you anywhere there's disorder."

Thatcher said, "That seems to make you nervous. I wonder how come."

Croft puffed up like an adder, but he faced Bill again. "You had just as well tell me who was in that ambulance. I'll wring it out of Dr. Perkins anyway. Save me the climb upstairs."

Bill relented. "A local woman was assaulted." Without going into detail, he told Croft what had happened.

"Jesus Christ," he said. "Who was she?"

"I'm keeping it quiet, Bernie, out of respect for the lady and her family's privacy."

"Very sensitive of you, Bill. But other ladies should be made aware that there's a rapist in our midst, don't you think?" He gave Thatcher a significant look.

Thatcher adjusted his stance to a more confrontational one. "Why don't you just come out and say it, Croft?"

"Say what?"

"Accuse me of preying on women."

"I already did."

"And it didn't stick."

"Gentlemen," Bill said quietly. "Let's not draw an audience, please."

The only audience they'd drawn that Thatcher could see was Hennessy, Croft's so-called chauffeur. Cap pulled low, he was leaning against the side of the mayor's car parked across the street, his posture a little too indolent to be genuine, his entire aspect one of menace.

Thatcher hadn't made out like he'd noticed him lurking there, but he was well aware.

Croft was adding to his list of complaints against the sheriff. "I just don't understand you. It's obvious to everyone except you, even to men in your department, that your judgment has become clouded of late. Mine hasn't. I'm responsible for the welfare of this town's citizenry, particularly those who can't defend themselves, our children, our female population."

"Oh, for godsake, Bernie," Bill snapped, "save the speech. The victim's name was Norma Blanchard."

The mayor reacted with a start.

"Obviously you knew her," Bill said.

"Not personally, but I knew of her. The pretty sister, correct?"

"She was pretty before today."

"Where was she attacked?"

"In her home."

Again he gave Thatcher a pointed glance. "Someone looking for a room to let?"

Thatcher moved in closer, wanting badly to knock this pompous hypocrite on his ass.

But Bill motioned for him to stay as he was, and for the sheriff's sake, Thatcher let the insult pass.

Bill said, "A vagrant is a possibility, of course. But initial indications are that she knew her assailant and let him inside the house. Her infant was asleep in the front room, so it was someone she trusted."

The mayor drew a frown and absently toyed with his watch chain.

"What is it, Bernie?"

He stopped fiddling with the chain, but his frown remained. "Something I wish I didn't know."

"About Miss Blanchard?"

"Yes, but I was told in the strictest confidence."

"If it's pertinent to the crime, then—"

"I'm not saying that," Croft said in a rush. "Not at all. It probably has no relevance whatsoever."

"Tell me and let me decide."

He sighed with seeming reluctance. "On the day following Mila Driscoll's disappearance, I spoke to Gabe by telephone. Mrs. Driscoll's relatives hadn't arrived yet, so while your deputy was using the bathroom, Gabe called me on the sly and confessed that he'd had a liaison with that Blanchard girl."

"Why would he have confessed that to you?"

"Because I had been his staunch proponent there in your office. I had promised to continue standing by him until his wife was found or her fate determined. Therefore, he felt I deserved to know that he harbored what he called 'a shameful secret.'

"I was thinking in terms of unsettled gambling debts, or blackmail, or fleecing hypochondriacs. Something like that. I never would have dreamed that Gabe Driscoll's dirty secret was a sexual fling. He's such a cold fish. I can't imagine him humping anybody, can you?"

Thatcher could tell that Bill was offended by Croft's terminology, but he pounced on the primary matter. "After that rousing sermon you just delivered about your civic responsibility, you tell me *this*? Why didn't you come to me with it before now? You didn't think an affair with another woman was pertinent to the sudden disappearance of the man's wife?"

"Calm down. It wasn't an *affair*. It was one afternoon of sexual congress that occurred the day after he and the Blanchard woman met."

"Only that one time?"

"That's what he told me. Tearfully. With contrition. Soon after this breach of his marriage vows, Mrs. Driscoll conceived. Gabe regarded her pregnancy as a sign of forgiveness from on high.

"Even though Mrs. Driscoll was blissfully unaware of his transgression, he atoned by lavishing attention on her. Pampered her with foot rubs. Picnics in her favorite spot near Pointer's Gap. Flowers and other romantic folderol. He never strayed again. I made him swear it on the Bible."

Mrs. Kemp had told Thatcher and Bill a completely different story, but it wasn't his place to cite that.

Bill said, "Although it's late in coming, thank you for this information, Bernie."

"I doubt it's relevant to what happened to the girl. If the rumor mill is credible, encounters such as the one she had with Gabe were not a rarity, but commonplace."

"Nevertheless, she suffered a brutal attack. I ask again for your discretion."

"Of course, Bill, of course. Good night." Croft tapped his thigh. The dog trotted up and rejoined his master, tongue lolling, tail wagging, ready to be off. As Croft came even with Thatcher, he said, "*Deputy* Hutton, don't think for a moment that badge on your chest makes me in any way nervous."

"I don't. But I don't wear it all the time. That's when you should be nervous."

Thatcher watched Hennessy hold open the backseat door of the town car for Croft and the bird dog. "Your mayor is the one who's got a shadow."

Bill looked over at the town car, then motioned Thatcher toward his own vehicle.

"I don't mind walking."

"I've got to go to the office anyway and finish the paperwork I started with Doc Perkins. But do you mind if I make a quick stop at home so I can give Daisy the stomach medication?"

"Not at all."

Once they were on their way, Bill said, "As bodyguards go, Bernie couldn't have hired a better one. Jimmy Hennessy—I doubt that's his real name—was in the IRA. Fought in the uprising in '17. Got a price put on his head for killing two British army officers. Outran his pursuers and made it to New York.

"Due to the large Irish population there, word got around, traitors talked, the city got too hot for him, he fled to Chicago. Same story there. Eventually he wound up here. All this is hearsay, you understand, probably embellished, but I believe the basics."

Bill made a corner, then said, "Only one afternoon of illicit romance? Do you believe that version?"

"No. Why would Mrs. Kemp exaggerate her sister's promiscuity in the wrong direction?"

"Exactly."

"And why did Driscoll do the opposite and swear on the Bible that he was with Norma Blanchard only once?"

"We'll ask him that tomorrow."

"Why not now?"

"I want to see what evidence the Kemp house yields. When we confront Gabe with this, I want to be as well-armed as possible."

When they arrived at the Amoses' house, Thatcher said he would wait in the car. "Take your time. I've got a lot to mull over."

Such as Laurel being a moonshiner, out of her league with big-time players like Landry and Croft, the Johnsons, and the unscrupulous couple at Lefty's.

Jesus.

Bill found Daisy in bed, listless and complaining of stomach cramps. He asked if she'd eaten anything, but she hadn't because she couldn't keep anything down. "Have you been drinking?"

"No, Bill." She reached for his hand and held it against her cheek. She was lying. He could smell whiskey on her breath, but he didn't want to start a row. She wasn't drunk, but she was obviously unwell.

He gave her half a dropper of the medicine. "Maybe it'll ease the cramping so you can sleep. I won't be long."

"I love you."

"I love you, too." He kissed her forehead. Her eyes drifted closed. It scared him how fragile she looked. Almost lifeless.

Shaking off that thought, he left the bedroom and had almost reached the front door when the telephone rang. He went back to answer it and could tell by the background noise coming through the earpiece that his long and strenuous day wasn't over yet.

Sixty seconds later, he strode to the car and climbed into the driver's seat. "Thatcher, do you have a gun belt?"

"At the boardinghouse."

"Then we'll stop there first."

"What's happened?"

"That moonshine war I knew was coming? Well, it's here."

FORTY-EIGHT

—◄●►—

Thatcher was putting the frisky mare through her paces in the corral when he saw Laurel come around the corner of the stable. She stopped there.

The sight of her made his heart jump and everything below his waist go tight, which didn't improve his dark mood this morning. He wanted to strangle her for being the damnedest woman he'd ever met. He wanted to make love to her for the same reason.

The mare was being her uncooperative self, but he stuck with the training for five more minutes, then, with a subtle motion of his right knee, directed her to the paddock gate where he dismounted. He led her out and over to the water trough near the stable.

He said to Laurel, "You're out early."

"I need to talk to you and figured I would find you here."

Her hair was hanging down her back in a long braid beneath the straw hat he recognized, the one with the wide brim that cast a criss-crossing pattern of shadows over her cheeks, her pert nose, her plump lower lip.

To distract himself from thoughts of biting that lip, he ran his hand along the horse's neck as she drank from the trough.

Laurel said, "What's her name?"

"Serena."

"Pretty."

"Yeah, but it doesn't fit her personality. She's high-stepping and willful, doesn't pay attention to anybody."

He could tell by Laurel's peeved expression that she knew he wasn't referring strictly to the mare. In a crisp voice, she said, "I wouldn't have bothered you, except that I need to tell you something the sheriff ought to know."

"Then why don't you go see him?"

"Are you going to be civil and talk to me or not?"

"I'll be civil and talk to you, but I can tell you right now that you won't want to hear what I have to say."

"And what is that?"

"Stay and find out."

He made a nicking sound with his mouth and gave the reins a gentle tug. The mare fell into step behind him as he led her into the stable. Laurel trailed behind.

The shade was welcome, but the air inside the building was stuffy and hot and added to his overall grouchiness. Only after the mare was unsaddled, unbridled, and munching oats in her stall did he turn his attention to Laurel, who'd been standing in the center aisle, tapping her hat against her leg with annoyance for having been kept waiting.

"You don't like horses?" he asked.

"I don't mind them."

"Do you ride?"

"Not with any skill. On the family farm, we had plow horses and one mule. I could sit astride and hold on. What is it you wanted to say that I don't want to hear?"

"Have a seat." He motioned to a bale of hay. She backed up to it and sat down. He took off his hat and hung it on a nail as he wiped his forehead with his sleeve. "I've got a bucket of well water. Are you thirsty?"

"No thanks."

He went over to the bucket, ladled himself a tin cup full, and drank it down. She set her hat on her lap. When he came back to her, he propped himself against a post between stalls. "Ladies first."

"There's something worth Sheriff Amos's knowing, especially after what happened to Elray Johnson."

"Why don't you tell him directly?"

"Because you're privy to certain things that he isn't."

"Like what?"

"My visit to Lefty's. Have you mentioned that to him?"

"No."

"Or that I've taken Corrine under my wing?"

"No."

She wet her lips, pulled that enticing lower one through her teeth, making it difficult for him to concentrate on what she was saying.

"...so last night, I tested my memory of what Corrine had told me before. She described again how furious Gert was with Wally over the beating. Not because she had any sympathy or concern for Corrine, but because she was going to lose money while Corrine was out of commission." She paused to take a breath. "It occurred to me that Gert might have killed Wally over it."

"Huh."

"You sound skeptical. Don't you think she's capable of murder?"

He thought back on his single experience with the woman and the fury she'd unleashed during the raid. "I don't doubt it for a minute."

"But what?"

"A lot of people are capable of murder. Gert has her own suspect in mind. She thinks Wally was killed by the woman who has put a cog in the local moonshining machine. Remember that's what Elray told me seconds before he got shot."

"Of course I remember. But does this mystery woman even exist? Gert probably made that up to deflect—"

"Laurel, stop. Just stop." He walked over, grabbed her hand, and pulled her to her feet, sending her hat into the dirt and shocking her into silence. "Do you think I'm just a cowboy too dumb to know what you're into?"

"What do you mean?"

"Fucking hell," he ground out, not caring if she was scandalized by his language. "Finding that hair clip where the still had been clinched it, but I already knew that you and Irv weren't living off pies and his handyman business. I know the O'Connor twins wouldn't be delivering baked goods—baked goods, for crissake—to the oil fields if there wasn't more at stake."

"They—"

"Don't say anything. I don't want to hear anymore. I *can't* hear anymore. I'm official now."

"Just because you made that grand gesture of pinning on the badge?"

"Because Sheriff Amos swore me in as a reserve deputy last night."

"Oh. I see."

She pulled her hand free of his grip, but he wrapped his hands around her upper arms and held her in place. "Know why he needed another deputy? To try to keep moonshiners from killing each other."

"Killing each other?"

"The war Bill Amos saw coming was declared."

"What happened?"

"Three stills belonging to members of the Johnson family were destroyed by rivals."

"Who?"

"Don't know yet. But the outbreak of violence went on for most of the night. Stills were busted up. The hills ran with rivers of whiskey that had been poured out, sometimes by the sheriff's men, sometimes by competing sides, and it was hard to tell who was who. There were several shootouts, them against each other, them against us."

"You were in on these shootouts?"

"Because men were shooting at me. At Bill. At all of us. One of the other reserve deputies got winged. Best I know, nobody died, but it wasn't for lack of trying. Sheriff's department arrested over twenty men. Bill had them scattered to different jails, in this county and neighboring ones. He did that for their own safety. Those who name names don't live long. If Elray was here, he'd vouch for that."

She had stopped trying to get free. In fact, she was gazing up at him with apprehension. "Do you know the names of those who were put in jail?"

Her face had gone pale. He knew what she was desperate to know, but couldn't come right out and ask. "There were no familiar names on the lists I saw." Only when he said that did she begin to breathe again.

"I've warned you before, Laurel, and it hasn't done a damn bit of good. Maybe because I've beat around the bush. But I'm going to tell you straight out this time." He drew her closer. "If you don't stop what you're dealing in, and making enemies with folks like Chester Landry, Gert, the Johnsons, you could wind up hurt or even dead."

"I—"

"Listen to me, dammit. Retaliation seems to be the only way these people know how to settle a disagreement or even a grudge." Thinking back on Norma Blanchard, he added, "Being a woman won't protect you from violence or cruelty. Believe that."

He rubbed her arms up and down once, then released her. "You've made it plain enough that I have no say in how you choose to live your life, and you don't want me to have a say. But the fear of something bad happening to you keeps me churned up and makes me mad as hell at you. That's why I acted like a jackass when you got here."

She looked down. "I thought you were mad because I made you stop the other night."

"I wasn't happy about it."

"I know. I'm sorry I—"

"Don't apologize. It was my fault. I read you wrong."

She tilted her head up, looked at him directly, and said softly, "I'm only sorry that I didn't see it through. I'd like to know what I missed."

He waited to make sure he hadn't imagined that she'd said that, but her green eyes reflected sincerity, regret, and yearning. He slid his hand beneath her braid and curved it around the back of her neck. "I damn near died. I'm damn near dying now." He lowered his head. Their lips barely touched.

"Thatcher? You in there?"

He and Laurel sprang apart. Standing in the wide stable opening was Sheriff Amos, silhouetted by blinding sunlight.

"Yeah. Here."

The sheriff came forward a few steps, spotted Laurel, and took in the situation immediately. "Oh. Excuse me."

"Just as well you're here." Thatcher bent down and picked up Laurel's hat and handed it to her. "Mrs. Plummer actually came to ask me to give you a message. Now she can deliver it herself."

Laurel looked up at him with consternation, but she went along without protest when he motioned her forward. They met Bill halfway.

"How's your father-in-law, Mrs. Plummer?" he asked.

"Much better, thank you."

"Glad to hear it."

Thatcher said, "Bill, you remember the young woman Wally Johnson beat up?"

"Of course. Corrine something."

"Well." Thatcher took a breath and told the sheriff about taking Corrine from Lefty's following the raid. "The Plummers sort of inherited her that night. They've given her a home in exchange for her helping out."

"Really?" Bill looked at Laurel. "That was a very kind gesture, Mrs. Plummer."

"Corrine was in an awful situation. Not one of her choosing."

"Tell Bill what she told you about Gert."

"She went on a tirade over the Wally Johnson incident." Laurel talked without interruption for the next several minutes. She finished by saying, "Isn't it possible Gert was angry enough to kill him over it?"

Bill didn't dismiss the conjecture out of hand, but he did make a valid point. "Could this be Corrine's way of getting revenge on Gert for mistreating her?"

"Corrine's not conniving, she's candid. She isn't lying about this. I'm sure of it."

"I don't believe she is either, Bill," Thatcher said.

"No, me neither, really," Bill said. "I questioned her myself." He chuckled. "She was very outspoken about her feelings over Wally's demise. And I wouldn't put anything past Gert, including cold-blooded murder. Her greediness is legendary." He stroked his mustache. "Only thing I can't reconcile is why Corrine didn't tell me about Gert's tirade when I questioned her."

"Probably because she feared reprisal. She didn't feel free to tell about it until she had gotten away from there. Her intention wasn't to implicate Gert. That's my notion. But if Gert were to find out that Corrine had talked about it at all, she could still retaliate."

"I'll definitely follow up, but I'll leave the girl out of it. I promise. Thank you for bringing it to my attention."

"You're welcome." Laurel put on her hat. "If you gentlemen will excuse me, I need to get to work."

The three of them left the stable together. Bill said, "Thatcher, we need to get to work, too. I'll meet you at the car." He struck out in the direction of the auto garage.

Thatcher asked Laurel where she'd parked.

"I walked over. I didn't want it to look like—"

"Like you were coming to see me."

She shrugged guilty. "People talk."

"People can go to hell."

He ducked his head under her hat brim and gave her a lingering kiss. When he pulled away he said, "I'm making you a promise, Laurel."

She looked at him quizzically.

"If I ever get you in bed again, you can count on finding out what you missed."

Excited by Thatcher's final words to her, but also shaken by what he had told her about last night's unrest, the arrests, the shootouts, Laurel swiftly walked home. She planned to hastily gather supplies and then to drive out to the stills. She feared what she might find when she got there, and was equally afraid of finding nothing.

By the time she reached her house, she was winded, but when she saw Irv's truck there, she ran inside. He was standing at the cook-stove cracking eggs into a skillet. She rushed over and hugged him from behind.

"Ouch! Mind my arm."

"Irv, I'm so relieved. My God! Last night—"

"Don't have to tell me about it. I lived through it." He flipped the frying eggs. "You want an over-easy?"

"No thank you. Are Corrine and Ernie all right?"

"They're fine. Pissed off because we couldn't do runs last night, just when we were rebuilding our inventory. By the way, I brought back crates packed with jars. I'll help you carry them down to the cellar once I've had a bite and a rest."

"Fine. Good. But what about last night?"

"We were all set to get both cookers going, but then we started hearing gunfire popping from every direction. Some of it might have been echoes, but there was enough of it, and close enough, to scare the bejesus out of us.

"We knew better than to light the fireboxes and become targets, so we scurried a distance away and took cover between rocks, huddled in the dark all night. Shootin' would break out every now and then. Didn't let up till almost dawn. We were glad to be alive to see the sunrise. Went back to the camp. Looked just like when we left it. They didn't find us."

He slid the eggs onto a plate, sprinkled both liberally with salt and pepper, and added a leftover biscuit. As he hobbled over to the table, he remarked, "Your color is hectic. What's the matter?"

"What's the matter?" She sat down across from him. "When you weren't here this morning, I thought you'd probably stayed at the stills all night because you were tired of being cooped up for so long. But when I heard about last night's ruckus—"

"Who'd you hear it from?" He mopped up egg yolk with half the biscuit and popped it into his mouth.

"Thatcher Hutton."

He gave a harrumph. "Figures."

"Why do you say that?"

"Did he come around to boast about all the men he killed?"

"He didn't kill anybody."

"Not what I heard. The boys at the filling station said—"

"The filling station?"

"Stopped there on my way into town. It's where you go to get a soda pop and the latest news. Word is that Hutton's the sheriff's new sharpshooter, said he dropped at least a dozen men last night. They say he's taken the sheriff's boy Tim's place in his daddy's affection. Said—"

"Nobody was killed."

"Then why'd he come over here if not to brag?" One of his eyebrows went up, the other down. "Or don't I know?"

She ignored the implication. "Actually, today I went looking for him to ask if he would pass along some information to the sheriff." She explained why she thought the blowout that Corrine had witnessed between Gert and Wally Johnson was important.

"Things were peaceful around here before that jug-eared runt was murdered," Irv said. "Now, look where we're at. Folks shootin' at each other." He crumbled the second half of the dry biscuit into the remaining egg yolk. "What about the O'Connors? Do you know how they fared last night?"

"They weren't around. They were making a delivery to Ranger."

"That was mighty convenient."

"Why are you still mistrustful of them?"

He waved his hand in dismissal. "They ain't at the top of my worry roster. Deputy Hutton holds that spot. Laurel, if you keep seeing him on a regular basis—"

"It's not on a regular basis."

"—he's going to find us out."

"He already has."

Irv wiped a napkin over his mouth, then held it there as she told him about Thatcher finding the barrette at the abandoned still site. "It was Corrine's, but it matched ones he'd seen me wear. A hair clip isn't conclusive evidence, of course, but even before he found it, he suspected."

"Has he come right out and accused you?"

"Not exactly."

"Not exactly?"

"We talk around it. For instance, he let me know that you and Corrine hadn't been arrested last night by saying he didn't recognize any names on the lists of arrests. He warns me to be careful."

"Of the likes of the O'Connors and that Chester Landry. But maybe he's the one you should be more careful of."

"He wears a badge now, but I truly believe he's looking out for us, Irv. He doesn't want us to get caught."

"For his sake as well as ours."

"How so?"

He thought over his answer. "Men like Hutton have this...fortitude. Honor. Whatever you want to call it. Unlike the most of us, it's hard to bend and damn near impossible to break. If he was put in a position of letting you off the hook, or enforcing the law he's now sworn to uphold, which do you figure he'd do?"

"I don't know, and neither do you."

"No, but I think *he* knows. That's why he doesn't want you to get caught."

FORTY-NINE

———⬥———

As Thatcher and Bill left Barker's garage, Bill told him they were headed for Gabe Driscoll's house.

"You're going to question him about the attack on Norma Blanchard."

"I am. But I should inform you that you're still Bernie's first choice suspect. He put in a call to me early this morning. He asked if I'd ascertained—his word—your whereabouts at the time Norma Blanchard was assaulted."

"Should I take that personally?"

Bill chuckled. "He's never going to like you, Thatcher."

"That doesn't hurt my feelings. I don't like him, either. We rubbed each other the wrong way from the start."

"Because you see through him. Also, he senses that you can't be corrupted or controlled." Bill gave him a sad look that said: *unlike me*.

"Gotta ask, Bill. Was he behind all that shit that happened last night?"

"I accused him."

"And?"

"What do you think?"

"He was walking his dog when it started." Thatcher swore. "We're his damn alibi."

"Hennessy's, too. Although Bernie wouldn't have wasted Hennessy on raiding other people's stills. But you can bet orders came from Bernie."

"What's he after?"

"The Johnsons' almost monopoly on the boom towns."

Thatcher said nothing for a time, thinking about the tightening web of danger being spun around Laurel. Then he asked Bill if Dr. Perkins's medicine had helped Mrs. Amos's stomach ailment.

Last night while Thatcher was retrieving his gun belt from his room, Bill had commandeered the boardinghouse telephone to call a woman in Daisy's bridge club, who had readily agreed to go sit with Mrs. Amos until Bill returned home, whenever that might be.

"The tincture seems to have helped. She hasn't thrown up again, but she was very weak this morning. I hope she can be persuaded to eat something. Her friend Alice Cantor said she would stay with her for however long she's needed."

"That's a huge relief."

"It is. My county was on fire last night, and probably will be again tonight. I've called in all my reserve deputies to help the regulars, but, hell, at least half of them make moonshine themselves or take graft from those who do. That mess, along with the Blanchard assault, it's like the damn sky is falling. Hated to pull you away from whatever you were doing at the stable."

Thatcher gave a half laugh. He didn't hate it near like Thatcher did. He'd have liked to have more time alone with Laurel.

Now, however, he needed to concentrate on the upcoming interview with Dr. Driscoll. Weeks ago, he'd realized that he would never be entirely cleared of suspicion in Mrs. Driscoll's disappearance until someone else was proved to be the culprit. Even though he'd joined the ranks on the side of the law last night, he still wasn't wholeheartedly accepted by the other men. The more Bill relied on him, consulted him on tactics and so forth, the more resentment Thatcher felt aimed his way.

This interrogation of Driscoll could turn that tide.

"I went out early to the Kemp house," Bill was saying. "Took a look around. It's as Mrs. Kemp described it. Norma's room looked like a tornado had hit it. There was blood on the bed. I left Scotty out there to try and lift fingerprints, but, if they do turn out to match Gabe Driscoll's, all that proves is that he's been there. Which we already know. Doesn't signify that he assaulted her."

"Where does that leave you?"

"Us. That's why I called you away from your work at the stable. You factor large in our approach."

"How?"

Bill took a sheet of folded paper from the breast pocket of his jacket and passed it to Thatcher, who unfolded the sheet and read the lines written in a spidery script. When he finished, he refolded the sheet and handed it back to Bill.

Thatcher said, "You're going to show this to Gabe Driscoll and gauge his reaction?"

"I'm going to show it to him," Bill said as he slowed his car in front of the Driscoll house. "*You're* going to gauge his reaction."

As they went up the walk, Thatcher noticed that without the kind-hearted lady of the house there to oversee its upkeep, the place was beginning to look neglected. Weeds were sprouting in the flower beds. The grass needed mowing.

The sign at the gate had indicated that the doctor was in, but there were no other autos there, and when Bill rang the doorbell, it echoed through empty rooms.

Thatcher hadn't seen Gabe Driscoll since the morning in the sheriff's office when the doctor had viciously accused him of abducting his wife. In the intervening weeks, his hairline had receded, he'd lost a considerable amount of weight, and his eyes were sunken into their sockets. He looked like a man who'd just crawled out of a hole or was about to crawl into one.

Upon seeing them, he clutched the doorjamb. "Mila?"

"No, Gabe, sorry," Bill said. "But we'd like to speak with you. Are you with a patient?"

He shook his head and, after a second's hesitation, stood aside and motioned them in. Bill removed his hat and used it to gesture toward Thatcher. "You remember Mr. Hutton?"

"I couldn't very well forget him." The doctor regarded him with hostility. "I thought you were on your way to the Panhandle."

"Change of plans."

Bill said, "I've made him a reserve deputy."

The doctor tilted his head as though the sheriff might be joking and would add a punch line. Realizing Bill was serious, he said, "If this isn't about Mila, why are you here?"

"We need your professional opinion on a matter."

Still looking puzzled and a bit uneasy, he said, "Let's talk in my office. The other rooms aren't...I haven't had anyone in to clean."

He led the way and pointed them into chairs facing his desk. The doctor went around and sat down behind it. They didn't make small talk. Bill leaned forward and passed Gabe the folded sheet of paper he'd shown Thatcher in the car.

He said, "Yesterday, a woman was brought to Dr. Perkins. She was unconscious, her condition life-threatening. She soon died. Since it was obvious that she had been the victim of a violent crime, at my request, Dr. Perkins compiled a comprehensive list of her more serious injuries."

As the doctor's eyes scanned down the sheet, his brow became increasingly furrowed. When he reached the final two notations, he murmured, "Good God."

Bill said, "I had her transported to Dallas for the autopsy."

"Why did you bring this to me?"

"Doc Perkins is earnest and hardworking, but he's the first to admit that he's not as knowledgeable in modern medicine as you are. I'd like to know if you agree with his hypothetical notes on how the victim's injuries were inflicted. I could wait on the autopsy report, but that may take days, if not weeks. I want to move on this. The perpetrator must be found."

"Without examining the woman myself—"

"I realize I'm placing you at a disadvantage. I'm asking for a general assessment only. Generally speaking, do you agree with Dr. Perkins's hypotheses?"

Looking dubious, Driscoll ran his finger down the page. "Well, yes. Based on his descriptions, I would say someone hit her in the face repeatedly and hard enough to break bones. Probably with his fist, but it could have been an instrument.

"And, if the infliction is violent enough, blunt force to an organ can cause it to bleed even if it doesn't rupture. Dr. Perkins's description of the bruise on her back above her kidney indicates to me that she was stomped on rather than kicked. In regards to the rape, I concur with him. It wasn't about sexual gratification. It was defilement and had to be sheer torture for the poor woman."

Bill said quietly, "It was Norma Blanchard, Gabe."

The doctor's face went as white as the sheet of paper that drifted out of his fingers as they went slack. He began breathing hard and fast through his mouth. He blinked rapidly. Thatcher thought he might be on the verge of passing out.

He tried to stand, but his knees buckled, and he dropped back into the seat of his chair. He planted his elbows on the surface of his desk and held his head between his hands.

"Gabe?" Bill said.

For the longest time, he didn't respond, then, "Who did it?"

"We don't know yet, but we intend to find out. We thought you might shed some light on that since you were well acquainted with Miss Blanchard."

Driscoll lowered his hands from his head and looked from Bill to Thatcher and then back to Bill. Their expressions must have been telling. His shoulders slumped. "You know."

"About your affair with her? Yes."

"Patsy told you?"

"We spoke with her before she left to accompany Miss Blanchard's body to Dallas."

His prominent Adam's apple bobbed. "What about the baby?"

"Mrs. Kemp arranged for a woman to look after him until further notice."

Looking dazed, the doctor listened as Bill gave him a summary of what Patsy Kemp had told them. "This morning, one of my deputies checked with the bank. The telephone call appears to have been a ruse to get Mrs. Kemp out of the house. This wasn't a crime of opportunity.

"Mrs. Kemp arrived home to find the door unlocked, Norma on her bed. The baby, thank God, was unharmed." Bill leaned forward in his chair and asked softly, "Is the child yours, Gabe?"

His voice was a croak, but his answer was swift, simple, and unequivocal. "Yes."

Bill let that settle, then asked, "Had you and Miss Blanchard planned to marry?"

He was about to speak, thought better of it, and finally said, "I'm married to Mila."

"But did Miss Blanchard have expectations of taking her place?"

"I told her that making our affair public would be regarded with scorn."

"Especially in light of Mrs. Driscoll's disappearance," Bill said. "You can understand why folks might jump to judgment."

He looked at each of them in turn as though pleading for absolution. "I'm not proud of committing adultery. I didn't go looking for it. I'm not like that."

"Like what?"

"A skirt chaser. A tomcat. I'd been faithful to Mila. But the moment I saw Norma, she took my breath."

"How soon before you became lovers?"

"The very next day." He gave an account that matched Patsy Kemp's.

"And you kept going back?"

He nodded morosely. "I couldn't stay away from her. She was like a drug. I couldn't get enough. She was so exotically beautiful and..." He looked down at the sheet of paper on his desk and made a choking sound. "Who would do that to her?"

"A rival for her affection?"

The doctor blinked several times. "What?"

"Meaning no disrespect to Miss Blanchard," Bill said. "And I hate to ask so bluntly, Gabe, but even after the two of you became involved, did she see other men?"

"No," he exclaimed. "No, we are—were—in love. She had a very passionate nature and expressed her affection for me without inhibition. There was no one else."

"Okay." Bill looked and sounded unconvinced. "When did you last see her?"

"About ten days ago. She showed up here unexpectedly. She brought Arthur with her. At first I was annoyed. It was the middle of the day."

"You were afraid of what people would think?"

"Yes. She laughed off my concern, said it would look like she was bringing the baby for treatment."

"How long did she stay?"

"About an hour. Maybe a little longer."

"Is that the first time you'd seen her since Mrs. Driscoll disappeared?"

The doctor's eyes darted furtively between Thatcher and Bill, then he confessed to the late-night visit Thatcher had witnessed. "She came uninvited then, too. I didn't want to let her in, but Norma could be persuasive. A little pushy, even."

"A little pushy." Bill assumed a thoughtful expression. "Did her pushiness ever lead to arguments? Did you part on good terms the last time you saw her?"

There was a noticeable hesitation, before he said, "Yes. I enjoyed having that time with my son." When Bill didn't continue, but only steadily watched him, he blurted, "But I told Norma that for appearance's sake, I would come to her from then on."

"Did you go to her yesterday afternoon, Gabe?"

Driscoll shot a look toward Thatcher, looking like a creature who'd just realized he'd been cornered.

Going back to Bill, he said, "You think *I* did that to Norma? That's what this is about?" He lurched to his feet and, with contempt, took a swipe at the sheet of paper on his desk and sent it flying. "I would never, could never, do that to her. I loved her."

"Sit down, Gabe."

"How can she be dead?" he said, his voice cracking. "I did not harm her."

"I'm glad to hear it. Sit down and tell me about yesterday. Where were you midafternoon, say between one-thirty and three-thirty?"

The doctor assumed a posture of righteous indignation. Bill waited him out. After half a minute, Driscoll lowered himself into his chair. "I haven't called on my rural patients since Mila's been missing. I resumed my route yesterday."

"Why yesterday? Any particular reason?"

"I felt it was time that I stopped dwelling on my...my personal tragedy and got back to work."

"Can you provide us with the names of the people you saw, and the route you took?"

"Of course." He took a fountain pen and paper from his lap drawer and began listing names. When he finished, Thatcher sat forward, took the paper from him and pocketed it.

"Thank you, Gabe," Bill said. "I've talked myself dry and could do with a glass of water. Mr. Hutton?"

"Sounds good."

Thatcher could tell that Driscoll saw through the ploy and didn't like leaving them, but his other choice was to appear overly nervous. "Of course." He got up and left the room. His footsteps echoed down the hallway toward the back of the house.

Bill leaned toward Thatcher, his eyebrows raised in an unspoken question.

"He believes the baby is his," Thatcher said quietly. "He's convinced that her love was true and that he was her only lover. He's lying about them parting on good terms, though. There was something there."

"I caught that, too. Maybe she was being pushy about marriage plans. He was afraid of public opinion. That would have given him a motive to shut her up, and yesterday's route gave him opportunity."

Thatcher stated flatly, "I don't think he did it."

Bill was taken aback. "Why not?"

"If he'd've inflicted those injuries, he'd've come apart while he was talking through them."

"He lied to Bernie about seeing Norma only one time. He gave a good performance of an hysterical husband the morning after Mila's disappearance."

"But he wasn't at the scene of the crime." Thatcher bent down and picked up Dr. Perkins's list from the floor. "This amounts to the scene of the crime. I don't believe he did these things."

"But?"

"But I think he got rid of Mrs. Driscoll."

"To be with Norma?"

"He admitted that he couldn't help himself, that she was a drug and he couldn't get enough. Guys in the trenches would say he was pussy whipped."

"What do you say?"

"That's my thinking, too."

Bill gave him a wry grin, but it was short-lived and turned into a frown. "We don't have a body, Thatcher. Not a solid clue as to what happened to Mila. As you know, the prosecutor won't indict on circumstantial evidence alone. A mistress, even an exotically beautiful, sexually uninhibited one, isn't evidence."

Thatcher said, "Well then, only one thing left to do."

"Let him get away with it?"

"Get him to confess."

Before Bill could comment, they heard Gabe returning. He walked into the room carrying a glass of water in each hand. He set one in front of Thatcher, the other in front of Bill, and returned to his chair behind the desk.

Then the three sat with nobody saying anything. Bill drank from his water glass, then smoothed his mustache as he did when muddling through a dilemma. This time, however, Thatcher believed it was more for effect.

Finally he said, "Gabe, the view from where I'm sitting doesn't look good. Within two months' time, your wife has gone missing, and your mistress died of injuries sustained during a brutal sexual assault."

Gabe swallowed audibly but didn't say anything.

Bill continued, "Now either the stars just really aren't lining up favorably for you, or an enemy is setting you up to do you in, or you're doing yourself in. Help me out here."

The doctor took several shallow breaths, like he was pumping up his courage. "I've owned up to having a passionate affair with Norma. Like all lovers, we had our spats. But I would never have done to her what was done."

"You were with her on two separate occasions the day Mrs. Driscoll disappeared."

Mention of that out of context momentarily flustered him. "I told you that myself."

"I remember." Bill looked down and seemed to study the pattern of the rug between his boots. When he raised his head, he said, "Do you want to change anything you've told me about your activities on that day and evening?"

"No."

Bill looked over at Thatcher, his expression pained. Going back to the doctor, he said, "What you told me about that day was that a patient, as of then unnamed, was going through a difficult breech birth. According to Mrs. Kemp, that's not true. She said Arthur was already a month old. Which one of you is lying?"

Gabe placed his elbow on his desk again and rubbed his forehead. "I thought it would make me look bad if you knew I'd been with my mistress that night."

"Well, you're right about that."

Thatcher cleared his throat. Bill said, "Mr. Hutton? Something on your mind?"

"Um-huh. I recall Mrs. Kemp's description of Dr. Driscoll when he went back to her house that second time late that night. She said he was frantic."

Bill said, "He's right, Gabe. She did say that. Why were you frantic?"

"Because Norma wasn't there, and I needed her."

"Needed her? For what?"

"I'd just come from that ratty roadhouse where I'd tended to that girl. I think her name was Corrine. It had been a long day. I was exhausted."

"You went seeking the womanly kind of comfort Miss Blanchard could give you?"

"You're putting words in my mouth."

"Then, in your words, why were you frantic?"

"Because Norma wasn't there."

"That's close, but not exactly what we were told," Thatcher said. "Mrs. Kemp's words were that when you got there, you were 'batshit crazy.' You didn't get upset after learning that Miss Blanchard wasn't there. You were unhinged when you arrived."

Softly, Bill said, "Why, Gabe?"

The crackup was gradual. It seemed to Thatcher that it started at his thinning hairline and worked its way down his long face. His brows drew together above the bridge of his nose. His eyes filled with tears. The tip of his nose turned red and dripped a bead of snot. Then his lower lip began to quiver and he blubbered, "I did something terrible."

FIFTY

Somewhere between his blubbered "I did something terrible" and the sheriff's office, Gabriel Driscoll grew a pair.

That was the only explanation Thatcher had for the doctor's change of heart. By the time he and Bill escorted him into the building, he had gone from a shattered man facing ruin to a haughty, self-righteous jerk.

Scotty and Harold, who were sharing a desk piled high with paperwork, stopped sorting through it and looked on with interest as Driscoll proclaimed that an affair was the only thing he had confessed to, and that if the sheriff and his fledgling deputy thought otherwise, they had misunderstood.

As though addressing a jury, he took the opportunity to profess his innocence. "When I said I'd done a terrible thing, I was referring to my infidelity. Nothing more. I sinned against my wife. And since you and your inept staff here haven't uncovered a single clue as to what happened to her, she'll never know how deeply I cared for her."

Looking at Thatcher with malice, he said, "You still haven't definitively accounted for yourself the night Mila disappeared." Then he turned to Bill. "I'm not saying another word without a lawyer present."

"Do you have one?"

"Not on retainer."

"I'll arrange for one, then. In the meantime, you'll wait in a cell." He instructed Harold to lock him up. As the deputy escorted Driscoll into the cell block, Bill quietly said to Thatcher, "I'm in no rush to call the public defender. Let's give him a while to ruminate on his sins against his wife."

When asked, Scotty gave Bill an update on the investigations being conducted relating to last night's events. "We ran down two more 'shiners trying to disassemble their still for relocation. I think they were relieved it was us who found them and not the Johnsons."

"Remember that the Johnsons were the targets and suffered the greatest losses," Bill said.

"Which is why they'll be primed for revenge," Scotty said. "I think we can look forward to another active night. Meanwhile..." He passed Bill a slip of paper. "Somebody from the governor's office. He's called twice. Asked you to call him back."

"He say what for?"

"He said the governor wants to know what the fuck is going on out here and what in holy hell you're doing about it. Says moonshine wars make the state look bad."

"The governor didn't have the guts to call and tell me himself?"

"He was giving the invocation at a prayer breakfast."

They all had a chuckle.

Harold returned. Bill asked him to put through the long-distance call to the governor's office. He asked Scotty to call the coroner's office in Dallas and ask about the timing of Norma Blanchard's autopsy, while Bill himself placed a call to his house and spoke with Mrs. Cantor about Daisy's condition.

While they were occupied, Thatcher wandered over to the county map tacked to the wall and began to study it. He half-listened as Bill conversed with his wife's friend and then spoke to the governor's toady. To an outlandish extent, Bill downplayed the seriousness of the previous night's crimes, even referring to it as "mischief."

When Bill hung up from that call, Thatcher said, "Mind if I get back to work? I've got horses to exercise."

"Of course. I've got plenty to do here while Gabe wallows in remorse. If I need you, I'll come find you."

Thatcher left, knowing that he might be hard to find for the next few hours. Neither the sheriff nor anyone else would know where to look.

Laurel and Irv transferred the crates he'd brought from the stills to the cellar where they would be stored until the O'Connors came for them that evening. Irv apologized for being unable to do his share of the lifting, carrying, and moving.

"I'd rather you let your arm heal," Laurel told him as she put the last crate in its place.

She also loaded supplies for Corrine and Ernie into Irv's truck. As he climbed up into the driver's seat, he said, "We'll have to wait and see if hell breaks loose again before we decide whether or not to do runs tonight."

"Don't take any chances. If there's the least sign of trouble, lay low. Promise."

"I promise. Keep your pistol handy."

She patted her skirt pocket and waved him off.

The kitchen was hot, and only got hotter from the ovens as she baked and the afternoon wore on. She had just taken the last pies out of the oven and set them to cool when there was a knock on her front door.

It was too early for Davy and Mike, and they always came around to the back. Pushing wisps of damp hair off her heated face, she went through the living room to the front door. The windowpane in its upper half gave her clear sight of the callers. Her heart stuttered, but since she'd been seen, she had no choice except to open the door.

In the background, a recent model car was parked in the street, a large man standing beside it. Out of reflex, she patted her skirt pocket, but she smiled. "Hello."

"Mrs. Plummer. You may not remember meeting me. It was a cursory introduction in—"

"The sheriff's office."

Mayor Bernie Croft said, "Your baby daughter was very ill. I heard about her passing. My condolences are long overdue."

"Thank you." Her gaze shifted to his companion, who removed his bowler hat.

The mayor said, "Mr. Landry says you two have met?"

"Briefly. How do you do, Mr. Landry?"

"Mrs. Plummer." He gave her a courtly little bow and a smile that flashed gold.

"What can I do for you gentlemen? Sell you a pie?"

The mayor laughed. "As delicious as that sounds, we'd rather you sell us your corn liquor."

Laurel called upon every reserve of discipline she had not to react. "I beg your pardon?"

"May we come in?" Landry said.

With the speed of comets, several options whizzed through her mind. None were good. But the worst of them would be to refuse them entry. That would only arouse suspicion.

"Of course." She stepped aside. Croft and Landry came in. Before shutting the door, she cast a furtive glance toward the car and chauffeur.

Her guests looked around at the empty front room. She said, "As you see, I haven't furnished the parlor yet, so I can't offer you a seat."

"Personally, I think furnishings would detract from that handsome spandrel," Landry said and moved to stand under it. "Craftsmanship like this is rare these days."

"Let's get to business, shall we?" Croft turned to her. "Mrs. Plummer, are you acquainted with a man by the name of Thomas Johnson?"

"No."

"You might never have met him, but you know who he is. He goes by the nickname of Tup."

...we found Cousin Tup. In a hole in the ground with his arm mangled... Thatcher's words echoed, but she tried to remain impassive. "I'm sorry. I don't know him."

Croft smiled. "Well, he knows you. His arm was caught in a bear trap set by you. He lost the arm."

"How terrible for him. But I still have no idea what you're talking about."

"I visited him in the hospital yesterday."

"So he's a friend of yours?"

"No. I paid him a courtesy call as a public servant."

"It must have cheered him to be so honored."

"Not in the slightest. Mr. Johnson used gutter language to denounce me and my elected office. But then, he wasn't in the best of moods. The nub is festering. They may have to do additional cutting."

She looked over at Landry, who still had his head back, admiring the room divider. Not a hair out of place.

"Mr. Johnson was also elaborately cursing the individual responsible for his misfortune." He smiled. "You, Mrs. Plummer."

"I?"

"You may think I've come to censure you."

"Censure me for what, Mr. Croft? For setting a bear trap, which I would have no earthly idea how to do? It sounds difficult and dangerous."

He pulled his watch out of his vest pocket and checked the time. "I have a schedule, so let's cut to the chase. You were brought to the attention of the disreputable Johnson clan by one Gertrude Atkins.

"She went to Hiram—I'm sure you've heard of him, as his name is widely known in moonshiner circles. Gert alleged that it was you who killed Hiram's kinsman, Wally."

"Obviously this woman is deranged."

"She also informed Hiram that you are poaching on his family business in the boom towns, and even in many local establishments, including her own. Tup and a younger Johnson, Elray, were sent to your still to teach you a lesson. How did they know where it was, you ask? Gert tracked a runaway whore to the shack once occupied by you and your father-in-law. From there it was easy to find the location of your industry. Is the purpose of Mr. Landry's and my visit becoming clearer now?"

"No, but this fanciful narrative is entertaining. However, I also have a schedule, mayor. I'd like for you to leave."

He said, "Don't mistake my reason for being here. I assure you I didn't come on behalf of the wretched Johnsons. I wish them all in hell. You see, the Johnsons and I are archrivals." He smiled again. "You've gotten yourself on their fighting side. I've come to offer you my protection."

"You have me at a complete loss. Protection from what?"

"Capture, incarceration. If you're lucky, that is. If the Johnsons don't get to you before the law does."

"Don't you represent the law, Mr. Mayor?"

"I represent the business interests of the community."

"As well as your own."

"If I prosper, everyone does."

"Hmm."

"Here's how it works. You give me your contacts in the boom towns. Together, Mr. Landry and I can increase that trade double-fold, triple-fold. You'll supply us with all the whiskey you can produce, but we'll take over the distribution. This system greatly decreases the risk to you, your operation, and your associates. We provide this protection for a percentage of the net."

"I say again, I have no idea what you're talking about."

"I'm talking about a ten percent take. Which is a token, really. You obviously have a very good distiller because your product sells so well. You're savvy, and you have backbone. Admirable qualities to be sure, especially in a fair lady.

"But your foremost asset is your *friend*, Thatcher Hutton, who is now serving as a reserve deputy sheriff. A lot of information could be acquired by sharing a mattress with someone inside the sheriff's office."

Heat rushed to her head. She looked over at Chester Landry, who was watching her with a smarmy smile, as though waiting to see how she was going to worm out of this.

She turned back to the mayor. "You insult me, sir. You also insult Mr. Hutton. I have pies delivered to the boom towns. Is that what you want a slice of? I didn't think so. Get out of my house."

He grinned, but the smile didn't reach his eyes. "Mrs. Plummer, you're quite charming and glib, but pleading ignorance is a waste of time. Many of the moonshiners already under my protection buy from the same suppliers of goods as you. I know exactly how many fruit jars and pounds of sugar your father-in-law purchases for you on a routine basis. I know the gentleman in Weatherford who sold him copper recently. In turn you've insulted me, my intelligence, by pretending that you aren't distilling illegal whiskey."

"I don't even drink."

"I'm familiar with this house," he said, seemingly out of context. "It has a sizable cellar."

Landry suddenly became animated. "I understand that it backs into the limestone hill," he said. "Is that right?"

"Yes."

"What an engineering marvel."

"Hardly, Mr. Landry," she said. "It's a rather crude construction, actually."

"Nevertheless, I would love to see it."

Laurel's heart was in her throat, but she said, "Follow me."

She led them through the dining room, the kitchen, and out the back door. As she began moving aside offshoots of the honeysuckle, Landry asked, "Is the cellar accessible only through this door?"

"Yes. But the fragrance is so nice I can't bring myself to prune the vine."

"Not only is it lovely to smell, it's useful. It partially conceals the door."

She saw another flash of gold in Landry's jaw when he smiled. She pushed open the door. At the top of the stairs, she said, "Please be careful. These steps are steep and rickety."

"Why not turn on the light?" the mayor said.

"It doesn't work."

He reached up and yanked on the string. The recently installed electric light, which had been one of the projects on Irv's list, came on.

"Voilà!" Landry said.

Laurel tried to look surprised and pleased. "My father-in-law must have changed the bulb. I've been after him to do it."

She preceded the men down the stairs. When she reached the bottom, she turned to face them. "Mr. Landry, note the inexpert connection of the rock wall to the interior.

"And, Mayor Croft, you're quite right about the goods that Irv purchases for me. He's a fix-it man, you know. He's made me copper pots, which I use when stewing fruit for my pie fillings. The recipes call for pounds of sugar. I can barely keep up with my demand for pies, so, while fresh fruit is in season, I've made provision for the fall and winter months by canning." She raised her hands to her sides, inviting them to take a look.

The surrounding walls were lined with shelves laden with fruit jars of pie fillings.

FIFTY-ONE

H e would pick the hottest day of the year to do this, Thatcher thought as he guided his mount into a shallow creek, where he reined in the pinto gelding so he could drink. Thatcher uncapped the canteen of water he'd brought with him and drank from it. After draping its strap back over the pommel, he dismounted, took off his bandana, dipped it into the creek water, then wrung it out before tying it back around his neck. The coolness was a welcome relief from the blistering heat and scorching sun.

The pinto was one of Fred Barker's horses for rent. Thatcher had asked if he could take him out for a couple of hours. He also asked to borrow a rifle from Barker, telling him he wanted to get in some target practice. Barker hadn't hesitated to grant both requests, but had remarked that it was one hell of a hot day to be either shooting or taking a pleasure ride.

Thatcher wasn't going on this ride for the fun of it. He'd chosen this particular horse because of his stamina. He also needed a stolid horse, one not easily spooked. He didn't know anything about his destination, but he'd envisioned it being desolate, rugged terrain, and he'd been right.

He'd ridden cross-country out of town, but had kept the roads in sight, using them and landmarks he'd seen on the county map to guide him to a pass between two sizable hills. He'd found it right where it was supposed to be. Pointer's Gap.

The pinto finished drinking and raised his head. Thatcher patted him on his neck and swung up into the saddle. "Let's go take a look-see."

He adjusted his hat to block the late-afternoon sun from his eyes. As he came out the other side of the creek, he pushed the responsive horse into a gallop to cover the last quarter mile of level ground. Before daylight ran out, he wanted to explore as much of the gap as he could.

When he reached the twin inclines and the narrow pass cleaving them, he slowed the horse to a walk. He flushed a covey of quail from a grove of mesquite trees. He saw a jackrabbit in a losing race against a bobcat, a nanny goat and two kids that had likely discovered an opening in their owner's fence, and countless horned toads skittering across the crusty earth. A foot-long lizard dozing on a flat rock slid to the ground when he and the pinto clomped past.

The wildlife were at home in this inhospitable landscape. They belonged to it and in it. Thatcher was searching for something that didn't belong.

Just as the sun was setting, he spotted it.

———————

Corrine hummed as she stirred the pot of beans suspended above the cookfire, which she'd let burn down to embers. The sun had set, but even though it wasn't full dark yet, flames would signal their location to anyone—lawmen or outlaws—who might be scouting the area.

Seated on side-by-side boulders several yards away from her, Irv and Ernie were watching Corrine, sharing a jar of moonshine, and discussing whether or not to risk distilling tonight.

"What do you think, Ernie?"

"Her beans are right tasty."

Irv growled with annoyance. "Not talking about her. What do you think about firing up the stills?"

Ernie took off his newsboy cap and fanned his face with it. "What's Laurel say?"

"She said to lay low at the first sign of trouble. Made me promise. But before that, she was expressing concern about our shortage caused by last night's shutdown."

"I hate to worry her about that."

"She'd hate to see us landed in jail or shot. So, tell me what you think?"

"I don't know, Irv. Might be imprudent."

"Where'd you get a word like imprudent?"

"My granddaddy used it whenever he got an itch on the back of his neck. Meant he sensed trouble. He'd say it might be imprudent to cook that night."

"Well, I wish he was here to tell us if his neck was itching. But since he ain't, what do you think?"

Ernie turned his gaze to Corrine. "If it was just you and me, I'd say to hell with it, let's take our chances. But it ain't just us two we've got to consider anymore."

Irv looked back and forth between Ernie and the girl, and clarity dawned. "Good God a'mighty. It's like that, is it?"

Ernie grinned. Rather stupidly, Irv thought. "She and me have took up."

"Hell, Ernie, you're old enough to be her—"

"Uncle. We figured it out."

"Have you figured out how you're going to support her?"

"She won't cost much. She don't take up hardly any room. She's little but carries her weight. Like an ant." He grabbed the jar of whiskey away from Irv, took a swig, and, keeping his eyes forward, said, "I know what's got your dander up. You're thinking how can I like her after she's been a whore."

"I don't judge the girl for that. You ought to know me better, Ernie. I just didn't see this coming. Took me by surprise, is all."

"You and me both," Ernie said, smiling in that stupid way again. "Me looking how I do, I never counted on having a woman. But

Corrine said she's no raving beauty, either. She looks fine to me, though. Appearances don't matter."

Irv shook his head and chuckled. "No, I guess they don't, or my Dorothy would never have taken to me."

"Beans are ready," Corrine called from across the clearing. "Are y'all gonna come eat or continue to talk about me like I ain't here?"

After gathering around the fire and filling their tin plates, Corrine said, "I got an opinion on whether or not we do a run." Snootily, she added, "If anybody's interested."

"Let's hear it," Irv said.

"How do you spell imprudent?" she asked Ernie.

As an aside to Irv, he said, "I'm helping her with her letters." Then to Corrine, "E-m-p-r-o-o-d-u-n-t. I think. It means—"

"I figured out what it means," she said. "And I think if your granddaddy was here, he'd say his neck was itching something fierce and we should lay low."

She tilted her head back and looked at the sky. "It was so hot today, the sky was almost white, hardly any blue. When it's this hot, people turn cranky, tempers get short. Things that've been simmering tend to boil over.

"If we don't cook tonight, Laurel will be disappointed we didn't make product. But if we got killed, she'd keel over herself. She's had enough people die on her. I don't want that lady to have more grief on account of me. That's my say."

"Irv?" Ernie said. "You get the last word."

He pondered it, then said, "I 'spect you're right, Corrine. After supper let's move to where we hid out last night. We'll be locked and loaded, prepared to defend ourselves, but let's hope we won't have to." He gazed off into the distance in the direction of town. "But I'm scared that no matter what we do, Laurel is going to come to grief."

"Jesus, Mary, and Joseph." Mike O'Connor's blasphemy echoed off the limestone wall of the cellar. "They came down here?"

"They invited themselves," Laurel said. "There was no graceful way to refuse. If we hadn't installed those false shelves, they would have caught me red-handed. All those evenings I spent stewing fruit and berries saved us."

It also had helped to have a father-in-law to whom nailing scrap lumber together to form shelving had been the work of only a few hours. The exertion had pained his wounded arm for days after, but he would be glad to hear that his effort had prevented a catastrophe.

"The mayor likes to push his weight around," Davy said. "He's a blowhard."

"Don't underestimate how sinister he is under all that bluster," Laurel said. "He frightened me, and so did Landry. At least with Croft you know where you stand. Landry lurked and listened, all the while smiling like a snake oil salesman."

Mike said, "Yeah, he's a sneaky one."

"How do you know Chester Landry?"

"We don't," Mike said, "but we've seen him around, usually at Lefty's. I know the smile you're talking about. Like he knows you're the one who farted."

Laurel said, "Thatcher warned me of him."

"When was this?"

"Oh, it's *Thatcher* now?"

Davy spoke over his brother, but Laurel addressed Mike's question. "That was Thatcher's purpose for coming here the night you saw him in the yard. He cautioned me about Landry. I didn't take him seriously. I should have. Croft made it clear that he and Landry are committed to squashing the Johnsons."

"Do they realize how many Johnsons there are?" Davy asked. "They're like cockroaches."

Musing aloud, Laurel said, "I wouldn't be surprised if Croft's and Landry's operation isn't just as large. They're more discreet, but ambitious and every bit as ruthless as any Johnson. I wouldn't be surprised to learn that they initiated all the trouble last night."

"Exactly what did Mr. Croft propose?"

"The upshot was that he and Landry have a pool of moonshiners producing for them, and they want me to become one of them. An 'or else' was implied."

"You're not thinking of joining them?"

"Absolutely not. I haven't worked this hard to pay middlemen ten percent. I suppose we should be flattered that they considered us enough of a threat to bother. Croft even admitted how good our liquor is and how well it sells."

"What happened after your grandstanding?"

"They complimented me on the pie business's expansion and left."

Mike frowned. "I don't like it. These men aren't fools, Laurel. They were too dignified to go tearing down shelving looking for your stockpile of 'shine. They backed off, but they're drawing up another plan of attack. Mark my words. Next time I doubt they'll be so polite."

"Then we've got to move our whiskey to another hiding place away from the house," Davy said. "Safer for the whiskey, safer for Laurel."

"That would require careful planning," she said. "First, we have to find a place, and we can't do that tonight. Not with the county already a powder keg. And forget delivering to Ranger tonight. It would be too risky."

"Don't worry about us," Davy said. "We know to be on the lookout."

"On the lookout for what?"

Mike smacked his twin on the side of his head. "You never could keep your friggin' mouth shut."

"On the lookout for *what?*"

Mike shot his brother a drop-dead look, then said to Laurel, "The other night, a truck loaded to the gills with whiskey was hijacked between here and Ranger. The poor bastard was dragged from his truck, blindfolded, manhandled into the woods, pushed to his knees, and told not to move or speak. He had a gun held to his head while all his whiskey was taken from his truck and put into the other vehicle.

"He never saw how many of them there were, but they made short work of it. When they were done, he thought he was dead for sure.

But he was threatened with the removal of body parts a man holds dear if he was seen on that road again. He was ordered to spread the warning to anyone whose ambition was to get rich selling 'shine in the boom towns. He was left there with a drained gas tank. But he lived to tell it."

Laurel said, "The Johnsons are hijacking now?"

Davy and Mike shared a look, then Davy said softly, "*He* was a Johnson."

"Lawmen don't terrorize," Mike said. "They would have identified themselves, confiscated the liquor, and placed him under arrest. Had to be a competitor who plans on taking over."

Laurel lowered herself into a chair at the kitchen table. Hearing of this on top of Thatcher's warnings this morning, and the visit from Croft and Landry this afternoon, left her rattled. She needed time to assimilate all this and plan her next course of action. But in the meantime, people for whom she was responsible were more vulnerable than she. "Lord, I hope our stills aren't cooking tonight. And you absolutely cannot make the trip to Ranger."

Mike said, "We're going."

"I forbid it."

"Our contact up there is waiting and watching for us," Davy said.

"He's not a patient man," Mike said.

Davy added, "Neither are his thirsty customers."

Laurel said, "Tonight they can get their whiskey from someone else."

"One of Croft's deliverymen would be waiting for just such an opportunity to wedge in. In which case, you'll be handing Croft exactly what he's after."

Davy nodded in agreement with Mike. "That would be bad for our business."

"So is being hijacked," she said.

Mike placed a hand on her shoulder. "We're making the delivery, as scheduled. Nothing to fret about. We've thought of a way to throw them off track."

Davy winked.

FIFTY-TWO

Darkness had fallen by the time Thatcher returned to Barker's from Pointer's Gap. The auto garage was closed for the night. He needed to return Barker's borrowed rifle, but he was relieved that he wouldn't be delayed any longer than necessary.

He stabled the pinto and saw to it that he was well rewarded for his patience and endurance that afternoon. He stored the saddle and tack, went down the row of stalls to make sure that all the horses were content. Not all were. He calmed the restless ones with soft talk and stroking, then secured the stable with his own sixth sense of uneasiness.

Taking Barker's rifle with him, he walked across the bridge into town. Martin's Café was open, but there were few diners tonight. For the most part, downtown was closed and locked up, as though braced for a storm.

With reason. One was brewing. Distant lightning brightened the sky just above the horizon. Every surface, whether natural or manmade, radiated the heat it had absorbed during the day. The air felt charged by something more ominous than low atmospheric pressure.

Thatcher entered the boardinghouse and went upstairs unnoticed.

By a stroke of luck the third-floor bathroom was available. He made quick work of bathing and exchanging his dusty work clothes for his black suit. He buckled on his gun belt, pinned the deputy badge to the lapel of his coat, and took Barker's rifle with him.

In and out of the boardinghouse in under ten minutes, he set out on foot again. Only Bill's car was parked in front of the sheriff's department. Inside, he was alone but on the telephone.

Thatcher propped Barker's rifle against the wall beneath the gun rack, took off his fedora, and slumped tiredly in a chair. Bill completed his call with a "Thank you very much," and hung the earpiece in its cradle. "Dennis Kemp checks out," he said to Thatcher. "Hasn't missed a day of work since he began the job. He was there yesterday."

"Mrs. Kemp told you you'd be barking up the wrong tree." Thatcher looked toward the door that led into the cell block. "How is he?"

"Sullen when I took him his supper. The public defender hasn't made it in yet."

"Have you called him?"

"Considering all the arrests last night, I'm sure he had his hands full today with arraignment hearings. Driscoll can sulk till morning."

"How's Mrs. Amos doing?"

The sheriff's forehead wrinkled with concern. "Still ailing. If she's not better by tomorrow, I may take her to a doctor in Stephenville. Mrs. Cantor agreed to stay with her overnight if I can't get home."

"You're expecting more trouble?"

He waved his hand to indicate the empty office. "I've got every full-timer plus a dozen reserves like you patrolling in pairs. I want to keep a lid on things if we can. Vain hope, probably."

Thatcher drew his long legs in, leaned forward, and placed his elbows on his knees. "You've got plenty of trouble right in here, Bill."

He reached into his pocket and pulled out a strip of cotton fabric roughly six inches in length and three inches wide. One side was flat, the other gathered. The weave was unraveling at both ends. The cloth had been weather-beaten, but under its coating of dust, the scarlet color was vibrant.

Thatcher set the piece of cloth on the edge of the sheriff's desk. He spoke softly so not to be overheard by the man in the cell. "I went exploring this afternoon and found this. I recognized it right off. When I talked to Mrs. Driscoll, she was wearing an apron made out of material printed with red and yellow apples. It had a red ruffled border."

Through the window, Thatcher saw a lightning bolt, closer this time, but it took the thunder a count of seven to reach them. The storm was headed this way but wasn't right on top of them yet.

Bill seemed not to notice the weather. He was fixated on the fabric scrap. "Where'd you find it?"

"Pointer's Gap. Caught between some rocks, piled up, but not by God or Mother Nature. They'd been stacked."

"Pointer's Gap. Where Gabe took his missus picnicking."

Thatcher scoffed. "The nearest I came to finding a picnic spot was a stream off the north fork of the Paluxy. No deeper than a foot at its deepest. It had a ripple, but not what I'd call a current. A few scraggly trees along its banks. If he was trying to romance his wife with a picnic, a prettier spot would have been in his own shady backyard."

"When Bernie told us that Gabe had taken her there, I remember thinking that same thing."

"That stream is about a quarter mile from the gap, and between them is wasteland. If he took her out there, it definitely wasn't to picnic."

Bill acknowledged that with a frown. "How'd you get out there?"

"Horseback."

"That's six, eight miles each way."

"I'm used to it. Or was," he said, wincing as he shifted in his chair. "I may be a bit saddle sore tomorrow."

Both of them smiled, but they quickly became serious again. Bill asked, "Did you disturb the pile of rocks?"

"No, just tugged that piece of cloth from between them. It ripped when I pulled, so there's more of it under there."

"Could you find the place again?"

"With no problem."

Bill smoothed his hand over his mustache a few times. "Gabe doesn't have a horse that I know of. How would he have gotten her out there?"

"There's a road, more like a trail, that comes in from the southwest on the other side of the hill. I figure he took care of Corrine at Lefty's—"

"With Mrs. Driscoll dead in his car?"

Thatcher shrugged. "This is just my guess, Bill."

"Go on."

"When he finished up at Lefty's, he drove out, circled back to the gap on that lonely road, carried her body the rest of the way until he found a suitable spot. Maybe he stumbled upon a natural depression, maybe he dug one. But he buried her and stacked those rocks on top. It was dark, so he missed that." He pointed to the remnant of ruffle. "As hiding a body goes, he chose a good spot. If that cloth had been dull in color, I would've missed it."

"Good work, Thatcher."

"Knowing what you're likely to find under those rocks, it doesn't feel good. Not good at all."

Bill waited a beat before continuing to theorize. "On his way back into town, Gabe's conscience grabbed hold."

"Or terror of being caught."

"Either way, he realized the magnitude of what he'd done and headed to his mistress for solace. Then what, Thatcher? Did Miss Blanchard know he'd killed Mila, or not? Did she calm him down and coach him on what to do next, what to say and how to perform when questioned?"

"Mrs. Kemp doesn't think so."

"She could be lying. She may know all too well that Norma was complicit."

"Could be."

"But you don't think so?"

"If Norma had lived, maybe her sister would've lied to cover for her. But why would she lie for her now?"

"To protect baby nephew Arthur from disgrace? Hell, I don't know." Sighing, he covered his face with both hands and pressed his middle fingers into his eye sockets, his weariness evident. "I don't know anything anymore."

"Two things you know," Thatcher said.

Bill lowered his hands and looked across at him.

"One. Norma Blanchard can't be held accountable even if she masterminded the murder. Second thing, you've finally got a piece of evidence. It's not a decomposed body, but that apron trim might be enough to bring Driscoll to his knees."

"He's proven to be mule-headed."

"Won't hurt to try."

Bill took the strip of cloth with him as he entered the cell block. Thatcher followed him to the last cell, where Driscoll was reclined on the cot, eyes closed, pale hands clasped over his stomach. "Unless you have a defense lawyer with you, go away."

"You'll want to see this, Gabe."

Thatcher and Bill waited him out, and his curiosity got the better of him. He opened his eyes and levered himself up on his elbows.

Bill dangled the strip of red cloth. "Recognize this?"

"No."

"Thatcher did." Bill explained how Thatcher remembered seeing the ruffle on Mila's apron.

Driscoll shrugged. "She wore an apron every day of her life."

"In the kitchen while baking shortbread," Bill said. "Around the house as she was dusting the furniture. But why would she wear one to Pointer's Gap?"

Mention of the landmark sparked a stunned reaction. His gaze darted to Thatcher, then back to Bill. "What was he doing out there?"

Bill ignored the question. "He found this caught in a pile of rocks. What do you know about it, Gabe?"

"Nothing."

"Explain to me how a ruffle off Mrs. Driscoll's apron got stuck between two rocks all the way out there in no-man's-land."

"Why are you asking me? Why don't you ask *him*?" He came off the cot and charged the cell bars, shoving his hand through two of them and grabbing Thatcher by his necktie. "Do you really think he just wandered out there and accidentally found this? Where's your common sense, sheriff? He knew where to find it, because he buried Mila's body out there. It was him all along. Don't you see?"

A crack of thunder startled them all. Driscoll actually let go of Thatcher's tie and fell back a step away from the bars, as though they'd suddenly been electrified.

The first clap was followed by a second, then a third. And then a salvo. Simultaneously, Thatcher and Bill realized that it wasn't thunder.

It was gunfire.

FIFTY-THREE

Chester Landry watched from the shadows as Laurel Plummer bade the O'Connor brothers goodbye. Even from this distance, he could tell she was anxious about sending them out tonight. She touched each of them on the arm, and clung for a moment, like a mother reluctant to wave her children off to school for the first time.

Final instructions were issued and goodbyes said, and the pair drove away in their truck. From the outside, it looked like a rattletrap held together with baling wire and crossed fingers.

But as it drove past Landry, he was close enough to feel the vibration of the new engine the twins recently had had installed. The swap-out had been done in a barn on a farm that had been foreclosed on years before. The mechanics, who'd helped themselves to the empty space, catered to moonshiners and bootleggers who were trying to outdo, or at least to equal, the horsepower had by lawmen, government agents, and each other.

He wondered if Mrs. Plummer was aware of the new oomph under the battered hood of the O'Connors' truck. He would guess she wasn't. The O'Connors were too cocksure of themselves by far. Brimming with piss and vinegar, they took needless chances, seemed to thrive on excitation, and routinely flirted with calamity.

But he couldn't fault them. He reveled in risk-taking.

Lights were on inside, affording him a view through the window into the kitchen. He watched Mrs. Plummer drink a glass of tap water at the sink. Then she moved about the room nervously, picking up this or that, setting it down, opening a cabinet door only to close it without putting anything in or taking anything out.

He saw her actually wring her hands. At one point, she lifted her pocketbook off a peg adjacent to the back door, as though she were about to leave, then changed her mind. She seemed troubled and restless, feeling compelled to do something, but unsure of what she should do.

His timing was perfect.

He emerged from the shadows and crossed the yard. The honeysuckle vine brushed his shoulder as he neared the back door. He knocked, but stood to one side, keeping himself concealed in the darkness until she appeared behind the screen.

He stepped into the light and tipped his bowler hat to her. "Mrs. Plummer."

Her lips tightened with dislike. "What are you doing here?"

Her hand moved to her side, where she no doubt secreted a firearm in the pocket of her skirt. Probably a Derringer. A whore's pistol. Small but lethal if fired at close range.

"May I come in?"

"No, you may not."

"You sound adamant."

"I am."

"Why?"

"It would be improper."

Amused by her hypocritical stance on propriety, he said, "Improper because your father-in-law isn't at home? He's away this evening?"

She realized that she'd trapped herself into admitting she was by herself, but rather than quail, she drew herself up taller. She looked above and beyond him at the lightning that streaked the sky.

"It's about to storm," she said over the boom of thunder that rattled the windows of her house. "You wouldn't want to get wet, so leave now and don't come back. You and Mr. Croft were fishing in the wrong pond today. In any case, I said everything I had to say. Now if you'll—"

"That's what I wanted to talk to you about. Our visit today." He gave her a look of rehearsed chagrin. "You have every right to be miffed."

"Don't talk down to me."

He held up his hand in a pacifying gesture. "Mr. Croft often gets carried away. His strident manner is a character flaw which I've pointed out to him on numerous occasions. Sadly, to no avail. His overbearing approach to you was tactless and clumsy. He came on like a buffalo when a swan would have been more effective. It's little wonder to me that you turned him down."

"Did he send you to make amends?"

"No, I came entirely on my own."

"I don't want your apology. I want you to leave."

"But I didn't come to apologize."

"To do what, then? Ask me to reconsider your deal?"

"No," he said smoothly, "I came to offer you a better one."

His statement startled her, but not as much as the gunshot that punctuated it.

Numerous blasts followed, the rapid popping sounding like the finale of a fireworks display.

Even before the barrage stopped, Laurel stunned him by shoving open the screen door. She shouldered him out of her way and began running in the direction from which the shots had come.

Landry went after her, shouting her name.

She didn't even slow down.

Bill locked the door between the office and the cell block while Thatcher retrieved Barker's rifle and took another from the rack for Bill. Moving swiftly and without a single word being spoken between them, they exited the building and got into Bill's car.

While Thatcher loaded and checked the weapons, the sheriff drove at top speed through downtown. Main Street was already filling up with curiosity-seekers streaming in the direction of the apparent shootout. Thatcher noticed that one man in the crowd still had his napkin from the café tucked into his collar.

Bill shouted at the onlookers and angrily waved them out of his way. He used his horn to bleat out warnings for them to move aside or get bowled over. Bill gave the car more gas as it trundled across the bridge.

On the far side of it, they rounded a bend to find the road blocked by a disabled truck. Both doors stood open. The radiator was spewing steam like a teakettle.

The truck had been riddled by bullets. The driver had made it out. He lay sprawled in the road. The passenger was still in his seat.

"Jesus." Bill used the handbrake to bring his car to a skidding stop. Thatcher, noticing movement in the underbrush to his right, was out of the car before inertia rocked it to rest. He leaped across the ditch in pursuit.

The woods were as dark as midnight. Bursts of lightning only served to momentarily blind him. But the brilliant flashes followed by complete darkness were reminiscent of nighttime battles, and he'd had plenty of experience with those. Conditioned reflexes took over. Rifle up, he ran on, dodging trees, ducking low branches, doing his best to avoid pitfalls in the undergrowth.

Ahead of him, men were shouting to each other. The words were indistinct, but their connotation was urgency. If they kept up the racket, they'd lead Thatcher straight to them. But then he heard the sound of an auto motor sputtering to life.

"Fuck, fuck." He pushed himself harder, but by the time he reached the road, all he saw of the retreating car was the wink of its taillights as it disappeared around a curve. Any attempt to run it down on foot would be futile.

He didn't even break stride as he reversed direction and ran back toward the site of an evident ambush. He cleared the woods and jumped the ditch again, then paused to catch his breath and take in the scene.

The crowd of onlookers had increased in number. Two more sheriff's department vehicles were parked on either side of Bill's car. Deputies had divided up. A few were grouped around the man lying face-up on the pavement. Others had formed a semicircle in the open passenger door.

Harold and another deputy Thatcher didn't know had the tailgate down and were shining flashlights into the back of the truck.

Thatcher lowered the rifle and made his way over to Bill, who was kneeling at the side of the man lying in the road. It was one of the O'Connor twins, although Thatcher couldn't have said which. He was bleeding from several wounds, but his lips were moving, and Bill was listening intently.

"His brother's dead." Thatcher turned. Harold elaborated without being asked to. "The twins came around the bend there, caught fire from the trees on both sides of the road. They didn't stand a chance. Somebody wanted to make a point."

"Whoever it was came through the woods from the road that parallels this one." Thatcher pointed. "I chased them, but they had too good of a head start. Didn't see how many, but all of them fit into one vehicle."

Harold nodded, then said, "Hell of it is, if this had to do with the illegal liquor trade, they got the wrong guys. All they were hauling was a bunch of pies and jars of fruit fillings."

"Get away from me!"

The voice was shrill but Thatcher recognized it instantly and spun around. Laurel was struggling to escape the grasping hands of Chester Landry. Thatcher was in motion before he even thought about it. He swung the rifle barrel to waist level and ran toward them, shouting, "Let her go!"

Laurel managed to wrestle herself free, but Landry reached for her again, catching hold of the back of her skirt and bringing her up short. She whirled around and slugged him in the face with her fist.

"Landry!" Thatcher yelled. "Let go of her!"

Seeing Thatcher bearing down on him, and recognizing the hellfire he represented, Landry immediately released Laurel and ran for his life, disappearing into the woods on the other side of the road.

Over his shoulder, Thatcher hollered to Harold, "Go after him." The deputy took off running.

Thatcher ran to close the remaining distance between him and Laurel, but she was on an undeterred path toward the truck, and she was in a crazed state.

Thatcher overcame her and grabbed hold of her arm with his free hand. She turned her head and looked up at him, wild-eyed and frantic. "That's the twins' truck. I heard the shooting."

She jerked free of his hold and continued on. Thatcher called her name, and, when he caught her again, they engaged in a tussle not unlike the one she'd been in with Landry.

"Laurel, stop it. Laurel!" He finally got her to stand still. "One is wounded but alive. The other is gone."

It took several seconds for the message to sink in, then she threw back her head and wailed, "Nooooo."

He tried to draw her to him, but she took in the badge, the gun belt around his hips, the rifle he still carried. When it all registered, she threw off his hands to free herself. "Damn you!" she yelled as she ran backward. "Stay away from me."

Realizing the conclusion she'd drawn, he said, "No, Laurel. It wasn't me. Wasn't us. This was—"

But he was talking to the empty space where she'd been standing. She knocked onlookers aside as she plowed through them to get to where Bill still knelt beside the wounded man. She gave another wail when she saw him and dropped to her knees.

Harold huffed up to Thatcher. "He was too fast. I lost him in the dark."

With cold determination, Thatcher said, "Don't worry. I'll find him."

Hiram Johnson sat in a filthy, upholstered armchair with his bare, bloated right foot propped on a stool. An open jar of moonshine was on the windowsill, along with a flyswatter, both within easy reach. A Bible lay open on his lap.

Mayor Bernard Croft had never seen such a disgusting sight in his life and doubted he ever would. The old man's rotting foot stank to high heaven. It was as though the walls of this house seeped the rancid odor of generations of Johnsons. The unmoving air smelled of dirty hair, dirty feet, decayed teeth, tobacco-laced expectorant, and baby shit.

The foulness of it all sickened Bernie. He could barely keep his dinner down.

Of course he'd known more or less what he was letting himself in for when he'd requested this meeting. He'd sent Hennessy to parley with Hiram, requesting an assemblage of the clan so that Bernie could address them collectively. Hennessy had been instructed to stress that Bernie would be assuming all the risks, because the meeting would take place on Hiram's turf.

Bernie would be walking into the lion's den, but the goal was to end the strife between his faction and the Johnsons. Give and take. Negotiation. Compromise. A fair division of territories. The goal being to end this silly and counterproductive war.

They had congregated. The house was overflowing with representatives of the myriad branches of the family. They had listened to Bernie's impassioned speech. It was time to make his final pitch and close the deal.

He stood before Hiram. "This feud would eventually play itself out, Mr. Johnson. You've lived long enough, been a businessman long enough, to know that ultimately things work themselves out and life returns to the way it was before.

"But in the meantime, this destructive bickering costs us both revenue. People get hurt. People die. It's a waste. If we stop fighting each other, we can devote ourselves to fighting our common enemy, which is this new goddamn federal law." He ended on a high note that elicited guffaws from many.

Not, however, from the old man, who spat into his coffee can. "You can have Ranger," Hiram said. "But I want Breckenridge and any other boom towns that spring up between here and the Red River. You can have anything south of here."

"There won't be any boom towns south of here because there's no oil south of here. Not for hundreds of miles. As you well know."

"West then," Hiram said. "Show him the map."

A man in greasy overalls stepped forward and passed Bernie a faded map. He studied the lines that had been drawn on it to demarcate territories. "This is attractive to me. They're already drilling out there west of Abilene, around Odessa."

"So more than fair, I think. Take it or leave it." He spat again.

"If I take it, it amounts to a cease-fire. Agreed?"

"Agreed."

"And it goes into effect immediately?"

Hiram nodded.

"Splendid." Bernie stepped forward, right hand extended. With an evil gleam in his eye, the rotting son of a bitch wiped tobacco spittle off his lip before clutching Bernie's hand. Despite his revulsion, Bernie gave him an enthusiastic handshake.

"I was so optimistic about the outcome of this meeting that I brought you a gift, Mr. Johnson." He signaled Hennessy, who'd been waiting out on the porch. "I've brought you a case of Kentucky bourbon, direct from my most trusted bootlegger in Dallas and Fort Worth."

Oohs and ahhs of appreciation rippled through the compacted gathering of bodies as the case was carried in and set on the floor in front of that putrid foot.

"Enjoy." Bernie's leave-taking was unceremonious. It was barely even noticed. Hiram was already swilling from a bottle of the whiskey. His relatives were greedily converging around the case.

Together Bernie and Hennessy walked toward the town car. Looking back over his shoulder at the party underway, Hennessy asked, "How long before the poison works?"

"I've decided it takes too long. Did you bring along some of your toys?"

"Always, boss."

Bernie grinned as he climbed into the driver's seat. "Give me ten minutes to get to the highway, then light her up."

FIFTY-FOUR

$$\longrightarrow \! \cdot \! \text{\ding{73}} \! \cdot \! \longrightarrow$$

Bernie entered his house through the front door, and automatically locked it behind him.

He had driven himself from Hiram's house to the intersection with the highway, where he'd gotten to enjoy the fireball. When Hennessy caught up with him, the Irishman had taken his traditional place in the driver's seat while Bernie got into the back and savored his success during the trip into town. The Johnsons not blown to smithereens in the blast would have been cooked to well done in the fire.

Both he and Hennessy were confident that they hadn't been followed. Hennessy had waited to be certain that Bernie made it safely inside his front door, then struck out on foot. He lodged in a seedier part of town. He didn't fear that on his walk home anyone would be fool enough to accost him.

Through the side window on the front door, Bernie checked the street one last time. It was empty, nothing moving save for Hennessy, disappearing into the downpour.

Tomorrow, when Mayor Croft was told the shocking news of the conflagration, he would publicly attribute it to a lightning strike. The old Johnson place would have been a tinder box, he would say.

The poor souls inside, a great number of the legendary clan including the patriarch, had stood little chance of escaping the flames.

For the town's biweekly gazette, he would wax poetic about the tragedy. He would milk it for all it was worth. But now, as he collapsed his umbrella and hung his hat on the coat tree, he wanted to cackle with delight over his triumph. He stepped into the parlor and reached for the light switch.

"Leave it."

Bernie fell back against the doorjamb and clapped his hand over his heart. "Jesus, Chester."

"Why, Mr. Mayor. You jumped like someone with a guilty conscience."

The darkness was relieved only by light from a streetlamp shining through the front window curtains. Bernie's eyes adjusted. Landry was sitting with his typical indolence in an easy chair, legs crossed.

He said, "Where have you and Hennessy been off to tonight?"

Bernie went over to a cabinet and took out a bottle of bourbon and two glasses. "A better question would be what are you doing inside my house at this hour, sitting in the dark?" He poured an inch of bourbon into each glass and carried one over to Landry.

"Thank you." He clinked his glass against Bernie's but didn't drink from it.

Bernie settled himself on the divan facing Landry's chair. "Well?"

Landry propped his drinking glass on his knee and stared into it for a moment. "My welcome in your little burg has worn thin, Bernie."

"You're leaving?"

"Tonight."

Bernie's eyebrows shot up. "Tonight? How long do you plan to be away?"

"Forever. I'm severing our partnership. As of now."

This was an unexpected turn, but not at all disappointing to Bernie. Landry's welcome had been wearing thin with him, too. Initially, he'd needed a man like Landry to grease the skids into the bootlegging trade.

But Bernie's own contacts in the cities were well established by now. The value of Landry's usefulness had decreased. It certainly wasn't worth the percentage he demanded. If Landry wanted out, Bernie wasn't at all sorry to bid him farewell.

Nevertheless, he attempted to look bemused. "Why?"

"Bad business practices."

"Whose?"

"Yours."

It was an effort for Bernie to conceal his outrage. "I don't ask for or require the approval of a slick dandy like you, but I am curious. Can you give me an example of the business practices you oppose?"

"Gladly. For example, with a little courting, a little finessing, Laurel Plummer might have been won over. Instead, you bullied her. That tactic didn't flatter you. It didn't cast a favorable light on me, either, which I resent. It also failed. Colossally."

"She'll come around."

"Oh, I seriously doubt that. Not after you had her errand boys ambushed and shot all to hell."

Bernie snickered. "How did the duo fare? Did they survive?"

"I don't know. I was spotted near the scene. Although I'm not proud to admit it, I ran." He swirled the whiskey in his glass, the only sign of his simmering anger. "You took that action upon yourself, Bernie. You executed that ambush without consulting me."

"Because you would have wavered when action was called for."

"I would have acted with more discretion, as I did with Randy. The problem was solved, but it was neat. Nobody's curiosity was aroused."

"We needed to make a splash," Bernie said. "We needed to do something that would get the lovely widow's attention."

"Well, you succeeded at that. But this bloody display will also draw the attention of people who aren't so lovely. Bad for business, Bernie. Bad for business. Because now, you're going to be in the bull's-eye of a crackdown, beginning with a thorough investigation by local law."

"I've made Bill Amos a eunuch, and his department is a joke."

"His newly appointed deputy isn't what I'd call a jolly sort."

"Hutton? I'm not scared of him."

"Another example of your foolishness."

"How dare—"

"If Hutton doesn't give you pause, the Texas Rangers are even less jocular than he is. The governor is a colorful character, granted. But he's been known to send in troops to help curtail a lucrative bootleg trade. When they all come gunning for the ringleader in this area of the state, I want to be far removed from you."

He set his glass on a small table at his elbow, then stood. "I let myself in through the back door. I'll go out the same way."

Bernie came to his feet. "You smug prick. Do you expect me to believe that you're just walking away, leaving money on the table, retiring?"

Landry stopped and turned back. "Did I say that?" He flashed the sly grin that Bernie had come to detest. "I've never met a woman who didn't love shoes. And there are women everywhere, who have men in their lives who enjoy a drink." The grin widened to reveal his gold tooth. "I won't have any trouble drumming up business." Then he whispered, "Watch your back, Bernie."

<hr />

Thatcher didn't see Chester Landry's car among those parked at the boardinghouse, but he didn't let that stop him from taking the front steps two at a time. The house was dark except for a few dim lights providing barely enough illumination for him to see his way up the staircase. He knew Landry occupied room number four on the second floor.

He knocked. Silence. He knocked again and put his ear to the door. He heard nothing.

Across the hall a door opened and a head popped out. He recognized the boarder, but didn't recall his name. He said, "He's not there. He left this afternoon."

"Did he say where he was going?"

"Nope. Just cleared out his stuff—"

"Cleared out? You mean he moved out?"

"Lock, stock, and barrel. Took all his shoe samples. Seemed to be on short notice."

Thatcher twisted the doorknob, but it was locked. He jerked on it harder. When it didn't give, he backed up a few steps.

"I don't believe Mrs. May would approve—"

Thatcher kicked in the door. The room was empty. The bed had already been stripped of sheets. Replacement bedding and a bath towel were folded and stacked, awaiting the next boarder.

Thatcher searched every drawer in the bureau, opened the closet, checked under the bed. He flipped back the mattress, but there was nothing beneath it except rusty bed springs.

"What the hell do you think you're doing?"

The landlady was standing in the open doorway, hands on her hips. She looked like a hag during daytime. The nighttime variant was worse.

Nevertheless, Thatcher moved in on her. "Did Landry say where he was going?"

"No, and I didn't ask," she said. "Ain't my business, is it?"

"He's moved out for good? He's not coming back?"

"Not your business, neither."

Thatcher tapped the badge on his lapel. "Sheriff Amos will disagree. Should I send him over to talk to you?"

She folded her housecoat closer around her and jutted out her pointy chin. "He said he was taking over a new sales territory and wouldn't be back. Paid me for a few extra days because he'd failed to give me notice. Packed up his automobile and headed out. That's all I know."

"What time did he leave?"

"I can't—"

"What *time*?"

"Four-thirty. Thereabouts. He interrupted me while I was busy setting up the sideboard." She sniffed. "Which I didn't appreciate one bit."

Thatcher stepped back into the hallway and addressed all the boarders who now were watching curiously from their open doorways, as they had the night he'd been taken into custody. Some shrank back. "Anybody know where Chester Landry was going? Did he ever say where he was from?"

"All I ever heard was Dallas," one said. That was followed with murmurs of agreement.

"He ever mention family?"

No one answered, but one asked, "Wha'd he do?"

Thatcher said, "If anyone hears anything from him, or about him, come get me. Sorry to have woken you up." He jogged down the stairs and out the front door.

Five minutes later, he stood dripping rainwater in the waiting room of Dr. Perkins's clinic, explaining to Bill what he'd learned. "Landry had prepared to run even before the ambush."

"Leading you to believe he may have been instrumental in that?"

"He might have planned it, but he didn't participate."

In unison Thatcher and the sheriff turned toward Laurel, who'd spoken from the chair that Patsy Kemp had occupied days before. Laurel looked small and defenseless, with shoulders hunched, hugging her elbows.

She said, "He was at my back door when the shooting started."

Bill walked over to her. "What was Chester Landry doing at your back door?"

She was about to answer, when Dr. Perkins came out of the interior room. His lab coat was bloodied. Laurel shot to her feet. He didn't keep them in suspense. "My nurse and I successfully removed two bullets. The third went through his lower left abdomen. I've done what I can. He's still with us."

"Is he out of danger?" Laurel asked.

"No, Mrs. Plummer. He survived the surgery, but he's not in the clear." Seeing her distress, he said, "But he's young and strong. His vitals are good. If he can stave off infection, he has a good chance of recovery. Men with far worse wounds have recovered."

Laurel covered her mouth and took a deep breath. "Does he know about Davy?"

"He demanded that I tell him," Bill said to her. "It was just before he lost consciousness, so it may not have sunk in."

"It did," Dr. Perkins said, looking bleak. "He came to and was most fretful over it before we sedated him."

Laurel gave a soft sob. "Can I see him?"

Dr. Perkins looked her over. Her dress, shoes, and stockings were spattered with mud and streaked with Mike's blood. "He's still out cold, Mrs. Plummer. He won't know you're there. And, uh, infection is a major concern. Tomorrow would be better."

Only then did she seem to realize how bedraggled she looked and the reason for the doctor's hesitancy to let her near his patient. But she stood proud and composed. "I'll be here first thing in the morning."

"I need to get back." Dr. Perkins retreated and shut the door.

The three of them filed out of the waiting area, Laurel leading the way. Bill and Thatcher had conferred briefly at the scene of the ambush before Thatcher had gone in search of Landry. At the time, the sheriff had dispatched men to comb the woods on both sides of the road in search of clues. They recovered dozens of shell casings from numerous weapons, but nothing else.

Bill had remarked then that he hoped the rain would hold off until daylight tomorrow when a more thorough search could be made of the woods and the road on which the getaway car had sped away.

Thatcher could tell how disheartened Bill was when they reached the exit of the office building to see that the lightning and thunder had moved east, but a hard rain was being driven sideways by a strong wind.

"So much for tire tracks and footprints," Bill said as he motioned Laurel and Thatcher toward his car. They dashed through the rain and piled in.

When they reached Laurel's house, it was in total darkness. "Thank you for the ride." She opened the backseat door herself, got out, and ran toward the house.

Thatcher watched her go inside, then turned his head and looked at Bill.

Bill gave him a knowing smile. "Busy day in store for tomorrow. Gabe Driscoll. Now this ambush with one man dead. You're only a reserve, Thatcher. I've got no claim on you. But I'd sure appreciate your help."

"I'll stop by the stable and see if Fred can spare Roger to tend to the horses tomorrow."

"Early then."

Thatcher nodded, got out, and ran through the torrent to Laurel's door.

FIFTY-FIVE

The electricity was out in Laurel's house. When Thatcher entered the kitchen through the back door, she was lighting a kerosene lamp. She blew out the match and situated the glass chimney.

She said, "You know what's funny?"

He propped Barker's rifle against the wall and hung his dripping hat on the wall peg. "I can't think of a thing."

"Davy would've been the first to laugh over being killed for a truckload of pies and fruit fillings. It was his and Mike's idea. They'd cooked it up even before I told them about Mayor Croft and Chester Landry visiting today. I was—"

"Hold on. The mayor and Landry came here?"

"To try to coerce me into joining their...I don't know the word. Syndicate? Did you know the mayor is a bootlegger? Anyway, they showed up at my front door this afternoon."

In a thready voice, she pieced together broken sentences to relate what the pair had proposed. Thatcher wasn't surprised by any of it except for Bernie Croft's brashness. "Who did the talking?" he asked.

"The mayor."

Up till now Croft had used his political office as cover. If he was stepping out from behind it, he must be feeling damned confident that he couldn't be touched. That was a troubling prospect.

"When they left," Laurel was saying, "I had the shakes. I knew I hadn't seen the last of them. But I didn't think their reprisal would come this soon or be so...deadly."

Tears filled her eyes. "When I told the twins about that visit and the reason behind it, they admitted that a truck had been hijacked just a few days ago." She described the incident to Thatcher.

"I suppose the only reason they let that Johnson man live was so he could put his family and the rest of us on notice. Nevertheless, the twins were keen on going tonight."

"But without whiskey."

She nodded. "They weren't selling just my whiskey. They had been dealing with another moonshiner, who's up closer to Ranger. They'd bought several crates from him and had hidden them someplace accessible, so the product would be on hand when they needed it.

"In view of this recent hijacking, they had counted on selling what was in that stockpile, but would continue to make the trip from here to there with pies only. In the event they were intercepted, the joke would be on whoever had stopped them.

"Their thinking was that after they were caught with only pies as cargo, they would be left alone. You see? Isn't that just like a prank the two of them would pull?"

She gave a dry, forced laugh, and she began to quiver like a shell-shocked trooper on the verge of cracking.

He spoke her name quietly, and when she'd blinked him into focus, he asked about Landry. "Tell me what happened with him."

"He must have been watching the house, because he came to the back door almost immediately after the twins left. He said Mayor Croft had been overbearing and tactless, and that he didn't blame me for turning them down. He said he had come, not at Croft's behest, but on his own, to make me a better offer. I don't know what he was going to propose, because that's when the shooting started. The instant I heard the gunfire, I had a premonition, a sick feeling."

She touched her stomach. "I took off running. Landry came after me, and caught up. From there, you know. You saw."

"The coward ran and got away."

"Mike was lying in the street, and Davy was dead. They made such easy targets as they came out of the curve in the road." She appeared to want to say more, but her throat seized up. She had difficulty swallowing.

"Laurel, it wasn't lawmen who ambushed them."

She looked down at the floor, but he didn't think it registered with her that the puddle around her muddy shoes had been formed by her dripping clothes.

"Sheriff Amos called it sabotage," she said. "Moonshiners mistaking the twins for rivals. And they were. They *were*. For me." She pressed her fist to her chest. "I let them go tonight, knowing the danger."

She covered her face with her hands and began to sob. "Irv kept telling me it wasn't a lark. You warned me. But, no, I was conceited and stubborn, and thought that I was above the fray, that I couldn't be touched. And because of that vanity, Davy died."

Sensing that she was about to collapse where she stood, Thatcher crossed over to her and enfolded her in his arms. "The O'Connors knew they were playing a dangerous game. They knew the risks."

"But it's my fault."

"No, Laurel. They loved the thrill. With or without you, they would have become part of this trade."

"I tried my best to talk them out of going tonight. Honestly, Thatcher, I did. But they were bent on it. If Mike lives, he will never get over losing his brother. Never." Her forehead dropped against his sternum and she began to sob harder. "I can't do this anymore. Even if I wanted to continue. I can't. I can't risk another life."

"You've got to stop risking your own." He scooped her up into his arms and headed for the staircase.

Feebly, she pushed against his chest. "Let me down."

"You're sopping wet. Your teeth are chattering, and you're about to drop."

He carried her into her bedroom, set her on her feet, and propped her against the wall. He went around the room pulling down the window shades and lit the lamp on her dresser, keeping the flame low. He folded back the bedcovers.

She hadn't moved from where he'd left her. For the longest time, they stood facing, staring into each other's eyes.

"You're fragile right now," he said. "I promised I would never take advantage of you, and I meant it. I'm putting you to bed. If you don't want me in there with you, say so now."

She didn't move or speak.

Keeping his eyes locked with hers, he reached down and untied the thong holding his holster against his thigh, then unbuckled the gun belt and set it in a chair. His coat was wet. It clung, but he worked himself out of it. He flipped his braces off his shoulders, opened several buttons of his shirt, then impatiently pulled it over his head. Shoes and socks went next. He unbuttoned his fly but stopped there.

He knelt in front of her and slipped off her shoes. Sliding his hands up her legs under her skirt, he found her garters, rolled down her stockings, and peeled them off her chilled feet.

When he stood up, he reached behind her head, pulled out what few pins remained in her hair, and dropped them to the floor. As her hair tumbled down her back, he combed his fingers through it.

"Thatcher, I—"

With abject misery, he moaned, "Please don't shy from me, Laurel."

"I'm not. It's just..." In a purely feminine, self-conscious gesture, she touched the tear tracks on her cheeks, then moved her hand down to her collar, which she drew closed over her throat. "I'm not very tidy."

His heart thumped with restored anticipation. Her voice was husky from weeping, and so seductive he wanted to trap it inside her mouth and taste it. "I don't need you tidy. I need you now."

He placed his hands flat against the wall on either side of her head, lowered his, and used his nose to nudge open the collar she'd closed. He pressed an open-mouth kiss on the side of her neck, nibbled up the slender column of it to her ear where he breathed, "I won't hold back."

"Please don't. Make me forget."

"What?"

"Everything."

That sighed consent unleashed a primal urge in him to claim, possess, mate. He came up against her and covered her face with kisses, then slanted his mouth over hers. He ate from it, unable to draw as much from it as he was yearning for, greedy for. He went back and back and back for more. He slid his hands from the wall to her breasts. There was no corset to prevent him from massaging and reshaping them. She leaned into the caresses in unshy offering.

Somehow he managed to keep their mouths fused as he pulled her blouse free of her waistband and unbuttoned it. The buttons were small and round and devils to work free of the wet material, but at last he got them undone, and her blouse was off.

He skimmed his hands over her front, feeling the warmth of her skin through her chemise. He compressed the tips of her breasts between his fingers and heard her breath flutter around his name as she sighed it.

After two failed attempts, he found the fastening of her skirt and undid it. The skirt, weighted with rainwater, crumpled to the floor. Laurel stepped out of it, leaving her in only her chemise and underpants.

He took her hands and tugged her forward as he backed up to the bed and sat down on the side of it, then wrapped her in his arms and pressed his face into the giving softness of her middle. Hands splayed over her back, he held her there and breathed her in.

Then he drew her down onto the bed, turned her to lie on her back, and, following her down, half covered her body as he kissed her. She clasped his head, digging her fingers into his hair.

His hands moved over her, charting the dips and swells of her body until he reached the hem of her chemise. He bunched it to her waist, pushed it up over her breasts, and pulled it over her head. She lifted her hair free of it, tossed it over the side of the bed, and lay back, drawing him back down to her.

He kissed her breasts, suckled them in turn as he stroked the plain of her stomach with the backs of his fingers, moving a little lower with each brush of skin over skin until he encountered the row of tiny buttons on her underpants. He toyed with them, plucked at them, then popped them free. He worked the garment over her hips, down her thighs, past her knees, and off.

The hair in the vee of her thighs was soft against his palm as he cupped her. Sliding his fingers deeper, he dipped into her and caressed, then rolled onto his hip, opened his fly, and made the head of his cock slick with the moisture his fingertips had collected.

He levered himself above her. Her thighs hugged his hips. His first probe found her tight, but yielding. He pressed inside, barely breaching but snugly securing himself in silky heat. He forced himself to hold there. But Laurel was looking up at him with lambent eyes, puffing soft and rapid breaths through her lips. Her fingers linked behind his neck. So he rocked into her incrementally, inch by intoxicating inch, until he was gloved by her.

His breath soughed loudly in the otherwise silent room. He bracketed her upper body with his forearms, leaving his hands free to touch her eyebrows, cheeks, lips. He kissed her gently. At least it started out that way, but her tongue tangled with his, and he resumed the hungry kisses of before.

She angled herself up against him, rubbing belly to belly, restlessly grazing her nipples against his chest. Her hands coasted down his spine to the small of his back, then into his loose trousers and onto his butt. For hands so small, they squeezed him with surprising strength, insistent on pulling him closer, deeper.

He heard the primal growl that came from his own throat as he began to move. Slow, penetrating glides. Near withdrawals before sinking deep, deeper. Shallow, rapid strokes that appealed to his carnal instinct to come. To come *now*.

He didn't. But he tilted his hips just enough to change the point of friction, to enable a prolonged grind against that elusive little bead that he had acquainted her with. Her first climax had alarmed her. She had resisted and rejected it. Now she was arching up in want of another.

He'd had wet dreams about just this, about Laurel's desperate reaching for the abandon he could give her.

His control slipping, he groaned her name in a plea, a prayer.

Her breath turned choppy, then stopped altogether as her body bowed and went taut. She gave a soft, startled cry, then began milking him with such perfection, he almost waited too late to pull out.

Really not since Derby had come home from Europe had Laurel felt completely at rest. This must be the way it felt when a beguiling narcotic channeled through one's veins, replacing distress, anger, grief, all things horrid with a honeyed peace. The languor was lovely. She had no wish to move.

Not until Thatcher did. And then she opened her eyes to watch as he walked over to the dresser and took off his pants. His tall frame was spared lankiness by wide shoulders, defined muscles and tendons, and a perfectly formed, firm backside.

"You mind me getting naked?"

She sought his eyes in the mirror above the dresser from which he'd obviously been watching her watch him.

A worry line appeared between his eyebrows. "Are you embarrassed now by what we did?"

"No. Only embarrassed that you caught me admiring the view."

The line faded and he grinned as he poured water onto a cloth and washed himself, then filled the bowl from the pitcher, got a fresh cloth off the towel rack, wet it, and brought it back to the bed. She couldn't keep herself from admiring the front view, too. He was generously apportioned.

He sat down on the side of the bed and washed her stomach

with the cloth, then passed it to her. Reaching beneath the sheet, she cleaned herself between her thighs.

"I'll get some Sheiks," he said. "But, except for the flu, I didn't catch anything over there."

Derby had explained to her why servicemen had been encouraged to use prophylactics. He'd assured her that he had.

Thatcher got back in the bed and stretched out beside her on his side, his elbow on the mattress, his fist supporting his cheek. He pulled back the sheet that she had draped over her hips and surveyed her with frank interest. His absorbed gaze made her turn rosier than she already was.

"You are embarrassed," he said.

"Bashful." She lowered her eyes and addressed his chin. "I've only been with Derby. I don't know how to act with you."

"Don't *act* at all. Just be you."

"Can I tell you something?"

"Something good, I hope."

"An admission." She reached out and placed her hand on the meaty part of his chest. Her fingers lightly stroked the dusting of hair. "I wanted to see you without your undershirt."

"What?"

"The night you brought Irv home. You'd used your shirt to stanch the wound and were wearing only a Henley. It fit so tight that I got some idea of what you must look like under it. I couldn't stop looking, imagining, and wishing I could see your bare chest."

He gave her a lopsided grin. "I was wishing I could see yours, too." He palmed her breast and ran his thumb across the nipple. "More than just see." He bent his head and caressed her nipple with his tongue then sucked each into his mouth before leaning away from her. "I've daydreamed for hours about doing that."

"You have?"

"Since I saw you wrestling with that sheet. Even that saggy dress you had on couldn't keep me from wondering what was underneath. Every time the wind kicked up, I got a fairly good idea."

"You gave no sign."

"I thought you were married."

"Have you ever been?"

"Married? Naw. There weren't any girls on the ranch except for one hand's mother, who cooked for Mr. Hobson. The girls in town were just, you know. Us cowboys made that house a stop on our alternating Saturday nights off."

She folded one arm beneath her head. "You never had a special girl, Thatcher? One who either got away, or who you left behind?"

"No."

She just looked at him.

"No," he repeated.

"You've never been in love?"

"No." He lifted a strand of her hair off the pillow and began winding it round and round his index finger. "There was a woman in France. Not one of the 'French girls' you referred to," he said wryly. "She was a nurse in the hospital. She was from Scotland. When she talked it sounded like bells jingling."

"Was she pretty?"

"In her way. Every soldier in the ward liked her. They'd flirt with her. She'd flirt back. All in fun. Whenever one would die, she took it hard, because she'd lost her fiancé during the first year of fighting. That's why she volunteered." He pulled his finger from the curl of hair he'd formed, laid it back on the pillow, then began to trace the shape of her eyebrow.

"She was crazy about horses, found out that I was a cowboy, wanted to know all about my life on the ranch in the wild, wild West. Sometimes after her shift, she'd come sit with me and we'd talk."

When he didn't continue, Laurel whispered, "There's more to this story, I think."

He gave a small shrug. "When I was discharged from the hospital, I was given a three-day leave before I had to report for duty. She invited me to stay with her. She had a small place. Only one room and a toilet, but she'd made it cozy."

"How often did you stay with her?"

"Just that once. After that three days, we said our goodbyes."

"Did you write to each other?"

"No."

"Did you see her after the war?"

"No."

"Did you try?"

"No. It wasn't like that, Laurel. She was a caring person. For all the cheer she gave her patients, she was sad. Still in love with her fiancé. We were a comfort to each other, that's all. Two people trying to take some pleasure where there was damn little to be found. Those three days were just a time-out from the hell going on around us."

"Like this is now?"

He quit concentrating on her eyebrow and met her gaze directly.

Placing his arm around her waist, he spread his hand wide over her bottom and pulled her against him. "Nothing like this. Nothing's ever been like this."

His deep kiss became a long, continual one that caused renewed arousal to spiral inside her sex. Gradually, the kiss changed character, taking on heat that melted any lingering inhibitions. Up till now the word "erotic" had hinted at dark and mysterious things of which she had no experience or knowledge. Now, she felt steeped in the essence of the word's definition.

Thatcher ended the kiss only to whisper against her lips, "I have to have you again."

Her desire for him had also risen to the level of need. "Yes."

He murmured indistinctly as he moved to lie between her legs. "I'm going to kiss you."

But he didn't do as he was wont to and cradle her face in his hands. Instead he clasped her hips between them and blazed a trail of wet kisses down the center of her body.

His hands assumed mastery over her movements, but their guidance was gentle and unrushed. He repositioned her legs to accommodate his shoulders, cupped her behind the knees and raised them, stroked the backs of her thighs, then slid his hands under her bottom. It was a delicious shock to feel the prickliness of whiskers against her navel, in the valleys under her hipbones, and on the insides of her thighs.

She couldn't hear everything he whispered directly against her, but she felt the words as they formed on his lips, felt the warm breath that wafted over her sensitive flesh as he spoke them.

She never would have imagined that his mouth could be both softly persuasive and aggressive at the same time, but it was. His tongue was simply wicked. It shattered her, and she surrendered to it utterly.

She was still in the throes of her orgasm when he braced himself above her. In a possessive push, he sheathed himself. He gave only a few more rapid thrusts before his body tensed and she felt his pulsing deep inside her. She closed around him as tightly as she could, and they held that way, until they both went listless.

Long moments later, he placed his hands at each side of her head and sank his fingers into her hair, tangling the strands around them as though he wanted to be ensnared.

He remained heavy and full inside her, filling her. His face was feverish against her neck. His breath, which had been gusting, eventually slowed. He inhaled deeply once and exhaled slowly.

Before he slept, he spoke a single word. "Laurel." Only that.

It was enough.

FIFTY-SIX

T hatcher's clothes were still damp, but he had no choice except to put them back on. He was moving quietly so not to waken Laurel, who was a damn tempting sight, hair streaming over her pillow, face relaxed in sleep. Her bare shoulder had escaped the covers. He thought of leaning down and kissing it but was afraid she would wake up. She needed her sleep.

Last night, after napping for a while, they'd gone downstairs to the bathroom and bathed together by the glow of a kerosene lamp. She had overcome some of her shyness and had asked delicate questions. His candid answers had made her blush. But not to be outdone by "French tarts," she'd asked him to coach her on how to please him. It was he who'd wound up in thrall of her ardor. And talent.

They'd fallen asleep, spooning, but he'd awakened an hour later, hard with wanting her again. She purred in permissive response to his hopeful nudges, but when she tried to turn, he reached across her and spread his hand over her middle, holding her in place.

"Ever since that damn rooster attacked, and your bottom bumped up against me..."

Just thinking about that slow, drowsy sex made him want to be coupled with her again. But each of them was facing a challenging day. She would be grieving Davy O'Connor and consoling his brother. Sheriff Amos was expecting him.

He gave her one last, longing look, then slipped out of the bedroom unheard.

Fred Barker was already in his shop when Thatcher arrived to return his rifle. "Why don't you keep it?" Barker said. "After what happened last night, I reckon you might need it."

"You heard about the ambush?"

"Heard the ambush as it happened. Wife and me thought firecrackers were going off. This morning, learned different from the milkman. That O'Connor boy was a hell-raiser. I'd've locked my daughter up was he to've come anywhere near her. But being gunned down like that..."

Barker shook his head in sorrow. "Somethin's gotta give around here, Thatcher. Hang on to that Springfield. It's not like it's the only rifle I have."

"Thanks. I'll take good care of it." He asked Fred if he could spare Roger to do the stable chores. "Sheriff wanted me to be on hand today."

Fred spat into the dirt. "He's gonna need all the men he can get. Do you believe a lightning strike caused that fire?"

"Fire?"

"Jesus, Thatcher. You ain't heard about that?"

The sheriff's office was more crowded than it had been since the morning the search for Mila Driscoll was organized. Then, Thatcher had only heard the commotion from his jail cell.

This morning, as he entered the building, he had to wedge himself between the interior wall and the throng of men surrounding Bill, who was standing in the center of the large room, fielding dozens of questions even as he issued assignments.

"We don't know how many confirmed dead yet," he was saying. "I'm afraid to calculate. Relatives we've talked to said that Hiram had called a clan conference. The only acceptable excuses for not attending were that you were being born or dying.

"There could have been dozens inside that house, including women and children. So far, we haven't come across any survivors. Which leaves us knowing squat about what happened during that meeting."

Thatcher listened as did everyone else as Bill shared what little he had learned. Hiram's nearest neighbor, with whom he wasn't on the best of terms, had heard a "loud bang" the night before.

"He took it for a lightning strike, rolled over and went back to sleep. This morning when he noticed several thin trails of smoke coming from the direction of Hiram's place, he thought he ought to go check."

When not a single Johnson appeared on their private road to challenge him for trespassing, the neighbor had become even more apprehensive of what he would find at the dead end.

"He said the house had been incinerated," Bill told those gathered around him. "Despite the rainstorm last night, parts of it were still smoldering. He drove to the nearest telephone and called me." Bill stared down at his boots for a moment. "All I can say is, it must've been a hell of a blaze. It's a scene out of hell."

Bill had left a team of deputies there to keep curiosity seekers away. Even those few Johnsons who hadn't attended the meeting, but had immediate family members who had, weren't allowed beyond a certain point.

"I've requested a team of state investigators specially trained in arson to come up from Austin. May be tomorrow before they can gather all their gear and make the drive. In the meantime, the rest of you continue investigating the ambush on the O'Connors. You have your duties. Get to them."

Many shuffled out. Others got on telephones. Bill came over to Thatcher, who said, "Sorry I wasn't here earlier."

"Be glad you missed it."

"The Johnson place?"

"Thatcher, if that fire wasn't an act of God, it was the work of Satan himself. There were kids in that house. Babies."

Thatcher had seen charred bodies of soldiers on the battlefield and of civilians in bombed-out villages. He had hoped never to see such a grotesque sight again. Neither he nor Bill said anything for a moment, then Thatcher asked if Mike O'Connor was still alive.

"Last word I got, he was holding on, but they're keeping him sedated. Doc Perkins said he'd let me know as soon as he's stable enough to be questioned."

Thatcher nodded absently, then asked about Gabe Driscoll's present frame of mind.

Bill said, "I haven't been in to see him this morning. Someone else took him breakfast."

Thatcher took a look around the room. It hadn't escaped others' notice that he and Bill were conferring privately, a privilege that Bill didn't afford everyone. Scotty and Harold tolerated Thatcher, but only to an extent. Most of the veterans of the department still regarded him with suspicion and hostility. He was sure that some held to the belief that he was guilty of doing something to Mila Driscoll. That continued to plague him. Whether or not they ever welcomed him into the fold, he had to lay that misconception to rest.

Which is why he wanted to speak to Bill alone. "Let's go take a look at that road where the getaway car was waiting for the shooters."

"I doubt we'll find any clues."

"I doubt we will, too, but I'm afraid these walls have ears."

Bill gave him a sharp look, then announced to the room at large that he would be back shortly.

Laurel woke up later than usual, with a fully risen sun lighting the bedroom through the shades Thatcher had lowered last night.

Thatcher. At the mere thought of him, warm happiness suffused her. She was a bit disappointed that he hadn't stayed until she woke up, but she knew the hard day he had in store.

At the same time, she was almost glad he wasn't facing her across the pillow just now. She blushed at the thought of ever looking him in the eye again. The things he'd taught her!

Derby had regarded himself as quite a Casanova. His lovemaking had been vigorous, and he'd strutted that as a sign of his virility. He'd always taken for granted that she was satisfied, when the gratification had been his alone. The sex had been for him, not her. To be fair, she didn't believe he'd been selfish. He simply hadn't known any better.

If not for Thatcher, neither would she.

He had awakened her to levels of sensuality she'd never known were available or would have dreamed possible. In response to her apprehension over what he expected, over what she could expect from him, he'd been patient and persuasive. His touch, knowing smile, and whispered words had been temptation made manifest. His tenderness, passion sanctified. Throughout the night, he'd given her rapturous pleasure and had taken his.

But in addition to the fervent lovemaking, he had also attended to her wracked emotions. Without words, he'd held her close against him. Just that. His quietude had assuaged her grief over Davy's murder, her anxiety over Mike's condition, her distress over the unknown future.

That thought prickled something at the back of her mind, some revelatory thought. But it had been fleeting, as elusive as the glimmer of a single firefly in a dark wood.

Once, when she was a young girl, she'd chased a lightning bug through the woods that bordered her daddy's cotton field. It had flickered only one time, but she'd been certain she'd seen it, not imagined it. She'd plunged after it in the hope of catching it to put in a jar near her bed. She'd darted through the trees and underbrush, had run in circles, until she had exhausted herself and had given up the chase in defeat.

She felt as frustrated and downcast now not to have netted that flash of clarity. It had been meaningful enough to give her instant pause, to raise goose bumps on her arms.

She closed her eyes, lay perfectly still, and strained to recapture it. But try as she might, she couldn't. It had retreated into the recesses of her subconscious. Maybe it would show itself at another time, probably in a moment when she wasn't searching for it.

Having been lazy long enough, she forced herself to get up. She washed and dressed, and was pinning up her hair when she heard the back door open and the scrape of footsteps in the kitchen.

Her heart swelled. Maybe Thatcher had come back for a good morning kiss after all.

More probably, though, it was Irv, returning from the stills. She dreaded having to tell him, Corrine, and Ernie about the O'Connors, but she also hoped that they hadn't heard the dreadful news from someone else first.

She pushed the last pin into her hair, and then started downstairs, calling as she went, "Irv?"

Once in Bill's car and on their way, Thatcher asked after Mrs. Amos.

"Not doing good, I hate to say. I'm worried, Thatcher. No ordinary bellyache lasts this long. With all these crises going on, if I can't take time off to get her to a doctor, I'm going to ask her friend to take her."

"What about Dr. Perkins?"

"He'd just give her more drops. She needs to be examined by somebody born *after* the Civil War. Have you heard of that sanitarium in Temple?"

Thatcher shook his head.

"Couple of doctors down there—names are Scott and White—

are building quite a reputation. I may look into getting her in down there."

They drove along the road where Thatcher had last seen the getaway car's taillights disappearing around a bend. Bill drove beyond that point, then pulled his car to the side of the road.

"This is pointless. What's on your mind?"

Thatcher said, "Have you sent anybody out to Pointer's Gap yet?"

"It was on my list of things to do today, but with the ambush, the fire, I haven't had the men to spare, and you'd have to go with them to show the way. So, no."

"Have you arranged for a lawyer for Driscoll?"

"It's not a priority."

Bill's expectant expression prompted Thatcher to get on with it. "This is going to sound like I'm beating around the bush but bear with me."

The sheriff checked his pocket watch. "It's a busy day. Five minutes, Thatcher."

"Last night when you dropped Laurel and me at her house, she was on the brink of a breakdown."

"Over Davy O'Connor."

"Sure. But also, yesterday afternoon she had an upsetting visit from Bernie Croft and Chester Landry."

"Let me guess. They wanted her to merge her business with theirs."

Thatcher said nothing. Bill waited a few seconds then sighed with exasperation. "They're bootleggers, Thatcher. They wouldn't have been interested in Mrs. Plummer's pie business."

"I'm not saying anything about her."

"You don't have to. I've known for years that old Irv dabbled. He didn't cause anybody trouble, so I looked the other way. Other moonshiners did, too, because he didn't put too deep a dent in their market. But the lady has gotten everybody riled."

"Croft and Landry for sure."

"She turned them down?" Again, Thatcher remained silent, but Bill nodded as though Thatcher had replied. "In return, they shot up her delivery boys."

"At the scene of the ambush, Harold said to me that somebody had wanted to make a point. I think he was right. I think it was Croft."

"What about Landry?"

"He was with Laurel when the shooting started, remember?"

"Now I do. I had asked her about it, but we got off on Mike O'Connor's condition, so I never received an answer. Was he a decoy, sent to keep her occupied while the O'Connors were being ambushed?"

"That's possible, I guess. But what Landry told Laurel was that he'd returned to make her a better offer."

"Behind Bernie's back? A double-cross?"

"Landry is weaselly enough."

"Oh, I agree. But are you suggesting that while he was negotiating with Mrs. Plummer, Bernie acted alone?"

"I don't think Landry is above removing somebody, but he wouldn't go about it like that. He wouldn't have made a spectacle."

"Like the ambush."

"And like a 'hell of a blaze.'"

Bill looked at him with raised brows. "Hiram's place?"

"Hennessy was in the IRA. They're famous for blowing things up. They make explosive devices out of tin cans. That fire at the Johnsons' place might not have been sparked by lightning."

"Christ, Thatcher. Do you have any idea of the shit you're wading into here? Bernie Croft isn't a man you trifle with."

"No, Bill, you can't *trifle*. You gotta hit him with more than a slap on the hand. You gotta kick him in the balls and then cut them off."

Bill lapsed into thought, tugging at the corner of his mustache. "We'd have a hell of a time proving that Bernie ordered that ambush or the fire. He's got loyal toadies. They would never give him up."

"They'd hang first?"

"I would."

Thatcher looked at him, stunned.

"You think I'm a coward? I guess I am," he said ruefully. "But it's not my skin I'm concerned about. Daisy's life is the bargaining chip Bernie holds over me. That's why I don't buck him, Thatcher. He doesn't even have to carry out his veiled threats. It's the fear that he will that keeps me—everybody—from crossing him beyond a certain point."

Thatcher turned his head forward and stared through the grimy windshield. "Maybe he carries out more threats than you know of. I told you this would sound like beating around the bush—"

"And time's winding down."

"Who told us about Pointer's Gap?"

"What's that got to do with—"

"Who, Bill?" The answer being obvious, Thatcher continued without pause. "Why did Croft drop that out-of-the-way place into the conversation? Like he just happened to think of it while explaining Driscoll's lust for Norma Blanchard?"

"Which we already knew about."

"Yes, but Croft didn't know we knew. He made certain we did."

"Bernie has been Gabe's advocate. Why would he plant in our minds the notion that Gabe could have assaulted Norma?"

"He did more than that," Thatcher said. "He beat us over the head with it. Makes me wonder why."

FIFTY-SEVEN

When Thatcher and Bill returned to the sheriff's department, it was still a beehive of activity. As soon as Bill came through the door, a dozen written messages were handed to him. He scanned the notes, then delegated various tasks to his deputies and staff.

Scotty approached and said under his breath, "The governor himself called this time."

"If he calls back, put him off. Tell him—"

"And the Texas Rangers are here."

Bill snorted. "Well, that was to be expected. Actually, I'm glad to have them. How many?"

"Two."

"Where are they?"

"Having a meal over at the café. Said they'd be back in thirty minutes."

"How long ago was that?"

Scotty checked the wall clock. "Twenty-seven minutes ago."

Bill turned to Thatcher. "Do you want to wait to confront Driscoll until we have more time?"

"Do you?"

By way of an answer, Bill said to Scotty, "When the Rangers come back, tell them we're trying to squeeze a confession out of a prisoner, and ask them to cool their heels a while longer."

"The governor?"

"Suggest he have a drink." Bill pushed open the door leading into the cell block. Thatcher followed him and closed the door behind them.

Driscoll was fit to be tied. "Where is my lawyer? What the hell is going on out there? It sounds like a carnival. I've been yelling for someone to get in here, but I've been ignored." Glaring at Thatcher, his voice went shrill. "And why is he still wearing a badge when he should be in here instead of me?"

In contrasting calmness, Bill said, "Because he's not a murder suspect, Gabe."

"I did not attack Norma. I would never have done that."

"No, we don't think you did. The patients on your rural route vouched for your whereabouts during the time frame when she was assaulted."

"Then why am I still locked up?"

"Because you killed Mila. Didn't you?"

"No." He gave an obstinate shake of his head.

"Did you plan it with Norma, or did you act alone?"

"I did *not kill my wife.*"

Disregarding the denial, Bill said, "I think Mrs. Driscoll's body was in the car with you when you went to Lefty's. Eleanor Wise just missed you loading it because you had parked around back."

Up till then, Thatcher had let Bill do all the talking. Now, he said, "I can't figure the murder weapon."

"Good point," Gabe said tightly. "Sheriff, are you listening? What did you use, Hutton?"

Unfazed, Thatcher said, "No obvious weapon was found inside the house. Either you used something commonplace that wouldn't be considered a weapon, or you took the weapon with you and tossed it somewhere along the way to Lefty's, or you buried it with Mrs. Driscoll's body at Pointer's Gap."

"I didn't—"

"And why Pointer's Gap?" Thatcher continued. "It's rugged country."

"You would know, wouldn't you?" Driscoll sneered. "You took Mila from our house that night and took her out there—"

"In what, Gabe?"

His head swiveled back to Bill. "What?"

"Thatcher was on foot. How would he have gotten her out there?"

Before the doctor could respond, Thatcher picked back up. "Why did you choose Pointer's Gap?"

"I didn't! I've never even been there."

"What about the picnics with your wife?"

Driscoll looked at Bill. "What is he talking about?"

"The picnics," Thatcher said, bringing Driscoll's attention back to him. "The ones you and Mrs. Driscoll went on at Pointer's Gap."

"That's absurd. First of all, I hate picnics. Where did you even get a crazy idea like that?"

Thatcher waited a beat, then said quietly, "From Bernie Croft."

The doctor looked like he'd been struck with a two-by-four right between the eyes. He gaped at Thatcher for a ten count, then took several short, shallow breaths. "Bernie told you that?"

Closely monitoring Driscoll's every reaction, Thatcher left it to Bill to explain how they'd come to hear about Pointer's Gap, when and where their seemingly casual conversation with the mayor had taken place. "To aid us in our investigation into the assault on Miss Blanchard, Bernie felt compelled to mention your affair with her, and then your earnest attempt to atone for it by paying more attention to your wife."

Gabe was swallowing convulsively.

Bill went on. "His offhanded mention of Pointer's Gap—"

"It wasn't offhanded," Driscoll blurted. He slumped forward against the bars, clutching two of them to help himself remain upright. "It was his idea."

"What was his idea?"

He remained silent and gave a mournful shake of his head.

"It was Bernie's idea to do what, Gabe? Say it."

"I can't. He'll kill me."

Thatcher leaned in and whispered to him, "If you betray Croft, he may very well kill you. But if you don't come clean, you have me to be scared of."

Gabe looked at him with fright. Thatcher gazed back, unblinking. The doctor was quick to yield. He turned to Bill and stammered, "B…Bernie took care of the body for me. He had men meet me at Lefty's. They took Mila."

"Was she dead, Gabe?"

He nodded.

"You killed her?"

"Yes." He lowered his head and began to cry.

Thatcher backed away from the bars separating them. He exchanged a glance with Bill. They'd gotten the confession they'd been after, but having Mila Driscoll's fate confirmed was a dismal triumph.

"How'd you kill her, Gabe?" Bill asked softly.

Just then Scotty came barging through the door at the end of the corridor. "Sheriff?"

"Not now," Bill said.

"It's—"

"Not now!"

"It's Mrs. Amos."

Bill spun around to his deputy. Scotty spoke so hastily, he tripped over his words. "Her friend Mrs. Cantor called, says Mrs. Amos is in pain something awful. Her stomach. Said it might've been, uh…whiskey. Said she caught her with a bottle of bourbon half empty."

"Jesus." Bill looked at Thatcher. "I have to go."

"And the Rangers are back," Scotty added.

"Screw them. Stay with Driscoll," Bill said to Thatcher. "Get it all on paper. Have him sign—"

"Wait! Your wife has severe stomach pains after drinking bourbon?" Gabe had stopped crying, but had turned whey-faced and his lips were rubbery. "He said it was for the Johnsons."

In a matter of seconds, Bill had the cell door unlocked, had grabbed Driscoll by the throat, and had backed him against the wall. "Who said? Bernie?"

Driscoll gave a wobbly nod.

"Said what was for the Johnsons?" Bill shook him, thumping him hard against the wall. "*What?*"

"Arsenic. In the bourbon."

With the regard one would give a rag doll, Bill dragged the doctor from the cell and pushed him down the hallway with the unstoppable propulsion of a cowcatcher.

Scotty had come along. He was with Bill as he burst through the front door of his house, shouting his wife's name. By the time Thatcher had towed Driscoll from the car, up the walk and into the house, Bill was on the landing, barging past a middle-aged woman who was wringing her hands with anxiety and saying repeatedly, "I don't know what to do for her."

Scotty hung back to explain the circumstances. "It'll be all right, Mrs. Cantor. We've brought Dr. Driscoll."

Thatcher, with a grip on the back of Driscoll's collar, pushed him up the stairs and into the bedroom. Bill was seated on the side of the bed, bending over his wife, who was writhing in apparent agony.

She reached out and clutched Bill's hand. "I think I'm dying."

"You're not going to die." He raised her hand and kissed the back of it, hard. "*You are not going to die.* I'm going to fix it."

He left the bed, walked over to Driscoll, drew his pistol, and pressed the barrel of it against the doctor's forehead. "If she doesn't survive this, I am killing you first, then Bernie Croft."

"Gastric lavage," Driscoll said.

"What?"

"Pump her stomach. I need to pump her stomach with salt water. I'll need my equipment."

"Describe it."

Thatcher was amazed by how suddenly Driscoll slipped into professional mode. In seemingly perfect control, he gave Scotty a description of the tubing device he required and told him in which cabinet it was stored in his office. "But the house is locked."

"Kick the damn door in. Shoot out the lock," Bill said to his deputy.

Scotty rushed out and thumped down the stairs.

Daisy groaned pitiably and extended her hand toward Bill, who holstered his pistol, but shouted to Driscoll, "Do something now!"

The doctor shrugged off his coat. "We need to induce vomiting."

"She's been vomiting for days."

"But she hadn't ingested half a bottle all at once. This is acute. We need to induce vomiting." He rolled up his shirtsleeves. "Where can I wash?"

"Across the hall."

Thatcher followed him as far as the door to the bathroom and watched as he lathered up and rinsed his hands. As he was drying them, his gaze met Thatcher's in the mirror above the sink. "Are you expecting an apology for my false accusations, Mr. Hutton?"

"I don't give a fuck in hell about an apology from you. But you owe your wife one. How'd you do it?"

"I hit her on the back of the head with an iron skillet. The skillet in which she baked the shortbread you enjoyed so much." He folded the hand towel and hung it just so on the metal bar, then went past Thatcher and returned to the bedroom.

Daisy was lying on her side, knees pulled to her chest, moaning and gripping her midsection. Bill was leaning over her, stroking her face and talking softly.

Thatcher noticed a half-full bottle of name-brand bourbon sitting on the bureau. He went over and got it, knowing it would be valuable evidence against both Driscoll and Croft.

As he left the bedroom unnoticed, Bill was holding back his beloved's hair as she retched into a basin held by the man who had poisoned her... at the direction of Bernie Croft.

Bernie said, "Hello, Gert."

"Ain't you heard? We're shut down. Good as anyway."

"I'd like to talk to you."

"We'll talk when you get the law off my back."

"In due time."

"Due time," she said scornfully. "No more graft, you hear me?"

"I'll get you back to normal soon."

"You been sayin' that, but in the meanwhile, Bill Amos is having our road patrolled nightly. All that attention is keepin' away customers too scared of being caught in another raid.

"Much longer, and we won't have any hooch to sell, 'cause Lefty's drinkin' it all up. Stays drunk, ain't no use to me. No pussy to sell, neither, 'cause all them twats upstairs has sneaked off one by one. Took their inspiration from that Corrine, I guess. I'm losing money by the hour, and you're doin' nothin' but takin' up space, Mr. Mayor."

He smiled. "I'm here to make it up to you, Gert."

She honked a laugh. "Ain't likely. Everybody knows you look after your ownself."

"This benefits us both."

She squinted at him through an exhalation of cigarette smoke. "Whut does?"

"I've brought you a present."

He turned. Hennessy was standing at the side of the town car. At a signal from Bernie, he opened the back door and pulled a bound and gagged woman from the car.

Croft said to Gert, "I believe you're acquainted with Mrs. Plummer."

Laurel had gone into the kitchen, expecting to find her father-in-law rummaging for the makings of breakfast.

Instead, Bernie Croft had been rifling through her recipe box.

Fanning one of the cards at her, he'd greeted her pleasantly. "Good morning, Mrs. Plummer. This lemon chess pie sounds delicious."

And then from behind her, a heavy hand had been clamped over her mouth at the same time an arm as strong as an iron band had encircled her waist.

She'd raked her nails across the hand over her mouth and knew by the profanities grunted near her ear that she'd drawn blood, or at least had caused pain. She'd struggled and kicked, but she'd been held fast while Croft had tied her hands behind her with a thin but sturdy cord that dug into her flesh. The hand over her mouth had been removed and replaced by a handkerchief, which had caused her to gag.

She'd been carried to the long, black car she'd seen parked in front of her house the day before. She'd been thrust into the backseat, no doubt by the burly chauffeur. Croft had climbed in beside her. They could have been out for a Sunday drive for all the attention she paid him until they'd made the turnoff to Lefty's.

She'd looked at him then, and his chuckle had been villainous. Or perhaps it had only sounded that way to her because she knew him to be a villain.

When they'd reached the roadhouse, Croft and Hennessy had gotten out. Croft had gone to the door, which had been answered by Gert. After a brief conversation, Croft had signaled Hennessy to get her from the car and bring her forward.

Now, upon seeing her, Gert stepped out onto the porch. She flicked her cigarette into the dirt and clapped her hands together. "Well, I be damned. You really did bring me a present, Bernie. It ain't even my birthday."

Laurel dug her heels in, kicked against the chauffeur's shins, twisted and turned her body, did anything she could think of to make his job more difficult. She didn't delude herself into thinking she could escape someone of his size, but she refused to meekly cooperate.

When they reached the porch steps, Croft instructed "Hennessy" to pat down her skirt pockets.

"Already did there in her kitchen."

He had, but with a sinking heart, Laurel had known he would come up empty, and he had. Irv would never let her hear the last of it. If she lived through this.

"Search again," Croft said now. "Right pocket. Yesterday, I saw her patting at it. Giveaway habit."

Hennessy did as told, even shoving his hands into her pockets and digging deep. "Nothing, boss."

Gert snickered. "Try her garters."

Laurel looked defiantly at Croft as he motioned for his muscle man to do as suggested. Hennessy knelt in front of her and ran his hands up and down both legs, higher than her garters. Being groped by him was a desecration of Thatcher's caresses. She wanted to scream.

As Hennessy came to his feet, he grinned at her. "Nothing but smooth skin."

She forced herself not to react either to his molestation or disgusting leer.

Croft then hitched his chin at Hennessy, who pushed her lower spine hard enough to knock her off balance. She fell forward onto the lowest porch step. Without her hands free to catch herself, she landed on her elbow. Pain sizzled up her arm and into her shoulder. She couldn't cry out for the handkerchief in her mouth. Even had she been able to, she wouldn't have given this trio of degenerates the satisfaction.

"No call for rough stuff, Hennessy," Croft said. "Yet."

He reached down and helped Laurel to her feet and guided her up the steps. But once they reached the porch, she yanked her arm free of his deceptively solicitous grip.

He took the white linen handkerchief from her mouth. It was monogrammed with his initials. Feeling her saliva on it, he frowned with distaste. She would have liked to spit in his eye, but reasoned that, at this point, her best defense was to show as little reaction as possible. But while her features remained composed and indifferent, she was quaking on the inside. No one knew where she was. Not Irv, Thatcher, no one.

Croft raised a hand to shade his eyes. "Gert, let's take her inside, get her and her delicate skin out of this sun. We wouldn't want her to burn."

Gert gave a phlegmy laugh as she pulled open the squeaky screened door. "Of course not, wouldn't want that to happen."

Hennessy stayed outside.

The room was as Laurel remembered: cavernous, dim, and hazy with cigarette smoke. There was no sign of Lefty. Only an ominous silence came from upstairs. The shotgun lay on the bar. Gert walked over to it, sat down on a stool, and lit a fresh cigarette as though settling in for the floor show.

Laurel realized she was it.

Croft pushed her into a chair, then dragged one over, stationed it directly in front of her, and sat down.

"Mrs. Plummer—can I call you Laurel?—where is Chester Landry?"

Of all the things he could have said, that question was the least expected.

Gert must have thought the same. She came off her stool with a thud. "Chester Landry, *my ass*. Ask her where my girl's at. Soon's I find that scheming little bitch, I'm gonna wring her neck, and let Miss High Horse here watch while I do it."

Croft acted as though he hadn't heard her and remained focused on Laurel. "Where was Landry headed when he slunk off last night?"

Laurel laughed. "You could have asked me that without going to all this elaborate trouble."

"Then tell me where he is."

"I have no earthly idea."

He sighed. Then, with shocking alacrity and force, he backhanded her across the face.

FIFTY-EIGHT

Following the stomach pumping procedure, Daisy Amos was resting more comfortably. Thatcher knew Bill hated leaving her side and resuming his duties, but he was hard pressed to do so on this of all days, when three major investigations demanded attention and action.

He asked Thatcher to escort the doctor downstairs to the parlor where he would soon join them. "Put these on him." He produced a pair of handcuffs.

Bill remained in the foyer with Scotty, who had been communicating with headquarters by telephone. He reported that the two Texas Rangers had divided up. One was getting information from the deputies who'd investigated the scene of the ambush. The other had gone to the Johnson homestead to assess the devastation there in advance of the arrival of the arson specialists.

Thatcher overheard Bill ask Scotty to locate Bernie Croft. "Don't approach him. Don't indicate that you're looking for him. Just let me know where he is. Me and me only."

"Yes, sir." The deputy left.

When Bill entered the parlor, Driscoll said, "I hope you can trust Mrs. Amos's friend to make her drink the water I prepared." He'd added honey to a large pitcher of water and had left it on the bed-side table.

"Even if she continues to throw up for a time, she needs the water. It will help flush the arsenic from her system naturally through urination. I've heard that the honey helps. Chemically, somehow. Also eggs. She should be fed eggs. The sulfur in them—"

Bill interrupted him. "You told Alice all that. I'm confident she'll follow your instructions to the letter."

Driscoll held up his cuffed hands. "Are these necessary?"

"They were for Thatcher when he was suspected of the crime you've confessed to. They stay on. You poisoned my wife."

"Bernie brought two cases of liquor to my office and left them to be spiked with a slow-working poison, so it wouldn't be immediately noticed. He told me those bottles were to be 'gifts' for members of the Johnson family. I had no way of knowing that Mrs. Amos would be allotted some, too."

Bill had admitted to Thatcher during his tell-all on the porch that Croft was Daisy's supplier of bootleg whiskey. That he'd given her bottles spiked with arsenic was indicative of the malice he felt toward Bill as well as Daisy for choosing Bill over him.

"Is she still in danger?" Bill was asking Driscoll. "And you had better not bullshit me."

"The arsenic will remain in her system, but for how long depends on a number of factors. That's why I emphasize flushing it out and neutralizing it as much as possible."

"Could she still die of it?"

"It can cause complications, organ damage and so forth, that can eventually prove fatal. It's a toxin, after all. Had I not acted so swiftly and given her the lavage, more than likely she would have succumbed."

To Thatcher, Driscoll was a complete mystery. He was like the doctor in that book. Two men with opposing personalities living inside the same body. One minute Driscoll was bawling like a child caught misbehaving, the next he was calm, detached, even defiant.

Within an hour the man had admitted to poisoning bottles of liquor he knew would be consumed by human beings and had confessed to murdering his wife and unborn baby. Thatcher rather agreed with Patsy Kemp, who'd said with bitterness: They ought to hang the bastard twice.

Bill was now asking Driscoll why he had agreed to poison the bourbon.

"Bernie had me over a barrel." He poured out the whole sordid story about Croft trying to recruit him to transport booze on his rural route. "I was offended. I'm a physician, not a bootlegger."

He looked down at his linked fingers. "But then, the night Mila... When I needed Bernie to see me through that crisis, he did so. He and that old bag at Lefty's quickly set up the incident with the prostitute so I would have a cover story for leaving the house at that hour of the night."

"Did Gert know about Mila?" Bill asked.

"I don't believe so. Bernie said she was a whore at heart and wouldn't ask questions so long as she was paid." He sighed deeply. "Anyway, after that night, he owned me body and soul. I was subjected to a lot of humiliation from him. I tolerated it, believing I had no other choice. But when I found out that he'd told Norma about Pointer's Gap, I—"

"What?" Bill held up his hand. "Run that past us again."

"Norma knew about Mila. She sprang it on me the afternoon she brought Arthur to the house. I was floored, flabbergasted. Bernie was the only person who could have told her, except for the men who actually buried the body, and they were all Mexicans who didn't even speak English.

"I had trusted Bernie to keep the secret. We'd made a pact. When I learned that he'd told Norma, I accosted him on the street." He described a volatile encounter in an alleyway. "I was livid."

Thatcher sat forward and placed his forearms on his thighs. "You were livid. What about Croft?"

"Smug. He said I was naïve to think that he wouldn't have held some collateral for doing me such a huge favor. I told him that Norma was using it to pressure me into marriage. He agreed that people would become suspicious if she and I married too soon, and that Norma should be made to understand that. He offered to speak to her on my behalf, but I told him I would handle it. I...I hadn't gotten around to it."

Thatcher looked over at Bill, who, like him, appeared to have realized the significance of Bernie Croft's offer to impress understanding upon Norma Blanchard.

Bill stood and pulled Driscoll out of his chair. "Just so we understand one another, Gabe. If Daisy gets well, you'll stand trial and be judged by a jury of your peers. If she *succumbs*, you won't live to see trial."

Driscoll jerked his arm free. "There's gratitude for you. I saved your wife's life, and you repay me by issuing threats? First him," he said, looking at Thatcher with scorn, "now you. Isn't it against the law to threaten a suspect in your custody? Doesn't that violate a lawman's code of ethics?"

"I don't give a damn." Bill hauled off and slammed his fist into Gabe's face. He fell backward and landed on the floor, out cold.

There was one knock on the front door before Scotty pushed it open and walked in. He looked down at Driscoll. "What happened?"

"He was trying to escape," Bill said. "When you get him back to the jail, put him in shackles, too. What about our mayor?"

"That's what I came to tell you. I know where he's at."

"What I think? We ought to go into town and check on her."

"We heard you the first dozen times you said that."

Corrine gave Irv a malevolent squint. "Well, apparently you ain't listening, old man. Miss Laurel said if she didn't come tomorrow, which was yesterday, she'd come the next day, which is today."

"Day ain't over, is it?"

Ernie looked up at the sun. "Noon or better. But she has a point, Irv."

"Aw, you're just horny. You'd agree with anything she said," Irv grumbled, shooting a glower toward Corrine.

"You said yourself you was scared Miss Laurel would come to grief," she said. "Didn't he say that, Ernie?"

Ernie tugged on his long earlobe. "Seems I do recollect—"

"I remember sayin' it," Irv snapped. "And I still hold to it. But you," he said to Corrine, "agreed that we should lay low till we got the all clear. Laurel wouldn't want us to show ourselves till it was safe. We've got no idea what all went on last night. I doubt much did on account of that storm. But still..."

Corrine stood and dusted off her seat. "Well, you can sit here till you become a fossil like in them rocks over yonder. I'm going." She marched off toward Irv's truck, which they'd camouflaged with cedar boughs.

"How are you going to get there?" he called after her. "You can't drive."

She started pulling the cedar branches off the truck and slinging them aside. "I can drive good enough. Ernie's been teaching me."

Irv turned an accusatory look on his friend. Ernie guiltily raised his bony shoulders. "In my spare time."

"Hell's bells." Irv started after Corrine. "I'll drive us." Over his shoulder, he said to Ernie, "You stay and guard the place. Don't do no cooking till we get back and keep those firearms within your reach."

"Y'all be careful."

Bill instructed Scotty to return Driscoll to the jail, leave a man there to guard him, then to bring a carload of deputies to Lefty's.

He also ordered Scotty not to leave town without obtaining an arrest warrant for Mayor Bernard Croft. Looking dubious, Scotty asked how the sheriff planned on arranging that. "I'm calling the judge now."

Scotty left with Driscoll, who had regained consciousness. His shouted protests over being treated inhumancly wcrc ignored.

Bill placed a call. Thatcher overheard him threatening a judge to expose both his bribe-taking and the mistress he kept in Stephenville if he didn't have the warrant ready by the time Scotty got to the courthouse to pick it up.

After completing the call, Bill went upstairs to check on Mrs. Amos. He didn't stay long. "She's better. Sleeping," he told Thatcher as they left the house.

Less than five minutes after Scotty's announcement that Bernie Croft had been seen heading for Lefty's, the sheriff and Thatcher were speeding toward it, having no idea if their quarry was still there.

Croft's notable town car, with Hennessy behind the wheel, had been spotted taking the turnoff to Lefty's by a deputy who'd come off guard duty at the Johnsons' property and was on his way back into town.

Bill took the turnoff now but didn't go far off the highway before stopping. As he checked his pistol to make sure it was loaded, he said, "I'm waiting for that warrant."

"I'll reconnoiter." Having checked his own Colt, Thatcher clicked the cylinder back into place and opened the passenger door. "Just in case I don't come back, that poisoned bottle of bourbon is in your kitchen cabinet behind a box of oatmeal."

"Only you would think of that right now."

"Could make the difference in a verdict." He hooked Barker's rifle onto his shoulder by the strap.

"Take these, too." Bill passed Thatcher a pair of binoculars. Thatcher recognized them as army issue and looked at Bill, who said, "They were among Tim's effects."

Thatcher left the car door ajar and jogged over to the trees that bordered the road. They were sparse, providing only marginal cover as he moved among them. The sun was high and hot. Last night's rain steamed up from the spongy ground. Thatcher was breathing heavily by the time the roof of the roadhouse came into view.

He proceeded in a crouch. Still about a hundred yards away

from the building, he spotted Croft's auto parked in front. A boulder provided him an advantageous spot from which to take a closer look. Situating himself behind the outcropping, he propped his elbows on it and looked through the binoculars.

He wasn't surprised to see Hennessy leaning against the front fender of Croft's car, smoking a cigarette. He whisked a fly off his face. He took a handkerchief from his pants pocket and wiped the back of his neck with it. He turned once and looked behind him down the road. Seeing nothing, he faced the building again.

Thatcher focused the binoculars on the screened entrance, and then on each of the front windows, but could see nothing through any of them. He watched for a couple more minutes. Nothing happened. He was about to turn away and return to report to Bill, when the screened door was pushed open and Gert appeared.

She called out something to Hennessy. Thatcher didn't catch her words, but the former IRA fighter responded immediately by tossing away his cigarette and climbing the steps to go inside.

Laurel had lost track of time under the barrage of Croft's questions, few of which she knew the answers to. He didn't believe that, so he continued relentlessly.

He hadn't hit her again, but the threat of his doing so filled her with dread. Her ears were still ringing. The side of her face throbbed. She could feel it swelling.

The blow had also fueled her contempt. She took pride in knowing that the only way the Honorable Mayor Croft had managed to subdue her was to strike her while her hands were bound. Some big man he was.

He never raised his voice. He ignored Gert's snorts of derision over his "going too easy on her." At her suggestion that she take a whack at Laurel, Croft had said, "I don't want her dead."

"I ain't gonna kill her till she tells me where she's hid that girl. She ain't reappeared at the shack."

"You see, Laurel?" Croft spoke with the dulcet tone and phony smile of a public official making a campaign promise. "If you'll just tell us what we want to know, we can end this unpleasantness."

What you'll end is me.

She feared she wouldn't live out this day, but she didn't know the answers to Croft's questions about Chester Landry. Why would he think she would? And she would never give Corrine over to Gert.

Croft asked her the same questions repeatedly, her answers never varied, but she began replying with mounting hostility. With her hands bound behind her, and Gert's evident affection for her shotgun, Laurel didn't have any means of fighting back except to show her loathing and defiance of both of them.

"Let's try one more time, Laurel," Croft said. "Landry went behind my back and offered to form a partnership with you, didn't he?"

"No."

"You've admitted that he returned to your house last night."

"Yes, but our conversation was interrupted by gunshots. We ran to the scene of the ambush. From there he disappeared. I've told you this a dozen times." Brazenly, she asked, "Did you have Davy O'Connor killed?"

Ignoring that, he said, "You never saw Landry again?"

"No."

"He just ran away."

"Yes."

"He didn't say where he was off to?"

"No. If you ordered my friend's execution, may God damn you," she yelled.

"Landry didn't lure you into a business arrangement that excluded me?"

"He couldn't have lured me into anything. He was slimy. I wanted nothing to do with either of you. If you want to know his whereabouts, go in search of him and stop wasting your time with me. I can't tell you something that *I don't know.*"

Croft sighed theatrically and looked over at Gert. "Get Hennessy."

Those two words caused Laurel's stomach to lurch, but she kept her expression impassive as the man came inside and took up a position to the left of and slightly behind Croft.

Laurel didn't acknowledge that he was there, didn't dare to look at him, not wanting to see on his ugly face either a fearsome threat or a taunting smile that would remind her of his groping hands.

Croft gave Hennessy a sidelong glance, then, when he came back around, slapped Laurel hard enough to knock her chair backward. Her head hit the floor with a crack. Hennessy stepped around, jerked her to her feet, righted the chair, firmly planted it in front of Croft, and pushed her down into it.

Croft's arrogant face swam into her vision through tears of pain and fury.

"One last time," he said softly. "Where is Chester Landry?"

"Go. To. Hell."

He heaved another sigh and gave her the look of a disappointed parent. "Since you're resistant to my rough handling, perhaps you'll be more receptive to Mr. Hennessy's sweet talk." He waited a beat before smiling and adding, "Upstairs."

Thatcher made his way back to where Bill was waiting. He got there just as a car bearing the sheriff's office insignia pulled off the highway and rolled to a stop behind Bill's car. Scotty, Harold, and three others got out. All were heavily armed with shotguns, rifles, and handguns.

Bill motioned for them to gather around Thatcher so he could brief them on what he'd observed. "I only saw Gert and Hennessy, but Croft is bound to be in there."

"No indication of what was going on inside?" Bill asked.

"No. I couldn't get close enough to hear anything without being seen. It was quiet, though. No ruckus."

Bill asked Scotty for the warrant and placed it in his breast pocket.

He addressed Harold and one of the other deputies. "You two set up a roadblock. Don't let anyone get past you, either going in or coming out." They nodded understanding.

"Scotty, and you other two, approach the house on foot. Flank it, cover the back. Stay in the trees and out of sight unless hell breaks loose. Thatcher and I will approach from the front in my car."

As Bill continued giving instructions, Thatcher took off his suit coat, rolled it up, and placed it on the floorboard of Bill's car. He didn't want anything between him and his holster, which he tied to his thigh.

Those in the group noticed and exchanged looks among themselves. Thatcher ignored the suspicion and resentment still directed at him, but Bill must've sensed it. He said, "Gabe Driscoll has confessed to killing his wife. He alleges that Bernie Croft arranged to have her buried out at Pointer's Gap. Thatcher was wronged."

To a man they shifted their gazes to him, but he gave a small shrug and kept his attention on Bill.

"Okay then," the sheriff said, as though a weighty matter had been settled. "We'll try to peacefully serve the warrant," he said, "but I don't expect Bernie to surrender without a fight. Thatcher, anything to add to what you've already told us of the situation?"

"Yeah. Croft's man Hennessy is no amateur. Given the chance, he'll kill you. If you get into it with him, don't hesitate. Put him down."

They acknowledged the advice with grim nods.

Bill said, "All right. Let's go."

"Who's that?" one of the deputies said.

They all turned. Irv Plummer's truck was rattling like a peddler's wagon up the road. It came to a stop behind the second department vehicle.

Bill swore. "Get him out of here."

But before anyone could act, Corrine hopped down from the passenger seat and came running toward Thatcher. "Mr. Hutton? What's going on?"

"We're serving an arrest warrant."

"For Gert?" She turned to Bill. "I hope it's for Gert."

"Not today."

"Fair warning, y'all. She keeps a loaded shotgun on the bar within reach."

Looking past Corrine, Bill said, "Mr. Plummer, you can't be here."

"It's a public road."

"Not now, it's not."

"Irv, you need to get going," Thatcher said.

"Oh, you think that badge gives you the right to order me around?"

"Take it up with me later, Irv. For right now, get Corrine and clear out."

Irv looked around at the group of solemn men, and the firepower they carried, and seemed to grasp the seriousness of the situation. He said to Thatcher, "The girl saw the marked cars, insisted on turning in and finding out if Gert was finally gonna get her comeuppance. But I see y'all got business, so we'll be on our way. Come on, girl." He put his hand in the crook of Corrine's elbow.

She shook him off, saying, "What the hell's *he* doing?"

They all followed her line of sight. Lefty was staggering out from a grove of mesquite trees. Seeing them, he stopped. Swaying on his feet, he slowly and unsteadily raised his hands in surrender. "I had no part in it. Didn't want no part in it."

The two deputies closest to him took him by his skinny arms, and half-dragged, half-carried him over to the group. "Swear to God, it was none of my doing." His protruding Adam's apple slid up and down. "I sneaked out the back while's they were occupied." His knees gave out, and he would have gone to the ground if the deputies hadn't been supporting him. "I'm kinda drunk."

Bill said sternly, "Well, you've got one second to sober up. What's going on back there? What don't you want any part of?"

"I'm scared 'fore it's over they're gonna kill her."

"Who?"

He rolled his eyes and finally blinked Irv into focus. "His daughter-in-law. Ain't that why all y'all are here?"

FIFTY-NINE

———◦◉◦———

Thatcher waited for no one. He tossed the rifle into the back of Bill's car, got behind the wheel, and, thanks to the electric starter, was already accelerating by the time Bill had caught hold of the open passenger door. He stood on the running board until he could clamber into the seat.

Scotty shouted, "All hell has broken loose." He and the other two deputies sprinted after the car, grasped whatever handhold they could get, and hopped onto the running boards.

Thatcher was merciless on the motor. He didn't spare the tires, either, making no attempt to dodge rain-filled potholes. When the roadhouse came into sight, he aimed the hood of Bill's car at the rear end of Croft's town car. As he braked behind it, mere inches away from colliding with it, the deputies leaped off and divided up as Bill had instructed them to. Scotty took off toward the left side of the building, the other two went right.

Thatcher pulled his pistol and hurdled the front steps, then flattened himself to one side of the screened door. "Laurel!"

No answer.

Bill made it to the porch and stationed himself on the other side of the door. "Bernie, we know you have Mrs. Plummer. Send her out unharmed."

Nothing.

"I have a warrant for your arrest, Bernie."

From within, Croft laughed. "That's hilarious."

Bill said, "You're right. Let's skip the official stuff, save taxpayers the money of trying you for the murder of Davy O'Connor and the arson murder of the Johnsons. I'll simply kill you for poisoning Daisy."

There was no response, and Thatcher was done fucking around. He signaled to Bill that he would open the screened door, since it opened out toward them, and he was on the left side. Bill nodded.

Thatcher reached for the handle and flung open the door toward Bill. Thatcher hit the ground and rolled across the threshold. He was greeted by two shotgun blasts. Gert must have fired both barrels. Thatcher registered that she would need time to reload. Bill must've had the same thought as he came through the opening with his pistol blazing.

He drew fire from two positions: behind the bar and from above. Thatcher looked up. Hennessy was on the landing at the top of the stairs, holding Laurel in front of him, one hand clamped over her mouth, his other aiming a pistol at Thatcher.

Don't hesitate. Put him down.

Sooner than Thatcher could think it, he fired at the bridge of Hennessy's nose. The man showed an instant of surprise, then fell back, dead before he hit the floor. But when he released Laurel, she went somersaulting down the stairs. Thatcher realized her hands were bound.

He shouted her name, but got no answer.

A bullet struck the floor within an inch of his face, sending up splintered wood. A chunk hit him on the cheekbone, barely missing his eye. He rolled away from where he was, came up in a crouch, and took cover behind a table.

"Bill, you okay?"

"I want these sons o' bitches."

"Hennessy's not a worry."

"Dead?"

"Yep."

"Hear that, Bernie?" Bill taunted. "Your hired gun is in hell."

Their repartee had given Thatcher time to scan the room. He couldn't see Gert, but figured she was behind the bar, reloading. It had to have been Croft's shot that had struck the floor near him, which gave him an idea of the mayor's accuracy. He wasn't a bad shot.

He waited, crazy to know where Laurel was. Was her neck broken, her back? Had she hit her head and was lying unconscious and defenseless?

Croft showed his head above the bar. Both Thatcher and Bill fired a volley. Soda pop bottles shattered against the back of the bar, but Thatcher got no indication that Croft had been hit.

Where was Gert and that goddamn shotgun?

Bill was off to Thatcher's left. When Croft raised his head again, Bill fired two shots. Thatcher used the cover to take up another position. He still couldn't see Laurel. He couldn't place Gert, either, and that bothered him. He would have expected another blast from the shotgun by now. Unless one of their shots had struck her and she was down.

Couldn't count on that. Too much to hope for.

He had to know where Laurel was and if she was hurt. From his present vantage point, he couldn't see the bottom of the staircase where he featured her crumpled, broken, bleeding.

Croft was keeping him and Bill pinned down.

A shadow fell across the screened door. Croft fired at it. The shadow disappeared.

Thatcher, who was nearest the door, whispered, "Who's that?"

"Scotty."

"Hennessy's dead. Croft's behind the bar. Have you seen Gert?"

"No. Mrs. Plummer?"

"Alive when we got here. Now..." Thatcher couldn't bring himself to venture a guess.

"What do you want me to do, Thatcher?"

"Stay put, but be ready."

While carrying on the whispered conversation with the deputy through the screen, Thatcher had reloaded. Bill, who'd been exchanging potshots with Croft, also had to pause to reload. Thatcher waited until he was done, then motioned to Bill that he was going to intentionally draw Croft's fire, giving Bill a chance at him.

Bill acknowledged.

Thatcher took a breath, then surged to his feet and ran toward the staircase, banging into tables, overturning chairs, reaching across his torso to fire back toward the bar.

Croft took the bait. As soon as he showed himself, he and Bill exchanged a barrage. From beneath his left arm, Thatcher turned and fired three rounds at Croft before diving beneath a table. He rolled onto his back and fired toward Croft again, but he had disappeared behind the bar.

Thatcher flipped the table onto its side and hunkered behind it so he could reload. "Bill?"

"Bernie's hit. Wounded, at least."

"Are you okay?"

"Yeah."

Thatcher knew that wasn't true. He was breathing like a man who'd been hit. But where? How bad? He couldn't ask without also giving Croft the advantage of knowing.

"Bill, can you cover me?"

There was a grunt, then, "Ready."

Thatcher sprang up and sprinted over to the staircase.

There was no sign of Laurel. Not below, midway, or above.

She tumbled. On her way down, one body part or another struck every tread of the steep staircase. She landed hard. The wind was knocked out of her.

"Laurel!"

The first time Thatcher had called out to her, Hennessy's hand had been over her mouth. She couldn't respond this time, either, because she hadn't regained her breath. And Gert had been waiting for her at the bottom of the staircase.

She crammed a sour dishcloth into Laurel's mouth and lifted her off the floor. The madam was more solidly built even than Hennessy and seemed twice as strong. She was certainly as mean and merciless.

Laurel struggled, but without the use of her arms, and with every inch of her body pulsing in pain, she was virtually defenseless. But she'd be damned before she gave up.

In an attempt to get Thatcher's attention, she banged her heels against the hardwood floor. But, as she did, gunfire exploded, seeming to come from all directions at once and drowning out the sound.

Gert hit her on the temple with the barrel of the shotgun, dazing her. She had the will but not the coordination to resist when she was dragged past the bar, into a narrow passage, and through a door. The area into which Gert shoved her was darker, cooler, and smelled of booze.

Head still reeling, she realized that she was in Lefty's infamous back room.

In the front room, Thatcher was in a gunfight. Thatcher could die.

That prospect was more terrifying to her than the actuality of Gert, who was standing over her, loading shells into her shotgun. When she snapped it closed, she crammed the barrels beneath Laurel's chin.

And Laurel's last thought: *I love Thatcher.*

Thatcher stared at the emptiness at the bottom of the staircase.

Laurel was unhurt. She'd gotten herself to safety.

No. If she'd been able to respond to his shouts, she would have. Unless she hadn't wanted to give away her position to . . . *Gert.*

Gert hadn't been behind the bar reloading. She'd abandoned

Bernie to fight it out with Bill while she was settling her grudge against Laurel.

But if Gert had fired the shotgun, he would have heard it. Laurel would be dead at the bottom of the stairs. Gert had a reason for keeping Laurel alive.

Hostage.

Okay, so where had Gert taken her?

The back room. Had to be.

Thatcher processed all this within a millisecond. By the time he'd completed the last thought, he was already moving in the direction of the back room. But as he reached the open space at the end of the bar, he was met with a hail of bullets.

He fell back and ducked under the counter. He waited, breathing hard but as quietly as possible. He would be no help to Laurel dead.

His mind tapered down to the single purpose of killing Bernie Croft. Now.

Gun hand extended, he stood up and moved into the space at the end of the bar, intentionally making himself an easy target. Croft was lying on his back in a pool of soda pop and his own blood. He must've spent all his bullets in that last barrage, because the pistol lay on the floor at his side.

Thatcher drew a bead on him.

Croft's eyes showed stark fear, but he couldn't speak for the blood bubbling from his mouth. He was frantically clawing with both hands at the multiple bullet wounds in his torso. His bloody watch fob kept getting in the way of his futile attempts to stanch the gushers of blood.

It would be a mercy kill. To hell with that. Thatcher lowered his gun. "Scotty!"

Scotty and the two other deputies rushed in, weapons drawn.

Already on the move, Thatcher said, "See to Bill. Croft's gut-shot."

"Dead?"

"Yeah. He just hasn't stopped breathing yet. Two of you follow me."

Thatcher ran into the dark, narrow passage behind the bar that led to the back room. "Laurel!" He tried the door. It was locked. "Laurel!"

He put his shoulder to the door. It burst open just as two gunshots were fired.

"You're my ticket out of here, princess." Gert yanked Laurel to her feet and began hauling her across the room toward a rear door.

Having taken several blows to the head, the sudden movement sickened her. Bile filled the back of her throat, but she knew that with that disgusting rag in her mouth, she would choke to death if she retched. She forced down the fiery bile.

The shooting in the front room had stopped. She heard scuffling footsteps and shouting, but the only distinct word she heard was her name.

Hearing Thatcher's voice coming nearer spurred her, imbued her with energy she would have thought unattainable. More than that, it filled her with die-hard determination not to let this ogress defeat her.

She jammed her feet against the floor, trying to halt or slow Gert's progress.

"Move! I'll shoot you!"

Laurel didn't believe she would. She was Gert's bargaining chip, but only for as long as she stayed alive.

A thumping noise came from beyond the door behind them. "Laurel!"

"Shit!" Gert muttered.

Try as she might, Laurel couldn't match Gert's strength, and they reached the back entrance. She still held the shotgun beneath Laurel's chin, but Laurel thought that if she could hold out for just a moment longer—

Gert reached around her and pulled open the door.

Corrine was standing within two feet of the threshold.

Taking advantage of Gert's surprise, Laurel lunged sideways.

Corrine stretched out her arm and fired two rounds point-blank into Gert's throat.

———

Thatcher crashed through the door in time to see Gert drop the shotgun. She clutched her throat with both hands and staggered backward as blood spurted from between her thick, tobacco-stained fingers. She landed on the floor like a felled redwood, her eyes wild.

Even before they went unseeing, Thatcher was kneeling beside Laurel and yanking a rancid dishcloth out of her mouth. In seconds, he had her hands untied. He ran his hands over her to reassure himself that she was intact.

She placed her hands on his chest, saying in a rush of breath, "She caught me at the foot of the stairs and stuffed that cloth in my mouth. I couldn't call out to you."

He pulled her to him and placed his chin on the crown of her head. He looked at Corrine. "How'd you get here?"

"Irv and them deputies setting up the roadblock got into an argument over who was moving what vehicle first. It got to be a real pissin' contest. Ain't that just like men? I run off while they weren't looking."

She grinned and extended her hand, palm up, on which lay the small Derringer. "I come to give Miss Laurel her pistol back."

SIXTY

The J.P. was summoned to declare Bernard Croft, Jimmy Hennessy, and Gertrude Atkins dead. Lefty, who seemed relieved rather than upset to learn that Gert had departed this life, was taken in for questioning and to sleep off his bender. He would keep Gabe Driscoll company in the cell block that night.

Bill had taken a bullet in the thigh. It had missed major blood vessels, but was buried in the muscle and would need to be surgically removed. Irv offered to transport him to town in the back of his truck. Deputies carried him over and placed him in it.

Laurel insisted she would be fine when her head cleared, but everyone else, especially Thatcher, was just as insistent that Dr. Perkins should check her over. He personally tucked her into the backseat of Bill's car, drove her to the clinic himself, and hand-delivered her to the doctor and a nurse.

They gowned her and left her lying on the table in the examination room, where Thatcher was granted a private moment with her while they assembled what they would need to treat her mild injuries.

She scooted over, creating a spot for Thatcher to sit. He clasped hands with her and looked her over. "Do you hurt anywhere?"

"A little bit everywhere. Bumps and bruises, mostly."

"Your head?" He wasn't sure she was aware of the large bruise on her temple.

"The nurse already gave me aspirin powder. What happened there?" Tenderly she touched the cut beneath his eye made by the wood splinter.

"Nothing."

She kissed her fingertip and barely touched it to the scrape. "I have some good news. Mike O'Connor is in a room down the hall. He's holding his own, Dr. Perkins said. He predicts a full recovery. But he also told me that, in a lucid moment, Mike vowed on his Saint Christopher medal to get revenge for Davy."

"Maybe he'll have a change of heart."

"I doubt it," she said wistfully.

So did Thatcher, actually.

To get her off that subject, he said, "You and Corrine will have to give your statements about what happened with Gert. It'll be a formality."

"Of course."

"But I have one question. Why did Corrine have your pistol?"

"When all the trouble started happening in the hills, I was afraid for her safety. Even though Ernie—"

"Who's Ernie?"

She smiled. "I'll tell you about him sometime."

He fingered a strand of her hair. "I think we both have a lot to tell each other."

"Give me a hint."

He softly kissed her lips.

As he eased away from her, she whispered, "I can't wait to hear the rest."

From the other side of the door, Dr. Perkins cleared his throat. "Mr. Hutton, they need your help with Sheriff Amos downstairs."

"Be right there." He stood and bent over Laurel. "I'll see you later."

"Yes. However late it is."

As he backed toward the door, they stretched out their arms, keeping their fingers touching for as long as possible before they fell away.

⚬

Thatcher exited through a door in the rear of the building, where Irv's truck was parked. As he approached it, he overheard Corrine saying to Irv, "Miss Laurel said you'd have a hissy fit if you knew she'd given me her little gun. But good thing she did. I can't wait to tell Ernie about Gert. He'll be so proud o' me."

Deputies were grouped around the tailgate, talking quietly among themselves. Thatcher felt a kick of apprehension. "What's the matter?"

"He won't come out," Scotty said.

"What do you mean? He can't walk. Lift him out and carry him."

"We tried. He threatened to fire all of us. He said he wouldn't go under the knife till he had talked to you."

"Thatcher," Bill called. "Get in here."

The others shuffled aside as Thatcher made his way to the raised tailgate and looked over it into the bed of the truck. Bill was lying on his back, sweating profusely and in obvious pain.

"What the hell, Bill? Doc's got everything ready for you upstairs."

"I need to talk to you. Get in. You others," he said, raising his voice, "make yourselves scarce."

Thatcher lowered the tailgate and stepped up onto it, saying over his shoulder, "Give us a few minutes."

"Uh, Thatcher?"

He paused and looked back. Harold was threading the brim of his hat through his fingers. It seemed he'd been appointed the spokesperson. "We, uh. You did okay out there today. I mean, damn good." The others nodded. "We'd all take you out for a beer, except, well, you know. This danged Prohibition."

The awkward invitation was their way of apologizing for the slights. Thatcher bobbed his chin. "A beer would go down real good. Some other time."

They all breathed a collective sigh. Scotty said, "We'll wait over here." They moved away as a group, giving Bill the privacy he'd asked for.

Thatcher hunkered down beside him. "What's this bullshit about?"

"Leg's hurting like a bastard."

"Then let us get you in there so the doc can fix you up."

"I'm scared of ether."

"You'll sleep it off."

"I sent one of the men to tell Daisy. Hated to. Alice Cantor sent back word that she's doing a lot better. Got some scrambled eggs down her. She'll bring her to see me tomorrow."

"That's good news. Let's go."

Bill caught Thatcher by the sleeve.

"Something else." He settled his head on the floor of the truck and stared at the tarpaulin stretched overhead. "Soon as I'm able, I'll be turning myself in. I took Bernie's bribes. Let Hiram...others...get away with murder. Like killing that boy Elray. He'll be on my conscience for a long time."

Thatcher wanted to say *Mine, too*, but Bill didn't give him a chance.

"Being lax kept things peaceful. But I'm a crook, same as the rest. Past time I owned up to it." He blinked sweat from his eyes and grimaced with pain.

"This confession can wait, Bill."

"No, it can't." He returned his gaze to Thatcher. "If I were to die on that table, you'd never know unless I tell you now. And that would be a tragedy."

"You're not in your right head, Bill. You're talking nonsense."

He clutched Thatcher's sleeve tighter.

"From the start, I saw in you..." He made a dismissive gesture. "I already told you why I wanted you to work with me. Tim. All that. I wanted it bad enough, I lied to keep you here."

His face contorted, and it wasn't sweat in his eyes, Thatcher now realized. It was tears.

He choked on his next words. "I told you that your Mr. Hobson had died."

SIXTY-ONE

The house was two-story, with a white clapboard exterior trimmed in sky blue. Thatcher was relieved to see that it was as nice a house as the growing city of Amarillo afforded.

He went through the gate of the iron picket fence and up to the front door. His knock was answered by a gray-haired gentleman with a benign smile and gentle brown eyes behind wire-rimmed eyeglasses. Thatcher had been told that he was a prosperous accountant.

"You must be Mr. Hutton." He extended his right hand and shook. "I'm George Maxwell. We received your telegram yesterday afternoon. Ever since, he's been watching the clock like a hawk."

Thatcher was led through the main rooms of a house that smelled like lemon oil and homemade bread. The bedroom he was ushered into was bright with sunlight filtered through gauzy curtains.

A woman who was bent over the bed adjusting the covers straightened up and turned as she heard Thatcher enter. "Welcome, Mr. Hutton. My name is Irma."

"Ma'am."

"Would you care for something to drink?"

"Thank you, but I'm okay for now."

She gave him an understanding smile. "Then I'll leave you to your reunion." As she passed him on her way out of the room, she said, "Bless you for coming." She and her husband withdrew and closed the door behind them.

Thatcher almost wouldn't have recognized the person on the bed. His memory was of an average-size man, but one who had seemed larger than life, a man robust enough to fit into the seemingly endless landscape that he'd lived on, worked on, and loved.

Propped against a stack of fluffy pillows, he looked diminished. The stroke had paralyzed his left side and distorted that half of his face. The eye was permanently closed, his mouth drawn downward.

No, Thatcher might not have recognized Mr. Henry Hobson Jr.

But Mr. Hobson recognized him.

His right eye was lit up with joy. He raised his right hand and reached out toward Thatcher. Although his countenance and reduced form were unfamiliar, Thatcher would have known that calloused, crusty hand anywhere. It had taught him how to rope and shoot and brand, how to pack a saddle bag, start a campfire and put it out safely, how to hold a poker hand, tie a necktie, and how to use his table manners. It had patted his shoulder in congratulations for achievements, and had squeezed it with encouragement following failures.

Just about anything worth knowing he had learned from Mr. Hobson, the principal lesson being that a man was only as good as his word. He crossed over to the bed and took Mr. Hobson's hand in his. "I promised you I'd be back."

In his mind, Thatcher had replayed the telephone conversation with Trey Hobson's secretary, and realized how the condolences he'd extended had been misconstrued as a reference to Mr. Hobson's debilitating stroke, not to his demise.

The Maxwells told him that following the major stroke, Mr. Hobson had suffered several minor ones, and that his doctor predicted a cerebral "event" from which he wouldn't recover.

"Irma has nursing experience," Mr. Maxwell explained. "Several years ago we began making our spare room available to patients in Mr. Hobson's condition. When he was dismissed from the hospital, we had a vacancy and invited him to move in. His son agreed that being with us was preferable to a nursing home."

And the kind couple were far preferable to Trey, Thatcher thought.

The Maxwells gave him a bedroom on the second floor and treated him like an honored guest, but largely he was left free to pass the time with Mr. Hobson.

His visit stretched into weeks.

He and his mentor spent hours together in the homey bedroom. For the most part, Mr. Hobson stayed in bed, but occasionally Thatcher would move him into a chair where he had a better view out the window. He couldn't converse, but he was an attentive listener and expressed himself eloquently by using his right hand to gesture and his right eye to blink twice for yes, once for no.

Thatcher read to him daily, either from the newspaper or from the dime novels he loved about the wild West, cattle drives, and shoot-'em'-ups. Thatcher shared war stories, some funny, some harrowing.

He told Mr. Hobson about his jump from the freight train and the unpredictable turn his life had taken since. He described in detail all the people with whom he'd become involved to one degree or another.

As he talked about them, Thatcher realized that even those with whom he'd barely crossed paths and would never see again had been woven tightly into his memory and would stay there forever.

He got angry all over again when he told Mr. Hobson about Bill's deception, the selfishness behind it, the betrayal of a man he'd come to respect. Mr. Hobson didn't immediately respond, and then he moved his right hand laterally, parallel to the ground, as though saying *Let it pass*.

And of course, Thatcher talked about Laurel. He described her physically but was frustrated by the inadequacy of his words. He groused about her stubborn streak but admitted to Mr. Hobson that he'd lost his heart to her sassiness. He could have sworn the old man chuckled.

Often Thatcher just sat with him, saying nothing, hoping that Mr. Hobson was as content simply being in his presence as much as Thatcher was simply being in his. It was during those quiet times that Thatcher reflected on his experience of the past several months, and began to realize that there might have been a purpose behind everything that had happened, a governing why for that he hadn't perceived while he was living it.

He wondered if Mr. Hobson, somehow, even in his limited capacity, had influenced that insight.

One morning, Thatcher asked Mr. Maxwell if he could borrow his car. "I'd like to drive out to the ranch."

Having spotted the car's wake of dust from a mile away, Jesse was waiting for it outside the bunkhouse, holding a shotgun across his chest. The dog, who was part wolf, sat growling at his side.

When Thatcher stepped out of the car, Jesse dropped the shotgun, called off the animal, and, although he was well past seventy, ran out to embrace him, thumping him on the back and laughing.

They opened a contraband bottle of mescal and spent the day sharing it and recollections. They laughed with hilarity over some. Others made them pensive or downright sad.

Thatcher was reunited with his saddle. It was on a stand inside the bunkhouse. Thatcher ran his hand over the smooth leather. "It's never looked better, Jesse. Thank you for keeping it in good condition."

When the old ranch hand asked about his former boss, Thatcher told him he'd considered packing Mr. Hobson into the car and bringing him along.

"But I think he's too frail to have made the drive out here." Thatcher gazed off into the distance, past the empty corrals and cattle pens where the dust had settled for good, and the whoops and hollers of rowdy cowboys would never be heard again. The magnificent span of the Panhandle's horizon was now interrupted by the silhouettes of drilling rigs. Thatcher added, "And it would have broken his heart."

When it came time for Thatcher to leave, his double-handed handshake with Jesse held for a long time in an unspoken acknowledgment that this was goodbye.

One afternoon Irma Maxwell knocked softly on the bedroom door then came in carrying a plate with a sandwich on it. "Since you didn't come to the table for lunch..." She halted midway across the room.

Thatcher's chair was pulled up close to the bed. His hand was wrapped around Mr. Hobson's. "He passed." He cleared his husky throat. "About ten minutes ago. No event. It was dignified and peaceful."

He spent that night with the Maxwells, but in the morning he came downstairs carrying his duffel bag already packed. He wanted to make a clean break before Trey arrived. Yesterday when notified of his father's death, he'd told Mr. Maxwell that he "couldn't get away" until this morning.

Thatcher didn't think he could be civil to the self-centered bastard, and it would be disrespectful to Mr. Hobson to create tension or cause a scene. Besides, attending a stuffy funeral, Mr. Hobson in a casket, him in a pew, didn't seem a fitting end to these meaningful weeks they had spent in each other's company.

He declined the Maxwells' offer of breakfast before he left. "Thank you, but there's a train at nine-forty. I'd like to make it."

"Before you go." Mr. Maxwell went over to a chest and took a shoe box from one of the drawers. "When Mr. Hobson was moved in here with us, this was among his things."

He handed the box to Thatcher. His name was written on top in Mr. Hobson's bold scrawl. Before he raised the lid, Thatcher heard the familiar jingle and knew what he would find inside: Mr. Hobson's spurs, still dirt-encrusted from his last ride.

SIXTY-TWO

Not entrusting his saddle to the baggage car, Thatcher boarded the train with it on his shoulder. He set it in the seat in front of him where he could keep an eye on it. He took the seat next to the window.

To discourage interaction with other passengers, he pulled his cowboy hat over his eyes, slumped in his seat, and pretended to be asleep. The train chuffed out of the station.

He must have dozed, because he was roused by someone asking, "Is this seat taken?"

Damn. Thatcher shook his head. "No."

"Aw, good. The cars are crowded."

The passenger settled into the seat. "Where are you headed?"

So much for discouraging conversation. Thatcher took off his hat and placed it on his knee. He put his thumb and middle finger into his eye sockets and rubbed them. "Abilene. Then east from there."

"Back to Foley?"

Surprised by that response, Thatcher glanced at his seat partner, did a double take, then his right hand automatically went for his pistol.

"You're not wearing your gun belt. I checked as you boarded. I didn't want you to shoot me before I could explain myself."

The smile he flashed was not that of a pimp. In place of the gold tooth was a normal white molar. "You thought you'd seen the last of Chester Landry, didn't you? Well, you have. And, God, what a jerk he was. I'm glad to be shed of him."

He had medium brown hair that was wavy and loose, not slicked back with pounds of pomade. He was dressed in a conservative dark suit, with a pinstripe vest and unremarkable necktie.

Thatcher looked around to see if they were being observed, possibly to reassure himself that he wasn't dreaming. No one was paying him any attention except the man seated next to him. Thatcher said, "Who the hell are you?"

"Lewis Mahoney, detective, Dallas PD. I'll show you my badge if you insist, but that can be awkward, because I'm presently on loan to another agency, working undercover."

"What agency?"

"I can't tell."

"That's convenient."

"Actually it's a nuisance. Because I would like for you to believe me, Mr. Hutton. I'm sure you have questions. I'll answer those I can."

"What happened to Randy?"

"He was drawing too much attention to himself. I was afraid that Croft was going to have him killed, so I had to get him out of there. I lured him to Dallas by promising him a position in my fictitious bootlegging operation. I took him to a speakeasy to celebrate his new employment. It was raided, as planned. Dallas police arrested him, as planned. I escaped arrest, as planned."

"Like at Lefty's."

He made a wry face. "No, that wasn't planned. I just got lucky that night. Anyway. Randy. Arresting officers promised him clemency in exchange for names. That of Chester Landry topped his list, of course. Not the most loyal of acquaintances, a young man of meager character, and negligible morals, but not deserving of having his throat cut by Jimmy Hennessy." He looked at Thatcher shrewdly. "By the way, congratulations on that outstanding display of marksmanship. You're already a legend. I'll bet Wyatt Earp is pea green."

Thatcher ignored that. "You know, some suspected me of being a secret agent."

"Croft was convinced. You bedeviled him, Mr. Hutton."

"I'm glad to hear it. But I'm talking about friends who figured me for a spy. I'd hate doing what you do, Mr. Mahoney."

"Yes, you would. The integrity thing."

"Doesn't it ever bother you to rat out people who've befriended you?"

"It would if I didn't stay focused on the big picture."

"Which is what?"

"First and foremost, I'm an officer of the law. I despise this Prohibition act, because it is already making lawbreakers out of law-abiding people, and turning petty criminals into villainous racketeers. Croft, for example."

"My understanding is that he was always corrupt."

"Yes, but he hadn't gone so far as to murder anyone. Greed rid him of restraint. Even in the short time I knew him, I saw it happening, and it was frightening. Mark my words, Hutton, the next war this country fights is going to be against violent crime syndicates that give no quarter."

"Like Davy O'Connor's assassination. Firing the Johnsons' house."

"Exactly like that. Jesus," he said, shaking his head. "For months I'd been coordinating a countywide raid. Several agencies, working together, we were going to nail Hiram Johnson and Bernie Croft." He made a helpless gesture.

"Croft moved first. Hard and fast and without my knowledge. Incidentally, we've identified the men who ambushed the O'Connors. All were on Croft's payroll. They've got prices on their heads. Somebody will turn. We'll get them."

"You went to Laurel Plummer that night and told her you wanted to make her an offer."

"I was going to reveal myself for who I am and ask her to become an informant for me. In exchange, I would see to it that she and her associates would be granted clemency for moonshining." He chuckled. "Looking back on it, it was a bad idea."

"For putting her in danger like that, I would have killed you."

"As I said, a bad idea." Again, he laughed softly. "I don't advise getting on her fighting side. She has a wicked right hook." He worked his jaw laterally.

When Thatcher didn't react, he said, "I can see that you're not amused." He paused as though seeking a better way to express himself. "Let me assure you that I'm often bothered about the betrayal aspect of my job. But I don't go after the small-timers like your Mrs. Plummer. I'm after the bad guys, the ones who would have ultimately gotten rid of her for no other reason than that she was becoming a pest."

"Croft."

"Or someone like a Chester Landry, but the real article."

"I was afraid that was exactly what was going to happen."

"I figured. Your *protectiveness* was apparent."

Thatcher didn't comment on that. "How'd you know I'd be on this train?"

"I knew you were in Amarillo, and the reason for your being here. I'm sorry about your friend."

"Thanks. But why were you keeping tabs on me?"

He smiled, a genuine, unaffected smile. "First because you're damned interesting. Then because the more I saw of you, the more I came to believe that you had missed your calling."

He withdrew a business card from the pocket of his vest and handed it to Thatcher. "There's a good man, a sheriff, in Bynum. Know it?"

"No."

"East Texas. Pretty country. Piney woods. Lakes full of fish. Bynum's a sleepy little town where not much happens. Except that, on the county line, there's a horse racetrack." He punched Thatcher in the arm as he said that. "Racetracks draw sinners like moths to flame. But now that there's no legal drinking or gambling, the sinners are restless, and the sheriff has more than he can handle. Think about it."

He scooted out of the seat. "My stop is coming up. It's been a pleasure chatting with you. I trust in your integrity to keep this meeting to yourself. And should we ever meet somewhere—"

"I wouldn't give you away."

"I know that." He extended his hand. Thatcher shook it. Looking directly into Thatcher's eyes, he said, "I've enjoyed making your acquaintance, Hutton. Take care."

Then he turned and walked to the end of the car, opened the door, and stepped through to the next car.

SIXTY-THREE

One morning Laurel woke up with a grasp on that missed flicker of illumination she'd had after her night of lovemaking with Thatcher. She couldn't let it go or even leave it to languish. It was so long overdue, she was compelled to share it without delay.

She dressed and went downstairs. Irv was finishing up his breakfast. "I left a pan of biscuits warming in the oven. Sit down, I'll pour you some coffee."

"Let's go for a ride."

He turned to her, a puzzled look on his face. "Now? Where to?"

"Just come, please."

She lifted her straw hat off the peg and put it on, took down her purse, and went out through the back door. Mumbling something about "nutty female notions," Irv followed.

Ten minutes later, Laurel sat down on the narrow strip of grass between Pearl's and Derby's graves. She motioned for Irv to join her on the ground.

"I won't be able to get back up."

"Yes, you will. I'll help you."

He lowered himself to the ground on the other side of his son's grave. "What's going on, Laurel? What's the matter? Are you sad over him?"

She knew he wasn't speaking of Derby. Thatcher had left without a word and hadn't come back. No one knew if he would. She cried herself to sleep most nights. She was in dire need of comforting. Yet, the person who could ease her misery was the source of it.

She was furious at him for that. But her yearning for him was like a sickness. "This isn't about him."

"Told you not to trust him."

"You did," she said softly. Idly, she began pulling up the dandelions that had begun sprouting on Pearl's grave. "Something's come to me recently."

"A package?"

"No," she said, smiling. "Nothing tangible, although I do consider it a gift of sorts."

"I think when Gert clouted you on the head, she knocked something loose."

She laughed softly. "You might be right. In which case, I have her to thank for this." He opened his mouth to say more, but she held up her hand. "It's enlightenment. It's been trying to worm its way into my consciousness. I think subconsciously I wanted it to stay put. I've resisted facing it. But I woke up this morning with it firmly seated in my mind. And please stop looking at me like I belong in a loony bin."

"Well, how am I supposed to be looking at you? You ain't making a lick of sense."

"Then I'll make it plainer." She dusted loose dirt off her hands. "Irv, you know how bitter I felt toward Derby for abandoning me."

"You had a right to be."

"Not really. Because I also abandoned him."

"What are you talking about?"

"I've never told you about our start. We met at a dance. Which was forbidden to me, of course. I sneaked out and went with a girl-friend. Derby was handsome and fun, someone I knew my parents would disapprove. I'll admit that was a large part of the attraction. Our whirlwind romance and hasty marriage was my deliverance. Just six weeks later, he left for Europe. I was a bride. Then the war ended, and he came home. To a wife.

"If he had returned with a shattered leg, I wouldn't have expected him to run sprints, would I? But in my selfishness and...and immaturity, I guess...I expected him to pick right back up where he'd left off. Giddy in love. Lighthearted, optimistic, oozing charm.

"But it soon became apparent that Derby was no longer that romantic hero. What's become clear to me is that I, unintentionally, applied pressure on top of the pressure he was already feeling. I didn't support him the way I should have."

"Laurel—"

"No, please. Let me get this out."

He dry-scrubbed his face with his hand and motioned for her to continue.

"I cleaned and cooked and slept with him like a dutiful wife. I begged him to talk to me about the things that were haunting him. I pushed him to try this, to do that, to get help. I swear to you that I did all of this out of love. I hated that he was suffering and seemingly unreachable.

"But I've come to realize that what I considered encouragement must have sounded like harping to him. He even said so just before he shot himself. 'I'm sick of you nagging me about every goddamn thing.'

"God knows I wanted to rescue him. But what he might have needed most was for me to stop flapping around him dispensing advice, and just to *be*. Be there. To hold him tight without saying anything. That's what I didn't do. I didn't allow him to face his fears within the cradle of my arms."

Irv frowned down at the turf over Derby's grave. There was still a slight mound that had yet to flatten out. "You're being too hard on yourself, Laurel. I told you Derby always had that darkness in him."

"I don't know that I could have fixed him, Irv. It's vain of me to think that I could have prevented him from taking his life if he was determined to do so. We'll never know. But, given how damaged he obviously was, I didn't give him credit for struggling through each day as well as he could.

"I laid all the blame on him for what he did. That was unfair." She reached across the grave and took Irv's hand. "You fault yourself for having to leave him when he was a boy. In your circumstances, you did the best you could. It was important for me to tell you that I could have done better by Derby."

He sat for a moment without saying anything, then squeezed her hand. "I couldn't have chosen a better daughter-in-law if I was to have picked you myself."

She had to clamp her lip between her teeth to keep it from quivering.

He cleared his throat noisily and said, "Now that's done, come hoist me up."

SIXTY-FOUR

———◆———

Thatcher walked from the train station straight to her back door, which stood open. He watched her through the screened door as she placed a circle of rolled-out dough into a pie tin and began working the edges with her fingers.

"Fluting."

She started at the sound of his voice. For a span of ten seconds, she held his gaze, then went back to what she was doing. "Go away."

"Didn't you get my telegram?"

With one flour-covered hand, she gestured toward the drainboard, where the torn-up pieces of a telegram lay scattered. "'I'm coming for you.' You have your nerve. Get away from my house. I'm busy."

"I had to go, Laurel."

She stopped fiddling with the dough, but kept her head down, looking at her handiwork rather than at him. "Sheriff Amos told me about Mr. Hobson."

"How'd that come about?"

"Well, after days of hearing nothing from you and not knowing where you were, if you were alive or dead, I went to see the one person who might know what had happened to you. He was still recovering from the surgery." Finished with the pie crust, she reached for a dishcloth and wiped her hands. "He told me about his lie."

She set down the cloth and looked at him sorrowfully. "That was an awful thing for him to do, Thatcher. Did you make it to Amarillo in time?"

He opened the screened door and went inside. "He passed last Wednesday."

"You got to see him?"

"Yeah." He searched her eyes. "Laurel, I know it must've looked like I had run out on you, but I had to go, and I had to go right then before anyone could try to talk me out of it, or delay it, or whatever.

"And I don't regret that decision. I loved the man, and I wouldn't give anything for the time we had together before he died. I don't blame you for being mad. Just please try to understand."

She had softened considerably. "Of course I understand, Thatcher. I was more afraid for your safety than mad." She covered a laugh with her hand. "No, I was furious."

He smiled. "You had reason."

She glanced at the telegram she'd ripped up. "Where have you been since last Wednesday?"

"I made a side trip to Bynum."

"In East Texas? That's more than a side trip."

"We can talk about it later. Is Irv here?"

"No."

"Are you expecting him?"

"He's staying out with Ernie and Corrine tonight."

Thatcher still didn't know who Ernie was. "Turn off the oven."

She placed her hands on her hips. "I'm in the middle of baking pies."

He went to her, put his hands at her waist, and drew her to him. "Turn off the oven."

———

Not long afterward, they lay naked and entwined, her hair as tangled around them as the bedsheet. He lay on his back with one knee raised, she with her head on his chest, which she lightly strummed with her fingertips. "I gave in way too easily."

"Easy, hell." He cupped her bottom and scooted her hip up against his. "It took me twenty whole seconds to get you up the stairs."

She laughed, then took his hand and nestled it between her breasts. "No teasing, I truly am sorry that you lost Mr. Hobson."

"I didn't lose him. He'll always be there."

"Will you tell me stories about him?"

He tilted his head down and tipped hers up so he could look into her face. He ran his thumb across her lips, but, being too moved to speak, only nodded.

She returned her cheek to his chest. After time, she asked, "What was in Bynum?"

"A job."

He felt her go still. "It's not a horse training job, is it?"

"No." He lifted her off his chest and turned onto his side to face her. He laid it all out and was more worried than he wanted to admit when she didn't immediately embrace the idea.

"It seems so random," she said. "Where'd you hear about it?"

He gave her a half smile. "I met a man on the train out of Amarillo. He told me about it."

"It sounds good, Thatcher, but you could have the same job here."

"It would be hard for me to work for Bill again."

"I get that, but—"

"And I can't wear a badge and be married to a local moonshiner."

"You haven't even asked me to marry you."

"Will you marry me?"

"No."

He laughed and nuzzled her neck. Sliding his hand into the vee of her thighs, he whispered, "You don't have to give me your answer right away."

He kept her occupied for the next half hour, rearranging her limbs to allow him access to enchanting spots, turning her this way and that to explore and entice, lazily mapping her sweet body with his hands and lips and tongue. He tormented her with his dalliances until she gasped *now*.

He pushed into her, and the fever pitch that he'd aroused in both of them combusted. He emptied all the sadness and disappointment, uncertainty and longing that he'd experienced in the past few weeks into her.

He was now convinced that everything that had happened since his leap from that freight car had been predestined. He'd been making his way home. But not to a place. To a person. He would only ever be home with this woman.

Still breathing hotly, he rested his forehead against hers and pushed his fingers up into her hair. "I love you, Laurel."

"I believe you do."

"And you love me."

"I'm thinking it over."

"Naw, you love me, and you're gonna marry me."

"You don't know that."

"Yeah, I do. I have a knack." He melded their mouths, and by the time he ended the kiss, he'd convinced her.

The next morning, over breakfast, he said, "On our way to Bynum, I thought we'd stop over in Dallas, and get married there. Spend a couple of nights in a hotel. In a hotel *bed*."

At the stove, she sent him a smile over her shoulder. "I've never been in a hotel. And I've only seen the skyline of Dallas from a distance. Tell me about Bynum."

"It's pretty. Green. Lots of trees. I looked at a house that has a barn."

"You could keep horses."

"I could teach you to ride."

She carried over a plate of hotcakes and set it in front of him. Lips smiling against his ear, she whispered, "You already did."

He pulled her onto his lap. "You took to it good, too." He lowered his head and snarled against her breast.

She pushed him away. "Stop that. Irv could come in. What's the kitchen in this house like?"

"Large and airy. You could bake to your heart's content. I'll bet you could sell slices of pie at the racetrack."

"There's a racetrack?"

"Um-huh." His hand had ventured inside her housecoat and was toying with her nipple through her nightgown. "It causes some excitement. But otherwise, it's a sleepy little town where nothing much happens."

His mouth replaced his plucking fingers. She leaned her head back and gave him access. Faintly, she said, "Your hotcakes..."

They got cold.

———

Thatcher went to the boardinghouse. Mrs. May greeted him with her characteristic geniality. "Don't think you're crawling back, 'cause I done rented your room." She'd packed everything in his trunk and put it in her root cellar. He retrieved his belongings and happily left the place for the last time.

He went from there to Fred Barker, literally with hat in hand, and profusely apologized for having left without notifying him. "I didn't even return the rifle you loaned me."

"No never mind," Barker said. "Sheriff sent a deputy over with the rifle and a note, explaining. 'Fraid some of the owners of the horses you were training came to get them."

"I don't blame them a bit."

That week, he worked at the stable several hours a day, exercising the horses belonging to Barker. On his last day, as he was about to leave, he said, "I'll always be in your debt for hiring me that first day."

"I ain't ever been sorry for it. Never saw a horseman good as you. I'm gonna miss havin' you around. Roger's plumb heartbroke." They shook hands. "Good luck to you, Thatcher."

Thatcher tipped his hat and walked away. Barker called after him. "I like them spurs."

Thatcher smiled back at him. "I'm gonna try to earn them."

———◇———

Bill was sitting in one of the rockers on his front porch when Thatcher drove up in Laurel's car. He got out and walked to the porch. As he sat down in the second chair, he motioned toward the cane propped against Bill's. "How's the leg?"

"Okay. Just aches. Some days worse than others."

For a time, neither said anything, then Thatcher asked after Mrs. Amos.

"I'm taking her to Temple. They've got a three-month program, but she hasn't had a drop since the arsenic thing. She wants to get well. We've been talking a lot about Tim. I think she's finally come to terms. The other day, we even laughed over something he'd done when he was a boy."

"That's good, Bill. That's real good. She'll be all right. I'm sure of it."

Bill waited a moment, then said, "Mila Driscoll's body was recovered."

"No trouble locating it?"

"Not after I passed along your description of that rock pile. Her uncle took her remains to New Braunfels for burial."

"Driscoll?"

"The sorry son of a bitch has fired two defense lawyers already, and they were glad of it. The judge granted a change of venue, so at least he's off our hands. If the state doesn't hang him, he'll spend the rest of his life behind bars." He looked over at Thatcher. "You'll probably be subpoenaed to testify when he comes up for trial."

"I'll be there."

"Patsy Kemp took Norma's baby boy and moved to Colorado to join her husband. They never could have kids, so they're happy to have him. I told her we suspected that Bernie Croft had fathered the boy, and that in all probability he'd been the one to assault Norma. She was shocked. She'd never met Bernie, only knew him to be the mayor."

"Miss Blanchard took that secret to her grave. I wish she'd kept the one that got her killed."

Bill gave a solemn nod, then said, "Still looking for Chester Landry. He's nowhere to be found. That one is slippery as owl shit."

"Yeah."

They rocked in silence until Bill said, "They charged me with misdemeanors only. Gave me one year and probated that."

"You're not a crook, Bill. You just got caught up and couldn't get out."

"Naturally, first thing I did was tender my resignation. But there's a group of county officials already urging me to run for reelection when the probation is up. Can you believe that?"

"Yeah, and I'd bet on you winning."

"How sure are you?"

"Royal flush sure. This is Texas."

The two laughed lightly, then Bill's smile gradually faded, until his mustache drooped. "I heard you're leaving."

"Tomorrow."

"Bynum? I've met the man you're going to be working with."

"He mentioned it. At a sheriff's association meeting?"

"In Austin. A while back. Before the war. He's a good man." He stared into the near distance. After a time he said, "You could stay here, Thatcher, take over while I'm on probation."

"No, that should be Scotty."

"You'd be leaving anyway, though, wouldn't you?" He hung his head. "For what I did, I apologize, Thatcher."

Thatcher made the gesture that Mr. Hobson had, a silent grant of forgiveness. "That's not the reason I'm going." Before continuing, he waited until Bill had raised his head and was looking straight at him. "This is your place, Bill. You found it, or it found you, but it's where you were meant. I need to make my own place."

"With Laurel Plummer? I trust she's going with you?"

"If I have to strap her to the back of the car."

"How will you two reconcile your job with her moonshining?"

"Davy O'Connor getting killed shook her to her core. When she started out, she underestimated the danger. But seeing firsthand all the blood spilt, she's sworn off. From now on, she wants to stick to pie-baking."

"Well, I wish you all the luck."

"Thanks. You, too." Thatcher stood.

Bill used his cane and pushed himself to his feet. They shook hands. Bill said, "I'm not proud of lying to you, Thatcher. But, God help me, I can't regret that I did."

Smiling at Bill from beneath the brim of his hat, Thatcher said, "Me neither."

Laurel returned home after running errands to find Irv and Mike O'Connor in conversation beside Irv's truck.

She had visited with him several times during his recovery. He was still paler and thinner than he'd been before he'd been shot. The twinkle in his eyes had dimmed, and it would probably be a while before they regained their full wattage, if they ever did.

But when she alighted from her car and walked toward them, the familiar dimple appeared in his cheek. "Ah, here's the lovely Laurel. I've been waiting on you."

Irv made his excuses and went into the house.

When they were alone, Mike said, "I understand that tomorrow's the big day. I thought I ought to come say my goodbyes to you now in private, while your sullen cowboy wasn't lurking about."

"You and I have nothing to hide from Thatcher."

"More's the pity." He slapped his hand over his heart like a wounded, rejected suitor, and she could have sworn he was Davy. "If that lucky bastard ever treats you bad, promise you'll come find me. I'll rub him out."

She laughed lightly. "I promise."

He reached into his pants pocket. "I have a going-away present for you." He took her hand and dropped a Saint Christopher medal and chain into her palm.

"Mike." Taken aback, she stared down at the gold necklace, then looked up at him, so touched her eyes turned misty. "Is it—?"

"Yes."

"I can't accept it. You should keep it."

"I have a matching one, and Davy would love knowing it was dangling around your pretty neck. He and Saint Chris are now your guardian angels." He lifted the necklace out of her hand and slipped it over her head. She pressed the medal against her chest.

They looked at each other, both unable to speak, so they hugged. When he released her, he said gruffly, "Be happy, Laurel." He tipped his cap and walked away.

———

Everything they were taking was piled up in the empty living room. Thatcher's saddle sat atop his trunk. Laurel had packed her clothing in the same suitcase she'd had with her the night she'd arrived at the shack with Derby. She was taking Pearl's baby clothes and all the recipes in her mother's handwriting. Most everything else she was leaving behind, because it would be needed. Corrine and Ernie had decided to move into the house.

"I love the idea," Laurel said to Corrine. "You couldn't stay out there during the winter months."

"Ernie and me could live in the shack and be just fine."

"But why would you when there's a whole upstairs here that would be going to waste. Stop trying to talk yourself out of it. The decision has been made. Besides, I'll feel better knowing that someone is here looking after Irv."

Corrine watched as Thatcher and Ernie—who had finally been introduced—began to load Laurel's car. "It's not going to be the same without you here, though," the girl said wistfully.

"No. But you have the post office box key. I'll be writing to you at least once a week, so don't forget to check it."

"If it weren't for you, I couldn't read them letters you'll send."

Laurel reached out and pulled the girl to her. "I'm going to miss you."

"Me too, Miss Laurel." Lowering her voice, she said, "I wouldn't trust you to nobody but him," she said, casting a glance at Thatcher as he swung his saddle onto his shoulder. "He's quality."

"Yes, he is."

As they broke their hug, Corrine dashed a tear from her eye, then said, "Oh hell, Ernie, you're gonna bust open that suitcase carrying it like that." She went over to instruct and assist him.

Laurel went in search of Irv and found him in his room. He was sitting on his barrel seat, staring at the floor.

"What are you doing in here?" she asked.

"The girl told me I was gettin' in the way more than helping. And she's right. Arm still hurts if I move it a certain way, and this damn bum hip." He muttered the rest, but she knew that his crankiness wasn't due to his ailments or Corrine's criticism.

She sat down on the end of his bed, facing him, and said softly, "I'm going to miss you, too. Terribly."

Frowning, he said, "It ain't too late to change your mind. I've worked the rails over there in East Texas. It ain't like here. It's humid. They got mosquitoes as big as turkeys. Alligators."

"I don't think there are any alligators in Bynum."

He harrumphed. She reached for his hands and held them. "Be careful with your new enterprise."

His bushy eyebrows shot up. "Enterprise?"

She gave him a look. "The first giveaway was catching you in a tête-à-tête with Mike O'Connor yesterday. I thought you didn't trust his dimples."

"Who said I do?"

She continued, "Another giveaway is all that busywork you and Ernie have been doing down in the cellar. Did you really think I would believe that you two are opening a machine shop?"

"Why not?"

"A machine shop with a mirror along one wall?"

He gave up the pretense. "With Gert dead, Lefty abandoned the roadhouse. Nobody knows where he ran off to. The county's condemned the building. The girl remembered that long mirror, so we helped ourselves to it and the gramophone. They'll give the place some class."

"I suppose you'll serve Ernie's moonshine. Is Mike supplying the bootlegged liquor?"

"He's got some good connections."

"I'm sure."

"The girl will make snacks to serve."

"When do you open?"

"Soon as you and Hutton clear town."

"Does this speakeasy have a name?"

"Blind Tiger."

She laughed. "Isn't that rather obvious?"

"The girl likes the way it sounds." He tipped his head toward the kitchen where Thatcher could be heard responding to Corrine's chatter. "Will you tell him?"

"He's going to be my husband."

"He's going to be a lawman."

"But he hasn't been sworn in yet. One thing, though. Will there be girls?"

"Hell no. I'm too old, Ernie's too much in love, and the girl would never hear of it."

"What about your fix-it business?"

"I'll keep it up for show."

"Just promise me that you'll be careful, Irv. Keep it exclusive. Locals only. People you know. No roughnecks."

"Like I said, classy. Discreet like. Hush-hush."

"Don't let Mike take unnecessary risks."

"None of us wants to get shot at again."

"If things get hot—"

"We'll head for the hills. Don't you worry none."

"I will."

"I know."

She patted him on the knee, then stood and placed her hands on either side of his face, tipped his head down, and kissed his bald pate. "You've become very dear to me, Irv. Thank you. For taking care of Pearl and me. For everything."

His eyes filled. He wiped his nose with the back of his hand and came off his barrel seat. "I'd better go see if I'm good for something."

<hr />

Another round of goodbyes was said outside.

As they pulled away, Thatcher reached across the seat and placed his hand on Laurel's knee, giving it a squeeze. "Are you sad?"

"Melancholy." She looked back to see the three of them still there, waving. Then, as one, they turned and filed back into the house. "But they're a family. I had become the odd man out."

As they drove past the cemetery, Thatcher switched the Model T into low gear. "Do you want to stop for one last visit?"

"No. Irv and I were here only a few days ago. He's promised to keep the graves well tended." She didn't share the conversation she'd had with Irv about Derby, but she said, "When I think about Pearl, I don't think of her being in the ground. I think of her sweet face looking up at me as she nursed. I'm not leaving her here. I'm taking her with me."

Thatcher pulled her closer, and she rested her head on his shoulder. "It was thoughtful of you to ask. Thank you."

They continued on their way. But she felt pressed to be candid with him. "Thatcher, we've joked about my accepting your proposal, but marrying you is a bigger step for me than you realize."

He pulled the car off the road onto the shoulder and gave her his undivided attention. "I've known that. But your past with Derby is your private business. I didn't want to dig into it until you invited me to."

"Which I appreciate, but you should know this."

"Okay."

"After he did what he did, I vowed that I would never again surrender control of my life to someone else."

"I don't want *control* over you, Laurel. I want *you*. If you're scared of marriage, we don't have to do it. A piece of paper isn't going to make me any more bound to you than I am."

"You'd be willing to do that?"

"Not overjoyed about it, but willing. I'd like it if you used my name, though. Not because I care what you call yourself, but because I wouldn't want people thinking bad of you, or our children."

She touched his face. "You really do love me."

He took her hand and kissed her palm. "I really do. But I can be stubborn, too. I'll never stop asking you to be my wife."

"I accept, Thatcher. I'll marry you today, because you're incredibly wonderful, and I love you with all my heart. But don't ever stop proposing. Ask me every day to marry you."

He grinned. "If you swear always to say yes."

"I will."

ACKNOWLEDGMENTS

Doing the research for *Blind Tiger* was some of the most fun I've had during my writing career.

Mired in the muck of 2020, I went back one hundred years, looking for something interesting to write about. *Prohibition*. It became law in January of 1920.

I soon became fascinated by the anecdotal personal histories of moonshiners, bootleggers, and the lawmen who doggedly chased them. No doubt many of these stories were embroidered for dramatic effect or the aggrandizement of the storyteller. But I got the feeling that, whether comic or tragic, they were too far-fetched *not* to be based on truth.

One fact is indisputable: for the thirteen years that Prohibition was in effect, alcohol and blood flowed in comparable quantities.

I want to give special thanks to former Garland Police Department detective Martin Brown, whose nonfiction book *The Glen Rose Moonshine Raid* (The History Press) acquainted me with a sliver of Texas history that I never knew, although I'm a native and have lived most of my life within an hour's drive of this small town that inspired my fictitious town of Foley.

Glen Rose earned the reputation of being the Moonshine Capital of Texas. In 1923, Texas Rangers, in conjunction with informers and local law enforcement, busted up one of the most profitable illegal liquor syndicates in the state—and that was saying something!

In this novel, I tried to capture the spirit of those wild times, and I hope you enjoy reading *Blind Tiger* as much as I enjoyed writing it.

Sandra Brown
May 2021

ABOUT THE AUTHOR

Sandra Brown is the author of seventy-three *New York Times* bestsellers. There are more than eighty million copies of her books in print worldwide, and her work has been translated into thirty-four languages. In 2008, the International Thriller Writers named Brown its Thriller Master, the organization's highest honor. She has served as president of Mystery Writers of America and holds an honorary doctorate of humane letters from Texas Christian University. She lives in Texas.

For more information you can visit:
SandraBrown.net
Facebook.com/AuthorSandraBrown
@Sandra_BrownNYT

READING GROUP GUIDE

DISCUSSION QUESTIONS

1. At the beginning of the novel, Derby tells Laurel that he's moving their young family from Sherman to Foley, Texas. Laurel is shocked and understandably anxious about what she feels is an impetuous decision. In your own life, have you ever had to make an abrupt change, one that required you to adapt very quickly to new circumstances? How did you cope with the transition?

2. Thatcher observes that Dr. Driscoll's wife, Mila—like many Germans before, during, and even after the war—was subjected to resentment and suspicion from her American peers. After experiencing Mrs. Driscoll's kindness toward Thatcher, how did this revelation make you feel? While the events of *Blind Tiger* take place more than a hundred years in the past, similar events are reported in present-day news. In your opinion, what steps can people take today to ensure this kind of discrimination doesn't happen in the future?

3. Under President Woodrow Wilson, in an attempt to create a more "temperate" American society, the Eighteenth Amendment—the legal prevention of the manufacture, sale, and transportation of alcohol in the United States from 1919 to 1933—went into effect. Instead of bringing about Wilson's admirable goal, Prohibition resulted in a rise of organized

crime and bootlegging became major business. Why do you think the institution of Prohibition failed?

4. In your view, were the men and women who distilled and sold alcohol throughout Prohibition doing what they could to feed their families? Or do you feel they were taking advantage of a difficult situation?

5. How did you feel when Thatcher was accused of abducting Mrs. Driscoll? The only evidence the sheriff had against him was the word of the Driscolls' neighbor, who distrusted Thatcher because he was a stranger. How did the neighbor's reaction mirror conflicts taking place today?

6. One of Thatcher's many talents is that he has a "knack" for reading people. Do you have a similar ability of your own, something that has helped you get a leg up or get out of trouble in your own life?

7. Thatcher believes "dumb fate" brought him to Foley. Do you believe in fate, predestination, or divine will? Or do you believe coincidence threw Thatcher and Laurel together?

8. Laurel experiences two very personal losses over the course of the novel. Initially, she feels her grief will break her, but she learns to love again, first with her stand-in father, Irv, then with her friendship with Corrine, and later with Thatcher. How did the characters support one another throughout the novel, especially when it came to grief and trauma?

9. The story is set in a dangerous, unpredictable time in Texas. Law enforcement was looking for bootleggers, bootleggers were competing for market share, and undercover agents

were active on both sides. How much did you know about Prohibition before reading *Blind Tiger?* Were you familiar with organizations like the Anti-Saloon League?

10. After Thatcher helps Laurel take care of Irv's arm, Laurel makes this observation on boundaries: "Once a boundary [is] breached, it [is] difficult, if not impossible, to reestablish." Have you ever had to reestablish a boundary with someone? How did you go about repairing the relationship?

11. After Norma is found badly injured, Bill, Thatcher, and Norma's sister, Patsy, discuss Norma's romantic relationships. Over the course of their conversation, Bill observes that big secrets tend to "erode" relationships, whether those relationships fall between siblings, married couples, or lovers. Do you share Bill's opinion? Or do you think some secrets are worth keeping—and may, perhaps, even preserve relationships?

12. In a time of great difficulty and poverty, Laurel, Gert, Corinne, and Norma worked, in their own ways, to achieve financial independence and stability. Discuss the industriousness of the women in the novel and the personality traits that helped them survive—and even thrive—in such an unforgiving time.

13. Discuss Sheriff Bill Amos's character. Given his actions throughout the novel—his motives for hiring Thatcher, the way he cared for his wife, the way he kept the peace in Foley as sheriff—would you consider him to be a good man or a bad one? Why?

14. At the end of the novel, Laurel sits down with Irv and apologizes to him, telling him she shouldn't have pushed Derby to

get over his inertia, but instead should have "[held] him tight without saying anything . . . allow[ed] him to face his fears within the cradle of [her] arms." Do you agree or disagree with the statement? Have you ever found yourself unsure of what to do in the face of a loved one's struggles?

15. After Derby's death, Laurel declares that she will "never again surrender control of [her] life to someone else." Did this declaration resonate or conflict with your personal views on marriage? Why or why not?

VISIT **GCPClubCar.com** to sign up for the **GCP Club Car** newsletter, featuring exclusive promotions, info on other **Club Car** titles, and more.

COLONEL RUTHERFORD B. HAYES, TWENTY-THIRD O. V. I.

From a photograph taken after recovery from wounds received September 14, 1862, at the battle of South Mountain, Maryland, in the Antietam Campaign.

DIARY AND LETTERS OF RUTHERFORD BIRCHARD HAYES

DIARY AND LETTERS OF
RUTHERFORD BIRCHARD HAYES

NINETEENTH PRESIDENT OF THE UNITED STATES

EDITED BY
CHARLES RICHARD WILLIAMS

VOLUME II
1861 — 1865

THE OHIO STATE ARCHÆOLOGICAL
AND HISTORICAL SOCIETY
1922

PRESS OF
The F. J. Heer Printing Company
Columbus, Ohio
1922

CONTENTS

(v)

ILLUSTRATIONS

(vii)

DIARY AND LETTERS OF
RUTHERFORD BIRCHARD HAYES

DIARY AND LETTERS OF RUTHERFORD BIRCHARD HAYES

CHAPTER XIV

SECESSION AND WAR — 1861

M R. HAYES did not perceive the full significance and implication of the Presidential contest of 1860 while it was in progress. The Southern extremists had been threatening disunion so long that, in common with most men of the North, Hayes attached little importance to their present mutterings. In his thought, apparently, it was just an ordinary Presidential canvass, complicated, to be sure, by the fact that there were four candidates, but not one to get excited over. He had figured out in June the probability of Lincoln's election, but hardly more than a month before election day he was anything but confident of the result. In a letter to his uncle of September 30, he wrote: "I have made a few little speeches in the country townships, and shall make a few more. I cannot get up must interest in the contest. A wholesome contempt for Douglas, on account of his recent demagoguery, is the chief feeling I have. I am not so confident that Lincoln will get votes enough as many of our friends. I think his chances are fair, but what may be the effect of fusions in such anti-Republican States as New Jersey and Pennsylvania, is more than I can tell or confidently guess until after the state elections."

On election day, November 6, he wrote in the Diary: "The Southern States are uneasy at the prospect of Lincoln's election today. The ultra South threatens disunion, and it now looks as if South Carolina and possibly two or three others would go out of the Union. Will they? And if so, what is to be the result? Will other slave States gradually be drawn after them, or will the influence of the conservative States draw back into the Union or. hold in the Union the ultra States? I think the latter. But at all events, I feel as if the time had come to test this question. If the threats are meant, then it is time the Union was dissolved or the traitors crushed out. I hope Lincoln goes in."

In the next few weeks of tense political excitement, with South Carolina openly moving toward secession and President Buchanan supinely looking on in a paralysis of inaction, the Diary is silent, as are also the extant letters, on the absorbing topic of the day. That he was not an indifferent observer of passing events, however, and that for the moment with large numbers of people of the North he contemplated calmly the possibility of the permanent disruption of the Union, the pages that follow clearly demonstrate.]

January 4, 1861. — South Carolina has passed a secession ordinance, and Federal laws are set at naught in the State. Overt acts enough have been committed. Forts and arsenal taken, a revenue cutter seized, and Major Anderson besieged in Fort Sumter. Other cotton States are about to follow. Disunion and civil war are at hand; and yet I fear disunion and war less than compromise. We can recover from them. The free States alone, if we must go on alone, will make a glorious nation. Twenty millions in the temperate zone, stretching from the Atlantic to the Pacific, full of vigor, industry, inventive genius, educated, and moral; increasing by immigration rapidly, and, above all, free — all free — will form a confederacy of twenty States scarcely inferior in real power to the unfortunate Union of thirty-three States which we had on the first of November. I do not even feel gloomy when I look forward. The reality is less frightful than the apprehension which we have all had these many years. Let us be temperate, calm, and just, but firm and resolute. Crittenden's compromise! *

* Hayes's disapproval of the Crittenden Compromise is indicated by the exclamation point. The venerable John J. Crittenden, Senator from Kentucky, sought by eloquent appeals to induce Congress to submit to the States for approval an amendment to the Constitution forbidding Congress to abolish slavery in the District of Columbia so long as it existed

Windham speaking of the rumor that Bonaparte was about to invade England said: "The danger of invasion is by no means equal to that of peace. A man may escape a pistol however near his head, but not a dose of poison."

CINCINNATI, January 6, 1861.

DEAR UNCLE: — We have had the usual fun and folly during the holidays and are safely through with them. Mother is almost perfectly well again and seems contented and happy. All the rest of the family are in usual health. I had a few days' influenza which passed off doing no harm.

I shall not be very busy, but employment enough for the next few weeks. I expect to spend some days at Columbus within two or three weeks. Mother wants to hear from you; thinks something wrong if you do not write often.

Sincerely,

R. B. HAYES.

S. BIRCHARD.

CINCINNATI, January 12, 1861.

DEAR UNCLE: — I will write oftener hereafter. I have some work, the days are short, and the state of the country is a never-ending topic which all you meet must discuss, greatly to the interruption of regular habits. I rather enjoy the excitement, and am fond of speculating about it.

We are in a revolution; the natural ultimate result is to divide us into two nations, one composed of free States, the other of slave States. What we shall pass through before we reach this inevitable result is matter for conjecture. While I am in favor of the Government promptly enforcing the laws for the *present,* defending the forts and collecting the revenue, I am not in favor of a war policy with a view to the conquest

in Virginia or Maryland, or to abolish it in national territory south of latitude 36° 30' — the southern line of Kansas. This was to be irrepealable by any subsequent amendment, as were also certain existing paragraphs in the Constitution relating to slavery. Further, Mr. Crittenden wished Congress to strengthen the Fugitive Slave Law and to appeal to the States and to the people for its thorough enforcement.

of any of the slave States; except such as are needed to give us a good boundary. If Maryland attempts to go off, suppress her in order to save the Potomac and the District of Columbia. Cut a piece off of western Virginia and keep Missouri and all the Territories.

To do this we shall not need any long or expensive war, if the Government does its duty. A war of conquest we do not want. It would leave us loaded with debt and would certainly fail of its object. The sooner we get into the struggle and out of it the better.

There, you can read that perhaps. If you can't, you lose nothing. If you can, it is no more worthless than the dispatches from Congress. . . .

Sincerely,

R. B. HAYES.

S. BIRCHARD.

January 27, 1861. — Six States have "seceded." Let them go. If the Union is now dissolved it does not prove that the experiment of popular government is a failure. In all the free States, and in a majority if not in all of the slaveholding States, popular government has been sucessful. But the experiment of uniting free states and slaveholding states in one nation is, perhaps, a failure. Freedom and slavery can, perhaps, not exist side by side under the same popular government. There probably is an "irrepressible conflict" * between freedom and slavery. It may as well be admitted, and our new relations may as well be formed with that as an *admitted* fact.

CINCINNATI, February 13, 1861.

DEAR UNCLE: — We are all well. Mother is in better health; went to church Sunday, and was able to enjoy the Lincoln reception yesterday. The great procession and crowd could be seen well from our windows and steps, and all had a good view

---

* This phrase had first been used by William H. Seward in a speech at Rochester, New York, October 25, 1858.

of the President.　He is in good health; not a hair gray or gone; in his prime and fit for service, mentally and physically.　Great hopes may well be felt.

Lucy and I went with a jolly party of friends to Indianapolis on Monday, and returned on the Presidential train to Cincinnati, seeing all the doings here and on the road.　We heard Lincoln make several of his good speeches, talked with [him], etc., etc.　Regards to all.

Sincerely,

R. B. HAYES.

S. BIRCHARD.

CINCINNATI, February 15, 1861.

DEAR UNCLE: — . . . The reception given to the President-elect here was most impressive.　He rode in an open carriage, standing erect with head uncovered, and bowing his acknowledgments to greetings showered upon him.　There was a lack of comfort in the arrangements, but the simplicity, the homely character of all was in keeping with the nobility of this typical American.　A six-in-hand with gorgeous trappings, accompanied by outriders and a courtly train, could have added nothing to him; would have detracted from him, would have been wholly out of place.　The times are unsuited to show.　The people did not wish to be entertained with a display; they did wish to see the man in whose hands is the destiny of our country.

You will read the speeches in the papers, and search in vain for anything to find fault with.　Mr. Lincoln was wary at all times, wisely so I think, and yet I hear no complaint.　Our German Turners, who are radical on the slavery question and who are ready to make that an issue of war, planned to draw from him some expression in sympathy with their own views. They serenaded him and talked at him, but they were baffled.* In private conversation he was discreet but frank.　He believes in a policy of kindness, of delay to give time for passions to cool, but not in a compromise to extend the power and the

---

* Mr. William Henry Smith happened to be present when the Germans serenaded Mr. Lincoln.　He made a shorthand report of Mr. Lincoln's reply.　The speech is preserved in print in Francis F. Browne's "Every-day Life of Lincoln," p. 385.

deadly influence of the slave system.   This gave me great satisfaction.   The impression he made was good.   He undoubtedly is shrewd, able, and possesses strength in reserve.   This will be tested soon. . . .

Sincerely,

R. B. HAYES.

S. BIRCHARD.

CINCINNATI, March 17, 1861.

DEAR UNCLE: — I received yours of the 13th yesterday.   I shall not come out for three or four weeks, perhaps not so soon.   It is not yet possible to guess how the [city] election will go, but the chances are decidedly against our side.   The Democrats and Know-nothings have united and will nominate their ticket this week.   If they nominate men tolerably acceptable to both wings of the fusion, they will succeed beyond all question.   Their majority at the last election over the Republicans was nearly three thousand.   We can't beat this.   Our chance is that there will be some slip or mistake which will upset the union.   I shall go under with the rest, but expect to run ahead of the ticket.   Of course, I prefer not to be beaten, but I have got out of the office the best there is in it for me. I shall get me an office alone, and start anew — a much pleasanter condition of things than the one I left with Corwine.

Yes, giving up Fort Sumter is vexing.   It hurts our little election, too; but I would give up the prospect of office, if it would save the fort, with the greatest pleasure.

Elinor Mead * leaves us on Tuesday to return home the last of the week.   She has enjoyed her visit, I think.   Mother is very well again; is able to go out, to shop and to church.   Little Ruddy (our brag boy now) has been sick, but is getting nearly well.   The other boys count largely on going to Fremont this summer. . . .

Sincerely,

R. B. HAYES.

S. BIRCHARD.

* A cousin from Vermont; later to become the wife of William Dean Howells, who that winter was a newspaper correspondent at Columbus.

Private Strictly.

CINCINNATI, March 22, 1861.

DEAR SIR: — I am on my way to Columbus and stopped at your house to say *for your own private ear, and as your friend, that* I would not [if in your place] consent to be a candidate for mayor in Eggleston's place. *This is not your best time.* I shall say this to nobody else, but as a looker-on and as one interested, I think what I say is true. Think of it well before you consent.

Sincerely,

R. B. HAYES.

To THOMAS H. WEASNER.

CINCINNATI, March 24, 1861.

DEAR UNCLE: — . . . All well here. Both parties have made their tickets for the election of the first of April. The chances are still against us, but somewhat better than when I wrote you last. . . .

Sincerely,

S. BIRCHARD.

R. B. HAYES.

CINCINNATI, March 29, 1861.

DEAR UNCLE: — I have received your favor, and suspect you are more anxious that I should be re-elected than the occasion calls for. I philosophize in this way: I have got out of the office pretty much all the good there is in it — reputation and experience. If I quit it now, I shall be referred to as the best, or one of the best solicitors, the city has had. If I serve two years more, I can add nothing to this. I may possibly lose. I shall be out of clients and business a little while, but this difficulty will perhaps be greater two years hence. So you see it is no great matter. Still, I should prefer to beat, and with half a chance, I should do it. . . .

I am not wasting much time looking after the election — none in mere personal electioneering. I am trying to so behave as to go out respectably.

Sincerely,

S. BIRCHARD.

R. B. HAYES.

CINCINNATI, April 2, 1861.

DEAR UNCLE: — Before this reaches you, you will no doubt learn that the Union-saving avalanche has overtaken us, and that my little potato patch went down with the rest. To prevent a general break-up of the Fusion, both wings agreed as far as possible, to vote an open ticket without scratching. By the aid of oceans of money and a good deal of sincere patriotism in behalf of Union, the plan was carried out with perfect success. It did not in the least disappoint me.

Now, what to do next and how to begin? My term expires next Monday. I shall keep my eyes open, and meditate making you a short visit before finally settling. I have enough cash on hand, or available, to support me for a year, even if I should fail to get business enough to do it, which I do not anticipate. Nothing unpleasant has occurred in the whole course of the canvass. I am quite as well content as one who has drawn a blank ever is, or can be.

Sincerely,

R. B. HAYES.

S. BIRCHARD.

CINCINNATI, April 10, 1861.

DEAR UNCLE: — You spoke too late. I am again settled in a respectable practice. I tried a case today and shall try another tomorrow. Mr. Hassaurek, the German who gets the highest office, viz., nine thousand feet above the sea at Quito, leaves a good German practice. I have taken it with his half-brother, a bright, gentlemanly, popular young German [Leopold Markbreit]. It will have both advantages and drawbacks, but it was the best that offered, and not getting a letter from you, I left the solicitor's office yesterday and entered my new quarters at once. I enclose my card for the German side of the house. I feel free and jolly.

Sincerely,

R. B. HAYES.

S. BIRCHARD.

CINCINNATI, April 15, 1861.

DEAR UNCLE: — . . . We are all for war. The few dissentients have to run like quarter-horses. A great change for two weeks to produce. As the Dutchman said, "What a beeples." Poor Anderson! What a chance he threw away. The Government may overlook or even whitewash it, but the people and history will not let him off so easily. I like it. Anything is better than the state of things we have had the last few months. We shall have nothing but rub-a-dub and rumors for some time to come.

All pretty well. Mother thinks we are to be punished for our sinfulness, and reads the Old Testament vigorously. Mother Webb quietly grieves over it. Lucy enjoys it and wishes she had been in Fort Sumter with a garrison of women. Dr. Joe is for flames, slaughter, and a rising of the slaves. All the boys are soldiers.

Sincerely,

R. B. HAYES.

S. BIRCHARD.

COLUMBUS, April 19, 1861.

DEAR UNCLE: — I came up last night to help Dr. James Webb get a place as surgeon, and for other purposes not warlike. The doctor left for the East as assistant surgeon of [the] Second Regiment with the soldiers this morning. I shall return home on [the] next train.

At the first, I put down my foot that I would not think of going into this first movement. This, of course, I shall stick to; but if this war is [to] go on, it is obvious that sooner or later thousands will be dragged into it who would now not contemplate doing so. Platt enjoys it hugely. So do all the old-style people who like a strong government. It took a great many delicate youngsters from our neighborhood; almost every other family on our street sent somebody — Wilson Woodrow, Wright, Schooley, of our near neighbors. I saw them in their tents last night — cold as Halifax, and compelled to get up at 2:30 this morning to go East. A sharp experience for tenderly reared boys.

Come down and see us.   All well here.

Sincerely,

R. B. HAYES.

S. BIRCHARD.

CINCINNATI, April 20, 1860 [1861].

DEAR UNCLE: — . . . I have joined a volunteer home company to learn drill. It is chiefly composed of the Literary Club. Includes Stephenson, Meline, John Groesbeck, Judge James, McLaughlin, Beard, and most of my cronies. We wish to learn how to "eyes right and left," if nothing more.

A great state of things for Christian people, and then to have old gentlemen say, as you do, "I am glad we have got to fighting at last." Judge Swan and Mr. Andrews and the whole Methodist clergy all say the same. Shocking! One thing: Don't spend much on your house or furniture henceforth. Save, save, is the motto now. People who furnish for the war will make money, but others will have a time of it.

Mother thinks it is a judgment on us for our sins. Henry Ward Beecher, who is now here, says it is divine work, that the Almighty is visibly in it.

Sincerely,

R. B. HAYES.

S. BIRCHARD.

CINCINNATI, April 23, 1861.

DEAR UNCLE: — No doubt the accounts sent abroad as to the danger we are in from Kentucky are much exaggerated. Kentucky is in no condition to go out immediately. If the war goes on, as I think it ought, it is probable that she will leave us, and that we shall be greatly exposed, but she has no arms, and almost no military organization. Even their secession governor is not prepared to precipitate matters under these circumstances. We are rapidly preparing for war, and shall be on a war footing long before Kentucky has decided what to do.

Lucy dislikes to leave here just now. She enjoys the excitement and wishes to be near her mother and the rest of us; but as for camping down in Spiegel Grove and roughing it, she thinks that will be jolly enough, and as soon as we are quiet here, she will be very happy to go into quarters with you. . . .

A great many gentlemen of your years are in for the war. One old fellow was rejected on account of his gray hair and whiskers. He hurried down street and had them colored black, and passed muster in another company.

Sincerely,

R. B. HAYES.

[Later.] — Yours of the 22nd just received. Fremont has done well. We are sending about four thousand [volunteers] from here, if all are accepted, besides [having] eight thousand more stay-at-homes. I am acting captain of our crack rifle company. I shall go into the ranks as a private in a week or two.

S. BIRCHARD.

[The following statement in Hayes's handwriting, evidently prepared about this time, shows what plans the citizens of Cincinnati were making to defend the city against possible attack from Kentucky.]

To be ready on the day that Kentucky secedes to take possession of the hills on the Kentucky side which command Cincinnati, or the approaches to it, and prepare to hold them against any force.

a. Regiments ready to cross on short notice with arms, ammunition, provisions, tools, etc., for entrenching; cannon, boats, and all essentials.

b. Cut off telegraphic communication south from Covington and Newport.

c. Also railroad communication.

d. Take all boats; fortify all hills, etc.

e. The prevention of raids to rob banks, etc.

Spies to Frankfort with passwords for dispatches, etc.

CINCINNATI, April 25, 1861.

DEAR UNCLE: — We are glad to hear from you often. I have written almost daily, and am surprised you do not hear from me more regularly. Your letters reach me in good time.

The point of interest here now is as to Kentucky. Her Legislature meets on the 6th of May. If a secession measure is passed we shall expect lively times here immediately afterwards. The chances are about equal in my upinion. If they were armed and ready they would go beyond all question; but their helpless condition will possibly hold them. Our people generally are quite willing to see them go. They prefer open enmity to a deceptive armed neutrality.

Sincerely,

R. B. HAYES.

P. S. — My company drills at 10 A. M. today — Sunday! I have two clergymen and the sons of two others in the ranks. I suspect they will not answer at roll-call.

S. BIRCHARD.

CINCINNATI, April 30, 1861.

DEAR UNCLE: — Your frequent letters are very acceptable. I am sorry, however, to be compelled to think that we are indebted to your ill health for the favor. Lucy says, "Why don't Uncle come down and make us a visit? If the house has a roof and floors, it is finished enough for war times and needs no further attention." You will find it almost as quiet as your own town. About five thousand men have left, and our streets show that even that number missing is noticeable. If any war news comes, we shall be lively enough soon. The first ten days of the war was as jolly and exciting as you could wish.

Sincerely,

R. B. HAYES.

S. BIRCHARD.

CINCINNATI, [May 27, 1861.]

DEAR UNCLE: — I have nothing in particular you to write. I heard a good war sermon today on the subject, "The Horrors of Peace"!

The weather is very unfavorable for troops in · camp — wet and chilly. The tents leak and the ground is low and flat. These things will gradually mend themselves. We shall have precious little business this summer, judging by present appearances. Come down when you feel like it.

Sincerely,

R. B. HAYES.

S. BIRCHARD.

CINCINNATI, May 8, 1861.

DEAR GUY: — I have just received and read your letter of the 27th ult. It does me good to hear from you again. I have thought of you often since these troubles began. Curiously enough, having a bad cold and a slight fever, I dreamed of many things last night. Among others I dreamed of seeing you at the Burnet House; that you wore on your cap some sort of secession emblem and that you were in danger of getting into difficulty with some soldiers who were in the rotunda, and that it was after some effort that I succeeded in getting you rid of them. I should have written you soon even if I had not heard from you.

Your predictions as to the course of things have indeed been very exactly fulfilled. I can recollect distinctly many conversations had twelve, perhaps even fifteen, years ago in which you pointed out the probable result of the agitation of slavery. I have hoped that we could live together notwithstanding slavery, but for some time past the hope has been a faint one. I now have next to no hope of a restoration of the old Union. If you are correct in your view of the facts, there is no hope whatever. In such case, a continued union is not desirable were it possible. I do not differ widely from you as to the possibility of conquering the South, nor as to the expediency of doing it even if it were practicable. If it is the settled and final judgment of any slave State that she cannot live in the Union, I should not think it wise or desirable to retain her by force, even if it could be done.

But am I, therefore, to oppose the war? If it were a war of conquest merely, certainly I should oppose it, and on the grounds you urge. But the war is forced on us. We cannot escape it. While in your State, and in others, perhaps in all the cotton-growing States, a decided and controlling public judgment has deliberately declared against remaining in the Union, it is quite certain that in several States rebellious citizens are bent on forcing out of the Union States whose people are not in favor of secession; that the general Government is assailed, its property taken, its authority defied in places and in a way not supported by any fairly expressed popular verdict. Undoubtedly the design to capture Washington is entertained by the Government of the Southern Confederacy. Undoubtedly that Confederacy has not by its *acts* sought a *peaceful* separation. Everything has been done by force. If force had been employed to meet force, I believe several States now out of the Union would have remained in it. We have an example before us. Two weeks ago Maryland was fast going out; now, aided by the power of the general Government, the Union men seem again to be in the ascendant. The same is true of Delaware, Kentucky, Missouri, and western Virginia, with perhaps allowances in some quarters.

I do not, of course, undertake to predict what will be the ultimate object of the war. I trust it will not be merely the conquest of unwilling peoples. Its present object, and its obvious present effect, is to defend the rights of the Union, and to strengthen the Union men in the doubtful States. We were becoming a disgraced, demoralized people. We are now united and strong.

If peaceful separation were to be attempted, it would fail. We should fight about the terms of it. The question of boundary alone would compel a war. After a war we shall make peace. It will henceforth be known that a State disappointed in an election can't secede, except at the risk of fearful war. What is left to us will be ours. The war for the purposes indicated — viz., for the defence of the capital, for the maintenance of the authority of the Government and the rights of the United States, I think is necessary, wise, and just. I know you honestly differ from me. I know that thousands — the great body of the people in some States, perhaps, — agree with you, and if we were only dealing with you and such as you, there would be no war between us. But if Kentucky, Virginia, and other States similarly situated leave the Union, it will be because they are forced or dragged out; and our Government ought not to permit it, if it can be prevented even by war.

I read your letter to Judge Matthews. We agree in the main respecting these questions. I shall be pleased to read it to George [Jones] when we meet. He has two brothers who have volunteered and gone to Washington. Lorin Andrews, President of Kenyon, our classmate, is colonel of a regiment. My brother-in-law, Dr. [James D.] Webb, has gone as a surgeon. I shall not take any active part, probably, unless Kentucky goes out. If so the war will be brought to our own doors and I shall be in it. If I felt I had any peculiar military capacity I should probably have gone to Washington with the rest. I trust the war will be short and that in terms, just to all, peace will be restored. I apprehend, and it is, I think, generally thought, that the war will [not] be a long one. Our whole people are in it. Your acquaintances Pugh, Pendleton, and Groesbeck, are all for prosecuting it with the utmost vigor. Vallandigham is silent, the only man I have heard of in any party. He has *not* been mobbed and is in no danger of it. I will try to send you Bishop McIlvaine's address on the war. It will give you our side of the matter.

We shall, of course, not agree about the war. We shall, I am sure, remain friends. There are good points about all such wars. People forget self. The virtues of magnanimity, courage, patriotism, etc., etc., are called into life. People are more generous, more sympathetic, better, than when engaged in the more selfish pursuits of peace. The same exhibition of virtue is witnessed on your side. May there be as much of this, the better side of war, enjoyed on both sides, and as little of the horrors of war suffered, as possible, and may we soon have an honorable and enduring peace!

My regards to your wife and boy. Lucy and the boys send much love.

As ever,

R. B. HAYES.

P. S. — My eldest thinks God will be sorely puzzled what to do. He hears prayers for our side at church, and his grandmother tells him that there are good people praying for the other side, and he asks: "How can He answer the prayers of both?"

Guy M. Bryan,
Texas.

May 10, 1861. — Great events the last month. April 12 and 13, Fort Sumter [was] attacked and taken by the South Carolina troops by order of the Government of the Confederate States at Montgomery. Sunday evening, April 14, news of Lincoln's call for 75,000 men [was] received here with unbounded enthusiasm. How relieved we were to have a Government again! I shall never forget the strong emotions, the wild and joyous excitement of that Sunday evening. Staid and sober church members thronged the newspaper offices, full of the general joy and enthusiasm. Great meetings were held. I wrote the resolutions of the main one, — to be seen in the *Intelligencer* of the next week. Then the rally of troops, the flags floating from every house, the liberality, harmony, forgetfulness of party and self — all good. Let what evils may follow, I shall not soon cease to rejoice over this event.

The resolutions referred to were published in the *Gazette* of the 16th [of] April and in the *Intelligencer* of the 18th.

[The resolutions were as follows:

"*Resolved,* That the people of Cincinnati, assembled without distinction of party, are unanimously of opinion that the authority of the United States, as against the rebellious citizens of the seceding and disloyal States, ought to be asserted and maintained, and that whatever men or means may be necessary to accomplish that object the patriotic people of the loyal States will promptly and cheerfully furnish.

"*Resolved,* That the citizens of Cincinnati will, to the utmost of their ability, sustain the general Government in maintaining its authority, in enforcing the laws, and in upholding the flag of the Union."]

May 15. 1861

Judge Matthews and ~~myself~~ I have agreed to go into the service for the war. if possible into the Same Regiment. I spoke my feelings to him which he said were his also viz that this was a just and necessary war and that it demanded the whole power of the Country. That I would prefer to go in to it [&] I knew to die or be killed in the course of it, than to live through and after it without taking any part in it—

19th

We find a good deal of difficulty in getting new Companies or Regiments accepted for the war, but we shall persevere —

FACSIMILE OF THE LAST PAGE OF THE DIARY OF RUTHERFORD B. HAYES BEFORE ENTERING THE UNION ARMY FOR THE WAR.

CINCINNATI, May 12, 1861.

DEAR UNCLE: —. . . The St. Louis and other news revives the war talk. We are likely, I think, to have a great deal of it before the thing is ended. Bryan writes me a long friendly secession letter, one-sided and partial, but earnest and honest. Perhaps he would say the same of my reply to it. I wish I could have a good talk with you about these days. I may be carried off by the war fever, and would like to hear you on it. Of course, I mean to take part, if there seems a real necessity for it, but I am tempted to do so, notwithstanding my unmilitary education and habits, on general enthusiasm and glittering generalities. But for some pretty decided obstacles, I should have done so before now.

All well at home. Lucy hates to leave the city in these stirring times. We hear that some of the Fremont men are at the camp near Milford. I shall see them one of these days, if this is so.

Sincerely,

R. B. HAYES.

S. BIRCHARD.

May 15, 1861. — Judge Matthews and I have agreed to go into the service for the war, — if possible into the same regiment. I spoke my feelings to him, which he said were his also, viz., that this was a just and necessary war and that it demanded the whole power of the country; *that I would prefer to go into it if I knew I was to die or be killed in the course of it, than to live through and after it without taking any part in it.*

CINCINNATI, May 16, 1861.

DEAR UNCLE: — I have got your favor of the 14th. . . . You say nothing about my going into the war. I have been fishing for your opinion in several of my late letters. Unless you speak soon, you may be too late.

My new business arrangement and my prospects, bad as times are, are evidently good. Whenever other lawyers have business, I shall easily make all that is needed; but still, as Billy Rogers

2

writes me, "This is a holy war," and if a fair chance opens, I shall go in; if a fair chance don't open, I shall, perhaps, take measures to open one. So don't be taken by surprise if you hear of my soldiering. All the family have been sounded, and there will be no *troublesome* opposition.

In view of contingencies, I don't like to leave home to visit you just now. I shall be able to leave money to support the family a year or two, without reckoning on my pay. Events move fast these days.

Since writing the foregoing, Judge [Stanley] Matthews called, and we have agreed to go to Columbus to lay the ropes for a regiment. There are a thousand men here who want us for their officers.

Sincerely,

R. B. Hayes.

S. Birchard.

May 19, 1861. — We find a good deal of difficulty in getting new companies or regiments accepted for the war, but we shall persevere.

Cincinnati, May 22, 1861.

Dear Uncle: — Your last is highly satisfactory. It is by no means certain that we shall get in, but we shall keep trying and sooner or later I suspect we shall succeed.

Lucy rather prefers, I think, not to go out to Fremont this summer if I should go away, but will of course do what we think best. I will come out before going away, even if I can stay only a day. If I should not leave, I shall of course visit you this summer and stay some time.

Sincerely,

R. B. Hayes.

S. Birchard.

Cincinnati, May 23, 1861.

Dear Uncle: — I received yours of the 17th this morning, and am glad to know that your views as to finishing and furnishing the house correspond with our own. If I should not go away during the summer, I will, of course, visit you several times, and we can arrange all these matters. . . .

I suspect you do not like to commit yourself on my warlike designs. We have often observed, that on some questions, advice is never asked until one's own purpose is fixed; so that the adviser is throwing away breath. Perhaps you think this is such a case, and perhaps you are right; but if the dispatches of this morning are correct, that the Government already has two hundred and twenty thousand men, and will accept no more, the question is settled.

It is raining again — disagreeable times for people in camp. I have not seen any Fremonters, but have written to Haynes* to come and see me, with any of the men.

Sincerely,

R. B. HAYES.

S. BIRCHARD.

CINCINNATI, May 26, 1861.

DEAR UNCLE: —. . . I have been watching the enlistments for the war during the last week with much interest, as the chance of our enterprise for the present depends on it. If twenty regiments enlist out of the twenty-six now on foot in the State, there will be no room for ours. If less than twenty go in for three years, we are safe. Until the news of the advance into Virginia arrived, and the death of Colonel Ellsworth, there was a good deal of hesitation in the various camps. The natural dissatisfaction and disgust which many felt, some with and some without adequate cause, were likely to prevent the quota from being filled out of the three-months men. But now all is enthusiasm again. Of course I like to see it, but for the present it probably cuts us out. Well, we shall be ready for next time. If all immediate interest in this quarter is gone, I shall likely enough come up and spend next Sunday with you.

Sincerely,

R. B. HAYES.

S. BIRCHARD.

* W. E. Haynes.   Later a colonel.   Long a prominent citizen of Fremont.   Member of Congress, etc.

CINCINNATI, May 31, 1861.

DEAR UNCLE: — I made my preparations to start for Fremont by way of Toledo tomorrow, as intimated in my letter of the early part of the week, but a gleam of light breaks in upon us in regard to our war project, and I concluded to wait; but if nothing turns up, I will come and see you a week hence. Mother is quite well again. All the rest of us in excellent health.

The times are no better, and I see nothing which indicates an early termination of the war. We must make up our minds for hard rations and little money.

Sincerely,

R. B. HAYES.

S. BIRCHARD.

CINCINNATI, June 5, 1861.

DEAR UNCLE: — I have received your letter of the 3rd. Am sorry to have disappointed you last Saturday. Shall try to come soon. I have just had a call from Buckland, * and went with him to the Burnet House and saw Miss Annie and Ralph.

A dispatch in the *Commercial* indicates that we are having better luck at Washington than at Columbus. If the authorities at Columbus do not interfere, we are likely to get in our regiment. We had a letter from Governor Chase a few days [ago], which encouraged us to hope that such would be the case.

Mother will probably go to Columbus next week or the week after. If the *Commercial* correspondent is correct, we shall probably be pretty busy for a few days or a week. I will advise you as soon as anything definite is known.

Sincerely,

R. B. HAYES.

S. BIRCHARD.

Ralph P. Buckland, of Fremont, Hayes's old law partner, later a general. Always a leading citizen.

CINCINNATI, June 10 [9], 1861.

DEAR UNCLE: — I shall go to Columbus in the morning *under orders*. I do not know what is intended, but by telegraph, Judge Matthews and myself are informed that we are to be in a regiment with Colonel Rosecrans — a West Pointer and intimate friend of Billy Rogers, and a capital officer, — Matthews as lieutenant-colonel and I as major. This is all we know about it. Buckland perhaps told you that I had got a dispatch asking if I would accept, and that I replied accepting the place. We have since been telegraphed that we were under orders accordingly, and must report at Columbus forthwith. This seems certain enough, but as red-tape is in the ascendant, we don't count positively on anything.

I shall try to visit you before definitely leaving home. Mother will return to Columbus soon. I hope this matter is as it appears. It is precisely what we wish, if we understand it.

Sincerely,

R. B. HAYES.

S. BIRCHARD.

COLUMBUS, June 10, 1861.

DEAR UNCLE: — Matthews and myself are here and find that the governor makes up a list of regimental officers, calls it a regimental organization and assigns to it companies as he pleases, preferring to select officers from one part of the State and men from another. We are the Twenty-third Regiment * and our companies will probably be from the north. The men indicated are said to be a superior body. We have seen the captains and are favorably impressed. Of course this policy is calculated to cause embarrassment, but the governor shoulders the responsibility and we are not involved in any personal unpleasantness. We shall be here probably a week before going down to make our final preparations.

I may not tbe able to visit Fremont. If not you will see me here. Sincerely,

R. B. HAYES.

S. BIRCHARD.

* The first three-years regiment organized in Ohio.

(Private — Don't show this out of the family.)

CINCINNATI [COLUMBUS], June 10, 1861.

DEAR DOCTOR: — We are not quite certain, but our matters probably stand this way. The governor makes up a regimental staff and assigns to it companies as far removed from it, usually, as possible. We are to be the Twenty-third Regiment and companies will be assigned, usually, from the north. The proposed companies are very fine ones. This policy naturally creates some embarrassment, and may, or may not, work well, but the governor takes the responsibility in a very manly way, and relieves *us* from all embarrassments. If there is trouble, it will be between the governor and the companies, not involving us in the least. We like our captains, and would get along with them well, if this policy don't interfere. Nothing can be said about surgeon at present. I suspect it is arranged, but can't guess how.

I can't say when I shall come down, but soon, to stay two or three days and fix up; probably about Saturday next. Lucy may gradually get ready my matters; not too many things; there will be time enough.

The camp is at the race-track four miles west. You need not talk much of my probable fix, as changes are possible. Love to all. I will write often.

Sincerely,

R. B. HAYES.

P. S. — Order at Sprague's a major's uniform for infantry; they have my measure; see Rhodes; also, a blue flannel blouse, regulation officer's; pants to be large and *very loose* about the legs; to be done the last of this week, or as soon as convenient. Blouse and pants first to be done.

DR. JOSEPH T. WEBB.

COLUMBUS, June 10, 1861.

DEAR FORCE: — I do not dispatch you as to matters here, because it is not certain what will be done, but our present impression is, that we can get no additional companies into our regiment. Full regiments have been made up, and the governor is assigning officers to them, or, rather, he makes up regimental staffs, and assigns companies from a list of accepted companies already in camp.   .   .   .   This mode of doing the thing creates some difficulty, and changes are possible, but not probable. I regret this, but we can't perhaps change it. The governor is doing it in a frank, manly way which relieves *us* from all embarrassment in the premises.

Sincerely,

R. B. HAYES.

M. F. FORCE, ESQ.
Cincinnati.

COLUMBUS, Monday, 10 P. M., June 10, 1861.

DEAREST LU : — I have just sent Judge Matthews to bed in the room over the library, and I thought I'd write a few words to my dear wife before sleeping. We have been at the camp all the afternoon. Our quarters are not yet built; all things are new and disorganized; the location is not nearly so fine as Camp Dennison, but with all these disadvantages, we both came away feeling very happy. We visited our men; they behaved finely; they are ambitious and zealous, and met us in such a good spirit. We really were full of satisfaction with it. We are glad we are away from the crowds of visitors who interfere so with the drills at Camp Dennison.

When we reached town, Judge Matthews learned that Bosley was elected over the Grays; he was more than content with it.

I shall not need things in a hurry; take time, and don't worry yourself. I shall probably be down the last of the week; I shall only be prevented by the absence of Colonel Rosecrans and Judge Matthews. The colonel has accepted and will be here Wednesday.

There is a good band in camp; several well drilled companies. We shall have four thousand men by Saturday. Ours is the best regiment: two companies from Cleveland, one from Sandusky, one from Bellefontaine and one from Ashtabula, under a son of J. R. Giddings — a pleasant gentleman and a capital company.

But I must stop this.   You know how I love you; how I love
the family all; but Lucy, I am much happier in this business
than I could be fretting away in the old office near the court-
house.   It is living.   My only regret is that you don't like our
location.   We shall probably spend the summer here, or a good
part of it, unless we go into Virginia.   No more tonight.   Much
love.

Sincerely,

R. B. Hayes.

Mrs. Hayes.

Columbus, June 12, 1861.

Dear Uncle: — We are in Camp Jackson — hot, busy, and
jolly. Colonel Rosecrans is an energetic, educated West Pointer,
very cheerful and sensible. Judge Matthews you know. We
are on good terms with our captains, and the whole thing pleases
me vastly; but I see no chance of getting out to see you; so
you must come here one of these days.   We are in the suds yet;
still I would enjoy a visit even now.   I cannot say more now.
Good-bye.

Sincerely,

R. B. Hayes.

P. S. — We were sworn in to-day; our commissions are from
the 7th.

S. Birchard.

Columbus, June 12, 1861.

Dear Force: — You can't regret more than I do the issue of
this business, so far as you are concerned.   I have tried to get
two companies (so as to include you and Company A of G. G.
[Guthrie Greys]) admitted. Failing in that, I tried one, but
the thing is all settled, and the governor fears to disturb the
elements again.

Our regiment promises to be an exceedingly pleasant one.
We are the first regimental officers on the ground.   Our colonel
will command in this camp until a brigadier-general arrives.
We are the best known persons, and the struggle is to get into
our regiment from all quarters.   The camp is yet higgledy-pig-

gledy and will require some labor to bring it up. But all goes on rapidly. We have been busy as bees a large part of the time in the scorching sun; but so far, it [is] great fun. I enjoy it as much as a boy does a Fourth of July.

Sincerely,

R. B. HAYES.

M. F. FORCE, ESQ.

CAMP JACKSON, NEAR COLUMBUS,
Friday P. M., June 14, 1861.

DEAR UNCLE: — I received from Cincinnati two letters from you, and am very sorry to hear of your ill health. If you are not likely to come here soon, let me know, and I will certainly visit Fremont, when I can get leave to go home. The business here will require attention for a few days yet, before we get into an established routine. I shall probably leave here in about a week, and can then, if you wish it, visit you one day. If you were well, you would enjoy a few days here. Laura could send you out in the morning, and there are hosts of conveyances back.

I enjoy this thing very much. It is open-air, active life, novel and romantic. Hotter than Tophet in the sun, but a good breeze blowing all the time.

Our arrangement of regimental matters has turned out to be a capital one so far. We are in command of the whole camp, and, as Colonel Rosecrans is absent, Matthews and I are starring it. What we don't know, we guess at, and you may be sure we are kept pretty busy guessing.

My want now is a good horse. A small or medium-sized animal of good sense, hardy and kind, good looking enough, but not showy, is what I want. A fast walk, smooth trot, and canter are the gaits. I don't object to a pacer if he can walk and gallop well. Don't bother yourself to find one, but if you happen to know any, let me know. I am busy or I would write more.

Sincerely,

R. B. HAYES.

S. BIRCHARD.

[The Diary gives the following narrative of the entrance into the service and the first few days in camp.]

June 7, 1861, I received a dispatch from Governor Dennison asking me if I would accept the majority in a regiment of which William S. Rosecrans was to be colonel and Judge Matthews lieutenant-colonel. I read it to Lucy, consulted with my old law partner [Ralph P. Buckland], who happened to be visiting Cincinnati, and thereupon replied that I would accept as proposed. Late in the afternoon of the next day I received a dispatch from the governor, addressed to Judge Matthews and myself, directing us to report to the adjutant-general at Columbus, Monday morning. Not being able to find Judge Matthews in the city, on the next day (Sunday, P. M.), I rode out to Judge Matthews' residence at Glendale, took tea with him and his family and friends (Mrs. Matthews and mother, and Mr. and Mrs. Todd), and rode into the city arriving a few minutes before 9 P. M. I bid good-bye to my family (my mother, mother-in-law, Mrs. Webb, Lucy, and the boys), and at 9:30 P. M. we took the cars by way of Dayton for Columbus.

June 10, Monday morning, after a few hours' rest at the Goodale or Capitol House, we went over to the governor's office and learned that the governor had made up a regiment composed of companies chiefly from the extreme northern and northeastern part of the East [State], the field officers being all from Cincinnati, to be the Twenty-third Regiment Ohio Volunteer Infantry, for the service of the United States during the war. This regiment was to be organized under General Order No. 15, issued by the adjutant-general of the United States, May 4, 1861, and was the first regiment in Ohio in which the regiment did not elect its own field officers. We feared there would be some difficulty in reconciling the men and officers to officers — strangers — not of their own selection. . . .

Several of these companies had been in camp in Camp Taylor, near Cleveland, together, and wished to remain and act together. All the captains came into the governor's office, soon after we entered, in a state of some excitement, or at least some feeling, at finding themselves placed under strangers from a distant part of the State. We were introduced to them. Colonel

Rosecrans unfortunately was not present, having not yet arrived from some military service at Washington. The governor explained to Matthews and myself that the field officers of the Twenty-third were fixed, that we were the Twenty-third Regiment, and that those captains could go into it or not as they saw fit. A little acquaintance satisfied us that our captains were not disposed to be unreasonable, that their feeling was a natural one under the circumstances, and that all ill feeling would disappear if we showed the disposition and ability to perform our duties. Captain Beatty, however, would not be content. He had been a senator in the Legislature, was fifty-five or sixty years old and not disposed to go under young men.

We took a hack out to Camp Jackson,* four miles west of Columbus on the National Road. Several companies were mustered into service by Captains Simpson and Robinson the same day. Colonel E. A. King, of Dayton, was, under state authority, in command of all the soldiers, some twenty-five hundred in number, not mustered into service. As rapidly as they were mustered in, they passed under Colonel Matthews, as the ranking field officer in United States service. Luckily, Captain Beatty was not ready for the mustering officer and we succeeded in getting Captain Zimmerman's fine company in his place. Ditto Captain Howard in place of Captain Weller.

Our mustering was completed June 11 and 12. We were guests of Colonel King (for rations) at the log headquarters and slept at Platt's. Both good arrangements. Wednesday evening, 12th, we got up a large marquee, fine but not tight, and that night I had my first sleep under canvas — cool but refreshing.

Thursday, June 13, Colonel William S. Rosecrans appeared and assumed the command. Our regiment was paraded after retreat had been sounded. The long line looked well, although the men were ununiformed and without arms. We were lucky in having a band enlisted as privates at Ashland.

Colonel Rosecrans is a spirited, rapid talker and worker and makes a fine impression on officers and men. Appointments of regimental staff officers were made. . . . Guards or sentinels

* Name changed a few days later to Camp Chase.

detailed. Men lectured on manners and behavior, etc., etc.

There are many good singers in camp, and as we are not reduced to order yet, the noises of the camp these fine evenings and the strangeness have a peculiar charm. How cold the nights are! I am more affected as I look at the men on parade than I expected to be; not more embarrassed. I am not greatly embarrassed, but an agreeable emotion, a swelling of heart possesses me. The strongest excitement was when I saw the spirit and enthusiasm with which the oath was taken.

Our captains impress me, as a body, most favorably. Captain McIlrath is a large, fine-looking man, six feet three and a half inches high; has been a chief of police in Cleveland — one of the best in his vocation; takes great pride in his company and has it in a fine state of discipline — the best of any in camp. Captain Skiles has served in Mexico, is apparently a man of fine character, a member of church. Captain Moore is a New England-farmer-like man, shrewd and trusty. Captain Zimmerman is a conscientious, amiable, industrious man and has a stout set of men from the iron region, Mahoning County.

Sunday [*June*] *16.* — Colonel Rosecrans and Matthews, having gone to Cincinnati, and Colonel King to Dayton, I am left in command of camp, some twenty-five hundred to three thousand men — an odd position for a novice, so ignorant of all military things. All matters of discretion, of common judgment, I get along with easily, but I was for an instant puzzled when a captain in the Twenty-fourth, of West Point education, asked me formally, as I sat in tent, for his orders for the day, he being officer of the day. Acting on my motto, "When you don't know what to say, say nothing," I merely remarked that I thought of nothing requiring special attention; that if anything was wanted out of the usual routine I would let him know.

CAMP JACKSON, Sunday, June 16, 1861.

DEAREST L—: — Morning work done and waiting till Dr. Hoge begins, I write to my darling wife and boys. Would you like to know our daily routine. (*Mem.:* — Colonel King commanding State troops and my superiors, Colonels Rosecrans and

Matthews, all having gone home, I am now in command of all at this post, eighteen companies United States troops and sixteen companies State troops, in all three thousand men and upwards. A sudden responsibility for a civilian, but the duties are chiefly such as a civilian can easily do, so it is strange rather in appearance than reality). First, at 5 A. M., gun fired and reveille sounded, calling all men to roll-call. I was up and dressing. Owing to bright light in a tent, sound sleeping in the cool air, etc., etc., this I did not find difficult. In a few minutes all the captains call at my tent to report themselves and the condition of their men.

I sit at a table looking towards the front entrance of the tent; an orderly on my right to go errands; a clerk at a table on the left to write; an adjutant ditto to give orders and help me *guess* what ought to be done in each case, and a sentinel slowly pacing back and forth in front of the entrance whose main employment is telling men to take off their hats before entering on the surroundings. The first business is looking over the orders of the day, and telling the adjutant to see them carried out. These are as to guards and sich, which are stereotyped with slight alterations to suit circumstances — such as guarding wells, fixing new sentinels where men are suspected of getting out, etc., etc. Next comes issuing permits to go out of camp to town and to parties to go bathing in the Scioto one and one-half miles distant. Then comes in, for an hour or more, the morning reports of roll-call, showing the sick, absent, etc., etc., all to be looked over and corrected; and mistakes abound that are curious enough. Once we got all the officers returned as "under arrest." One captain lost a lieutenant, although he was present as plainly as Hateful W. Perkins was in Pease's anecdote. Then rations are returned short; on that point I am strong, and as the commissary is clever, we soon correct mistakes. Then we have difficulties between soldiers, very slight and easily disposed of; but troubles between soldiers and the carpenters whose tools disappear mysteriously, and farmers in the neighborhood who go to bed with roosts of barnyard fowl and wake up chickenless and fowlless, are more troublesome. The accused defenders of their country can always prove an *alibi* by their comrades, and that the thing is impossible by the sentinels whose beat they must have passed.

Since writing the above, I have waited under a tree, with a flag raised, three quarters of an hour for Dr. Hoge's congregation, but for some reason he did not come, and an audience of one thousand were disappointed, possibly(?), however, not all disagreeably. I have sent five men and a sergeant to arrest two deserters in Columbus (not of our regiment) belonging to Captain Sturgess' company of Zanesville; one sergeant and two men to see safely out of camp two men who were about to have their heads shaved for refusing to take the oath of allegiance; a lieutenant and ten men to patrol the woods back of the camp, to prevent threatened depredations on a farmer. This all since I began writing. The wind is rising and the dust floats in on my paper, as you see. As yet, we eat our meals at Colonel King's quarters — plain good living. Guard-mounting is a ceremonious affair at 9 A. M. At 12 M., drum-beat and roll-call for dinner; at 6 P. M., ditto for supper; at 7 P. M., our band calls out the regiment for a parade; not yet a "dress parade," but a decidedly imposing affair, notwithstanding. The finale is at 10 P. M.

The evenings and night are capital. The music and hum, the cool air in the tent, and open-air exercise during the day, make the sleeping superb. We have cots about like our lounge, only slighter and smaller, bought in Dayton. Our men are fully equal to the famous Massachusetts men in a mechanical way. They build quarters, ditches, roads, traps; dig wells, catch fish, kill squirrels, etc., etc., and it is really a new sensation, the affection and pride one feels respecting such a body of men in the aggregate.

We are now feeling a good deal of anxiety about Colonel Rosecrans. He is said to be appointed a brigadier. If it were to take effect six weeks or three months hence, we would like it if he should be promoted; but now we fear some new man over us who may not be agreeable, and we do not like the difficulties attendant upon promotion. The governor says we shall not lose Colonel Rosecrans, and we hope he is right.

I enclose a letter in the Cleveland *Herald* written by some one in one of our Cleveland companies. With Colonel Rosecrans in command, we should have no trouble with our men. We have reconciled them as, I think, perfectly, or as nearly so as men ever are with their officers. But if Colonel Rosecrans goes, we are between Scylla and Charybdis you know — officers at our head whom we may not like, or men under us who do not like us; but it will all come right. I am glad I am here, and only wish you were here.

I was in at Platt's last evening an hour or so. Laura was expecting Platt by the late train, but as he has not yet come out here, I suspect he did not arrive. Love to all. Kiss the boys. I enjoyed reading your talk about them and their sayings.

Affectionately,

R. B. HAYES.

MRS. HAYES.

June —, 1861. — Early in the second week of our camping out in service, Colonel Rosecrans returned and set vigorously to work organizing the regiment. The evening of the day he returned we were closing up matters in our tent preparatory to going to bed, when two gentlemen rode up with a dispatch which announced the appointment of Colonel Rosecrans to the post of brigadier-general, and ordering him to repair to western Virginia to take command of Ohio troops moving in that direction. We rode into Columbus and saw the colonel now general, off about midnight. Good-bye to our good colonel. A sorry thing for us. May it prove all he hopes to him. I shall never forget how his face shone with delight as he read the dispatch.

CAMP CHASE, June 20, 1861.

DEAR UNCLE: — I now expect to leave here on Saturday and come to Fremont to stay over Sunday with you. On Monday I will go down to Cincinnati to stay one or two days, and then I return to devote myself to the instruction and exercises of my post. Matthews returned yesterday, having finished his home preparations.

We have been in camp almost two weeks, and were getting on finely when we lost our colonel. Rosecrans has been promoted to a brigadier-generalship, and left us night before last to command the Virginia expedition to the Kanawha. We are helping the governor find some competent military man to take his place. If Matthews had had two months' teaching and experience, he would be willing to take the place, and I should have perfect confidence in him, but as it is, he prefers not to take the responsibility.

Mother has returned. She was out here a few days ago, in good health for her and spirits. I shall see you so soon, that I need not write further. I enjoy this life, and it is going to be healthy for me. I shall hardly be more exposed to cold than in a very open tent the two cold nights a few days ago; but I am gaining in strength and spirits.

                                    Sincerely,
                                                R. B. HAYES.
S. BIRCHARD.

                                    CAMP CHASE, June 20, 1861.

DEAREST L—:— Your letter filled me with joy — as your letters will always do. I write to say that my present purpose is to go to Fremont Saturday, to remain over Sunday, and Monday, to go down home and stay one or two days only. You will find it so pleasant up here that I do not go down except for business. Make little *mem.'s* of all things you want me to attend to. Recollect about any thin duds I have, especially coats. I am now well provided with most things.

Yes, the loss of our colonel did trouble us. Matthews does not yet wish the responsibility of command. With a few weeks' experience I would prefer his appointment; in fact, I would anyhow, but we are casting about and the governor will consult our wishes. Our present preference is either Colonel [Eliakim Parker] Scammon or Colonel George W. McCook, the latter if he would take it. It will probably be satisfactory. If the new man is competent, he will be a very mean man if he does not get on well with us.

                                    Affectionately,
MRS. HAYES.   R.

CAMP CHASE, June 22, 1861.

DEAREST LU: — I start for Fremont this morning. . . . As to surgeons, four only are to be appointed; it will not be possible to get two of them from Cincinnati. Either Clendenin or Dr. Joe will not get appointed. I mention this merely to show the facts. I want the doctor to do nothing at all about it, nor to say anything about it. Dr. Clendenin can probably get an appointment from Washington as brigade surgeon. It will be some days before the appointments will be made. There is a good disposition to accommodate us at headquarters, and I think the prospect fair for his [Dr. Joe's] appointment.

I shall want towels, sheets, and three table-cloths, one and one-half dozen napkins, two comforts. *Don't buy them, or any of them,* but if you have them to spare, I will take them. I would advise the spending of as little as possible. We do not know the future, and economy is a duty. These things are merely luxuries. Love to all.

Affectionately,

R.

P. S. — You will enjoy looking at us here, and I shall be glad to have you come up. You can hardly live out at camp; but possibly, we can keep you a night or two, and you can stay here through the day. It is pleasant living here. Colonel Scammon is our colonel. This will do. It has advantages which I need not explain which would not occur to an outside looker-on.

MRS. HAYES.

CAMP CHASE, June 27, 1861, Thursday, A. M.

DEAREST L—: — At my leisure, I have looked over the little what-you-may-call-it and its chapter of contents. It is so nice, and has everything needful that I have thought of, and more too. Much obliged, dearest. With all my boots, I find I have no slippers; forgot, also, my pepper-and-salt vest.

Found mother and all well and happy, and most glad that you are coming up. . . . We shall probably be here some time longer than I supposed. Matthews says Colonel Scammon turns

3

out to be *socially* and *individually* a most agreeable person to be associated with.

We have chosen a Methodist chaplain, Amos Wilson, of Bucyrus. The governor could not appoint but one of these four surgeons from Cincinnati, and took Clendenin as first on the list, and first applied for by Colonel Fyffe. If Dr. Clendenin declines, he will appoint Dr. Joe for us, and says he shall be the next appointed from Cincinnati. He has appointed a good man for us, but will transfer him to make room for Joe if Clendenin does not accept. We can't complain of the governor's disposition in the matter. He wishes to know Dr. Clendenin's intentions as soon as possible. If he declines, Dr. Joe must be ready to come up forthwith. Dr. Jim will pretty certainly be retained as assistant, in any event, but he must pass an examination, if he is in this region when the new appointment is to be made.

Love to "all the boys," and much for Grandma and yourself, from your loving and affectionate.

R.

Mrs. Hayes.

Camp Chase, June 28, 1861.

Dear Uncle: — I found all well at home and at Columbus — all feeling anxious about you. I gave as favorable an account of your health as I could conscientiously.

I am again in camp. Our new colonel is personally an agreeable gentleman to be associated with; in experience and education, equal to the place; but probably deficient in physical health and energy. . . .

Sincerely,

R. B. Hayes.

S. Birchard.

Camp Chase, June 30, 1861.

Dearest: — Sunday morning, according to army regulations, there is to be a mustering and inspection of all men, visiting of sick quarters, etc., etc., on the last Sunday of each month. We have gone through with it, and have found, with a few exceptions, matters in good sort. Our colonel is fond of pleasantry, amiable and social. He enjoys the disposition of Matthews and myself to joke, and after duty, we get jolly. But he has not a happy way of hitting the humors of the men. Still, as we think him a kind-hearted, just man, we hope the men will learn to appreciate his good qualities, in spite of an unfortunate manner.

I have had some of the jolliest times the last week I have any recollection of. A camp is a queer place; you will enjoy being here. Matthews writes his wife not to come until the men are uniformed. This will be in about ten days we suppose. I don't want you to wait on that account, but would like to have you stay until after we get on our good "duds." Mother and Platt were out with Ruddy last night. He wanted to stay with us very much, but his father objected; he promised to let him stay out here with Birch.

I have heard nothing from Clendenin, but our colonel says he *thinks* Dr. Joe will be our physician, even if Clendenin concludes to accept the post he is offered in the Twenty-sixth. I hope he is right, and as he has had some talk with Governor Dennison on the subject, I am inclined to put faith in his conjecture.

Affectionately, your

R.

Mrs. Hayes.

Camp Chase, July 2, 1861.

Dearest: — The comet, or the storm, or something makes it cold as blazes this morning, but pleasant. Speaking of shirts, did I leave my shirts at home? I have but two or three here now. Have they been lost here, or how? You need not make me any if they are gone. I intend to wear flannel or mixed goods of some sort, but if there are a few tolerably good ones or collars, you may let Dr. Joe bring them up when he comes.

By the by, you know Dr. Joe has been appointed to our regiment, Dr. Clendenin having declined the Twenty-sixth. I wrote Dr. Joe a scolding letter in reply to his note abusing the governor. I did so because I felt confident that he was to be appointed in some way, and I didn't want him to kick the fat in the fire by getting in a sensation about it before the matter was finally determined.   Matthews and all are very glad.   I am more interested in it than in anything else connected with the regiment.

I believe I told you it would be in good point if you could fix up one or two of my thick vests.   I shall take away from here nothing but my gray travelling suit and thick vests.   The military coats will conceal the vests, so they are as good as any other.   Dr. Joe better get a good ready before he comes up. It may be difficult for him to get away.   As for clothing and fixings, they can all be sent to him; but his business arrangements better be made, if possible, before he leaves.   If he keeps well, as I think he will, he will enjoy this life very much.   His rank and pay will be the same as mine.   He is *allowed* two or three horses, and *should have* at least one.   There is no stabling here at present, so he need not now bring his horse, if he would prefer not to keep him at the hotel or in Columbus.

Love to Grandma and all.   Kisses for the dear boys.   They will mourn the loss of their Uncle Joe.   I should not be much loss to them now; when they get older I will try to help in their education.   Birch, if possible, should be a soldier; Webb will do for a sailor; Ruddy will do for either or 'most anything else. I am sorry you are to be left with so much responsibility; but, with your mother's advice, do what you both agree is best and it will perfectly satisfy me.

Affectionately, yours ever,

RUTHERFORD.

MRS. HAYES.

CAMP CHASE, July 5, 1861.

DEAR UNCLE: — I have so little to write that I have, perhaps, neglected you. . . . . We are getting on very pleasantly here. It is a gentlemanly, social life, with just business and exercise enough to pass the time.

I have probably engaged a horse for one hundred dollars — a dark sorrel, good stock, neat, graceful, and of good temper.

Dr. Joe has been appointed our surgeon.   We have not heard from home since he received the appointment, but I expect him to accept it. It will please Lucy and mother particularly. Let me hear of or from you often.

Sincerely,

R. B. HAYES.

S. BIRCHARD.

CAMP CHASE, July 6, 1861.

DEAREST: — I have written to John Herron to supply you with what money you need for the present, and I suppose it will be convenient for him to do so out of a loan I made him some time ago. It does not seem like Saturday. The Fourth was like Sunday here. Colonel Matthews and I formed the regiment into a hollow square (rather oblong, in fact). I read the Declaration and he made a short pithy speech and wound up with cheers for the Union; and no more duty during the day. In the evening there were fire-balls and a few fireworks. A little shower this morning laid the dust, a fine thing in our little Sahara.

Colonel Matthews came in last night from Columbus, saying he rode out with the surgeon of the Twenty-sixth — the one intended for us — "and what an escape we have made. He is a green, ignorant young doctor who has all to learn." I suppose Dr. Joe is getting ready to come; we hear nothing from him; I hope we shall see him soon. I am seeing to his hut which is building today. Uncle is rather better but not decidedly so. We have a lot of Secessionists from Virginia — a good camp sensation. I went in late last night after ball-cartridges, which stirred up the soldiers with its warlike look. I esteem these armed sentinels about as dangerous to friends as to foes. ·Here is our style of countersign. Done up Know-nothing fashion. Love to all and much for your own dear self.

Affectionately,

R. B. HAYES.

MRS. HAYES.

CAMP CHASE, July 8, 1861.

DEAR UNCLE: — Lucy came up to Columbus with Birtie Saturday evening. They have both been out once, and Birch twice to see me in camp. It is very pleasant to see them about. We are jogging on in routine duties. The only variation is the advent of twenty-three Secessionists, held as hostages for Union men seized in Virginia. On the release of the Union men, our prisoners were sent home yesterday.

I fear from the tenor of McLelland's letters, and what Hale told me, that you are not getting rid of your cough. I hope you will do so soon. It is too bad that you should be unwell now. You would enjoy a little campaigning with me very much, and I would so enjoy having you along. . . . — Good-bye.

R. B. Hayes.

S. Birchard.

Camp Chase, July 11, 1861.

Dear Uncle: — I am now almost at home. Lucy is at Platt's with Birch and Webb. Dr. Joe came yesterday bringing Webb with him. We shall have the boys out here a good deal. It is a good place for them. Birch was infinitely disgusted to meet me without my uniform on.

I have my horse here and ride him all about the camp and parade ground. Although young, he is sensible to the last. I shall probably not need Ned, Jr. A horse must canter or lope well to be of any account in a camp. The colonel and Matthews have both been disappointed in theirs. Matthews sent his back home yesterday. My sorrel cost one hundred dollars. He is called the cheapest and one of the best horses in camp. . . .

Sincerely,

R. B. Hayes.

S. Birchard.

Camp Chase, July 18, 1861.

Dear Uncle: — I have just read your letter of the 16th. I hope it is good proof that you are mending rapidly. It is pleasant to see your own handwriting again.

Our men are uniformed and we are daily receiving our needful equipments. The indications are that we shall soon move. In what direction and under whose command, we do not know. We are not very particular. We prefer the mountainous region of Virginia or Tennessee.

If Ned, Jr. was down here, I would try what could be done

with him. But the travelling is done so much by rail, that I hardly need two horses. My sorrel is a good one.

My notion is that we shall go within a fortnight. Lucy and the two boys will stay until we go with Platt. Come down if you can, but not at the risk of health. Write often. No letters are so good as yours.

Sincerely,

R. B. HAYES.

S. BIRCHARD.

COLUMBUS, Sunday morning, July 21, 1861.

DEAR UNCLE: — I came in last evening to attend a little tea gathering at Mr. Andrews'; shall return this morning. We are now in condition to move on a few days' notice, and expect to go soon — say a week or two. I constantly at camp am reminded of you. You would enjoy the company we have and the amusing incidents which are occurring. The colonel [Jacob Ammen] of the Twenty-fourth next us is a character. He has been an army officer (West Pointer) many years, a teacher of mathematics, etc., in different colleges, and has seen all sorts of life. He is a capital instructor in military things, and finding Matthews and myself fond of his talk, he takes to us warmly. Dr. Joe is now settled with us, and we are made up. We have had good visits from Mr. Giddings, David Tod, and other State celebrities. . . .

It would have been a great happiness to have spent the summer and fall fixing up around Spiegel Grove. But in this war I could not feel contented if I were not in some way taking part in it. I should feel about myself as I do about people who lived through the Revolution, seeing their neighbors leaving home, but doing nothing themselves — a position not pleasant to occupy.

I hope you will be well enough to come down. If not, I do not doubt we shall be together again one of these days. All well here.

Sincerely,

R. B. HAYES.

S. BIRCHARD.

July 22. — Just received news of a dreadful defeat at Manassas, or beyond Centreville. General McDowell's column pushed on after some successes, were met apparently by fresh troops, checked, driven back, utterly routed! What a calamity! Will not the secession fever sweep over the border States, driving out Kentucky, Missouri, (Baltimore) Maryland, etc., etc.? Is not Washington in danger? I have feared a too hasty pushing on of McDowell's column into ground where the Rebels have camped and scouted and entrenched themselves for months. My brother-in-law, as surgeon, is with the Second Ohio Regiment in advance, and is doubtless among those in the worst position. But private anxieties are all swallowed up in the general public calamity. God grant that it is exaggerated!

Our regiments are now likely, I think, to be speedily needed at Washington or elsewhere. I am ready to do my duty, promptly and cheerfully. Would that I had the military knowledge and experience which one ought to have to be useful in my position! I will do my best, my utmost in all ways to promote the efficiency of our regiment. It is henceforth a serious business.

July 23. 6 A. M. — This extra* was handed me on our parade ground last evening about 6 P. M. by my brother-in-law, Dr. Joe Webb, who had just galloped out from the city on my sorrel. We had heard the first rumor of a great defeat, but this gave us the details. A routed army, heavy loss, demoralization, on our side; a great victory, confidence, and enthusiasm, on the other, were the natural results to be expected. Washington in danger, its capture probable, if the enemy had genius. These were the ideas I was filled with.

But so far as we were concerned all was readiness and energy. Colonel Matthews and myself superintended the opening and distribution of cartridge-boxes, etc., etc., until late at night that our regiment might be ready to march at a moment's warning. Slept badly. Meditated on the great disaster. On Lucy prob-

* Pasted in the Diary is the report of the disaster at Manassas Junction and the retreat of the Union army, clipped from the *Ohio State Journal* extra.

ably hastening to Cincinnati to comfort and be with her mother. I dreamed I was in Washington, Union men leaving in haste, the enemy advancing to take the city, its capture hourly expected. My own determination and feelings when awake were all as I would wish. A sense of duty excited to a warmer and more resolute pitch.

This morning I rose at the first tap of reveille and went out on the parade-ground. Soon came the morning papers correcting and modifying the first exaggerated reports. There was a great panic, but if the morning report is reliable, the loss is not very heavy; the army is again in position. The lesson is a severe one. It may be a useful one. Raw troops should not be sent to attack an enemy entrenched on its own ground unless under most peculiar circumstances. Gradual approach with fortifications as they proceeded would have won the day.

Last evening Adjutant-General Buckingham took tea with Colonel Scammon. My mind was full of the great disaster. They talked of schoolboy times at West Point; gave the bill of fare of different days — beef on Sunday, fish on etc., etc. — anecdotes of Billy Cozzens, the cook or steward, never once alluding to the events just announced of which we were all full.

July 12, Lucy and Birch and Webb came up to Columbus. They spent a few days in camp, she remaining over night but once. They will probably remain until we leave here.

Mrs. Matthews and Willie left today (23rd). With her daughter Jennie, they have spent two or three days in camp.

Continuing my narrative. — In the place of Colonel Rosecrans, promoted to brigadier-general, Colonel Scammon is appointed to command our regiment. He is a gentleman of military education and experience. Amiable and friendly with us — an intelligent, agreeable gentleman; but not well fitted for volunteer command; and I fear somewhat deficient in health and vigor of nerve. We shall find him an entertaining head of our mess of field officers. — After some ups and downs we have succeeded in getting for our surgeon my brother-in-law, Dr. Joseph T. Webb. Our field officers' mess consists of Colonel Scammon, Lieutenant-Colonel Matthews, Dr. Webb, and myself.

CAMP CHASE, July 23, 1861.

DEAR UNCLE: — We are in the midst of the excitement produced by the disastrous panic near Washington. We expect it will occasion a very early movement of our regiment. We shall, perhaps, be ordered to the Kanawha line. We certainly shall, unless the recent defeat shall change the plan of the campaign. Colonel DePuy's regiment is on that line, so that the Fremont companies are likely to be in the same body with us. Their association will be pleasant enough, but there are two or three regiments with them in which I have very little confidence; viz., the Kentucky regiments "falsely so called." We are yet raw troops, but I think we shall soon grow to it.

The Washington affair is greatly to be regretted; unless speedily repaired, it will lengthen the war materially. The panic of the troops does not strike me as remarkable. You recollect the French army in the neighborhood of the Austrians were seized with a panic, followed by a flight of many miles, caused merely by a runaway mule and cart and "nobody hurt." The same soldiers won the battle of Solferino a few days ago [later]. But I do think the commanding officers ought not to have led fresh levies against an enemy entrenched on his own ground. Gradual advances, fortifying as he went, strikes me as a more prudent policy. But it is easy to find fault. The lesson will have its uses. It will test the stuff our people are made of. If we are a solid people, as I believe we are, this reverse will stiffen their backs. They will be willing to make greater efforts and sacrifices.

We worked late last night getting our accoutrements ready. In the hurry of preparations to depart, I may not be able to write you before I go. Good-bye.

Sincerely,

R. B. HAYES.

S. BIRCHARD.

CAMP CHASE, July 24, 1861.

DEAR UNCLE: — I am surrounded by the bustle and confusion attendant upon a hurried leaving of camp. We go tomorrow at 5 A. M. to Zanesville by railroad, thence down the Muskingum on steamboats to Marietta, and on the Ohio to Ripley Landing, a short distance from Point Pleasant in Virginia. We are to be a part of General Rosecrans' force against Wise.

Last night I had a good chat with Frémont. He is a hero. All his words and acts inspire enthusiasm and confidence. He and the governor reviewed our regiment today. Lucy, Laura, and many friends were present. It was a stirring scene. I wish you could have been here. You would subscribe heartily to General Frémont. Good-bye. My saddest feeling — my almost only sad feeling — is leaving you in such bad health.

Affectionately,

R. B. HAYES.

P. S. — Always send me full sheets of paper — the blank sheet is so useful. The use and scarcity of paper is appalling.

S. BIRCHARD.

July 25 [24]. — A. M. our regiment was reviewed by the Governor and Major-General Frémont. It was a gratifying scene. The Colonel (Frémont — I must always think of the man of fifty-six [as] the colonel) looked well. How he inspires confidence and affection in the masses of people! The night before I was introduced to him at the American. He is a romantic, rather perhaps than a great, character. But he is loyal, brave, and persevering beyond all compare. Lucy and Laura were present.

July 26 [25]. — Last night I went in to Columbus to bid good-bye to the boys; on the road met Lucy, Laura, and Mother Webb; advised them to return. After we were at home (Platt's), Lucy showed more emotion at my departure than she has hitherto exhibited. She wanted to spend my last night with me in Camp Chase. I took her out. We passed a happy evening going around among the men gathered in picturesque groups, cooking rations for three days at the camp fires. Early in the morning, as she was anxious Mother Webb should see the camp before I left, I sent her in by a hack to return with Mother Webb which she did, and they saw us leave the camp.

I marched in with the men afoot; a gallant show they made as they marched up High Street to the depot. Lucy and Mother Webb remained several hours until we left. I saw them watching me as I stood on the platform at the rear of the last car as long as they could see me. Their eyes swam. I kept my emotion under control enough not to melt into tears. — A pleasant ride to Bellaire; staid in the cars all night.

BELLAIRE, July 26, 1861,
Friday morning, 7:30 A. M.

DEAR BROTHER WILLIAM: — I write for you and Lucy. Please send this note to her. We were ordered at Zanesville to change our destination to this point and Grafton. Whether we are to go from Grafton to the Kanawha country or to Oakland, Maryland, is uncertain; we think Oakland is our point; we hope so. It is to hold in check a rising secession feeling and to sustain Union men. We reached here at midnight and slept in the cars until morning. All in good spirits. I will advise you as to the ultimate determination of our course.

If my pistols come to the express office, send them to me by express when you ascertain where we are. You can probably learn at the governor's office, if not direct from me. The express to the armies is very safe usually. Love to all.

Yours,

R. B. HAYES.

W. A. PLATT.

CHAPTER XV

CAMPAIGNING IN WEST VIRGINIA — 1861

JULY 27, 1861. — From Bellaire to Clarksburg in Virginia. All the way, one hundred and thirty miles, in Virginia, greeted by shouts and demonstrations of joy. The people had seen many three-months men going, leaving western Virginia for home. This, with the defeat at Washington perhaps, led the people to fear that the Union men were left to the Rebels of the eastern part of the State. Our coming relieved them and was hailed with every demonstration of joy. [Today], Saturday, at 2 P. M. [A. M.] reached Clarksburg. Worked like a Turk in the rain all the morning laying out a camp and getting it up, on a fine hill with a pretty scene before us. Clearing off towards the close of the day. Tried to dry clothes. A busy day but a jolly.

In the evening General Rosecrans came over here and ordered Lieutenant-Colonel Matthews to march at 2 A. M. with the right wing in seventy-five waggons, leaving us with left wing and baggage to move at 7 A. M. to Weston. Order of march for our column, ten pioneers, three hundred or four hundred yards in advance of main body; advance guard of thirty, one hundred yards in advance of main body; next, main body; waggon train with baggage, twenty-eight wagons; rear guard of thirty, one hundred and eighty yards in rear of wagons.

(I write one letter for all friends and want Lucy to keep all these scrawls for future reference.)

CLARKSBURG, VIRGINIA, July 27, 1861 (?) (I
believe) Saturday (I know).

DEAR WIFE: — Our second day, from Bellaire to this place, was an exceedingly happy one. We travelled about one hundred and thirty miles in Virginia, and with the exception of one

(45)

deserted village of Secessionists (Farmington), we were received everywhere with an enthusiasm I never saw anywhere before. No such great crowds turned out to meet us as we saw from Indianapolis to Cincinnati assembled to see Lincoln, but everywhere, in the corn and hay fields, in the houses, in the roads, on the hills, wherever a human being saw us, we saw such honest spontaneous demonstrations of joy as we never beheld elsewhere. Old men and women, boys and children — some fervently prayed for us, some laughed and some cried; all did something which told the story. The secret of it is, the defeat at Washington and the departure of some thousands of three-months men of Ohio and Indiana led them to fear they were left to the Rebels of eastern Virginia. We were the first three-years men filling the places of those who left. It was pleasant to see we were not invading an enemy's country but defending the people among whom we came. Our men enjoyed it beyond measure. Many had never seen a mountain; none had ever seen such a reception. They stood on top of the cars and danced and shouted with delight.

We got here in the night. General Rosecrans is with us. No other full regiment here. We march tomorrow up the mountains. All around me is confusion — sixteen hundred horses, several hundred wagons, — all the preparations for a large army. Our own men in a crowded camp putting up tents. No time for further description.

Captain McMullen will go to Columbus to return. He will get my pistols of Mr. Platt, if they come to Columbus in time.

You would enjoy such a ride as that of yesterday as much as I did. It was perfect. Now comes the hard work. Good-bye; love to all.

Affectionately,

R. B. HAYES.

P. S. — Colonel Matthews showed me a letter from his mother received at the moment of his leaving. She said she rejoiced she was the mother of seven sons all loyal and true, and that four of them were able to go to the war for the national rights.

The view from where I sit is most beautiful — long ranges of hills, a pleasant village, an extensive sweep of cultivated country, the fortified hill where an Indiana regiment prepared to defend itself against overwhelming odds, etc., etc.

Direct all letters and express matters to Clarksburg, Virginia, with my title and regiment until further directions. This is the great depot for operating in western Virginia, and all letters, etc., will be sent from here forward to me.

MRS. HAYES.

July 28. Sunday. — Busy from 4 A. M. packing baggage, striking tents, and preparing to move. Baggage enormous and extra; great delays; great stew. Our new Irish quartermaster — a failure so far. Got off about 11 A. M., in a great shower. I rode backwards and forwards; got wet; weather hot after the showers; face and nose, softened by the rain, begin to scorch; a peeling time in prospect. Still it was novel, scenery fine. Blackberries beyond all experience line the road; road good. Camped at night in a meadow by the road. Rain-storm soon followed. Many put up no tents; wearied with the day's march, they threw themselves on the ground and slept through. I got wet through trying to get them sheltered.

In the enemy's country, although all we meet are Union men. Many fancied threatening dangers in all novel sights. A broken limb in a tree top was thought to be a spy looking down into the camp; fires were seen; men riding by were scouts of the enemy, etc., etc.

July 29. Monday. — A bright, warm day. Marched yesterday fourteen miles; today, nine miles to Weston, which we reached soon after noon. A pretty county town of one thousand people or so, surrounded by hills, picturesque and lovely. Encamped on a hill looking towards the town, my tent where I now sit opening upon a sweet scene of high hills, green smooth sward, or forests. The west fork of the Monongahela flows at the bottom of the hill, just below the rear of the field officers' tents.

July 30. Tuesday. — Warm, bright morning. Damp in the tent with the fogs of the night. Hang out my duds to dry.

Have met here divers Cincinnati acquaintances and Lieutenant Conger and Dr. Rice, of Fremont. Just now a fine young first-lieutenant (Jewett of Zanesville) was accidentally shot by a gun falling on the ground out of a stack. A great hole was torn through his foot. The ball passed through three tents, barely missing several men, passed through a knapsack and bruised the leg of one of Captain McIlrath's men.

WESTON, VIRGINIA, Tuesday Morning, July 30, 1861.

DEAR UNCLE: — If you look on the map you can find this town about twenty-five miles south of Clarksburg, which is about one hundred miles east of Parkersburg on the Northwest Virginia Railroad. So much for the general location; and if you were here, you would see on a pretty sidehill facing towards and overlooking a fine large village, surrounded by lovely hills, almost mountains, covered with forest or rich greensward, a picturesque encampment, and on the summit of the hill overlooking all, the line of field officers' tents. Sitting in one of them, as [Henry] Ward Beecher sat in the barn at Lenox, I am writing you this letter.

I have seen Conger, acting assistant quartermaster of [the] Tenth Regiment. He wishes a place. I ventured to suggest that he could perhaps raise a company in your region by getting an appointment from the governor. All here praise him both as a business man and as a soldier. He must, I think, get some place. His reputation is so good with those he is associated with.

Dr. Rice also called to see me; he looks well and is no doubt an efficient man. Dr. Joe has had a consultation with him and thinks him a good officer.

We enjoy this life very much. So healthy and so pretty a country is rarely seen. After a month's campaign here the Tenth has lost no man by sickness and has but seven sick. General Rosecrans takes immediate command of us and will have us with him in his operations against Wise. We shall have mountain marches enough no doubt. So far I stand it as well as the best. . . .

This is the land of blackberries. We are a great grown-up armed blackberry party and we gather untold quantities.

Here there are nearly as many Secessionists as Union men; the women avow it openly because they are safe in doing so, but the men are merely sour and suspicious and silent. . . .

Men are at work ditching around my tent preparatory to a thunder-shower which is hanging over the mountain west of us. One of them I hear saying to his comrade: "This is the first time I ever used a spade and I don't like it too well."

But you have had enough of this incoherent talk. Colonel Scammon and Matthews have both been absent and left me in command, so that I have been exposed to numberless interruptions.

Good-bye. Direct to me by my title "Twenty-third Regiment, Ohio troops, Clarksburg, Virginia," and it will be sent me.

R. B. HAYES.

Send this to Lucy.

S. BIRCHARD.

CAMP ON WEST FORK OF MONONGAHELA RIVER, WESTON, VIRGINIA, Tuesday, P. M.,
July 30, 1861.

DEAREST: — We are in the loveliest spot for a camp you ever saw — no, lovelier than that; nothing in Ohio can equal it. It needs a mountainous region for these beauties. We do not know how long we shall stay, but we suppose it will be three or four days. We have had two days of marching — not severe marching at all; but I saw enough to show me how easily raw troops are used up by an injudicious march. Luckily we are not likely to suffer in that way. We are *probably* aiming for Gauley Bridge on the Kanawha where Wise is said to be fortified. General Rosecrans is engaged in putting troops so as to hold the principal routes leading to the point.

The people here are divided. Many of the leading ladies are Secessionists. We meet many good Union men; the other *men* are prudently quiet. Our troops behave well.

4

We have had one of those distressing accidents which occur so frequently in volunteer regiments. You may remember that a son of H. J. Jewett, of Zanesville, President of [the] Central Ohio Railroad, was on the request of his father appointed a first-lieutenant in Captain Canby's company. He joined us at Grafton in company with his father. He had served in Colonel ———'s regiment of three-months men in all the affairs in western Virginia and is very promising. A loaded gun was thrown down from a stack by a careless sentinel discharging a Minié ball through young Jewett's foot. I was with him in a moment. It is a painful and severe wound, perhaps dangerous. There is a hope he may not be crippled. He bears it well. One of his exclamations was, "Oh, if it had only been a secession ball I wouldn't have cared. Do you think you can save my leg," etc., etc. The ball after passing through his foot passed through three of McIlrath's tents, one full of men lying down. It cut the vest of one over his breast as he lay on his back and stirred the hair of another; finally passed clean through a knapsack and struck a man on the leg barely making a slight bruise and dropping down. Dr. Joe has the flattened bullet now to give to Jewett.

My horse came over the hills in good style. —— Pshaw! I wish you were here; this *is* a camp. The field officers' tents are on a high greensward hill, the other tents spreading below it in the sweetest way. As I write I can turn my head and from the entrance of the tent see the loveliest scene you can imagine. . . .

Affectionately,

R. B. HAYES.

Mrs. Hayes.

July 31. Wednesday. — Another warm, bright day. Orders from General Rosecrans direct Colonel Lytle to go with his regiment to Sutton and put this place in command of Colonel Scammon. This is supposed to indicate that we are to remain here for some weeks.

PRESIDENT LINCOLN AND OHIO SUPPORTERS IN THE WAR FOR THE UNION, 1861–1865.

SALMON P. CHASE,
Secretary of the Treasury and Chief Justice of the United States.

WILLIAM DENNISON,
War Governor of Ohio, 1860–1862, and Postmaster General.

JOHN BROUGH,
War Governor of Ohio, 1864–1865.

ABRAHAM LINCOLN,
President.

JOHN SHERMAN,
United States Senator.

EDWIN M. STANTON,
Secretary of War.

DAVID TOD,
War Governor of Ohio, 1862–1864.

BENJAMIN F. WADE,
United States Senator.

CAMP NEAR WESTON, VIRGINIA,
Wednesday, P. M., July 31, 1861.

DEAR MOTHER: — How you would enjoy sitting by my side on this beautiful hill and feasting your eyes on the sweep of hills that surrounds us. Nothing in Vermont is finer. The great majority of the people here are friendly and glad to have us here to protect them from the Secessionists. This is agreeable; it puts us in the place of protectors instead of invaders. The weather is warm, but a good breeze is blowing. The water is good; milk and blackberries abundant, and the location perfectly healthy. . . .

The village is a pretty one with many good residences and nice people. The State is, or *was,* building near where we are encamped a large lunatic asylum — an expensive and elegant structure. The war stops the work. This part of Virginia naturally belongs to the West; they are now in no way connected with eastern Virginia. The only papers reaching here from Richmond come by way of Nashville, Louisville, and Cincinnati. The courthouse and several churches are creditable buildings, and the shrubbery and walks in the private grounds are quite beautiful.

Do not allow yourself to worry if you do not hear often. I think of you often. Love to Laura and all.

Affectionately, your son,

R. B. HAYES.

MRS. SOPHIA HAYES.

[WESTON], July 31, [1861], Wednesday P. M.
DEAREST: — We are to stay here and keep in countenance the Union people for several days — or a week or more — until others come in to take our places. It is safe, which would please Mother; it is pleasant as a camping ground. I wish you were here.

I tell Mr. Schooley to bring me an India-rubber havelock and cape to keep water out of neck — or some such thing; also strong black buttons — a few — and a pair of yellow spurs, regulation style.

Young Jewett sleeps well and is in no great pain — so far doing well. His chance of saving his foot is about even — a sad case. We are to be alone in this locality; possibly we may be divided so as to occupy two or three places. Kisses for the boys.

Affectionately,

R.

MRS. HAYES.

August 1, [1861]. — Another hot, moist day; deep fogs in the night. Two gentlemen, suspected of secession proclivities, clerks of the courts, were required to take the oath of allegiance to the new State Government of Virginia and to the United States.

They say it is not always so rainy here; they lay it to the presence of our troops.

Colonel Matthews left with the five right-wing companies for Bulltown and Sutton at 1 P. M. today. I felt a little melancholy to see the fine fellows leaving us.

A year ago today was with Lucy travelling from Detroit on the Grand Trunk Railroad eastwardly for pleasure. A telegraph line is completed to this point connecting us with all the world.

Governor Wise, it is said, has continued his retreat up the Kanawha towards eastern Virginia. It is said that he has left Gauley River and burnt the bridge. If so western Virginia is now in our undisputed possession. But it is also said that General Lee is coming with a large force to look after General Rosecrans. I suspect that all the movements of the Southern army look to operations about Washington and Baltimore, and that all movements of troops in other directions are merely feints.

WESTON, August 1, 1861.

DEAREST: — Do you remember a year ago today we were riding on the Grand Trunk Railroad from Detroit by Sarnia eastwardly? Jolly times those. If you were here, these would be as pleasant. The water in the river below our camp flows past you in the Ohio; in these low water days, about a month after they leave here.

We are now in telegraphic communication with the world. Dr. Joe receives dispatches about medicines and Colonel Scammon about military matters from Columbus and Cincinnati. We had the two county court clerks before the colonel taking the oath of allegiance to the United States and to the new Government of Virginia. They squirmed a little, but were required to do it or go to Camp Chase.

Colonel Matthews left this noon with five companies — right wing — for Sutton, a place forty-four miles south of this place. We suspect that Wise has left western Virginia. If so, our campaigning here is likely to be pacific and uninteresting.

August 2. — I have been out to report myself at reveille, and not feeling like resuming my nap, am seated on my trunk jotting down these lines to my darling. Colonel Jewett arrived last night from Zanesville. He finds his boy doing well. It is still very uncertain what is to be the result. It is probable that no amputation will be necessary, and there is hope that he may not be more than very slightly crippled, He will be unable to use his foot, however, for perhaps months.

Our news is that Wise has continued his retreat burning the bridges after him. This confirms our suspicions as to his abandoning all west of the mountains. There is, however, a report from the East that General Lee is to be sent out here to look after General Rosecrans, with a considerable force. I do not believe it, but if so, we shall have lively times. Colonel Ammen with the Twenty-fourth is reported in our neighborhood. We shall be glad to be with them again.

Puds, here it is Saturday, the 3d, and my foolishness isn't off yet and won't be until Monday. It is so hot and pleasant. I am so lazy and good-natured. Joe says, "I wish Webb was here"; I say, I wish you were all here. We may be ordered to move any hour, and it may be [we] shall be here a week hence. We have got our camp into good order — clean and pretty. Joe was pretty sick last night, but is under a nice shade today, as lazy and comfortable as possible. The effect is curious of this fine mountain air. Everybody complains of heat, but everybody is in a laughing humor. No grumbling reaches me today.

I have called on divers leading lawyers and politicians, generally Union men, and find them agreeable people. The courthouse here is a good one and is used as a hospital for all these regiments. About one hundred sick are there. When Joe gets perfectly well, which I advise him not to do, he will have charge of all of them. We have four or six there. . . .

Very affectionately, your

R.

"Love me?" I have heard nothing from Ohio except an occasional newspaper. Write about Uncle and everybody. Our men sing beautifully tonight.

Mrs. Hayes.

August 2, 1861. — A. M. fired pistol with Captain Zimmerman and P. M. Enfield rifle with Captain Sperry. My pistol shooting rather poor. Rifle shooting at one hundred yards good, at three hundred yards, tolerable. Weather hot. In the evening passed the sentinels to try them, back and forth several times. Found them generally defective; they took instruction kindly and I hope they may do well yet.

August 3, 1861. — Called on James T. Jackson, a Secessionist, for a map of Virginia — one of the Board of Public Works maps. He said he once had one but his brother had sold it to a captain in [the] Seventh Regiment. Called then on William E. Arnold, a lawyer and Union man. He offered every facility for getting information and gave such as he could; also lent us a good map. Hottest day yet. Dr. Joe ailing. Young Jewett doing well, but getting tired and sore.

August 4. Sunday. — Visited the hospital. It is airy and comfortable — the court-house of the county, a large good building. The judge's bench was full of invalids, convalescent, busily writing letters to friends at home. Within the bar and on the benches provided for the public were laid straw bedticks in some confusion, but comfortable. A side room contained the very sick, seven or eight in number. The total inmates about seventy-five. Most of them are able to walk about and are improving;

very few are likely to die there. One poor fellow, uncomplaining and serene, with a good American face, is a German tailor, Fifth Street, Cincinnati; speaks little English, was reading a history of the Reformation in German. I inquired his difficulty. He had been shot by the accidental discharge of a musket falling from a stack; a ball and several buckshot pierced his body. He will recover probably. My sympathies were touched for a handsome young Canadian, Scotch or English. He had measles and caught cold. A hacking cough was perhaps taking his life. Nobody from the village calls to see them!

A hot day but some breeze. We hear that Colonel Matthews with the right wing was, on the morning of the third day from here, near Bulltown, twenty-seven miles distant. Governor Wise is somewhere near Lewisburg in Greenbrier County. Cox [General J. D.] is in no condition to engage him and I hope will not do it. I rather hope we shall raise a large force and push on towards Lynchburg and east Tennessee. Jewettt is doing well.

WESTON, VIRGINIA, August 4, 1861.

DEAR MOTHER: — I write often now, as we soon pass out of reach of mails. We hear the news by telegraph here now from all the home towns, but mails are uncertain and irregular. We are very healthy, but the weather is hotter than any I have known in a great while. Our wounded lieutenant, Jewett, is doing well. His father is here nursing him. The fine large hospital for all this region of country, having one hundred patients belonging to different regiments, is in charge of Dr. Joe. It is the courthouse. The people here do not find us much of a nuisance. Of course, in some respects we are so, but all things considered, the best of the people like to see us. I mean to go to church this pleasant Sunday. My only clerical acquaintance here is an intelligent Catholic priest who called to see Colonel Scammon. I have been cross-examining a couple of prisoners — one a Methodist preacher — both fair sort of men, and I hope not guilty of any improper acts. Good-bye.

Affectionately,

R. B. HAYES.

MRS. SOPHIA HAYES.

NEAR WESTON, VIRGINIA, August 4, 1861.

DEAR LAURA: — As we ride about this exceedingly pretty country and through this reasonably decent village, I am reminded of young ladies in Ohio by occasionally meeting a damsel wearing a stars-and-stripes apron, or by seeing one who turns up her nose at the said stars, etc.

We are leading camp life again — watching Secessionists, studying geography, sending and receiving scouts and couriers and sich like. Colonel Matthews has gone with the five companies of the right wing forty-four miles further up into the hills. We shall follow him if there are any hostile signs up there, and he will return to us if such sign fail him.

You and Jeanie A— have been of use. The bandages are used in dressing the shocking wound of young Jewett of Zanesville — a lieutenant, handsome, gallant, and intelligent. Just the person you would wish to serve in this way. Dr. Joe hopes he will not be crippled. At first it seemed that he must lose his foot; but your bandages or something else are bringing him up. It will be perhaps months before he can walk.

The court-house here (about like yours) is a hospital for the sick and wounded of all the regiments hereabouts. It would be a glorious thing if some Florence Nightingales would come here. They could be immensely useful, and at the same time live pleasantly in a pretty mountain village, safe as a bug in a rug. Won't you come? It is easy getting here and cheap staying. Too hot under canvas to write much. Love to all.

Your uncle,

R.

MISS LAURA PLATT,
   Columbus.

August 5. — Cloudy and showery and sunny at intervals this Monday morning. Went out shooting pistol with Adjutant C. W. Fisher. No good shooting by either. I did the worst, pistol dirty — cleaned it. — More couriers, more rumors of Wise down towards Greenbrier County.

August 6. — Warm, beautiful weather. A busy day, settling disputes between citizens and their quarrels. I held a sort of police court. Dr. Joe also decided cases. The parties under arrest, we hear their stories and discharge or put on bread and water as the case seems to require. All local tribunals suppressed or discontinued. We also are full of courier and express duty. Colonel Withers, a Union citizen of the old-fashioned *Intelligencer* reading sort, called. He is a true patriot. We sent out a courier to meet Colonel Ammen with the Twenty-fourth, preparatory to greeting and escorting him. But he isn't coming yet. Colonel Scammon is policing and disciplining in a good way. The colonel improves. As soon as taps sounds he has the lights put out and all talk suppressed.

When we came to Weston, Colonel Lytle was here with four companies. The Seventeenth returning home (three-months men) passed through here about the second or third. The Nineteenth about the first. Colonel E. B. Tyler with the Seventh is beyond Sutton. Colonel Bosley with the Sixth is at Beverly.

WESTON, VIRGINIA, Tuesday P. M., August 6, 1861.

DEAR MOTHER: — I have just read your letter, with Brother William's of the 2nd, — the first I have had from anybody since we came to Virginia. I am sitting in my tent looking out on the same beautiful scene I have so often referred to. It is a bright and very warm afternoon, but a clear, healthful mountain air which it is a happiness to breathe. . . .

My horse shows a little weakness in the fore shoulders, but as he can probably work well in an ambulance, I can exchange him for a good government horse, if he gets worse. We have plenty of business. A good deal of it is a sort of law business. As all civil authority is at an end, it is our duty to keep the peace and do justice between the citizens, who, in these irregular times, are perhaps a little more pugnacious than usual. Dr. Joe and I, under direction of the colonel, held courts on divers cases all the forenoon. It was rather amusing, and I think we dispensed very exact justice. As there is no appeal, a case decided is for good and all.

I am so glad you and Uncle are both getting well. If Uncle wishes to travel, and we remain here, he couldn't please himself better than by a trip this way. He would enjoy a few days very much in our camp, or at the hotel in the village.

Young Jewett leaves with his father for Zanesville tonight. I hope he will stand the trip well. I will hand them this letter to mail when they get out of these woods. Send me sometime a neat little New Testament. I have nothing of the sort. I have clothes enough. I am cut short by business. Good-bye.

Affectionately,

R. B. HAYES.

MRS. SOPHIA HAYES.

August 7, Wednesday. — Another bright, warm day. With Adjutant Fisher pistol shooting this A. M. Tolerably good firing. Last night a picket shot through the hand; said he fired twice at his assailant; doubted. Supposed to be an accidental wounding. Letters from Ohio.

August 8. Thursday. — Rumors of the approach of a great army under Lee from eastern Virginia are still rife. The enemy is said to be near Monterey, the other side of the Alleghanies and aiming to come in this direction to reoccupy western Virginia, capture our stores, and to dash the war if possible into Ohio. The United States ought promptly to push into western Virginia an army of at least fifty thousand men to repel any such attack if made and to push on to the railroad leading from Richmond southwesterly through Lynchburg towards east Tennessee. This would cut off Richmond from the southwestern States and be otherwise useful. Horsemen and waggons are now passing towards Bulltown. This is the hottest day yet; it must rain before night.

WESTON, VIRGINIA, August 8, 1861.

DEAR UNCLE: — I am glad to learn by a letter from Mother that you are getting well enough to ride about town. I hope you will continue to gain. If you should want to take a short trip this fall, I am not sure but a journey this way would be as enjoyable as any you could make. By getting a note from Governor Dennison, you could travel on railroad (now run by the Government) to Clarksburg, and thence, there are all sorts of conveyances, from a teetering ambulance to an old-fashioned Pennsylvania six-horse waggon.

Our regiment is divided for the present. One half under Colonel Matthews has gone forty-four miles south. We remain in charge of a great supply depot, and charged with keeping in order the turbulent of this region. The Union men are the most numerous, but the other side is the more wealthy and noisy. We are kept busy enough with them.

This town is about as large as Fremont was ten years ago, has a fine court-house and other county buildings. A lunatic asylum for the State of great size was building when the war broke out. It is a healthy hilly country, very picturesque, and hotter today than the Cincinnati landing. We are so busy that we do not complain much of the tediousness of camp life. We are now constantly hearing of the approach of General Lee from eastern Virginia with a force large enough to drive us out and capture all our stores, if one-fourth that is told is true. He is said to be about seventy-five miles southeast of us in the mountains. Whether there is truth in it or not, I have no doubt that troops will be urged into this region to hold the country. At any rate, as it is on the route to east Tennessee, and on a route to cut off the railroads from the southwest, I am sure there ought to be a splendid Union army assembled here. I suppose it will be done.

Lucy and the boys are in Pickaway County. Dr. Jim was taken prisoner at Manassas, but escaped; lost his carpet-sack, but captured a secession horse which he brought home. Dr. Joe enjoys it well. Colonel Scammon is an agreeable gentleman to associate with. We have a great deal of amusement. Dr. Joe visits the secession folks, and reports a great many good things. They say that in two weeks they will see us scattering like sheep before the great army of Lee and Wise.

When you write, direct to me, "Twenty-third Regiment, Ohio Volunteers, Clarksburg, Virginia," and it will be sent wherever

I may chance to be. We are now connected by telegraph with the whole country. A dispatch to or from Weston, is more certain of delivery than a letter. Love to all.

Sincerely,

R. B. HAYES.

S. BIRCHARD.

August 9. Friday. — The colonel is out of humor with Lieutenant Rice for letting men on guard go to their tents to sleep and scolds him severely in the presence of his men. A little less grumbling and more instruction would improve the regiment faster. The men are disconcerted whenever the colonel approaches; they expect to be pitched into about something. A good man, but impatient and fault-finding; in short, he is out of health, nervous system out of order. Would he had sound health, and all would go well. He gives no instruction either in drill or other military duties but fritters away his time on little details which properly belong to clerks and inferior officers. — Begun to rain at noon, refreshing rather.

Our men returning from Sutton report our right wing under Lieutenant-Colonel Matthews gone on to Summersville. Also that a party in ambush fired on two companies of Colonel Lytle's regiment, killing one and wounding four. This sort of murder must be stopped. The colonel is busy issuing passes to citizens, the patrol or picquets having been ordered to stop all persons travelling on the roads without passes. This must be a great annoyance to the inhabitants. Is there enough benefit to be gained for all the hate we shall stir up by it?

The mother of our adjutant at Camp Chase seeing a boy walking up and down on his sentinel's beat took pity on him, sent him out a glass of wine and a piece of cake with a stool to sit on while he ate and drank. She told him not to keep walking so, to sit down and rest! She also advised him to resign!

More rumors of the approach of Lee with fifteen thousand men to attack our forces at Buchanan [Buckhannon]. Lieutenant Reichenbach with his party of twenty men marched yesterday twenty-eight miles and today, by noon, fifteen miles.

Joe Holt* makes the best war speeches of any man in the land. It always braces my nerves and stirs my heart when I read them. At Camp Joe Holt, near Louisville, he said: "Since the sword flamed over the portals of Paradise until now, it has been drawn in no holier cause than that in which you are engaged."

CAMP NEAR WESTON, VIRGINIA, August 9, 1861.

Friday Afternoon.

DEAREST: — I have just read your letter postmarked the 5th at Kingston. Right pleased with you. Very happy to get your good letter. It has been bright, warm (hot) weather since Sunday, but today at noon a fine rain began to fall, and this afternoon I was loafing about in the tents, hard up for occupation. Lying alone in my tent, your letter came in with one from Uncle written Sunday. Wasn't it so lucky? I've nothing to tell you, I believe. Dr. Joe is well — perfectly — again; busy changing his hospital from the court-house and jail to a secession church which doesn't run now. The colonel is busy giving passes to citizens wishing to travel roads guarded by our picquets.

Colonel Matthews under Colonel Tyler has gone to Summersville about seventy miles south of this. They are looking for Wise. In the meantime we have rumors that General Lee is marching over the mountains to push the Union forces in this region out of the State, and to seize the stores so abundantly gathered hereabouts. We have no means of knowing the truth here; if there is anything in it, we shall be called to Buchanan [Buckhannon], sixteen miles east, where the first attack is expected. There is a little more activity among the enemy in this quarter since these rumors became rife. Our party from the

---

*Joseph Holt, born in Breckinridge County, Kentucky, January 6, 1807; died in Washington, August 1, 1894. Famous as a jurist and an orator. He was Postmaster-General in Buchanan's Cabinet for a time and in 1860, when John B. Flood resigned, he became Secretary of War. He was a vigorous Union man, urging his fellow Kentuckians "to fly to the rescue of their country before it is everlastingly too late." In September, 1862, President Lincoln appointed him Judge-Advocate General of the army, in which capacity he served long with great distinction.

south, returning today, report that an attack was made up the road on two companies of Colonel Lytle's men by a party in ambush, who fired one volley and ran off into the hills. One man killed and four wounded. Captain Gaines (our prosecutor) called to see me last night. His company is detached from his regiment, guarding a party putting up telegraph wires. Mr. Schooley returned from Cincinnati with late news last night. He says, it [was] so lonely he really wished to get back to camp. I am sorry to have Colonel Matthews and the right wing gone, but except that we are doing nicely. Colonel Scammon is in better health and things go on very smoothly.

The soldiers fare very well here, and stand in little need of sympathy, but when I have an opportunity to smooth matters for them, I try to do it, always remembering how you would wish it done. What a good heart you have, darling. I shall try to be as good as you would like me to be.

Young Jewett got safely home. He is likely to have a long and serious time getting well, but will probably be very slightly, if at all, crippled. Colonel Ammen is at Clarksburg. If we have any force sent against us, we shall be with him; otherwise, not at present.

I am glad you are visiting at Aunt Margaret's this hot weather. Do you recollect when we were up [the] Saguenay a year ago at this time? Here Colonel Scammon came in full of pleasant gossip, feeling happy with letters from his wife and daughters. No more chance to write in time for tonight's mail. Continue to address me at Clarksburg until I direct otherwise. Love to all at Elmwood. Kiss the boys all around.

Affectionately,

R. B. Hayes.

Mrs. Hayes.

———————

August 10. Saturday. — Rained a good part of the night. We learned that while the right wing of our regiment occupied the court-house at Sutton, many records, etc., etc., were torn up. It is said the old clerk cried when he saw what had been done. Disgraceful! What a stigma on our regiment if true! We have had and deserved to have a good name for our orderly conduct, respect for rights of citizens, etc., etc. I hope nothing has been done to forfeit our place.

August 11. Sunday. — Raining this morning, very warm. Arrested, on complaint of a Union man, H. T. Martin, a secession editor, who is charged with holding communication with James and William Bennett, leaders of a guerrilla party. He was formerly from Ohio. Is a Southern state's-right Democrat in talk, and makes a merit of holding secession opinions. Having been engaged in getting up troops for the Southern army, the colonel will probably send him to Ohio.

Colonel Lytle's men fired on near Bulltown; one killed, four wounded; guerrilla party in the hills out of reach. Our regiment did not destroy records. We have sent two captains and eighty men after the guerrillas.

August 12. Monday. — Showery all day. Sent to Clarksburg H. T. Martin. He will probably be sent to Columbus for safe keeping. I gave him a letter to my brother-in-law to insure him attention there in case he should need. It is impossible to avoid mistakes in these cases. Union men may make charges merely to gratify personal animosity, knowing that in the nature of things a full investigation is impossible.

During Monday night a squad of the Tenth Regiment returned from the Buckhannon road with the body of one of the wild men of the mountains found in this country. He followed their regiment, shooting at them from the hills. They took him in the Bulltown region. He wore neither hat nor shoes, was of gigantic size — weighing two hundred and thirty pounds; had long hooked toes, fitted to climb — a very monster. They probably killed him after taking him prisoner in cold blood — perhaps after a sort of trial. They say he was attempting to escape.

WESTON, VIRGINIA, August 12, 1861.

DEAR UNCLE: — We are still getting on nicely. We have a good deal more excitement now than usual. Wagon and cattle trains and small parties are fired on by guerrillas from the hills on two of the roads leading from here. Dr. Joe has about eight or ten in charge who have been wounded in this way. Two only have been killed. None in our regiment. The men all laugh at "squirrel guns" and the wounds they make. Several would have been killed if shot in the same part by the conical balls of our military guns. The "deadly rifle" of olden times shoots too small a bullet, and is too short in its range; but as Cassio says, it is often "sufficient." We send out parties who bring in prisoners — sometimes the right men, sometimes not. All this keeps up a stir. In a week or two we shall get up a regular system of scouring the country to get rid of these rascals. The Union men here hate and fear them more than our men.

The threatened invasion by Lee from eastern Virginia hangs fire. They will hardly venture in, unless they come in a few days, as we are daily getting stronger. I hope you are still getting better.

Good-bye,

R. B. HAYES.

S. BIRCHARD.

August 13. — Still rain. My horse hitched to a tree on the brow of a hill very near my tent broke loose during the night, and, it is said, rolled down the steep hill and swam the river. This morning he was seen trotting about in high feather on the opposite side of the river. He was caught and brought back *unhurt,* to the surprise of all who saw the place he must have gone down. Our right wing has been sent for to return to Bulltown. Captains Drake and Woodward who are out guerrilla hunting are still absent and not heard from for twenty-four hours. — P. M. Still raining. Captains Drake and Woodward have returned. They caught two of the pickets of the guerrilla party they were after but failed in surprising them, owing to a boy who gave information of their coming. They found a few good Union men; the mass of the people most ignorant. [They] describe the country in the edge of Webster County as precipitous and difficult; the people timid but cunning. They also brought two other prisoners, men who have been in the secession army.

August 14. Wednesday. — The weather has changed to cool, and although the sky is still clouded I hope this long rain is now over. Our prisoners turn out to be Hezekiah and Granville Bennett, cousins of the notorious James and William Bennett, aged forty-nine and twenty-two, father and son, and Moss and George W. Brothers, aged fifty-eight and forty-eight. Our information is not definite as to their conduct. One or more of them belonged to the Southern army, and all are accused by their Union neighbors with divers acts of violence against law-and-order citizens.

Last evening Lieutenant Milroy came over from Glenville reporting that Captain R. B. Moore feared an attack from three companies of well armed Secessionists in the region west of them, say Spencer, and was fortifying himself. The people immediately around him are friendly, he having conducted himself with great prudence and good sense and by kindness and justice made friends of the people of all parties.

August 15. Thursday. — A bright, lovely day and the prettiest evening of the month. The bright moonlight exhibits the landscape enough to show its loveliness and the lights and shadows. The hills and woods are very picturesque. It makes me long for wife and boys and friends behind. How Lute would enjoy roaming with me through camp tonight.

More rumors of attacks by guerrillas, or "bushwhackers" as they are here called, on our couriers and trains. A courier and captain and some wagoners are reported killed or taken below Sutton.

My box containing pistols and sash, etc., by mistake sent from Clarksburg to Buckhannon. Made arrangements to send Lieutenant Richardson and two men with ambulance after it.

Weston, Virginia, August 15, 1861.
Thursday Morning.

Dearest L — : — We had four days of rain ending yesterday morning — such rain as this country of hills and mountains can afford. It was gloomy and uncomfortable but no harm was done.

It cleared off beautifully yesterday morning and the weather has been most delicious since. This is a healthful region. Nobody seriously sick and almost everybody outrageously healthy. I never was better. It is a luxury to breathe. Dr. Joe — but don't he go into the corn? He has it three times a day, reminding me of Northampton a year ago and your order for supper on our return from Mount Holyoke.

Our regiment has had divers duties which keep up excitement enough to prevent us from stagnating. Colonel Matthews and right wing is fifty miles south. Captain Drake and Captain Woodward, with their companies, spent the four rainy days scouring the steepest hills and deepest gullies for the rascals who waylay our couriers and wagon trains. They captured three or four of the underlings, but the leaders and main party dodged them. Captain Zimmerman and his company have gone west forty miles to escort provisions to Colonel Moor (Second German Regiment of Cincinnati in which Markbreit is Lieutenant) and to clean out an infected neighborhood between here and there. A sergeant and six men are at Clarksburg escorting a prisoner destined for Columbus. Lieutenant Rice and twenty men are escorting cattle for Colonel Tyler's command south of here. A part of our cavalry are gone west to escort a captain and the surgeon of the Tenth to Glenville, thirty-seven miles west. On Saturday I go with Captain Drake's company to meet Captain Zimmerman's company returning from the west, and with the two companies, to go into the hills to the south to hunt for a guerrilla band who are annoying Union men in that vicinity. I shall be gone almost a week so you will not hear from me for some time. The telegraph is now extended south to a station near where I am going to operate, so that we are in reach of humanity by telegraph but not by mail.

Dr. Joe has got the hospital in good condition. A church (Methodist South) in place of the court-house for the merely comfortable, and a private house for the very sick. None of our regiment are seriously ill. The sick are devolved upon us from other regiments — chiefly lung complaints developed by marching, measles, or exposure. Very few, if any, taken here. Divers humane old ladies furnish knickknacks to the hospital and make glad the poor fellows with such comforts as women can best provide.

We find plenty of good Union men, and most of our expeditions are aided by them. They show a good spirit in our behalf. A large part of our friends in the mountains are the well-to-do people of their neighborhoods and usually are Methodists or other orderly citizens.

Good-bye, dearest. I love you very much. Kiss the boys and love to all. Tell Webby that during the rain the other night, dark as pitch, my horse, Webb, fell down the hill back of the camp into the river. Swam over to the opposite shore, and at daylight we saw him frisking about in great excitement trying to get back to his companion Birch. When we got him he was not hurt or scratched even. He stumbles a little, which doesn't do for a riding horse, so I have taken a government horse which looks very much like him; same color and size but not quite so pretty, and given Webb to Uncle Joe for an ambulance horse. I shall call my new horse Webb, so there are to be two Webbys in the regiment. My next horse I shall call Ruddy. Love to Grandma.

Affectionately,

R.

Mrs. Hayes.

August 16. Friday. — A morning of small excitements. A wagon train stopped on its way towards Sutton to search for arms or ammunition concealed in boxes of provisions. . . . Drake, Captain, and Woodward search train in vain for contraband.

August 17. Saturday. — Dispatches came last [night] from Colonel Matthews. He can't return as ordered for fear of losing his command between Summersville and Sutton; rumors of Wise, etc., etc. Colonels Tyler and Smith go with him nine miles back towards Gauley Bridge to fortify. The colonel thinks this is a mistake of judgment and is disgusted with it. I think Colonel Scammon is right.

Lieutenant Rice's men report that three men named Stout were taken near Jacksonville by some of Captain Gaines' men and part of his command and that afterwards Gaines' men killed them, alleging orders of Captain Gaines, etc., etc. This is too bad. If any of my men kill prisoners, I'll kill them.

Captain McMullen with four mountain howitzers arrived this morning — 12-pounders. Good! My horse, not Webb first but Webb second, by hard riding foundered or stiffened. *Mem.:* — Lend no horse; see always that your horse is properly cared for, especially after a hard ride.

HEADQUARTERS 23D REG'T, O. V. INF., U. S. A.,
August 17, 1861. -

DEAR UNCLE: — We are kept very busy, hunting up guerrillas, escorting trains, etc., etc. Attacking parties are constantly met on the roads in the mountains, and small stations are surrounded and penned up. We send daily parties of from ten to one hundred on these expeditions, distances of from ten to forty miles. Union men persecuted for opinion's sake are the informers. The Secessionists in this region are the wealthy and educated, who do nothing openly, and the vagabonds, criminals, and ignorant barbarians of the country; while the Union men are the middle classes — the law-and-order, well-behaved folks. Persecutions are common, killings not rare, robberies an every-day occurrence.

Some bands of Rebels are so strong that we are really in doubt whether they are guerrillas or parts of Wise's army coming in to drive us out. The Secessionists are boastful, telling of great forces which are coming. Altogether, it is stirring times just now. Lieutenant-Colonel Matthews is nearly one hundred miles south of us with half our regiment, and is not strong enough to risk returning to us. With Colonels Tyler and Smith, he will fortify near Gauley Bridge on [the] Kanawha.

Dr. Rice is here sick in charge of Dr. Joe. He got in safely from a post that was invested about thirty miles west. He will get well, but has been very sick. This is the healthiest country in the world. I have not been in such robust health for a great while. My horse is not tough enough for this service. I had better have taken Ned Jr., I suspect, although there is no telling. The strongest horses seem to fail frequently when rackabones stand it well. The Government has a good many horses, and I use them at pleasure. When I find one that will do, I shall keep it. . . .

Sincerely,

R. B. HAYES.

S. BIRCHARD.

WESTON, VIRGINIA, August 17, 1861.

DEAR MOTHER: — Nothing new to tell you. We are kept more busy than heretofore with watching and hunting after the robbers who are plundering the Union men in our neighborhood. We have rumors of invading forces from eastern Virginia strong enough to drive us out, but we know nothing definite about them. Captain McMullen arrived safely with my box. His company of artillery is a great addition to our strength.

Our men are very healthy and busy enough to keep them out of mischief. Dr. Joe finds a number of old ladies who do all in their power to make our sick soldiers comfortable. One poor fellow who was thought to be gone with consumption is picking up under their nursing and strengthening food, and will, perhaps, get well. None of our regiment are seriously ill. We were never in so healthy a country. . . . .

The war brings out the good and evil of Virginia. Some of the best and some of the worst characters I ever heard of, have come under our notice during the last fortnight. It is not likely that we shall move from here for some weeks. We are required to send expeditions to protect Union neighborhoods and wagon trains, and to drive off scamps almost every day. We are probably doing some good to the better sort of people in this country, besides the general good which we are supposed to be doing in the cause of the country.

My love to all. — Affectionately,

R. B. HAYES.

MRS. SOPHIA HAYES.

HEADQUARTERS, 23D REG'T, O. V. INF., U. S. A.,
August 17, 1861.

DEAREST: — Your letter to Dr. Joe did me much good. Bless the boys. I love to read your talk about them.

I had just started this letter when a dispatch came from Captain Zimmerman. He had a little brush with some guerrillas in the mountains twenty-five miles from here and had three men wounded. This is the first blood of our regiment shed in fight. He scattered the rascals without difficulty, making some prisoners. We have had a picquet wounded on guard and accidental wounding but no fighting blood-letting before. This is the expedition I expected to go with when I wrote you last, but the accounts of the enemy not justifying the sending of more than one company, I was not sent.

There is a general rising among the Rebels. They rob and murder the Union men, and the latter come to us for help. We meet numbers of most excellent people. We have out all the time from two to six parties of from ten to seventy-five or one hundred men on scouting duty. There are some bloody deeds done in these hills, and not all on one side. We are made happy today by the arrival of Captain McMullen with an excellent company of artillery — four mountain howitzers and complete equipments. They will be exceedingly useful. Lieutenant-Colonel Matthews is nearly one hundred miles south of us with Colonel Tyler and others. The road between here and there is so infested with "bushwhackers" that we have no communication with him except by way of Gallipolis in Ohio. He has been ordered to return here but deems it unsafe to attempt it.

Colonel Scammon has fallen in love with Joe. He says if his qualities were known he would get a high place in the Regular Army medical staff, and brags on him perpetually. We have very few of our own men sick, but numbers in the hospital of other regiments.

My new horse doesn't turn out any tougher than the other. But Captain McMullen says he has one which I am to try tonight. I shall get a "Webby" that can stand hard work and poor fare one of these days.

How about the pants? If they are reasonably good blue, put a light blue stripe down the outside seam and send them to me when you have a chance. I don't care about the color. The blue stripe is enough uniform for this latitude. Hard service for duds. I am well supplied — rather too much of most things.

August 18. Sunday P. M. — Since writing the above we have received word that the enemy in force is coming towards us through the mountains to the southeast, and have been ordered to prepare three days' rations and to be ready to march at a moment's notice to attack the enemy. I am all ready. My little knapsack contains a flannel shirt, one of those you gave me, two pairs of socks, a pair of drawers, a towel, the what-you-may-call-it you made for me to hold scissors, etc., etc. This is enough. We are to go without tents or cooking utensils. A part of Colonel Moor's Second German Regiment are to go with us. Markbreit is among them. They reached here last night.

It will be a stirring time if we go, and the result of it all by no means clear. I feel no apprehension — no presentiment of evil, but at any rate you know how I love you and the dear boys and Grandma and all will take care that I am not forgotten. You will know by telegraph long before this reaches you what comes of the anticipated movements. I suspect we are misinformed. At any rate, good-bye, darling. Kisses for all.

Affectionately,

R.

Mrs. Hayes.

August 18. Sunday. — Last night, about ten or eleven, five companies of Colonel Moor's (Second German Regiment) Twenty-eighth Regiment arrived from Clarksburg under Lieutenant-Colonel Becker. My partner, L. Markbreit, is sergeant-major. This morning, raining hard. Exciting rumors and news. A Tennessee regiment and force coming through the mountains east of Sutton — a battery of four guns, one thirty-two-pounder!! What an anchor to drag through the hills! Absurd! Danger of all provisions below here with vast stores being taken by the enemy. We are ordered to cook three days' rations and be ready, to move at a moment's warning, with forty rounds of ammunition. All trains on the route to Sutton are ordered back or to take the way to Buchanan [Buckhannon] via Frenchtown. Eighty thousand rations are ordered to same place from here. All is war. I pack my portmanteau and prepare to move. Oh, for a horse which wouldn't founder, or get lame, or stumble! At night no order to move yet.

August 19. Monday. — No more rumors. A tolerably pretty day. At 12 M. [midnight] got orders to quietly strike tents and with three days' rations and the minimum amount of baggage move to Buckhannon. Two companies, Captain Drake's and Captain Zimmerman's, had just returned from a scouting expedition to Walkersville, etc. No rest yet. After a world of confusion, aggravated by an incompetent quartermaster, we got off at daylight.

August 20. Tuesday. — After marching three miles we stopped for water and to let the teams come up. One man reclining was accidentally shot by another hitting his foot against the hammer of a musket. Poor Carr received the ball in the heel of his shoe; it passed up his leg, grazing it merely, grazed his body and arm and shoulder, and left him without a serious wound! Fortunate. Reached Buckhannon about 3:30 P. M. — so sleepy; no rest or sleep the night before. Stopped at noon — got good bread and milk, honey and blackberry jam, and slept nearly an hour in a barn. Buckhannon a pretty place.

August 21. — Changed camping place at Buckhannon to a fine spot one and one-half miles on road to Cheat Mountain. Got settled with McMullen's Battery just as rain set in at night. Had letters from Jim and Will Scott and Uncle George.

BUCKHANNON, VIRGINIA, August 21, 1861.

DEAR MOTHER: — You may send this letter, showing my whereabouts, to Lucy. I have no time to write much. On Sunday night, about 12 o'clock, we were ordered to quietly pack and march rapidly to this place. Some of our men had just returned from long scouting expeditions. They were weary with marching over the hills in rain and mud, and here was another march without sleeping. It was borne cheerfully — the men supposing it was to meet an enemy.

We find this a lovely spot, superior in some respects to the scenery about Weston. We have a beautiful camp about one and one-half miles from the village. There are here parts of five regiments — all but this from Cincinnati. Men are constantly arriving, showing the rapid concentration at this point of a large body of troops. We are ignorant of its purpose, but suppose it to be for service. We are all so healthy. I meet many Cincinnati friends and enjoy the greetings.

I received a letter from Uncle, directed to Clarksburg. I suppose that is still the best place to direct my letters. Write often. Let Uncle know where I am and how lately you have heard from me. Love to all.

Affectionately,

R. B. HAYES.

MRS. SOPHIA HAYES.

[*August*] *22. Thursday.* — At our nice camp. P. M. rained and blew violently. In the midst of it we got orders from General Rosecrans to prepare to march to Beverly. "Early" in the morning would do. Slept in my wet boots. Wrote home and to mother and Uncle.

BUCKHANNON, August 22, 1861.

DEAR JIM: — I have written hastily to Mr. Warren. I hope he will not be so much disturbed after he reflects on matters. Have you had a formal application before the governor for a place? It should be done by *yourself or by a friend in person.* I suppose examination may be required. If so, attend to it. Dr. Joe is well. We are expecting an enemy soon.

Sincerely,

R. B. HAYES.

DR. JAMES D. WEBB.

BUCKHANNON, VIRGINIA, August 22, 1861.

DEAREST: — It is a cold, rainy, dismal night. We are all preparing for an early march. I have made up a large bundle of duds — all good of course — which must be left here, to be got possibly some day but not probably. All are cut down to regulation baggage. Many trunks will stop here. A tailor sits on one end of my cot sewing fixings. All is confusion. The men are singing jolly tunes. Our colonel takes his half regiment, the left wing, and half of McCook's Germans, and we push off for the supposed point of the enemy's approach. We shall stop and camp at Beverly a while, and then move as circumstances require.

How are the dear boys? Will Scott writes me that he goes into the Kentucky Union regiments.

Good-bye, darling. Joe wishes to write and wants my pen.

Affectionately,

R. B. HAYES.

MRS. HAYES.

Friday 23. — Clear, bright day; mud and water in the road but a bracing air and blue sky overhead. Men marched with spirit. Lovely mountain views and clear mountain streams always in sight. Camped on the mountainside in the road; no tents pitched. Colonel and Dr. Joe slept in ambulance. I fixed up our cots under the blue canopy, near a roaring mountain stream, and with Adjutant Fisher watched the bright star near the Great Bear, perhaps one of that constellation, which I conjectured was Arcturus, until the moon came in sight. Slept in snatches and was refreshed.

Saturday 24. — Doctor and I laughed at a soldier who said it was Saturday. We thought it was Thursday. The finest day's march yet. Streams, mountain views, and invigorating air! Reached Buckhannon [Beverly] at 2 P. M.; greeted by friends in the Guthries warmly — Captain Erwin, Captain Bense, Captains Tinker, Clark. Saw Tatem, sick, Charles Richards, Tom Royse, and others. Danger here; men killed and an enemy coming or near Cheat River. Ambulance guide and men of

"Guthries" killed. We camped on a pretty spot. Captain Mc-Mullen's howitzers and one-half of McCook's regiment with us on the march. Ours the only band here.

BEVERLY, VIRGINIA, August, Saturday, 24 or 23, 1861.

DEAREST: — Your letters are all directed right — to Clarksburg, Virginia — got one from you, one from Uncle and one from Mother with a nice Testament today.

We marched from Buckhannon as I wrote you; but the rain stopped, the air was delicious, the mountain scenery beautiful. We camped at night in the hills without tents. I looked up at the stars and moon — nothing between me and sky — and thought of you all. Today had a lovely march in the mountains, was at the camp of the enemy on Rich Mountain and on the battlefield. Reached here today. Saw Captain Erwin and friends enough. It is pleasant. We had one-half of our regiment, one-half of McCook's German regiment and McMullen's Field Battery. Joe and I led the column. The Guthrie Greys greeted us hospitably. Men are needed here, and we were met by men who were very glad to see us for many reasons. We go to the seat of things in Cheat Mountain perhaps tomorrow.

I love you so much. Write about the dear boys and your kindred — that's enough. Your letter about them is so good.

Affectionately,

[R.]

P. S. — My favorite horse has come out fine again (Webby first, I mean) and Webby second is coming out.

Joe and I vote these two days the happiest of the war. Such air and streams and mountains and people glad to see us.

MRS. HAYES.

BEVERLY, VIRGINIA, August 24, 1861.

DEAR UNCLE: — Thank you for the postage stamps. The traitors at home, you need not fear. . . . We are needed here. Shall march towards the enemy tomorrow again. I am better pleased with this than with the main army at Washington. . . .

Affectionately,

R. B. HAYES.

S. BIRCHARD.

BEVERLY, August 24, 1861.

DEAR MOTHER: — Fifty miles further in the mountains. Most lovely streams and mountains. My tent now looks out on a finer scene than any yet. Thank you for the Testament. I see war enough. I prefer to read something else. We expect to move on soon. We are at the jumping-off place. You will not hear often now.

Affectionately,

R. B. HAYES.

MRS. SOPHIA HAYES.

Beverly, August 25. Sunday. — A cold night. Clear but foggy this A. M. No orders to march yet. Good! Provisions and provender, i. e. rations and forage, scarce and poor. Captain Clark, a spirited German (Prussian) officer of the "Greys," dined us yesterday at Widow What's-her-name's hotel, Got letters here from Lute, Uncle, and Mother, with a Testament from Mother. Shall read it "in course" — through I mean; begin now.

BEVERLY, VIRGINIA, August 25, 1861, Sunday A. M.

DEAREST: — Supposing I might have to go on towards Cheat Mountain this morning, I wrote you a very short note last night I now write so soon again to show you how much I love you and how much my thoughts are on the dear ones at home.

I never enjoyed any business or mode of life as much as I do this. I really feel badly when I think of several of my intimate friends who are compelled to stay at home. These marches and campaigns in the hills of western Virginia will always be among the pleasantest things I can remember. I know we are in frequent perils, that we may never return and all that, but the feeling that I am where I ought to be is a full compensation for all that is sinister, leaving me free to enjoy as if on a pleasure tour.

I am constantly reminded of our trip and happiness a year ago. I met a few days ago in the Fifth Regiment the young Moore we saw at Quebec, who went with me to see the animals at Montreal one Sunday. Do you remember the rattlesnakes?

Young Bradford goes to Cincinnati today. — We have our troubles in the Twenty-third of course, but it is happiness compared with the Guthries — fine fellows and many fine officers, but, etc., etc.

We saw nothing prettier [last year] than the view from my tent this morning. McCook's men are half a mile to the right, McMullen's Battery on the next hill in front of us. The Virginia Second a half mile in front, and the Guthries to the left. We on higher ground see them all; then mountains, meadow, and stream. Nothing wanting but you and the boys.

I want to say to you it will be impossible often, as we get further in the hills, to write, and when I do write it will be only a few lines. Don't think I am getting weaned from you and home. It is merely the condition of things compels me.

I saw young Culbertson, looking strong and healthy, Channing Richards, the Andersons, etc., etc., all ditto. Young Culbertson is now in a scouting party that is after guerrillas who murdered some of their men in an ambulance.

I have got a new boy — a yellow lad in Guthrie Gray uniform, aged about sixteen, named Theodore Wilson.

Sunday evening. — Just got orders to go to Huttonsville. Look on my map of Virginia and you will see it geography style, but the beautiful scenery you will not see there. We are to be for the present under General Reynolds, a good officer, and then General Benham or General Rosecrans. All good. The colonel takes our one-half and the German half of McCook and the battery of McMullen. The soldiers are singing so merrily tonight. It is a lovely sweet starlit evening. I rode over to Colonel Sandershoff (I think that is the name of McCook's soldierly and gentlemanly lieutenant-colonel) to tell him about the march, and from his elevated camp I could see all the camps, "sparkling and bright." I thought of the night you walked with me about Camp Chase.

Good-night. Our most advanced outpost is connected by telegraph, so that in Cincinnati you will know what happens at an early date; earlier far than any letter of mine can reach you. Kisses to all the boys. Love to Grandma and affection enough for you, dearest.

Affectionately,

R. B. HAYES.

P. S. — It would do mother good to know that I read three chapters in the Testament she sent me. Send a quarter's worth of postage stamps in your next.

MRS. HAYES.

Monday evening, August 26. — Marched today up the beautiful valley, "Tygart's Valley" I believe, to this pretty camp in the hills, eighteen miles. Saw our general. About forty-five, a middle-sized, good-looking man, educated at West Point. An army man, good sense, good talker — General Reynolds. Oh, what a lovely spot!

August 26, 1861.

DEAR UNCLE: — We are camped somewhere near, I think, the head of Tygart's Valley, near Cheat Mountain Pass. Several regiments are in sight, and the enemy under Lee so near that our outposts have fights with his daily. We are under a capital general, and are fast getting ready. I think we are safe; if not, we shall be within a very short time. We expect to stay here until we or the enemy are whipped, or back out for fear of a whipping — probably weeks.

We are in [a] lovely little valley on a fine clear trout stream, with high mountains on all sides and large trees over us. A perfect camp, perfectly protected by entrenchments for miles up the valley, pickets and scouts in all directions, etc., etc. A telegraph finished to headquarters of our general from General Rosecrans' at Clarksburg, and rapid mail carriers daily to the same place. For instance, your letter of the 19th was handed to me at my tent by the courier within half an hour after our arrival here.

Glad Fanny is with you. Lee will not whip us unless we attack him with a force too small. If he attacks us, we are the best off. The postage stamps are all gone.

Sincerely,

R. B. HAYES.

I got four Fremont *Journals*. Much obliged.

S. BIRCHARD.

SOMEWHERE IN TYGART'S VALLEY, NEAR CHEAT
MOUNTAIN PASS, VIRGINIA,

August 26, Monday evening, 8:30
P. M., after a march of eighteen miles, 1861.

DEAREST : — You will think me insane, writing so often and always with the same story : Delighted with scenery and pleasant excitement.

We are camped tonight in a valley surrounded by mountains on a lovely stream under great trees. With the Third Ohio, Thirteenth Indiana, one-half of McCook's Ninth and the Michigan artillery, which Mother remembers passed our house one Sunday about the last of May, and McMullen's Battery, all in sight. Our General Reynolds makes a good impression. We are disposed to love him and trust him. We expect to remain here and hereabouts until the enemy, which is just over the mountain, either drives us out, which I think he can't do, or until we are strong enough to attack him. A stay of some weeks, we suppose.

What a lovely valley! Joe and I will always stick by Ohio River water. It must be in the summer chiefly made up of these mountain streams than which nothing can be purer. Our mails will come here daily. I got a letter from Uncle delivered at my tent within half an hour after it was up, dated 19th and directed as all letters should be, Clarksburg.

We sent back our band to escort in the Germans who were

three hours behind us. I built a bridge for them, etc., etc. How polite they were. We like them so much.

Affectionately,

R. B. HAYES.

Have the daily *Commercial* sent me directed, "Maj. R. B. Hayes, 23d Ohio Regiment, Clarksburg."

MRS. HAYES.

Tuesday, [August] 27. — Ordered to make a forced march, without tents, knapsacks, or cooking utensils, to French Creek by a mountain path scarcely practicable for horsemen. At about 3 P. M. set out. I led the column afoot, Captain Sperry on Webby. Reached a river over the mountain after dark; kindled fires and slept on ground. Thirteen miles.

Wednesday, 28. — A long march over a bad path — thirty miles — to French Creek, or Scotchtown. Boarded with Mrs. Farrell. A fine Union settlement. Forty years ago a Massachusetts colony came here, and their thrift, morality, and patriotism are the salt of this region. Slept in tent of Culbertson and Lieutenant —— of Captain Remley's Fifth Regiment. Noble and generous treatment from them.

Thursday, 29. — Moved into the Presbyterian church to await our tents and train.

Friday, 30. — Last night Dr. Joe and I did our best to house in Mrs. Sea's barn (a good Union lady, two sons in the army), the Germans of the Ninth, who lay in the mud, without shelter. Spent today in a jolly way, resting.

FRENCH CREEK, August 30, 1861, Friday Night.

DEAREST: — "The best laid schemes of mice and men," etc., especially in war. That beautiful camp at the head of the valley, where we were to stay so long, had just been gotten into fine order, when the order to leave came: "Make a forced march to French Creek by a mountain path, leaving tents, baggage, and knapsacks to be sent you." We obeyed, and are yet alive. A queer life. We are now as jolly as if we never saw trouble or hardship. Two nights ago and three nights ago we lay in the rain in the woods without shelter, blankets, and almost without food, and after such hard days' toil that we slept on the mountains as soundly as logs. All the horses used up, Uncle Joe's Birch among the rest, except my pretty little sorrel, Webby, which came through better than ever.

Let me describe my kit: Portmanteau containing two pair socks, one shirt, a towel containing bread and sugar, a tin cup, a pistol in one holster and ammunition in the other, a blanket wrapped in the India-rubber you fixed, and a blue (soldier's) overcoat. Seven miles we made after 2:30 P. M. on a good road to Huttonsville, then by a bridle-path part of the way and no path the rest, following a guide six miles over a steep, muddy, rocky mountain. At the foot of the mountain I put Captain Sperry, who was footsore, on Webby, and pushed ahead afoot. I could see we would not get over the mountain to a stream we wished to camp on until after night, unless we pushed. I put on ahead of [the] guide and reached the top with Lieutenant Bottsford, the keen-eyed snare-drummer, Gillett (Birch remembers him, I guess), a soldier, and the guide alone in sight. We waited till the head of the column came in sight, got full instructions from the guide, directed him to wait for the column, and leaving him, re-enforced, however, by the silver cornet player, we hurried down. In half an hour it was dark as tar. I led the little party blundering sometimes, but in the main, right, until we could hear the river. Long before we reached it, all sound of the column was lost, and the way was so difficult that we agreed they could not get down until daylight. We got to the river at 9:15 with three matches and a Fremont *Journal* to kindle fire with, no overcoats and no food. It was a wet night. Didn't we scratch about and whittle to get dry kindling, and weren't we lucky to get it and start a great fire with the first precious match?

Now for the column: It reached almost over the mountain single file. 1st, Pioneers under a sergeant, ten men; 2nd, Lieutenant Smith with advance guard of thirty men; 3d, Colonel Scammon and the five companies, Twenty-third; 4th, Captain

6

McMullen and his four mountain howitzers and mules and eighty men; 5th, Lieutenant-Colonel Sandershoff with five companies of McCook's regiment. The head of the column got down to us to our surprise at 10 P. M. McMullen gave it up at 11 P. M. half-way up the mountain, and the Germans were below him. The next day we toiled on thirteen and a half hours' actual marching over the hills to this place, thirty miles. About three hundred of our men reached here at 8 P. M. — dark, muddy, rainy, and dismal — hungry, no shelter, nothing. Three companies of the Fifth under Captain Remley (part of Colonel Dunning's Continentals) were here. They took us in, fed us, piled hay, built fires, and worked for us until midnight like beavers, and we survived the night. Our men will always bless the Cincinnati Fifth. A friend of the doctor's, Davis, named Culbertson, looked after [me] and Dick Wright and others took care of Joe. Those who seemed unable to keep up, I began to order into barns and farmhouses about 6:30 o'clock. The last six miles was somewhat settled and I took care of the rear.

In the morning we found ourselves in a warm-hearted Union settlement. We got into a Presbyterian church. We made headquarters at a Yankee lady's and fared sumptuously; but McMullen and the Germans were still behind. They got in twenty-four hours after us in another dark wet night. Dr. Joe was in his glory. He and I took charge of the Germans. They were completely used up. The worst off we took into a barn of Mrs. Sea. I mention the old lady's name for she has two sons and a son-in-law in the Union army of Virginia and gave us all she had for the Germans. We got through the night work about 12 M. [midnight] and today have enjoyed hugely the comparing notes, etc., etc. Our tents reached us just now, and I am writing in mine. The colonel was used up; Joe and I are the better for it. The move is supposed to be to meet the enemy coming in by a different route. We march on tomorrow but on good roads (reasonably so) and with tents and rations.

I love you so much. Kisses for all the boys and Grandma. Good night.

R.

Tell Mother, Uncle, Laura, etc., that I get all letters, papers, Testament, etc., that are sent. I have lost nothing, I am sure. Such things are carefully forwarded from Clarksburg.

I am in command of the battalion and write this in the bustle of pitching tents preparatory to marching again as soon as fairly settled.

MRS. HAYES.

Saturday, [August] 31. — Mustered today. I called the roll of our five companies and of McMullen's Battery.

Sunday, 1 [September]. — Drummed three men (youngsters) out of Captain Drake's company, by [the] colonel's order. The men all approve it but it makes me sick. The boys all probably confirmed thieves before they joined the army, but it makes me sick. Also sent back a waggon-master and drivers. This pleased me. The rascals refused to drive further unless certain conditions were complied with. Sent off, all right! Took the mutinous waggon-master off his horse.

Tuesday, September 2 [3]. — Twelve miles from Walkersville to Bulltown. Found McCook and had a good time with him.

Wednesday, 3 [4]. — Saw General Rosecrans and staff. Caught our guard without a salute. We go with him south today. A good time with McCook and his Ninth. Marched from Bulltown to Flatwoods on road to Sutton, about ten or eleven miles. Camped on a hill with Captain Canby's Company F of our right wing and Captain Moore's Company I, ditto. How pleasant to meet them after our long (five weeks) separation. They have had troubles, hard marches, and fun; one man shot resisting a corporal, two men in irons for a rape, and one man arrested for sleeping on post (third offence penalty death!)

BULLTOWN, September 3, [4], 1861. Wednesday Morning.

DEAREST: — Let me say first that the army mail arrangement is perfect. All letters are got promptly here. We march forty or sixty miles to a new point. We are hardly stopped at our destination on a sidehill, in a wood or meadow, before a courier steps up and hands us, privates and all, letters just from Clarksburg. For instance, we are seventy miles over mountains from our last camping place. I had not got off of Webby before a fellow came up, "Are you the Major?" and handed me a letter from you, 27th, from Mother, 26th, from Uncle, 26th, and half a dozen others all late. The same thing is happening all the time.

We have had a forced march without tents, cooking utensils, or knapsacks over a mountain road — bridle path. I came out first best. All the horses injured except Webby. . . .

Good time here. McCook gathered his whole regiment. They serenaded us and we them. The Ninth and Twenty-third swear by each other. They Dutch, we Yankees. General Rosecrans takes command here. We go south to Sutton, etc., until we meet the enemy. Shall not write often now.

Good-bye. Blessings, love, and kisses for all.

Affectionately,

R. B. Hayes.

Mrs. Hayes.

Bulltown, September 3, [4], 1861.

Dear Uncle: — All your letters come safely; got one of the 26th yesterday. Mail facilities coming this way are perfect.

We are now under General Rosecrans in person going south toward Summersville, through Sutton, until we meet the enemy unless he leaves western Virginia. Unless overwhelming[ly] superior in numbers, we shall beat him, accidents always excepted. Our numbers are not, perhaps, as great as we would wish, but you must remember we are over one hundred miles from a railroad and bad roads (not very bad) to haul supplies. It is physically impossible to supply a very large army without a very long preparation. The wagon-trains would actually impede each other, if you were to attempt to crowd too fast, faster than we are now doing.

Take it easy, we shall clean them out in time, if the people at home will hold on and be persevering and patient.

We have had the severest experience soldiers are required to bear, except a defeat; viz, forced marches without shelter, food, or blankets over mountain bridle-paths, in the night and rain. Many fail. My little horse came out well and sound again, the best in the regiment. The doctor's gave out and was left. I gain strength and color; a little flesh perhaps. Never before so healthy and stout. You will hear first of our welfare in the [Cincinnati] *Commercial*. Their "special correspondent" wrote a letter in my tent this A. M. Good-bye.

Sincerely,

R. B. HAYES.

S. BIRCHARD.

ON ROAD TO SUTTON, SOUTH FROM
WESTON, September 3 [4], 1861.

DEAR MOTHER: — We are having great times with forced marches over the hills. It agrees with me. I get all letters by couriers very promptly. . . .

We go south under General Rosecrans. All things look encouragingly. We meet friends constantly and unexpectedly. . . . On Sunday we had church in camp, with a Presbyterian Congregation of Yankees who came here forty-five years ago. We occupied their church for shelter. They treated us most hospitably. All from Massachusetts and retaining the thrift, morality, and loyalty of their native State, or rather of the State of their fathers, for most of them were born here.

Affectionately,

R. B. HAYES.

MRS. SOPHIA HAYES.

SUTTON, OR SUTTONVILLE, VIRGINIA, September 5, 1861.

DEAREST: — We are in another camp of fine views. This is the last stronghold of our army as we advance toward the enemy. We are now part of an army of from six to eight thousand and are pushing towards an advancing enemy stronger in numbers, it is said. Some time will perhaps elapse before we meet, but we are pretty certain to meet unless the enemy withdraws. This,

I think, they will do. I like the condition of things. Our force, although not large, is of good regiments for the most part: McCook's Ninth, Colonel Smith's Thirteenth, Lytle's Tenth (Irish), are all here; also Colonel Moor's Twenty-eighth (Markbreit's regiment), Colonel Lowe's Twelfth, our regiment, and Colonel Porshner's Forty-ninth (Wilstach regiment) coming; also one part company of Regulars; four companies artillery, four companies cavalry. An army about as large as can well manœuvre in these mountains. General Rosecrans is in command in person with General Benham of the Regular Army to second him. We are camped on both sides of Elk River, connected by a beautiful suspension bridge. Camps on high hills; fortifications on all the summits. "A gay and festive scene," as Artemus Ward would say, especially about sundown when three or four fine bands are playing in rivalry.

Elk River empties into Kanawha, so that the water now dripping from my tent will pass you, perhaps, about a fortnight hence; the clearest, purest water it is too. From the tops of the high hills you can see the rocks in the river covered by ten or twenty feet of water. Nothing finer in Vermont or New Hampshire.

I have just got a letter from Dr. James [D. Webb]. Say to him, let all my letters be opened, and if any are important, send them; otherwise, not, unless from some especial friend. Send me some stamps and tell me how you are off for cash. We expect to be paid soon; if so, I can send you some three hundred to six hundred dollars.

We are to have a bore here in a few days — a court-martial on some officer in the Tenth or Twelfth, and I am to be judge-advocate, unless I can diplomatize out of it, which I hope to do.

We got today papers from Cincinnati — the *Times* of the 28th and the *Commercial* of the 2d. Think of it; only three days old! It has rumors that General Rosecrans is captured. Well, not quite. He is in good health, and the Twenty-third Regiment is his especial guard. No force can get him here without passing my tent.

Among the interesting things in camp are the boys. You recollect the boy in Captain McIlrath's company; we have another like unto him in Captain Woodward's. He ran away from Norwalk to Camp Dennison; went into the Fifth, then into the Guthries, and as we passed their camp, he was pleased with us, and now is "a boy of the Twenty-third." He drills, plays officer, soldier, or errand boy, and is a curiosity in camp. We are getting dogs too, some fine ones; almost all the captains have horses and a few mules have been "realized" — that's the word — from Secessionists.

It is clearing off, so we shall be happy again. I am sorry you are unwell. Don't get down-spirited. We shall get through and come home again. Love and kisses for all the boys. Affectionate regards to Grandma. Jim's letters will be very acceptable. Good-bye, darling.

Affectionately,

R. B. HAYES.

P. S. — If you could see the conveniences (?) I have for writing, you would see how such a scrawl as this becomes a possibility. I have found out the day of the week and month; it is Thursday, the 5th September, 1861.

MRS. HAYES.

Friday, [September] 5 [6]. — As judge-advocate, with General Benham, Colonels Scammon, Smith, *et al.,* I tried two cases. J. W. Trader, etc.

Saturday, 6 [7]. — Marched to Birch River.

Sunday, 7 or 8. — As officer of the day, I rode all day — up Birch, crossing it forty times and going fifty to sixty miles. Rode out to pickets with General Benham.

Monday, 9. — Marched over Powell Mountain and camped eight miles from Summersville. Enemy near us; a battle to come soon.

Tuesday, 10. — Marched seventeen miles, drove enemies' pickets out of Summersville, followed nine miles to Gauley river. Enemy entrenched on a hill, high, steep, and hidden by bushes, three to six thousand strong. We get ready to attack. We have been divided into three brigades: First, General Benham's, consisting of Tenth (Colonel Lytle's Irish), Twelfth (Colonel Lowe's), and Thirteenth (Colonel Smith's) regiments; Second, Colonel McCook's — the Ninth, Twenty-eighth, and Forty-ninth; Third, — Twenty-third and Thirtieth and Mack's Battery. McMullen's Battery attached to McCook. Stewart's Cavalry, West's to headquarters, and Schaumbeck's Cavalry to McCook's.

First Brigade led the attack. We stood near half an hour listening to the heavy cannon and musketry, then were called to form in line of battle. My feelings were not different from what I have often felt before beginning an important lawsuit. As we waited for our turn to form, we joked a great deal. Colonel Matthews, Scammon, Captains Drake and Woodward, and privates — all were jolly and excited by turns.

Finally our turn came. I was told to take four companies and follow one of General Rosecrans' staff. I promptly called off Seventh, Eighth, Ninth and Tenth companies. We marched over a hill and through a cornfield; the staff officer and myself leading on, until we reached the brow of a high hill overlooking the Gauley River and perhaps three-quarters of a mile from the entrenchments of the enemy. He [the officer] then said to me that I was to be on the extreme left of our line and to march forward guided by the enemy's guns, that he had no special orders to give, that I was an officer and must use my own judgment. He never had been over the ground I was to pass over; thought the enemy might retreat that way.

I marched to the wood; found it a dense laurel thicket on the side of a steep hill, rocky and cavernous; at the bottom a ravine and river and up the opposite hill seemed to be the enemy. I formed the four companies into order of battle, told them to keep together and follow me; in case of separation to push forward in the direction of the declining sun and when the firing could be heard to be guided by it. I handed my horse to one of the unarmed musicians, and drawing my sword crept, pushed, and struggled rapidly down the hill. When I reached the bottom but four or five of Company K (Captain Howard) were in sight. Soon men of Captain Zimmerman's came up and soon I gathered the major part of the four companies. I had sent Captain Woodward and twenty scouts or skirmishers ahead; they were among the unseen.

By this time it was getting late. I formed a line again extending from the river up the hill and facing towards the enemy, as we supposed. The firing had ceased except scattered shots. We pushed slowly up, our right up hill, where I was soon encountered [by] the Twenty-eighth — lost. Had a laugh and greeting with Markbreit who was on the left of the Twenty-eighth (he was my partner). The head of my column was near enough to be fired on. Two were wounded, others hit; none seriously hurt. The face of the hill on which the enemy was posted was towards precipitous rock. We could only reach them by moving to the right in front of the Twenty-eighth, Forty-seventh, and Thirteenth.

I have heard nothing clear or definite of the position, either of the enemy or ourselves. The above [drawing] is no doubt very erroneous, but is my guess. I got up nearer than anybody except the Tenth and Twelfth but was down a steep hill or precipice and concealed. Some of my men bore to the right and pushing in front of the Twenty-eighth and Forty-seventh mixed with the Thirteenth. It soon got dark; all firing ceased. I drew off single file, Captain Sperry leading; got up the hill just at complete dark; found messengers ordering us to return to the rest of our regiment, on the extreme right. Some thirty of my men were missing — Captain Woodward, Lieutenant Rice, etc., etc. I left ten sentinels along the brow of the hill to direct them where to find us. The greater part soon overtook us. We marched through lost fragments of regiments — Germans mostly, some Irish, talking of the slaughter, until we got into an old field near our regiment. There we waited. Nobody seemed nervous or anxious — all wishing for light. Talked with McCook who criticized the orders, but was in good temper; had lost three horses. Finally found our regiment and all marched off to bivouac. In the morning great cheering near the fort. Enemy had run away in a panic by a road over the hill back of their works, leaving flag, etc.

GAULEY RIVER, 8 MILES SOUTH OF SUMMERSVILLE,
September 11, 1861.

DEAR LUCY: — Well, darling, we have had our first battle, and the enemy have fled precipitately. I say "we," although it is fair to say that our brigade, consisting of the Twenty-third, the Thirtieth (Colonel Ewing), and Mack's Battery had little or nothing to do, except to stand as a reserve. The only exception to this was four companies of the Twenty-third, Captains Sperry, Howard, Zimmerman, and Woodward, under my command, who were detailed to make an independent movement. I had one man wounded and four others hit in their clothing and accoutrements. You will have full accounts of the general fight in the papers. My little detachment did as much real work — hard work — as anybody. We crept down and up a steep rocky mountain, on our hands and knees part of the time, through laurel thickets almost impenetrable, until dark. At one time I got so far ahead in the struggle that I had but three men. I finally gathered them by a halt, although a part were out all night. We were near half an hour listening to the cannon and musketry, waiting for our turn to come.

You have often heard of the feelings of men in the interval between the order of battle and the attack. Matthews, myself, and others were rather jocose in our talk, and my actual feeling was very similar to what I have when going into an important trial — not different nor more intense. I thought of you and the boys and the other loved ones, but there was no such painful feeling as is sometimes described. I doubted the success of the attack and with good reason and in good company. The truth is, our enemy is very industrious and ingenious in contriving ambuscades and surprises and entrenchments but they lack pluck. They expect to win, and too often do win, by superior strategy and cunning. Their entrenchments and works were of amazing extent. During the whole fight we rarely saw a man. Most of the firing was done at bushes and log and earth barricades.

We withdrew at dark, the attacking brigades having suffered a good deal from the enemy and pretty severely from one of those deplorable mistakes which have so frequently happened in this war — viz., friends attacking friends. The Tenth and Twenty-eighth (Irish and Second German of Cincinnati) fired on each other and charged doing much mischief. My detachment was in danger from the same cause. I ran upon the Twenty-eighth, neither seeing the other until within a rod. We mutually recognized, however, although it was a mutual surprise. It so happened, curiously enough, that I was the extreme right man of my body and Markbreit the left man of his. We had a jolly laugh and introductions to surrounding officers as partners, etc.

The enemy were thoroughly panic-stricken by the solid volleys of McCook's Ninth and the rifled cannon of Smith's Thirteenth. The Tenth suffered most. The enemy probably began their flight by a secret road soon after dark, leaving flag, ammunition, trunks, arms, stores, etc., etc., but no dead or wounded. Bowie knives, awful to look at, but no account in war; I have one. One wagon-load of family stuff — a good Virginia plain family — was left. They were spinning, leaving rolls of wool, knitting, and making bedquilts. I enclose a piece; also a pass — all queer.

They [the enemy] crossed the Gauley River and are said to be fortifying on the other side. We shall probably pursue. Indeed, Colonel Matthews and [with] four of our companies is now dogging them. We shall probably fight again but not certainly.

I have no time to write to other friends. The men are now talking to me. Besides, I want to sleep. Dearest, I think of you and the dear ones first, last, and all the time. I feel much encouraged about the war; things are every way looking better. We are in the midst of the serious part of a campaign. Good-bye, dearest. Pass this letter around — bad as it is. I have no time to write to all. I must sleep. On Sunday last, I rode nineteen hours, fifty to sixty miles, crossed a stream with more water than the Sandusky at this season at Mr. Valette's from thirty to forty times — wet above my knees all the time and no sleep for thirty-six hours; so "excuse haste and a bad pen", as Uncle says.

Affectionately,

R. B. Hayes.

P. S. — Joe and his capital assistants are trumps.

Mrs. Hayes.

BIRCH RIVER, BETWEEN SUMMERSVILLE AND
SUTTON, VIRGINIA, September 14, 1861.

DEAR UNCLE: — I have no time to write letters. We are getting on finely. Our battle on the 10th at Gauley River, you have no doubt heard all about. Nothing but night prevented our getting Floyd and his whole army. As it was, we entirely demoralized them; got all their camp equipage even to their swords, flag, and trunks (one of the best of which the general gave me). I had an important and laborious part assigned me. An independent command of four companies to be the extreme left of our attacking column. We worked down and up a steep rocky mountain covered with a laurel thicket. I got close enough just at dark to get two men wounded and four others struck in their garments.

This is not a dangerous business; after tremendous firing of cannon and musketry, we lost only thirteen killed, about fifteen badly wounded and fifty or sixty slightly wounded. The enemy are no match for us in fair fighting. They feel it and so do our men. We marched rapidly seventeen miles, reaching their vicinity at 2:30 or 3 P. M. We immediately were formed and went at them. They were evidently appalled. I think not many were killed. Governor Floyd was wounded slightly.

On yesterday morning I was sent on a circuitous march to head off parties hastening to join Wise or Floyd. Four companies of my regiment, two companies of Colonel Ewing's, and a squadron of Chicago cavalry are under my command. We marched up Gauley River to Hughes Ferry. There we were fired on by a lot of guerrillas concealed in rocks. It was more dangerous than the battle. Three of us who were mounted and in advance were decidedly objects of attention, but fortunately none were hit. We chased them off, getting only one.

I am now here relieving a small party of our folks who are entrenched and who have been in constant dread of an attack. We are without tents and expect to return to the battle-ground in six days.

In the battle only one commissioned officer was killed, Colonel Lowe. One acquaintance of yours, Stephen McGroarty, an

Irish Democratic orator, formerly of Toledo, now of Cincinnati (a captain), was shot through the body, but kept on his feet until the fight was stopped by the darkness. He will recover. One of my comforts is that my horse has come out in better plight than ever. I think he never looked so well and spirited as he did today as we marched over Birch Mountain.

If no disaster overtakes us at Washington, we shall soon see signs of yielding by the South. The letters, diaries, etc., etc., found in Floyd's trunks and desks, show that their situation is desperate. Thousands are in their army who are heartily sick of the whole business.

We retook a large part of the plunder taken from Colonel Tyler as well as prisoners. The prisoners had been well treated, very. The young men in Floyd's army of the upper class are kind-hearted, good-natured fellows, who are [as] unfit as possible for the business they are in. They have courage but no endurance, enterprise, or energy. The lower class are cowardly, cunning, and lazy. The height of their ambition is to shoot a Yankee from some place of safety.

My regards to all. Send this to Mother and Lucy.

Sincerely,

R. B. HAYES.

P. S. — The enclosed picture of a lieutenant in the army we routed is for Laura.

S. BIRCHARD.

BIRCH RIVER, EIGHTEEN MILES NORTH OF SUM-
MERSVILLE, Sunday, September 15, 1861.

DEAREST: — We are as happy and care-for-nothing [a] set of fellows here today as you could find anywhere. I have now for a while an independent command of four companies, Twenty-third, Captain Moore, Captain Lovejoy, Woodward, and Drake, two companies of the Thirtieth and a squadron of the Chicago Dragoons. We are now about thirty miles from the battlefield, heading off (if there are any, which I doubt), reinforcements for the enemy. The men are jolly, the anxieties of the battle all forgotten. We seem to be in most prosperous circumstances. I shall rejoin the main army in three or four days.

You have heard about the fight. It was a very noisy but not dangerous affair. . . . Where I was a few balls whistled forty or fifty feet over our heads. The next day, however, with Captain Drake's company I got into a little skirmish with an outpost and could see that the captain and myself were actually aimed at, the balls flying near enough but hurting nobody. The battle scared and routed the enemy prodigiously. . . .

I hardly think we will [shall] have another serious fight. Possibly, Wise and Floyd and Lee may unite and stiffen up the Rebel back in this quarter. If so we shall fight them. But if not encouraged by some success near Washington, they are pretty well flattened out in this region. We shall be busy with them for a few weeks, but as I remarked, unless we meet with some serious disaster near Washington, they will not, I think, have heart enough to make a stiff battle.

My "Webby," tell the boys, pricked up his ears and pranced when he heard the cannon and volleys of musketry. He is in excellent condition.

Dr. Joe and McCurdy were very busy with the sick and wounded during and after the battle. Our troops who were taken from Colonel Tyler and retaken by us say they were very well treated by the enemy. McCurdy is now with me. Colonel Scammon couldn't spare Joe.

The last week has been the most stirring we have had during the war. If in all quarters things go on as well as here we shall end the war sometime. The captured letters show that Governor Floyd's army were getting tired of the business.

Did I tell you General Benham gave me an awful bowie knife and General Rosecrans a trunk out of the enemy's spoil? The last much needed.

Well, dearest, this is one of the bright days in this work. I am prepared for all sorts of days. There will be dark ones of course, but I suspect there is a gradual improvement which will continue with occasional drawbacks until we are finally successful. Love and kisses for all. Good-bye, darling.

Affectionately,
R. B. HAYES.

P. S. — Captain McMullen who was wounded is well enough for another battle. Since writing in comes a mail carrier out on this road and your letter of the 5th and postage stamps is in his budget. So I put a stamp on it and if I had another envelope would direct it again.

Tell Webb that my pretty horse is the original Camp Chase "Webby," the finest horse in the regiment. I tried one or two others, but Webb plucked up and beats them all.

Glad, very, you are at home and happy. We are here happy, too. This is all Cincinnati nearly — this army. Yes, Joe, is a great favorite with the colonel and with all. The colonel leans upon [him] entirely. He is really surgeon of the brigade and should Colonel Scammon be a brigadier, Dr. Joe will become his brigade surgeon permanently. All glad to get letters. I love you so much. Good-bye.

Affectionately,

R.

MRS. HAYES.

September 19. — Offered the place of judge-advocate general by General Rosecrans. Have served in five cases — [on the] 5th and 6th at Sutton, 16th, 17th and 18th at Cross Lanes (also the 12th) — and a few days between those dates preparing reports of proceedings.

CROSS LANES, NEAR GAULEY RIVER, BELOW
SUMMERSVILLE, VIRGINIA, September 19,
Thursday A. M., [1861].

DEAREST: — I fear you do not get the letters I have written the last ten days, as we are out of the reach of mail facilities. I got your letter of the 5th about forty miles north of here out of a waggon-train that I stopped. You can always know of my welfare from the correspondence in the *Gazette* and [the] *Commercial*. They are informed directly from headquarters. I see their correspondents daily. Colonel Scammon being at the head of a brigade (a very little one), Colonel Matthews commands our regiment. On the day of the fight, and most of the time since, I have had an independent command. Most [of] the time almost a regiment, made up from our regiment, the Thirtieth, and small parties of cavalry. I have thus far been the sole judge-advocate also of this army; so I am very busy. We tried three cases yesterday. It is a laborious and painful business. And after writing so much I would not write you but for my anxiety to have you know how much I think of and love you. Love and kisses to all the boys.

My impression is that the enemy has left our bailiwick entirely, but there are rumors of re-enforcements, etc., etc. If so, we shall have another fight within ten days. With anything like management and decent luck, we shall surely beat them. But there is a great deal of accident in this thing. Not enough to save them unless they do better than heretofore.

Dr. Joe is well. All of us getting thin and tough. Matthews has lost twenty-five pounds, Dr. Joe five pounds. I have lost five to eight. The soldiers generally from ten to twenty pounds. I never was so stout and tough. You need not send my pants unless you see somebody coming direct or get a chance with Mr. Schooley's things. I am well fixed. Dr. McDermott is here, one week from Ohio. We now get news by way of Kanawha in two days from Cincinnati.

You need have no fear of my behaviour in fight. I don't know what effect new dangers might have on my nerves, but the other day I was several minutes under a sharp guerrilla fire — aimed particularly at Captain Drake and myself (being on horseback), so I know somewhat of my capacity. It is all right. In the noisy battle, for it was largely noise, none of our regiment was under fire except the extreme right wing of my little command; two were wounded, and I could hear the balls whistle away up in the air fifty feet over my head; but it amounted to nothing. A portion of Colonel Lytle's men caught nearly all the danger, and they were under a very severe fire.

It is beautiful weather — lovely moonlight nights. A great many well cultivated farms; plenty of fruit, vegetables, and food. Good-bye again. The paymaster is expected soon. I shall be able to send you lots of money if he does [come], as I now spend next to nothing. Kisses for all. Dearest, I love you so much.

Affectionately,

RUTHERFORD.

P. S. — This letter is so incoherent by reason of interruptions. Joe wants me to say that we had peaches and cream just now.

MRS. HAYES.

CROSS LANES, September 19, 1861.

DEAREST: — It is a lovely moonlight evening. I mailed you a letter this morning, but as Lieutenant Wall of Captain McIlrath's company has resigned to go with the navy, and will go to Cincinnati tomorrow, I thought I would say a word further while our band plays its finest tattoo tunes. They are sweet, very. You see by the enclosed the scrape I am in. I have tried four or five cases on general orders, and here comes an order making me permanently a J. A. [judge-advocate]. It is not altogether agreeable. I shall get out of it after a while somehow. For the present I obey. It is pleasant in one respect as showing that in my line I have done well. Lieutenant Wall will, I hope, call and see you. He is a good soldier and we are sorry to lose him. If this reaches you before other letters from here and Birch River, you may know that two older and longer ones are after you.

One thing in the new appointment: If I can't get out of it, you may see me one of these days, sooner than you otherwise would, as it confers some privileges, and that would be sweet. Love to all.

Affectionately,

R. B. HAYES.

P. S. — We hear tonight of the death of Colonel Lorin Andrews at Kenyon.* We feel it more deeply than in most cases.

* Lorin Andrews born at Ashland, Ohio, April 1, 1819. Studied law, but soon gave up the practice to devote himself to work of education. He was President of Kenyon College at the outbreak of the war and was the first man in Ohio to offer his services to the country. He was colonel of the Fourth O. V. I. in the first campaign of the war and "died, a martyr to the Union, September 18, 1861."

He was my classmate — a fellow student of Colonel Matthews. He took a great interest in our efforts to get a place in the war, and rejoiced with us when we got a fine regiment. McCook gave me Andrews' spurs when he left for home, to wear until his return. Alas! we are not to see him. He was an earnest, true man. Hail and farewell! We have been so full of humor tonight and this saddens us. Good-bye again, dearest.

MRS. HAYES.   R.

CROSS LANES, NEAR GAULEY RIVER,
SOUTH OF SUMMERSVILLE, VIRGINIA,
September 19, 1861.

DEAR MOTHER: — I am in the best possible health. Since the retreat of the enemy I have been too busy to write. You must look in the correspondence of the *Commercial* or *Gazette* for my welfare. If I should lose a little toe, it will be told there long before a letter from me would reach [you]. Their correspondents send by telegraph and couriers every day from this army. Their accounts, making proper allowance for sensational exaggeration, are pretty truthful.

Dr. Joe and his assistant performed their duty and the duty of about half a dozen other surgeons during and after the fight. Everybody was well cared for — even the enemy. The number of killed and badly wounded did not exceed twenty-five; other wounds about seventy-five, mostly very slight. The suffering is not great. Gunshot wounds are accompanied with a numbness which relieves the wounded. Laura's bandages figured largely.

We are now enjoying ourselves very much; beautiful weather; fine fruit, vegetables, and other food, also pretty nights. Love to all.

Affectionately your son,

R. B. HAYES.

P. S. — You must excuse my short letter. I have a prodigious amount of writing to do. I am acting judge-advocate and have tried five cases lately. — H.

MRS. SOPHIA HAYES.

OHIO GENERALS AND GENERALS APPOINTED FROM OHIO — ALL WEST POINT GRADUATES.

MAJOR-GENERAL DON CARLOS BUELL, 1818-98.

MAJOR-GENERAL IRWIN McDOWELL, 1818-85.

MAJOR-GENERAL JOHN POPE, 1822-92.*

MAJOR-GENERAL WILLIAM S. ROSECRANS, 1819-98.

MAJOR-GENERAL GEORGE B. McCLELLAN, 1826-1885.*

MAJOR-GENERAL A. McD. McCOOK, 1831-1903.

* Appointed from Ohio.

September 20. — I am ordered to the place of judge-advocate and to be attached to headquarters. I dislike the service but must obey, of course. I hope to be released after a few weeks' service. In the meantime I will try to qualify myself for an efficient discharge of my new duties. I agree with General Rosecrans that courts-martial may be made very serviceable in promoting discipline in the army. I shall try to introduce method and system into the department. I will keep a record of cases, collect a list of sentences proper for different cases, etc., etc.

September 21, 1861. — Equinoctial storm today. Our regiment does not move. I am getting ready for my new quarters and duties. Just got ready for bed; a dark, dismal, rainy night. Visited the hospital tonight. Saw several of Colonel Tyler's men who were wounded and taken prisoners in his surprise a month ago and were retaken by us after the fight at Carnifax Ferry. Intelligent men from Oberlin, one Orton; one from Cleveland. They have suffered much but are in good spirits. The enemy boasted that they would soon drive us out and would winter in Cincinnati.

September 22. Sunday. — Cold, raw, and damp — probably will rain. I must get two flannel or thick shirts with collars, also one or two pairs of thick gloves.

CROSS LANES, VIRGINIA, September 22, [1861].
Sunday morning, before breakfast.

DEAREST: — It is a cold, drizzly, suicidal morning. The equinoctial seems to be a severe storm. Part of our force has crossed [the] Gauley to operate in conjunction with General Cox who is near us. The enemy have retreated in a broken and disheartened condition twenty or thirty miles to near Lewisburg. Unless largely reinforced, they will hardly make another stand. The first fair day our regiment will cross [the] Gauley and the rest will follow as weather permits. We have such a long line of transportation and as the wet fall months are at hand, I suspect we shall not attempt to go further than Lewisburg, possibly to the White Sulphur Springs, before we go into winter quarters.

You know I am ordered to be attached to headquarters. As soon as my regiment moves they will leave me. This is hard, very. I shall feel badly enough when they march off without me. There are some things pleasant about it, however. In the first place, I shall probably not be kept away more than a month or two before I shall be relieved. Then, I shall be in much more immediate communication with you. I can at any time, if need be, dispatch you; so you are within an hour of me. I shall travel a good deal and may possibly go to Ohio. I began my new duties by trying to do a good thing. I have sent for Channing Richards to be my clerk. He is a private in the Guthries. Enough said. If he comes as he is ordered to by the general, and as no doubt he will, I can easily see how his education, brought to notice as it will be, will get him into the way of promotion. I have also a soldier of the Twenty-third, who has been a sailor, an ostler, and a cook, and will be able to look after me in his several capacities. . . .

The wounded are all doing well. The number now in the hospital is small. The doctor has been getting discharges or furloughs for our sick. The rest are getting hardened to this life and I hope we shall continue healthy. Colonel Matthews has been slightly, or even worse, sick, not so as to confine him to his quarters except one morning. His health generally has been excellent. The "poor blind soldier," as Birtie called him, is perfectly well again. . . .

It is coming out a bright warm day. Weather is a great matter in camp. A man so healthy and independent of weather as I am can keep up spirits in bad weather; but [to] a camp full, on wet ground, under wet tents, hard to get food, hard to cook it, getting homesick, out of money, out of duds, weather becomes an important thing.

Speaking of duds, I ought to have a neckerchief, a pair of officers' thick gloves, two soldiers' shirts with collars, flannel collars same as the shirt. I have worn but one white shirt in two months, and as only one of my thick shirts has a collar,

I am more or less bored for the want of them. I shall get soldiers' shirts by the first arrival.

Love to the dear boys. I am hoping to send you money soon. If the paymaster will only come! Love to all the rest as well and bushels for your own dear self.

Affectionately,

R. B. HAYES.

P. S. — Dr. Clendenin arrived today and is brigade surgeon of *our* (Colonel Scammon's) brigade. This pleases Joe and all. We are lucky in doctors. Colonel Scammon says, "No doubt Dr. Clendenin is a good man, but I would prefer Dr. Webb."

MRS. HAYES.

CROSS LANES, VIRGINIA, Sunday, September 22, 1861.

DEAR MOTHER: — . . . We are waiting for good weather to go in pursuit of the enemy. Unless some calamity occurs to us at Washington, so as to enable the Rebels to reinforce Wise and Floyd, I do not think they will fight us again. We shall probably not pursue more than forty miles to Lewisburg or White Sulphur Springs, and then our campaign closes for the season. You see, probably, that I am appointed judge-advocate for the department of the Ohio. This includes the State of Ohio, and, should I continue to hold the place, I shall probably be required to go to Columbus and Cincinnati in the course of my duties. But I shall get out of it, I hope, in a month or so. It will separate me from my regiment a good deal, and the increase of pay, about forty or fifty dollars per month, and increase of honor, perhaps, is no compensation for this separation. I have acted in all the cases which have arisen in General Rosecrans' army. I shall be with my regiment soon again, I hope. While the general is in the same army with them, we are together, of course. I am constantly interrupted. I am today in command of the regiment, Colonel Matthews being unwell, so I am perpetually interrupted. Good-bye.

Affectionately,

R. B. HAYES.

MRS. SOPHIA HAYES.

MT. SEWELL ON PIKE FROM LEWISBURG DOWN GAULEY
AND KANAWHA RIVERS, THIRTY MILES FROM LEWIS-
BURG, CAMP SEWELL, September 25, 1861.

DEAR L —: — I am now in General Cox's camp, twenty-five miles from the Carnifax. Ferry. The regiment is back about twenty miles. I am here as J. A. [judge-advocate]. Came over yesterday. This camp is on the summit of a high hill or mountain which affords a most extensive view of mountain scenery. The enemy is on a hill about one or two miles from us under Wise. Their strength is not known. Firing continued between the pickets yesterday a good part of the day. Many cannon shot and shell also were let off without much result. One man (Major Hise) slightly wounded on our side. We are ordered not to fight the enemy, not to attack, I mean, until General Rosecrans arrives with our regiment and other forces. McCook is here. If the enemy does not retire, I think there will be a battle in a few days, but I think they will retreat again. They left a strongly fortified position day before yesterday. I found it yesterday. Well, all these matters you read in the papers.

Tell uncle I would write him, but I don't know where he is, and I suppose he sees my letters often enough. I am in the best possible health and spirits. I trust you are also. It seems to me we are gradually getting better off in the war. It may, and will last some time, but the prospect improves steadily.

I merely write this morning to tell you of my present whereabouts, and that I love you dearly. Kisses and love for the boys and all.

Affectionately,

R.

MRS. HAYES.

SEWELL MOUNTAIN, GENERAL COX'S CAMP,
September 27 (Saturday or Friday, I am told), 1861.

DEAR L —: — We are in the midst of a very cold rain-storm; not farther south than Lexington or Danville and on the top of a high hill or small mountain. Rain for fifteen hours; getting colder and colder, and still raining. In leaky tents, with worn-out blankets, insufficient socks and shoes, many without over-coats. This is no joke. I am living with McCook in a good tent, as well provided as anybody in camp; better than either General Cox or Rosecrans.

I write this in General Cox's tent. He sits on one cot read-ing, or trying to read, or pretending to read, Dickens' new novel, "Great Expectations." McCook and General Rosecrans are in the opposite tent over a smoke, trying to think they are warmed a little by the fire under it. Our enemy, far worse provided than we are, are no doubt shivering on the opposite hill now hidden by the driving rain and fog. We all suspect that our campaign in this direction is at an end. The roads will be miry, and we must fall back for our supplies. My regiment is fourteen miles back on a hill. When clear we can see their tents.

Just now my position is comparatively a pleasant one. I go with the generals on all reconnaissances, see all that is to be seen, and fare as well as anybody. We were out yesterday P. M. very near to the enemy's works; were caught in the first of this storm and thoroughly soaked. I hardly expect to be dry again until the storm is over.

Good-bye, dearest.

Affectionately,

R.

Mrs. Hayes.

Sewell Mountain, September 29, 1861.

Dearest L —: — A beautiful bright Sunday morning after a cold, bitter, dismal storm of three days. It finds me in perfect health, although many a poor fellow has succumbed to the weather. The bearer of this goes home sick — a gentlemanly German. I am still living with McCook, my regiment being back ten miles. We are in doubt as to whether we shall fight the enemy ahead of us or not. We are compelled now by roads and climate to stop and return to the region of navigable waters or railroads. No teams can supply us up here much longer. In this state of things we shall probably be content with holding the strong points already taken without fighting for more until another campaign.

We have three generals here. Rosecrans, Cox, and Schenck. General Cox is a great favorite, deservedly I think, with his men. We suppose, but don't know, that there are three generals in the enemy's camp, viz: Lee, Wise, and Floyd. Their force is believed to be much larger than ours, and many more cannon, but they dare not attack. They are industriously fortifying hills which we care nothing about.

My regards to the family. Love and kisses to the boys. The bearer, Mr. Harries, will, I hope, call on you.

Affectionately as ever, your

R.

Mrs. Hayes.

Camp Sewell, October 1, 1861. — About a week ago I left Camp Scott, or Cross Lanes, and came over to General Cox's camp on the top of Sewell Mountain. Our Secesh friends are fortifying in sight. I staid with McCook. General Cox is an even-tempered man of sound judgment, much loved by his men. McCook and he both wanted to occupy Buster's Knob on the left of our enemy's camp, but a dispatch from General Rosecrans prevented. The next day the enemy were fortifying it. General Schenck takes command of our brigade. I have tried five cases the last two days. We had a rain-storm, cold, windy, and awful. Must go to winter quarters. The enemy still fortifying. Our pickets killed a colonel or lieutenant-colonel of the enemy who rode among them. All wrong and cruel. This is too like murder. Shooting pickets, etc., etc., ought to be put down. Another cold night. Jolly times we have in camp.

Camp Sewell, October 3, 1861.

Dearest: — This is a pleasant morning. I yesterday finished the work of a court-martial here; am now in my own tent with my regiment "at home." It does seem like home. I have washed and dressed myself, and having nothing to do I hope to be able today to write to all. I begin, of course, with my darling wife, of whom I think more and more affectionately the longer we are separated. And the dear boys too — kiss and hug them warmly.

We are evidently at the end of our campaign in this direction for this season. The bad roads and floods make it impossible longer to supply an army so far from railroads and navigable waters. How soon we shall begin our backward march, I do not know. If the enemy were not immediately in front of us we should leave instantly but, no doubt, our leaders dislike to make a move that will look like a retreat from an enemy that we care nothing about. But there is nothing to be gained by staying so far in the mountains, and the danger of starving will send us back to Gauley Bridge long before this reaches you. We shall, no doubt, garrison and fortify the strong points which control western Virginia, and the question with us all is, who is to stay and who go to some pleasanter scene.

We are now in General Schenck's brigade, and hope he will have influence enough to get us a place in the Kentucky or some other army. We are, no doubt, the crack American regiment of all this region, and think we should have the conspicuous place. I think we shall get out of here, but we shall see. I think there will be no battle here. The enemy are strongly entrenched and far superior to us in numbers. Besides there is no object in attacking them. They have twenty-two pieces of artillery. They will not attack us, unless encouraged to do so by our apparent retreat. If they come out of their entrenchments to fight us we think we have got them. So if our retreat is prudently managed, I suspect there will be nothing but skirmishing. That we have a little of daily.

Since we passed into the mountains, we are out of reach of mails. It is almost a month since the date of your last letter. I am still on General Rosecrans' staff although with my regiment, and you can direct letters as heretofore, except instead of "Clarksburg" put "Gauley Bridge," and ask Dr. James W. [Webb] to leave the new direction at the *Commercial* office.

I am in the best of health. I speak of this always because it is now a noticeable thing. No man in our regiment has been healthier than I have, perhaps none so healthy. I have not been laid up a moment, hardly felt even slightly unwell.

It is singular how one gets attached to this life with all its hardships. We are a most jovial happy set. Our mess now is Colonel Scammon, Lieutenant-Colonel Matthews, Dr. Clendenin, Dr. Joe, and myself. I doubt if anywhere in the country a happier set gather about the table. Joe is full of life, occasionally unwell a little, but always jovial. Matthews has had some of his old troubles — nothing serious — but is a most witty, social man. Colonel Scammon takes medicines all the time, but is getting fat, and is in the best of temper with *all of us.* General Schenck and his staff are also here. Donn Piatt is one of them. The general and Donn add greatly to our social resources. Indeed I have seen no regiment that will at all compare with us in this respect. . . .

I shall be thirty-nine years old, or is it thirty-eight, tomorrow? Birthdays come along pretty fast these days.

Do the boys go to school? I hope they will be good scholars, but not study at the expense of growth and health. . . .

If the paymaster ever gets along I shall be able to send home money enough to pay debts, taxes, and keep you going for some time.

We have news of a victory by McClellan. We hope it is true. Whatever may befall us, success at Washington if followed up secures our country's cause. Love to all.

Affectionately, as ever,

R.

Mrs. Hayes.

Up Gauley River, Camp Sewell, October 3, 1861.

Dear Uncle: — I should have written you, if I had known where you were. We are in the presence of a large force of the enemy, much stronger than we are, but the mud and floods have pretty much ended this campaign. Both the enemy and ourselves are compelled to go back to supplies soon. I think, therefore, there will be no fight. We shall not attack their entrenchments now that they are reinforced, and I suspect they will not come out after us. Donn Piatt just peeped in. He always has funny things. I said, quoting Webster, "I still live." "Yes," said he, "Webster — Webster. He was a great man. Even the old Whigs about Boston admit that!" And again, speaking of the prospect of a fight, he said: "This whistling of projectiles about one's ears is disagreeable. It made me try to think at Bull Run of all my old prayers; but I could only remember, 'Oh Lord, for these and all thy other mercies, we desire to be thankful.'"

We shall soon go into winter quarters at posts chosen to hold this country, Gauley Bridge, Charleston, etc., etc. Who will get into a better place, is the question. We all want to go to Washington or to Kentucky or Missouri. We are in General Schenck's brigade, and hope he will make interest enough to get us into good quarters. There is much sickness among officers and men. My health was never better than during these four months. I hope you will continue to improve.

I am still in General Rosecrans' staff; but having just finished an extensive tour of court-martial, am again in camp with my regiment in good order. It is like going home to get back. Still this practicing on the circuit after the old fashion, only more so — an escort of cavalry and a couple of wagons with tents and grub — has its attractions. I shall get out of it soon, but as a change, I rather enjoy it.

Between you and Platt, I must get a strong, fleet, sure-footed horse for the next campaign. If the paymaster comes, I shall be able to pay from one hundred and fifty to two hundred dollars. My present horse turns out well, very well, but the winter will probably use him up, and I must get another.

Hereafter, direct to me, Gauley Bridge, instead of Clarksburg.

We have just learned that McClellan has had a success at Washington. If so, whatever happens here, the cause is safe. I hope the news is true.

Sincerely,

R. B. HAYES.

S. BIRCHARD.

CHAPTER XVI

IN WINTER QUARTERS, WEST VIRGINIA — 1861

OCTOBER 4, 1861. — My birthday. At Camp Scammon, one and one-half miles from Camp Sewell. A warm day with clouds gathering. General Schenck has assumed command of our brigade — Twenty-third and Thirtieth [Regiments]. Dined with General Schenck — a birthday dinner. His birthday also — he fifty-one.

CAMP LOOKOUT, Monday, October 7, 1861.

DEAREST: — The mails are in order again. Letters will now come promptly. On the day after I wrote you last we got all the back letters — lots of papers and dates up to October 1. One queer thing, a letter from Platt of *July 31* and one from Mother of October 1 got up the same day.

Our campaign is closed. No more fighting in this region unless the enemy attack, which they will not do. We are to entrench at Mountain Cove, eight miles from here, at Gauley Bridge, twenty miles off, and [at] Summersville, about the same. These points will secure our conquest of western Virginia from any common force, and will let half or two-thirds of our army go elsewhere. I hope we shall be the lucky ones to leave here.

The enemy and ourselves left the mountains about the same time; the enemy first, and for the same reason, viz., impossibility of getting supplies. We are now fourteen miles from Mount Sewell and perhaps thirty miles from the enemy. Our withdrawal was our first experience in backward movement. We all approved it. The march was a severe one. Our business today is sending off the sick, and Dr. Joe is up to his eyes in hard work. We have sixty to send to Ohio. This is the severest thing of the campaign. Poor fellows! We do as well as we can with them; but road-wagons in rain and mud are poor places.

Very glad — oh, so glad — you and Ruddy are well again. You did not tell me you were so unwell. I felt so badly to hear it. Do be very careful.

Don't worry about the war. We are doing our part, and if all does not go well, it is not our fault. I still think we are sure to get through with it safely. The South may not be conquered, but we shall secure to the Nation the best part of it.

We hope to go to Kentucky. If so, we shall meet before a month. Our regiment is a capital one. But we ought to recruit. We shall be about one hundred to one hundred and fifty short when this campaign is ended.

Tomorrow is election day [in Ohio]. We all talked about it today. We are for Tod and victory.

Good-bye. Much love to all.

Affectionately, yours ever,

R.

Tuesday morning, 6 A. M., October 8.

Your election day.

DEAREST: — This wet dirty letter and its writer have had considerable experience in the last twenty-four hours, and since the above was written. In the first place we have had another bitter storm, and this cold raw morning we shiver unless near the fires. At one time yesterday I thought I should have to take back a good deal of what I said in the letter I had just started for Cincinnati. I was at the hospital three-quarters mile from camp, helping Dr. Joe and Captain Skiles put the sick into wagons to be transported to Gallipolis and Cincinnati, when firing was heard and word came that the enemy in force had attacked our camp. The doctor and I hurried back leaving Captain Skiles to look after the sick. All the army, seven regiments (five to six thousand men), were forming in line of battle. I joined my regiment, and after waiting a half hour or so we were ordered to quarters with word that it was only a scouting party driving in our pickets. This was all in a rain-storm. The poor fellows in hospital — many of them — panic-stricken, fled down the road and were found by Dr. Joe on his return three or four miles from the hospital. Three of our regiment got up from their straw piles, got their guns and trudged up the road and took their places in line of battle. The behavior of the men was for the most part perfectly good. The alarm was undoubtedly a false one. No enemy is near us.

We shall go, if the sun comes out, seven miles nearer home, to Mountain Cove, and begin to build quarters and fortifications for a permanent stronghold. This brings us within an easy day's ride of the navigable waters of the Kanawha. Thence a steamboat can take us in about a day or so to Cincinnati. Pretty near to you. Telegraph also all the way.

Speaking of telegraph makes me think I ought to say Captain Gaines (our prosecuting attorney) has done as much, I think more, useful service, dangerous too, than any other officer in western Virginia. The history of his company, protecting the telegraph builders, would be a volume of romantic adventures.

Lieutenant Christie, of General Cox's staff, tells me Union Chapel has had a division, and troubles. Sorry to hear it. If you are compelled to leave, be in no haste to choose a new church. I want to confer on that subject. I think it important to be connected with a church, and with the right one. Mere nearness is important. This would favor the church near Seventh and Mound, if you can consent to go to a Presbyterian [church]. But of this hereafter.

I somehow think we shall meet within a month or two. I am very well and very full of fun this morning. A credit to be jolly.

Affectionately,

R. B. Hayes.

Captain Howard goes home in broken health. I shall send this, dirty as it is, by some sick officer or soldier. You must see some of them.

Mrs. Hayes.

CAMP EWING, MOUNTAIN COVE, SIX MILES ABOVE
GAULEY BRIDGE, Wednesday, October 9, 1861.

DEAREST: — Captain Zimmerman and I have just returned from a long stroll up a most romantic mountain gorge with its rushing mountain stream. A lovely October sun, bright and genial, but not at all oppressive. We found the scattered fragments of a mill that had been swept away in some freshet last winter, and following up came to the broken dam, and near by a deserted home — hastily deserted lately. Books, the cradle, and child's chair, tables, clock, chairs, etc., etc. Our conjecture is they fled from the army of Floyd about the time of [the] Carnifax fight. We each picked up a low, well-made, split-bottom chair and clambered up a steep cliff to our camp. I now sit in the chair. We both moralized on this touching proof of the sorrows of war and I reached my tent a little saddened to find on my lounge in my tidy comfortable quarters your good letter of October 1, directed in the familiar hand of my old friend [Herron]. Love to him and Harriet. How happy it makes me to read this letter.

Tell Mother Webb not to give up. In the Revolution they saw darker days — far darker. We shall be a better, stronger nation than ever in any event. A great disaster would strengthen us, and a victory, we all feel, will bring us out to daylight.

No, I don't leave the Twenty-third. I have been with them all the time except six days. I am privileged. In the Twenty-third I am excused from duty as major being judge-advocate general. On the staff I am free to come and go as major of the Twenty-third. This of course will not relieve me from labor, but it makes me more independent than any other officer I know of.

Dr. Clendenin and Joe tent together and mess with us. Dr. Clendenin's connection with us is permanent. We are in General Schenck's brigade. He lives in our regiment and we like him.

We are now in easy two days' ride of Cincinnati by steamboat, all but thirty or forty miles. We shall stay at this place ten days at least. We are building an entrenched camp for permanently holding this gateway of the Kanawha Valley. . . .

I feel as you do about the Twenty-third, only more so. There are several regiments whose music and appearance I can recognize at a great distance over the hills, as the Tenth, Ninth, and so on, but the Twenty-third I know by instinct. I was sitting in the court-house at Buckhannon one hot afternoon, with windows up, a number of officers present, when we heard music at a distance. No one expected any regiment at that time. I never dreamed of the Twenty-third being on the road, but the music struck me like words from home. "That is the band of my regiment," was my confident assertion. True, of course.

We have lost by death about six, by desertion four, by dismissal three, by honorable discharge about twenty-five to thirty. About two hundred are too sick to do duty, of whom about one-fifth will never be able to serve.

I was called to command parade this evening while writing this sheet. The line is much shorter than in Camp Chase, but so brown and firm and wiry, that I suspect our six hundred would do more service than twice their number could have done four months ago. . . .

You need not get any shirts or anything. We get them on this line, very good and very cheap. I bought two on the top of Mount Sewell for two dollars and forty cents for the two — excellent ones. I am now wearing one of them.

One of the charms of this life is its perpetual change. Yesterday morning we were in the most uncomfortable condition possible at Camp Lookout. Before night I was in a lovely spot with most capital company at headquarters. . . .

[R.]

Mrs. Hayes.

Headquarters 23d Reg't., O. V. Inf., U. S. A.,
Mountain Cove, six miles above Gauley
Bridge, October 9, 1861.

Dear Brother: — We are now near or at the point where an entrenched camp for winter quarters is to be established. It will command the main entrance to the head of the Kanawha Valley, and can be held by a small force; is within a day's ride of navigable waters connecting with Cincinnati, and telegraphic communication nearly completed. From half to two-thirds of the men in western Virginia can be spared as soon as a few days' work is done. Indeed, green regiments just recruited could take care of this country and release soldiers who have been hardened by some service. Our regiment is second to no other in *discipline,* and equal in *drill* to all but two or three in western Virginia. We think it would be sensible to send us to Kentucky, Missouri, or the sea coast for the winter. We can certainly do twice the work that we could have done four months ago, and there is no sense in keeping us housed up in fortifications and sending raw troops into the field. In Kentucky, disciplined troops — that is, men who are obedient and orderly — are particularly needed. A lot of lawless fellows plundering and burning would do more hurt than good among a Union people who have property. We have met no regiment that is better than ours, if any so good.

Now, the point I am at is, first, that a large part of the soldiers here can be spared this winter; second, that for service, the best ought to be taken away. With these two ideas safely lodged in the minds of the powers that be, the Twenty-third is sure to be withdrawn. If you can post the Governor a little, it might be useful.

We are pleasantly associated. My mess consists of Colonel Scammon, Lieutenant-Colonel Matthews, Drs. Clendenin and Webb. The general (Schenck) and staff quarter in our regiment, so that we have the best of society. My connection with General Rosecrans' staff, I manage to make agreeable by a little license. I quarter with my regiment, but am relieved from all but voluntary regimental duty. I think I have never enjoyed any period of my life as much as the last three months. The risks, hardships, separation from family and friends are balanced by the notion that I am doing what every man, who possibly can, ought to do, leaving the agreeable side of things as clear profit. My health has been perfect. A great matter this is. We have many sick, and sickness on marches and in camps is trebly distressing. It makes one value health. We now have our sick in good quarters and are promised a ten days' rest.

The weather today is beautiful, and I don't doubt that we shall get back to good condition in that time.

Your election yesterday, I hope, went overwhelmingly for "Tod and Victory." We talked of holding an election here, but as we liked Jewett personally, it was not pushed. We should have been unanimous for the war ticket.

Letters now should be sent to Gauley Bridge. Love to all.

Sincerely,

R. B. HAYES. *

WM. A. PLATT.

October 10, Camp Ewing, seven miles above Gauley Bridge. — A pretty day in a pleasant camp, surrounded by mountain scenery. We had a false alarm in Camp Lookout; formed in line of battle. I was at the hospital but rode rapidly up and was on hand before the line was ready. Some men at hospital fled. Some were suddenly well and took [their] place in line of battle.

October 11, Camp Ewing. — Wet, cold. We hear of enemy back at Camp Lookout and rumors of, over New River. On this road are many deserted homes — great Virginia taverns wasted. The people are for the most part a helpless and harmless race. Some Massachusetts people have come in and made pleasant homes. We are on a turnpike leading up the Kanawha to White Sulphur Springs and so on to eastern Virginia.

October 12. At Camp Ewing. — Rode down to Hawk's Nest with General Schenck and Colonel Scammon and Lieutenant Chesebrough; a most romantic spot. A cliff seven hundred feet perpendicular projects out over New River; a view of New River

* This letter was placed in the Governor's hands for his information. It was then sent to Mrs. Hayes, who on October 23 forwarded it to Mr. Birchard. In her accompanying letter Mrs. Hayes wrote that she had seen Colonel Matthews, who had told her that "Rutherford was almost the only man who had not been sick or affected some by the campaign, that he was perfectly well and looking better than ever." Mrs. Hayes tries bravely to conceal her sense of loneliness, but it appears unmistakably in her closing paragraph where she writes: "We would be so glad to see you. Yours and Rutherford's room is waiting — the books are lonely and everybody and everything would meet you so gladly."

for a mile or two above and below the cliff, rushing and foaming between the mountains.   On the top was a small entrenchment built by Wise.   A Union man (like other Union men) wishing to move to Ohio, says he means to burn his house to keep it from falling into secession hands.

October 14.   Camp Tompkins, General Rosecrans' Headquarters, near Gauley Bridge. — I came down here to hold court today.   Left my regiment about eight miles up the pike.   Mrs. Tompkins lives here in a fine large white house.   Her husband, a graduate of West Point, is a colonel in the secession army.   Why devastate the homes and farms of poor deluded privates in the Rebel army and protect this property?   Treat the lady well, as all women ought always to be treated, but put through the man for his great crime.

NEAR GAULEY BRIDGE, October 15, 1861.

DEAR UNCLE: — I am practicing law on the circuit, going from camp to camp.   Great fun I find it.   I am now in General Rosecrans' headquarters, eight miles from my regiment.   This is the spot for grand mountain scenery.   New River and Gauley unite here to form the Kanawha.   Nothing on the Connecticut anywhere equals the views here.

Glad Ohio is sound on the goose.   Sandusky County for once is right.   We shall beat the Rebels if the people will only be patient.   We are learning war.   The teaching is expensive and the progress slow, but I see the advance.   Our army here is safe and holds the key to all that is worth having in western Virginia.   . . .

Sincerely,

R. B. HAYES.

P. S. — Send letters, etc., care of General Rosecrans as heretofore.   How about Treasury notes?   Patriotism requires us to take and circulate them, but is there not a chance of their sharing, sooner or later, in a limited degree, the fate of the Continental money of Revolutionary times?

S. BIRCHARD.

CAMP TOMPKINS, GAULEY BRIDGE, October 15, 1861.

DEAR MOTHER: — You will be pleased to hear that I am here practicing law. The enemy having vanished in one direction and our army having retired to this stronghold in the other, I, yesterday, left my regiment about seven miles up the river and am here at General Rosecrans' headquarters, looking after offenders. It is safe enough in all this region. Our soldiers occupy all the leading roads and strong places. We hear of nobody being fired on, even by murderous bushwhackers. . . .

We are in the midst of glorious mountain scenery. Hawk's Nest and Lover's Leap are two of the most romantic spots I have ever seen. A precipitous cliff over seven hundred feet high, with high mountains back of it, overlooks a wild rushing river that roars and dashes against the rocks, Niagara fashion. The weather too has been, and is, lovely October weather. Love to all.

Affectionately, your son,

RUTHERFORD.

MRS. SOPHIA HAYES.

October 17, 1861. Camp Tompkins, near New River, two and one-half miles above Gauley Bridge, at General Rosecrans' Headquarters. — A threatening morning, a steady rain, fall fashion, in the afternoon. Received a letter by Mr. Schooley, dated 9th, from Lucy. Ruddy had been sick with a chill and Lucy not so well. Dear wife! She is troubled in her present trials that I am absent, but stoutly insists that she can bear up, that she is "a good soldier's wife." She sends me pants, etc., etc. A great many papers today in the court-martial line. Dr. Menzies called. Somewhat gloomy but not more so than is his wont.

CAMP TOMPKINS, NEAR GAULEY BRIDGE, October 17, 1861.

DEAREST: — I am practicing law again. My office is pleasantly located in a romantic valley on the premises of Colonel Tompkins of the Rebel army. His mansion is an elegant modern house, and by some strange good luck it has been occupied by his family and escaped uninjured while hundreds of humbler homes have been ruined.   Mrs. Tompkins has kept on the good side of our leaders, and has thus far kept the property safe.

The Twenty-third is seven miles or so up the valley of New River.   I was there last evening.   Dr. Joe has been sick a couple of days but is getting well.   Very few escape sickness, but with any sort of care it is not dangerous.   Not more than one case in a hundred has thus far proved fatal.

Colonel Matthews has gone home for a few days.   You will see him, I hope.   If he succeeds in one of the objects of his trip, I shall probably visit you for a few days within six weeks or so.

Our campaign here is ended, I think without doubt.   We hear stories which are repeated in your papers which look a little as if there might be an attempt to cut off our communications down the Kanawha, but I suspect there is very small foundation for them.   We are strongly posted.   No force would dare attack us.   To cut off supplies is the most that will be thought of, and any attempts to do that must meet with little success, if I am rightly informed about things.

We have had the finest of fall weather for several (it seems many) days.   The glorious mountains all around us are of every hue, changing to a deeper red and brown as the frosts cut the foliage.   I talk so much of the scenery, you will suspect me to be daft.   In fact I never have enjoyed nature so much. Being in the open air a great part of each day and surrounded by magnificent scenery, I do get heady I suspect on the subject. I have told you many a time that we were camped in the prettiest place you ever saw.   I must here repeat it.   The scenery on New River and around the junction of Gauley and New River where they form the Kanawha, is finer than any mere mountain and river views we saw last summer.   The music and sights belonging to the camps of ten thousand men add to the effect.

Our band has improved and the choir in McIlrath's Company would draw [an] audience anywhere.   The companies, many of them, sound their calls with the bugle, which with the echoes heightens the general charm.

I wish you and the boys were over in the Tompkins house. How you would be happy and wouldn't I? I do hope you will keep well, all of you. Kiss the little fellows all around and the big boy Birch too. Tell Webby the horse Webb is in excellent plight. I suppose "Birch" (the horse) has got home. Love to Grandma and all.

Affectionately,

R. B. HAYES.

MRS. HAYES.

CAMP TOMPKINS, October 18, 1861.

DEAREST: — Soon after I had sent off my letter yesterday, Mr. Schooley stopped with your bundle and letter. All most acceptable, gloves, etc., particularly. I get all your letters. . . .

Don't worry about the country. Things are slowly working around. For a first campaign by a green people, we have done well. The Rebellion will be crushed even at this rate by the time our three years are up. McClellan is crowding them. They must fight or run soon, and I think either is death.

We have a little excitement every day over some guerrilla story. But the rumors as they are sifted vanish rapidly into smoke.

Dr. Menzies was here today. He is troubled about his family, about his colonel, and so on. Very queer how some clever people manage to keep in a worriment under all circumstances.

One paymaster has come up. We hope to see ours some day. I shall send you funds as soon as they are paid me.

It is raining — a settled fall rain. But we are in a valley (not on top of Mount Sewell). I have a board floor to my tent. Who cares for the rain? — especially if my wife and bairns are safe under a tight roof by a warm fire. Keep up good courage. Kiss the boys, give my love to all, and continue to have happy dreams about your

Affectionate husband,

RUTHERFORD.

MRS. HAYES.

CAMP TOMPKINS, October 19, 1861.

DEAREST : — I got your letter of last Sunday yesterday. You can't be happier in reading my letters than I am in reading yours. Very glad our little Ruddy is no worse.

Don't worry about suffering soldiers, and don't be too ready to give up President Lincoln. More men are sick in camps than at home. Sick [men] are not comfortable anywhere, and less so in armies than in *good* homes. Transportation fails, roads are bad, contractors are faithless, officials negligent or fraudulent, but notwithstanding all this, I am satisfied that *our army is better fed, better clad, and better sheltered than any other army in the world.* And, moreover, where there is want, it is not due to the general or state Government half as much as to officers and soldiers. The two regiments I have happened to know most about and to care most about — McCook's Ninth and our Twenty-third — have no cause of complaint. Their clothing is better than when they left Ohio and better than most men wear at home. I am now dressed as a private, and I am well dressed. I live habitually on soldiers' rations, and I live well.

No, Lucy, the newspapers mislead you. It is the poor families at home, not the soldiers, who can justly claim sympathy. I except of course the regiments who have mad officers, but you can't help their case with your spare blankets. Officers at home begging better be with their regiments doing their appropriate duties. Government is sending enough if colonels, etc., would only do their part. McCook could feed, clothe, or blanket half a regiment more any time, while alongside of him is a regiment, ragged, hungry, and blanketless, full of correspondents writing home complaints about somebody. It is here as elsewhere. The thrifty and energetic get along, and the lazy and thoughtless send emissaries to the cities to beg. Don't be fooled with this stuff.

I feel for the poor women and children in Cincinnati. The men out here have sufferings, but no more than men of sense expected, and were prepared for, and can bear.

I see Dr. S— wants blankets for the Eighth Regiment. Why isn't he with it, attending to its sick? If its colonel and quartermaster do their duties as he does his, five hundred miles off, they can't expect to get blankets. I have seen the stores sent into this State, and the Government has provided abundantly for all. It vexes me to see how good people are imposed on. I have been through the camps of eight thousand men today, and I tell you they are better fed and clothed than the people of half the wards in Cincinnati. We have sickness which is bad enough, but it is due to causes inseparable from our condition. Living in open air, exposed to changes of weather, will break down one man in every four or five, even if he was "clad in purple and fine linen and fared sumptuously every day."

As for Washington, McClellan and so on, I believe they are doing the thing well. I think it will come out right. Wars are not finished in a day. Lincoln is, perhaps, not all that we could wish, but he is honest, patriotic, cool-headed, and safe. I don't know any man that the Nation could say is under all the circumstances to be preferred in his place.

As for the new governor, I like the change as much as you do. He comes in a little over two months from now.

A big dish of politics. I feared you were among croakers and grumblers, people who do more mischief than avowed enemies to the country.

It is lovely weather again. I hope this letter will find you as well as it leaves me. Love and kisses for the dear ones.

Affectionately, ever,

R. B. HAYES.

MRS. HAYES.

CAMP TOMPKINS, NEAR GAULEY BRIDGE, October 19, 1861.

DEAR UNCLE: — It is late Saturday night. I am away from my regiment at General Rosecrans' headquarters and feel lonesome. The weather is warm, threatening rain. We are waiting events, not yet knowing whether we are to stay here or go to some other quarters for the winter. I can't help suspecting that important events are looked for near Washington which may determine our course for the winter. All things in that direction have, to my eye, a hopeful look. A victory there if decisive will set things moving all over. We know the enemy *we* have been after is heartily sick of this whole business, and only needs a good excuse to give it up. A party of our men, bearing a flag of truce, spent a night with a party of Lee's men a few days ago, and the conversations they report tell the story.

Matthews has gone home for a fortnight. It is quite probable that I shall go home during the fall or winter for a short visit.

We have done no fortifying yet. We occasionally hear of a little guerrilla party and scamper after them, but no important movements are likely to occur here, unless a road should be opened from Washington to Richmond.

I see that Buckland is in the war. That is right. The noticeable difference between North and South in this war is, that South, the leading citizens, the lawyers and public men of all sorts, go into the fight themselves. This has not been so with us in the same degree. I am less disposed to think of a West Point education as requisite for this business than I was at first. Good sense and energy are the qualities required. . . .

Sincerely,

R. B. HAYES.

S. BIRCHARD.

CAMP TOMPKINS, October 21, 1861.

Monday morning before breakfast.

DEAREST: — Dr. Clendenin goes home this morning and I got up early to let you know how much I love you. Isn't this a proof of affection? I dreamed about you last night so pleasantly.

The doctor will give you the news. I see Colonel Tom Ford has been telling big yarns about soldiers suffering. They may be true — I fear they are — and it is right to do something; but it is not true that the fault lies with the Government alone. Colonel Ammen's Twenty-fourth has been on the mountains much more than the G. G — s [Guthrie Greys], for they have been in town most of the time; but nobody growls about them. The Twenty-fourth is looked after by its officers. The truth is, the suffering is great in all armies in the field in bad weather.

It can't be prevented. It is also true that much is suffered from neglect, but the neglect is in no one place. [The] Government is in part blamable, but the chief [blame] is on the armies themselves from generals down to privates.

It is certainly true that a considerable part of the sick men now in Cincinnati would be well and with their regiments, if they had obeyed orders about eating green chestnuts, green apples, and green corn. Now, all the men ought to be helped and cared for, but in doing so, it is foolish and wicked to assail and abuse, as the authors of the suffering, any one particular set of men. It is a calamity to be deplored and can be remedied by well directed labor, not by indiscriminate abuse.

I am filled with indignation to see that Colonel Ewing is accused of brutality to his men. All false. He is kind to a fault. All *good* soldiers love him; and yet he is published by some lying scoundrel as a monster.

I'll write no more on this subject. There will be far more suffering this winter than we have yet heard of. Try to relieve it, but don't assume that any one set of men are to be blamed for it. A great share of it can't be helped. Twenty-five per cent of all men who enlist can't stand the hardships and exposures of the field if suddenly transferred to it from their homes, and suffering is inevitable. Love to all.

Affectionately,

R. B. HAYES.

MRS. HAYES.

Sunday morning before breakfast,

TOMPKINS' FARM, THREE MILES FROM GAULEY BRIDGE,

October 27, 1861.

DEAR UNCLE: — It is a bright October morning. Ever since the great storms a month ago, we have had weather almost exactly such as we have at the same season in Ohio — occasional rainy days, but much very fine weather. We are still waiting events. Our winter's work or destination yet unknown. Decided events near Washington will determine our course. We shall wait those events several weeks yet before going into winter quarters. If things remain there without any events, we shall about half, I conjecture, build huts here and hereabouts, and the rest go to Ohio, and stay there, or go to Kentucky or Missouri as required.   I hope and expect to be of the half that leaves here.   But great events near Washington are expected by the powers that be, and it looks, as you see, some like it.

I have been occupied the whole week trying cases before a court-martial.   Some painful things, but on the whole, an agreeable time.   While the regiment is in camp doing nothing, this business is not bad for a change.

The paymasters are here at last, making the men very happy with their pretty government notes and gold.   The larger part is taken (seven-eighths) in paper on account of the bother in carrying six months' pay in gold.   Each regiment will send home a very large proportion of their pay — one-half to three-fifths.

The death of Colonel Baker is a national calamity, but on the whole, the war wears a favorable look.   Lucy says you are getting ready to shelter us when driven from Cincinnati. All right, but if we are forced to leave Cincinnati, I think we can't stop short of the Canada line.   There is no danger.   These Rebels will go under sooner or later.   I know that great battles are matters of accident largely.   A defeat near Washington is possible, and would be disastrous enough, but the Southern soldiers are not the mettle to carry on a long and doubtful war. If they can get a success by a dash or an ambuscade, they do it well enough, but for steady work, such as finally determines all great wars, our men are far superior to them.   With equal generalship and advantages, there is a perfect certainty as to the result of a campaign.   Our men here attack parties, not guerrillas merely, but uniformed soldiers from North Carolina, Georgia, South Carolina, etc., of two or three times their number with entire confidence that the enemy will run, and *they do*. They cut us up in ambuscades sometimes, and with stratagems of all sorts.   This sort of things delays, but it will not prevent, success if our people at home will pay the taxes and not tire of it.   Breakfast is ready.

Sincerely,

R. B. HAYES.

P. S. — You hear a great deal of the suffering of soldiers. It is much exaggerated. A great many lies are told. The sick do suffer. A camp and camp hospitals are necessarily awful places for sickness, but well men, for the most part, fare well — very well. Since I have kept house alone as judge-advocate, my orderly and clerk furnish soldiers' rations and nothing else. It is good living. In the camp of the regiment we fare worse than the rest, because the soldiers are enterprising and get things our lazy darkies don't.

Warm bedding and clothing will be greatly needed in the winter, and by troops guarding mountain passes. The supply should be greater than the Government furnishes. Sewing Societies, etc., etc., may do much good. The Government is doing its duty well. The allowance is ample for *average* service; but winter weather in mountains requires more than will perhaps be allowed.

S. BIRCHARD.

CAMP TOMPKINS, October 27, 1861.

DEAREST: — I have had a week's work trying twenty cases before a court-martial held in one of the fine parlors of Colonel Tompkins' country-seat. I have profaned the sacred mansion, and I trust that soon it will be converted into a hospital for our sick. My pertinacity has accomplished something towards that end. My week's work has had painful things, but many pleasant ones. I trust no life will be lost, but I fear it. Still I have done my duty kindly and humanely.

The weather generally has been good. The paymasters are here and general joy prevails. I expect to remain at this camp about a week or ten days. Whether I shall return to my regiment or go around to Grafton is not yet certain, probably the latter.

I see that the Sixth Street ladies are at work for the Tenth. All right. Clothing, but blankets and bedding comforts, etc., still more, will be needed this winter. Army blankets are small and are getting thin and worn-out. As cold weather comes on the well, even, will need all they can get.   As yet, in this region, nobody but sick men have any business to complain.

Dr. Joe has an order from General Rosecrans to Jim to come out and assist him.   If he comes let him bring a good blanket or comfort for me.   If I am away it can be kept for me till I return or used by somebody else.   During the next ten days I shall get money plenty to send you for all debts, etc., etc.

I can quite certainly make you a visit, but I hardly know when to do it.   Dr. Joe will want to visit home sometime this fall or winter and you better "maturely consider," as the court-martial record says, when you would prefer him to come.   Of course he must wait for Dr. Clendenin and I for Colonel Matthews.   My preference is about December.

Mother and Jim both seem to think letters never reach us. We get all your letters now, and quite regularly.   There was a period after Carnifax when we were out of reach, but now we are in line again.   We see Cincinnati papers of the 24th on the 26th.   By the by, you need not renew my subscription to the *Commercial*.   No use to send papers.   We get them from the office sooner in another way.

If Jim comes let him get an assortment of late papers, *Harper's, Atlantic,* etc., etc., and *keep them till he gets to our camp.* We are the outermost camp and people are coaxed out of their literature before they get to us. . . .

I dined in a tent with fourteen officers and *one* lady on Wednesday.   Her husband was formerly a steamboat captain, now a major in [the] First Kentucky.   She evidently enjoyed her singular position; bore her part well. . . .

Affectionately, your

RUTHERFORD.

Things I would like before winter sets in — I am not sure that Dr. Jim better bring them — there is no hurry:

1. A good large blanket; 2. An India-rubber coat, common black, — Dr. J—'s size; 3. A pair of gloves, riding, buckskin or sich; 4. A thick dark blue vest, military buttons and fit; my size at Sprague's; 5. Enough blue cord for seams of one pair

of pants; Dr. Joe's poem, "Lucile"; 6. Two blank books, **size** of my diaries — good nice ruled paper, 6 or 8 inches by 4 or 5; 7. A pocket memorandum book.

I could make a big list, but I'll quit.

MRS. HAYES.

Camp Tompkins, Tuesday morning, October 29, 1861. — A bright, cold October morning, before breakfast. This month has been upon the whole a month of fine weather. The awful storm on Mount Sewell, and a mitigated repetition of it at Camp Lookout ten days afterward, October 7, are the only storms worth noting. The first was unprecedented in this country and extended to most of the States. On the whole, the weather has been good for campaigning with this exception. Camp fever, typhus or typhoid, prevails most extensively. It is not fatal. Not more than four or five deaths, and I suppose we have had four or five hundred cases. Our regiment suffers more than the average. The Tenth, composed largely of Irish laborers, and the Second Kentucky, composed largely of river men, suffer least of any. I conjecture that persons accustomed to outdoor life and exposure bear up best. Against many afflictions incident to campaigning, men from comfortable homes seem to bear up best. Not so with this.

I have tried twenty cases before a court-martial held in Colonel Tompkins' house the past week. One conviction for desertion and other aggravated offenses punished with sentence of death. I trust the general will mitigate this.

We hear that Lieutenant-Colonel Matthews, who left for a stay of two weeks at home about the 18th, has been appointed colonel of a regiment. This is deserved. It will, I fear, separate us. I shall regret that much, very much. He is a good man, of solid talent and a most excellent companion, witty, cheerful, and intelligent. Well, if so, it can't be helped. The compensation is the probable promotion I shall get to his place. I care little about this. As much to get rid of the title "Major" as anything else makes it desirable. I am prejudiced against "Major." Doctors are majors and (tell it not in Gath) Dick

Corwine is major! So if we lose friend Matthews, there may be this crumb, besides the larger one of getting rid of being the army's lawyer or judge, which I don't fancy.

Colonel Baker, gallant, romantic, eloquent soldier, senator, patriot, killed at Edwards Ferry on the upper Potomac! When will this thing cease? Death in battle does not pain me much. But caught surprised in ambush again! After so many warnings. When will our leaders learn? I do not lose heart. I calmly contemplate these things. The side of right, with strength, resources, endurance, must ultimately triumph. These disasters and discouragements will make the ultimate victory more precious. But how long? I can wait patiently if we only do not get tricked out of victories. I thought McClellan was to mend all this. "We have had our last defeat, we have had our last retreat," he boasted. Well, well, patience! West Pointers are no better leaders than others.

October 29, 1861. Evening. — This is the anniversary of the Literary Club — the society with which so much of my life is associated. It will be celebrated tonight. The absent will be remembered. I wish I was there. How many who have been members are in the tented field! What a roll for our little club! I have seen these as members: General Pope, now commanding in Missouri; Lieutenant-Colonel Force of the Twentieth, in Kentucky; Major Noyes of the Thirty-ninth, in Missouri; Lieutenant-Colonel Matthews, Twenty-third, in Virginia; Secretary Chase, the power (brain and soul) of the Administration; Governor Corwin, Minister to Mexico; Tom Ewing, Jr., Chief Justice of Kansas; Ewing Sr., the great intellect of Ohio; Nate Lord, colonel of a Vermont or New Hampshire regiment; McDowell, a judge in Kansas; McDowell (J. H.), a senator and major in Kansas; Oliver and Mallon, common pleas judges; Stanton, a representative Ohio House of Representatives; and so on. Well, what good times we have had! Wit, anecdote, song, feast, wine, and good fellowship — gentlemen and scholars. I wonder how it will go off tonight.

Queer world! We fret our little hour, are happy and pass away. Away! Where to? "This longing after immortality!

These thoughts that wander through eternity"! I have been and am an unbeliever of all these sacred verities. But will I not take refuge in the faith of my fathers at last? Are we not all impelled to this? The great abyss, the unknown future, — are we not happier if we give ourselves up to some settled faith? Can we feel safe without it? Am I not more and more carried along, drifted, towards surrendering to the best religion the world has yet produced? It seems so. In this business, as I ride through the glorious scenery this loveliest season of the year, my thoughts float away beyond this wretched war and all its belongings. Some, yes many, glorious things, as well as all that is not so, [impress me]; and [I] think of the closing years on the down-hill side of life, and picture myself a Christian, sincere, humble, devoted, as conscientious in that as I am now in this — not more so. My belief in this war is as deep as any faith can be; — but thitherward I drift. I see it and am glad.

All this I write, thinking of the debates, the conversations, and the happiness of the Literary Club. It has been for almost twelve years an important part of my life. My best friends are among its members — Rogers, Stephenson, Force, James. And how I have enjoyed Strong, McConkey (alas!), Wright, McDowell, Mills, Meline, and all! And thinking of this and those leads me to long for such communion in a perfection not known on earth and to hope that in the future there may be a purer joy forever and ever. And as one wishes, so he drifts. While these enjoyments are present we have little to wish for; as they slip from us, we look forward and hope and then believe with the college theme, "There is more beyond." And for me to believe is to act and live according to my faith.

CAMP TOMPKINS, VIRGINIA, October 29, 1861.

Tuesday morning after breakfast.

MY DEAR BOY: — If I am not interrupted I mean to write you a long birthday letter. You will be eight years old on the 4th of November — next Monday, and perhaps this letter will get to Cincinnati in time for your mother or grandmother to read it to you on that day.

If I were with you on your birthday I would tell you a great many stories about the war. Some of them would make you almost cry and some would make you laugh. I often think how Ruddy and Webby and you will gather around me to listen to my stories, and how often I shall have to tell them, and how they will grow bigger and bigger, as I get older and as the boys grow up, until if I should live to be an old man they will become really romantic and interesting. But it is always hard work for me to write, and I can't tell on paper such good stories as I could give you, if we were sitting down together by the fire.

I will tell you why we call our camp Camp Tompkins. It is named after a very wealthy gentleman named Colonel Tompkins, who owns the farm on which our tents are pitched. He was educated to be a soldier of the United States at West Point, where boys and young men are trained to be officers at the expense of the Government. He was a good student and when he grew up he was a good man. He married a young lady, who lived in Richmond and who owned a great many slaves and a great deal of land in Virginia. He stayed in the army as an officer a number of years, but getting tired of army life, he resigned his office several years ago, and came here and built an elegant house and cleared and improved several hundred acres of land. The site of his house is a lovely one. It is about a hundred yards from my tent on an elevation that commands a view of Gauley Bridge, two and a half miles distant — the place where New River and Gauley River unite to form the Kanawha River. Your mother can show you the spot on the map. There are high hills or mountains on both sides of both rivers. and before they unite they are very rapid and run roaring and dashing along in a very romantic way. When the camp is still at night, as I lie in bed, I can hear the noise like another Niagara Falls.

In this pleasant place Colonel Tompkins lived a happy life. He had a daughter and three sons. He had a teacher for his daughter and another for his boys. His house was furnished in good taste; he had books, pictures, boats, horses, guns, and dogs. His daughter was about sixteen, his oldest boy was fourteen, the next twelve, and the youngest about nine. They lived

9

here in a most agreeable way until the Rebels in South Carolina attacked Major Anderson in Fort Sumter. Colonel Tompkins wished to stand by the Union, but his wife and many relatives in eastern Virginia were Secessionists. He owned a great deal of property which he feared the Rebels would take away from him if he did not become a Secessionist. While he was doubting what to do and hoping that he could live along without taking either side, Governor Wise with an army came here on his way to attack steamboats and towns on the Ohio River. Governor Wise urged Colonel Tompkins to join the Rebels; told him as he was an educated military man he would give him the command of a regiment in the Rebel army. Colonel Tompkins finally yielded and became a colonel in Wise's army. He made Wise agree that his regiment should be raised among his neighbors and that they should not be called on to leave their homes for any distant service, but remain as a sort of home guards. This was all very well for a while. Colonel Tompkins stayed at home and would drill his men once or twice a week. But when Governor Wise got down to the Ohio River and began to drive away Union men, and to threaten to attack Ohio, General Cox was sent with Ohio soldiers after Governor Wise.

Governor Wise was not a good general or did not have good soldiers, or perhaps they knew they were fighting in a bad cause. At any rate, the Rebel army was driven by General Cox from one place to another until they got back to Gauley Bridge near where Colonel Tompkins lived. He had to call out his regiment of home guards and join Wise. General Cox soon drove them away from Gauley Bridge and followed them up this road until he reached Colonel Tompkins' farm. The colonel then was forced to leave his home, and has never dared to come back to it since. Our soldiers have held the country all around his house.

His wife and children remained at home until since I came here. They were protected by our army and no injury done to them. But Mrs. Tompkins got very tired of living with soldiers all around, and her husband off in the Rebel army. Finally a week or two ago General Rosecrans told her she might go to eastern Virginia, and sent her in her carriage with an escort of ten dragoons and a flag of truce over to the Rebel army about thirty miles from here, and I suppose she is now with her husband.

I suppose you would like to know about a flag of truce.   It is a white flag carried to let the enemy's army know that you are coming, not to fight, but to hold a peaceful meeting with them.   One man rides ahead of the rest about fifty yards, carrying a white flag — any white handkerchief will do.   When the pickets, sentinels, or scouts of the other army see it, they know what it means.   They call out to the man who carries the flag of truce and he tells them what his party is coming for. The picket tells him to halt, while he sends back to his camp to know what to do.   An officer and a party of men are sent to meet the party with the flag of truce, and they talk with each other and transact their business as if they were friends, and when they are done they return to their own armies.   No good soldier ever shoots a man with a flag of truce.   They are always very polite to each other when parties meet with such a flag.

Well, Mrs. Tompkins and our men travelled till they came to the enemy.   The Rebels were very polite to our men.   Our men stayed all night at a picket station in the woods along with a party of Rebels who came out to meet them.   They talked to each other about the war, and were very friendly.   Our men cooked their suppers as usual.   One funny fellow said to a Rebel soldier, "Do you get any such good coffee as this over there?"   The Rebel said, "Well, to tell the truth, the officers are the only ones who see much coffee, and it's mighty scarce with them."   Our man held up a big army cracker.   "Do you have any like this?" and the Rebel said, "Well no, we do live pretty hard," — and so they joked with each other a great deal.

Colonel Tompkins' boys and the servants and tutor are still in the house.   The boys come over every day to bring the general milk and pies and so on.   I expect we shall send them off one of these days and take the house for a hospital or something of the kind.

And so you see Colonel Tompkins didn't gain anything by joining the Rebels.   If he had done what he thought was right, everybody would have respected him.   Now the Rebels suspect him, and accuse him of treachery if anything occurs in his regiment which they don't like.   Perhaps he would have lost property, perhaps he would have lost his life if he had stood by the Union, but he would have done right and all good people would have honored him.

And now, my son, as you are getting to be a large boy, I want you to resolve always to do what you know is right. No matter what you will lose by it, no matter what danger there is, always do right.

I hope you will go to school and study hard, and take exercise too, so as to grow and be strong, and if there is a war you can be a soldier and fight for your country as Washington did. Be kind to your brothers and to Grandmother, and above all to your mother.   You don't know how your mother loves you, and you must show that you love her by always being a kind, truthful, brave boy; and I shall always be so proud of you.

Give my love to all the boys, and to Mother and Grandmother.

Affectionately, your father,

R. B. Hayes.

Birchard A. Hayes,

October 30.   Tompkins Farm. — [I] walked with Captain Gaines two and one-half or three miles down to Gauley Bridge. Called on Major William H. Johnston and Swan, paymaster and clerk for our regiment [for] Cracraft, quartermaster sergeant, who wanted Dr. McCurdy's pay.   To get it, drew my own and sent him two hundred and sixty dollars and blank power-of-attorney to me to draw his pay.   The doctor is sick and wants to go home.   Our regiment suffers severely with camp fever. About one hundred and twenty absent, mostly sick, and as many more prescribed for here.   This out of nine hundred and fifty. Severe marches, ill-timed, in rain, etc., etc., is one great cause. Then, most of our men have been used to comfortable homes, and this exposed life on these mountains is too much for them.

Well, we dined at a Virginia landlady's, good coffee, good biscuit; in short, a good homelike dinner.   Walked immediately back.

October 31.   Tompkins Farm. — Smoky, foggy, and Indian-summery in the morning; clear, warm, and beautiful in the afternoon. I rode up to the regiment at Camp Ewing, gave some directions as to making out the new muster-rolls. Saw several of the officers sick with the camp fever.

Poor "Bony" Seaman, it is said, will die. What a good-hearted boy he was! His red glowing face, readiness to oblige, to work — poor fellow! He was working his way up. Starting as private, then commissary sergeant, then sergeant-major, and already recommended and perhaps appointed second-lieutenant. I shall never forget his looks at the battle of Carnifax. We were drawn up in line of battle waiting for orders to go down into the woods to the attack. The First Brigade had already gone in and the firing of cannon and musketry was fast and furious. "Bony" rode ahead to see, and after an absence of twenty minutes came galloping back, his face radiant with joyous excitement and his eyes sparkling. He rode up to Colonel Scammon and myself calling out: "I've been under fire, the bullets were whistling all about me, and I wasn't scared at all!" He looked like my Birtie when he is very happy and reminded me of him. His dress was peculiar too — a warm-us and a felt grey hat like mine. Good boy, noble, true, must he die?

Captain Drake and Captain McIlrath had a quarrel last night. Captain Drake had been drinking (not enough to hurt). Captain McIlrath, putting his face close to Captain Drake's mouth to smell his breath, said: "Where did you get your whiskey?" And so it went, the plucky Captain Drake striking the giant McIlrath, but no fight followed. McIlrath as captain of company A was first in line of promotion for major and Captain Drake had been just recommended for the place. This fact had nothing to do with it, merely a coincidence.

Returned to camp in the evening; rode part way with Colonel McCook, open and minatory against Rosecrans. At eight P. M. a dispatch from Adjutant-General Buckingham announced my promotion to lieutenant-colonel *vice* Matthews, and J. M. Courtly [Comly] as major. The latter is I fear an error. He is a stranger to the regiment. It will make a fuss, and perhaps ought to. Captain Drake is a brave, generous old fellow, excitable and furious, but when the heat is off sound to the core, with the instincts of a gentleman strong in him.

November 1. Camp Tompkins. — Cold, gusty, but sunshiny. The fine band of the Second Kentucky does discourse glorious music. A dapper little fellow with a cane, "a nice young man," fit for Fourth Street in piping times of peace, walked by my tent just now. Not a fellow in camp with his army blue, tattered or not, who does not feel above him.

The enemy have just begun to fire on the ferry and on the teams and passers between here and Gauley Bridge. They have cannon and riflemen on the opposite side of New River. Went with Sweet scouting to ascertain exact position of enemy. Followed up rills and ravines, running imminent risk of breaking necks; discovered tolerable views of the enemy. The echoes of the cannon and bursting shells were grand in these defiles. Two of our men slightly wounded. The ferry stopped during daylight (but doing double duty at night), is all that was accomplished. Great waste of ammunition, great noise, excitement among soldiers. *Vox præterea nihil.* Got home at night, tired enough, in the rain.

CAMP TOMPKINS, VIRGINIA, November 2, 1861.

DEAREST LUCY: — I am about to return to my regiment, six or eight miles up New River at Camp Ewing. I shall probably be comfortably settled there tonight.

Colonel Matthews having been promoted to the colonelcy of the Fifty-first, I have been promoted to the lieutenant-colonelcy of the Twenty-third and relieved, for the present at any rate, of the duties of judge-advocate. I of course regret very much the loss of Colonel Matthews. But you know we have been separated more than half the time since we came to Virginia; so it is more a change in name than in fact. I hope he has a good regiment. If he has decent materials he will make it a good one. I am pleased, as people in the army always are, with my promotion. I confess to the weakness of preferring (as I must hereafter always be called by some title) to be called Colonel to being styled Major.

We had a noisy day yesterday. A lot of Floyd's men (we suppose) have got on the other side of the river with cannon. They tried to sink our ferry-boats and prevent our crossing Gauley River at the bridge (now ferry for Wise destroyed the bridge). They made it so hazardous during the day that all teams were stopped; but during the night the ferry did double duty, so that the usual crossing required in twenty-four hours was safely done. Both sides fired cannon and musketry at each other several hours, but the distance was too great to do harm. We have two wounded and thought we did them immense damage. They probably suffered little or no loss, but probably imagined that they were seriously cutting us. So we all see it. Our side does wonders always. We are not accurately informed about these Rebels, but appearances do not make them formidable. They can't attack us. The only danger is that they may get below on the Kanawha and catch a steamboat before we drive them off.

I wish you could see such a battle. No danger and yet enough sense of peril excited to make all engaged very enthusiastic. The echoes of the cannon and bursting shells through the mountain defiles were wonderful. I spent the day with two soldiers making a reconnaissance — that is to say trying to find out the enemies' exact position, strength, etc., etc. We did some hard climbing, and were in as much danger as anybody else, that is, none at all. One while the spent rifle balls fell in our neighborhood, but they hadn't force enough to penetrate clothing, even if they should hit. It's a great thing to have a rapid river and a mountain gorge between hostile armies. . . .

Affectionately,

R. B. Hayes.

P. S. — I have been paid half of my pay, and will send you two or three hundred dollars at least, the first chance. I wish you would get Dr. Jim to buy one or two pairs of lieutenant-colonel's shoulder-straps to send with the privilege of returning if they don't suit. We expect Dr. Clendenin daily.

Mrs. Hayes.

Camp Ewing, Virginia, November 3. Sunday. — Yesterday and today it has been rainy, stormy, and disagreeable. I came up to my regiment yesterday as lientenant-colonel. The men and officers seem pleased with my promotion. All regret the loss of Colonel Matthews and say that if I go their interest in the regiment is gone. The paymaster has paid me up to the 31st [of] August, four hundred and ninety-six dollars. Lieutenant Richardson has also collected for me two hundred and fifty dollars of money lent the company officers. I can send home seven hundred dollars and still have two months' pay due me. I have been very economical in order to a fair start for my family. I shall now feel relieved from anxiety on that score and will be more liberal in my expenditures.

A Mr. Ficklin, of Charlottesville, Virginia, a brother-in-law of Mrs. Colonel Tompkins, came with her bearing a flag of truce. He staid with us last night. He is an agreeable, fair-minded, intelligent gentleman of substance, formerly and perhaps now a stage proprietor and mail-carrier. He says he entertains not the shadow of a doubt that the Confederate States will achieve independence. He says the whole people will spend and be spent to the last before they will yield. On asking him, "Suppose on the expiration of Lincoln's term a state-rights Democrat shall be elected President, what will be the disposition of the South towards him?" he replied hesitatingly as if puzzled, and seemed to feel that the chief objection to the Union would be removed. So it's Lincoln, Black Republican, prejudice, a name, that is at the bottom of it all. His account of things goes to show that great pains have been taken to drill and discipline the Rebel troops, and that their cavalry are especially fine.

All the sick sent over Gauley last night. A new lot appear today. We have had three deaths by the fever.

I now enter on new duties. I must learn all the duties of colonel, see that Colonel Scammon does not forget or omit anything. He is ready to all but so forgetful. He loves to talk of West Point, of General Scott, of genteel and aristocratic people; and if an agreeable person is found who will seem to be entertained, he can talk by the hour in a pleasant way to the omission of every important duty.

Camp Ewing up New River. November 4. Monday. — Cold and clear; rain probably over. My boy's birthday — eight years old. It was such a morning as this eight years ago. I hope they are all well and happy at home. They will think of me today as they eat the birthday dinner and give him the birthday presents. Dear boy!

This morning four yawls were hauled into camp. It shows that it is intended to cross the river and attack the enemy. The blunder is in hauling them up in daylight. The enemy have thus been told of our design and will guard the few practicable ferries, as I fear, to our serious loss if not defeat. Stupid! stupid!

About seven hundred and fifty men are present this morning. Sixty-nine are sick. This, after sending off one hundred and fifty-nine sick men. Only one second-lieutenant for duty — a bad showing. Sun shining at 11 A. M. All the company officers gloomy and grumbling. The paymaster coming just at this time is all that makes endurable this state of things.

3:30 P. M. — Cannon firing heard. Shelling McCook's camp on the hills below. I order out Captain McIlrath and company to go with Mack's Battery.

CAMP EWING, November 4, 1861.

DEAR UNCLE: — Your letter of October 21 came to hand the day before yesterday. I am very glad you are so much better. If you will now be careful, I hope you will be able to get comfortably through the winter. You have no doubt heard that Matthews has been promoted to a colonelcy and has left us. I have been promoted to his place of lieutenant-colonel. We regret to lose him. He is a good officer. I have now been relieved from duty as judge-advocate, and will hereafter be with my regiment. The colonel of our regiment is a genial gentleman, but lacks knowledge of men and rough life, and so does not get on with the regiment as well as he might. Still, the place is not an unpleasant one.

The enemy has appeared in some force, with a few cannon, on the opposite side of New River at this point, and on the left bank of Kanawha lower down, and are, in some degree, obstructing our communications with the Ohio. To get rid of this, we are canvassing divers plans for crossing and clearing them out. The river here is rapid, the banks precipitous rocks, with only a few places where a crossing, even if not opposed, is practicable; and the few possible places can be defended successfully by a small force against a large one. We are getting skiffs and yawls from below to attempt the passage. If it is done, I shall do what I can to induce the generals to see beforehand that we are not caught in any traps.

This is Birch's birthday — a cold, raw November morning — a dreadful day for men in tents on the wet ground. We ought to be in winter quarters. I hope we shall be soon. We are sending from this army great numbers of sick. Cincinnati and other towns will be full of them. . . .

[R. B. Hayes.]

S. Birchard.

Camp Ewing, November 5. — Six hundred and fifty-seven present for duty; sixty-nine sick. Total strength nine hundred and thirty-six. Absent one hundred and ninety-three — all sick but about forty on detached service. Captain Woodward worse and in great danger. Enemy firing again on McCook's camp. No casualties at 10:30 o'clock.

Camp Ewing, November 5, 1861. Tuesday morning.

Dearest Lucy: — . . . We are having stirring times again. The enemy on the other side of New River are trying to shell such of our camps as lie near the river bank. We are just out of reach of their shot. McCook, in sight of us below, is camped in easy range, and they are peppering at him. I hear their guns every two or three minutes as I write. He doesn't like to move, and probably will not until they do him some serious harm. They fired all day yesterday without doing any other mischief than breaking one tent pole. A ball or shell would hardly light before his men would run with picks to dig it up as a trophy. It is probable that we shall cross the river to attempt to drive them off in a day or two. You will know the result long before this letter reaches you.

I had a note from Jim yesterday, saying he had reached the steamboat landing below here. We look for him today. I hope he will get up so as to be here to help take care of things here while we cross the river.

I have nearly one thousand dollars, seven hundred or eight hundred dollars of which I will send you the first good chance. Two months' more salary is due me besides about eighty-five dollars as judge-advocate. So we shall have funds plenty for this winter.

I thought of you all yesterday, and wished I could look in on you at Birch's birthday dinner. You were thinking of the absent father and uncles. * So it is. We love each other so much that on all sad or joyous occasions we shall always have each other in mind. . . . Good-bye. Love to all.

Lovingly,

RUTHERFORD.

MRS. HAYES.

Camp Ewing, November 8. — A beautiful fall day. About six hundred and fifty for duty, about two hundred and twenty-five

---

* Mrs. Hayes, writing November 4, said: "All we lacked of happiness was your presence. Not much time passes that you are not thought of, talked of, and sometimes cried over, but that is always done *decently* and in *order*, so I think I pass for one of the most cheerful, happy women imaginable. I do not dare to let Birchie see me downcast for he has so much sympathy that it is very touching to see him, and I do not want to cloud his young life with sorrow. Today is his birthday. He is very happy. Uncle George brought him an air-pistol, and he started to school, all of which, makes him really happy. The book which I get for him from you will complete his joy. . . . I felt finely this morning. Every thing right. . . . But this afternoon, felt almost down. Ruddy's chill is one cause, Birchie's absence another and *Frémont* the last and greatest. I cannot give him up, yet it looks dark and forbidding. It will be the last moment that I give up his honor, patriotism, and power to successfully command an army."

sick, present and absent.   All sent off who are in hospital but four; nine hundred and twenty-nine men still in regiment. *

We are getting ready to leave. I send home all I can, preparatory for rapid movements with weak trains of transportation. Still we have thirty-nine waggons, thanks to Gardner.

Captain Woodward died Tuesday, our hardiest officer. Industrious, faithful soldier, he has made his company from the poorest to almost the best. A sad loss. We send his remains home. Our fourth death in camp.

CAMP EWING, November 8, 1861, Thursday A. M.

DEAREST: — Mr. Fuller, our waggon-master, goes to Cincinnati today. We are [so] busy preparing to send expeditions against the enemy, sending off sick and baggage, that I have no time to write.

I send you a few things that I would not want lost. My Diary, up to date, for your eye alone, etc., etc. Drs. Joe and Jim are busy as bees also.

We shall go into winter quarters in a fortnight or so I think, when we shall have plenty of leisure.

I see the papers are full of foolish stories, sent by frightened people to terrify without rhyme or reason. Nobody is hurt by all this cannonading. One killed and three wounded covers the casualties of five days. Our provisions are plenty and we are in no peril here.

"Love to all the boys" and Grandma. Bushels — no, oceans for yourself.

Affectionately,

R.

P. S. — Jim laughs when he sees me and says I must send home my picture to show you that I tell the truth about health.

You need not buy any lieutenant-colonel's shoulder-straps or send me anything more to this region.

MRS. HAYES.

* For some weeks after this date, nearly every entry in the Diary contained a report similar to the one in this paragraph.

Camp Ewing, November 9, 1861. — A wet disagreeable morning. Anticipating hasty movements — expeditions without baggage against the enemy and the like — I yesterday sent home my jottings up to this time and begin today a new book. We were yesterday expecting to use four skiffs or yawls and two boat frames built here covered with canvas in crossing New River at a point five miles above here. It was hoped to surprise the enemy. Indications yesterday showed that the enemy were preparing to meet us. The passage to the water is down precipitous rocks six or seven hundred feet. The stream is very rapid and deep. McCook says one hundred yards wide by one hundred and fifty yards deep! The ascent on the opposite side is equally difficult. One hundred men could resist the passage of one thousand. We were not ordered over in view of these facts. What will be done is yet unknown.

Last night ate a turkey supper at commisary building [with] Captains Skiles and Drake and Lieutenant Avery and others. Yesterday I drew resolutions on occasion of death of Captain Woodward; today, on leaving of Colonel Matthews. Last night Sergeant Blish of Company I, a very competent, good officer, died — making, I think, the fifth death in camp in our regiment.

CAMP EWING, November 9, 1861.

DEAR MOTHER: — It is a rainy disagreeable November day. I have done up all the little chores required, have read the article in November number of the *Atlantic Monthly* on "Health in Camp," and hope not to be interrupted until I have finished a few words to you.

I wish you could see how we live. We have clothing and provisions in abundance, if men were all thrifty — food enough and good enough in spite of unthrift. Blankets, stockings, undershirts, drawers, and shoes are always welcome. These articles or substitutes are pretty nearly the only things the soldiers' aid societies need to send. India-rubber or oilcloth capes, or the like, are not quite abundant enough. Our tents are floored with loose boards taken from deserted secession barns and houses. For warmth we have a few stoves, but generally fires in trenches in front of the tents or in little ovens or furnaces in the tents formed by digging a hole a foot deep by a foot and a half wide and leading under the sides of the tent, the smoke passing up through chimneys made of barrels or sticks crossed cob-house fashion, daubed with mud.

There is not much suffering from cold or wet. The sickness is generally camp fever — a typhoid fever not produced, I think, by any defect in food, clothing, or shelter. Officers, who are generally more comfortably provided than the privates, suffer quite as much as the men — indeed, rather more in our regiment. Besides, the people residing here have a similar fever. Exposure in the night and to bad weather in a mountain climate to which men are not accustomed, seems to cause the sickness irrespective of all other circumstances. We have nine hundred and twenty-five men and officers, of whom two hundred and thirty are sick in camp, in hospitals in Virginia and in Ohio. Less than one-fourth of the privates are sick. One-half the captains, and one-half the lieutenants are or lately have been sick. Few are seriously or dangerously sick. Almost all are able to walk about. Only five out of about as many hundred cases have died. Three of them were very excellent men. Overwork and an anxiety not [to] give up had much to do with the fatal nature of their attacks. One was one of our best and hardiest captains, and one a most interesting youngster who somehow always reminded me of Birch — Captain Woodward, of Cleveland, and Bony Seaman, of Logan County.

I never was healthier in my life. I do not by any means consider myself safe from the fever, however, if we remain in our present location — higher up in the mountains than any other regiment. If I should find myself having any of the symptoms, I shall instantly come home. Those who have done so have all recovered within a week or two and been able to return to duty. I do not notice any second attacks, although I suppose they sometimes occur. Other regiments have had more deaths than we have had, but not generally a larger sick-list.

Our men are extremely well-behaved, orderly, obedient, and cheerful. I can think of no instance in which any man has ever been in the slightest degree insolent or sullen in his manner towards me.

During the last week the enemy have made an attempt to dislodge us from our position by firing shot and shell at our camps from the opposite side of New River. For three days there was cannonading during the greater part of daylight of each day. Nothing purporting to be warfare could possibly be more harmless. I knew of two or three being wounded, and have heard that one man was killed. They have given it up as a failure and I do not expect to see it repeated.

Dr. Jim Webb came here a few days ago, on a dispatch from the general, and will aid in taking charge of the sick in some part of the army, not in our regiment. He brought many most acceptable knickknacks and comforts from home. . . .

The newspapers do great mischief by allowing false and exaggerated accounts of suffering here to be published. It checks enlistments. The truth is, it is a rare thing for a good soldier to find much cause of complaint. But I suppose the public are getting to understand this. I would not say anything to stop benevolent people from contributing such articles of clothing and bedding as I have described. These articles are always put to good use. — Love to all.

Affectionately, your son,

R. B. HAYES.

MRS. SOPHIA HAYES.

Camp Ewing, November 10, 1861. Sunday morning. — I am officer of the day today and interested in the weather. It stopped raining towards evening yesterday. It is foggy and damp this morning — will probably be pleasant during the day. I have to visit all the pickets; the stations are ten or twelve in number and it takes about three hours' riding to visit them. They are on the Lewisburg pike for three or four miles, on the Chestnutburg road about the same distance, and on suitable points commanding views of the country on either side and of the river.

Went with Colonel Scammon, Captain Crane [Company A, Twenty-sixth Ohio], [and] Lieutenant Avery to Pepperbox

Knob and looked over into enemy's camps on [the] south side of New River; thence with Avery to Townsend's Ferry, the proposed crossing place. Most romantic views of the deep mountain gorge of New River, near the ferry. Climbed down and up the hill by aid of ropes. Two Rebel soldiers got up an extempore skiff, just opposite where our men were getting our skiffs, and crept down the cliffs. They came over and were caught by our men as they landed. They were naturally surprised and frightened. A third was seen on the other bank who escaped. So our scheme is by this time suspected by the enemy.

CAMP EWING, November 10 (Sunday night late), 1861.

DEAREST: — I have just returned from a hard day's work examining the romantic mountain gorge of New River which we are preparing to cross, but which I suspect we shall not cross. A glorious day — exciting, and delightfully spent.

Got your letter by Dr. Clendenin on my return at dark. A good letter, darling. Write 'em often.

Yes, Frémont's removal hurts me as it does you. I hate it as much as I did the surrender of Sumter. It may be justified and required by the facts; but I don't see it in anything yet published against him.

Mrs. Herron is misinformed about Matthews. I know *all* about it. The colonel would have returned and expected to return. He wished a change *immensely,* but he would not have resigned. I am sorry to lose him. I know he did his best to get me with him. He got a promise which he thought would please me even better. — It is all agreeable with me here — perfectly so. I can't say when I shall be able to go home. Not for some weeks, but sometime during December or January, I see no reason to doubt that I shall see you. . . .

We sent home a lot of things and would send more if we could. (Take care of the soldier with the scalded hand. You will, of course.*) The reason is, the roads are bad and when

---

* Mrs. Hayes wrote November 19: "We had kept the soldier, Harvey, here. His hand was badly burnt, but mother has dressed it every day, and now it is well."

we move as we must do often, we shall be compelled to leave or destroy all surplus baggage.

Affectionately,

RUTHERFORD.

MRS. HAYES.

Camp Ewing, November 11.   Monday. — Today private Roach, Company I, was killed by a pistol shot accidentally discharged by a comrade. Rode down to reconnoitre enemy's position up the river. Saw Captain Mack fire at them with Parrott six-pound guns.

Camp Ewing, Virginia, up New River, twelve miles above Gauley. November 12. Tuesday. — Officer of the day. Rode to Townsend's Ferry to see Major Crawford's folly. Saw it. Preparations to cross New River although the enemy must be aware of our purpose — a thing difficult if unopposed, impossible and ruinous if opposed. Why don't these generals have common sense?

FAYETTEVILLE, VIRGINIA,

November 19, 1861. (Tuesday).

DEAREST: — We are housed comfortably in a fine village deserted by its people, leaving us capital winter quarters. Floyd intended to winter here, but since his retreat we are left in possession.

We have had severe marching; two nights out without tents — one in the rain and one on the snow. We stood it well. Not a man sick of those who were well, and the sick all improving — due to the clear frosty weather.

Dr. Joe is reading with much satisfaction the news of the success of our fleet. It is most important. We are hoping to stay here for the winter if we do not leave Virginia. It is much the best place we have been in. All, or nearly all, people gone, fine houses, forage, healthy location, etc., etc. Direct to Gauley as usual. I think of you almost constantly these days.

We are now entirely clear of the enemy. I met a party of

10

Georgians yesterday with a flag of truce; had a good friendly chat with them. They are no doubt brave fine fellows but not hardy or persevering enough for this work. They really envied us our healthy and rugged men. They are tired of it heartily.

I can't yet tell when Dr. Joe or Jim or myself will come home, but one of us will pretty certainly come within a fortnight. No, *I* shall not be able to come so soon, but one of the doctors, will I think. Love to the dear boys and Grandma and *so much for your own dear self.*

Affectionately,

R.

MRS. HAYES.

CAMP UNION, FAYETTEVILLE, VIRGINIA,

November 25, 1861.

DEAR MOTHER: — I have just read your letter written at Delaware, and am glad to know you are so happy with Arcena and the other kind friends. You may feel relieved of the anxiety you have had about me.

After several days of severe marching, camping on the ground without tents, once in the rain and once on the snow, we have returned from a fruitless chase after Floyd's Rebel army, and are now comfortably housed in the deserted dwellings of a beautiful village. We have no reports of any enemy near us and are preparing for winter. We should quarter here if the roads to the head of navigation would allow. As it is we shall probably go to a steamboat landing on the Kanawha. Snow is now three or four inches deep and still falling. We are on high ground — perhaps a thousand feet above the Kanawha River — and twelve miles from Gauley Mountain.

Our troops are very healthy. We have here in my regiment six hundred and sixty-two men of whom only three are seriously ill. Perhaps fifteen others are complaining so as to be excused from guard duty. The fever which took down so many of our men has almost disappeared. . . .

This is a rugged mountain region, with large rushing rivers of pure clear water (we drink it at Cincinnati polluted by the Olentangy and Scioto) and full of the grandest scenery I have

OHIO MAJOR-GENERALS, 1861-1865.

MAJOR-GENERAL O. M. MITCHEL,* 1810-62.

MAJOR-GENERAL D. S. STANLEY,* 1828-1902.

MAJOR-GENERAL GODFREY WEITZEL,* 1835-84.

MAJOR-GENERAL JACOB D. COX, 1828-1900.

MAJOR-GENERAL Q. A. GILLMORE,* 1825-88.

MAJOR-GENERAL JAMES A. GARFIELD, 1831-81.

MAJOR-GENERAL M. D. LEGGETT, 1831-96.

MAJOR-GENERAL ROBERT C. SCHENCK, 1807-82.

MAJOR-GENERAL JAMES B. STEEDMAN, 1818-83.

* West Point graduate.

ever beheld. I rode yesterday over Cotton Hill and along New River a distance of thirty miles. I was alone most of the day, and could enjoy scenes made still wilder by the wintry storm.

We do not yet hear of any murders by bushwhackers in this part of Virginia, and can go where we choose without apprehension of danger. We meet very few men. The poor women excite our sympathy constantly. A great share of the calamities of war fall on the women. I see women unused to hard labor gathering corn to keep starvation from the door. I am now in command of the post here, and a large part of my time is occupied in hearing tales of distress and trying to soften the ills the armies have brought into this country. Fortunately a very small amount of salt, sugar, coffee, rice, and bacon goes a great ways where all these things are luxuries no longer procurable in the ordinary way. We try to pay for the mischief we do in destroying corn, hay, etc., etc., in this way.

We are well supplied with everything. But clothes are worn out, lost, etc., very rapidly in these rough marches. People disposed to give can't go amiss in sending shoes, boots, stockings, thick shirts and drawers, mittens or gloves, and blankets. Other knickknacks are of small account.

Give my love to Arcena, Sophia, and to Mrs. Kilbourn.

Affectionately,

R. B. Hayes.

Fayetteville (Camp Union), Virginia, November 27. Wednesday. — We left all baggage on the morning of the 13th early, except what the men could carry, and started down to Gauley to pursue Floyd or rather to attack him. My memo[randa] are as follows: —

November 13. — Had a good march down to Gauley — the whole Third Brigade under General Schenck. Weather warm as summer, almost hot. Crossed New River at ferry near its mouth, worked by Captain Lane and his good men, thence down left bank of the Kanawha to the road from Montgomery Ferry to Fayetteville, thence about two miles to Huddleston's farm, where we bivouacked among briars and devil's-needles — officers in corn fodder in a crib. The band played its best tunes as we crossed New River, Captain Lane remarking, "I little hoped to see such a sight a week ago when the enemy were cannonading us." About 10:30 o'clock General Schenck got a dispatch from General Benham saying Floyd was on the run and he in pursuit, and urging us to follow. At midnight the men were aroused and at one we were on the way.

November 14, Thursday. — A dark, cold, rainy morning. Marching before daylight in pitchy darkness. (*Mem.*: — Night marches should only be made in extremest cases; men can go farther between daylight and dark than between midnight and dark of the next day, and be less worn-out.) We stopped in the dark, built fires, and remained until daylight, when we pushed on in mud and rain past enemy's entrenchments on Dickinson's farm to Fayetteville where we arrived about eight or nine A. M. After passing enemy's works, [we found] the road strewed with axes, picks, tents, etc., etc. — the debris of Floyd's retreating army. Fayetteville, a pretty village, deserted by men and by all but a few women. We quartered with Mrs. Mauser; her secession lord gone with Floyd. We heard P. M. of General Benham's skirmishers killing Colonel St. George Croghan today — colonel of Rebel cavalry and son of Colonel George Croghan of Fort Stephenson celebrity. Died in a bad cause; but Father O'Higgins, of the Tenth, says he behaved like a Christian gentleman. Colonel Smith wears his sword. Shot through the sword-belt.

November 15. Friday. — General Benham's brigade return from the pursuit of Floyd. He runs like a quarter-horse. One of the servants says that when Floyd was here, Mrs. Mauser said she hoped he wouldn't leave. He replied: "I assure you, madam, I'll not leave Cotton Hill until compelled by death or the order of the Secretary of War"; and, added the darkey, "The next I saw of him he was running by as fast as he could tar." At night, a fierce snow-storm; no shelter for many of the troops; bivouac in it!

Saturday, November 16. — General Benham's brigade marched back towards Gauley, leaving here with cheers after their inclement night! Colonel Scammon went on reconnaissance towards Raleigh, in command; nothing to do. Present for duty four hundred and nine. No sick; all sick and weakly gave out before we reached here; a number left to guard property, do work at Gauley, etc.

November 17. Sunday. — I was sent in command of one hundred men of Twenty-third and one hundred of Twenty-sixth six miles towards Raleigh to Blake's to watch a road on which it was thought Colonel Jenkins' Rebel cavalry might pass with prisoners and plunder from Guyandotte. We bivouacked on the snow in fence corners — ice half inch thick — and passed the night not uncomfortably at all. A party of Rebels from Floyd's army met us here with a flag of truce. Had a good little chat with several of them. They did not seem at all averse to friendly approaches. It seemed absurd to be fighting such civil and friendly fellows. I thought they were not so full of fight as our men — acted sick of it. One youngster, a lieutenant in Phillips' Legion, T. H. Kennon of Milledgeville, Georgia, wanted to buy back his little sorrel mare which we had captured — a pleasant fellow. They were after Croghan's body.

Monday, 18. — No signs of Jenkins last night. Heard cannon firing down Kanawha and got ready some rail barricades under direction of Colonel Ewing — rather shabby affairs; could see it gave confidence to men. Ordered back to Fayetteville; returned at dark.

Tuesday, 19. — General Schenck and staff left today. General Schenck sick — not health enough for this work. We are rejoiced reading news of the naval expedition to Port Royal. It looks well. I hope the present anticipations will be fully realized.

Wednesday, 20. — A wet disagreeable day. Captain Reynolds returned from a trip to Raleigh with a flag of truce. Town of Raleigh abandoned. Floyd on beyond. They treated the captain and his party well. The impression is they are not averse to peace. Once taught to respect the North, they will come to terms gladly, I think.

Thursday, 21. — Colonel Ewing bent on a quarrel with Avery about an old secesh horse; a nice gentleman, Colonel Ewing, but so "set in his way." Lieutenant Hunter returned. Lieutenant Warren gone to headquarters to be captain of ordnance.

Friday, 22. — Rode alone down to Gauley over Kanawha and Gauley Rivers, up New River, and stayed at headquarters of General Rosecrans. Always treated well there. Ate pickled oysters immoderately and foolishly; drank mixed drinks slightly but foolishly. But spent an agreeable night with General Rosecrans, Major Crawford, and Captain Reynolds and Major Jos. Darr. Good men all. Cold, desperately windy night; slept coldly in Captain Hartsuff's tent.

Saturday, 23. — Rode up to Captain Mack's (Regular-army artillery officer) ten miles up N[ew River] and near our old Camp Ewing. Business: To appraise under order from General Rosecrans damage done citizens by our men. Board consisted of Colonel McCook, self, and Captain Mack. Met McCook mending road. [He] said he would sign what we should agree to. Did the work and slept with Captain Mack in his new Sibley tent, warmed by a stove. A good institution, if [tent is] floored, for winter.

Sunday, 24. — Rode in rain and snow, chiefly snow, down to Gauley over Kanawha and back to Fayetteville; a hard ride in such a day and alone, too. How I enjoy these rides, this scenery, and all! Saw a teamster with a spike team (three horses) stalled; got on to his leader and tried to help through; gave it up; took a pair of his socks — he had a load.

FAYETTEVILLE, VIRGINIA, November 27, 1861.

DEAREST: — I sent you a rifle for Birch. It was loaded, as I learn. The lieutenant promised to take the load out. If he has forgotten it, have our neighbor of all work, corner of Longworth and Wood, take out the load before Birch plays with or handles it. You may send my vest by anybody coming direct to my regiment. We expect to move two or three days nearer to you the last of this week. The point is not yet known — perhaps Cannelton or Charleston on the Kanawha. I have got a "contraband," a bright fellow who came through the mountains a hundred miles, hiding daytime and travelling nights to get to us. Daniel Husk is his name. His story is a romantic one, if true, as it probably is.

I would have Mr. Stephenson invest in Government 7 3/10 per cent five hundred or six hundred dollars. I shall send you three hundred or four hundred dollars more, as soon as the paymaster comes again. . . . Colonel Scammon is absent. I command the regiment and the post, so I am busy. Excuse brevity, therefore. Love to the boys.

Affectionately,

R.

Mrs. Hayes.

Fayetteville, Virginia, Thursday, 28. — Thanksgiving at home. Dear boys and wife! I hope they are enjoying a happy dinner at home. Here it is raining and gloomy. We do not yet know where we are to winter; men are growing uneasy and dissatisfied. I hope we shall soon know; and if we are to stay here I think we can soon get into good case again. — Decided that we are to stay here for the winter. Wrote to Uncle and Laura humorous letters — attempts — describing our prospects here. Two small redoubts to be built soon. Quarters to be prepared. Rain, mud, and cold to be conquered; drilling to be done, etc., etc.

FAYETTEVILLE, VIRGINIA, November 29, 1861.

DEAR UNCLE: — We have just got our orders for the winter. We are to stay here, build a little fort or two, keep here fifteen hundred men or so — sixty horsemen, a battery of four or six small cannon, etc., etc. We shall live in comfortable houses. The telegraph will be finished here in a day or two. We shall have a daily mail to the head of navigation — sixteen miles down the Kanawha. On the whole a better prospect than I expected in western Virginia. Our colonel will command. I am consequently in command of the Twenty-third Regiment. This is the fair side.   The other side is, sixteen miles of the sublimest scenery to travel over.   We get supplies chiefly, and soon will wholly, by pack mules.   We have a waggon in a tree top ninety feet high.   If a mule slips, good-bye mule!   This is over the "scenery," and where there is no scenery, the mud would appal an old-time Black Swamp stage-driver.   If rations or forage give out, this is not a promising route, but then we can, if forced, march the sixteen miles in one day — we have done it — and take the mouths to the food if the food can't be carried to the mouths.

If the river gets very low, as it sometimes does, the head of navigation will move thirty or forty miles further off; and if it freezes, as it does once in six or eight years, there will be no navigation, and then there will be fifteen hundred souls hereabouts anxiously looking for a thaw.

You now have the whole thing.   I rather like it.   I wish you were in health.   It would be jolly for you to come up and play chess with the colonel and see things.   As soon as we are in order, say four or five weeks, I can come home as well as not and stay a short time. . . .

Sincerely,

R. B. HAYES.

S. BIRCHARD.

FAYETTEVILLE, VIRGINIA, November 29, 1861.

DEAR LAURA: — Thanks for your letter.   I hope I may think your health is improved, especially as you insist upon the pair of swollen cheeks.   We are to stay here this winter.   Our business for the next few weeks is building a couple of forts and getting housed fifteen hundred or two thousand men.   We occupy a good brick house, papered and furnished, deserted by its secession proprietor on our approach.   Our mess consists of Colonel Scammon, now commanding [the] Third Brigade, Colonel Ewing of [the] Thirtieth, Dr. Joe, and a half dozen other officers.

The village was a fine one — pretty gardens, fruit, flowers, and pleasant homes.   All natives gone except three or four families of ladies — two very attractive young ladies among them, who are already turning the heads or exciting the gallantry of such "gay and festive" beaux as the doctor.

We are in no immediate danger here of anything except starvation, which you know is a slow death and gives ample time for reflection. All our supplies come from the head of navigation on the Kanawha over a road remarkable for the beauty and sublimity of its scenery, the depth of its mud, and the dizzy precipices which bound it on either side. On yesterday one of our bread waggons with driver and four horses missed the road four or six inches and landed ("landed" is not so descriptive of the fact as lit) in the top of a tree ninety feet high after a fall of about seventy feet. The miracle is that the driver is here to explained that one of his leaders hawed when he ought to have geed.

We are now encouraging trains of pack mules. They do well among the scenery, but unfortunately part of the route is a Serbonian Bog where armies whole might sink if they haven't, and the poor mules have a time of it. The distance luckily to navigable water is only sixteen to twenty miles. If, however, the water gets low, the distance will increase thirty to forty miles, and if it freezes — why, then we shall all be looking for the next thaw for victuals.

We are to have a telegraph line to the world done tomorrow, and a daily mail subject to the obstacles aforesaid, so we can send you dispatches showing exactly how our starvation progresses from day to day.

On the whole, I rather like the prospect. We are most comfortably housed, and shall no doubt have a pretty jolly winter. There will be a few weeks of busy work getting our forts ready, etc., etc. After that I can no doubt come home and visit you all for a brief season.

So the nice young lieutenant is a Washington. Alas! that so good a name should sink so low.

I am interrupted constantly. Good-bye. Love to all. Can't write often. Send this to Lucy.

Affectionately, your uncle,

RUDDY.

MISS LAURA PLATT.

Fayetteville, Virginia, Saturday, 30. — Snow on the ground; not cold, but raw and disagreeable. Granting furloughs to four men from each company keeps me busy. A week or two ago the colonel sent a recommendation to appoint Sergeant Haven, of Company A, a captain, for services in connection with our naval expedition across New River. His services were probably important, but the jump over the heads of lieutenants is rather too big.

FAYETTEVILLE, CAMP UNION, November 30, 1861.

DEAREST: — We are now engaged in getting winter quarters fixed comfortably. There are not houses enough to lodge all the men without too much crowding. We hope soon to have elbow-room. We ease it off a little by being very liberal with furloughs. We allow four men — "men of family preferred — " to go from each company for twenty days. As a consequence, there must be daily some of our men going through Cincinnati. The bearer will bring (probably) besides this letter, the accoutrements which go with Birt's Mississippi rifle, and a couple of gold pieces, one for a present for you and one for Grandma Webb.

We are doing well. Today is bright and warm after a three-days storm of rain and sleet. I had a letter from Laura. You may send my vest; also "Lucile." All sorts of reading matter finds grabbers, but I think of nothing except any stray *Atlantic* or *Harper's* of late date. I do not wish to go home for some weeks, but if necessary, I can now go home at any time. I prefer that every other officer should go before I do. Dr. Joe is now acting as brigade surgeon, Colonel Scammon as brigadier, and I as colonel; Dr. Jim, as temporary surgeon of the Thirtieth.

All the people hereabouts are crowding in to take the oath of allegiance. A narrow-chested, weakly, poverty-stricken, ignorant set. I don't wonder they refuse to meet our hardy fellows on fair terms. Captain Sperry says: "They are too ignorant to have good health."

Love to "all the boys," to Mother Webb, and ever so much for your own dear self.

Affectionately,

MRS. HAYES.   R.

Sunday, December 1, [1861]. — A dry, cold day, no sun, leaden sky, — threatens snow. About noon gets gusty, wintry and colder. No severe cold yet. Am preparing to have regular lessons and drills. P. M. Began to drizzle — a wintry rain. Loup Creek or Laurel, up yesterday, prevented our waggons crossing. Today fifteen wagons with food came in. Read Halleck's "Lectures on the Science and Art of War." Goodish. Youth, health, energy are the qualities for war. West Point good enough, if it did not give us so much of the effete.

Monday, 2. — Snows all day in the mud. Letter from Lucy dated 24th. Seems in pretty good heart. Kanawha ferry stopped — flood wood too much for the rope. Men engaged fixing quarters as well as they can in such bad weather.

FAYETTEVILLE, VIRGINIA, December 2, 1861.

DEAREST: —   . . .   Dr. Joe made up his mind to go by the first wagon to Gauley on his way to Cincinnati. Won't the boys jump to see him!

I should like a first-rate pair of military boots — not so high as common — *high in the instep and large.* Two or three military books — good reading books. We have Halleck ["Elements of Military Art and Science"] and Scott's dictionary and don't want them. . . .

Affectionately,

MRS. HAYES.   R.

Fayetteville, Virginia, Thursday, December 5. — Another bright, warm day; the afternoon was like spring. Held the first meeting of regimental officers in the adjutant's office last evening. Went over guard duty in the "Regulations." I learned something and think the others did.

Today a foolish young countryman came in with apples, pies and bread, [and] tobacco. Undertook to sell apples at ten cents per dozen, pies twenty cents. The soldiers got mad and robbed the apple cart in the streets. I got mad; paid the F. F. V. five dollars out of my own pocket; got Colonel Eckley to do likewise; had the colonel informed and the thing suitably noticed.

Drilled after parade in a few simple movements; got along tolerably.

Friday, December 6. — A warm, bright day. The chaplain returned today; not an agreeable or useful person. He has been absent over two months. I wish he had not returned.

Colonel Scammon gave me a good, long confidential talk. Like all men having some trifling peculiarities which are not pleasant but who are sterling in all important things, he is best liked when best known. He is a gentleman by instinct as well as breeding and is a most warm-hearted, kindly gentleman; and yet many of the men think him the opposite of all this. I must take more pains than I have [taken] to give them just ideas of him.

Saturday, December 7. — Another warm, bright day — the roads improving. People come twenty-five miles to take the oath. How much is due to a returning sense of loyalty and how much to the want of coffee and salt, is more than I know. They are sick of the war, ready for peace and a return to the old Union. Many of them have been Secessionists, some of them, soldiers.

Rode Schooley's high-tailed, showy horse twice. Drilled after evening parade. Met the sergeants for instruction tonight.

Sunday, December 8. — A cloudy morning, threatening rain. After ten A. M. cleared up and a bright, warm day. Inspected quarters informally with Lieutenant-Colonel Eckley. Favorable impressions of his disposition confirmed; dined with him and his adjutant, Lieutenant James, of Urbana, and Rev. Long, ditto. Wrote letters — very short — to Uncle, mother, and Lucy.

Had a good drill after evening parade. Colonel Scammon, Lieutenant Gardner, quartermaster, and Major Comly play whist in the other room. . . . We have intimations that Jenkins and his cavalry are coming in here again. The colonel is taking precautions against surprise. I shall see that my regiment is ready, if possible.

CAMP UNION, December 8, 1861.

DEAREST: — It is Sunday — inspection day. Visited all quarters and hospital. All in improving condition. Tell Dr. Joe we have had five bright warm lovely days and a fair prospect for as many more. Roads improving; telegraph wire here, and will be in working order tomorrow or day after.

Have the daily *Commercial* mailed to me here from the office for one month. If it comes as often as twice a week, I will renew the subscription, otherwise not.

A trunk full of nice doings, socks, mittens, small looking-glasses, needle doings, etc., etc., came up from Gauley among our baggage. Nothing to show who from or who to. I assumed that it was an instalment from Cleveland for the Twenty-third and Dr. McCurdy disposes of it accordingly. . . .

I am feeling anxious about you. Write often all about yourself. Love to the dear boys and all. Ever so much for yourself.
Affectionately,

R.

MRS. HAYES.

Tuesday, December 10. — A little warm rain last night; cloudy and threatening rain in morning; turned off bright and clear. Had a good drill after evening parade. Moved into a good room in a pretty cottage house owned by J. H. Phillips, a drygoods dealer, who has left with the Rebels. His store was burned by McCook's men because he was a persecutor of Union men. Captain Sperry and Lieutenant Kennedy are my co-tenants. We shall take good care of the premises and try to leave them in as good condition as we find them.

Wednesday, January [December] 11. — A cold morning, threatening rain; rained a little last night. Turned off bright, clear, and cold in the afternoon. Had a headache in morning, drank a little bad wine last night; all right after dinner. Living so cozily in my new quarters. Oh, if Lucy was here, wouldn't it be fine! How she would enjoy it! Darling! I think of her constantly these days. A drill; formed squad in four ranks; marched, closed in mass.

Thursday, December 12. — A bright, pretty, cold winter morning; *our eighth fine day!!* Ground froze in the morning; dry and warm all day after sun got one-third up. In [the] morning walked with Lieutenant-Colonel Eckley around southern part of town, in the woods, visiting pickets and noticing the lay of the land. He agrees with me that the chief danger of an attack is a hasty assault to burn the town; that for this purpose a stockade or log entrenchment should be thrown up at the lower end of town. Drilled P. M. — No letters or news.

Friday, December 13. — Another beautiful winter day — cold, quiet. Sun strong enough to thaw all mud and ice. No ice on streams yet that will bear a man. Building redoubts at either end of town. Since I came to Virginia in July, I have not shaved; for weeks at a time I have slept in all clothes except boots (occasionally in boots and sometimes with spurs), a half dozen times on the ground without shelter, once on the snow. I have wore [worn] no white clothing (shirts, drawers, etc.) for four months; no collar or neckerchief or tie of any sort for two months; and have not been the least unwell until since I have taken winter quarters here in a comfortable house. Now I have but a slight cold.

December 14, Saturday. — A fine day, warm and bright, — the tenth! Western Virginia is redeeming itself. Our men think there is something wrong. The nights are clear, frosty, and moonlit.

Camp Union, Fayetteville, Virginia. Sunday, December 15. — Another fine day. Had a review this morning — fine spectacle. Received a letter from Dr. Joe, dated 10th, last night. All well at home. Lucy looking for her troubles to be over soon. Dear Lute! I hope she will get on well. Some fleecy clouds in the sky; the good weather must end soon.

Camp Union, Fayetteville, Virginia,
December 15, 1861.

Dear Uncle:— I have often wished since I have been in Virginia that you were well enough to come and spend a few weeks with me. I have never wished it more than now. I am quartered alone in a pleasant cottage house, with plenty to run and do whatever I want done. The weather is lovely. We are drilling our men, building forts, etc., etc., and are undisturbed by the world. The people hereabouts, many of them fresh from the Rebel armies, come in, take the oath, and really behave as if they were sick of it, and wanted to stop. Nothing but ill luck, or a great lack of energy, will prevent our wiping out the Rebellion, The common people of this region want to get back to coffee and salt and sugar, etc., etc., none of which articles can now be got through whole extensive districts of country.

If nothing occurs to prevent, I shall come home in January for thirty days. Will visit you at Fremont, if you do not happen to be in Cincinnati or Columbus. . . .

Good-bye,

R. B. Hayes.

S. Birchard.

Camp Union, Monday, December 16, 1861. — A beautiful day. Rode with Colonel Scammon to Townsend's Ferry. That is we rode to the top of the cliffs on New River; thence with six men of Company B we scrambled down by the path to the river, perhaps by the path three-quarters of a mile. A steep rocky gorge, a rushing river, the high precipices, all together make a romantic scene.

It was here we intended to cross with General Schenck's brigade to cut off Floyd's retreat. Boats were prepared, four skiffs brought from Cincinnati, but the river rose, just as we were about to cross, making it impossible. It has always been a question since whether the enemy were aware of our purpose and would have opposed our crossing. I supposed that so much work preparing could not have escaped their notice, and that they were ready for us. Opposition on such a path would have been fatal. From all I saw at the ferry, I am inclined to think they knew nothing of our purpose. There are no signs of pickets or ambuscades to be found on this side. The distance from the river to this village is only two miles and we could probably have taken it and held it.

The bold enterprises are the successful ones. Take counsel of hopes rather than of fears to win in this business.

FAYETTEVILLE, VIRGINIA, December 16, 1861.

DEAREST:— . . . I think of you constantlty now. Keep up good courage. Let me know all about you all the time. I will send you a dispatch from here as soon as our operator is at work just to show you that we are not far apart.

We are very healthy and contented here. The sick are less and less daily.

I see somebody knits woollen gloves for soldiers. That's sensible. A few stockings, gloves, woolen shirts, and the like are always wanted at this season.

I write this by Captain Howard. He is probably to resign on account chiefly of ill health.

Kisses for all the boys and "love you much."

Affectionately,

R.

Did you get the gold pieces, etc?

MRS. HAYES.

Camp Union, Tuesday, December 17, 1861. — Our thirteenth fine day. The frost still coming out of the ground; freezes hard nights, thaws all day in the sun. Mud deeper in many places than it was a week ago; on the hills and ridges getting dry. . . . Drilled as usual at night. Men improving in drill. Lieutenant Durkee returned yesterday or day before — health restored; weighs one hundred and eighty [pounds], looks well; left Camp Ewing over the river in October, apparently a doomed man. Captain Moore returned today, apparently in good health. Talks gloomily of the regiment; thinks Captain Drake, Lieutenant

Avery, etc., will not return; that he and most of the officers will resign. Chief difficulty is the governor appointed Major Comly in my place as major. It [the appointment] ought to have been made from our own regiment. Captain Drake was recommended and would have been satisfactory to a majority. But Major Comly has shown himself so diligent, gentlemanly, and reasonably [reasonable], withal so well acquainted with tactics and the duties of a soldier, that those who have been here the last six weeks are reconciled to his appointment and think it is well for the regiment. Captain Moore also reports an impression he got that I was to be a colonel soon and leave the regiment. I don't believe it.

Camp Union, Tuesday, December 17, A. M., 1861.

Dearest: — I can't let another chance slip without a letter to show you I am thinking of you.

Still lovely weather. Rode to the scene of the naval expedition on this side of New River, a romantic place.

I send this by Lieutenant Kennedy's father. He brought from Bellefontaine gloves, socks, blankets, and shirts — enough and to spare all around — for Captain Canby's company. I get something every time anything comes.

We are in glorious trim now. Some of the companies still lack comforts, but we drill with life. The paymaster is here and it is white days with us.

The Rebels are getting sick of it. Nobody but Jenkins holds out in all this country. Rebel soldiers come and give up their arms, etc.

Dearest, good-night. Love to all the boys and Grandma. . . . I do hope you will get along well. You shall keep Dr. Joe till the trouble is over.

Affectionately,

R. B. Hayes.

Mrs. Hayes.

Fayetteville, Virginia, Camp Union. Wednesday, December 18. — Another fine day. Sergeant John McKinley, Company

G, left for Mount Vernon this morning; took a letter to Lucy and a watch to be repaired. He is a character, an erect, neat, prompt old soldier. English of Lancaster, or rather Irish of England, he talks the most profuse flattery, but it does win, fulsome as it is. He does his whole duty. As he left me he said "I want to see that 'Lieutenant' from before your name. Every good man should go up."

Drilled as usual. Weather very warm at evening. "Jeff Davis," a boy who came into Camp Chase with Company A and who drilled like an old sergeant, though aged but thirteen, returned yesterday from Cleveland.

CAMP UNION, FAYETTEVILLE, VIRGINIA, December 18, 1861.

DEAREST: — You will think I have nothing to do but to write to you. I can't let a good chance slip without sending you word that "I am well and doing well and hope, etc." Sergeant McKinley, an old soldier, or rather I ought to say an experienced soldier, offers so generously to go and see you that I must let him. Birch ought to hear him talk. He has many scars received in battle, and Birt would like to hear about them. He is trusty.

Love to all the boys and ever so much for yourself. I suspect I am getting more anxious about you than the people at home. You must keep up good heart. We shall be together pretty soon again. If we have another little boy, we will have enough *for a file in four ranks* — which Birtie knows, I suppose, is requisite for a march by the flank. "Companions in battle" they are called. If it is a daughter, why bless you darling, won't we have a nice family? . . .

This is our fourteenth beautiful day and prospects of more, tell Joe. — Love to all.

Affectionately, dearest, your

R.

MRS. HAYES.

CAMP UNION, FAYETTEVILLE, VIRGINIA, December 19, 1861.

DEAR UNCLE: — Yesterday morning, a party of contrabands started for Ohio. It is not unlikely that some of them will find their way to Fremont. Allen, a mulatto, with his wife and one or two children, is one of a thousand — faithful, intelligent, and industrious, — will do for a house servant — would just answer your purpose. His wife can cook — is neat and orderly — a most valuable family, you will find them, if you put them into the new house, or anywhere else. If you don't want them, you can safely recommend them. Quite a number have come to me, but these are the pick of the lot. They have another black man and wife with them who are well spoken of; I do not know them. It is, of course, doubtful whether Allen will find you; I think he will. I send him because I think he will just answer your purpose.

They will all be entitled to freedom, as I understand the rule adopted by our Government. Their master is a Rebel, and is with Floyd's army as quartermaster, or the like, being too old for a soldier. These people gave themselves up to me, and I let them go to Ohio. The rule is, I believe, that slaves coming to our lines, especially if owned by Rebels, are free. Allen gave me valuable information as to the enemy. These facts, if necessary hereafter, can be proved by members of Captain McIlrath's Company A, Twenty-third Regiment, Cleveland, or of Captain Sperry's Company H, Ashtabula County. Of course, there is little present danger of attempt to recapture them under the Fugitive Bill, but it may be done hereafter.

You, perhaps, know that Dr. Joe took a contraband to Cincinnati. These people do not go to Cincinnati, preferring the country, and fearing relatives of their master there. The party start for Galion in company with the servant of one of our men; from there, they will probably get to you.

Sincerely,

R. B. HAYES.

S. BIRCHARD.

Camp Union, Fayetteville, Virginia. Friday, December 20. — A. M., before breakfast, some clouds and wind but sun now shining. Change threatened. We have here Twenty-sixth Regiment, now under Lieutenant-Colonel Eckley, who also commands the post; Thirtieth Regiment, five companies, under Colonel Ewing; Twenty-third, now under my command; McMullen's Battery, and a Pennsylvania cavalry company, stationed on the road towards Raleigh. Twenty-third here 550, Twenty-sixth, 600, Thirtieth, 200, battery, 40, cavalry, 40 — 1430 men. Building two forts on hill northeast of town, one on hill southwest of town. Wind and clouds during the day, but the sun shone brightly on our dress parade, making this our sixteenth good day.

Saturday, 21. — A cold, bright winter day. Sent a dispatch home to Lucy. Paymaster here getting ready to pay our men. The James D. (Devereux) Bulloch* was a good friend of mine at Middletown, Connecticut, (Webb's school) in 1837-8 from Savannah, Georgia — a whole-hearted, generous fellow. A model sailor I would conjecture him to be. Rebel though he is, I guess him to be a fine fellow, a brave man, honorable and all that.

It is rumored that Great Britain will declare war on account of the seizure of Slidell and Mason. I think not. It will blow over. First bluster and high words, then correspondence and diplomacy, finally peace. But if not, if war, what then? First, it is to be a trying, a severe and dreadful trial of our stuff. We

---

* Pasted in the Diary is the following clipping from the Richmond *News* of November 30: — "Captain James D. Bulloch, who lately successfully ran the blockade while in command of the steamship *Fingal,* has arrived in Richmond. He thinks there is a likelihood of Lord Palmerston's proving indifferent to the question involved in the seizure, by Captain Wilkes, on the high seas, from a British vessel, of Messrs. Mason and Slidell."

Captain James D. Bulloch was the "Naval Representative of the Confederate States in Europe" during the Civil War. It was under his direction and through his energy that the *Alabama* and other cruisers were built and equipped to prey on American commerce. In 1883 Captain Bulloch published in two volumes a most interesting narrative, entitled "The Secret Service of the Confederate States in Europe, or How the Confederate Cruisers Were Equipped." It may also be recalled that Captain Bulloch was a brother of President Roosevelt's mother.

shall suffer, but we will stand it. All the Democratic element, now grumbling and discontented, must then rouse up to fight their ancient enemies the British. The South, too, will not thousands then be turned towards us by seeing their strange allies? If not, shall we not with one voice arm and emancipate the slaves? A civil, sectional, foreign, and servile war — shall we not have horrors enough? Well, I am ready for my share of it. We are in the right and must prevail.

Six companies paid today. Three months' pay due not paid. A "perfectly splendid" day — the seventeenth!!

Sunday, December 22. — The Forefathers' day — Pilgrim day. We are at the same high call here today — freedom, freedom for all. We all know that is the essence of this contest.

Cold, but the sun gilds the eastern sky as I write, and a few thin clouds gathered during the night are rolling away. . . . At 3:30 P. M. a cold rain begins to fall — the end of our fine weather. How long shall we now be housed up by stormy weather? . . .

Monday, December 23. — Wet, cold, windy; sleet last night. Five companies of the Thirtieth came up last night. Little or no preparations to shelter them — all their field officers gone. A sorry plight.

At dinner today with Captain Sperry and Lieutenant Kennedy, I was handed the following dispatch:

"Cincinnati, December 23, 1861.

"Lieutenant-Colonel R. B. Hayes, Twenty-third Regiment.

"Wife and boy doing well. Stranger arrived Saturday evening, nine o'clock P. M.

J. T. Webb."

Good! Very! I preferred a daughter, but in these times when women suffer so much, I am not sure but we ought to rejoice that our girls are boys. What shall I call him? What will Birt say, and Webb, and Babes? "Babes" no longer. He is supplanted by the little stranger. Cold wind and snow-storm outside. Dear Lucy! I hope she will keep up good heart. I replied by telegraph: "Congratulations and much love to mother and son. All well."

CAMP UNION, December 23, 1861.

DEAREST: — I am so happy to hear today by telegraph that your troubles are over (at least the worst, I hope) and that "mother and son are doing well." Darling, I love you so much and have felt so anxious about you. The little fellow, I hope, is healthy and strong. It is best it was not a daughter. These are no times for women. . . . What do the boys say? . . . Tell me all about him.

Captain Sperry will take this. I shall time it so as to come about the time that Dr. Joe will leave — say, the 15th to 20th January, unless something occurs to stop it.

I shall send either to you or to Platt five hundred dollars by Captain Sperry. Get all you want — Christmas presents for the boys and all.

Kiss *the boy,* yes, "all the boys" for me.

Affectionately,

R.

MRS. HAYES.

FAYETTEVILLE, VIRGINIA, December 23, 1861.

DEAR UNCLE: — I have just heard by telegraph of the birth of my fourth son. In these times, boys are to be preferred to girls. Am glad to hear Lucy is doing well. . . .

Yes, we are in winter quarters, most comfortable quarters. I have to myself as nice a room as your large room, papered, carpeted, a box full of wood, and with a wild snow-storm blowing outside to make it more cheerful by contrast. We have had eighteen days of fine weather to get ready in, and are in pretty good condition. We have our telegraph line running down to civilization; get Cincinnati papers irregularly from four to ten days old. I have enjoyed the month here very much. Busy fortifying — not quite ready yet, but a few more days of good weather will put us in readiness for any force. The enemy are disheartened; the masses of the people want to stop. If England does not step in, or some great disaster befall us, we shall conquer the Rebellion beyond doubt, and at no distant period. . . .

I shall go home about the time Dr. Joe starts back here —
say the 15th to 20th January, if nothing new occurs to prevent.
If you can't come down to Cincinnati, I shall go to Fremont.

Sincerely,

R. B. HAYES.

S. BIRCHARD.

HEADQUARTERS 23D REG'T. O. V. INF. U. S. A.,
December 23, 1861.

DEAR DOCTOR: — Thanks for your letter of the 16th. You
will of course stay with Lucy until after she is out of all danger,
if it is a month or more, and all will be well. Some arrangement, or no arrangement, it will be all right. I will come home
unless something turns up to prevent, which I do not anticipate,
so as to reach there just before you leave. McCurdy would
like to go home during the next month, but it can all be arranged.

I will make Jim assistant at any time if it is thought best,
but I do not wish to put him over McCurdy. This, however,
need not trouble you. You can stay as long as you please, and
I will see it duly approved.

You have authority to send home our men, but to stop all
cavil I send you an order which you can fill up with the name
of any officer, commissioned or non-commissioned, who you
think can be trusted, directing him to bring here all men who
are able to come.

At dinner just now I got your dispatch as to the boy. . . .
Welcome to the little stranger! I hope he will be stout and
healthy. . . .

Did Lucy get a draft for eighty-seven dollars by Captain
Drake or Lieutenant Richardson, and two gold twenty-dollar
pieces by a Company A man? Get Lucy for me some ring or
"sich" thing that she will like — something nice.

Sincerely,

R. B. HAYES.

DR. J. T. WEBB.

Tuesday, December 24. — Good weather. Moderately cold; ground frozen so it will bear teams, whitened with a thin sprinkling of snow. Captain Sperry left this morning with Sergeant Hall and Private Gillet for home via Cincinnati. . . .

Fayetteville, Virginia, Wednesday, 25. — A beautiful Christmas morning — clear, cool, and crisp (K. K. K.), bright and lovely. The band waked me with a serenade. How they improve! A fine band and what a life in a regiment! Their music is better than food and clothing to give spirit to the men. . . .

Dined with McIlrath's company — sergeants' mess; an eighteen-pound turkey, chickens, pies, pudding, doughnuts, cake, cheese, butter, coffee, and milk, all abundant and of good quality. Poor soldiers! A quiet orderly company under good discipline; speaks well for its captain.

In the evening met at the adjutant's office the commissioned officers of the regiment. Much feeling against the promotion from third sergeant to captain of Company G of Sergeant Haven, Company A. It was an ill-advised act. I think highly of Sergeant Haven. He will, I think, make a good officer. But the regular line of promotion should [be departed from] only in extraordinary cases, and then the promotion should be limited to the merits of the case. The lieutenants passed over — all the first and second-lieutenants — are much dissatisfied and the captains who are not yet reconciled to the major are again excited. They have a story that the colonel recommended Sergeant McKinley for promotion to a first lieutenancy. It can't be possible, and if not, the other case will lead, I think, [to] no unpleasant action.

We adjourned to my quarters. I sent for oysters to the sutler's; got four dollars and fifty cents' worth and crackers. They were cooked by Lieutenants Warren and Bottsford. A good time; Bottsford, a little merry and noisy. Present, Major Comly, Captains Canby and Moore, First-Lieutenants Warren, Hood, and Rice and Naughton, Second-Lieutenants Bottsford, Hastings, Ellen, Adjutant Kennedy, Stevens. Retired at 11 P. M.

CAMP UNION, Christmas morning, 1861.

DEAREST: — A merry Christmas to you and the little stranger (I suppose he is a stranger to you no longer) — and to all at home. At this home-happiness season, I think of you constantly. . . . Oh the boys, how they must enjoy Uncle Joe and the presents! You will see they get some from "Uncle Papa" too.

A Dr. Hayes is here as brigade surgeon. Scarcely any sick in our regiment, so Dr. Joe can feel easy about his absence.

Beautiful weather again. Only one bad day. The rest of the Thirtieth has come up. It is now the strongest regiment here. *This* half is better stuff too and had some service.

Captain Zimmerman takes this. I sent a chair and five hundred dollars, by Captain Sperry. Let Joe tell me what money you have received from me. It is all right, I suppose, but I would like to know. . . .

Affectionately, darling,

MRS. HAYES.

R.

Thursday, December 26. — A cloudy day — thawing and muddy. The colonel is planning an expedition through Raleigh to Princeton to capture what is there of the enemy, — viz. six hundred sick with a guard of about one hundred men, arms and stores, with a possibility of getting Floyd who is said to be without guard at —— and to burn the railroad bridges near Newbern. The plan is to mount one-half the force on pack mules and ride and tie — to make a forced march so as to surprise the enemy. He does not seem willing to look the difficulties in the face, and to prepare to meet them. He calls it forty or fifty miles. It is sixty-seven and one-half. He thinks men can move night and day, three of four miles an hour. Night in those muddy roads will almost stop a column. With proper preparations, the thing is perhaps practicable. Let me study to aid in arranging it, if it is to be.

Dear wife! how is she? — Soon after breakfast the sun chased the clouds away and we had a warm spring day. The bluebirds are coming back if they ever left. Our twenty-first fine day this month.

Friday, December 27. — A cold and windy but clear morning — good winter weather. It was warm last night until 2 [A. M.], wind veered around from south to north and [it was] cold as blazes (why blazes?). Rode with Major Comly down to Captain McIlrath's. He preferred remaining in his quarters to a trip to Raleigh. Five companies to be sent to Raleigh to occupy it, — to push further if best to do so.

Drilled in a clear, brisk air. Colonel Scammon is preparing to send to Raleigh in the hope that a party of the enemy at Princeton may be surprised; also that railroad bridges near Newbern may be destroyed.

Harvey Carrington and T. S. Dickson, Company C, complain of Sergeant Keen and Thomas Mason for keeping two hundred and ten dollars won at "Honest John." They say the agreement was that whatever was lost or won was to be returned and that they played merely to induce others to play. I told them that as they, by their own stories, were stool-pigeons, they were entitled to no sympathy. They admitted that much of the money had been won gaming. I declined to order the money returned to them. I sent for Sergeant Keen and Mason, who denied the story of Carrington and Dickson, but admitted winning the money. I ordered them to pay the money into the company fund of Company C where it will be used to buy gloves and such other comforts as the Government does not furnish for all the company.

Saturday, December 28. — Cold very, but still and clear — good weather. Warm in the afternoon. Rode with Colonel Scammon to the different works. They are well done as works, not very necessary, and not perhaps in the *very* best localities, but well enough. They are, I suspect, creditable to Colonel Scammon as military earthworks of no great pretension. Attended the funeral of another man of Company B. Sad and solemn. The lively music after all is over offends my taste. — A good, lively drill.

Camp Union, Fayetteville, Virginia, Sunday, December 29. — Major Comly (J. M.) with five companies marched today to occupy Raleigh twenty-five miles south of here. Companies F and G, Twenty-third, two companies of Thirtieth, and one company, Twenty-sixth. Weather, bright and clear; ground, frozen hard; roads, good. Success attend them! Company inspection.

CAMP UNION, FAYETTEVILLE, VIRGINIA, December 29, 1861.

DEAREST: — I have no letter from home since *the* boy was born. I have by mail *Commercials* of several days later date and hoped for a letter; but I comfort myself by thinking that all is going well with you, or the telegraph would inform me.

I now begin to think anxiously of coming home. If nothing occurs unforeseen, I must get home before the next month runs out. We have sent Major Comly with a detachment to occupy Raleigh, twenty-five miles further into the bowels of the land, and his absence may prevent my coming so soon as I hope, but I shall come if possible.

Dr. McCurdy is sick, and will probably go home soon. *Dr. Hayes,* the brigade surgeon, seems to be a nice gentleman, and gets along well with Dr. Jim, as surgeon of the Twenty-third. Colonel Scammon has been unwell, and says that while he likes Dr. Hayes as a gentleman, he would prefer to be doctored by Dr. Joe, and inquires often as to his coming. I tell him Dr. Joe will in no event return before the 10th and not then unless you are out of all danger.

Make Joe tell me all about "the boy." Does "the face of the boy indicate the heart of the boy"? Do you love him as much as the others? Do you feel sorry the fourth was not a daughter? I think it's best as it is. — Love to "all the boys" and kiss the little one.

Affectionately,

R. B. HAYES.

MRS. HAYES.

Monday, December 30. — A "magnificent splendid" day — the twenty-fifth fine day this month; twenty-five out of the last twenty-six!! The companies at Raleigh diminish our strength. Five hundred and twenty present. Total in companies here seven hundred and forty-three.

Tuesday, December 31, 1861. — New Year's Eve — the last day of the year — a busy day with me. A review, an inspection, and a muster of the regiment all by me; also an inspection of McMullen's Battery. Yesterday received letters from Platt and Dr. Joe. The little stranger is more like Birt than the others and smaller than Rud. Birch indignant that he isn't big enough to drill! — A lovely day today. Twenty-six fine days this month; a few [of] them cold, not severely so, but all good weather. Lucy getting on well. Good, all!

CHAPTER XVII

CAMP Union, Fayetteville, Virginia, Wednesday, New Year's Day, 1862. — Sun shone brightly an hour or two; mild winter weather, then windy and threatening. Rode with Colonel Scammon four or five miles southwest of town. Wind blew all day as if a storm were by brewing, but no rain or snow. I set it down as a pleasant day. Number 1 for January 1862.

At dinner, speaking of naming my boy, I said: "The name was all ready if I had heard that a daughter was born." "Fanny Lucy" or "Lucy Fanny" — linking together the names of the two dear ones, wife and sister. Dear Fanny! what an angel she was, and, may I hope, now is.

Heard from home. Sergeant [John] McKinley, with letter and watch — tight, drunk, the old heathen, and insisting on seeing the madame! I didn't dream of that. He must be a nuisance, a dangerous one too, when drunk. A neat, disciplined, well-drilled soldier under rule, but what a savage when in liquor! Must be careful whom I send home.

Thursday, January 2, 1862. — Cleared off moderately cold; quiet and beautiful weather. Remarkable season. Rode with Colonel Scammon about the works. Major Comly reports finding about one hundred and twenty muskets, etc., concealed in and about Raleigh; also twelve or fifteen contrabands arrived. What to do with them is not so troublesome yet as at the East. Officers and soldiers employ them as cooks and servants. Some go on to Ohio.

Nobody in this army thinks of giving up to Rebels their fugitive slaves. Union men might perhaps be differently dealt with — probably would be. If no doubt of their loyalty, I suppose they would again get their slaves. The man who repudiates all obligations under the Constitution and laws of the

United States is to be treated as having forfeited those rights which depend solely on the laws and Constitution. I don't want to see Congress meddling with the slavery question. Time and the progress of events are solving all the questions arising out or slavery in a way consistent with eternal principles of justice. Slavery is getting death-blows. As an "institution," it perishes in this war. It will take years to get rid of its debris, but the "sacred" is gone.

FAYETTEVILLE, VIRGINIA, January 2, 1862.

DEAREST: — I hope you all enjoyed New Year's Day. I dispatched you "a happy New Year's" which I suppose you got. We had nothing unusual. The weather still good. Twenty-six fine days in December, and a start of two for the new year.

Dr. Jim got a letter from Joe yesterday. Sergeant McKinley was drunk. I doubted him somewhat, but thought if trusted with an errand, he would keep straight until it was done. A good soldier in camp — somewhat obtrusive and talkative, but always soldierlike. He got into the guard-house for raising Ned at Gallipolis.*

For convenience of forage, and at the request of Union citizens, a detachment of five companies — two of Twenty-third, one of Twenty-sixth, and two of Thirtieth — have occupied Raleigh. All quiet there. One or two other places may be occupied in the same way, in which case I shall go with the next detachment. This all depends on the continuance of good weather and roads. I do not mean to let it prevent my going home the latter part of this month, and it will not unless the enemy wakes up again. At present their attention is so occupied on the seacoast and elsewhere that we hear nothing of them. . . . Dr. Hayes is a quiet, nice gentleman. Jim likes him very much. Jim is now acting surgeon of the Twenty-third under employment by Dr.

---

* Mrs. Hayes wrote, January 5: "Your Sergeant McKinley is a curiosity. . . . Don't say anything about the sergeant's condition when he called, for getting home had overcome him and it did not affect me in the least."

Hayes as "a private physician" — that is, at a hundred dollars per month.

As detachments are likely to be sent off if this good weather lasts, Dr. Joe better return when it is perfectly safe for him to do so — not before.

I shall come home as soon as possible. Nothing but these good roads and fine weather keeps me here now. If the weather and roads were bad I would start within a week; but in such weather I don't feel that it would be safe to leave. We may be required to move forward, or to be ready for movements of the enemy. Such weather puts us into a campaign again. We have had men sixty miles further south and forty east within a week or ten days. No symptom of enmity anywhere. . . .

Affectionately,

R.

Mrs. Hayes.

Friday, January 3. — Last evening threatened snow but too cold. Today cold and dry. P. M. 4 o'clock began to rain; may rain for a month now.

Charles, an honest-looking contraband — six feet high, stout-built, thirty-six years old, wife sold South five years ago, — came in today from Union, Monroe County. He gives me such items as the following: Footing boots $9 to $10. New boots $18 to $20. Shoes $4 to $4.50. Sugar 25 to 30 [cents a pound], coffee 62½, tea $1.50, soda 62½, pepper 75, bleached domestic 40 to 50 [cents a yard.] Alex Clark [his master], farmer near Union (east of it), Monroe County, one hundred and fifty (?) miles from Fayetteville — fifty miles beyond (?) Newbern. Started Saturday eve at 8 P. M., reached Raleigh next Monday night; crossed New River at Packs Ferry. (Packs a Union man.)

Companies broken up in Rebel army by furloughs, discharges, and sickness. Rich men's sons get discharges. Patrols put out to keep slaves at home. They tell slaves that the Yankees cut off arms of some negroes to make them worthless and sell the rest in Cuba for twenty-five hundred dollars each to pay cost of war. "No Northern gentlemen fight — only factory men thrown out of employ." They (the negroes) will fight for the North if they find the Northerners are such as they think them.

Union is a larger and much finer town than Fayetteville. William Erskine, keeper of Salt Sulphur Springs, don't let Rebels stay in his houses. Suspected to be a Union man. Lewisburg three times as large as Fayetteville. Some Fayetteville people there. People in Greenbrier [County] don't want to fight any more.

General Augustus Chapman the leading military man in Monroe. Allen T. Capelton, the other mem[ber] of Legislature, Union man, had his property taken by them. Named Joshua Seward, farmer. Henry Woolwine, ditto, for Union, farmer, [living] near Union — three and three and one-half miles off. Dr. Ballard a good Union man (storekeeper) on the road from Giles to Union, twelve miles from Peterstown, also robbed by Floyd. Wm. Ballard and a large connection, all Union men — all in Monroe. Oliver Burns and Andrew Burns contributed largely to the Rebels. John Eckles in Union has a fine brick house — a Rebel colonel. Rebels from towards Lynchburg and Richmond would come by way of Covington, forty-five miles from Union. Landlords of principal hotel Rebels — one at Manassas. Two large, three-story high-school buildings, opposite sides of the street, on the hill this end of town. "Knobs," or "Calder's Peak," three miles from town. A hilly country, but more cleared and better houses than about Fayetteville.

They "press" poor folks' horses and teams not the rich folks'. Poor folks grumble at being compelled to act as patrols to keep rich men's negroes from running off. "When I came with my party, eleven of us, in sight of your pickets, I hardly knew what to do. If you were such people as they had told us, we would suffer. Some of the party turned to run. A man with a gun called out halt. I saw through the fence three more with guns. They asked, 'Who comes there?' I called out 'Friends.' The soldier had his gun raised; he dropped it and said: 'Boys, these are some more of our colored friends,' and told us to 'come on, not to be afraid,' that we were safe. Oh, I never felt so in my life. I could cry, I was so full of joy. And I found them and the major (Comly) and all I have seen so friendly — such perfect gentlemen, just as we hoped you were, but not as they told us you were."

Saturday, January 4, 1862. — Major Comly calls his camp at Raleigh "Camp Hayes." It rained last night as if bent to make up for the long drouth. Foggy this morning; warm and muddy enough to stop all advances. Besides, yesterday the Twenty-sixth Regiment was ordered from here to Kentucky. Two other regiments go from below. Ten regiments from New York in same direction. Such an immense force as is gathering ought to open the Mississippi River, capture Memphis, New Orleans, and Nashville before the heat of summer closes operations on that line. Oh, for energy, go-ahead! With horses here we could do wonders, but such a rain as last night forbids any extensive movement.

Sent today as recruiting officers for the regiment Captains Lovejoy and Skiles, Sergeants Hicks and Powers, privates Seekins and Lowe, to report at Camp Chase to Major McCrea, U. S. A.

No rain today, but mist and clouds with occasional flakes of snow.

Camp Union, Fayetteville, Virginia, January 4, 1862.

Dear Mother: — I have a chance to send letters direct to Columbus by a recruiting officer this morning and write in great haste. We are still in good quarters and good health. The people we meet are more and more satisfied that it is best to return to their allegiance. Our men, pickets and outposts, are daily pushed out further into what *has been* the enemy's country, and everywhere they meet friends, or at least people who no longer behave like enemies. Part of our regiment is fifty miles south of here, and no signs even of hostility from anybody. Not a man has been fired at in this brigade for more than a month. If no disaster befalls our armies on the Potomac or in Kentucky, the masses of the people in Virginia are ready — would be glad — to submit. England out of the way, and a little patience and determination will crush the Rebellion.

12

You say you are glad I am coming home — that you didn't expect it. I hope to start the latter part of this month. All the officers but five have been home and returned or are now absent. My turn is next to the last. I shall go before Colonel Scammon. Of course, events may occur to prevent my leaving, but I don't anticipate them.

Affectionately, your son,

R. B. HAYES.

MRS. SOPHIA HAYES.

CAMP UNION, January 4, 1862.

DEAR DOCTOR: — You have probably learned that Dr. McCurdy has gone home to recruit his health. If Dr. Jim does not break down (I have some fears on that score) this absence of Dr. McCurdy need not hasten your departure. Our men are generally very healthy; the sick are daily returning, for the most part well. Captain Skiles and Captain Lovejoy are to recruit in Ohio. It is possible that I may not come, if Lucy gets on well, until you return. If we do not move the Twenty-third on to Raleigh, I would prefer to wait, if possible, until you get here. If we go on to Raleigh where Major ——. At this point, I learned that the Twenty-sixth is ordered to Kentucky. If so, it will stop our going on to Raleigh; besides, it has just begun to rain, so I suppose we are fixed. If so, I shall be coming home in two or three weeks, I think. Possibly not. You need send me nothing except newspapers. The *Commercial* via Gallipolis by mail comes in good time.

We have some interesting contrabands coming in daily. Eleven came in yesterday. The rain seems to be a "settled" one. If so, all movements in this quarter are at an end. Sorry, but it can't be helped. . . .

Yours,

R.

DR. J. T. WEBB.

———

Fayetteville, Virginia, Sunday, January 5, 1862. — Ground frozen, moderately cold. A slight swelling of the left gland of the throat — the first symptom of influenza since I came to war. Generally with the first cold weather in November and frequently again in the latter part of the winter, I have a week's pretty severe influenza. I think I shall escape it this year, notwithstanding this slight symptom. Orders issued for a march to Raleigh early Tuesday morning — Twenty-third and Thirtieth to go, with intention to push farther if possible. But I suspect the weather and roads forbid. In the evening rain and sleet.

Monday, January 6. — Snow on the ground. Rainy and blustering — turning into a big fall of snow soon after noon. . . . A big snow-storm — wind whistling in its wintriest way. Not so severe as the northwest storms of the lake shore, but respectable.

FAYETTEVILLE, VIRGINIA, January 6, 1862.

DEAR JOE: — I yesterday received yours of the 26th; at the same time the *Commercial* of the first — six days later. Am glad to know you are doing so well at home. . . .

We go up to Raleigh tomorrow. A considerable march in the winter, if the mud thaws, as now seems likely. There is no difficulty in teams reaching [there] with goods and stores, but footing it, is, to say the least, disagreeable. Don't buy a new chest for me or anybody now. In the spring will be time enough.

It is possible you will start for here before this reaches Cincinnati; if not, come on, unless you hear by telegraph, without delay, if the condition of the family will allow. Love to all the dear ones — "wee" one and all.

Yours,

R.

DR. J. T. WEBB.

FAYETTEVILLE, January 6, 1862.

DEAR MOTHER: — I yesterday received your letter dated Christmas. It was very welcome. I also got a letter from home of one day's later date. Glad to know you are all well. It is impossible yet to fix the time of my visit home. It may be a month yet. If the weather allows, we are going tomorrow to Raleigh — twenty-five miles further from the steamboat landing, and rendering our communications with home somewhat more precarious. We are now in a region where the resident population is friendly, and we are urged to come to Raleigh by Union citizens for protection. We have established a camp there, and may, perhaps, push our movements further toward the interior. . . . I am busily engaged getting ready to move.

January 7. — It has been snowing steadily for several hours, and all thought of going further is indefinitely postponed. We shall stay in our comfortable quarters until the snow melts, and the floods abate, and the weather again allows the roads to settle. This, very likely, will not be until after my visit home, so I shall not see "Camp Hayes," as my friend Major Comly has called the post at Raleigh, until after I see some other Hayeses who are in another direction. I suspect I shall get home in between three and four weeks. I know no reason which will prevent my visiting you at Delaware and uncle at Fremont for a day or two each.

Affectionately,

YOUR SON.

MRS. SOPHIA HAYES.

Tuesday, January 7, 1862. — Snowing scattered flakes. Not more than three inches of snow has fallen. The weather is not cold for the season. Seven companies here now.

Joseph Bean resides nine miles from Boyer's Ferry on the old road between pike and river, five miles from Sewell (Mount) Camp; a Union man. . . . Mr. Bean is on the common errand, justice (possibly, vengeance or plunder) against his Rebel neighbors. Very unreliable stories, these.

The day before Christmas private Harrison Brown, Company B, stole a turkey from a countryman who came in to sell it. I made Brown pay for it fifty cents and sent him to the guard-house over Christmas. I hated to do it. He is an active, bright soldier, full of sport and lawless, but trusty, brave and strong. He just came in to offer me a quarter of venison, thus "heaping coals of fire on my head." He probably appreciated my disagreeable duty as well as any one and took no offense.

Lieutenant Avery (Martin P.) and Lieutenant Kennedy are

my messmates. Avery is a capital soldier. He joined the regular army as a private, five or six years ago, before he was of age, served a year and a half; joined the Walker expedition to Nicaragua, was in several fights and saw much severe service. He joined a company in Cleveland as a private — was made a second lieutenant and has since been promoted to first and was by me appointed adjutant. He is intelligent, educated, brave, thoroughly trained as a soldier and fit to command a regiment.

Kennedy is of Bellefontaine, an agreeable, gentlemanly youngster, dead in love, reads novels, makes a good aide, in which capacity he is now acting. Took a long walk with Avery in the snow.

Tuesday, January 7, 1862.

DEAREST L—: — The enclosed letter to Dr. Joe did not get off yesterday and thinking it likely *he* may be off, I enclose it with this to you.

Since writing yesterday a deep snow has fallen postponing indefinitely all extensive movements southward. We shall have a thaw after the snow, then floods, bad roads for nobody knows how long, and so forth, which will keep us in our comfortable quarters here for the present at least. Write me one more letter if you can before I come home. I shall not leave for home in *less* than three weeks. I trust my absence will not continue much *longer* than that time. Take care of yourself and you will be able to be up with me and about long before I leave. I must visit Columbus, Delaware, and Fremont (unless Uncle happens to be at Cincinnati) while at home, besides doing a great many chores of all sorts. I don't expect you to be able to go with me, but I hope you will be well enough to be with me a good deal while we are in Cincinnati.

I just ran out in the snow to detail four men to run down a suspicious character who is reported as hanging around the hospital and lower part of the village. A queer business this is.

I sent Laura some letters written by lovers, wives, and sisters to Rebels in Floyd's army. The captured mails on either side afford curious reading. They are much like other folks — those Rebel sweethearts, wives, and sisters.

I trust we shall crush out the Rebellion rapidly. The masses South have been greatly imposed on by people who were well informed. I often wish I could see the people of this village when they return to their homes. On the left of me is a pleasant cottage. The soldiers, to increase their quarters, have built on three sides of it the awkardest possible shanty extensions — one side having a prodigious stone and mud chimney, big enough for great logs ten feet in length. On three of the prominent hills of the village considerable earthworks have been built. There are no fences in sight except around the three buildings occupied by leading officers. Such is war. One young lady writing to her lover speaks of a Federal officer she had met, and laments that so nice a gentleman should be in the Union army.

. . . . You must be ever so careful for a good while yet. Good night, dearest. Much love to all and, as about forty affectionate Rebels say, a large portion for yourself.

Affectionately,

R.

Mrs. Hayes.

Wednesday, January 8. — "New Orleans," "The Union — it must and shall be preserved," "Old Hickory forever." These are the watchwords of today. This is our coldest day — clear, bright, and beautiful. Not over three inches of snow.

Rode with Adjutant Avery and two dragoons to Raleigh, twenty-four miles. A cold but not disagreeable day. The village of Raleigh is about ten to twelve years old; three or four hundred inhabitants may have lived there before the war; now six or eight families. Two churches, two taverns, two stores, etc., etc., in peaceful times. Our troops housed comfortably but too scattered, and too little attention to cleanliness. (*Mem.:* — Cooking ought never to be allowed in quarters.) I fear proper arrangements for repelling an attack have not been made.

Thursday, January 9, 1862. Raleigh, Virginia, (Beckley's Court-house). Cloudy; rained during last night, thawing, foggy, etc., etc. Rode with Avery to the mill of young Mr. Beckley on Piney River. Found it a most romantic spot. Beckley's family, a pretty wife and daughter, there in a cabin by the roaring torrent in a glen separated from all the world. I shall long remember that quiet little home. — One man of company —— died at Fayetteville.

Friday, January 10. — Heard rumors from Fayetteville of a great battle and victory at Bowling Green. Three thousand of our men killed and wounded. Enemy driven into the river — camp taken. One adds thirteen thousand taken prisoners. Floyd captured, says another. Fort Sumter retaken, says a third, and so on. Rode to Raleigh [slip of the pen for Fayetteville] with Avery, — very muddy — twenty-five miles in five to six hours. Rumors of the battle varied and conflicting. We ask all pickets and all we meet. As we approach Fayetteville the rumor loses strength. At Fayetteville, "Nothing of it, Colonel," says a soldier. So we go.

Fayetteville, Camp Union, January 11. Saturday. — Pleasant weather — warm and *very* muddy. A soldier of Company C died last night. Few cases of sickness but very fatal; calls for great care. Must see to clean livers at once. Made the commander of the post *vice* Colonel Eckley who is to leave with the Twenty-sixth (he to command the Eightieth) in a day or two. Sergeant McKinley brings me a letter from Lucy, the first since her confinement. She says she is well again; calls, as she speaks of him, the little fourth "Joe." Well, Joe it shall be — a good name, after the best of brothers and uncles.

Reports of preparations southward to meet and cut off our expedition to the railroad and the impassable roads have fast bound our intended enterprise.

Sunday, January 12, 1862. — Very warm, threatening rain all day. Three of our men died yesterday and today — two of them just recruited. Good letter from Dr. Joe. Bothered about our not going to Kentucky and such nonsense, but full of interesting particulars about the boys and family.

FAYETTEVILLE, VIRGINIA, Sunday A. M., January 12, 1862.

DEAREST LUCY: — I was made very happy by your letter of the 6th per Sergeant McKinley, and again this morning by a capital account of the boys — rose-colored by his affectionate partiality, but very enjoyable — from Dr. Joe. Such letters from home are next to meeting you all again. You speak of the fourth boy as "Joseph." Well, "Joe" it shall be if you wish it. Indeed, I thought of suggesting that name but I didn't know what you might have thought of, and one dislikes sometimes to disregard suggestions even on such subjects, and I thought to be, like Lincoln on the Mason and Slidell question, prudently silent. I hope you are not getting about the house so early as to put in hazard your health. Do be very careful.

We are letting a good many of our soldiers go home now that the snow, rain, and thaw have spoiled the roads. Joe seems worried that we are not holding somebody's horses in the "grand army" (a foolish phrase) in Kentucky. We are, or rather, have been, having our share of enterprises towards the jugular vein of Rebeldom — the Southwestern Virginia Railroad, and have captured arms, etc., in quantity.

I was out beyond Raleigh ("Camp Hayes") last week and returned the day before yesterday. Such consternation as spread among the Rebels on the advance of our troops was curious to behold. The advance party went fifty miles from here. People prepared to go as far up as Dublin Depot. Regiments were sent for to Richmond. Rumor said two bodies of Yankees, one thousand strong, were approaching, one on each bank of New River. The militia of five counties were called out, and a high time generally got up. There are many Union men south of here who kept us well posted of Rebel movements. Major Comly is left at Raleigh, and I feel somewhat apprehensive about him. Since the Twenty-sixth has been recalled, I am put in command of the post here.

I just stopped writing to give a pass to Ohio for a man belonging to the sutler department of the Thirtieth who turned out to be a Kinsell of Delaware. He promised to see mother.

I wrote a short note to you or Joe this morning, saying he had better come home (camp is always spoken of as *home*) if he can safely leave you. Colonel Scammon is really quite unwell, and while he likes Dr. Hayes as a gentleman, would prefer Dr. Joe as a physician. Dr. Jim or I can *perhaps* go to Cincinnati on his return. My going is rendered doubtful for the present by the departure of Colonel Eckley of the Twenty-sixth and the sickness of Colonel Scammon. Colonel Ewing of the Thirtieth will not return until the first week in February. I may possibly be obliged to await his return.

13th. — The newspapers from the *Commercial* office still get here three or four days in advance of other news, except dispatches. I shall send home a sabre captured by Company G on the late trip up New River towards the railroad. It is one of about a dozen taken, which belonged to a company of Richmond cavalry commanded by Captain Caskie. I send you the letter I got from Major Comly with the sabre.

You will send Joe off as soon as it is safe for him to go. I am always amused with his talk on one subject. He is resolved to consider our regiment as a much abused and neglected one. We were in about the only successful campaign made the past summer. We have the best winter quarters in the United States. He thinks we can't be favorites of General Rosecrans because he don't send us away to Kentucky or somewhere else! And so on. But old bachelors must grumble at something, and as he seems now to be enjoying everything else, it is perhaps right that he should be unhappy about the regiment. . . .

I feel a little embarrassed about Joe. He says, "Telegraph if you want me," etc., etc. Now, the truth is, he ought not to be absent without or beyond his leave. I have constantly said that if it was not safe to leave you he ought to stay, and I would see it [made] all right. This I repeat. But what annoys me is, Joe seems to feel as if something was wrong about the regiment; as if he would like to leave it, etc., etc. Now, if he isn't satisfied with it, I will do all I can to get him a place in another regiment. Don't let him stay in *this* on my account. I am liable to leave it at any time, and I really don't want anybody in high position in the regiment who is dissatisfied, and particularly if he is a friend or relative of mine. I feel a duty in this matter.

The happiness of several hundred men is affected more or less if one of the prominent officers allows himself to be habitually out of sorts about things. You may show this to Joe. Don't let there be any misunderstanding. I prefer greatly that Dr. Joe should be our surgeon, but if he feels that he can't return to western Virginia, or go anywhere else that the chances of war may take us, without feeling injured and soured, then my preference is that he do not come. I will do all I can to get him another place, as I said before, but I don't want to see him with us if he feels "snubbed" because we are not sent to Kentucky.

I ought not to trouble you with this, but it is written and you will not think me unkind, will you? Love to all the dear boys, *little* Joe and all. Very glad Mother Webb is so well.

Affectionately, as ever your

R.

Mrs. Hayes.

Sunday, January 12, 1862.

Dear Joe: —. . . Generally healthy; less sickness than ever, but more fatal. Come as soon as you safely can. Jim or I will return as soon as you get here. Can't come now.

Don't think our position an insignificant one. We make more captures and do more than any regiment I have yet heard of in Kentucky. Worrying on such subjects is simply *green*. It makes me laugh.

I was much interested in your account of the boys; very glad to have such favorable stories of them all. Love to 'em.

Sincerely,

R. B. Hayes.

Dr. J. T. Webb.

Monday, January 13, 1862.— As commander of the post have charge of the pass business. Have deputized —— to do the clerkly part, and private Gray, Company I, to do the orderly and department part, an erect, neat, fine old soldier; like him much. . . .

The Twenty-sixth preparing to leave.   Will take William Smith, a crack shot and well known bushwhacker, to Charleston or Columbus.   James Phillips the owner of this cottage was in the habit of going to Miller's Ferry to shoot at our men.   Mr. Mauser opposed it, said the town would be burned.   To no purpose.   Phillips kept at the business.

Tuesday, January 14, 1862. — My old veteran orderly, Gray, says *it makes his flesh creep to see the way soldiers enter officers' quarters, hats on, just as if they were in civil life!*   [The] Twenty-sixth Regiment left today.   Three or four inches snow.   Some winter!

Spent the afternoon looking over a trunk full of letters, deeds, documents, etc., belonging to General Alfred Beckley. They were buried in the graveyard near General Beckley's at Raleigh.   Some letters of moment showing the early and earnest part taken by Colonel Tompkins in the Rebellion.   The general Union and conservative feeling of General Beckley shown in letters carefully preserved in his letter-book.   Two letters to Major Anderson, full of patriotism, love of Union and of the Stars and Stripes — replies written, one the day after Major Anderson went into Sumter, the other much later.   His, General Beckley's, desire was really for the Union.   He was of West Point education.   Out of deference to popular sentiment he qualified his Unionism by saying, "Virginia would stay in the Union as long as she could consistently with honor."

General Beckley's note from "J. C. Calhoun, Secretary of War," informing him of his appointment as a cadet at West Point, and many other mementos, carefully preserved, were in the trunk.   Title papers and evidence relating to a vast tract of land, formerly owned by Gideon Granger and now by Francis Granger and brother, were also in it.   All except a few letters as to the Rebellion were undisturbed.

January 15.   Wednesday. — A swashing rain is falling on top of the snow.   What floods and what roads we shall have! No more movements in this quarter.   Yesterday a party from Camp Hayes went out after forage to the home of a man named Shumate who had escaped from the guardhouse in Raleigh a few days ago. They stopped at his house. As one of the men were [was] leaving, he said he would take a chunk along to build a fire. Mrs. Shumate said, "You'll find it warm enough before you get away." The party were fired on by about thirty bushwhackers; two horses badly wounded. Four men had narrow escapes, several balls through clothing.

Two more contrabands yesterday. These runaways are bright fellows. As a body they are superior to the average of the uneducated white population of this State. More intelligent, I feel confident. What a good-for-nothing people the mass of these western Virginians are! Unenterprising, lazy, narrow, listless, and ignorant. Careless of consequences to the country if their own lives and property are safe. Slavery leaves one class, the wealthy, with leisure for cultivation. They are usually intelligent, well-bred, brave, and high-spirited. The rest are serfs.

Rained all day; snow gone. I discharged three suspicious persons heretofore arrested; all took the oath. Two I thought too old to do mischief, Thurman and Max; one I thought possibly honest and gave him the benefit of the possibility. He was from Logan County. Knew Laban T. Moore and my old friend John Bromley. John, he says, is "suspect" of Secesh.

Thursday, January 16, 1862. — Bright, warm weather. Colonel Scammon moved from Mrs. Manson's house to Dr. Stites'. Lieutenants Warren and Smith start for Ohio. *I send letters to Mother, Uncle, and Lucy.* Warm and so muddy. The Kanawha up. Three steamboats at Loup Creek. Navigation good. Not having written "Thursday" above until this moment I thought it was Wednesday, and by a bet with Lieutenant Reichenbach lost a bottle of wine and the sardines. Present Dr. Jim W. [James Webb]; Lieutenants Reichenbach, Avery, and Kennedy. I fear Avery loves liquor "not wisely but too well." Major Comly says he has captured two hundred and five law books.

FAYETTEVILLE, January 16, 1862.

DEAR LUCY: — Lieutenants Warren and Smith leave today. We are very well. Mud awful deep and streams overflowing.

I shall apply for leave of absence soon after Captains Sperry and Zimmerman return, provided Dr. Joe is here. Of course it would not do for two prominent officers of the same family to be absent at the same time. These leaves of absence are so abused, that in the absence of some great necessity, I would not leave my regiment unless plenty of officers remain. I shall leave about the last of the month, I think, unless Dr. Joe should be detained on your account.

I am writing in much haste with a host of citizens growling. Love to all.

Good-bye, dearest.

R. B. HAYES

MRS. HAYES.

FAYETTEVILLE, VIRGINIA, January 16, 1862.

DEAR UNCLE: — I am in receipt of your favor of New Year's. So Allen got along. I hope he will not cause you more bother than he is worth. He was a good man here. I shall not be at all surprised if some day his owners undertake to recover him. You need not say this to him. His master still refuses to come in and take the oath of allegiance although an opportunity has been given him. He is a Rebel in the Rebel service.

We are doing well in all respects. I was at Camp Hayes, twenty-five miles further south, last week. They have pretty active times there with a few Rebel bushwhackers that infest the roads. Men are occasionally slightly wounded, but the shooting is from such great distances, and with common rifles, that no serious harm is done. The vast majority of the people are friendly.

As soon as four or five absent officers return, I shall ask for leave of absence. Say, in about three weeks.

Sincerely,

R. B. HAYES.

S. BIRCHARD.

Friday, January 17, 1862. — Froze last night to harden mud; cold and clear this morning; warm and bright all day. We feel rather lonely — so many gone. One regiment departed.

We hear of the resignation of Cameron and Welles. What does this mean? I think we must gain by it. I hope such men as Holt and Stanton will take their places. If so, the Nation will not lose by the change.

Read Nat Turner's insurrection of 1831. I suspect there will be few such movements while the war continues. The negroes expect the North to set them free, and see no need of risking their lives to gain what will be given them by others. When they discover their mistake and despair of other aid, *then* troubles may come.

Saturday, January 18, 1862. — Attempting to rain this morning. All important movements everywhere stopped by the rain and mud already. Still further "postponement on account of weather." How impatiently we look for action on Green River [and] at Cairo. As to the Potomac, all hope of work in that quarter seems to be abandoned. Why don't they try to flank the Rebels — get at their communications in the rear? But patience! Here we are in a good position to get in the rear via two railroads. Suppose two or even three or four bodies of men were to start, one by way of Lewisburg for White Sulphur Springs and Jackson Depot, one via Peterstown and Union, east side of New River, for Central Depot, one via Princeton and Parisburg [Pearisburg] right bank of New River, for Dublin, and another via Logan Court-house for some point lower down on the railroad.

A heavy rain falls — warm, spring-like, copious. The scenery of New River is attractive. The river runs in a deep gorge cut through the rock to a depth of one thousand to two thousand feet. The precipitous cliffs, occasionally cut through by streams running into the river, the rapid rushing river, and brawling mountain streams furnish many fine views. The Glades, a level region near Braxton and Webster Counties, where streams rise, and a similar region, called the Marshes of Cool, are the cattle grounds of this part of western Virginia. Braxton and Webster are the haunts of the worst Rebel bushwhackers of the country. Steep mountains, deep gorges and glens afford them hiding-places. They are annoying but not

dangerous except to couriers, mail-carriers, and very small par·
ties. They shoot from too great a distance at large parties to
do much harm. . . .

Fayetteville, Virginia, January 19, Sunday A. M. — It rained
almost all night; still falling in torrents. A great freshet may
be expected. . . .

Great war news expected. Burnside's expedition sailed; near
Cairo, a great movement forward; Green River, ditto. What we
need is greater energy, more drive, more enterprise, not unac-
companied with caution and vigilance. We must not run into
ambuscades, nor rush on strongly entrenched positions. The
battle of New Orleans and many others in our history teach
the folly of rushing on entrenchments defended by men, raw
and undisciplined it may be, but all of whom are accustomed
to the use of firearms. Such positions are to be flanked or
avoided.

*Camp Union, Fayetteville, Virginia, January 20, 1862. Mon-
day.* — This is the birthday of sister Fanny. Dear, dear sister,
so lovely, such a character! She would have been forty-two
years old today. Now six years — six years next June — since
she left us.

Rained during the night. Warm, and probably more rain
today. This is the January thaw. The mud is beaten down by
the rain. The thunder roaring now. Very few thunder-storms;
not more than three or four since we came to western Virginia.

A pleasant lull in the storm gave me a chance for a parade
last evening, or rather the adjutant asked if we should have
one. I, supposing him to be joking, said, "Yes, the weather is
so favorable." He ordered it and I was caught. I got a captured Caskie Cavalry sabre, slung it across my shoulder, and
went through with [it]. We returned in column by companies
closed in mass. The men marched well in the mud and it went
off with spirit.

Spent the evening reading the [Cincinnati] *Gazette* of the
16th, eating *peaches* with Avery and Gardner, and listening to
their tales of life on the plains and in Mexico. Avery's story

of the Navajos running off goats and sheep and his killing an Indian will do to tell Birch.

Tuesday, January 21, 1862. — Colder, but still raining. What a flood this will cause if it's general, as I think it is.

After being aroused by Thomas building a fire, I fell into a doze and dreamed. I thought Lucy had come and was in the room opposite to mine. I seemed to be partially asleep, and couldn't awake. She came in and stood by the bedside, not very affectionate in manner. I tried to arouse and succeeded in telling her how much I loved her. She was kind but not "pronounced." I thought, as I happened to see little Joe in her arms, that she was waiting to see me notice him and was hurt that I had not done so sooner. I spoke up cheerfully, held out my arms for him. I saw his face. He was a pretty child — like Webb, with sister Fanny's eyes, a square forehead, but his face looked too old, bright, and serious for a boy of his age; looked as a child of two or three years who had lost flesh.

I also dreamed during the night of being at home — anxiously, so anxiously, looking at the newspapers for news from the Cairo expedition; feared it would be defeated; reflected on the advantages the enemy had in their fortifications over an attacking party, and began to feel that the news must be disastrous.

Wednesday, January 22, 1862. — Cold, threatening rain or snow all day. . . . In the evening reports from Raleigh. Three of Company K, Thirtieth, and young Henderson, scout Company H, captured by the enemy. Report says no fighting except by Henderson. No other fired a gun. Rumor says they were drunk.

A great bushwhacker captured with three others. In the night bushwhacker taken with pains in his bowels — rolled over the floor, etc., etc., suddenly sprang up, seized two muskets and escaped! This is the official (false!) report. The other prisoners report that the sentinels were asleep, and the bushwhacker merely slipped out, taking two muskets with him.

Report says that three thousand milish of Mercer [County] are on or near Flat Top Mountain twenty miles from Raleigh and thirteen hundred cavalry!!

Three prisoners brought down last night. Captain McVey, a bushwhacking captain, armed with sword and rifle, was approaching a Union citizen's house to capture him, when [the] Union man, hearing of it, hid behind a log, drew a bead on Secesh as he approached, called out to him to lay down his arms, which Secesh prudently did, and thereupon the victor marched [him] to our camp at Raleigh. Another prisoner, a son of General Beckley, aged about sixteen. Why he was taken I don't understand. He carried dispatches when the militia was out under his father, but seems intelligent and well-disposed. Disliking to see one so young packed into a crowded guardhouse (thinking of Birch and Webb, too), I took him to my own quarters and shared my bed with him last night. He talked in his sleep incoherently, otherwise a good bedfellow.

Thursday, [January] 23. — A pretty fair day, warm and no rain. Dr. Joe arrived.

Friday, [January] 24, 1862. — A cold morning, ground frozen; promises to be a fine day. Snowed all the afternoon. A busy day. Had a good confidential talk with Colonel Scammon. He gains by a close and intimate acquaintance.

Alfred Beckley, Jr., left with a pledge to return if he failed to get exchanged for young Henderson, Company H, Twenty-third, the captured scout.

Two women wanted me to compel a neighbor to pay for tobacco and hogs he had stolen from them. One had a husband in the Secesh army and the other in the Union army.

An old man who had been saved by our soldiers because he was a Mason, so he thought, wanted pay for rails, sheep, and hogs; another, for hogs; another would give security for his good behavior, having been discharged, on condition he would do so, from Columbus, Ohio.

Sixteen Rebels captured in Raleigh County by Captain Haven sent in. Thirteen of our men found thirteen of them in a house armed to the teeth. They surrendered without firing a shot!! A mail-carrier caught with letters of the 17th. Many from soldiers of the Twenty-second Virginia to their friends in Boone County.

13

Dr. Joe in a stew and much laughed at by Dr. Jim and myself because he left his trunk, etc., on the river in a big skiff in charge of a blacksmith he had never seen before.

Saturday, January 25. — Snow thawing into the deepest mud and slush imaginable. Thawed into water; sky cleared off; a drying wind and a pleasant evening. Examined the eighteen prisoners; generally gave me truthful answers; a queer lot of people.

Yesterday had pictures taken — Avery, Sperry, Adjutant Bottsford, Thomas (our colored man), and Gray, the Scotch veteran orderly, at dinner table and fencing. Great news of a victory at Cumberland Gap. I hope it is true.

Sunday, [January] 26. — A lovely winter day, frozen in the morning, warm and thawing before noon. Inspected with Adjutant Avery the quarters; creditably clean. Feel happy today; fine weather, good health, the probable victory over Zollicoffer, the prospect — this chiefly — by next Sunday of seeing my darling Lucy and the boys — "all the boys."

A pleasant trip with Lieutenants Avery and Ellen and two riflemen of Company B to Long Point, with its romantic views of New River. The only dash to this pleasure is the report that my friend Bob McCook is seriously wounded. —— Later, not seriously only gloriously wounded. Good! He and I were friends before the war and more intimately since. His regiment and ours also fraternized very cordially — Yankees and Germans. Sperry went to Raleigh last night with Company B.

Monday, [January] 27, 1862. — Snow, sleet, finally rain. Rumors of "Secesh" cavalry and troops in various directions. Six hundred crossing Packs Ferry, threatening Raleigh. A like number of cavalry crossing to Princeton, ditto. Colonel Tompkins and a regiment above Camp Lookout, etc., etc. All probably with very slight foundation in fact. Two howitzers sent to Camp Hayes. Houses prepared to resist an attack by Major Comly. The major is plucky beyond question. All safe in that quarter.

Tuesday, January 28, 1862. — Dr. Jim left this morning for home, taking letters to Lute, Mother, Uncle, Platt, and others. Warm and bright all day, but oh, so muddy! Called on by two really good-looking ladies — Mrs. Thurman (husband Secesh soldier) and Miss Mary Mars.

General Rosecrans replies to my application for thirty days' leave: "Ask Hayes if thirty days isn't too long for these times?" I construe this as friendly, but the colonel thinks it is another instance of injustice to him. He thinks after he has recommended it, and in view of the fact that Colonel Ewing has over sixty days, Colonel Fyffe ditto, Lieutenant-Colonel Eckley about the same, Majors Ferguson and Degenfeld and Lieutenant-Colonel Jones, all of this brigade, and *all* our company officers, it looks unfair.

"Ah, but," said I, "circumstances may have changed." "Yes," said he, "but I have judged of that in asking the leave, and he don't take my judgment."

Well, well, I have made up my mind to do my duty and do it cheerfully in this war, and if orders don't suit me I shall obey them without demur.

Captain Gunckle, ordnance officer, Gauley, will furnish new bright muskets, shoulder-straps and plates, and ball and buck cartridge.

[FAYETTEVILLE], January 28, 1862.

Tuesday A. M. — before breakfast.

DEAR LUTE: — I am getting impatient to be with you. I have sent for leave of absence during the month of February. I expect to get a favorable answer so as to leave here by the last of the week. If so, nothing but some inroad of the enemy south of us will delay my coming. They are threatening "Camp Hayes" — mustn't let *that* be taken — and we sent Captain Sperry's company and two of McMullen's Battery there in the night, last night. I suspect that will settle the thing. I am delighted with the Kentucky victory, and particularly that my friend McCook and his regiment take the honors. We were good friends before the war, but much more intimately so since we came into service.   Our regiments, too, fraternized more cordially with each other than with anybody else.

Do not give it up, if I should not come quite so soon as I wish.   'I am bent on coming as soon as possible — am getting ready.   Sold my horse.   Sorry to do it, but he was unsafe — would sometimes stumble.   Will get another in Ohio.   I *do* want to see you "s'much," and I love you "s'much."   Good-bye.

Affectionately,

R.

Mrs. Hayes.

Fayetteville, Western Virginia, January 28, 1862.

Dear Brother William : — The excellent glass has reached me.   It is all I could ask.   I will settle with you when I see you. In the meantime, accept thanks.

I have applied for leave of absence during February, and if granted, shall leave for home the last of the week.   We are a good deal in the field just now, and have made some good moves lately, considering the weakness of our forces, and that we have but forty cavalrymen.   I see in the papers a good deal said about "too much cavalry accepted."   If we had only five hundred now, we could do more injury to the enemy than has yet been done by the Port Royal expedition.   We are elated with the victory in Kentucky.   I am especially pleased that McCook gets the plumes.

Sincerely,

R. B. Hayes.

W. A. Platt,
Columbus, Ohio.

Thursday, January 30, 1862. — Rained heavily last night, nearly all night; cloudy this morning.   Received permission for twenty-one days to go home, from headquarters, seven days additional from Colonel Scammon, and an assurance of three days' grace.   Total thirty-one.

People constantly come who are on their way to Ohio, Indiana, or other Western States.   Many of them young men who

are foot-loose, tired of the war.   No employment, poor pay,
etc., etc., is driving the laboring white people from the slave
States.

Mr. Ellison and his wife and little boy are here to see their
son John R., who is a prisoner in our guardhouse; to be sent
to the government prison at Columbus as a prisoner of war.
They seem glad to find their son safe out of the Rebel ranks
and not at all averse to his going to Columbus as a prisoner of
war.   Their only fear seems to be that he will be exchanged into
the Rebel army again.

Spent the evening in a jolly way at headquarters with Avery,
Kennedy, Hunter, etc.   Colonel Scammon gone to Raleigh; expected his return but didn't come.   Read the "Island," in "Lady
of the Lake," to Avery.

Camp Union, January 31, 1862. — Inspection day.   Good
weather until dark when a rain "set in."   Had a review and
inspection.   Satisfactory.   Cannon firing with a new brass six-
pounder, cast by Greenwood.   First two shots four hundred
and fifty yards, plumb in line, two and one-half feet below the
centre of the target.   At parade, had practice in musket firing —
six rounds — eight hundred shots.   Put one hundred and fifty-
four balls in a board five feet high by twenty inches broad — one
hundred yards.   Very good.   A jolly evening.   Read the letters
in the 27th and 28th *Commercials* to Avery, Bottsford, Captain
Moore, Dr. Webb, etc.; then a talk and laugh at campaign jokes.
Colonel Scammon returned from Raleigh; thinks the mud too
deep for forward movements for a month or six weeks.

Camp Union, Fayette, Virginia, February 1, 1862. — Rain all
night last night; mud indescribable and unfathomable.   Lieutenant Avery and Secesh prisoners start today.

At 2 P. M., having heard that General Schenck would perhaps
reach camp in a day or two, and fearing that he would object
to my absence (he having himself been away two months
and over!!) I started on the doctor's stumbling gray for Loup
Creek Landing.   It rained a cold storm, mud deep.   Thomas,
the gay, dramatic colored servant of Dr. Webb, and my orderly
(Barney) in a waggon with my baggage.   I got to Loup Creek

Landing, sixteen miles, after dark alone. Stayed there in a cabin, fitted up with bunks for soldiers, with Lieutenant Avery's guard of the seventeen Secesh prisoners. Bill Brown the life of the party. Poor accommodations for sleeping. Little sleeping done. So ends the first.

Loup Creek Landing, five miles below Landing, February 2. — Sunday morning finds us waiting for a steamboat to get down Kanawha River. *General Meigs* took us aboard about 12 M. A cold ride — occasional gleams of sunshine — down the Kanawha to Charleston. A picturesque valley, high hills, ruins of salt-works, etc., etc., a fine river, make up the scene. A servant girl of Mrs. Mauser, apparently under the auspices of Thomas (he passed her on the steamer as his wife!), was met by our team yesterday and taken aboard a half mile out of Fayetteville. She must have been there by preconcert with Thomas. The feeling of the soldiers, a sort of indifferent satisfaction, easily roused to active zeal, expressed itself, "Another shade of Mrs. Mauser's lost." Not another syllable by way of comment in a circle of six around the camp-fire.

Reached Charleston before dark. Avery and I took quarters at the Kanawha House, a good hotel. Visited General Cox; a good talk; a sound man; excellent sense. I wish he commanded our brigade. . . . Heard the church bells at Charleston — the first for six months; a home sound.

Monday, February 3. Charleston, Virginia.—Leave this morning on the steamboat —— for Gallipolis. Reached there at 2 P. M. A drizzly, cold day, snow on the hills, mud, snow, and slush at Gallipolis. With Avery and Bill Brown over town; oysters, eggs, and ale. At nine P. M. on *Dunleith* down the Ohio.

Steamboat Dunleith, Ohio River, Tuesday, February 4, 1862. — A bright cold winter day; a good sail down the Ohio. Banks full. Beautiful river.

Reached home as the clock finished striking 12 midnight. A light burning in front room. Wife, boys, Grandma, all well. "Perfectly splendid."

[The entries in the Diary for the next few days are very brief. Tuesday, February 11, Hayes went to Columbus to visit his brother-in-law, W. A. Platt, and family; two days later to Delaware where he remained two days with his mother. The week-end he spent "happily at Fremont with Uncle. All the talk is of battles — the late victories at Roanoke Island, Fort Henry, and the pending struggle at Donelson." Monday, the 17th, returning to Cincinnati, he hears "of the decisive victory at Fort Donelson as we reached Crestline and Galion. Joy and excitement, cannon, flags, crowds of happy people everywhere." The following days at home in Cincinnati "getting ready to return to his regiment."]

DELAWARE, February 14, 1862. Friday morning.

DEAREST LUCY: — I reached here last night. Mother, Mrs. Wasson, and Sophia, all well and happy. *Old* Delaware is gone; the bright new town is an improvement on the old.

Snow deep, winter come again. Old times come up to me — Sister Fanny and I trudging down to the tanyard with our little basket after kindling. All strange; you are Sister Fanny to me now, dearest.

I go to Fremont this evening. Mother sends love. Write to her. Love to all.

Affectionately,

R.

MRS. HAYES.

CINCINNATI, February 18, 1862.

DEAR UNCLE: — It will be agreeable to Lucy to go to Fremont with the family as soon as you wish. She proposes to take all of our furniture that may be wanted there — to store the rest, and to rent the house — thus in effect moving to Fremont until the war is ended. This or any other plan you prefer will suit. Our furniture will be enough for all purposes — unless you wish to show off in some one room or something of that sort.

All well here. The great victory is a crusher.

Sincerely,

S. BIRCHARD.

R. B. HAYES.

CINCINNATI, February 22, 1862.

DEAR MOTHER: — I am ready to start back to Virginia on the first steamer for the Kanawha River. I expect to get off tomorrow or next day.

I found Uncle in good health for him. The other friends were as usual. . . . I returned home Monday finding all here as 1 left them.

The recent victories convince everybody that the Rebellion can be conquered. Most people anticipate a speedy end of the war. I am not so sanguine of a sudden wind-up, but do not doubt that the Confederacy is fatally wounded. We are having a gaudy celebration of the 22nd here with the usual accompaniments which delight the children.

Affectionately, your son,

RUTHERFORD.

MRS. SOPHIA HAYES.

Cincinnati, February 25, 1862. Tuesday. — A. M., 8:30, bright, cold, gusty, started in cars on Marietta Railroad; reached Hamden, junction of railroad to Portsmouth, about 2 P. M.; twenty-five miles to Oak Hill on this railroad; Cuthbert, in quartermaster department under Captain Fitch at Gauley Bridge, my only acquaintance. Took an old hack — no curtains, rotten harness, deep muddy roads — for Marietta [Gallipolis]. The driver was a good-natured, persevering youngster of seventeen, who trudged afoot through the worst holes and landed us safely at Gallipolis [at] three-thirty A. M., after a cold, sleepless, uncomfortable ride. He said he had joined three regiments; turned out of two as too young and taken out of the third by his father. Poor boy! His life is one of much greater hardship than anything a soldier suffers.

Wednesday, 26. — Spent in Gallipolis waiting for a steamboat going up the Kanawha. Quartermaster Cuthbert and I slept, walked, and watched the clouds and rain.

GALLIPOLIS, February 26, 1862.

DEAR UNCLE: — On my way to the wars again. Left all well and happy at home. Your letters reached me. There will be no difficulty about "camping down" in your house. Lucy could get up out of her furniture a camp chest which will be ample for comfort without buying anything.

I shall be away from mails soon. Shall not write often. You will hear all important things by telegraph.

Sincerely,

R. B. HAYES.

S. BIRCHARD.

Thursday, [February] 27. — Clear, cold, windy. On steamer *Glenwood* passed up to Camp Piatt. Left Gallipolis about 9 A. M., reached Charleston 7 P. M., Camp Piatt at 10 P. M.

Fayetteville, Virginia, Febraury 28, 1862. Friday. — Reached here after a hard ride of forty miles from Camp Piatt. Found the Twenty-third men pleased to see me; felt like getting home. Had been absent four weeks, less one day, on furlough. Road from Camp Piatt a good part of the way very good; but from the ferry to Fayetteville execrable. The weather moderate, windy, threatening a storm.

CINCINNATI — NO, FAYETTEVILLE, VIRGINIA,

Saturday, March 1, 1862.

DEAR L—: — I reached here in good condition last night. Find Dr. Joe very well. How he loves the boys! All things look bright and cheerful.

Colonel Scammon goes home today. People seem glad to see me, and I am glad to see the Twenty-third again. They greet me a good deal as the boys did at home.

Darling, you will be pleased to know, and so I tell you, I never loved you more than I do as I think of you on my late visit, and I never *admired* you so much. You are glad I feel so? Yes; well, that's "pretty dood." No time to write much. Love to Grandma and kisses for all the boys.

I brought all the grub in my haversack except three biscuits clear here. More welcome here than on the road. Ask Dr. Jim to see that my *Commercial* and Joe's *Gazette* are sent. They don't come.

Affectionately,

R.

Mrs. Hayes.

Monday, March 3. — Still raining, some sleet, cold as blazes at night. Ride my new horse, a yellow sorrel of Norman stock; call him Webby.

Tuesday, 4. — Bright, cold, snow on ground. Ride with Dr. Joe, A. M. Webby doesn't like the bit; it brings the blood. A good horse, I think.

Today a German soldier, Hegelman, asks to marry a girl living near here. She comes in to see me on the same subject; a good-looking girl, French on her father's side, name, Elizabeth Ann de Quasie. A neighbor tells me she is a queer girl; has belonged to the Christian, Baptist, and Methodist church, that she now prefers the Big Church. She has a doubtful reputation. When Charles Hegelman came in to get permission to go to Gauley to get married by the chaplain of the Twenty-eighth, I asked him why he was in a hurry to marry; if he knew much about her; and what was her name. He replied, "I like her looks"; and after confessing that he didn't know her name, that he thought it was Eliza Watson(!), he admitted that the thing was this: Eight hundred dollars had been left to him payable on his marriage, and he wanted the money out at interest!

A jolly evening with Drs. Webb and McCurdy and Lieutenants Avery and Bottsford at my room. Bottsford giving his California experience — gambling, fiddling, spreeing, washing clothes, driving mules, keeping tavern, grocery, digging, clerking, etc., etc., rich and poor, in debt and working it out; all in two or three years.

News on the wires that the Rebels have Murfreesboro; that Pope takes four or six guns from Jeff Thompson; that there is appearance of a move at Centreville and also of a move on Charleston, Virginia, and the capture of six hundred barrels of flour.

Fayetteville, Virginia, Wednesday, March 5. — Snow, raw weather. Rode with Dr. Joe four or five miles. The new horse doesn't seem to care for pistol firing. Open-air exercise agrees with me so well that I often feel as if an indoor life was unworthy of manhood; outdoor exercise for health! Read news of the 28th and [March] 1, Cincinnati. Rebel papers afford good reading these days.

Thursday, 6. — Snow two or three inches deep on top of the mud. Dr. Webb and Adjutant Avery started for Raleigh in the storm, or rather on the snow and mud. There is no storm, merely snowing. P. M., with Captain McMullen and Lieutenant Bottsford rode out toward Bowyer's Ferry; horses "balled" badly; fired a few pistol shots. My Webby (new) shies some and was decidedly outraged when I fired sitting on his back. Practiced sabre exercise. Evening, heard the telegraphic news; General Lander's death, the only untoward event. How many of the favorites are killed! General Lyon, Colonel Baker, Major Winthrop, and now General Lander. I should mention Colonel Ellsworth also. He was a popular favorite, but by no means so fine or high a character as the others. Army in Tennessee "marching on." The newspapers and the telegraph are under strict surveillance. Very little of army movements transpire[s]. On the upper Potomac a movement seems to be making on the enemy's left in the direction of Winchester. Night, very cold — very.

FAYETTEVILLE, March 6, 1862.

DEAREST: — Dr. Joe has been in his happiest mood every since my return — all the regiment are perfectly healthy. Avery and he started for Raleigh with Thomas this morning. Snowing — snow three inches on mud twelve inches. All of the Twenty-third goes up soon. We shall be "to ourselves" a little while up there. . . . The telegraph line will extend to Raleigh soon.

Lieutenant Bottsford says the picture I bring of you is **not** so pretty as you are! What do you say to that?

Affectionately,

R.

Mrs. Hayes.

Saturday, March 8. — Ground frozen; sun came out bright and warm, speedily thawing all snow. Company C and four wagons carry all the "plunder" of the company and the adjutant's office to Raleigh.

P. M. A glorious ride to the scenery of New River at and about Long Point; a rapid ride back; Doctors McCurdy, Twenty-third, and Potter, Thirtieth, Lieutenant-Colonel Jones, and Adjutant-General Hunter for companions. How the blood leaps and thrills through the veins as we race over the hills! Physical enjoyments of this sort arc worth a war. How the manly, generous, brave side of our people is growing! With all its evils war has its glorious compensations.

News by telegraph this evening very meagre. A fine, affectionate letter from my dear wife, written last Sunday. She is so distressed at my absence but would not have me do otherwise.

FAYETTEVILLE, March 9, 1862. Sunday P. M.

DEAREST: — I received your letter last night — sent by Mr. Schooley. You wrote it a week ago. A rainy, gloomy day here too, but made rather jolly by Dr. Joe's good nature, with Avery and Bottsford to help me laugh. Dr. Joe is in his best humor these days and makes all around him happy. Today is a lovely spring day — but getting lonely here. I am a hen with one chicken. All but one company, I have sent to Raleigh since Colonel Scammon left. We have been here almost four months. The men are pleased to go. I shall start in a day or two when the hospital goes. No sickness — not a man who can't go about, and only four who need a hospital. Eight hundred well men here and at Raleigh.

There is a real gloom among the men caused by a report that

I am to be colonel of the Sixth. It is no doubt a repetition of an idle rumor I heard in Cincinnati. But as the thing may come up, I wish you and Stephenson to know that I would not want the place unless it was agreeable generally that I should have it. Young Anderson is probably entitled to it, and I would not want it in opposition to him or his friends. The place is, perhaps, not preferable to my present position and I do not desire it, unless it is all smooth — particularly with Anderson. If I were sure of continuing my present command of the Twenty-third, I would not wish a colonelcy of any other regiment; but in the present uncertainty I am willing to take a certainty in any good regiment.

My new horse performs beautifully. I am in the best of health. There is only one thing: You are not here. Don't you think I love you as much as you do me? Why, certainly. There, I have fixed this letter so you can't show it to "Steve." I'll write him a note. . . .

> Affectionately,
>
> R. B. HAYES.

MRS. HAYES.

Monday, 10. — Captain Moore (R. B.), of Willoughby, has resigned. I yesterday invited him to quarter with me, his company (I) having gone to Raleigh. The weather is warm and threatening rain. Last night there was a thunder-storm.

Tuesday 11. — A warm bright day. Dined at the hospital with our excellent assistant surgeon, Dr. McCurdy. Sent Company E to Raleigh. The last of the Twenty-third quartered in Fayette is gone. Camp Hayes, Raleigh, headquarters henceforth.

Heard of the evacuation of Manassas by the Rebels. If so, it is evidence of a breaking away that almost decides the contest. But how did they do it undisturbed? *What was McClellan doing?* A great victory over the combined forces of Van Doren, Price, McCulloch, and McIntosh reported to have occurred in Arkansas.

Wednesday, March 12. — A bright warm day. I go to Raleigh, bidding good-bye to Fayetteville. We entered Fayetteville either the 13th or 14th of November; four months in one home, not unpleasant months, considering the winter weather of this region. Rode to Fayetteville [slip of pen for Raleigh] on my new bright bay — a good ride. Reached Fayetteville [Raleigh] just as our regiment was forming for dress parade. Eight companies in line looked large. Was greeted warmly. I gave them the news of the evacuation of Manassas and the victory in Arkansas. Three cheers given for the news; three more for General Curtis, and three for the colonel! All seemed pleased to be again together. How well they looked. The band is in capital condition. How I love the Twenty-third. I would rather command it as lieutenant-colonel than to command another regiment as colonel.

Camp Hayes, Raleigh, Virginia, Thursday, [March] 13.— Spent the day arranging quarters, guards, etc., etc. I room with Avery. Messed three meals with Colonel Burgess. Hash — such hash! Colonel Burgess was a venomous Secesh but is now mollified and so strong a Union man that with a body of our troops he attacked a gang of his old Secesh friends at Jumping Branch and killed one of them! Before noon it began to rain. Cleared a little in time for evening parade.

Read confirmation of good news of yesterday. Five, only think, five!! Secesh prisoners captured! Negligence in the Potomac army. A new division and assignment of commands gives great satisfaction to us all. General McClellan no longer acts as Commander-in-Chief. Three great divisions created. General McClellan commands the Potomac, General Halleck the Mississippi, and General Frémont the Mountains (supposed to be our case). General Frémont has a strong hold on the hearts of the people and of the soldiers. We all feel enthusiasm and admiration for him.

Camp Hayes, Raleigh, Virginia, March 13, 1862.

Dearest: — I came up last night just as the regiment was forming for dress parade. For the first time in months we are all together; health good; ranks very full. Oh! it was a beautiful sight; we had plenty of cheering, music, and our best marchnig.

The men were never in finer condition. You would enjoy seeing the Twenty-third now; well dressed, bravely looking, and soldier-like.

We expect to remain here until a forward movement is made — perhaps two to four weeks, possibly longer. Dr. Joe very well and in good spirits. My new Webby still does finely. It is just daylight. Captain Slocum who left us at Camp Chase, has visited us and goes home this morning. Love to all.

Most affectionately, your

R.

Mrs. Hayes.

Camp Hayes, Raleigh, Virginia, Friday, March 14, 1862. — A fine pleasant morning. About 11 A. M. Captain Gilmore of Company [C, First] Pennsylvania [Virginia] Cavalry, came in, saying, "My scouts sent out this morning have all been killed or captured"; two only returned. It turned out that eight cavalry patrols of his company, who left here about 8:30 A. M., this morning, were fired upon by a gang of men concealed in the woods about seven miles from here on the Princeton Road near Hunly's. Two were killed, two wounded, one taken prisoner. One of the wounded men and two unhurt galloped into camp, having taken a circuitous route over the hills and through the woods. At this writing our loss is two killed and one taken prisoner.

I think the manner of this scouting or patrolling very objectionable. Six to ten men every morning about the same hour have been in the habit of riding out six to ten miles on this road. Nothing was easier than to lay an ambush for them. I suspect that the enemy fled instantly, that they are bushwhackers or militia. I sent out the whole cavalry company under Captain Gilmore and Companies B, H, and K, under Captain Drake, to get the bodies of the dead and the wounded man. Hunly is suspected to communicate intelligence to the enemy. None of these people are perfectly reliable. They will do what is necessary to protect their property.

Henderson, of Company H, taken prisoner last January, returned last night. He was exchanged and left Richmond February 23. He is called "Cleveland" by his company from the place of his enlistment. Others call him the "Pet Lamb," from his delicate and youthful appearance. He is a quiet, observing, enterprising youngster; slender, sickly-looking, amiable; runs all risks, endures all hardships, and seems to enjoy it. A scout in fact, he is in constant danger of being taken for a spy. I must watch him. I suspect he is a genius. His father and mother died when he was a child.

HEADQUARTERS, CAMP HAYES, RALEIGH, VIRGINIA,

March 14, 1862.

SIR: — A scouting party consisting of Sergeant A. H. Bixler, and seven men belonging to Captain George W. Gilmore's Company C, First Virginia Cavalry, was this morning attacked about seven miles from Raleigh on the pike leading to Princeton, by about fifty bushwhackers. Sergeant Bixler and Private James Noble were killed. Privates Jacob McCann and Johnson Mallory were dangerously wounded, and Private Thomas B. Phillips was taken prisoner. Three escaped unhurt. The attacking party rendezvous on Flat Top Mountain. Major Hildt will, perhaps, recognize the names of some of them. Christ Lilley, Daniel Meadows, and Joshua Rowls were certainly of the party.

On hearing of the affair I dispatched Captain Gilmore with his cavalry, and Captain Drake with three companies of infantry to the scene of the occurrence. They found that the bushwhackers had instantly fled to their fastnesses in the hills, barely stopping long enough to get the arms of the dead and to rob them of their money. Captain Drake followed them until they were found to have scattered. Two horses were killed, one captured, one wounded, and one lost. Vigilant efforts will be made to ascertain the hiding-places of the bushwhackers and when found, unless orders to the contrary shall be received, all houses and property in the neighborhood which can be destroyed by fire, will be burned, and all men who can be identified as of the party will be killed, whether found in arms or not.

Will you direct the brigade quartermaster to procure tents enough for Captain McIlrath's Company A, Twenty-third Regiment O. V. I., as soon as practicable, and send that company here as soon as the tents arrive. There will be no quarters for them until the tents are obtained.

I desire to have your views in the premises.

Respectfully,

R. B. HAYES,

LIEUTENANT-COLONEL TWENTY-THIRD REGIMENT O. V. I.,
COMMANDING.

[GENERAL J. D. COX (?)]

Saturday, March 15. — Changed the manner of scouting. Hereafter the cavalry are to scout at irregular intervals on routes changed daily, and an infantry scouting party of twenty-five to a full company will be sent in the general direction of apprehended danger to skirmish the woods and by-roads. Lieutenant Hastings with twenty-five men of Company I does this duty today.

P. M. Rained and cleared up half a dozen times during the day; a heavy thunder-storm. April weather. Lieutenant Hastings with a man he found four or five miles out on the Princeton Road, named —— Hull, scoured the country near the scene of the attack on the cavalry patrol; found where about twelve to fifteen of the bushwhackers staid during the night after the affair at an empty house owned by Saulsbury; burned it, also burned two other houses owned by bushwhackers. Captain Drake burned three. James Noble buried yesterday.

Sunday, 16, A. M. — Another change — a snow-storm; March fuss and fury. Received a note from Lieutenant-Colonel Jones, directing vigilance and to be in readiness for an attack by the enemy or for a forward movement, — the abandonment by the Rebels of eastern Virginia on the Potomac rendering it likely that the enemy will come here or we go there!! . . .

CAMP HAYES, RALEIGH, VIRGINIA, March 16, 1862.

DEAR UNCLE: — I am in most respects pleasantly fixed here. I am here in command of nine companies of the Twenty-third,

14

one section (two guns) of an artillery company (thirty men) and one company of cavalry. We are quartered in the courthouse, churches, and deserted dwellings. It is near the spurs of the Alleghany Mountains, which about twenty miles from here are filled with militia. A few regulars and bushwhackers are just in front of us. We are kept on the alert all the time by such events as the one referred to in the enclosed notes. As a general rule, we get the better of the bushwhackers in these affairs. There is no hesitation on our part in doing what seems to be required for self-protection. Since writing the note enclosed, have done a good deal towards punishing the cowardly bushwhackers.

We have April weather, for the most part — thunder-storms, rain, and shine. Today we are having a winter snow-storm. Since the rumored abandonment of Manassas, we have been notified to be in constant readiness to move. My letters will probably be more irregular than usual after we get started, but all important events occurring with us will be sent you by telegraph. We take the wires with us. Love to all.

Sincerely,

R. B. HAYES.

S. BIRCHARD.

Camp Hayes, Raleigh, Virginia, Monday A. M., March 17, 1862. — Cold raw morning; snow at last lying on the ground enough to whiten it. Stormy (rather Aprilish) and bright by turns all day.

Mrs. Beckley (General) called (with another lady) in tears saying her husband, the general, was at home. Had concluded to surrender himself; that she hadn't seen or heard from him for three months, hoped we would not send him to Columbus, etc., etc. In his letter he pledged his honor not to oppose the United States; to behave as a loyal citizen, etc., etc. I called to see him; found him an agreeable old gentleman of sixty; converses readily and entertainingly; told an anecdote of General Jackson capitally; he said, Old Hickory's hair bristled up, his eyes shot fire, and his iron features became more prominent, as, in a passion, raising both hands, he said (speaking of a postmaster General Beckley wished to retain in office, and who had himself taken no active part against General Jackson but whose clerks had been against the general) : "What if the head is still when both hands are at work against me!" — shaking his hands outstretched and in a tearing passion. The lieutenant (then) subsided in the presence of such wrath.

General Beckley thinks western Virginia is given up to us, and that his duty is to go with his home — to submit to the powers that be. I agreed to his views generally and told him I would recommend General Cox to assent to his surrender on the terms proposed.

Sent Captain Zimmerman and company out scouting the woods in our vicinity; Captain Harris out to break up a bushwhacking party he thinks he can surprise.

Tuesday, March 18. — A. M., very cold but looks as if the storm was at an end and bright weather come again. P. M., a lovely day. Rode with Avery on the Logan Road three miles to Evans' and Cook's. Drilled the regiment. Adjutant Avery drilled skirmish drill. P. M., drilled sergeants in bayonet exercise, and regiment in marching and squares. Spent the evening jollying with the doctors and reading Scott.

A queer prisoner brought in from New River by Richmond. Richmond, a resolute Union citizen was taken a prisoner at his house by three Rebels — two dragoons and a bushwhacker. One of the dragoons took Richmond up behind him and off they went. On the way they told Richmond that he would have to ———— ——— ———. Thereupon Richmond on the first opportunity drew his pocket-knife slyly from his pocket, caught the dragoon before him by his hair behind and cut his throat and stabbed him. Both fell from the horse together. Richmond cut the strap holding the dragoon's rifle; took it and killed a second. The third escaped, and Richmond ran to our camp.

Jesse Reese brought in as a spy by Richmond, says he is a tailor; was going to Greenbrier to collect money due him. Says he married when he was about fifty; they got married because they were both orphans and alone in the world!

[Dr. J. T. Webb, in a letter, of March 12, to his sister (Mrs. Hayes), tells the story of Richmond's feat in the following graphic recital:

"About thirty miles from here, on New River, lives an old man (Richmond) and several sons. His boys are all grown and living to themselves, some four and five miles from the old man. They have lived out there many years and for this country are all rich. Besides being wealthy they are all very powerful (physically) and are the leaders, as it were, of society. They have the *best* horses, cattle, etc. of any one out here. They are noted for their fine horses. They are all strong Union men, and have been very much angered by the Rebels taking their cattle, sheep, etc. — stealing them. A few days since some Rebel cavalry concluded they would arrest the squire and take his horses. Accordingly day before yesterday, just at daybreak, three Rebel cavalry called at the squire's and took him prisoner. They also took three of his fine horses. They put the squire on a horse behind one of the cavalrymen, and started off with him. After they had gone some ten miles, they came to a noted Rebel's house, and all cheered at the capture of the squire. This was too much for him, and he determined to make his escape. They had gone but a short distance when the Rebel behind whom he was riding fell back behind the other two some distance. Now was the time for the squire. So drawing a long knife from his pocket, he caught the Rebel by his hair, drew him back, and *cut his throat*. Both fell off the horse together. As they fell he plunged the knife into the Rebel's bowels. Then he took the Rebel's gun, and got behind a tree when one of the others returned, and the squire *shot him dead*. The third took to his heels and left the squire *victor* of the field. There is no mistake about this; he came to camp with their two guns. His knife and coat-sleeve is covered with blood. Richmond is a trump and two hundred such men would clean out this country of Rebels."]

Camp Hayes, Raleigh, Virginia, March 19, 1862. — Before breakfast. A lovely day. Captain Haven returned last night after an extensive scout; burned seven empty houses — occupants gone bushwhacking. Burned none with women in them.

About noon a gentleman rode up and inquired for the colonel commanding. He turned out to be Clifton W. Tayleure, a local editor, formerly of Baltimore *American,* lately of Richmond *Enquirer.* Left Richmond a week ago to avoid the draft. All between eighteen and forty-five to be drafted to fill up the old regiments; all between sixteen and eighteen and forty-five and fifty-five to be enrolled as home guards to protect the homes and guard the slaves. He is a South Carolinian by birth; lived there until he was fifteen; came North; has been a "local" in various cities since; has a family in Baltimore; went to Richmond to look after property in August last; couldn't get away before; got off by passes procured by good luck, etc., etc.; is a Union man by preference, principle, etc., etc. This is his story. He is about thirty-three years of age, of prepossessing appearance, intelligent and agreeable. Gives us interesting accounts of things in the Capital of Secession. Says the tradespeople are anxious for peace — ready for the restoration of the old Union. He seems to be truthful. I shall give him a pass to General Cox there to be dealt with as the general sees fit. — Will he visit them (Colonel Jones and General Cox) and report himself, or will he hurry by?

Thursday, 20. — Cold; no rain falling this morning, but the storm not over. Frémont at the head of our department, the Mountain District, western Virginia and east Tennessee. Good! I admire the general. If he comes up to my anticipations, we shall have an active campaign.

Colonel Scammon returned, also Major Comly, to Fayetteville. They send no news and bring no newspapers. Thoughtless fellows! No, I must not call the colonel *fellow.* He put down a countryman who came in with, "Are you the feller what rents land?" Colonel Scammon: "In the first place I am not a feller; in the second place, take off your hat! and in the third place, I don't rent land. There is the door"!

Friday, 21. — Storm not over yet; snows P. M. . . . News of retreat of enemy after leaving Manassas. If McClellan pursues vigorously he will thrash or destroy them. A victory that crushes the Rebellion as a power. It may be a great annoyance afterwards but nothing more. Vigor, energy now for a few weeks and the thing is done. He (McClellan) ought not to have allowed them to steal away from him, but if he now crushes them he redeems it all and becomes the Nation's idol. I hope he will do it. I do not quite like his views of slavery if I understand them; but his cautious policy if now followed by energy will be vindicated by the event.

Saturday, 22. — Still snowing. I write home and to Mother this morning.

Captain R. B. Foley, of Mercer County signs himself Captain of Confederate Company; Captain Michael Hale, Raleigh, ditto; Joel F. Wood, James N. Wood, Wm. A. Walker, Geo. A. Walker, [and] Charles Walker (Rev.), all of Raleigh.

The foregoing people agree to remain peaccably at home if we will not molest them. I wrote as follows: "No citizen who remains peaceably at home and who neither directly nor indirectly gives aid or comfort to the enemies of the United States will be molested in person or property by the troops under my command."

RALEIGH, VIRGINIA, March 22, 1862.

DEAREST: — Your letters, 13th and 15th, reached me yesterday. Also the gloves and [percussion] caps. They suit perfectly.

You don't know how I enjoy reading your accounts of the boys. Webb is six years old. Dear little fellow, how he will hate books. Don't be too hard with him. Birch's praying is really beautiful.

We are in the midst of one of the storms so frequent in these mountains. We call it the equinoctial and hope when it is over we shall have settled weather. It is snowing in great flakes which stick to the foliage of the pine and other evergreen trees on the hills, giving the scene in front of the window near me a strangely wintry appearance.

To kill time, I have been reading "Lucile" again, and you may know I think of you constantly and oh, so lovingly as I read. When I read it first we were on the steamer in the St. Lawrence River below Quebec. What a happy trip that was! It increased my affection for you almost as much as my late visit home. Well, well, you know all this. You know "I love you so much."

We are all feeling very hopeful. We expect to move soon and rapidly, merely because Frémont is commander. I do not see but this war must be soon decided. McClellan seems determined, and I think he is able to force the retreating Manassas army to a battle or to an equally disastrous retreat. A victory there ends the contest. I think we shall be months, perhaps even years, getting all the small parties reduced, but the Rebellion as a great peril menacing the Union will be ended.

General Beckley, whose sword-belt Webby wears, came in and surrendered to me a few days ago. Mrs. Beckley brought me his note. She is a lady of good qualities. Of course, there were tears, etc., etc., which I was glad to relieve. The old general is an educated military gentleman of the old Virginia ways — weak, well-intentioned, and gentlemanly; reminds one of the characters about Chillicothe, from Virginia — probably of less strength of character than most of them. A citizen here described him to Dr. McCurdy as "light of talent but well educated."

Gray, "the blind soldier" you saw at Camp Chase, is, I notice, on duty and apparently perfectly well. Gray, the orderly, you saw drunk is in good condition again, professing contrition, etc. McKinley is bright and clean, looking his best. Inquires if you see his wife.

So, you go to Fremont. You will once in a while see our men there, too. Some five or six Twenty-third men belong in that region.

You ought to see what a snow-storm is blowing. Whew! I had a tent put up a few days ago for an office. Before I got it occupied the storm came on and now it is split in twain. . . .

Our regiment was never so fine-looking as now. It is fun to see them. No deaths, I believe, for two months and no sickness worth mentioning. Chiefly engaged hunting bushwhackers.

Our living is hard, the grub I mean, and likely not to improve. Salt pork and crackers. The armies have swept off all fresh meats and vegetables. A few eggs once in a great while.

Love to Grandma and all the boys.

Affectionately, as ever,

R.

MRS. HAYES.

CAMP HAYES, RALEIGH, VIRGINIA, March 22, 1862.

DEAR WEBBY: — You are six years old — a big boy. I want you to be a very good boy; tell the truth, and don't be afraid. Learn to read and write, and you shall have horses to ride and a gun when you get a little bigger. You must learn to spell well, too. A man is ashamed if he can't spell.

Tell Birch that the tall fifer that took Spencer is now playing the bugle, and plays well. His name is Firman. Good-bye.

Your father,

R. B. HAYES.

MASTER WEBB HAYES.

RALEIGH, VIRGINIA, March 22, 1862.

DEAR MOTHER: —. . . We are in the midst of one of the storms so common in this mountain region. We hope it is the equinoctial and will be followed by good weather. It is a driving snow-storm. The pine trees are crusted with it giving a peculiarly wintry appearance to the hills. Fortunately we are all comfortably housed, except two companies who are on a scout in the mountains after bushwhackers. I hope they will find some sort of shelter these stormy nights.

We all feel more hopeful than ever about an early close of the war. It looks to us as if General McClellan must succeed in forcing a battle that will decide the fate of the Rebellion. I do not expect we shall be released from duty for months, perhaps years, but it seems almost certain that a victory in eastern Virginia will decide the war.

I hope you will be able to see the little folks all gathered at Fremont as you anticipate. The boys look forward to it impatiently. Webb was six years old the day before yesterday.

He is now to go at his books. His mind runs on horses more than on books. Birch is a very sincere believer in the efficacy of prayer in our common affairs and is finishing the war in that way, famously, as he thinks.   .   .   .

Love to all. — As Frémont is commander of this division, we expect prompt and rapid movements. I shall write to you rarely when we once set out. All important events occurring to me or this army you will know by telegraph. The wires still follow us wherever we go.

Affectionately, your son,

RUTHERFORD.

MRS. SOPHIA HAYES.

Monday, A. M., Raleigh, March 24, 1862. — It is snowing still. What a climate! This storm began Wednesday last.   .   .   .

Captain Drake returned. He was very lucky — caught fifteen bushwhackers, captured twelve horses, eighteen rifles and muskets, fifteen hundred pounds bacon, ten sacks flour, six canoes; destroyed the Rebel headquarters and returned safely. Abram Bragg and Wm. C. Richmond with fifteen or twenty Union men joined them and acted as guides, etc., etc.

RALEIGH, VIRGINIA, March 24, 1862.

DEAR UNCLE: — Your letter of the 14th came to hand the day before yesterday. We all feel pleased to be in Frémont's division. The only drawback is that it seems to keep us in the mountains, and we have had about enough of the snows, winds, and rains of the mountains. We have had a five-days snowstorm. It seems to be now clearing off bright. We occupy ourselves in these storms very much as you do, reading newspapers and discussing the war news. The recent victories convince a great many in the region south of us that the game is up. On the other hand, the Government at Richmond is making desperate efforts to get out under arms nearly the whole male population of military age. Many are running away from the drafting. Being the extreme outpost we see daily all sorts of queer characters. They sometimes come in boldly, sometimes with fear and trembling. I am often puzzled what to do with them, but manage to dispose of them as fast as they come.

An odd laughable incident occurred to Joe the other day. You know his fondness for children. He always talks to them and generally manages to get them on his knee. Stopping at a farm-house he began to make advances towards a little three-year old boy who could scarcely talk plain enough to be understood. The doctor said, "Come, my fine little fellow. I want to talk to you." The urchin with a jerk turned away saying something the doctor did not comprehend. On a second approach the doctor made it out "Go to Hell, you dam Yankee!" This from the little codger was funny enough. . . .

I send you a dime shinplaster. — Good-bye.

Sincerely,

R. B. HAYES.

S. BIRCHARD.

Thursday, March 27. — A wintry morning — snow two or three inches deep, ground frozen; the ninth day since this equinoctial set in. P. M. The sun came out bright and warm about 9 A. M.; the snow melted away, and before night the ground became [began] to dry off so that by night we had a very fair battalion drill.

News of a battle near Winchester in which General Shields was wounded. Union victories. I am gradually drifting to the opinion that this Rebellion can only be crushed finally by either the execution of all the traitors or the abolition of slavery. Crushed, I mean, so as to remove all danger of its breaking out again in the future. Let the border States, in which there is Union sentiment enough to sustain loyal State Governments, dispose of slavery in their own way; abolish it in the premanently disloyal States, in the cotton States — that is, set free the slaves of Rebels. This will come, I hope, if it is found that a stubborn and prolonged resistance is likely to be made in the cotton States. President Lincoln's message recommending the passage of a resolution pledging the aid of the general Government to States which shall adopt schemes of gradual emancipation, seems to me to indicate that the result I look for is anticipated by the Administration. I hope it is so.

Camp Hayes, Raleigh, Virginia, March 28, 1862. Friday. — . . . Dr. Webb received an order from the medical director on General Rosecrans' staff to report for examination before a medical board at Wheeling. If he is singled out, it is an indignity and I do not blame him for resigning rather than submit. I have written to see what it means. I hope we are not to lose him.

Captain Sperry returned with thirteen prisoners and a few horses. Several of the prisoners wished to come in but feared to [do] so. The Rebels are vindictive in punishing all who yield. Abram Bragg and Wm. C. Richmond with other Union men never sleep at home; they hide up on the hills during the night. This they have done for two months past. . . .

Saturday, March 29. — Raining like fun again, Two fine days in ten. I dispatched Dr. Clendenin that Dr. Webb had been ordered to Wheeling for examination and asked him if they were aware he had already been examined. He replied: "Yes, and I have remonstrated; rather than submit, he ought to resign." The doctor will leave me his resignation, go to Wheeling, and if he finds the examination insisted on, will resign by telegraphing me to that effect.

RALEIGH, March 30, 1862. Sunday night.

DEAREST: — I received your good letters tonight. I will recollect Will De Charmes and do what I can properly, and more too. I wish you and the boys and Grandma were here tonight to enjoy the sacred music of our band. They are now full (eighteen) and better than ever. The regiment is also strong and looks big and effective. Eight companies on dress parade looked bigger than the regiment has ever seemed since we left Camp Chase. The service performed the last ten days, breaking up bushwhackers and Governor Letcher's militia musters, is prodigious. They have marched in snow four to six inches deep on the mountains sixty-five miles in three days, and look all the better for it. — Much love to Grandma and the dear boys.

Ever so lovingly yours,

R.

I hear of Lippett's arrest and Whitcomb's death; both sad for families, but Lippett better have gone into the army and been killed.

MRS. HAYES.

Monday, 31. — A lovely day; a glorious inspection! How finely the men looked! Dr. Webb left us today. I hope so much that he will return. We are being paid off today. Mr. Walker, clerk of Major Cowan, attends to it. I send home by Dr. Webb three hundred and fifty dollars for my wife. . . .

Took advantage of the fine day to march off to a field half a mile or more and drill "charge bayonet, with a yell." Good — very; first-rate! Will do it more. Saw the moon accidentally and honestly over the right shoulder!

CHAPTER XVIII

ADVANCE AND RETREAT — WEST VIRGINIA — SPRING OF 1862

TUESDAY, April 1. — Cloudy and threatening this morning. . . . All Fools' day. Soldiers sent companies to get pay out of time; bogus dispatches and the like.

I hear that Dr. Joe is in his trouble by consent of Scammon. Was he induced to ask for his examination? If so, how foolish! I can hardly be angry, and yet [I am] vexed outrageously. He [Scammon] has been operated on, used. Surely he wouldn't do such a thing if he was wide-awake.

April 2. Wednesday. — A windy day; roads drying rapidly. Rode out with Avery. Saw the companies drill skirmish drill. The militia called out to be enrolled in this county on the Union side. About a hundred queer-looking, hollow-chested, gaunt, awkward fellows in their tattered butternut garments turned out. A queer customer calls our scouts "drives," another calls it "drags." A fellow a little sick here calls it "trifling." He says, "Yes, I feel 'trifling,' " meaning unwell.

Sent Captain Zimmerman with Company E and Lieutenant Bottsford, Company C, the scout Abbott, and two or three citizens out towards Wyoming. Will be gone two or three days.

CAMP HAYES, RALEIGH, VIRGINIA, April 2, 1862.

DEAR MOTHER: — I received your letter yesterday, just one day after it was written. Very glad you are so well and happy. You do not seem to me so near seventy years old. I think of you as no older than you always were. I hope you may see other happy birthdays.

Our men stationed here, nine companies, were paid for the third time yesterday. They send home about thirty thousand dollars. Many families will be made glad by it. A small proportion of our men have families of their own. The money goes chiefly to parents and other relatives. . . .

I send you two letters showing the business [we] are in. General Beckley is the nabob of this county; commanded a regiment of Rebels until we came and scattered [it]. He is now on his parole at home. The other is from an old lady, the wife of the Baptist preacher here. Her husband preached Secession and on our coming fled South.

We are all in the best of health. Love to Sophia and Mrs. Wasson.

Your affectionate son,

RUTHERFORD.

P. S. — The total amount sent home from our regiment figures up thirty-five thousand dollars.

MRS. SOPHIA HAYES.

Raleigh, Virginia, Thursday, April 3. — The rain last night was merely an April shower. It has cleared off bright and warm. The grass looks fresh and green. I have one hundred and fifty dollars in treasury notes. Last night Lieutenant Hastings with Company I started for the Marshes of Cool to protect the election and if possible catch the Trumps. . . . .

Election day for West Virginia. One hundred and eight votes polled here, all for the new Constitution. I doubt its success. Congress will be slow to admit another slave State into the Union. The West Virginians are blind to interest as well as duty, or they would abolish slavery instantly. They would make freedom the distinguishing feature of West Virginia. With slavery abolished the State would rapidly fill up with an industrious, enterprising population. As a slave State, slaveholders will not come into it and antislavery and free-labor people will keep away.

Camp Hayes, Raleigh, Virginia, April 4, 1862. Friday. — Very warm, windy. Mud drying up rapidly. Dr. Webb has returned. Dr. Hayes was at the bottom of the affair. Colonel Scammon telegraphed that Dr. Webb couldn't be spared and ordered him to return here. I suspect that Dr. Hayes made such representations to Colonel Scammon as induced him to report Dr. Webb for examination. On reflection Colonel Scammon no doubt felt that he had yielded too much and will now, I presume, put a stop to further proceedings.

About 4 or 5 P. M. yesterday I received an order requiring Lieutenant Stevens and a corporal and six men to arrest General Beckley and take him to Wheeling. The arrest was made. General Beckley's wife and family felt badly enough. The general said he recognized the propriety of it and did not complain.

A thunder-storm last night. Will it clear off or give us "falling weather"? The natives with their queer garments and queerer speech and looks continue to come in.

Camp Hayes, Raleigh, Virginia, April 5, 1862. Saturday. — Windy, cloudy, threatening more rain. Captain Haven in command of companies G and K started for the Bragg and Richmond settlement this morning to defend that Union stronghold and to operate if practicable against a force of cavalry and bushwhackers who are reported to be threatening it. They will remain at least three days.

Lieutenant Stevens, Sergeant Deshong, a corporal, and six men started this morning with General Beckley for Fayetteville and probably Wheeling.

Company A came up about 3 P. M. Hardy, well drilled. Camp in Sibley tents in court-house yard in front of my quarters.

Captain Zimmerman with Companies C and E and ten prisoners returned at 4 P. M. Marched fifty miles; burned the residence of Pleasant Lilly. Lieutenant Hastings came in about same time; had protected the election in the Marshes, and marched forty miles.

Sunday, [April] 6. — A lovely morning. Sent Sergeant Abbott to Fayetteville with five prisoners. Company A look splendidly; drill well, sing well, and, I doubt not, fight well. Received orders to be ready to move by Wednesday night. We need canteens, a quartermaster, ammunition. Must see that captains are all ready.

CAMP HAYES, RALEIGH, VIRGINIA, April 6, 1862.

DEAREST: — . . . We are to move southward this week. You will not hear from me so often as heretofore. At any rate, you will get shorter letters — none but the shortest; but you will feel and know that I am loving you as dearly as ever, and think of you and the dear boys with so much affectionate sympathy.

The poor Lippetts! How sad! I did not doubt it. A man who always spends more than he earns is on the downward road. I advised him to go into the army, but he said his family would not listen to it. Far better to be in the place of Mrs. Whitcomb and child. Pshaw! it is absurd to make the comparison. After the sharpness of the first grief is over, its bitterness will be mixed with a just pride that in time will be a gratification rather. Children would be sure to so regard it.

Corwine married to a girl of twenty-two! Joe tells a story of a Lexington gate-keeper's remark to General Coombs about his marriage: "Men must have been scarce where she comes from."

. . . Affectionately ever,

R.

MRS. HAYES.

CAMP HAYES, April 6, 1862.

DEAR MOTHER: — . . . We are to move southward before this will reach you, and before you will hear from me again. . . . We are now about beginning our campaign. Your philosophy as to what befalls us is the true one: What is best for us will occur. I am satisfied that we are doing an important duty, and do not, therefore, feel much anxiety about consequences. . . .

The pleasantest thing in this part of our work is that, in this region, the best people are on our side. We are not in an enemy's country.

[R. B. HAYES.]

MRS. SOPHIA HAYES.

———

Monday, April 7. — Rained violently all day. Visited all officers to see if they were provided with canteens, etc., etc. All very nearly ready.   Streams will rise and roads deepen so that no movement can now be made.   A gloomy day to pass in camp, especially after getting ready to move.   Set at liberty two citizens in guardhouse.

Tuesday, 8. — A. M.   Still raining!   Have borrowed "Jack Hinton" to read to pass time.   Rained all day.   At night heard a noise; found the sutler was selling whiskey; ordered two hundred bottles poured out.

CAMP HAYES, RALEIGH, VIRGINIA, April 8, 1862.

DEAR UNCLE: — We are getting ready to move south.   Our first halt, unless the enemy stops us, will be at Princeton, forty-two miles from here, the county-seat of Mercer County.   We shall stop there for supplies, etc., etc., and to suppress Rebel recruiting and guerrilla bands probably a fortnight, then on to the railroad at Wytheville, Dublin, or some other point.   The enemy will try to stop us.   They will do their best, as the railroad is of the utmost importance to their grand army in eastern Virginia.

Colonel Scammon has a brigade consisting of [the] Twenty-third, Thirtieth, and Thirty-seventh Ohio Regiments, a fine battery of eight pieces, and a small force of cavalry.   I command the Twenty-third which has the advance.   General Cox commands the division consisting of three brigades.   At present only one brigade (ours) moves up this side of New River.

We should move tomorrow, but heavy rains yesterday and today have filled the streams so that they can't be forded.   I have got two companies cut off by the freshet, and have been taxing the Yankee ingenuity of a company from Ashtabula in getting grub to them.   I think it has succeeded.

It is much pleasanter carrying on the war now than last campaign.   *Now* the people, harried to death by the Rebel impressment of provisions and also of men, welcome our approach, receive us gladly, send us messages to hurry us forward, and a few turn out to fight.   Guides are plenty, information furnished constantly, etc.   All which is very different from carrying on an invasion of a hostile people.

15

I can't think that the new armies of the South will fight as well as the old ones. Besides being raw, large numbers are unwilling. Our troops have improved beyond all expectation. Our regiment is now a beautiful sight. The Thirtieth too has become, under the drilling of the last two months, a capital body in appearance. The Thirty-seventh is a German regiment — has companies from Toledo, Sandusky, and Cleveland. I have not yet seen it.

I prefer Lucy should let the house remain empty this summer, or rented to some [family] to take care of it with my name on the door, etc., and in the fall we will see as to permanent arrangements.

The war will certainly last another campaign — I mean through this summer and until next fall. Even with victories on the Potomac and at Corinth and Memphis, it will take months, if not a year or two, to crush out the Rebellion in all quarters.

Sincerely,

R. B. Hayes.

S. Birchard.

April 9, 1862. Wednesday. — Rain; cooler than yesterday. Company B sent off to effect a crossing over Piney. Ten refugees from Monroe [County], escaping [Governor] Letcher's draft, just in. A crossing over Piney effected. Captain Haven, with [Companies] G and K, reported to have fifteen prisoners and twenty-five horses. Kept back by the high water. P. M. Cold and windy, but still raining. Have read "Jack Hinton" these two gloomy days with Avery.

How pleased I am to hear from Lucy that Birtie has been a good scholar; that at the school exhibition he was called up to speak and spoke Logan's speech very well. . . .

Captain Drake returned tonight. Sent my money by the paymaster to my wife. He reports that the Thirtieth Regiment is under marching orders for this point; that the Thirty-fourth is at Fayetteville, and that a cavalry regiment, the Second Virginia, is to form part of our brigade.

April 10. Thursday. — A. M. Ground whitened with snow; still threatening bad weather.

3. P. M. Captain Haven, Company G, and Lieutenant Bacon, Company K, have just returned. They bring fifteen prisoners and about fifteen horses, with a number of saddles and bridles. They were captured over New River in Monroe County.

At 8 P. M. F. M. Ingram (the silent telegrapher) came in saying we had gained a victory at Corinth; Major-General Lew Wallace killed; [Albert] Sidney Johnston, ditto; Beauregard lost an arm. Later told me that Island Number 10 was taken with six thousand prisoners. Glorious, if true! Night, clear and cold.

Friday, April 11. — Clear and cold. Bet with Avery that five men could not put a great log across Piney. Rode out to see the work. The pine log was water-soaked, long, large, and very heavy. Five men from Company C worked resolutely at it two or three hours, when Avery gave it up. — Threatening again.

Further news shows that on Sunday our men near Pittsburg [Landing] were surprised by the Rebel army in great force from Corinth, Mississippi. They were driven from their camps with heavy loss, took shelter near the river under protection of the gunboats. Early next day Buell came up and attacked the enemy, routing him. Sidney Johnston reported killed and Beauregard wounded — lost an arm. We barely escaped an awful defeat, if these first accounts are true.

Island [Number] 10 was a great capture. Cannon, stores, etc., etc., in prodigious quantities were taken. These victories if followed up give us Memphis and New Orleans. — Nothing said about our moving the last three or four days.

Camp Hayes, Raleigh, Virginia, April 12, 1862. Saturday. — Windy, cold, and cloudy — another storm impending. Cleared up towards noon. Had two good drills. A first-rate ride, — new horse getting up to it.

Further news confirms the victory at Pittsburg or Corinth. The first day, last Sunday, our men [were] surprised and badly whipped; the second day, the fresh troops redeemed the day and gained a great victory. Island Number 10, a most important capture; now said to have taken six thousand prisoners.

Nothing as to our future movements. Perhaps we are waiting to see what effect these victories will have. — Blowing up a storm again.

Sunday, 13. — Rain begins at guard-mounting. A year ago today Sumter was taken. Great events, great changes, since then. The South was eager, prepared, "armed and equipped." The event found the North distracted, undecided, unarmed, wholly unprepared, and helpless. Then came the rousing up of the lion-hearted people of the North. For months, however, the superior preparation of the South triumphed. Gradually the North, the Nation, got ready; and now the victory over Beauregard and [that] at [Island] Number 10, following Fort Donelson, put the Nation on firm ground, while the Rebellion is waning daily. Tonight received *Commercial* of the 10th, with pretty full accounts of the great battles.

Captain Haven and Lieutenant Bacon, Companies G and K, marched seventy miles on their late scout into Monroe. Scout Jackson, Company B, gone one week today toward Logan. I hope he is all right.

Monday, 14, 1862. — Still raining. No further knowledge of movements. Lieutenant Reichenbach's party that went to Columbus with prisoners, returned this evening. We hear of the taking of Huntsville, Alabama, today, the death of Beauregard, and news of the siege of Yorktown.

Tuesday 15. — Still rain! — Read Bulwer's "Strange Story." One idea I get: "We have an instinctive longing for a future existence"; ergo, there is a future. "Jack Hinton" and "Strange Story" both read in these days of rain and suspense. I think often of my wife and mother as I read news which seems to point to an early termination of the war. How happy peace will make many families!

Lieutenant Harris, [a] corporal, and seven men go with prisoners to Fayetteville. Two will go on to Ohio.

P. M. Cleared off enough to have a parade in the evening. Evening, read *Commercial* of 11th containing more particulars of the fight, the great battle at Pittsburg Landing. What a complete success General Pope's operations against Island Number 10 turned out to be! Complete. It must weaken the enemy more than any blow they have yet received.

April 16. Wednesday. — A. M. Sun shining brightly. I have hopes of weather now that will allow us to move forward. A fine day at last! Major Comly drilled the non-commissioned officers as a company, A. M. and P. M. I drilled the regiment after parade. In the evening the new sutler, Mr. Forbes, brought me [a] letter from Lucy and portrait. Dear wife, the "counterfeit presentment" is something. Also papers of 12th. The victory at Pittsburg [Landing] was not so decisive as I hoped. The enemy still holds Corinth, and will perhaps fight another battle before giving it up.

Captain Bragg came in tonight, reporting a gang of bushwhackers in his neighborhood. Would send out a company if I were not afraid that orders to move would catch me unprepared.

Thursday, April 17. — Another fine day; very warm this A. M. Drilled three times. Heard that Colonel Scammon and McMullen's Battery were on the way here from Fayetteville; that we must get ready for them.

RALEIGH, VIRGINIA, April 17, 1862.

DEAREST: — I was made happy by your letter and the fine picture of you it contained. You seem undecided which you intended should have it, Uncle Joe or your husband. But I shall keep it. You will have to send another to Joe.

Very glad the money and everything turned out all right. I get the *Commercial* quite often — often enough to pay for taking it. And you paid Mr. Trenchard! Why, you are getting to be a business woman. I shall have to let the law out to you when I come home again. I do not know that I shall have an opportunity to do much for Will De Charmes, but I shall bear him in mind. If Frémont ever comes along here I may succeed.

We are still hunting bushwhackers, succoring persecuted

Union men, and the like. Our intended advance was stopped by a four-days rain which, like the old four-days meeting, I began to think never would end. We are now getting ready to go on — in fact we *are* ready, but waiting for others. A great battle at Pittsburg [Landing] and probably not a very great victory. It will all come right, however. We are told that Captain Richardson of the Fifty-fourth was killed. You will perhaps remember him as a gigantic lieutenant of Company D, whose wife was at Camp Chase when you were there.

18th, A. M. — We shall make a short march today. Letters, etc., may be directed as heretofore. Very glad to hear your talk about the boys. It is always most entertaining to me. You will be a good instructor for them. Let me hear from you as often as you can. You need not feel bound to write long letters — short ones will do. I always like your letters to be long, but I don't want you to put off writing because your time will not allow you to write long ones.

It begins to look like spring at last. We are on very elevated ground. The season is weeks later than in the valley of the Kanawha.

Kiss all the boys. Love to Grandma. I wish so much to be with you all. I think of you constantly and with much happiness and love. Good-bye.

Affectionately, your

R.

P. S. — 18th, P. M. I am ordered to advance to Princeton tomorrow morning, in command of [the] Twenty-third, a section of McMullen's Battery, and a squadron of cavalry. We are all delighted with this plan.

MRS. HAYES.

Friday, 18. — A. M. Finished letter to Lucy. Must get ready to move. Put all the regiment into tents today, by one o'clock. A shower fell just after the tents were up.

Colonels Scammon and Ewing [arrived]; Lieutenant Kennedy, A. A. A. G. to Colonel Scammon, and Lieutenant Muenscher, aide, with an escort of horsemen came with them. The Thirtieth began to arrive at 2:30 P. M. They came in the rain. Major Hildt came to my quarters. I joined the regiment out in camp — the camp in front of General Beckley's residence one mile from Raleigh. Rainy all night. Our right rest on the road leading southwardly towards Princeton, the left on the graveyard of Floyd's men. The graves are neatly marked; Twentieth Mississippi, Phillips' Legion, Georgia, Fourth Louisiana, furnished the occupants. Four from one company died in one day! (November 2, 1861.)

Slept in Sibley tent. Received orders to proceed with Twenty-third, thirty [of] Captain Gilmore's Cavalry, and a section of McMullen's Battery to Princeton tomorrow at 7 A. M.

Saturday, April 19. — Rained violently; starting postponed. Order modified to marching by easy stages to Flat Top Mountain, there to choose strong position. General Frémont speaks of our forces as his right wing; the left must be up towards Cheat Mountain. We are now at the pivot; to proceed slowly until the left wheels so as to face southwardly with us. Rained all day; couldn't move. At evening looked slight*eously* like clearing off.

Sunday, 20. — Rained four or five hours, part very violently. I fear we can't cross Piney. Sent to Piney; find it too high to cross teams, but not so high as to preclude the hope that it will run down in a few hours after the rain stops falling.

A cold rain coming; men sing, laugh, and keep mirthful. I poke about from [the] major's tent to my own, listen to yarns, crack jokes, and the like. Avery won a knife and fifty cents of Dr. McCurdy (a cool-head Presbyterian) today at (what is it?) freezing poker! The doctor couldn't play himself and sent for Bottsford to play his game. This, Sunday! Queer antics this life plays with steady habits!

Received by Fitch, Company E, a *Commercial* of 16th. Pittsburg battle not a decided victory. Beauregard in a note to Grant asks permission to bury his dead; says that in view of the reinforcements received by Grant and the fatigue of his men after two days' hard fighting, "he deemed it his duty to withdraw his army from the scene of the conflict." This is proof enough that the enemy was repulsed. But that is all. Two or three Ohio regiments were disgraced; [the] Seventy-seventh mustered out of service, [the] Seventy-first has its colors taken from it, etc., etc. Lieutenant De Charmes, the brother of Lucy's friend, killed.

What a day this is! Cold rain, deep mud, and "Ned to pay." Cold and gusty. Will it snow now?

CAMP NEAR BECKLEY'S, Easter Sunday, April 20, 1862.

DEAREST: — We left Raleigh the day before yesterday and came here intending to continue our march at least as far south as Flat Top Mountain. But just as we had got our tents up the rain began to fall and by morning all movement was out of the question. It has rained ever since. The streets of the camp are trodden into mortar-beds, the weather is getting cold, and you would naturally think that a gloomier set of fellows could hardly be found. But we are jolly enough. A year ago we used to read of these things and sympathize with the suffering soldiers. But a year of use has changed all that. Like sailors in a storm, the soldiers seem stimulated to unnatural mirth by the gloomy circumstances. We are guessing as to when it will stop. We hope this is the last day of the storm, but there is no trusting to experience in the Virginia mountains. Every new storm has a new set of phenomena. The men sing a great deal, play fiddle, banjo, etc. At the stated calls, the fifer, buglers, and band exert themselves to play their liveliest airs, and so we manage to get on.

I (when alone) get out your two pictures and have a quiet talk with you. Joe is in the next tent with Major Comly and Dr. McCurdy singing sacred music. I am alone in a tall Sibley tent writing this on a book on my knee, my ink on my trunk. The mess-chest open is before me; next to it, saddle, etc., then India-rubber cloth and leggings, old hat, haversack, glass, and saddle-bags; by my side, trunk; behind me cot with overcoat and duds, and on the other side of the tent Avery's truck in similar disorder. We have a sheet-iron stove in the centre —

no fire now. So you see us on a muddy sidehill. I can't find time to write often now. If we are resting I don't feel like writing; when going, of course I can't.

Send this to Mother Hayes. She is seventy years old this month, about these days. She will think I am forgetting her if I don't send her some "scrabble" (western Virginia for "scribbling") of mine. — Love to all at home.

Affectionately, your

R.

Mrs. Hayes.   _____

Beckley's farm near Raleigh, Virginia, Monday, April 21. — A. M. All night a high wind and driving cold rain; mud in camp deep. Like the Mount Sewell storm of September last. All day rain, rain — cold, cold rain. Rode to Raleigh, called on Colonel Scammon and Lieutenant-Colonel Jones and Major Hildt of Thirtieth. Talked over the troubles between the men of the Twenty-third and the men of [the] Thirtieth. The talk very satisfactory.

_____

Camp South of Raleigh, Virginia, April 22, 1862.

Dear Uncle: — The ugly chap on the enclosed bill is Governor Letcher of Virginia. He is entitled to our lasting gratitude. He is doing more for us in this State than any two brigadiers I can think of. He has in all the counties, not occupied by our troops, little squads of volunteers busily engaged in hunting up and "squadding in," as they call it, all persons capable of military duty. Thousands who wish to escape this draft are now hiding in the mountains or seeking refuge in our lines. Meantime the rascals are plundering and burning in all directions, making friends for the Union wherever they go. The defeat of the enemy in eastern Virginia sends this cobhouse tumbling very fast.

We left Raleigh last week and have been struggling against storms and freshets ever since. Today it has snowed, rained, sleeted, and turned off bright but gusty a dozen times. Camp muddy, tents wet, but all glad to be started.

I have for the present an independent command of the

Twenty-third Regiment, a section of McMullen's Battery, and a small body of horse. We are the advance of Frémont's column. We are directed to move by "easy marches" forward south. The design being, I suppose, to overtake us in force by the time we meet any considerable body of the enemy. We meet and hear of small bodies of enemy now constantly, but as yet nothing capable of serious resistance.

I see that Buckland's Seventy-second was in the great battle at Pittsburg. Glad they are not reported as sharing the disgrace which seems to attach to some of the other new regiments. There was shocking neglect there, I should guess. Generals, not the regiments, ought to be disgraced. A sudden surprise by a great army with cavalry and artillery can't be had without gross negligence. The regiments surprised ought not [to] be held up to scorn if they are stricken with a panic in such a case. A few thousand men can slip up unperceived sometimes, but for an army of fifty or sixty thousand men to do it — pshaw! it's absurd. What happened to Buckland's regiment? Send your newspapers of Fremont giving letters from the regiment.

I see that your friend McPherson * is one of the distinguished. Good.

Colonel Scammon is back with the brigade, Thirtieth, Thirty-fourth, and a regiment of cavalry.

Good-bye,

R. B. HAYES.

April 23. — Since writing the foregoing I have received *Commercials* of 17th and 18th containing the doings of Buckland and the Seventy-second. They did well. It is absurd to find fault with men for breaking away under such circumstances. The guilty officers ought to be punished — probably Grant or Prentiss, or both. — H.

S. BIRCHARD.

---

* James B. McPherson, a native of Sandusky County. He was at that time chief engineer on General Grant's staff. A brilliant and able officer who rose to the position of corps commander. He was killed in battle at Atlanta, July 22, 1864, — the officer highest in rank and command killed during the war. His grave is at Clyde, Ohio, marked by an imposing monument. One of the entrances to Spiegel Grove bears his name.

OHIO GENERALS, 1861-1865.

MAJOR-GENERAL C. R. WOODS,* 1827-85.

BRIGADIER-GENERAL W. S. SMITH,* 1830-1902.

MAJOR-GENERAL JAMES W. FORSYTH,* 1836-1906.

MAJOR-GENERAL KENNER GARRARD,* 1830-79.

BRIGADIER-GENERAL JOSHUA W. SELL,* 1831-62.

MAJOR-GENERAL ROBERT S. GRANGER,* 1816-94.

BRIGADIER-GENERAL J. S. MASON,* 1824-97

MAJOR-GENERAL WAGER SWAYNE, 1834-1902.

* West Point graduate.

Price's Farm, four miles south of Raleigh, Virginia, April 24, 1862. Thursday. — Left camp at Beckley's at 10:30 A. M. with Twenty-third, a section of McMullen's Battery under Lieutenant Crome, twenty horse under Captain Gilmore and his first lieutenant, Abraham. Reached here at 1:30 P. M. A short march but crossed two streams somewhat difficult. Broke one whiffletree. All right, with this exception. Camp on fine ground, sandy, rolling and near to Beaver Creek. Floyd camped here on his retreat from Cotton Hill. The men carried their knapsacks; shall try to accustom them to it by easy marches at first. They are in fine spirits; looked well.

A hostile feeling exists toward the Twenty-third by the Thirtieth. Had a talk with Colonel Jones, Major Hildt, and Colonel Ewing. All agree that Major Comly and myself have treated them well, but the company officers of the Twenty-third have not behaved fraternally towards them. The immediate trouble now is some defilement of the quarters we left for the Thirtieth in Raleigh. This must be looked into and punished if possible.

This is one of the finest camping spots I have seen. Soil sandy, surface undulating, in the forks of two beautiful mountain streams; space enough for a brigade and very defensible. It began to rain within half an hour after our tents were pitched and was "falling weather" (west Virginia phrase for rainy weather) the rest of the day. This is the sixth day of falling weather, with only a few streaks of sunshine between.

Friday, April 25. Camp Number 2, Price's Farm, four miles. — Rained in torrents all night. The windows of heaven were indeed opened. By midnight the streams we crossed with teams yesterday swum a courier's horse. At 7:30 this morning they were impassable — swollen to rushing rivers. About seven this morning rain ceased to fall.

Received orders last evening to send party to New River to crush one hundred and twenty-five Rebels who crossed Monday evening. In view of the storm, order countermanded this A. M. Hereafter the camps of this detachment will be known by their number. This is Number 2. Men catch fish this morning —

a species of chub. We have a corps of scouts organized, Sergeant Abbott commanding, composed chiefly of citizens — six or eight citizens. Names: Russell G. French, Mercer County farmer, and Thos. L. Bragg, Wm. C. Richmond, —— Maxwell, and —— Simpkins, all of Raleigh.

Prepared during the afternoon to send four companies, A, E, G, and H, to the junction of New River and Bluestone to "bag" (favorite phrase with officers) a party of one hundred and twenty-five Rebels supposed to be there on this side, shut in by the high water. They left in the night under Major Comly, Dr. Webb accompanying. Had a dress parade and a spirited little drill after it. The sun set bathing the western sky and its fleecy clouds in crimson. Said to indicate fair weather. I hope so. The streams still too high to be crossed.

Camp Number 2, near Raleigh, Virginia, Saturday, April 26, 1862. — The sky is still overcast. We shall move on five miles today if it clears up.

At General Beckley's residence are the females of three families. Mrs. Beckley and all cried when we left. One young lady, Miss Duncan, has a lover in Company F; Miss Kieffer, in hospital staff, and all the other damsels in the like category. They all speak of our regiment as such fine men! We burned all their rails! Will pay for them if General Beckley is discharged.

At 10 o'clock marched to Shady Spring; camped on a fine sandy piece of ground belonging to Dr. McNutt. The Secesh burned the dwelling, the doctor being a Union man. Floyd camped here also. A large spring gives the name to the place. The water gushes out copiously, runs on the surface a few rods and runs again into the earth. The grass is starting. The horses of the cavalry were turned loose on it and played their liveliest antics. The sun came out bright, a clear, bracing breeze blowing. Altogether a fine afternoon and a happy time.

Camp Number 3, Shady Spring, nine miles' march from Raleigh. Sunday, April 27. — A shower during the night; clear and beautiful again this morning. *Scrubbed* all over; arrayed in the glories of clean duds!

Six fugitives from Wyoming [County] came in today. Major Comly returned. No enemy at the point where expected. Expedition a "water-haul."

Monday, 28. — A fine, warm spring day. Drills as usual. . . . . Four of Company I, a sergeant, two corporals, and one private, left on Sunday to forage. They have not returned. Their leave of absence extended a *few* hours — not to [be] longer than the evening dress parade. They stayed last night with two of Company B near Flat Top and in the morning separated from the Company B men saying they would not return until they got something, but would be in by the Monday dress parade "which period has now expired." I much fear that they are taken. Sergeant Abbott's party of scouts were fired on last evening; "nobody hurt." We must break up the gang (Foley's) near Flat Top before we shall be rid of them.

Camp 3, Shady Spring, Tuesday, April 29, 1862. — Rain fell at intervals last night; falling in a "drizzling manner" this morning. Colonel Scammon says we have rifled muskets at Gauley. If good long-range pieces, this is good. We must have pieces that will carry half a mile, or we shall never hit these fellows in western Virginia. Sent Lieutenant Bottsford with Company C sixteen miles after Foley's bushwhackers.

CAMP NUMBER 3, SHADY SPRING, April 29, 1862.

DEAREST : — We are camped in a beautiful healthy place at the foot of Flat Top Mountain, on the line between Raleigh and Mercer Counties, Virginia. The whole "surroundings" are exhilarating — just enough of enemy's guerrillas to keep men awake. We are in the advance, the only grumbling being because we are not allowed to push on as fast as we would like. . . . Our only drawback is the frequency of rain-storms. I don't know but they prepare our minds to appreciate more keenly the bright bracing air that succeeds them.

I need not say that I read all the accounts of the great battle. We made a narrow escape there. It will probably save us from similar disasters in the next two or three engagements.

We fear we have lost four good men in a scout a few days back. They disobeyed or neglected a positive order and have, I fear, been captured or worse.

You must, I suppose, be getting ready for a move northwardly. I hope you will enjoy the new home as much as we have the old one. I do not quite feel like giving up the old home yet, but when I think of the boys, I think of it as a duty we owe to them. . . .

Affectionately, dearest, your loving husband,

R.

P. S. — Our four lost men escaped. They were fired on but have got back safely. It is hard to punish men over whose escape we are so rejoiced, but it must be done.

Mrs. Hayes.

Camp 4, Miller's Tannery, twelve miles from No. 3, April 30, 1862. — Mustered the men before breakfast at reveille; marched for this camp twelve miles; arrived in good condition. Rained P. M. Joined by Lieutenant-Colonel Paxton and Major Curtis, Second Virginia Cavalry, with four companies, fine horses and men. Report from Bottsford that he found Foley's nest but the bird gone.

Camp 5, Princeton, May 1, 1862. Thursday. — Marched at 6 A. M. Heard firing in advance. Turned out to be Company C on Camp Creek, attacked by Lieutenant-Colonel Fitzhugh with four companies, dismounted, Jenkins' Cavalry and Foley's bushwhackers. The company was in line ready to move off to return to camp when they saw a party of bushwhackers coming down the road who called out (Captain Foley called): "Don't fire; we are Richmond's men." Immediately after, a volley was fired into our men from all sides. They were surrounded by three hundred Secesh. Finding the attack so heavy, Company C was ordered by Lieutenant Bottsford to take shelter in the log house where they had quartered. They kept up such a spirited fire that the enemy retreated, leaving four dead, four mortally [wounded], four more dangerously. All these we *got*. Captain Foley had his shoulder broken. The enemy fled in confusion leaving their dead and wounded on the field. This was a splendid victory for Lieutenant Bottsford and Sergeant Ritter, of Company C, and Sergeant Abbott, Company I. They were the prominent officers. Our loss was a German, Pfeffer, killed; Lenox and another mortally wounded, three severely wounded, and fifteen others slightly. Sergeant Ritter had a bullet shot into his head lodging between the scalp and skull. He fell, but instantly jumped up saying, "You must shoot lower if you want to kill me." It was a gallant fight. Company C wears the honors.

I came up to the scene of the conflict soon after the enemy fled. They say our coming drove them away. I couldn't speak when I came up to the gallant little company and they presented arms to me. I went around shaking hands with the wounded. They all spoke cheerfully. We immediately pushed on in mud and rain after the retreating foe. Captain McIlrath's company (A) [led]. At a house where three cavalrymen were leaving two of the enemy's wounded, they killed one and captured his horse and shotgun, etc. I then sent the cavalry under Lieutenant-Colonel Paxton in advance. They soon were fired on by a gang of bushwhackers from a hill and their horses badly stampeded. One horse threw his forelegs over Colonel Paxton's horse's neck. The cavalry dismounted, charged up the hill, and caught one dragoon.

Finding the cavalry would dismount and skirmish all the bad hillsides (and they were abundant — being twelve miles of defiles), I again put the Twenty-third in advance. At Ferguson's we saw Captain Ward, quartermaster Rebel army, badly wounded and another young soldier.

We pushed on rapidly, crossing Wolf Creek, Camp Creek, and wading Bluestone waist-deep — rain falling, mud deep and slippery. We came in sight of the wagons of the retreating foe, but for want of cavalry familiarized to the business, we were unable to overtake them. We were told of great reinforcements at Princeton or soon to be at Princeton. The Forty-fifth [Virginia] there or coming. Captain Ward, a pleasant gentleman, said we would probably "get thunder at Princeton." We kept ahead. On approaching town we saw great clouds. Some thought it smoke, some supposed it was clouds. Within two miles we knew the Rebels were burning the town. We hurried forward; soon reached an elevated ground overlooking the place. All the brick buildings, court-house, churches, etc., were burning. I ordered up the howitzers to scatter out the few Rebel cavalry who were doing it; deployed the regiment by a file right into a field and marched forward by battalion front. The town was soon overrun. Some fires were put out; four or five tolerably fine dwellings were saved; a number of small buildings and some good stables were also saved.

And so ended the first of May — twenty-two miles in mud and rain. An exciting day. Five enemy killed, nine badly wounded that we *got;* three unwounded prisoners, and about a dozen Rebels wounded. Total five killed, three prisoners, twenty-one wounded. A good day's work.

Camp No. 5, Princeton, May 2, 1862. Friday. — A fine day. The cavalry yesterday took the Bluff Road and came into [the] road from Princeton to Giles five miles. They came across tracks leading *to* Princeton. Soon saw soldiers, opened fire and had a fusillade of wild firing, the enemy fleeing to the mountains. It was the Forty-fifth Virginia coming to reinforce Princeton. Slightly "too late." Spent A. M. organizing detachment of occupation.

Camp Number 5, Princeton, May 2, 7:30 A. M., 1862.

Sir: — Your strictures on the expedition under Lieutenant Bottsford are very severe. I wrote you my account of it hastily during a momentary delay of the column and am perhaps blamable for sending to you anything so imperfect as to lead to such misapprehension. I was, however, compelled to write such an account or none at all. I trusted to your favorable judgment of what was done rather than to the fulness and accuracy of what I was writing. I thought that a most meritorious thing in *all respects* had been done and did not imagine that it could be so stated as to give you such a view of it as you have taken. You seem to think that the expedition was an improper one and that Lieutenant Bottsford or his men must have been guilty of great negligence. I think the expedition was strictly according to the spirit and letter of instruction given by both you and General Frémont and that no blame ought to attach to any one for the manner of it in any particular. I knew by reliable information, which turned out to be perfectly correct, that Captain Foley and his notorious gang of bushwhackers were camped within sixteen or eighteen miles of the camp at Shady Spring where I was stationed; that Foley's force was from thirty to sixty men, and that the only way of catching him was by surprising his camp at night or early daylight. I sent Lieutenant Bottsford with about seventy-five men of Company C, aided by Sergeant Abbott and his scouts, six in number, to do this service. I was satisfied that the enemy had no force worth naming nearer than Princeton, and at Princeton their force was small, probably not over two hundred or three hundred. All this information has turned out to be correct. Lieutenant Bottsford left camp at 9 P. M., April 29, and reached Foley's about daylight. He found the nest warm but the bird was gone. I can find no blame in this. He was compelled to move slowly in a strange country at night. A scout could easily give the required warning without fault on our part.

On the 30th, Lieutenant Bottsford scouted the country for the bushwhackers; camped in a house very defensible within four to six miles of where he knew I was to camp with the regiment. In the meantime Lieutenant-Colonel Fitz Hugh, or Fitzhugh, had marched with the whole force at Princeton, four companies of Jenifer's Cavalry, dismounted, numbering over two hundred, to aid Foley. This was done on the morning of the 30th, and on that evening Foley with bushwhackers and militia, to the number of seventy-five or one hundred, joined Fitzhugh. During the night they got as near Lieutenant Bottsford as they could without alarming his pickets, not near enough to do any mischief. In the morning Lieutenant Bottsford prepared to return to camp. He drew in his pickets, formed his line, and then for the first time, the enemy came within gunshot. Bottsford's men, in line of battle in front of a log house, saw the enemy approaching. A volley was fired on each side, when

16

Lieutenant Bottsford, finding the strength of the attack, took shelter in the house and fired with such spirit and accuracy as to drive the enemy out of gunshot, leaving his dead and four of his wounded on the field, all of whom were taken possession of by Lieutenant Bottsford's men immediately, besides four wounded prisoners who didn't run far enough before hiding.

This attack was in no blamable sense "a surprise." It found Lieutenant Bottsford perfectly prepared for it.

You seem to think there was nothing gained by this affair; that it is a "disaster" and that "we lost twenty men." Surely I could have said nothing to warrant this. Of the twenty wounded over two-thirds were able and desired to march to Princeton with us. Our loss was one killed, two dangerously, perhaps mortally, wounded, and two, possibly three, others disabled, — perhaps not more than one. The enemy's loss was thirteen dead and disabled that "we got." Captain Foley was disabled and we know of four others in like condition and I know not how many slightly wounded. This is not a disaster, but a fight of the sort which crushes the Rebellion.

You speak of Company C as advanced beyond "supporting distance." We heard the firing and if the enemy had been stubborn should have been in good time to help drive him off. He reported here that our advance did in fact drive him off. If this is not supporting distance, parties cannot leave camp without violating an important rule. Lieutenant Bottsford had retreated to within four miles of us.

Upon the whole, I think that the affair deserves commendation rather than censure, and I take blame to myself for writing you a note under circumstances which precluded a full statement; such a statement as would prevent such misapprehension as I think you are under.

Respectfully,

R. B. Hayes,
Lieutenant-Colonel 23rd Regiment, O. V. I.,
Commanding.

[Colonel Scammon.]

CAMP NUMBER 5, PRINCETON, May 2, 8 A. M., [1862.]

SIR: — Lieutenant-Colonel Paxton with the cavalry reached here by the Giles Road about dark. He left the direct road to Princeton at Spanishburg and took the Bluff Road, which strikes the road from Giles to Princeton four miles from Princeton. We found it impossible to send the cavalry to the Tazewell or Wytheville Road, at least in time, and they went to the Giles Road hoping to catch the enemy retreating on that road. The enemy took the Wytheville Road to Rocky Gap and escaped. The cavalry on entering the Giles Road found a great number of fresh tracks leading to Princeton. Hastening on, they came suddenly on the Forty-fifth Virginia coming to the relief of Princeton. As soon as the cavalry came in sight there was a "skedaddling" of the chivalry for the hills and a scattering of knapsacks very creditable to their capacity to appreciate danger. There was a good deal of hurried firing at long range, but nobody hurt on our side and perhaps none on the other. The regiment seemed to number two or three hundred. We suppose they will not be seen again in our vicinity, but shall be vigilant.

This is a most capital point to assemble a brigade. The best camping for an army I have seen in western Virginia. Stabling enough is left for all needful purposes, two or three fine dwellings for headquarters, and smaller houses in sufficient numbers for storage. The large buildings were nearly all burned, all of the brick buildings included. Churches all gone and public buildings of all sorts. Meat — sheep, cattle, and hogs — in sufficient quantities to keep starvation from the door. If you will send salt we shall be able to live through the bad roads. Forage I know nothing of — there must be some. Our couriers were fired on at Bluestone. They report Foley's gang is scattered along the road. There should be a strong force at Flat Top under an enterprising man like Colonel Jones. The country we passed over yesterday is the most dangerous I have seen; at least twelve miles of the twenty-two [miles] needs skirmishing.

If quartermasters are energetic there ought to be no scarcity here. The road can't get worse than it was yesterday and our trains kept up to a fast-moving column nearly all the way. The

Twenty-third marched beautifully. A steady rain, thick slippery mud, and twenty-two miles of travelling they did, closed up well, without grumbling, including wading Bluestone waist-deep. The section of the battery behaved well. I have already praised the cavalry. You see how I am compelled to write — a sentence and then an interruption; you will excuse the result. I am very glad the telegraph is coming; we shall need it. I have just heard that the train and one piece of artillery was in rear of the point where our cavalry came on the Forty-fifth. I would be glad to pursue them *but am bound to obey instructions in good faith.* Rest easy on that point. The men are praying that they [the enemy] may be encouraged yet to come to us.

Respectfully,

R. B. HAYES,

LIEUTENANT-COLONEL 23D REGIMENT O. V. I.

P. S. — Lieutenant-Colonel Paxton will act as provost marshal. He is admirably fitted for it and is pleased to act.

[COLONEL SCAMMON.]

CAMP NUMBER 5, PRINCETON, May 2, 1862. 4:30 P. M.

SIR: — Company B and a company of cavalry scouted the road towards Wytheville several miles today. They report the enemy all gone to Rocky Gap. None, bushwhackers, or others, anywhere in the direction near here. Numbers of militia who were in service here yesterday are reported escaped to their homes and willing to take the oath of allegiance and surrender their arms. A cavalry company scouted the road towards Giles. They report the Forty-fifth retreated in great haste to Giles, saying they found Princeton just occupied by two thousand cavalry and eight thousand infantry. Their panic on falling in with Colonel Paxton's cavalry was even more complete than was supposed. They left knapsacks, blankets, and baggage. They had marched over twenty miles yesterday to get here and were worn-out.

There was a mistake as to the enemy firing on our couriers. No bushwhackers have been seen between here and Flat Top since we passed. Three parties have passed the entire distance since baggage trains. Negro servants of officers straggling along alone, etc., etc., and nobody disturbed by the enemy. The courier rode past a picket post of one of my scouting parties refusing to halt, and was therefore fired on.

Captain Gilmore is here with his company. Lieutenant Cooper and property left at Shady Spring is here. Forage is turning up in small quantities in a place but amounts to an important item in the aggregate. Fifteen head of cattle have been gathered up. There are sheep and hogs of some value.

Only twelve men reported excused from duty out of seven hundred Twenty-third men who came up. Company C I left behind to look after their wounded. They will come up tomorrow. Russell G. French will perhaps be crippled for life, possibly die. Can't he be put in the position of a soldier enlisted, or something, to get his family the pension land, etc., etc.? What can be done? He was a scout in our uniform on duty at the time of receiving his wound.

If the present indications can be relied on, this region will soon return to its allegiance. If nothing new of interest transpires, will not one dispatch each day be sufficient hereafter, with the understanding that on any important event occurring a messenger will be sent?

Respectfully,

R. B. HAYES,
LIEUTENANT-COLONEL 23D REGIMENT O. V. I.

[COLONEL SCAMMON.]

CAMP NO. 5, PRINCETON, MERCER COUNTY, VIRGINIA,

May 2, 1862.

DEAREST: — I reached yesterday this town after a hard day's march of twenty-two miles through deep, slippery mud and a heavy rain, crossing many streams which had to be waded — one, waist-deep. The men stood it bravely and good-humoredly. Today, only twelve are reported as excused from duty. Our advance company (C), Lieutenant Bottsford in command, had a severe battle. Seventy-five of them were attacked by two hundred and forty of Jenkins' Cavalry, now Jenifer's, with seventy-seven of Foley's guerrillas. The battle lasted twenty minutes, when the Rebels fled, leaving their killed and wounded on the ground. One of our men was killed outright, three mortally wounded, and seventeen others more or less severely injured. The whole regiment came up in a few moments, hearing the firing. Didn't they cheer us? As I rode up, they saluted with a "present arms." Several were bloody with wounds as they stood in their places; one boy limped to his post who had been hit three times. As I looked at the glow of pride in their faces, my heart choked me, I could not speak, but a boy said: "All right, Colonel, we know what you mean." The enemy's loss was much severer than ours.

We pushed on rapidly, hearing extravagent stories of the force waiting for us at Princeton. Prisoners, apparently candid, said we would catch it there. We would have caught Lieutenant-Colonel Fitzhugh and his men, if our cavalry had had experience. I don't report to their prejudice publicly, for they are fine fellows — gentlemen, splendidly mounted and equipped. In three months they will be capital, but their caution in the face of ambuscades is entirely too great. After trying to get them ahead, I put the Twenty-third in advance and [the] cavalry in the rear, making certainly double the speed with our footmen trudging in the mud, as was made by the horsemen on their fine steeds. We caught a few and killed a few. At the houses, the wounded Rebels would be left. As we came up, the men would rush in, when the women would beg us not to kill the prisoners or the wounded. I talked with several who were badly wounded. They all seemed grateful for kind words, which I always gave them. One fine fellow, a Captain Ward, was especially grateful.

This work continued all day; I, pushing on; they, trying to keep us back. The fact being, that General Heth had sent word that he would be in Princeton by night with a force able to hold it. As we came on to a mountain a couple of miles from Princeton, we saw that the Rebels were too late. The great clouds were rolling to the sky — they were burning the town. We hurried on, saved enough for our purposes, I think, although the best buildings were gone. The women wringing their hands and crying and begging us to protect them with the fine town in flames around us, made a scene to be remembered. This was my May-day. General Heth's forces got within four miles; he might as well have been forty [miles away]. We are in possession, and I think can hold it.

Joe and Dr. McCurdy had a busy day. They had Secesh wounded as well as our own to look after. Dr. Neal of the Second Virginia Cavalry (five companies of which are now here in my command), a friend of Joe's, assisted them.

Saturday morning. — I intended to send this by courier this morning, but in the press of business, sending off couriers, prisoners, and expeditions, I forgot it. Telegraph is building here. Anything happening to me will be known to you at once. It now looks as if we would find no enemy to fight.

The weather yesterday and today is perfect. The mountains are in sight from all the high grounds about here, and the air pure and exhilarating. The troubles of women who have either been burnt out by Secesh or robbed of chickens and the like by us, are the chief thing this morning. One case is funny. A spoiled fat Englishwoman, with great pride and hysterics, was left with a queer old negro woman to look after her wants. Darky *now* thinks she is mistress. She is sulky, won't work, etc., etc. Mistress can't eat pork or army diet. There is no other food here. The sight of rough men is too much for her nerves! All queer.

We are now eighty-five miles from the head of navigation in time of flood and one hundred and twenty-five in ordinary times; a good way from "America," as the soldiers say.

"I love you so much." Kiss the dear boys. Love to Grandma. Ever so affectionately,

Yours,

Mrs. Hayes.   R.

Camp 5, Princeton, May 3. Saturday. — The Forty-fifth Regiment had marched twenty miles through the rain to reach here, were very tired and straggled badly. They were regularly stampeded, panic-stricken, and routed. They report three killed in one party of stragglers. They had a cannon drawn by six horses, but our men "yelled so" and "fired so fast" that it was no place for cannon; so they wheeled it about and fled with it. All queer! Company C killed eleven, Colonel Jenifer burned Rocky Gap (four houses) and continued his flight towards Wytheville. The Rebels report us two thousand cavalry and eight thousand infantry!! Got our tents today; got into a good camp overlooking the town.

Camp 5, Princeton, May 4, 1862. Sunday. — A fine day. Rode with Avery out two or three miles. This is a fine country. Mountainous but with much good land and tolerably well cultivated. A train of waggons with eight or ten thousand rations arrived about 2 P. M. escorted by Captain Townsend's Company B, Thirtieth. Captains Hunter and Lovejoy arrived from Cincinnati bringing good letters from Lucy — all about the dear boys. . . . She takes a great interest in Will De Charmes; I have today written Corwine of Frémont's staff to get him a place if possible. A pleasant night — the men sitting around their fires and in tents on the fine hillside, laughing, joking, singing so happily! A more happy lot of men can't be found. It is everywhere cheerfulness and mirth.

CAMP NUMBER 5, PRINCETON, May 4, 6 A. M. [1862].

SIR: — At this time I have received no communication from [you] written after you heard of the capture of this point. I shall hold this until 10 o'clock if I don't sooner hear from you.

I send you enclosed a list of Captain Foley's men, the "Flat Top Copperheads," taken from the pocket of one killed by Lieutenant Bottsford's men. You have the precious document with spelling, etc., etc. It should be copied for all who are likely to catch any of the scamps. Foragers yesterday found considerable quantities of well-cured bacon and fresh meat. With the new grass coming on and this meat, an enterprising army is not going to starve. This move was not made a day too soon; a further advance while the panic prevails is a plain duty and I doubt not you will order it as soon as you arrive. Company C will be very anxious to come here to be ready to go forward with us. If a guard is required when you reach them for their wounded, I suggest that you order a detail of say two men from each company of this regiment, to do that duty and thus relieve the company.

Two citizens of Kanawha County fled here with their slaves soon after our forces entered the valley, — Colonel Ward and Blain, or some such names. They hesitated about taking the oath to support Governor Pierpont's Government. They will take the oath to the United States. This simply means secession. One of them got a pass from General Cox, dated December 17.

I think these wealthy scoundrels ought to be treated with the same severity as other Rebels. They want food for their slaves. We have none to spare to such men. Colonel P. [Paxton] will perhaps pass them to you. If you allow quartermaster Gardner to furnish them, let them pay sutler's prices the same as our soldiers do. If I hear that you put them in the guard-tent, I shall be pleased. They may not leave here until you come.

I have stricken Rev. Amos Wilson's name from the rolls. If he sends his resignation, all well; if not the order will be published if you approve. I enclose Major Comly's remarks on the Foley list.

Respectfully,

R. B. HAYES,
LIEUTENANT-COLONEL 23D REGIMENT O. V. I.,
COMMANDING.

[COLONEL SCAMMON.]

Camp 5, Princeton, May 5, 1862. Monday. — A rainy day. Very interesting today. The citizens admitted freely. Militia-men, Union men, and all, coming in taking the oath. The enemy reported running with a big scare, hurrying through Rocky Gap, burning it, their tents and arms even. Tazewell Court-house, deserted by troops, reported burned. Giles Court-house reported ditto!!! Got a fine Mississippi rifle, brought in today by a repentant Rebel. My orderly, Gray, will carry it for me. The Narrows of New River deserted, too.

CAMP NUMBER 5, PRINCETON, May 5, 8 A. M. [1862].

SIR: — There will be no difficulty in turning the enemy's position at the Narrows of New River. There are paths or open woods accessible to infantry leading across the mountains to the right of the Narrows into the valley of Wolf Creek; thence by good roads to the mouth of Wolf Creek, four to six miles from Giles Court-house, and in the rear of the Narrows. This you will understand by looking at any map of this region. Guides can be procured who will undertake to pilot us across, a circuit of perhaps ten or twelve miles. I doubt whether the enemy will attempt to hold the Narrows. Their force was the Forty-fifth Regiment, and about eight hundred militia of Giles, Montgomery, and ———— Counties.

The Forty-fifth has a large part of it scattered over towards the Wytheville Road, a part missing, and the remnant at the Narrows will run on the first excuse. The force now here can take the Narrows on your order in forty-eight hours. They are said to have some artillery — three to six pieces. I have sent reliable scouts to try to get accurate information. A Rebel captain of the Forty-fifth said: "No man could stand the yelling of the Yankees, especially as they fired so fast!!" Twenty wagons [with] provisions and Company B, Thirtieth, arrived at 2 P. M. They report the roads hence to Raleigh very good and improving; the trouble is from Raleigh to Gauley.

Captains Hunter and Lovejoy have arrived. They report Captain Foley died of his wounds. This will be a death-blow to the "Copperheads." All the people tell us we need apprehend no bushwhacking this side of that gang, either here or in front of us.

I am much gratified with the order and messages you send. I know I have not given you as full and explicit reports of things as would have been desirable. But when actually engaged in an enterprise I am so occupied in trying to *do* the best thing that I can't *write* satisfactorily. I think in this matter every important thing was right, save possibly one which I will explain when we meet. We can get here and in the country in front considerable meat — some cured but mostly fresh. In sending forward provision trains this can to some extent be considered. More salt and less meat can be sent.

Will you dispatch General Cox that our long-range muskets are much needed in the present service. Our experience the last few days satisfies everyone that a man who can kill at four hundred yards is worth three or four men with common muskets. The quartermaster will never, send them unless General Cox orders it.

It rained during the night and is cloudy this morning. I think we shall not have another "smart spell of falling weather," however. In the house intended for your headquarters are ten or fifteen rooms of all sorts, some chairs and tables but *no bedding*, a good kitchen cooking stove, two *negro* women and all appendages. Thomas will be able to make it a good establishment in a few hours for everybody you want and room for hospitality. If, however, you prefer smaller quarters, there are three or four others that will do as well, and the house in question can be a hospital if needed. No sick here now. You must have your bedding with you when you arrive if possible.

Respectfully,
R. B. HAYES,
Lieutenant-Colonel 23d Regiment O. V. I.,
Commanding Detachment.

[Colonel Scammon.]

Camp Number 5, Princeton, May 5, 1862.

Sir: — This whole region is completely conquered. Rapid movement is all that is needed to take possession of the railroad and several good counties without opposition. Militiamen are coming in glad to take the oath and get home "to work crops." A part of Jenifer's force retreated through Tazewell, abandoning Jeffersonville and it is *reported* burning it. Humphrey Marshall is reported on the railroad and near or at Wytheville. The Forty-fifth retreated on to Giles abandoning the Narrows, leaving the position deserted. These are the reports. Not perfectly reliable, but I am inclined to credit them. At the Rocky Gap many muskets even were burned, the militiamen thinking it safer to return home unarmed. There is a report from Tazewell that a battalion of cavalry is approaching through Logan and McDowell, the other part of the Second Virginia. If so they will meet with no opposition worth naming. It is about certain that the enemy had but one cannon at the Narrows. All I give you is rumor, or the nature of rumor, except the conduct and disposition of the new militia. I hear that from their own lips. An active command can push to the railroad, taking coffee, salt, and sugar, and subsist itself long enough to get the railroad from Newbern a hundred miles west. I speak of the future in the way of suggestion that your thoughts may turn towards planning enterprises before the *scare* subsides. The rations I speak of because we ought to have a larger supply of some things, counting upon the country for the others. Colonel Little will send in reports perfectly reliable as to the Narrows tomorrow. I hear a report that the enemy — the Forty-fifth — didn't stop at Giles but kept on towards Newbern! I give these reports as showing the drift of feeling in this country, and [as] hints at truth rather than truth itself.

Monday night. — I now have reliable information of the enemy, I think. It differs in many respects from rumors mentioned in the foregoing. The Forty-fifth Regiment during Friday and Saturday straggled back to its camp at the mouth of Wolf Creek, a short distance above the Narrows. About four-fifths of the force got back foot-sore, without hats, coats, knapsacks, and arms in many cases. In the course of Friday and Saturday a considerable part (perhaps half) of the cavalry we drove from here reached the same point (mouth of Wolf Creek) having passed through Rocky Gap and thence taken the Wolf Creek and Tazewell Road easterly. On Saturday evening they were preparing to leave camp; the Forty-fifth to go to Richmond whither they had just been ordered, and the cavalry and the few militia were to go with them as far as Dublin. The militia were uncertain whether they were to remain at Dublin or go west to the Salt Works in Washington and Wythe Counties. They all expected to be gone from Wolf Creek and the Narrows during Sunday. There would be no fighting the Yankees this side of Dublin — possibly at Dublin a fight. The militia of Wythe, Grayson, and Carroll, seven hundred strong, are the force [at] Wytheville. At Abbington, one thousand [of] Floyd's men. In Russell County Humphrey Marshall is still reported with three thousand men badly armed and worse disciplined. The great Salt Works (King's) work four hundred [men], ten furnaces, and turn out seventeen hundred bushels every twenty-four hours. No armed force there. All this from contrabands and substantially correct.

Later. — Seven more contrabands just in. They report that on Sunday the Forty-fifth and other forces, except about thirty guards of baggage, left the vicinity of the Narrows arriving at Giles Court-house Sunday afternoon on their way to Dublin Depot; that from there they expected to go west to Abbington. The contrabands passed the Narrows; only a small guard was there with a few tents and wagons. No cannon were left there. I do not doubt the general truthfulness of the story. It confirms the former. The enclosed letters perhaps contain something that ought to be known to General Frémont; if so you can extract a fact or two to telegraph. They were got from the last mail sent here by the Rebels. The carrier stopped seven miles south of here and the mail [was] picked up there.

I wish to send three companies or so to the Narrows immediately to see if we can catch the guard and baggage left behind. If you approve send me word back immediately and I will start the expedition in the morning.

Latest. — Two more contrabands!! We can surely get the baggage in six hours (eighteen miles) without difficulty. *Do send* the order.

Respectfully,

R. B. HAYES,
LIEUTENANT-COLONEL 23D REGIMENT O. V. I.,
COMMANDING DETACHMENT.

[COLONEL SCAMMON.]

Princeton, May 6, 1862. Tuesday evening. — A clear, cold, bright day. Got a letter from my dear wife, very patriotic, very affectionate. An angel of a wife, I have. And the boys, dear little fellows! I hope we shall be together again before many months.

I have been rather anxious today. We heard from contra-bands and others that the Narrows [of New River] was deserted except by a small guard for property and tents. Major Comly with Companies H, I, and K and Captain Gilmore's Cavalry was dispatched to the point eighteen to twenty-two miles distant. No tidings yet, although a courier ought to have reached here before this time if they and he travelled rapidly. I suggested that if necessary to secure property they go to Giles Town.

In the meantime I hear that a foraging party of six of our men as guards under Corporal Day, with three battery men and a waggon, have been taken by a large party of cavalry on the Tazewell Road, ten miles. Jenifer's Cavalry have gone to Tazewell; got their horses and are now in the saddle ready to cut off our men. Oh, for an enterprising cavalry force!

I have looked for a messenger since 5 o'clock from Major Comly. At midnight received a message from Major Comly that the party finding the Narrows deserted and all property gone, had gone on to Giles and taken it completely by surprise, capturing some prisoners and a large amount of stores, — two hundred and fifty barrels of flour and everything else. Very lucky! and Colonel Scammon thereupon approved of the whole expedition, although it was irregular and in violation of the letter of orders. The enemy just out of Giles were at least eleven hundred and had forces near to increase it to fifteen hundred. Our party was only two hundred and fifty! The colonel fearing the capture of our little party ordered me to proceed at daylight with two companies Second Virginia Cavalry and the rest of [the] Twenty-third Regiment to reinforce Giles.

Giles Court-house, or Parisburg [Pearisburg], Camp Number 6, May 7, 6:30 P. M. Wednesday. — Just reached here from Princeton after a fatiguing march of twenty-eight miles. Found the major very glad to see us. All anxious, hearing reports of [the] Forty-fifth reinforced by [the] Thirty-sixth or [the] Twenty-second with artillery, etc., etc. Now all safe if we are vigilant. The country after the road strikes New River is romantic, highly cultivated, and beautiful. Giles Court-house is

[a] neat, pretty village with a most magnificent surrounding country both as regards scenery and cultivation. The people have all been Secesh, but are polite and intelligent. When Major Comly, Captain Gilmore, and Captain Drake entered town, the people were standing on the corners, idly gossiping — more numerous than the invaders. They did not at first seem to know who it was; then such a scampering, such a rushing into the streets of women, such weeping, scolding, begging, etc., etc.

Spent the night posting pickets and arranging against an attack so as to prevent a surprise. At midnight a citizen came in saying the enemy were preparing to attack us — the Forty-fifth and Twenty-second — when he was at their camp, twelve miles from here at Cloyd's Mountain. I doubled the pickets, dressed myself and kept about quietly all the rest of the night.

CAMP NUMBER 6, GILES, May 7, 1862, 6:30 o'clock.

SIR: — We arrived here after a pretty severe march of twenty-eight miles. We know really very little of the enemy. It is reported that the Jenifer Cavalry is at Newbern, the Forty-fifth at Cloyd's Mountain, thirteen miles distant, also the Twenty-second. We are without artillery and perhaps you would do well to send us some. We are told that the enemy are informed of our strength and of the large amount of property of theirs in our hands. There is no reason other than this fact for apprehending an attack. The current rumor is that they intend fortifying Cloyd's Mountain. You can judge from these facts what is required. My opinion is we are perfectly safe. The property is *valuable, very* valuable, especially for us here. It is worth here not less than five thousand dollars.

Respectfully,

R. B. HAYES,
LIEUTENANT-COLONEL 23D REGIMENT O. V. I.,
COMMANDING.

P. S. — General Heth is nowhere near here.

[COLONEL E. P. SCAMMON.]

Parisburg [Pearisburg], Virginia, May 8, 1862. Thursday. — A perfectly splendid day. No attack or approach last night. Passed out at daylight a mile and a half in direction of enemy. Selected my ground in case of an approach of the enemy. Talked with Mr. Pendleton [and] Colonel English. Find more intelligence and culture here than anywhere else in Virginia. Today Sergeant Abbott found a Rebel picket or scouting party on the mountain overlooking the village, peering into us with a fine glass. A reconnaissance today discovered three regiments in line marching coolly and well to the front as our men crossed Walker's Creek, ten or twelve miles from here. They are said to have three pieces of artillery and some cavalry.

We get no reinforcements today and hear of none on the way. I have asked for artillery two or three times and get none. No message even today. It is a great outrage that we are not reinforced. We are losing stores all the time which the enemy slips away, — not [to] speak of the possibility of an attack by an overwhelming force. Shameful! Who is to blame? I think we shall not be attacked, but I shall have an anxious night.

CAMP NUMBER 6, GILES COURT-HOUSE,
May 8, 1862, 4:30 A. M.

SIR: — A citizen came in from Dublin last [night] about 11 o'clock. He reports no troops there except a few guards, and the enemy engaged in removing all stores to Lynchburg; they commenced removing before we came here. He came over Cloyd's Mountain and in the Gap, posted strongly, he found the Forty-fifth and its militia, perhaps five hundred strong, and the Thirty-sixth, which had just joined them from the other side of New River (they had been at Lewisburg), three hundred strong, with five (5) pieces artillery, one large and four small. They had ascertained that the "advance guard of Yankees" which took Giles was only two hundred and fifty strong and were then getting ready to march against us to attack last night, with one cannon. He heard when he came within four miles that we were being reinforced; the negro reporting it thought there must be fifteen thousand now in Giles. He said if they heard of the reinforcements it would certainly stop their coming. They had hope of reinforcements to stop us at Cloyd's Mountain from the men on furlough from Floyd's Brigade. The brigade is to be reorganized immediately. It will form part of three regiments. No other reinforcements hoped for in the camp talk of the enemy.

This is the substance of the information given me. I *think* it reliable. I doubled the pickets at 12 last night and sent cavalry patrols four miles to the front. I could not help wishing, if our information was correct, that the enemy would be discovered approaching. But all is reported quiet. I suspect they will let us alone. If they had approached in the force reported we should have flogged them well. As to reinforcements, we should have some artillery. All others should bring tents with them. The houses are all occupied. If the Thirtieth comes let them take two days, it is too severe on feet to march twenty-eight miles on stones and hard knobs. The necessity for strengthening this post lies here: The country has a great deal of forage, and we can't get it unless we are strong. The enemy yesterday ran off six hundred bushels of shelled corn from near here. We have two hundred and fifty barrels of flour, nine barrels cornmeal, six barrels salt, sugar, drugs, some corn, and a vast variety of stuff such as ammunition, tools, harness, material of wear in stuff, etc., etc., all hauled into town and under guard. But a great deal is slipping through our fingers for want of force to take and hold it.

This is a lovely spot, a fine, clean village, most beautiful and romantic surrounding country, and *polite* and *educated* Secesh people. It is the spot to organize your brigade. For a week or two we are almost independent of quartermasters. The road from you to this place has some *very* bad places — perhaps five miles in all; the rest is hard, smooth, and dry, a good road. Our teams broke down a good deal but got within twenty miles. I left a guard at Wolf Creek Bridge. That is where the road from Tazewell comes to the river and the bridge is very important. We got Rebel papers to the 5th. Notice the article marked in the Lynchburg paper mentioning our advance. Also

17

letters, etc., which you will find interesting; also important list of captured stores. Our prisoners, the officers and militia, nice gentlemen but of no importance. I found [turned?] them out on parole. You will not greatly disapprove of this when you know the facts. In short, if you can get the permission you want to come here with your brigade, do so by all means as fast as you can get tents for them. We are in no need of reinforcements for defense, if our information is correct, *as yet,* but the point is too important to lose. You will see some beginnings at fortifying the Narrows. It was a strong place.

I still retain Gilmore's Cavalry. It is a necessity. Captain Gilmore and his two lieutenants pretty much captured this town. They have behaved admirably. Do get a revocation of the order sending them to the rear, at least for the present. You will need them *very* much. Will you send up their tents and baggage today? *They must* stay for the present. They can send tents, etc., up with their own teams now there. I say nothing about the major and his command. They deserve *all praise.* Say what you please that is good of them, and it will be true. The taking of Giles Court-house is one of the boldest things of the war. It was *perfectly impudent.* There were more Secesh standing on the corners than were in the party with Major Comly and Captain Gilmore when they *dashed in.*

Respectfully,

R. B. HAYES,
LIEUTENANT-COLONEL 23D REGIMENT O. V. I.,
COMMANDING.

COLONEL E. P. SCAMMON,
COMMANDING THIRD BRIGADE.

CAMP NUMBER 6, GILES COURT-HOUSE,
May 8, 1862. 7 P. M.

SIR: — We are getting on very prosperously gathering up forage, etc. We have in town six hundred bushels corn in addition to amount heretofore reported. Our stores of all sorts exceed anything this side of Fayette. We are in much need of shoes. We have got a lot of Secesh which though inferior will help until our quartermaster gets a supply. It is ascertained that the enemy is fortifying beyond Walker's Creek in a gap of Cloyd's Mountain, twelve or thirteen miles from here; that they have the Forty-fifth, Thirty-sixth, and probably the Twenty-second Virginia, also a small number of cavalry and three to six pieces of cannon. They advanced to within four miles of us last night, but learning of our reinforcements they retreated. Their advance guard was seen by my patrols and promptly reported, but on scouting for them, they were found to have turned back. Today I sent Captain Gilmore with half of his men and a company of the Second Virginia cavalry to make a reconnaissance. They drove in the enemy's pickets, crossed Walker's Creek, and went within a mile of the enemy's position. The whole force of the enemy was marched out and formed in order of battle. The *apparent* commander with a sort of body-guard of twenty or so rode up to Lieutenant Fordyce drawing a revolver when he was shot from his horse by Colonel Burgess. He was certainly an important officer. No one on our side hurt. The cavalry quietly fell back when the enemy burned the bridge over Walker's Creek after our cavalry had turned back.

This indicates to my mind that *as yet* the enemy is disposed to act on the defensive, but it is certain *we ought to be promptly and heavily reinforced.* I do not doubt you have men on the way. We shall not be attacked, I think, in advance of their coming; if so we shall be ready, *but* the stores and position are too valuable to be left in any degree exposed. With a large force we can get much more property. Today while our scouting party of cavalry was in front, about twenty of the enemy under an officer with a large glass was seen by Sergeant Abbott and a scout, examining the village from a very high mountain whose summit, two miles distant, overlooks the whole town.

8:30 P. M. — Couriers have arrived bringing messages for the cavalry, but none for me. No words of any reinforcements either. In any event, the want of force will prevent us gathering all the provisions and forage our position here entitles us to have. Major Comly says a conversation with the family he boards in, satisfies him that the enemy has three regiments at Walker's Creek. We shall be vigilant tonight, and shall be astonished tomorrow if we do not hear of the battery, at least, moving to us before another of these clear moonlight nights has to be watched through.

Respectfully,

R. B. HAYES,
LIEUTENANT-COLONEL 23D REGIMENT O. V. I.,
COMMANDING.

[COLONEL E. P. SCAMMON.]

Parisburg, [*Pearisburg*], *May 9. Friday.* — A lovely day. — No reinforcements yet; have asked for them in repeated dispatches. Strange. I shall be vigilant. Have planned the fight if it is to be done in the houses at night, and the retreat to the Narrows, if in daylight with artillery against us. The town can't be held if we are attacked with artillery. Shameful! We have rations for thirty days for a brigade and tents and other property.

CAMP NUMBER 6, GILES COURT-HOUSE,
May 9, 1862. A. M.

SIR: — Your dispatch of yesterday reached me about 10:30 o'clock P. M. Its suggestions and cautions will be carefully heeded. If in any important respect my reports are defective, I shall be glad to correct the fault. The novelty of my situation and the number and variety of claims upon my attention must be my apology for what may seem negligence. Our men and horses are getting worn-out with guard, picket, and patrol duty, added to the labor of gathering in forage and provisions. You say nothing of the forward movement having been disapproved, nor of abandoning or reinforcing this point. I *infer* that we may look for reinforcements today. It is of the utmost importance that we get prompt and large additions to our strength. The facts are these: Large amounts of forage and provisions which we might have got with a larger force are daily going to the enemy. The enemy is recovering from his panic, is near the railroad and getting reinforcements. He is already stronger than we are, at least double as strong. But all this you already know from repeated dispatches of mine and I doubt not you are doing all you can to bring up the needed additions to our force.

I learn from contrabands that there is a practicable way for foot and horse, not teams, up Walker's Creek on this side, by which a force can pass over the mountains, five or seven miles from the road and reach the rear or turn the enemy's position. From the general appearance of the hills near here I think that some such passage can be found. The enemy has destroyed the boats at the ferries, or removed them from this side wherever it was possible to do so. The quartermaster is rigging up mule teams and ox teams to do the extra hauling with considerable success. There is of course some grumbling among owners of wagons, etc., but I tell them it is a military necessity. The morning papers of Lynchburg are received here frequently the evening of the same day and regularly the next day. This shows how near we are to the centre of things.

Respectfully,

R. B. HAYES,
LIEUTENANT-COLONEL 23D REGIMENT O. V. I.,
COMMANDING.

P. S. — Details are constantly made from the force ready for battle to take care of prisoners, guard bridges, etc., etc., until our force here is reduced to a very small figure. *Instant action is required one way or the other.*

COLONEL E. P. SCAMMON,
  COMMANDING THIRD BRIGADE.

CAMP NUMBER 6, GILES COURT-HOUSE,
May 9, 1862, 10:30 (P. M.)

SIR: — You will have to hurry forward reinforcements rapidly — as rapidly as possible — to prevent trouble here. This is not a defensible point without artillery against artillery. No news of a movement by the enemy but one may be expected soon. Shall we return to the Narrows if you can't reinforce?

Respectfully,

R. B. HAYES,

LIEUTENANT-COLONEL 23D REGIMENT O. V. I.,

COMMANDING.

P. S. — A party the other side of the river is firing on our men collecting forage and provisions.

COLONEL E. P. SCAMMON,
    Princeton.

Adair's, ten and one-half miles from Parisburg [Pearisburg], Saturday, May 10, 4 P. M. — We were attacked at 4 o'clock this morning. I got up at the first faint streak of light and walked out to see the pickets in the direction of the enemy. As I was walking alone I heard six shots. "No mistake this time," I thought. I hurried back, ordered up my own and the adjutant's horse, called up the men and officers, [and] ordered the cavalry to the front. [I ordered] Captains Drake and Sperry to skirmish before the enemy and keep them back; the rest of the regiment to form in their rear. Led the whole to the front beyond the town; saw the enemy approaching — four regiments or battalions, several pieces of artillery in line of battle approaching. The artillery soon opened on us. The shell shrieked and burst over [our] heads, the small arms rattled, and the battle was begun. It was soon obvious that we would be outflanked. We retreated to the next ridge and stood again. The men of the Twenty-third behaved gloriously, the men of Gilmore's Cavalry, ditto; the men of Colonel Paxton's Cavalry, not so well. I was scratched and torn on the knee by a shell or something, doing no serious injury. I felt well all the time. The men behaved so gallantly! And so we fought our way through town, the people rejoicing at our defeat, and on for six hours until we reached the Narrows, five and one-half miles distant. The time seemed short. I was cheered by Gilmore's Cavalry at a point about three and one-half miles from Giles Court-house, and we were all in good humor. We had three men killed, a number wounded, none severely, and lost a few prisoners.

In the Narrows we easily checked the pursuit of the enemy and held him back until he got artillery on to the opposite side of New River and shelled us out. Reached here about 1 P. M. safely. A well-ordered retreat which I think was creditable.

Camp near Adair's, Giles County, Virginia, Sunday (?) May 11. — This is the first Sunday that has passed without my knowing the day of the week since childhood. The men bivouacked on a sidehill near New River. Nothing exciting during the day. The enemy in the Narrows, but not coming through. Our masterly retreat of yesterday lost the Twenty-third one killed, Hoyt C. Tenney, Company B, and three missing — prisoners and mostly drunk; perhaps eight or ten wounded, generally slightly. The cavalry, one killed, three missing, and some wounded. Gilmore's Cavalry, one killed and one wounded. The Twenty-third behaved admirably, cool, steady, obedient. A few cowards — a corporal or two in Company H, the most exposed company, a sergeant of Company ——, etc., etc.; but men of the Twenty-third with teams, etc., from Raleigh hastened to share our fate; five for every one who left. *The Second Virginia Cavalry left us!* Bad state of things.

CAMP AT ADAIR'S, NEAR NARROWS OF NEW RIVER,
May 11, 1862.

SIR: — Yesterday morning, 10th inst., at dawn, our mounted pickets three miles south of Parisburg [Pearisburg] gave notice that the enemy was approaching in order of battle. It was soon discovered that his force was from twenty-five hundred to three thousand, and that he had a battery of five pieces. In pursuance of your order and according to a plan previously arranged, the following disposition of my command was made. All our teams and all the teams we could press were loaded and started for the Narrows of New River. The cavalry under Captain Gilmore, numbering thirty-five, and detachments of two companies of the Second Virginia V. C. [Volunteer Cavalry] under Captains Emmons and Scott respectively were dispatched to the front with instructions to harrass and delay the enemy. Company H, Captain Drake, and Company B, Captain Sperry of the Twenty-third Regiment O. V. I. were assigned a similar duty. The remaining seven companies (Company C not having joined the regiment) of the Twenty-third Regiment were drawn up in line of battle on a ridge in the rear of the village and about a half a mile in rear of our skirmishers. My whole force did not exceed six hundred men.

The enemy on approaching the first line of skirmishers halted and opened upon it with their artillery. The enemy, soon after the firing commenced, sent detachments right and left to flank our skirmishers. The skirmishers slowly and in good order withdrew keeping up a constant and galling fire upon the advancing lines. The enemy continued to press forward slowly and occasionally halting until they reached the seven companies of the Twenty-third Regiment in line of battle. Our whole force was gradually pushed back, the enemy following with his whole force, halting frequently to place his guns in position. In this way the fight was kept up four or five hours when we reached the Narrows of New River five and a.half miles north of Parisburg [Pearisburg]. Here we were able to take advantage of the narrow pass and brought the enemy to a stand. He made no serious effort to enter the Narrows in the face of the force I had posted at the extreme southern entrance of the Narrows at Wolf Creek Bridge.

After perhaps two hours' delay the enemy succeeded in getting two guns on the opposite bank of New River and at a distance of two hundred and fifty or three hundred yards began to throw shell into the detachment defending the pass. Our force drew back to a new position out of range. The enemy again advanced his guns, and thus gradually we were forced to the lower entrance of the Narrows. No part of the enemy's force succeeded in getting through the Narrows. About the time the enemy ceased to push forward, the cavalry under your command came up. The fighting lasted seven or eight hours during which time the detachment under my command retreated about seven miles.

Our loss was two killed and ten wounded and six missing.

Of these the Twenty-third O. V. I. lost Private Hoyt C. Tenney, Company B, killed; and Privates Thomas Redmond, Company I, John Leisure, Company D, and Henry Ward, Company B, missing and probably taken prisoners. The wounded are all doing well. Sergeant-Major Eugene L. Reynolds was hit in the head by a fragment of shell while fighting in the front line of skirmishers and knocked down. He had a narrow escape, but was not seriously hurt. A severe wound was received by Sergeant O. H. Ferrell, Company H. The other wounds are all slight. The names of the injured in the Second Virginia Cavalry have not been sent in.

We brought off our prisoners taken when we entered Parisburg [Pearisburg] and carried away all our quartermaster stores and ammunition. We lost the provisions we had previously captured from the enemy (except what we had consumed), of which there was a large quantity. The enemy's loss in killed and wounded is not known.

The officers and men of Captain Gilmore's Cavalry behaved with the greatest gallantry during the entire day. The two companies of the Second Virginia Cavalry rendered important service when dismounted and acting as skirmishers on the right of our line in the morning. The Twenty-third Regiment, officers and men, were cool and steady and the whole retreat in the face, and for the most part under the fire, of an overwhelming superior force was conducted without the slightest confusion or haste on their part.

It is much to be regretted that reinforcements which I had so frequently and urgently requested could not be sent in time to save Parisburg [Pearisburg], as the loss of position and property is very serious. *

Respectfully,

R. B. HAYES,
LIEUTENANT-COLONEL 23D REGIMENT O. V. I.,
COMMANDING.

Copy [of] report to Colonel Scammon of retreat from Giles C. H. May 10, submitted May 11.

* [This paragraph] erased before signing on request of Colonel Scammon — not because I did not deem it true, but because he wished it, and I did not want to embarrass him.

CAMP AT MOUTH OF EAST RIVER, GILES COUNTY,
VIRGINIA, May 11, 1862.

DEAREST: — Since I wrote you last I have lived a great deal. Do you know that Giles Court-house was captured with a large amount of stores, etc., etc., by a party sent by me from Princeton? It was so bold and impudent! I went with six companies of the Twenty-third to reinforce. I soon found that unless further reinforced we were gone up. The enemy, three thousand strong, were within ten miles of us with a battery of artillery. We had none. The place, a lovely mountain village, was wholly indefensible except by a large force. I sent two couriers a day to beg for reinforcements for three days. None came. At the last moment the order came that I should retreat if attacked by a largely superior force. This was easy to say, but to do it safely, after waiting till the enemy is on you, is not a trifle. I was up every night. Had guards and pickets on every point of approach. Well, yesterday morning, I got up before daylight, and visited the outposts. Just at dawn, I heard the alarm guns. The enemy were coming even in greater force than we expected. Four regiments, a battery of guns, and a small force of cavalry. I had only nine companies of the Twenty-third, much weakened by detachments guarding supply trains, etc., and two weak companies of cavalry. Not more than one-fourth of the enemy's strength. But all went on like clockwork. Baggage was loaded and started. Captains Drake and Sperry undertook to hold the enemy with their companies and Captain Gilmore's Cavalry until the rest could take position in rear of the town. I went out with Captains Drake and Sperry.

Just before sunrise, May 10, a lovely morning, we saw the advancing battalions in line of battle in beautiful order. They were commanded, it is said, by General Heth. They opened first with cannon firing shell. The first personal gratification was to find that my horse stood it well. Soon I saw that the men were standing it well. As they came in range of our skirmishers, some fatal firing checked them; but they were rapidly closing around us. Now was the first critical moment: Could our men retreat without breaking into confusion or a rout?

They retired slowly, stubbornly, in good spirits and in order! I got a scratch on the right knee, just drawing blood but spoiling my drawers. But what of that? Things were going well. The enemy now approached our main line. Could it retreat also in order, for I knew it must be forced back. Here was the crisis of our fate. They stood firmly. The enemy halted to get his guns in position again. Soon we were in a fair way to be surrounded.

The men were ordered to retire slowly, firing as they went, to a ridge forty rods back, and then to form again. They did it to perfection, and I knew we were safe. From that time, for five hours, it was only exciting fun. The fight lasted seven hours, we retreating six and one-half miles until we came to a narrow pass where three of our companies could hold back any number. Here we were safe. The Twenty-third looked gloriously after this. We got off as by a miracle. We lost one killed, one wounded badly and a host slightly, in the regiment; about the same in the cavalry. Applause was never so sweet as when right in the midst of the struggle, Gilmore's Cavalry gave me three cheers for a sharp stroke by which I turned the column out of range of the enemy's guns, which, with infinite trouble, he had placed to sweep us.

It was a retreat (which is almost a synonym for defeat) and yet we all felt grand over it. But warn't the men mad at somebody for leaving us? We were joined by a battery and the Thirtieth Regiment at 4 P. M. under Colonel Scammon, starting at the seasonable hour of 7 A. M.! We are now strong again, but driven from a most valuable position with a loss of stores we had captured worth thousands.

I am reported dangerously wounded by some of the cowardly cavalry (not Gilmore's) who fled forty miles, reporting us "routed," "cut to pieces," and the like. Never was a man prouder of his regiment than I of the Twenty-third. I keep thinking how well they behaved. — Love to all.

Affectionately,   R. B. HAYES.

12th, A. M. — Since writing the foregoing, we have got information which leads me to think it was probably well we were not reinforced. There would not have been enough to hold the position we had against so great a force as the enemy brought against us. You see we were twenty miles from their railroad, and only six to twelve hours from their great armies. . . .

MRS. HAYES.

Monday, May 12. Camp at north of East River near line between Giles and Mercer Counties, eleven miles from Giles Courthouse. — We moved here to a strong position. The whole brigade as now organized is with us. This is the First Brigade of the Army of the District of Kanawha — General Cox. It consists of [the] Twelfth, Twenty-third, and Thirtieth Ohio Regiments, McMullen's Battery (two brass six-pounders and four howitzers), and four companies [of] Paxton's or Bowles' Second Virginia Cavalry; with Captain Gilmore's Cavalry for the present. Brigade commanded by Colonel Scammon.

Colonel White of [the] Twelfth a clever gentleman. Lieutenant-Colonel Hines, ditto, but a great talker and a great memory for persons and places.

Fine weather since Sunday the 4th. Out of grub, out of mess furniture. Rumors of the defeat of Milroy and of overwhelming forces threatening us. Great news by telegraph: The capture of Norfolk, blowing up the Merrimac, and the like! Corinth being abandoned. York peninsula falling into McClellan's hands. If all that this indicates comes to pass, the Rebellion is, indeed, on its last legs.

HEADQUARTERS 23D REGT. O. V. I., CAMP AT MOUTH
OF EAST RIVER, GILES COUNTY, VIRGINIA,

May 12, 1862.

SIR: — Enclosed I send you the proceedings of the company commanders of the Twenty-third Regiment O. V. I. nominating Rev. Russell G. French, a clergyman of the Methodist Episcopal Church, to the office of chaplain of the regiment. I have to request that Mr. French may be immediately commissioned — *his commission to bear date May 1, 1862.*

Rev. Amos Wilson was the former chaplain. He resigned on the 30th of April. His resignation was accepted and I directed his name to be stricken from the roll of officers of the Twenty-third Regiment.

Mr. French is a loyal citizen of Mercer County, of unblemished character, and with a fair reputation as a Christian and clergyman. He was driven from his home because he was a Union man; joined my command at Raleigh to act as guide and scout. We found him a most valuable man. He served without compensation. When serving with Company C in the late fight at Camp Creek he had his right thigh shattered to pieces by a Rebel ball. He is probably mortally wounded; in any event, he is crippled for life. Lieutenant Bottsford, who commanded Company C, says he behaved with great gallantry. He has a large family and small means. Officers and men all desire his appointment as herein requested.

Respectfully,

R. B. Hayes,
Lieutenant-Colonel 23d Regiment O. V. I.,
Commanding.

Brigadier-General C. P. Buckingham,
   Adjutant-General.

Copy [of] letter to Governor Tod asking a commission for Russell G. French, our wounded scout, etc., etc., as chaplain Twenty-third Regiment O. V. I.

Tuesday, [May] 13, Same Camp, Giles County, Virginia. — Still dry and *dusty!* We shall soon need rain! Queer need in Virginia! No bread in camp today, but beans and beef and some bacon. Had an evening parade. The regiment looked strong and well. Our camp, on a hill overlooking New River in front and East River in the rear — the Twelfth and Thirtieth in the valley of East River, McMullen's Battery near by — is very picturesque. High mountains all around; some finely cultivated country in sight.

The Second Virginia Cavalry, out foraging, came rushing in covered with foam; reported a great force of Rebel cavalry near by! Turned out to be our own—Gilmore's Cavalry! What a worthless set they are proving to be.

Camp near Mouth East River, Giles County, May 14, 1862. Wednesday. — Rained violently last night; not a bad morning, however. Rumors of defeat of General Milroy up northeast by Stonewall Jackson. Don't believe it. If true, it is not very important, if the taking of Norfolk holds out. We ought to catch the whole Rebel army near Richmond. With gunboats at West Point up York River, up James River, and so on, we must have that whole region soon. We now have a base of operations close up to the enemy's right. — Rain in violent storms during the day two or three times.

No bread; men want crackers. Transportation insufficient. But for the large quantities of bacon we get in this neighborhood, we should suffer. General Cox with Second Brigade is at Napoleon French's, six or seven miles from here. Will be here tomorrow. General McClellan within twenty miles of Richmond! The crisis is now at hand. If no serious disaster occurs in the next ten days, the Rebel cobhouse tumbles speedily and forever!

Same Camp, Thursday, May 15, 1862. — Cloudy and threatening rain. Several warm showers during the day. Firing between pickets constantly going on two or three miles down the river. We send out two or three companies and a howitzer or six-pounder to bang away, wasting ammunition. If the enemy is enterprising he will capture some of these parties and perhaps a cannon.

CAMP, MOUTH OF EAST RIVER, GILES COUNTY, VIRGINIA,

May 15, 1862.

DEAR MOTHER: — We have marched a great many miles through this mountain region since I last wrote you. We have had some fighting, some excitement, and a great deal to do. We are now in a strong position. General Cox commands the army, about five thousand strong, in this vicinity. We feel pretty safe, although the success of our arms at the East seems to be driving the enemy to these mountains in greater strength than before.

The scenery is finer than any we have before seen. How you would enjoy the views from my tent. In sight, at the bottom of the hill the Twenty-third is camped on, runs New River, a stream larger than the Connecticut at Brattleboro, then a beautiful cultivated country along its banks, and steep high mountains bounding the scene on all sides. I am afraid I am ruined for living in the tame level country of Ohio.

The reports indicate that the Rebellion is going under very rapidly. If no serious disaster befalls us the struggle will hardly outlast the summer.

I shall write very rarely. You will hear by telegraph all important news of us. I think of you and all the dear ones often —*constantly.*

Affectionately,

R. B. HAYES

MRS. SOPHIA HAYES.

Saturday, May 17. — A very hard day, — muddy, wet, and sultry. Ordered at 3 A. M. to abandon camp and hasten with whole force to General Cox at Princeton. He has had a fight with a greatly superior force under General Marshall. We lost tents, — we slit and tore them, — mess furniture, blankets, etc., etc., by this hasty movement. I was ordered with the Twenty-third, Gilmore's Cavalry, and two pieces McMullen's Battery, to cover the retreat to Princeton. We did it successfully, but oh, what a hard day on the men! I had been up during the night, had the men out, etc., etc. We were all day making it. Found all in confusion; severe fighting against odds and a further retreat deemed necessary. Bivouacked on the ground at Princeton.

Mem. : — I saved all my personal baggage, tent included; but no chance to use it at Princeton.

Sunday!! Came again unawares upon me at Princeton. At 1 or 2 A. M. aroused to prepare to move. Moved off quietly; got off, again unmolested, to this point, viz., Bluestone River,

Mercer County, Virginia. I hope this is the last of the retreat. We have [the] Thirty-fourth, Twenty-eight, Twelfth, Twenty-third, Thirtieth, Thirty-seventh O. V. I.; Second Virginia Cavalry; and Simmonds' and McMullen's Batteries. The enemy reported to have three thousand or so under General Heth and five thousand or so under General Humphrey Marshall. The numbers are nothing, but at present our communications can't well be kept up. All will soon be remedied under Frémont. Then, forward again! In the fights we have lost in our army, chiefly Thirty-seventh and Thirty-fourth, near one hundred killed, wounded, and prisoners.

Camp on Flat Top Mountain, May 20, 1862. — Monday, 19th, marched from camp on Bluestone River to this point (yesterday) — a hot dry march — with knapsacks. I supposed we were to go only five miles; was disappointed to find we were retreating so far as this point. Being out of humor with that, I was out of sorts with all things; scolded "some" because the column was halted to rest on the wrong side of a stream which had to be crossed single file; viz., the near instead of the opposite side; mad because Colonel Scammon halted us in the sun half an hour — no water — without telling us how long we were to halt, etc., etc. But got good-humored again soon. Must swear off from swearing. Bad habit. Met Dr. Jim Webb, assistant surgeon of [the] Twelfth, yesterday as we approached here. March fourteen miles.

[Today], Tuesday, 20th, rains occasionally — a cold rain. No tents, some trouble, but men are patient and hardy. Heard of Ike Nelson's wounds, four to six in number and twenty bullet holes in his clothing. Left for dead but got well.

Avery and Captain Drake go to Raleigh this morning. We are holding on, waiting for supplies in the place of the tents, etc., we have lost. No news yet of Richmond's having been taken, but it is likely soon to fall unless we are defeated.

CAMP ON FLAT TOP MOUNTAIN ON LINE BETWEEN
MERCER AND RALEIGH COUNTIES, May 20, 1862.

DEAR UNCLE: — The last three weeks has been a period of great activity with us — severe marching, sharp fighting, and all sorts of strategy and manœuvring. I had command of the advance southward and marched to within ten miles of the railroad, seventy miles south of this. This was ten days ago. On the morning of the 10th the enemy attacked us in greatly superior numbers and with artillery. In *obedience to orders* we have been falling back ever since. I was much vexed that we were not reinforced. Perhaps I was wrong. It is now believed that the enemy, since their reverses in eastern Virginia, have been sending heavy bodies of troops this way; that our force is wholly inadequate to its task, and must wait here until largely strengthened. I am not sure about this, but accept it without much grumbling. As I had command of the advance, I also had command of the rear-guard during the two most perilous days of the retreat. I am glad to know that nobody blames me with anything. Perhaps nobody ought to be blamed, *certainly* not if the force of the enemy is correctly reported. We have got off very well, having the best of all the fighting, and losing very little property in the retreat, and conducting it in good order.

General Cox and staff narrowly escaped capture. My command had a narrow escape. With any common precautions we should have been captured or destroyed, but luckily I had mounted pickets two miles further out than usual and got notice of the trap in time. The total loss of my command up to yesterday since May 1 inclusive is seven killed, six missing, and thirty-five wounded. We have killed forty to fifty of the enemy, captured about fifty, and wounded a large number. We have captured and destroyed many arms, and lived on the enemy's grub a week. We also took several teams and waggons. We have lost our tents (except headquarters) and part of our mess furniture.

We shall remain here and hereabouts some time to get reinforced and to get supplies. We are in telegraphic communication with the world and only sixty miles from navigation.

18

Dr. James Webb is now in this brigade, assistant surgeon of the Twelfth Regiment O. V. I. Dr. Joe is brigade surgeon. We shall enjoy a few days' rest here. The Twenty-third is a capital set. They always stood up squarely to the work and enjoyed it. A vast difference between raw troops and those who have tried it enough to be at home.

Love to all. Good-bye.

R. B. Hayes.

S. Birchard.

Camp on Flat Top Mountain,
May 20, (Tuesday), 1862.

Dearest: — Here we are "back again" — fifty or sixty miles in rear of the advanced position we had taken. The short of it is, since the Rebel disasters in eastern Virginia they have thrown by the railroad a heavy force into this region, forcing us back day by day, until we have gained a strong position which they are not likely, I think, to approach. I do not think there is any blame on the part of our leaders. We were strong enough to go ahead until recent events changed the plans of the enemy, and made it impossible [for us] to reinforce sufficiently. I was much vexed at first, but I suspect it is all right. We have had a great deal of severe fighting — fragmentary — in small detachments, but very severe. We have had narrow escapes. My whole command was nearly caught once; the Twenty-eighth barely escaped. General Cox and staff got off by the merest chance. Colonel Scammon's brigade was in close quarters, etc., etc. And yet by good luck, we have had no serious disaster. We have lost tents and some small quartermaster stores, but nothing important. In the fighting we have had the best of it usually. The total loss of General Cox's command is perhaps two hundred to three hundred, including killed, wounded, prisoners, and missing. The enemy has suffered far more. In my fight at Giles, the enemy had thirty-one killed and many wounded; our total casualties and missing, about fifteen. We shall remain here until reinforced or new events make it possible to move.

I see the *Thirty-third*, not the *Twenty-third*, gets the credit of taking Giles. Such is fame. No Thirty-third in this country. [The papers also said] Major *Cowley* not *Comly*, and so on. Well, all right. General Frémont complimented *me* for "energy and courage" and the Twenty-third for "gallantry" to this division. So it is all right.

Jim is here in our brigade (the Twelfth Regiment) looking very well. Dr. Joe well. Adjutant Avery is to take this to Raleigh only twenty miles off. We are connected by telegraph with you too, so we are near again for a season.

Affectionately,

R.

Show this to Steve [Stephenson].

Mrs. Hayes.

Camp Flat Top, May 21, 1862. Wednesday.—A warm, windy, threatening day. Drilled the regiment this morning; marched to the summit of Flat Top, thence along the summit to the Raleigh Road, and so back to camp. Men looked well. Companies A, E, and K, under Major Comly, with a howitzer, marched to Packs Ferry to hold it, build boats, and the like. They take about twenty carpenters from the Twenty-third, also six cavalrymen and a howitzer.

Camp Flat Top, May 22, 1862. Thursday. — Today Colonel Scammon with a small escort went over to Packs Ferry to look after affairs with Major Comly and his boat-builders. A Captain Jenkins, of Kentucky, came from General Williams to negotiate as to exchange of prisoners. General Cox detailed Lieutenant-Colonel Hines and myself to meet him. After some reflection, I suggested that it was honoring Captain Jenkins too much to send two lieutenant-colonels, and the programme was changed.

I have caught a bad cold, the worst I have had since I came into the army, caused chiefly by changing underclothes and stockings from thick to thin.

Called on Colonel Moor of the Twenty-eighth. The German officers are neater and more soldierly in dress and accoutrements than ours. The Twenty-eighth has a fine band, twenty or twenty-four musicians. Wrote to Lucy a short letter — no flow in it; but how I love my wife and boys! All the more tenderly for these separations.

CAMP FLAT TOP MOUNTAIN, May 22, 1862.

DEAREST: — I have written you one or two letters which I suspect fell into the hands of the enemy, but ere this, I do not doubt, you have received dispatches and word by Thomas which relieves you of all trouble on my account.

We have had a good deal of war this month. More than half the time during two weeks we were in the presence of the enemy. Most of the time they [we] were either pursuing them or they were crowding us. The number killed and wounded, considering the amount of firing, was not large. I suppose the total loss of this army would not exceed two hundred. Our force is not strong enough to do the work before us. We have so many points to garrison and so long a line of communications to protect, that it leaves a very small force to push on with. . . .

Before this reaches you, the great battles of the war will probably be fought. If successful, we shall not meet with much determined opposition hereafter. I was sent to meet a flag of truce sent by General Williams and Humphrey Marshall this morning. The officers talk in a high tone still, but the privates are discouraged, and would be gladly at home on any terms. . . .

Affectionately,

R.

MRS. HAYES.

Flat Top Mountain, May 23, 1862. Friday. — Warm and dry; getting dusty!! Mr. French lies here wounded — his thigh bone shattered by a ball that passed clear through his leg. Dr. McCurdy thinks he will not survive more than three or four weeks. . . . Our regiment elected him chaplain a week or two ago to date from the day of battle, May 1, 1862. I hope the Governor will commission [him] promptly. . . .

The *Commercial* is reported as saying that people may "act as if they had heard some very good news" from General Halleck's army.

It is dusty!! A cold wind blowing. The plan of going to Packs Ferry and crossing New River, uniting with Colonel Crook, and thence through Union to Christiansburg, is not yet fixed upon.

Flat Top Mountain, May 24, 1862. Saturday. — Cold, rainy, and windy, — an old-fashioned storm. Men bivouacking! Colonel Crook, of [the] Third Brigade, was attacked yesterday morning by General Heth with the same force which drove me out of Giles. Colonel Crook had parts or the whole of three regiments. He defeated Heth and captured four of his cannon. Our loss, ten killed and forty wounded. Enemy routed and one hundred prisoners. What an error that General Cox didn't attack Williams and Marshall at Princeton! Then *we* should have accomplished something.

CAMP FLAT TOP MOUNTAIN, May 24, 1862.

DEAR MOTHER: — I have written you twice this month, but am not sure as to your getting my letters. The enemy have captured some of our mails, and possibly your letters are in Secession. . . .

We are having pretty busy times in the mountains. One of our brigades, under Colonel Crook, gained an important victory over the Rebels under General Heth yesterday morning at Lewisburg, capturing cannon, etc., etc. We shall not remain long in the same place. Our force is not so large as that of the enemy, and we must make up the difference by activity. They are very sick of the contest, and if our great armies are successful, we shall soon be over the worst of the Rebellion. . . .

Affectionately, your son,

R.

MRS. SOPHIA HAYES.

Camp Flat Top Mountain, May 25, 1862. Sunday. — Bright, clear, and bracing. My cold no better yet, but no worse. I hope it has reached the turning-point. All suspense in military matters, awaiting result at Corinth and Richmond. The three Companies, A, E, and K of Twenty-third, sent to Packs Ferry were ordered in yesterday, as if much needed. They marched in the rain and darkness seventeen miles last night and six this morning; the severest trial they have had. It was too bad, too bad.

Sacred music by the band at sundown. Captain Evans, a Cincinnati boy of [the] Thirty-fourth Zouaves, called to see me. Queer people meet here. The Thirty-seventh and the Thirty-fourth (Zouaves) suffered badly in the skirmishing about Princeton. About sixty wounded (of ours) came up tonight, having been exchanged, from Princeton.

CAMP FLAT TOP MOUNTAIN, May 25, 1862.

DEAREST : — Dr. Joe has a letter from McCabe in which he speaks of your anxiety on my account. I hope that it has not been increased by my dispatch. You will always hear the precise truth from me. You may rely on it that you hear exactly the state of things. It would be idle to say that we have been in no danger, or that we are not likely to be in peril hereafter. But this is certain, that there is not half the danger for officers in a regiment that can be trusted to behave well, as there would be in a regiment of raw troops; besides, the danger on this line is much diminished by a victory which one of our brigades under Colonel Crook gained day before yesterday at Lewisburg. He routed the army under General Heth, which drove me out of Giles Court-house, captured their cannon, etc., etc. Now the drift is again all in our favor.

This is a lovely Sunday morning, after a cold storm of about thirty hours. It brings great relief to men bivouacking on the ground without tents, to have the sun shining out bright and warm. The weather, except two days, has been good this whole month. This is *the* department to spend the summer in — healthier and pleasanter than any other.

I received Uncle's letter written when he was with you. I am rather gratified to hear that you are not going to Fremont this summer. It pleases me that Uncle likes the boys so well. Dear little fellows, they must be so interesting. I think of them often.

We expect to move from here southward in a few days. Our army is under General Cox, and consists of the First Brigade, Twelfth, Twenty-third, and Thirtieth under Colonel Scammon; Second Brigade, Twenty-eighth, Thirty-seventh, and Thirty-fourth under Colonel Moor; Third Brigade, Eleventh, Thirty-sixth, Forty-fourth, and Forty-seventh under Colonel Crook, besides a due proportion of cavalry and artillery. It is a good army, but too small for the magnificent distances we have to operate over. We expect to be able to unite with Frémont's larger body in about three or four weeks. In the meantime, good luck at Richmond and Corinth may pretty nearly take away our occupation.

P. M. — Recent news indicate [indicates] that we shall see no enemy for some time. I believe I told you my *Commercial* has stopped again. Try to start it so it will hold out. It comes to subscribers here pretty regularly and promptly.

Tomorrow a couple of men leave here for Camp Chase with a prisoner. I shall send a Mississippi rifle with them. This is the most formidable weapon used against us in this region by the Rebels; they will leave it either with you or at Platt's in Columbus.

I enclose for Uncle a fifty-dollar bill. It was worth fifty dollars when I got it. I could buy a pretty fair horse with it.

Love to all the boys and kisses all round. Ever so much affection for your own dear self.

R.

Mrs. Hayes.

Camp Flat Top Mountain, May 26, 1862. Monday. — Clear and cool. A private dispatch informs General Cox that General

Banks has been driven back by the Rebel Jackson, probably to Harpers Ferry. This is a long move to the rear. If true, it indicates a pretty heavy disaster; places in jeopardy the Baltimore and Ohio Railroad, etc. So we go.

CAMP FLAT TOP, May 26, 1862.

DEAREST: — Your excellent letters of [the] 17th and 19th came this morning — only a week in getting to me. I wrote you yesterday by the soldiers, Corporal West and Harper, but I must give you another by the sutler who goes in the morning, just to show how much I think of you and your letters.

We are now at rest on a mountain top with no immediate prospect of anything stirring. We stand for the moment on the defensive, and are not likely to be disturbed. We have been having exchanges of wounded and prisoners with the enemy. They have behaved very well to our men, and were exceedingly civil and hospitable in our negotiations with them. They feel a good deal discouraged with the general prospect, but are crowding our small armies under Banks and Frémont pretty severely. All will be well if we carry the pivots at Richmond and Corinth. Enough of this.

I still feel just as I told you, that I shall come safely out of this war. I felt so the other day when danger was near. I certainly enjoyed the excitement of fighting our way out of Giles to the Narrows as much as any excitement I ever experienced. I had a good deal of anxiety the first hour or two on account of my command, but not a particle on my own account. After that, and after I saw we were getting on well, it was really jolly. We all joked and laughed and cheered constantly. Old Captain Drake said it was the best Fourth of July he ever had. I had in mind Theo. Wright singing "The Star-Spangled Banner." "The bombs bursting in air" began before it was quite light, and it seemed to me a sort of acting of the song, and in a pleasant way, the prayer would float through my thoughts, "In the dread hour of battle, O God, be thou nigh!"

A happy thing you did for the sick soldiers, good wife! *
"I love you so much." Well, that is all I wrote to tell you. I must repeat again, send the *Commercial* "for the war." Tell Webb Lieutenant Kennedy was delighted with the picture, and will try to send his to Webb some day. Send me one of all the boys if you get them — Webb's of course. I am much pleased that you are to stay in Cincinnati. Love to all the boys and Grandma. Send me by sutler *Harper* and *Atlantic* for June. Good-bye, dearest.

Affectionately ever,

R.

P. S. — I enclose you a letter which I wish Dr. Murphy [to read] or somebody to read to him. He behaves badly, I sus-

---

* Mrs. Hayes, in her letter of May 19, had written: "Our hospitals are all full of sick and wounded. A great difference can be seen between the sick and [the] wounded. The sick appear low-spirited — downcast, while the wounded are quite cheerful, hoping soon to be well. I felt right happy the other day, feeling that I had made some persons feel a little happier. Going down to Mrs. Herron's I passed four soldiers, two wounded and two sick. They were sitting on the pavement in front of the office where their papers are given to them. I passed them, and then thought, well, anyhow, I will go back and ask them where they are going. A gentleman who I saw then was with them, said he had just got in from Camp Dennison, and found they were too late to get their tickets for that evening. I asked, 'Where will you take them?' He said he did not know, but must get them to the nearest place, as they were very weak. I said, 'Doctor, (the wounded man had told me he was his family doctor and had come to take him home), if you will take them to my house I will gladly keep them and have them taken to the cars. There is the street-car which will take you near my house.' He was very thankful, and he put sick and wounded on, and I started them for Sixth Street, while I finished my errand, took the next car, and found my lame man hobbling slowly along. We fixed them in the back parlor. The doctor I asked to stay also, to attend to them. He said he could not thank me enough, that he was a stranger here and was almost bewildered as to what to do or where to take them. Mary was up early and we had a cup of coffee for them before five. I thought of you in a strange country, wounded and trying to get home. The cases were not exactly alike, but if anyone was kind to you, would I not feel thankful?"

pect. In short, darling, all men who manage to keep away from their regiments are to be suspected. They are *generally* rascals.

MRS. HAYES.

Flat Top, May 27, 1862. Tuesday. — A warm, fine day. My cold is still very bad. I call to see Mr. French, the wounded citizen of Lieutenant Bottsford's fight, now our Twenty-third chaplain, daily. He is in good spirits, but [the] doctors talk discouragingly of his case.

News today that General Halleck has taken Corinth and twenty thousand prisoners! Is it true? I hope so.

Flat Top, May 28, 1862. Wednesday. — No news yet from Corinth; none from Richmond; all in suspense yet. We almost fear to hear the news. Many rumors indicate that the Rebels are leaving Richmond. The gathering of great forces opposite to General Banks, and to Frémont all look that way. A large force is reported near Tazewell or at Tazewell, also. The air is full of rumors. The great events will soon clear the air, and we shall see where we are.

Flat Top, May 30, 1862. Friday. — A hot summer day. A very singular thing happened this afternoon. While we were at supper, 5:30 P. M., a thunder-storm broke out. It was pretty violent. Avery and Dr. McCurdy got up a warm discussion on electricity. As the storm passed away we all stepped out of the tent and began to discuss the height of the clouds, the lapse of time between the flash and the thunder. While we were talking, Avery having his watch out and I counting, there came a flash and report. It seemed to me that I was struck on the top of the head by something the size of a buckshot. Avery and McCurdy experienced a severe pricking sensation in the forehead. The sentinel near us was staggered as by a blow. Captain Drake's arm was nearly benumbed. My horse Webb (the sorrel) seemed hit. Over a hundred soldiers felt the stun or pricking. Five trees were hit about a hundred yards off and some of them badly splintered. In all the camps something similar was felt; but "no harm done."

The news not decisive but favorable. Lost a bet of twenty-five cents with Christie, Company C, that either Richmond or Corinth would be taken today.

May 31, 1862. Saturday. — Clear and bracing. Had a very satisfactory inspection on the hill back of General Cox's head-quarters. The men were many of them ragged and their clothes and caps faded, but they looked and marched like soldiers.

We hear of the retreat of Beauregard's great army from Corinth. This is probably a substantial victory, but is not so decisive as I hoped it would be. The Rebels have a talent for retreating. Our generals do not seem to be vigilant enough to prevent their slipping away. A thunder-storm last night.

CHAPTER XIX

HOLDING THE FRONT LINE — WEST VIRGINIA — JUNE-AUGUST 1862

*F*LAT TOP, *June 1, 1862.   Sunday.* — We got our new rifled muskets this morning.   They are mostly old muskets, many of them used, altered from flint-lock to percussion, rifled by Greenwood at Cincinnati.   We tried them on the hill one and a half miles east of camp, spending three hours shooting.   At two hundred yards about one shot in eight would have hit a man; at four hundred yards, or a quarter of a mile, about one shot in ten would have hit; at one-third to one-half mile, say seven hundred yards, about one shot in eighty would have hit.   The shooting was not remarkably accurate, but the power of the gun was fully as great as represented.   The ball at one-fourth mile passed through the largest rails; at one-half mile almost the same.   The hissing of the ball indicates its force and velocity. I think it an excellent arm.

Companies B and G went out to Packs Ferry to aid in building or guarding a boat, built to cross New River

Flat Top Mountain, June 2, 1862.   Monday. — A clear, hot, healthy summer day.   General McClellan telegraphs that he has had a "desperate battle"; a part of his army across the Chickahominy, is attacked "by superior numbers"; they "unaccountably break"; our loss heavy, the enemy's "must be enormous"; enemy "took advantage of the terrible storm."   All this is not very satisfactory.   General McClellan's right wing is caught on the wrong side of a creek raised by the rains, loses its "guns and baggage."   A great disaster is prevented; this is all, but it will demonstrate that the days of Bull Run are past.

FLAT TOP MOUNTAIN, June 3, 1862.

DEAREST: — I am made happy by your letter of the 24th and the picture of Webb. Enclosed I send Webb a letter from Lieutenant Kennedy.

I am not surprised that you have been some puzzled to make out our movements and position from the confused accounts you see in the papers. Our log-book would run about this way: Flat Top Mountain, twenty miles south of Raleigh, is the boundary line between America and Dixie — between western Virginia, either loyal or subdued, and western Virginia, rebellious and unconquered. [Here follows an account of the movements and activities of the regiment during May, which is a repetition in brief of previous letters and Diary entries.] Here we are safe as a bug in a rug — the enemy more afraid of us than we are of them — and *some* of us do fear them quite enough. My opinion was, we ought to have fought Marshall at Princeton, but it is not quite certain.

All our regiments have behaved reasonably well except [the] Thirty-fourth, Piatt's Zouaves, and Paxton's Cavalry. Don't abuse them, but they were pretty shabby. The zouaves were scattered seventy miles, reporting us all cut to pieces, etc., etc. Enough of war.

The misfortune of our situation is, we have not half force enough for our work. If we go forward the enemy can come in behind us and destroy valuable stores, cut off our supplies, and cut through to the Ohio River, — for we are not strong enough to leave a guard behind us.

We look with the greatest interest to the great armies. Banks' big scare will do good. It helps us to about fifty thousand new men. . . .

I nearly forgot to tell you how we were all struck by lightning on Saturday. We had a severe thunder-storm while at supper. We were outside of the tent discussing lightning — the rapidity of sound, etc., etc., Avery and Dr. McCurdy both facing me, Dr. Joe about a rod off, when there came a flash and shock and roar. The sentinel near us staggered but did not fall. Dr. McCurdy and Avery both felt a pricking sensation on the forehead.

I felt as if a stone had hit me in the head. Captain Drake's arm was benumbed for a few minutes. My horse was nearly knocked down. Some horses were knocked down. Five trees near by were hit, and perhaps one hundred men more or less shocked, but strange to say "nobody hurt."

All things still look well for a favorable conclusion to the war. I do not expect to see it ended so speedily as many suppose, but patience will carry us through.

I thought of you before I got up this morning, saying to myself, "Darling Lucy, I love you so much," and so I do.

Affectionately,

R.

Mrs. Hayes.

Flat Top Mountain, June 5, 1862. Thursday. — Rained most of the day. Want of exercise these rainy days begets indigestion, indigestion begets headache, blue devils, ill nature, sinister views, and general disgust. Brightened up a little by news that General Pope has taken ten thousand men and fifteen thousand stand of arms from Beauregard's retreating army. It looks as if Beauregard's army was breaking up. Later. News of the taking of Memphis and Fort Pillow.

General Cox read me a letter from General Garfield in which he speaks of the want of sympathy among army officers with the cause of the war; that they say Seward, Chase, and Sumner are more to blame than Davis and Toombs! General Sherman said he was "ashamed to acknowledge that he had a brother (Senator John Sherman) who was one of these damned Black Republicans"!

These semi-traitors must be watched. — Let us be careful who become army leaders in the reorganized army at the end of the Rebellion. The man who thinks that the perpetuity of slavery is essential to the existence of the Union, is unfit to be trusted. The deadliest enemy the Union has is slavery — in fact, its only enemy.

FLAT TOP MOUNTAIN, June 5, 1862.

SIR:—Colonel Little wishes to procure the release of James McKenzie, of Mercer County, Virginia, now a prisoner of war at Columbus. McKenzie was taken by Lieutenant Bottsford, Company C, Twenty-third Regiment, at the time of the fight at Clark's house, May 1. Colonel Little says he knows McKenzie was always a Union man, and believes his assertion that he joined the militia under compulsion, that he intended to desert to our forces, and at Clark's availed himself of the first opportunity to do so. I therefore recommend that steps be taken to procure the release of McKenzie.

Respectfully,

R. B. HAYES,
LIEUTENANT-COLONEL 23D REGIMENT O. V. I.,
COMMANDING.

COLONEL E. P. SCAMMON,
COMMANDING FIRST BRIGADE.

Flat Top Mountain, June 6, 1862. Friday. — Rained a great part of the night; a cold, foggy morning; but I feel vigorous and well. . . . I climbed to the top of the mountain to the right of the camp through the wet bushes and fog and feel the better for it. We have scarcely tents enough for the officers. The men build shelters of bark, rail pens, and the like. I call this "Woodchuck Camp." Our new chaplain, Russell G. French, is gaining strength and will probably recover. There is a loose piece of bone still in his leg, but it does not seem to distress him a great deal. Five of Company C were either killed or have died of their wounds received in the recent fight at Camp Creek.

Flat Top Mountain, June 7, 1862. Friday [Saturday] A. M. — Still cloudy with hopes of clearing off. This has been a bad storm, lasting almost a week. No prospect of moving yet. Read the "Bride of Lammermoor." — I don't like the conclusion of it —lame and impotent.

Flat Top Mountain, June 8, 1862. Sunday. — A bitterly cold morning — too cold to snow! Gradually warmed up. P. M. rode with Avery four or five miles. Our horses rested and fed up were in high spirits. We are all heartily tired of staying here. When shall we go? — Dear Lucy, I think of her very often these dull days. It looks as if the war would soon be ended, and then we shall be together again.

Flat Top Mountain, June 9, 1862. Monday. — Still cold weather. . . . Heard of the taking of Memphis after a battle of gunboats lasting an hour and twenty minutes. As reported it was a brilliant victory.

Flat Top Mountain, June 10, 1862. Tuesday. — Still cold. A month ago we were driven out of Giles. Over three weeks of inaction! No news for two or three days either from McClellan or Halleck. Frémont is pushing ahead with energy.

Flat Top Mountain, June 12, 1862. Thursday. — A warm, bright, seasonable morning. Heard of Frémont's battle near Port Republic. As yet doubtful as to the result; shall look anxiously for the next news. . . . The battle before Richmond looks better, the more we see of it.

CAMP ON FLAT TOP, VIRGINIA, June 12, 1862.

DEAREST: — I began a letter to you yesterday intending to finish it after the mail came in; I can't find it. No loss. I recollect I told you to [give] Mrs. Sergeant McKinley ten dollars on account of the sergeant, which please to do. I probably also said that up on this mountain the weather is colder than Nova Zembla, and that since the enemy left us we have been in a state of preparation to go ahead — which means do-nothingness, so far as soldiers are concerned. I have now an expedition out under Major Comly, not important enough for a regimental commander, so I am here in inglorious idleness.

A day's life runs about thus: — At 5 A. M., one or the other of our two Giles County contrabands, Calvin or Samuel, comes in hesitatingly and in a modest tone suggests, "Gentlemen, it is 'most breakfast time." About ten minutes later, finding no results from his first summons, he repeats, perhaps with some slight variation. This is kept up until we get up to breakfast, that is to say, sometimes cold biscuits, cooked at the hospital, sometimes army bread, tea and coffee, sugar, sometimes milk, fried pork, sometimes beef, and any "pison" or fraudulent truck in the way of sauce or pickles or preserves (!) (good peaches sometimes), which the sutler may chance to have. After breakfast there is a little to be done; then a visit of half an hour to brigade headquarters, Colonel Scammon's; then a visit to division ditto, General Cox's, where we gossip over the news, foreign and domestic (all outside of our camps being foreign, the residue domestic), then home again, and novel reading is the chief thing till dinner. I have read "Ivanhoe," "Bride of Lammermoor," and [one] of Dickens' and one of Fielding's the last ten days.

P. M., generally ride with Avery from five to ten miles; and as my high-spirited horse has no other exercise, and as Carrington (Company C boy) is a good forager and feeds him tip-top, the way we go it is locomotive-like in speed. After this, more novel reading until the telegraphic news and mails, both of which come about the same hour, 5:30 P. M. Then gossip on the news and reading newspapers until bedtime — early bedtime, 9 P. M. We have music, company drills, — no room for battalion drills in these mountains, — and target practice with other little diversions and excitements, and so "wags the world away."

We get Cincinnati papers in from four to six days. My *Commercial* is running again. Keep it going. Write as often as you can. I think of you often and with so much happiness; then I run over the boys in my mind — Birt, Webb, Ruddy. The other little fellow I hardly feel acquainted with yet, but the other three fill a large place in my heart.

Keep up good heart. It is all coming out right. There will be checks and disappointments, no doubt, but the work goes forwards. We are much better off than I thought a year ago we should be. — A year ago! Then we were swearing the men in at Camp Chase. Well, we think better of each other than we did then, and are very jolly and friendly.

"I love you s'much." Love to all.

Affectionately,

R.

Since writing this we have heard of Frémont's battle the other side of the Alleghanies in the Valley of Virginia. It will probably set us a-going again southward. — H.

MRS. HAYES.

Camp Jones, Flat Top, June 15, 1862. Sunday. — Had our first dress parade in five or six weeks last night. No room or opportunity for it this side of Princeton, May 5. . . . Wrote to General Hill requesting the commissions of Russell G. French and Martin V. Ritter. Red-tape is a great nuisance unless everybody acts with promptness and accuracy in all departments. This we know will not be done. Red-tape must therefore be cut or important rights and interests [suffer].

CAMP ON FLAT TOP MOUNTAIN, June 15, 1862.

DEAR MOTHER: — It is a beautiful Sunday morning. We are on the summit of a range of mountains, perhaps one-third to half a mile high, giving us extensive views of mountains and valleys for thirty or forty miles south, east, and west of us. The nights are cool, often cold, and the brisk breezes make even the hottest part of the day agreeable. We are exceedingly healthy and with just enough to do to keep blood circulating, and occasionally a little flowing.

I hear from home very often, letters usually reaching me about seven days after they are written. I am rather glad that Lucy will remain in Cincinnati this summer. By next summer the war will, perhaps, be ended and we can all spend it in Fremont together. The boys seem to be doing well in the city and can afford to wait.

I hope Uncle's health is again as good as usual. It will not surprise me if he goes up to seventy as you have [done]. It does n't seem such a great age as it once did. You are no older, or but little older, as I think of you, than you were many years ago. — My love to Laura and all.

Affectionately, your son,

R. B. HAYES,

MRS. SOPHIA HAYES.

Camp Jones, Flat Top, June 16, 1862. Monday. — A cold morning and a cloudy, clearing off into a bright, cool day.

Last night walked with Captain Warren down to General Cox's headquarters. Talked book; the general is a reader of the best books, quite up in light literature; never saw the Shakespeare novels; must try to get him "Shakespeare and his Friends." . . .

The extracts from Richmond papers and Jeff Davis' address to the soldiers indicates that the Rebels are making prodigious efforts to secure the victory in the approaching struggle. I trust our Government will see that every man is there who can possibly be spared from other quarters. I fear part of Beauregard's army will get there. Can't we get part of Halleck's army there?

Camp Jones, Flat Top Mountain, June 19, 1862. Thursday. — Cold, dull, and P. M., rainy. Drilled A. M. Rode with Adjutant Avery and practiced pistol firing in the P. M.

Lieutenant-Colonel Paxton of the cavalry called to see me about Lieutenant Fordyce. Would he do for captain? Is he not too fond of liquor? My reply was favorable. He says he has three vacancies in the regiment. Captain Waller seduced Colonel Burgess' daughter; had to resign in consequence. I recommended both Avery and Bottsford for captains of cavalry; both would make good captains. Only one will probably be commissioned. While I dislike to lose either, I feel they are entitled to promotion and are not likely to get it here.

Ditto, Ditto, June 20, 1862. Friday. — Cold and wet. We wear overcoats, sit by fires in front of tents, and sleep under blankets! Had a very satisfactory drill. Am reading "St. Ronan's Well." Rode down the mountain towards New River On returning found R. S. Gardner giving a blow-out on receiving news of his appointment as captain and quartermaster. Lieutenant-Colonel Paxton, Bottsford, and Lieutenant Christie, of General Cox's staff, all a little "how-come-ye-so." . . .

Camp Jones, Flat Top, June 21, 1862. —. . . Rather agreeable social evenings with the officers at my quarters, the band enlivening us with its good music.

Dr. McCurdy having been appointed inspector of hospitals for this division, we had a Dr. Hudson, of Medina, a new state surgeon, assigned to us as assistant surgeon in Dr. McCurdy's place. Dr. Hudson turns out to be a thin-skinned, nervous, whimsical, whining Yankee. He has just heard of the death of a favorite daughter. His grief loses all respectability, coupled as it is with his weaknesses and follies. We agreed today with Dr. Holmes (the medical head man) to swap our Dr. Hudson "unsight, unseen" for any spare doctor he could turn out. We find we caught a Dr. Barrett, lately of Wooster, a young man of good repute. We take him, pleased well with the bargain.

CAMP JONES, FLAT TOP MOUNTAIN, June 21, 1862.

DEAR UNCLE: — We have been here and hereabouts almost a month. Our line of defense extends twenty to thirty miles from New River southwesterly along a mountain range. We have mountain weather. If the wind happens to lull when the sun shines we get a taste of summer heat. At all other times it is very cold. We have fires, wear overcoats, and sleep under winter blankets every night. Our men from the lake shore say it is very much like April and May weather in the neighborhood of home. The men are very healthy; not over a dozen or so unfit for duty out of eight hundred. We have frequent reconnaisances and scouting expeditions against the enemy, not amounting to any great matter. We have not seen or heard of a guerrilla in these mountains since we passed here about the first of May. We get and meet parties of the enemy occasionally, but they are regular soldiers. We suppose the savage treatment administered when we went across a month ago finished bushwhacking in this vicinity. We do not expect any important movement until the event at Richmond is known. Then, whatever the result, we expect to be busy enough.

Soon after we came on to this mountain, I caught a bad cold — the worst I have had in some years. Since I have been in camp I had not had a severe cold before. It held on two weeks, but is now nearly gone without doing any mischief.

Both sides appear to be fighting well in all parts of Virginia now. It seems to be reduced pretty nearly to a question of numbers — I mean, of course, numbers of *drilled* soldiers. I do not reckon the enemy's recent conscripts nor our own new regiments as amounting to much yet. It seems therefore as if, with the superior numbers which we ought to have at the critical points, we would crush them out during the next six weeks in Virginia. Virginia gone, with what the Rebels have already lost, and the Rebellion is a plain failure. But I think we shall need *all* our soldiers a long time after that. I hope we shall not be needed another winter, but I greatly suspect we shall.

Sincerely,

R. B. Hayes.

S. Birchard.

"Same as before," June 22, 1862. *Sunday.* — A warm, beautiful, Sunday morning; all things bright and cheerful. Inklings and hints of matters before Richmond are more encouraging. But these delays of McClellan are very wearisome.

Ditto, Ditto, June 25, 1862. Wednesday. — Dined with General Cox. He has a plan of operations for the Government forces which I like: To hold the railroad from Memphis through Huntsville, Chattanooga, Knoxville [and] southwest Virginia to Richmond; not attempt movements south of this except by water until after the hot and sickly season. This line is distant from the enemy's base of supplies; can therefore by activity be defended, and gives us a good base.

Camp Jones, Flat Top Mountain, June 27, 1862. Friday. — Took the men to Glade Creek to wash. Water getting scarce in this quarter. The men danced to the fiddle, marched to music, and had a good time generally. Rode, walked, and read "Seven Sons of Mammon."

Read the account of the disaster on White River, Arkansas, to the gunboat, Mound City. The enemy sent a forty-two-pound ball through her boiler and a horrible slaughter followed, scalding and drowning one hundred and fifty men!

General Pope appointed to "the Army of Virginia" — being the combined forces of Frémont, Shields, Banks, and McDowell, now in the Valley of Virginia. Sorry to see Frémont passed over but glad the concentration under one man has taken place. General Pope is impulsive and hasty, but energetic, and, what is of most importance, patriotic and sound — *perfectly sound.* I look for good results. — Rained in the evening.

Camp Jones, June 28, 1862 — . . . Spent the evening with General Cox. He gave me some curious items about the last campaign from the diary of an officer of the Rebel army.

We hear General Pope is to command the Army of Virginia and that Frémont has, on his own request, been relieved from the command of [the] First Army Corps. — Sorry Frémont is so cuffed about, but am glad one mind is to control the movements in the Valley.

We have rumors of "tremendous fighting" before Richmond; that we have achieved a success, etc., etc. What suspense until the truth is known!

FLAT TOP MOUNTAIN, June 30, 1862.

DEAREST: — I write by Captain Gardner, who having been promoted to captain in [the] quartermaster's department, now leaves our regiment. I send a package of your letters, some Secesh letters, etc., etc. I do not wish to lose the letters and official documents, and send them to you for safety.

"We are well and doing well at this present time and hope these few lines will find you enjoying the same blessing." Why, that is a good letter. No wonder the uninitiated ride that formula so hard. It says a great deal. . . .

As ever, affectionately, your

R.

MRS. HAYES.

Camp Jones, July 1, 1862. Tuesday. — Cloudy and rainy. Our water on this mountain top is giving out. Avery and I rode six miles towards New River in the rain but could find no good camping ground where water could be had. This rain will perhaps give us enough here again.

Nothing definite from Richmond. There was some fighting and an important change of position on Friday. There are rumors of disaster and also of the burning of Richmond, but telegraphic communication is reported cut off between Washington and McClellan. This is the crisis of the Nation's destiny. If we are beaten at Richmond, foreign intervention in the form perhaps of mediation is likely speedily to follow. If successful, we are on the sure road to an early subjugation of the Rebels. The suspense is awful. It can't last long. — Night; raining steadily.

Camp Jones, July 2, 1862. Tuesday [Wednesday]. — Rained all night; weather cold. Water must again be abundant. Gradually cleared off about 3 or 4 P. M.

Dispatches state that McClellan has swung his right wing around and pushed his left towards James River, touching the river at Turkey Island, fifteen miles from Richmond. Is this a voluntary change of plan, or is it a movement forced by an attack? These questions find no satisfactory response in the dispatches. Some things look as if we had sustained a reverse. (1.) It is said the move was "necessitated by an attack in great force on Thursday." (2.) All communication with Washington was cut off for two or three days. (3.) We have had repeated reports that the enemy had turned our right wing. (4.) The singular denial of rumors that our army had sustained a defeat, viz., that "no information received indicated a serious disaster." (5.) The general mystery about the movement.

It may have been according to a change of plan. I like the new position. If we are there uninjured, with the aid of gunboats and transports on James River, we ought soon to cripple the enemy at Richmond.

Camp Jones, July 3, 1862. Wednesday [Thursday]. — A fine bright day. General Cox is trying to get our army transferred to General Pope's command in eastern Virginia.

The dispatches received this beautiful afternoon fill me with sorrow. We have an obscure account of the late battle or battles at Richmond. There is an effort to conceal the extent of the disaster, but the impression left is that McClellan's grand army has been defeated before Richmond!! *If so, and the enemy is active and energetic,* they will drive him out of the Peninsula, gather fresh energy everywhere, and push us to the wall in all directions. Foreign nations will intervene and the Southern Confederacy be established.

Now for courage and clear-headed sagacity. Nothing else will save us. Let slavery be destroyed and this sore disaster may yet do good.

Flat Top, July 4, 1862. Friday. — A fine day. No demonstrations in camp except a National salute and a little drunkenness. Quietness of the Sabbath reigned.

The *Commercial* of the first puts a different face on the news of McClellan's recent movements near Richmond. The change of position seems to have been well planned — a wise change — and it is not certain that any disaster befell us during its execution. There was fierce fighting and heavy loss, but it is quite possible that the enemy suffered more than we did.

My orderly, Gray, good old veteran Irish soldier, "drunk and disorderly" yesterday. All right; he shall be released today.

July 5, 1862. Saturday. — A fine, warm day. I rode with Avery and an escort of twelve dragoons under Captain Harrison (a Union doctor of Monroe County), to look for a new camping ground, ten or twelve miles from here, at or near Jumping Branch, on the pike leading from Raleigh to Packs Ferry. The village last winter was the rendezvous of the enemy who were threatening Raleigh and was burnt, except two or three houses, by Major Comly to get rid of the nest. We dined with an intelligent Union farmer, a Mr. Upton, whose house was spared. A good spring for the men's use and a tolerable stream for the animals and washing. But no camping ground which we would take in exchange for Flat Top as long as water can be got here.

While at Mr. Upton's, we heard from an artilleryman that after we left camp news was received at headquarters that McClellan had entered Richmond yesterday! Prior advices led us strongly to hope, almost to believe, it was true. We all said we believed it. How suddenly McClellan loomed up into a great general — a future (not distant future) President! We thought of a speedy end of the war and a return home; of the loved ones' happiness at home! I could toast McClellan, "slow but sure," "better late than never," and the like.

On reaching camp our hopes were cruelly dashed. The only dispatches received, meagre, ambiguous, and obscure, indicate disaster rather than victory! That after six days' hard fighting McClellan has lost fifteen to twenty thousand [men] and is twenty or thirty miles further distant from Richmond than when the battle began! No disaster is told other than this; but if it is true that he has been beaten back to a point thirty-five or forty miles from Richmond, we are where I feared we were on the third. But these dispatches are so deceptive as to complicated and extensive movements that I must hear further before I give up to such gloomy anticipations. But I am anxious!

Camp Jones, Flat Top Mountain, July 6, 1862. Sunday. —
. . . It seems on reflection that McClellan has been forced back in seven days — six of them days of fighting — about fifteen to twenty-five miles; that he has probably not lost very heavily in artillery or stores; that the weight of the attacks on him have [has] been too heavy and have [has] forced him back. Well, then, our columns must be rapidly made heavier. We shall see!
. . . Nothing new from Richmond today. What is the condition there? Is our army merely pushed back by superior numbers or has it been defeated?

FLAT TOP MOUNTAIN, July 6, 1862.

DEAREST: — Sunday afternoon about 4 P. M. — hotter than ever. I have just finished reading your letter written last Sunday at Chillicothe. I am very glad you are so happily *homed* at Uncle Scott's. It is far better up on that beautiful hill with such kind friends, young and old, than in a hot and dirty city. You cannot think oftener of me than I do of you and the dear ones around you; no, nor more lovingly.

I knew you would be troubled when Frémont was relieved from duty, and perhaps still more when you hear of McClellan's repulse before Richmond. These things appear to postpone the termination of the war; but are such disasters as must be looked for in such a contest. We must make up our minds that we have a heavy work, and that reverses must frequently occur.

We have no right to complain of our lot. We have a beautiful and healthy camp, with the enemy in front, strong enough to keep us busy holding our position, without much danger of losing it. It is the common opinion that if the reverse before Richmond has been serious, we shall be sent to eastern Virginia, and I may add that it is the universal wish that we may see some of the movements that are going on there.

Drs. Joe and Jim are both very well and with little to do. Our loss by sickness during the last three months is only three.

Dr. Joe and I sent early in June to your address nine hundred and fifty dollars. Did you get it? It is important we should know if it has failed to reach you. As letters miscarry sometimes, be sure to speak of it in two or three letters.

I got from Mr. Stephenson a *Harper* and *Atlantic* for July today. All reading matter is in the greatest demand. . . .

It is not of much consequence to Boggs whether he returns or not; yet he ought to be allowed to do it. If a soldier is well enough to be a nurse he can be useful with his regiment. If he can neither nurse nor march, he can get his pay or a discharge easier here than elsewhere. But we will do our best for the man.

Think of it, the Fourth was a lovely day but we sat around a fire in the evening and slept under blanket and coverlid. . . .

Good-bye, darling. Don't get downhearted about the war and our separation. It will all come right, and then how happy we shall be — happier than if we had not known this year's experience.

Affectionately ever, your

R.

Mrs. Hayes.

Camp Jones, Flat Top, July 7, 1862. Monday. — The warmest day of the season. The men are building great bowers over their company streets, giving them roomy and airy shelters. At evening they dance under them, and in the daytime they drill in the bayonet exercise and manual of arms. All wish to remain in this camp until some movement is begun which will show us the enemy, or the way out of this country. We shall try to get water by digging wells.

The news of today looks favorable. McClellan seems to have suffered no defeat. He has changed front; been forced (perhaps) to the rear, sustained heavy losses; but his army is in good condition, and has probably inflicted as much injury on the enemy as it has suffered. This is so much better than I anticipated that I feel relieved and satisfied. The taking of Richmond is postponed, but I think it will happen in time to forestall foreign intervention.

There is little or no large game here. We see a great many striped squirrels (chipmunks), doves, quails, a few pigeons and pheasants, and a great many rattlesnakes. I sent Birch the rattles of a seventeen-year-old yesterday. They count three years for the button and a year for each rattle.

There is a pretentious headboard in the graveyard between here and headquarters with the inscription "Anna Eliza Brammer, *borned* ——"

Camp Jones, July 8, 1862. Tuesday. — A fine breezy day on this mountain top. Bathed three miles from here in Glade Creek. I find this sitting still or advancing age (good joke!) is getting me into old gentlemen's habits. My breath is shorter than it used to be; I get tired easier and the like.

Very little additional from Richmond, but that little is encouraging. Our forces have not, I think, been discouraged or in any degree lost confidence, by reason of anything that has occurred before Richmond. Our losses are not greater than the enemy's — probably not so great. The Rebel reports here are that our loss is thirty-eight thousand killed and wounded and two thousand prisoners; that *they* left fourteen thousand dead on the field! This is all wild guessing; but it indicates dreadful and probably nearly equal losses on both sides.

July 10, 1862. Thursday.—. . . I wrote this morning a cheerful letter to Mother. I think often these days of the sad loss six years ago; my dear, dear sister, — so —. But it is perhaps for the best. How she would suffer during this struggle!

I have just read the *Commercial's* story of the six days' battles. What dreadful fighting, suffering, weariness, and exhaustion were there! The letters in the paper of the 5th are agonizing in the extreme. The telegraphic news diminishes our loss in the battles before Richmond, and gives, I think, exaggerated reports of the enemy's loss. They are said to have lost from thirty to sixty thousand!!

FLAT TOP MOUNTAIN, July 10, 1862.

DEAR MOTHER: — I think you would enjoy being here. We have a fine cool breeze during the day; an extensive mountain scene, always beautiful but changing daily, almost hourly. The men are healthy, contented, and have the prettiest and largest bowers over the whole camp I ever saw. They will never look so well or behave so well in any settled country. Here the drunkards get no liquor, or so little that they regain the healthy complexion of temperate men. Every button and buckle is burnished bright, and clothes brushed or washed clean. I often think that if mothers could see their boys as they often look in this mountain wilderness, they would feel prouder of them than ever before. We have dancing in two of the larger bowers from soon after sundown until a few minutes after nine o'clock. By half-past nine all is silence and darkness. At sunrise the men are up, drilling until breakfast. Occasionally the boys who play the female partners in the dances exercise their ingenuity in dressing to look as girlish as possible. In the absence of lady duds they use leaves, and the leaf-clad beauties often look very pretty and always odd enough.

We send parties into the enemy's lines which sometimes have strange adventures. A party last Sunday, about forty miles from here, found a young Scotchman and two sisters, one eighteen and the other fourteen, their parents dead, who have been unable to escape from Rebeldom. They have property in Scotland and would give anything to get to "the States." One officer took one girl on his horse behind him and another, another, and so escaped. They were fired on by bushwhackers, the elder lady thrown off, but not much hurt. They were the happiest girls you ever saw when they reached our camp. They are now safe on the way to Cincinnati, where they have a brother.

We are expecting one of these days to be sent to eastern Virginia, if all we hear is true.

I have just received an invitation to Rogers' wedding. If you see him or his bride tell them I regret I shall not be able to be at Columbus on the first of this month. . . . Love to all.

Affectionately, your son,

R. B. Hayes.

Mrs. Sophia Hayes,
   Columbus, Ohio.

Flat Top Mountain, July 11, 1862. Thursday [Friday]. — Wrote to Platt about promotion to colonelcy in one of the new regiments. I would dislike to leave the Twenty-third under any circumstances and would not be willing to do it to be taken from active service. But I certainly wish the command of a regiment before the war closes.

Today, to my surprise, Rev. A. Wilson made his appearance. He could not get his pay on the pay sheets furnished because there was no certificate of his resignation having been accepted. He was directed to return to the regiment by General Frémont's adjutant-general. So he came. One of the men, seeing him, said to me with a knowing look: "Have you any chickens in your coop, Colonel?" A pretty reputation for a chaplain truly! — A fine rain last night and this forenoon.

July 12, 1862. Saturday. — Received orders today to move to Green Meadows tomorrow. It is said to be a fine camping place, and although our present camp is the prettiest I have ever seen, we are glad for the sake of change to leave it.

Camp Green Meadwos, July 13, 1862. Sunday. — Struck tents this morning on Flat Top at 5 A. M. and marched to this place, reaching here at 11:30 A. M., fourteen miles; a jolly march down the mountain under a hot sun. Many sore feet.

Band played its lively airs; the men cheered, and all enjoyed the change. We are east of Camp Jones and about three miles from the mouth of Bluestone River and New River, within six miles of camp at Packs Ferry on New River. The camp being one thousand to fifteen hundred feet lower than Flat Top is warmer. We shall learn how to bear summer weather here. Our waggons arrived about 6:30 P. M. We relieved here two companies of the Thirtieth under Captain Gross. I command here six companies Twenty-third, Captain Gilmore's Cavalry, a squad of Second Virginia, a squad of McMullen's Battery, and a squad on picket of Captain Harrison's Cavalry.

Ditto, July 14, 1862. Monday. — I rode today with Captain Gilmore and Avery to the mouth of Bluestone and a ford on New River. The pickets are so placed that an enterprising enemy would by crossing New River and passing by mountain paths to their rear, cut them off completely.

CAMP GREEN MEADOWS, July 14, 1862.

DEAREST: — I am so pleased with your affectionate letter, that I sit down merely to "jaw back," as the man said of the responses in the Episcopal service.

I love you just as much as you love me. There now! Yes, dearest, this separation so painful does, I think, make us both dearer and better. I certainly prize you more than ever before, and am more solicitous about your happiness. . . .

We came here yesterday. It is a fine camp, but warm and summery compared with Flat Top. There is no noticeable scenery in view from camp, but we are near New River at the mouth of Bluestone River where the scenery is truly grand. I rode down there this morning to enjoy it. We marched fifteen miles yesterday — the happiest gang of men you ever saw. We are nearer the enemy, and have more of the excitement incident to such a position than at Flat Top. I am in command here, having six companies of the Twenty-third, Captain Gilmore's Cavalry (the men who behaved so well when we fought our way out of Giles), and a section of McMullen's Artillery, besides two squads of First and Second Virginia Cavalry. Everyone seems to be happy that we are out by ourselves. Besides, Major Comly with the other four companies Twenty-third is only five miles from us.

Drs. Joe and Jim are still at Flat Top. Dr. Joe will join us in a day or two. Colonel Scammon is not expected here to stay.

I sent off Captain Drake and two companies with a squad of cavalry just now to effect a diversion in favor of Colonel Crook who is threatened by a force said to be superior to his own. The captain is instructed to dash over and "lie like a bulletin" as to the immense force of which he is the advance and then to run back "double-quick." Risky but exciting.

Richmond is not so bad as it was. Our men, *certainly,* and our general, *perhaps,* did admirably there. . . . Don't worry about the country. "It's no good." We can't help it if things go wrong. We do our part and I am confident all will come right. We can't get rid of the crime of centuries without suffering. So, good-bye, darling.

Lovingly, as ever,

R.

Mrs. Hayes.

Green Meadows, July 15, 1862. Tuesday. — Captain Drake with Companies H and I returned this morning. The mounted men crossed the ford just above Bluestone on New River. The water was too deep and current too strong for footmen. They (the horsemen) called at Landcraft's, Young's, etc., etc. They learned that the only enemy now in Monroe is probably the Forty-fifth [Virginia], some cavalry, and artillery; and they have withdrawn from the river towards Centreville or some other distant part of the county. All others gone to or towards the Narrows or railroad.

At 9 o'clock I took four companies, A, C, E, and K, and the band and went to Packs Ferry. There the men went in swimming. Crossed 262 of them in the flying bridge — an affair like this [a crude pen sketch is given] — which swings from side to side of the river by force of the current alone. The bow (whichever way the boat goes) is pulled by means of a windlass up the stream at a small angle. The men enjoyed the spree.

We returned at 6:30 P. M. The scenery is of the finest; the river is a beautiful clear river. Strange, no fish except catfish, but they are of superior quality and often of great size.

The enemy shows signs of activity in Tennessee again. Our men will have a hard time during the next two or three months trying to hold their conquests. We will have our day when cold weather and high water return, not before. About Richmond there is much mystery, but supposed to be favorable.

Camp Green Meadows, July 16, 1862. Wednesday. — A warm, beautiful day. The men busy building shades (bowers or arbors) over their streets and tents, cleaning out the springs, and arranging troughs for watering horses, washing, and bathing. The water is excellent and abundant.

I read "Waverley," finishing it. The affection of Flora McIvor for her brother and its return is touching; they were orphans. And oh, this is the anniversary of the death of my dear sister Fanny — six years ago! I have thought of her today as I read Scott's fine description, but till now it did not occur to me that this was the sad day. Time has softened the pain. How she would have suffered during this agonizing war! Perhaps it was best — but what a loss!

Camp Green Meadows, Mercer County, Virginia,

July 17, 1862.

Dear Uncle: — . . . I am not satisfied that so good men as two-thirds of this army should be kept idle. New troops could hold the strong defensive positions which are the keys of the Kanawha Valley, while General Cox's eight or ten good regiments could be sent where work is to be done.

Barring this idea of duty, no position could be pleasanter than the present. I have the Twenty-third Regiment, half a battery, and a company of cavalry under my command stationed on the edge of Dixie — part of us here, fourteen miles, and part at Packs Ferry, nineteen miles from Flat Top, and Colonel Scammon's and General Cox's headquarters. This is pleasant. Then, we have a lovely camp, copious cold-water springs, and the lower camp is on the banks of New River, a finer river than the Connecticut at Northampton, with plenty of canoes, flat-boats, and good fishing and swimming. The other side of the river is enemy's country. We cross foraging parties daily to their side. They do not cross to ours, but are constantly threatening it. We moved here last Sunday, the 13th. On the map you will see our positions in the northeast corner of Mercer County on New River, near the mouth of and north of Bluestone River. Our camps five miles apart — Major Comly commands at the river, I making my headquarters here on the hill. We have pickets and patrols connecting us. I took the six companies to the river, with music, etc., etc., to fish and swim Tuesday.

It is now a year since we entered Virginia. What a difference it makes! Our camp is now a pleasanter place with its bowers and contrivances for comfort than even Spiegel Grove. And it takes no ordering or scolding to get things done. A year ago if a little such work was called for, you would hear grumblers say: "I didn't come to dig and chop, I could do that at home. I came to fight," etc., etc. Now springs are opened, bathing places built, bowers, etc., etc., got up as naturally as corn grows. No sickness either — about eight hundred and fifteen to eight hundred and twenty men — none seriously sick and only eight or ten excused from duty. All this is very jolly.

We have been lucky with our little raids in getting horses, cattle, and prisoners. Nothing important enough to blow about, although a more literary regiment would fill the newspapers out of less material. We have lost but one man killed and one taken prisoner during this month. There has been some splendid running by small parties occasionally. Nothing but the enemy's fear of being ambushed saved four of our officers last Saturday. So far as our adversaries over the river goes, they treat our men taken prisoners very well. The Forty-fifth, Twenty-second, Thirty-sixth, and Fifty-first Virginia are the enemy's regiments opposed to us. They know us and we know them perfectly well. Prisoners say their scouts hear our roll-calls and that all of them enjoy our music.

There are many discouraging things in the present aspect of affairs, and until frost in October, I expect to hear of disasters

20

in the Southwest. It is impossible to maintain our conquests in that quarter while the low stage of water and the sickness compel us to act on the defensive, but if there is no powerful intervention by foreign powers, we shall be in a condition next December to push them to the Gulf and the Atlantic before winter closes. Any earlier termination, I do not look for.

Two years is an important part of a man's life in these fast days, but I shall be content if I am mustered out of service at the end of two years from enlistment. — Regards to all.

Sincerely,

R. B. HAYES.

S. BIRCHARD.

Camp Green Meadows, July 18, 1862. Friday. — Rained last night and drizzled all this morning. . . . I feel dourish today; inaction is taking the soul out of us.

I am really jolly over the Rebel Morgan's raid into the blue-grass region of Kentucky. If it turns out a mere raid, as I suppose it will, the thing will do great good. The twitter into which it throws Cincinnati and Ohio will aid us in getting volunteers. The burning and destroying the property of the old-fashioned, conservative Kentuckians will wake them up, will stiffen their sinews, give them backbone, and make grittier Union men of them. If they should burn Garrett Davis' house, he will be sounder on confiscation and the like. In short, if it does not amount to an uprising, it will be a godsend to the Union cause. It has done good in Cincinnati already. It has committed numbers who were sliding into Secesh to the true side. Good for Morgan, as I understand the facts at this writing!

Had a good drill. The exercise and excitement drove away the blues. After drill a fine concert of the glee club of Company A. As they sang "That Good Old Word, Good-bye," I thought of the pleasant circle that used to sing it on Gulf Prairie, Brazoria County, Texas. And now so broken! And my classmate and friend, Guy M. Bryan — where is he? In the Rebel army! As honorable and true as ever, but a Rebel! What strange and sad things this war produces! But he is true and patriotic wherever he is. Success to him personally!

July 19. Saturday. — Some rain. Ride with Quartermaster Reichenbach to the scene of [the] Jumping Branch fight. Read with a good deal of levity the accounts of John Morgan's raid into the blue-grass region of Kentucky. It strikes me that the panic and excitement caused in Cincinnati and Indiana will stimulate recruiting; that Secesh sentiment just beginning to grow insolent in Ohio will be crushed out, and indirectly that it will do much good. All this is on the assumption that Morgan is routed, captured, or destroyed before he gathers head and becomes a power.

Camp Green Meadows, Mercer County, Virginia, July 20, 1862. Sunday. — Morgan's gang, or Rebels encouraged by him, have got into Warrick County, Indiana. This is the first successful (if it turns out successful) invasion of free soil. I regret it on that account. I wished to be able to say that no inch of free soil had been polluted by the footstep of an invader. However, this is rather an incursion of robbers than of soldiers. I suppose no soldiers have yet set foot on our soil.

I wish we were near or amidst the active movements. We ought to be sent somewhere.

July 21. Monday. — We are target firing now. The Enfields are a little better sighted than the muskets; the muskets have most power and the longest range. Company C does rather the best shooting, Companies E and A coming next.

A zouave at the Flat Top camp found tied to a tree with five bullet holes through him! Naked too! An enemy's cavalry patrol seen two miles outside of our pickets. Secesh, ten or twelve in number.

July 23. Wednesday. — Marched four companies to Blue-stone; bathed. A good evening drill.

Last evening I fell into a train of reflection on the separation of the regiment, so long continued, so unmilitary, and so causeless, with the small prospect of getting relief by promotion or otherwise in the Twenty-third, and as a result pretty much determined to write this morning telling brother William [Platt] that I would like a promotion to a colonelcy in one of the new regiments. Well, this morning, on the arrival of the mail, I get a dispatch from W. H. Clements that I am appointed colonel of the Seventy-ninth, a regiment to be made up in Hamilton, Warren, and Clinton Counties. Now, shall I accept? It is hard to leave the Twenty-third. I shall never like another regiment so well. Another regiment is not likely to think as much of me. I am puzzled. If I knew I could get a chance for promotion in the Twenty-third in any reasonable time, I would decline the Seventy-ninth. But, then, Colonel Scammon is so queer and crotchety that he is always doing something to push aside his chance for a brigadiership. Well, I will postpone the evil day of decision as long as possible.

———————

CAMP GREEN MEADOWS, July 23, 1862.

DEAREST: — I today received a dispatch from Captain Clements that I have been appointed colonel of the Seventy-ninth Regiment to be made up in Warren and Clinton Counties. I shall make no definite decision as to acceptance until I get official notice of it. I suppose it is correct. I shall much hate to leave the Twenty-third. I can't possibly like another regiment as well, and am not likely to be as acceptable myself to another regiment. If there was a *certainty* of promotion to the command of the Twenty-third, I would certainly wait for it. But between you and I [me], Colonel Scammon is not likely to deserve promotion, and will perhaps fail to get it. If he gets it he will probably keep command of the Twenty-third — that is, have it in his brigade. Besides, I begin to fear another winter in these mountains. I could stand it after two or three months' vacation with *you* in Ohio, but to go straight on another year in this sort of service is a dark prospect. Altogether, much as I love the Twenty-third, I shall probably leave it. I shall put off the evil day as long as I can, hoping something will turn up to give me this regiment, but when the decision is required, I shall probably decide in favor of the new regiment and *a visit to you and the boys*. I know nothing of the Seventy-ninth except that a son of the railroad superintendent, W. H. Clements, is to be major. I knew him as a captain in the Twelfth, a well-spoken-of youngster. It will be a sad day all around when I leave here.

Last night various doings at headquarters of brigade disgusted me so much, that before I went to sleep I pretty much resolved to get up this morning and write in the most urgent manner soliciting promotion in a new regiment to get out of the scrape. But when this morning brings me the news that I have got what I had determined to ask, I almost regret it. "Such is war!"

Write me all you learn, if anything, about the new regiments — what sort of people go into them, — are they likely ever to fill up? Etc., etc.

24th, A. M. — A year ago tonight you and I walked about Camp Chase looking at the men cooking their rations to be ready to leave the next morning. A short and a long year. Upon the whole, not an unhappy one. Barring the separation from you, it has been a healthy fine spree to me.

Since writing to you yesterday I learn from Dr. Joe, who is now here, that there really seems to be a fair prospect of Colonel Scammon's promotion. This will probably induce me to hold off as long as I can about the Seventy-ninth business. You can simply say you don't know if you are asked before hearing further as to what I shall do. — Love to all the boys.

Affectionately,

R.

Mrs. Hayes.

Camp Green Meadows, July 24, 1862. Thursday. — I got a lame, halting permission from Colonel Scammon to go on an errand of mercy over New River into Monroe [County] after the family of Mr. Caldwell, a Union man, who has been kept away from home and persecuted for his loyalty. The colonel says I may go *if* and *if;* and warning me of the hazards, etc., etc., shirking all responsibility. It is ridiculous in *war* to talk this way. If a thing ought to be done according to the lights we have, let us go and do it, leaving events to take care of themselves. This half-and-half policy; this do-less waiting for certainties before action, is contemptible. I rode to the ferry and arranged for the trip with Major Comly.

Six companies go over the ferry tonight and go on towards

Indian Creek. Two stop at the Farms Road, to protect our rear from that approach; four companies and the cavalry will go to Indian Creek take post at the cross-roads, and the waggons and cavalry will push on to Mr. Caldwell's and get his family before daylight and start back. The whole party will retire to the ferry if possible before night of the 26th.

July 25, 1862. — Friday. — Preparations for the trip. We go from this camp immediately after dinner.

July 26, 1862. — Had a good trip. Got out from under the noses of heavy forces of the enemy the wife and four children of Mr. Archibald Caldwell. He will settle in Indiana. We left camp with Companies A, I, C, and E at half past twelve and marched to within a mile of the ferry; halted in a valley out of sight of the river and of the river hills until 7:30. We were joined by Captain Gilmore, Lieutenant Abraham, and Lieutenant Fordyce with their excellent company of cavalry about 7 P. M. We marched to the ferry just at dark and were there joined by Companies B and F and by Lieutenant Croome with a squad of Captain McMullen's artillery company and one howitzer. We crossed New River on the flying bridge built by Captain Lane of the Eleventh. We had three loaded wagons and an ambulance. Four trips, fifteen minutes each, crossed us. At the Farms Road, five miles from the ferry, Company B, Captain Sperry, and Company I, Captain Warren, were detailed to take position to hold that road and prevent any enemy's force from coming into our rear.

Soon after passing the ferry, it was found that the road had in places been washed away, in others, filled by slides, and in others, cut into deep gullies. The waggons and ambulances were turned back; the column pushed on. Near Indian Creek, at Mrs. Fowler's, about 1:30 P. M. [A. M.], Captain Gilmore and myself with Captain Drake being in advance, we stopped and these officers and myself went in. Mrs. Fowler refused to get a light, saying she had none; refused to tell whether there was a man about the house; said she didn't know Mr. Caldwell and was very uncommunicative generally. She persisted in asking us who we were, what we wanted, and the like. Just as she had said there was no candle or light in the house, I struck a light with a match when we saw the candle she had blown out on going to bed not two yards off! It was lit and a man was discovered peeping through a door! We got from her the fact that no soldiers were at Indian Creek and very few at Red Sulphur or Peterstown.

I ordered the cavalry to push rapidly on to Mr. Caldwell's house, and bring off his wife and children on horseback. I rode back to the infantry and artillery and directed them to bivouac — to sleep on the ground. Lieutenant Hastings was officer of the guard. I told him he *need station no pickets or guard!* A year ago we camped our first night in Virginia. It was near Clarksburg in the midst of a Union region. No enemy anywhere near, and we had *one hundred and sixteen men on guard!* My reason for not worrying anybody with guard duty was that our position was concealed; and as we had just taken it after a night march no one could know that we were there. The camp was inaccessible, by reason of [the] river on one side and impassable mountains on the other, except by the road up and down the river. [Companies] B and I were on this road at the first road leading into it, eight miles off, and the cavalry were passing up in the other direction. So I made up my mind that as I was not sleepy I would keep awake and would be guard enough. I lay down on an India-rubber blanket — my sheepskin for a pillow — with only an overcoat on, Dr. Joe sleeping by my side; and in this position where I could hear every sound, remained comfortable but watchful until morning. The stars disappeared towards morning, covered by fleecy clouds.

In the morning we built fires, got warm coffee, and felt well; we were opposite Crump's Bottom. We hailed a man on the bank at Crump's and made him bring over a canoe, but learned little from him. About 5:30 the cavalry returned having Mrs. Caldwell and the children on their horses. We immediately set out on our return. The first eight miles in the cool of the morning was done in two and one-fourth hours; after that leisurely to the ferry. Six men of Company A waded New River near the mouth of Bluestone. A long, tedious wade they had of it. Stopped at the ferry two hours; men all had a good swim. Got back to camp here safe and sound. Cavalry marched almost fifty miles in about twelve hours; artillery with mountain howitzer twenty-five miles in nine hours' marching time and thirteen hours altogether; infantry thirty-six in fourteen hours' marching time and twenty hours altogether. A pretty jolly expedition! Horses fell down, men fell down; Caldwell got faint-hearted and wanted to give it up. Lieutenant Abraham was cowed and I sent him with the infantry to bivouac. As they returned, the cavalry took all of Mrs. Fowler's new blackberry wine and honey! All sorts of incidents; — funny good time.

July 28, 1862. Monday. — Received letters from Mother, *June* 3 and July 17, and from Platt, July 22. Platt says Governor Tod will not appoint men now in the field because he needs the officers at home to aid in recruiting the regiments. This is foolish. If volunteering has to be hired(?) and forced, we had better resort to drafting. That is the true course! Draft!

Rode with Major Comly to Flat Top. No news there of much note. Colonel Scammon was nominated for a brigadiership by the President but there are seventy others of whom eighteen were confirmed, making it is said the two hundred allowed by law. So the thing seems to be up. Whether the Governor will confirm the nomination of the Hamilton County committee does not yet appear.

Camp Green Meadows, July 29, 1862. Tuesday. — Returned from [to] Camp Green Meadows today. General Cox thinks Colonel Scammon will be ordered to act as brigadier by the President; that a vacancy in the colonelcy of the Twenty-third will thus occur; that I had better hold on for the present before accepting the Eighty-third [Seventy-ninth]. As I have no notice that the Governor has made the appointment, I shall have nothing to act on for some days, if at all. But drafting is the thing!

CAMP GREEN MEADOWS, July 29, 1862.

DEAR MOTHER: — I received a letter from you dated the 17th July — one from William dated 22d July, and another from you dated June 3, yesterday. I begin to have hopes that your birthday letter may yet turn up. Letters are rarely lost, even in this region. The Rebels captured one of our mails early in May, and may have got your letter.

I am glad you are enjoying so much. It is not at all unlikely that I may have an opportunity to visit you in August or September for a day or two. I shall do so if it is possible without neglecting duty.

We are not as busy here as we would like to be, but we are delightfully camped, and among a friendly people. The greater part of them are preparing to move to Ohio and Indiana, fearing that we may go off and let the Rebels in to destroy them. We receive many letters at this camp from Rebels who are in Camp Chase as prisoners. Their wives and relatives call almost daily to inquire about them and for letters.

Last Sunday I dined at a Union citizen's near here. There were eleven women there whose husbands or brothers were at Camp Chase. I took over a lot of letters for them. Some were made happy, others not so. There had been sickness and death at the prison, and the letters brought tears as well as smiles.

Good-bye. — Affectionately, your son,

RUTHERFORD.

MRS. SOPHIA HAYES.

July 30, 1862. Wednesday. — I set the men to drilling in the new target practice. Rode with Bottsford over to see Mrs. Lilley, an old lady whose husband, James Lilley, lately died at Camp Chase in prison. Her son James is still there. As the only male member of the family old enough to do work, I am inclined to ask for his release. Her daughter Emily, a well-appearing young woman, is accused of giving the information which led to bushwhacking Captain Gilmore's cavalry. I hope it is not so.

I received today letters from Stephenson and Herron and an order from Columbus "authorizing" me to assist in raising a regiment, the Seventy-ninth. I don't know what to think of all this. Am I required to go home and assist?

July 31, 1862. Thursday. — Rained almost all day, clearing up the after part of the day. Received *Commercial* of 28th. It looks as if they were getting ready to draft. The *Commercial* finds fault with the rule which practically excludes from the new regiments officers already in the field: no one to be appointed unless he can be present to aid in recruiting, and no officer to have leave of absence unless he is actually commissioned over a regiment already filled up!! Well, I am indifferent. The present position is too agreeable, to make [me] regret not getting another. — I saw the new moon square in front.

HEADQUARTERS 23D REGT. O. V.,
CAMP GREEN MEADOWS, MERCER COUNTY, VIRGINIA,
July 31, 1862.

SIR: — I am this day in receipt of Special Orders No. 716, dated Adjutant-General's Office, Columbus, Ohio, July 21, 1862, directed to me at Cincinnati, authorizing me to assist in raising one of the new regiments now forming in Ohio. I shall apply for leave of absence by today's mail for the purpose of entering upon the service indicated in the order.

It is proper to add that, although fully sensible of the importance of rapid recruiting, I would not ask leave of absence from duty in the field for that purpose, if there was any immediate prospect of active operations here.

Respectfully,
R. B. HAYES,
LIEUTENANT-COLONEL TWENTY-THIRD REGT., O. V.
COMMANDING.

BRIGADIER-GENERAL C. W. HILL,
ADJUTANT-GENERAL OHIO.

August 1, 1862. Friday. — A good little drill. Mr. Landcraft, one of the three slaveholders of Monroe County who were true to the Union, and a Mrs. Roberts were arrested and brought into my camp in obedience to orders from headquarters. Mrs. Roberts is a ladylike woman; her husband, a Secesh, is a prisoner at Raleigh. Mrs. Roberts and her uncle, Mr. Landcraft, came over New River and passed into our lines, the pickets admitting them, without proper passes. If this is the whole offense, the arrest is on most insufficient and frivolous grounds. In the case of Mrs. Roberts, who has a nursing child at home, it is as cruel as it is unnecessary. I shall do my best to get them out of the trouble. These needless persecutions of old men and of women, I am ashamed of.

August 2, 1862. Saturday. — . . . From General Cox I hear that I can't send captains on recruiting service. This disappoints Captains Drake and Sperry. I have named Lieutenants Avery and Hastings. I also learn that I can't go home to recruit the Seventy-ninth Regiment whose colonel I am to be if and if. Well I don't care much. I should never find such a regiment as the Twenty-third.

August 3, 1862. Sunday. — . . . Was glad to be able to release Mr. Landcraft and Mrs. Roberts. This arrest was a foolish business.

[August] 4, 1862. Monday. — Company I, Greenwood muskets, fired at target one hundred yards. Best string, thirty-seven inches (4 shots); the muskets not so accurate for short ranges as the Enfields; not so well sighted. Possibly the men are somewhat afraid of them is one reason. I keep the men busy to prevent rusting. This target practice seems to interest them very much.

August 5, 1862. Tuesday. — Target practice continues. I did a thing that worried me this A. M. I saw two *soldiers sitting* on post. It was contrary to orders. I directed that they should carry knapsacks one hour. I do not often punish. They turned out to be two good quiet soldiers. But the order was given before I knew who they were. One of them felt badly, wanted to be excused; but the order was out and I had it executed. I trust it will cure the evil. . . .

Camp Green Meadows, August 6, 1862. Wednesday. — This has been a day of excitement and action. Before I was out of bed a courier came saying our pickets on New River above Bluestone were probably cut off; that firing had been heard near there, and none had come in to the picket station. I ordered Companies C and E to go down and look them up, supposing some small party of the enemy had attempted to cut them off. Before the companies could get away another courier came reporting that the enemy in force, three thousand to four thousand, had passed down New River on the other side. Of course this was to attack the ferry. I sent word to the ferry and to Flat Top, directed the men to put one day's rations in haversacks, forty rounds of ammunition in boxes, and fill canteens. Then word came that the forces were smaller than supposed and *no cannon.* I dispatched Flat Top, Colonel Scammon to that effect, and that reinforcements were not needed.

Soon after a courier from [the] ferry [reported] that the enemy in large force were firing cannon rifled at them. I sent this to Flat Top. Then called up Companies E, C, and K to go to reinforce the ferry. I sent the band to give them music and told the men: "Fighting battles is like courting the girls: those who make most pretension and are boldest usually win. So, go ahead, give good hearty yells as you approach the ferry, let the band play; but don't expose yourselves, keep together and keep under cover. It is a bushwhacking fight across the river. Don't expose yourself to show bravery; we know you are all brave," etc., etc. The men went off in high spirits.

A courier came from Bluestone saying the enemy were at the ford with a cannon in some force. I sent Company I down there to watch them and hinder them if they attempted to cross. Under what he deemed obligatory written orders, Major Comly destroyed the large ferry-boat. Soon after, the enemy ceased firing and made a rapid retreat. They ran their horses past the ford at Bluestone. Whether they left because they heard our band and reinforcements coming or because *they saw the major had done their work,* is problematical.

My couriers reached Flat Top in from one hour ten to one hour thirty minutes: viz., at 7:10, 8:30, and 9 A. M. The colonel with [the] Thirtieth and artillery, cavalry (Thirty-fifth), *starting* at 12 M! Rather slow business. The artillery and Thirtieth halted at Jumping Branch, reaching there two and one-half miles back at 4 P. M. Slow aid. It beats Giles!

A singular and almost fatal accident occurred about 5:30 P. M. In the midst of a severe thunder-storm the guard-tent was struck by lightning. Eight men were knocked flat, cartridge boxes exploded, muskets were shattered, etc., etc. The eight were all badly hurt, but dashing cold water on them they revived. They were playing "seven-up." They thought it was shell. One said as he came to "Where are they? Where are they?" Another spoke up repeating the question, "Where is Colonel Hayes? Where is the colonel?"

GREEN MEADOWS, August 6 [5], 1862.

DEAREST: — Adjutant Avery, Lieutenant Hastings, and some good men go home on recruiting service.

I have nothing to say this hot day. I have still some hope that things will so work together as to allow me to see you during the next month or two. At present no leaves of absence are granted to officers appointed in new regiments. I do not know how this will affect the appointees for the Seventy-ninth. If they choose to turn us out, all right. I am indifferent. Indeed, leaving the Twenty-third is an unpleasant thing to contemplate. When I look at the neat, hardy, healthy, contented young fellows who make up nine-tenths of the regiment, and contrast their appearance with a mob of raw recruits — dirty, sickly, lawless, and complaining, I can't help feeling that I should be a great fool to accept the new position.

But there are other considerations which influence me in the other direction, and so I quietly dodge the question for the present. To see "all the boys" and your own dear self, that is a great matter, and I think, if things go on as I anticipate, that circumstances will decide me for the Seventy-ninth, always provided these stringent orders as to absence don't cut me out of the chance.

Dr. Joe has been for three or four days quite sick. He is now up and about again. He complains that he gets no letters.

Later. — Dr. Joe is content. He has got two letters — one from you and one from Mother. I have yours of the 26th. Yes, we feel a good deal alike about leaving the Twenty-third. Well,

I have no official notice as to what I am to do. But I *have* official notice that *no* leave of absence is granted for the purpose of recruiting new regiments. So the question as to whether I go or stay is likely to decide itself. So let it do. . . . Love to all the boys.

Affectionately ever,

R.

August 7 [6].

DEAREST: — I wrote this last night — today has been a day of excitement. All has *not* been quiet on New River. This morning at daylight I was aroused by a courier saying our most distant picket had been fired on and as no one had come in, they were believed to be all cut off. I got out two companies to see to it. In twenty minutes another came in saying that the enemy three thousand to four thousand strong, with artillery, were coming to attack our four companies at Packs Ferry, under Major Comly. I sent word to the major and three companies, [and] word to Flat Top for help. Well, they made the attack both at the ferry and the ford — but it was across a broad river. Cannon shots barely missed many times. Shell lit in close proximity and failed to explode, and our sharpshooters getting bold and skilful, the enemy retreated, running the gauntlet of our sharpshooters on the river bank for three miles. Not a man of ours killed or wounded. Reinforcements reached us under Colonel Scammon at 4 P. M., just four hours after the last Rebel had disappeared six miles above here. Our courier carried the news to Flat Top in one hour and ten minutes. The "aid" did it in six hours!

We had a terrific thunder-storm about six P. M. The lightning struck our guard-tent. Five men were laid out apparently dead. Dr. Joe and all of us were there in an instant. The men are all restored and I think will all get well. They all appeared dead, and but for instant aid would have died. . . .

[R.]

MRS. HAYES.

August 7. — *Thursday.* — Colonel Scammon who came down with the battery and the Thirtieth Regiment, returned to Flat

Top this A. M.   The colonel is too nervous and fussy to be a good commander.   He cut around like a hen with one chicken after getting news of our being attacked three hours or four before he started his troops.   They reached the place where they camped, twelve miles from Flat Top, about 5 P. M.   They would have got to the ferry, if at all, after dark.   The enemy could have fought a battle and escaped before aid would have come.

Lieutenants Avery and Hastings, Sergeant Abbott, Corporal Bennett, and two privates left today on recruiting service.

Camp Green Meadows, Friday, August 8, 1862. — Captains Drake and Skiles of [the] Twenty-third and Captain Gilmore of the cavalry returned today.   They brought fourteen head [of] good cattle got from Secesh.   Captain Drake is very much irritated because he and Captain Sperry were not detailed on my recommendation to go on recruiting service, the reason given being that captains in the opinion of [the] general commanding, General Cox, ought not to be sent.   Since that, a number of captains have been sent from this division.   This looks badly.   Captain Drake tenders his resignation "immediate and unconditional."   I requested the captain not to be too fast.   He is impulsive and hasty, but gallant and brave to a fault, honorable and trustworthy. I prefer to send him on any dangerous service to any man I ever knew.   I hope he will remain in the regiment if I do.

I ordered camp changed today to get rid of old leaves, soured ground, dirty tents, and the like.   Have succeeded in getting more room for tents and more room for drill.

CAMP GREEN MEADOWS, MERCER COUNTY, VIRGINIA,
August 8, 1862.

DEAR UNCLE: —.   .   .   .   I have not yet decided as to the Seventy-ninth Regiment.   I would much prefer the colonelcy of this [regiment, the Twenty-third], of course.   At the same time there are some things which influence me strongly in favor of the change.   I shall not be surprised if the anxiety to have the colonel present to aid in recruiting will be such that I shall feel it my duty to decline.   You know I can't get leave of absence until my commission is issued, and the commission does not issue until the regiment is full. By this rule, officers in the field are excluded. I shall leave the matter to take care of itself for the present.

We have had a good excitement the last day or two. A large force, about two thousand, with heavy artillery and cavalry, have been attacking the positions occupied by the Twenty-third. They cannonaded Major Comly at the ferry four and one-half miles from here, and a post I have at the ford three and one-half miles from here, on Wednesday. Tents were torn and many narrow escapes made, but strangely enough nobody on our side was hurt. With our long-range muskets, the enemy soon found they were likely to get the worst of it.

The same evening our guard-tent was struck by lightning. Eight men were knocked senseless, cartridge boxes, belted to the men, were exploded, and other frightful things, but all are getting well.

The drafting pleases me. It looks as if [the] Government was in earnest. All things promise well. I look for the enemy to worry us for the next two months, but after that our new forces will put us in condition to begin the crushing process. I think another winter will finish them. Of course there will be guerrilla and miscellaneous warfare, but the power of the Rebels will, I believe, go under if [the] Government puts forth the power which now seems likely to be gathered.

I am as anxious as you possibly can be to set up in Spiegel Grove, and to begin things. It is a pity you are in poor health, but all these things we need not grieve over. Don't you feel glad that I was in the first regiment originally raised for the three-years service in Ohio, instead of waiting till this time, when a man volunteers to escape a draft? A man would feel mean about it all his days.

I wish you were well enough to come out here. You would enjoy it to the top of town. Many funny things occur in these alarms from the enemy. Three shells burst in our assistant surgeon's tent. He was out but one of them killed a couple of live rattlesnakes he had as pets! One fellow, an old pursy fifer, a great coward, came puffing up to my tent from the river and began to talk extravagantly of the number and ferocity of the enemy. Said I to him, "And, do they shoot their cannon pretty rapidly?" "Oh, yes," said he, "very rapidly indeed — they had fired *twice* before I left the camp"!

It is very hot these days but our men are still healthy. We have over eight hundred men, and only about ten in hospital here. . . . .

Sincerely,

R. B. Hayes.

P. S. — Wasn't you pleased with the Morgan raid into Kentucky? I was in hopes they would send a shell or two into Cincinnati. It was a grand thing for us.

S. Birchard.

August 9. Saturday. — Am planning an expedition to go to Salt Well and destroy it; also to catch old Crump if he is at home. Jacobs, Company G, a scout, went up yesterday to Crump's Bottom. Reports favorably. All safe now. Curious, quiet fellow, Jacobs. He takes no grub, wears moccasins; passes himself for a guerrilla of the Rebels, eats blackberries when he can't get food; slips stealthily through the woods, and finds out all that is going.

Old Andy Stairwalt, a fat, queer-looking old fifer with a thin voice, and afflicted with a palpitation of the heart (!) — a great old coward, otherwise a worthy man — was one of the first men who reached here from the ferry after the attack of Wednesday. He was impressed that the enemy were in great force. I asked him if they fired their cannon rapidly. "Oh, yes," said he, "very rapidly; they fired *twice* before I left the camp"!

Sad news. The dispatch tells us that "General Bob McCook was murdered by guerrillas while riding in front of his brigade in Tennessee." He always said he did not expect to survive the war. He was a brave man, honest, rough, "an uncut diamond." A good friend of mine; we have slept together through several stormy nights. I messed with him in his quarters on Mount Sewell. Would that he could have died in battle! Gallant spirit, hail and farewell!

21

I send out today Company E, thirty-nine men, K, twenty-seven men, H, about thirty men, and a squad of men from A, I, and C of twenty-seven men, and about twenty-five cavalry to stop the salt well in Mercer, twenty miles above here. Total force about one hundred and fifty men. They go up to Crump's Bottom, catch him if they can, take his canoe and the ferry-boat and destroy the Mercer salt well. This is the programme.

A charming affectionate letter from my dear wife. She speaks of her feelings on the night before the regiment left for the seat of war, a year ago the 24th of July.* Dear Lucy, God grant you as much happiness as you deserve and your cup will indeed be full! She speaks of the blue-eyed beautiful youngest. He is almost eight months old. A letter from mother Hayes, more cheerful than usual, religious and affectionate. She is past seventy, and fears she will not live to see the end of the war. I trust she will, and to welcome me home again as of old she used to from college.

Sunday, August 10, 1862, 9:30 A. M. — Captain Drake and Gilmore's Cavalry have returned. The infantry are bathing in Bluestone. The expedition was completely successful, and was of more importance than I supposed it would be. They reached the salt well about 2:30 A. M.; found the works in full blast — a good engine pumping, two pans thirty feet long boiling, etc., etc. The salt is good; considerable salt was on hand. All the works were destroyed by fire. A canoe found at Crump's was taken to the ferry.

I spent an anxious night. Jackson, Major Comly's scout, reported that the salt well was guarded. This came to me after I

* Mrs. Hayes had written from Chillicothe, August 2: "The 24th of July a year ago was a happy, and yet, oh, sad night, and yet the thought that I was with you to the last moment of that sad parting sends such a thrill of joy through my heart. I think of it so often. 'Twas bitter to know that when morning dawned, instead of joy and happiness, 'twould bring such heavy sorrow, such bitter tears. We stood and gazed after the cars holding all that was dearest to us, but I was a soldier's wife, I must not cry yet. While standing there, an old woman spoke to Mother, asking who was gone; then she turned to me, 'You had better take a good cry, my dear, 'twill lighten your heart.' How freshly everything comes before me now!"

was in bed and too late to send the word to the expedition. I anticipated trouble there and felt anxious enough. I slept little, was up often. But luckily all went well. Not a man was in sight. This morning, as they were returning, the cavalry were bushwhacked, horses wounded, clothes cut, but no man hurt.

Received a "secret" order to be ready to move on one-half hour's notice. Rode post to the ferry; set the men to preparing for one of General Pope's minute and practical inspections.

CAMP GREEN MEADOWS, August 10, 1862.

DEAREST LUTE: — All your names are sweet. "Lu" is good; I always think of the girls at Platt's saying "Aunt Lu." "Lute" and "Luty" is Joe; and "Lucy darling," that's me. All pretty and lovable.

Your letter of the 2nd came last night. A great comfort it was. Several things last night were weighing on me, and I needed a dear word from you. I had got a reluctant permission to send a party to attempt to destroy the salts-works at the Mercer salt well twenty-five miles from here, over a rough mountain country full of enemies, and uncertain who might be at the well. I started the party at 6 P. M. to make a night march of it to get there and do the work and get fairly off before daylight. Captains Drake and Zimmerman were in command with twenty of Gilmore's gallant cavalry and one hundred and thirty of our best men. I had got all the facts I could before they left, but after they were gone three hours, a scout I had given up came in with information that the works were strongly guarded. I slept none during that night. Then too, the sad news that McCook was murdered was in the evening dispatches, casting a deep shadow over all. It needed your letter to carry me through the night.

I was out at early dawn, walking the camp, fearing to hear the gallop of a horse. Time went on slowly enough, but it was a case where no news was good news. If they had run into trouble the word would have returned as fast as horseflesh could bring it. By breakfast time I began to feel pretty safe; at eight I visited the hospital and talked cheerfully to the sick, feeling pretty cheerful really. About half past nine Captain Drake rode in. The fifty miles had been travelled, and the Secesh salt well for all this saltless region was burned out root and branch. Three horses were badly wounded; many [men] had their clothes cut, but not a man was hurt. They reached the well at 2 A. M., found it in full blast, steam on, etc., etc., received one feeble volley of rifle balls and the thing was done. So much good your letter did.

Yes, I get all your letters about one week after you mail them. I got a letter from Mother of same date at same time. This happens almost always.

As to the Seventy-ninth, I agree with you. The greatest inducements are to visit you and to get out of these mountains before another winter. I may, and probably will, find worse places, but I am getting tired of this. Another thing, a sense of duty. I do not know that it *clearly* inclines either way. In such case we usually manage to persuade ourselves that it points the way we wish. But it strikes me that the Twenty-third is as near right as I can make it. It can't get much more out of me, while possibly my experience might be more useful in a new regiment than anywhere else. Do you see where I am coming out?

As I am writing a messenger from headquarters comes with a significant order headed "secret." I am ordered to place all things in readiness to move on thirty minutes' notice — to have baggage, etc., etc., in such condition that it can be done on that notice any time after tomorrow at 3 P. M. This means what? I *suspect* a move to the east by way of Lewisburg and White Sulphur Springs. It may be a move to eastern Virginia. It may be towards Giles and the railroad again.

Well, I have galloped to the ferry five miles and back. I am likely to be settled some way soon, but at any rate, in the Seventy-ninth or Twenty-third, I have got the best wife of any of them. This war has added to my confidence in you, my love for you, and my happiness that I have so dear a wife. The character you have shown in bearing what was so severe a trial, the unselfish and noble feeling you constantly exhibit, has endeared you to me more than ever before.

Joining the army when I did is now to be thought fortunate. Think of my waiting till forced by the fear of a draft to volunteer!

Good-bye, darling. Love and kisses to the dear boys, the little blue-eyed favorite, and all.

                    Affectionately ever, your

                                                        R.

I enclose a literary specimen.*

MRS. HAYES.

Monday, August 11, 1862. — Received a note from Major [Comly] that the enemy was moving from Red Sulphur either towards us or Colonel Crook. Kept the men preparing for the "secret" inspection or movement. Got a letter from the major, rather obscurely intimating that I did wrong in sending him aid at the time of the attack on him, and showing that he is offended about it, or hurt about it, at any rate. He says I lent official color to the rumor that he had abandoned the place by doing it, etc., etc. I replied that he was in error in thinking I had said I sent reinforcements to him instead of sending to Bluestone *because* of a rumor that went to Raleigh that he had abandoned the ferry without firing a gun. I had not heard the rumor then; but I *did fear he was losing,* AS I heard from couriers that he was destroying boats, and that the column a mile or more out was still marching this way.

Tuesday, August 12, 1862. — I sent this morning to J. C. Dunlevy, Lebanon, the following dispatch: "I am glad to hear that the Seventy-ninth is likely to be promptly filled without drafting. If so I shall join it as soon as leave can be obtained." So I am committed!

* The "specimen" was a scrap of paper reading: "Mr. Kernel hase I Want a Pass to go to see Wilson Lilly he has Sent for me he is Just at the Point of death

                                    "EMILY LILLY"

A fine rain this P. M. — A most gorgeous picture was presented by the sky and clouds and the beautiful hills surrounding, as I sat looking at our dress parade.

CAMP GREEN MEADOWS, August 12, 1862.

DEAR UNCLE: — I write merely to say that I have concluded to accept [the] colonelcy of the Seventy-ninth if it is filled without drafting. I love this regiment, but must leave it. I was pretty evenly balanced on the question. I have decided it rightly. It will take me to Cincinnati, I conjecture, in about three or four weeks. I shall no doubt be kept closely at work, but will manage some way to see you, if but for a night. Possibly you can come down.

I am sad over McCook's death. From the first he always told me — I suppose he said the same thing to many — that he would certainly not survive the war. He expected confidently to be killed. I suppose all men have notions one way or the other of that sort.

Quite a batch of the new colonels are persons with whom I am on agreeable terms. Anderson, Haynes, Lee Stem, Moore, Longworth, Tafel, and a bunch of others. But they will be a funny lot for a while. I suspect I shall enjoy the thing. I can now appreciate the difference between an old seasoned regiment and the same people raw. Nothing is nicer than a good old regiment. The machine runs itself — all the colonel has to do is to look on and see it go. But at first it's always in a snarl, and a thousand unreasonable men make such a big snarl. I have no doubt I shall see times when I would like to see around me the quiet, neat, hardy youngsters who are with me now.

Well, good-bye. I feel like shedding tears when I think of leaving these men, but I at once get into a quiet laugh when I think of what I am going to — a thousand-headed monster!

Sincerely,

R. B. HAYES.

P. S. — I forgot to say anything about the war. My command is scattered from fourteen to twenty miles from any succor, and if attacked it's doubtful if any would reach in time. We must fight or go under, perhaps both. Well, on the 6th, the enemy three times our whole and six times our detachment at the ferry, with rifle, cannon, etc., etc., attacked. We had a busy day but by stratagem and good luck we got off with slight damage. They thought we were the strongest and after firing two hours retreated. Next day but one, we destroyed their salt works twenty-five miles from here. Last night I was up all night riding and manœuvring to keep them off; but it makes a man feel well to have something to do.

S. BIRCHARD.

CAMP GREEN MEADOWS, August 12, 1862.

DEAR MOTHER: — I received your good letter of the 2d the day before yesterday. On same day received one from Lucy of same date.

We have had some fighting and a good deal of excitement and night riding and duty of various sorts during the last week. We have been exceedingly lucky, losing, so far as I know, but one man. We had two accidents — one man drowned and eight struck with lightning. All were senseless and most of them seemed dead for a short time, but all are living and probably all will recover entirely. It was the same day that we were attacked, after the enemy had retreated. The men all supposed that a shell of the enemy had burst. The enemy were in great force and had artillery superior to ours, but the security of our position was soon apparent, and after less than an hour's firing they retired, having lost a few killed and wounded.

I have agreed to accept [the] colonelcy of [the] Seventy-ninth regiment if it is filled without drafting. I suppose this will take me to Cincinnati and home in three or four weeks. I shall no doubt be in duty bound to devote all my time to the new regiment, but I shall of course manage to see you if it is but for a day or night.

The weather is seasonable — that is hot as Tophet. We have a few more sick than usual but nothing serious.

I am pleased with the war prospects. We may meet with disasters to give things a gloomy look before the new troops are ready for the field, but it certainly seems as if we could, with the new army, put a speedy end to the Rebellion. I trust you will live to see the country again at peace. But war isn't the worst thing that can happen to a country. It stirs up a great deal of good. I see more kindness, more unselfish generosity around me than would probably be found among these young men if they were plodding along in ordinary selfish pursuits. . . .

Affectionately, your son,

R.

Mrs. Sophia Hayes.

On Steamer Monitor, Kanawha River,
August 18, [1862]. Evening.

Dear Wife: — I am four hard days' marching, and a few hours' travel on a swift steamer nearer to you than I was when I last wrote you, and yet I am not on my way home. You will see in the newspapers, I suppose, that General Cox's Division (the greater part of it) is going to eastern Virginia. We left our camps Friday, the 15th, making long and rapid marches from the mountains to the head of navigation on this river. We now go down to the Ohio, then up to Parkersburg, and thence by railroad eastwardly to the scene of operations. My new regiment fills slowly, I think, and it may be longer than I anticipated before I shall be called for at Cincinnati, if at all. There is talk of an order that will prevent my going to the new regiment, but I think it is not correctly understood, and the chance, it seems to me, is that I shall go home notwithstanding this change of plan.

Our men are delighted with the change. They cheer and laugh, the band plays, and it is a real frolic. During the hot dusty marching, the idea that we were leaving the mountains of west Virginia kept them in good heart.

You will hereafter direct letters to me "General Cox's Division, Army of Virginia."

August 19. Evening. Same steamer on the Ohio River. —
DEAREST : — We have had a particularly jolly day. The river
is very low, and at many of the bars and shoals we are compelled
to disembark and march the troops around. In this way we have
marched through some villages, and fine farming neighborhoods
in Meigs County. The men, women, and children turned out with
apples, peaches, pies, melons, pickles (Joe took to them), etc., etc.,
etc., in the greatest profusion. The drums and fifes and band all
piped their best. The men behaved like gentlemen and marched
beautifully. Wasn't I proud of them? How happy they were!
They would say, "This is God's country." So near you and
marching away from you! That was the only sad point in it for
me. Only one man drunk so far; his captain put him under
arrest. He insisted on an appeal to me, and on my saying, "It's
all right," he was sober enough to submit, saying, "Well, if the
colonel says it's right, it must be right," so he made no trouble.

I shall write daily until we get to Parkersburg — that is on
the line of railroad to Chillicothe, I believe. No more tonight.

[R. B. HAYES.]

MRS. HAYES.

CHAPTER XX

*M*ONDAY, [*August*] *25 and Tuesday, 26.* — In Washington. Here all arrangements connected with army matters are perfect. An efficient military police or patrol arrests all men and officers not authorized to be absent from their regiments, and either returns them to their regiments or puts them under guard and gives notice of their place. A good eating-house feeds free of expense and *sleeps* all lost and stray soldiers. An establishment furnishes quartermasters of regiments with *cooked* rations at all times; fine hospitals, easily accessible, are numerous. The people fed and complimented our men (*chiefly* the middling and mechanical or laboring classes) in a way that was very gratifying. We felt proud of our drill and healthy brown faces. The comparison with the new, green recruits pouring in was much to our advantage. Altogether Washington was a happiness to the Twenty-third.

WASHINGTON CITY, August 25, 1862.

DEAREST: — We arrived here after ten days' marching and travelling, this morning. We go over to Alexandria in an hour or two to take our place in General Sturges' Army Corps of General Pope's Command. Colonel Scammon leads the First Brigade of General Cox's Division in the new position. If the enemy press forward, there will be fighting. It is supposed they are trying to push us back. Reinforcements for us are pouring in rapidly.

In case of accident, Joe and I will be reported at the Kirkwood House in this city. I feel a presentiment that all will be right with us. If not, you know all the loving things I would say to you and the dear boys. My impression is that the enemy will be in no condition to hurry matters fast enough to get ahead of the new legions now coming in. They must act speedily or they are too late.

Direct to me as in my last.

Affectionately ever,

R.

MRS. HAYES.

WASHINGTON CITY, August 25, 1862.

DEAR UNCLE: — Our men are in the cars expecting to cross to the scene of war (Warrenton) every moment. Aften ten days' marching, etc., etc., we got here this A. M. Things here look improving. The troops are pouring in from all directions, and unless the enemy get some success soon, they will be too late. There seems to be some fighting in the front. We shall be in it, if it continues. I think it will all go well. We are gaining strength every hour.

The Kirkwood House here is the place where Dr. Webb and I will be reported in case of accident.

Sincerely,

R. B. HAYES.

S. BIRCHARD.

Wednesday, [August] 27 [and Thursday, 28th,] at Alexandria. No great difference from time in Washington, but much less agreeable. Friday, 29th, marched to Munson's Hill and bivouacked. Saturday, 30th, put up our tents between Forts Ramsay and [Buffalo] at Upton's Hill. On Friday, fighting heard west and southwest of us — supposed to be at Manassas. All day Saturday, ditto. At Alexandria first saw McClellan's Grand Army. They do not look so efficient as General Cox's six regiments, but are no doubt good.

The Thirtieth got here in time to get through to Pope. [The] Eleventh and Twelfth [Ohio] went forward under Colonel Scammon to try to do the same thing. At Bull Run Bridge, beyond Fairfax, united with First, Second, Third, and Fourth New Jersey, under General Taylor, and pushed on, New Jersey regiments in advance; ran into a battery and heavy force of the enemy. New Jersey broke, fled, and never rallied; [the] Eleventh and Twelfth pushed on and fought gallantly, Colonel Scammon *cool* and *steady!* Won praise from all. Good! Honor of Ohio sustained. Eastern correspondents fail to tell the facts.

Camp near Upton's Hill, near Falls Church, on road to Manassas, August 30, 1862. — All or nearly all day we have heard cannon firing, as is supposed, in direction of Manassas Junction. It is believed that General Jackson is fighting Pope. The firing was heard yesterday a considerable part of the day. We all listen to it, look at the couriers; anybody moving rapidly attracts a thousand eyes. For a long time the thing was not very much attended to. Now it gets exciting. We feel anxious; we wish to know whether the battle is with us or with our foes. It is now 5 or 5:30 P. M. The decision must come soon. It is not a bright nor a dark day. It is neither hot nor cool for the season. A fair fighting day. The only report we hear is that a Union man eight miles out says we got possession of Manassas yesterday, and that the Rebels today are trying to get it back; that they have been repulsed three times. The firing seems to be in the same direction as heretofore and not differing much in loudness. Anxious moments these are! I hear the roar as I write.

7:30 P. M. — A lovely quiet sunset; an exhilarating scene around us; the distant booming growing more faint and more distant, apparently, till at early dark it died away. With us or with our foes?!! It is said Jackson was west of Pope and being driven back; if so, probably "with us." That Jackson made a speech saying they must win this fight, that it would decide the fate of the Confederacy! Well, we wait. The suspense is less dreadful since the cannon no longer roar.

9:30 P. M. — No news. This I interpret to mean that there has been no decided victory — no decided defeat — a drawn battle. Why not mass tonight all the thousands of troops to overwhelm Jackson tomorrow? It could have been done in time to have flogged him today. He is *the* rebel chieftain. His destruction destroys the Rebel cause?

CAMP ON MUNSON'S HILL, NEAR WASHINGTON,
(SAY EIGHT MILES), August 30, 1862.

DEAR LUCY: — Things all seem to be going well with General Pope and the rest. I am not sure, but I think the day for an important Rebel success in this region is past. Colonel Scammon with the Eleventh and Twelfth Ohio had a severe fight at Bull Run Bridge with a superior foe. They behaved gallantly and saved our arms from a disgrace which was imminent in consequence of the ill conduct of four New Jersey regiments. Colonel Scammon behaved with unexpected coolness and skill. He was good-natured and self-possessed, both unexpected.

Well, we *do* enjoy the change. We, of course, are full of perplexity, getting into the new schoolhouse, but we feel pretty proud of ourselves. All of McClellan's army is near us, but we see nothing superior to General Cox's six Ohio regiments.

We were in Washington two or three days. All arrangements there are capital; fine hospitals, good police for arresting stray soldiers; a soldiers' retreat, where all lost and sick are lodged and fed well, and a place where all were furnished with cooked rations to carry on marches. The people near our camp furnished us with fruit, melons, and nice things unlimited. We staid in Alexandria two or three days. Not like Washington, but so-so. We are here with other troops looking after three fine forts built here by the Rebels, intending, I suppose, to occupy them if the Rebels should get near Washington again.

The Rebels have been making a strong effort to rush on to Washington and Baltimore, but as I have said, I think they are just too late. It looks to me as if we would remain here a few days, perhaps a few weeks, until the new army is gathered and organized. I feel hopeful of the future.

Well, I love you so much. I wrote you a loving letter from Flat Top or Green Meadows, which I wish you to think of as my good[-bye] words for you in case of accident. — Love to the boys.

Affectionately,

R.

P. S. — The Eastern correspondents do no sort of justice to the gallantry of the Eleventh and Twelfth Ohio, nor to the poltroonery of the First, Second, Third, and Fourth New Jersey.

MRS. HAYES.

[In a letter of the same date and place as the preceding, Dr. J. T. Webb writes his mother: —

"We are in hearing of a battle that is progressing some ten or fifteen miles distant. The cannonading has been kept up pretty steady all day long; at times it is quite brisk; what would you think of it were you here? This country presents the same appearance as western Virginia, save only on a grander scale. There is not a *fence* between here and Alexandria, although it is almost a continuous village; splendid residences line this road that have had fine parks of trees around, all of which have been cut down to clear the way for the artillery; every mile almost, you come upon a line of forts. This point was for some time held by the Rebels, and between the armies this section is pretty badly used up. Many of the finest residences are deserted, some have been burnt. It is a sorry sight to witness it."]

Upton's Hill (near Washington), August 31. — Mustered the men for July and August. A rainy, cool day. The great battle of yesterday and the day before, so near here that we heard the roar distinctly, is *supposed* to have resulted favorably to our arms. How decisively is not yet known here. We hear all sorts of rumors, such as the capture of Jackson and sixteen thousand men and the like; but nothing definite is known. The appearances are favorable. We inquire of every one to get *facts* and get only vague rumors.

This Sunday evening the reports from the battlefield are less favorable than the morning rumors. There is talk of "no result," a "drawn battle," and the like; that our army has fallen back four miles to Centreville. Another [report] says McDowell withdrew a division from one outlet and let Jackson escape. A report says our loss is ten thousand; the enemy's much heavier.

No firing all day today. This evening after dark firing of heavy guns was heard for a few minutes, apparently in the same place as before.

Received a dear letter from Lucy dated August 13 and directed to Flat Top. She says she is happy in the thought that we are doing our duty. This is good. Darling wife, how this painful separation is made a blessing by the fine character it develops, or brings to view! How I love her more and more!

September 1. — A coolish, cloudy day. Wrote letters to Mother and Lucy. Nothing definite from the battlefield. Rumors of good and bad. Many complaints of McDowell; that he let Jackson slip off by withdrawing a division from an important point. On the whole, the result seems to be a draw yet. Our army in great strength, rumor says two hundred thousand, is on this side of the old Bull Run battlefield; the enemy one hundred and eighty thousand strong on the identical ground. No firing today until about 5:30 or 6 o'clock when there was a grand uproar until *after* dark near the old place, possibly further north; rumored or conjectured to be an attempt to our right. A thunderstorm came on about the same time when there was a fierce rivalry between the artillery of earth and heaven, the former having a decided advantage. A fierce storm of wind and rain all night, blowing down some tents and shaking all in a threatening way. About 9 P. M. received orders from brigade headquarters to be especially vigilant and to have the men ready to form line of battle without confusion. All which was done.

UPTON'S HILL, NEAR WASHINGTON,

September 1, 1862.

DEAREST: — Very severe battles were fought day before yesterday and the day before that a few miles west of here. The roar could be heard in our camp the greater part of each day. We are six or eight miles west of Washington over the Potomac in Virginia between Forts Ramsay and Buffalo — strong works which we, I conjecture, are to hold in case of disaster in front. The result of the battles, although not decisive, I think was favorable. The enemy's advance was checked, and as our strength grows with every hour, the delay gained is our gain.

You have no doubt heard of the battles, and perhaps feel anxious about us. One thing be *assured* of, after such affairs *no news of us is good news.* The reason of this is, if we are well we shall not be allowed to leave, nor send communications; if injured or worse, officers are taken instantly to Washington or Alexandria and tidings sent. I write this to relieve, if possible, or as much as possible, your anxiety on hearing of battles. At present I see no prospect of our being engaged, but I look for battles almost daily until the enemy is driven back or gives up his present purpose of carrying the war into our territory. I feel hopeful about the result.

Your letter of the 13th August, directed to me Raleigh, etc., I got last night. We shall now get one another's letters in three or four days. I was made happy by your sensible and excellent talk about your feelings. A sense of duty or a deep religious feeling is all that can reconcile one to the condition we are placed in. That you are happy notwithstanding this trial, adds to my appreciation and love and to my happiness. Dearest, you are a treasure to me. I think of you more than you suppose and shall do so more here than in western Virginia. Here I have far less care and responsibility. I am now responsible for very little. The danger may be somewhat greater, though that I think doubtful.

By the by, we hear that Raleigh and our camps in west Virginia were occupied by the enemy soon after we left. No difference. There is one comfort here. If we suffer, it is in the place where the *decisive* acts are going on. In west Virginia, success or failure was a mere circumstance hardly affecting the general cause. . . .

Well, love to all. Dearest be cheerful and content. It will all be well.

Affectionately,

R.

P. S. — I was near forgetting to say that I think I shall not be permitted to join the Seventy-ninth. That matter I suppose is settled. The prospect of Colonel Scammon being brigadier is *good*.

———

September 1. Evening. — About five o'clock this P. M. heavy firing began in the old place — said to be near Centreville or at Bull Run. A fierce rain-storm with thunder set in soon after, and for the last ten hours there has been a roaring rivalry between the artillery of earth and heaven. It is now dark, but an occasional gun can still be heard. The air trembles when the great guns roar. The place of the firing indicates that our forces still hold the same ground or nearly the same as before. It is queer. We really know but little more of the fights of two or three days ago than you do; in the way of accurate knowledge, perhaps less, for the telegraph may give you official bulletins. We have seen some, a great many, of our wounded; some five or six hundred of the enemy taken prisoners, and a few of our men paroled. Some think we got the best of it, some otherwise. As yet I call it a tie.

I am very glad to be here. The scenes around us are interesting, the events happening are most important. You can hardly imagine the relief I feel on getting away from the petty warfare of western Virginia. Four forts or field works are in sight, and many camps. The spire of Fairfax Seminary (now a hospital), the flags on distant hills whose works are not distinguishable, the white dome of the capitol, visible from the higher elevations, many fine residences in sight — all make this seem a realization of "the pride and pomp of glorious war." The roar of heavy artillery, the moving of army waggons, carriages, and ambulances with the wounded, marching troops, and couriers hastening to and fro, fill up the scene. Don't think I am led to forget the sad side of it, or the good cause at the foundation. I am thinking now of the contrast between what is here and what I have looked on for fifteen months past.

Dearest, what are you doing tonight? Thinking of me as you put to sleep the pretty little favorite? Yes, that is it. And my thought in the midst of all this is of you and the dear ones.

I just got an order that I must be "especially vigilant tonight

22

to guard against surprise, or confusion in case of alarm." I don't know what it indicates, but that I have done so often in the mountains that it is no great trouble. So I go to warn the captains. — Good night, darling.

Ever yours most lovingly,

R.

September 2, A. M. — A stormy night but no surprise. A bright cold morning, good for the poor fellows who are wounded.

Mrs. Hayes.

Upton's Hill (six or eight miles from Washington), Virginia, September 1, 1862.

Dear Mother: — We are in the midst of the great acts. The roar of the battles of the 30th and 31st was perfectly distinct here. We were in readiness to join in if needed. We are placed here, however, I conjecture, for a few days with a few other old regiments, to hold Forts Ramsay and Buffalo in case of disaster in front. I think the result thus far, though not at all decisive, upon the whole, favorable.

You will feel some anxiety when you hear of battles, but I tell Lucy *no news, after a fight, from me is good news.* If safe I have no opportunity to communicate. If injured or worse, officers are taken to Washington and tidings sent. I am glad to say all things pertaining to soldiers, sick or wounded, in Washington are managed most admirably. Few private families could provide equal comforts and accommodations. I write this for Uncle as well as for you.

I saw Captain Haynes the day before yesterday. He is thin and worn, but gaining. He was uncertain whether he could join his regiment (the *new* one) or not. I suppose it is settled that old officers can't go to the new regiments. This settles' my chance for the Seventy-ninth also. All right, as far as I am personally concerned. The rule is a bad one — a very bad one — so bad that it will perhaps be changed, but it is no hardship to me personally. I see no regiment here that I would prefer to the Twenty-third. General Cox's six regiments from Ohio are among the crack troops of the army in the opinion of everybody.

Colonel Scammon distinguished himself the other day and will, I doubt not, be made a brigadier.   .   .   .

Affectionately, your son,

RUTHERFORD.

MRS. SOPHIA HAYES.

Tuesday, September 2, 1862.   Upton's. — A clear, cold, windy day; bracing and *Northern.*   No news except a rumor that the armies are both busy gathering up wounded and burying dead; that the enemy hold rather more of the battlefield than we do.

12:30 P. M. — I have seen several accounts of the late battles, with details more or less accurate.   The impression I get is that we have rather the worst of it, by reason of superior generalship on the part of the Rebels.

9:30 P. M. — New and interesting scenes this P. M.   The great army is retreating, coming back.   It passes before us and in our rear.   We are to cover the retreat if they are pursued.   They do not look or act like beaten men; they are in good spirits and orderly.   They are ready to hiss McDowell.   When General Given announced that General McClellan was again leader, the cheering was hearty and spontaneous.   The camps around us are numerous.   The signal corps telegraphs by waving lights to the camps on all the heights.   The scene is wild and glorious this fine night.   Colonel White of the Twelfth and I have arranged our plans in case of an attack tonight.   So to bed.   Let the morrow provide for itself.

Wednesday, September 3. — No alarm last night.   Enemy quiet in front.   A little firing near [the] chain bridge, supposed to be feeling of our position.   It is rumored that the main body is going up the Potomac to cross.   Many men last evening in the retreating ranks were ready to hiss McDowell.

P. M.   After supper.   I am tonight discouraged — more so than ever before.   The disaster in Kentucky is something, but the conduct of men, officers, generals and all, in the late battles near Bull Run is more discouraging than aught else.   The Eastern troops don't fight like the Western.   If the enemy is now energetic and wise, they can take great advantages of us. Well, well, I can but do my duty as I see it.

EIGHT MILES WEST OF WASHINGTON,
UPTON'S HILL, September 3, 1862.

DEAR UNCLE: — The fighting at and near Bull Run battlefield is finished and our army has withdrawn to the fortifications near Washington, leaving General Cox's force here on the outposts. The general result I figure up as follows: We lose ten to fifteen cannon, five thousand to eight thousand killed, wounded, or prisoners, a large amount of army stores, railroad stock, etc., destroyed, and the position. The enemy lose a few cannon, about the same or a greater number killed and wounded, not so many prisoners by about half, and hold the position. It is not a decided thing either way. We had decidedly the advantage in the fighting of Thursday and Friday, 28th and 29th. At the close of the 29th Jackson was heavily reinforced, and worsted us on Saturday. Saturday evening our reinforcements reached General Pope and we were about equal in the subsequent skirmishing. I get some notions of the troops here, as I look on and listen, not very different from those I have had before.

The enemy here has a large force of gallant and efficient cavalry. Our cavalry is much inferior. The Rebel infantry is superior to ours gathered from the cities and manufacturing villages of the old States. The Western troops, are, I think, superior to either. The Rebels have as much *good* artillery as we have. We have largely more than they have, but the excess is of poor quality. In generalship and officers they are superior to us. The result is we must conquer in land warfare by superior numbers. On the water we have splendid artillery, and are masters. High water, deep rivers, heavy rains, are our friends.

General Sigel is a favorite with troops. General Banks and Schenck are praised by them. General McDowell is universally denounced. General Pope is coldly spoken of. General McClellan is undoubtedly a great favorite with men under him. Last night it was announced that he was again in command at this the critical region now. Everywhere the joy was great, and was spontaneously and uproariously expressed. It was a happy army again.

There is nothing of the defeated or disheartened among the men. They are vexed and angry — say they ought to have had a great victory, but not at all demoralized. I speak, of course, only of those I see, and I have seen some of the most unfortunate regiments. Everyone now recognizes the policy of standing on the defensive until the new levies are organized and ready. All that we can save is clear gain. Unless the enemy gets decided and damaging advantages during the next fortnight or so, it is believed we can push them back with heavy loss and with a fair prospect of crushing them. I see you are having another demonstration at Cincinnati and Louisville. I can't think it can end successfully. The great number of new troops must be able to hold them in check until they will be compelled to fall back. Once let the enemy now begin a retrograde movement with our great wave after them and I think they must go under.

We are here a good deal exposed. Anything that shall happen to me, you will know at once. I feel very contented with my personal situation. Your certain aid to my family relieves me from anxiety on their account. It is an immense relief to be here away from the petty but dangerous warfare of west Virginia.

Direct General Cox's Division, via Washington. I already get the *Sentinel* here of late date — the last published.

P. M. — Since writing the foregoing I received your letter of the 28th inst. [ult.] Your letters will come to me with great certainty, I do not doubt, and quicker than when I was in west Virginia.

We see that a strong Rebel force occupies Lexington, Kentucky. All the river towns are threatened. This is our dark hour. We will [shall] weather it, I think. Generalship is our great need.

Glad you will write often. — I shall stay with the Twenty-third. — I saw Haynes and told him I supposed we were cut out by the orders. I care nothing about it. Haynes was looking thin.

Sincerely,

R. B. Hayes.

Since writing I have been in a caucus of the major-generals. It is curious, but a large number of truthful men say Sigel is an accomplished military scholar, but such a coward that he is of no account on the battle-field! Funny! We don't know all about things and men from the newspapers.

S. BIRCHARD.

Thursday, September 4. — A cheerful bright morning and a sound sleep dispels the gloom resting on my views of the future. During the night a courier came to my tent saying that two thousand of our wounded are in the hands of the enemy and are starving! The enemy is in bad condition for food.

Siege guns were put in the fort on our right (Ramsay) during the night; the preparations are advancing which will enable us to hold this post and "save Washington."

10 A. M. — The rumor is that the enemy is directing his course up the Potomac, intending to cross into Maryland. We now hear cannon at a great distance, in a northern direction.

About 4:30 P. M. the enemy began to fire at our cavalry picket, about three miles out. Waggoners rolled in, horsemen ditto, in great haste. The regiments of General Cox's Division were soon ready, not one-fourth or one-third absent, or hiding, or falling to the rear as seems to be the habit in this Potomac army, but all, all, fell in at once; the Eleventh, Twelfth, Twenty-third, Twenty-eighth, Thirtieth, and Thirty-sixth Ohio can be counted on. After skedaddling the regiment of cavalry, who marched out so grandly a few hours before, the firing of the enemy ceased. A quiet night followed.

Cincinnati is now threatened by an army which defeated our raw troops at Richmond, Kentucky. Everywhere the enemy is crowding us. Everywhere they are to be met by our *raw* troops, the veterans being in the enemy's country too distant to be helpful. A queer turning the tables on us! And yet if they fail of getting any permanent and substantial advantatge of us, I think the recoil will be fatal to them. I think in delaying this movement until our new levies are almost ready for the field, they have let the golden opportunity slip; that they will be able to annoy and harass but not to injure us; and that the reaction will push them further back than ever. We shall see! A rumor of a repulse of the enemy at Harpers Ferry by Wool. Hope it is true!

———

Upton's Hill, Fairfax County, Virginia,
September 4, (P. M.), 1862.

Dearest: — I received your good letter of the 29th yesterday. Our situation now is this: Washington is surrounded for a distance of from seven to fifteen miles by defensive works, placed on all the commanding points. For the present the thing to be done is to keep the enemy out of the capital until our new army is prepared for the field and the old one is somewhat recruited. We (that is General Cox's Division, viz.: Eleventh, Twelfth, Twenty-third, Twenty-eighth, Thirtieth, and Thirty-sixth regiments of infantry, Captains McMullen's and Simmond's Batteries, Gilmore's, West's, and Schaumbeck's Cavalry, all from western Virginia) are placed to guard important roads and points of which Upton's Hill and Munson's Hill, Forts Ramsay, Buffalo, and "Skedaddle," all in the same vicinity, are the chief. We are about seven miles from Washington, in sight of the capitol, and eight miles from Alexandria.

For a few days after the retreat of our forces from Centreville and Bull Run, these were points of peril. In case of an advance of the Rebels we would be first attacked. I slept in boots and spurs with my horse saddled. But now all the forts are manned and I do not expect to see the enemy approach in this direction. They could easily storm our positions with a strong force, but it would cost so many lives to storm all the works between here and Washington that they would be ruined to attempt it.

I therefore look for quiet camp life for some time to come, unless the enemy makes such advances to Washington from other directions as will make these works worthless, when we should probably go to Washington. This I do not anticipate. We shall drill, brush and burnish up, sleep and get fat.

Things have had a bad turn lately, but I don't give it up. Something far more damaging than anything which has yet happened must occur, or these attempts to carry the war into our territory must recoil heavily on the Rebels. Failing to hold their advanced conquests, they must go back vastly weakened and disheartened, while our following wave will be a growing and resistless one. It will be a few weeks yet before the evil time and the occurrence of sinister events will cease. But frosts and rains are coming and when they come will be our day. We can only hope to get off as easily as possible until that time.

The Kentucky disaster I fear injured many of your friends; but if not made permanent, it will do good.

Well, this is talk about public affairs. I sent my trunk today via Washington to Platt. If not intercepted (no unlikely event) I will mail one key to Mother and the other to you.

An old gentleman — too old to stand this "biz"— named Kugler, called to see me just now, saying that my commission in the Seventy-ninth was made out; that he was a captain in the Seventy-ninth and was trying to get the War Department to let me go. I said "nix" either way. At present I prefer to stay here, but no odds. While he was talking, the enemy began to fire on one of our cavalry pickets with shell. He said to me: "When do you start in such a case?" I told him, "When I got orders." He seemed much astonished at the quiet reigning in camp, while the teamsters were tearing in like mad. He is a wealthy distiller at Milford who gave twenty-five hundred dollars to raise a company which he intends to turn over to a son or nephew. He seems determined to get permission for me to join the regiment and may possibly succeed.

A lovely sunset on a most animating scene. Troops are getting into shape and things look better. McClellan is indeed a great favorite with the army. He is no doubt the best man to take the defense of the capital in hand. He is the only man who can get good fighting out of the Potomac Army. McDowell is detested by them. Pope coldly regarded. McClellan is loved. Not thinking him a first-class commander, I yet in view of this feeling, think him the best man now available.

There, darling, is a long letter and yet not a word of love in it. But I do you love so much, dearest. You may emphasize every word of that sentence.

I hope they will whip Kirby Smith and his Rebel horde. But, at any rate, he will soon get to the end of that rope.

Affectionately,

MRS. HAYES.   R.

Friday, September 5, 1862, 9 A. M. — Distant firing heard towards Leesburg and up the Potomac. A warm fine day.

P. M. Received orders to be ready to march immediately; to cook three days' rations, etc. Understood to be to join Burnside.

September 6. Saturday. — Left Upton's Hill at 7:30 A. M. Marched through Georgetown and Washington to the outskirts of Washington towards Leesboro Road, a very dusty, hot, oppressive day; Twenty-third in the rear. Men kept well closed up through Washington but stopped at a grove, near where we stopped to camp, in large numbers. Lieutenant Christie reported that only three hundred of the Twenty-third marched into camp. This was substantially true, but conveyed an erroneous impression that we fell out and straggled badly. All corrected however soon.

WASHINGTON CITY, September 6, 1862.

DEAREST: — We have had a very hot, dusty, and oppressive march from our camp at Upton's Hill. Some of McDowell's demoralized men are thought good enough to take care of the field-works out there, and General Cox's six regiments of Ohio men are now attached to General Burnside's Corps. What is to be our duty and where, we do not yet know. We suppose we are to meet the invasion threatened by the Rebels into Maryland. We may be destined for other service; but you will hear from us often. We all hear favorable impressions of General Burnside, and are glad to be assigned to his corps.

You will not allow yourself to be too anxious, I trust, on my account. Rejoice when it rains or gets cold. We are victimized by the drouth. Well, good-bye. Love to the dear boys. I thought of them often today; little fellows very like them followed us as we marched through the streets today.

Affectionately, ever your

MRS. HAYES.   R.

WASHINGTON CITY, September 6, 1862.

DEAR UNCLE: — We left Upton's Hill and its earthworks to be guarded by less serviceable troops than ours, and marched here through heat and dust today. We (that is General Cox's six Ohio regiments and the artillery and cavalry that we had on [the] Kanawha) are attached to General Burnside's Army Corps. Pope is under a cloud; promised and boasted too much, and has failed in performance. We like General Burnside and his reputation.

We suppose we are destined for the defense of Maryland, but don't know. Being with General Burnside, you can keep the run of us. I am told that my commission as colonel of the Seventy-ninth has issued, and that influences are at work to get me released here. I do and say nothing in the premises.

It is very touching, the journey of Father Works, mentioned in a letter I got from you last night, to see his friends at Fremont. His desire, under such circumstances, to see you all, and his anxiety not to put you to the trouble of visiting him. He is a noble old man. It would be well if we had many like him. Regards to all. I am gratified that you approve my being here.

Sincerely,

R. B. HAYES.

S. BIRCHARD.

Sunday, September 7. Washington City. — Left the suburbs of Washington to go on Leesboro Road about twelve to fifteen miles. Road full of horse, foot, and artillery, baggage and ambulance waggons. Dust, heat, and thirst. "The Grand Army of the Potomac" appeared to bad advantage by the side of our troops. Men were lost from their regiments; officers left their commands to rest in the shade, to feed on fruit; thousands were straggling; confusion and disorder everywhere. New England troops looked well; Middle States troops badly; discipline gone or greatly relaxed.

On coming into camp Major-General Reno, in whose corps we are, rode into the grounds occupied by General Cox's troops in a towering passion because some of the men were taking straw or wheat from a stack. Some were taking it to feed to horses in McMullen's Battery and to cavalry horses; some in the Twenty-third Regiment were taking it to lie upon. The ground was a stubble field, in ridges of hard ground. I saw it and made no objection. General Reno began on McMullen's men. He addressed them: "You damned black sons of bitches." This he repeated to my men and asked for the colonel. Hearing it, I presented myself and assumed the responsibility, defending the men. I talked respectfully but firmly; told him we had always taken rails, for example, if needed to cook with; that if required we would pay for them. He denied the right and necessity; said we were in a loyal State, etc., etc. Gradually he softened down. He asked me my name. I asked his, all respectfully done on my part. He made various observations to which I replied. He expressed opinions on pilfering. I remarked, in reply to some opinion, substantially: "Well, I trust our generals will exhibit the same energy in dealing with our foes that they do in the treatment of their friends." He asked me, as if offended, what I meant by that. I replied. "Nothing — at least, I mean nothing disrespectful to you." (The fact was, I had a very favorable opinion of the gallantry and skill of General Reno and was most anxious to so act as to gain his good will.) This was towards the close of the controversy, and as General Reno rode away the men cheered me. I learn that *this,* coupled with the remark, gave General Reno great offense. He spoke to Colonel Ewing of putting colonels in irons if their men pilfered! Colonel Ewing says the remark "cut him to the quick," that he was "bitter" against me. General Cox and Colonel Scammon (the latter was present) both think I behaved properly in the controversy.

Monday, September 8. Camp near Leesboro, Maryland. — Nothing new this morning. Men from Ohio all in a talk about General Reno's abusive language. It is said that when talking with me he put his hand on his pistol; that many standing by began to handle their arms also! I am sorry the thing goes so far.

CAMP FIFTEEN MILES NORTH OF WASHINGTON, IN
MARYLAND, September 8, 1862.

DEAR UNCLE: — I write you about a difficulty I had yesterday
with Major-General Reno, not because it gives me any trouble
or anxiety but fearing that false and partial accounts of it may
get into the Eastern papers and give you trouble.

As we were camping last night, the general rode into my regiment in a towering passion, using most abusive language to my
men for taking a little straw to put on the hard, rough, ploughed
ground they were to lie on. I defended the men and in respect-
ful language gave him my opinion of the matter. He gradually
softened down and the affair seemed to end pretty well. But
the men cheered me, and this he seems to lay up against me. He
couples this with a remark I made that, "I trusted our generals
would exhibit the same energy in dealing with our foes that
they did in the treatment of their friends," and has talked of
putting me in irons, as is said. General Cox, Colonel Scammon,
and all the Ohio colonels and troops sustain me fully and justify
the cheering, saying the men have the same right to cheer their
colonel that they have to cheer General McClellan. I think it
will stop where it is, except in the newspapers. Whatever is
reported, you may feel safe about the outcome. They are doing
some hasty things at Washington, but I have no doubt in any
event that Governor Chase and the President will see justice
done at the end to all our Ohio men.

We are supposed to be here in readiness to operate against
the enemy invading Maryland. At *present* we are in General
Reno's Corps, General Cox's Division, Colonel Scammon's Brigade, of General Burnside's Army. On the march, the Ohio troops
have shown the best discipline and the most endurance of any
body. New England furnishes the next best. Some of the
Yankee troops are capital, *all* are good. The Middle States
(New Jersey, New York, and Pennsylvania) are many of them
abominable.

I have seen Colonel Ewing, who called on General Reno. He
says General Reno was "cut to the quick"' by the remark I have
quoted, and is exceedingly "bitter" about it. Well, it's all in a

lifetime. General Cox means to get us transferred if possible to General Sigel's Corps, on the ground that General Reno has given such offense to the Ohio troops that they will serve under him with reluctance.

Things have a bad look just now, but I still think they will mend before any crushing calamity comes. They will, if proper system and energy is adopted.

Sincerely,

R. B. HAYES.

P. S. — You may send this to Platt to set him right if he hears any lies about it. — H.

S. BIRCHARD.

September 9. Tuesday. — Marched about eight miles in a westerly direction through a fine-looking, well-improved region. Men very jolly. All came in together, "well closed up," at night. Major Comly sent with five companies to Seneca Bridge, three-fourths mile west of camp, to "hold it." Kelly, Company A, a witty Dutch-Irishman, kept up a fusillade of odd jokes in English German. The men cheered the ladies, — joked with the cuffys, and carried on generally.

Wednesday, September 10, 1862. — We camped near Seneca Bridge, about twenty-five to thirty miles from Washington. The order cutting down baggage trains leaves us eight waggons; — one for headquarters, i. e. field and staff; one for hospital; two for stores; four for company cooking utensils and the like. The band trouble breaks out again. We enjoy these short marches among great bodies of moving troops very much. Tonight the sutler sold brandy peaches making about ten or a dozen of our men drunk. I thereupon made a guard-house of the sutler's tent and kept all the drunken men in it all night! A sorry time for the sutler! Got orders to move at the word any time after 10 o'clock. I simply did nothing!

Camp near Rich or Ridgefield [Ridgeville], about forty miles from Baltimore, about thirty from Washington, about seventeen from Frederick. Marched today from ten to fourteen miles.

Occasionally showery — no heavy rain; dust laid, air cooled. Marched past the Fifth, Seventh, Twenty-ninth, and Sixty-sixth Ohio regiments. They have from eighty to two hundred men each — sickness, wounds, prisoners, etc., etc., the rest. This looks more like closing the war from sheer exhaustion than anything I have seen. Only four commissioned officers in the Seventh. A lieutenant in command of one regiment; an adjutant commands another! Saw General Crawford today, he was very cordial.

CAMP NORTHWEST OF BROOKVILLE, MARYLAND,

September 10, 1862.

DEAREST: — We are now about twenty-five or thirty miles northwest of Washington, about thirty miles from Baltimore, in Maryland. The army is gradually moving up to operate against the Rebels who have crossed the Potomac. We march about eight to twelve miles a day — General Cox's Division always near the front, if not in front. We are now in front. Captured a Rebel patrol last night. We subordinates know less of the actual state of things than the readers of the *Commercial* at home. Order is coming out of chaos. The great army moves on three roads five or eight miles apart. Sometimes we move in the night and at all other hours, moving each subdivision about six or eight hours at a time in each twenty-four hours. Some large body is moving on each road all the time. In this way the main body is kept somewhere in the same region. General Burnside is our commander. I have not yet seen him. He was cheered heartily, I am told, yesterday when he met his troops below here. His Yankee regiments are much the best troops we have seen East. "The Grand Army of the Potomac" suffers by comparison with General Cox's or General Burnside's men. It is not fair, however, to judge them by what we now see. They are returning form a severe and unfortunate service which of necessity has broken them down.

We march through a well-cultivated, beautiful region — poor soil but finely improved. I never saw the Twenty-third so happy as yesterday. More witty things were said as we passed ladies, children, and negroes (for the most part friendly) than I have heard in a year before. The question was always asked, "What troops are those," or "Where are you from?" The answers were "Twenty-third Utah," "Twenty-third Bushwhackers," "Twenty-third Mississippi," "Drafted men," "Raw Recruits," "Paroled prisoners," "Militia going home," "Home Guards," "Peace Men," "Uncle Abe's children," "The Lost Tribes," and others "too numerous, etc." Nearly all the hands are mustered out of service; ours therefore is a novelty We marched a few miles yesterday on a road where troops have not before marched. It was funny to see the children. I saw our boys running after the music in many a group of clean, bright-looking, excited little fellows.

What a time of it they have in Cincinnati? I got a dispatch from Mr. Clements yesterday saying I was discharged ten days ago by the War Department to take command of the Seventy-ninth, but I get no official notice of it, and at present can't get leave to go and see to it. If the place is not filled by somebody else I shall join the new regiment before the end of the month, I suspect. I have no particular preference or wish about it, but having said that I will join if leave is given, I shall do so unless in the meanwhile some change in affairs takes place to justify a different course.

I can hardly think the enemy will carry his whole or main force into Maryland and risk all upon a battle here. If not he will probably withdraw on the approach of our army. If he does, I can then get leave of absence.

Kisses and love to all the boys. Love to Grandma and the dear friends you are among. I feel very grateful for their kindness to you and the boys. I think of you now almost as constantly as you do of me.

I have very little care or responsibility. The men behave well, and are always ready. I got into an angry altercation with Major-General Reno who was in a passion and abusive to some of my men; the men cheered me as he rode off, which made a little difficulty, but I am told he is ashamed of it, and it led to no trouble.

Good-bye, darling. "I love you so much."

Affectionately, yours ever,

Mrs. Hayes.   R.

FREDERICK, MARYLAND, September 13, 1862, A. M.

DEAREST: — Yesterday was an exciting but very happy day. We retook this fine town about 5:30 P. M. after a march of fourteen miles and a good deal of skirmishing, cannon firing and uproar, and with but little fighting. We marched in just at sundown, the Twenty-third a good deal of the way in front. There was no mistaking the Union feeling and joy of the people — fine ladies, pretty girls, and children were in all the doors and windows waving flags and clapping hands. Some "jumped up and down" with happiness. Joe enjoyed it and rode up the streets bowing most gracefully. The scene as we approached across the broad bottom-lands in line of battle, with occasional cannon firing and musketry, the beautiful Blue Ridge Mountains in view, the fine town in front, was very magnificent. It is pleasant to be so greeted. The enemy had held the city just a week. "The longest week of our lives," "We thought you were never coming," "This is the happiest hour of our lives," were the common expressions.

It was a most fatiguing day to the men. When we got the town, before the formal entry, men laid [lay] down in the road, saying they couldn't stir again. Some were pale, some red as if apoplectic. Half an hour after, they were marching erect and proud hurrahing the ladies!

Colonel Moor, Twenty-eighth, of Cincinnati, was wounded and taken prisoner in one of the skirmishes yesterday. The enemy treat our men well — very well. We have of sick and wounded five hundred or six hundred prisoners taken here.

Well, Lucy dearest, good-bye. Love to all. Kiss the boys.

Affectionately, ever,

R.

MRS. HAYES.

FREDERICK, MARYLAND, September 13, 1862.

DEAR UNCLE: — We retook "Old Frederick" yesterday evening. A fine town it is, and the magnificent and charming reception we got from the fine ladies and people paid us for all the hardships endured in getting it.

BATTLE OF SOUTH MOUNTAIN, MARYLAND, SEPTEMBER 14, 1862

Where Colonel Hayes was severely wounded

The enemy has gone northwest. They are represented as in great force, filthy, lousy, and desperate. A battle with them will be a most terrific thing. With forty thousand Western troops to give life and heartiness to the fight, we should, with our army, whip them. I think we shall whip them, at any rate, but it is by no means a certainty. A defeat is ruin to them, a retreat without a battle is a serious injury to them. A serious defeat to us is bad enough. They left here, for the most part, a day or two ago, saying they were going to Pennsylvania. They behaved pretty well here, but avowed their purpose to ravage Pennsylvania. We had a good deal of skirmishing and a little fighting to get this town. General Cox's Division did it. We lost Colonel Moor of [the] Twenty-eighth Ohio, Cincinnati, wounded and taken prisoner. We captured five hundred to six hundred sick and wounded Rebels. A few of our men killed and wounded. The whole body (Ohio *infantry*) behaved splendidly.

Sincerely,

R. B. Hayes.

P. S. — Cannon firing now in front.

S. Birchard.

(*Telegram.*)

Frederick, Maryland, September 15, 1862.

To W. A. Platt, *Columbus, Ohio.*

I am seriously wounded in the left arm above the elbow. The Ohio troops all behaved well.

R. B. Hayes.

Middletown, Frederick County, Maryland,

September 15, [1862].

Dear Mother: — I was wounded in the battle yesterday. A musket-ball passed through the centre of the left arm just above the elbow. The arm is of course rendered useless and will be so for some weeks. I am comfortably *at home* with a very kind and attentive family here named Rudy — not quite Ruddy.

23

The people here are all, or nearly all, Union people and give up all they have to the wounded. The ladies work night and day. We are doing well so far in the fighting.

You see I write this myself to show you I am doing well, but it is an awkward business sitting propped up in bed nursing a useless arm. Lucy will find me here if she comes. Or if I go to Frederick, [let her] inquire at provost or military headquarters. If I go to Baltimore, she must have inquiry made at same places there. — Love to all.

Affectionately,

R. B. HAYES.

P. S. — Send this to Mother Hayes also. I write you thinking Lucy may leave before this gets there.

MRS. WEBB.

MIDDLETOWN, September 16, 1862.

DEAR MOTHER: — It would make you very happy about me if you could see how pleasantly and comfortably I am cared for. Imagine Mrs. Wasson and two or three young ladies doing all in their power to keep me well nursed and fed, and you will get a good idea of my situation.

The worst period of my wound is now over. I am, when still, free from pain. A little boy, about Ruddy's age, (eight or nine) named Charlie Rudy, sits by the window and describes the troops, etc., etc., as they pass. I said to him, "Charlie, you live on a street that is much travelled." "Oh," said he, "it isn't always so, it's only when the war comes." Mrs. Rudy's currant jellies remind me of old times in Delaware.

I hope Lucy will be able to come out to see me. At any rate, I shall probably come home and stay a few weeks when I shall see you. Thus far, the best of the fighting is with us. My regiment has lost largely but has been victorious. — Love to all.

Affectionately,

R.

MRS. SOPHIA HAYES.

Thursday, September 18, 1862. — [At] Captain Rudy's (Jacob Rudy, merchant), Middletown, Maryland. Here I lie nursing my shattered arm, "as snug as a bug in a rug."

September 12, entered Frederick amidst loud huzzahs and cheering — eight miles. Had a little skirmish getting in; a beautiful scene and a jolly time.

September 13, marched to this town, entered in night — Middletown, Maryland.

September 14, Sunday. Enemy on a spur of Blue Ridge, three and one-half miles west. At 7 A. M. we go out to attack. I am sent with [the] Twenty-third up a mountain path to get around the Rebel right with instructions to attack and take a battery of two guns supposed to be posted there. I asked, "If I find six guns and a strong support?" Colonel Scammon replies, "Take them anyhow." It is the only safe instruction. General Cox told me General Pleasanton had arranged with Colonel Crook of [the] Second Brigade as to the support of his (General Pleasanton's) artillery and cavalry, and was vexed that Colonel Scammon was to have the advance; that he, General Cox, wished me to put my energies and wits all to work so that General Pleasanton should have no cause to complain of an inefficient support. The First Brigade had the advance and the Twenty-third was the front of the First Brigade.

Went with a guide by the right flank up the hill, Company A deployed in front as skirmishers. Seeing signs of Rebels [I] sent [Company] F to the left and [Company] I to the right as flankers. Started a Rebel picket about 9 A. M. Soon saw from the opposite hill a strong force coming down towards us; formed hastily in the woods; faced by the rear rank (some companies inverted and some out of place) towards the enemy; pushed through bushes and rocks over broken ground towards the enemy; soon received a heavy volley, wounding and killing some. I feared confusion; exhorted, swore, and threatened. Men did pretty well. Found we could not stand it long, and ordered an advance. Rushed forward with a yell; enemy gave way. Halted to reform line; heavy firing resumed.

I soon began to fear we could not stand it, and again ordered a charge; the enemy broke, and we drove them clear out of the woods. Our men halted at a fence near the edge of the woods and kept up a brisk fire upon the enemy, who were sheltering themselves behind stone walls and fences near the top of the hill, beyond a cornfield in front of our position. Just as I gave the command to charge I felt a stunning blow and found a musket ball had struck my left arm just above the elbow. Fearing that an artery might be cut, I asked a soldier near me to tie my handkerchief above the wound. I soon felt weak, faint, and sick at the stomach. I laid [lay] down and was pretty comfortable. I was perhaps twenty feet behind the line of my men, and could form a pretty accurate notion of the way the fight was going. The enemy's fire was occasionally very heavy; balls passed near my face and hit the ground all around me. I could see wounded men staggering or carried to the rear; but I felt sure our men were holding their own. I listened anxiously to hear the approach of reinforcements; wondered they did not come.

I was told there was danger of the enemy flanking us on our left, near where I was lying. I called out to Captain Drake, who was on the left, to let his company wheel backward so as to face the threatened attack. His company fell back perhaps twenty yards, and the whole line gradually followed the example, thus leaving me between our line and the enemy. Major Comly came along and asked me if it was my intention the whole line should fall back. I told him no, that I merely wanted one or two of the left companies to wheel backward so as to face an enemy said to be coming on our left. I said if the line was now in good position to let it remain and to face the left companies as I intended. This, I suppose, was done.

The firing continued pretty warm for perhaps fifteen or twenty minutes, when it gradually died away on both sides. After a few minutes' silence I began to doubt whether the enemy had disappeared or whether our men had gone farther back. I called out, "Hallo Twenty-third men, are you going to leave your colonel here for the enemy?" In an instant a half dozen or more men sprang forward to me, saying, "Oh no, we will carry you wherever you want us to." The enemy immediately opened fire on them. Our men replied to them, and soon the battle was raging as hotly as ever. I ordered the men back to cover, telling them they would get me shot and themselves too. They went back and about this time Lieutenant Jackson came and insisted upon taking me out of the range of the enemy's fire. He took me back to our line and, feeling faint, he laid me down behind a big log and gave me a canteen of water, which tasted so good. Soon after, the fire having again died away, he took me back up the hill, where my wound was dressed by Dr. Joe. I then walked about half a mile to the house of Widow Kugler. I remained there two or three hours when I was taken with Captain Skiles in an ambulance to Middletown — three and a half miles — where I stopped at Mr. Jacob Rudy's.

I omitted to say that a few moments after I first laid [lay] down, seeing something going wrong and feeling a little easier, I got up and began to give directions about things; but after a few moments, getting very weak, I again laid [lay] down. While I was lying down I had considerable talk with a wounded [Confederate] soldier lying near me. I gave him messages for my wife and friends in case I should not get up. We were right jolly and friendly; it was by no means an unpleasant experience.

Telegraphed Lucy, Uncle, Platt, and John Herron, two or three times each. Very doubtful whether they get the dispatches. My orderly, Harvey Carrington, nurses me with the greatest care. Dr. Joe dresses the wound, and the women feed me sumptuously.

Don't sleep much these nights; days pretty comfortable.

[Yesterday, the] 17th, listened almost all day to the heavy cannonading of the great battle on the banks of the Antietam, anxiously guessing whether it is with us [or] our foes. [Today, the] 18th, write letters to divers friends.

MIDDLETOWN, MARYLAND, September 18, 1862, (P. M.)

DEAR MOTHER: — I am steadily getting along. For the most part, the pain is not severe, but occasionally an unlucky move of the shattered arm causes a good deal of distress. I have every comfort that I could get at home. I shall hope to see Lucy in two or three days.

The result of the two great battles already fought is favorable, but not finally decisive. I think the final struggle will occur soon.

We feel encouraged to hope for a victory from the results thus far. We have had nearly one-half our fighting men in the Twenty-third killed or wounded. Lieutenant-Colonel Jones of Thirtieth Ohio, in our Brigade, of Columbus, is missing; supposed to be wounded. Colonel —— of the Eleventh Ohio, killed. Love to all. — Send this to Uncle.

Affectionately, your son,

R.

Mrs. Sophia Hayes.

Middletown, Maryland, September 18, (P. M.), 1862.

Dear Mother: — I hope to see Lucy in a few days. She will find me here in good hands and improving fast. I suffer a good deal at times, but for the most part get on well. Drs. Joe and Jim both safe and very busy. The Twenty-third has suffered heavily, nearly one-half our fighting men killed or wounded. Two battles already fought; result not yet decided. So far, the advantage is rather with us.

Affectionately,

R. B. Hayes.

Mrs. Webb.

September 19. — Begin to mend a little.

September 20. — Got a dispatch from Platt. Fear Lucy has not heard of my wound; had hoped to see her today, probably shan't. This hurts me worse than the bullet did.

September 21. — Battle of Antietam rather with us. The Twenty-third has done nobly. Very gratifying. But alas, thirty or forty dead, and one hundred and thirty or one hundred and forty wounded.

Middletown, Monday, September 22, 1862.

Dear Uncle: — I am still doing well. I am looking for Lucy. My only anxiety is lest she has trouble in finding me. Indeed, I am surprised that she is not here already. I shall stay here about ten days or two weeks longer, then go to Frederick and a few days afterwards to Washington. About the 15th or 20th October, I can go to Ohio, and if my arm cures as slowly as I suspect it will, I may come via Pittsburgh and Cleveland to Fremont and visit you. I do not see how I can be fit for service under two months.

The Eighth Regiment was in the second battle and suffered badly. You must speak well of "old Frederick" hereafter. These people are nursing some thousands of our men as if they were their own brothers. McClellan has done well here. The Harpers Ferry imbecility or treachery alone prevented a crushing of the Rebels. Love to all. Send me papers, etc., here "care Jacob Rudy."

Do you remember your Worthington experience in 1842? Well this is it. I don't suffer as much as you did, but like it.

Middletown is eight miles west of Frederick on the National Road. The nearest telegraph office is at Frederick. Two-thirds of the wounded men of my regiment have gone to Frederick. The worst cases are still here. In my regiment, four captains out of eight present were wounded, thirty-nine men killed, one hundred and thirty-seven wounded, and seven missing. I expect about twenty to twenty-five of the wounded to die. The New York *Times* account gives us the nearest justice of anybody in its details of the Sunday fight but we are all right. Everybody knows that we were the first in and the last out, and that we were victorious all the time. How happy the men are — even the badly wounded ones. One fellow shot through the body has gathered up a banjo and makes the hospital ring with negro songs!

Good-bye,

H.

S. Birchard.

Middletown, Maryland, September 26, 1862.

Dear Uncle: — Lucy is here and we are pretty jolly. She visits the wounded and comes back in tears, then we take a little refreshment and get over it. I am doing well. Shall, perhaps, come home a little sooner than I expected to be able to. I am now in a fix. To get me for the Seventy-ninth, some of its friends got an order to relieve me from the Twenty-third from the War Department. So I am a free man, and can go or come as I see fit. I expect, however, to stay with [the] Twenty-third.

Shall probably start home in ten days or so. I got your letter of the 18th. You need have no anxiety about me. I think I shall come home by way of Cleveland and Fremont, stopping a few days with you. Love to all.

H.

S. BIRCHARD.

MIDDLETOWN, MARYLAND, September 26, 1862.

DEAR MOTHER: — Lucy is making me very happy and comfortable. She visits the wounded and is much interested in them. I am doing well, and shall probably get home in three or four weeks. Many of the wounded are starting home, and all hope to get leave to go before they return to service. I am not suffering much. The weariness from lying abed is the chief annoyance. Dr. Smith was here with Mr. Sessions and others. You need not send fruit and things. I get all I need without trouble. Love to all.

Affectionately,

R.

MRS. SOPHIA HAYES.

MIDDLETOWN, October 1, 1862.

DEAR UNCLE: — Lucy is here; we are rather enjoying it. The rascally arm is very uncertain; sometimes I think it is about well, and then I have a few hours of worse pain than ever. It is, however, mending prosperously. I think I can travel comfortably by the first of next week.

I get all of your letters. Those sent to Washington have all been forwarded here.

Lejune, who has a brother in Fremont (grocery keeper), *captured twenty-five rebels on the 14th!!* He surrounded them! He was afterwards wounded — I think not dangerously.

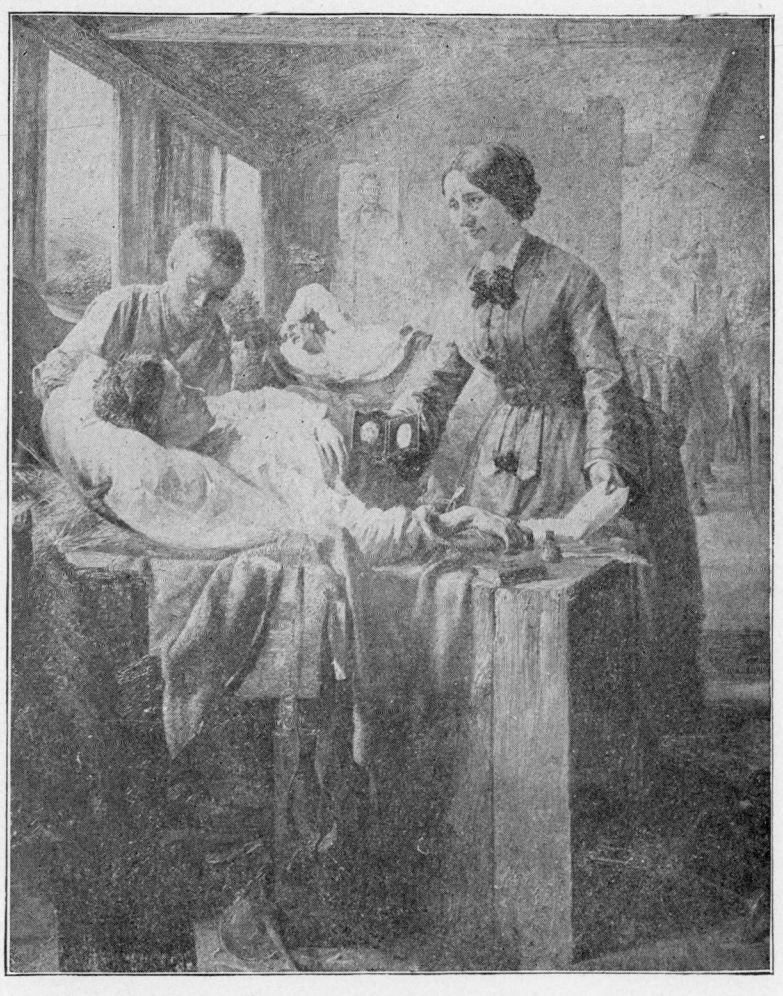

WOMAN'S MISSION IN WAR.

Lucy Webb Hayes in Hospital at Middletown, Maryland, after the Antietam Campaign of 1862.

You will like the President's [Emancipation] Proclamation. I am not sure about it, but am content.

McClellan is undoubtedly the general for this army. If he is let alone, I think he may be relied on to do well. One element we of the West overlook: These troops are not any better (if so good) than the Rebels. We must have superior numbers to make success a sure thing. All things look well to me now. If we don't divide too much among ourselves, I think we get them this winter.

We shall probably go to Columbus at first. Our boys at Uncle Boggs' will draw us that way. My stay in Ohio will probably be about fifteen to twenty days. We must meet, of course. If necessary, I will come out to Fremont.

H.

S. BIRCHARD.

MIDDLETOWN, MARYLAND, October 1, 1862.

DEAR MOTHER: — We are getting on very well. The arm mends slowly but is doing well. I think I can move by the first of next week.

I receive your letters and was much obliged for the dainties you *intended* to send, but we don't need them. Lucy visits the hospital daily. We rather enjoy this life. For the most part, I am very comfortable, but an hour or two a day I suffer more than ever. I shall come to Columbus first; probably the last of next week, say about the 12th of October. Love to all.

Your son,

R. B. HAYES.

MRS. SOPHIA HAYES.

October 4, 1826. — Visited the battle-field with Lucy, Mr. Rudy, Corporal West, and Carrington this [my] fortieth birthday, Hunted up the graves of our gallant boys.

[The next day Hayes had a letter from Dr. J. T. Webb, who was with the Twenty-third at Sharpsburg, Maryland, informing him that General Cox had been ordered back to western Virginia. The letter said: "We all expect to be on our way back in a few days. There is much dissatisfaction at the prospect of returning to western Virginia. For my part, I will not remain in western Virginia another winter for any consideration whatever, if there is any way to avoid it."

Dr. Webb added these words about a young man some day to be President: "Our young friend, William McKinley, commissary sergeant, would be pleased with a promotion, and would not object to your recommendation for the same. Without wishing to interfere in this matter, it strikes me he is about the brightest chap spoken of for the place."

A few days later Colonel and Mrs. Hayes returned to Ohio. October 17, Miss Laura Platt, Hayes's niece, wrote Mr. Sardis Birchard announcing her approaching marriage to Mr. John G. Mitchell. To this letter Hayes added the following postscript: "I know Mr. Mitchell (Colonel Mitchell) well. He is a young lawyer, educated at Kenyon, of good family, entered the war as lieutenant, then adjutant, then captain, and now lieutenant-colonel of [the] One Hundred and Thirteenth. A member of the Episcopal Church, and a *capital fellow.* He is neither *tall* nor *slim,* but good-looking. He is taller than Laura and about as 'chunky.' "]

COLUMBUS, October 23, 1862.

DEAR UNCLE: — Laura married and off yesterday — all sensible and happy. We had a delightful visit to the boys and kin at Pickaway and Ross Counties. Lucy drove young Ned to Chillicothe and back from here. He is a safe horse and Platt expects to send him back to you when he begins to use his colt. My arm mends very slowly. Mother and all here well. I am to be colonel of [the] Twenty-third and to go to western Virginia. Shan't go for some weeks. Lucy goes home to Cincinnati next week — about the last of the week. My regards to all.

Sincerely,

S. BIRCHARD.   R. B. HAYES.

COLUMBUS, October 31, 1862.

DEAR UNCLE: — Lucy has had a pretty severe attack of diphtheria. For three or four days she was in a good deal of pain and could neither swallow nor talk. Yesterday and today she has been able to sit up, and is in excellent spirits. We expect to return to Cincinnati next week, and in a week or ten days after I shall probably go to the Twenty-third. My arm has improved the last week more than any time before.

You are glad to hear so good an account of Ned! Lucy says you ought to be glad to hear so good an account of her! That she drove him so skillfully, she thinks a feat.

Unless you come down here by Monday next, we shall be gone home. Laura is looked for with her spouse tomorrow.

Sincerely,

R.

S. BIRCHARD.

CINCINNATI, November 8, 1862.

DEAR UNCLE: — Lucy and I came down Tuesday and are now comfortably home again. My arm improves rapidly, and I think in two or three weeks I shall return to the regiment. All the boys came down with their grandma and Aunt Lucy. They are very healthy and happy. In haste.

Sincerely,

R. B. HAYES.

S. BIRCHARD.

CINCINNATI, November 12, 1862.

DEAR UNCLE: — Your letter, also the apples, came safely to hand. The apples were finer than usual. The family are settled down with a girl that starts off well. The elections don't worry me. They will, I hope, spur the Administration to more vigor. The removal of McClellan and the trial of Buell and Fitz-John Porter, the dismissal of Ford, and substituting Schenck for Wool, all look like life. General Burnside may not have ability for so great a command, but he has energy, boldness, and luck on his side. Rosecrans, too, is likely to drive things. All this is more than compensation for the defeat of a gang of *our* demagogues by the demagogues of the other side. As to the Democratic policy, it will be warlike, notwithstanding Vallandigham and others. Governor Seymour has made a speech in Utica *since* his election indicating this. Besides, that party must be, *in power,* a war party.

I *expect* to return next week, middle or last of the week. My arm does well, but is not of much use. If I find anything injurious or difficult in campaigning, I will get assigned to some light duty for a few months.

Sincerely,

R. B. Hayes.

S. Birchard.

Cincinnati, November 24, 1862.

Dear Mother: — I took passage on a steamboat and left for my regiment at Gauley Bridge on Saturday, but after going a few miles, we got cast on a bar, and can't get off until a rise of water. Luckily, I was in reach of the street railroad cars, and so came home to await the coming rise. It is expected tonight. I am sorry not to visit Columbus again, but we had a good visit with you, and we should not feel more reconciled to a separation if I were to stay a month. You will be glad to learn from Uncle that I am likely to stay in winter quarters where my arm can be cared for as well as if I were at home. You will direct letters to me at "Gauley Bridge, Virginia, via Gallipolis."

The children were to see us yesterday and seemed very happy. They would like to go home before Christmas, but will not mourn much, as they suppose they are sure to be relieved then. We had an excellent visit from Uncle. I hope he enjoyed it as much as we did. Good-bye. Love to Ruddy.

Affectionately,

R. B. Hayes.

Mrs. Sophia Hayes.

GALLIPOLIS, November 28, 1862 (P. M.)

DEAREST: — Had a nice trip up the river. All accounts from the Twenty-third seem favorable for a tolerably decent winter. I go up in the morning. Met Captain Hood here. He goes up with me, also two or three soldiers.

Mr. French and eight men in hospital, all glad to see me. I wished you were with me on the way.

Love to all the boys and Grandma. Write often. With much love.

Yours,

R.

MRS. HAYES.

CHAPTER XXI

CAMP MASKELL, GAULEY BRIDGE, December 1, 1862.

D EAREST LU: — We are on the south side of the Kanawha —
same side as the Eighty-ninth — at the ferry below and
in sight of the falls, two miles below Gauley Bridge. There, do
you know where we are? It is a muddy — bad slippery mud —
place, and as it rains or sleets here all winter, that is a serious
objection. Now you have the worst of it. In all other respects,
it is a capital place. Beautiful scenery — don't be alarmed, I
won't describe; no guard or picket duty, scarcely; good water
and wood; convenient to navigation; no other folks near enough
to bother, and many other advantages. The men are building
cabins without tools or lumber (sawed lumber, I mean,) and will
be at it some weeks yet before we look like living.

It was jolly enough to get back with the men — all healthy and
contented, glad to be back in western Virginia by themselves.
They greeted me most cordially. It was like getting home after
a long absence. The officers all came in, twenty-four in number,
and around the wine, etc., you saw packed, talked over the funny
and sad things of the campaign — a few sad, many funny. We
resolved to build a five-hundred-dollar monument to the killed,
etc., to be put in cemetery ground at Cleveland.

A story or two. Bill Brown, as he rushed forward in the bayonet charge at South Mountain, said to his lieutenant behind him:
"I'll toss the graybacks over my head to you, and you must
wring their necks." In Washington a lady asked Bill if he
wouldn't have his handkerchief scented: "Yes, yes," said he and
tore off about four inches square of his shirt and handed it to
her. She took the hint and gave him a fine handkerchief.

In Maryland, Colonel Scammon dressed up in a splinter-new
unform. He met a fellow hauling into camp a load of rails to

burn. Colonel Scammon said: "Where did you get those rails?" "On a fence down by the creek." "Who authorized you to take them?" "I took them on my own hook." "Well, sir," said the colonel, "just haul them back and put them where you got them." The fellow looked at the colonel from head to heel and drove ahead merely remarking: "A bran' new colonel by G—d!" The doctor asked Bill Brown where he was wounded: "Oh, in the place where I'm always ailing." . . .

Comly is urged by leading officers in this brigade to be made colonel of the Eighty-ninth. He would be a capital man for the place.

My mess are eating up the good things with a relish. It consists of Comly, Doctor Joe, McIlrath, and myself. We have Company A's fine tenor singer for cook — a good cook and a nice gentleman he is. My orderly, Carrington, and Doctor's ditto are the only servants, all soldiers — contrary to law, but much better than having darkies. Dr. Joe has built a bed today wide enough to have Webb and Birch both sleep with him! He really thinks of it.

Dr. Jim resigned today on a surgeon's certificate. Joe thought it best and I concurred. He is not in danger, but was evidently breaking down in this climate. Old Gray is with his company. Dr. Joe saw him today carrying mud to a couple of men building a chimney, and asked him what he was doing now. Gray replied: "I am clark to these gentlemen!"

The Eighty-ninth were camped on this ground. When the Twenty-third moved up alongside of them, the officer of the day in the Eighty-ninth was heard by some of our men telling in his camp that they were near an old regiment now and they must be watchful at night or the Twenty-third would steal whatever they wanted! That night cook-stoves, blankets, a tent from over the sleepers' heads, and a quantity of other property mysteriously disappeared from the Eighty-ninth notwithstanding their vigilance. Our men sympathized, our camp was searched, but, of course, nothing was found. After the Eighty-ninth moved, men were seen pulling out of the river stoves and other plunder by the quantity. The Eighty-ninth's surgeon was a friend of Captain Canby. He called on the captain a few days ago and was surprised to find his cooking stove doing duty in Captain Canby's tent. The best of it was the Eighty-ninth appeared to take it in good part.

Bottsford and Kennedy, both captains and A. A. G's — Bottsford for General Scammon and Kennedy for General Crook. Hood came up with me from Gallipolis. . . .

Affectionately ever,

R.

Mrs. Hayes.

Camp Maskell, near Gauley Bridge, West Virginia, December 2, 1862. — November 21, went on board [the] *Izetta* bound up the Ohio; 22d, grounded on a bar (crawfish) and stayed there until Wednesray, 26th. Found on board Captain Patterson, of General Morgan's staff, and family, and other agreeable passengers. Bid good-bye to Lucy, boys, and all, four times on different days. Reached camp Sunday P. M. with Captain Hood and Mr. Stover. A cold morning, but Indian-summer-like in the afternoon. Sunday evening, November 30, a jovial festive meeting in my shanty of all the officers, twenty-four or twenty-five in number. Fought over South Mountain and Antietam, with many anecdotes, much laughter, and enjoyment.

Monday, December 1, a wet, raw day. Visited the men, all at work on their new quarters — cabins sixteen by eighteen feet square; four for a company and a kitchen or two. Rode out to General Scammon's headquarters and dined with him. In my shanty are Dr. Webb, Lieutenant-Colonel Comly, and Major McIlrath. Mess, same. Frank Alpin [Halpin], cook, Harvey Carrington, ostler, Bill (colored), bootblack. I am to pay Alpin [Halpin] five dollars, Bill three dollars and fifty cents, and Carrington seven dollars and fifty cents.

[Today], Tuesday, December 2, a cold morning, but a warm, pleasant day. Sun shone about four hours. Only four men sick in hospital.

REGIMENTAL HEADQUARTERS MESS TWENTY-THIRD O. V. I. IN WESTERN VIRGINIA, 1862.

Left to right, Colonel Rutherford B. Hayes. Surgeon J. T. Webb, Major J. P. McIlrath, Adjutant M. P. Avery.   Insert Master Webb Hayes, Aged Six Years.

CAMP MASKELL, NEAR GAULEY BRIDGE, December 2, 1862.

DEAR MOTHER: — I am again with my friends and am enjoying camp life more than ever. The men are so hardy and healthy (only four in hospital) and so industrious (all hard at work building log cabins for winter quarters) and contented that I feel very happy with them. We are in a quiet place by ourselves, surrounded by fine scenery. Six miles only from the head of navigation, and no drawbacks except mud and a good deal of wet weather. Other regiments are on all the roads leading into "Dixie," leaving us very little guard duty to do. A great relief in winter. . . . .

Affectionately, your son,

RUTHERFORD.

P. S. — Please send this to Uncle, as I have no time now for writing. — H.

MRS. SOPHIA HAYES.

————————

Wednesday, December 3. — A bright, fine winter day. We moved our quarters fifty yards up the river into a house lately occupied by a daughter of Mr. Riggs. Its windows on the north side afford a good view of the river and of the Falls of the Kanawha. With our new cooks, two soldiers, we are living sumptuously — better than ever before since I have been in camp.

Signed a recommendation for Sergeant Chamberlain, Company A, as second lieutenant. Introduced to Captain Rigdon Williams, of the Twelfth. While at Middletown, Maryland, wounded, I heard he was killed, and on my return to Ohio I reported him killed. It was a Captain Liggett who was shot at South Mountain in the head.

The Rebels did *not* carry the American flag at Antietam to enable them to get into the rear of the Ohio troops. It was their battle-flag. Yet I have reported this, on good authority, as I thought. Our sergeant-major was probably killed attempting to escape from the enemy, although Lieutenant Ritter thinks — and I have reported — that he was killed pushing ahead of the regi-

24

ment. So difficult it is with the best intentions and no motive to deceive, to get the truth of these battle incidents even from eye-witnesses. The men are building the new city very rapidly.

Thursday, December 4, 1862. — A clear fine day. In the morning I walked, or climbed rather, to the top of the hill near the camp, just east of us. On the top I could see east of me the camp of the Forty-seventh [Ohio] at Tompkins farm, the camp of the Fourth Virginia, and other camps on the west side of Kanawha to the west, and the road to Fayette south. A hard scramble but I stood it well. My arm is still weak and easily hurt. Queer feeling, to think I can reach up to grasp a limb of a tree, and find it impossible to raise my hand above my head. In the afternoon I walked with Captain Haven up to Gauley Bridge. He explained to me the dwarf and giant laurel and the beautiful holly. The dwarf laurel grows from three to five feet high, is usually in thickets, and has an oval leaf. The giant laurel grows fifteen or twenty feet high and has a long leaf. The holly grows as high as apple trees and has a prickly leaf.

I give Colonel Comly drill and discipline, Major McIlrath, supplies of all sorts, and I attend to general interests of the regiment. I have sinks dug, look to camp drainage, and the like. The exercise agrees with me.

Friday, December 5. — Making sand walks around quarters. A threatening morning and a snowy day. General Scammon passed today with his staff for Fayette: Captain James L Bottsford, First Lieutenant A. C. Reichenbach, [and] Headington, of Thirtieth. A good staff. Captain Hildt, of Twelfth, provost marshal. Bottsford and Reichenbach of Twenty-third dined with us on their way up to Fayette. General Scammon commands all south and east of Kanawha River; General Crook all north of same; both under Major-General Cox.

CAMP MASKELL, NEAR GAULEY BRIDGE, December 5, 1862.

DEAR UNCLE: — I am enjoying myself here, looking after the new town we are building. We are putting up about a hundred log cabins, generally sixteen by twenty feet square. We are furnished with no nails, very little sawed lumber, and no tools. Somewhat over one-half the work is done, but cutting timber, splitting shakes and puncheons, and putting them together is the great business. We are on a piece of muddy bottom-land on a beautiful bend of the Kanawha, with high mountains pressing close up to us on all sides. We are on the side of the river where no enemy can come without first running over three or four other regiments, so that we have very little guard duty to do. The men are strong, healthy, and happy. I yesterday climbed the mountain just east of us, making a journey of four miles before dinner. I walked six miles in the afternoon. The ten miles was done easily. You may judge of my health by this. Today it snows and blows. Tomorrow it will probably thaw. We shall have some trouble with the mud, but I think with proper ditching, and the use of sand, we can conquer the trouble.

Read in December *Atlantic Monthly,* "Hunt for the Captain," by Holmes. It is good.

Sincerely,

R. B. HAYES.

S. BIRCHARD.

———

Saturday, 6. — A cold morning. Snow, two to four inches, on the ground and more falling. Five wounded men returned last night, restored and ready for duty. Captain Haven's resignation having been accepted on account of ill health, he left us today He goes home to Bedford, Cuyahoga County. He exhibited great courage at Antietam and South Mountain. Appointed captain from sergeant, in violation of the rule of seniority, he encountered bitter prejudice as an officer, but his courage and good conduct overcame it. Success to him!

This morning I climbed the hill above the falls on this side of the Kanawha. Fine views of the wintry mountains, snow-clad and with dark green holly, laurel, and pine along their sides. The beautiful cold river beneath. Lucy thinks I am "dazed" on scenery.

Sunday, 7. — Very cold, but pleasant winter weather. There is talk of the Kanawha freezing over. The river is low and a severe "spell" will do it. Cotton Mountain so slippery as to be dangerous to cross with teams or on horseback. Dr. Joe went over today to the Eighty-ninth to see Captain Brown of Chillicothe, whose mother is there. She was charged thirty dollars by a liveryman to bring her from Charleston, a distance of forty-six miles. Dr. Parker, of Berea, Cuyahoga County, agent of Sanitary Commission, visits us. We are in no condition for inspection, but he is a sensible man and will make proper allowances. Our sick in hospital is two, and excused from duty by surgeon eight. — Snow lying all around.

Monday, 8. — A cold morning, but a bright warm sun melts the snow on all the low ground. Lieutenant Smith says some of our prisoners at South Mountain heard my speech as we went into the fight. He says the colonel rode up, his eyes shining like a cat's, [and said:] "Now boys, remember you are the Twenty-third, and give them hell. In these woods the Rebels don't know but we are ten thousand; and if we fight, and when we charge yell, we are as good as ten thousand, by ——."

WANTS.

A paymaster. Not paid since August and then only to June 30.

A Sawmill — *or* lumber (ten thousand feet); none yet, except eighteen hundred feet and old drift, etc., etc.

Window sash and nails.

Mess stores at *Charleston* and *Gallipolis;* privilege to send.

CAMP MASKELL, December, 8, 1862. Monday morning.

DEAREST: — I have been here a week yesterday. The knocking about among the men, getting out lumber, building cabins, ditching and cleaning camp and sich, agrees with me spiritually and physically. We have pretty good living and splendid appetites and digestion. . . .

Comly is reading a novel, McIlrath a newspaper, Dr. Joe is visiting, and I am writing you before a huge log fire in a great old-fashioned fireplace. I wish you were here. It's really jolly living so; you would be delighted with it. I love you ever so much. Kiss the boys. Love to Grandma.

Affectionately, your

R.

Mrs. Hayes.

Camp Maskell, near Gauley,
Monday Morning,, December 8, 1862.

Dear Mother: — I got your letter, mailed the 2nd, yesterday morning. It was my first letter since I left home and was very welcome. I like the coolness of the old Yankee colonel and admire his earnestness. My speech at South Mountain was not quite so religious, but I suppose it answered very much the same purpose. I don't value what comes out of the mouth on such occasions so much as the spirit of it.

We are having severe, but pleasant and healthful winter weather. The men work hard getting up our log village and enjoy it much. I spent Thanksgiving on the Ohio River very pleasantly with an intelligent crowd of passengers. . . .

Affectionately, your son,

Rutherford.

Mrs. Sophia Hayes.

Camp Maskell, near Gauley, December 12. — Ninth to twelfth bright, warm days; cold nights; snow scarcely melted at all on the north side of the hills. The river is low and freezes in the pools clear across. A single very severe night would close navigation on the Kanawha. Nothing will save us from this calamity but a mild winter or a freshet in the river. With this low water a cold winter will bother us exceedingly. Well, well, our camp is growing; a few nails have come to us; no sawed lumber yet.

Yesterday (11th) received a good letter from Lucy. She has read Wendell Holmes' "Search After the Captain" in [the] December number of [the] *Atlantic* and thinks I must not laugh at her any more about her efforts to find me — I being at Middletown and she at Washington searching the hospitals for me.

Today got news of the capture of a brigade of our troops in Tennessee by four thousand of John Morgan's men! Either a surprise or a disgraceful thing of some sort! Also the crossing of the river at Fredericksburg after heavy cannonading.

Saturday, December 13. — The hottest day of the winter; a hot sun made the shady side of the house the most comfortable. Our new second lieutenant, [William] McKinley, returned today — an exceedingly bright, intelligent, and gentlemanly young officer. He promises to be one of our best.   . . .

Camp Maskell, December 14, 1862.

Dearest: — Very glad to have a good letter from you again. Very glad indeed the bag is found — glad you read the article of Dr. Holmes in the *Atlantic Monthly*. It is, indeed, a defense pat for your case. I knew you would like it. You must keep it. When we are old folks it will freshly remind us of a very interesting part of our war experience.

If the enchanted bag contains my spurs, and if they are both alike (which I doubt), you may send them to me when a good chance offers. The pair I now use are those worn by Lorin Andrews and given me by McCook. I don't want to lose them.

The fine weather of the past week has been very favorable for our business and we are getting on rapidly. The river is so low that a cold snap would freeze it up, and leave us "out in the cold" in a very serious way — that is, without the means of getting grub. This would compel us to leave our little log city and drive us back towards Ohio. . . .

One of our new second lieutenants — McKinley — a handsome, bright, gallant boy, got back last night. He went to Ohio to recruit with the other orderly sergeants of the regiment. He tells good stories of their travels. The Thirtieth and Twelfth sergeants stopped at second-class hotels, but the Twenty-third boys "splurged." They stopped at the American and swung by the big figure. Very proper. They are the generals of the next war.

I rode over to the Eighty-ninth. Promising boys over there. I like the cousins much. Ike Nelson is a master spirit. The others will come out all right.

Yes, darling, these partings don't grow any easier for us, but you don't regret *that*, I am sure. It will be all the pleasanter when it is all over. How is your health? *Is all right with you?* Your sake, not mine. Thanks for the *Harper* and *Atlantic*, mailed me by Stephenson. Love to all.

Conners whom we saw at Frederick is *not* dead. He returned safely last night. All the wounded are gathering in except the discharged. Sergeant Tyler whom we saw with his arm off at Frederick is in a bad way — others doing well. .   .   .

Affectionately yours, ever,

R.

P. S. — Three months ago the battle of South Mountain. We celebrated it by climbing the mountain on the other side of the river to the castle-like-looking rocks which overlook the Falls of the Kanawha. Captains Hood, Zimmerman, Canby, Lovejoy and Lieutenant Bacon were of the party. Hood and I beat the crowd to the top. Hood, the worst wounded, up first. When I saw him shot through that day I little thought I would ever see him climbing mountains again.

Mrs. Hayes.

———

Monday, 15. — A hot, clear day. Lieutenant McKinley and his party work hard clearing our parade. Rode the little sorrel up the river two miles. Threatens rain at night but we all vote for another fine day. Fire in the mountains.

Tuesday, 16. — Rained last night; raw and cloudy with a little snow this morning. Sun shone in the afternoon. We hear today of the crossing by General Burnside of the Rappahannock at Fredericksburg.

Wednesday, 17. — Rode with Major McIlrath to General Ewing's camp near Loup Creek to see about "wants." Generally satisfactory results. Dined with the general and Mrs. Ewing. A rough day with gusts of snow and the like.

Thursday, 18. — A cold, bitterly cold, night but a bright, fine day. Major McIlrath and Dr. Webb left for Ohio today.

Major under orders from General Ewing goes to Camp Chase with prisoner. Doctor got a leave from General Ewing for twenty days to look after medicines, but this morning came a thirty-day leave from Washington.

Sinister rumors from General Burnside. Telegraph operator reported to say, "Burnside whipped like the Devil"! Ah, if so, sad hearts in the North! Intervention again. So much blood shed in vain! I confess to feeling much anxiety. The crossing of the river at Fredericksburg with so little resistance, looks as if the enemy was willing to let Burnside cross — as if they were leading him into a trap. I trust the sinister report is false.

CAMP, December 18, 1862.

DEAREST: — Joe goes this morning, thanks to General Ewing for the leave, contrary to general orders. Don't let him spend more than two weeks at home.

I love you all to pieces this cold morning. Kiss the boys. Merry Christmas 'em for me. I mean to have the cousins to dine with me on Christmas. We shall have a good dinner. Our cooks are splendid. . . .

Send me about two or three yards carpet (old will do) to light out on these frosty mornings. Thunder, but it's cold this morning! If the water doesn't rise, we freeze up "shore," as darkies say.

Well, dearest, think of me lovingly during the holy days.

Affectionately,

R.

MRS. HAYES.

Friday, 19. — Captain Bottsford and his father stayed with me this evening; a pleasant time. Captains Zimmerman and Rice, also from Mahoning County, helped drink an egg-nog of Mr. Bottsford's mixing.

Saturday, 20. — Burnside has retreated across the Rappahannock. The Rebels can now set off the battle of Fredericksburg against the battle of Antietam.   They retreated back across the Potomac.   But I suspect they have a great advantage in having suffered much less than we have.   They fought behind entrenchments.   When will our generals learn not to attack an equal adversary in fortified positions?   Burnside will now perhaps have to yield to McClellan.   It looks as if in the East neither army was strong enough to make a successful invasion of [the territory of] the other.   If so conquest of [the] Rebellion is not to be.   We have now the Emancipation Proclamation to go upon.   Will not this stiffen the President's backbone so as to drive it through?   Desperate diseases require desperate remedies.

CAMP MASKELL, NEAR GAULEY BRIDGE, December 20, 1862.

DEAR UNCLE: — Dr. Webb went home on a thirty-day furlough a few days ago.   Our good health here makes a surgeon almost unnecessary.   We now have only one man in hospital — a chance case of erysipelas.   Our camp is improving.   We are almost out of the mud and the greater part of our cabins finished.

Another serious reverse.   Burnside's repulse at Fredericksburg is bad enough as it looks from my point of view.   It would seem as if neither party in eastern Virginia was strong enough to make a successful invasion of the territory of the other—which is equivalent to saying that the Rebellion can there sustain itself as long as it stands on the defensive.   I don't like two things in this campaign of General Burnside.   (1) It looks as if his first delay opposite Fredericksburg was an error.   (2) To attack an enemy of equal (or nearly equal strength) behind entrenchments is always an error.   This battle is a set-off for Antietam.   That forced the Rebels back across the Potomac.   This forces us back across the Rappahannock.   We suffer, I fear, a larger proportionate loss.   I suspect the enemy lost but little, comparatively.   Now remains our last card, the emancipation of the slaves.   That may do it.   Some signs of wavering are pointed out by the correspondents, but I trust the President will now stand firm.   I was not in a hurry to wish such a policy adopted, but I don't now wish to see it abandoned.   Our army is not seriously weakened by the affair at Fredericksburg and very slight events will change the scale in our favor. Push on the emancipation policy, and all will yet go well.

Our partisanship about generals is now rebuked. General McClellan has serious faults or defects, but his friends can truly claim that if he had retained command, this disaster would not have occurred. The people and press would perhaps do well to cultivate patience. It is a virtue much needed in so equal a struggle as this. If the people can hold out, we shall find the right man after [a] while.

But I bore you with reflections that must occur to every one.

Sincerely,

R. B. HAYES.

S. BIRCHARD.

LOG CABIN CAMP, December 21, 1862. Sunday evening.

DEAREST: — Dr. Jim got his proper resignation papers today and will leave in the morning. Dr. Joe's leave of absence from Washington for thirty days from December 18 came to hand a half an hour after he had left on General Ewing's twenty-day leave. He will not regret the ten day's extension. . . .

I cannot answer all your inquiries about the wounded. Ligget is doing well; is probably at home ere this. I got a letter from Joel tonight. He is the Jew who got eight bullet holes in his person and limbs. He says he thinks he can stand service in a couple of months. He don't want to be discharged. Ritter writes me in good spirits.

Very interesting, all talk about the boys. . . . Webb's surprise that learning is needed in western Virginia hits the position of matters more closely than he knew. Sound teeth and a good digestion are more required than education. I do not know but fear to risk the boys in this eager mountain air; not at present, at any rate. So, of your coming, —

Almost ten years. How happy we have been. But you don't say a word about your *health*. If that requires you to come, you shall come. Otherwise you perhaps "better not." Do you comprehend the solicitude I feel? Enough for tonight. — Love [to] all the boys and to Grandma.

Affectionately,

R.

MRS. HAYES.

Monday, 22. — Warm, a shower in the morning. Finished reading "Mysteries of Paris" last night. Not a wicked or obscene novel by a good deal.

CAMP NEAR GAULEY, December 22, 1862.

DEAR MOTHER: — I received your letter of the 10th. Yes, the Vermont colonel's speech, etc., at Bennington came safely. A cool old colonel he was, as well as pious. I see that the One Hundred and Thirteenth Regiment is consolidated with some other. How does it affect Colonel Mitchell? I hope he does not lose his position. . . .

Dr. Joe Webb has gone home on thirty-days leave of absence. Colonel Comly, on an order from General Scammon, is with him at Fayette. Major McIlrath has gone home for a twenty-day visit. This leaves me the only field officer here, but there is very little to do. The men still busy with their quarters and all quiet in front. My health is perfect; I was never so heavy as now.

You will enjoy the return of the children, or the young ladies rather. What charming girls they are! My love to them and Ruddy and all. I hope you will have happy holidays.

Affectionately, your son,

RUTHERFORD.

MRS. SOPHIA HAYES.

December 23. Tuesday. — Soft weather. Reading Buckle's second volume. What a deep impression his mode of collecting authorities and heaping up facts produces! It shakes one's faith in the old orthodox notions to read his chapters on Scotch superstitions.

THE DEAD OF SOUTH MOUNTAIN AND ANTIETAM.

Sergeant-Major Eugene L. Reynolds, of Bellefontaine. A bright, handsome, ambitious, soldierly youngster; brave as a lion; so game in appearance and conduct; cheerful, happy, and full of promise! Killed at the close of the day on the mountain top. Taken prisoner, says Captain Williams of the Twelfth, and attempting to escape, shot in the bowels and afterwards bayonetted through the forearm.

Corporal Bull, Company A. A fine-looking, amiable boy, always smiling. Killed at Antietam.

Wilson B. Harper, Franklin County. A Mark Tapley for jollity, large, healthy, industrious, and so anxious to please, he always agreed with you. Wounded badly in thigh at South Mountain and died after amputation a few days after. Cheerful to the last. [List not completed.]

Sunday, 28. — On Christmas my wife's cousins, Lieutenant Nelson and privates Ed and Ike Cook and Jim McKell* dined with me; all of Company D, Eighty-ninth Regiment. A. M. of that day the regiment fired by battalion and file. P. M. I offered a turkey to the marksman who would hit his head, and a bottle of wine and a tumbler to next best shot, and a bottle of wine to third best. A bright, warm day and a jolly one — a merry Christmas indeed.

[The] 26th and 27th, mild days and cloudy but only a few drops of rain. Dr. Kellogg spent the 26th with us — surgeon on General Scammon's staff. Talked free-thinking talk with him in a joking vein. A clever gentleman. Major Carey stopped [the] 27th with us — of the Twelfth. Told a good one; the Thirty-fourth got a good lot of lumber; put a sentinel over it. After dark the Twelfth got up a relief — relieved the Thirty-four sentinel and carried off the lumber!

---

* Willie McKell. He died at Andersonville 1864. — This written on margin by Mr. Hayes.

CAMP MASKELL, December 28, 1862.

DEAREST : — Sunday evening. Captain Hunter brings me the spurs and pictures; for which, thanks. I will send the old spurs home the first chance. There will be a good many [chances] soon. Don't let Dr. Joe forget to bring back his sword-belt for me, and a piece of *old* carpet or backing.

General Ewing has *ordered* one officer, three non-commissioned officers, and ten privates to go home a week from today! And what is still stranger our men are asking not to be sent home so soon! The explanation of this latter wonder is that a paymaster is pretty certain to be along about the 10th of January and the men want to see him before going home. Unless General Ewing's orders are changed you will soon see some of our men. My orderly (cook), William T. Crump, will stop with you. If you are curious to know how we live, put him in the kitchen a day or two. The children will like him.

We have had no serious accidents with all our chopping, logging, and hauling. On Christmas I was alarmed. John Harvey (the boys remember him) driving a team with a big log at the sawmill was thrown off and the wheel ran across his ankle. It was thought to be a crusher but turns out merely a slight sprain.

Nobody sick in the hospital and only *four* excused from duty by Dr. Barrett!

I dined the four cousins on Christmas day. Had a good time. The regiment fired volleys in the morning. In the afternoon I gave a turkey and two bottles of wine to the three best marksmen. Target firing all the afternoon. A week more [of] pleasant weather will put us entirely "out of the suds," or out of the mud.

We had our first dress parade this evening. The old flag was brought out with honors. The companies look smaller than they did at the last parade I saw on Upton's Hill, near Washington, almost four months ago, but they looked well and happy.

The weather here is warm and bright. Very favorable for our making camp. I am thinking how happy the boys are with their uncles. It would be jolly to see you all. I love you ever so much. Tell me about the Christmas doings. Love to all.

Affectionately ever,

MRS. HAYES.   R.

Tuesday, 30. — Yesterday was a fine, warm, spring-like day. This month has been generally good weather. We are getting our camp in good condition. Yesterday General Ewing received orders to "go South" (as General Banks said) with the Thirtieth and Thirty-seventh Ohio and the Fourth and Eighth Virginia. This breaks up our brigade. We were not very well suited with it. General Ewing has many good qualities but thinks so well of his old regiment (the Thirtieth) that he can do no sort of justice to its rival, the Twenty-third. We are glad also to have no longer any connection with the Thirtieth. The brigade now consists of the Twenty-third, Eighty-ninth, and Ninety-second. Two new regiments with ours. Colonel Nelson H. Van Vorhes will command the brigade. He is a gentleman of character and capacity without any military experience.

I can't help feeling the injustice in that point of view of putting him over me; but as he is my senior as colonel of a new regiment, it is according to rule and I shall cheerfully submit. Yet it looks hard that he shall get the credit or glory of what Comly, myself, and my regiment may do. For in any emergency it would be to us that all would look for action and advice. But "such is war," and I am here to do my duty wherever I may be placed — and I mean to do it fully and cheerfully, wherever the credit may go. My impressions of Colonel Van Vorhes are favorable. I have yet to make his acquaintance. General Ewing, it is said, goes down the Mississippi. Good-bye, Thirtieth! We have been with them since they joined us at Sutton, September 8, 1861 — a year and a quarter ago.

CAMP, December 31, 1862.

DEAREST: — This is New Year's eve. Dancing and merriment seem to prevail. Many men and a few officers are expecting to go home soon. Sergeant-Major Sweet will take you this, and the McCook and Andrews spurs. We have had a great change this week. Colonel Ewing — I mean General Ewing — has gone South, taking with him the Thirtieth, Thirty-seventh, and Forty-seventh Ohio and Fourth Virginia. The Eighty-ninth goes into the fine camp left by the Thirtieth, ten miles below here; a great gain to the Eighty-ninth. The Ninety-second goes to Tompkins Farm, the camp left by the Forty-seventh, and are great losers by the change; mad about it, too. We get rid of divers old troubles, but remain in our log-cabin camp, and are content, or rather pleased, upon the whole.

Now good night. Happy New Years to all. If no further changes occur, and Uncle Joe would like to bring you up here with one or two boys, I suspect you would like to come. Think of it, and I will try to see you part of the way home, or all of the way. Let him start about the middle of the month, so as to reach here by the 20th. It will probably rain and be muddy enough, but it will be funny and novel.

Good night. If Grandma wants to come, she will be welcome, she knows, but I mistrust the peculiar climate we have. Our weather this month has been much better than in Ohio.

Affectionately,

R.

Mrs. Hayes.

Camp Reynolds, January 4, 1863

Dearest: — The same old camp, but "Reynolds," after our gallant Sergeant-Major Eugene M., [L. Reynolds] who was killed at South Mountain.

I am glad you are all *well* and *happy* with the uncles and "all the boys." Yes, I confess I did forget the 30th [the tenth anniversary of his marriage]. Strange, too. I had thought of it a few days before. I did not neglect to think of *you*. That I do daily; but nothing occurred to call to mind the happy day. A white day in my calendar — the precursor of the ten happiest years. On the 30th we were all agog with the order and movements connected with General Ewing's departure with four of our regiments. This may have caused the lapse.

We had none of your bad weather. This [the] morning opened rainy, windy, and turbulent, but by 2 P. M. it was warm, bright, and serene. At our evening parade I made a little address on the New Year and the past. I'll send you it to be put in the archives.

It is Sunday evening and our cook, Frank Halpin (the best tenor going), with three or four Company A comrades are singing in the kitchen. "Magnif!"

In the very worst of the rain-storm this morning, an ambulance passed with Mrs. Brown, her son, and Ed Cook. Ed is sick, decidedly, not as yet dangerously. He refuses to go home because he has been home sick already. Plucky. Perhaps it's as well, although I rather urged his going. He will go to Cannelton, where the regiment is now stationed, and will be well cared for. Mrs. Brown takes the captain home. I suspect Ike [Nelson]* will soon be captain of the company. Brown is not able to stand service, I think. Ike now commands the company.

Send me Rud's picture, and another installment of mine, for distribution.

If not costing more than about a couple of dollars, I wish Joe would bring me Adam Smith's "Wealth of Nations," also "Lucile." The first large print. At Gallipolis or somewhere he better get three or four split-bottomed or other cheap chairs — none but cheap — [and] a cheap *square* looking-glass.

I am still busy trying to conquer the mud. We are very comfortable but a sprinkling of snow or rain makes us ankle-deep where the sand is not put on. This and our little town gives me plenty to do. The lieutenant-colonel and major are both absent.

I shall be very glad to have you here. My only fear is possible ill health for the boys. There is less sickness than last year and by keeping carefully housed if the weather is bad, you will be safe. — Darling, much love for you and the dear ones at home.

Affectionately,

R.

MRS. HAYES.

———

[The address mentioned in the letter follows.]

COMRADES: — We have just closed an eventful year in our soldier life. During the year 1862 the Twenty-third Regiment

---

*Cook and Nelson, cousins of Mrs. Hayes.

has borne well its part in the great struggle for the Union. The splendid fight of Company C at Clark's Hollow, the daring, endurance, and spirit of enterprise exhibited in the capture of Princeton and Giles Court-house, the steadiness, discipline, and pluck which enabled you, in the face of an overwhelming force of the enemy, to retreat from your advanced position without panic or confusion and almost unharmed, the conspicuous and acknowledged achievements of the regiment at the battles of South Mountain and Antietam, amply justify the satisfaction and pride which I am confident we all feel in the regiment to which we belong.

We recall these events and scenes with joy and exultation. But as we glance our eyes along the shortened line, we are filled with sadness that we look in vain for many forms and faces once so familiar! We shall not forget them. We shall not forget what they gave to purchase the good name which we so highly prize. The pouring out of their lives has made the tattered old flag *sacred*.

Let us begin the new year — this season to us of quiet and of preparation — with a determination so to act that the future of our regiment shall cast no shadow on its past, and that those of us who shall survive to behold the opening of another new year shall regard with increased gratification the character, history, and name of the gallant old Twenty-third!

Camp Reynolds, near Gauley, Virginia, January 4, 1863.

Dear Uncle: — First of all, my arm gives me no trouble at all ordinarily. Getting on or off from a horse, and some efforts remind me once in a while that it is not quite as good as it was. Perhaps it never will be, but it is good enough, and gives me very little inconvenience.

I am learning some of your experience as to the necessity of overseeing all work. I find I must be out, or my ditches are out of shape, too narrow or wide, or some way wrong, and so of roads, houses, etc., etc. We are making a livable place of it. I put off my own house to the last. Fires are now burning in it, and I shall occupy it in a day or two. It is a double log cabin,

25

two rooms, eighteen by twenty each, and the open space under the same roof sixteen by eighteen; stone fireplaces and chimneys. I have one great advantage in turning a mudhole into a decent camp. I can have a hundred or two men with picks, shovels, and scraper, if I want them, or more, so a day's work changes the looks of things mightily. It is bad enough at any rate, but a great improvement.

We have rumors of heavy fighting in Tennessee and at Vicksburg, but not enough to tell what is the result. I hope it will be all right. I tell Dr. Joe to bring out Lucy if he thinks best, and I will go home with her.

Sincerely,

R. B. HAYES.

S. BIRCHARD.

Tuesday, January 6. [1863]. — Very fine weather for a week past, and I am busy digging ditches, building walks, roads, bridges, and quarters. A pleasant occupation. Great fighting at Murfreesboro; heavy losses on our side, but the general result not yet known. Rainy today. I must build a skiff to get over to the brick house to headquarters easily.

During past year we have received sixty-eight recruits; discharged sixty-six; killed in action forty-seven; died of wounds twenty; died of disease fifteen. [Total] deaths eighty-two. Total loss aggregates one hundred and forty-eight. Net loss eighty.

CAMP REYNOLDS, NEAR GAULEY BRIDGE, January 6, 1863.

DEAR MOTHER: — This is a rainy day — the first we have had in a great while. I never saw finer weather than we have had. It has enabled us to finish our log cabins and we are now in most comfortable quarters. It would surprise you to see what tidy and pretty houses the soldiers have built with very little except an axe and the forest to do it with. My house is a double cabin under a roof about sixty feet long by twenty wide with a space between the cabins protected from weather.

I see that the One Hundred and Thirteenth is ordered off, so I suppose Laura is at home again. I shall write to her in reply to her good letter soon. I think not less but more of her since she has made so valuable an addition to the kinship.

I am writing to Dr. Joe to bring Lucy out here, if he thinks well of it. There are three or four officers' wives in this quarter now. . . .

Affectionately,

RUTHERFORD.

MRS. SOPHIA HAYES.

Wednesday, January 7, [1863]. — Appointed to command First Brigade, Second Kanawha Division. Rather a small affair — Twenty-third Regiment and Eighty-ninth Regiment, Captain Harrison's Cavalry, Captain Gilmore's ditto.

Reports, after several days' desperate fighting, General Rosecrans has taken Murfreesboro and defeated Bragg.

Sunday, 11. — Moved into my new quarters last night. Ratherish damp; roof and gables of "shakes," a little open; no ceiling or flooring above; altogether cool but not unpleasant. A letter from Dr. Joe. Lucy and Birch and Webb to come up and give me a visit. Right jolly! A letter from Uncle also.

Rosecrans by his fiery and energetic courage at Murfreesboro or Stone River saved the day. Not intellectually an extraordinary man, but his courage and energy make him emphatically the fighting general of this war.

CAMP REYNOLDS, NEAR GAULEY BRIDGE, January 12, 1863.

DEAR UNCLE: — Yours of the 6th came duly to hand. The death of Magee is indeed a public calamity. No community has such men to spare. There is, I judge, no doubt of the death of Leander Stem. More of my acquaintances and friends have suffered in that than in any battle of the war except those in which my own regiment took part. It was Rosecrans' personal qualities that saved the day. He is not superior intellectually or by education to many of our officers, but in headlong daring, energy, and determination, I put him first of all the major-generals. He has many of the Jackson elements in him. Another general, almost any other, would, after McCook's misfortune, have accepted a repulse and turned all his efforts to getting off safely with his shattered army.

Sherman has been repulsed, it seems. No doubt he will get aid from below and from Grant. If so, he will yet succeed.

I do not expect a great deal from the [Emancipation] Proclamation, but am glad it was issued.

Notice Governor Seymour's message. It shows what I anticipated when I was with you — that the logic of the situation will make a good enough war party of the Democracy *in power*. If you want to see eyes opened on the slavery question, let the Democracy have the power in the nation. They would be the bitterest abolitionists in the land in six months. I am perfectly willing to trust them.

I received a letter from Dr. Joe saying he would bring Lucy and Birch and Webb back with him. They will enjoy it, I do not doubt.

I am now in command of [the] First Brigade of [the] Second Kanawha Division. General Ewing has gone South with six regiments from this quarter. This leaves us none too strong, but probably strong enough. I shall probably have command of the extreme outposts. I am not yet in command at *Gauley Bridge*. I say this because I think it very insufficiently garrisoned, and if not strengthened a surprise would not be remarkable. If I am put in command, as seems likely, I shall see it fixed up very promptly.

Sincerely,

R. B. HAYES.

S. BIRCHARD.

Tuesday, [January] 14. — A warm, pleasant day. Sent three companies late last night to Tompkins Farm under Captain Sperry; a dark, muddy march — just out of good quarters too. Colonel Hatfield of [the] Eighty-ninth Regiment makes a singular point as to my rank compared with his. He was appointed colonel about December 1, and has a commission of that date; that is, at the bottom are the words "issued this day of December" and also sealed, etc., this day of December. My commission in like manner was of November 1. Colonel Hatfield was major before and acted as *second* in command until he received his commission. But his commission in the body of it has a clause to take rank from *October 2, 1862,* which is twelve days earlier than mine. He claims this is the *date* of his commission. Not so, the date is at the bottom as above. A note dated December 1 with interest from October 2 is still a note of December 1. But what is the effect of the clause or order in the body of the commission? I say nothing. The governor of a State has no power to give rank in the army of the United States prior to either *appointment* or *actual service* in such rank. If he could confer rank two months prior to appointment or service, he could two years. He could now appoint civilians to outrank all officers of same grade now in service from Ohio or from any other State. But this is absurd. A commission being merely *evidence* of appointment, the governor may perhaps date it back to the time of actual appointment or service. The President of the United States, as Commander-in-Chief of [the] United States army, can, perhaps, give rank independent of service or actual appointment. But if a state governor is authorized to do so, the Act of Congress or lawful order for it can be shown. Let us see it.

The President's power to appoint and to *discharge* officers embraces all power. It is supreme. But the governor has no power of removal. He can only appoint according to the terms of his authority from Congress or the War Department. What is that authority?

The appointments are often made long before the issuing of commissions. The commission may *then* well specify the date from which rank shall begin. But I conclude there can be no rank given by a governor prior to either commission, appointment, or actual service. Else a citizen could now be appointed colonel to outrank every other colonel in the United States, and be entitled to pay for an indefinite period in the past, which is absurd.

The governor has no authority to put a junior over a senior of the same grade. He may promote or rather appoint the junior out of order, because the power to appoint is given him. But to assign rank among officers of [the] same grade is no part of his duties. Why is such a clause put in commissions? (1) Because appointments are often made (always so at the beginning of the war) long before the commissions issue. (2) In recruiting also, the appointment is conditional on the enlistment of the requisite number of men. Of course the rank dates from the appointment and actual service.

But the great difficulty lies here. Is not this clause the *highest* evidence — *conclusive* evidence — of the date of the appointment? Can we go behind it? I say no, for so to hold is to give the governor the power to determine rank between officers of [the] same grade after appointment.

The order of appointment is highest (see Regulations). The governor's order may be written, as Governor Dennison's were, or verbal as Governor Tod's are — to be proved in one case by the order, in the other verbally.

Thursday, 15. — Rained last night; warm and cloudy today, threatening rain. Yesterday warm and sunny but threatening. Captain Gilmore dined with me. Says Colonel Hatfield reported that he was to command the brigade; says he [Gilmore] and his men are mad about it, that they want this brigade commanded as it is.

Lucy and the boys to start today if possible. I hope it will be more cheerful weather when they reach here.

Saturday evening, 17. — The two wintriest days yet, yesterday and today. Snowed and blowed yesterday all day. My open shake roof let the snow through in clouds; felt like sitting by my fire with an umbrella over me. Read Victor Hugo's new book, "Les Miserables." Good, very.

Kanawha river rose fast — about three feet yesterday, all from the Gauley. New River doesn't rise until Gauley runs out.

Lieutenant Hastings and some of the new lieutenants, viz.,

Abbott, Seamans, and part of the sergeants, returned today. They tell of strong "Secesh" feeling and talk in Ohio. The blunder at Vicksburg, the wretched discords at the North, and the alarming financial troubles give things a gloomy appearance tonight. But Lucy and the boys are coming! That will be a happiness.

Sunday, 18. — Last night the coldest of the winter. Today clear and bright. Rode over to see Captain Simmonds about the Rebel mail supposed to run from Charleston via Lick or Rich Creek above Gauley, across Gauley River to Lewisburg Pike. Walked P. M. on this side up to Gauley with Lieutenant Hastings and Lieutenant (formerly sergeant) Abbott. Both been absent on recruiting service since August 7. Am thinking of the coming of my wife and boys.

HEADQUARTERS OUTPOST.

FIRST BRIGADE, SECOND KANAWHA DIVISION,

January 20, 1863.

SIR: — I am instructed by General Scammon to inform Major-General Jones through you that he regards his sending two flags of truce at the same time by different routes to our outposts upon the same business, viz., the admission of ladies into our lines, as using the flag for a purpose as obvious as it is improper, and that such an abuse of it is not to be permitted.

Not to subject the lady in your charge to hardship, she will be admitted into our lines on the representation of Lieutenant Norvell that she is the wife of a citizen loyal to the United States.

R. B. HAYES,

COLONEL TWENTY-THIRD REGIMENT, O. V. I.

CAMP REYNOLDS, WEST VIRGINIA, January 25, 1863.

DEAR MOTHER: — Lucy with Birch and Webb arrived here last night safe and sound. We shall enjoy the log-cabin life very much — the boys are especially happy, running about where there is so much new to be seen. . . . I write merely to relieve anxiety about the new soldiers. — Love to all.

Affectionately,

RUTHERFORD.

MRS. SOPHIA HAYES.

CAMP REYNOLDS, February 8, 1863.

DEAR UNCLE: — Your tracts came yesterday and were distributed. They will do instead of sermons today. Lucy and the boys are enjoying it much. They add much to our happiness this bad weather.

I shall go with [the] Twenty-third to Charleston in a few weeks. We are pretty well thinned out — only three old regiments left. Lucy says she thinks the Rebels can't get her. I am not so sure. She rode outside of the lines four or five miles yesterday.

Sincerely,

R. B. HAYES.

S. BIRCHARD.

February 18, [1863]. — Lucy, Birch, and Webb came up here on the 24th of January. We have had a jolly time together. We have rain and mud in abundance but we manage to ride a little on horseback or in a skiff; to fish a little, etc., etc. I was more than two weeks housed up with left eye bloodshot and inflamed. Birch read "Boy Hunters and Voyageurs," and Lucy the newspapers.

February 19. — [Companies] G and B marched to Loup Creek to take steamboat to Charleston; the rest to go soon.

A sort of pike called here salmon, a fine fish, caught at the Falls, weighing from three to ten pounds. A large live minnow is the bait.

CAMP REYNOLDS, VIRGINIA, February 24, 1863.

DEAR UNCLE: — We are all well. Lucy and the boys enjoy camp life and keep healthy. Two of our companies have gone down the river to Charleston preparatory to moving the Twenty-third there. We expect to follow in two or three weeks. We care nothing about the change. It brings us into easier communication with home and has other advantages. We shall possibly remain there the whole spring. If so, after weather settles in May, it will be a pleasant trip for you to visit us if you can spare time.

I have no idea when Lucy will return home. The boys are doing well here.

Sincerely,

R. B. Hayes.

S. Birchard.

Camp Reynolds, Virginia, March 4, 1863.

Dear Uncle: — Getting on finely. The boys busy and very happy. Webb, I fancy, is a good deal such a boy is [as] Lorenzo was. He is to be seen driving some soldier's team or riding whenever there is a chance. Lucy will probably leave in a fortnight or so, probably about the time we go to Charleston.

The new conscription law strikes me as a capital measure. I hope it will be judiciously and firmly administered.

I have an offer for my Hamilton property one thousand dollars cash, one thousand dollars in six months, and the balance of fifteen hundred in three equal annual payments. Before the war I would have taken it quickly enough, but I am not sure now but the real estate is best. It pays taxes and about one hundred dollars a year rent. What could I do with the money?

Sincerely,

R. B. Hayes.

S. Birchard.

Camp Reynolds, March 9, 1863.

Dear Uncle: — Yours of last Sunday came to hand yesterday. Wife and boys still here — very happy. They fish and row skiff and ride horseback. They can all row. Webb and Birch rowed a large load of soldiers across the river and back — a large roaring river, almost like the Ohio in a fair fresh. They will go home in a week or two probably. We shall remain here two or three weeks and then probably go to Charleston.

The new conscript act strikes me as the best thing yet, if it is only used. I would only call enough men to recruit up weakened regiments, and compel the return of the shirks and deserters. Make our commanders give more time to drill and discipline; make the armies regulars — effectives; stand on the defensive except when we can attack in superior numbers; send no more regiments or gunboats to be gobbled up one at a time. Mass our forces and we shall surely conquer.

Sincerely,

R. B. HAYES.

S. BIRCHARD.

March 15, 1863. — Left our log-cabin camp at the Falls of the Kanawha. Camp Reynolds was a happy abiding place. Lucy came with Birch and Webb on the 24th of January. They rowed skiffs, fished, built dams, sailed little ships, played cards, and enjoyed camp life generally. We reached Charleston at dark [this] Sunday evening. The men went to the churches to stay.

March 18-19, [*1863*]. — Went into Camp White (after Colonel White of the Twelfth), opposite the mouth of the Elk.

Saturday 21. — Lucy and boys on the *Allen Collier* home.

CAMP WHITE, March 21, 1863.

DEAREST: — You left this morning. Don't think I am going daft after you. I am in my tent facing the parade between the captains and companies. McKinley is in his. The doctor, Avery, and [the] major will come over tomorrow. I shall sleep in a tent tonight for the first time since the night before South Mountain — over six months ago. . . .

Did you see us crossing in our boat before your steamer passed? I saw you and swung my hat, but whether you saw me I could not tell.

Our house flag must come out to go on a high pole near headquarters if it is militarily proper, and I think it is. . . . Goodbye, darling.

As ever,

R.

Mrs. Hayes.

Sunday, March 22, 1863. — Have gone into camp. My headquarters here. My brigade is Twenty-third Ohio, Fifth Virginia, Colonel Ziegler, Thirteenth Virginia Cavalry, Colonel Brown, Captain Gilmore's Cavalry, Lieutenant Gonseman's ditto, and Lieutenant ——; also Captain Simmond's Battery. Gonseman at Loup and Tompkins Farm. Gilmore, here. Battery at Gauley Bridge; Twenty-third here. Thirteenth at Coal's Mouth and Hurricane Bridge; Fifth at Ceredo.

The boys will never forget their visit to papa and the Twenty-third. It will be a romatic memory. Webb was a greater favorite than Birch. Mischievous but kind-hearted and affectionate. Birch more scholarly and more commanding. Dear boys, how I love them! They were with me nearly two months in my log-cabin camp. Great happiness in log cabins.

Camp White, near Charleston, Virginia, March 22, 1863.

Dear Uncle: — We came out of the wilderness a week ago today. We are now pleasantly located on the left bank of the Kanawha, just below (opposite) Charleston. We are almost at home, and can expect to see anxious friends soon. You would, I think, enjoy a trip up here in a few weeks. You can get on a steamer at Cincinnati and land at our camp, and be safely and comfortably housed here. Lucy and the boys, after a most happy time, went home yesterday. We shall expect to see them again while we are here.

We seem intended for a permanent garrison here. We shall probably be visited by the Rebels while here. Our force is small but will perhaps do. My command is Twenty-third Ohio, Fifth and Thirteenth Virginia, three companies of cavalry, and a fine battery. I have some of the best, and I suspect some of about the poorest troops in service. They are scattered from Gauley to the mouth of Sandy on the Kentucky line. They are well posted to keep down bushwhacking and the like, but would be of small account against an invading force. We have three weak, but very good regiments, Twenty-third, Twelfth, and Thirty-fourth Ohio, some, a small amount, of good cavalry and good artillery, and about three or four regiments of indifferent infantry. So we shall probably see fun, if the enemy thinks it worth while to come in. Come and see me.

Sincerely,

R. B. HAYES.

S. BIRCHARD.

CAMP WHITE, NEAR CHARLESTON, March 22, 1863.

DEAR MOTHER: — One week ago today we started bag and baggage for this place. We are within five or six hours' travel by steamboat from Ohio (Gallipolis). Steamers pass our camp daily two or three times for home. We are within fifteen hours of Cincinnati and the communication frequent and regular. . . .

We shall remain here probably a good while. The Twenty-third is the only regiment in the vicinity. My command is stretched from Gauley to the Kentucky line. I make my headquarters here but shall go in both directions often. Quite likely, if present arrangements continue, I may run up to Columbus in a month or two. . . . Love to all.

Affectionately, your son,

R. B. HAYES.

MRS. SOPHIA HAYES.

Monday, [*March*] *23.* — Rained during the night. Rained 19th and 20th all day; looks like rain all day today. This is a beautiful valley from Piatt down to its mouth. Make west Virginia a free State and Charleston ought to be a sort of Pittsburgh.

P. M. Warm and bright until 6 P. M. An April shower. Camp getting into order; gravel walks building, streets making. Muddy now, but it is a loose porous soil and will turn out well.

Tuesday, 24. — Rain all night and this A. M.! Army movements very slow. Vicksburg the great point of interest for a month past. Things looking like fight in Rosecrans' vicinity; Charleston also a point of attack.

In the North a reaction favorable to the war is taking place. The peace men, sympathizers with the Rebels, called Copperheads or Butternuts, are mostly of the Democratic party. They gained strength last fall by an adroit handling of the draft, the tax-law arrests, the policy favorable to the negro, and the mistakes and lack of vigor in prosecuting the war. This led to overconfidence, and a more open hostility to the war itself. The soldiers in the field considered this a "fire in the rear," and "giving aid and comfort to the enemy." They accordingly by addresses and resolutions made known their sentiments. Loyal Democrats like John Van Buren [and] James T. Brady begin to speak out in the same strain. A considerable reaction is observable. The late acts of Congress, the conscription, the financial measures, and [the] *Habeas Corpus* Act, give the Government great power and the country more confidence. If the conscription is wisely and energetically administered, there is much reason to hope for good results.

In the meantime the Rebels are certainly distressed for want of provisions. The negro policy doesn't seem to accomplish much. A few negro troops give rise to disturbances where they come in contact with our men and do not as yet worry the enemy a great deal.

Thursday, 26. — A cold, rainy day. Last night the coldest of the season. Yesterday with Dr. Joe and four oarsmen rowed in his large skiff up Elk, three or four miles; caught in a wild storm of rain and sleet.

Had a dispatch today from Captain Simmonds at Gauley; he reports rumors of an early advance on all our posts. "Sensational!" General Scammon in a "stew" about it.

Friday, 27. — Bitterly cold last night; a bright, frosty morning. Election yesterday in all these counties on accepting the conditions which Congress affixes to the admission as a State of West Virginia. The condition is abolition of slavery. The people doubtless have acquiesced.

Rumors of enemy in Boone and Logan [Counties], also on the Sandy. All pointing to an attempt to take this valley and the salt-works.

Saturday, 28. — Rain all night. Yesterday, a clear, cold morning; a white frost; cloudy and hazy all day; rain at night.

P. M. Rode with Dr. Webb, Lieutenant McKinley, and a dragoon out on road to Coal Forks as far as Davis Creek, thence down the creek to the Guyandotte Pike (river road), thence home. Crossed the creek seven times; water deep and bottom miry.

Today a fight between four hundred Jenkins' or Floyd's men and two hundred and seventy-five Thirteenth Virginia [men] at Hurricane Bridge. Rebels repulsed. Our loss three killed and six wounded, one mortally. Floyd's men coming into Logan, Boone, Wayne, Cabell, and Putnam [Counties], reporting Floyd dismissed and his troops disbanded. The troops from being state troops refuse to go into Confederate service but seem willing to fight the Yankees on their own hook.

CAMP WHITE, March 28, 1863.

DEAREST: — I received yours last night. It is a week this morning since you left. We have had rain every day, and in tents in the mud it is disagreeable enough. The men still keep well. We have plenty of rumors of forces coming in here. It does look as if some of the posts below here might be attacked.

You went away at just the right time as it has turned out. A few weeks hence it will be good weather again and you would enjoy it if we are not too much annoyed with the rumors or movements of the enemy.

Nothing new to talk about. General Cox is quite certainly not confirmed, ditto his staff officers, Bascom, Conine, and Christie. It is now a question whether they revert to their former rank or go out of service. At any rate, we are *probably* not to be under them. At present we are *supposed* to report to General Schenck at Baltimore. We like General Schenck but he is too distant and we prefer on that account to be restored to the Department of the Ohio under General Burnside.

We have had two bitterly cold nights the last week; with all my clothes and overcoat on I could not keep warm enough to sleep well. But it is healthy!

Love to all the boys, to Grandma and "a smart chance" for your own dear self.

Same as before, yours lovingly,

R.

Mrs. Hayes.

Sunday, [March 29]. — Last night Lieutenant Austin came into camp with thirty-three men and two guns; a ten-pound Parrott and a three-inch Rebel gun captured by Colonel Crook at Lewisburg last summer. Cleared off cold last night; a strong northwest wind all night and today; bitterly cold. No fun in tent life in such weather. Rumors of the fight at Hurricane Bridge represent the Rebels as Jenkins' men, four hundred to seven hundred strong.

Monday, 30. — A cold, clear night last night; a fine morning, *but a white frost* — light. Report that the steamer which left here yesterday morning with Quartermaster Fitch, Paymaster Cowen, etc., on board was fired into nearly opposite Buffalo. Said to be ten companies of Jenkins' men, some crossing Kanawha, a few with horses. Lieutenant-Colonel Comly with five companies [of the] Twenty-third went down [the] river in [a] steamboat to Coal's Mouth to defend that point.

4 P. M. — Reported that Point Pleasant is in possession of the Rebels.

6 P. M. — Dispatch from Captain Fitch says [that a] company of [the] Thirteenth Virginia holds out in court-house at Point Pleasant; with impromptu gunboats from Gallipolis drove the Rebels out of Point Pleasant; can certainly hold it until dark.

9 P. M. — Dispatch: Rebels driven back, twelve killed, fourteen taken prisoners. Our loss one killed, one wounded, three officers (?) taken prisoners. Stores all safe.

10 P. M. — Rebels retreated up Kanawha; starving, out of shoes, and ammunition.

Colonel Comly ordered to rig up steamboat so as to protect men and go down the river to prevent Jenkins from recrossing the river.

[*March 31*]. — *7:30 A. M.* — Colonel Comly started from Coal's Mouth down [the] river at daylight.

8:30 A. M. — Dispatch from Colonel Comly at Red House says, "Jenkins supposed to have recrossed the river five miles above Point Pleasant." Our telegraphic communications via Gauley and Clarksburg with the outside world cut off between Gauley and Clarksburg! Bottsford says now: "Keep your powder dry and trust in God!" I advised to send word to Captain Fitch at Gallipolis to run his steamboats up Kanawha and prevent a recrossing of the Rebels, but it was too late or seems not to have been heeded.

CAMP WHITE, April 1, 1863.

DEAR UNCLE: — We have had most disagreeable weather for a week. Part of the time we were cut off from outside world by General Jenkins' raid below. He has thus far made nothing. He has attacked two of the posts garrisoned by men under my command and been whipped both times with a loss to him of seventy killed and prisoners. Our loss is six. We could take the whole party with cavalry enough. As it is, he will get off.

All fools' day is a bright cold windy day. We are in tents rather too early for comfort or health. We are glad to see warm weather coming.

Sincerely,

R. B. HAYES.

S. BIRCHARD.

CAMP WHITE, April 1, 1863.

DEAREST: — We are again in communication with America after being cut off about four or five days by General Jenkins. He attacked two posts garrisoned by [the] Thirteenth Virginia — and one had Lieutenant Hicks, the color sergeant and six men of Twenty-third. In both cases General Jenkins was badly worsted losing seventy men killed or captured, while we lost only four killed and five wounded. A sorry raid so far.

Judge Matthews, I see, is to be superior court judge. I suppose his health is the cause. He had a difficulty before he left the Twenty-third which at times unfitted him for service in the field.

Awful weather for tent life the last week — snow, rain, and wind "all to once." I am really glad you left when you did. A few weeks hence if Jenkins lets us alone we shall be in condition to enjoy your presence.

Love to the dear boys. Webb will, I am sure, study hard when he hears how much I want him to be a scholar. Birch and the others are right of course.

The Prince's [Prince of Wales] wedding you read, I know. No happier than ours!

Affectionately,

R.

MRS. HAYES.

Friday, [April] 3. — Monday's fight at Point Pleasant was a fine affair; twenty Rebels killed and fifty taken prisoners, of whom twenty-four were wounded. Colonel Comly returned with [Companies] E and K on Tuesday or Wednesday.

Jackson Smith [a prisoner] says: "[The] Eighth Virginia is commanded by Colonel Corns; Colonel Ferguson [commands] the Sixteenth Virginia. We took a near cut from Marion to Jeffersonville, crossing Holston River and Brush, Poor Valley and Rich Mountains, about twenty-eight miles in two days, leaving Marion, March 14. Waggons followed by turnpike from Wytheville. [On the] 16th, camped at Jeffersonville. [The]

26

17th, twelve miles to Abbs Valley; 18th, twelve miles into Mc-
Dowell County; 19th, twelve miles to Tug Fork in McDowell
County. Eight days' rations issued, crackers and dried beef.
[The] 20th, three miles up Tug and crossed. [The] 21st, twelve
or fourteen [miles] to Cub Creek; crossed [the] Guyandotte in
canoes. [The] 24th, passed Logan Court-house; 25th I came up
Big Creek to Turtle Creek; down Turtle Creek to Coal."

CAMP WHITE, April 5, 1863.

DEAREST: — The weather is good, our camp dry, and everybody happy. Joe has got a sail rigged on his large skiff and he
enjoys sailing on the river. It is pleasant to be able to make
use of these otherwise disagreeable spring winds to do our
rowing.

Visited the hospital (it being Sunday) over in town this morning. It is clean, airy, and cheerful-looking. We have only a
few there — mostly very old cases.

Comly heard a couple of ladies singing Secesh songs, as if
for his ear, in a fine dwelling in town. Joe has got his revenge
by obtaining an order to use three rooms for hospital patients.
The announcement caused grief and dismay — they fear small-
pox (a case has appeared). I think Joe repents his victory now.

Enclosed photographs, except Comly's, are all taken by a
Company B man who is turning a number of honest pennies by
the means — Charlie Smith, Birch will recollect as Captain
Avery's orderly.

Five companies of the Twenty-third had a hard race after
Jenkins. They got his stragglers. Colonel Paxton and Gilmore are after him with their cavalry. General Jenkins has had
bad luck with this raid. He came in with seven hundred to eight
hundred men. He will get off with four hundred to five hundred,
badly used up, and nothing to pay for his losses. We lost half
a dozen killed. They murdered one citizen of Point Pleasant, an
old veteran of 1812, aged eight-four. They will run us out in a
month or two, I suspect, unless we are strengthened, or they
weakened. General Scammon is prepared to destroy salt and
salt-works if he does have to leave.

I think of you and the boys oftener than ever. Love to 'em and oceans for yourself.

Affectionately ever,

R.

P. S. — I sent by express three hundred and fifty dollars in a package with two hundred dollars of Joe's. It ought to reach Mother Webb in a day or two after this letter. Write if it *doesn't* or *does.*

MRS. HAYES.

CAMP WHITE, April 9, 1863.

DEAR UNCLE: — Yours of the 3rd received. Yes, Jenkins made a dash into Point Pleasant, but he dashed out before doing much mischief with a loss of seventy-five killed and prisoners. He attacked one other post garrisoned by men under my command but was repulsed. His raid was a failure. He lost about one hundred and fifty men while in this region and accomplished nothing. But we expect repetitions of this thing, and with our present force we shall probably suffer more another time.

I do not look for an end of the war for a long time yet. I am glad the late elections show the second sober thought to be right. We can worry them out if we keep at it without flagging.

Come on, it will be good weather in a few weeks.

I send you a soldier's photograph of our log-cabin camp near Gauley. It is not good. You can see the falls beyond the camp and the high cliffs on the opposite side of the Kanawha. My quarters were at the long-roofed cabin running across the street towards the back and right of the picture.

Sincerely,

S. BIRCHARD.   R. B. HAYES.

CAMP WHITE, April 10, 1863.

DEAREST: — Your most welcome letter reached me this morning. Tell Webby the little rooster is in fine feather. He has had a good many fights with a big rooster belonging to the family near our camp, but holds his own very bravely.

Yes, a coat of course. I am afraid about pants — they should be long and wide in the legs for riding if you get them. No vest is wanted. — Did the cash come to hand?

Our large flag at home would look well flying over this camp if you will send it by Mr. Forbes. As for the new regimental flag, you shall get it some day if you wish to do it.

The fine weather of a few days past has brought us out. We are very happy here again.

Colonel Matthews is perfectly right. He no doubt leaves the army on account of the impossibility of serving in the field. He was barely able to get through his first campaign. . . .

I am as glad as anybody that the Union ticket [in Cincinnati] was carried. The soldiers all feel happy over the recent indications at home. A few victories over the Rebels now would lift us on amazingly. — Yes, "cut off" sounds badly, but it was a very jolly time.

I have Captain Gilmore and Lieutenant Austin and two rifled guns camped here, besides four howitzers with gun squads on the steamboats. General Jenkins and about eight hundred men left the railroad at Marion, Smith County, southwestern Virginia, and crossed the mountains to the head waters of Sandy River and so across towards the mouth of Kanawha. They reached our outpost twenty-four miles from here and demanded a surrender. Captain Johnson with four companies of [the] Thirteenth Virginia declined to surrender and, after a good fight, repulsed General Jenkins. He then crossed Kanawha twenty miles from the mouth or less and attacked Point Pleasant at the mouth. Captain Carter and one company of [the] Thirteenth Virginia occupied the court-house. They could not keep the whole town clear of Rebels but defended themselves gallantly until relieved from Gallipolis. General Jenkins then retreated. Colonel Paxton and Captain Gilmore followed by different routes, worrying him badly and getting about forty prisoners.

Does Birch remember Captain Waller, a cavalry captain who took care of Colonel Paxton and sat opposite us at table often? Perhaps he recollects his little boy. Well he, the boy, rode with his father in the pursuit and captured two armed men himself!

Captain Stevens and all the others are commissioned. Naughton is wroth at Dr. Webb and me! . . . More photographs. Preserve with the war archives, and be sure of one thing, I love you so much.

As ever,

R.

MRS. HAYES.

CAMP WHITE, April 15, Evening.

DEAREST: — Your short business letter came this afternoon. I do not yet know about your coming here during the campaigning season. If we fortify, probably all right; if not, I don't know.

Lieutenant Ellen is married. His wife sent me a fine big wedding cake and two cans of fruit. Good wife, I guess, by the proofs sent me.

You speak of Jim Ware. What does he think of the prospects? I understand Jim in a letter to Dr. Joe says Dr. Ware gives it up. Is this so?

I send you more photographs. The major's resignation was not accepted and he is now taking hold of things with energy.

We are having further disasters, I suspect, at Charleston and in North Carolina. But they are not vital. The small results (adverse results, I mean,) likely to follow are further proofs of our growing strength.

What a capital speech Everett has made. He quite redeems himself.

Always say something about the boys — their sayings and doings.

Affectionately ever,

R.

MRS. HAYES.

CAMP WHITE, April 19, 1863.

DEAR MOTHER: — I received the letter written on your birthday yesterday. It found me very well and pleasantly employed.

Today is Sunday. We had a meeting this morning which you would have enjoyed. We had the first sermon to the soldiers we have heard in many months. A Presbyterian clergyman, educated at Granville and Hudson, named Little, a man well adapted to talk to soldiers, preached, sang, etc., etc., most acceptably to a fine audience of troops. He dined with me and promises to come often. He belongs to one of the regiments under my command, posted about forty miles from here.

My eyes are perfectly good — my arm good enough for my use. — The weather here is beautiful — rather too hot. Health good with us generally. — Love to all.

Affectionately, your son,

RUTHERFORD.

MRS. SOPHIA HAYES.

Wednesday, [April] 22. — A good spell of weather just ended. Drilling, boating, ball-playing, and the like make the time pass pleasantly. Last Sunday had a Mr. Little preach to us on the bank of the river. Several young ladies, a good audience of soldiers, and a good sermon. Mr. Little brought a sort of hand organ and was the chief musician — an eccentric, witty man, capable and zealous.

CAMP WHITE, April 22, 1863.

DEAR UNCLE: — We have a pleasant camp, just enough for men to do to keep them out of mischief. About as easy soldiering as we ever had. You can stay on the opposite side of the river at a fair hotel for seven dollars per week, or on this side in a comfortable tent, better grub, for nothing. If you can do better at home, we can make up the difference in novelty. So come soon. We shall have a superior foe driving us out or worrying us badly in a month or two, and at your time of life that might be uncomfortable. I think we shall be let alone now until after the first of June. General Jenkins learned that a small force had no fun coming in here and a large force can't live here until the first of June or after.

I hope we shall soon see the drafting begin. It ought not to be delayed a day now.

Sincerely,

R. B. HAYES.

S. BIRCHARD.

CAMP WHITE, WEST VIRGINIA, April 30, 1863.

DEAR UNCLE: — I have received yours of the 25th. I am not surprised to hear you are going into business under Governor Chase's Bank Law. I thought of suggesting it, but knew so little about it that I could form no intelligent opinion.* . . .

You can come here well enough. There is of course a possibility of being cut off, but very small probability of it. I do not doubt that the Rebels will get in below us, but we shall certainly hear of it in time to ship off all who are not ready to stay. Lucy would like to come with you, but you will not bring her unless you find it quite convenient to do so.

Sincerely,

R. B. HAYES.

S. BIRCHARD.

CAMP WHITE, May 2, 1863.

DEAREST L—: — Yours and the monthlies were handed me last night. No hurry about the "duds." As for shoulder-straps, it would make no difference how it's done if it's according to custom or regulations. I don't want to *start* a new fashion. Regulations require straps of a certain size, color, etc., a *silver* eagle, etc., etc. I would sooner have simply the eagle than a strap twice as big as the rule, but of no importance. Glad to get the monthlies.

We are fortifying, partly to occupy time, partly to be safe. Will [shall] be at it some time.

---

* Mr. Birchard was promptly taking steps to convert his bank into a national bank under the new law. It became the First National Bank of Fremont, and was the fifth bank in the country to be chartered by the Government.

Uncle talks of coming up. If he does, you may bring one or more of the boys if you can do so conveniently, and if he asks you. . . .

Affectionately,

MRS. HAYES.   R.

May 7, [1863]. — Another movement of the army of the Potomac, this time under General Hooker, a man of energy and courage. Whether able and skilful enough to handle so great an army is the question. He is confident and bold. His crossing the Rappahannock was sudden and apparently successful. It looked a little like separating his army. The great fighting [at Chancellorsville] was on Saturday and Sunday, reported vaguely as "indecisive." Again this suspense — "with us or with our foes?" All day Sunday I was thinking and talking of the battle. The previous news satisfied me that about that time fighting would be done.

CAMP WHITE, May 7, 1863.

DEAREST: — The boxes came safely. The flag will not be cut. The coat fits well. Straps exactly according to regulations or none. The eagles are pretty and simple and I shall keep them until straps can be got of the size and description prescribed, viz., "Light or sky-blue *cloth*, one and three-eighths inches wide by four inches long; bordered with an embroidery of gold one-fourth of an inch wide; a *silver* embroidered spread eagle on the center of the strap." I am content with the eagles as they are but if straps are got, let them be "according to red-tape." The pants *fit Avery* to a charm and he keeps them. What is the price? I'll not try again until I can be measured. I do not need pants just now.

We have a little smallpox in Charleston. Lieutenant Smith has it, or measles. Also raids of the enemy threatened. I wouldn't come up just now; before the end of the month it may be all quiet again. Bottsford's sister and other ladies are going away today.

We are building a fort on the hill above our camp — a good position. We are in suspense about Hooker. He moves rapidly and boldly. If he escapes defeat for the next ten days he is the coming man. — Pictures O. K., etc., etc. — Love to all.

Affectionately,

R. B. Hayes.

Mrs. Hayes.

CAMP WHITE, May 17, 1863.

DEAREST: — Things look well for quiet in our vicinity for a time to come. We have had a good deal of excitement for the past fortnight, but it is over now. Any time you think best to come or send Grandma or any of the family, advise me as you start and we will be ready for you and glad to see you. Comly brings his new wife here soon. Ellen (Lieutenant Ellen), ditto. Mrs. Zimmerman, an agreeable lady, is here now.

My whole brigade except two or three detached companies, is now here. Delany, Simmonds, the Fifth and Thirteenth Virginia and a new cavalry company were sent for during the recent scare. We have nearly finished a tolerable fort, and have a gunboat. I have thirteen pieces of artillery.

I am most agreeably disappointed in my Virginia regiments. The Thirteenth is new and composed of West Virginians, but it has capital officers and they promise well in all respects. I reviewed them this Sunday morning. Their appearance would be creditable to an old regiment.

The Fifth was in all battles under Frémont and Pope last summer and behaved well, but was unfortunately officered. *This* has been corrected. Their present commander is an excellent man and I look for good things from them.

It perhaps would be better for you not to come until you are ready to leave Cincinnati for the summer, if you do leave for the summer. But you and Mother Webb will make your own arrangements and it will suit me.

As ever, affectionately,

R. B. Hayes.

Mrs. Hayes.

CAMP WHITE, May 17, 1863.

DEAR UNCLE:—. . . We are in no danger here. We have built a tolerably good fort which we can hold against superior forces perhaps a week or two or more. We have a gunboat which will be useful as long as the river is navigable. My whole brigade has been here. The most of it is good and the rest is improving.

I like your bank project.

The Richmond hoax was a severe one. It did not reach us in a way to command belief. I still stick to Hooker. The Rebel loss of Jackson gives us the best of that effort. I hope the Potomac Army will get a victory sometime.

Sincerely,

R. B. HAYES.

S. BIRCHARD.

CAMP WHITE, WEST VIRGINIA, [May 20 (?)], 1863.

DEAR UNCLE:— If I wrote you two or three days ago after getting your last, I take this one back; or let it go to my credit on future account. We are expecting to have our communications cut with the outside world soon again. We are tolerably fixed for it, and can worry through, if not too long continued.

We do not know accurately yet what has happened to Hooker. He is repulsed and his movement a failure. I hope he is left relatively as well off as he was before. If so, he is still, for all I see, our general. I can perceive nothing injurious to him personally in the failure. He has shown his disposition to do something, and, for all that appears, capacity. This is all we can demand. The radical vice is, as I have said to you before, I fear, in the army. Somebody behaves badly. This is always to be expected in all armies. But in this army it seems always to be at the vital point, where it is ruinous. I always feel when the Potomac Army moves, that if they are not routed, we are to be glad. So now, from present accounts, I feel happy that it is no worse. If our army under Hooker can keep employed the largest and best Rebel army, they are probably fulfilling their mission.

To do more than this, would speedily end the Rebellion. To do merely this, will end it in time.

Perhaps I better take stock in your bank. I could now pay one or two thousand cash, and by selling my Hamilton property, could increase it soon to five thousand dollars. What say you?

Sincerely,

R. B. HAYES.

S. BIRCHARD.

CAMP WHITE, WEST VIRGINIA, May 25, 1863.

DEAREST : — If Vicksburg is taken it will perhaps take us to some other field. At least, important changes in our military policy may be looked for. Therefore, darling, I want you to visit me when you can, with such of the boys as you choose. All this is supposing Vicksburg ours. If not there will be time enough, I think, when you get ready to quit the city for the summer a few weeks hence.

Comly has his wife here. Captains Zimmerman and Sperry theirs, and more are expected — *mine* among the rest. — Love to all.

Affectionately,

R.

P. S. — Tell Stephenson I am now ready to sell the Hamilton property as proposed, if the offer can still be had.

MRS. HAYES.

CAMP WHITE, May 25, 1863.

DEAR UNCLE: — The Rebels don't make much progress towards getting us out. We are tolerably well fortified here and at Fayette. At the latter place they tried it, banging away three or four days and doing nothing.

I will see to the bank stock and try to pay a little at any rate.

Grant seems to be doing well. If all we hear is true, I think he will get Vicksburg soon.

I have sent to Lucy to come up as soon as Vicksburg is taken, thinking it probable that such an event may soon send us further out.

Sincerely,

R. B. HAYES.

S. BIRCHARD.

CAMP WHITE, May 27, 1863.

DEAR MOTHER: — I received your letter and Laura's a few days ago. . . . You seem to suppose Lucy and the boys are here. This is a mistake. I did not send for Lucy until yesterday. If the reports of General Grant's victories at Vicksburg are true, I shall expect to see important changes in the location of troops in this quarter. I therefore tell Lucy that her best chance to visit me is now. . . .

We have had a good deal of marching, but little fighting, during the recent attempts of the enemy to get into this valley. They failed entirely in their efforts. We are sufficiently fortified to keep our positions against anything but greatly superior forces. If Grant is successful, at Vicksburg, as seems now probable, the whole prospect is changed and changed favorably.

Affectionately, your son,

RUTHERFORD.

MRS. SOPHIA HAYES.

CAMP WHITE, June 2, 1863.

DEAR UNCLE: — Yes, I vote for you bank president. Signing the bills will be a bore, but then the signature can't be counterfeited. . . .

Vicksburg appears to be a hard nut to crack. But with proper efforts to reinforce and supply Grant, he must, I think, succeed. The more obstinate the resistance, the more valuable will be the victory if we finally gain it. We are stronger here than we were. I now have a full brigade, four regiments infantry, a battery, and three campanies cavalry. We fortify all points deemed important.

Sincerely,

S. BIRCHARD.   R. B. HAYES.

CAMP WHITE, June 14, 1863.

DEAR UNCLE: — I received yours dated the 4th last night. I see by the *Sentinel* that you are a bank president, one of the "moneyed aristocracy" of the land.

No taking of Vicksburg yet. I still think we must get it soon. Vallandigham for governor? Pretty bold move. Rather rash if it is considered that forty to sixty thousand soldiers will probably vote. I estimate that about as many will vote for Vallandigham as there are deserters in the course of a year's service — from one to five per cent. A foolish (or worse) business, our Democratic friends are getting into. I don't like arbitrary or military arrests of civilians in States where the law is regularly administered by the courts, but no issue can be made on such questions while the Rebellion is unconquered, and it's idle to attempt it.

Lucy and all the family are on a steamboat a few miles below here, and will be up this afternoon. We have had no trouble from Rebels since their repulse at Fayette, so I think they will be quite comfortable here.

15th. — Mother Webb and Lucy, with all the boys, are here. Boys are delighted.

Sincerely,

R. B. HAYES.

S. BIRCHARD.

CAMP WHITE, June 19, 1863.

DEAR MOTHER: — . . . Mother Webb, Lucy and the four boys all got here in good health last Monday. They are housed in a pleasant little cottage on the river bank — plenty of fruit and flowers and not over fifty steps from my tent.

General Scammon's wife left yesterday. Four of [or] five officers' wives are here, making society enough. It is not likely they will remain in the present stirring times more than a week or so.

Lucy had a long letter from Nellie Howells (Mead) just before she left Cincinnati. Nellie is very happy in her European home. — Love to all.

Affectionately,

Mrs. Sophia Hayes.

R. B. Hayes.

Camp White (opposite Charleston), West Virginia, June 25, 1863. — Last Monday, the 15th, Lucy, Mother Webb, and "all the boys" came here from Cincinnati on the *Market Boy.* A few happy days, when little Joseph sickened and died yesterday at noon (12:40). Poor little darling! A sweet, bright boy, "looked like his father," but with large, handsome blue eyes much like Webb's. Teething, dysentery, and brain affected, the diseases. He died without suffering; lay on the table in our room in the Quarrier cottage, surrounded by white roses and buds all the afternoon, and was sent to Cincinnati in care of Corporal Schirmes, Company K [D], this morning. I have seen so little of him, born since the war, that I do not realize a loss; but his mother, and still more his grandmother, lose their little dear companion, and are very much afflicted.

Camp White, June 25, 1863.

Dear Uncle: — Our little Joseph died yesterday after a few days' severe illness. He was eighteen months old — bright and very pretty. I have hardly seen him, and hardly had a father's feeling for him. To me, the suffering of Lucy and the still greater sorrow of his grandmother, are the chief afflictions. His brain was excessively developed, and it is probable that his early death has prevented greater suffering. He was the most excitable, nervous child I ever saw. We have sent his body home for burial. Lucy and the rest will leave here in a few days for Chillicothe. This has dashed the pleasure of their visit here.

I have one thousand dollars for your bank (at Cincinnati), and will [shall] have fifteen hundred dollars more in two or three weeks. I want stock to that amount. I have one thousand dollars' worth of 7:30 bonds, but I will keep them in preference to the stock.

I like Brough's nomination [for governor of Ohio.]   We everywhere lack energy.   He will have enough.

Sincerely,

R. B. HAYES.

S. BIRCHARD.

July 1, [1863]. — Lucy and the family left on the *Marwood* today.   The visit has been a happy one, saddened though it is by the death of our beautiful little Joseph.   Lucy has been cheerful since — remarkably so — but on leaving today without him she burst into tears on seeing a little child on the boat.   The boys, the three, all lovable.   Birchie is delicate, looks like Billy Rogers.   Must take care of his training.

Little "Jody" died in the Quarrier house, a little frame cottage on the bank of the Kanawha opposite the lower end of Charleston.   Camp White was on the same premises.

CAMP WHITE, WEST VIRGINIA, July 1, 1863.

DEAR UNCLE: — Lucy and family left here today.   They go to Ross County.   They will probably visit Delaware during the summer.   Unless we should have more active duty, I shall be quite lonely for a while without them.

The invasion of Pennsylvania is likely to work important changes; possibly to take us East again.   The Army of the Potomac has another commander.   I still suspect that in the case of that army, the soldiers are more in fault for their disasters than the generals.   I dread to hear of a battle there.   They will do better, however, on our own soil.   If Grant could only get Vicksburg in time to spare a corps or two of his troops for the campaign in the East, we should be safe enough.   If Lee really is pushing into Pennsylvania in full force, it ought to prove his ruin; but we shall see.   I think, as you do, that it will do much to unite us.

Sincerely,

R. B. HAYES.

S. BIRCHARD.

CAMP WHITE, July 6, 1863.

DEAREST: — Dr. Joe got back yesterday — twenty-four hours from Chillicothe. Very glad to hear his cheerful account of you.

I am in the tent occupied by Captain Hood and wife in front of the cottage. We all miss you. You could not have felt the loss of me more than I did of you. Notwithstanding the loss of the dear little boy, your visit leaves a happy impression. I love you more than ever, darling.

The Ninth has gone to Fayette. If the good news from the East holds out, I think the Twenty-third will follow soon.

We had a good Fourth. Salutes from Simmonds and Austin. A good deal of drinking but no harm. We let all out of the guard-house.

I send you a deed to execute and send to Stephenson. Do it before a notary. I will ask Uncle to put twenty-five hundred dollars stock in his bank in your name.

I am sorry to hear Uncle Scott is in poor health. I think the news from the East will be a good tonic. We shall whip the rascals some day. — Love to all.

Affectionately,

R. B. HAYES.

MRS. HAYES.

CAMP WHITE, July 6, 1863.

DEAR UNCLE:—. . . I propose to take in your bank twenty-five hundred dollars stock in Lucy's name. Please see *when* you get the cash to put the stock in her name. I have in Stephenson's hands one thousand dollars and expect fifteen hundred dollars more in three weeks. I send you an order for it.

Reports from the East look well. If true, we shall perhaps go forward here. The Rebels found fighting in the enemy's country a different thing from battling on their own ground.

Sincerely,

R. B. HAYES.

S. BIRCHARD.

CAMP WHITE, CHARLESTON, WEST VIRGINIA, July 8, 1863.

DEAR MOTHER: — . . . We received the news of the capture of Vicksburg last night. I hope it will not turn out as so many reports — stock-jobbers' lies. We have thus far had encouraging success in Pennsylvania. If it is continued the Rebels will hardly repeat the experiment of invading our soil. Altogether things wear a hopeful appearance, but I do not expect an early end of the war. A great deal remains to be done, and it is gratifying that the people seem determined to be patient and firm. . . .

Affectionately, your son,

RUTHERFORD.

MRS. SOPHIA HAYES.

July 7. P. M. — Heard the news of Vicksburg captured. Fired one hundred guns and had a good time.

July 9. P. M. — Left Charleston on steamboat for upper river.

10 — At Loup Creek all day.

11. — Moved to foot of Cotton Hill, Fayette side.

CHAPTER XXII

MORGAN'S RAID AND MINOR OPERATIONS — WEST VIRGINIA — JULY-DECEMBER 1863

CAMP Joe Webb, Near Fayetteville, West Virginia, Sunday, July 12, 1863. — We are starting on an expedition to Raleigh County and perhaps further. I do not fully approve of the enterprise. We are too weak to accomplish much; run some risks; and I see no sufficient object to be accomplished.

I wrote to Lucy yesterday. I shall not write to Mother or Uncle until my return. It would only cause them anxiety and do no good. Of course this book will be sent home in case of accident, and they will here see that they were not forgotten. Dear boys, darling Lucy, and all, good-bye! We are all in the hands of Providence and need only be solicitous to do our duty here and leave the future to the Great Disposer.

[July 16, 1863]. — We reached Raleigh Tuesday, 14th, about 12:30 P. M. Found the enemy strongly fortified at Piney River. It was deemed unsafe to assault in front, and finding it would take much time to turn the position, it was resolved to leave without attempting to storm the works. During the night the Rebels kindly relieved us by running away! P. M. We started for Fayette on the 15th.

FAYETTEVILLE, July 16, P. M., 1863.

DEAREST: — We reached here today; left Raleigh yesterday. The Rebels were fortifying beyond Raleigh on Piney. They were already annoying us a good deal from there. We reached their works Tuesday, 14th. After feeling for their position we withdrew for the night. In the morning they were gone. A force is destroying their works and we are so far on our way back. We may go on another expedition before returning to Charleston, but not one involving much risk.

Morgan is in Ohio. I wish we were there also. Possibly we may be if he remains long. Very queer, these last struggles of the Rebs. They are dying hard, but it seems like the convulsive and desperate efforts of the dying. . . . Love to all.

Affectionately, dear one, your

R.

Mrs. Hayes.

FAYETTEVILLE, July 16, 1863.

DEAR MOTHER: — We have been into Dixie and are safe out again into our own lines — a very lively and pleasant raid.

I see Morgan is raiding in Ohio. I hope he will be caught. It will not surprise me if we are called home to look after him. I regard this as one of the reckless efforts of a despairing and lost cause. Certainly the Rebel prospects were never before so dark, nor ours so cheering.

I am very well. No time to say more.

Affectionately,

R. B. Hayes.

Mrs. Sophia Hayes.

FAYETTEVILLE, July 16, 1863.

DEAR UNCLE: — We are on our return from beyond Raleigh. Rebs we were after left their stronghold without a fight, and our troops destroyed their works. Shall probably return to Charleston soon. Morgan in Ohio! I wish we were there also. All things look well. The escape of Lee does not disappoint me. To get rid of him so easily is a success. We shall get him some day. I enjoyed this last little campaign very much indeed.

Sincerely,

R. B. Hayes.

S. Birchard.

[*July 22, 1863*]. — [On the] 16th, at Fayette, heard that Morgan was in Ohio at Piketon, leaving there for Gallipolis. General Scammon wisely and promptly determined to head him [off] by sending me. (This was after a sharp controversy.) [The] Seventeenth with [the] Twenty-third and Thirteenth took steamboats from Loup Creek for Gallipolis. [The] 18th at Gallipolis heard Morgan had pushed by up the Ohio as if to cross at Pomeroy.

Sunday, 19th, [at] Pomeroy. Halted; found the militia waiting in position for Morgan. About noon he came; the Twenty-third went out to meet him; found him in force; sent for [the] Thirteenth; formed lines of battle. Morgan ditto. Seeing we were "regulars and not militia" (words of inspection of Rebels), he hurried off, with some loss. We had one wounded, in his hand — Clemens, Company B.

[The] 20th, at daylight, found Morgan at Buffington Island. He was here attacked by General Judah's cavalry and the gunboats. Not much fighting by Rebels, but great confusion, loss of artillery, etc., etc.

On to Hockingport; guarded the ferries over the Ohio at Lee's Creek, Belleville, and Hocking.

[The] 21st, back to Gallipolis. Morgan's army gone up. We got over two hundred prisoners. Everybody got some. No fight in them. The most successful and jolly little campaign we ever had.

[The] 22nd, Wednesday, home again in Camp White. [The] Thirteenth left at Point Pleasant; [the] Fifth sent to Gauley Bridge.

STEAMBOAT VICTRESS, OHIO RIVER, July 22, 1863.

DEAR UNCLE: — We have been after Morgan for a week. The Twenty-third was in all the fighting at Pomeroy and Buffington and took two hundred and six prisoners. The Rebs couldn't fight *soldiers* at all. We lost one man. We had a most glorious time. We go up the Kanawha again today.

Sincerely,

S. BIRCHARD. R. B. HAYES.

OHIO GENERALS, 1861-1865.

BRIGADIER-GENERAL
R. L. McCOOK, 1827-62.

BRIGADIER-GENERAL
WILLIAM H. LYTLE,
1826-63.

BRIGADIER-GENERAL
DANIEL McCOOK, 1834-64.

BRIGADIER-GENERAL
JOHN G. MITCHELL,
1838-94.

BRIGADIER-GENERAL
RALPH P. BUCKLAND,
1812-92.

MAJOR-GENERAL
J. WARREN KEIFER,
1836 —

BRIGADIER-GENERAL
JOHN BEATTY, 1828-1914.

CAMP WHITE, July 22, 1863.

DEAREST: — Home again after an absence of two weeks, marching and hurrying all the time. The last week after Morgan has been the liveliest and jolliest campaign we ever had. We were at all the skirmishes and fighting after he reached Pomeroy. It was nothing but fun — no serious fighting at all. I think not over ten killed and forty wounded on our side in all of it. Unluckily McCook, father of Robert and the rest, was mortally wounded. This hurt me but all the rest was mere frolic. Morgan's men were only anxious to get away. There was no fight in them when attacked by us. You will no doubt see great claims on all sides as to the merits of his captors. The cavalry, gunboats, militia, and our infantry each claim the victory as their peculiar property. The truth is, all were essential parties to the success. The cavalry who pursued him so long deserve the lion's share. The gunboats and militia did their part. *We* can truly claim that Morgan would have crossed and escaped with his men at Pomeroy if we had not headed him there and defeated his attempt. It is not yet certain whether Morgan himself will be caught. But it is of small importance. His force which has so long been the terror of the border, and which has kept employed all our cavalry in Kentucky is now gone. Our victorious cavalry can now operate in the enemy's country.

I thought of you often. We were quartered on steamboats — men were singing, bands playing. *Our* band was back and with us, and such lively times as one rarely sees. Almost everybody got quantities of trophies. I got nothing but a spur and two volumes captured from the Twentieth Kentucky, Captain H. C. Breman, and now recaptured by us. Morgan's raid will always be remembered by our men as one of the happiest events of their lives.

Love to the dear boys and Grandmother. Joe is unwell and is in a room in town.

Affectionately,

R.

MRS. HAYES.

CAMP WHITE, July 24, [1863].

DEAREST : — The happiness of this week's operations is dashed by the death of Captain Delany and the probable loss of a number of other good officers and men in our cavalry. Captains Delany [and] Gilmore, the Thirty-fourth mounted infantry, and Second Virginia Cavalry left Raleigh, on the day we returned from there, to cut the Tennessee Railroad at or near Wytheville. On the very day *we* (the infantry) were gaining bloodless (or almost bloodless) victories over Morgan on the Ohio, our cavalry were fighting a most desperate battle with superior numbers three hundred miles off at Wytheville. Our men were victorious, carried the town by storm, but they lost Colonel Toland, Thirty-fourth killed, Colonel Powell, Second Virginia, mortally wounded, Captain Delany, killed, his two lieutenants, mortally wounded (you know them both), and four other lieutenants, wounded; thirteen privates, killed, and fifty, wounded or prisoners. It was a most creditable but painful affair.

I am expecting my two companies, the survivors, back tomorrow. Wytheville has been one of the most violent Rebel towns from the first. They always talked of "no quarter," "the black flag," etc. The citizens fired from their houses on the troops as they rode in. Colonel Powell was shot in the back. The town was burned to ashes. I will write you more about it when they get in.

We are cleaning camp and getting settled again. The old lady moved into the cottage when we left; I occupy the tent Captain and Mrs. Hood were in. Captain Zimmerman went today to relieve Captain Hunter as commandant of post at Gallipolis.

Uncle Scott and Uncle Moses will feel very hopeful in view of this month's work. We have taken, as I reckon it, seventy thousand prisoners this month besides killing or disabling perhaps fifteen thousand to twenty-thousand more. A pretty big army of Rebels disposed of.

Morgan is not yet caught. He may get off, but his ruin is very complete. — Love to all.

Affectionately, your

MRS. HAYES.   R.

Sunday, [July] 26. — The cavalry of General Scammon's command left Raleigh on Wednesday, 15th, to cut the [Virginia and] Tennessee Railroad. On the [18th] they reached Wytheville and had a desperate and bloody encounter. The Rebels occupied the houses firing from them on our men. Our loss is serious. Colonel Toland, Thirty-fourth Ohio Mounted Infantry, killed. Colonel Powell, Second Virginia Cavalry, wounded mortally. Captain Delany, a brave and valuable officer of my brigade, killed. He was wounded in the body as he rode into town; dismounted and stood by his horse firing his revolver when he was shot through the head and killed instantly. The ball came from a house hitting the eagle ornament on the side of his hat. Two of his lieutenants badly wounded. The Rebels used the houses as fortifications. They were burned.

Captain Delany was killed at Wytheville on the 18th. It was near the entrance to the town from the northwest. His horse had been killed and he stood by her firing his revolver. He reloaded after firing all his shots. A ball from a second-story window struck through the eagle ornament on his hat and ranging down through his head came out at his lower jaw on the opposite side. Colonel Toland was at the bottom of the ascent leading up into town, urging the men to go in and fire the town, when he was shot through the breast. It is thought the same citizen, a man of wealth living in a brick house at that end of town, shot both Colonel Toland and Captain Delany. He (the citizen) was killed by a [man of the] Thirty-fourth. His house was burned. One citizen, a large fleshy man, in specs, was killed.

The Second Virginia Cavalry behaved shamefully. They would not go in to the support of Captains Gilmore and Delany. The Thirty-fourth did nobly. Major Huffman, Second Virginia, said with a smile as Lieutenant-Colonel Franklin and the Thirty-fourth passed in: "That's right Colonel, go in"! but [he] didn't offer to go in himself.

CAMP WHITE, WEST VIRGINIA, July 26, 1863.

MRS. DELANY: — I have seen several officers and men who were with your husband at Wytheville. His company led the attack on the town. Captain Delany's horse was killed under him and some think he was slightly wounded soon after the attack began. Captain Delany continued the attack, encouraging his men by his example until he was killed instantly by a ball in his head. His body was taken to a house outside of the town, and it is a gratification to know that it was left in charge of Father Heidekamp, a friend of your husband, who is in charge of a parish at Wytheville.

I will get together the property of your husband and send it to you as soon as practicable.

A flag of truce will be sent towards Wytheville when further particulars will be known.

Sincerely,

R. B. HAYES,

COLONEL COMMANDING FIRST BRIGADE.

CAMP WHITE, July 26, 1863.

DEAREST:— I got yours of the 18th last night. Morgan's embargo having been removed, we may now expect less delay in our correspondence. . . . Your description of the militia doings is amusing enough. We saw the same things on our route in Ohio, but they were really very useful in blocking roads, carrying information, and the like.

Dear little Joe, it will be a long, long time before you will even know in how many ways he was dear to you. There will be a loneliness in the house at Cincinnati greater than anywhere else. It was fortunate for your present feelings that we lost him as we did, instead of at home. The other boys are, I hope, enjoying themselves.

We are likely, I think, to remain here some time. The great successes of this month, if the Potomac Army meets with no great reverse, will be likely, I think, to substantially end the Rebellion during my original term of service. It is two years ago yesterday since we left Camp Chase. — Good-bye, dearest. Love to all.

Affectionately,

MRS. HAYES.   R.

CAMP WHITE, July 28, 1863.

DEAR UNCLE: — . . . We are again in our old camp. We have lost some valuable officers and men since we left. Captain Delany, commanding one of my cavalry companies, was killed in storming Wytheville. He was a man to trust. He received his promotion on my recommendation and was one of my best friends. . . .

We hear Morgan is himself taken at last. This is important. At least ten thousand of our mounted men have heretofore been kept busy watching him. They will now be at liberty to push against the weakened enemy.

It now seems probable enough that the war will be substantially ended with our original enlistment.

Sincerely,

R. B. HAYES.

S. BIRCHARD.

August 1, [1863]. — Our best scout, Corporal Jacobs, and Private Fenchard, Company F, were murdered last night at Morris' mill on Gauley River, twelve miles above Gauley Bridge. Jacobs was an awkward, pigeon-toed youngster, cool, shrewd, brave; could walk fifty miles a day, go without food or sleep longer than most men; very fond of scouting. Poor fellow! I have long feared that he would be caught in this way. He was made one of the color-guard but was so awkward — never could keep step — that we usually let him be excused from all ordinary duty. Ordered Morris arrested, to be kept if no proof against him; hung if guilty of the murder in any way.

CAMP WHITE, August 5, 1863.

DEAREST: — Yours from Elmwood, dated 2nd, reached me this morning. You were not in as good heart as it found me. I am feeling uncommonly hopeful. The deaths of officers and men to whom I am attached give me pain, but they occur in the course of duty and honorably, and in the prosecution of a war which now seems almost certain to secure its object. If at any time since we were in this great struggle there was cause for thanksgiving in the current course of things, surely that time is now.

Our prisoners left at Wytheville were well treated, and a chaplain has been allowed to go there to see if the bodies of Colonel Toland and Captain Delany can be removed.

I am grieved to hear that Uncle Scott is in trouble about Ed. If he recovers from his present sickness it is likely he will be able to stand it better hereafter. The process of acclimating must have been run through with him by this time. If he gets good health he will soon recover from the trouble about the promotion. Let him make himself a neat, prompt, good soldier and there need be no worry about promotions. It was not lucky to put so many cousins in one company. I could have managed that better, but as it's done they ought to be very patient with each other. Ike Nelson was placed in a delicate position, and while he perhaps made a mistake, it was an error, if error at all, on the right side. Too much kinship in such matters does not do, as Governor Dennison found out a year or two ago.

I am glad you are going to Columbus. I had a chance to send one hundred and eighty dollars by Colonel Comly to Platt where you can get it as you want.

By the by, who has the money left at Cincinnati? I sent an order to Stephenson and he had none.

Poor boys, they will get to have too many homes. I fear they will find their own the least agreeable. Very glad Birch is getting to ride. Webb will push his way in such accomplishments, but Birch must be encouraged and helped. Rud will probably take care of himself.

Yes, darling, I love you as much as you can me. We shall be together again. Time is passing swiftly. . . .

Joe was never so jolly as this summer. He is more of a treasure than ever before. — Love to all.

Affectionately,

R.

Mrs. Hayes.

CAMP WHITE, CHARLESTON, WEST VIRGINIA, August 6, 1863.

DEAR UNCLE: — I received yours of the first yesterday morning. Lucy writes that she expects to go to Delaware and Columbus about the middle of this month, and to visit you before her return. I begin to feel about those visits to you a good deal as mother does — that the care and trouble they make for you more than overbalances your pleasure in them; but you ought to know best.

The money that I supposed was in Stephenson's hands, is *somewhere*, and I'll inquire until I find it and let you know.

I think it probable that we shall remain in West Virginia. The enemy has become alarmed by our movements against the Tennessee Railroad, and has been strengthening their posts in front of us until now we have twice our numbers watching us. To keep *them* out of mischief, it is more likely that our force will be increased rather than diminished. A gunboat has come up to help us within the last half-hour. Our Wytheville raid did the Rebels more harm than was reported. Five thousand suits of clothing, over four thousand new arms, and quantities of supplies were burned. I think they will not attempt to drive us out in their present scarcity of men and means.

The Kentucky election pleases me. I hope Ohio will do as well.

Sincerely,

S. BIRCHARD.   R. B. HAYES.

CAMP WHITE, CHARLESTON, WEST VIRGINIA,
August 9 (Sunday), 1863.

DEAR MOTHER: — It is a quiet, pleasant Sunday morning. A large number of the officers and men have gone over to town to church, leaving a few of us here "to keep house."

Our Rebel friends are gathering in pretty strong force in our front. Many think it is with the intention of driving us out as soon as the roasting-ears are in condition to afford them food. I think, however, that they are merely concentrating to prevent us from making raids to destroy their important railroad to the Southwest. Whatever they mean, it is a comfort to know that we are giving occupation to a larger force of Rebels that they can well spare at this time.

Uncle writes that he expects to meet Lucy at Delaware or Columbus, and as she intends to visit you soon, I suppose you will see them all in a few days or weeks. I would be glad to be with you, but I am not expecting to be my own master before another year. — Love to all.

Affectionately, your son,

RUTHERFORD.

MRS. SOPHIA HAYES.

CAMP WHITE, August 15 (Saturday afternoon), 1863.

DEAREST : — Hottest day yet. All busy trying to keep cool. A dead failure all such attempts. A year ago today we set out for Maryland and east Virginia. A swift year.

You don't write often these days. You don't love me so much as you did. Is that it? Not much! You are as loving as ever, I know, only it is a bore to write. I know that. So it's all right and I am as fond of you as I was when you were only my sweetheart. Yes, more too. Well, write when you can comfortably.

I am going to inspect the Thirteenth at Coal's Mouth tomorrow; take the band along for the fun of it.

I ride about, read novels, newspapers, and military books, and sleep a power. We shall go up to Lewisburg, I guess, in two or three weeks to see after the Rebels in that quarter. All quiet in our borders now. . . . Love to all.

Yours, with *great warmth*,

R.

MRS. HAYES.

CAMP WHITE, August 17, 1863.

DEAR UNCLE:— . . . It looks as if we should be very quiet here for two or three weeks, after which it is probable we shall push up into the mountains again for a campaign of three or four weeks. . . .

Sincerely,

S. BIRCHARD. R. B. HAYES.

August 19. — Mrs. Comly returned with her husband a few days ago. I wish Lucy was here also. Foolish business to send away our wives as was done. A very queer man when he gets into a state of mind on any subject!

The hottest of weather for the past three weeks or so. Mother made a visit to Fremont with Laura and Colonel Mitchell.

———

CAMP WHITE, August 23, 1863.

DEAREST : — Very glad to get your good letter from Columbus. I wish I could travel with you a few weeks now. Everybody praises our nephew and his wife. That last phrase means Laura.

You must tell me more particulars about Fanny and Minnie, or do they call her Emily now? If she is growing into a young lady as fast as I suppose she is, Emily is the best name.

I got a letter from Mother at the same time with yours. She is very contented and happy at Fremont. You will be together soon. I hope you will manage to have the boys like her. She is not likely to have much time to enjoy with her grandsons, and I hope the most will be made of it.

I see that our beautiful little lost one is in your thoughts a great deal — much more perhaps than you thought he would be when you left here. If it does not sadden your life, as I think it does not, I am not sorry that you remember him so often. He was too lovely to be forgotten. Your moralizing on your want of dignity and all that doesn't disturb me. You'll do for your husband, and I love you so much, darling. Be cheerful and happy. Do as well as you can by the boys, but don't worry about them. They will come out sometime. — Love to all.

Affectionately yours,

R.

MRS. HAYES.

CAMP WHITE, August 24, 1863.

DEAREST : — I write you again so soon to speak of a man we lost on Saturday. Joseph Kramer was drowned while sailing on the river. The sailboat (that pretty one of Captain Warren's) was swamped by a severe gale and poor Kramer sank after swimming several rods. You will remember him as a good-natured sailor who rowed boat with Archie at Camp Reynolds. He got a furlough to see his family near Columbus. He was a good soldier; leaves a wife and three or four children. They live near Georgesville on the farm of the Harpers, a few miles southwest of Columbus. Lieutenant Abbott was nearly lost with him. He sank near shore and was senseless for a time.

Kramer is buried on the beautiful hill above the White monument. He was so good a man that I hope his family will not be forgotten by those who are interesting themselves at Columbus in the welfare of soldiers' families. His widow will need the aid of a lawyer or claim agent to get her allowances from [the] Government. Platt can perhaps name the right person and otherwise assist her. — No news. — Love to all.

Affectionately,

R.

Mrs. Hayes.

Camp White, August 25, 1863.

Dear Uncle:— . . . I keep my cavalry moving as much as possible. The infantry has little to do. The prisoners taken and deserters coming in all talk in a way that indicates great despondency in Dixie. If the movements of Rosecrans on Chattanooga, Burnside towards Cumberland Gap, and Gilmore at Charleston are reasonably successful, the Rebellion will be nearer its end by the middle of October than I have anticipated. A great contrast between the situation now and a year ago, when Lee was beating Pope out of the Valley and threatening Washington. Beat the peace men in your elections and the restoration of the Union is sure to come in good time.

. . . There will be no need of your going to Delaware or Columbus merely to get Lucy. If she goes to Fremont she will be able to travel without other escort than the boys. — Love to Mother. I enjoy her letters.

Sincerely,

S. Birchard.   R. B. Hayes.

CAMP WHITE, August 30, 1863.

DEAREST: — . . . These cold nights and autumn storms remind us of winter quarters. If we remain in this region I mean to have you with me if possible all winter, and I feel like beginning winter in good season. Already men are putting chimneys in their tents. A few weeks will probably settle the question as to where we shall spend the cold weather, and I shall send for you at the earliest possible moment.

My little sorrel in a savage fit bit Carrington very severely yesterday. In one snap he cut ten large gashes, several of them to the bone, in the muscular part of the right arm between the shoulder and elbow. The bone is not broken, but he will be disabled for a month. He shook him as a rat is shaken by a terrier dog. Charley Smith and two others were looking on, and jumped in, or it is possible he would have been killed. As soon as he was taken out of his stall the sorrel was as good-natured as usual.

I see it stated that very few are to be drafted in Ohio on this call. I am glad if it is really not necessary, although it would be pleasant to see our ranks full again. If we are not filled up we shall of course be mustered out of service at the end of our three years. — My love to all. Good-bye.

Affectionately, ever your

R.

MRS. HAYES.

CAMP WHITE, September 4, 1863.

DEAREST: — Yours mailed 31st came last night. McKinley (the former sergeant), tearfully and emotionally drunk, has been boring me for the last half-hour with his blarney. He uttered a great many prayers for "madame and those little boys, God bless them." So, of course, I was civil to him.

We are less and less likely to be moved from here as the fall weather sets in. The change to cold weather was a most grateful one in our hot camp. It takes the long cold rain-storms of November to make our camps put on their most cheerless aspect.

You inquire about Mrs. Comly and how we like her. She is an excellent sweet young woman, and all who get acquainted with her like her. She is affable and approachable, but of course she can't make friends as you do. Your gifts are rare enough in that line. The colonel is not well. He is living too luxuriously!

I would be glad enough to see you enjoying a faith as settled and satisfactory as that of Mrs. Davis, but really I think you are as cheerful and happy as she is, and that is what is to be sought, a cheerful and happy disposition.

Tell the boys that Dick and Guinea are still fast friends. They travelled with us up into Dixie as far as Raleigh, and down into Ohio after Morgan. Dick has a battle with each new rooster which is brought to headquarters, and with the aid of Guinea, and perhaps a little from Frank or Billy, manages to remain "cock of the walk." . . .

Love to all — girls and boys. Tell Fanny [Platt] if she ever gets time in her Yankee school to write to outsiders, I wish her to remember me.

Affectionately ever,

R.

Mrs. Hayes,
   Columbus.

September 5, 1863. 8 P. M. — Lieutenant Abbott, Sergeant Clark, Sergeant Stoner, and seventeen other Twenty-third men go into Dixie to destroy iron-works, bridges, etc., etc. A perilous task. Great hardships and exposures to be encountered. Good luck to them!

Headquarters 1st Brigade, 3d Division, 8th Army Corps, Camp White, West Virginia,

September 5, 1863.

Editor Catholic Telegraph: — In the *Catholic Telegraph* of August 26, I am mentioned as the commander of the expedition to Wytheville in which Captain Delany lost his life. This is an error. The expedition was planned by General Scammon and was under the command of Colonel Toland until he was killed early in the action at Wytheville, when (Colonel Powell, the next officer in rank, having been disabled by a severe wound) the command devolved upon Lieutenant-Colonel Franklin of the Thirty-fourth Regiment, O. V.   This daring enterprise was so ably conducted, not only in the advance and attack, but also in the retreat, that it is due both to the living and the dead that this correction should be made.   Captain Delany was in the brigade under my command until temporarily detached for this dangerous service.   Upon hearing of his death I sent the melancholy intelligence of the loss of this most gallant and meritorious officer to his friends in Cincinnati.   It was no doubt in consequence of this that the mistake of the *Telegraph* as to the leadership of the Wytheville expedition occurred.

Respectfully,

R. B. HAYES,
COLONEL COMMANDING.

CAMP WHITE, September 6, 1863.

DEAREST: — How will it suit you to come out here as soon as you have visited Fremont, say in two or three weeks?   I would like to have you here before the weather gets too bad.   You can leave the boys with their grandmother somewhere and after it is known where we are to winter, I can send for Grandmother and the boys to come also.   If we stay here, I will want to keep house for "you all" this winter.   If we go too far into the bowels of the land for you to follow, you can return to Grandma and the boys after a suitable visit here.

As things are now it would be very agreeable for you here. I prefer not to have the boys come out until it is quite certain they can stay.   If you only staid a week or two, it would be worth while to come.   If any change occurs to make it not desirable for you to come, I will write you.   In the meantime I hope you will be able to cut your visits short so as to get here by the last week in this month, or sooner if convenient.

I send you enclosed a letter from Mrs. Delany as one of the memorials to be kept with slips from the *Catholic Telegraph.*

28

I shall direct this to Columbus hoping however you have started for Fremont. — Love to all.

Affectionately, your

R.

Mrs. Hayes,
   Columbus, Ohio.

Camp White, September 11, 1863.

Dearest: — Glad to get letters both from you and Mother last night. Bless the boys, how they must enjoy their first family visit to their new home! I would be as happy as any of them to be there.

We hear good news from Burnside in Tennessee. If true it makes it more desirable that you should come here soon. If he moves along the railroad into southwestern Virginia, we are likely to push forward to coöperate, in which case we shall probably get too far into Dixie for our families to winter with us. I will notify you if anything occurs to make it imprudent for you to be here a couple of weeks hence. This is the month in which the Rebels can come into the valley with the least difficulty on the score of supplies, but I don't think they will come. If there is a probability of it, I will telegraph Uncle Scott in time to stop your coming, or have Captain Zimmerman stop you at Gallipolis. I do not decide against the boys coming, but as you will be compelled to come to Gallipolis by railroad and stage (steamers don't run on the Ohio now) and will perhaps only remain a fortnight or so, it will perhaps be as well not to bring them. If after you reach here it turns out that we shall winter in the valley, I shall send for Mother Webb and all the boys and keep house, or you can go back after them. In that case you can rent the house, or if you prefer to winter at Fremont or in Chillicothe, in case you can't do so here, you may rent the house at once.

My reason for wanting you to come here as soon as you are through visiting at Fremont, is, that perhaps we shall be ordered forward as soon as east Tennessee is firmly in our possession.

I think, however, the chances are in favor of our wintering on the Kanawha.

Get me a lot of silk handkerchiefs and about three or four pair stockings, not very heavy, but so-so. You can get them at Fremont and do it before you forget.

Mrs. Comly is greatly pleased with the prospect of your coming so soon. Mrs. Ellen is expected soon. She is supposed to be on some sandbar between here and Cincinnati on the Ohio, praying for a rise of water. Mrs. Barrett is the only other officer's wife now here and she talks of going home in a fortnight. . . .

Let me know by telegraph when you will be at Gallipolis and the doctor or some one will come there after you.

Since writing we have further news of gratifying successes in east Tennessee. If all continues to go well there, it increases the chances of a forward movement here, and furnishes additional reason for you to come on soon before it is too late. — Love to all.

Affectionately,

R.

P. S. — You may get me a good pair of gloves — citizens', not gauntlets — warm.

MRS. HAYES,
  Fremont, Ohio.

September 13. — Sunday a year ago was the 14th. South Mountain and its losses and glories. How the sadness for the former fades and the satisfaction with the latter grows!

General Burnside has east Tennessee. Knoxville ours; Cumberland Gap taken, and our forces on the railroad nearly to Bristol. Knoxville to Bristol one hundred and thirty miles; Bristol to depot at bridge one hundred and seven; total two hundred and thirty-seven. Charleston to bridge one hundred and sixty-six.

September 20. — Abbott and party returned. Found the mountains filled with deserters and refugees, the roads and paths patrolled by Rebel soldiers in pursuit of them. Food scarce; returned in consequence of difficulty of getting food and the great number patrolling all routes. Many very desperate gangs of Union men in the mountains.

September 21, P. M. — "Rosecrans [at Chickamauga] has been badly beaten"! Such is the shock the dispatch gives us this evening. After months of success one of our great armies is defeated. A concentration of Rebel armies has overwhelmed our noble Army of the Cumberland. How these blows strike my heart! I had just read a joyous dispatch from "L. W. H.", "Billy Rogers has a baby." But nerve ourselves, we must. We shall recover from the blow.

I have thought over it and feel easier. I suffer from these blows more than I did from the loss of my sweet little boy. But I suffer less now than I did from Bull Run, or even Fredericksburg. Can Rosecrans hold Chattanooga? Has he lost his army? Will he be driven across the Tennessee? He ought to have stopped his campaign with the capture of Chattanooga, fortified the place, and awaited events. Easy to say so now, but impossible before, I suppose. Jim McKell, Lieutenant Nelson, Colonel Mitchell (Laura's husband), all with Resecrans. Anxious hearts at home.

September 23. — News better. Rosecrans defeated but not badly. Enemy probably suffered too much to take advantage of their victory.

GALLIPOLIS, September 24, [1863].

DEAR UNCLE: — Lucy arrived here safely last night. We shall go up the Kanawha tomorrow.

I hope that Rosecrans will be able to hold Chattanooga after all. If he does, this struggle will be a most serious disaster to the Confederacy, even if they have gained the battle, as a mere military result.

I hope Birchie will not give you trouble. It gratifies me to hear that he can chop so well, and that he is learning the names of the trees.

Sincerely,

R. B. HAYES.

S. BIRCHARD.

CAMP WHITE, WEST VIRGINIA, September 28, 1863.

DEAR MOTHER: — . . . Your letter from Delaware dated the 20th came this morning. I am glad you are safely back to Mrs. Wasson's pleasant home. I always feel uneasy when you have a journey before you.

Lucy left Webb and Ruddy with their Grandmother Webb at Mrs. Boggs'. Birch went with Uncle back to Fremont.

I am in no hurry about having my boys learn to write. I would much prefer they would lay up a stock of health by knocking around in the country than to hear that they were the best scholars of their age in Ohio.

I am glad to see that Laura's husband has distinguished himself in the recent great battle and has escaped without injury. His good fortune will be gratifying intelligence at Columbus.

Lucy is in camp with me. Mrs. Comly (late Libby Smith) and Dr. Barrett's wife are also in camp and make a pleasant little circle. She sends love. — Remember me to Sophia and Mrs. Wasson.

Affectionately, your son,

R.

MRS. SOPHIA HAYES.

September 30, [1863]. — Today I explained to the Twenty-third Order Number 191 respecting the re-enlistment of veteran volunteers. I told them I would not urge them to re-enlist; that my opinion was that the war would end soon after the inauguration of a new President or of Lincoln for a second term, say within one year after the expiration of their present term, i. e., June 1865, unless foreign nations intervened, in which case they would all expect to fight again. About sixty re-enlisted.

CAMP WHITE, WEST VIRGINIA, October 2, 1863.

MY DEAR SON : — I received a letter today from Uncle Birchard. He says you appear to be very happy learning to chop and work, and that you are helping Allen. Your mother tells me, too, that you have learned the names of a good many trees, and that you know them when you see them. I am very glad to hear so much good of you. It is an excellent thing to know how to work — to ride and drive and how to feed and hitch up a team. I expect you will know more about trees than I do. I did not learn about them when I was a little boy and so do not now know much about such things. There are a great many things that are learned very easily when we are young, but which it is hard to learn after we are grown. I want you to learn as many of such things now as you can, and when you are a man you will be able to enjoy and use your knowledge in many ways.

Your mother took a ride on Lieutenant McKinley's horse this morning, and enjoyed herself very much.

Uncle Joe has a big owl, such a one as Lucy saw at Uncle Birchard's. A corporal in Company E shot its wing off, so it couldn't escape. It snaps its beak very fiercely when we poke sticks at it. The band boys have a 'possum and there is a pet bear and deer.

I think Uncle Birchard will find a way to stop his chimney from smoking. If he doesn't, you must tell him to build campfires in front of his house as we do here. We find them very pleasant.

I am sure you will be a good boy and I hope you will be very happy.

Your affectionate father,

R. B. HAYES.

BIRCHARD A. HAYES,
    Fremont, Ohio.

October 7. — A rain a few days ago gave us a rise of two or three feet in the Kanawha River. It is falling again, but is raining today again with prospects of water.

Another order to give no passes and take up all old ones. Funny business, this pass business. "Finds something still for idle hands to do."

CAMP WHITE, October 7, 1863.

DEAR UNCLE: — I am very glad to hear that you are having so little trouble with Birchie. He is of an affectionate disposition, conscientious and truthful. His natural sense of duty is, I think, unusually strong. . . . I much prefer that he should work or ride or hunt in the open air than read in the house or go to school. I do not care if he is far behind other boys of his age in what is taught in schools. If he has health enough to become a scholar or prepare himself for a learned profession at sixteen, he will have enough time to do it then. If he hasn't a constitution that will bear a sedentary life, there is more reason for trying to build it up now by work and exercise in the open air.

Lucy is well and enjoys our camp life as well as she could be expected to do away from her boys. In about a week from now I shall probably be able to settle the question as to our winter quarters and as to whether it will be worth while to send for the boys. It looks as if the coming winter would be one of active operations, and if so any plan I may form is likely to be interrupted before spring. Indeed, is liable to be interrupted at any time. In any event, I think we shall stay here watching the gaps in front of us for six or eight weeks longer. After that I think a somewhat smaller force will suffice to defend this region, and we may be sent elsewhere. I think there is no danger of our being seriously disturbed here. . . .

Sincerely,

R. B. HAYES.

S. BIRCHARD.

CAMP WHITE, October 10, 1863.

DEAR MOTHER: — I have just received your good long letter from Delaware on [of] the 3d. . . . There was no time for Lucy to stop at Delaware on her way here. We were likely to be sent South immediately after the battle in Georgia, and I telegraphed her to come at once if she wished to see me. Our going was not ordered as expected, and now we are more likely to go to Ohio to recruit this winter than South. The Twenty-third was the first original three-year regiment and its time will be out in a few months. The men are re-enlisting for another three years and there is a fair prospect of continuing the regiment if we can get a little while at home this winter.

In the present uncertainty as to our winter campaign, I can make no arrangements for my family. In the meantime Lucy is enjoying a visit here. We have a number of agreeable ladies in camp, and are making pleasant acquaintances among the citizens. Charleston was a fine town before the war, and had a very cultivated society. The war broke it up, but now the town is gaining again and will ultimately recover its former prosperity. Give my love to friends.

Affectionately,

R.

Mrs. Sophia Hayes.

October 15, [1863]. — No rise of water on account of the rain of the 7th. — A fine time, election day (13th). The Twenty-third — five hundred and fourteen — unanimous for Brough. I went to bed like a Christian at 9 P. M. McKinley waked me at eleven with the first news — all good and conclusive. My brigade unanimous for Brough; Twelfth Regiment, ditto. A few traitors in [the] Thirty-fourth. McMullen's Battery, one for Vallandigham. State forty or fifty thousand on home vote. A victory equal to a triumph of arms in an important battle. It shows persistent determination, willingness to pay taxes, to wait, to be patient.

Camp White, October 19, 1863.

Dear Uncle: — You are a prophet. Brough's majority is "glorious to behold." It is worth a big victory in the field. It is decisive as to the disposition of the people to prosecute the war to the end. My regiment and brigade were both unanimous for Brough.

Lucy will go to Chillicothe and home this week. She will fix up matters, gather the chickens, and return in two or three weeks, if all things look well, for the winter. She will, in that case, rent the house in Cincinnati. Love to Birch.

Sincerely,

R. B. HAYES.

S. BIRCHARD.

October 21. — General Duffie with about one thousand men, cavalry, and two guns of Simmonds' off last night; supposed to be after the railroad bridge again.

Lee followed Meade until he was near the defenses of Washington, when Lee is reported retiring again.

CAMP WHITE, October 21, 1863.

DEAR UNCLE: — I received yours of the 17th this morning; also one from mother of the 16th. Lucy left for home this morning with Dr. Joe. She will rent our house in Cincinnati, and return with our family two or three weeks hence, if things remain as now. I gave her a letter to send for the pony, as well as Birch, if agreeable to you. I am now entitled to two more horses than I am keeping, and if we remain here, would like the pony both for Birch and myself. I find little horses, if they are stout, much better for the mountains. My sorrell stallion I want to sell, because he is troublesome sometimes. He is a beauty and good stock; worth two hundred or three hundred dollars.

Sincerely,

R. B. HAYES.

S. BIRCHARD.

CAMP WHITE, WEST VIRGINIA, October 21, 1863.

DEAR MOTHER: — I received your letter of the 17th this morning. Our soldiers rejoice over the result of the Ohio election as much or more than the good people at home. They felt afraid last winter that the people were getting disheartened and that there was danger that the war would be abandoned just as we were about to succeed. They saw, too, how much the Rebels were encouraged by our divisions in the North. The men of my regiment and my brigade were both unanimous for the Union ticket. The brigade cast over eight hundred votes all one way. I have seen no account of any equal body of troops who did as well. . . .

It is very uncertain what our movements this winter will be, but I think I shall be able to come and see you by midwinter. The time of mustering out my regiment is approaching and we shall perhaps be sent home to recruit. At any rate I think I shall see you this winter. — Love to all.

Affectionately,

R. B. HAYES.

MRS. SOPHIA HAYES.

CAMP WHITE, October 25, (Sunday), 1863.

DEAR MOTHER: — I received your letter of the 19th last evening. We have been very busy here the last week, worrying the Rebels in our front to prevent their sending reinforcing the Rebels who are opposing General Burnside, and getting ready for apprehended attacks from them. It is now quiet again and the rain and snow in the mountains are fortifications getting stronger every day.

We are not allowed to build winter quarters yet, but the men are fixing up all sorts of shelters and fireplaces to find comfort these cold nights.

I heard from Lucy after she was well on her way to Chillicothe. . . . I think it almost certain that she will come back to stay in a fortnight or so.

I hope you will stand the cold winter well. — Love to all.

Affectionately, your son,

RUTHERFORD.

MRS. SOPHIA HAYES.

CHARLESTON, October 30, 1863.

DEAREST : — General Kelley was here and reviewed the troops on Wednesday. General Duffie's review was a beautiful and interesting sight. Generals Kelley, Scammon, and Duffie with their staffs have gone to Fayette — Miss Scammon, Miss Jones and Miss Smith with them. I am now in command of their troops here *pro tem.*, and Avery and I run the machine on the town side.

We have got the regiment and brigade tents on stockade for winter weather. They look well and will be comfortable. Mrs. Comly is in the house, and Mrs. Graves will vacate the rest in a day or two. It now looks favorably for our family arrangements to be carried out as we planned them. Can tell certainly after General Kelley leaves.

Uncle is so urgent for Birtie's staying longer with him that I wish to consent unless you are very anxious to the contrary. Birch says he would like to see us all but prefers to stay longer at Fremont. — Love to all.

Affectionately,

MRS. HAYES.   R. B. HAYES.

October 31. — On the 28th General Kelley reviewed the Third Brigade, [and] General Duffie's cavalry. A beautiful day; a fine spectacle. I had only nine companies of the Twenty-third here — a small affair. General Kelley is a gentlemanly man of fifty to sixty; not an educated man — nothing particularly noticeable about him. [The] 29th, the three generals with their young ladies, Miss Jones, Miss Scammon, and Miss Smith and staffs went to Fayette. I [am] left in command here at Charleston. [The] 29th, got into new quarters — wall-tents on boards.

CAMP WHITE, (Sunday), November 1, 1863.

DEAR MOTHER : — It is a lovely morning. I have just got into new quarters, two tents together on a stockade, making two good little rooms with a coal stove. As cozy as need be. . . .

We had preaching in our camp last Sunday by the chaplain of

the Thirty-fourth, Mr. Collier, a rather entertaining speaker, and have been promised meetings every other Sunday hereafter. It is so unusual a thing that the novelty makes it attractive, if there were nothing else to recommend it. . . .

Affectionately, your son,

RUTHERFORD.

MRS. SOPHIA HAYES.

November 5, 1863. — A warm fall evening. How I am moved as I read the letter below. My own dear boys, and my feelings towards the soldiers who are kind to them; Willie too — the name of sister Fanny's lost boy. Oh, and my dear sister too. How many will love General Sherman for that letter who would never care for any laurels he might earn in battle.

[Pasted in the Diary is a copy of General Sherman's famous letter to Captain C. C. Smith of the Thirteenth Regulars, thanking the regiment — in which his little son Willie had fancied himself a sergeant — for the "kind behavior" of its officers and soldiers to his "poor child." "Please convey to the battalion," the letter says in conclusion, "my heartfelt thanks, and assure each and all that if in after years they call on me or mine, and mention that they were of the Thirteenth Regulars, when poor Willy was a sergeant, they will have a key to the affections of my family that will open all it has, that we will share with them our last blanket, our last crust."]

November 7, [1863]. — I am asked if I would not be gratified if my friends would procure me promotion to a brigadier-generalship. My feeling is that I would rather be one of the *good* colonels than one of the *poor* generals. The colonel of a regiment has one of the most agreeable positions in the service, and one of the most useful. "A good colonel makes a good regiment," is an axiom.

Two things make me sometimes think it desirable to have the promotion, viz., the risk of having a stupid brigadier put over me, and the difficulty and uncertainty of keeping up my regiment — that is the risk of losing my colonelcy.

CAMP WHITE, November 8, 1863.

DEAR UNCLE: — I received your letter of the 4th last night. Very glad to hear Birch is still contented. The tool-chest would just hit his fancy. He ought to learn the use of tools, but I don't imagine he has any mechanical turn. The only decent thing I could ever make was a bow, and that was rather from a knowledge of the best material than from any skill in whittling. . . .

Stormy weather here. A large part of our forces is out after a fight with a considerable Rebel force in the mountains. We are anxiously waiting the result. Only two companies of my immediate command is [are] out. This probably the last of our campaigning in this quarter for a season.

Sincerely,

R. B. HAYES.

S. BIRCHARD.

November 9. — The ground is white with snow for the first time this year. Drs. Mussey and Blaney called Saturday. It is intimated that there will be difficulty, or is danger of difficulty, on account of Dr. Webb's long absence.

November 21. Saturday. — Went to Gallipolis to meet the family, — Lucy, Webb, and Rud with Grandma Webb.

25. — Lucy and I came up on the *Viola.*

26. — Thanksgiving Day. Reports of fighting at Knoxville, Chattanooga, and with Lee. If the result is generally favorable, we shall see daylight plainer than ever; if otherwise, darkness again but not so "visible" as before.

December 3, [1863]. — The recent victory of Grant near Chattanooga seems to be very complete. We have not heard from Burnside, besieged in Knoxville by Longstreet, since the 24th or 25th. We have some apprehensions, but hope that he has been relieved by Grant's success. Meade has pushed into the heart of eastern Virginia after Lee. I fear the result. The Army of the Potomac has been as unlucky on Virginia soil as the army of Lee on our soil.

Company B left today for home, over three-fourths, fifty-four, having enlisted as veteran volunteers. Companies A, E, and F are likely to follow suit.

CAMP WHITE, December 3, 1863.

DEAR MOTHER: — We are all here living very comfortably. Webb and Ruddy are learning lessons daily. Webb is a little backward and hates books. The other little fellow is like Birch and takes to larnin'."

Lucy writes very few letters to anybody and avoids it when she can. She finds a sympathizing friend on this subject in Mrs. Comly, who dislikes it equally. When I am with Lucy, I do the writing.

We are likely to be engaged in pretty active operations here this winter. We are doing all that the weather allows, and have been pretty lucky so far. It will not surprise me if we have some rather severe fighting.

My regiment is re-enlisting daily. There is no doubt that it will be reorganized for three years more before the winter is over. There is a general disposition with officers and men to see the end of the war in the field, if our lives and health are spared. Your letter mailed 30th came last night. Quick time! — My love to all.

Affectionately, your son,

R.

MRS. SOPHIA HAYES.

CAMP WHITE, December 4, 1863.

DEAR UNCLE: — Lucy and I have considered your bulletin announcing your determination to hold Birch. I now write to give you fair warning that the Twenty-third has re-enlisted for the war. We are entitled therefore under a late order to be furloughed in a body. One company has gone to Ohio already, and more are preparing to go as soon as the situation here will allow. Now, if you want war we can give it to you. I can take companies enough of veteran volunteers to recapture our boy. So be on your guard.

We are threatened with a Rebel invasion again. If they don't come after us it looks now as if we should go after them. When this is over our men will generally go home, and I am pretty likely to go also. About the last of this month or early in January if matters go well I shall probably visit you. All well here.

Let Birch write to his Grandma Hayes as often as he is disposed to write at all. She is very much pleased with his letters. — Good-bye.

R. B. HAYES.

S. BIRCHARD.

[*December 18, 1863*]. — December 8. Started P. M. for Gauley (a campaign to Lewisburg). Avery, Mather, McKinley, Dr. Webb; one hundred men under Captain Warren of Twenty-third, whole of Fifth Virginia under Colonel Tomlinson, Ninety-first and Twelfth of Colonel White's brigade, General Duffie's Cavalry, General Scammon and staff, to co-operate with General Averell in an attack on the railroad at Salem. Stopped at Clark Wyeth's, five miles above Piatt, evening of 9th [8th]. 9th to Gauley Bridge at Mrs. Hale's, Warren and Twenty-third — twenty-six and one-half miles. 10th, nineteen miles to Lookout (Mrs. Jones's). 11th, twenty-two miles to Hickman's. 12th, twenty-three miles to Lewisburg, to Mrs. Bell's. 13th, return thirteen miles to Jesse Thompson's, where my pistol was stolen by young ladies; got it back by threat of sending father and mother to Camp Chase. 14th, three miles to Meadow Bluff. Stopped with Sharp. 15th, at Meadow Bluff. 16th, returned twenty-seven miles to Mrs. Jones'. 17th, to Gauley, Loup Creek, and steamer *Viola* to Charleston. — A good trip for the season. What of Averell?

December 30, [*1863*]. — Eleven years ago married. Lucy and I talked of it and lived it over on this eleventh anniversary. A happy day.

[In the] evening, spoke to the men again about re-enlisting as veterans. I want three-fourths of the present. We have two hundred and fifty-five. Our present total five hundred; of these we deduct officers twenty-five, invalids fifteen, recruits having more than one year to serve seventy-five — total one hundred and fifteen, [leaving] three hundred and eighty-five. Three-fourths [would be] two hundred and eighty-eight.

CHAPTER XXIII

WINTER RECRUITING—ADVANCE AND RETREAT—CLOYD'S MOUNTAIN — LEXINGTON — WESTERN MARYLAND — JANUARY-JULY 1864

CAMP WHITE, January 1, 1864.

DEAR UNCLE: — . . . This is New Year's day. Bright but very cold and windy. My regiment has re-enlisted and a majority of the men and part of the officers have gone home. I expect to go to Ohio towards the last of this month.

Sincerely,

S. BIRCHARD.   R. B. HAYES.

January 5, 1864. — Last day of bounties. Got about three hundred veterans. The Twenty-third may now be counted as a veteran regiment. Very absurd in Congress repealing bounties.

CAMP WHITE, January 17, 1864.

DEAR MOTHER: — We are all very well and have enjoyed the cold snap. We had good sleighing about ten days. The river was closed, cutting us off completely from the civilized world. Provisions were pretty plenty, however, and we felt independent of the weather.

It is not quite certain yet when I can get off. I hope to do so by the last of this month. Lucy will come with me. We shall go first to Cleveland where some of our veterans are recruiting; from there to Fremont, thence to Delaware and Columbus, and return by the way of Cincinnati. . . .

Affectionately, your son,

R.

MRS. SOPHIA HAYES.

Monday, [January] 18. P. M. — Raining the first time this month. New Year's Eve change came about midnight. January 1 cold and windy, "very, very indeed"; snow about [the] 3rd. Two weeks of unusual cold weather. Kanawha frozen; navigation suspended about a week; a week's good sleighing. Now a thaw for a few days; snow going off.

Captain Gilmore out after Rebel Colonel Ferguson, Sixteenth Virginia Cavalry; fourth day out.

CAMP WHITE, January 24, 1864.

DEAR UNCLE: — The extension of the bounties and postponement of the draft will postpone my visit home a week or two. I shall not leave here probably before the second week in February.

We are all very well. It is very lonesome here now. All the Twenty-third company officers but four or five are at home, half of the men, besides a good many of all other organizations hereabouts. Recruiting seems to be progressing favorably. I trust we shall have stronger and more efficient armies in the field this spring than ever before. I think it likely that the Rebels with their unsparing conscription of young and old will for a time outnumber us again. But a few weeks' campaigning will send to the rear the old men and boys in vast numbers.

I am growing anxious to see Birch and his mother talks of him constantly.

Sincerely,

S. BIRCHARD.   R. B. HAYES.

January 26, 1864. — Another large squad of veterans and the most of the remaining officers left for Ohio yesterday. Recruiting seems to be active in Ohio. I think we shall get our share.*

*A Columbus dispatch of February 14, in the Cincinnati *Gazette*, had this paragraph: — "It has been ascertained at the muster-in office, that the Twenty-third Ohio, Colonel R. B. Hayes, Department of West Virginia, was the first regiment from this State to enlist as veterans. Several regiments have claimed that honor."

Plan of spring campaign from Kanawha Valley. — Ten or fifteen thousand men can move from the head of navigation on the Kanawha River (Loup Creek) via Fayette, Raleigh, Flat Top, and Princeton to the Virginia and Tennessee Railroad between New River and Wytheville, a distance of one hundred and thirty-nine miles, in a week or ten days; spend a week on the railroad destroying New River Bridge and the track for twenty-five miles; return to Loup Creek in one week more and be carried in steamers into the Ohio, and thence East or South for other operations. One week is time enough to convey such a force to Loup Creek from the Potomac or the West. The roads and weather will ordinarily allow such a column to move April 20. Supplies and transportation should be provided at Fayette during February and March. The utmost secrecy should be observed so that the first information the Rebels would have would be the approach of the force. Such a destruction of the railroad would effectually cut the communications of Longstreet and Jones in east Tennessee and compel him [the enemy] to abandon that country. The Rebels could not reconstruct the railroad during the next campaign. It would perhaps compel the evacuation of Richmond.

CAMP WHITE, February 7, 1864.

DEAR UNCLE: — The capture of General Scammon and two of his staff, will postpone my coming a few days, only a few days, I hope. I must be cautious what I say, but to you I can write that his capture is the greatest joke of the war. It was sheer carelessness, bad luck, and accident. It took a good many chances, all lost, to bring it about. Everybody laughs when he is alone, and very intimate friends laugh in concert when together. General Scammon's great point was his caution. He bored us all terribly with his extreme vigilance. The greatest military crime in his eyes was a surprise. Here he is caught in the greenest and most inexcusable way.

We shall come, I think, in a week or so via Cleveland.

Sincerely yours,

S. BIRCHARD.   R. B. HAYES.

COLUMBUS, February 29, 1864.

DEAR MOTHER: — We are having a pleasant visit. The new Mrs. Platt we like well. Her presence will be a good thing for the little folks and Laura receives and treats her in a very sensible and happy way.

I go to Cincinnati tomorrow or day after, and early next week leave for the Kanawha. . . .

Affectionately,

RUTHERFORD.

MRS. SOPHIA HAYES.

CAMP WHITE, March 11, 1864.

DEAR UNCLE: — Home again with Lucy and all the boys — well and happy. Birch did not meet his brothers until he saw them here last night. Three happier boys I never saw. They are all very well. — Love to all.

Sincerely,

R. B. HAYES.

S. BIRCHARD.

CAMP WHITE, March 26, 1864.

DEAR MOTHER: — We are now having a cold rain-storm, but are all well. There is considerable sickness among our new recruits of the usual sort — measles, mumps, and a little small-pox and fever. Nothing very serious so far, and as the weather gets warmer we hope to get clear of it altogether.

Mrs. Ellen, a nice lady, wife of our quartermaster, is teaching the two smaller boys regularly and speaks very encouragingly of her scholars. Lucy schools the larger boy with a young soldier who is a good deal older than Birch, but not so far advanced. . . .

I hope you will get through the raw weather of spring without serious illness. — Love to all.

Affectionately, your son,

R.

MRS. SOPHIA HAYES.

CAMP WHITE, April 3, 1864.

DEAR UNCLE: — . . . I have spent the last week visiting the five posts between here and Sandy occupied by my men. We are picking up a good many Rebels in small squads. Things look like active operations here as everywhere else, but nothing definite yet.

Sincerely,

R. B. HAYES.

S. BIRCHARD.

CAMP WHITE, April 9, 1864.

DEAR MOTHER: — It is wet and stormy weather, but we are all safely sheltered and care nothing for wind or rain.

I am very glad you can write so cheerfully as you did in your last letter. If you could see what I see every day you would think the people of the North were blessed indeed. I feel confident that we are more than half through with the work of crushing [the] Rebellion.

I send you this time the writing of my grandfather [about his ancestors]. It will interest you a great deal. I would be glad if you would preserve it or send it to Uncle Birchard for him to keep for me. I wish you would write me a similar account of your ancestors. Mrs. Wasson's excellent memory of dates and names may aid you.

Affectionately, your son,

RUTHERFORD.

MRS. SOPHIA HAYES.

CAMP WHITE, April 20, 1864.

DEAR UNCLE: — It now seems certain that we are to take an active part in the summer's campaign. We expect to see some of the severe fighting. The Rebel troops in our front are as good as any, and we shall attempt to push them away. My brigade is three large regiments of infantry, containing a good many new recruits. They have been too much scattered (at ten or twelve places) to be properly drilled and disciplined. Still we have some of the best men in service. Of course, if they should break or falter in action, I will be a good deal exposed, otherwise, not so much as heretofore. Still I have no misgivings on my own account, and even if I had, you know my views of such things well enough to know that it would not disturb me much.

Lucy and the boys will soon go to Chillicothe to stay in that vicinity with or near her relatives. Birch would like to go to Fremont, if his mother could go with him.

Sincerely,

R. B. HAYES.

S. BIRCHARD.

CAMP WHITE, April 24, 1864.

DEAR MOTHER: — We are very busy, and of course happy getting ready for campaigning. General Averell is here and large additions are daily arriving to our force. The Thirty-sixth Ohio is at present added to my command, I hope permanently.

Lucy and the other ladies are preparing to go to Ohio. The weather is favorable and everything is cheering and full of life. . . .

Your affectionate son,

R.

MRS. SOPHIA HAYES.

April 26, 1864. — All things point to early action. [The] Thirty-sixth Ohio came up and entered our camp yesterday morning; now below us. The enlisted men gave General Crook a seven-hundred-dollar sword on our parade this morning.

Avery, a major, on his way to Annapolis with the Sixtieth. Glad he is getting his deserts; sorry to lose him. I hope the Thirty-sixth is to be with us. General Duffie and others dined with me today. All talked action.

CAMP REYNOLDS, NEAR GAULEY BRIDGE, May 1, 1864.

DEAR MOTHER: — We have been marching now three days. We have a considerable force and are setting out on a campaign.

We expect our full share of active service. We are under the immediate command of General [George] Crook. We all feel great confidence in his skill and good judgment. General Averill is also with us in command of the cavalry. I have the First Brigade of Infantry, consisting of [the] Twenty-third and Thirty-sixth Ohio, Fifth and Thirteenth Virginia Volunteers. The last named is not yet with us.

Lucy and the boys left on a steamboat at the same time I did. You will perhaps not hear from me often for a while. — Goodbye.

Your affectionate son,

R.

Mrs. Sophia Hayes.

Camp Reynolds, May 1, [1864]. 12 M.

Dearest: — I am in the old log cabin at a desk where our bed stood. The troops are on the hill overlooking the Falls. The Fifth has gone to Tompkins Farm. I write you merely to finish the good-bye so hastily spoken on the steamboat. Your visit has been the greatest possible happiness to me. I carry with me the pleasantest recollections of you dear ones all. Goodbye.

Affectionately,

R.

Mrs. Hayes.

May 2. — March at 6 A. M. to Fayetteville. Reached camp on Raleigh road in a cold driving rain at 1 P. M. Camped on wet ground in snow. A rough opening of our campaign.

Fifth and Seventh [Virginia Cavalry], six hundred men, [under] Major Slack, attached to [the] First Brigade. [The] Thirty-fourth [Ohio], Major Furney, two hundred and seventy men, ditto. — Twelve miles.

May 3, Tuesday. — Marched to Blake's, thirteen miles. Called with Colonel White on Colonel Sickles. Get an order from division headquarters regulating halts. General Crook orders, "No rails to be burned." Hard to enforce but am doing my best. The Thirty-sixth obey promptly. Others grumble. General Crook is testing our discipline!

May 4, Wednesday. — Marched 5:30 A. M. from Blake's to Prince's, fifteen miles; Third Brigade, Colonel Sickles, in advance. Fine, bright weather. Soldiers call out to General Beckley: "Now bring on your militia!" A laugh rings out.

May 5, Thursday. — From Prince's to Camp Creek, twenty-five miles. Road blocked by chopping trees. Cleared by thirty or forty of our axemen as fast as the column needed to pass. We led off reaching Flat Top at 11 o'clock A. M.

May 6. Friday. — To Princeton sixteen miles. Very hot and dusty. Enemy left yesterday evening except a small camp guard. Camps and baggage of officers all left; apparently deceived by our manœuvres or [they] trusted too much to the blockade. General Crook's strategy has succeeded perfectly in deceiving the Rebels. Main force [under] Colonel McCausland, said to have gone to meet us towards Lewisburg. Rebels had begun pretty extensive and well-constructed works. We burn their camps. Foolish business to entrench this point at this stage of the game. In green sods on the parapet was the name "Fort Breckinridge." Our boys changed it to "Fort Crook."

May 7. — A hard day's march. Left Princeton at 4 A. M., crossed East River Mountain and passed through Rocky Gap. To cross roads nine miles, to Gap, eighteen — a twenty-mile march.

May 8. Sunday. — Rocky Gap to Poplar Hill (Sharmon's), twenty-four miles. — Ten from Giles; ten and one-half from Dublin. Rebels probably ahead of us getting ready.

May 9. — Battle of Cloyd's Mountain, or as Rebs call it "Cloyd Farm." Lasted one hour and a half. The Twenty-third and Thirty-sixth, under the immediate direction of General Crook, charged across a meadow three hundred yards wide, sprang into a ditch and up a steep wooded hill to Rebel breastworks, carried them quickly but with a heavy loss. Captain

Hunter killed. Lieutenant Seaman ditto. Abbott's left arm shattered. Rice a flesh wound. Eighteen killed outright; about one hundred wounded — many mortally. This in [the] Twenty-third. [The] Thirty-sixth less, as the Twenty-third led the column. Entered Dublin Depot, ten and one-half miles, about 6:30 P. M. A fine victory. Took some prisoners, about three hundred, [and] five pieces [of] artillery, many stores, etc., etc. A fine country; plenty of forage. My loss, two hundred and fifty [men].

Tuesday, [*May*] *10.* — Went to New River Bridge. They shelled the woods filled with our men killing three or four. A fine artillery duel between our guns on the high ground on the west side of the river, theirs on the east. The Rebel effort was to keep our men from firing the bridge. It was soon done. A fine scene it was, my band playing and all the regiments marched on to the beautiful hills hurrahing and enjoyed the triumph. Marched thence to Pepper's Ferry and spent the afternoon and night fording and ferrying the river. Sixteen miles.

Wednesday, [*May*] *11.* — To Blacksburg, nine miles, through a finely cultivated country; constant pursuit of mounted videttes. We caught Colonel Linkus, formerly of [the] Thirty-sixth [Virginia], as he was leaving town. Camped about 2 P. M. on a fine slope in a fierce rain-storm. No comfort.

I protect all the property in my vicinity. I take food and forage and burn rails, but all pillaging and plundering my brigade is clear from. I can't say as much for the Pennsylvania regiments, Third and Fourth, etc. Their conduct is most disgraceful. An officer may be excused for an occasional outrage by some villain in his command, but this infamous and universal plundering ought to dispose of shoulder-straps. Camped on Amos' farm — engaged in the Rebellion.

Thursday, *12.* — A most disagreeable rainy day. Mud and roads horrible. Marched from Blacksburg to Salt Pond Mountain. My brigade had charge of the train. I acted as wagonmaster; a long train to keep up. Rode all day in mud and rain back and forth. Met "Mudwall" Jackson and fifteen hundred

[men] — a poor force that lit out rapidly from near Newport. Got to camp — no tents — [at] midnight. Mud; slept on wet ground without blankets. A horrible day, one of the worst of all my experience. Fifteen miles.

Friday, 13. — From Salt Pond Mountain to Peters Mountain. A cold rainy morning. Afternoon, weather good. Bivouacked on east side of Peters Mountain very early. Sun and rest make all happy. Caught a Rebel train and a cannon at the foot of the hill. [At] 3 P. M. ordered to cross Peters Mountain to get forage for animals. A good little march — fifteen miles. Bivouacked at foot of Peters Mountain northeast side.

Monroe County, in Bivouac, May 13, 1864.

Dearest: — We are all right so far. Burned New River Bridge, etc., etc. A most successful campaign. The victory of Cloyd's Mountain was complete. The Twenty-third and Thirty-sixth and part of Thirty-fourth fought under me. All behaved well. The Twenty-third led the charge over an open meadow to the enemy's works and carried them with a will. It cost us one hundred and twenty killed and wounded. . . . This is our best fight. [The] Twenty-third captured two cannon and other trophies. General Jenkins and other officers and men captured. — Love to all.

H.

Mrs. Hayes.

Saturday, 14. — A rainy night. No march this A. M. Sergeant Ogden here wounded twice — not dangerously. Given by Captain Hastings a pair of spurs from Cloyd's Mountain said to have been worn by General Jenkins.

12 M. Ordered to march. [The] Fifth and Seventh Virginia dismounted men report to me under Major Slade; Captain Reynolds, quartermaster.

P. M. Marched in a driving rain over execrable roads to near Salt Sulphur Springs, three or four miles south of Union. The question is, Can the train pass over such roads? — six miles. Out of grub; live off of the country. General Averell and his cavalry a failure.

May 15. Sunday. — Marched four miles from south of Salt Sulphur Springs to north of Union — a beautiful grazing country. Salt Sulphur a pleasure. resort in good condition; Union a fine village. A bushwhacker killed by [the] Thirty-sixth. Slept last night on the ground; rained all night; roads still worse. Slept well. Greenbrier River reported unfordable. Starvation only to be kept off by energetic and systematic foraging. General Crook anxious; works himself like a Turk.

Four men of Company F, who went out foraging at Blacksburg, reported to have been seen dead on the road. They went out foolishly unarmed. Washed, shirted, and cleaned up.

MEMORANDA.

1. A better pioneer party.
2. A provost guard to look after stragglers, prevent plundering, etc.
3. A better arrangement for sick and wounded.
4. A guard to feed and keep prisoners.

We have now been fifteen days away from all news except of our own successful movements.

We have here two hundred and fifty Rebel prisoners of [the] Thirty-sixth, Forty-fifth, Sixtieth Virginia, etc. They are well-behaved, civil fellows; have had very little to eat for some days. We are trying to feed them. A good Secesh mother is now feeding some of them.

May 16. Monday. — Ordered to march at 8 A. M. on road to Alderson's Ferry. We guard the trains. Before trains [were] all out, General Averell requests that I detain one regiment; his pickets fired on or approached on Sweet Springs Road. At his request remain until 11 A. M. Marched one hour and fifteen minutes to [within] about four and one-half miles from Union. There shown a dispatch from General Crook by an aide-de-camp of General Averell authorizing him to detain me but no orders given. Told the aide I would halt there until he could send orders from General Averell if I was wanted. Waited one and one-fourth hours; sent a messenger to Captain Bottsford for orders. Reports from Union indicate no force. After 3 P. M. marched slowly on after the infernally slow train. Soon overtook it at Little Flat Top. After crossing met my orderly (Heckler, Company C, wounded severely) from Captain Bottsford directing me to remain at place I sent from. I rode rapidly forward towards ferry to get further orders. Met Lieutenant Patton and got from him verbal orders and also a written order to camp near ferry. A bad road over Little Flat Top and also near the river. The rest of the road good. Three or four wagons broken; men tired, weak and hungry. "Living on the country"; showery still, muddy of course.

May 17. Tuesday. — Rained last night of course. Camp at Alderson's Ferry on Centreville road; very wet. Ordered to send a regiment to Union to report to General Averell. Sent five companies from Colonel Duval's command [and] five companies of Twenty-third, all under Lieutenant-Colonel Comly; Major Adney also went with [the] Thirty-sixth companies, [and] Dr. Barrett, surgeon. I don't believe the enmy is in force near Union. All busy with a small ferry-boat getting over wagons, etc.; horses and mules swim. General Crook and staff all at work, clubbing mules into the river. Considerable quantities of corn, etc., got here. Corn in the ear issued to men. Some parch, some boil, some pound up. Regular rations all gone long ago. A prodigious rain-storm about noon; no escape from the flood of falling and running water. The river we are crossing fell two feet last night. This will fill it booming full again.

We are now nearly three weeks without news from the outside or inside world. Great movements have taken place, we know, but "with us or with our foes," we can't answer. The Rebels we see seem to have heard news which they construe in their own favor, but there is no elation of feeling as we would expect if they had met with decided success. We are so absorbed in our own fate that the more important operations of Grant do not fill us with anxiety.

Lieutenant Hamlin, Thirty-sixth, goes with twenty-two men, three seregants, etc., on Centreville Road.

May 18.   Wednesday. — A foggy morning. Teams still slowly crossing. Brigade flag carried by Brigdon hit two or three times in battle of Cloyd's Mountain. Once struck out of Brigdon's hands.

May 19.   Thursday. — From three miles north of Greenbrier River to Meadow Bluff ten miles. Forgot a picket of twenty men on south side of Greenbrier River; got them up all right. Reached Meadow Bluff at 12:30 P. M. Found Colonel Enochs with three companies of Fifth Virginia. Rest at Lewisburg. The Fifth did its duty well. They divided into two regiments, built fires, and played tattoo, as if a division were coming, and deceived the Rebels completely. We camp here as if for time enough to refit, etc., etc. Lieutenant-Colonel Comly tells me that —— is disposed to find fault with me and my doings. Very well. I shall do my duty to the best of [my] ability and give myself as little trouble as possible about faultfinders and grumblers.

MEADOW BLUFF, May 19, 1864.

DEAREST : — We got safely to this point in our lines, two hours ago, after twenty-one days of constant marching, frequent fighting, and much hardship, and some starvation. This is the most completely successful and by all odds the pleasantest campaign I have ever had. Now it is over I hardly know what I would change in it except to restore life and limbs to the killed and wounded.

My command in battles and on the march behaved to my entire satisfaction. None did, none could have done better. We had a most conspicuous part in the battle at Cloyd's Mountain and were so lucky. You will see the lists of killed and wounded. We brought off two hundred of our wounded in our train and left about one hundred and fifty. But we have good reason to think they will fare well. . . .

We took two cannon which the regiment has got along here by hard work. The Thirty-sixth and Twenty-third are the only regiments which went into the thickest of the fight and never halted or gave back. The Twelfth did well but the "Flatfoots" backed out. The Ninety-first well, but not much exposed. The Ninth Virginia did splendidly and lost heavier than any other. The Potomac Brigade, (Pennsylvania Reserves, etc., etc.,) broke and fled. I had the dismounted men of the Thirty-fourth. They did pretty well. Don't repeat my talk. But it is true, the Twenty-third was *the* Regiment. The Thirty-sixth I know would have done as well if they had had the same chance. The Twenty-third led and the Thirty-sixth supported them. General Crook is the best general I have ever known.

This campaign in plan and execution has been perfect. We captured ten pieces of artillery, burned the New River Bridge and the culverts and small bridges thirty in number for twenty miles from Dublin to Christiansburg. Captured General Jenkins and three hundred officers and men; killed and wounded three to five hundred and routed utterly his army.*

We shall certainly stay here some days, perhaps some weeks, to refit and get ready for something else. You and the boys are remembered and mentioned constantly.

One spectacle you would have enjoyed. The Rebels contested our approach to the bridge for two or three hours. At last we drove them off and set it on fire. All the troops were

---

*Dr. J. T. Webb in a letter to his mother from Meadow Bluff, May 24, 1864, says: —

"The more we learn of the Rebels, etc., at Cloyd's Mountain, the greater was our victory. It is well ascertained now that in addition to their strong position and works, they had more men in the fight than we had, and also more killed and wounded. They not only expected to *check* us there, but fully counted on *capturing* our whole force. Their officers whom we captured complain bitterly of their men not fighting. Our *new recruits,* whom we were disposed to smile at, did splendidly. One of them, whom Captain Hastings on inspection at Camp White told he must cut off his hair, as men with long hair could not fight, meeting the captain in the midst of the fight, the fellow at the head of his company, playfully remarked, shaking his locks at the captain: 'What do you think of long-hair fighting now?'"

marched up to see it — flags and music and cheering. On a lovely afternoon the beautiful heights of New River were covered with our regiments watching the burning bridge. It was a most animating scene.

Our band has been the life of the campaign. The other three bands all broke down early. Ours has kept up and played their best on all occasions. They alone played at the burning of the bridge and today we came into camp to their music.

I have, it is said, Jenkins' spurs, a revolver of the lieutenant-colonel of [the] Rebel Thirty-sixth, a bundle of Roman candles, a common sword, a new Rebel blanket, and other things, I would give the dear boys if they were here. — Love to all.

Affectionately ever

R.

Mrs. Hayes.

Meadow Bluff, Greenbrier County, West Virginia,
May 19, 1864.

Dear Uncle: — We are safely within what we now call "our own lines" after twenty-one days of marching, fighting, starving, etc., etc. For twelve days we have had nothing to eat except what the country afforded. Our raid has been in all respects successful. We destroyed the famous Dublin Bridge and eighteen miles of the Virginia and Tennessee Railroad and many depots and stores; captured ten pieces of artillery, three hundred prisoners, General Jenkins and other officers among them, and killed and wounded about five hundred, besides utterly routing Jenkins' army in the bloody battle of Cloyd's Mountain. My brigade had two regiments and part of a third in the battle. [The] Twenty-third lost one hundred killed and wounded. We had a severe duty but did just as well as I could have wished. We charged a Rebel battery entrenched in [on] a wooded hill across an open level meadow three hundred yards wide and a deep ditch, wetting me to the waist, and carried it without a particle of wavering or even check, losing, however, many officers and men killed and wounded. It being the vital point General Crook charged with us in person. One brigade from the Army of the Potomac (Pennsylvania Reserves) broke and fled from the field. Altogether, this is our finest experience in the war, and General Crook is the best general we have ever served under, not excepting Rosecrans.

Many of the men are barefooted, and we shall probably remain here some time to refit. We hauled in wagons to this point, over two hundred of our wounded, crossing two large rivers by fording and ferrying and three ranges of high mountains. The news from the outside world is meagre and from Rebel sources. We almost believe that Grant must have been successful from the little we gather.

Sincerely,

R. B. HAYES.

S. BIRCHARD.

May 20. Friday. — Settled weather at last; cold nights. One of the most interesting and affecting things is the train of contrabands, old and young, male and female — one hundred to two hundred — toiling uncomplainingly along after and with the army. They with our prisoners and the trains left for Gauley this morning.

May 21. Saturday. — Rations of coffee, sugar, hard bread, etc., filled our camp with joy last night. It now looks as if Grant had failed to crush Lee merely on account of rain and mud. We *seem* to have had the best of the fighting and to have taken the most prisoners. I suspect we have gained the most guns and lost the most killed and wounded. General Crook thinks Grant will force the fighting until some definite result is obtained.

Sunday, [May] 22. — President of court martial to try the Rebel quartermaster (Jenkins), of [the] Fifteenth Virginia, for pillaging. Sat at Sharpe's; Lieutenant-Colonel Bukey, Major Carey, Major Cadot, Captain Henry, Sweet, etc., etc.

News from Grant confirms my impression that the storm, mud, and rain prevented a decisive victory.

[*May*] *23. Monday.* — Court martial continues. Prosecution closed yesterday. Defense opens this A. M. Adjourned until tomorrow, 9 A. M., after hearing all the testimony the accused had [to] present. Two captains and several men captured near here by guerrillas.

[*May*] *24. Tuesday.* — Finished Jenkins' trial. No definite news lately. Charlie Hay, Sergeant Heiliger, and Sergeant Clark returned. Hay and Clark get from Casey's Board captaincies of first class. Heiliger gets second lieutenant of second class. A queer result. The three are probably nearly equal in merit. Major McIlrath reported near with detachments for all regiments. Captain Hood sick.

[*May*] *25. Wednesday.* — Major McIlrath with seven hundred of various regiments came in at 10 A. M.; Lieutenant Hicks, Dr. McClure, and forty men of [the] Twenty-third; about three hundred of [the] Thirty-sixth. Wrote to mother and Lucy.

———

Meadow Bluff, May 25, 1864.

Dearest : — We are preparing for another move. It will require a week's time, I conjecture, to get shoes, etc., etc. It looks as if the route would be through Lewisburg, White Sulphur, Covington, Jackson River, etc., to Staunton. The major came up this morning with a few recruits and numbers of the sick, now recovered. They bring a bright new flag which I can see floating in front of [the] Twenty-third headquarters. I suspect it to be your gift. Three hundred more of the Thirty-sixth also came up. The Fifth and Thirteenth are coming, so I shall have my own proper brigade all together soon. . . .

Brigdon carried the brigade flag. It was knocked out of his hands by a ball striking the staff only a few inches from where he held it. It was torn twice also by balls.

I see the papers call this "Averell's raid." Very funny! The cavalry part of it was a total failure. General Averell only got to the railroad at points where we had first got in. He was driven back at Saltville and Wytheville. Captain Gilmore is pleased. He says the Second Virginia was the best of any of them! . . .

I am now on most intimate and cordial terms with General Crook. He is a most capital commander. His one fault is a too reckless exposure of himself in action and on the march — not a bad fault in some circumstances.

I shall probably send my valise back to Gallipolis from here to Mr. James Taylor. It will contain a leather case with Roman candles for the boys, a sabre will go with it for one of them, a wooden-soled shoe, such as we destroyed great numbers of at Dublin, and very little else. If it is lost, no matter. . . .

May 26. — Just received your welcome letters of the 6th and 14th. Very glad you are so fortunate. Write to Uncle and Mother when you feel like it.

We shall start soon — perhaps in the morning. We take only one wagon to a regiment. The Fifth is now coming into camp. The general is pleased with Colonel Tomlinson's conduct and Colonel Tomlinson will remain. The Thirteenth will be here tonight. All my brigade together. The rest of the Thirty-sixth is here, six hundred and fifty in all. We feel well about the future. General Crook is more hopeful than ever before.

You need not believe the big stories of great victories or defeats at Richmond. But I think we shall gradually overcome them.

Good-bye, darling,

R.

MRS. HAYES.

———

[*May*] *26. Thursday.*— . . . Trains arriving; looks like moving on Staunton soon. News from Grant rather favorable.

———

MEADOW BLUFF, May 26, 1864.

DEAR UNCLE: — I get two letters from you today. We all believe in General Crook. I am on the best of terms with him. He is the best general I have ever been with, no exceptions.

We have all sorts of rumors from Grant, but it is all clear that we shall finish them soon, if our people and leaders do their duty. They are at the end of their means, and failure now is failure for good.

My brigade is all here, or near here, now. We are getting ready to move towards Staunton soon; tomorrow, I think. I have the two best regiments to be found and two others which promise well. Good-bye.

Sincerely,

R. B. HAYES.

S. BIRCHARD.

[*May*] *27. Friday.* — Read Colonel Gilbert's pamphlet on Governor Brough's rule as to promotion. I do not quarrel with it as a general rule, but Colonel Gilbert and the Forty-fourth should have had their officers as desired. To make such a rule *inflexible* is very foolish.

Saturday, [*May*] *28.* — Colonel Brown and [the] Thirteenth came up last night; seemed glad to be with the brigade all at one camp. I was certainly glad.

Sunday, [*May*] *29.* — Heard preaching of Mr. Harper, Thirteenth, on the hill in front of [the] Thirty-sixth; so-so. Fine day. At night news that Grant had crossed the Pamunkey, fifteen miles from Richmond. Sherman at Dallas, Georgia.

MEADOW BLUFF, May 29, 1864.

DEAR UNCLE: — Contrary to my expectation when I wrote you a few days ago, we are still here. We are detained, I suppose, by different causes, but I suspect we shall move soon towards Staunton. We may drift into the army of Grant before a month. My proper brigade is now here and all of it camped in sight of where I now sit, viz., Twenty-third and Thirty-sixth Ohio, Fifth and Thirteenth Virginia. I have seen them all in line today. They form a fine body of troops. We are soon to lose the enlisted men of the Twenty-third who did not become veterans. I think a good many officers will leave at the same time. It is probable that the veterans of the Twelfth will go into the Twenty-third. If so it will make the regiment better and stronger than ever before.

We are not informed how Grant succeeds in getting into Richmond. You know I have always thought he must get the Western Army there before he can whip Lee. It looks a little now as if he might do it without Western help. We shall see,

Sincerely,

R. B. Hayes.

I hear from Lucy that she is settled in a good boarding-house at Chillicothe.

S. Birchard.

Meadow Bluff, Sunday, May 29, 1864.

Dearest: — Still here getting ready — probably delayed some by the change in Department commanders, but chiefly by rains and delays in obtaining supplies. All the brigade now here, camped in sight of where I now sit. We hardly know where we are to come out, but there is a general feeling that unless Grant succeeds soon, we shall turn up in his army.

You notice the compliment to Major Avery, "bravest of the brave." A good many officers of [the] Twenty-third are talking of going out at the end of the original term, ten days hence. Major McIlrath bid us good-bye this morning. Major Carey is likely to take his place with the veterans of the Twelfth. . . .

My staff now is Lieutenant Hastings, adjutant-general, [Lieutenant William] McKinley, quartermaster, Lieutenant Delay, Thirty-sixth, commissary, and Lieutenant Wood, Thirty-sixth, aide — all nice gentlemen. I enclose Colonel Tomlinson's photograph which he handed me today.

Well, this is a happy time with us. — You must not feel too anxious about me. I shall be among friends.

A flag of truce goes in the morning after our wounded left at

Cloyd's Mountain. There were four doctors and plenty of nurses left with them. . . . Love to all the boys.

Affectionately ever,

R.

Mrs. Hayes.

Monday, [May] 30. — No move today; hot and sultry. Saw [the] Fifth drill; [the] Thirteenth, ditto. News that Grant's prospects are fair.

Tuesday, May 31, 1864. — We move today. Colonel Sickles and the reserve, except veteran volunteers, go home today. They passed with slow sad music this morning. A bad time to go to the rear. Marched to Bunger's Mill, ten and one-half miles from Meadow Bluff and five miles from Lewisburg. Camped on left of Second Brigade in a pleasant glen.

Wednesday, June 1. — Marched thirteen miles to [within] one mile of White Sulphur Springs. A hot day; easy march. Waded Greenbrier. A good camp on Howard's Creek, headquarters on a knoll, left-hand side going east. Mr. Caldwell at White Sulphur very civil. Sold me two teams. A fine, beautiful place. Rumors of Rebels at Callaghan, Jackson River, etc., etc.; a patrol or picket at White Sulphur.

Thursday, June 2. — March at 5 A. M. White Sulphur to Callaghan, about fourteen miles; a cloudy, good marching day. Nothing of interest today. Bill Jackson left Callaghan three days ago.

Friday, [June] 3. — From Callaghan to near Hot Springs in Bath County, nineteen miles. Yesterday crossed Allegheny Mountain; good road. Waters this side flow to the James River. A good day's march; forded Jackson River at Mr. Porter's. A young lady says Richmond papers of 27th contain news favorable to *them.*

Saturday, [June] 4. — From the vicinity of Hot Springs to the east side of Warm Springs Mountain, beyond the alum-works, sixteen miles. My brigade in advance drove a small squad of Rebels from Warm Springs — said to be McNeil's and Marshall's Cavalry. No resistance offered but a few trees cut to blockade the road. Rumors of a fight at Harrisonburg; as usual reports are two-faced. Papers of the 27th to 31st inclusive [from] Richmond.

Sunday, [June] 5. — From three miles west of Millboro to one mile beyond Goshen; about thirteen to fourteen miles. Rained last night. Our march today impeded by a small body of Rebel cavalry. Rumors of Jackson, McCausland, and General Morgan, all hurrying to Staunton to oppose Hunter or our command. Perhaps both in detail. Bad strategy to propose to unite two forces in the enemy's lines. Struck the Virginia Central one hundred and seventy-five [miles] from Richmond near Goshen. Our route through narrow valleys or cañons where a small force can easily hold a large one.

Now (3 P. M.) we are waiting as rear brigade, on a pretty stream, for the leading brigade, Colonel White's, to drive a party of Rebels through a narrow gap on railroad from Millboro to Goshen. They turn the position and we go on. We lose two or three slightly wounded and capture four or five Rebels and wound three others badly. Goshen a pretty place in the mountains. We cross no high mountain today.

Monday, June 6. — From one mile east of Goshen to two miles west of Craig [Craigsville] on Central Railroad, six miles — 10 A. M. to 1 P. M. Still halted, destroying Central Railroad. A big squad of men turn it over, rails and ties, and tumble it down the embankment; burn culverts and ties as far as possible. The railroad can be destroyed by troops marching parallel to it very fast. Easier to destroy than to build up, as our Rebel friends are learning to their cost. Camped in a big thunder-shower, all wet as drowned rats. Slept well.

June 7. Tuesday. — From two miles west of Craig [Craigsville] to within six or eight of Staunton. A fine day. At Pond Gap crossed Central Railroad and over a mountain — a detour which let us into [the] Valley of Virginia, avoiding the Rebel position in Buffalo Gap. A lovely valley; we dine now (12 M.) on a beautiful farm in this lovely valley — all happy to get here so easily. Reports say Hunter is in Staunton; got there last night. The general (Crook) found a four-leafed clover yesterday. I saw the new moon over my right shoulder. Funny how a man of sense can think for an instant even of such follies. We crossed the mountain to Summerdean, a little pretty hamlet. Skirmished into Middlebrook, a beautiful country. Supplies are abundant. Hunter flogged the Rebels badly and took Staunton yesterday. Eighteen miles today.

June 8. Wednesday. — Marched ten miles in a northeast direction to Staunton, a fine town of five thousand inhabitants or so. General Hunter here. He had a good victory.

STAUNTON, VIRGINIA, June 8, 1864.

DEAR UNCLE: — We have had another very fortunate campaign. Everything lucky — except Hunter got the victory instead of Crook. But that is all right, of course. The march, destruction of railroads and stores, so far, have made this a most useful expedition. We know nothing of Grant for many days, but we think he must be doing well.

We shall be at work immediately again. Now out of West Virginia for good, I suppose.

I had a letter from you the day we crossed the Allegheny Mountains. Nothing from Mother for more than a month.

Our march for five days has been in counties where Yankee soldiers were never seen before, Bath, Rockbridge, and Augusta. We have visited many watering-places, White Sulphur, Hot, and Warm Springs, etc., etc. An active campaign leaves little chance for writing or hearing. I think you had better direct hereafter to Crook's Division, Hunter's Army, via Martinsburg, Virginia.

[R. B. HAYES.]

S. BIRCHARD.

STAUNTON, June 8, 1864.

DEAREST: — We reached the beautiful Valley of Virginia yesterday over North Mountain and entered this town this morning. General Hunter took the place after a very successful fight on the 6th. We seem to be clear of West Virginia for good. We shall probably move on soon.

Our march here over the mountains was very exciting. We visited all the favorite resorts of the chivalry on our route, White Sulphur, Blue Sulphur, Warm, and Hot Springs, etc., etc. Lovely places, some of them. I hope to visit some of them with you after the war is over.

We know nothing of Grant but conjecture that he must be doing well. We are now in Crook's division, Hunter's Army, I suppose. General Crook is the man of all others. I wish you could have seen the camps the night we got our last mail from home. It brought me two letters from you, one of [the] 26th. I told General Crook, Webb sent his love. "Yes," said he, "Webb is a fine boy; he will make a soldier."

We have enjoyed this campaign very much. I have no time to write particulars. It is said that the prisoners will be sent to Beverly tomorrow and that the men and officers of [the] Twenty-third whose time expires will go as guard. I shall perhaps send my sorrel horse by Carrington and if he can't sell him for two hundred dollars to take him to Uncle Moses to do just what he pleases with him. If he can't keep him he may give him away or shoot him. He is a fine horse and behaved admirably at Cloyd's Mountain, but he is too fussy and noisy.

I feel the greatest sympathy for you during these long periods of entire ignorance of my whereabouts. I trust it will soon be so that I can hear from you and send news to you often.

[R. B. Hayes.]

Mrs. Hayes.

Staunton, Virginia, June 9, 1864.

Dearest: — I wrote you yesterday a letter which if it reaches you at all, will be some days in advance of this. I send this by the men whose term of service has expired and who go to "America" in charge of prisoners captured a few days ago by General Hunter at the battle of Piedmont or "New Hope."

All operations in this quarter have been very successful. We reached here yesterday morning after an exciting and delightful march of nine days from Meadow Bluff. . . .

The men not enlisting (one hundred and sixty) with nine officers left our camp this morning to start tomorrow in charge of Colonel Moore. The band played "Home, Sweet Home." The officers who leave are Captains Canby, Rice, Stevens, Sperry, and Hood; First Lieutenants Stephens, Chamberlain, Smith, Jackson, and Hicks. We have left seven full companies and twelve good officers. The old flags go to Columbus to the governor by the color-bearer. We shall quite certainly get more men from the Twelfth in a couple of weeks than we now lose.

I send Carrington with the little sorrel to sell or leave with Uncle Moses if he fails to sell him, and Uncle Moses can do what he pleases with him.

I send a pistol captured at Blacksburg from Lieutenant-Colonel Linkus, Thirty-sixth Virginia, Rebel. Also pencil memorandum of no account. Preserve the handbill showing Lee's appeal to the people of this (Augusta) county.

I have just visited the very extensive hospitals here. They are filled with patients, two-thirds Secesh, one-third our men. Nothing could be finer. In a fine building (Deaf and Dumb Asylum), in a beautiful grove — gas and hydrants — shade, air, etc. The Secesh were friendly and polite; not the slightest bitterness or unkindness between the two sorts. If I am to be left in hospital this is the spot.

Direct to "Second Infantry Division (or General Crook's Division), Department West Virginia, via Martinsburg."

Love to all. — Affectionately ever,

R.

Mrs. Hayes.

[*Lexington*], *Sunday, June 12.* — General Hunter burns the Virginia Military Institute. This does not suit many of us. General Crook, I know, disapproves. It is surely bad. No move today. [Marched] thirteen miles yesterday.

LEXINGTON, ROCKBRIDGE COUNTY, June 12 (Sunday), 1864.

DEAREST: — I just hear that a mail goes tomorrow. We captured this town after an artillery and sharpshooter fight of three hours, yesterday P. M. My brigade had the advance for two days and all the casualties, or nearly all, fell to me. [A] first lieutenant of [the] Fifth Virginia killed and one private; three privates of [the] Thirty-sixth killed and ten to fifteen wounded. [The] Twenty-third had no loss. Very noisy affair, but not dangerous.

This is a fine town. Stonewall Jackson's grave and the Military Institute are here. Many fine people. Secesh are not at all bitter and many are Union.

I am more pleased than ever with General Crook and my brigade, etc., but some things done here are not right. General Hunter will be as odious as Butler or Pope to the Rebels and not gain our good opinion either. You will hear of it in Rebel papers, I suspect.

Weather fine and all our movements are successful. The Rebels have been much crippled already by our doings. We are probably moving towards Lynchburg. If so you will have heard of our fortunes from other sources before this reaches you.

I got a pretty little cadet musket here which I will try to send the boys. Dear boys, love to them and the tenderest affection for you. — Good-bye.

[R. B. HAYES.]

MRS. HAYES.

[*Camp Piatt, West Virginia,*] *Thursday, June 30, 1864.* — This [has been] the hardest month of the war; hot and dusty long marches; hungry, sleepy night marches; many skirmishes; two battles. Men worn out and broken down.

Tuesday, June 14, [we] marched [from Lexington] to Buchanan. A hot, dusty march, twenty-four miles. Bathed in James River. The next day [we pushed on] to "Fancy Farm," Bedford County, near Liberty, sixteen miles. Fine views of Peaks of Otter. [Thence], Thursday, (16th), to Liberty and beyond on railroad towards Lynchburg. Worked on the railroad, tearing up and burning, etc. [We heard] various rumors, generally good.

Friday (17th), Colonel White's brigade cleaned out Rebels handsomely to [within] three miles of Lynchburg. The next day [the] Rebels [inside the] works [were] re-inforced. [There was] skirmishing and fighting but no general attack. [At] 8:30 P. M., we back out via Liberty Road, [Hunter's attempt to capture Lynchburg having proved a failure].

Sunday (19th), *en route* to Liberty, sleepy, tired; hot, and dusty. All goes well however so far. Twenty-six miles. Monday (20th), still on, night and day! Sleepy and tired. Enemy following attacked our cavalry at Liberty yesterday evening with some loss to us. Today at Buford Gap we got ready for battle, but Rebels not ready.

Tuesday (21st), on to four miles beyond Salem. Rebels attack often, but their feeble skirmishes do no hurt to Crook. They however get nine guns of Hunter! Wednesday (22d), fifteen miles to Newcastle. We (First Brigade) guarded the wagon train; poor business. Thursday (23d), [from] Newcastle to Sweet Springs — a beautiful watering-place — twenty-two miles, over two high ranges of the Alleghenies. [Thence, by] night march, seventeen miles to White Sulphur, [arriving] at 2:30 P. M., Friday (24th). Night marches bad unless there is good moonlight.

From White Sulphur, Saturday (25th), [we marched] to Meadow Bluff, twenty-four miles, [reaching there] long after midnight, starved and sleepy. The hardest [march] of the war. The next day [starting] at sunrise, many without sleeping a wink, we march to Tyrees, twenty miles, [at the] foot of Mount Sewell. Monday (27th), at 4 A. M., [we] march and meet a train of provisions at or near Mountain Cove. A jolly feeding time. Camp at old Camp Ewing. The next day, march to Loup Creek, fourten miles; and yesterday to Piatt, twenty-two miles.

CAMP PIATT, June 30, 1864.

DEAREST: — We reached here ten miles above Charleston last night. Dr. Joe will tell you all the news. It has been a severe but very pleasant campaign. We did not do as much as we think might have been done, but we did enough to make our work of great importance.

We are now talking of *rumors* that we are to go East via [the] Ohio River and [the] Baltimore and Ohio Railroad. It is generally believed to be true, although as yet we have no other evidence of it than camp rumor.

I thought of you often while I was gone — of your anxiety about me and the suffering that all rumors of disaster to us would cause you. But I hoped you would keep up good courage and live it through. Oh, darling, I love you so tenderly. You must always think of me pleasantly. You have been the source of such happiness to me that I can't bear to think that anything that may befall me will throw a permanent gloom over your life.

The Twenty-third was lucky on this campaign, losing less than any other regiment, etc. The Fifth lost most, [the] Thirty-sixth next. All together, killed, wounded, and missing, my brigade does not lose over one hundred, if so much [many].

I am very fortunate in my brigade. It is now to me like my own regiment, and is really a very good one, perhaps the best to be found, or one of the best, in the army. General Crook is the favorite of the army. We hope to be organized into an independent command with Colonel Powell's Cavalry Brigade and two batteries. Then we can raid to some purpose.

If we are not sent East, we shall stay here three or four weeks recruiting, etc. — My love to the boys. Dr. Joe will have plenty of stories to tell them. The doctor was a most important person in this raid. He did more for the wounded than anybody else. Colonel Turley had his thigh broken at Lynchburg and was hauled over two hundred miles over all these mountains. His admirable pluck and cheerfulness has saved him. Nothing can exceed the manliness he has exhibited. — Love to friends all.

Affectionately,

R.

Mrs. Hayes.

CAMP PIATT, TEN MILES ABOVE CHARLESTON,
WEST VIRGINIA, June 30, 1864.

DEAR UNCLE: — Back home again in the Kanawha Valley. Our raid has done a great deal; all that we at first intended, but failed in one or two things which would have been done with a more active and enterprising commander than General Hunter. General Crook would have taken Lynchburg without doubt. Our loss is small. [The] Twenty-third had nobody killed. My brigade loses less than one hundred. Our greatest suffering was want of food and sleep. I often went asleep on my horse. We had to go night and day for about a week to get out. We are all impressed with the idea that the Confederacy has now got all its strength of all sorts in the field, and that nothing more can be added to it. Their defeat now closes the contest speedily. We passed through ten counties where Yankees never came before; there was nothing to check us even until forces were drawn from Richmond to drive us back.

There are rumors that we are to go East soon, but nothing definitely is known. We hope we are to constitute an independent command under General Crook. We have marched, in two months past, about eight hundred miles; have had fighting or skirmishing on over forty days of the time.

My health, and my horse's (almost of equal moment) are excellent.

Send letters to the old direction, via Charleston, for the present.

Sincerely,

R. B. HAYES.

S. BIRCHARD.

CAMP [PIATT], TEN MILES ABOVE CHARLESTON,
WEST VIRGINIA, June 30, 1864.

DEAR MOTHER: — We got safely back to this point yesterday after being almost two months within the Rebel lines. . . . We have had a severe and hazardous campaign and have, I think, done a great deal of good. While we have suffered a good deal from want of food and sleep, we have lost very few men and are generally in the best of health. . . . General Crook has won the love and confidence of all. General Hunter is not so fortunate. General Averell has not been successful either. We had our first night's quiet rest *all* night for many weeks.

Dr. Joe went to Ohio with our wounded yesterday and will see Lucy. He has been a great treasure to our wounded.

We have hauled two hundred [wounded men] over both the Blue Ridge and the Alleghenies and many smaller mountains, besides crossing James River and other streams. Our impression is that the Rebels are at the end of their means and our success now will speedily close the Rebellion.

Affectionately,

R. B. Hayes.

Mrs. Sophia Hayes.

Charleston, Camp Elk, July 2, 1864.

Dearest : — Back again to this point last night. Camped opposite the lower end of Camp White on the broad level bottom in the angle between Elk and Kanawha. My headquarters on one of the pretty wooded hills near Judge Summers'.

Got your letter of 16th. All others gone around to Martinsburg. Will get them soon. Very much pleased to read about the boys and their good behaviour.

Dr. Joe went to Gallipolis with our wounded, expecting to visit you, but the rumors of an immediate movement brought him back. We now have a camp rumor that Crook is to command this Department. If so we shall stay here two or three weeks; otherwise, only a few days, probably.

You wrote one thoughtless sentence, complaining of Lincoln for failing to protect our unfortunate prisoners by retaliation. All a mistake, darling. All such things should be avoided as much as possible. We have done too much rather than too little. General Hunter turned Mrs. Governor Letcher and daughters out of their home at Lexington and on ten minutes' notice burned the beautiful place in retaliation for some bushwhackers' burning out Governor Pierpont [of West Virginia.]

And I am glad to say that General Crook's division officers and men were all disgusted with it.

I have just learned as a fact that General Crook has an independent command or separate district in the Department of West Virginia, which practically answers our purposes. We are styled the "Army of the Kanawha," headquarters in the field.

I have just got your letter of June 1. They will all get here sooner or later. The flag is a beautiful one. I see it floating now near the piers of the Elk River Bridge.

Three companies of the Twelfth under Major Carey are ordered to join the Twenty-third today — Lieutenants Otis, Hiltz and ——— command them, making the Twenty-third the strongest veteran regiment. Colonel White and the rest bid us good-bye today. What an excellent man he is. I never knew a better.

You use the phrase "brutal Rebels." Don't be cheated in that way. There are enough "brutal Rebels" no doubt, but we have brutal officers and men too. I have had men brutally treated by our own officers on this raid. And there are plenty of humane Rebels. I have seen a good deal of it on this trip. War is a cruel business and there is brutality in it on all sides, but it is very idle to get up anxiety on account of any supposed peculiar cruelty on the part of Rebels. Keepers of prisons in Cincinnati, as well as in Danville, are hard-hearted and cruel. . . .

Affectionately,

R.

MRS. HAYES.

CHARLESTON, WEST VIRGINIA, July 2, 1864.

DEAR MOTHER: — We got back here yesterday. I find a letter from you [of] June 11. No doubt others are on the way from Martinsburg — the point to which all our letters were forwarded for some weeks.

I am glad you are back at Columbus again and in tolerable health. We have had altogether the severest time I have yet known in the war. We have marched almost continually for two months, fighting often, with insufficient food and sleep, crossed the three ranges of the Alleghenies four times, the ranges of the Blue Ridge twice, marched several times all day and all night without sleeping, and yet my health was never better. I think I have not even lost flesh.

We all believe in our general. He is a considerate, humane man; a thorough soldier and disciplinarian. He is hereafter to have the sole command of us. I mean, of course, General Crook. General Hunter *was* chief in command, and is not much esteemed by us. . . . I think Colonel Comly will get home a few days. His health has not been very good during the latter part of our campaign.

I hope you will not be overanxious about me. What is for the best will happen. In the meantime I am probably doing as much good and enjoying as much happiness here as I could anywhere. — Love to all. I knew you would like Mrs. Platt.

Affectionately, good-bye,

R.

P. S. — I expect to remain here a fortnight or more.

Mrs. Sophia Hayes.

Charleston, West Virginia, July 2, 1864.

Dear Uncle: — We are told this morning that General Crook is to have the command of the "Army of the Kanawha," independent of all control below Grant. If so, good. I don't doubt it. This will secure us the much needed rest we have hoped for and keep us here two or three weeks. My health is excellent, but many men are badly used up. . . .

I do not feel sure yet of the result of Grant's and Sherman's campaigns. One thing I have become satisfied of. The Rebels are now using their last man and last bread. There is absolutely nothing left in reserve. Whip what is now in the field, and the game is ended.

Sincerely,

R. B. Hayes.

S. Birchard.

CAMP CROOK, CHARLESTON, July 5, 1864.

DEAREST: — Your last from Elmwood, June 16, reached me last night. Very glad to get so good and cheerful talk.

It is not yet quite certain whether I shall be able to come and see you for a day or two or not. I think it is hardly best for you to attempt coming here now, but if I can't come to you, we will see about it.

Sunday morning the veterans of the Twelfth under Major Carey were united to the Twenty-third and that evening your flag was formally presented to the regiment at dress parade. The hearty cheers given for Mrs. H— (that's you) showed that you were held in grateful remembrance. I do not know whether you will get any letters from Colonel Comly or not. You certainly will if he does not think it will be a bore to you.

You have no doubt seen the proceedings of the non-veterans on giving the old flag to the governor at Columbus. I send a slip containing them to be kept with *our* archives. Secretary [of State, William Henry] Smith's allusion to me was awkward and nonsensical; but as it was well meant I, of course, must submit to be made ridiculous with good grace.

The fracture of Abbott's arm turned out like mine, a simple fracture without splintering and he saves his arm in good condition. He is doing well.

Our prisoners wounded at Cloyd's Mountain were well treated by the citizens of Dublin and Newbern, etc., and by the Rebel soldiers of that region. Morgan and his men, however, behaved badly towards them — very badly — but as they were with them only a few hours, they were soon in better hands again. At Lynchburg the people behaved well also.

Don't let Uncle Scott be pestered with the little sorrel. He may give him away if he can't dispose of him otherwise.

We are gradually getting over our sore feet and weak stomachs and shall be in good condition shortly. Captain Hood is here again in command of his company. Major McIlrath, Captain Warren, Lieutenants Deshong and Nessle and perhaps one or two others leave us here. The Twenty-third is now a large and splendid regiment again, better than ever, I suppose. — Love to all.

Affectionately, ever,

R.

MRS. HAYES.

Thursday, July 7, 1864. — Ordered to Parkersburg and East tomorrow. I go on steamboat with Third and Fourth Reserves, Captain Moulton, to Gallipolis.

PARKERSBURG, WEST VIRGINIA, July 12, 1864.

DEAR MOTHER : — We are here on our way East. I managed to slip ahead of my command and spend Sunday with Lucy and the boys at Chillicothe. I should have been very glad to get to Columbus and would have done so if it had been possible. But we are being hurried forward as fast as possible to aid in putting an end to the trouble in Maryland. I know very little about it but hope it will turn out much less serious than is now represented.

I found my family well homed and in good health. It was an unexpected but very happy meeting.

My love to all the family. Letters directed to me in Crook's Division, via Cumberland, will probably find me. I think all your letters have finally reached me.

My health, after all our severe campaigning, is excellent.

Your affectionate son,

RUTHERFORD.

MRS. SOPHIA HAYES.

MARTINSBURG, July 17 (Sunday), 1864.

DEAREST : — A week ago, about this time, we were enjoying our pleasant ride like young lovers on the Kingston Pike. Now we are widely separated.

I am semi-sick — that is the boil I told you I was threatened with on my hip is actively at work. The worst is over with it. I am lying on my blankets in the barroom of a German drinking saloon that was gutted by the Rebels. The man is a refugee but his excellent *frau* is here ready to do anything in the world for a bluecoat. She wants me to go [to] a chamber and a clean bed, but I like the more public room better.

Half my brigade went this morning to General Crook, thirty miles east. We go in a day or two. The combinations to catch the Rebels seem to me good, but I expect them to escape. Raiding parties always do escape. Morgan was foolhardy and Streight lacked enterprise. They are the only exceptions.

You will probably see some correspondence about your flag gift in the papers. Don't blush, it's all right. — "S'much." Love to all.

Ever, darling, your

R.

Mrs. Hayes.

Martinsburg, Virginia, July 17 (Sunday), 1864.

Dear Mother: — I am much obliged for your letter by Colonel Comly. Glad you still are in good health. We are pretty busy now trying to prevent the escape of the Rebel raiders who have plundered Maryland. . . . The weather is very warm but we have good breezes and excellent water in this region so that campaigning is not unpleasant.

I notice Mitchell's name is often mentioned in connection with Sherman's army. He has a fine position. I trust he will come safely out of it. — Love to all.

Affectionately, your son,

R.

Mrs. Sophia Hayes.

[The Diary for the last few months of 1864 is for the most part hardly more than a line a day, entered in a pocket memorandum book, "The Southern Almanac for 1864," which Hayes's orderly, William Crump, had got hold of at Middlebrook, Virginia, early in June. Many of the entries were originally made with a pencil and subsequently inked over. Usually the entries give only a bald statement of the movement of the day. In some cases entries are omitted here entirely; in other cases several are combined in a single paragraph.]

Sunday afternoon, July 17, [the] Fifth [Virginia] and Twenty-third [Ohio] [marched from Martinsburg] to near Charlestown. Slept in a farmyard. Twelve miles. The next day, march toward Harpers Ferry and [the] Shenandoah at Keys Ferry. Whole brigade together. Fine river and valley. Skirmish all P. M. Heavy cannonading at Snickers Ford. Twenty-three miles. Spent Tuesday (19th) skirmishing with Bradley Johnson's Cavalry between camp on Bull Skin and Kabletown. Rodes' Division try to take us in and fail after a brisk fight. Six miles. Wednesday (20th), back to Keys Ferry and Harpers Ferry [and] thence to Charlestown; ordered to join General Crook. Ten miles.

HARPERS FERRY, July 20, 1864.

DEAREST: — I am here with my brigade, merely to get ammunition and grub. Have been fighting and marching three days; lost only three killed and twelve wounded. Shall remain all day. All well. My boil does me no harm, but it is an awful hole. Doctor well. Can't give you much news. I am on a scout after Crook who is lost to the bureau! It is very funny. He has caught some Rebels and many wagons, I know, and I think he has got a good victory, but I don't yet know. . . .

In our hunt we have had hard marching and plenty of fighting of a poor sort. Rebel cavalry is very active and efficient, but it don't fight. Our losses are ridiculously small for so much noise. . . .   Affectionately,

R.

MRS. HAYES.

Thursday (21st), marched to near Snickers Ford. Camped near Colonel Ware's. Fifteen miles. The next day, marched to Winchester. A fine town before the war. Eleven and one-half miles. Saturday (23d), enemy reported in force approaching Winchester. Skirmished all day. Small force of Rebel cavalry fool ours. Seven miles. Sunday (24th), defeated badly at Winchester near Kernstown by Early with a superior force. My brigade suffered severely. Rebels came in on my left. Poor cavalry allowed the general to be surprised. Seven miles. All [that] night marching, twenty-two miles, to Martinsburg. My brigade covered the retreat. Retreated from Martinsburg; turned on Rebels and drove them out. Monday night to Potomac at Williamsport, [Maryland], twelve miles, a severe, sleepy job. Camped on Antietam near battle-ground.

CAMP NEAR SHARPSBURG, MARYLAND,
Tuesday evening, July 26, 1864.

DEAREST: — We reached here today after two nights and one day of pretty severe marching, not so severe as the Lynchburg march, and one day of very severe fighting at Winchester. We were defeated by a superior force at Winchester. My brigade suffered most in killed and wounded and not so much in prisoners as some others. The Twenty-third lost about twenty-five killed and one hundred wounded; [the] Thirty-sixth, eleven killed, ninety-nine wounded; [the] Thirteenth, fifteen killed, sixty wounded (behaved splendidly — its first battle) ; [the] Sixth, four killed, twenty-seven wounded. In [the] Twenty-third, six new officers wounded and two killed — Captain McMillen late of [the] Twelfth and Lieutenant Gray, a sergeant of Company G. Morgan again wounded, not dangerously. Comly very slightly. Lieutenant Hubbard, late commissary sergeant, fell into [the] hands of Rebels. The rest all with us. Lieutenant Kelly slightly three times. Lieutenant Clark (late sergeant) not badly. All doing well. Lieutenant-Colonel Hall (Thirteenth) twice badly but not dangerously — a brave man, very. My horse wounded. This is all a new experience, a decided defeat in battle. My brigade was in the hottest place and then was in condition to cover the retreat as rear-guard which we did successfully and well for one day and night.

Of course the reason, the place for blame to fall, is always asked in such cases. I think the army is not disposed to blame the result on anybody. The enemy was so superior that a defeat was a matter of course if we fought. The real difficulty was, our cavalry was so inefficient in its efforts to discover the strength of the enemy that General Crook and all the rest of us were deceived until it was too late.*

We are queer beings. The camp is now alive with laughter and good feeling; more so than usual. The recoil after so much toil and anxiety. The most of our wounded were brought off and all are doing well. — Colonel Mulligan, commanding [the] brigade next to mine was killed. Colonel Shaw of [the] Thirty-fourth killed.

As we were driven off the field my pocket emptied out map, almanack, and [a] little photographic album. We charged back ten or twenty yards and got them!

There were some splendid things done by those around me. McKinley and Hastings were very gallant. Dr. Joe conspicuously so. Much that was disgraceful was done, but, on the whole, it was not so painful a thing to go through as I have thought it would be.

This was Sunday, about 2 P. M., that we all went up. We shall stay here some time if the Rebels don't invade Maryland again and so give us business.

I thought of you often, especially as I feared the first reports by frightened teamsters and cavalry might carry tidings affecting me. It was said my brigade was crushed and I killed at Martinsburg. By the by, the enemy followed us to that place

* Dr. J. T. Webb, in a letter of July 28 to his mother, writes: — "All this misfortune was occasioned by the *infernal* cavalry. They were sent out to guard our flanks and failed to do so. Had they done their duty, Crook would never have thought of fighting. There were about twenty thousand Rebels, while we had some six or eight thousand, all told. Our calvary is a miserable farce. They are utterly useless, in fact they were in our way. Had we not depended on them, we never would have been caught. They (cavalry) cut loose from their artillery and we, with our infantry, hauled off their guns, at the same time driving, or rather keeping, back the Rebels."

where we turned on them and flogged their advance-guard handsomely.

So much, dearest, as ever.

Affectionately,

R.

Mrs. Hayes.

[August 27, Hayes's command marched fourteen miles down the river road toward Harpers Ferry and camped below Sandy Hook. The next day the Potomac was crossed and a camp was established in the woods near Halltown, Virginia, a good location except that it was "too far from water." Here the weary soldiers rested two days. Then, Saturday night, July 30, they marched back in the darkness, through dust, heat, and confusion, fourteen miles into Maryland; and Sunday ten miles farther on through Middletown to a wooded camp. Hayes writes: "Men all gone up, played out, etc. Must have time to build up or we can do nothing. Only fifty to one hundred men in a regiment came into camp in a body."]

Camp near Halltown, Virginia, Four miles south of Harpers Ferry, July 29, 1864.

Dearest: — A fine day in a pleasant shady camp, *resting*. That sentence contains a world of comfort to our weary, worn-out men. All are clothed and shod again, and general good feeling prevails.

We are joined by a large force under General Wright, who commands the whole army. It looks as if we would move up the Valley of Virginia again. If so the papers will inform you of our movements and doings.

I sent you a dispatch and letter after our return from the reverse at Winchester, but am not certain that either was forwarded.

I can only repeat what I have written so often, my love and esteem for my darling and my wish that she may be as happy as she has always made me. — Love to the boys and all the dear ones.

Affectionately ever,

R.

MRS. HAYES.

CAMP FIVE MILES SOUTH OF HARPERS FERRY, VIRGINIA,
July 30, 1864.

DEAR UNCLE: — I received your letter of the 13th last night. I hardly know what to think about your bank. It seems likely enough that greenbacks may get lower as compared with gold, and perhaps all property employed in banking may depreciate correspondingly. But I am not thinking much of these things now and have no opinions on them which I think of any value.

As to that candidacy for Congress, I care nothing at all about it, neither for the nomination nor for the election.* It was merely easier to let the thing take its own course than to get up a letter declining to run and then to explain it to everybody who might choose to bore me about it.

We are gathering an army here apparently to drive the Rebels out of the Valley. I hope we shall be long enough about it to give the men rest and to heal their sore feet. We have had now three months of hard campaigning — marched one thousand to one thousand two hundred miles, besides [travelling] seven hundred [miles] by railroad and steamboat. Much night marching, four or five pitched battles, and skirmishing every other day.

My health is good — perfect; bothered with boils from constant riding in hot weather, but of no importance.

I wish you to send my letters to Mother. It will be a comfort to her to hear oftener than I have time to write. . . .

Colonel Mulligan was shot down very near me. We were side by side conversing a few moments before. My orderly was wounded, also my horse. *Lieutenant* Kelly had the narrowest

---

* Hayes had received numerous letters from friends in Cincinnati, William Henry Smith, R. H. Stephenson, E. T. Carson, and others, urging him to be a candidate. He was too busy in the field to bother about politics. But he was nominated August 6, and elected in November, without having taken any part in the canvass.

possible escapes — several — balls grazing his head, ear, and body — Mrs. Zimmerman's brother, you know.

Sincerely,

R. B. HAYES.

Sunday, 31st. — I write this at Middletown, at the table of my old home when wounded — Jacob Rudy's. They are so cordial and kind. Dr. Webb and I are at the breakfast table. All inquire after Lucy and all. Send this to Lucy. Such is war — now here, tomorrow in Pennsylvania or Virginia. — Goodbye. — R.

S. BIRCHARD.

CAMP NEAR WOLFSVILLE, MARYLAND, August 2, 1864.

MY DARLING: — We are having a jolly good time about sixteen miles north of Middletown, resting the men, living on the fat of the land, among these loyal, friendly people. We are supposed to be watching a Rebel invasion. Our cavalry is after the Rebel cavalry and I hope will do something. Averell is a poor stick. Duffie is willing and brave and will do what he can. Powell is the real man and will do what a small force can do. I suspect there is nothing for us to do here — that is, that no [Rebel] infantry are here.

I saw Colonel Brown. — Hayes Douglass was, I am told, to be in our division. I am sorry he is not. I have not seen him.

The Rudys I saw Sunday. They were so kind and cordial. They all inquired after you. The girls have grown pretty — quite pretty. Mr. Rudy said if I was wounded he would come a hundred miles to get me. Queer old neighborhood this. They sell goods at the country store at old prices and give silver in change! Dr. Joe bought good shoes for two dollars and twenty-five cents a pair.

We are in the Middletown Valley, by the side of a fine mountain stream. We get milk, eggs, and good bread. All hope to stay here *always* — but I suppose we shall soon dance. We have campaigned so long that our discipline and strength are greatly deteriorated.

I read the correct list of killed, wounded, etc., of [the] Twenty-third this A. M. It contains scarcely any names you would know. With two-thirds of the regiment composed of new recruits and Twelfth men this would of course be so. — The band astonished our rural friends with their music last night. They never saw Federal soldiers here before. They have twice been robbed by Rebel raiders and so are ready to admire all they see and hear. — Love to all.

Affectionately ever,

R.

MRS. HAYES.

Friday, August 5, 1864. — Wednesday, marched eighteen to twenty miles across the Catoctin (Blue) Ridge, [and on] through Frederick to the left bank of the Monocacy, one and one-half miles below [Frederick] Junction [where we camped]. Yesterday [there arrived] ninety recruits for [the] Twenty-third, a deserter from Charleston among them. Providential ! —[I] rode into Frederick with General Crook, and dined with Dr. Steele, of Dayton. Today [was the] trial [drumhead court-martial] of deserter Whitlow. He was shot at sundown before all the troops.

CHAPTER XXIV

FIGHTING IN THE SHENANDOAH VALLEY, OPEQUON,
FISHER'S HILL, AND CEDAR CREEK —
AUGUST-OCTOBER 1864

CROOK'S weary army had been summoned to the East because of Early's activities. As soon as Hunter's forces, after their failure at Lynchburg, were well in the mountains, Early had started for the Shenandoah Valley, now left unguarded. He moved rapidly down the Valley, meeting practically no resistance, crossed over into Maryland, and levying contributions as he went, hurried on towards Washington which was in a fever of apprehension. Lew Wallace, with an inadequate force, strove bravely but in vain to block his way at Monocacy. The most he could do was to delay Early and the delay saved Washington. By the time Early came in sight of the dome of the Capitol, knowledge of the arrival of troops from Grant's army deterred him from any serious attempt to take the city. He turned back the night of July 12 and crossed the Potomac to Leesburg with all the booty his raiders had gathered in Maryland.

"Then followed three weeks of perpetual fighting, raiding, marching, and countermarching in the lower Shenandoah Valley and western Maryland, with frequent changes of commanders of departments and corps, with clashings of authority and conflicting orders, resulting in dissipating the strength of the Union forces and giving the alert and clear-headed Early almost constant success. At last (August 5) Grant solved the perplexing problem by insisting on a consolidation of the Middle, Washington, Susquehanna, and West Virginia Departments and placing General Sheridan with an adequate army in command. Then began the brilliant campaign in the Valley which finally crushed the Confederate strength in that quarter."* This chapter records Hayes's share in that campaign.]

CAMP PLEASANT VALLEY, MARYLAND,
August 8 (Monday), 1864.

DEAREST: — We have had pretty good times the last week or ten days. Easy marching, plenty to eat, and good camps. We are, for the present, part of a tolerably large army under Sheridan. This pleases General Crook and suits us all. We are likely to be engaged in some of the great operations of the autumn. But service in these large armies is by no means as severe as in our raids.

Hayes Douglass is commissary on General Crook's staff. I have not yet seen him. He is spoken of very favorably.

My staff is Captain Hastings, Lieutenant Wood and Delay of Thirty-sixth, and Comstock of Thirteenth. I was sorry to lose McKinley but I couldn't as a friend advise him to do otherwise. He is taken *out* of [the] quartermaster's department and *that* is good, and *into* [the] adjutant-general's office, and that is good.

One of the scamps who deserted the Rebels and then deserted Hicks' company (you remember) was captured at Cloyd's Mountain in the Rebel ranks. He escaped and by a remarkable providence enlisted as a substitute in Ohio and was sent to the Twenty-third Regiment. He was tried anl shot within twenty-four hours. His execution was in [the] presence of General Crook's command. Men of the Twenty-third shot him. They made no mistake. Eight out of ten balls would either of them have been instant death. We are getting a considerable number of substitutes — many good men, but many who are professional villains who desert of course.

We seem to be going up the Valley of the Shenandoah again. We get no letters. None from you since I saw you. But I know you are loving me and only feel anxious lest you are too anxious about me.

* "Life of Hayes," Vol. I, p. 227.

One of the best officers in my command wrote an article on the Winchester fight which will appear in the Gallipolis *Journal* which you would be happy to read.

Well, time is passing rapidly. The campaign is half over. If we can only worry through the Presidential election I shall feel easier. I hope McClellan will be nominated at Chicago. I shall then feel that, in any event, the integrity of the Union is likely to be maintained. A peace nomination at Chicago would array the whole party against the war.

Love to all. Much for thyself, darling.

Ever your

R.

MRS. HAYES.

SHENANDOAH VALLEY, NEAR STRASBURG,
August 14 (Sunday), 1864.

DEAREST: — You see we are again up the Valley following Generals Early and Breckinridge who are in our front. I know nothing as to prospects. I like our present commander, General Sheridan. Our movement seems to relieve Maryland and Pennsylvania. Whether it means more and what, I don't know. We are having rather pleasant campaigning. The men improve rapidly.

Put Winchester down as a Christian town. The Union families took our wounded off the field and fed and nursed them well. Whatever town is burned to square the Chambersburg* account, it will not be Winchester.

Several in my brigade supposed to be dead turn out to be doing well. There are probably fifty families of good Union people (some quite wealthy and first-familyish) in Winchester. It is a splendid town, nearly as large as Chillicothe.

Much love to all. Good-bye, darling.

Ever lovingly, your

R.

MRS. HAYES.

* General McCausland had recently been on a raid in Pennsylvania; had captured Chambersburg, and the citizens being unable to pay the exorbitant levy he demanded, had burned it to the ground.

SHENANDOAH VALLEY, CAMP NEAR STRASBURG, VIRGINIA,
August 14, 1864.

DEAR UNCLE: — You see we are again up the famous Valley; General Sheridan commands the army; General Early and Breckinridge are in our front; they have retired before us thus far; whether it is the purpose to follow and force a battle, I don't know; the effect is to relieve our soil from Rebels.

My health is excellent. Our troops are improving under the easy marches. We shall get well rested doing what the Sixth and Nineteenth Corps of the Potomac ([who] are with us) regard as severe campaigning.

I have heard nothing from home since I saw Lucy on the 10th [of] July. Direct to me: "First Brigade, Second Division, Army of West Virginia, via Harpers Ferry."

Sincerely yours,

R. B. HAYES.

S. BIRCHARD.

Monday, August 15, 1864. — Rebels attacked our picket line and drove it after a brisk skirmish. [The] Twenty-third and Thirty-sixth supporting soon check the Rebels. Our loss two killed, ten wounded. I had some narrow escapes.

CEDAR CREEK, NEAR STRASBURG, August 16, 1864.

DARLING: — We are still here observing the enemy and skirmishing with him daily. Yesterday with [the] Twenty-third and Thirty-sixth had a very brisk skirmish; lost two killed, twelve wounded. One of [the] color corporals in Twenty-third (Corporal Hughes) killed. We are gaining in strength and spirits daily. Numbers supposed to have been killed at Winchester turn out to be only wounded. . . . Love to all.

Affectionately, ever,

R.

MRS. HAYES.

CAMP NEAR CHARLESTOWN SIX MILES (OR FOUR) FROM
HARPERS FERRY, August 23, 1864.

DEAREST: — For the first time since I saw you I received letters from you the day before yesterday. I hope I shall not be so cut off again. It almost pays, however, in the increased gratification the deferred correspondence gives one. You can't imagine how I enjoy your letters. They are a feast indeed.

I had hardly read your letter when we were called out to fight Early. We skirmished all day. Both armies had good positions and both were too prudent to leave them. So, again yesterday. We are at work like beavers today. The men enjoy it. A battle *may* happen at any moment, but I think there will be none at present. Last evening the Twenty-third, Thirty-sixth, and Fifth surprised the Rebel skirmish line and took a number of prisoners, etc., without loss to us. It is called a brilliant skirmish and we enjoyed it much.

You recollect "Mose" Barrett. He was taken prisoner at Lynchburg while on a risky job. I always thought he would get off. Well, he came in at Cumberland with a comrade bringing in *twelve* horses from the Rebel lines!

Colonel Tomlinson was slightly wounded in the skirmish last night, just enough to draw blood and tear his pants below the knee. — One corporal of the color-guard was killed at Winchester — George Hughes, Company B. He died in five minutes without pain.

Winchester is a noble town. Both Union and Secesh ladies devote their whole time to the care of the wounded of the two armies. Their town has been taken and retaken two or three times a day, several times. It has been the scene of five or six battles and many skirmishes. There are about fifty Union families, many of them "F. F.'s." But they are true as steel. Our officers and men all praise them. One queer thing: the whole people turn out to see each army as it comes and welcome their acquaintances and friends. The Rebels are happy when the Secesh soldiers come and vice versa. Three years of this sort of life have schooled them to singular habits.

I have heard heavy skirmishing ever since I began to write.

Now I hear our artillery pounding, but I anticipate no battle here as I think our position too good for Early to risk an assault and I suppose it is not our policy to attack them.

Interrupted to direct Captain Gillis about entrenching on our left. Meantime skirmish firing and cannonading have almost ceased.

I believe you know that I shall feel no apprehension of the war being abandoned if McClellan is elected President. I therefore feel desirous to see him nominated at Chicago. Then, no odds how the people vote, the country is safe. If McClellan is elected the Democracy will speedily become a war party. A great good that will be. I suspect some of our patriots having fat offices and contracts might then on losing them become enamored of peace! I feel more hopeful about things than when I saw you. This Presidential election is the rub. That once over, without outbreak or other calamity, and I think we save the country.

By the by, I think I'll now write this to Uncle Scott. So good-bye. Love to chicks. Ever so much for their grandmother and more for you, darling.

Ever yours,

R.

Mrs. Hayes.

Camp between Harpers Ferry and Charlestown,
Virginia, August 23, 1864.

Dear Mother: — We have a pretty large Rebel army just in front of us. We drove it before us several days until it was reinforced when it slowly drove us back to this point. Here we are in a pretty good position and there seems to be a purpose to fight a general battle here if the enemy choose to attack. Of course, there are frequent skirmishes and affairs in which parts of the army only are engaged which are small battles. So far our success in such affairs has been quite as good as the enemy's. I am inclined to think that there will be no general engagement here. It looks as if we were so well prepared that the Rebels would move in some other direction.

Paine

Camp of Sheridan's Army near Charlestown Va
Aug 24. 1864

Friend S.

Your favor of the 7th came to hand on Tuesday. It was the first I had heard of the doings of the 2 Dist Convention. My thanks for your attention and service in the premises. I cared very little about being a candidate, but having consented to the use of my name I prefered to succeed ———— Your suggestion about getting a furlough to take the Stump was certainly made without reflection. An officer fit for duty who at this crisis would absent himself by hook to electioneer for a

sure I shall do no such thing ———— We are, and for
two weeks past, have been in the immediate presence of
a large Rebel Army. We have skirmishing and similar
affairs constantly. I am not partial in the policy deem —
will not set Halleny and court grant as to the prospect of
a general engagement. The condition and spirit of this
army is good and are growing. I suspect the enemy is
sliding around us towards the Potomac. If they
cross we shall pretty certainly have a meeting ————

Sincerely

Wm H Smith Esq

R B Hayes

"Ought to be Scalped," Letter.

I am now longer without a letter from you than ever before. I know you write but we have had no mails. — My health is good. I heard from Lucy and Uncle Sunday. The weather is now delightful. We have had good rains. — Love to all.

Affectionately, your son,

R.

Mrs. Sophia Hayes.

Camp of Sheridan's Army, August 24, 1864.

Friend Smith: — Your favor of the 7th came to hand on Monday. It was the first I had heard of the doings of the Second District Convention. My thanks for your attention and assistance in the premises. I cared very little about being a candidate, but having consented to the use of my name I preferred to succeed. Your suggestion about getting a furlough to take the stump was certainly made without reflection.

An officer fit for duty who at this crisis would abandon his post to electioneer for a seat in Congress ought to be scalped. You may feel perfectly sure I shall do no such thing.

We are, and for two weeks have been, in the immediate presence of a large Rebel army. We have skirmishing and small affairs constantly. I am not posted in the policy deemed wise at headquarters, and I can't guess as to the prospects of a general engagement. The condition and spirit of this army are good and improving. I suspect the enemy is sliding around us towards the Potomac. If they cross we shall pretty certainly have a meeting.

Sincerely,

R. B. Hayes.*

Wm. H. Smith, Esq.,
   Cincinnati, Ohio.

* This letter was lithographed and widely used as an effective campaign document during the Presidential canvass of 1876.

CAMP SHERIDAN'S ARMY NEAR HALLTOWN, VIRGINIA,
August 27, 1864.

DEAR UNCLE: — I am getting letters at last; heard nothing from anybody for six weeks until last Sunday.

We are entrenching a fine camp here as if a strong Rebel attack was expected. We have the enemy directly in front — supposed to be in force. We have fighting daily. My brigade and the other brigade of Crook's old division are in the front and do the most of it. We had quite a little battle last night — our loss seventy — Rebel about [the] same in killed and wounded and we captured a small South Carolina Rebel regiment entire (one hundred and four [men]). This is the third time we have dashed back on them and picked up their skirmish line. The Rebs *did* intend to go into Maryland and Pennsylvania. *Perhaps* we have stopped them. We don't know yet.

Sheridan's cavalry is splendid. It is the most like the right thing that I have seen during the war.

Discipline and drill have been woefully neglected in our army. General Crook's army is about one-third of the force of Sheridan. Half of his (Crook's) force is capital infantry — the old Kanawha Division and two or three other regiments. The rest is poor enough — as poor as anything here. This is what hurt us at Winchester. The Nineteenth Corps, another third of Sheridan's army, are Yankee troops just returned from Louisiana. We have not seen them fight yet, but they look exceedingly well. We are pretty certain to have heavy fighting before long.

We are having capital times in this army — commanders that suit us (we are rid of Hunter), plenty to eat and wear, and beautiful and healthy camps, with short marches. The best times we have had since our first raid under Crook.

My old regiment keeps up notwithstanding the losses. We have filled up so as to have in the field almost six hundred men — more than any other old regiment.

I see Buckland is nominated [for Congress.] I suppose that will please him much. My college friend, from Michigan, Trowbridge, is a candidate also.

I hope McClellan will be nominated at Chicago. I shall then feel that in any event the war is to be prosecuted until the Union is restored.

Sincerely,

R. B. HAYES.

S. BIRCHARD.

Monday, August 29, 1864. — In camp, five miles to south of Charlestown, lazily listening to heavy firing on our right. McClellan probably nominated. I suspect he will be elected. Not so bad a thing if he is. Reading "Harry Lorrequer."

CAMP SHERIDAN'S ARMY BETWEEN CHARLESTOWN AND
WINCHESTER, August 30, 1864.

DEAREST: — A lucky day. A big mail — letters (all of July) from you, Uncle, Mother, soldiers, their wives, fathers, etc., etc., and newspapers (all July) without end. So I must write short replies. . . .

We are slowly (I think) pushing the enemy back up the Valley. We have some fighting, but no general engagement. Sheridan's splendid cavalry does most of the work. Heretofore, we (the infantry, especially [the] First and Second Brigades) have had to do our own work and that of the cavalry also. Now, if anything, the cavalry does more than its share. It is as if we had six or eight thousand such men as Captain Gilmore's; only better drilled. A great comfort this. Indeed, this is our best month.

The men are fast getting their Kanawha health and spirits back, now that we are rid of Hunter, hard marching night and day, and nothing to eat.

The paymaster, Major Wallace (he inquires after Mrs. Hayes of course), has found us at last. The color-company of [the] Twenty-third is Twelfth men — a fine company of veterans. The color-sergeant is Charles W. Bendel of Maysville, Kentucky, of the Twelfth. He loves the flag as if he thought it his sweetheart — kisses it, fondles it, and bears it proudly in battle.

I hope things turn out so I can be with you about the time you would like me to be at home. Perhaps they will. Love to all.

Affectionately ever, your

R.

Mrs. Hayes.

Camp beyond Charlestown, August 30, 1864.

Dear Uncle: — We got a big mail today; letters from you, Lucy, Mother, and everybody, all written in July. We have had no general engagement, but a world of small affairs the last week. I think the enemy are giving it up. We are slowly pushing them back up the Valley. General Sheridan's splendid cavalry do a great share of the work; we look on and rest. This has been a good month for us. We are a happy army.

I see it is likely McClellan will be nominated. If they don't load him down with too much treasonable peace doctrine, I shall not be surprised at his election. I can see some strong currents which can easily be turned in his favor, provided always that his loyalty is left above suspicion. I have no doubt of his personal convictions and feelings. They are sound enough, but his surroundings are the trouble. We have a paymaster at last.

Sincerely,

R. B. Hayes.

S. Birchard.

[Dr. J. T. Webb, in a letter to his mother from "Camp Charlestown, August 30, 1864," writes: "This is the place the chivalry hung old John Brown some four years since. It has been a *beautiful* place, many elegant residences, fine stores, printing press, and public halls. Now how changed! Not a store in the place, in fact nothing but the women and children and a few old men live here; a few of the fine residences look as though they were kept up, but everything around is sad and gloomy, and then to add to all, the Sixth Corps (some fifteen or twenty thousand troops) as they passed through the place, had all their bands, some twenty, play 'John Brown.'

"I met an old man the other day in the street, and said to him,

'This is the place you hung old John Brown.' 'Yes,' he replied. 'How long since?' said I. 'Four years since and,' added he, 'never had no *peace* since.' "]

Wednesday, August 31, 1864. — McClellan nominated. A happy month in the main. The prospect is much less gloomy than at the beginning of the month. Grant will probably be able to keep his position before Richmond.

CAMP OF SHERIDAN'S ARMY, September 1, 1864.

DEAREST : — Enclosed find state receipt for seven hundred dollars payable at county treasury of Ross County. You can sign the receipt on the back and send it to the treasurer of Ross County by any friend. I suppose it will get around in about four weeks from this time.

The Rebs are reported all gone. With Sheridan's fine cavalry and General Crook's shrewdness they had no business so far from home. We were picking them up in detail. Their loss in the last two weeks was sixteen hundred — mostly prisoners; our loss not over four hundred.

Your two letters in which you speak of Ike Cook [a cousin of Mrs. Hayes] just reached me. I do not see how he can be commissioned as Mr. Hough proposes, but if he can get him commissioned and mustered in any regiment and get him leave to come here, I will get him a good place as aide (aide-de-camp) to myself or somebody else. Of course the regiments in the field need all their promotions. If he is drafted, Mr. Hough can arrange it probably so he can join the Twenty-third or Thirtysixth. I will then make him an orderly which will give him a horse and very easy duty — nothing harder usually than the care of his horse. If he wishes to volunteer, or go as a substitute, he can get big bounties, and as long as I retain my present position he shall be mounted.

All well. Soldiers so jolly. Birch and Webb would like it here. The men are camped in a wooded ravine, officers' quarters on the edge of the wood looking out upon fine open fields and mountains. About a dozen men of Company B, Twenty-third, with their hats swinging ran yelling up to the open ground crying, "See the prisoners! Mosby a prisoner." Of course those next to them ran, the thing took and the whole camp clear to army headquarters a mile off or more, perhaps ten thousand men, followed their example. Officers of course ran, major-generals and all. Then the "sell" was discovered, and such laughing and shouting I never heard before. — A squirrel is started; up the trees go the soldiers and fun alive until he is caught. A mule or a dog gets into camp, and such a time! I am constantly saying, "How the boys would like this."

Well, good-bye dearest. We feel that *this* Valley campaign has been a lucky one, though not very eventful. We shall, I think, go up the Valley again to Winchester and beyond. — Love to all.

Ever affectionately, your

R.

McKinley is a captain now on General Crook's staff.

September 2, A. M. — Your letter of 22nd came last night. You are doing me such a favor in writing often. I now get letters. In [the] September *Harper* is an article "First Time Under Fire" which is very like my case. — Truthful.

Mrs. Hayes.

Camp near Berryville, September 4, [1864].

Sunday evening.

Dearest: — We had one of the fiercest fights yesterday I was ever in. It was between the South Carolina and Mississippi Divisions under General Kershaw and six regiments of the Kanawha Division. My brigade had the severest fighting, but in loss we none of us suffered as might have been expected. We were under cover except when we charged and then darkness helped. We whipped them, taking about one hundred prisoners and killing and wounding a large number. Captain Gillis was killed, shot near the heart, Captain Austin dangerously wounded through the right shoulder, George Brigdon, my color-bearer, bearing the brigade flag, mortally wounded. Only ten others of [the] Twenty-third hurt. Sixty in the brigade killed or wounded. Captain Gillis was a noble, brave man, a good companion, cheerful and generous — a great loss to us. The Rebel army is again just before us.

It was a pleasant battle to get through, all except the loss of Gillis and Brigdon and Austin. I suppose I was never in so much danger before, but I enjoyed the excitement more than ever before. My men behaved so well. One regiment of another division nearly lost all by running away. The Rebels were sure of victory and run [ran] at us with the wildest yells, but our men turned the tide in an instant. This was the crack division of Longstreet. They say they never ran before.

Darling, I think of you always. My apprehension and feeling is a thousand times more for you than for myself. I think we shall have no great battle. We are again entrenched here. Our generals are cautious and wary. — Love to all. The dear boys, God bless them.

Affectionately ever, your

R.

MRS. HAYES.

CAMP OF SHERIDAN'S ARMY NEAR BERRYVILLE, VIRGINIA,
September 6, P. M., 1864.

DEAR UNCLE: — Saturday evening (September 3) my brigade and two regiments of the other brigade of the Kanawha Division fought a very fierce battle with a division of South Carolina and Mississippi troops under Kershaw. We whipped them handsomely after the longest fight I was ever in. Took seventy-five officers and men prisoners and inflicted much severer loss than we suffered. Prisoners say it is the first time their division was ever flogged in fair fight.

My color-bearer was killed and some of the best officers killed or wounded. We have fought nine times since we entered this valley and have been under fire, when men of my command were killed and wounded, probably thirty or forty times since the campaign opened. I doubt if a brigade in Sherman's army has fought more. None has marched half as much. I started with twenty-four hundred men. I now have less than twelve hundred, and almost none of the loss is stragglers.

I hope they will now get Sherman's army to Richmond. It will be taken if they do it promptly, otherwise I fear not for some time.

McClellan would get a handsome soldiers' vote if on a decent platform; as it is, he will get more than any other Democrat could get.

I am glad that you feel as you do about my safety. It is the best philosophy not to borrow trouble of the future. We are still confronted by the enemy. I can't help thinking that the fall of Atlanta will carry them back to Richmond. What a glorious career Sherman's army has had! That is the best army in the world. Lee's army is next. There is just as much difference between armies, divisions, brigades, etc., as between individuals. Crook, I think, has the best and the worst division in this army. Of the one you can always count upon it, that it will do all that can be expected, and of the other that it will behave badly. Sincerely,

R. B. HAYES.

September 8. — Nothing new except that the Rebels have drawn back perhaps ten miles from our front, possibly gone back to Richmond.

S. BIRCHARD.

CAMP AT SUMMIT POINT, VIRGINIA, September 9, 1864.

DEAREST: — I received today your good letter of the 30th. I think I have got the most, perhaps, all of your back letters.

. . .

Speaking of politics: It is quite common for youngsters, adopting their parents' notions, to get very bitter talk into their innocent little mouths. I was quite willing Webb should hurrah for Vallandigham last summer with the addition, "and a rope to hang him." But I feel quite different about McClellan. He is on a mean platform and is in bad company, but I do not doubt his personal loyalty and he has been a soldier, and what is more a soldier's friend. No man ever treated the private soldier better. No commander was ever more loved by his men. I therefore want my boys taught to think and talk well of General McClellan. I think he will make the best President of any Democrat. If on a sound platform, I could support him. Do not be alarmed. I do not think he will be elected. The improved condition of our military affairs injures his chances very materially. He will not get so large [an] army vote as his friends seem to expect. With reasonably good luck in the war, Lincoln will go in.

Have you any picture of Captain Gillis and Brigdon? Captain Austin had his arm amputated at the shoulder and died the night after. There was no saving him. Lieutenant Hubbard, supposed killed at Winchester, escaped from the Rebels and is now with us, well and strong. About half of the Fifth Virginia Volunteers leave us today. Colonel Enochs, Captain Poor, and others remain.

I do not know where the enemy is today. They were still in our front the day before yesterday. . . .

As ever your

MRS. HAYES.   R.

[Dr. J. T. Webb writing to his nephews, the Hayes boys, from Camp Summit Point, Virginia, September 11, 1864, says:— "Since we left Charleston in April last, the Twenty-third Regiment has had three captains killed and three wounded, two lieutenants killed and three wounded, and about four hundred and fifty privates killed and wounded. We have *marched on foot* twelve hundred miles, travelled on steamboats and cars five hundred; fought six or eight battles, (*worsted* in but one — at Winchester), [and] skirmished with the enemy in front or rear *sixty* days. Since we came into Sheridan's Army we have had comparatively easy times, as far as marching is concerned. In the way of skirmishing our division has had more than its share. Every few days an order came for us to go out and see where and what the enemy was doing. On one of these expeditions we killed and captured quite a number of the enemy without losing a man. This was fun for me. It was quite a battle, and our friends, back in camp, from the amount of firing, supposed we were having a hard time, and sent out thirty ambulances to carry in our wounded. Imagine their surprise when we returned them all empty. In our other skirmishes we lost more or less each time, but invariably worsted the enemy."]

HEADQUARTERS FIRST BRIGADE, SECOND DIVISION, ARMY OF WEST VIRGINIA, SUMMIT POINT, VIRGINIA, September 12, 1864.

DEAR UNCLE: — We have had no severe fighting since the third. The frequent rains have filled the Potomac so it is no longer fordable. I look for no attempt now on the part of the Rebels to get over the river and think there will be very little fighting unless we attack. We are gaining strength daily. Our policy seems to be not to attack unless the chances are greatly in our favor. Military affairs wear a much better look. Our armies are rapidly filling up. I shall not be surprised if Grant should soon find himself able to make important moves.

I like McClellan's letter. It is an important thing. It is the best evidence to Europe and the South that the people intend to prosecute the war until the Union is re-established. Still, if things continue as favorable as they now are, I think Lincoln will be elected.

I see that Mr. Long is not renominated. I supposed he would be and that my election over him was quite a sure thing. Against Mr. Lord the result will depend on the general drift matters take. I am not a-going to take it to heart if I am beaten. "It's of no consequence at all," as Mr. Toots would say. Mr. Lord's wife and family are particular and intimate friends of my wife and family. His wife is a sister of Stephenson's wife. Divers friends of his and mine will be in a worry how to vote, I suspect.

I am glad you are out of debt — a good place to be out of in the times a-coming. . . .

Sincerely,

R. B. HAYES.

S. BIRCHARD.

CAMP NEAR SUMMIT POINT, VIRGINIA, September 13, 1864.

DEAREST: — We have had heavy fall rains and are now having windy, cold fall weather. We are, however, very comfortably camped, clad, and fed.

No fighting of importance since the third. The enemy was still in our front yesterday morning. A division is now out feeling of their lines — the cannonading indicates that they have not all gone.

McClellan, I see, has written a pretty good war letter. I suspect it will make him trouble among the genuine copperheads. Mr. Lord declines running in the Second District and Mr. Butler is put in his place! I think both of them are good war men and that they do not differ much from me. A funny mix it is.

We have had two votes in this camp. The Thirteenth Virginia, Colonel Brown, gave three hundred and seventy-five for Lincoln, fifteen for McClellan. The Ninth Virginia two hundred and seventy for Lincoln, none (!) for McClellan. The platform and Pendleton destroys his chances in the army.

I dreamed about you and the boys last night. I hope you are as well as I thought you looked. . . . Love to all

Affectionately ever

R.

MRS. HAYES.

CAMP NEAR SUMMIT POINT, VIRGINIA, September 17, 1864.

DEAREST: — Did Carrington leave a revolver (pistol) with you when he left [the] little sorrel? I have forgotten about it.

General McClellan has written a pretty good Union and war letter, which I see is bringing the Democratic party over to our side on the war question. If he should be elected, — an event not now seeming probable, — I have no doubt that the war will go right on. The chief difference between us is on slavery, and I have no doubt that when the burden and responsibility of the war is on the Democracy, they will rapidly "get religion," as Sam Cary would say, "on that subject."

General Grant is now here in consultation with General Sheridan. The recruits and convalescents will soon fill up his ranks and I look for an active fall campaign.

September 18. Sunday P. M. — As usual the order to move comes on Sunday. We go on [in] what direction or why I don't know. But, darling, I love you and the dear ones. — Good-bye.

Ever affectionately,

R.

Mrs. Hayes.

Monday, September 19, 1864. — Marched fifteen miles and gained the battle of Winchester. Colonel Duval and Captain Hastings wounded near the close of the battle. I took command of the Second (old "Kanawha") Division at end of day.

Tuesday, September 20. — Marched fifteen miles to Cedar Creek (near Strasburg). Early badly beaten yesterday; twenty-six hundred prisoners taken, swords, guns, and flags. Rebels halt at Fisher's Hill. We hide in the woods after dark.

Wednesday, September 21. — In camp at Cedar Creek. Crook's troops concealed in woods. Rebels in a strong position on Fisher's Hill beyond Strasburg with strong works; we are trying to turn it.

Camp near Strasburg, Virginia, September 21, 1864.

Dearest: — As I anticipated when I added a few words in pencil to a half finished letter last Sunday, we left camp to seek General Early and give him battle. We met him at Winchester and, as I telegraphed, gained a great victory. General Crook's command in general, and my brigade and the Second (Kanawha) Division in particular, squared up the balance left against us on the 24th of July at the same place. The fighting began at daylight Monday (19th), with our cavalry. Then the Sixth Corps fighting pretty well, joined in; and about 10:30 A. M. the Nineteenth [Corps] took part — some portions of it behaving badly, losing ground, two guns, and some prisoners. We in the meantime were guarding the wagons (!). Since the fight they say Crook's command was the *reserve!*

By noon the battle was rather against [us]. The Rebels were jubilant and in Winchester were cheering and rejoicing over the

BRIGADIER-GENERAL RUTHERFORD B. HAYES (BREVET MAJOR-GENERAL) AND STAFF.

JOSEPH T. WEBB, SURGEON.   LIEUTENANT WILLIAM   LIEUTENANT O. J. WOOD.

LIEUTENANT JAS. W. DELAY.   MCKINLEY, JR.   CAPTAIN RUSSELL HASTINGS.

BRIGADIER-GENERAL RUTHERFORD B. HAYES.

victory. We were sent for. General Crook in person superintended the whole thing. At one o'clock, having passed around on to the Rebel left, we passed under a fire of cannon and musketry and pushed direct for a battery on their extreme flank. This division was our extreme right. My brigade in front, supported by Colonel White's old brigade. As soon as we felt their fire we moved swiftly forward going directly at the battery. The order was to walk fast, keep silent, until within about one hundred yards of the guns, and then with a yell to charge at full speed. We passed over a ridge and were just ready to begin the rush when we came upon a deep creek with high banks, boggy, and perhaps twenty-five yards wide.

The Rebel fire now broke out furiously. Of course the line stopped. To stop was death. To go on was probably the same; but on we started again. My horse plunged in and mired down hopelessly, just as by frantic struggling he reached about the middle of the stream. I jumped off, and down on all fours, succeeded in reaching the Rebel side — but alone. Perhaps some distance above or below others were across. I was about the middle of the brigade and saw nobody else, but hundreds were struggling in the stream. It is said several were drowned. I think it not true. (N. B. I just received the enclosed with orders to have it read to every man in my division. I send you the original. Save it as precious.)* The next man over (I don't know but he beat me — but —) was the adjutant of the Thirty-sixth.

Soon they came flocking, all regiments mixed up — all order gone. [There was] no chance of ever reforming, but pell-mell, over the obstructions, went the crowd. Two cannons were cap-

---

* Two yellow flimsies. One giving a despatch of September 20 from Secretary Stanton to General Sheridan, reading: "Please accept for yourself and your gallant army the thanks of the President and the Department for your great battle and brilliant victory of yesterday. . . . One hundred guns were fired here at noon today in honor of your victory."

The other a despatch of the same date from General Grant, reading: "I have just received the news of your great victory and ordered each of the army corps to fire a salute of one hundred guns in honor of it at 7 o'clock tomorrow morning."

tured; the rest run off. The whole of Crook's Command (both divisions) were soon over, with the general swinging his sword, and the Rebel position was successfully flanked, and victory in prospect for the first time that day.

We chased them three to five hundred yards, when we came in sight of a second line, strongly posted. We steadily worked towards them under a destructive fire. Sometimes we would be brought to a standstill by the storm of grape and musketry, but the flags (*yours* as advanced as any) would be pushed on and a straggling crowd would follow. With your flag were [the] Twenty-third, Thirty-fourth, Thirty-sixth, and Seventy-first men, and so of all the others. Officers on horseback were falling faster than others, but all were suffering. (*Mem.:* — Two men got my horse out and I rode him all day, but he was ruined.)

Things began to look dark. The Nineteenth Corps next on our left were in a splendid line, but they didn't push. They stood and fired at long range! Many an anxious glance was cast that way. They were in plain sight, but no, or very little, effective help came from that handsome line. It was too far off. At the most critical moment a large body of that splendid cavalry, with sabres drawn, moved slowly around our right beyond the creek. Then at a trot and finally with shouts at a gallop [they] charged right into the Rebel lines. We pushed on and away broke the Rebels. The cavalry came back, and an hour later and nearly a mile back, the same scene again; and a third time; and the victory was ours just at sundown.

My division [was] entering Winchester as the Rebels were leaving, far in advance of all other troops. My division commander had fallen (Colonel Duval) badly, not dangerously, wounded, and I commanded the division in the closing scenes. The colonel of the other brigade, Captain Hastings, one of my orderlies (Johnny Kaufman), and hosts of others [were] wounded. You will see the lists. No intimate friends killed.

It was a great victory, but a much greater battle to take part in than the results would indicate. I certainly never enjoyed anything more than the last three hours. Dr. Joe was perfectly happy, the last two hours at least — always after the first cavalry charge. We felt well. The sum of it is, [the] Sixth Corps fought well; [the] Nineteenth only so-so. Crook's skill and his men turned the Rebel left making victory possible, and the cavalry saved it when it was in danger of being lost.

Of course this is imperfect. I saw but little of what occurred. For that reason I would never have a letter of mine shown outside of the family. There is too much risk of errors. For instance, crossing the creek, I could only see one hundred yards or so up and down. Forty men may have beaten me over, but I didn't see them.

Colonel Duval has gone home. I command the division. Colonel Devol of the Thirty-sixth commands the First Brigade in my stead. We are following the retreating Rebels. They will get into an entrenched position before fighting again, and I suspect we shall not assault them in strong works. So I look for no more fighting with General Early this campaign. — Love to all.

Affectionately,

R.

Send this to Mother and Uncle with request to return it to you.

P. S. — A comment on this letter. I am told that the creek we crossed was a swail or "sloo" [slough] three hundred yards long, and that my line above and below me crossed it easily — thus separating still more the different parts of my line. No one knows a battle except the little part he sees.

Friday, September 23. — Marched twelve miles to Woodstock. Rebels outran the first Bull Run great rout. Woodstock a pretty reigon. Bath and clean woollen today.

WOODSTOCK, VIRGINIA, September 23, 1864.

DEAREST: — We fought the enemy again [yesterday] at Fisher's Hill near Strasburg. They had fortified a naturally strong position with great industry. It seemed impregnable, but General Crook contrived an attack, by going up a mountainside, which turned their position. My *division* led the attack. The victory was [as] complete as possible and, strangest of all, our loss is almost nothing.

Captain Douglass sits near me in excellent health. We are following the enemy. Shall be out of hearing for some time.

In the rush after the Rebels no flag was so conspicuous as yours. It seems a trifle larger than others, is bright and new, and as it went double-quick at the head of a yelling host for five miles, I thought how you would enjoy the sight. The color-bearer told me he should go to see you when the war was over. He is an American German, with a dark Indian face, full of spirit.

Captain Hastings' wound is severe but not dangerous. Captain Stewart, the best captain in [the] Thirteenth, ditto. Captain Slack killed. In the fight yesterday none were killed of your friends or acquaintances and very few hurt.

A train goes in a minute and I must send a line to Mother. — Dr. Joe perfectly triumphant. He was at the head of the host yesterday. — Love to all.

Affectionately ever,

R.

P. S. — Since the wounding of Colonel Duval, I command the splendid old Kanawha Division — two brigades, now not over three thousand strong, but no better fighters live.

MRS. HAYES.

WOODSTOCK, VIRGINIA, September 23, 1864.

DEAR MOTHER: — We have gained two great victories this week. The first was after a fierce and long battle, in which we lost heavily. The last unwounded man of my staff was badly wounded; one orderly ditto; two horses killed, rode by my aides. I am unhurt and in good health. We are in pursuit and will soon get out of the reach of mails. — In haste. Love to all.

Affectionately, your son,

R.

MRS. SOPHIA HAYES.

Saturday, September 24. — Marched five [miles] to Edinburg, seven to Mount Jackson, seven and one-fourth to New Market — nineteen and one-fourth [in all]. A fine day; fine scenery.

Rebels stood a short time at Reed's Hill near Mount Jackson, but soon retreated; admit a bad defeat — loss of seventeen pieces of artillery and five thousand men. Camp facing the gap into Luray Valley.

Sunday, September 25. — March nine [miles] to Sparta and nine to Harrisonburg — eighteen. A fine town and a fine day. General Early reported [to have] gone over into Luray Valley to go through Blue Ridge. I conjecture he will go to railroad and Lynchburg. This is a splendid day, a fine town.

Monday, September 26. — At camp near Harrisonburg. Receive Sheridan's telegraphic report of our last battle. Crook's command gets proper credit for once.

HARRISONBURG, VIRGINIA, September 26, 1864.

DEAREST: — Another victory and almost nobody hurt. The loss in my division (you know I now command General Crook's old Division, Twenty-third and Thirty-sixth Ohio and Fifth and Thirteenth Virginia, Thirty-fourth and Ninety-first Ohio and Ninth and Fourteenth Virginia) is less than one hundred. Early's Rebel veterans, Jackson's famous old corps, made our Bull Run defeat respectable. They ran like sheep. The truth is, General Crook outwitted them. The other generals opposed his plan but Sheridan trusts him absolutely and *allowed* him to begin the attack on his own plan. But I have written all this.

Love to the boys. Regards to Uncle Scott and all on the hill. I got his good letter just before our last fight.

Affectionately ever,

R.

MRS. HAYES.

HARRISONBURG, VIRGINIA, September 26, 1864.

DEAR UNCLE: — You have heard enough about our great victories at Winchester and Fisher's Hill. I will say only a word. No one man can see or know what passes on all parts of a battle-field. Each one describes the doings of the corps, division, or what not, that he is with. Now, all the correspondents are

33

with the Sixth and Nineteenth Corps and the cavalry command. General Crook has nobody to write him or his command up. They are of course lost sight of. At Winchester at noon, the Sixth and Nineteenth Corps had been worsted. In the afternoon, General Crook (who is the brains of the whole thing) with his command turned the Rebel left and gained the victory. The cavalry saved it from being lost after it was gained. My brigade *led* the attack on the Rebel left, but *all* parts of Crook's command did their duty. The Sixth Corps fought well, the Nineteenth failed somewhat, and the cavalry was splendid and efficient throughout. This is my say-so.

My division entered the fight on the extreme right of the *infantry*, Merritt's splendid cavalry on our right, and Averell still further on our right. We ended the fight on the extreme left. The Rebels retreated from our right to our left, so that we went in at the rear and came out at the front, my flag being the first into and through Winchester. My division commander was wounded late in the fight and I commanded the division from that time. It is the Second, General Crook's old division.

At Fisher's Hill the turning of the Rebel left was planned and executed by General Crook against the opinions of the other generals. *My division led* again. General Sheridan is a whole-souled, brave man (like Dr. Webb) and believes in Crook, his old class and roommate at West Point. Intellectually he is not General Crook's equal, so that, as I said, General Crook is the brains of this army.

The completeness of our victories can't be exaggerated. If Averell had been up to his duty at Fisher's Hill, Mr. Early and all the rest would have fallen into our hands. As it is, we have, I think, from the two battles five thousand Rebel prisoners unhurt — three thousand wounded, five hundred killed; twenty-five pieces of artillery, etc., etc.

In the Fisher's Hill battle, the Sheridan Cavalry was over the mountains going around to the rear. This, as it turned out, was unfortunate. If they had been with us instead of Averell, there would have been nothing left of Early. *General Averell is relieved*.

I lost one orderly, my adjutant-general, Captain Hastings, and field officers in *all* regiments, wounded.   No officers especially intimate with me killed.   I had my scene which I described in a letter to Lucy.

Sincerely,

R.

S. BIRCHARD.

ONE HUNDRED MILES SOUTH OF THE POTOMAC,
HARRISONBURG, VIRGINIA, September 27, 1864.

DEAREST: — We have left the further pursuit of Early's broken army to cavalry and small scouting parties.   We are resting near a beautiful town like Delaware.   We suspect our campaigning is over and that we shall ultimately go back towards Martinsburg.

It has been a most fortunate and happy campaign for us all — I mean, for all who are left!   For no one more so than for me. My command has been second to none in any desirable thing. We have had the best opportunity to act and have gone through with it fortunately.

My chief anxiety these days is for you.   I hope soon to hear that your troubles are happily over. — Much love to the dear ones and oceans for yourself.

Affectionately ever, your

R.

MRS. HAYES.

ONE HUNDRED MILES SOUTH OF THE POTOMAC,
September 27, 1864.

DEAR UNCLE: — Our work seems to be done for the present. The cavalry and small scouting parties are after the scattered and broken army.   It looks as if we should, after [a] while, return towards the Potomac.   We are resting in the magnificent Valley of Virginia.   A most happy campaign it has been.   Our chance to act has been good, and it has been well improved. My immediate command is one of the very finest, and has done all one could desire.

There are five or six brigadier-generals and one or two major-generals, sucking their thumbs in offices at Harpers Ferry and elsewhere, who would like to get my command. One came out here yesterday to ask for it, but General Crook tells them he has all the commanders he wants and sends them back. There is not a general officer in General Crook's army and has not been in this campaign.

Things look well in all directions. Lincoln must be re-elected easily, it seems to me. Rebel prisoners — the common soldiers — all talk one way: "Tired of this rich man's war; determined to quit if it lasts beyond this campaign."

                              Sincerely,

                                        R. B. HAYES.

S. BIRCHARD.

                    HARRISONBURG, VIRGINIA, September 27, 1864.

DEAR MOTHER: — We are now one hundred miles south of Harpers Ferry. Our victories have so broken and scattered the Rebel army opposed to us that it is no use for infantry to pursue further, except in small parties scouting the woods and mountains. The cavalry are going on. We are resting in a lovely valley. I rather think that our campaigning is over for the present. It has been exceedingly fortunate. General Crook's whole command has done conspicuously well. I commanded in the last fighting the fine division formerly commanded by General Crook. We led the attack on both days. It is the pleasantest command a man could have. Half of the men are from Ohio, the rest from West Virginia.

I *think* we shall stay here some time and then go back towards Martinsburg. — Love to all.

                              Affectionately,

                                        R. B. HAYES.

MRS. SOPHIA HAYES.

                    ————————

[Dr. J. T. Webb, in a letter from "Camp nigh Harrisonburg, Virginia, September 28, 1864," describes the battle of Fisher's Hill in a graphic way:

"[After the battle on the Opequon] the enemy fell back to Fisher's Hill, some eighteen miles from Winchester. This was supposed to be impregnable, the key to the Valley. Here they fortified themselves and boasted, as you will see by the Richmond papers, that they could not be ousted. We followed on. At this point the Valley is quite narrow, North Mountain and Middle Mountain approaching each other, say within three miles of each other. The mountainsides are steep and rough. Now, just here, a creek runs directly across the valley, whose banks are steep and high on which the Rebels have erected strong earthworks. To attack these would be worse than death. The Rebels felt quite secure. We could see them evidently enjoying themselves. After looking about a day or so, Crook proposed to flank them on their left again, this time climbing up the side of the mountain. So after marching all day, at four P. M., we found ourselves entirely inside of their works, and they knew nothing of it. Again Crook orders a charge, and with yells off they go, sweeping down the line of works, doubling up the Rebels on each other. They were thunderstruck; swore we had crossed the mountain. The men rushed on, no line, no order, all yelling like madmen. [The] Rebs took to their heels, each striving to get himself out of the way. Cannon after cannon were abandoned (twenty-two captured). Thus we rushed on until we reached their right. Here again [as on the 19th] darkness saved them once more. Such a foot-race as this was is not often met with. The Rebs say Crook's men are devils.

"It was after this charge, as we were encamped on the roadside, [that] the Sixth and Nineteenth [Corps] passing gave us three cheers. Crook had given Averell his orders to charge just so soon as the enemy broke, but as usual he was drunk or something else and failed to come to time. Thus he wasted the grandest opportunity ever offered for capturing the enemy and gaining credit for himself. Sheridan ordered him to the rear, relieving him of his command. This same Averell was the sole cause of Crook's disaster at Winchester. He failed constantly on the Lynchburg raid; now he lost everything almost, and is merely relieved. Had he followed up the enemy after they were dispersed, he could have captured all their train, cannon, etc., besides scattering and capturing all of the men. Sheridan's Cavalry proper had been sent round to turn their flank through

Luray Valley, but the Rebs had fortified the pass and they could not reach us. As it is, however, we have whipped the flower of the Rebel army; they are scattered in all directions. We have captured about four thousand prisoners (sound) and three thousand wounded, killing some five or seven hundred.

"Our cavalry are still pursuing. All this day we can hear artillery firing. It is reported that yesterday we captured or caused them to burn one hundred waggons. I presume the infantry will not move much farther in this direction.

"The men all feel fine. We have 'wiped out' Winchester. Notwithstanding the Rebs had choice of position, [the number of] our killed and wounded does not equal theirs. They have lost four or five generals; colonels and majors, any quantity. Many are coming in from the mountain. All say they are tired of this war. The people are getting tired, and many noted Rebels are willing and anxious to close this out."]

HARRISONBURG, VIRGINIA, September 28, (5 A. M.), 1864.

DEAREST: — We have marching orders this morning. Where to, etc., I don't yet know. I think we shall have no more heavy fighting. You will know where we are before this reaches you through the papers. We shall probably be out of the reach of you for several days.

My thoughts are of you these days more than usual and I always think of my darling a good deal, as I ought to do of such a darling as mine. You know I am

Your ever affectionate

MRS. HAYES.   R.

HARRISONBURG, VIRGINIA, September 29, P. M., 1864.

DEAREST: — The cavalry and part of our infantry are in Staunton and on the road to Gordonsville. They are merely keeping up the big scare. The Sixth and Nineteenth Corps are eight miles on the Staunton Road. We are enjoying ourselves. We rather *expect* and *prefer* to start back towards Winchester soon, but we *know* nothing.

I write so often these days because I feel anxious about you and because I am uncertain about the delivery of my letters within our lines. — Love to all. Much for your own private self, my darling.

Affectionately, your

R.

P. S. — It is now universally conceded in this army that Crook and his men *did it*.

Mrs. Hayes.

Harrisonburg, Virginia, October 1, 1864.

Dearest : — The First Brigade has gone out six miles to grind up the wheat in that neighborhood — three mills there — and Dr. Joe has gone with them.

Colonel Powell just returned from Staunton. They burned all wheat stacks, mills, and barns with grain, and are driving in all cattle and horses. Large numbers of families are going out with us. Dunkards and Mennonites, good quiet people, are generally going to Ohio. I hope we shall move back in a day or two.

Our wounded all doing well. Only seven deaths in all the hospitals at Winchester. Miss Dix and Presidents of Christian and Sanitary Commissions with oceans of luxuries and comforts there, and the good people of Winchester to cook and help. [The] Sixth Corps take one street; [the] Nineteenth, the Main Street; and Crook's, the Eastern. Rebel [wounded] and ours now there about three thousand. Twenty-third, thirty-three; Fifth, eight; Thirty-sixth, thirteen, and Thirteenth, twenty. All the rest gone home. Captain Hiltz, Twelfth-Twenty-third, lost his leg. As soon as the operation was over and the effect of the chloroform passed off, he looked at the stump and said: "No more eighteen dollars for boots to sutler now; nine dollars [will] shoe me!" Captain Hastings doing well; heard from him last night.

General Lightburn came up a day or two ago with staff and orderlies and asked General Crook for the command of my division. He had reported along the road that he was going out to take General Crook's old division. General Crook told him the division was officered to his satisfaction and ordered him back to Harpers Ferry to await orders.

Colonel Duval is doing well and hopes to return by the last of this month (October).

Colonel Comly keeps a pretty full diary. He has sent extracts containing the two battles home. They will probably appear in the Cincinnati *Gazette*.

I shall send a Rebel's diary to the *Commercial*. It was taken from his pocket at Winchester.

We rather expect to go into something like winter quarters soon after getting back to Winchester or Martinsburg. Of course there will be extensive campaigning done yet, but we think we shall now be excused. I speak of Crook's Command. — Love to all. Affectionately ever,

R.

MRS. HAYES.

Harrisonburg, Sunday, October 2, 1864. — A fine day. First Brigade six miles out grinding; came in after dark. Cannonading in front. A hegira of Dunkards and others. Grant orders all provisions destroyed so "a crow flying from Staunton to Winchester must carry his rations."

HARRISONBURG, VIRGINIA, Sunday, October 2, 1864.

DEAREST: — I am writing to you so often these days because I am thinking of you more anxiously than usual, and on account of the great uncertainty of our communications. There are some indications today that we shall push on further south. You will know if we do by the papers. If so we shall be cut off from friends more than ever.

Dr. Joe has gone with the First Brigade out about six miles to grind up the wheat at some mills in that quarter. It seems to be a great place for sport. They are having a jolly time.

We hear from Winchester today. One of our orderlies, Johnny Kaufman, died of his wound. Captain Hastings and the rest are all doing well.

Great droves of cattle and sheep are going past us north. Everything eatable is taken or destroyed. No more supplies to Rebels from this valley. No more invasions in great force by this route will be possible.

P. M. — Indications look more like going on with our campaign. I would prefer going towards my darling and the chicks. Still, I like to move. We came here a week ago. After this active year I feel bored when we stop longer than a day or two. I have tried all available plans to spend time. I read old *Harpers*, two of Mrs. Hall's novels, — you know I don't "affect" women's novels. I find myself now reading "East Lynne." Nothing superior in it, but I can read anything.

For the first time in five or six days, we are just startled by cannon firing and musketry, perhaps four or five miles in our front. It is probably Rebel cavalry pitching into our foraging parties, or making a reconnaisance to find whether we have left.

"Have your men under arms," comes from General Crook. I ask, "Is it thought to be anything?" "No, but General Sheridan sends the order to us." Well, we get under arms. This letter is put in my ammunition box. I mount my horse and see that all are ready. The firing gets more distant and less frequent. "We have driven them," somebody conjectures, and I return to my tent, "East Lynne," and my darling, no wiser than ever.

I am in receipt of yours of [the] 13th. The mail goes back immediately. Good-bye. Blessings on your head.

Affectionately ever,

R.

Mrs. Hayes.

Camp south of Harrisonburg, Virginia,
Sunday, October 2, 1864.

Dear Mother: — I have supposed that we would soon go back, at least as far as Winchester. We have destroyed the railroad from Richmond to Staunton in several places, and all the provisions and stores at Staunton and for a considerable distance south of that point. It would seem to be impossible for the Rebels to get supplies from this valley, or even to march a large force through it for the purpose of invading Maryland and Pennsylvania. There are now some appearances which would indicate that we may push on further south. We have no regular communication now with the States, and if we go further we shall probably be for some time out of hearing of friends.

All things with us are going on prosperously. The people here are more inclined to submit than ever before.

I have heard nothing from Ohio later than the 8th — almost a month. I still *hope* that we shall be allowed to return north. — Love to all.   Affectionately, your son,

R.

MRS. SOPHIA HAYES.

Tuesday, October 4. — My birthday — forty-two. Wrote to mother. Lieutenant Meigs killed last night by guerrillas, three miles south of camp. Houses on the road for five miles burned by order of General Sheridan. Not according to my views or feelings.*

HARRISONBURG, VIRGINIA, October 4, 1864.

DEAR MOTHER: — I celebrate my forty-second birthday by writing a few letters.

We have had a few gloomy days — wet, windy, and cold — but this morning it cleared off bright and warm. The camps look prettier than usual. Many flags are floating gaily and every one seems hopeful and happy. There is a universal desire to return towards the Potomac. We shall probably soon be gratified, as we have pretty nearly finished work in this quarter.

I am in excellent health. This life probably wears men out a little sooner than ordinary occupations, even if they escape the dangers from battle and the like, but I am certain that we are quite as healthy as people who live in houses. — My love to all.

Affectionately, your son,

R.

MRS. SOPHIA HAYES.

* The order was mitigated. Only a few houses near the scene of the murder were burned.

[Thursday, October 6, the Union forces began to retire down the Valley. That day Hayes's division marched north twenty-four miles to Mount Jackson. The next day it made Woodstock, fourteen miles. Then]

Saturday, October 8. — Marched eleven miles to Fisher's Hill. Ascended Round Top Mountain, Rebel signal station. A fine view of the Valley, marred by the fires and smoke of burning stacks and barns. A bitter, windy, cold afternoon and night. Rebel cavalry harrassing our rear.

Sunday, October 9. — Felt a great repugnance to fighting another battle last night; all right this morning. Our cavalry flogged the Rebels handsomely today. Took nine pieces of artillery and many prisoners and train. Captain H. J. Farnsworth. a quartermaster, reported to my division.

HEADQUARTERS SECOND INFANTRY DIVISION A. W. VA., CAMP NEAR FISHER'S HILL, SOUTH OF STRASBURG, VIRGINIA,

October 10, 1864.

DEAREST: — I am very anxious to hear from you. I hope you are doing well.

We have slowly returned from our splendid campaign to this point. The Rebel cavalry impudently undertook to harass us as we approached here. General Sheridan halted his army and sent his cavalry back supported by two of my infantry regiments (Ninth and Fourteenth Virginia) and gave them a complete flogging, capturing their cannon (nine), train, and many prisoners. They were chased from the field at a run for twenty miles.

I don't know when we shall return to Winchester, but probably soon. This valley will feed and forage no more Rebel armies. It is completely and awfully devastated — "a belt of desolation," as Sherman calls it for one hundred and twenty-five miles or more from our lines. — My love to all.

Ever affectionately,

R.

P. S. — Just heard through Captain Douglass (10 A. M.) that I am the father of another boy. God bless the boy — *all* the boys — and above all the mother. — H.

MRS. HAYES.

CAMP NEAR STRASBURG, VIRGINIA, October 12, 1864.

DEAR UNCLE SCOTT: — I am much obliged for your letter announcing the arrival of the big boy and the welfare of his mother. I had been looking for news somewhat anxiously. I intended to have had a daughter, but I failed to see the new moon over my right shoulder. I am glad to hear he promises to be a good boy, as Aunt Phœbe writes Dr. Joe.

We had a quiet election here yesterday. My old brigade, Ohio voters, were unanimous — the two veteran regiments voting as follows: Twenty-third — two hundred and sixty-six Union; Thirty-sixth — two hundred and fifty-nine ditto, and no Copperheads. The whole of Crook's Command stands fourteen hundred Union and two hundred Democrats in round numbers — three-fourths of the Democrats being in companies from Monroe and Crawford [counties].

Our campaign in the Valley is supposed to be ended. It winds up with a most signal cavalry victory. It is believed that the Sixth and Nineteenth Corps with Sheridan's splendid cavalry will join Grant and that Crook's hard-worked command will have the duty of guarding the Baltimore and Ohio Railroad in winter quarters. We hope this is correct. If so, I shall probably get home by Christmas for a good visit.

I am compelled to write this on the half sheet of your letter. — Love to all.

                                  Sincerely,
                                            R. B. HAYES.

MATTHEW SCOTT COOK.
    Chillicothe, Ohio.

Thursday, October 13. — Today Rebels surprised us. The first intimation we had of them, a battery opened on my Second Brigade marching to put a signal station on Massanutten Mountain. Colonel Thoburn made a reconnaisance, was forced back losing Colonel Wells, Thirty-fourth Massachusetts, and one hundred and fifty men, after a great fight.

Friday, October 14. — I had five killed and six wounded by the Rebel battery yesterday. Colonel Brown, Thirteenth, went out and established a picket line easily. General Early very timid. Captain Little, five days in Libby [Prison, at Richmond], says Mosby's men are gentlemen.

Saturday, October 15. — Rebels still in front. Election said to be favorable. Captain Hastings I fear is worse. Mosby captures a railroad train. General Angus gets Mosby's artillery. Mosby gets three hundred thousand [dollars].

CEDAR CREEK NEAR STRASBURG, VIRGINIA, Saturday
Morning before breakfast, October 15, 1864.

MY DARLING WIFE: — Oceans of love for you and the fine new boy — yes, and for the boys all. You may be sure I shall come to see you as soon as affairs here will allow. . . .

Early with a large re-inforcement came up to us on Thursday evening. He evidently supposed that the Sixth and Nineteenth Corps were gone. The Sixth was gone. He came up very boldly. But after a brisk affair, learning that the Nineteenth was still here, he hastily withdrew and took up his old entrenched position on Fisher's Hill. Yesterday he was at work fixing his left on North Mountain where we turned him before. The Sixth came back yesterday. This morning the Sixth and Nineteenth are moving out as if for battle.

In any event, you know all I would wish to say. So, think of me, dearest, as ever your

LOVING HUSBAND, R.

MRS. HAYES.

CAMP NEAR STRASBURG, VIRGINIA, October 15, 1864.

DEAR MOTHER: — We have remained quiet in camp during this week with the exception of one afternoon's skirmishing. Early, or somebody with a considerable force, is entrenched near us. We may fight another battle with him, but I have no information as to the intention.

Colonel Comly is very well. He has had great luck to get through all this fighting with so little injury. He and the Twenty-third have been in all the hottest places. Over twenty officers in the regiment have been killed or wounded since the first of May. . . . My love to all.

Affectionately, your son,

R.

Mrs. Sophia Hayes.

Camp near Strasburg, Virginia, October 15, 1864.

Dear Uncle: — We are resting. Early, reinforced, came up a few days ago, evidently thinking a good part of our army had gone to Grant. Finding his mistake, he moved back to his old fortifications on Fisher's [Hill], and is now there digging and chopping like mad. What we are to do about it, I can't tell. It must be a serious business for the Rebels to feed an army there now.

I have not yet heard from the Ohio election. The two Ohio regiments in my old brigade (Twenty-third and Thirty-sixth Ohio) gave five hundred and fifteen votes for the Union state and county ticket, and *none at all* for the Democrats. People at home can't beat that!

Give my regards to Father Works and to Mr. and Mrs. Valette. My sympathies or congratulations, *perhaps,* should be given to Mr. Oscar Valette. I see he is drafted. Of course, his health will be reason enough not to go. Jim Webb was drafted; ill health excused him.

Sincerely,   R.

S. Birchard.

_____

Monday, October 17. — My election [to Congress] reported. Seventeen [Republican] to two [Democratic] members of Congress in Ohio; sixteen to eight in Pennsylvania. Better than all, Governor Morton elected by a good majority in Indiana.

Tuesday, October 18. — A letter from Stephenson congratulating me on my election by twenty-four hundred majority. [In the] First District, Eggleston has seventeen hundred majority. Still busy on entrenchments.

Wednesday, October 19. — Before daylight under cover of a heavy fog Rebels attacked the left. Colonel Thoburn's First Division was overwhelmed. His adjutant, Lieutenant —— brought me the word. We hurried up, loaded our baggage, and got into line. [The] Nineteenth Corps went into the woods on right (one brigade). General Sheridan was absent. General Wright, in command, directed my division to close up on [the] Nineteenth. Too late; the fugitives of the First Division and the Nineteenth's brigade came back on us. The Rebels broke on us in the fog and the whole line broke back. The Rebels did not push with energy. We held squads of men up to the fight all along. My horse was killed instantly. I took Lieutenant Henry's, of my staff. We fell back — the whole army — in a good deal of confusion but without panic. Artillery (twenty-five pieces) fell into Rebel hands and much camp equipage. About two and one-half miles back, we formed a line. [The] Rebels failed to push on fast enough.

P. M. General Sheridan appeared; greeted with cheering all along the line. His enthusiasm, magnetic and contagious. He brought up stragglers. "We'll whip 'em yet like hell." he says. General Crook's men on left of pike. — Line goes ahead. A fine view of the battle. [The] rebels fight poorly. Awfully whipped. —Cannon and spoils now on our side. Glorious!

CAMP AT CEDAR CREEK NEAR STRASBURG, VIRGINIA,
October 21, 1864.

MY DARLING: — We have had another important victory over General Early's oft-defeated army. Reinforced by a division or two of Longstreet's Corps, he was foolish enough to follow and attack us here on the 19th. In the darkness and fog of early morning he was successful in doubling up our left flank, held by General Crook's little First Division, and so flanking our whole army out of its position, capturing for the time our camps, a good many cannon, and perhaps fifteen hundred prisoners. But soon after it got light, we began to recover and finally checked and held them.

In the afternoon we took the offensive and without much difficulty or loss flogged them completely, capturing all their cannon, trains, etc., etc., and retaking all we had lost besides many prisoners. The Rebels marched off a part of our prisoners. For a time things looked squally, but the truth is, all the fighting capacity of Early's army was taken out of it in the great battle at Winchester a month ago. My loss was small. In the Thirteenth Lieutenant-Colonel Hall, a conspicuously brave and excellent officer, was killed. Lieutenant McBride (of [the] Twelfth) was wounded in [the] Twenty-third; two officers of [the] Fifth [Virginia] ditto.

As usual with me I had some narrow escapes. While galloping rapidly, my fine large black horse was killed instantly, tumbling heels over head and dashing me on the ground violently. Strange to say I was only a little bruised and was able to keep the saddle all day. (*Mem.*: — I lost all my horse trappings, saddle, etc., including my small pistol.) I was also hit fairly in the head by a ball which had lost its force in getting (I suppose) through somebody else! It gave me only a slight shock. — I think serious fighting on this line is now over.

. . . I suppose you are pleased with the result of the election. Of course, I am, on *general* reasons. My *particular* gratification is much less than it would be, if I were not so much gratified by my good luck in winning "golden opinions" in the more stirring scenes around me here. My share of *notoriety* here is nothing at all, and my *real* share of merit is also small enough, I know, but the consciousness that I am doing my part in these brilliant actions is far more gratifying than anything the election brings me.

Love to all. I am more than anxious to see you again.

Affectionately ever, your

R.

MRS. HAYES.

CAMP NEAR STRASBURG, VIRGINIA, October 21, 1864.

DEAR UNCLE: — Early reinforced by a division or two of Longstreet's Corps was foolish enough to attack us again on the 19th. It was a foggy morning, and the attack before daylight. One of General Crook's divisions (the *First*) was doubled up and our whole army flanked out of its position in confusion. But after daylight, order was gradually restored and in the afternoon, General Sheridan attacked in turn; retook all we had lost and utterly ruined Early. It was done easily and with small loss.

The fact is, all the *fight* is out of Early's men. They have been whipped so much that they can't keep a victory after it is gained. This is the last of fighting on this line, I am confident. My horse was killed under me instantly, dashing me on the ground violently. Luckily, I was not hurt much. I was hit fairly in the head with a spent ball. Narrow escapes! The Rebels got my saddle, pistol, etc.

The elections also are encouraging. In haste.

Sincerely,

R. B. HAYES.

P. S. — General Max Weber, a "veteran of European reputation," and one of the senior brigadiers in our service, came out yesterday with the intention of taking command of this division. General Crook sent him to Hagerstown, Maryland, to await orders!

S. BIRCHARD.

CAMP NEAR STRASBURG, VIRGINIA, October 25, 1864.

MY DARLING: — . . . . We expect to remain here some time yet. I suspect that apprehension is felt at Washington that the Rebels will try to get up a raid into Maryland or Pennsylvania to create a panic about the time of the Presidential election, and that we are kept here to prevent it. I can't think that after the complete defeat of Early's Army on the 19th, any serious attempt will be made to drive us back. I regard the fighting on this line as at an end for this year. I suspect that about the 10th [of] November we shall move north, and I hope go into winter quarters soon afterwards.

34

We are having fine weather. Camped on a wooded ridge, we are very comfortable. This life is a good deal like that of the fall of 1861 when General Rosecrans' Army was camped around Tompkins' Farm. The men were then very sickly. Now there is no sickness. We now talk of our killed and wounded. There is however a very happy feeling. Those who escape regret of course the loss of comrades and friends, but their own escape and safety to some extent modifies their feelings.

Laura has a daughter! I must write her a congratulatory note. But how much I prefer a boy. Well stocked as our house is with boys, I almost rejoice that our last is not a girl.

My regards and love to all the good friends who are so kind to you. Kiss all the boys.

Affectionately ever, your

R.

P. S. — Had a good letter from Force. He is returning to the Georgia front.

Mrs. Hayes.

Camp at Cedar Creek, Virginia, October 27, 1864.

My Darling: — Yours of the 18th — the first since the boy — reached me last night. Very glad you were able to write so soon. I don't want you to make any exertion to write — just write one line and it will be enough. Half a page of your little note sheet will be a long letter now. . . .

We have had so far fine weather. Our camps are as comfortable as possible. We expect to stay here until the season is too far advanced to admit of any formidable raids into Maryland or Pennsylvania. The Rebels, it is known, have been resolved to create a panic if possible in time to affect the Presidential election.

Some of the foolish fellows in the Sixth and Nineteenth Corps, feeling envious of our laurels in previous battles, have got the Eastern correspondents to represent the rout of Crook's Corps as worse than theirs, etc., etc. There is not a word of truth in it. A sentence in General Sheridan's dispatch was no doubt *intended to correct this in a quiet way.* "Crook's Corps lost seven pieces of artillery, the Nineteenth, eleven, and the Sixth Corps, six." We were attacked before them, and of course under more unfavorable circumstances, and yet we lost no more. In fact *I* lost nothing. My division fell back, but brought *everything* we had — our *two cows*, tents, and everything. Of course we lost *no* artillery, but did save an abandoned piece of the Nineteenth Corps.

I hope to see you soon. It is impossible now to tell when we shall be in a situation to ask for leaves of absence, but I suspect it will be within a month or six weeks. If we get on the railroad, I can go for a few days and not be missed.

The Rebels have not shown their heads since the last crushing defeat. Nothing but a determination to interfere with the election will bring back their forces. — Love to all.

Affectionately ever,

MRS. HAYES.   R.

Friday, October 28. — Rained hard last night; gusty and cold this A. M. *Mem.*: —Buy Lowell's "Fireside Travels." Barry, of Hillsboro, and West, of Cincinnati, bring poll-books for all and tickets for both sides. General Crook anxious to have Comly write our side of battle of Cedar Creek.

Saturday, October 29. — Bright and warm. Read "John Phoenix." A new tent put up in good style. Bunk and fireplace.

Sunday, October 30. — Another beautiful October day. We are having delicious weather. The only shadow on my spirits now is the critical condition of Captain Hastings. So brave, so pure, so good! God grant him life!

Monday, October 31. — [The] Fifth and Ninth Virginia consolidated as First Veterans West Virginia Volunteer Infantry. A splendid regiment it will be. Rode with Captain Hicks to Strasburg and down the Shenandoah below [the] railroad bridge and back to camp. Rebels at New Market with six pieces of artillery left! A month of splendid weather for campaigning. In a court-martial case for cowardice at Winchester a soldier testifies of the accused: "He is a good soldier in camp, but does not relish gunpowder well from what I saw."

CHAPTER XXV

IN GARRISON — END OF THE WAR — NOVEMBER 1864- MAY 1865

CEDAR CREEK, November 1, 1864. — Saw the new moon over my right shoulder. Thar! "Thinking of absent wife and boys will blanch a faithful cheek." God bless the dear ones! I never was so anxious to see them before. Another fine day; cold nights.

Wednesday, November 2. — Papers of 31st with much good news; small victories in West Virginia, east Tennessee, and over Price in Missouri. Early scolds his army.

CEDAR CREEK, November 2, 1864.

DEAR UNCLE: — We are waiting for the fall rains and the Presidential election before withdrawing for the season. A drizzle today gives us hope that our work is almost over for this year. I am more impatient than usual to see my family.

The campaign, if it closes now, will remain a most satisfactory one. I have only one drawback. I fear that Captain Hastings, my adjutant-general, will die of the wound got at Winchester, September 19. He is a man of the Rogers and Jesse Stem stamp. I can't bear to lose him, but his chance is less from day to day. — My health is excellent as usual.

Sincerely,

R.

S. BIRCHARD.

CAMP AT CEDAR CREEK, VIRGINIA, NOVEMBER 2, 1864.

MY DARLING: — We get trains through from Martinsburg regularly once in four days. We return them as often. I try to write you by every regular train. We hope to get mails with each train.

We have had most charming weather all the fall. Our camps are healthful and pleasant, but we all are looking forward to the "going into winter quarters" with impatience. We suppose a week or two more here will finish the campaign. Then a week or two of disagreeable marching and delays and *then* rest.

My tent and "fixin's" are as cozy as practicable. If my darling could share them with me, I could be quite content. I never was so anxious to be with you. This has been one of the happy periods with me. I have had only one shadow over me. You know Captain Hastings was severely wounded at the battle of Winchester, September 19. For three or four weeks he has been in a most critical condition. I have had a feeling that he would get well. I still *hope,* but all agree that his chance is very slight. He may live a month or die at any time. He is the best man whose friendship I have formed since the beginning of the war.

Doctor is well and has a great deal of enjoyment. We still think we shall have no more heavy fighting this fall. General Duffie was captured by Mosby! He was to marry Miss Jeffries soon (the younger).

R.

MRS. HAYES.

CAMP CEDAR CREEK, VIRGINIA, November 4, 1864.

MY DEAR SON: — This is your birthday — eleven years old today — almost a man. In less than eleven years more, everybody will call you a man, you will have a man's work to do and will be expected to know as much as men know. But you are a good student and an industrious boy, and I have no fears of your being an ignorant or a lazy man.

I wish I could be with you today. I would buy you something that don't cost much, for I mustn't spend much now or I shan't have anything left for that new little brother of yours. Besides, I would tell you about the battles. Uncle Joe has all the good stories now. He says up in Winchester the people work for the soldiers to make a living — they wash and mend and bake. The soldiers say they bake two kinds of pies, "pegged" and "sewed"! The difference is the "pegged" have no *sugar* in them.

One boy in the Twenty-third was shot in the face. The ball entered near his nose and passed over or through the cheekbone up towards the outer corner of his eye. The surgeon thought it was a small bullet and fearing it would injure his eye to probe for it, let it alone. He got along very well for three weeks, when they cut it out near his temple. They were astonished to find that it was an *iron grape-shot* over an inch in diameter — as large as one of your India-rubber balls! He is well and never did suffer much!   .   .   .

There have been a good many changes in the Twenty-third and the First Brigade since you saw them last at Loup Creek. Captain McKinley is on General Crook's staff. He has not been wounded, but every one admires him as one of the bravest and finest young officers in the army. He has had two or three horses shot under him. General Crook said his mess was starving for want of a good cook, so we let him have Frank. Frank is doing well there. Billy Crump has been so faithful that a short time ago he was given a furlough, and is now with his wife. He is coming back soon. Lieutenant Mather is on my staff as provost marshal. He is the only one you are acquainted with.   .   .   .

The band is full; all of them safe and well. I hear them now playing for guard-mounting. We have many fine bands in this army, but none better than ours.

I have lost three horses killed or disabled since I saw you in July. I am now riding a "calico" horse lent to me by Captain Craig. My John horse is with me still, but he will never get fit to use again.

My orderly in the place of Carrington is Underhill of [the] Twenty-third, an excellent young man; you would like him better than Carrington.

Did I write your mother that I found my opera-glass again? It was lost at the battle of Fisher's Hill. I got it about three weeks afterwards from a Thirty-fourth soldier who found it near the first cannon we captured.

It is getting very cold. We build a sort of fireplace in our tents and manage to be pretty comfortable. You and Webb would enjoy being in this camp. There is a great deal to see and always something going on.

You must learn to write me letters now. My love to all the family, "Puds" and all.

> Affectionately, your father,
>
> R. B. HAYES.

MASTER S. B. HAYES [BIRCHARD A. HAYES],
Chillicothe, Ohio.

Tuesday, November 8, — Went with Generals Sheridan and Crook and Colonel Forsythe to polls of [the] Thirty-fourth Regiment. All vote for Lincoln. General Sheridan's "maiden vote." All of this A. M. under arms.

Wednesday, November 9. — Marched eleven miles to camp south of Kernstown. Whole army glad to move towards winter quarters. — Result of election in this division: Lincoln, 575; McClellan, 98.

Thursday, November 10. — Rode to Winchester; saw Hastings; he is better! Very great hopes of his recovery. Lincoln probably gets all the States but three! Good. General Duval returns improved from his wound.

Friday, November 11. — Clear and cold. Skirmishing all P. M. on our right. What does it mean? We don't want to fight any more battles this fall, but if we do we shall probably whip them.

Saturday, November 12. — November weather; like snow, only it doesn't. Captain Blazer and his scouts make some captures; a deserter from Sixth Corps was married in ten days after.

Sunday, November 13. — Windy and very cold. General Powell on Front Royal road captures from McCausland two guns, two colors, and two hundred prisoners! A fine affair. Rode to the front. Rebels gone.

CAMP FOUR MILES SOUTH OF WINCHESTER, VIRGINIA,
> November 13, 1864. — Sunday.

MY DARLING: — You see we have made one day's march towards civilization, and, as we hope, towards our much wished for winter quarters. The weather has been and still is very favorable for the season — cold and windy to be sure, but very little rain. We do not know how far north we shall go. No doubt as far as some railroad and telegraphic communication. We have halted here for four days past, probably on account of reports that the Rebel army, reinforced and reorganized, is following after us. We do not know how it is, but if they wish to try conclusions with us again, it is likely General Sheridan will meet them.

My first brigade went to Martinsburg a week ago. It was hoped that they would not have to come back, but the probability now is that they will return. If so, I shall assume command of them again. General Duval has returned cured of his wound. I could perhaps keep a division, but under the circumstances I much prefer my old brigade. It has been greatly improved by the addition of the Ninth Virginia Veterans, who now with the Fifth form the First Virginia Veterans under Lieutenant-Colonel Enochs — a splendid regiment.

We are rejoiced that Captain Hastings is improving; he is still low but decidedly improving. His sister, whom you know, and a brother are with him.

Lincoln's election was so confidently expected that it does not cause so much excitement as we sometimes see, but it gives great satisfaction here.

Generals Sheridan and Crook both voted for him. It was General Sheridan's *first* vote!

I have no decided feeling about the little soldier's name. But I can't help thinking, suppose he should die after living long enough to become very dear to all of you. Would it not be awkward to think of the dear lost ones by the same name? And is not the idea of death now associated with the nickname "Little Jody"? But I am quite indifferent. Decide as you wish, or leave it to be decided by the boys.

Give my love to the kind friends.

Captain Reed, who sent you the dispatch, is an officer on Colonel Thoburn's staff — who was thoughtful enough to contradict the false report.*

Affectionately ever, your   R.

* See "Life of Hayes," Vol. I, page 257.

P. S. — Doctor and I rode to the front this P. M., a very cold, windy, raw day. From the best information I can get, nothing but cavalry has been seen. I think the Rebel army is not a-going to disturb us again. General Powell took two guns, two flags, and two hundred prisoners from General McCausland last night. A very handsome affair. The Second Virginia Cavalry is getting as good as any of them under General Powell.

Mrs. Hayes.

Monday, November 14. — Cold, windy day. This morning the First Brigade returned from Martinsburg. I assumed command again and camped them pleasantly in a wood on the extreme left. Slept cold.

Tuesday, November 15. — General Crook gone to Cumberland. General Duval takes his place. I today return to Second Division. Not so good quarters nor arrangements as at the brigade.

Wednesday, November 16. — A fine November day. Had my tent floored, banked up, and a chimney. [The] Sixth and Nineteenth Corps building winter quarters. P. M. rode to cavalry camp on Front Royal Road. Night, a wine-drinking.

Thursday, November 17. — Read speculations on Sherman's new move. Great hopes of his success. Rode into Winchester with Colonel Harris and Captain McKinley; called at Mr. Williams' law office; read the constitutional provisions as to amendments.

Camp near Winchester, Virginia, November 17, 1864.

Dearest: — When I wrote last I was in some doubt whether this Valley campaign was ended or not. It seems to be now settled. Early got a panic among his men and left our vicinity for good, I think.

The Sixth and Nineteenth Corps are building winter quarters. A telegraph line is put up and the railroad from Winchester to Harpers Ferry is nearly rebuilt. The location is a good one for a large body of troops. *We* are very pleasantly camped, but having no orders to put up winter quarters, have not fixed up for winter. We are very comfortable, however. My tent is floored, banked up, a good tent flue built, etc., etc. We get daily papers now regularly. The Baltimore *American,* a sound Republican paper, sells several thousand copies, — more than all other papers put together. The Philadelphia *Inquirer,* also sound, sells next in number. The New York *Herald,* sound on the war in a sort of guerrilla style, sells one thousand to two thousand copies. No other newspapers have any large circulation, but the pictorials, *Harper's Weekly* having the preference, sell immensely — nearly as many copies, I judge, as the Baltimore *American.* The Christian Commission distributes a vast amount of religious reading matter gratuitously. The sutlers sell dime novels and the thunder-and-lightning style of literature, in large quantity.

The Sixth and Nineteenth Corps have built fine fieldworks. The weather has been good and a great many squads and regiments are drilling. There are a score or two of bands. Possibly two are better than ours — not more than that. There is a good deal of horse-racing with tolerably high betting. The scenes at the races are very exciting. You would enjoy them. Nothing so fine of the kind is anywhere to be sene in civil life. Here the subordination of rank, the compulsory sobriety of the great crowds, etc., rid these spectacles of such disagreeable accompaniments as rioting, drunkenness, and the like. — We are beginning to have oyster and wine suppers and festive times generally.

General Crook has gone to Cumberland, and it is thought that my command will be ordered there for the winter, but this is all guess. I am again in command of the division after going back to the brigade for one day. How we shall be organized ultimately is not settled. I prefer the brigade. It now has three fine veteran regiments and the Thirteenth. The First Virginia Veterans (old Fifth and Ninth) is splendid.

I mean to ask for a leave as soon as we get housed in *our* winter quarters. I hope to see you by Christmas.

Tell Birch I am greatly pleased to have a letter from him. He will soon be one of my chief correspondents. — Love to all.

Affectionately ever, your   R.

P. S. — Hastings is getting better slowly. There are now hopes of his recovery. His sister is with him.

Mrs. Hayes.

CAMP RUSSELL, VIRGINIA, November 20, 1864.

DEAR UNCLE: — I tonight received yours of the 14th. We have had no battle for a month, and it is a week yesterday since I heard Rebel firing! This is wonderful. It is more than six months since I could say the same. We do not feel settled here, but are getting very comfortable. It is *probable* that we shall have a rest sometime this winter, but not yet *certain*. The Sixth and Nineteenth Corps may be needed at Richmond or somewhere, but I think the Army of West Virginia will do guard duty merely. What an interest the country now feels in Sherman! It looks as if he might strike some vital blows. If we get settled in time, I mean to get home by Christmas, if it is possible.

Sincerely,

R. B. HAYES.

November 23. — Awful weather. *Linen tents,* like a fiish seine for shelter, mud bottomless, cold and cheerless. All *that* yesterday and day before made many of us cross and gloomy — not me — but today is clear and bright and bracing. The turkeys, etc., sent from the Christian land [have arrived] and everyone is happy and jolly. This is camp life. We are sure we shall make another move back in a few days.

24th. — Thanksgiving Day. Good winter weather and no news.

S. BIRCHARD.

CAMP RUSSELL, VIRGINIA, November 20, 1864.

MY DARLING: — You see the Army of the Shenandoah has a name for its camp. Named after the General Russell who was killed at the battle of Winchester, September 19.

We have had no battle for a month! No Rebel firing for a week! Wonderful. But we don't feel settled yet. We are quite comfortable, nevertheless. We are I think waiting to see the issue of Sherman's daring campaign in Georgia. At present no furloughs or leaves of absence are granted except for sickness.

November 23. — Colder than any huckleberry pudding I know of! Whew, how it blew and friz last night! I took my clothes off in Christian style last night. No enemy near for a week and more makes this the correct thing. It got windy, flue disgusted smoked, let the fire go out, then grew cold; put on pants, coat, and vest, in bed. Cold again, put on overcoat and in bed again. Colder than ever, built up the fire, [it] smoked. So I *wanted* to be cold, and soon was. Tent-pins worked loose from the wind flapping the fly; fixed them after much trouble; to bed again, and wished I was with my wife in a house of some sort!

Today the men *were* to have had overcoats, stockings, shirts, etc., which they greatly need, but behold, we learn that the clothing couldn't come because all the transportation was required to haul up the turkeys and Thanksgiving dinner! We must wait until next train, eight days! And we all laugh and are very jolly in spite of it.

8 P. M. — The clothing has come after all. The turkeys are issued at the rate of a pound to a man. Very funny times we are having! When the weather is bad as it was yesterday, everybody, *almost* everybody, feels cross and gloomy. Our thin linen tents — about like a fish seine, the deep mud, the irregular mails, the never-to-be-seen paymasters, and "the rest of mankind," are growled about in "old-soldier" style. But a fine day like today has turned out brightens and cheers us all. We people in camp are merely big children, wayward and changeable.

Believe me, dearest, your ever loving husband,

R.

Mrs. Hayes.

Camp Russell, Monday, November 21, 1864. — Cavalry camp on our left broken up. Said to be gone to Stephenson's Depot, five miles north of Winchester. Rode out to works on Front Royal Road. Review of Sixth Corps in a cold rain-storm; eight brigades — ten thousand [men].

Tuesday, 22. — Snow on the mountains low down; ground frozen; "sky, chill and drear." Rode with Roberts to Winchester and the battle-field, to where I crossed Red Bud Creek. An ugly place to cross, it is.

Saturday, 26. — Rode with Generals Crook and Duval, Colonel Harris, of [the] Tenth, and Wells, of [the] Fourteenth, to works. A jolly wine-drinking in the evening with Captains Stanley and Stearns, Thirty-sixth, who leave on resignation.

Sunday, 27. — A ride with Colonel Comly; a visit to General Crook. A fine day; a brigade dress parade. All pleasant.

CAMP RUSSELL, November 27, [1864].   Sunday.

DEAR MOTHER: — We are not in winter quarters yet. The continued presence of the Rebel army in our front, or Sherman's campaign, or Grant's, or something else, keeps us in suspense. But we are gradually improving our condition and quarters until now we are pretty comfortable, and if we finally stay here for the winter, I, for one, shall not grumble.

We had a jovial Thanksgiving. A fair supply of turkeys and other good things from the cities, together with good weather, made the day cheerful.

The railroad, it is supposed, will be finished to within four or five miles of us this week. We shall then have mails and supplies with some regularity.

I still hope to get settled in time to visit [home] during the holidays. My kind regards to Mrs. Wasson and Sophia.

Affectionately, your son,

R.

MRS. SOPHIA HAYES.

CAMP RUSSELL, ARMY OF THE SHENANDOAH, VIRGINIA,
November 30, 1864.

MY DEAR SON: — I received a letter from your mother today in which she says that you are expecting a letter from me. . . . I am very glad to hear that you are studying your lessons very well. . . . What a funny name your mother has for your brother "the Little Soldier." She thinks of calling him after one of her ancestors, Captain Bilious Cook. I would prefer George Crook to such a queer name as "Bilious."

We are having pleasant weather, and drill the officers and men every day. All the officers of the brigade were out today and we began with the musket drill, shoulder arms, etc. You would like to see our brigade have dress parade. The four regiments are formed in one line — the band and brigade flag in the middle. It makes a fine display. . . .

December 2. — You would have enjoyed being here yesterday. It was a fine warm day and we moved camp. One division of the Sixth Corps left to go south via Washington, perhaps to Grant. We moved our camp about a mile over to their ground. We are getting well fixed again. We hauled over our flooring and bunks, and they left a great deal of material, so we rather made by the change.

Your little letter pleased me very much. If you study hard you will soon be able to write a good long one. Give my love to Grandma, "the Little Soldier," and all the rest of your friends. If I don't get home by New Year's, you must write me about the holidays. — Good-bye.

Your affectionate father,

R. B. Hayes.

Master James Webb Hayes,
    Chillicothe.

Thursday, December 1, 1864. — An Indian-summer-like day. [The] First Division, Sixth Corps, go back — where? We change camp to their place — a pleasant enough change — west side of Valley Pike one and one-half miles south of Kernstown.

Friday, 2. — Another good day. All thought is of Sherman and Hood's army. Hopeful. Busy fixing new camp for cold and wet weather.

Saturday, 3. — Still fair weather. [The] Third Division, Sixth Corps, leave us. Rode around our works. Too numerous for our force. Too extensive for less than forty thousand infantry or more. A battle at Franklin. Reports look well.

Sunday, 4. — A fine day. All talk is of Sherman and Georgia or Hood and Tennessee. This week is likely to inform us of their movements and so determine our own. Will Early on hearing that the Sixth Corps has left visit us?

Tuesday, 6. — Good weather. The battle at Franklin, Tennessee, was a fortunate escape from a disastrous defeat. It was probably also a damaging blow, perhaps severely so. Nashville can probably hold out. The situation there is interesting with a favorable look for us.

Camp Russell, December 6, 1864.

My Darling: — We are very comfortable and very jolly. No army could be more so. We have had no orders to build winter quarters, but we have got ready for rough weather, and can now worry through it. . . .

We have horse-races, music, church (*sic!*), and all the attractions. No fighting, which makes me hope I shall get off the last of this month to see my darling and the dear ones.

Affectionately,

R.

Mrs. Hayes.

Camp Russell near Winchester, Virginia,

December 6, 1864.

Dear Mother: — I received your cheerful letter on Sunday. It finds us in the best of spirits and so comfortably camped that we all would be glad to know that our winter quarters would be at this camp. We have the railroad finished to within eight miles; daily mails and telegraphic communication with the world. The men have built huts four feet high, eight or nine feet square, of logs, puncheons, and the like, banked up with earth and covered with their shelter blankets. My quarters are built of slabs and a wall tent. Tight and warm. We are in woods on a rolling piece of ground. It will be muddy but we are building walks of stone, logs, etc., so we can keep out of the dirt. — I have a mantel-piece, a table, one chair, one stool, an ammunition box, a trunk, and a bunk for furniture.

We get *Harper's Monthly* and *Weekly*, the *Atlantic*, daily papers from Baltimore, New York, and Philadelphia. The Christian Commission send a great many religious books. I selected "Pilgrim's Progress" from a large lot offered me to choose from a few days ago.

Our living is, ordinarily, bread (baker's bread) and beef, and coffee and milk (we keep a few cows), or pork and beans and coffee. *Occasionally* we have oysters, lobsters, fish, canned fruits, and vegetables. The use of liquor is probably less than among the same class of people at home. All kinds of liquor can be got, but it is expensive and attended with some difficulty.

The chaplains now hold frequent religious meetings. Music we have more of and better than can be had anywhere except in the large cities. We have very fine horse-racing, much better managed than can be found anywhere out of the army. A number of ladies can be seen about the camps — officers' wives, sisters, daughters, and the Union young ladies of Winchester. General Sheridan is particularly attentive to one of the latter. General Crook is a single man — fond of ladies, but very diffident. General Custer has a beautiful young wife, who is here with him.

I have just seen a case of wonderful recovery — such cases are common, but none more singular than this. Captain Williams of my command was shot by a Minié ball on the 24th of July in the center of the back of his neck, which passed out of the center of his chin, carrying away and shattering his jaw in front. He is now perfectly stout and sound (his voice good) and not disfigured at all. But he can chew nothing, eats only spoon victuals!

Dr. Webb is a great favorite. The most efficient surgeon on the battle-field in this army. He is complimented very highly in General Crook's official report. He hates camp life, especially in bad weather, when he suffers from a throat disease.

My love to the household.

Affectionately, your son,

R.

Mrs. Sophia Hayes.

Wednesday, December 7, 1864. — Fine weather. We still inquire as to Early's position, not feeling sure but that he will visit us. Sherman is reported to have taken Millen. If so he is safe; quite sure to reach the sea.

Thursday, 8. — Windy and very cold, but dry. Rode with Dr. Joe around the works on our left. Bitterly cold. Some things look as if we were to move up the Valley to stop Early from going to Richmond, so as to give Grant a fair field.

Friday, 9. — Cold and raw all day. First snow fell this evening. General Crook gave me a pair of his brigadier-general shoulder-straps this afternoon. A rank cheapened by poor appointments. I feel it an honor, conferred as it is at the close of a bloody campaign on the recommendation of General Crook approved by General Sheridan.

Camp Russell, Virginia, December 9 (Evening), 1864.

My Darling: — We have had two winter days. It has been snowing for the last hour or two. We feel that this ends our campaigning for this year. The last of the Sixth Corps left this morning. One "grapevine" (our word for camp rumor) says they have gone to Kentucky or Tennessee by way of the Ohio River, and another that they passed through Washington on the way to Grant. I conjecture the last is the truth.

General Crook gave me a very agreeable present this afternoon — a pair of his old brigadier-general straps. The stars are somewhat dimmed with hard service, but will correspond pretty well with my rusty old blouse. Of course I am very much gratified by the promotion. I know perfectly well that the rank has been conferred on all sorts of small people and so cheapened shamefully, but I can't help feeling that getting it at the close of a most bloody campaign on the recommendation of fighting generals like Crook and Sheridan is a different thing from the same rank conferred — well, as it has been in some instances.

Dr. Joe is busy court-martialling one of his brethren, who as medical chief of our hospitals at Winchester turned into private

35

profit the medicines, stimulants, chickens, eggs, etc., which had been provided for our wounded.

We hope to get home together the last of this month or early next, but no one can yet tell what is to be our fate. We are waiting on Sherman and the weather. — My love to all.

Affectionately ever, your

R.

P. S. — I am ever so glad that Governor Chase is Chief Justice. I had given up all hope of his appointment.

I sent to Gallipolis directing my trunk or valise to be expressed to Chillicothe care of William McKell. If he is put to expense, as he will be, perhaps, have it paid. Get into it — my duds may need airing. — I shall want two or three pairs knit woollen socks.

MRS. HAYES.

Saturday, December 10, 1864. — A cold day; deep snow (eight inches) on the ground. [I] am the centre of congratulations [on promotion to generalship] in the camp. General Duval and staff, Colonel Comly, etc., drink poor whiskey with me! A rational way of doing the joyful, but all we have!

Sunday 11. — Snow still on the ground. Wind high and very cold. Men must suffer on picket. Three deserters came in from Early. Early going to Staunton — perhaps to Richmond. Sherman and Hood "as they were." Am getting anxious about Sherman.

Monday, 12. — A bright, cold day, less wind. Miss Hastings and Miss Defendrefer came out with Captain Hastings' nurse (Miss Wilber) in a sleigh. Their first visit to a winter camp. I give them wine and warm up. A pleasant call, the first from ladies.

CAMP RUSSELL, VIRGINIA, December 12, 1864.

DEAR UNCLE: — The snow is at least eight inches deep. A fierce northwester has been blowing for the last fifteen hours and the cold is intense. I fear that men on the picket line will perish of cold. We probably notice severe weather more when living as we are in rather poor tents, but I certainly have seen nothing worse than this even on the shore of the lake.

The campaign in the Valley has closed. The Rebel infantry has all been withdrawn. Our own is leaving rapidly. It goes to Grant. The destination of Crook's command is not yet known. It probably waits news from Sherman.

I shall ask for a leave of absence as soon as we get orders to go into winter quarters, which may come any day.

I have been promoted to brigadier-general. The honor is no great things, it having been conferred, particularly at the first part of the war, on all sorts of men for all sorts of reasons; but I am a good deal gratified, nevertheless. It is made on the recommendation of General Crook, approved by Sheridan. This at the close of such a bloody campaign is something; besides, I am pleased that it seems so well received by officers and men of the command. It has not yet been officially announced, and will not be for perhaps a week or so.

I am very glad Governor Chase is Chief Justice. I had almost given up his appointment. I received letters from Swayne's friends urging me to write in his behalf. I heard nothing of the kind from the friends of Governor Chase. I suppose they felt safe. I replied to Perry and others that I was for Governor Chase.

It seems I have a place at West Point at my disposal. It is quite encouraging to know that my district abounds in young Napoleons. I hear of a new one almost every mail. The claim of one is based largely on the fact that he has two brothers in the service. I happen to know that they (both officers) have been so successful in finding soft places in the rear that neither of them after more than three years' service, has ever been in a battle!

I begin to feel very anxious about Sherman. His failure would be a great calamity in itself. Besides, it would bring into favor the old-fogy, anaconda style of warfare. Boldness and enterprise would be at a discount. If he has made a mistake, it is in not moving with more celerity.

We ought to have another draft without delay — or rather another call for troops, to be followed by a draft if volunteering failed to produce the required number within a reasonable period.

Sincerely,

R. B. Hayes.

S. Birchard.

Tuesday, December 13, 1864. — Snow still on the ground; very cold. Sleigh-ride with Captain McKinley to Winchester Depot. Run against hay team. Hastings improving decidedly. News from Sherman encouraging but meagre. Hood as he was, before Nashville. Early gone.

Wednesday, 14. — Snow going off rapidly; sun shining at intervals. In quarters almost all day. News from Sherman favorable. He is near Savannah and can probably avoid a fight and go to the sea if he wishes to do so. Nothing new from Nashville.

Thursday, 15. — Cold, a little sleet. This evening we get the first message from Sherman's army. "So far all well," says General Howard from camp five miles from Savannah. Rebel news is that a battle for the possession of Savannah was raging on the 12th. God protect the right!

Friday, 16. — A thawing, raw day; no rain. General Thomas attacks Hood's left with good results. We hope for a complete victory. Nothing new from Sherman. . . . Fifty guns fired.

Saturday, 17. — An inspection of First Brigade. [The] Twenty-third looked well, but alas! very few of the old men. I shed tears as I left the line. It never looked better. Abbott, wounded at Cloyd's Mountain and a prisoner for months, joined us today. General Thomas completed his victory at Nashville. One hundred guns fired here. General Crook fears that one division will go to Grant.

CAMP RUSSELL, December 17, 1864.

MY DARLING: — No certainty about things yet. We fired fifty guns yesterday and one hundred more today over General Thomas' great victories. How happy our men are. We had an inspection today of the brigade. The Twenty-third was pronounced the crack regiment in appearance, etc. It looks very finely — as large as you used to see it at Camp White, but so changed in officers and men. A great many new ones at Camp White; then three hundred of the Twelfth in July; and three hundred conscripts, volunteers, and substitutes since. I could see only six to ten in a company of the old men. They all smiled as I rode by. But as I passed away I couldn't help dropping a few natural tears. I felt as I did when I saw them mustered in at Camp Chase.

Captain Abbott joined us today — a prisoner since Cloyd's Mountain. He is very happy to be back. He looks in good health, his arm not perfectly well.

Lieutenant McBride, the brave fellow who took Lieutenant-Colonel Edgar and forty-two others at Winchester, is here again. Sweet and Snyder are back. Hastings is in capital spirits; says he will be well long before next spring campaign. Heiliger writes me that he wants to get a commission in Hancock's Veterans.

The band is playing its finest tonight. It contains all the old members and some good additions.

I have written the boys. I asked them how they would like to call the little soldier George Crook; they don't reply. — Love to all.

Affectionately ever,

R.

MRS. HAYES.

CAMP RUSSELL, VIRGINIA, December 18, 1864.
Sunday morning before breakfast.

DEAR MOTHER: — We have as yet received no orders as to winter quarters. I begin to suspect I shall not get home during the holidays.

We are feeling very happy over the good news from the other armies. Salutes were fired yesterday and the day before in all our camps in honor of General Thomas' victory at Nashville.

We are living on the fat of the land now. The sutlers are now again allowed to come to the front and they bring all manner of eatables, wholesome and otherwise, but chiefly otherwise.

I wish you could visit our camps. I know what you would exclaim on coming into my quarters, "Why, Rutherford, how comfortably you are fixed. I should like to live with you myself." I am getting books and reading matter of all sorts against rainy weather. Unless the weather is atrocious, I take a ride daily of a couple of hours or more. We yesterday had an inspection of my brigade. The Twenty-third was in the best condition. Notwithstanding our heavy losses, we have managed to get so many new men during the summer that the regiment is about as large as it was in the spring. It is larger than it was at this time last year.

A large number of men and officers who fell into Rebel hands, wounded, are now coming back, having been exchanged. They are all happy to be back and full of determination to fight it out.

I have been made a brigadier-general, but it is not yet officially announced. It was on the recommendation of Generals Crook and Sheridan.

Affectionately, your son,

R.

MRS. SOPHIA HAYES.

CAMP AT STEPHENSON'S DEPOT, VIRGINIA,
December 20, 1864.

DEAR UNCLE: — We broke camp at Camp Russell yesterday at early daylight and marched to this place on the railroad from Harpers Ferry towards Winchester. It rained, snowed, "blew, and friz" again. Awful mud to march in and still worse to camp in. But today it is cold and none of us got sick, so far as I know. Our First Division took cars to join Grant. It is said we shall follow in a day or two. This is not certain, but I shall not be surprised if it is true. I prefer not to go, and yet one feels that it is almost necessary to be present at the taking of Richmond. I am content, however, to go. I believe in pushing the enemy all winter if possible. Now that we have a decided advantage is the time to crowd them. Things look as if that were to be the policy.

I like the new call for troops. What good fortune we are having. If Sherman takes Savannah and then moves north, this winter will be the severest by far that our Rebel friends have had.

I received today your letter of the 14th enclosing Uncle Austin's about the sad fate of Sardis. I will do what I can to get further information, but we are no longer with the Nineteenth Corps and may not again see them.

I am sorry to hear you have a severe cold. I am getting more nervous when I hear of your taking cold. Don't try to visit Lucy or anybody else in the winter.

I am afraid I shall not get to visit you this winter.

Sincerely,

R. B. HAYES.

P. S. — There is a short but tolerably fair account of the battle of Winchester in *Harper's Monthly* of January. It is written by somebody in the Nineteenth Corps. You will hardly read it with such emotion as I do. The writer calls our force "the Eighth Corps." When you read on the 199th page his account of our battle-yell as we advanced, and of the Rebel musketry which met it, you will remember that I led the advance brigade of the advance division, and that perhaps the happiest moment of my life was then, when I saw that our line *didn't* break and that the enemy's *did*.

23d. — It is pretty certain [that] we do not go to Grant; probably in a week or two to Cumberland or West Virginia.

S. BIRCHARD.

Thursday, December 22, 1864. — Last night the worst of my experience. A new camp; slight shelter; very cold; tent smoky. In all respects we are badly fixed. Issue a ration of whiskey to all.

Friday, 23. — A clear, cold, fine winter day. Began to move into a house; changed back. Visited Mr. Joseph Jolliffe, the only man who voted for Lincoln in 1860! A brother of Mr. Jolliffe of Cincinnati. Read with great pleasure the story of Thomas' victories and Sherman's great march.

Saturday, 24. — A fine day; a pleasant chatty Christmas eve with the gentlemen of my staff in the hospital tent of the adjutant: viz., Captain Nye (R. L.), Captain Delay, Lieutenants Turner and Stanley — all of Thirty-sixth O. V. I. and good men.

Sunday, 25. — A pleasant and "merry Christmas." A good dinner. Captain Nye, Lieutenants Turner and Stanley, Dr. Webb, Majors Carey, Twenty-third, and McKown, Thirteenth. Wine, oysters, turkey, etc., etc. Read through [General Winfield] Scott's "Autobiography." Weak and vain beyond compare.

Monday, 26. — A dull, foggy day; snow thawing rapidly. Savannah captured by Sherman on the 21st, Hardee making a hasty retreat across the river to South Carolina. Some important captures. Salute of one hundred guns fired. We expect to go to New Creek soon.

Tuesday, 27. — A bright, warm day; snow turns to water and mud; mud everywhere! Rode into Winchester with Captain Abbott and Dr. Joe. Hastings in good plight and heart, but improving so slowly. General Crook says he has written for my missing appointment as brigadier-general. No increase of pay till it comes. No news today.

Wednesday, 28. — Thawing and muddy. General Crook and staff go by railroad to Cumberland. We hope to follow soon. Rain this eve. Attack on Fort Fisher by Porter, etc.; no results as yet. We hope Wilmington will be closed — but?

Friday, 30. — A cold morning, but ground thaws during day. March seventeen miles to Martinsburg. Men in fine spirits. Camp in the snow!

Saturday, 31. — Staid at Mr. Allen's, Martinsburg, last night. At 9 or 10 A. M., [the] Thirty-sixth and Thirteenth by cars to

Cumberland. With staff at 3 P. M. to Cumberland. Supper and good time at Cumberland. Winter quarters here.

CUMBERLAND, MARYLAND, January 1, 1865.

DEAREST: — We reached here last night. We shall build winter quarters and soon settle down. I shall apply for a leave of absence as soon as we are all fixed, and then to see the dear ones!

On the 30th we were marching from Stephenson's Depot to Martinsburg. I often thought of the twelve-years-ago day [wedding-day], and of the happiness my darling has been to me since. I do hope I shall see you soon. — Love to all.

Affectionately, your

MRS. HAYES.   R.

Revere House, Cumberland, Maryland, Monday, January 2, 1865. — A fine day. Rode to camp, out one mile north of railroad, east of town. Men all busy getting up huts. Scenery, mountains, etc., around the "Mountain City" very pretty.

Eagle adopted as our badge. Red Eagle for my division. Army of West Virginia in three divisions; General Duval, the First; Kelley, Second; Stephenson, Third. I have First Brigade, First Division.

Tuesday, 3. — Bright day. Walked up Wills Creek to the Narrows. Received appointment as brigadier-general, dated November 30, to rank from October 19, "for gallantry and meritorious servies in the battles of Opequon, Fisher's Hill, and Middletown." Put on shoulder-straps worn by General Crook in Tennessee. Changed quarters from Revere House to St. Nicholas.

Thursday, 5. — Fine winter day. All goes well at camp. Shall call it Camp Hastings. Eve with Generals Crook [and] Duval and doctors at Mr. Thurston's. The old gentleman a fine staunch Unionist. Miss Tidball, a cousin of doctor's sang Secesh songs. **Pretty girl.**

CUMBERLAND, MARYLAND, January 5, 1865.

DEAREST: — I am just in receipt of yours of the 21st. It has probably been on the hunt of me a week or more.

I am very glad you are pleased to call the little soldier George Crook. I think it is a pretty name, aside from the agreeable association.

We are most pleasantly located here. In the midst of fine mountain scenes, plenty of wood and water, and no duty for the men. They are already in their new huts and are very jolly over it.

The publication of my appointment has been made. I have not yet got the original document. It was missent to New York City and will go from there to Chillicothe. If it gets there before I do you will open it. It gives as the reason of the appointment, gallantry and good conduct in the late battles in the Shenandoah Valley and dates from the Battle of Cedar Creek, October 19, 1864. Aside from the vanity which goes always with brass buttons, I have other reasons for wanting the grounds of the appointment published. No flourish of trumpets, no comment, but simply, "Colonel R. B. Hayes, Twenty-third Regiment O. V. I., has been apopinted brigadier-general" for (here quote the exact words of the appointment). Show this to Uncle Scott and request him to have the paragraph published in the Chillicothe paper when the letter of appointment gets there. I may be there first, but it is still doubtful.

The doctor is very happy — young ladies, a pretty town, parties, balls, etc.

I hope to get home within a fortnight. — Love to all.

Affectionately, ever,

R.

MRS. HAYES.

CUMBERLAND, MARYLAND, January 6, 1865.

DEAR UNCLE: — We are getting into very pleasant quarters. The town is a fine one, plenty of parties, balls, etc., etc., for the beaux — fine mountain scenery — good water and wood convenient.

OHIO GENERALS, GRADUATES FROM WEST POINT WHO WON THE WAR FOR THE UNION.

MAJOR-GENERAL PHILIP H. SHERIDAN, 1831-88.

MAJOR-GENERAL GEORGE CROOK, 1828-1890.

LIEUTENANT-GENERAL WILLIAM T. SHERMAN, 1820-91.

GENERAL ULYSSES S. GRANT, 1822-85.

MAJOR-GENERAL JAMES B. MCPHERSON, 1828-64.

MAJOR-GENERAL GEORGE A. CUSTER, 1839-76.

There are still odds and ends of business to be finished, and then no reason that I can see why I should not go home. I expect quite confidently to be at home within two weeks. . . .

The reason for my promotion, etc., has been officially announced "for gallantry and meritorious services in the Battles of Opequon, Fisher's Hill, and Cedar Creek" and dates from the Battle of Cedar Creek, October 19. All very satisfactory.

Sincerely,

R. B. HAYES.

S. BIRCHARD.

CAMP HASTINGS, NEAR CUMBERLAND, MARYLAND,

January 8, 1865.

DEAR UNCLE: — I am now in our winter camp. All things seem to be about as they should be. My leave of absence for twenty days has been granted, and I shall start home in two or three days. I shall probably not be able to stay with you more than one day. I can't yet tell, but I suppose about the 25th I shall get around to Fremont. I hope to reach Chillicothe on the 12th. Yours of the first I got last night. I will stay with Mother one or two days at Delaware.

Sincerely,

R. B. HAYES.

P. S. — My adjutant, Captain Hastings, is getting well. He is at Winchester and can't yet be moved from his bed. He will be major of [the] Twenty-third and in two or three months can probably ride. I have named my camp after him.

S. BIRCHARD.

Monday, January 9. — Spent the day getting ready to visit home, signing approval of applications for furloughs and leaves, and reading Heine. His wit not translatable; ratherish vulgar and very blasphemous.

[Tuesday evening, January 10, Hayes started for Ohio by railway. He reached the Ohio River the next day at Benwood and there took a steamer, filled with "oil or petroleum speculators," for Parkersburg. He arrived at Chillicothe January 12, where he found Mrs. Hayes afflicted with rheumatism. A month was spent in Ohio with wife and children at Chillicothe and in visits to relatives and friends at Columbus, Delaware, Fremont, and Cincinnati. He was back at Cumberland, Thursday, February 9.]

CHILLICOTHE, Sunday morning, January 22, 1865.

DEAR MOTHER: — We returned here yesterday afternoon. . . . I read your journal of the family and your early times in Ohio to Uncle Sardis. It was very interesting. It reminded him of many things which he had entirely forgotten. I am very glad you wrote it. I shall always preserve and prize it. I do not wish to impose any labor on you, but it would gratify me very much if you would occasionally put down in the same way anything you happen to think of.

Aunt McKell's oldest son (a captain) returned from Sherman since I was here. He is out of service. His time was out three months ago, but he remained to go through the Georgia campaign. . . .

One of our officers from Cumberland tells me he thinks we shall see very little more hard service during the war. — Love to all.

Affectionately, your son,

RUTHERFORD.

MRS. SOPHIA HAYES.

CHILLICOTHE, OHIO, February 1, 1865.

DEAR HASTINGS: — I returned here from Cincinnati last night and find your letter of the 23d ult. I am surprised and very glad to hear of your arrival home. If the journey has not hurt you it is a capital thing. I shall return to Cumberland in a few days via Columbus. . . .

You will of course be promoted. If the governor should remain fixed in his feelings against [Major Edward M.] Carey, you will be lieutenant-colonel. I hear it said that you would not accept. I can't suppose this is so. It surely ought not to be. I shall ask Governor Brough to promote Carey. If he will not do it, there is no propriety in your declining the promotion.

My wife joins in regards to your sister and yourself.

Sincerely,

R. B. HAYES.

CAPTAIN RUSSELL HASTINGS,
  Willoughby, Ohio.

CAMP HASTINGS, Sunday, February 12, 1865.

DEAREST: — We reached here after a pleasant journey Thursday evening on time. No important changes here. The remnant of the unlucky Thirty-fourth is now in my camp to be consolidated with the Thirty-sixth. General Duval is quite unwell, and will go to Cincinnati to be treated for troubles affecting his hearing. General Crook has had a ball. I send you a ticket. He inquired after you all, particularly Webb and George. He is in fine health and spirits. He has become a convert to negro soldiers — thinks them better than a great part of the sort we are now getting. . . .

It is cold, windy, and snowy. My tent groans, squeaks, and flaps. The sleeping is not so *comfortable* as in a house these days, but is more refreshing and invigorating. The Shenandoah army is all gone. Part of Nineteenth Corps is at Savannah; the Sixth at Richmond and the most of ours. I had a brigade drill yesterday. The regiments are full, and in fine condition. The First Veterans [Twenty-third Regiment] are *rather* the crack men in appearance. Major Carey has resigned.

Mrs. Comly is here, that is, in town. I have not yet seen her. The cars upset with her near Newark, but she kept on this way instead of going back home. Good stuff. — Love to all.

Affectionately ever,

R.

MRS. HAYES.

Shriver Mansion, Cumberland, Tuesday, January 14. — Took command of First Division today. General Duval gone to Cincinnati for treatment of his hearing. Came down in a sleigh; sleighing almost all winter.

Wednesday P. M., February 15, [1865].

DEAREST: — You notice the last sentence.* Is it prudent or possible even for you to drop little George for a fortnight? I have of course no fears about the boy. His grandmother seems to have the full charge of him, but will it do for you? If so, you come to see your husband at Cumberland. Washington is not to be named. We are such little people that we can go "strictly incog." Bring on two hundred to three hundred dollars — no care about dress — and we can manage it.

Write soon so I can get the leave if you say so. — Love to all.

Affectionately ever,

R.

MRS. HAYES.

CUMBERLAND, MARYLAND, February 15, 1865.

DEAR MOTHER: — We are jogging along in the usual style of a winter camp. The thing about us which you would think most interesting is the doings of our chaplain. We have a good one. He is an eccentric, singular man — a good musician — very fond of amusement and as busy as a bee. He is a son of a well-known Presbyterian minister of Granville, Mr. Little. Since I left he has had built a large log chapel, covered with tent cloth. In this he has schools, in which he teaches the three R's, and music, and has also preaching and prayer-meetings and Sunday-school. The attendance is large. The number of young men and boys from the mountains of West Virginia, where schools are scarce, in my command makes this a useful thing. He has also got up a revival which is interesting a good many.

* This refers to the last sentence of a letter to Hayes from his friend Judge William Johnston, written from Washington, on the blank page of which Hayes was writing. The sentence read: "Say whether you will be here at the inauguration. I have sent home for my family to be here. It will be the greatest demonstration the world ever saw, and I think both you and Mrs. Hayes ought to be here."

Since my return itinerant preachers of the Christian Commission have held two or three meetings in our chapel.

Affectionately, your son,

R.

Mrs. Sophia Hayes.

Cumberland, Maryland, February 17, 1865.

Dear Uncle: — I send for safe keeping my original appointment as brigadier-general. It was confirmed by the Senate a few days ago. . . .

No movements here. It seems to be the expectation that Lee will attempt something desperate to get out of the net forming around him. We are having a gay time. Balls, etc., of the fastest sort are common. . . .

Sincerely,

R. B. Hayes.

S. Birchard.

Cumberland, Maryland, February 19, 1865.

Dear Uncle: — Yours of [the] 17th received today. I will send you five hundred dollars by express tomorrow. It is in interest-bearing notes. Are they worth any more to you than other funds? We are paid a good deal of it.

A cripple of my regiment from Fremont goes home in [a] day or two. I think he is a first-rate man — Lejune. [He] captured twenty-five Rebels at South Mountain. He was badly wounded at Antietam, and got well just in time to get awfully hurt at Cloyd's Mountain.

Sincerely,

R. B. Hayes.

S. Birchard.

Shriver Mansion, January 21. — At 3:30 A. M. Captain McNeal and fifty or so of his band kidnapped Generals Kelley and Crook from their hotel on Baltimore Street. Daring and well executed. They inquired for me but on learning that I quartered in camp did not look further.

CUMBERLAND, February 21, 1865.

DEAR LUCY: — You will be sorry to hear that the Rebels got General Crook this morning. A party of perhaps fifty or so dashed into town in the night, went direct to the hotels where General Crook (the Revere) and General Kelley (the St. Nicholas) quartered, took them prisoners and hurried off. All possible pains to recapture them have been taken, but I have no confidence of success. No special blame will attach to anyone, I suppose. General Kelley commanded the post and had such guards posted as he deemed necessary — the same I suppose he has had for the last year or more. The picket post was not blamable, I think, — at least not flagrantly so. It is a very mortifying thing to all of us. I have been in the habit of staying at my camp out a mile or so, and so was not looked for. The fact was, I had received an order to get quarters in town and was in town that night at General Duval's headquarters. But he, having left as everybody knew a week before, his quarters were not searched. A narrow chance for me. The only other officer taken was Captain Melvin, adjutant-general of General Kelley. The only possible danger to General Crook is the chance of his attempting to escape and failing. — Love to all.

Affectionately ever

MRS. HAYES.

R.

Shriver Mansion, Wednesday, January 22. — Sherman took Columbia Friday, the 18th. Rebels evacuated Charleston Tuesday, 15th. Today at noon national salute here and everywhere because "the old flag floats again over Sumter."

CAMP HASTINGS, NEAR CUMBERLAND, February 22, 1865.

DEAR MOTHER: — I suppose you have heard of the kidnapping of General Crook and General Kelley. . . . The exchange of prisoners is now so prompt that the matter is not regarded as a very serious calamity. General Crook's reputation is so good that it will not affect him much. Besides, such bold attempts may be successful in any town where a general is likely to have his quarters.

The success of Sherman's splendid operations give[s] us all reason to hope that we are getting near the end of the Rebellion. As long as Lee's fine army remains, there is, of course, a chance that he may succeed in doing something that will postpone the final blow. But no defeat or disaster now could long delay our triumph. . . . . Love to all.

Affectionately, your son,

R.

Mrs. Sophia Hayes.

Cumberland, Maryland, February 23, 1865.

My Dearest: — . . . As to the visit to Washington, the capture of General Crook may change my chance of getting permission to go there. The expense is of no importance, if it is prudent in view of the state of your health. I think I can get permission to go, but it is more questionable than it was. You should start so as to reach here by the 28th (or first of March). Stop, if you are not met by me or Dr. Joe, at the St. Nicholas, Cumberland. Telegraph me once when you start, and again when you are on the Baltimore and Ohio Railroad. Captain McKinley, Major Kennedy, and many other of your friends are at the St. Nicholas, if I happen not to be there.

General Crook is of course in Libby by this time. If he can be exchanged soon, it will not, I think, injure him. His reputation is of the solid sort. He is spoken of by officers and men always in the right spirit.

General Kelley had command of the town and of all the troops on picket. I do not hear him censured in regard to it. He should have had cavalry here, but I suppose it is not his fault that there was none. The truth is that all but "a feeble few" are taken to the coast from Savannah to Richmond, leaving these posts to take their chances. I think it is wise policy, but at the same time *we* are exposed to surprise and capture at any time.

You need not be surprised to hear that the enemy are across the Baltimore and Ohio Railroad at any time. I have great faith in my troops, my vigilance, and my luck, but I shall be much mistaken if the Rebels don't overwhelm a number of our posts during the next six weeks or two months.   Nothing but their extreme weakness will prevent it.

How gloriously things are moving!   Columbia, Charleston, Sumter!   Lee must act speedily.   I should think he would gather up all the scattered forces and attack either Grant or Sherman before Sherman gets within supporting distance of Grant.   But it is all guess.   The next two months will be more and more interesting with the *hopes,* at least, in our favor largely. If Lee evacuates Richmond and moves towards Lynchburg or Danville or North (?) it merely prolongs the struggle.   The evacuation of Richmond is a confession of defeat.

General Stephenson temporarily commands the Department. Well enough.   If Lee leaves Richmond I shall then feel like resigning the moment things don't suit me.   The war will be substantially over and I can honorably quit. — Love to all.

Affectionately ever

R.

P. S. — The Rebels inquired for me, but were informed that I quartered with my troops.   If it could be without stain I would rather like now to be captured.   It would be a good experience.

Mrs. Hayes.

Cumberland, Maryland, March 2, 1865.

Dear Uncle: — It is a rainy, dismal day.   General Hancock is in command of this Department.   Sheridan has collected all his cavalry, and it is on a big raid to cut and slash the railroads west of Richmond, or to capture Gordonsville, or something of the sort.   I doubt whether *we see* any more battles.   I shall consider myself discharged as soon as my four years are up and Richmond taken.   I shall be surprised if the latter does not occur first.

Great preparations are making for the inauguration.   If nothing *disastrous* happens to our armies, it will be the greatest thing of the sort that ever has been witnessed in the country. Write often.

Sincerely,

R. B. HAYES.

S. BIRCHARD.

CUMBERLAND, MARYLAND, March 2, 1865.

DEAR HASTINGS: — Glad to get yours of the 27th and to find you are sound on the question of promotion. There is some danger that your absence over sixty days may in the War Office induce your discharge, but the chances are that it will not be known. I want you to get the new title at least. The commander of a scow on the canal is called *captain,* but colonel is the best sounding title I know of.

Yes, General Crook's capture is a great loss, as well as an especial calamity to all serving in this command. General Hancock takes the Department of West Virginia and General (brevet major) Carroll formerly of the Eighth Ohio, the District of Cumberland.

General Sheridan, with an immense force of cavalry, is on a raid towards Gordonsville or Charlottesville, or *somewhere* — probably to distract the attention of Lee. We are all in suspense as to Sherman and Grant. I look forward to the capture of Richmond as my discharge from service. . . .

A great many staff officers are in a state of mind about these days; also divers brigadier-generals "of whom I am not which." Webster is often quoted — "Where am I to go?" — in a very despondent way. General Lightburn, Colonel Comly, and Captain Sweet are running an examining board as usual, much to the disgust of the Thirteenth. Mrs. Comly is here with a fine boy. The colonel makes a pretty fair "nuss." — My regards to your sister.

Sincerely,

R. B. HAYES.

CAPTAIN RUSSELL HASTINGS,
   Willoughby, Ohio.

HEADQUARTERS FIRST INFANTRY DIVISION,
DEPARTMENT OF WEST VIRGINIA,
CAMP HASTINGS, NEAR CUMBERLAND, March 4, 1865.

DEAR SIR: — I am just in receipt of yours of the 25th. As to going to Washington, if it is so important to our friend's success, I must strain a point to get there.

The kidnapping of our two generals and the state of things growing out of Sheridan's absence with all the mounted men of this region makes it imperative that I should for the *present* stay where I am. A few weeks will probably change all this — possibly a few days. Who am I to look to for the truth when I get to Washington? I think you told me that Barrett was both friendly and well informed in these matters. I have written to him today on this supposition.

Write to me frequently and fully and oblige.

Sincerely,

R. B. HAYES.

WILLIAM HENRY SMITH,
SECRETARY OF STATE,
Columbus, Ohio.

CUMBERLAND, MARYLAND, March 5, 1865.

DEAREST: — General Sheridan has got together all the four-footed beasts of this region and mounted his last trooper. They are gone to try to destroy railroads and stores if possible all the way to Lynchburg. We are thinking of nothing else just now. The only danger is the mud and high waters from the rains and melting snows. He is reported to have had a good little success at Woodstock, taking four guns and four hundred prisoners.

A few weeks will probably produce great changes in the situation. Even a considerable disaster to our arms now will hardly enable the Rebels to hold Richmond much longer.

Judge Johnston was here yesterday morning. He did not take his family to the inauguration. As things now are, I am glad you did not come. The railroad is in a wretched condition and our forces are so weak that we are liable to interruption at any time. General Duval will return, it is supposed, in a few days, when I can be better spared, if I wish to go anywhere.

I do not see any notice of Mitchell's appointment or confirmation. I fear the announcement was premature.

Wager Swayne lost a leg in South Carolina and is promoted to brigadier-general. General Hancock takes General Crook's place. We rather like the new regime. General Carroll takes General Kelley's shoes. We all like him, so far, very much. He takes to Dr. Joe almost as much as Crook did. — Love to all the boys and Grandma.

Affectionately, ever,

R.

Mrs. Hayes.

Cumberland, March 5, 1865.

Dear Mother: — We are feeling a good deal of anxiety now to hear from our cavalry. General Sheridan with all the mounted men of the Department left last Monday to make a raid on the Rebel towns south of us. If successful, he will do much towards compelling the evacuation of Richmond. The rains and swollen streams are regarded as the chief danger.

So many troops have left us that those who remain are kept almost constantly on duty. The men never were so cheerful when overworked before. They all think the end is so near that they can stand anything during the rest of the struggle. . . .

Affectionately, your son,

R.

Mrs. Sophia Hayes.

Monday, March 6. — Sheridan last Monday with a large cavalry force went towards Staunton, Charlottesville, and Lynchburg to destroy stores and connections with Richmond. Mud and water his chief enemies.

Tuesday, 7. — Sheridan whips Early near Staunton, takes eleven cannon and over one thousand prisoners. "The boy Jube ran away from the subscribers."

Wednesday, 8. — Busy replying to letters from divers officeseekers. They come by the dozens.

CAMP HASTINGS, March 11, 1865.

DEAR MOTHER: — Nothing of interest in this particular locality. As part of Sheridan's command, we feel a good deal of interest in his cavalry raid. He has already sent back about fourteen hundred prisoners. We hope to hear further.

Major-General Hancock is now our immediate commander. He is a very large, noble-looking man — not less than six feet three inches high, and very large. All his new arrangements are very satisfactory to our division. He will hardly be so great a favorite as General Crook, but is making a most favorable impression. . . .

Affectionately,

R. B. HAYES.

MRS. SOPHIA HAYES.

CAMP HASTINGS, March 12, 1865.

MY DARLING: — I am very glad to have heard from or of you several times during the last week. While your rheumatism stays with you I naturally feel anxious to hear often. If you should be so unlucky as to become a cripple, it will certainly be bad, but you may be sure I shall be still a loving husband, and we shall make the best of it together. There are a great many worse things than to lose the ability of easy locomotion. Of course, you will have to use philosophy or something higher to keep up your spirits. I think of Mrs. Little as giving more happiness to her household by her cheerfulness and agreeable ways than most of the walking women I know off.

It is lucky you didn't come to the inauguration. The bad weather and Andy Johnson's disgraceful drunkenness spoiled it.

I have bought a "Gulliver's Travels" which I will give to Webb if he can read it. I remember he was very fond of my telling it, and with his sweet voice often coaxed me to tell him about "the little people."

We are under General Hancock now, and like him. He is [a] noble man in his physical get-up — six feet three and handsomely proportioned. So far as he has arranged, matters are satisfactory to me. I keep my brigade.

Sheridan is still absent. Of course some solicitude will be felt until he gets through. The last accounts are favorable. . . .

Hastings is promoted lieutenant-colonel, Thompson, major. Good! McKinley and Watkins, Twenty-third, have gone with Hancock to Winchester or somewhere else up the Valley. Dr. Joe visits the "Pirates" (Semmes family, but intensely loyal), but not with any reputed designs. — Chaplain Little runs with his wife all sorts of schools and is useful and a favorite with all sensible people. . . . Love to all.

Affectionately ever,

R.

Mrs. Hayes.

Tuesday, March 14. — Sheridan tearing up railroads, burning bridges, and destroying the James River Canal very successfully; goes near Lynchburg, Gordonsville, and beyond Staunton. I hope he will in spite of high water get over James River and cut the Danville Railroad and join Grant.

Camp Hastings, March 17, 1865.

My Darling: — . . . You will feel relieved about General Crook. General Kelley is here. General Crook is at Baltimore and will return here in a few days. They were treated in the kindest and most liberal way by the Rebels. The only exception was old Early; he was drunk and insolent. They were furnished with all the money they needed. Crook had no money. His pocketbook was left under his pillow where I found it. Their captors were civil and accommodating. The people at Richmond are whipped and confess it. The West Virginia Rebels at Richmond couldn't do enough for the generals and in fact, all prisoners there now are *courted* by the Secesh.

It is an early spring here. We are now enjoying ourselves very much. — Love to all.

Affectionately,

R.

March 18. — Great fun — a fine bright night, wind rose un-heard of and blew down several hundred tents, etc., etc. Billy's kitchen, Uncle Joe's hat, etc., etc., still "absent without leave."

MRS. HAYES.

CAMP HASTINGS, March 18, 1865.

DEAR UNCLE: — I have very little care or responsibility. My command is exclusively a fighting command. I have nothing to do with guards, provost or routine duty connected with posts. Mine is the only movable column west of Winchester. If an enemy threatens any place, I am to send men there when ordered. My time is wholly occupied drilling and teaching tactics and the like. My brigade furnishes details for guard and provost when needed, but I am not bothered with them when on such duty. My regiments are all large; nearly four thousand men in the four, of whom twenty-five hundred are present at least. General Crook is again out, and we hope he will return to this command. We like Hancock very well. He behaved very handsomely with Crook's staff, and all of the troops and officers which [that] were particularly favorites with Crook. We were all left in our old positions, although some pressure was brought against it.

I see gold is tumbling. If no mishap befalls our armies, the downward tendency will probably continue. Then *debtors* must look out. It will not be so easy to pay debts when greenbacks are worth eighty to ninety [cents] on the dollar. My four years are up about the first of June.

Sincerely,

R. B. HAYES.

S. BIRCHARD.

CAMP HASTINGS, March 21, 1865.

DEAREST: — You would have boiled over with enjoyment if you had been here today. General Crook came out to my quarters. Both bands were out and *all* the men. We had about forty rousing cheers, a speech from Chaplain Collier, a good talk from the general, a little one from me, and lots of fun. It is four weeks today since the capture.

We are having the finest possible time. The Twenty-third is

not camped with me now. It is two and one-half miles off in the prettiest camp they ever had the other side of town. But the brigade is a *unit* now. The mountain scenery is glorious; the men happy and well behaved. Chaplain Little and his wife get up something good at the log chapel daily. . . .

Affectoinately

R.

We have an old fellow, hard-looking and generally full of liquor, who brings in our wood and builds fires — of the Thirteenth. He says, "I was glad to see old Uncle George."

MRS. HAYES.

CAMP HASTINGS, March 24, 1865.

DEAR UNCLE: — Crook was all right with Grant, but Stanton was angry. Grant however rules matters where he really attempts it. Stanton refused to make an effort for a special and privileged exchange. Grant, however, had it done. Crook stopped at Grant's headquarters. Grant wanted him to stay and take an important active command in his army before Richmond. Crook told him he wanted to be restored to the Department of West Virginia, if for only one day, to show the public that he was not in disfavor. It was accordingly so arranged. Crook returned here, took command, came out to my camp and had a happy meeting with the men, and the next day left for Grant's Army. It is supposed he will take the cavalry of the Army of the Potomac. It is probably better for his reputation that it is so.

Hancock is a very fair man, but nervous, excitable, and hasty. Would not act badly except from want of reflection.

Your suggestion as to Mother is, I think, correct. She is probably happier than her letters would indicate. As people get along in life, their feelings and mode of talking and writing get into channels; they have *habits* of talking, etc., which do not mean much. If mother was perfectly happy she would write in a strain of melancholy. She is in the *habit* of thinking that she would like to be with her grandchildren all the time. This is a mistake. Their noise and childish acts and talking would in one week weary her into greater discomfort than she is now in for want of them. For a litle while she enjoys them very much. My only effort is to treat her affectionately and try to turn her thoughts in some incidental way into pleasanter paths. If I were keeping house, I know she would soon become more tired of my home than she is now of Mrs. Wasson's. Her intellect is twisted into a habit of thinking and meditating too much on herself instead of occupying her mind with external affairs. It can't be helped. *Indirectly* we may do a good deal to contribute to her happiness, but scarcely anything in the common way. Suppose I should say, "What do you prefer as your mode of life?" and she should reply, I would do her no favor by complying exactly with her wishes.

I shall try to go to Washington [for] a few days soon.

Sincerely,

R. B. Hayes.

S. Birchard.

Camp Hastings, March 25, 1865.

Dear Mother: — We have had a sudden and severe change of weather. For the first time this month the ground is white with snow, and the mountains look like midwinter. The wind blows our tents down once in a while, and makes a little trouble. In other respects the change does not trouble us much.

General Crook has been exchanged and given a command under Grant before Richmond. He was placed in command of his old Department a few days to show that Grant had not lost confidence in him. He came out to my camp, where the troops gave him a most enthusiastic reception. . . .

We are ready to move from here at any time. It is not known, I think, by anybody where [and] when we shall go. . . .

Affectionately, your son,

R.

Mrs. Sophia Hayes.

Camp Hastings, April 3, 1865.

Dear Mother: — . . . I am to have a new command in Hancock's Corps. Either veterans or a brigade of new Ohio troops. I shall probably prefer the latter, as it is not likely to continue a great while. I leave Cumberland tomorrow. The new command is near Harpers Ferry. Letters addressed to me via Harpers Ferry will reach me.

Affectionately,

R.

MRS. SOPHIA HAYES.

CAMP HASTINGS, April 3, 1865.

DEAR COLONEL: — That sounds better, don't it? Your commission was sent three weeks ago, as I was told by Harry Thompson. There has been some oversight or negligence. I know Colonel Comly would not purposely withhold it.

The Twenty-third is in a nice camp near town, doing provost duty. You could enjoy yourself with them as soon as you can hobble about a little. . . .

General Crook has command of the cavalry of the Army of the Potomac. Just for the name of the thing, he took command of this Department for a day or two. He came out to our camp. We gave him a regular jolly mass-meeting sort of reception, which he and all of us enjoyed. I think it better for *him* as it is.

We are all ready to move. The talk is that we shall go soon. Hancock has at Halltown about ten thousand to fifteen thousand men, six or eight new Ohio regiments of the number. . . .

Sincerely,

R. B. HAYES.

LIEUTENANT-COLONEL RUSSELL HASTINGS,
   Willoughby, Ohio.

NEW CREEK, [WEST] VIRGINIA, April 5, 1865.

DEAR LUCY: — I am assigned to a new command of cavalry, infantry, and artillery — mostly West Virginia troops. I hated to leave my old command and at first was disposed to rebel. I am ordered to take command of an expedition through the mountains towards Lynchburg. It is over awful mountain roads, through a destitute country, and is in all respects a difficult, if not impossible, thing to do. I hope that Lee in his retreat will take such a direction as will make it plainly useless. If so, it will be abandoned, I trust. There will be little danger or hardship to me, but great hardships for the men. I will write you often till I start. I am to make my headquarters here while getting ready. I am to start from Beverly in Randolph County. Warm Springs, Staunton, and Lexington are named as points. — Love to all.

Affectionately ever,

R.

General Crook had the advance of Sheridan [in] the late movement at Petersburg.

Mrs. Hayes.

New Creek, [West] Virginia, April 8, 1865.

Dearest : — The glorious news is coming so fast that I hardly know how to think and feel about it. It is so just that Grant, who is by all odds our man of greatest merit, should get this victory. It is very gratifying too that Sheridan gets the lion's share of the glory of the active fighting. The clique of showy shams in the Army of the Potomac are represented by Warren. We do not know the facts, but I suspect Warren hung back, and after the Potomac fashion, didn't take hold with zeal when he found Sheridan was to command. So he was sent to the rear! General Crook wrote me the day before the battle that the *men* were in superb condition and eager for the fray, but that some of the *generals* were half whipped already. No doubt he meant Warren. Crook commanded the advance of Sheridan's attack. No doubt his strategy had much to do with it.

Personally, matters are probably as well as they could be, considering that we are in the hands, as Joe says, of the Yankees. The fall of Richmond came the day before we all left Camp Hastings. We had a glorious time. All the men gathered, all the bands; Chaplain Collier and I talked. I did not then of course say good-bye, but I said about all I would have said if just parting. The Thirty-sixth is about as near to me, the officers possibly more so, than the Twenty-third. I am in a command of all sorts now, a good regiment of cavalry, the old Pennsylvania Ringgold Cavalry, two batteries of Ohio men, one of them Captain Glassier's (the old Simmonds Battery), one of the veteran West Virginia regiments (Second Veterans), and a lot of others of less value. It was intended to send me in command of about five thousand men, quite a little army, by mountain routes towards Lynchburg. We are still preparing for it, but I have no idea *now* that we shall go. I wish to remain in service until my four years is up in June. Then I shall resign or not, as seems best. If matters don't suit me, I'll resign sooner.

Now, if things remain here *in statu quo,* would you like [to] come here? It is a most romantic spot. I have Captain Nye and Lieutenant Turner of Thirty-sixth as part of my staff, Charley Smith, Billy Crump, and two other Twenty-third men as orderlies. We have speedy communication by rail and telegraph and with a little more company it would be very jolly. — Love to all.

Affectionately,

R.

Mrs. Hayes.

New Creek, [West] Virginia, April 9 (Sunday), 1865.

Dear Mother: — The good news is coming so fast and so much of it that I hardly know how to think or feel about it. I expect to see no more fighting with any part of my command, and in all quarters the severe fighting must, I think, soon cease. I was assigned to the command of an independent expedition through the mountains towards Lynchburg some days ago. We are still preparing for it, but I now think it will not go. In the meantime my headquarters are temporarily at this place. I do not much care where I am during the short time I shall probably now remain in the army. I want to stay a little while longer until the smoke of these great events blows away enough to let us see what the Rebels will try to do next. I expect to see many of them give up, but the Rebel organization will hold on I suspect some time longer. My four years is up in June; after that I feel at liberty to resing. Sooner if matters [don't (?)] suit.

Write me at this place for the present.

Affectionately, your son,

R.

Mrs. Sophia Hayes.

CUMBERLAND, MARYLAND, April 10, 1865.

DEAR JUDGE: — I am told that my application for leave has come back without approval. I am sending it again today. At this rate it will be ten days before I see it again. The War Department wants to know my business. They mustn't be too crotchety or I'll get naughty on their hands.

I hope this cruel war is over. I shall resign *probably* in about six weeks.

Sincerely,

R. B. HAYES.

[JUDGE WILLIAM JOHNSTON (?),
Washington.]

NEW CREEK, WEST VIRGINIA, April 12, 1865.

DEAR UNCLE: — I am just beginning to fully realize and enjoy our great victories. I am more glad to think my fighting days are ended than I had expected. Grant deserves his great victory. Crook, too, had a conspicuous place. It was his immediate command which captured the wagon train, Armstrong guns, prisoners, etc., which figure so largely in Sheridan's reports.

I am still preparing for my expedition, but I am confident it is given up and will never be undertaken; it is rendered useless. I think it not improbable that there will be an extra session of Congress; if so, I go out of service then, of course. I am pretty well pleased with matters now. Pecuniarily, I shall gain by staying in service as long as possible. That consideration aside, I am ready to quit now almost any time. Address me at this place.

Sincerely,

R. B. HAYES.

S. BIRCHARD.

NEW CREEK, WEST VIRGINIA, April 12, 1865.

DEAREST: — I wonder if you feel as happy as I do. The close of the war, "home again," darling and the boys and all to be together again for good! And the manner of it too! Our best general vindicated by having the greatest victory. General Crook too. Did you see, it was his immediate command that captured so much, which Sheridan telegraphs about — the wagons, Armstrong guns, etc., etc.? All most gratifying.*

My expedition into the mountains will no doubt be given up, although we are still preparing.

I am well satisfied with present matters personally, and think I am rather fortunate, all things considered. I decide nothing at present. I wish you to be ready to join me on very short notice. It is not likely I shall send for you, but I may do so any day if you would like to come.

My notion is that an extra session of Congress soon is a likely thing to occur. That will be known in a week or two. — Love to all. "So much."

As ever

R.

P. S. — My pictures being in demand, I have got another.

MRS. HAYES.

New Creek, Saturday, April 15. — 8 A. M. startled by report that Lincoln, Seward and ——— were assassinated. Somehow felt it was true.

NEW CREEK, WEST VIRGINIA, April 16, 1865.

DEAR UNCLE: — I am in receipt of yours of the 11th. My mountain expedition is given up. If I go at all from here, it will be directly up the valleys to occupy Staunton. In any event, I think I shall see no more active campaigning.

I have been greatly shocked by the tragedy at Washington.

* Dr. J. T. Webb writing to his mother from Winchester, April 13, 1865, says: — "It must be pleasant to those worthies who put on so much style to reflect that while there was fighting to be done here in this valley, Sheridan and Crook were here; now that the fighting has been transferred to Richmond, they [the worthies] are sent here and Crook and Sheridan taken off down there. *It's all style and airs* — very offensive to sensible people, but as the war is about over, it matters but little who commands. Were there an enemy in our front, I should not fancy our generals. As it is they are very good for *fuss and feathers,* great on revers, etc., — about all they are suited for."

At first it was wholly dark. So unmerited a fate for Lincoln! Such a loss for the country! Such a change! But gradually, consolatory topics suggest themselves. How fortunate that it occurred no sooner! Now the march of events will neither be stopped nor changed. The power of the Nation is in our armies, and they are commanded by such men as Grant, Sherman, and Thomas, instead of McClellan, Hooker, or, etc., etc. Lincoln's fame is safe. He is the Darling of History evermore. His life and achievements give him titles to regard second to those of no other man in ancient or modern times. To these, this tragedy now adds the crown of martyrdom.

Sincerely,

R.

S. Birchard.

New Creek, West Virginia, April 16 (Sunday), 1865.

Dearest: — When I heard first yesterday morning of the awful tragedy at Washington, I was pained and shocked to a degree I have never before experienced. I got onto the cars, then just starting, and rode down to Cumberland. The probable consequences, or rather the possible results in their worst imaginable form, were presented to my mind one after the other, until I really began to feel that here was a calamity so extensive that in no direction could be found any, the slightest, glimmer of consolation. The Nation's great joy turned suddenly to a still greater sorrow! A ruler tested and proved in every way, and in every way found equal to the occasion, to be exchanged for a new man whose ill-omened beginning made the Nation hang its head. Lincoln for Johnson! The work of reconstruction requiring so much statesmanship just begun! The calamity to Mr. Lincoln; in a personal point of view, so uncalled for a fate! — so undeserved, so unprovoked! The probable effect upon the future of public men in this country, the necessity for guards; our ways to be assimilated to those of the despotisms of the Old World. — And so I would find my mind filled only with images of evil and calamity, until I felt a sinking of heart hardly equalled by that which oppressed us all when the defeat of our army at Manassas almost crushed the Nation.

But slowly, as in all cases of great affliction, one comes to feel that it is not all darkness; the catastrophe is so much less, happening now, than it would have been at any time before, since Mr. Lincoln's election. At this period after his first inauguration; at any of the periods of great public depression; during the pendency of the last Presidential election; at any time before the defeat of Lee, such a calamity might have sealed the Nation's doom. Now the march of events can't be stayed, probably can't be much changed. It is possible that a greater degree of severity in dealing with the Rebellion may be ordered, and *that* may be for the best.

As to Mr. Lincoln's name and fame and memory, — all is safe. His firmness, moderation, goodness of heart; his quaint humor, his perfect honesty and directness of purpose; his logic, his modesty, his sound judgment, and great wisdom; the contrast between his obscure beginnings and the greatness of his subsequent position and achievements; his tragic death, giving him almost the crown of martyrdom, elevate him to a place in history second to none other of ancient or modern times. His success in his great office, his hold upon the confidence and affections of his countrymen, we shall all *say* are only second to Washington's; we shall probably *feel* and *think* that they are not *second* even to his.

My mountain expedition is at an end. If I go on any more campaigning, it will be an easy march to occupy some point on the Central Virginia Railroad — Staunton or Charlottesville. I anticipate, however, an early call of an extra session of Congress. In any event, I shall probably not see any more active service.

I enclose my good-bye to my old First Brigade.* I now regard the order separating us as not unfortunate. It must have been soon, and could not have been in a better way.

Direct your letters to this point — Second Brigade, First Division, Department West Virginia. — Love to all.

Affectionately,

R.

Mrs. Hayes.

* See "Life," Vol. I, p. 269, footnote.

*37

New Creek, West Virginia, April 16, 1865.

Dear Mother: — I am as much shocked as I ever was by any calamity by the awful tragedy at Washington. Still I can discover many topics of consolation. It is fortunate that it did not occur before. We are fortunate in now having such good men as Grant, Sherman, and Thomas commanding our armies, for there is the power in this country. Mr. Lincoln's fame is safe. He is the "Darling of History" evermore. To titles to regard and remembrance which equal those of any man in ancient or modern times growing out of the events and achievements of his life, his tragic death now adds the crown of martyrdom.

Affectionately,

R.

Mrs. Sophia Hayes.

Wednesday, April 19. — Sheridan evidently did the decisive fighting at Five Forks; but for him it would have been a failure again.

New Creek, West Virginia, April 19, 1865.

My Darling: — I have just returned from Cumberland to meet Dr. Joe from Winchester and to see the funeral ceremonies, etc., at department headquarters.

Had a good time. I feel the national loss, but even that is nothing compared to the joy I feel that this awful war is ended in our favor. Joe and I moralized over it, and agreed that no one man, not even so great a one as Lincoln, was anything by the side of the grand events of the month.* We are to leave

* Dr. Webb wrote his mother the next day (April 20) from Cumberland as follows: —

"We are all well. The time passes slow now that there is no work in view. The Rebels all feel disposed to quit; the women, if possible, more insolent than ever. It is a bitter pill for the First Families. Most of the 'Gorillas' have signified their desire to quit, but the Union people who have suffered from their atrocious acts, do not feel exactly disposed to receive the murderers back into their arms. The Union citizens who have suffered everything during this war feel outraged at the service hereafter when things take shape a little, if possible at the same time.

I asked you in a late letter to be ready to come to me on short notice. I, or somebody, will meet you at Parkersburg or somewhere. Come without much baggage ready *to travel*. We will perhaps take a journey of three weeks or so when I quit. Joe will go along and possibly two of my staff. Can we take Birch without Webb? Can you leave George?

I am so anxious to be with you. Your letter of the 5th, which I find here, is the first I have from you in a great while. I am so happy in the prospect of being with you for good soon. — Reply at once.

Affectionately, ever,

R.

Mrs. Hayes.

New Creek, West Virginia, April 21, 1865.

Dear Uncle: — I am amused by your anxiety about General Hayes being relieved. "Tardiness" in the presence of the enemy was quite the opposite of *my* difficulties. Sheridan in one of his dispatches, spoke of Crook "with his usual impetuosity." As my command led in the affair, it meant me. There are five General Hayes[es] in our service and two in the Rebel that I know of. Alexander, a gallant officer killed under Grant, William, who has charge of the draft in New York City, Ed of Ohio, and Joseph who had charge of exchange of prisoners. *He* is the *tardy* one who is reported relieved.

My command is [the] Second Brigade, First Division, Army of West Virginia — a large brigade of calvary, artillery, and in-

the disposition evinced by the powers that be to take back as erring brethren these fiendish villains.

"While I think the President a good honest man, none better, I am not so certain that his loss at this time is so great a public calamity as many are disposed to think. He was entirely too forgiving. He appeared to have forgotten the thousands of honest, brave, and true men either in their graves or limping about cripples, etc.

"So we go, the world moves on, one man succeeds another. This country is too great, its aim too holy to fail at this period on account of the death of any one man."

fantry. We are now busy paroling guerrillas and the like. All, from Mosby down, seem disposed to quit and surrender. If the feeling continues, we shall soon have peace throughout Virginia, at least.

Sincerely,

R. B. Hayes.

S. Birchard.

New Creek, April 28, 1865.

My Darling: — Yours came yesterday. I can't yet decide anything, either as to your coming here, or as to my quitting service. As soon as the Government, in any official way, says officers of my grade, or generally, are no longer needed in their present numbers, I am ready to go.

I am a little bored, at the same time that I am pleased, by the doings of the Ohio soldiers of my old division.* I tried to stop the proceedings getting into print, but am now told that I was too late. I have letters from all the colonels of a very pleasant sort, as to their feelings, etc., etc.

I have a leave to go to Washington, and shall go there early next week, to spend the week. I shall then probably decide all matters as to your coming out or my going home. I think three weeks will be long enough for your absence if you come.

I have a long letter from Crook written soon after Lee's surrender. He thanks the guerrillas for his capture, as it got him into active service. — Sheridan by his personal efforts secured the victory of Five Forks, which decided the fate of Richmond, Lee, and all. — Love to all.

Affectionately ever,

R.

Mrs. Hayes.

Saturday, April 29. — Johnston's surrender I regard as the end of the war. Celebrate it by wearing a white collar, first time in service, four years!

* A meeting, April 20, which adopted resolutions urging the Union party to nominate Hayes for Governor of Ohio. See "Life," Vol. I, p. 290.

WASHINGTON, May 5, 1865.

DEAREST: — I am here in Judge Johnston's pleasant quarters, established in a homelike way. Dined with Charley Anderson at Governor Dennison's yesterday. All talk of you. . . .

I am yet undecided as to when I go out, etc., etc., but *soon*. My trip with you is not any more probable, but keep ready a little while longer. We shall be together very soon somewhere. If at Chillicothe, you must get an extra room for a short time.

I am meditating *this,* to quietly *determine,* for my own and your knowledge, to quit public life as soon as my term in Congress ends. That *fixed,* then at once either open a law office in Cincinnati as soon as I resign, or prepare a home at Fremont. Don't worry over it, but think of it and when we meet we will confer. — Love to the dear ones.

Ever affectionately,

R.

MRS. HAYES.

WASHINGTON, May 7, 1865.

DEAR UNCLE: — I am spending a few days very pleasantly here. I have had two talks with the President. He strikes me favorably.

The great armies are gathering here. Grant is here; also Sheridan. Sherman is expected soon. I am waiting a little while to see how the cat will jump. June early is still my time for leaving — possibly sooner. I return to New Creek in a few days.

Sincerely,

R. B. HAYES.

S. BIRCHARD.

WASHINGTON, May 7, 1865.

DEAR MOTHER: — . . . The President impresses me more favorably than I anticipated. He strikes one as a capable and sincere man — patriotic and with a great deal of experience as a public man.

The great armies are getting back from the South to this

city in great numbers. Grant and Sheridan are here. Sherman is soon coming. All think the war at an end. . . .

Affectionately, your son,

R.

Mrs. Sophia Hayes.

Washington, May 9, 1865.

Dearest: — I am here looking on at the closing scenes. I wish you were here with me. I shall know in a few days how long I shall stay. If I am to remain long you must come here.

I now think it probable I shall stay in service just a month longer. If so, I will send for you. Otherwise, you will see me at home within a fortnight.

I could *talk* to you a great deal about things, but I don't care to write them.

I am a very *little* bored by having my name mentioned for governor. The answer is simply, *I have accepted another place*, and that is reason enough for not looking further.

I send you Bishop Simpson's excellent address on Lincoln. — The foolish talk about your husband was not paid for I assure you.

Affectionately ever,

R.

Mrs. Hayes.

Washington, D. C., May 9, 1865.

Dear Laura: — I suppose from what I hear of your gallant husband that he will be here in a few days. I guess also that after the grand doings of the army, when it gets here, that he will resign, as I mean to do, and go home. Now, why shouldn't our wives come after us? I hereby empower you to order Lucy to come with you to Washington about the 20th or 25th. Write me what you think of it.

Affectionately,

R.

Mrs. Laura Mitchell,
    Columbus.

NEW CREEK, May 12, 1865.

DEAR MOTHER: — I have returned from Washington, and shall start this afternoon for Chillicothe. I do not leave the army for a few days until I know what is to be done with my favorite troops. As soon as that is known I quit. I shall bring Lucy here to await events.   .   .   .

Affectionately, your son,

R.

MRS. SOPHIA HAYES.

MARIETTA, OHIO, May 14, 1865.

DEAR MOTHER: — Having business on this end of the Baltimore and Ohio Railroad, I came on this far to meet Lucy. She will go back to New Creek with me, and remain as long as I stay in the army — that is about two weeks.

The weather is very fine, and I never saw the Ohio River and its hills and bottoms looking so well. We shall probably go up the Ohio to Wheeling, and thence by railroad back. I now intend to leave the army so as to get settled up and ready for home by the 10th to 15th of June. I shall go to Delaware and Fremont before Cincinnati.

Affectionately, your son,

R.

NEW CREEK, WEST VIRGINIA, May 20, 1865.

DEAR MOTHER: — I got here safely with Lucy last night. I have resigned to take effect the week after next, and will probably be at Delaware within three weeks to see you. We shall travel about a few days before starting West.

The soldiers are leaving for home very rapidly. They are all in excellent spirits and glad to go. I have no idea that many of them will ever see as happy times again as they have had in the army. — I shall perhaps return by way of Fremont.

Affectionately, your son,

R.

NEW CREEK, WEST VIRGINIA, May 20, 1865.

DEAR UNCLE: — Lucy arrived here last night with me from Chillicothe. We expect to go to Washington in a few days, and after a little run about, home probably by way of Fremont about the 5th to 10th of June. I have sent my resignation, and shall be out of service just four years after entering it. My chest will go to Fremont by express; my horse and equipments, flag, sword, etc., etc., start tomorrow with my orderlies. If they need cash, please let them have it

Sincerely,

R. B. HAYES.

S. BIRCHARD.

NEW CREEK, WEST VIRGINIA, May 20, 1865.

DEAR COLONEL: — My wife came here last evening. I have sent in my resignation and asked to be relieved. I hope to get to Washington to the great doings to come off next week.

I take "Old Whitey" home (to Fremont, Ohio,) and hope you will be able to ride him again.

It is not yet known when troops of the class of Twenty-third, Thirty-sixth, and First West Virginia Veterans will be mustered out. They are all now at Staunton and appear to enjoy it much.

I have had the Cincinnati papers withdraw my name from the candidate list. I am of course much obliged to the brigade, but it would not be the thing for me to allow it.

My wife says she is glad you have sound views on the treatment of Rebels. She doubts her husband.

If Sherman did it with an eye to political advancement, as some say, of course it is bad, but if he thought to follow the policy of Lincoln as indicated by Weitzell's programme (and this I believe), he surely ought not to be abused for it.

My wife sends regards to your sister and yourself. Excuse haste.

Sincerely,

R. B. Hayes.

LIEUTENANT-COLONEL RUSSELL HASTINGS.

WASHINGTON, D. C., May 28, 1865.

DEAR MOTHER: — Mr. and Mrs. Phelps of Fremont joined us here this morning. We expect to finish our trip together. I suppose that week after next I shall start home, done with the war. Laura and Lucy are enjoying themselves very much. General Mitchell and myself have been busy a large part of the time, leaving our wives to follow their own plans. We shall probably leave here tomorrow to visit Richmond, and will come West soon after. Mitchell will perhaps stay in service a few weeks or months longer. — Love to friends.

Affectionately, your son,

R.

MRS. SOPHIA HAYES.

CHILLICOTHE, June 11, 1865.

DEAR MOTHER: — We are once more all together in good health. The three larger boys are all going to school and are improving in their books. Little George is a very fine-looking and promising child.

We had a pleasant trip to Richmond. . . . I expect to go to Cincinnati in a few days and will probably be at Delaware to spend Sunday with you. I am now out of the army. Laura and General Mitchell will come home soon. General Mitchell has also resigned and will be out of the army in a few days.

I am very happy to be through with the war.

Affectionately, your son,

RUTHERFORD.

MRS. SOPHIA HAYES.

END OF VOLUME II.